Praise for
THE INHERITANCE TRILOGY

"A complex, edge-of-your-seat story with plenty of funny, scary, and bittersweet twists."

—*Publishers Weekly* (Starred Review)

"An offbeat, engaging tale by a talented and original newcomer."

—*Kirkus*

"An astounding debut novel...the worldbuilding is solid, the characterization superb, the plot complicated but clear."

—*RT Book Reviews* (Top Pick!)

"A delight for the fantasy reader."

—*Library Journal* (Starred Review)

"*The Hundred Thousand Kingdoms*...is an impressive debut, which revitalizes the trope of empires whose rulers have gods at their fingertips."

—io9.com

"N. K. Jemisin has written a fascinating epic fantasy where the stakes are not just the fate of kingdoms but of the world and the universe."

—sfrevu.com

"Many books are good, some are great, but few are truly important. Add to this last category *The Hundred Thousand Kingdoms*, N. K. Jemisin's debut novel...In this reviewer's opinion, this is the must-read fantasy of the year."   —*BookPage*

"A similar blend of inventiveness, irreverence, and sophistication—along with sensuality—brings vivid life to the setting and other characters: human and otherwise....*The Hundred Thousand Kingdoms* definitely leaves me wanting more of this delightful new writer."   —*Locus*

"A compelling page-turner."   —*The Onion A.V. Club*

"An absorbing story, an intriguing setting and world mythology, and a likable narrator with a compelling voice. The next book cannot come out soon enough."   —fantasybookcafe.com

"*The Broken Kingdoms*...expands the universe of the series geographically, historically, magically and in the range of characters, while keeping the same superb prose and gripping narrative that made the first one such a memorable debut."
—*Fantasy Book Critic*

"*The Kingdom of Gods* once again proves Jemisin's skill and consistency as a storyteller, but what sets her apart from the crowd is her ability to imagine and describe the mysteries of the universe in language that is at once elegant and profane, and thus, true."   —*Shelf Awareness*

Also by N. K. Jemisin

The Inheritance Trilogy

The Hundred Thousand Kingdoms

The Broken Kingdoms

The Kingdom of Gods

The Awakened Kingdom (brand-new sequel)

Dreamblood

The Killing Moon

The Shadowed Sun

THE INHERITANCE TRILOGY

INCLUDES:
THE HUNDRED THOUSAND KINGDOMS,
THE BROKEN KINGDOMS,
THE KINGDOM OF GODS,
THE AWAKENED KINGDOM

N. K. JEMISIN

orbit

www.orbitbooks.net

Orbit
Hachette Book Group
1290 Avenue of the Americas, New York, NY 10104
HachetteBookGroup.com

First Edition: December 2014

Orbit is an imprint of Hachette Book Group, Inc. The Orbit name and logo are trademarks of Little, Brown Book Group Limited.

The Hachette Speakers Bureau provides a wide range of authors for speaking events. To find out more, go to www.hachettespeakersbureau.com or call (866) 376-6591.

The publisher is not responsible for websites (or their content) that are not owned by the publisher.

The characters and events in this book are fictitious. Any similarity to real persons, living or dead, is coincidental and not intended by the author.

Library of Congress Control Number: 2014951263

ISBN: 978-0-316-33400-6

10 9 8

LSC-C

Printed in the United States of America

Contents

THE
HUNDRED
THOUSAND
KINGDOMS

BOOK ONE OF
THE INHERITANCE TRILOGY

1

Grandfather

I AM NOT AS I ONCE WAS. They have done this to me, broken me open and torn out my heart. I do not know who I am anymore.

I must try to remember.

My people tell stories of the night I was born. They say my mother crossed her legs in the middle of labor and fought with all her strength not to release me into the world. I was born anyhow, of course; nature cannot be denied. Yet it does not surprise me that she tried.

My mother was an heiress of the Arameri. There was a ball for the lesser nobility—the sort of thing that happens once a decade as a backhanded sop to their self-esteem. My father dared ask my mother to dance; she deigned to consent. I have often wondered what he said and did that night to make her fall in love with him so powerfully, for she eventually abdicated her position to be with him. It is the stuff of great tales, yes? Very romantic. In the tales, such a couple lives happily ever after. The tales do not say what happens when the most powerful family in the world is offended in the process.

*   *   *

But I forget myself. Who was I, again? Ah, yes.

My name is Yeine. In my people's way I am Yeine dau she Kinneth tai wer Somem kanna Darre, which means that I am the daughter of Kinneth, and that my tribe within the Darre people is called Somem. Tribes mean little to us these days, though before the Gods' War they were more important.

I am nineteen years old. I also am, or was, the chieftain of my people, called *ennu*. In the Arameri way, which is the way of the Amn race from whom they originated, I am the Baroness Yeine Darr.

One month after my mother died, I received a message from my grandfather Dekarta Arameri, inviting me to visit the family seat. Because one does not refuse an invitation from the Arameri, I set forth. It took the better part of three months to travel from the High North continent to Senm, across the Repentance Sea. Despite Darr's relative poverty, I traveled in style the whole way, first by palanquin and ocean vessel, and finally by chauffeured horse-coach. This was not my choice. The Darre Warriors' Council, which rather desperately hoped that I might restore us to the Arameri's good graces, thought that this extravagance would help. It is well known that Amn respect displays of wealth.

Thus arrayed, I arrived at my destination on the cusp of the winter solstice. And as the driver stopped the coach on a hill outside the city, ostensibly to water the horses but more likely because he was a local and liked to watch foreigners gawk, I got my first glimpse of the Hundred Thousand Kingdoms' heart.

There is a rose that is famous in High North. (This is not a digression.) It is called the altarskirt rose. Not only do its petals unfold in a radiance of pearled white, but frequently it grows an incomplete secondary flower about the base of its stem. In its most prized form, the altarskirt grows a layer of overlarge petals that drape the ground. The two bloom in tandem, seedbearing head and skirt, glory above and below.

This was the city called Sky. On the ground, sprawling over a small mountain or an oversize hill: a circle of high walls, mounting tiers of buildings, all resplendent in white, per Arameri decree. Above the city, smaller but brighter, the pearl of its tiers occasionally obscured by scuds of cloud, was the palace—also called Sky, and perhaps more deserving of the name. I knew the column was there, the impossibly thin column that supported such a massive structure, but from that distance I couldn't see it. Palace floated above city, linked in spirit, both so unearthly in their beauty that I held my breath at the sight.

The altarskirt rose is priceless because of the difficulty of producing it. The most famous lines are heavily inbred; it originated as a deformity that some savvy breeder deemed useful. The primary flower's scent, sweet to us, is apparently repugnant to insects; these roses must be pollinated by hand. The secondary flower saps nutrients crucial for the plant's fertility. Seeds are rare, and for every one that grows into a perfect altarskirt, ten others become plants that must be destroyed for their hideousness.

At the gates of Sky (the palace) I was turned away, though not for the reasons I'd expected. My grandfather was not present, it seemed. He had left instructions in the event of my arrival.

Sky is the Arameri's home; business is never done there. This is because, officially, they do not rule the world. The Nobles' Consortium does, with the benevolent assistance of the Order of Itempas. The Consortium meets in the Salon, a huge, stately building—white-walled, of course—that sits among a cluster of official buildings at the foot of the palace. It is very impressive, and would be more so if it did not sit squarely in Sky's elegant shadow.

I went inside and announced myself to the Consortium staff, whereupon they all looked very surprised, though politely so. One of them—a very junior aide, I gathered—was dispatched to escort me to the central chamber, where the day's session was well under way.

As a lesser noble, I had always been welcome to attend a Consortium gathering, but there had never seemed any point. Besides the expense and months of travel time required to attend, Darr was simply too small, poor, and ill-favored to have any clout, even without my mother's abdication adding to our collective stain. Most of High North is regarded as a backwater, and only the largest nations there have enough prestige or money to make their voices heard among our noble peers. So I was not surprised to find that the seat reserved for me on the Consortium floor—in a shadowed area, behind a pillar—was currently occupied by an excess delegate from one of the Senm-continent nations. It would be terribly rude, the aide stammered anxiously, to dislodge this man, who was elderly and had bad knees. Perhaps I would not mind standing? Since I had just spent many long hours cramped in a carriage, I was happy to agree.

So the aide positioned me at the side of the Consortium floor, where I actually had a good view of the goings-on. The

Consortium chamber was magnificently apportioned, with white marble and rich, dark wood that had probably come from Darr's forests in better days. The nobles—three hundred or so in total—sat in comfortable chairs on the chamber's floor or along elevated tiers above. Aides, pages, and scribes occupied the periphery with me, ready to fetch documents or run errands as needed. At the head of the chamber, the Consortium Overseer stood atop an elaborate podium, pointing to members as they indicated a desire to speak. Apparently there was a dispute over water rights in a desert somewhere; five countries were involved. None of the conversation's participants spoke out of turn; no tempers were lost; there were no snide comments or veiled insults. It was all very orderly and polite, despite the size of the gathering and the fact that most of those present were accustomed to speaking however they pleased among their own people.

One reason for this extraordinary good behavior stood on a plinth behind the Overseer's podium: a life-size statue of the Skyfather in one of His most famous poses, the Appeal to Mortal Reason. Hard to speak out of turn under that stern gaze. But more repressive, I suspected, was the stern gaze of the man who sat behind the Overseer in an elevated box. I could not see him well from where I stood, but he was elderly, richly dressed, and flanked by a younger blond man and a dark-haired woman, as well as a handful of retainers.

It did not take much to guess this man's identity, though he wore no crown, had no visible guards, and neither he nor anyone in his entourage spoke throughout the meeting.

"Hello, Grandfather," I murmured to myself, and smiled at him across the chamber, though I knew he could not see me.

The pages and scribes gave me the oddest looks for the rest of the afternoon.

I knelt before my grandfather with my head bowed, hearing titters of laughter.

No, wait.

There were three gods once.

Only three, I mean. Now there are dozens, perhaps hundreds. They breed like rabbits. But once there were only three, most powerful and glorious of all: the god of day, the god of night, and the goddess of twilight and dawn. Or light and darkness and the shades between. Or order, chaos, and balance. None of that is important because one of them died, the other might as well have, and the last is the only one who matters anymore.

The Arameri get their power from this remaining god. He is called the Skyfather, Bright Itempas, and the ancestors of the Arameri were His most devoted priests. He rewarded them by giving them a weapon so mighty that no army could stand against it. They used this weapon—weapons, really—to make themselves rulers of the world.

That's better. Now.

I knelt before my grandfather with my head bowed and my knife laid on the floor.

We were in Sky, having transferred there following the Consortium session, via the magic of the Vertical Gate. Immediately upon arrival I had been summoned to my grandfather's audience chamber, which felt much like a throne room. The chamber was roughly circular because circles are sacred to

Itempas. The vaulted ceiling made the members of the court look taller—unnecessarily, since Amn are a tall people compared to my own. Tall and pale and endlessly poised, like statues of human beings rather than real flesh and blood.

"Most high Lord Arameri," I said. "I am honored to be in your presence."

I had heard titters of laughter when I entered the room. Now they sounded again, muffled by hands and kerchiefs and fans. I was reminded of bird flocks roosting in a forest canopy.

Before me sat Dekarta Arameri, uncrowned king of the world. He was old; perhaps the oldest man I have ever seen, though Amn usually live longer than my people, so this was not surprising. His thin hair had gone completely white, and he was so gaunt and stooped that the elevated stone chair on which he sat—it was never called a throne—seemed to swallow him whole.

"Granddaughter," he said, and the titters stopped. The silence was heavy enough to hold in my hand. He was head of the Arameri family, and his word was law. No one had expected him to acknowledge me as kin, least of all myself.

"Stand," he said. "Let me have a look at you."

I did, reclaiming my knife since no one had taken it. There was more silence. I am not very interesting to look at. It might have been different if I had gotten the traits of my two peoples in a better combination—Amn height with Darre curves, perhaps, or thick straight Darre hair colored Amn-pale. I have Amn eyes: faded green in color, more unnerving than pretty. Otherwise, I am short and flat and brown as forestwood, and my hair is a curled mess. Because I find it unmanageable otherwise, I wear it short. I am sometimes mistaken for a boy.

As the silence wore on, I saw Dekarta frown. There was an odd sort of marking on his forehead, I noticed: a perfect circle of black, as if someone had dipped a coin in ink and pressed it to his flesh. On either side of this was a thick chevron, bracketing the circle.

"You look nothing like her," he said at last. "But I suppose that is just as well. Viraine?"

This last was directed at a man who stood among the courtiers closest to the throne. For an instant I thought he was another elder, then I realized my error: though his hair was stark white, he was only somewhere in his fourth decade. He, too, bore a forehead mark, though his was less elaborate than Dekarta's: just the black circle.

"She's not hopeless," he said, folding his arms. "Nothing to be done about her looks; I doubt even makeup will help. But put her in civilized attire and she can convey…nobility, at least." His eyes narrowed, taking me apart by degrees. My best Darren clothing, a long vest of white civvetfur and calf-length leggings, earned me a sigh. (I had gotten the odd look for this outfit at the Salon, but I hadn't realized it was *that* bad.) He examined my face so long that I wondered if I should show my teeth.

Instead he smiled, showing his. "Her mother has trained her. Look how she shows no fear or resentment, even now."

"She will do, then," said Dekarta.

"Do for what, Grandfather?" I asked. The weight in the room grew heavier, expectant, though he had already named me granddaughter. There was a certain risk involved in my daring to address him the same familiar way, of course—powerful men are touchy over odd things. But my mother had indeed trained me well, and I knew it was worth the risk to establish myself in the court's eyes.

Dekarta Arameri's face did not change; I could not read it. "For my heir, Granddaughter. I intend to name you to that position today."

The silence turned to stone as hard as my grandfather's chair.

I thought he might be joking, but no one laughed. That was what made me believe him at last: the utter shock and horror on the faces of the courtiers as they stared at their lord. Except the one called Viraine. He watched me.

It came to me that some response was expected.

"You already have heirs," I said.

"Not as diplomatic as she could be," Viraine said in a dry tone.

Dekarta ignored this. "It is true, there are two other candidates," he said to me. "My niece and nephew, Scimina and Relad. Your cousins, once removed."

I had heard of them, of course; everyone had. Rumor constantly made one or the other heir, though no one knew for certain which. *Both* was something that had not occurred to me.

"If I may suggest, Grandfather," I said carefully, though it was impossible to be careful in this conversation, "I would make two heirs too many."

It was the eyes that made Dekarta seem so old, I would realize much later. I had no idea what color they had originally been; age had bleached and filmed them to near-white. There were lifetimes in those eyes, none of them happy.

"Indeed," he said. "But just enough for an interesting competition, I think."

"I don't understand, Grandfather."

He lifted his hand in a gesture that would have been grace-ful, once. Now his hand shook badly. "It is very simple. I have named three heirs. One of you will actually manage to succeed me. The other two will doubtless kill each other or be killed by the victor. As for which lives, and which die—" He shrugged. "That is for you to decide."

My mother had taught me never to show fear, but emotions will not be stilled so easily. I began to sweat. I have been the target of an assassination attempt only once in my life—the benefit of being heir to such a tiny, impoverished nation. No one wanted my job. But now there would be two others who did. Lord Relad and Lady Scimina were wealthy and powerful beyond my wildest dreams. They had spent their whole lives striving against each other toward the goal of ruling the world. And here came I, unknown, with no resources and few friends, into the fray.

"There will be no decision," I said. To my credit, my voice did not shake. "And no contest. They will kill me at once and turn their attention back to each other."

"That is possible," said my grandfather.

I could think of nothing to say that would save me. He was insane; that was obvious. Why else turn rulership of the world into a contest prize? If he died tomorrow, Relad and Scimina would rip the earth asunder between them. The killing might not end for decades. And for all he knew, I was an idiot. If by some impossible chance I managed to gain the throne, I could plunge the Hundred Thousand Kingdoms into a spiral of mis-management and suffering. He had to know that.

One cannot argue with madness. But sometimes, with luck and the Skyfather's blessing, one can understand it. "Why?"

He nodded as if he had expected my question. "Your mother deprived me of an heir when she left our family. You will pay her debt."

"She is four months in the grave," I snapped. "Do you honestly want revenge against a dead woman?"

"This has nothing to do with revenge, Granddaughter. It is a matter of duty." He made a gesture with his left hand, and another courtier detached himself from the throng. Unlike the first man—indeed, unlike most of the courtiers whose faces I could see—the mark on this man's forehead was a downturned half-moon, like an exaggerated frown. He knelt before the dais that held Dekarta's chair, his waist-length red braid falling over one shoulder to curl on the floor.

"I cannot hope that your mother has taught you duty," Dekarta said to me over this man's back. "She abandoned hers to dally with her sweet-tongued savage. I allowed this—an indulgence I have often regretted. So I will assuage that regret by bringing you back into the fold, Granddaughter. Whether you live or die is irrelevant. You are Arameri, and like all of us, you will serve."

Then he waved to the red-haired man. "Prepare her as best you can."

There was nothing more. The red-haired man rose and came to me, murmuring that I should follow him. I did. Thus ended my first meeting with my grandfather, and thus began my first day as an Arameri. It was not the worst of the days to come.

2

The Other Sky

THE CAPITAL OF MY LAND is called Arrebaia. It is a place of ancient stone, its walls overgrown by vines and guarded by beasts that do not exist. We have forgotten when it was founded, but it has been the capital for at least two thousand years. People there walk slowly and speak softly out of respect for the generations that have trodden those streets before, or perhaps just because they do not feel like being loud.

Sky—the city, I mean—is only five hundred years old, built when some disaster befell the previous Arameri seat. This makes it an adolescent as cities go—and a rude, uncouth one at that. As my carriage rode through the city's center, other carriages went past in a clatter of wheels and horseshoes. People covered every sidewalk, bumping and milling and bustling, not talking. They all seemed in a hurry. The air was thick with familiar smells like horses and stagnant water amid indefinable scents, some acrid and some sickly sweet. There was nothing green in sight.

What was I—?

Oh, yes. The gods.

Not the gods that remain in the heavens, who are loyal to Bright Itempas. There are others who were not loyal. Perhaps I should not call them gods, since no one worships them anymore. (How does one define "god"?) There must be a better name for what they are. Prisoners of war? Slaves? What did I call them before—weapons?

Weapons. Yes.

They are said to be somewhere in Sky, four of them, trapped in tangible vessels and kept under lock and key and magic chain. Perhaps they sleep in crystal cases and are awakened on occasion to be polished and oiled. Perhaps they are shown off to honored guests.

But sometimes, sometimes, their masters call them forth. And then there are strange new plagues. Occasionally the population of an entire city will vanish overnight. Once, jagged, steaming pits appeared where there had been mountains.

It is not safe to hate the Arameri. Instead we hate their weapons, because weapons do not care.

My courtier companion was T'vril, who introduced himself as the palace steward. The name told me at least part of his heritage at once, but he went on to explain: he was a halfbreed like me, part Amn and part Ken. The Ken inhabit an island far to the east; they are famous for their seacraft. His strange red-colored hair came from them.

"Dekarta's beloved wife, the Lady Ygreth, died tragically young more than forty years ago," T'vril explained. He spoke briskly as we walked through Sky's white halls, not sounding particularly broken up about the tragedy of the dead lady. "Kinneth was just a child at the time, but it was already clear she would grow up to be a more-than-suitable heir, so I suppose Dekarta felt no pressing need to remarry. When Kinneth, er, left the family fold, he turned to the children of his late brother.

There were four of them originally; Relad and Scimina were the youngest. Twins—runs in the family. Alas, their elder sister met with an unfortunate accident, or so the official story goes."

I just listened. It was a useful, if appalling, education about my new kin, which was probably why T'vril had decided to tell me. He had also informed me of my new title, duties, and privileges, at least in brief. I was Yeine Arameri now, no longer Yeine Darr. I would have new lands to oversee and wealth beyond imagining. I would be expected to attend Consortium sessions regularly and sit in the Arameri private box when I did so. I would be permitted to dwell permanently in Sky in the welcoming bosom of my maternal relatives, and I would never see my homeland again.

It was hard not to dwell on that last bit, as T'vril continued.

"Their elder brother was my father—also dead, thanks to his own efforts. He was fond of young women. Very young women." He made a face, though I had the sense he'd told the story often enough that it didn't really trouble him. "Unfortunately for him, my mother was just old enough to get with child. Dekarta executed him when her family took exception." He sighed and shrugged. "We highbloods can get away with a great many things, but...well, there are rules. We were the ones to establish a worldwide age of consent, after all. To ignore our own laws would be an offense to the Skyfather."

I wanted to ask why that mattered when Bright Itempas didn't seem to care what else the Arameri did, but I held my tongue. There had been a note of dry irony in T'vril's voice in any case; no comment was necessary.

With a brisk efficiency that would have made my no-nonsense grandmother jealous, T'vril had me measured for new clothing, scheduled for a visit to a stylist, and assigned quarters all in the span of an hour. Then came a brief tour, during which T'vril chattered endlessly as we walked through corridors lined with white mica or mother-of-pearl or whatever shining stuff the palace was made of.

I stopped listening to him at about this point. If I had paid attention, I probably could have gleaned valuable information about important players in the palace hierarchy, power struggles, juicy rumors, and more. But my mind was still in shock, trying to absorb too many new things at once. He was the least important of them, so I shut him out.

He must have noticed, though he didn't seem to mind. Finally we reached my new apartment. Floor-to-ceiling windows ran along one wall, which afforded me a stunning view of the city and countryside below—far, far below. I stared, my mouth hanging open in a way that would have earned me a scold from my mother, had she still been alive. We were so high that I couldn't even make out people on the streets below.

T'vril said something then that I simply did not digest, so he said it again. This time I looked at him. "This," he said, pointing to his forehead. The half-moon mark.

"What?"

He repeated himself a third time, showing no sign of the exasperation he should have felt. "We must see Viraine, so that he can apply the blood sigil to your brow. He should be free from court duty by now. Then you can rest for the evening."

"Why?"

He stared at me for a moment. "Your mother did not tell you?"

"Tell me what?"

"Of the Enefadeh."

"The Enewhat?"

The look that crossed T'vril's face was somewhere between pity and dismay. "Lady Kinneth didn't prepare you for this at all, did she?" Before I could think of a response to that, he moved on. "The Enefadeh are the reason we wear the blood sigils, Lady Yeine. No one may pass the night in Sky without one. It isn't safe."

I pulled my thoughts away from the strangeness of my new title. "Why isn't it safe, Lord T'vril?"

He winced. "Just T'vril, please. Lord Dekarta has decreed that you are to receive a fullblood mark. You are of the Central Family. I am a mere halfblood."

I could not tell if I had missed important information, or if something had been left unsaid. Probably several somethings. "T'vril. You must realize nothing you're saying makes any sense to me."

"Perhaps not." He ran a hand over his hair; this was the first sign of discomfort he'd shown. "But an explanation would take too long. There's less than an hour 'til sunset."

I supposed that this, too, was one of those rules the Arameri insisted on being sticklers for, though I could not imagine why. "All right, but…" I frowned. "What of my coachman? He's waiting for me in the forecourt."

"Waiting?"

"I didn't think I'd be staying."

T'vril's jaw flexed, containing whatever honest reply he might have made. Instead he said, "I'll have someone send him away and give him a bonus for his trouble. He won't be needed; we have plenty of servants here."

I had seen them throughout our tour—silent, efficient figures bustling about Sky's halls, clad all in white. An impractical color for people whose job it was to clean, I thought, but I didn't run the place.

"That coachman traveled across this continent with me," I said. I was irked and trying not to show it. "He's tired and his horses are, too. Can he not be given a room for the night? Give him one of those marks and then let him leave in the morning. That's only courteous."

"Only Arameri may wear the blood sigil, my lady. It's permanent."

"Only—" Understanding leapt in my head. "The servants here are *family*?"

The look he threw me was not bitter, though perhaps it should have been. He had given me the clues already, after all: his roaming father, his own status as the steward. A high-ranking servant, but still a servant. He was as Arameri as I, but his parents had not been married; strict Itempans frowned on illegitimacy. And his father had never been Dekarta's favorite.

As if reading my thoughts, T'vril said, "As Lord Dekarta said, Lady Yeine—all descendants of Shahar Arameri must serve. One way or another."

There were so many untold tales in his words. How many of our relatives had been forced to leave their homelands, and whatever future they might have had, to come here and mop floors or peel vegetables? How many had been born here and never left? What happened to those who tried to escape?

Would I become one of them, like T'vril?

No. T'vril was unimportant, no threat to those who stood to inherit the family's power. I would not be so lucky.

He touched my hand with what I hoped was compassion. "It's not far."

On its upper levels, Sky seemed to have windows everywhere. Some corridors even had ceilings of clear glass or crystal, though the view was only of the sky and the palace's many rounded spires. The sun had not yet set—its lower curve had only touched the horizon in the past few minutes—but T'vril set a more brisk pace than before. I paid closer attention to the servants as we walked, seeking the small commonalities of our shared lineage. There were a few: many sets of green eyes, a certain structure of the face (which I lacked completely, having taken after my father). A certain cynicism, though that might have been my imagination. Beyond that, they were all as disparate as T'vril and I, though most seemed to be Amn or some Senmite race. And each of them bore a forehead marking; I had noticed that before but dismissed it as some local fashion. A few had triangles or diamond shapes, but most wore a simple black bar.

I did not like the way they looked at me, eyes flicking near and then away.

"Lady Yeine." T'vril stopped a few paces ahead, noticing that I had fallen behind. He had inherited the long legs of his Amn heritage. I had not, and it had been a very trying day. "Please, we have little time."

"All right, all right," I said, too tired to be strictly polite anymore. But he did not resume walking, and after a moment I saw that he had gone stiff, staring down the corridor in the direction we were to go.

A man stood above us.

I call him a man, in retrospect, because that is what he seemed at the time. He stood on a balcony overlooking our corridor, framed perfectly by the ceiling's arch. I gathered he had been traveling along a perpendicular corridor up there; his body still faced that direction, frozen in midpace. Only his head had turned toward us. By some trick of the shadows, I could not see his face, yet I felt the weight of his eyes.

He put a hand on the balcony railing with slow, palpable deliberation.

"What is it, Naha?" said a woman's voice, echoing faintly along the corridor. A moment later she appeared. Unlike the man, she was clearly visible to me: a reedy Amn beauty of sable hair, patrician features, and regal grace. I recognized her by that hair as the woman who'd sat beside Dekarta at the Salon. She wore the kind of dress that only an Amn woman could do justice to—a long straight tube the color of deep, bloody garnets.

"What do you see?" she asked, looking at me although her words were for the man. She lifted her hands, twirling something in her fingers, and I saw then that she held a delicate silver chain. It dangled from her hand and curved back up; I realized that the chain was connected to the man.

"Aunt," T'vril said, pitching his voice with a care that let me know at once who she was. The lady Scimina—my cousin and rival heir. "You look lovely this evening."

"Thank you, T'vril," she replied, though her eyes never left my face. "And who is this?"

There was the faintest pause. By the taut look on T'vril's face, I gathered he was trying to think of a safe answer. Some quirk of my own nature—in my land, only weak women allowed men to protect them—made me step forward and incline my head. "My name is Yeine Darr."

Her smile said that she'd already guessed it. There could not have been many Darre in the palace. "Ah, yes. Someone spoke of you after Uncle's audience today. Kinneth's daughter, are you?"

"I am." In Darr, I would have drawn a knife at the malice in her sweet, falsely polite tone. But this was Sky, blessed palace of Bright Itempas, the lord of order and peace. Such things were not done here. I looked to T'vril for an introduction.

"The lady Scimina Arameri," he said. He did not swallow or fidget, to his credit, but I saw how his eyes flicked back and forth between my cousin and the motionless man. I waited for T'vril to introduce the man, but he did not.

"Ah, yes." I did not try to mimic Scimina's tone. My mother had tried, on multiple occasions, to teach me how to sound friendly when I did not feel friendly, but I was too Darre for that. "Greetings, Cousin."

"If you'll excuse us," T'vril said to Scimina almost the instant I closed my mouth, "I'm showing Lady Yeine around the palace—"

The man beside Scimina chose that moment to catch his breath in a shuddering gasp. His hair, long and black and thick enough to make any Darre man jealous, fell forward to obscure his face; his hand on the railing tightened.

"A moment, T'vril." Scimina examined the man thought-fully, then lifted her hand as if to cup his cheek under the curtain of hair. There was a click, and she pulled away a deli-cate, cleverly jointed silver collar.

"I'm sorry, Aunt," T'vril said, and now he was no longer both-ering to hide his fear; he caught my hand in his own, tight. "Viraine's expecting us, you know how he hates—"

"You will wait," Scimina said, cold in an instant. "Or I may forget that you have made yourself so useful, T'vril. A good little servant…" She glanced at the black-haired man and smiled indulgently. "So many good servants here in Sky. Don't you think, Nahadoth?"

Nahadoth was the black-haired man's name, then. Something about the name stirred a feeling of recognition in me, but I could not recall where I'd heard it before.

"Don't do this," T'vril said. "Scimina."

"She has no mark," Scimina replied. "You know the rules."

"This has nothing to do with the rules and you know it!" T'vril said with some heat. But she ignored him.

I felt it then. I think I had felt it since the man's gasp—a shiver of the atmosphere. A vase rattled nearby. There was no visible cause for this, but somehow I knew: somewhere, on an unseen plane, a part of reality was shifting aside. Making room for something new.

The black-haired man lifted his head to look at me. He was smiling. I could see his face now, and his mad, mad eyes, and I suddenly knew who he was. *What* he was.

"Listen to me." T'vril, his voice tight in my ear. I could not look away from the black-haired creature's eyes. "You must get to Viraine. Only a fullblood can command him off now, and Viraine is the only one—Oh, for demons' sake, look at me!"

He moved into my line of sight, blocking my view of those eyes. I could hear a soft murmur, Scimina speaking in a low voice. It sounded like she was giving instructions, which made a peculiar parallel with T'vril in front of me doing the same. I barely heard them both. I felt so cold.

"Viraine's study is two levels above us. There are lifting

chambers at every third corridor juncture; look for an alcove between vases of flowers. Just—just get to one of those, and then think *up*. The door will be straight ahead. While there's still light in the sky you have a chance. Go. Run!"

He pushed me, and I stumbled off. Behind me rose an inhuman howl, like the voices of a hundred wolves and a hundred jaguars and a hundred winter winds, all of them hungry for my flesh. Then there was silence, and that was most frightening of all.

I ran. I ran. I ran.

3

Darkness

SHOULD I PAUSE TO EXPLAIN? It is poor storytelling. But I must remember everything, remember and remember and remember, to keep a tight grip on it. So many bits of myself have escaped already.

So.

There were once three gods. The one who matters killed one of the ones who didn't and cast the other into a hellish prison. The walls of this prison were blood and bone; the barred windows were eyes; the punishments included sleep and pain and hunger and all the other incessant demands of mortal flesh. Then this creature, trapped in his tangible vessel, was given to the Arameri for safekeeping, along with three of his godly children. After the horror of incarnation, what difference could mere slavery make?

As a little girl, I learned from the priests of Bright Itempas that this fallen god was pure evil. In the time of the Three, his followers had been a dark, savage cult devoted to violent midnight revels, worshipping madness as a sacrament. If that one had won the war between the gods, the priests intoned direly, mortalkind would probably no longer exist.

"So be good," the priests would add, "or the Nightlord will get you."

I ran from the Nightlord through halls of light. Some property of the stuff that made up Sky's substance made it glow with its own soft, white luminescence now that the sun had set. Twenty paces behind me charged the god of darkness and chaos. On the one occasion that I risked a glance back, I saw the gentle glow of the hallway fade into a throat of blackness so deep looking that way hurt the eye. I did not look back again.

I could not go straight. All that had saved me thus far was my head start, and the fact that the monster behind me seemed incapable of moving faster than a mortal's pace. Perhaps the god retained a human form somewhere within all that dark; even so, his legs were longer than mine.

So I turned at nearly every juncture, slamming into walls to brake my speed and give me something to push against as I sprinted away. I say this as if the wall slamming was deliberate on my part; it was not. If I had been able to reason through my abject terror, I might have retained a general sense of which direction I was going in. As it was, I was already hopelessly lost.

Fortunately, where reason failed, blind panic served well enough.

Spying one of the alcoves that T'vril had described, I flung myself into it, pressing against the back wall. He had told me to think *up*, which would activate the lifting spell and propel me to the next level of the palace. Instead I thought AWAY AWAY AWAY, not realizing the magic would oblige that, too.

When the coach had brought me from the Salon to Sky-the-palace, I'd had the curtains closed. The coachman had simply driven us to a particular spot and stopped; my skin had prickled; a moment later the coachman opened the door to reveal we were there. It had not occurred to me that the magic had pulled me through half a mile of solid matter in the blink of an eye.

Now it happened again. The little alcove, which had been growing dim as the Nightlord closed in, suddenly seemed to stretch, its entrance moving impossibly farther away while I remained still. There was an inbreath of tension, and then I shot forward as if from a sling. Walls flew at my face; I screamed and flung my arms over my eyes even as they passed through me. And then everything stopped.

I lowered my arms slowly. Before I could muster my wits enough to wonder whether this was the same alcove or another just like it, a child thrust his face through the opening, looked around, and spied me.

"Come on," he said. "Hurry up. It won't take him long to find us."

The Arameri magic had brought me to a vast open chamber within the body of Sky. Dumb, I looked around at the cold, featureless space as we hurried through it.

"The arena," said the boy ahead of me. "Some of the high-bloods fancy themselves warriors. This way."

I glanced back toward the alcove, wondering if there was some way to block it off so the Nightlord couldn't follow.

"No, that won't work," said the boy, following my gaze. "But the palace itself inhibits his power on a night like this. He can hunt you using only his senses." (*As opposed to what else?* I wondered.) "On a moonless night you'd be in trouble, but tonight he's just a man."

"That was not a man," I said. My voice sounded high and shaky in my own ears.

"If that were true, you wouldn't be running for your life right now." And apparently I wasn't running fast enough. The boy caught my hand and pulled me along faster. He glanced back at me, and I caught a glimpse of a high-cheekboned, pointed face that would one day be handsome.

"Where are you taking me?" My ability to reason was returning, though slowly. "To Viraine?"

He uttered a derisive snort. We left the arena and passed into more of the mazelike white halls. "Don't be foolish. We're going to hide."

"But that man—" Nahadoth. Now I remembered where I'd heard the name. *Never whisper it in the dark,* read the children's tales, *unless you want him to answer.*

"Oh, so now he's a man? We just have to keep ahead of him and everything will be fine." The boy ran around a corner, more nimble than me; I stumbled to keep up. He darted his eyes around the corridor, looking for something. "Don't worry. I get away from him all the time."

This did not sound wise. "I w-want to go to Viraine." I tried to say it with authority, but I was still too frightened, and winded now besides.

The boy responded by stopping, but not because of me. "Here!" he said, and put his hand against one of the pearlescent walls. "*Atadie!*"

The wall opened.

It was like watching ripples in water. The pearly stuff moved away from his hand in steady waves, forming an opening—a hole—a door. Beyond the wall lay an oddly shaped, narrow chamber, not so much a room as a *space between*. When the door was big enough for us both, the boy pulled me inside.

"What is this?" I asked.

"Dead space in the body of the palace. All these curving corridors and round rooms. There's another half a palace in between that no one uses—except me." The boy turned to me and flashed an up-to-no-good grin. "We can rest for a little while."

I was beginning to catch my breath, and with it came a weakness that I recognized as the aftermath of adrenaline. The wall had rippled shut behind me, becoming as solid as before. I leaned back against it gingerly at first, then gratefully. And then I examined my rescuer.

He wasn't much smaller than me, maybe nine years old, with the spindly look of a fast grower. Not Amn, not with skin as dark as mine and sharpfold eyes like those of the Tema people. They were a murky, tired green, those eyes—like my own, and my mother's. Maybe his father had been another wandering Arameri.

He was examining me as well. After a moment, his grin widened. "I'm Sieh."

Two syllables. "Sieh Arameri?"

"Just Sieh." With a child's boneless grace, he stretched his arms above his head. "You don't look like much."

I was too tired to take offense. "I've found it useful," I replied, "to be underestimated."

"Yes. Always good strategy, that." Lightning-quick, he straightened and grew serious. "He'll find us if we don't keep moving. *En!*"

I jumped, startled by his shout. But Sieh was looking up. A moment later, a child's yellow kickball fell into his hands.

Puzzled, I looked up. The dead space went up several floors, a featureless triangular shaft; I saw no openings from which the ball could have come. There was certainly no one hovering above who could have thrown the ball to him.

I looked at the boy and suffered a sudden, chilling suspicion.

Sieh laughed at my face and put the ball on the floor. Then he sat on it, cross-legged. The ball held perfectly still beneath him until he was comfortable, and then it rose into the air. It stopped when he was a few feet above the ground and hovered. Then the boy who was not a boy reached out to me.

"I won't hurt you," he said. "I'm helping you, aren't I?"

I just looked at his hand, pressing myself back against the wall.

"I could have led you in a circle, you know. Right back to him."

There was that. After a moment, I took his hand. His grip left no question; this was not a child's strength.

"Just a little ways," he said. Then, dangling me like a snared rabbit, he floated us both up through the shaft.

There is another thing I remember from my childhood. A song, and it went...How did it go? Ah, yes. *"Trickster, trickster / Stole the sun for a prank. / Will you really ride it? / Where will you hide it? / Down by the riverbank . . ."*

It was not *our* sun, mind you.

Sieh opened two ceilings and another wall before finally setting me down in a dead space that was as big as Grandfather Dekarta's audience chamber. But it was not the size of this space that made my mouth gape.

More spheres floated in this room, dozens of them. They were fantastically varied—of all shapes and sizes and colors—turning slowly and drifting through the air. They seemed to be nothing more than a child's toys, until I looked closely at one and saw clouds swirling over its surface.

Sieh hovered near as I wandered among his toys, his expression somewhere between anxiety and pride. The yellow ball had taken up position near the center of the room; all the other balls revolved around it.

"They're pretty, aren't they?" he asked me, while I stared at a tiny red marble. A great cloud mass—a storm?—devoured the nearer hemisphere. I tore my eyes from it to look at Sieh. He bounced on his toes, impatient for my answer. "It's a good collection."

Trickster, trickster, stole the sun for a prank. And apparently because it was pretty. The Three had borne many children before their falling-out. Sieh was immeasurably old, another of the Arameri's deadly weapons, and yet I could not bring myself to dash the shy hope I saw in his eyes.

"They're all beautiful," I agreed. It was true.

He beamed and took my hand again—not pulling me anywhere, just feeling companionable. "I think the others will like you," he said. "Even Naha, when he calms down. It's been a long time since we had a mortal of our own to talk to."

His words were gibberish strung together without meaning. Others? Naha? Calm?

He laughed at me again. "I especially like your face. You don't show much emotion—is that a Darre thing, or your mother's training?—but when you do, all the world can read it."

My mother had warned me of the same thing long ago. "Sieh—" I had a thousand questions and couldn't decide where to begin. One of the balls, a plain green one with bright white poles, went past us, tumbling end over end. I didn't register it as an anomaly until Sieh saw it and stiffened. That was when my own instincts belatedly sent a warning.

I turned to find that Nahadoth stood behind us.

In the instant that my mind and body froze, he could have had me. He was only a few paces away. But he did not move or speak, and so we stared at each other. Face like the moon, pale and somehow wavering. I could get the gist of his features, but none of it stuck in my mind beyond an impression of astonishing beauty. His long, long hair wafted around him like black smoke, its tendrils curling and moving of their own volition. His cloak—or perhaps that was hair, too—shifted as if in an unfelt wind. I could not recall him wearing a cloak before, on the balcony.

The madness still lurked in his face, but it was a quieter madness now, not the rabid-animal savagery of before. Something else—I could not bring myself to call it humanity—stirred underneath the gleam.

Sieh stepped forward, careful not to move in front of me. "Are you with us yet, Naha?"

Nahadoth did not answer, did not even seem to see Sieh. Sieh's toys, I noticed with the fragment of my mind that wasn't frozen, went wild when they came near him. Their slow, graceful orbits changed: some drifted in a different direction, some froze in place, some sped up. One split in half and fell broken to the floor as I watched. He took a step forward, sending more of the colored balls spinning out of control.

That one step was enough to jar me out of my paralysis. I stumbled back and would have fled screaming if I'd known how to make the walls open.

"Don't run!" Sieh's voice snapped at me like a whip. I froze.

Nahadoth stepped forward again, close enough that I could see a minute shiver pass through him. His hands flexed. He opened his mouth; struggled a moment; spoke. "P-predictable, Sieh." His voice was deep, but shockingly human. I had expected a bestial growl.

Sieh hunched, a sulky little boy again. "Didn't think you'd catch up that fast." He cocked his head, studying Nahadoth's face, and spoke slowly, as if to a simpleton. "You are here, aren't you?"

"I can *see* it," whispered the Nightlord. His eyes were fixed on my face.

To my surprise, Sieh nodded as if he knew what such ravings meant. "I wasn't expecting that, either," he said softly. "But perhaps you remember now—we need this one. Do you remember?" Sieh stepped forward, reaching for his hand.

I did not see that hand move. I was watching Nahadoth's face. All I saw was the flash of blind, murderous rage that crossed his features, and then one of his hands was 'round Sieh's throat. Sieh had no chance to cry out before he was lifted off the ground, gagging and kicking.

For a breath I was too shocked to react.

Then I got angry.

I *burned* with anger—and madness, too, which is the only possible explanation for what I did then. I drew my knife and cried, "Leave him alone!"

As well a rabbit threaten a wolf. But to my utter shock, the Nightlord looked at me. He did not lower Sieh, but he blinked. Just that quickly, the madness left him, replaced by a look of astonishment and dawning wonder. It was the look of a man who has just discovered treasure beneath a pile of offal. But he was still choking the life out of Sieh.

"Let him go!" I crouched, shifting my stance the way my Darren grandmother had taught me. My hands shook—not with fear, but with that mad, wild, righteous fury. Sieh was a *child*. "Stop it!"

Nahadoth smiled.

I lunged. The knife went into his chest, going deep before lodging in bone with such a sudden impact that my hand was jarred free of the hilt. There was an instant in which I braced myself against his chest, trying to push away. I marveled that he was solid, warm, flesh and blood despite the power writhing about him. I marveled even more when his free hand wrapped around my wrist like a vise. So fast, despite the knife in his heart.

With the strength in that hand, he could have crushed my wrist. Instead he held me in place. His blood coated my hand, hotter than my rage. I looked up; his eyes were warm, gentle, desperate. *Human.*

"I have waited so long for you," the god breathed. Then he kissed me.

Then he fell.

4

Magician

WHEN THE NIGHTLORD SAGGED to the ground, dropping Sieh in the process, I nearly fell with them. I had no idea why I was still alive. The tales of the Arameri's weapons are full of them slaughtering whole armies. There are no stories of crazed barbarian girls fighting back.

Sieh, to my great relief, immediately pushed himself up on his elbows. He seemed fine, though his eyes went very round at the sight of Nahadoth's motionless form. "Look what you did!"

"I . . ." I was shaking, almost too hard to talk. "I didn't mean . . . He was killing you. I couldn't"—I swallowed hard—"let him."

"Nahadoth would not have killed Sieh," said a new voice behind me. My nerves did not like this. I jumped and grabbed for the knife that was no longer tucked into my back-sheath. A woman resolved out of the silent drift of Sieh's toys. The first thing I noticed was that she was huge, like the great sea ships of the Ken. She was built like one of those ships, too, broad and powerful and astonishingly graceful; none of it was fat. I could not guess her race, because no woman of any race I knew was that damned big.

She knelt to help Sieh up. Sieh was shaking, too, though with excitement. "Did you see what she did?" he asked the newcomer. He pointed at Nahadoth; he was grinning.

"Yes, I saw." Setting Sieh on his feet, the woman turned to

regard me for a moment. Kneeling, she was taller than Sieh standing. Her clothing was simple—gray tunic and pants, a gray kerchief covering her hair. Maybe it was her *grayness* after the unrelenting black of the Nightlord, but there was something about her that seemed fundamentally gentle to me.

"There is no greater warrior than a mother protecting her child," the woman said. "But Sieh is far less fragile than you, Lady Yeine."

I nodded slowly, not allowing myself to feel foolish. Logic had not been part of what I'd done.

Sieh came over and took my hand. "Thank you anyway," he said shyly. The purpled, ugly handprint around his throat was fading even as I watched.

We all looked over at Nahadoth. He sat on his knees as he had fallen, the knife still hilt-deep in his chest, his head slumped. With a soft sigh, the gray woman went to him and pulled the knife out. I had felt it lodge in bone, but she made the withdrawal look easy. She examined it, shook her head, then offered it to me hilt first.

I made myself take it, getting more god's blood on my hand. I thought that she held the blade more firmly than necessary because my hand was shaking so badly. But as I got a better grip on the hilt, the woman's fingers trailed down the blade. When I had the knife again, I realized that not only was it clean of blood, but it was a different shape—curved now—and finely honed.

"That suits you better," said the woman, giving a solemn nod at my stare. Unthinking, I put the knife into its sheath at the small of my back, though it should no longer have fit. It did; the sheath had changed, too.

"So, Zhakka, you like her." Sieh leaned against me, wrapping his arms around my waist and resting his head on my breast. Immortal or not, there was such innocence in the way he did it that I did not push him away. I put my arm around him without thinking, and he uttered a deep, contented sigh.

"Yes," said the woman without prevarication. She leaned forward, peering into Nahadoth's face. "Father?"

I did not jump, not with Sieh leaning against me, but he felt me stiffen. "Shhh," he said, rubbing my back. That touch was not quite childlike enough to be truly soothing. A moment later, Nahadoth stirred.

"You're back," said Sieh, straightening with a bright smile. I took that opportunity to step away from Nahadoth. Sieh caught my hand quickly, all earnestness. "It's all right, Yeine. He's different now. You're safe."

"She will not believe you," said Nahadoth. He sounded like a man waking from a deep sleep. "She will not trust us now."

"It isn't your fault." Sieh sounded unhappy. "We just need to explain, and she'll understand."

Nahadoth looked at me, which made me jump again, though it seemed the madness was indeed gone. Nor did I see that other look—when he'd held my hand in his heartblood and whispered soft, longing words. And that kiss...no. I had imagined it. That was clear, as the Nightlord who sat before me now was detached, regal even on his knees, and contemptuous. I was reminded painfully of Dekarta.

"Will you understand?" he asked me.

I could not help taking another step back in answer. Nahadoth shook his head and rose, nodding gracefully to the woman Sieh had called Zhakka. Though Zhakka towered over

Nahadoth, there was no question which was the superior and which the subordinate.

"We have no time for this," Nahadoth said. "Viraine will be looking for her. Mark her and be done with it." Zhakka nodded and came toward me. I stepped back a third time, unnerved by the intent in her eyes.

Sieh let go of me and stood between us, a flea confronting a dog. He barely came up to Zhakka's waist. "This isn't the way we were supposed to do it. We agreed to try and win her over."

"That isn't possible now," said Nahadoth.

"What's to stop her from telling Viraine about this, then?" Sieh put his hands on his hips. Zhakka had stopped, waiting patiently for the dispute to be resolved. I felt forgotten and supremely unimportant—as I probably should, given that I stood in the presence of three gods. The term *former* gods just didn't seem to fit.

Nahadoth's face showed something less than a smile. He glanced at me. "Tell Viraine and we'll kill you." His gaze returned to Sieh. "Satisfied?"

I must have been tired. After so many threats that evening, I didn't even flinch.

Sieh frowned and shook his head, but he stepped out of Zhakka's path. "This wasn't what we'd planned," he said with a hint of petulance.

"Plans change," said Zhakka. Then she stood before me.

"What are you going to do?" I asked. Somehow, despite her size, she did not frighten me near as much as Nahadoth.

"I will mark your brow with a sigil," she said. "One that cannot be seen. It will interfere with the sigil Viraine intends to put on you. You will look like one of them, but in truth you'll be free."

"Are they..." All the sigil-marked Arameri? Was that who she meant? "...not free?"

"No more than we, for all they think otherwise," said Nahadoth. There was, for just that moment, a hint of the softness in him that I'd seen before. Then he turned away. "Hurry up."

Zhakka nodded, and touched my forehead with the tip of a finger. Her fists were the size of dinner plates; her finger seemed to sear like a brand when it touched me. I cried out and tried to slap her finger away, but she lifted her hand before I could. She was done.

Sieh, his sulk forgotten, peered at the spot and nodded sagely. "That will do."

"Take her to Viraine, then," said Zhakka. She inclined her head to me in courteous farewell, then turned away to join Nahadoth.

Sieh took my hand. I was so confused and shaken that I did not fight when he led me toward the nearest of the dead space's walls. But I did glance back over my shoulder once, to watch the Nightlord walk away.

My mother was the most beautiful woman in the world. I say that not because I am her daughter, and not because she was tall and graceful, with hair like clouded sunlight. I say it because she was strong. Perhaps it is my Darre heritage, but strength has always been the marker of beauty in my eyes.

My people were not kind to her. No one said it in front of my father, but I heard the murmurs when we walked through Arrebaia sometimes. *Amn whore. Bone-white bitch.* They would spit on the ground after she passed, to wash the streets of her Arameri taint. Through all this she maintained her dignity and was never less than polite to people who were anything but. My father, in one of the few clear memories of him that I have, said this made her better than them.

I am not sure why I remember this now, but I am certain it is somehow important.

Sieh made me run after we left the dead space, so that I would be out of breath when we arrived at Viraine's workshop.

Viraine opened the door after Sieh's third impatient knock, looking irritated. The white-haired man from Dekarta's audience, who had judged me "not hopeless."

"Sieh? What in demons—ah." He looked at me and raised his eyebrows. "Yes, I'd rather thought T'vril was taking too long. The sun went down nearly an hour ago."

"Scimina sicced Naha on her," said Sieh. Then he looked up at me. "But the game was to end if you made it here, right? You're safe now."

This was my explanation, then. "That was what T'vril said." I glanced back down the hall as if I was still afraid. It was not difficult to pretend.

"Scimina would have given him specific parameters," Viraine said, which I suppose was meant to reassure me. "She knows what he's like in that state. Come in, Lady Yeine."

He stepped aside, and I entered the chamber. Even if I hadn't been bone tired I would have stopped there, for I stood in a room like nothing I had ever seen. It was long and oval-shaped, and there were floor-to-ceiling windows down both of the longer walls. Twin rows of workbenches had been placed along either side of the room; I saw books, flasks, and incomprehensible contraptions on each. Along the far wall were cages, some containing rabbits and birds. In the center of the chamber was a huge white orb set on a low plinth. It was as tall as me and completely opaque.

"Over here," Viraine said, heading toward one of the workbenches. Two stools sat in front of it. He chose one of them and patted the other for me. I followed him, but then hesitated.

"I'm afraid you have the advantage of me, sir."

He looked surprised, then smiled and gave me an informal, not-quite-mocking half bow. "Ah, yes, manners. I am Viraine, the palace scrivener. Also a relative of yours in some way or another—too distant and convoluted to determine, though Lord Dekarta has seen fit to welcome me into the Central Family." He tapped the black circle on his forehead.

Scriveners: Amn scholars who made a study of the gods' written language. This scrivener did not look like the cold-eyed ascetics I'd imagined. He was younger, for one—perhaps a few years younger than my mother had been. Certainly not old enough for such stark white hair. Perhaps he was like T'vril and me, part Amn of a more exotic variety.

"A pleasure," I said. "Though I cannot help but wonder why the palace needs a scrivener. Why study the gods' power when you have actual gods right here?"

He looked pleased by my question; perhaps few people asked him about his work. "Well, for one thing, they can't do everything or be everywhere. There are hundreds of people in this palace using small magics on an everyday basis. If we had to stop and call an Enefadeh every time we needed something, very little would get done. The lift, for example, that carried you to this level of the palace. The air—this far above the ground, it would ordinarily be thin and cold, hard to breathe. Magic keeps the palace comfortable."

I sat down carefully on one of the stools, eyeing the bench beside me. The items there were laid out neatly: various fine paintbrushes, a dish of ink, and a small block of polished stone, incised on its face with a strange, complicated character of spikes and curlicues. The character was so fundamentally alien, so jarring to the eye, that I could not look at it long. The urge to look away was part of what it was, because it was gods' language; a sigil.

Viraine sat opposite me while Sieh, unbidden, claimed a seat across the bench and rested his chin on his folded arms.

"For another thing," Viraine continued, "there are certain magics that even the Enefadeh cannot perform. Gods are peculiar beings, incredibly powerful within their sphere of influence, so to speak, but limited beyond that. Nahadoth is powerless by day. Sieh cannot be quiet and well-behaved unless he's up to something." He eyed Sieh, who gave us both an innocent smile. "In many ways, we mortals are more . . . versatile, for lack of a better term. More *complete*. For example, none of them can create or extend life. The simple act of having children— something any unlucky barmaid or careless soldier can do—is a power that has been lost to the gods for millennia."

From the corner of my eye, I saw Sieh's smile fade.

"*Extend* life?" I had heard rumors about what some scriveners did with their powers—terrible, foul rumors. It occurred to me suddenly that my grandfather was very, very old.

Viraine nodded, his eyes twinkling at the disapproval in my tone. "It is the great quest of our profession. Someday we might even achieve immortality..." He read the horror in my face and smiled. "Though that goal is not without controversy."

My grandmother had always said the Amn were unnatural people. I looked away. "T'vril said you were going to mark me."

He grinned, openly amused now. Laughing at the prudish savage. "Mmm-hmm."

"What does this mark do?"

"Keeps the Enefadeh from killing you, among other things. You've seen what they can be like."

I licked my lips. "Ah. Yes. I...didn't know they were..." I gestured vaguely, unsure how to say what I meant without offending Sieh.

"Running around loose?" Sieh asked brightly. There was a wicked look in his eye; he was enjoying my discomfiture.

I winced. "Yes."

"Mortal form is their prison," Viraine said, ignoring Sieh. "And every soul in Sky, their jailer. They are bound by Bright Itempas to serve the descendants of Shahar Arameri, His greatest priestess. But since Shahar's descendants now number in the thousands..." He gestured toward the windows, as if the whole world was one clan. Or perhaps he simply meant Sky, the only world that mattered to him. "Our ancestors chose to impose a more orderly structure on the situation. The mark confirms for the Enefadeh that you're Arameri; without it they will not obey you. It also specifies your rank within the family. How close you are to the main line of descent, I mean, which in turn dictates how much power you have to command them."

He picked up a brush, though he did not dip it in the ink; instead he reached up to my face, pushing my hair back from my forehead. My heart clenched as he examined me. Clearly

Viraine was some sort of expert; could he truly not see Zhakka's mark? For an instant I thought he had, because his eyes flicked down to hold mine for half a breath. But apparently the gods had done their work well, because after a moment Viraine let my hair go and began to stir the ink.

"T'vril said the mark was permanent," I said, mostly to quell my nervousness. The black liquid looked like simple writing ink, though the sigil-marked block was clearly no ordinary inkstone.

"Unless Dekarta orders it removed, yes. Like a tattoo, though painless. You'll get used to it."

I was not fond of a permanent mark, though I knew better than to protest. To distract myself I asked, "Why do you call them Enefadeh?"

The look that crossed Viraine's face was fleeting, but I recognized it by instinct: calculation. I had just revealed some stunning bit of ignorance to him, and he meant to use it.

Casually, Viraine jabbed a thumb at Sieh, who was surreptitiously eyeing the items on Viraine's worktable. "It's what they call themselves. We just find the label convenient."

"Why not—"

"We don't call them gods." Viraine smiled faintly. "That would be an offense to the Skyfather, our only true god, and those of the Skyfather's children who stayed loyal. But we can't call them slaves, either. After all, we outlawed slavery centuries ago."

This was the sort of thing that made people hate the Arameri—truly hate them, not just resent their power or their willingness to use it. They found so many ways to lie about the things they did. It mocked the suffering of their victims.

"Why not just call them what they are?" I asked. "Weapons."

Sieh glanced at me, his gaze too neutral to be a child's in that instant.

Viraine winced delicately. "Spoken like a true barbarian," he said, and though he smiled, that did nothing to alleviate the insult. "The thing you must understand, Lady Yeine, is that like our ancestress Shahar, we Arameri are first and foremost the servants of Itempas Skyfather. It is in His name that we have imposed the age of the Bright upon the world. Peace, order, enlightenment." He spread his hands. "Itempas's servants do not use, or need, weapons. Tools, though..."

I had heard enough. I had no idea of his rank relative to mine, but I was tired and confused and far from home, and if barbarians' manners would serve better to get me through this day, then so be it.

"Does 'Enefadeh' mean 'tool,' then?" I demanded. "Or is it just 'slave' in another tongue?"

"It means 'we who remember Enefa,'" said Sieh. He had propped his chin on his fist. The items on Viraine's workbench looked the same, but I was certain he had done something to them. "She was the one murdered by Itempas long ago. We went to war with Him to avenge her."

Enefa. The priests never said her name. "The Betrayer," I murmured without thought.

"She betrayed no one," Sieh snapped.

Viraine's glance at Sieh was heavy-lidded and unreadable. "True. A whore's business can hardly be termed a betrayal, can it?"

Sieh hissed. For an eyeblink there was something inhuman about his face—something sharp and feral—and then he was a boy again, sliding off the stool and trembling with fury. For a moment I half-expected him to poke out his tongue, but the hatred in his eyes was too old for that.

"I will laugh when you're dead," he said softly. The small hairs along my skin prickled, for his voice was a grown man's now, tenor malevolence. "I will claim your heart as a toy and kick it for a hundred years. And when I am finally free, I will hunt down all your descendants and make their children just like me."

With that, he vanished. I blinked. Viraine sighed.

"And that, Lady Yeine, is why we use the blood sigils," he said. "Silly as that threat was, he meant every word of it. The sigil prevents him from carrying it out, yet even that protection is limited. A higher-ranking Arameri's order, or stupidity on your part, could leave you vulnerable."

I frowned, remembering the moment when T'vril had urged me to get to Viraine. *Only a fullblood can command him off now.* And T'vril was a—what had he called it?—a halfblood.

"Stupidity on my part?" I asked.

Viraine gave me a hard look. "They must respond to any imperative statement you make, Lady. Consider how many such statements we make carelessly, or figuratively, with no thought given to other interpretations." When I frowned in thought, he rolled his eyes. "The common folk are fond of saying 'To the hells with you!' Ever said it yourself, in a moment of anger?" At my slow nod, he leaned closer. "The subject of the phrase is implied, of course; we usually mean 'You should go.' But the phrase could also be understood as 'I want to go, and you will take me.'"

He paused to see if I understood. I did. At my shudder, he nodded and sat back.

"Just don't talk to them unless you have to," he said. "Now. Shall we—" He reached for the ink dish and cursed as it toppled the instant his fingers touched it; Sieh had somehow lodged a brush underneath. The ink splattered across the tabletop like

like

and then Viraine touched my hand. "Lady Yeine? Are you all right?"

That was how it happened, yes. The first time.

I blinked. "What?"

He smiled, all condescending kindness again. "Been a hard day, has it? Well, this won't take long." He'd cleaned up the ink spill; there was enough left in the dish that apparently he could continue. "If you could hold your hair back for me..."

I didn't move. "Why did Grandfather Dekarta do this, Scrivener Viraine? Why did he bring me here?"

He raised his eyebrows, as if surprised that I would even ask. "I'm not privy to his thoughts. I have no idea."

"Is he senile?"

He groaned. "You really are a savage. No, he isn't senile."

"Then why?"

"I just told you—"

"If he wanted to kill me, he could have simply had me executed. Trump up an excuse, if he even bothered. Or he could have done what he did to my mother. An assassin in the night, poison in my sleep."

I had finally surprised him. He grew very still, his eyes meeting mine and then flicking away. "I would not confront Dekarta with the evidence, if I were you."

At least he hadn't tried to deny it.

"I hardly needed evidence. A healthy woman in her forties doesn't die in her sleep. But I had her body searched by the physician. There was a mark, a small puncture, on her forehead. On the—" I trailed off for a moment, suddenly understanding something I'd never questioned in my life. "On the scar she had, right here." I touched my own forehead, where my Arameri sigil would be.

Viraine faced me full-on now, quiet and serious. "If an Arameri assassin left a mark that could be seen—and if you expected to see it—then, Lady Yeine, you understand more of Dekarta's intentions than any of us. Why do *you* think he brought you here?"

I shook my head slowly. All along the journey to Sky, I'd suspected. Dekarta was angry at my mother, hated my father. There could be no good reason for his invitation. In the back of my mind I'd expected to be executed at best, perhaps tortured first, maybe on the steps of the Salon. My grandmother had been afraid for me. If there'd been any hope of escape, I think she would have urged me to run. But one does not run from the Arameri.

And a Darre woman does not run from revenge.

"This mark," I said at last. "It will help me survive this place?"

"Yes. The Enefadeh won't be able to hurt you unless you do something stupid. As for Scimina, Relad, and other dangers..." He shrugged. "Well. Magic can only do so much."

I closed my eyes and traced my mother's face against my memory for the ten thousandth time. She had died with tears on her cheeks, perhaps knowing what I would face.

"Then let's begin," I said.

5

Chaos

THAT NIGHT AS I SLEPT, I dreamt of him.

It is an ugly, stormcloud-choked night.

Above the clouds, the sky is lightening with the approach of dawn. Below the clouds, this has made absolutely no difference in the battlefield's illumination. A thousand torches burning amid a hundred thousand soldiers are more than enough light. The capital, too, is a gentle radiance nearby.

(It is not the Sky that I know. This city sprawls across a floodplain rather than over a hill, and the palace is embedded at its heart, not hovering overhead. I am not me.)

"A respectable force," says Zhakka, beside me. Zhakkarn, I know now, goddess of battle and bloodshed. In place of her usual headscarf is a helm that fits her head almost as closely. She wears shining silver armor, its surface a glory of engraved sigils and incomprehensible designs that glow red as if hot. There is a message written in the gods' words there. Memories I should not possess tease me with its meaning, though in the end they fail.

"Yes," I say, and my voice is male, though high-pitched and nasal. I know myself to be Arameri. I feel myself to be powerful. I am the family head. "I would have been offended if they had come with even one soldier less."

"Then since you are not offended, perhaps you can parley with them," says a woman beside me. She is sternly beautiful: her hair is the color of bronze, and a pair of enormous wings feathered in gold, silver, and platinum are folded on her back. Kurue, called Wise.

I feel arrogance. *"Parley? They're not worth the time."*

(I do not think I like this other me.)

"What then?"

I turn to look at the ones behind me. Sieh sits cross-legged on his floating yellow ball. He has propped his chin on his fist; he is bored. Beyond Sieh lurks a smoking, pent presence. I had not noticed this one move behind me. He watches me as if he has been imagining my death.

I make myself smile, unwilling to reveal how he unnerves me. *"Well, Nahadoth? How long has it been since you had any fun?"*

I have surprised him. It gratifies me to realize that I can. An eagerness fills his face that is chilling to behold, but I have given no command, and so he waits.

The others are surprised, too, less pleasantly. Sieh straightens and glares at me. *"Are you out of your mind?"*

Kurue is more diplomatic. *"That is unnecessary, Lord Haker. Zhakkarn or even I can take care of this army."*

"Or me," says Sieh, stung.

I look at Nahadoth and consider how the stories will go when word spreads that I unleashed the Nightlord on those who dared to challenge me. He is the most powerful of my weapons, yet I have never witnessed any significant display of his capabilities. I am curious.

"Nahadoth," I say. His stillness and the power I have over him are thrilling, but I know to keep my head. I have heard the stories, passed

down from previous family heads. It is important to give just the right instructions. He thinks in loopholes.

"Go onto the battlefield and dispose of this army. Do not allow them to advance on this position, or Sky. Do not allow survivors to escape." I almost forget but quickly add, "And do not kill me in the process."

"Is that all?" he asks.

"Yes."

He smiles. "As you wish."

"You're a fool," says Kurue, abandoning politeness. The other me ignores her.

"Keep him safe," says Nahadoth to his children. He is still smiling as he walks onto the battlefield.

The enemy are so numerous that I cannot see the end of them. As Nahadoth walks toward their front line he seems tiny. Helpless. Human. I can hear, echoing across the flat expanse of the plain, some among their soldiers laughing. The commanders at the center of the line are silent. They know what he is.

Nahadoth holds his hands out from his sides, and a great curved sword appears in each. He runs at the line, a black streak, and pierces it like an arrow. Shields split; armor and swords shatter; body parts fly. The enemy dies by the dozen. I clap and laugh. "What a marvelous show!"

Around me, the other Enefadeh are tense and afraid.

Nahadoth cuts a swath through the army until he reaches its general center. No one can stand against him. When he finally stops, having carved a circle of death 'round himself, the enemy soldiers are falling over themselves trying to get away. I cannot see him well from here, even though the black smoke of his aura seems to have flared higher in the intervening minutes.

"The sun comes," says Zhakkarn.

"Not soon enough," says Kurue.

At the center of the army, there is a sound. No, not a sound, a vibration. Like a pulse, except that it shakes the whole earth.

And then a black star blazes to life at the army's heart. I can think of no other words to describe it. It is a sphere of darkness so concentrated that it glows, so heavy with power that the earth groans and sags beneath it. A pit forms, radiating deep cracks. The enemy fall inward. I cannot hear their screams because the black star sucks in the sound. It sucks in their bodies. It sucks in everything.

The earth shakes so violently that I fall to my hands and knees. There is a hollow, rushing roar all around me. I look up to see that the very air is visible as it flies past, sucked down into the pit and the ravening horror that Nahadoth has become. Kurue and the others are around me, murmuring in their tongue to command the winds and whatever other terrible forces their father has unleashed. Because of that we are safe, enclosed in a bubble of calm, but nothing else is. Above us, the very clouds have bent, funneling down into the star. The enemy army is gone. All that remains is the land we stand on, and the continent around it, and the planet beneath that.

I finally realize my error: with his children protecting me, Nahadoth is free to devour it all.

It takes all my will to overcome my own choking fear. "S-stop!" I shout. "Nahadoth, stop!" The words are lost in the howling wind. He is bound by magic even more powerful than himself to obey my commands, but only if he can hear me. Perhaps he intended to drown me out—or perhaps he is simply lost in the glory of his own power, reveling in the chaos that is his nature.

The pit beneath him erupts as he strikes molten rock. A tendril of fiery lava rises and swirls about the blackness before it, too, is swallowed. Tornado above, volcano below, and at the heart of it, the black star, growing ever larger.

It is, in a terrible way, the most beautiful thing I have ever seen.

At the end, we are saved by the Skyfather. The torn clouds reveal a light-streaked sky, and in the instant that I feel the stones beneath my hands shiver, ready to fly away, the sun peeks above the horizon.

The black star vanishes.

Something—charred, pitiful, not enough of a human form to be called a body—hovers in the star's place for a moment, then falls toward the lava below. Sieh curses and streaks off on his yellow ball, breaking the bubble, but the bubble is no longer necessary. The air is hot and thin around me; it is hard to breathe. Already I can see stormclouds forming in the distance and rushing this way to fill the void.

The nearby capital . . . oh. Oh, no.

I see the broken shells of a few buildings. The rest has been devoured. Part of the land has fallen into the churning red pit; the palace was on that land.

My wife. My son.

Zhakkarn looks at me. She is too much the soldier to show her contempt, though I know she feels it. Kurue helps me to my feet, and her face, too, is blank as she faces me. You have done this, *her eyes say.*

I will think it over and over as I mourn.

"Sieh has him," says Zhakkarn. "It will take him years to recover."

"He had no business calling on that kind of power," Kurue snaps. "Not in human flesh."

"It doesn't matter," I say, and for once I am right.

The earth has not stopped shaking. Nahadoth has broken something deep within it. This was once beautiful country, the perfect seat for the capital of a global empire. Now it is ruined.

"Take me away," I whisper.

"Where?" asks Zhakkarn. My home is gone.

I almost say anywhere, but I am not a complete fool. These beings are not as volatile as Nahadoth, not as hateful, but neither are they my friends. One colossal folly for the day is enough.

"To Senm," I say. "The Amn homeland. We will rebuild there."

So they carry me away. Behind me, over the next few days, the continent breaks apart and sinks into the sea.

6

Alliances

Yeine." My mother, murdered by jealousy, grasps my hand. I hold the hilt of a dagger that has been thrust into my own breast. Blood hotter than rage coats my hand; she leans close to kiss me. "You're dead."

You lie, Amn whore, bone-white bitch. I will see all your lying kind swallowed into the darkest depths of

myself

There was another Consortium session the next morning. Apparently this was the body's peak season, in which they met every day for several weeks trying to resolve fiscal business before a lengthy winter break. T'vril arrived early that morning to wake me for the occasion, which took some doing. When I got up, my feet ached dully, as did the bruises I'd sustained running from Nahadoth the night before. I'd slept like death, exhausted emotionally and physically.

"Dekarta attends nearly all the sessions, when his health permits," T'vril explained, while I dressed in the next room. The tailor had worked an overnight miracle, delivering me an entire rack of garments deemed appropriate for a woman of my station. He was very good; instead of simply hemming the long Amn styles, he'd given me a selection of skirts and dresses that complemented my shorter frame. They were still far more decorative and less practical than I was used to, not to mention constricting in all the oddest places. I felt ridiculous. But it would not do for an Arameri heir to look like a savage—even if she was one—so I asked T'vril to convey my thanks for the tailor's efforts.

Between the foreign garments and the stark black circle on my forehead, I barely recognized myself in the mirror.

"Relad and Scimina aren't required to attend—and they often don't," T'vril said. He'd come in to give me a shrewd once-over as I stood in the mirror; by his pleased nod, I evidently met with his approval. "But everyone knows them, while you're an unknown quantity. Dekarta asks that you attend today in particular, so that all can see his newest heir."

Which meant that I had no choice. I sighed and nodded. "I doubt most of the nobles will be pleased," I said. "I was too minor to be worth their time before this whole mess. I imagine they'll resent having to be nice to me now."

"You're probably right," T'vril said, airily unconcerned. He crossed the room to my windows, gazing out at the view while I fussed with my unruly hair in a mirror. This was just nerves on my part; my hair never looked any better.

"Dekarta doesn't waste his time with politics," T'vril continued. "He considers the Central Family above such things. So naturally, any nobles with a cause tend to approach Relad or Scimina. And now you."

Lovely. I sighed, turning to him. "I don't suppose there's any chance I might be disowned if I get myself involved in a scandal or two? Maybe then I could be banished to some backwater land up north."

"More likely you'd end up like my father," he said, shrugging. "That's the usual way the family deals with embarrassments."

"Oh." For a moment I felt uneasy for reminding him of tragedy, but then I realized he didn't care.

"In any case, Dekarta seems determined to have you here. I imagine that if you cause enough trouble, he'll simply have you trussed up and delivered to the succession ceremony at the appropriate time. Though for all I know, that's how the ceremony usually goes."

That surprised me. "You don't know?"

"About the ceremony?" T'vril shook his head. "Only members of the Central Family are allowed to witness that. There hasn't been one for forty years, anyhow—not since Dekarta's ascension."

"I see." I put aside this information to consider later. "All right, then. At the Salon, are there any nobles I should beware of?" He threw me a wry look, and I amended myself. "Any *in particular?*"

"You'll learn that before I will," he said. "I imagine both your allies and your enemies will introduce themselves rather quickly. In fact, I suspect *everything* will happen rather quickly, now. So, are you ready?"

I was not. And I wanted badly to ask him about his last comment. Things would happen even more quickly than they had been? Was that possible?

But my questions would have to wait for later. "I'm ready."

So T'vril led me out of the apartment and through the white corridors. My apartment, like that of most fullbloods, was on the topmost floor of Sky's main bulk, though I understood there were apartments and chambers within the spires as well. There was another, smaller Vertical Gate on this level, intended solely for fullblood use. Unlike the Gate in Sky's forecourt, T'vril explained, this Gate had more than one terminus; it apparently went to a number of offices in the city below. That way the full-bloods could conduct family business without getting rained or snowed upon—or without being seen in public, if they so wished.

No one else was about. "Has my grandfather already gone down?" I asked, stopping on the edge of the Gate. Like the main Gate and the palace lifts, it consisted of black tiles set into the floor in a mosaic that formed a gods' sigil. This one resembled nothing so much as a huge spiderwebbed crack in the floor: an uncomfortably suggestive similarity that made me look away more quickly than usual.

"Probably," T'vril said. "He likes to be early. Now, Lady Yeine, remember: at the Consortium you must not speak. The Ara-meri merely advise the nobles, and only Dekarta has the right to address them. He doesn't do it often. Don't even speak to him while you're there. Your task is simply to observe and be observed."

"And...introduced?"

"Formally? No, that will happen later. But they'll notice you, never fear. Dekarta won't need to say a word."

And with that, he nodded, and I stepped onto the mosaic.

One blurring, terrifying transition later, I found myself in a lovely marble room, standing atop a mosaic of inlaid blackwood. Three Consortium aides—not so junior this time, or so surprised—stood waiting to greet and escort me. I followed them through a shadowed corridor and up a carpeted ramp to find myself in the Arameri private box.

Dekarta sat in his customary place; he did not turn as I arrived. Scimina sat on his right side. She glanced around and smiled at me. I managed not to stop and glare, though it took a powerful effort on my part. But I was very aware of the gathering nobles, who milled around the Salon floor as they waited for the Overseer to begin the session. I saw more than a few glances directed toward the private box; they were watching.

So I inclined my head to Scimina in greeting, though I could not bring myself to return her smile.

Two chairs stood unoccupied at Dekarta's left. Assuming the nearer seat was for my yet-unseen cousin Relad, I moved to take the farther of the two. Then I caught Dekarta's hand movement; he did not look at me, but he beckoned me closer. So I took the nearer seat instead—just in time, as the Overseer called the meeting to order.

This time I paid more attention to what was going on. The meeting proceeded by region, beginning with the Senmite nations. Each region had its representative—nobles appointed by the Consortium to speak for themselves and their neighboring lands. The fairness of this representation varied widely, however, and I could not make heads or tails of how it was organized. The city of Sky had its own representative, for example, yet all the High North continent had only two. The latter did not surprise me—High North had never been highly regarded—but the former did, because no other single city had its own speaker. Sky wasn't *that* important.

But then, as the session went on, I saw that I'd misundertood. As I paid close attention to the edicts that Sky's representative put forth and supported, I realized that he spoke not just on behalf of Sky the city, but Sky the palace as well. Understandable, then, if unfair; Dekarta already commanded the entire world. The Consortium existed only to do the ugly, messy work of world governance, with which the Arameri couldn't be bothered. Everyone knew that. What was the point in being overrepresented on a governing body that was little more than a puppet show to begin with?

But perhaps that was just the way of power: no such thing as too much.

I found the High North representatives more interesting. I had never met either of them, though I recalled hearing complaints about them from the Darre Warriors' Council. The first, Wohi Ubm—I think the latter name was a title of some sort—came from the largest nation on the continent, a sleepy agrarian land called Rue, which had been one of Darr's strongest allies before my parents' marriage. Since then any correspondence that we sent her got returned unopened; she certainly didn't speak for my people. I noticed her glancing at me now and again as the session went on, and looking extremely uncomfortable as she did so. Had I been a more petty woman, I would have found her unease amusing.

The other High Norther was Ras Onchi, a venerable elder who spoke for the easterly kingdoms and the nearer islands. She didn't say much, being well past the usual age of retirement and, as rumor had it, a bit senile—but she was one of the few nobles on the floor who stared directly at me, for nearly the whole session. Her people were relatives of my own, with similar customs, and so I stared back as a show of respect, which seemed to please her. She nodded once, minutely, in a moment when Dekarta's head was turned away. I didn't dare nod back with so many eyes watching every move I made, but I was intrigued by the gesture all the same.

And then the session was over, as the Overseer rang the chime that closed the day's business. I tried not to exhale in relief, because the whole thing had lasted four hours. I was hungry, in dire need of the ladies' room, and restless to be up and moving about. Still, I followed Dekarta's and Scimina's lead and rose only when they rose, walking out with the same unhurried pace, nodding politely when a whole phalanx of aides descended upon us in escort.

"Uncle," said Scimina, as we walked back to the mosaic chamber, "perhaps Cousin Yeine would like to be shown around the Salon? She can't have seen much of it before."

As if anything would induce me to agree, after that patronizing suggestion. "No, thank you," I said, forcing a smile. "Though I would like to know where the ladies' room is."

"Oh—right this way, Lady Yeine," said one of the aides, stepping aside and gesturing for me to lead the way.

I paused, noting that Dekarta continued onward with no indication that he'd heard either me or Scimina. So that was how things went. I inclined my head to Scimina, who'd also stopped. "No need to wait on my account."

"As you like," she said, and turned gracefully to follow Dekarta.

I followed the aide down the longest hallway in the city, or so it felt, because now that I'd stood my bladder had become most insistent about being emptied. When we at last reached the small chamber—the door was marked *Private* in Senmite, and I took it to mean "for the highest-ranking Salon guests only"— it took all my willpower not to rush undignified into the very large, roomlike stall.

My business completed, I was beginning the complicated process of reassembling my Amn underclothes when I heard the outer chamber door open. *Scimina,* I thought, and stifled both annoyance and a hint of trepidation.

Yet when I emerged from the stall, I was surprised to see Ras Onchi beside the sinks, obviously waiting for me.

For a moment I considered letting my confusion show, then decided against it. I inclined my head instead and said in Nirva—the common tongue of the north long before the Arameri had imposed Senmite on the world—"Good afternoon to you, Auntie."

She smiled, flashing a mouth that was nearly toothless. Her voice lacked for nothing, though, when she spoke. "And to you," she said in the same language, "though I'm no auntie of yours. You're Arameri, and I am nothing."

I flinched before I could stop myself. What does one say to something like that? What did Arameri say? I didn't want to know. To break the awkwardness, I moved past her and began to wash my hands.

She watched me in the mirror. "You don't look much like your mother."

I frowned up at her. What was she about? "So I've been told."

"We were ordered not to speak to her, or your people," she said quietly. "Wohi and I, and Wohi's predecessor. The words came from the Consortium Overseer, but the sentiment?" She smiled. "Who knows? I just thought you might want to know."

This was rapidly beginning to feel like an entirely different conversation. I rinsed my hands, picked up a towel, and turned to her. "Have you got something to say to me, Old Aunt?"

Ras shrugged and turned to head for the door. As she turned, a necklace that she wore caught the light. It had an odd sort of pendant: like a tiny gold treenut or cherrystone. I hadn't noticed it before because it was half-hidden on a chain that dipped below her neckline. A link of chain had caught on her clothing, though, pulling the pendant up into view. I found myself staring at it rather than her.

"I have nothing to tell you that you don't already know," she said, as she walked away. "If you're Arameri, that is."

I scowled after her. "And if I'm not?"

She paused at the door and turned back to me, giving me a very shrewd look. Unthinkingly I straightened, so that she would think better of me. Such was her presence.

"If you're not Arameri," she said after a moment, "then we'll speak again." With that, she left.

I went back to Sky alone, feeling more out of place than ever.

I had been given three nations to oversee, as T'vril reminded me that afternoon, when he came to continue my hurried education in Arameri life.

Each of the three lands was bigger than my Darr. Each also had its own perfectly competent rulers, which meant that I had very little to do with regard to their management. They paid me a regular stipend for the privilege of my oversight, which they probably resented deeply, and which instantly made me wealthier than I'd ever been.

I was given another magic thing, a silvery orb that would,

on command, show me the face of any person I requested. If I tapped the orb a certain way, they would see my face, hovering in the air like some sort of decapitated spirit. I had been the recipient of such messages before—it was how I'd gotten the invitation from Grandfather Dekarta—and I found them unnerving. Still, this would allow me to communicate with my lands' rulers whenever I wished.

"I'd like to arrange a meeting with my lord cousin Relad as soon as possible," I said after T'vril finished showing me how to use the orb. "I don't know if he'll be any friendlier than Scimina, but I take heart in the fact that he hasn't tried to kill me yet."

"Wait," T'vril muttered.

Not promising. Still, I had a half-formed strategy in my head, and I wanted to pursue it. The problem was that I did not know the rules of this Arameri game of inheritance. How did one "win" when Dekarta himself would not choose? Relad knew the answer to that question, but would he share it with me? Especially when I had nothing to offer in return?

"Tender the invitation anyhow, please," I said. "In the meantime, it might be wise for me to meet with others in the palace who are influential. Who would you suggest?"

T'vril considered for a moment, then spread his hands. "You've already met everyone here who matters, except Relad."

I stared at him. "That can't be true."

He smiled without humor. "Sky is both very large and very small, Lady Yeine. There are other fullbloods, yes, but most of them waste their hours indulging all sorts of whims." He kept his face neutral, and I remembered the silver chain and collar Scimina had put on Nahadoth. Her perversity did not surprise me, for I had heard rumors of far worse within Sky's walls. What astounded me was that she dared play such games with that monster.

"The few fullbloods, halfbloods, and quarters who bother to do any legitimate work are often away from the palace," T'vril continued, "overseeing the family's business interests. Most of them have no hope of winning Dekarta's favor; he made that clear when he named his brother's children potential heirs rather than any of them. The ones who stay are the courtiers—pedants and sycophants for the most part, with impressive-sounding titles and no real power. Dekarta despises them, so you'd do better to avoid them altogether. Beyond that there are only servants."

I glanced at him. "Some servants can be useful to know."

He smiled unselfconsciously. "As I said, Lady Yeine—you've already met everyone who matters. Though I'm happy to arrange meetings for you with anyone you like."

I stretched, still stiff after the long hours of sitting at the Salon. As I did so, one of my bruises twinged, reminding me that I had more than earthly problems to worry about.

"Thank you for saving my life," I said.

T'vril chuckled with a hint of irony, though he looked pleased. "Well, as you suggested...it could be useful to have influence in certain quarters."

I inclined my head to acknowledge the debt. "If I have the power to help you in any way, please ask."

"As you like, Lady Yeine."

"Yeine."

He hesitated. "Cousin," he said instead, and smiled at me over his shoulder as he left my apartment. He really was a superb diplomat. I supposed that was a necessity for someone in his position.

I went from the sitting room into my bedroom and stopped.

"I thought he'd never leave," said Sieh, grinning from the middle of my bed.

I took a deep breath, slowly. "Good afternoon, Lord Sieh."

He pouted, flopping forward onto his belly and regarding me from his folded arms. "You're not happy to see me."

"I'm wondering what I've done to deserve such attention from a god of games and tricks."

"I'm not a god, remember?" He scowled. "Just a weapon. That word was more fitting than you know, Yeine, and how it burns these Arameri to hear it. No wonder they call you a barbarian."

I sat in the reading chair beside the bed. "My mother often told me I was too blunt," I said. "Why are you here?"

"Do I need a reason? Maybe I just like being around you."

"I would be honored if that were true," I said.

He laughed, high and carefree. "It *is* true, Yeine, whether you believe me or not." He got up then and began jumping on the bed. I wondered fleetingly whether anyone had ever tried to spank him.

"But?" I was sure there was a *but*.

He stopped after his third jump and glanced at me over his shoulder, his grin sly. "But it's not the only reason I came. The others sent me."

"For what reason?"

He hopped down from the bed and came over to my chair, putting his hands on my knees and leaning over me. He was still grinning, but again there was that indefinable something in his smile that was not childlike. Not at all.

"Relad isn't going to ally with you."

My stomach clenched in unease. Had he been in here

all along, listening to my conversation with T'vril? Or was my strategy for survival just so painfully obvious? "You know this?"

He shrugged. "Why would he? You're useless to him. He has his hands full dealing with Scimina and can't afford distractions. The time—of the succession, I mean—is too close."

I had suspected that as well. That was almost surely why they'd brought me here. It was probably why the family kept a scrivener in-house, to ensure that Dekarta didn't die off schedule. It might even have been the reason for my mother's murder after twenty years of freedom. Dekarta didn't have much time left to tie up loose ends.

Abruptly Sieh climbed into the chair with me, straddling my lap, knees on either side of my hips. I flinched in surprise, and again when he flopped against me, resting his head on my shoulder.

"What are you—?"

"Please, Yeine," he whispered. I felt his hands fist in the cloth of my jacket, at my sides. The gesture was so much that of a child seeking comfort that I could not help it; the stiffness went out of me. He sighed and snuggled closer, reveling in my tacit welcome. "Just let me do this a moment."

So I sat still, wondering many things.

I thought he had fallen asleep when he finally spoke. "Kurue—my sister, Kurue, our leader inasmuch as we have one—invites you to meet."

"Why?"

"You seek allies."

I pushed at him; he sat back on my knees. "What are you saying? Are you offering yourselves?"

"Maybe." The sly look was back. "You have to meet with us to find out."

I narrowed my eyes in what I hoped was an intimidating look. "Why? As you said, I'm useless. What would you gain from allying with me?"

"You have something very important," he said, serious now. "Something we could force you to give us—but we don't want to do that. We are not Arameri. You have proven yourself worthy of respect, and so we will *ask* you to give that something to us willingly."

I did not ask what they wanted. It was their bargaining chip; they would tell me if I met with them. I was rabidly curious, though—and excited, because he was right. The Enefadeh would make powerful, knowledgeable allies, even hobbled as they were. But I dared not reveal my eagerness. Sieh was nowhere near as childish, or as neutral, as he pretended to be.

"I will consider your request for a meeting," I said in my most dignified voice. "Please convey to the Lady Kurue that I will give you a response in no more than three days."

Sieh laughed and jumped off me, returning to the bed. He curled up in the middle of it and grinned at me. "Kurue's going to *hate* you. She thought you'd jump at the chance, and here you are keeping her waiting!"

"An alliance made in fear or haste will not last," I said. "I need a better understanding of my position before I do anything that will strengthen or weaken it. The Enefadeh must realize that."

"I do," he said, "but Kurue is wise and I'm not. She does what's smart. I do what's fun." He shrugged, then yawned. "Can I sleep here, sometimes, with you?"

I opened my mouth, then caught myself. He played innocent so well that I'd almost said yes automatically.

"I'm not sure that would be proper," I said at last. "You are very much older than me, and yet clearly underage. It would be a scandal, either way."

His eyebrows flew up almost into his hairline. Then he burst out laughing, rolling onto his back and holding his middle. He laughed for a long time. Eventually, a bit annoyed, I got up and went to the door to summon a servant and order lunch. I ordered two meals out of politeness, though I had no idea what, or whether, gods ate.

When I turned, Sieh had finally stopped laughing. He sat on the edge of the bed, watching me, thoughtful.

"I could be older," he said softly. "If you'd rather have me older, I mean. I don't have to be a child."

I stared at him and did not know whether to feel pity, nausea, or both at once.

"I want you to be what you are," I said.

His expression grew solemn. "That isn't possible. Not while I'm in this prison." He touched his chest.

"Do—" I did not want to call them my family. "Do others ask you to be older?"

He smiled. It was, most horribly, very much a child's smile. "Younger, usually."

Nausea won. I put a hand to my mouth and turned away. Never mind what Ras Onchi thought. I would never call myself Arameri, never.

He sighed and came over, wrapping arms around me from behind and resting his head on my shoulder. I did not understand his constant need to touch me. I didn't mind, but it made me wonder who he cuddled when I was not around. I wondered what price they demanded of him in exchange.

"I was ancient when your kind first began to speak and use fire, Yeine. These petty torments are nothing to me."

"That's beside the point," I said. "You're still…" I groped for words. *Human* might be taken as an insult.

He shook his head. "Only Enefa's death hurts me, and that was no mortal's doing."

In that moment there was a deep, basso shudder throughout the palace. My skin prickled; in the bathroom something rattled for an instant, then went still.

"Sunset," Sieh said. He sounded pleased as he straightened and went to one of my windows. The western sky was layered clouds, spectrum-painted. "My father returns."

Where had he gone? I wondered, though I was distracted by another thought. The monster of my nightmares, the beast who had hunted me through walls, was *father* to Sieh.

"He tried to kill you yesterday," I said.

Sieh shook his head dismissively, then clapped his hands, making me jump. "*En. Naiasouwamehikach.*"

It was gibberish, spoken in a singsong lilt, and for an instant while the sound lingered, my perception changed. I became aware of the faint echoes of each syllable from the room's walls, overlapping and blending. I noticed the way the air felt as the sounds rippled through it. Along my floor into the walls. Through the walls to the support column that held up Sky. Down that column to the earth.

And the sound was carried along as the earth rolled over like a sleepy child, as we hurtled around the sun through the cycle of seasons and the stars around us did a graceful cartwheel turn—

I blinked, momentarily surprised to find myself still in the room. But then I understood. The earliest decades of the scrivening art's history were littered with its founders' deaths, until they'd restricted themselves to the written form of the language. It amazed me now that they'd even tried. A tongue whose meaning depended upon not only syntax and pronunciation and tone, but also one's position in the universe at any given moment—how could they even have imagined mastering that? It was beyond any mortal.

Sieh's yellow ball appeared out of nowhere and bounced into his hands. "Go and see, then find me," he commanded, and threw the ball away. It bounced against a nearby wall, then vanished.

"I'll deliver your message to Kurue," he said, heading toward the wall beside my bed. "Consider our offer, Yeine, but do it quickly, will you? Time passes so swiftly with your kind. Dekarta will be dead before you know it."

He spoke to the wall and it opened before him, revealing another narrow dead space. The last thing I saw was his grin as it closed behind him.

7

Love

How strange. I have only now realized that this whole affair was nothing more than one family squabble pitted against another.

*   *   *

From my window in Sky, it seemed as though I could see the
whole of the Hundred Thousand Kingdoms. That was a fallacy,
I knew; scriveners have proven that the world is round. Yet it
was easy to imagine. So many winking lights, like stars on the
ground.

My people were audacious builders once. We carved our cities into mountainsides and positioned our temples to make a
calendar of the stars—but we could never have built anything
like Sky. Nor could the Amn, of course, not without the aid
of their captive gods, but this is not the main reason Sky is
deeply, profoundly wrong in Darre eyes. It is blasphemy to separate oneself from the earth and look down on it like a god. It is
more than blasphemy; it is dangerous. We can never be gods,
after all—but we can become something less than human with
frightening ease.

Still…I could not help drinking in the view. It is important
to appreciate beauty, even when it is evil.

I was very tired. I had been in Sky for little more than a day,
and so much of my life had changed. In Darr, I was effectively
dead. I had left no heirs, and now the council would appoint
some other young woman, of some other lineage, as *ennu*. My
grandmother would be so disappointed—and yet this was nothing more than what she had feared all along. I was not dead, but
I had become Arameri, and that was just as bad.

As an Arameri, I was expected to show no favoritism to my
birthland and consider the needs of all nations equally. I had
not done so, of course. As soon as T'vril and Sieh were gone,
I had contacted each of my assigned nations and suggested—
knowing full well that a suggestion from an Arameri heir is not

a suggestion—that they consider resuming trade with Darr. It had not been an official trade embargo, the lean years since my mother's defection from the Arameri. We could have protested an embargo to the Consortium, or found ways to circumvent it. Instead, every nation that hoped to curry favor with our rulers simply chose to ignore Darr's existence. Contracts were broken, financial obligations abandoned, lawsuits dismissed; even smugglers avoided us. We became pariah.

So the least I could do with my newfound, unwanted Arameri power was to accomplish part of my purpose in coming here.

As for the rest of my purpose...well. The walls of Sky were hollow, its corridors a maze. This left many places wherein the secrets of my mother's death could hide.

I would hunt them down, every one.

I had slept well my first night in Sky. Worn out by shock and running for my life, I didn't even remember lying down.

On the second night, sleep stubbornly refused to come. I lay in the too-big, too-soft bed of my quarters, staring up at the glowing ceiling and walls that made my room bright as day. Sky embodied the Bright; the Arameri allowed no darkness here. But how did the other members of my illustrious family get any sleep?

After what felt like hours of tossing, I finally managed a sort of half doze, but my mind never settled. In the silence I was free to think of all that had happened in the past days, and to wonder about my family and friends back in Darr, and to worry whether I had a hope in the Maelstrom of surviving this place.

Presently, however, it came to me that I was being watched.

My grandmother had trained me well; I came fully awake. But though I mastered the urge to open my eyes or otherwise react, a deep voice said, "You are awake."

So I opened my eyes and sat up, and had to suppress an entirely different urge when I saw the Nightlord standing not ten paces away.

It would do no good to run. So I said, "Good evening, Lord Nahadoth." I was proud that my voice did not quaver.

He inclined his head to me, then just stood there smoldering and looking ominous at the foot of my bed. Realizing that a god's sense of time was probably very different from a mortal's, I prompted, "To what do I owe the honor of this visit?"

"I wanted to see you," he said.

"Why?"

To this he did not answer. But he moved at last, turning and pacing over to the windows, his back to me. He was harder to see there, with the night view as a backdrop. His cloak? hair?— the nimbus of dark that constantly shifted 'round him—tended to blend with the black starry sky.

This was neither the violent monster that had hunted me nor the coldly superior being who had threatened to kill me afterward. I could not read him, but there was a softness to him now that I had glimpsed only for an instant before. When he had held my hand, and bled on me, and honored me with a kiss.

I wanted to ask him about that, but too many things about the memory disturbed me. So instead I asked, "Why did you try to kill me, yesterday?"

"I wouldn't have killed you. Scimina commanded me to leave you alive."

That was curious, and even more disturbing. "Why?"

"I assume because she didn't want you dead."

I was dangerously close to growing annoyed. "What would you have done to me, then, if not kill me?"

"Hurt you."

This time I was glad he was so opaque.

I swallowed. "As you hurt Sieh?"

There was a pause, and he turned to me. The moon, half-full, shone through the window above him. His face had the same faint, pale glow. He said nothing, but abruptly I understood: he did not remember hurting Sieh.

"So you truly are different," I said. I wrapped my arms around myself. The room had grown chilly, and I wore only a thin shirt and pantlets for sleep. "Sieh said something to that effect, and T'vril, too. 'While there's still light in the sky…'"

"By day I am human," said the Nightlord. "At night I am… something closer to my true self." He spread his hands. "Sunset and dawn are when the transition takes place."

"And you become… that." I carefully did not say *monster*.

"The mortal mind, imbued with a god's power and knowledge for even a few moments, rarely reacts well."

"And yet Scimina can command you through this madness?"

He nodded. "Itempas's compulsion overrides all." He paused then, and his eyes abruptly became very clear to me—cold and hard, black as the sky. "If you don't want me here, command me to leave."

Consider: An immensely powerful being is yours to command. He must obey your every whim. Wouldn't the temptation to diminish him, to humble him and make yourself feel powerful by doing so, be almost irresistible?

I think it would be.

Yes, it definitely would be.

"I would rather know why you've come in the first place," I said. "But I won't force you to explain."

"Why not?" There was something dangerous in his voice. Why was he angry? Because I had power over him and chose not to use it? Was he worried that I would?

The answer to his question came to my mind at once: *because it would be wrong.* I hesitated to say that, however. The answer wasn't even correct—he had entered my room unbidden, a breach of manners in any land. If he had been human, I wouldn't have hesitated to order him out.

No; not human. If he had been *free.*

But he was not free. Viraine had explained further the evening before, during the painting of my sigil. My commands to the Enefadeh had to be simple and precise. I was to avoid metaphors or colloquialisms, and above all *think* about whatever I told them to do, lest I trigger unintended consequences. If I said something like, "Nahadoth, get out," he would be free to leave not only my room, but the palace entire. Skyfather knew what he'd get up to then, and only Dekarta could summon him back. Or if I said, "Nahadoth, be silent," he would be rendered mute until I or some other fullblooded Arameri rescinded the order.

And if I were ever so careless as to say, "Nahadoth, do as you please," he would kill me. Because killing Arameri pleased him. It had happened before, many times over the centuries, according to Viraine. (A service, he called it, as stupider Arameri were usually eliminated before they could breed or embarrass the family further.)

"I won't command you because I'm considering the alliance proposed by your Lady Kurue," I said at last. "An alliance should be based on mutual respect."

"Respect is irrelevant," he said. "I am your slave."

I could not help wincing at the word. "I'm a captive here, too."

"A captive whose every command I must obey. Forgive me if I feel little sympathy."

I did not like the guilt his words triggered in me. Perhaps that was why my temper slipped, before I could think to rein it in. "You are a god," I snapped. "You're a deadly beast on a leash who has already turned on me once. I may have power over you, but I would be a fool to think that makes me safe. Far wiser to offer you courtesy, *ask* for what I want, and hope for your cooperation in return."

"Ask. And then command."

"Ask, and if you say no, accept that answer. That, too, is part of respect."

He fell silent for a long while. In that silence I replayed my words in my head, praying I had left him no opening to exploit.

"You cannot sleep," he said.

I blinked in confusion, then realized it was a question. "No. The bed . . . the light."

Nahadoth nodded. Abruptly the walls went dim, their light fading until shadows shrouded the room, and the only illumination came from the moon and stars and the lights of the city. The Nightlord was a darker shadow etched against the windows. He had put out the unlight of his face as well.

"You have offered me courtesy," he said. "I offer cooperation in return."

I could not help swallowing, remembering my dream of the black star. If it was true—it had felt true, but who could say with dreams?—then Nahadoth was more than capable of destroying the world, even diminished as he was. Yet it was his simple gesture of putting out the lights that filled me with awe. Tired as I was, I suppose that mattered more to me than the whole of the world.

"Thank you," I managed at last. "And—" There was no subtle way to say it. "Will you leave now? Please?"

He was a silhouette. "All that happens in darkness, I see," he said. "Every whisper, every sigh, I hear. Even if I leave, some part of me will remain. That cannot be helped."

Only later would his words disturb me. For now, I was just grateful. "It will be enough," I said. "Thank you."

He inclined his head, then vanished—not all at once, as Sieh had done, but fading over the space of several breaths. Even after I could no longer see him, I felt his presence, but eventually that faded, too. I felt, properly or not, alone.

I climbed back into bed and was asleep in a span of minutes.

There is a tale of the Nightlord that the priests allow.

Once long ago, before the war between the gods, the Nightlord descended to earth, seeking entertainment. He found a lady in a tower—the wife of some ruler, shut away and lonely. It was not difficult for him to seduce her. Some while later, the woman gave birth to a child. It was not her husband's. It was not human. It was the first of the great demons, and after it and others like it were born, the gods realized they had made a terrible mistake. So they hunted their own offspring, slaying them down to the tiniest infant. The woman, who had been turned out by her husband and was now deprived of her child as well, froze to death alone in a snowy forest.

My grandmother told me a different version of the tale. After the demon-children were hunted down, the Nightlord found the woman again and begged her forgiveness for what he'd done. In atonement he built her another tower and gave her riches so that she might live in comfort, and he visited her ever afterward to see that she was all right. But she never forgave him, and eventually she killed herself for grief.

The priests' lesson: beware the Nightlord, for his pleasure is a mortal's doom. My grandmother's lesson: beware love, especially with the wrong man.

8

Cousin

THE NEXT MORNING, a servant arrived to help me dress and groom myself. Ridiculous. Still, it seemed appropriate to at least try to behave like an Arameri, so I bit my tongue while she fussed about me. She did my buttons and shifted my clothing minutely as if that would somehow make me look more elegant, then brushed my short hair and helped me put on makeup. The last I did actually need help with, as Darre women do not wear cosmetics. I could not help feeling some consternation as she turned the mirror to show me all in paint. It didn't look bad. Just...strange.

I must have frowned too much, because the servant grew anxious and began rummaging in the large bag she'd brought with her. "I have just the thing," she said, and lifted out something that I thought at first was a party masque. It certainly looked like one, with a wire eyeframe attached to a satin-wrapped rod. But the masque itself was peculiar, seeming to consist only of a pair of bright blue feathery objects like the eyes of a peacock's tail.

Then they blinked. I started, looked closer, and saw that they were not feathers at all.

"All the highblood ladies use these," said the servant eagerly. "They're very fashionable right now. Watch." She lifted the frame to her face so that the blue eyes superimposed her own rather pretty gray ones. She blinked, lowered the frame—and suddenly her eyes were bright blue, surrounded by long, exotically thick black lashes. I stared, then saw that the eyes in the frame were now gray, staring blankly and fringed with the servant's own very ordinary lashes. Then she put the frame back to her face, and her eyes were her own again.

"You see?" She held the rod out to me. Now I could see the tiny black sigils, barely visible, etched along its length. "Blue would look lovely with that dress."

I recoiled, and it took me another few seconds to speak through my revulsion. "Wh-whose eyes were they?"

"What?"

"The eyes, the eyes. Where did they come from?"

The servant stared at me as if I'd asked where the moon had come from. "I don't know, my lady," she said after a flustered pause. "I could inquire, if you like."

"No," I said, very softly. "There's no need."

I thanked the servant for her assistance, praised her skill, and let her know I would have no further need of a dressing servant for the remainder of my stay in Sky.

Another servant arrived shortly afterward with word from T'vril: as expected, Relad had declined my request for a meeting. As it was a rest day, there was no Consortium meeting, so I ordered breakfast and a copy of the latest financial reports on my assigned nations.

As I studied the reports over raw fish and poached fruit—I did not dislike Amn food, but they never seemed to know what to cook and what to leave alone—Viraine dropped by. To see how I was doing, he said, but I had not forgotten my earlier sense that he wanted something of me. I felt that more strongly than ever as he paced about my room.

"Interesting to see you taking such an active interest in governance," he said, as I set aside a sheaf of papers. "Most Arameri don't bother even with basic economics."

"I rule—ruled—a poor nation," I said, draping a cloth over the remains of my breakfast. "I've never had that luxury."

"Ah, yes. But you've taken steps to remedy that poverty, haven't you? I heard Dekarta commenting on it this morning. You ordered your assigned kingdoms to resume trade with Darr."

I paused in the midst of drinking my tea. "He's watching what I do?"

"He watches all his heirs, Lady Yeine. Very little else entertains him these days."

I thought of the magic orb I'd been given, through which I had contacted my nations the night before. I wondered how difficult it would be to create an orb that would not alert the person being observed.

"Have you secrets to hide already?" Viraine raised his eyebrows at my silence, amused. "Visitors in the night, secret trysts, conspiracies afoot?"

I have never possessed the innate talent for lying. Fortunately, when my mother realized this, she taught me alternative tactics. "That would seem to be the order of business here," I said. "Though I haven't tried to kill anyone yet. I haven't turned the future of our civilization into a contest for my amusement."

"If those small things trouble you, Lady, you won't last long here," Viraine said. He moved to sit in a chair across from me, steepling his fingers. "Would you like some advice? From someone who was once a newcomer here himself?"

"I welcome your counsel, Scrivener Viraine."

"Don't get involved with the Enefadeh."

I considered whether to stare at him or feign ignorance and ask what he meant. I chose to stare.

"Sieh seems to have taken a liking to you," he said. "He does that sometimes, like a child. And like a child, he's affectionate; he amuses and exasperates; he's very easy to love. Don't."

"I'm aware that he's not truly a child."

"Are you aware that he's killed as many people over the years as Nahadoth?"

I could not help flinching. Viraine smiled.

"He *is* a child, mind you—not in age, but in nature. He acts on impulse. He has a child's creativity... a child's cruelty. And he is Nahadoth's, blood and soul. Just think about that, Lady.

The Nightlord, living embodiment of all that we who serve the Bright fear and despise. Sieh is his firstborn son."

I did think about it. But strangely, the image that came most clearly to mind was Sieh's utter contentment when I'd put an arm around him that first night. Later I would understand that I had already begun to love Sieh, possibly in that very moment. Some part of me agreed with Viraine: to love such a creature was beyond foolish, edging into suicidal. Yet I did.

Viraine saw me shudder. With perfect solicitousness he came over and touched my shoulder. "You aren't entirely surrounded by enemies," he said gently, and so discomfited was I that for a moment I actually took comfort from his words. "T'vril seems to like you, too—though that isn't surprising, given his history. And you have me, Yeine. I was your mother's friend before she left Sky; I can be yours as well."

If he had not spoken those last words, I might have indeed considered him a friend.

"Thank you, Scrivener Viraine," I said. For once, thank the gods, my Darre nature did not assert itself. I tried to sound sincere. Tried not to show my instant dislike and suspicion. Judging by his pleased look, I succeeded.

He left, and I sat silent in his wake for a long time, thinking.

It would occur to me shortly thereafter that Viraine had warned me off only Sieh, not Nahadoth.

I needed to know more about my mother.

Viraine had said he was her friend. Everything I knew of my mother said this was a lie. Viraine's strange mix of solicitousness and nonchalance, his callous help and false comfort—no. My mother had always valued people who were straightforward in their dealings with others. I could not imagine her being friendly toward, much less close to, someone like Viraine.

But I had no idea where to begin learning more about my mother. The obvious source for information was Dekarta, though I had no desire to ask him for the intimate details of my mother's past in front of the entire Salon. A private meeting, though...yes. That would suffice.

Not yet, though. Not until I understood better why he had brought me to Sky in the first place.

That left other members of the Central Family, some of whom were more than old enough to have remembered the days when my mother was heir. But T'vril's warning lingered in my mind; any of the Central Family who truly had been friends to my mother were off doing family business, no doubt to keep themselves apart and safe from the viper pit that was life in Sky. No one who remained would speak honestly to me. They were Dekarta's people—or Scimina's, or Relad's.

Ah, but there was an idea. Relad.

He had refused my request for a meeting. Protocol dictated that I not try again—but protocol was a guideline, not an absolute, and among family protocol took whatever form its members permitted. Perhaps a man used to dealing with someone like Scimina would value a direct approach. I went in search of T'vril.

I found him in a spacious, neat little office on one of the palace's lower levels. The walls glowed down here, even though it was a bright day outside. This was because the lower levels of the palace were underneath the broadest part of its bulk and cast into perpetual shadow as a result. I could not help noticing that I saw only servants on these levels, most of them wearing the blood sigil that looked like a simple black bar. Distant relatives, I knew now, thanks to Viraine's explanations. Six generations or more removed from the Central Family.

T'vril was giving instructions to a group of his staff when I arrived. I stopped just beyond the open door, listening idly but not interrupting or making my presence known, as he told a young woman, "No. There won't be another warning. When the signal comes, you'll have one chance. If you're still near the shaft when it comes…" He said nothing more.

The grim silence that fell in the wake of his words was what finally caught my attention. This sounded like more than the usual instructions to clean rooms or deliver food more quickly. I stepped closer to the doorway to listen, and that was when one of T'vril's people spotted me. He must have made some sort of signal to T'vril, because T'vril immediately looked my way. He stared at me for half a breath, then told his people, "Thank you; that's all."

I stood aside to let the servants disperse through the doorway, which they did with a brisk efficiency and lack of chatter that I found unsurprising. T'vril had struck me as the type to run a tight ship. When the room was clear, T'vril bowed me inside and shut the door behind us in deference to my rank.

"How may I help you, Cousin?" he asked.

I wanted to ask him about the shaft, whatever that was, and the signal, whatever that was, and why his staff looked as though he had just announced an execution. It was obvious, though, that he preferred not to speak of it. His movements were ever so slightly forced as he beckoned me to a seat in front of his desk and offered me wine. I saw his hand tremble as he poured it, until he noticed me watching and set the carafe down.

He had saved my life; for that I owed him courtesy. So I said only, "Where do you think Lord Relad might be about now?"

He opened his mouth to reply, then paused, frowning. I saw him consider attempting to dissuade me, then decide against it. He closed his mouth, then said, "The solarium, most likely. He spends most of his idle time there."

T'vril had shown me this the day before, during my tour of the palace. Sky's uppermost levels culminated in a number of plat-forms and airy spires, most of which contained the apartments and entertainments of the fullbloods. The solarium was one of the entertainments: a vast glass-ceilinged chamber of tropical plants, artfully made couches and grottoes, and pools for bath-ing or...other things. T'vril had not led me far inside during our tour, but I'd caught a glimpse of movement through the fronds and heard a cry of unmistakable ardor. I had not pressed T'vril for a further look, but now it seemed I would have no choice.

"Thank you," I said, and rose.

"Wait," he said, and went behind his desk. He rummaged through the drawers for a moment, then straightened, holding a small, beautifully painted ceramic flask. He handed this to me.

"See if that helps," he said. "He could buy himself bucketsful if he wanted, but he likes being bribed."

I pocketed the flask and memorized the information. Yet the whole exchange raised a new question. "T'vril, why are you helping me?"

"I wish I knew," he replied, sounding abruptly weary. "It's clearly bad for me; that flask cost me a month's wages. I was sav-ing it for whenever I needed a favor from Relad."

I was wealthy now. I made a mental note to order three of the flasks sent to T'vril in compensation. "Then why?"

He looked at me for a long moment, perhaps trying to decide the answer for himself. Finally he sighed. "Because I don't like what they're doing to you. Because you're like me. I honestly don't know."

Like him. An outsider? He had been raised here, had as much connection to the Central Family as me, but he would never be a true Arameri in Dekarta's eyes. Or did he mean that I was the only other decent, honorable soul in the whole place? If that was true.

"Did you know my mother?" I asked.

He looked surprised. "Lady Kinneth? I was a child when she left to be with your father. I can't say I remember her well."

"What do you remember?"

He leaned against the edge of his desk, folding his arms and thinking. In the Skystuff light his braided hair shone like copper rope, a color that would have seemed unnatural to me only a short time before. Now I lived among the Arameri and consorted with gods. My standards had changed.

"She was beautiful," he said. "Well, the Central Family are all beautiful; what nature doesn't give them, magic can. But it was more than that with her." He frowned to himself. "She always seemed a little sad to me, somehow. I never saw her smile."

I remembered my mother's smile. She had done it more often while my father was alive, but sometimes she had smiled for me, too. I swallowed against a knot in my throat, and coughed to cover it. "I imagine she was kind to you. She always liked children."

"No." T'vril's expression was sober. He had probably noticed my momentary lapse, but thankfully he was too much the dip-lomat to mention it. "She was polite, certainly, but I was only a halfblood, being raised by servants. It would have been strange if she'd shown kindness, or even interest, toward any of us."

I frowned before I could stop myself. In Darr, my mother had seen to it that all the children of our servants got gifts for their birthing days and light-dedication ceremonies. During the hot, thick Darr summers, she had allowed the servants to take their rest hours in our garden, where it was cooler. She'd treated our steward like a member of the family.

"I was a child," T'vril said again. "If you want a better recol-lection, you should speak to the older servants."

"Is there anyone you'd recommend?"

"Any of them will speak to you. As for which one might remember your mother best—that I can't say." He shrugged.

Not quite what I'd hoped for, but it was something I'd have to look into later. "Thank you again, T'vril," I said, and went in search of Relad.

In a child's eyes, a mother is a goddess. She can be glorious or terrible, benevolent or filled with wrath, but she commands love either way. I am convinced that this is the greatest power in the universe.

My mother—

No. Not yet.

In the solarium the air was warm and humid and fragrant with flowering trees. Above the trees rose one of Sky's spires—the centralmost and tallest one, whose entrance must have been somewhere amid the winding paths. Unlike the rest of the spires, this one quickly tapered to a point only a few feet in diameter, too narrow to house apartments or chambers of any great size. Perhaps it was purely decorative.

If I kept my eyes half-lidded, I could ignore the spire and almost imagine I was in Darr. The trees were wrong—too tall and thin, too far apart. In my land the forests were thick and wet and dark as mysteries, full of tangled vines and small hidden creatures. Still, the sounds and smells were similar enough to assuage my homesickness. I stayed there until the sound of nearby voices pushed my imagination away.

Pushed *sharply*; one of the voices was Scimina's.

I could not hear her words, but she was very close. Somewhere in one of the alcoves ahead, concealed behind a copse of brush and trees. The white-pebbled path beneath my feet ran in that direction and probably branched toward it in some way that would make my approach obvious to anyone there.

To the infinite hells with obviousness, I decided.

My father had been a great huntsman before his death. He'd taught me to roll my feet in a forest, so as to minimize the crackle of leaf litter. And I knew to stay low, because it is human nature to react to movement at eye level, while that which is higher or lower often goes unnoticed. If this had been a Darren forest, I would have climbed the nearest tree, but I could not easily climb these skinny, bare-trunked things. Low it was.

When I got close—just barely close enough to hear, but any closer and I risked being seen—I hunkered down at the foot of a tree to listen.

"Come, Brother, it's not too much, is it?" Scimina's voice, warm and cajoling. I could not help shivering at the sound of it, both in remembered fear and anger. She had set *a god* on me, like a trained attack dog, for her own amusement. It had been a long time since I'd hated anyone so fiercely.

"Anything you want is too much," said a new voice—male, tenor, with a petulant edge. Relad? "Go away and let me think."

"You know these darkling races, Brother. They have no patience, no higher reason. Always angry over things that happened generations ago..." I lost the rest of her words. I could hear occasional footsteps, which meant that she was pacing, toward me and away. When she moved away, it was hard to hear her. "Just have your people sign the supply agreement. It's nothing but profit for them and for you."

"That, sweet Sister, is a lie. You would never offer me anything solely for my benefit." A weary sigh, a mutter I didn't catch, and then: "Go *away*, I said. My head hurts."

"I'm sure it does, given your indulgences." Scimina's voice had changed. It was still cultured, still light and pleasant, but the warmth had left it now that Relad clearly meant to refuse her. I marveled that such a subtle change could make her sound so different. "Very well; I'll come back when you're feeling better. —By the way. Have you met our new cousin?"

I held my breath.

"Come here," Relad said. I knew at once he was speaking to someone else, perhaps a servant; I couldn't imagine him using that peremptory tone with Scimina. "No. I hear you tried to kill her, though. Was that wise?"

"I was only playing. I couldn't resist; she's such a serious little thing. Do you know, she honestly believes she's a contender for Uncle's position?"

I stiffened. So, apparently, did Relad, because Scimina added, "Ah. You didn't realize?"

"You don't know for sure. The old man loved Kinneth. And the girl is nothing to us."

"You really should read more of our family history, Brother. The pattern..." And she paced away. Infuriating. But I did not dare creep closer, because only a thin layer of branches and leaves separated me from them. This close, they would hear me breathing if they listened hard enough. All I had to count on was their absorption in the conversation.

There were a few more comments exchanged between them, most of which I missed. Then Scimina sighed. "Well, you must do as you see fit, Brother, and I shall do the same, as always."

"Good luck." Was this quiet wish sincere or sarcastic? I guessed the latter, but there was something in it that hinted at the former. I could not tell without seeing him.

"And to you, Brother." I heard the click of her heels along the path stones, rapidly fading.

I sat where I was against the tree for a long while, waiting for my nerves to settle before I attempted to leave. My thoughts, too, though that took longer, as they whirled in the aftermath of what I'd heard. *She honestly believes she's a contender.* Did that mean I wasn't? Relad apparently believed I was, but even he wondered, as I did: why had Dekarta brought me to Sky?

Something to ponder for later. First things first. Rising, I began to make my careful way back through the brush—but before I could, the branches parted not five feet away, and a man stumbled through. Blond, tall, well-dressed, with a full-blood mark: Relad. I froze, but it was too late; I was standing in plain sight, caught in midcreep. But to my utter amazement, he didn't see me. He walked over to a tree, unfastened his pants, and began voiding his bladder with much sighing and groaning.

I stared at him, unsure what to be more disgusted by: his choice to urinate in a public place, where others would smell his reek for days; his utter obliviousness; or my own carelessness.

Still, I had not been caught yet. I could have ducked back down, hidden myself behind a tree, and probably gone unnoticed. But perhaps an opportunity had presented itself. Surely a brother of Scimina would appreciate boldness from his newest rival.

So I waited until he finished and fastened his clothing. He turned to go, and probably still wouldn't have seen me if I hadn't chosen that moment to clear my throat.

Relad started and turned, blinking blearily at me for a full three breaths before either of us spoke.

"Cousin," I said at last.

He let out a long sigh that was hard to interpret. Was he angry? Resigned? Both, perhaps. "I see. So you were listening."

"Yes."

"Is this what they teach you in that jungle of yours?"

"Among other things. I thought I might stick to what I know best, Cousin, since no one has seen fit to tell me the proper way Arameri do things. I was actually hoping you might help me with that."

"Help you—" He started to laugh, then shook his head. "Come on, then. You might be a barbarian, but I want to sit down like a civilized man."

This was promising. Already Relad seemed saner than his sister, though that wasn't difficult. Relieved, I followed him through the brush into the clearing. It was a lovely little spot, so meticulously landscaped that it looked natural, except in its impossible perfection. A large boulder, contoured in exactly the right ways to serve as a lounging chair, dominated one side of the space. Relad, none too steady on his feet to begin with, slumped into this with a heavy sigh.

Across from the seat was a bathing pool, too small to hold more than two people comfortably. A young woman sat here: beautiful, nude, with a black bar on her forehead. A servant, then. She met my eyes and then looked away, elegantly expressionless. Another young woman—clothed in a diaphanous gown so sheer she might as well have been nude—crouched near Relad's lounge, holding a cup and flask on a tray. I made no wonder that he'd had to relieve himself, seeing this; the flask was not small, and it was nearly empty. Amazing he could still walk straight.

There was nowhere for me to sit, so I clasped my hands behind my back and stood in polite silence.

"All right, then," Relad said. He picked up an empty glass and peered at it, as if checking for cleanliness. It had obviously been used. "What in every demon's unknown name do you want?"

"As I said, Cousin: help."

"Why would I possibly help you?"

"We could perhaps help each other," I replied. "I have no interest in becoming heir after Grandfather. But I would be more than willing to support another candidate, under the right circumstances."

Relad picked up the flask to pour a glass, but his hand wavered so badly that he spilled a third of it. Such waste. I had to fight the urge to take it from him and pour properly.

"You're useless to me," he said at last. "You'd only get in my way—or worse, leave me vulnerable to her." Neither of us needed clarification on who he meant by *her*.

"She came here to meet with you about something completely different," I said. "Do you think it's a coincidence she mentioned me in the process? It seems to me that a woman does not discuss one rival with another—unless she hopes to play them against each other. Perhaps she perceives us both as threats."

"Threats?" He laughed, then tossed back the glass of whatever-it-was. He couldn't have tasted it that fast. "Gods, you're as stupid as you are ugly. And the old man honestly thinks you're a match for her? Unbelievable."

Heat flashed through me, but I had heard far worse in my life; I kept my temper. "I'm not interested in matching her." I said it with more edge than I would have preferred, but I doubted he cared. "All I want is to get out of this godsforsaken place alive."

The look he threw me made me feel ill. It wasn't cynical, or even derisive, just horrifyingly matter-of-fact. *You'll never get out*, that look said, in his flat eyes and weary smile. *You have no chance.*

But instead of voicing this aloud, Relad spoke with a gentleness that unnerved me more than his scorn. "I can't help you, Cousin. But I will offer one piece of advice, if you're willing to listen."

"I would welcome it, Cousin."

"My sister's favorite weapon is love. If you love anyone, anything, beware. That's where she'll attack."

I frowned in confusion. I'd had no important lovers in Darr, produced no children. My parents were already dead. I loved my grandmother, of course, and my uncles and cousins and few friends, but I could not see how—

Ah. It was plain as day, once I thought about it. Darr itself. It was not one of Scimina's territories, but she was Arameri; nothing was beyond her reach. I would have to find some means of protecting my people.

Relad shook his head as if reading my mind. "You can't

protect the things you love, Cousin—not forever. Not completely. Your only real defense is not to love in the first place."

I frowned. "That's impossible." How could any human being live like that?

He smiled, and it made me shiver. "Well. Good luck, then."

He beckoned to the women. Both of them rose from their places and came over to his couch, awaiting his next command. That was when I noticed: both were tall, patrician, beautiful in that flat, angular Amn way, and sable-haired. They did not look much like Scimina, but the similarity was undeniable.

Relad gazed at them with such bitterness that for a moment, I felt pity. I wondered whom he had loved and lost. And I wondered when I had decided that Relad was as useless to me as I was to him. Better to struggle alone than rely on this empty shell of a man.

"Thank you, Cousin," I replied, and inclined my head. Then I left him to his fantasies.

On my way back to my room, I stopped at T'vril's office and returned the ceramic flask. T'vril put it away without a word.

9

Memories

THERE IS A SICKNESS CALLED the Walking Death. The disease causes tremors, terrible fever, unconsciousness, and in its final stages a peculiar kind of manic behavior. The victim is compelled to rise from the sickbed and walk—walk anywhere, even back and forth in the confines of a room. Walk, while the fever grows so great that the victim's skin cracks and bleeds; walk while the brain dies. And then walk a little more.

There have been many outbreaks of the Walking Death over the centuries. When the disease first appeared, thousands died because no one understood how it spread. The walking, you see. Unimpeded, the infected always walk to wherever healthy people can be found. They shed their blood and die there, and thus the sickness is passed on. Now we are wise. Now we build a wall around any place the Death has touched, and we close our hearts to the cries of the healthy trapped within. If they are still alive a few weeks later, we let them out. Survival is not unheard of. We are not cruel.

It escapes no one's notice that the Death afflicts only the laboring classes. Priests, nobles, scholars, wealthy merchants... it is more than that they have guards and the resources to quarantine themselves in their citadels and temples. In the early years there were no quarantines, and they still did not die. Unless they rose recently from the lower classes themselves, the wealthy and powerful are immune.

Of course such a plague is nothing natural.

When the Death came to Darr a little while before I was born, no one expected my father to catch it. We were minor nobility, but still nobility. But my paternal grandfather had been a commoner as Darre reckon it—a handsome hunter who caught my grandmother's eye. That was enough for the disease, apparently.

Still... my father survived.

I will remember later why this is relevant.

* * *

That night as I readied myself for bed, I came out of the bath to find Sieh eating my dinner and reading one of the books I'd brought from Darr. The dinner I did not mind. The book was another matter.

"I like this," Sieh said, throwing me a vague wave by way of greeting. He never lifted his eyes from the book. "I've never read Darre poetry. It's strange—from talking with you I'd thought all Darre were straightforward. But this: every line is full of misdirection. Whoever wrote this thinks in circles."

I sat down on the bed to brush my hair. "It's considered courteous to ask before invading others' privacy."

He didn't put the book down, though he did close it. "I've offended you." There was a contemplative look on his face. "How did I do that?"

"The poet was my father."

His face registered surprise. "He's a fine poet. Why does it bother you to have others read his work?"

"Because it's mine." He had been dead a decade—a hunting accident, such a typically male way to die—and still it hurt to think of him. I lowered the brush, looking down at the dark curls caught in the bristles. Amn curls, like my Amn eyes. I wondered, sometimes, whether my father had thought me ugly, as so many Darre did. If he had, would it have been because of my Amn features—or because I did not look *more* Amn, like my mother?

Sieh gazed at me for a long moment. "I meant no offense." And he got up and replaced the book on my small shelf.

I felt something in me relax, though I resumed brushing to cover it. "I'm surprised you care," I said. "Mortals die all the time. You must grow tired of dancing around our grief."

Sieh smiled. "My mother is dead, too."

The Betrayer, who betrayed no one. I had never thought of her as someone's mother.

"Besides, you tried to kill Nahadoth for me. That earns you a little extra consideration." He shifted to sit on my vanity table, his rump shoving aside my few toiletries; the extra consideration apparently did not extend that far. "So what is it you want?"

I started. He grinned.

"You were glad to see me until you saw what I was reading."

"Oh."

"Well?"

"I wondered…" Abruptly I felt foolish. How many problems did I have right now? Why was I obsessing over the dead?

Sieh drew up and folded his legs, and waited. I sighed.

"I wondered if you could tell me what you know of…of my mother."

"Not Dekarta, or Scimina, or Relad? Or even *my* peculiar family?" He cocked his head, and his pupils doubled in size in the span of a breath. I stared, momentarily distracted by this. "Interesting. What brings this on?"

"I met Relad today." I groped for words to explain further.

"Quite a pair, aren't they? Him and Scimina. The stories I could tell you about their little war…"

"I don't want to know about that." My voice was too sharp as I said it. I hadn't meant to let him see how much the meeting with Relad had troubled me. I had expected another Scimina, but the drunken, bitter reality was worse. Would I become another Relad if I did not escape Sky soon?

Sieh fell silent, probably reading every thought on my face.

So it did not entirely surprise me when a look of calculation came into his eyes, and he gave me a lazy, wicked smile.

"I'll tell you what I can," he said. "But what will you give me in return?"

"What do you want?"

His smile faded, his expression changing to one of utter seriousness. "I said it before. Let me sleep with you."

I stared at him. He shook his head quickly.

"Not as a man does with a woman." He actually looked revolted by the notion. "I'm a child, remember?"

"You aren't a child."

"As gods go, I am. Nahadoth was born before time even existed; he makes me and all my siblings combined look like infants." He shifted again, wrapping arms around his knees. He looked terribly young, and terribly vulnerable. Still, I was not a fool.

"Why?"

He uttered a soft sigh. "I just like you, Yeine. Does there have to be a reason for everything?"

"I'm beginning to think so, with you."

He scowled. "Well, there isn't. I told you; I do what I like, whatever feels good, as children do. There's no logic to it. Accept that or not, as you please." Then he put his chin on one knee and looked away, doing as perfect a sulk as I'd ever seen.

I sighed, and tried to consider whether saying yes to him would somehow make me susceptible to Enefadeh trickery or some Arameri plot. But at last it came to me: none of that mattered.

"I suppose I should be flattered," I said, and sighed.

Instantly Sieh brightened and bounded over to my bed,

pulling back the bedcovers and patting my side of the mattress. "Can I brush your hair?"

I could not help laughing. "You are a very, very strange person."

"Immortality gets very, very boring. You'd be surprised at how interesting the small mundanities of life can seem after a few millennia."

I came to the bed and sat down, offering him the brush. He all but purred as he took hold of it, but I held on.

He grinned. "I have a feeling I'm about to have my own bargain thrown back in my face."

"No. But it only seems wise, when bargaining with a trickster, to demand that he hold up his end of the deal first."

He laughed, letting go of the brush to slap his leg. "You're *so* much fun. I like you better than all the other Arameri."

I did not like that he considered me Arameri. But... "Better than my mother?" I asked.

He sobered, then settled against me, leaning on my back. "I liked her well enough. She didn't often command us. Only when she had to; other than that she left us alone. The smart ones tend to do that, exceptions like Scimina notwithstanding. No sense getting to know your weapons on a close personal basis."

I did not like hearing such a casual dismissal of my mother's motives, either. "Perhaps she did it on principle. So many of the Arameri abuse their power over you. It isn't right."

He lifted his head from my shoulder and looked at me for a moment, amused. Then he lay back down. "I suppose it could have been that."

"But you don't think so."

"Do you want truth, Yeine? Or comfort? No, I don't think

it was principle that made her leave us alone. I think Kinneth simply had other things on her mind. You could see that in her eyes. A drive."

I frowned, remembering. There had been a driven look to her, yes; a grim, unyielding sort of resolve. There had been flickers of other things, too, especially when she'd thought herself unobserved. Covetousness. Regret.

I imagined her thoughts when, sometimes, she had turned that look on me. *I will make you my instrument, my tool, to strike back at them,* perhaps, though she would have known far better than me how slim my chances were. Or perhaps, *At last, here is my chance to shape a world, even if it is only that of a child.* And now that I had seen what Sky and the Arameri were like, a new possiblity came to me. *I will raise you sane.*

But if she had also worn that look during her days in Sky, long before my birth, then it had nothing whatsoever to do with me.

"There was no contest in her case, was there?" I asked. "I thought she was the sole heir."

"No contest. There was never any question Kinneth would be the next head of the clan. Not until the day she announced her abdication." Sieh shrugged. "Even after that, for a time, Dekarta expected her to change her mind. But then something changed, and you could taste the difference in the air. It was summer that day, but Dekarta's rage was ice on metal."

"That day?"

Sieh did not answer for a moment. Abruptly I knew, with an instinct that I neither understood nor questioned, that he was going to lie. Or, at least, withhold some part of the truth.

But that was fine. He was a trickster, and a god, and when all was said and done I was a member of the family that had kept him in bondage for centuries. I could not expect complete trust from him. I would take what I could get.

"The day she came to the palace," Sieh said. He spoke more slowly than usual, palpably considering each word. "A year or so after she married your father. Dekarta ordered the halls empty when she arrived. So that she could save face, you see; even then he looked out for her. He met her alone for the same reason, so no one knows what was said between them. But we all knew what he expected."

"That she was coming back." Fortunately she had not, or I might never have been born.

But why *had* she come, then?

I needed to find that out, next.

I offered Sieh the brush. He took it, sat up on his knees, and very gently began working on my hair.

Sieh slept in a sprawl, taking over much of the very large bed. I had expected him to cuddle close, but he seemed content merely to have some part of his body in contact with me—a leg and a hand this time, tossed over my own leg and belly respectively. I did not mind the sprawl, nor the faint snoring. I did, once again, mind the daylight-bright walls.

Despite that, I dozed off anyhow. I must have been tired. Sometime later I half-woke and opened my eyes, bleary, to see that the room had gone dark. Since dark rooms at night were normal to me, I thought nothing of it and drifted off again. But in the morning I would recall something—a taste in the air, as Sieh had termed it. That taste was something I had little experience with, yet I knew it the way an infant knows love, or an animal knows fear. Jealousy, even between father and son, is a fact of nature.

That morning I turned over and found Sieh awake, his green eyes dark with regret. Wordlessly he rose, smiled at me, and vanished. I knew that he would never sleep with me again.

10

Family

AFTER SIEH LEFT I ROSE EARLY, intent upon finding T'vril before the day's visit to the Salon. Despite his reassurance that I'd already met everyone who mattered, that had been in reference to the contest of heirs. In the matter of my mother, I hoped someone might know more about the night of her abdication.

But I turned left where I should have turned right, and didn't take the lift far enough down, and instead of T'vril's office I found myself at the palace entrance, facing the forecourt where my life's most unpleasant saga had begun.

And Dekarta was there.

When I was five or six, I learned about the world from my Itempan tutors. "There is the universe, ruled by the gods," they told me. "Bright Itempas is chief among these. And there is the world, where the Noble Consortium rules with the guidance of the Arameri family. Dekarta, the Lord Arameri, is chief among them."

I had said to my mother, later, that this Lord Arameri must be a very great man.

"He is," she'd said, and that was the end of the conversation.

It was not the words that had stuck in my mind, but the way she said them.

Sky's forecourt is the first sight that visitors see, so it is calculated to impress. Besides the Vertical Gate and the palace entrance—a cavernous tunnel of concentric arches, around which stands the intimidating bulk of Sky itself—there is also the Garden of the Hundred Thousand, and the Pier. Of course nothing docks at this Pier, as it juts out from the forecourt over a half-mile drop. It has a thin, elegant railing, about waist-high. This railing would do nothing to stop a person intent on suicide, but I suppose it provides some reassurance to everyone else.

Dekarta stood with Viraine and several others at the foot of the Pier. The group was some ways off, and they had not yet seen me. I would have turned at once and headed back into the palace if I hadn't recognized one of the figures with Dekarta and Viraine. Zhakkarn, the warrior goddess.

That made me pause. The other people present were Dekarta's courtiers; I remembered some of them vaguely from my first day. Another man, not nearly as well-dressed as the rest, stood a few paces onto the Pier, as if gazing at the view—but he was shivering. I could see that even from where I stood.

Dekarta said something, and Zhakkarn lifted a hand and conjured a gleaming silver pike. Pointing this at the man, she took three steps forward. The pike's tip hovered, rock-steady despite the wind, a few inches from the man's back.

The man took a step forward, then looked back. Wind

whipped his hair in a wispy cloud about his head; he looked Amn, or of some sister race. I recognized his manner, though, and his wild, defiant eyes. A heretic, flouter of the Bright. Once there had been entire armies like him, but now there were only a few left, hiding in isolated pockets and worshipping their fallen gods in secret. This one must have been careless.

"You cannot keep them chained forever," the man said. The wind carried his words toward me and away, teasing my ears. The protective magic that kept the air warm and calm within Sky apparently did not operate on the Pier. "Not even the Sky-father is infallible!"

Dekarta said nothing to this, though he leaned forward and murmured something to Zhakkarn. The man on the Pier stiffened. "No! You can't! You can't!" He turned and tried to move past Zhakkarn and the jutting pike, his eyes fixed on Dekarta.

Zhakkarn merely moved the pike's tip, and the man impaled himself.

I cried out, putting my hands to my mouth. The palace entrance amplified the sound; Dekarta and Viraine both glanced back at me. But then came a sound that dwarfed my cry, as the man began to scream.

It went through me like Zhakkarn's pike. Hunched around the pike and clutching its shaft, the man's body shivered even harder than before. Belatedly I realized that some other force besides his cry shook him, as his chest began to glow red-hot around the pike's tip. Smoke rose from his sleeves, his collar, his mouth and nose. His eyes were the worst of it, because he was aware. He knew what was happening to him, knew it and despaired, and that, too, was part of his suffering.

I fled. Skyfather help me, but I could not bear it; I ran back into the palace and ducked around a corner. Even that did not help, for I could still hear him screaming, screaming, *screaming* as he burned from the inside out, on and on until I thought I would go mad and hear nothing more for the rest of my life.

Thank all the gods, even Nahadoth, that it eventually ended.

I don't know how long I crouched there with my hands over my ears. After a time I became aware that I was no longer alone, and I lifted my head. Dekarta, leaning heavily on a dark polished cane whose wood might have come from Darr's forests, stood watching me, Viraine beside him. The other courtiers had dispersed down the corridor. Zhakkarn was nowhere to be seen.

"Well," said Dekarta, his voice thick with derision, "we see the truth of it now. It is her father's cowardice that flows strongest in her, not Arameri courage."

That replaced my shock with fury. I leapt up from my crouch.

"The Darre were famous warriors once," said Viraine, before I could speak and damn myself. Unlike Dekarta, his expression was neutral. "But centuries under the Skyfather's peaceful rule have civilized even the most savage races, my lord, and we cannot blame her for that. I doubt she has ever seen a man killed."

"The members of this family must be stronger," said Dekarta. "It is the price we pay for our power. We cannot be like the darkling races, who gave up their gods to save their necks. We must be like that man, misguided though he was." He pointed back toward the Pier, or wherever the dead heretic's corpse was now. "Like Shahar. We must be willing to die—and kill—for our Lord Itempas." He smiled; my skin crawled. "Perhaps I should have you deal with the next one, Granddaughter."

I was too upset, too angry, to even try to control the hatred in my face. "What strength does it take to kill an unarmed man?

To order *someone else* to kill him? And like that—" I shook my head. The scream still rang in my ears. "That was cruelty, not justice!"

"Was it?" To my surprise, Dekarta actually looked thoughtful. "This world belongs to the Skyfather. That is indisputable. That man was caught distributing forbidden books, books which denied this reality. And every one of those books' readers—every good citizen who saw this blasphemy and failed to denounce it—has now joined in his delusion. They are all criminals in our midst, intent on stealing not gold, not even lives, but *hearts*. Minds. Sanity and peace." Dekarta sighed. "True justice would be to wipe out that entire nation; cauterize the taint before it spreads. Instead, I've merely ordered the deaths of everyone in his faction, and their spouses and children. Only those who are beyond redemption."

I stared at Dekarta, too horrified for words. Now I knew why the man had turned back to impale himself. Now I knew where Zhakkarn had gone.

"Lord Dekarta did give him a choice," Viraine added. "Jumping would have been the easier death. The winds usually spin them into the palace's support column, so nothing hits the ground. It's…quick."

"You…" I wanted to put my hands over my ears again. "You call yourselves servants of Itempas? You're rabid beasts. Demons!"

Dekarta shook his head. "I am a fool to keep looking for anything of her in you." He turned away then and began moving down the hall, slow even with the cane. Viraine fell in beside him, ready to assist if Dekarta stumbled. He looked back at me once; Dekarta did not.

I pushed myself away from the wall. "My mother lived truer to the Bright than you ever could!"

Dekarta stopped, and for a heartbeat I felt fear, realizing I had gone too far. But he did not turn back.

"That is true," Dekarta said, his voice very soft. "Your mother wouldn't have shown any mercy at all."

He moved on. I leaned back against the wall and did not stop trembling for a long time.

I skipped the Salon that day. I couldn't have sat there beside Dekarta, pretending indifference, while my mind still rang with the heretic's screams. I was not Arameri and would never be Arameri, so where was the point in my acting like them? And for the time being, I had other concerns.

I walked into T'vril's office as he was filling out paperwork. Before he could rise to greet me, I put a hand on his desk. "My mother's belongings. Where are they?"

He closed his mouth, then opened it again to speak. "Her apartment is in Spire Seven."

It was my turn to pause. "Her apartment is intact?"

"Dekarta ordered it kept that way when she left. After it became clear that she would not return..." He spread his hands. "My predecessor valued his life too much to suggest that the apartment be emptied. So do I."

He added then, diplomatic as ever, "I'll have someone show you the way."

My mother's quarters.

The servant had left me alone on my unspoken order. With the door closed, a stillness fell. Ovals of sunlight layered the floor. The curtains were heavy and had not stirred at my entrance. T'vril's people had kept the apartment clean, so not even dust motes danced in the light. If I held my breath I could almost believe I stood within a portrait, not a place in the here and now.

I took a step forward. This was the reception room. Bureau, couch, table for tea or work. A few personal touches here and there—paintings on the wall, sculpture on small shelves, a beautifully carved altar in the Senmite style. All very elegant.

None of it felt like her.

I went through the apartment. Bathchamber on the left. Bigger than mine, but my mother had always loved bathing. I remembered sitting in bubbles with her, giggling as she piled her hair on top of her head and made silly faces—

No. None of that, or I would soon be useless.

The bedchamber. The bed was a huge oval twice the size of mine, white, deep with pillows. Dressers, a vanity, a hearth and mantel—decorative, since there was no need for fire in Sky. Another table. Here, too, were personal touches: bottles carefully arranged on the vanity to put my mother's favorites at the front. Several potted plants, huge and verdant after so many years. Portraits on the walls.

These caught my eye. I went to the mantel for a better look at the largest of them, a framed rendering of a handsome blonde Amn woman. She was richly dressed, with a bearing that spoke of an upbringing far more refined than mine, but something about her expression intrigued me. Her smile was only the barest curve of lips, and although she faced the viewer, her eyes were vague rather than focused. Daydreaming? Or troubled? The artist had been a master to capture that.

The resemblance between her and my mother was striking. My grandmother, then, Dekarta's tragically dead wife. No wonder she looked troubled, marrying into this family.

I turned to take in the whole room. "What were you in this place, Mother?" I whispered aloud. My voice did not break the stillness. Here within the closed, frozen moment of the room, I was merely an observer. "Were you the mother I remember, or were you an Arameri?"

This had nothing to do with her death. It was just something I had to know.

I began to search the apartment. It went slowly because I could not bring myself to ransack the place. Not only would I offend the servants by doing so, but I felt that it would somehow disrespect my mother. She had always liked things neat.

Thus the sun had set by the time I finally found a small chest in the headboard cabinet of her bed. I hadn't even realized the headboard had a cabinet until I rested my hand on its edge and felt the seam. A hiding space? The chest was open, stuffed with a bouquet of folded and rolled papers. I was already reaching for it when my eyes caught a glimpse of my father's handwriting on one of the scrolls.

My hands shook as I lifted the chest from the cabinet. It left a clean square amid the thick layer of dust on the cabinet's inside; apparently the servants hadn't cleaned within. Perhaps they, like me, hadn't realized the headboard opened. Blowing dust off the topmost layer of papers, I picked up the first folded sheet.

A love letter, from my father to my mother.

I pulled out each paper, examining and arranging them in

order by date. They were all love letters, from him to her and a few from her to him, spanning a year or so in my parents' lives. Swallowing hard and steeling myself, I began to read.

An hour later I stopped, and lay down on the bed, and wept myself to sleep.

When I awakened, the room was dark.

And I was not afraid. A bad sign.

"You should not wander the palace alone," said the Nightlord.

I sat up. He sat beside me on the bed, gazing at the window. The moon was high and bright through a smear of cloud; I must have slept for hours. I rubbed my face and said, greatly daring, "I would like to think we have an understanding, Lord Nahadoth."

My reward was his smile, though he still did not turn to me. "Respect. Yes. But there are more dangers in Sky than me."

"Some things are worth the risk." I looked at the bed. The pile of letters lay there, along with other small items I'd taken from the chest: a sachet of dried flowers; a lock of straight black hair that must have been my father's; a curl of paper that held several crossed-out lines of poetry in my mother's hand; and a tiny silver pendant on a thin leather cord. The treasures of a woman in love. I picked up the pendant and tried again, unsuccessfully, to determine what it was. It looked like a rough, flattened lump, oblong with pointed ends. Familiar, somehow.

"A fruitstone," said Nahadoth. He watched me now, sidelong.

Yes, it did look like that—apricot, perhaps, or gingko. I

remembered then where I'd seen something similar: in gold, around Ras Onchi's neck. "Why...?"

"The fruit dies, but within lies the spark of new life. Enefa had power over life and death."

I frowned in confusion. Perhaps the silver fruitstone was Enefa's symbol, like Itempas's white-jade ring. But why would my mother possess a symbol of Enefa? Or rather—why would my father have given it to her?

"She was the strongest of us," Nahadoth murmured. He was gazing out at the night sky again, though it was clear his thoughts were somewhere else entirely. "If Itempas hadn't used poison, He could never have slain her outright. But she trusted Him. Loved Him."

He lowered his eyes, smiling gently, ruefully, to himself. "Then again, so did I."

I nearly dropped the pendant.

Here is what the priests taught me:

Once upon a time there were three great gods. Bright Itempas, Lord of Day, was the one destined by fate or the Maelstrom or some unfathomable design to rule. All was well until Enefa, His upstart sister, decided that she wanted to rule in Bright Itempas's place. She convinced their brother Nahadoth to assist her, and together with some of their godling children they attempted a coup. Itempas, mightier than both His siblings combined, defeated them soundly. He slew Enefa, punished Nahadoth and the rebels, and established an even greater peace—for without His dark brother and wild sister to appease, He was free to bring true light and order to all creation.

But—

*   *   *

"P-poison?"

Nahadoth sighed. Behind him his hair shifted restlessly, like curtains wafting in a night breeze. "We created the weapon ourselves in our dalliances with humans, though we did not realize this for some time."

The Nightlord descended to earth, seeking entertainment— "The demons," I whispered.

"Humans made that word an epithet. The demons were as beautiful and perfect as our godborn children—but mortal. Put into our bodies, their blood taught our flesh how to die. It was the only poison that could harm us."

But the Nightlord's lover never forgave him— "You hunted them down."

"We feared they would mingle with mortals, passing on the taint to their descendants, until the entire human race became lethal to us. But Itempas kept one alive, in hiding."

To murder one's own children...I shuddered. So the priests' story was true. And yet I could sense the shame in Nahadoth, the lingering pain. That meant my grandmother's version of the story was true, too.

"So Lord Itempas used this...poison to subdue Enefa when she attacked Him."

"She did not attack Him."

Queasiness. The world was tilting in my head. "Then... why...?"

He lowered his gaze. His hair fell forward to obscure his face, and I was thrown back in time three nights to our first meeting. The smile that curved his lips now was not mad, but held such bitterness that it might as well have been.

"They quarreled," he said, "over me."

For half an instant, something changed in me. I looked at Nahadoth and did not see him as the powerful, unpredictable, deadly entity that he was.

I wanted him. To entice him. To control him. I saw myself naked on green grass, my arms and legs wrapped around Nahadoth as he shuddered upon me, trapped and helpless in the pleasure of my flesh. Mine. I saw myself caress his midnight hair, and look up to meet my own eyes, and smile in smug, possessive satisfaction.

I rejected that image, that feeling, almost as soon as it came to my mind. But it was another warning.

"The Maelstrom that begat us was slow," Nahadoth said. If he sensed my sudden unease, he gave no sign. "I was born first, then Itempas. For uncountable eternities He and I were alone in the universe—first enemies, then beloved. He liked it that way."

I tried not to think of the priests' tales. Tried not to wonder if Nahadoth was lying, too—though there was a feel of truth to his words that rang within me on an almost instinctive level. The Three were more than siblings; they were forces of nature, opposed yet inextricably linked. I, an only child and a mortal who had never had a beloved of her own, could not begin to understand their relationship. Yet I felt compelled to try.

"When Enefa came along…Lord Itempas saw her as an interloper?"

"Yes. Even though before her we felt our incompleteness. We were made to be Three, not two. Itempas resented that, as well."

Then Nahadoth glanced at me sidelong. In the shadow of my

body, for just an instant, the uncertain shift of his face resolved into a singular perfection of lines and features that made my breath catch. I had never seen anything so beautiful. At once I understood why Itempas had killed Enefa to have him.

"Does it amuse you to hear that we can be just as selfish and prideful as humankind?" There was an edge to Nahadoth's voice now. I barely noticed it. I could not look away from his face. "We made you in our image, remember. All our flaws are yours."

"No," I said. "A-all that surprises me are...the lies I've been told."

"I would have expected the Darre to do a better job of preserving the truth." He leaned closer, slow, subtle. Something predatory was in his eyes—and I, entranced, was easy prey. "Not every race of humankind worships Itempas by choice, after all. I would have thought their *ennu* at least would know the old ways."

I would have thought so, too. I clenched my hand around the silver fruitstone, feeling light-headed. I knew that once my people had been heretics. That was why the Amn called races like mine *darkling*: we had accepted the Bright only to save ourselves when the Arameri threatened us with annihilation. But what Nahadoth implied—that some of my people had known the real reason for the Gods' War all along and had *hidden it from me*—no. That I could not, did not want to, believe.

There had always been whispers about me. Doubts. My Amn hair, my Amn eyes. My Amn mother, who might have inculcated me with her Arameri ways. I had fought so hard to win my people's respect. I thought I had succeeded.

"No," I whispered. "My grandmother would have told me..."

Wouldn't she?

"So many secrets surround you," the Nightlord whispered. "So many lies, like veils. Shall I strip them away for you?" His hand touched my hip. I could not help jumping. His nose brushed mine, his breath tickling my lips. "You want me."

If I had not already been trembling, I would have begun. "N-no."

"So many lies." On the last word, his tongue licked out to brush my lips. Every muscle in my body seemed to tighten; I could not help whimpering. I saw myself on the green grass again, under him, pinned by him. I saw myself on a bed—the very bed on which I sat. I saw him take me on my mother's bed, his face savage and his movements violent, and I did not own him or control him. How had I ever dared to imagine that I might? He used me and I was helpless, crying out in pain and want. I was his and he devoured me, relishing my sanity as he tore it apart and swallowed it in oozing chunks. He would destroy me and I would love every minute of it.

"Oh gods—" The irony of my oath was lost on me. I reached up, burying my hands in his black aura to push at him. I felt cool night air and thought my hands would just go on, touching nothing. Instead I encountered solid flesh, a warm body, cloth. I clutched at the latter to remind me of reality and danger. It was so hard not to pull him closer. "Please don't. Please, oh gods, please don't."

He still loomed over me. His mouth still brushed mine, so that I felt his smile. "Is that a command?"

I was shaking with fear and desire and effort. The last finally paid off as I managed to turn my face away from his. His cool breath tickled my neck and I felt it down my whole body, the most intimate of caresses. I had never wanted a man so much, never in my whole life. I had never been so afraid.

"Please," I said again.

He kissed me, very lightly, on my neck. I tried not to moan and failed miserably. I *ached* for him. But then he sighed, rose, and walked over to the window. The black tendrils of his power lingered on me a moment longer; I had been almost buried in his darkness. But as he moved away the tendrils released me—reluctantly, it seemed—and settled back into the usual restlessness of his aura.

I wrapped my arms around myself, wondering if I would ever stop shivering.

"Your mother was a true Arameri," said Nahadoth.

That shocked me out of desire, as suddenly as a slap.

"She was all that Dekarta wanted and more," he continued. "Their goals were never the same, but in every other way, she was more than a match for her father. He loves her still."

I swallowed. My legs were shaky so I did not stand, but I made myself straighten from the hunch that I had unconsciously adopted. "Then why did he kill her?"

"You think it was him?"

I opened my mouth to demand an explanation. But before I could, he turned to me. In the light from the window his body was a silhouette, except for his eyes. I saw them clearly, onyx-black and glittering with unearthly knowing and malice.

"No, little pawn," said the Nightlord. "Little tool. No more secrets, not without an alliance. That is for your safety as well as ours. Shall I tell you the terms?" Somehow I knew that he smiled. "Yes, I think I should. We want your life, sweet Yeine. Offer it to us and you'll have all the answers you want—and, too, the chance for revenge. That's what you truly want, isn't it?" A soft, cruel chuckle. "You're more Arameri than Dekarta sees."

I began to tremble again, not out of fear this time.

As before, he faded away, his image disappearing long before his presence did. When I could no longer feel him, I put away my mother's belongings and straightened the room so that no one would know I had been there. I wanted to keep the silver fruitstone, but I could think of nowhere safer to hide it than the compartment where it had lain undiscovered for decades. So I left it and the letters in their hiding place.

When I was finally done, I went back to my room. It took all my willpower not to run.

11

Mother

T'VRIL TOLD ME THAT sometimes Sky eats people. It was built by the Enefadeh, after all, and living in a home built by angry gods necessarily entails some risk. On nights when the moon is black and the stars hide behind clouds, the stone walls stop glowing. Bright Itempas is powerless then. The darkness never lingers—a few hours at most—but while it lasts, most Arameri keep to their rooms and speak softly. If they must travel Sky's corridors, they move quickly and furtively, always watching their step. For you see, wholly at random, the floors open up and swallow the unwary. Searchers go into the dead spaces underneath, but no bodies are ever found.

I know now that this is true. But more important—

I know where the lost ones have gone.

"Please tell me about my mother," I said to Viraine.

He looked up from the contraption he was working on. It looked like a spidery mass of jointed metal and leather; I had no inkling of its purpose. "T'vril told me he sent you to her room last night," he said, shifting on his stool to face me. His expression was thoughtful. "What is it you're looking for?"

I made note: T'vril was not entirely trustworthy. But that did not surprise me; T'vril doubtless had his own battles to fight. "The truth."

"You don't believe Dekarta?"

"Would you?"

He chuckled. "You have no reason to believe me, either."

"I have no reason to believe anyone in this whole reeking Amn warren. But since I cannot leave, I have no choice but to crawl through the muck."

"Oh, my. You almost sound like her." To my surprise he seemed pleased by my rudeness. Indeed, he began smiling, though with an air of condescension. "Too crude, though. Too straightforward. Kinneth's insults were so subtle that you wouldn't realize she'd called you dirt until hours afterward."

"My mother never insulted anyone unless she had good reason. What did you say to provoke her?"

He paused for only a heartbeat, but I noted with satisfaction that his smile faded.

"What do you want to know?" he asked.

"Why did Dekarta have my mother killed?"

"The only person who could answer that question is Dekarta. Do you plan to talk to him?"

Eventually, I would. But two could play the game of answering a question with a question. "Why did she come here, that last night? The night Dekarta finally realized she wasn't coming back?"

I had expected the surprise in Viraine's face. What I had not expected was the cold fury that followed swiftly on its heels.

"Who have you been talking to? The servants? Sieh?"

Sometimes the truth can throw an opponent off-balance. "Nahadoth."

He flinched, and then his eyes narrowed. "I see. He'll kill you, you know. That's his favorite pastime, to toy with any Arameri foolish enough to try and tame him."

"Scimina—"

"—has no intention of taming him. The more monstrous he becomes, the happier she is. He spread the last fool who fell in love with him all over the centeryard, I hear."

I remembered Nahadoth's lips on my throat and fought to suppress a shudder, only half-succeeding. Death as a consequence of lying with a god wasn't something I had considered, but it did not surprise me. A mortal man's strength had limits. He spent himself and slept. He could be a good lover, but even his best skills were only guesswork—for every caress that sent a woman's head into the clouds, he might try ten that brought her back to earth.

Nahadoth would bring me into the clouds and keep me there. He would drag me further, into the cold airless dark that was his true domain. And if I suffocated there, if my flesh burst or my mind broke…well. Viraine was right; I'd have only myself to blame.

I gave Viraine a rueful smile, letting him see my very real fear. "Yes, Nahadoth probably will kill me—if you Arameri don't beat him to it. If that troubles you, you could always help me by answering my questions."

Viraine fell silent for a long moment, his thoughts unfathomable behind the mask of his face. Finally he surprised me again, rising from his workbench and going to one of the enormous windows. From this one we could see the whole of the city and the mountains beyond.

"I can't say I remember the night well," he said. "It was twenty years ago. I had only just come to Sky then, newly posted by the Scriveners' College."

"Please tell me all you can recall," I said.

Scriveners learn several mortal tongues as children, before they begin learning the gods' language. This helps them understand the flexibility of language and of the mind itself, for there are many concepts that exist in some languages that cannot even be approximated in others. This is how the gods' tongue works; it allows the conceptualization of the impossible. And this is why the best scriveners can never be trusted.

"It was raining that night. I remember because rain doesn't often touch Sky; the heaviest clouds usually drop below us. But Kinneth got soaked just between her carriage and the entrance. There was a trail of water along the floor of every corridor she walked."

Which meant that he had watched her pass, I realized. Either he'd been lurking in a side corridor while she went by, or he'd followed close enough in her wake that the water hadn't dried. Hadn't Sieh said Dekarta emptied the hallways that night? Viraine must have disobeyed that order.

"Everyone knew why she had come, or thought they did. No one expected that marriage to last. It seemed unfathomable that a woman so strong, a woman raised to rule, would give it all up for nothing." In the reflection of the glass, Viraine looked up at me. "No offense meant."

For an Arameri, it was almost polite. "None taken."

He smiled thinly. "But it *was* for him, you see. The reason she came that night. Her husband, your father; she didn't come to reclaim her position, she came because *he* had the Walking Death, and she wanted Dekarta to save him."

I stared at him, feeling slapped.

"She even brought him with her. One of the forecourt servants glanced inside the coach and saw him in there, sweating and feverish, probably in the third stage. The journey alone must have stressed him physically, accelerating the disease's course. She gambled everything on Dekarta's aid."

I swallowed. I'd known that my father had contracted the Death at some point. I'd known that my mother had fled from Sky at the height of her power, banished for the crime of loving beneath herself. But that the two events were linked— "She must have succeeded, then."

"No. When she left to return to Darr, she was angry. Dekarta was in such a fury as I've never seen; I thought there would be deaths. But he simply ordered that Kinneth was to be struck from the family rolls, not only as his heir—that had already been done—but as an Arameri altogether. He ordered me to burn off her blood sigil, which can be done from a distance, and which I did. He even made a public announcement. It was the talk of society—the first time any fullblood has been disowned in, oh, centuries."

I shook my head slowly. "And my father?"

"As far as I could tell, he was still sick when she left."

But my father had survived the Walking Death. Surviving was not unheard of, but it was rare, especially among those who had reached third stage.

Perhaps Dekarta had changed his mind? If he had ordered it, the palace physicians would have ridden out after the carriage, caught up to it and brought it back. Dekarta could have even ordered the Enefadeh to—

Wait.

Wait.

"So that's why she came," Viraine said. He turned from the window to face me, sober. "For him. There's no grand conspiracy to it, and no mystery—any servant who'd been here long enough could've told you this. So why were you so anxious to know that you'd ask *me*?"

"Because I thought you'd tell me more than a servant," I replied. I struggled to keep my voice even, so that he would not know my suspicions. "If sufficiently motivated."

"Is that why you goaded me?" He shook his head and sighed. "Well. It's good to see you've inherited *some* Arameri qualities."

"They seem to be useful here."

He offered a sardonic incline of the head. "Anything else?"

I was dying to know more, but not from him. Still, it would not do to appear hasty.

"Do you agree with Dekarta?" I asked, just to make

conversation. "That my mother would have been more harsh in dealing with that heretic?"

"Oh, yes." I blinked in surprise, and he smiled. "Kinneth was like Dekarta, one of the few Arameri who actually took our role as Itempas's chosen seriously. She was death on unbelievers. Death on anyone, really, who threatened the peace—or her power." He shook his head, his smile nostalgic now. "You think Scimina's bad? Scimina has no vision. Your mother was purpose incarnate."

He was enjoying himself again, reading the discomfort on my face like a sigil. Perhaps I was still young enough to see her through the worshipful eyes of childhood, but the ways I'd heard my mother described since coming to Sky simply did not fit my memories. I remembered a gentle, warm woman, full of wry humor. She could be ruthless, oh yes—as befitted the wife of any ruler, especially under the circumstances in Darr at the time. But to hear her compared favorably against Scimina and praised by Dekarta... that was not the same woman who had raised me. That was another woman, with my mother's name and background but an entirely different soul.

Viraine specialized in magics that could affect the soul. *Did you do something to my mother?* I wanted to ask. But that would have been far, far too simple an explanation.

"You're wasting your time, you know," Viraine said. He spoke softly, and his smile had faded during my long silence. "Your mother is dead. You're still alive. You should spend more time trying to stay that way, and less time trying to join her."

Was that what I was doing?

"Good day, Scrivener Viraine," I said, and left.

*   *   *

I got lost then, figuratively and literally.

Sky is not generally an easy place in which to get lost. The corridors all look the same, true. The lifts get confused sometimes, carrying riders where they *want* to be rather than where they *intend* to go. (I'm told this was especially a problem for lovesick couriers.) Still, the halls are normally thick with servants who are happy to aid anyone wearing a highblood mark.

I did not ask for help. I knew this was foolish, but some part of me did not want direction. Viraine's words had cut deep, and as I walked through the corridors I worried at the wounds with my thoughts.

It was true that I had neglected the inheritance contest in favor of learning more about my mother. Learning the truth would not bring the dead back to life, but it could certainly get me killed. Perhaps Viraine was right, and my behavior reflected some suicidal tendency. It had been less than a turn of the seasons since my mother's death. In Darr I would have had time and family to help me mourn properly, but my grandfather's invitation had cut that short. Here in Sky I hid my grief—but that did not mean I felt it any less.

In this frame of mind I stopped and found myself at the palace library.

T'vril had shown me this on my first day in Sky. Under ordinary circumstances I would have been awed; the library occupied a space larger than the temple of Sar-enna-nem, back in my land. Sky's library contained more books, scrolls, tablets, and spheres than I had seen in my entire life. But I had been in need of a more peculiar kind of knowledge since my arrival in

Sky, and the accumulated lore of the Hundred Thousand Kingdoms could not help me with that.

Still... for some reason, I now felt drawn to the place.

I wandered through the library's entrance hall and was
greeted only by the sounds of my own faintly echoing footsteps.
The ceiling was thrice the height of a man, braced by enormous
round pillars and a maze of floor-to-ceiling bookcases. Both
cases and pillars were covered by shelf upon shelf of books and
scrolls, some accessible only by the ladders that I saw in each
corner. Here and there were tables and chairs, where one might
lounge and read for hours.

Yet there seemed to be no one else around, which surprised
me. Were the Arameri so inured to luxury that they took even
this treasure trove for granted? I stopped to examine a wall of
tomes as thick as my head, then I realized I couldn't read a single one. Senmite—the Amn language—had become the common tongue since the Arameri's ascension, but most nations
were still allowed their own languages so long as they taught
Senmite, too. These looked like Teman. I checked the next
wall; Kenti. Somewhere in the place there was probably a Darren shelf, but I had no idea of where to begin finding it.

"Are you lost?"

I jumped, and turned to see a short, plump old Amn woman
a few feet away, peering around the curve of a pillar. I hadn't
noticed her at all. By the sour look on her face, she'd probably
thought herself alone in the library, too.

"I—" I realized I had no idea what to say. I hadn't come in for
any purpose. To stall, I said, "Is there a shelf here in Darren? Or
at least, where are the Senmite books?"

Wordlessly, the old woman pointed right behind me. I turned

and saw three shelves of Darren books. "The Senmite starts around the corner."

Feeling supremely foolish, I nodded thanks and studied the Darren shelf. For several minutes I stared at them before realizing that half were poetry, and the other half collections of tales I'd heard all my life. Nothing useful.

"Are you looking for something in particular?" The woman stood right beside me now. I started a bit, since I hadn't heard her move.

But at her question, I suddenly realized there *was* something I could learn from the library. "Information about the Gods' War," I said.

"Religious texts are in the chapel, not here." If anything, now the woman looked more sour. Perhaps she was the librarian, in which case I might have offended her. It was clear the library saw little enough traffic as it was without being mistaken for someplace else.

"I don't want religious texts," I said quickly, hoping to placate her. "I want...historical accounts. Death records. Journals, letters, scholarly interpretations...anything written at the time."

The woman narrowed her eyes at me for a moment. She was the only adult I'd seen in Sky who was shorter than me, which might have comforted me somewhat if not for the blatant hostility in her expression. I marveled at the hostility, for she was dressed in the same simple white uniform as most of the servants. Usually all it took was the sight of the fullblood mark on my brow to make them polite to the point of obsequiousness.

"There are some things like that," she said. "But any *complete* accounts of the war have been heavily censored by the priests. There might be a few untouched resources left in private collections—it's said Lord Dekarta keeps the most valuable of these in his quarters."

I should have known. "I'd like to see anything you have." Nahadoth had made me curious. I knew nothing of the Gods' War that the priests hadn't told me. Perhaps if I read the accounts myself, I could sift some truth from the lies.

The old woman pursed her lips, thoughtful, and then gestured curtly for me to follow her. "This way."

I followed her through the winding aisles, my awe growing as I realized just how truly big the place was. "This library must hold all the knowledge of the world."

My dour companion snorted. "A few millennia worth, from a few pockets of humanity, nothing more. And that picked and sorted, trimmed and twisted to suit the tastes of those in power."

"There's truth even in tainted knowledge, if one reads carefully."

"Only if one knows the knowledge is tainted in the first place." Turning another corner, the old woman stopped. We had reached some sort of nexus amid the maze. Before us, several bookcases had been arranged back-to-back as a titanic six-sided column. Each bookcase was a good five feet wide, tall and sturdy enough to help support the ceiling that was twenty feet or more above; the whole structure rivaled the trunk of a centuries-old tree. "There is what you want."

I took a step toward the column and then stopped, abruptly uncertain. When I turned back, I realized the old woman was watching me with a disconcertingly intent gaze. Her eyes were the color of low-grade pewter.

"Excuse me," I said, spurred by some instinct. "There's a lot here. Where would you suggest I begin?"

She scowled and said "How should I know?" before turning away. She vanished amid the stacks before I could recover from the shock of such blatant rudeness.

But I had more important concerns than one cranky librarian, so I turned my attention back to the column. Choosing a shelf at random, I skimmed the spines for titles that sounded interesting, and began my hunt.

Two hours later—I had moved to the floor in the interim, spreading books and scrolls around myself—exasperation set in. Groaning, I flung myself back amid the circle of books, sprawling over them in a way that would surely incense the librarian if she saw me. The old woman's comments had made me think there would be little mention of the Gods' War, but this was anything but the case. There were complete eyewitness accounts of the war. There were accounts of accounts, and critical analyses of those accounts. There was so much information, in fact, that if I had begun reading that day and continued without stopping, it would have taken me months to read it all.

And try as I might, I could not sift the truth from what I'd read. All of the accounts cited the same series of events: the weakening of the world, in which every living thing from forests to strong young men had grown ill and begun to die. The three-day storm. The shattering and re-formation of the sun. On the third day the skies had gone quiet, and Itempas appeared to explain the new order of the world.

What was missing were the events leading up to the war. Here I could see the priests had been busy, for I could find no descriptions of the gods' relationship prior to the war. There were no mentions of customs or beliefs in the days of the Three. Those few texts that even touched on the subject simply cited what Bright Itempas had told the first Arameri: Enefa was instigator and villain, Nahadoth her willing coconspirator, Lord Itempas the hero betrayed and then triumphant. And I had wasted more time.

Rubbing my tired eyes, I debated whether to try again the next day or just give up altogether. But as I mustered my strength to get up, something caught my eye. On the ceiling. I could see, from this angle, where two of the bookcases joined to form the column. But they were not actually joined; there was a gap between them perhaps six inches wide. Puzzled, I sat up and peered closer at the column. It appeared as it always had, a set of huge, heavily laden bookcases arranged back-to-back in a rough circle, joined tight with no gaps.

Another of Sky's secrets? I got to my feet.

The trick was amazingly simple, once I took a good look. The bookcases were made of a heavy, dark wood that was naturally black in color—probably Darren, I guessed belatedly; once upon a time we'd been famous for it. Through the gaps I could see the backs of the other bookcases, also blackwood. Because the edges of the gaps were black, and the backs of the bookcases were black, the gaps themselves were all but invisible, even from a few steps away. But knowing the gaps were there...

I peered through the nearest gap and saw a wide, white-floored space corraled by the bookcases. Had someone tried to hide this space? But that made no sense; the trick was so simple that someone, probably many someones, must have found the inner column before. That suggested the goal was not to conceal, but to misdirect—to prevent casual browsers and passersby from finding whatever was within the column. Only those who knew the visual trick was there, or who spent enough time looking for information, would find it.

The old woman's words came back to me. *If one knows the knowledge is tainted in the first place . . .* Yes. Plain to see, if one knew something was there to find.

The gap was narrow. I was grateful for once to be boy-shaped, because that made it easy to wriggle between the shelves. But then I stumbled and nearly fell, because once I was inside the column, I saw what it *truly* hid.

And then I heard a voice, except it wasn't a voice, and he asked, "Do you love me?"

And I said, "Come and I will show you," and opened my arms. He came to me and pulled me hard against him, and I did not see the knife in his hand. No, no, there was no knife; we had no need of such things. No, there was a knife, later, and the taste of blood was bright and strange in my mouth as I looked up to see his terrible, terrible gaze . . .

But what did it mean that he made love to me first?

I stumbled back against the opposite wall, struggling to breathe and think around blazing terror and inexplicable nausea and the yawning urge to clutch my head and scream.

The final warning, yes. I am not usually so dense, but you must understand. It was a bit much to deal with.

"Do you need help?"

My mind latched on to the voice of the old librarian with the ferocity of a drowning victim. I must have looked a sight as I whipped around to face her; I was swaying on my feet, my mouth hanging open and dumb, my hands outstretched and forming claws in front of me.

The old woman, who stood bracketed by one of the bookcase gaps, gazed in at me impassively.

With an effort, I closed my mouth, lowered my hands, and straightened from the bizarre half crouch into which I'd sunk. I was still shaking inside, but some semblance of dignity was returning to me.

"I . . . I, no," I managed after a moment. "No. I'm . . . all right."

She said nothing, just kept watching me. I wanted to tell her to go away, but my eyes were drawn back to the thing that had shocked me so.

Across the back of a bookcase, the Bright Lord of Order gazed at me. It was just artwork—an Amn-style embossing, gold leaf layered onto an outline chiseled in a white marble slab. Still, the artist had captured Itempas in astounding, life-size detail. He stood in an elegant warrior's stance, His form broad and powerfully muscled, His hands resting on the hilt of a huge, straight sword. Eyes like lanterns pinned me from the solemn perfection of His face. I had seen renderings of Him in the priests' books, but not like this. They made Him slimmer, thin-featured, like an Amn. They always drew Him smiling, and they never made His expression so cold.

I put my hands behind me to push myself upright—and felt more marble under my fingers. When I turned, the shock was not so great this time. I half-expected what I saw: inlaid obsidian and a riot of tiny, starlike diamonds, all of it forming a lithe, sensual figure. His hands were flung outstretched from his sides, nearly lost amid the flaring cloak of hair and power. I could not see the exulting? screaming? figure's face, for it was tilted upward, dominated by that open, howling mouth. But I knew him anyhow.

Except...I frowned in confusion, reaching up to touch what might have been a swirl of cloth, or a rounded breast.

"Itempas forced him into a single shape," said the old woman, her voice very soft. "When he was free, he was all things beautiful and terrible." I had never heard a more fitting description.

But there was a third slab to my right. I saw it from the corner of my eye. Had seen it from the moment I'd slipped between the shelves. Had avoided looking at it, for reasons that had nothing to do with my rational self and everything to do with what I now, deep down in the unreasoning core of my instincts, suspected.

I made myself turn to face the third slab, while the old woman watched me.

Compared to her brothers, Enefa's image was demure. Undramatic. In gray marble profile she sat, clad in a simple shift, her face downcast. Only on closer observation did one notice the subtleties. Her hand held a small sphere—an object immediately recognizable to anyone who had ever seen Sieh's orrery. (And I understood, now, why he treasured his collection so much.) Her posture, taut with ready energy, more *crouch* than *sit*. Her eyes, which despite her downturned face glanced up, sidelong, at the viewer. There was something about her gaze that was...not seductive. It was too frank for that. Nor wary. But...

evaluative. Yes. She looked at me and through me, measuring all that she saw.

With a shaking hand, I reached up to touch her face. More rounded than mine, prettier, but the lines were the same as what I saw in mirrors. The hair was longer, but the curl was right. The artist had set her irises with pale green jade. If the skin had been brown instead of marble...I swallowed, trembling harder still.

"We hadn't intended to tell you yet," said the old woman. Right behind me now, though she should've been too fat to fit through the gap. Would've been, if she had been human. "Pure chance that you decided to come to the library now. I suppose I could've found a way to steer you elsewhere, but..." I heard rather than saw her shrug. "You would have found out eventually."

I sank to the floor, huddling against the Itempas wall as if He would protect me. I was cold all over, my thoughts screaming and skittering every which way. Making that first, crucial connection had broken my ability to make others.

This is how madness feels, I understood.

"Will you kill me?" I whispered to the old woman. There was no mark on her forehead. I had missed that, still used to the absence of a mark, not its presence. I should have noticed. She'd had a different shape in my dream, but I knew her now: Kurue the Wise, leader of the Enefadeh.

"Why would I do that? We've invested far too much in creating you." A hand fell on my shoulder; I twitched. "But you're no good to us insane."

So I was not surprised to feel darkness close over me. I relaxed and, grateful, let it come.

12

Sanity

Once upon a time there was a
Once upon a time there was a
Once upon a time there was a
Stop this. It's undignified.

ONCE UPON A TIME THERE WAS A little girl who had two older siblings. The oldest was dark and wild and glorious, if somewhat uncouth. The other was filled with all the brightness of all the suns that ever were, and he was very stern and upright. They were much older than her, and very close to one another even though in the past they had fought viciously. "We were young and foolish then," said Second Sibling, whenever the little girl asked him about it.

"Sex was more fun," said First Sibling.

This sort of statement made Second Sibling very cross, which of course was why First Sibling said it. In this way did the little girl come to know and love them both.

This is an approximation, you realize. This is what your mortal mind can comprehend.

Thus went the little girl's childhood. They had no parents, the three of them, and so the little girl raised herself. She drank glimmering stuff when she was thirsty and lay down in soft places when she got tired. When she was hungry, First Sibling showed her how to draw sustenance from energies that suited her, and when she was bored Second Sibling taught her all the lore that had come into being. This was how she came to know names. The place in which they lived was called EXISTENCE— as opposed to the place from which they had come, which was a great shrieking mass of nothingness called MAELSTROM. The toys and foods she conjured were POSSIBILITY, and what a delightful substance that was! With it she could build anything she needed, even change the nature of EXISTENCE—though she quickly learned to ask before doing this, because Second Sibling got upset when she altered his carefully ordered rules and processes. First Sibling did not care.

Over time it came to be that the little girl spent more time with First Sibling than with Second, because Second did not seem to like her as much. "This is difficult for him," First Sibling said, when she complained. "We have been alone, he and I, for so very long. Now you are here, and that changes everything. He does not like change."

This the little girl had already come to understand. And this was why her siblings so often fought with each other, because First Sibling loved change. Often First Sibling would grow bored with existence and transform it, or turn it inside out just to see the other side. Second Sibling would rage at First Sibling whenever this happened, and First Sibling would laugh at his fury, and before the little girl could blink they would be on each other, tearing and blasting, until something changed and then they would be clutching and gasping, and whenever this

happened the little girl would patiently wait for them to finish
so they could play with her again.

In time the little girl became a woman. She had learned to
live with her two siblings, each in their own way—dancing
wild with First Sibling and growing adept at discipline alongside Second. Now she made her own way beyond their peculiarities. She had stepped in between her siblings during their
battles, fighting them to measure her strength and loving them
when the fighting turned to joy. She had, though they did not
know it, gone off to create her own separate EXISTENCES, where
sometimes she pretended that she had no siblings. There she
could arrange POSSIBILITY into stunning new shapes and mean-
ings that she was sure neither of her siblings could have created
themselves. In time she grew adept at this, and her creations so
pleased her that she began to bring them into the realm where
her siblings lived. She did this subtly at first, taking great care to
fit them into Second Sibling's orderly spaces and arrangements
in a way that might not offend him.

First Sibling, as usual delighted by anything new, urged
her to do far more. However, the woman found that she had
developed a taste for some of Second Sibling's order. She incorporated First Sibling's suggestions, but gradually, purposefully,
observing how each minute change triggered others, sometimes causing growth in unexpected and wonderful ways.
Sometimes the changes destroyed everything, forcing her to
start over. She mourned the loss of her toys, her treasures, but
she always began the process again. Like First Sibling's darkness and Second Sibling's light, this particular gift was something only she could master. The compulsion to do it was as

essential to her as breathing, as much a part of her as her own soul.

Second Sibling, once he got over his annoyance at her tinkering, asked her about it. "It is called 'life,'" she said, liking the sound of the word. He smiled, pleased, for to name a thing is to give it order and purpose, and he understood then that she had done so to offer him respect.

But it was to First Sibling that she went for help with her most ambitious experiment. First Sibling was, as she had expected, eager to assist—but to her surprise, there was a sober warning as well. "If this works, it will change many things. You realize that, don't you? Nothing in our lives will ever be the same." First Sibling paused, waiting to see that she understood, and abruptly she did. Second Sibling did not like change.

"Nothing can stay the same forever," she said. "We were not made to be still. Even he must realize that."

First Sibling only sighed and said no more.

The experiment worked. The new life, mewling and shaking and uttering vehement protests, was beautiful in its unfinished way, and the woman knew that what she had begun was good and right. She named the creature "Sieh," because that was the sound of the wind. And she called his type of being a "child," meaning that it had the potential to grow into something like themselves, and meaning, too, that they could create more of them.

And as always with life, this minute change triggered many, many others. The most profound of them was something even she had not anticipated: they became a family. For a time, they were all happy with that—even Second Sibling.

But not all families last.

*   *   *

So there was love, once.

More than love. And now there is more than hate. Mortals have no words for what we gods feel. *Gods* have no words for such things.

But love like that doesn't just disappear, does it? No matter how powerful the hate, there is always a little love left, underneath.

Yes. Horrible, isn't it?

When the body suffers an assault, it often reacts with a fever. Assaults to the mind can have the same effect. Thus I lay shivering and insensible for the better part of three days.

A few moments from this time appear in my memory as still-life portraits, some in color and some in shades of gray. A solitary figure standing near my bedroom window, huge and alert with inhuman vigilance. Zhakkarn. Blink and the same image returns in negative: the same figure, framed by glowing white walls and a black rectangle of night beyond the window. Blink and there is another image: the old woman from the library standing over me, peering carefully into my eyes. Zhakkarn stands in the background, watching. A thread of conversation, disconnected from any image.

"If she dies—"

"Then we start over. What's a few more decades?"

"Nahadoth will be displeased."

A rough, rueful laugh. "You have a great gift for understatement, sister."

"Sieh, too."

"That is Sieh's own fault. I warned him not to get attached, the little fool."

Silence for a moment, full of reproach. "There is nothing foolish about hope."

Silence in reply, though this silence feels faintly of shame.

One of the images in my head is different from the others. This one is dark again, but the walls, too, have gone dark, and there is a *feeling* to the image, a sense of ominous weight and pressure and low, gathering rage. Zhakkarn stands away from the window this time, near a wall.

Her head is bowed in respect. In the foreground stands Nahadoth, gazing down at me in silence. Once again his face has transformed, and I understand now that this is because Itempas can only control him so much. He must change; he *is* Change. He could allow me to see his fury, for it weighs the very air, making my skin itch. Instead he is expressionless. His skin has turned warm brown and his eyes are layered shades of black, and his lips make me crave soft, ripe fruit. The perfect face for seducing lonely Darre girls—though it would work better if his eyes held any warmth.

He says nothing that I recall. When my fever breaks at last and I awaken, he is gone and the weight of rage has lifted— though it never goes away entirely. That, too, Bright Itempas cannot control.

Dawn.

I sat up, feeling heavy and thick-headed. Zhakkarn, still near the window, glanced back at me over her shoulder.

"You're awake." I turned to see Sieh curled in a chair beside the bed. Bonelessly he unfolded himself and came to me, touching my forehead. "The fever's broken. How do you feel?"

I responded with the first coherent thought my mind could muster. "What am I?"

He lowered his eyes. "I'm...not supposed to tell you."

I pushed away the covers and got up. For a moment I was dizzy as blood rushed to my head and away, but then it passed and I stumbled toward the bathroom.

"I want you both out of here by the time I'm done," I said over my shoulder.

Neither Sieh nor Zhakkarn responded. In the bathroom I stood over the sink for several painful moments, debating whether to vomit, though the emptiness of my stomach eventually settled the matter. My hands shook while I bathed and dried myself, and drank some water straight from the tap. I came out of the bathroom naked and was not at all surprised to find both Enefadeh still there. Sieh had drawn up his knees to sit on the edge of my bed, looking young and troubled. Zhakkarn had not moved from the window.

"The words must be phrased as a command," she said, "if you truly want us to leave."

"I don't care what you do." I found underthings and put them on. In the closet I took the first outfit I saw, an elegant Amn sheath-dress with patterns meant to disguise my minimal curves. I picked boots that didn't match it and sat down to work them onto my feet.

"Where are you going?" Sieh asked. He touched my arm, anxious. I shook my arm as I would to get rid of an insect, and he drew back. "You don't even know, do you? Yeine—"

"Back to the library," I said, though I picked that at random because he'd been right; I hadn't had a destination in mind other than *away*.

"Yeine, I know you're upset—"

"*What am I?*" I stood with one boot on and rounded on him. He flinched, possibly because I'd bent to scream the words into his face. "*What? What? What am I, gods damn you? What*—"

"Your body is human," interrupted Zhakkarn. Now it was my turn to flinch. She stood near the bed, gazing at me with the same impassivity she'd always shown, though there was something subtly protective in the way she stood behind Sieh. "Your mind is human. The soul is the only change."

"What does that mean?"

"It means you're the same person you always were." Sieh looked both subdued and sullen. "An ordinary mortal woman."

"I look like her."

Zhakkarn nodded. She might have been reporting on the weather. "The presence of Enefa's soul in your body has had some influence."

I shivered, feeling ill again. Something inside me that was not me. I rubbed at my arms, resisting the urge to use my nails. "Can you take it out?"

Zhakkarn blinked, and I sensed that for the first time I'd surprised her. "Yes. But your body has grown accustomed to two souls. It might not survive having only one again."

Two souls. Somehow that was better. I was not an empty thing animated solely by some alien force. Something in me, at least, was me. "Can you try?"

"Yeine—" Sieh reached for my hand, though he seemed to think better of it when I stepped back. "Even we don't know what would happen if we take the soul out. We thought at first that her soul would simply consume yours, but that clearly hasn't happened."

I must have looked confused.

"You're still sane," said Zhakkarn.

Something inside me, *eating me.* I half-fell onto the bed, dry-heaving unproductively for several moments. The instant this passed, I pushed myself up and paced, limping with my one boot. I could not be still. I rubbed at my temples, tugged at my hair, wondering how much longer I would *stay* sane with such thoughts in my mind.

"And you're still *you,*" Sieh said urgently, half-following me as I paced. "You're the daughter Kinneth would have had. You don't have Enefa's memories or personality. You don't think like her. That means you're strong, Yeine. That comes from *you,* not her."

I laughed wildly; it sounded like a sob. "How would you know?"

He stopped walking, his eyes soft and mournful. "If you were her," he said, "you would love me."

I stopped, too, pacing and breathing.

"And me," said Zhakkarn. "And Kurue. Enefa loved all her children, even the ones who eventually betrayed her."

I did not love Zhakkarn or Kurue. I let out the breath I'd held.

But I was shaking again, though part of that was from hunger. Sieh's hand brushed mine, tentative. When I did not pull away this time, he sighed and took hold of me, pulling me back to the bed to sit down.

"You could have gone your whole life never knowing," he said, reaching up to stroke my hair. "You would have grown older and loved some mortal, maybe had mortal children and loved those, too, and died in your sleep as a toothless old woman. That was what we wanted for you, Yeine. It's what you would have had if Dekarta hadn't brought you here. That forced our hand."

I turned to him. This close, the impulse was too strong to resist. I cupped his cheek in my hand and leaned up to kiss his forehead. He started in surprise but then smiled shyly, his cheek warming under my palm. I smiled back. Viraine had been right; he was so easy to love.

"Tell me everything," I whispered.

He flinched as if struck. Perhaps the magic that bound him to obey Arameri commands had some physical effect; perhaps it even hurt. Either way, there was a different kind of pain in his eyes as he realized I had issued the command deliberately.

But I had not been specific. He could have told me anything—the history of the universe from its inception, the number of colors in a rainbow, the words that cause mortal flesh to shatter like stone. I had left him that much freedom.

Instead, he told me the truth.

13

Ransom

WAIT. SOMETHING HAPPENED BEFORE THAT. I don't mean to get things so mixed up; I'm sorry, it's just hard to think. It was the morning after I found the silver apricotstone, three days before. Wasn't it? Before I went to Viraine, yes. I got up that morning and readied myself for the Salon, and found a servant waiting for me when I opened the door.

"Message for you, Lady," he said, looking immensely relieved.

I had no idea how long he'd been standing out there. Servants in Sky knocked only when the matter was urgent.

"Yes?"

"Lord Dekarta isn't feeling well," he said. "He will not be joining you for today's Consortium session, should you choose to attend."

T'vril had intimated that Dekarta's health played a factor in his attendance at the sessions, though I was surprised to hear it now: he had seemed fine the day before. And I was surprised he'd bothered to send word. But I hadn't missed that last bit; a subtle reprimand for my skipping the session the day before. Suppressing annoyance, I said, "Thank you. Please convey my wishes for a swift recovery back to him."

"Yes, Lady." The servant bowed and left.

So I went to the highbloods' gate and transferred myself down to the Salon. As I had expected, Relad was not there. As I had feared, Scimina was. Once again she smiled at me, and I merely nodded back, and then we sat beside each other, silent, for the next two hours.

The session was shorter than usual that day because there was only a single item on the agenda: the annexation of the small island nation Irt by a larger kingdom called Uthr. The Archerine, former ruler of Irt—a stocky, red-haired man who reminded me vaguely of T'vril—had come to lodge a protest. The king of Uthr, apparently unconcerned about this challenge to his authority, had sent only a proxy on his behalf: a boy who looked not much older than Sieh, also red-haired. Both the Irti and the Uthre were offshoots of the Ken race, a fact that apparently had done nothing to foster genial relations between them.

The core of the Archerine's appeal was that Uthr had filed no petition to begin a war. Bright Itempas detested the chaos of war, so the Arameri controlled it strictly. The lack of a petition meant the Irti had had no warning of their neighbor's aggressive intent, no time to arm, and no right to defend themselves in any way that would have caused deaths. Without the petition, any enemy soldiers killed would be treated as murders and prosecuted as such by the law-keeping arm of the Itempan Order. Of course, the Uthre could not legally kill, either—and they hadn't. They had simply marched into the Irtin capital in overwhelming numbers, literally forced its defenders to their knees, and booted the Archerine out into the street.

My heart went out to the Irti, though it was clear to me they had no hope of succeeding in their appeal. The Uthre boy defended his people's aggression simply: "They weren't strong enough to hold their land against us. We have it now. It's better that a strong ruler hold power here than a weak one, isn't it?"

And that was what the whole matter boiled down to. What was *right* mattered far less than what was *orderly*, and the Uthre had proven their ability to keep things orderly by the simple fact that they'd taken Irt without shedding a drop of blood. That was how the Arameri would see it, and the Order, too, and I could not imagine the Nobles' Consortium daring to disagree.

In the end, to no one's surprise, they did not: the Irt appeal was rejected. No one even proposed sanctions against Uthr. They would keep what they had stolen, because making them give it back was too messy.

I could not help frowning as the final vote was read. Scimina, glancing over at me, let out a soft amused snort that reminded me of where I was; quickly I schooled my expression back to blankness.

When the session ended and she and I descended the steps, I kept my eyes forward so that I would not have to look at her, and I turned toward the bathroom so I would not have to travel back to Sky with her. But she said, "Cousin," and at that point I had no choice but to stop and see what in the unknown demons' names she wanted.

"When you've had time to settle in back at the palace, would you be interested in having lunch with me?" She smiled. "We could get to know each other better."

"If you don't mind," I said carefully, "no."

She laughed beautifully. "I see what Viraine meant about you! Well, then; if you won't come out of courtesy, perhaps curiosity will draw you. I have news of your homeland, Cousin, that I think will interest you greatly." She turned and began walking toward the gate. "I'll see you in an hour."

"What news?" I called after her, but she did not stop or turn back.

My fists were still clenched by the time I got to the bathroom, which was why I reacted badly to the sight of Ras Onchi sitting in one of the parlor's plush chairs. I stopped, my hand reaching automatically for a knife that was not in its usual place on my back. I'd chosen to strap it to my calf, under my full skirts, since it was not the Arameri way to go armed in public.

"Have you learned yet what an Arameri should know?" she asked, before I could recover.

I paused, then pushed the bathroom's door firmly closed. "Not yet, Auntie," I said at last. "Though I'm not likely to, since

I'm not truly Arameri. Perhaps you could tell me, and stop rid-
dling about."

She smiled. "So very Darre you are, impatient and sharp-
tongued. Your father must have been proud."

I flushed, confused, because that had sounded suspiciously
like a compliment. Was this her way of letting me know that
she was on my side? She wore Enefa's symbol around her
neck... "Not really," I said, slowly. "My father was a patient,
cool-headed man. My temper comes from my mother."

"Ah. It must serve you well, then, in your new home."

"It serves me well everywhere. Now will you *please* tell me
what this is about?"

She sighed, her smile fading. "Yes. There isn't much time.
Forgive me, Lady." With an effort that made her knees crack—I
winced in sympathy—she pushed herself up out of the chair. I
wondered how long she'd been sitting there. Did she wait for me
after every session? Again I regretted skipping the previous day.

"Do you wonder why Uthr didn't file a war petition?" she
asked.

"I imagine because they didn't need to," I said, wondering
what this had to do with anything. "It's nearly impossible to get
a petition approved. The Arameri haven't allowed a war in a
hundred years or more. So the Uthre gambled on being able
to conquer Irt without bloodshed, and fortunately they were
successful."

"Yes." Ras grimaced. "There will be more of these 'annexa-
tions,' I imagine, now that the Uthre have shown the world
how to do it. 'Peace above all; this is the way of the Bright.'"

I marveled at the bitterness in her tone. If a priest had heard
her, she'd have been arrested for heresy. If any other Arameri

had heard her—I shuddered, imagining her skinny frame walking onto the Pier with Zhakkarn's spear at her back.

"Careful, Auntie," I said softly. "You won't live to a ripe old age, saying such things out loud."

Ras laughed softly. "True enough. I'll be more careful." She sobered. "But think of this, Lady Not-Arameri: maybe the Uthre didn't bother to petition because they knew another petition had *already* been approved—quietly, mingled in with other edicts the Consortium has passed in the past few months."

I froze, frowning. "*Another* petition?"

She nodded. "As you said, there hasn't been a successful petition for a century, so of course two petitions would never be approved back-to-back. And perhaps the Uthre even knew that other petition was more likely to pass, since it served the purposes of someone with a great deal of power. Some wars, after all, are useless without death."

I stared at her, too thrown to hide my confusion or shock. An approved war petition should have been the talk of the entire nobility. It should have taken the Consortium weeks to discuss it, much less approve it. How could anyone get a petition through without half the world hearing of it?

"Who?" I asked. But I was already beginning to suspect.

"No one knows the petition's sponsor, Lady, and no one knows what lands are involved, either as invader or target. But Uthr borders Tema on its eastern side. Uthr is small—bigger now—but their ruling family and the Teman Triadice have links of marriage and friendship going back generations."

And Tema, I realized with a belated chill, was one of the nations beholden to Scimina.

Scimina, then, had sponsored the war petition. And she

had kept its approval quiet, though that had probably required a masterwork of political maneuvering. Perhaps helping Uthre conquer Irt had been part of that. But that left two very crucial questions: *why* had she done it? And what kingdom would soon fall victim to the attack?

Relad's warning: *If you love anyone, anything, beware.*

My mouth and hands went dry. I now wanted, very badly, to go and see Scimina.

"Thank you for this," I said to Ras. My voice was higher than usual; my mind was already elsewhere, racing. "I'll make good use of the information."

She nodded and then hobbled her way out, patting my arm in passing. I was too lost in thought to say good-bye, but then I recalled myself and turned, just as she opened the door to leave.

"What is it that an Arameri should know, Auntie?" I asked. It was something I had wondered since our first meeting.

She paused, glanced back at me. "How to be cruel," she said very softly. "How to spend life like currency and wield death itself as a weapon." She lowered her eyes. "Your mother told me that, once. I've never forgotten it."

I stared at her, dry-mouthed.

Ras Onchi bowed to me, respectfully. "I will pray," she said, "that you never learn this for yourself."

Back in Sky.

I had regained most of my composure by the time I went in search of Scimina's apartment. Her quarters were not far from my own, as all fullbloods in Sky are housed on the topmost level of the palace. She had gone one step further and claimed one of Sky's greater spires as her domain, which meant that the lifts did me no good. With a passing servant's aid I found the carpeted stairs leading up the spire. The stairway was not a great height—perhaps three stories—but my thighs were burning by the time I reached the landing, and I wondered why she'd chosen to live in such a place. The fitter highbloods would have no trouble and the servants had no choice, but I could not imagine someone as infirm as, say, Dekarta, making the climb. Perhaps that was the idea.

The door swung open at my knock. Inside I found myself in a vaulted corridor, lined on either side by statues, windows, and vases of some sort of flowering plant. The statues were of no one I recognized: beautiful young men and women naked and in artful poses. At the end the corridor opened out into a circular chamber that was furnished with cushions and low tables—no chairs. Scimina's guests were clearly meant to either stand or sit on the floor.

At the center of the circular room, a couch sat on an elevated dais. I wondered whether it was intentional on Scimina's part that this place felt so much like a throne room.

Scimina was not present, though I could see another corridor just beyond the dais, ostensibly leading into the apartment's more private chambers. Assuming she meant to keep me waiting, I sighed and settled myself, looking around. That was when I noticed the man.

He sat with his back propped against one of the room's wide windows, his posture not so much casual as insolent, with one leg drawn up and his head lolling to the side. It took me a moment to realize he was naked, because his hair was very long and draped over his shoulder, covering most of his torso. It took me another moment to understand, with a jarring chill, that this was Nahadoth.

Or at least, I thought it was him. His face was beautiful as usual, but strange somehow, and I realized for the first time that it was *still*—just one face, one set of features, and not the endlessly shifting melange that I usually saw. His eyes were brown, and not the yawning pits of black I recalled; his skin was pale, but it was a human pallor like that of an Amn, and not the glow of moonshine or starlight. He watched me lazily, unmoving except to blink, a faint smile curving lips that were just a shade too thin for my tastes.

"Hello," he said. "It's been a while."

I had just seen him the night before.

"Good morning, Lord Nahadoth," I said, using politeness to cover my unease. "Are you...well?"

He shifted a little—just enough for me to see the thin silver collar 'round his neck and the chain that dangled from it. Abruptly I understood. *By day I am human*, Nahadoth had said. No power save Itempas Himself could chain the Nightlord at night, but by day he was weak. And...different. I searched his face but saw none of the madness that had been there my first night in Sky. What I saw instead was calculation.

"I am very well," he said. He touched his tongue to his lips, which made me think of a snake testing the air. "Spending the afternoon with Scimina is usually enjoyable. Though I do grow bored so easily." He paused, just for a breath. "Variety helps."

There was no doubt as to what he meant—not with his eyes stripping my clothing as I stood there. I think he meant for his words to unnerve me, but instead, strangely, they cleared my thoughts.

"Why does she chain you?" I asked. "To remind you of your weakness?"

His eyebrows rose a touch. There was no true surprise in his expression, just a momentary heightening of interest. "Does it bother you?"

"No." But I saw at once by the sharpening of his eyes that he knew I was lying.

He sat forward, the chain making the faintest of sounds, like distant chimes. His eyes, human and hungry and so very, very cruel, stripped me anew, though not sexually this time. "You're not in love with him," he said, thoughtful. "You're not that stupid. But you want him."

I did not like this, but I had no intention of admitting it. There was something in this Nahadoth that reminded me of a bully, and one did not show weakness before that.

While I considered my response, however, his smile widened. "You can have me," he said.

I worried, for the briefest of instants, that I would find the thought tempting. I needn't have worried; all I felt was revulsion. "Thank you, but no."

He ducked his eyes in a parody of polite embarrassment. "I understand. I'm just the human shell, and you want something more. I don't blame you. But..." And here he glanced up at me through his lashes. Never mind bully; what lurked in his face was *evil*, pure and plain. Here was the sadistic glee that had gloried in my terror that first night, all the more disturbing because this time it was sane. This version of Nahadoth gave truth to the priests' warning tales and children's fears of the dark.

And I did not like being alone in the room with him. Not one bit.

"You do realize," he drawled, "that you can never have him? Not that way. Your weak mortal mind and flesh would shatter like eggshells under the onslaught of his power. There wouldn't be enough left of you to send home to Darr."

I folded my arms and gazed pointedly at the corridor beyond Scimina's couch-throne. If she kept me waiting much longer I was going to leave.

"Me, though…" Abruptly he was on his feet and across the room and entirely too close. Startled, I lost my pose of indifference and tried to face him and stumble back all at once. I was too slow; he caught me by the arms. I had not realized until then how very *big* he was, taller than me by more than a head and well-muscled. In his night form I barely noticed his body; now I was very, very aware of it, and all the danger that it posed.

He demonstrated this by spinning me around and pinning me again from behind. At this I struggled, but his fingers tightened on my arms until I cried out, my eyes watering from the pain. When I stopped struggling, his grip eased.

"I can give you a taste of him," he whispered in my ear. His breath was hot on my neck; all over my body my skin crawled. "I could ride you all day—"

"Let go of me right now." I gritted the command through my teeth and prayed it would work.

His hands released me, but he did not move away. I danced away instead, and hated myself for it when I turned to face his smile. It was cold, that smile, which made the whole situation somehow worse. He wanted me—I could see that plainly enough now—but sex was the least of it. My fear and disgust pleased him, as had my pain when he'd bruised my arms.

And worst of all, I saw him relish the moment when I realized he had not lied. I had forgotten: night was the time not just of seducers but rapists; not just passion but violence. This creature *was* my taste of the Nightlord. Bright Itempas help me if I were ever insane enough to want more.

"Naha." Scimina's voice made me jump and spin. She stood beside the couch, one hand on her hip, smiling at me. How long had she been there, watching? "You're being rude to my guest. I'm sorry, Cousin; I should have shortened his leash."

I was feeling anything but gracious. "I haven't the patience for these games, Scimina," I snapped, too angry and, yes, frightened to be tactful. "State your business and let's be done."

Scimina lifted an eyebrow, amused by my rudeness. She smiled over at Nahadoth—no, *Naha*, I decided. The god's name did not fit this creature. He went to stand beside her, his back to me. She grazed the knuckles of one hand along his nearer arm and smiled. "Made your heart race a bit, did he? Our Naha can have that effect on the inexperienced. You're welcome to borrow him, by the way. As you've seen, he's nothing if not exciting."

I ignored this—but I did not miss the way Naha looked at her, beyond her line of sight. She was a fool to take that thing into her bed.

And I was a fool to keep standing there. "Good day, Scimina."

"I thought you might be interested in a rumor I heard," Scimina said to my back. "It concerns your homeland."

I paused, Ras Onchi's warning suddenly ringing in my mind.

"Your promotion has won your land new enemies, Cousin. Some of Darr's neighbors find you more threatening than even Relad or I. I suppose that's understandable—we were born to this, and have no antiquated ethnic loyalties."

I turned back, slowly. "You are Amn."

"But Amn superiority is accepted the world over; there is nothing surprising about us. You, however, are from a race that has never been more than savages, no matter how prettily we dress you."

I could not ask her outright about the war petition. But perhaps— "What are you saying? That someone may attack Darr simply because I've been claimed by the Arameri?"

"No. I'm saying someone may attack Darr because you still *think* like a Darren, though you now have access to Arameri power."

My order to my assigned nations, I realized. So that was the excuse she meant to use. I had forced them to resume trade with Darr. Of course it would be seen as favoritism—and those who saw it as such would be completely right. How could I not help my people with my new power and wealth? What kind of woman would I be if I thought only of myself?

An Arameri woman, whispered a little, ugly voice in the back of my mind.

Naha had moved to embrace Scimina from behind, the picture of an amorous lover. Scimina absently stroked his arms while he gazed murder at the back of her head.

"Don't feel bad, Cousin," Scimina said. "It wouldn't have mattered what you did, really. Some people would've always hated you, simply because you don't fit their image of a ruler. It's a shame you didn't take anything after Kinneth, other than those eyes of yours." She closed her eyes, leaning back against Naha's body, the picture of contentment. "Of course the fact that you *are* Darre doesn't help. You went through their warrior initiation, yes? Since your mother wasn't Darre, who sponsored you?"

"My grandmother," I answered quietly. It did not surprise me that Scimina knew that much of the Darre's customs. Anyone could learn that by opening a book.

Scimina sighed and glanced back at Naha. To my surprise, he did not change his expression, and to my greater surprise, she smiled at the pure hate in his eyes.

"Do you know what happens in the Darre ceremony?" she asked him conversationally. "They were quite the warriors once, and matriarchal. We forced them to stop conquering their neighbors and treating their men like chattel, but like most of these darkling races, they cling to their little traditions in secret."

"I know what they once did," Naha said. "Capture a youth of an enemy tribe, circumcise him, nurse him back to health, then use him for pleasure."

I had schooled my face to blankness. Scimina laughed at this, lifting a lock of Naha's hair to her lips while she watched me.

"Things have changed," she said. "Now the Darre aren't permitted to kidnap and mutilate their boys. Now a girl just survives alone in the forest for a month, and then comes home to be deflowered by some man her sponsor has chosen. Still barbaric, and something we stop whenever we hear about it, but it happens, especially among the women of their upper class. And the part they think they've hidden from us is this: the girl must either defeat him in public combat and therefore control the encounter, or be defeated—and learn how it feels to submit to an enemy."

"I would like that," Naha whispered. Scimina laughed again, slapping his arm playfully.

"How predictable. Be silent now." Her eyes slid to me, sidelong. "The ritual seems the same in principle, does it not? But so much has changed. Now Darre men no longer fear women—or respect them."

It was a statement, not a question; I knew better than to answer.

"Really, when you consider it, the earlier ritual was the more civilized. That ritual taught a young warrior not only how to survive but also how to respect an enemy, how to nurture. Many girls later married their captives, didn't they? So they even learned to love. The ritual now . . . well, what *does* it teach you? I cannot help but wonder."

It taught me to do whatever was necessary to get what I wanted, you evil bitch.

I did not answer, and after a moment Scimina sighed.

"So," she said, "there are new alliances being formed on Darr's borders, meant to counter Darr's perceived new strength. Since Darr in fact *has* no new strength, that means the entire region is becoming unstable. Hard to say what will happen under circumstances like that."

My fingers itched for a sharpened stone. "Is that a threat?"

"Please, Cousin. I'm merely passing the information along. We Arameri must look out for one another."

"I appreciate your concern." I turned to leave, before my temper slipped any further. But this time it was Naha's voice that stopped me.

"Did you win?" he asked. "At your warrior initiation? Did you beat your opponent, or did he rape you in front of a crowd of spectators?"

I knew better than to answer. I really did. But I answered anyway.

"I won," I said, "after a fashion."

"Oh?"

If I closed my eyes, I would see it. Six years had passed since that night, but the smell of the fire, of old furs and blood, of my own reek after a month living rough, was still vivid in my mind.

"Most sponsors choose a man who is a poor warrior," I said softly. "Easy for a girl barely out of childhood to defeat. But I was to be *ennu*, and there were doubts about me because I was half Amn. Half Arameri. So my grandmother chose the strongest of our male warriors instead."

I had not been expected to win. Endurance would have been sufficient to be marked as a warrior; as Scimina had guessed, many things had changed for us. But endurance was not sufficient to be *ennu*. No one would follow me if I let some man use me in public and then crow about it all over town. I needed to win.

"He defeated you," Naha said. He breathed the words, hungry for my pain.

I looked at him, and he blinked. I wonder what he saw in my eyes in that moment.

"I put on a good show," I said. "Enough to satisfy the requirements of the ritual. Then I stabbed him in the head with a stone knife I had hidden in my sleeve."

The council had been upset about that, especially once it became clear I had not conceived. Bad enough I had killed a man, but to also lose his seed and the strength it might have given future Darre daughters? For a while victory had made things worse for me. *She is no true Darre*, went the whispers. *There is too much death in her.*

I had not meant to kill him, truly. But in the end, we were warriors, and those who valued my Arameri murderousness had outnumbered my doubters. They made me *ennu* two years later.

The look on Scimina's face was thoughtful, measuring. Naha, however, was sober, his eyes showing some darker emotion that I could not name. If I had to put a word to it, it might have been bitterness. But that was not so surprising, was it? I was not so Darre as, and so much more Arameri than, I seemed. It was something I had always hated about myself.

"He's begun to wear a single face for you, hasn't he?" Naha asked. I knew at once who "he" was. "That's how it starts. His voice grows deeper or his lips fuller; his eyes change their shape. Soon he's something out of your sweetest dreams, saying all the right things, touching all the right places." He pressed his face into Scimina's hair, as if seeking comfort. "Then it's only a matter of time."

I left, goaded by fear and guilt and a creeping, hateful sense that no matter how Arameri I was, it was not enough to help me survive this place. Not Arameri enough by far. That is when I went to Viraine, and that is what led me to the library and the secret of my two souls, and that is how I ended up here, dead.

14

The Walking Dead

WE CURED YOUR FATHER," said Sieh. "That was your mother's price. In exchange she allowed us to use her unborn child as the vessel for Enefa's soul."

I closed my eyes.

He took a deep breath in my silence. "Our souls are no different from yours. We expected Enefa's to travel onward after she died, in the usual manner. But when Itempas...When Itempas killed Enefa, he kept something. A piece of her." It was difficult to catch, but he was rushing his words ever so slightly. Distantly I considered soothing him. "Without that piece, all life in the universe would have died. Everything Enefa created—everything except Nahadoth and Itempas himself. It is the last vestige of her power. Mortals call it the Stone of Earth."

Against my closed eyelids images formed. A small, ugly lump of bruise-dark flesh. An apricotstone. My mother's silver necklace.

"With the Stone still in this world, the soul was trapped here, too. Without a body it drifted, lost; we only discovered what had happened centuries later. By the time we found it the soul had been battered, eroded, like a sail left on a mast through a storm. The only way to restore it was to house it again in flesh." He sighed. "I will admit the thought of nurturing Enefa's soul in the body of an Arameri child was appealing on many levels."

I nodded. That I could certainly understand.

"If we can restore the soul to health," Sieh said, "then there is a chance it can be used to free us. The thing that subdues us in this world, trapping us in flesh and binding us to the Arameri, is the Stone. Itempas took it not to preserve life, but so that he could use Enefa's power against Nahadoth—two of the Three against one. But he could not wield it himself; the Three are all too different from one another. Only Enefa's children can use Enefa's power. A godling like me, or a mortal. In the war, it was both—some of my siblings, and one Itempan priestess."

"Shahar Arameri," I said.

The bed moved slightly with his nod. Zhakkarn was a silent, watching presence. I drew Zhakkarn's face with my mind, matching it against the face I'd seen in the library. Zhakkarn's face was framed like Enefa's, with the same sharp jaw and high cheekbones. It was in all three of them, I realized, though they didn't look like siblings or even members of the same race. All of Enefa's children had kept some feature, some tribute, to their mother's looks. Kurue had the same frank, dissecting gaze. Sieh's eyes were the same jade color.

Like mine.

"Shahar Arameri." Sieh sighed. "As a mortal, she could wield only a fraction of the Stone's true power. Yet she was the one who struck the deciding blow. Nahadoth would have avenged Enefa that day, if not for her."

"Nahadoth says you want my life."

Zhakkarn's voice, with a hint of irritation: "He told you that?"

Sieh's voice, equally irritated, though at Zhakkarn: "He can only defy his own nature for so long."

"Is it true?" I asked.

Sieh was silent for so long that I opened my eyes. He winced at the look on my face; I did not care. I was through with evasions and riddles. I was not Enefa. I did not *have* to love him.

Zhakkarn unfolded her arms, a subtle threat. "You haven't agreed to ally with us. You could give this information to Dekarta."

I gave her the same look that I had Sieh. "Why," I said, enunciating each word carefully, "would I possibly betray you to *him*?"

Zhakkarn's eyes flicked over to Sieh. Sieh smiled, though there was little humor in it. "I told her you'd say that. You do have one advocate among us, Yeine, however little you might believe it."

I said nothing. Zhakkarn was still glaring at me, and I knew better than to look away from a challenge. It was a pointless challenge on both sides—she would have no choice but to tell me if I commanded her, and I would never earn her trust merely by my words. But my whole world had just been shattered, and I knew of no other way to learn what I needed to know.

"My mother sold me to you," I said, mostly to Zhakkarn. "She was desperate, and perhaps I would even make the same choice in her position, but she still did it and at the moment I am not feeling well-inclined towards any Arameri. You and your kind are gods; it doesn't surprise me that you would play with mortal lives like pieces in a game of *nikkim*. But I expect better of human beings."

"You were made in our image," she said coldly.

An unpleasantly astute point.

There were times to fight, and times to retreat. Enefa's soul inside me changed everything. It made the Arameri my enemies in a far more fundamental way, because Enefa had been Itempas's enemy and they were his servants. Yet it did not automatically make the Enefadeh my allies. I was not actually Enefa, after all.

Sieh sighed to break the silence. "You need to eat," he said, and got up. He left my bedroom; I heard the apartment door open and close.

I had slept nearly three days. My angry declaration that I would leave had been a bluff; my hands were shaking, and I did not trust my ability to walk far if I tried. I looked down at my unsteady hand and thought sourly that if the Enefadeh had infected me with a goddess's soul, the least they could have done was give me a stronger body in the process.

"Sieh loves you," said Zhakkarn.

I put my hand on the bed so it would no longer shake. "I know."

"No, you don't." The sharpness in Zhakkarn's voice made me look up. She was still angry, and I realized now that it had nothing to do with the alliance. She was angry about how I'd treated Sieh.

"What would you do, if you were me?" I asked. "Surrounded by secrets, with your life dependent on the answers?"

"I would do as you have done." That surprised me. "I would use every possible advantage I had to gain as much information as I could, and I would not apologize for doing so. But I am not the mother Sieh has missed for so long."

I could tell already that I was going to become very, very sick of being compared to a goddess.

"Neither am I," I snapped.

"Sieh knows that. And yet he loves you." Zhakkarn sighed. "He is a child."

"He's older than you, isn't he?"

"Age means nothing to us. What matters is staying true to one's nature. Sieh has devoted himself fully to the path of childhood. It is a difficult one."

I could imagine, though it made no sense to me. Enefa's soul seemed to bring me no special insight into the tribulations of godhood.

"What do you want me to do?" I asked. I felt weary, though that might've been the hunger. "Shall I cuddle him to my breast when he comes back, and tell him everything will be all right? Should I do the same for you?"

"You should not hurt him again," she said, and vanished.

I gazed at the spot where she had stood for a long while. I was still staring at it when Sieh returned, setting a platter in front of me.

"The servants here don't ask questions," he said. "Safer that way. So T'vril didn't know you'd been unwell until I showed up and asked for food. He's tearing a strip out of the servants assigned to you right now."

The platter held a Darren feast. Maash paste and fish rolled in callena leaves, with a side of fire-toasted golden peppers. A shallow boat of serry relish and thin, crisp-curled slices of meat. In my land it would've been the heart of a particular species of sloth; this was probably beef. And a true treasure: a whole roasted gran banana. My favorite dessert, though how T'vril had found that out I would never know.

I picked up a leafroll, and my hand trembled with more than hunger.

"Dekarta doesn't mean for you to win the contest," Sieh said softly. "That isn't why he's brought you here. He intends for *you* to choose between Relad and Scimina."

I looked sharply at him, and recalled the conversation I'd overheard between Relad and Scimina in the solarium. Was this what Scimina had meant? "Choose between them?"

"The Arameri ritual of succession. To become the next head of the family, one of the heirs must transfer the master sigil—the mark Dekarta wears—from Dekarta's brow to his own. Or her own. The master sigil outranks all the rest; whoever wears it has absolute power over us, the rest of the family, and the world."

"The rest of the family?" I frowned. They had hinted at this before, when they altered my own sigil. "So that's it. What do the blood sigils really do? Allow Dekarta to read our thoughts? Burn out our brains if we refuse to obey?"

"No, nothing so dramatic. There are some protective spells built in for highbloods, to guard against assassins and the like, but among the family they simply compel loyalty. No one who wears a sigil can act against the interests of the family head. If not for measures like that, Scimina would have found a way to undermine or kill Dekarta long ago."

The leafroll smelled too good. I bit off a piece, making myself chew slowly as I mulled over Sieh's words. The fish was strange—some local species, similar to but not the same as the speckled ui usually used. Still good. I was ravenous, but I knew better than to bolt my food after days without.

"The Stone of Earth is used in the succession ritual. Someone—an Arameri, by Itempas's own decree—must wield its power to transfer the master sigil."

"An Arameri." Another puzzle piece slipped into place. "Anyone in Sky can do this? Everyone, down to the lowliest servant?"

Sieh nodded slowly. I noticed he did not blink when he was intent on something. A minor slip.

"Any Arameri, however distant from the Central Family. For just one moment, that person becomes one of the Three."

It was obvious in his wording. That person. For one moment.

It would be like striking a match, I imagined, having that much power course through mortal flesh. A bright flare, perhaps a few seconds of steady flame. And then...

"Then that person dies," I said.

Sieh gave me his unchildlike smile. "Yes."

Clever, so clever, my Arameri foremothers. By forcing all relatives however distant to serve here, they had in place a virtual army of people who could be sacrificed to wield the Stone. Even if each used it only for a moment, the Arameri—the highbloods, at least, who would die last—could still approximate the power of a goddess for a considerable time.

"So Dekarta means for me to be that mortal," I said. "Why?"

"The head of this clan must have the strength to kill even loved ones." Sieh shrugged. "It's easy to sentence a servant to die, but what about a friend? A husband?"

"Relad and Scimina barely knew I was alive before Dekarta brought me here. Why did he choose me?"

"That, only he knows."

I was growing angry again, but this was a frustrated, directionless sort of anger. I'd thought the Enefadeh had all the answers. Of course it wouldn't be that easy.

"Why in the Maelstrom would *you* use me, anyhow?" I asked, annoyed. "Doesn't that put Enefa's soul too close to the very people who would destroy it if they could?"

Sieh rubbed his nose, abruptly looking abashed. "Ah... well...that was my idea. It's always easier to hide something right under a person's nose, you see? And Dekarta's love for Kinneth was well known; we thought that would make you safe. No one expected him to kill her—certainly not after twenty years. All of us were caught off guard by that."

I made myself take another bite of the leafroll, chewing on more than its fragrant wrapping. No one had expected my mother's death. And yet, some part of me—the still-grieving, angry part of me—felt they should have known. They should have warned her. They should have prevented it.

"But listen." Sieh leaned forward. "The Stone is what's left of Enefa's body. Because you possess Enefa's soul, you can wield the Stone's power in ways that no one but Enefa herself could do. If *you* held the Stone, Yeine, you could change the shape of the universe. You could set us free like that." He snapped his fingers.

"Then die."

Sieh lowered his eyes, his enthusiasm fading. "That wasn't the original plan," he said, "but yes."

I finished the leafroll and looked at the rest of the plate without enthusiasm. My appetite had vanished. But anger—slow-building and fierce, almost as hot as my anger over my mother's murder—was beginning to take its place.

"*You* mean for me to lose the contest, too," I said softly.

"Well...yes."

"What will you offer me? If I accept this alliance?"

He grew very still. "Protection for your land through the war that would follow our release. And favor forever after our victory. We keep our vows, Yeine, believe me."

I believed him. And the eternal blessing of four gods was indeed a powerful temptation. That would guarantee safety and prosperity for Darr, if we could get through this time of trial. The Enefadeh knew my heart well.

But then, they thought they already knew my soul.

"I want that and one thing more," I said. "I'll do as you wish, Sieh, even if it costs me my life. Revenge against my mother's killer is worth that. I'll take up the Stone and use it to set you free, and die. But not as some humbled, beaten sacrifice." I glared at him. "I want to win this contest."

His lovely green eyes went wide.

"Yeine," he began, "that's impossible. Dekarta and Relad and Scimina...they're all against you. You haven't got a chance."

"You're the instigator of this whole plot, aren't you? Surely the god of mischief can think of a way."

"*Mischief*, not politics!"

"You should go and tell the others my terms." I made myself pick up the fork and eat some relish.

Sieh stared at me, then finally let out a shaky laugh. "I don't believe this. You're crazier than Naha." He got to his feet and rubbed a hand over his hair. "You—gods." He seemed not to notice the strangeness of his oath. "I'll talk to them."

I inclined my head formally. "I shall await your answer."

Muttering in his strange language, Sieh summoned his yellow ball and left through the bedroom wall.

They would accept, of course. Whether I won or lost, they would get the freedom they wanted—unless, of course, I chose not to give it to them. So they would do whatever it took to keep me agreeable.

Reaching for another leafroll, I concentrated on chewing slowly so that my ill-used stomach would not rebel. It was important that I recover quickly. I would need my strength in the time to come.

15

Hatred

I SEE MY LAND BELOW ME. It passes underneath, as if I am flying. High ridges and misty, tangled valleys. Occasional fields, even rarer towns and cities. Darr is so green. I saw many lands as I traveled across High North and Senm on the way to Sky, and none of them seemed half as green as my beautiful Darr. Now I know why.

I slept again. When I woke, Sieh still had not returned, and it was night. I did not expect an answer from the Enefadeh anytime soon. I had probably annoyed them by my refusal to trudge obediently to death. If I were them, I would keep me waiting awhile.

Almost as soon as I woke, there was a knock at the door. When I went to answer, a bony-faced servant boy stood very straight and said, with painful formality, "Lady Yeine. I bear a message."

Rubbing sleep from my eyes, I nodded permission for him to continue, and he said, "Your grandsire requests your presence."

And suddenly I was very, very awake.

The audience chamber was empty this time. Just me and Dekarta. I knelt as I had that first afternoon, and laid my knife on the floor as was customary. I did not, to my own surprise, contemplate using it to kill him. Much as I hated him, his blood was not what I wanted.

"Well," he said from his throne. His voice sounded softer than before, though that may have been a trick of perception on my part. "Have you enjoyed your week as an Arameri, Granddaughter?"

Had it been only a week?

"No, Grandfather," I said. "I have not."

He uttered a single laugh. "But now, perhaps, you understand us better. What do you think?"

This I had not expected. I looked at him from where I knelt, and wondered what he was up to.

"I think," I said slowly, "the same thing that I thought before I came here: that the Arameri are evil. All that has changed is that now I believe most of you are mad as well."

He grinned, wide and partially toothless. "Kinneth said much the same thing to me once. She included herself, however."

I resisted the immediate urge to deny this. "Maybe that's why she left. Maybe, if I stay long enough, I'll become as evil and mad as the rest of you."

"Maybe." There was a curious gentleness in the way he said this that threw me. I could never read his face. Too many lines.

Silence rose between us for the next several breaths. It plateaued; stalled; broke.

"Tell me why you killed my mother," I said.

His smile faded. "I am not one of the Enefadeh, Granddaughter. You cannot command answers from me."

Heat washed through me, followed by cold. I rose slowly to my feet. "You loved her. If you had hated her, feared her, that I could have understood. But you loved her."

He nodded. "I loved her."

"She was crying when she died. We had to wet her eyelids to get them open—"

"You will be silent."

In the empty chamber, his voice echoed. The edge of it sawed against my temper like a dull knife.

"And you love her *still*, you hateful old bastard." I stepped forward, leaving my knife on the floor. I did not trust myself with it anymore. I moved toward my grandfather's highbacked not-throne, and he drew himself up, perhaps in anger, perhaps in fear. "You love her and mourn her; it's your own fault and you *mourn* her, and you want her back. Don't you? But if Itempas is listening, if he cares at all about order and righteousness or any of the things the priests say, then I pray to him now that you keep loving her. That way you'll feel her loss the way I do. You'll feel that agony until you die, and I pray that's a long, long time from now!"

By this point I stood before Dekarta, bent down, my hands on the armrests of his chair. I was close enough to see the color of his eyes at last—a blue so pale that it was barely a color at all. He was a small, frail man now, whatever he'd been in his prime. If I blew hard, I might break his bones.

But I did not touch him. Dekarta did not deserve mere physical pain any more than he deserved a swift death.

"Such hate," he whispered. Then, to my shock, he smiled. It looked like a death rictus. "Perhaps you are more like her than I thought."

I stood up straight and told myself that I was not drawing back.

"Very well," said Dekarta, as if we'd just exchanged pleasant small talk. "We should get down to business, Granddaughter. In seven days' time, on the night of the fourteenth, there will be a ball here in Sky. It will be in your honor, to celebrate your elevation to heir, and some of the most noteworthy citizens of the world will join us as guests. Is there anyone in particular you'd like invited?"

I stared at him and heard an entirely different conversation. *In seven days the most noteworthy citizens in the world will gather to watch you die.* Every mote of intuition in my body understood: the succession ceremony.

His question hovered unanswered in the air between us.

"No," I said softly. "No one."

Dekarta inclined his head. "Then you are dismissed, Granddaughter."

I stared at him for a long moment. I might never again have the chance to speak with him like this, in private. He had not told me why he'd killed my mother, but there were other secrets that he might be willing to divulge. He might even know the secret of how I might save myself.

But in the long silence I could think of no questions to ask, no way to get at those secrets. So at last I picked up my knife and walked out of the room, and tried not to feel a sense of shame as the guards closed the door behind me.

This turned out to be the start of a very bad night.

I stepped inside my apartment and found that I had visitors.

Kurue had appropriated the chair, where she sat with her fingers steepled, a hard look in her eyes. Sieh, perched on the edge of my parlor's couch, sat with his knees drawn up and his eyes downcast. Zhakkarn stood sentinel near the window, impassive as ever. Nahadoth—

I felt his presence behind me an instant before he put his hand through my chest.

"Tell me," he said into my ear, "why I should not kill you."

I stared at the hand through my chest. There was no blood, and as far as I could tell there was no wound. I fumbled for his hand and found that it was immaterial, like a shadow. My fingers passed through his flesh and waggled in the translucence of his fist. It did not hurt exactly, but it felt as though I'd plunged my fingers into an icy stream. There was a deep, aching coldness between my breasts.

He could withdraw his hand and tear out my heart. He could leave his hand in place but make it tangible, and kill me as surely as if he'd punched through blood and bone.

"Nahadoth," Kurue said in a warning tone.

Sieh jumped up and came to my side, his eyes wide and frightened. "Please don't kill her. Please."

"She's one of them," he hissed in my ear. His breath was cold as well, making the flesh of my neck prickle in goose bumps. "Just another Arameri convinced of her own superiority. We *made* her, Sieh, and she dares to command us? She has no right to carry my sister's soul." His hand curled into a claw, and suddenly I realized it was not my flesh that he meant to damage.

Your body has grown used to containing two souls, Zhakkarn had said. *It might not survive having only one again.*

But at that realization, completely to my own surprise, I burst into laughter.

"Do it," I said. I could hardly breathe for laughing, though that might've been some effect of Nahadoth's hand. "I never wanted this thing in me in the first place. If you want it, take it!"

"Yeine!" Sieh clutched my arm. "That could kill you!"

"What difference does it make? You want to kill me anyway. So does Dekarta—he's got it all planned, seven days from now. My only real choice lies in *how* I die. This is as good as any other method, isn't it?"

"Let's find out," Nahadoth said.

Kurue sat forward. "Wait, what did she—"

Nahadoth drew his hand back. It seemed to take effort; the arm moved through my flesh slowly, as if through clay. I could not be more certain because I was shrieking at the top of my lungs. Instinctively I lunged forward, trying to escape the pain, and in retrospect this made things worse. But I could not think, all my reason having been subsumed by agony. It felt as though I was being torn apart—as, of course, I was.

But then something happened.

Above, a sky out of nightmare. I could not say if it was day or night. Both sun and moon were visible, but it was hard to say which was which. The moon was huge and cancerously yellow. The sun was a bloody distortion, nowhere near round. There was a single cloud in the sky and it was black—not dark gray with rain but black, like a drifting hole in the sky. And then I realized it was a hole, because something fell through—

Tiny figures, struggling. One of them was white and blazing, the other black and smoking; as they tumbled, I could see fire and hear cracks like thunder all around them. They fell and fell and smashed into the earth nearby. The ground shook, a great cloud of dust and debris kicked up from the impact; nothing human could have survived such a fall, but I knew they were not—

I ran. All around me were bodies—not dead, I understood with the certainty of a dream, but dying. The grass was dry and dessicated, crackling beneath my bare feet. Enefa was dead. Everything was dying. Leaves fell around me like heavy snow. Ahead, just through the trees—

"Is this what you want? Is it?" Inhuman fury in that voice,

echoing through the forest shadows. Following it came a scream of
such agony as I have never imagined—

I ran through the trees and stopped at the edge of a crater and
saw—

O Goddess, I saw—

"Yeine." A hand slapped my face lightly. "Yeine!"

My eyes were open. I blinked because they were dry. I was on
my knees on the floor. Sieh crouched before me, his eyes wide
with concern. Kurue and Zhakkarn were watching, too, Kurue
looking worried and Zhakkarn soldier-still.

I did not think. I swung around and looked at Nahadoth, who
stood with one hand—the one that had been in my body—still
raised. He stared down at me, and I realized he somehow knew
what I had seen.

"I don't understand." Kurue rose from the desk chair. Her
hand, on the chair's back, tightened. "It's been twenty years.
The soul should be able to survive extraction by now."

"No one has ever put a god's soul into a mortal," said Zhakkarn. "We knew there was a risk."

"Not of *this*!" Kurue pointed at me almost accusingly. "Will
the soul even be usable now, contaminated with this mortal
filth?"

"Be silent!" Sieh snapped, whipping around to glare at her.
His voice dropped suddenly, a young man's again; instant
puberty. "How dare you? I have told you time and again—
mortals are as much Enefa's creations as we ourselves."

"Leftovers," Kurue retorted. "Weak and cowardly and too
stupid to look beyond themselves for more than five minutes.
Yet you and Naha will insist on putting your trust in them—"

Sieh rolled his eyes. "Oh, *please*. Tell me, Kurue, which of your proud, god-only plans has gotten us free?"

Kurue turned away in resentful silence.

I barely saw all this. Nahadoth and I were still staring at each other.

"Yeine." Sieh's small, soft hand touched my cheek, coaxing my head around to face him. His voice had returned to a childish treble. "Are you all right?"

"What happened?" I asked.

"We're not certain."

I sighed and pulled away from him, trying to get to my feet. My body felt hollowed out, stuffed with cotton. I slipped and settled onto my knees again, and cursed.

"Yeine—"

"If you're going to lie to me again, don't bother."

A muscle worked in Sieh's jaw; he glanced at his siblings. "It's true, Yeine. We *aren't* certain. But... for some reason... Enefa's soul has not healed as much as we hoped it would in the time since we put it in you. It's whole," and here he glanced at Kurue significantly. "Enough to serve its purpose. But it's very fragile— too fragile to be drawn out safely."

Safely for the soul, he meant, not for me. I shook my head, too tired to laugh.

"No telling how much damage has been done," Kurue muttered, turning away to pace the room's small confines.

"An unused limb withers," Zhakkarn said softly. "She had her own soul, and no need for another."

Which I would happily have told you, I thought sourly, *if I'd been able to protest at the time.*

But what in the Maelstrom did all this mean for me? That the

Enefadeh would make no further attempt to draw the soul from my body? Good, since I had no desire to experience that pain ever again. But it also meant that they were committed to their plan now, because they couldn't get the thing out of me otherwise.

Was that, then, why I had all these strange dreams and visions? Because a goddess's soul had begun to rot inside me?

Demons and darkness. Like a compass needle seeking north, I swung back around to look at Nahadoth. He turned away.

"What did you say earlier?" Kurue suddenly demanded. "About Dekarta."

That particular concern seemed a million miles away. I pulled myself back to it, the here and now, and tried to push from my mind that terrible sky and the image of shining hands gripping and twisting flesh.

"Dekarta is throwing a ball in my honor," I replied, "in one week. To celebrate my designation as one of the possible heirs." I shook my head. "Who knows? Maybe it's just a ball."

The Enefadeh looked at each other.

"So soon," murmured Sieh, frowning. "I had no idea he would do it this soon."

Kurue nodded to herself. "Canny old bastard. He'll probably have the ceremony at dawn the morning after."

"Could this mean he's discovered what we've done?" asked Zhakkarn.

"No," Kurue said, looking at me, "or she'd be dead and the soul would already be in Itempas's hands."

I shuddered at the thought and finally pushed myself to my feet. I did not turn to Nahadoth again.

"Are you done being angry with me?" I asked, brushing wrinkles out of my skirt. "I think we have unfinished business."

16

Sar-enna-nem

THE PRIESTS DO MENTION THE GODS' WAR sometimes, mainly as a warning against heresy. Because of Enefa, they say. Because of the Betrayer, for three days people and animals lay helpless and gasping for air, hearts gradually slowing and bellies bloating as their bowels ceased to function. Plants wilted and died in hours; vast fertile plains turned to gray desert. Meanwhile the sea we now call Repentance boiled, and for some reason all the tallest mountains were split in half. The priests say that was the work of the godlings, Enefa's immortal offspring, who each took sides and battled across the earth. Their fathers, the lords of the sky, mostly kept their fight up there.

Because of Enefa, the priests say. They do not say, because Itempas killed her.

When the war finally ended, most of the world was dead. What remained was forever changed. In my land, hunters pass down legends of beasts that no longer exist; harvest songs praise staples long lost. Those first Arameri did a great deal for the survivors, the priests are careful to note. With the magic of their war-prisoner gods they replenished the oceans, sealed the mountains, healed the land. Though there was nothing to be done for the dead, they saved as many as they could of the survivors.

For a price.

The priests don't mention that, either.

There had in fact been very little business to discuss. In light of the looming ceremony, the Enefadeh needed my cooperation more than ever, and so—with palpable annoyance—Kurue agreed to my condition. We all knew there was little chance I could become Dekarta's heir. We all knew the Enefadeh were merely humoring me. I was content with that, so long as I did not think about it too deeply.

Then one by one they vanished, leaving me with Nahadoth. He was the only one, Kurue had said, who had the power to carry me to and from Darr in the night's few remaining hours. So in the silence that fell, I turned to face the Nightlord.

"How?" he asked. The vision, he meant, of his defeat.

"I don't know," I said. "But it's happened before. I had a dream once, of the old Sky. I saw you destroy it." I swallowed, chilled. "I thought it was just a dream, but if what I just saw is what really happened..." Memories. I was experiencing Enefa's memories. Dearest Skyfather, I did not want to think about what that meant.

His eyes narrowed. He wore that face again—the one I feared because I could not help wanting it. I fixed my eyes on a point just above his shoulder.

"It is what happened," he said slowly. "But Enefa was dead by then. She never saw what he did to me."

And I wish I hadn't. But before I could speak, Nahadoth took a step toward me. I very quickly took a step back, and he stopped.

"You fear me now?"

"You did try to rip out my soul."

"And yet you still desire me."

I froze. Of course he would have sensed that. I said nothing, unwilling to admit weakness.

Nahadoth moved past me to the window. I shivered as he passed; a tendril of his cloak had curled 'round my calf for just an instant in a cool caress. I wondered if he was even aware of this.

"What exactly do you hope to accomplish in Darr?" he asked.

I swallowed, glad to be on another subject. "I need to speak with my grandmother. I thought of using a sigil sphere, but I don't understand such things. There could be a way for others to eavesdrop on our conversation."

"There is."

It gave me no pleasure to be right. "Then the questions must be asked in person."

"What questions?"

"Whether it's true what Ras Onchi and Scimina said, about Darr's neighbors arming for war. I want to hear my grandmother's assessment of the situation. And...I hope to learn..." I felt inexplicably ashamed. "More about my mother. Whether she was like the rest of the Arameri."

"I have told you already: she was."

"You will forgive me, Lord Nahadoth, if I do not trust you."

He turned slightly, so that I could see the side of his smile. "She was," he repeated, "and so are you."

The words, in his cold voice, hit me like a slap.

"She did this, too," he continued. "She was your age, perhaps younger, when she began asking questions, questions, so many questions. When she could not get answers from us with politeness, she commanded them—as you have done. Such hate there was in her young heart. Like yours."

I fought the urge to swallow, certain he would hear it.

"What sort of questions?"

"Arameri history. The war between my siblings and me. Many things."

"Why?"

"I have no idea."

"You didn't ask?"

"I didn't care."

I took a deep breath and forced my sweaty fists to unclench. This was his way, I reminded myself. There had been no need for him to say anything about my mother; he just knew it was the way to unsettle me. I had been warned. Nahadoth didn't like to kill outright. He teased and tickled until you lost control, forgot the danger, and opened yourself to him. He made you ask for it.

After I had been silent for a few breaths, Nahadoth turned to me. "The night is half over. If you mean to go to Darr, it should be now."

"Oh. Ah, yes." Swallowing, I looked around the room, anywhere but at him. "How will we travel?"

In answer, Nahadoth extended his hand.

I wiped my hand unnecessarily on my skirt, and took it.

The blackness that surrounded him flared like lifting wings, filling the room to its arched ceiling. I gasped and would have stepped back, but his hand became a vise on my own. When I looked at his face I felt ill: his eyes had changed. They were all black now, iris and whites alike. Worse, the shadows nearest his body had deepened, so much that he was invisible beyond his extended hand.

I stared into the abyss of him and could not bring myself to go closer.

"If I meant to kill you," he said, and his voice was different, too, echoing, shadowed, "it would already be too late."

There was that. So I looked up into those terrible eyes, mustered my courage, and said, "Please take me to Arrebaia, in Darr. The temple of Sar-enna-nem."

The blackness at his core expanded so swiftly to envelop me that I had no time to cry out. There was an instant of unbearable cold and pressure, so great I thought it would crush me. But it stopped short of pain, and then even the cold vanished. I opened my eyes and saw nothing. I stretched out my hands—including the hand that I knew he held—and felt nothing. I cried out and heard only silence.

Then I stood on stone and breathed air laden with familiar scents and felt warm humidity soak into my skin. Behind me spread the stone streets and walls of Arrebaia, filling the plateau on which we stood. It was later in the night than it had been at Sky, I could tell, because the streets were all but empty. Before me rose stone steps, lined on either side by standing lanterns, at the top of which were the gates to Sar-enna-nem.

I turned back to Nahadoth, who had reverted to his usual, just-shy-of-human appearance.

"Y-you are welcome in my family's home," I said. I was still shivering from our mode of travel.

"I know." He strode up the steps. Caught off guard, I stared at his back for ten steps before remembering myself and trotting to follow.

Sar-enna-nem's gates are heavy, ugly wood-and-metal affairs—a more recent addition to the ancient stone. It took at least four women to work the mechanism that swung them open, which made a vast improvement over the days when the gates had been made of stone and needed twenty openers. I had arrived unannounced, in the small hours of the morning, and knew that this meant upsetting the entire guardstaff. We had not been attacked in centuries, but my people prided themselves on vigilance nonetheless.

"They might not let us in," I murmured, drawing alongside the Nightlord. I was hard-pressed to keep up; he was taking the steps two at a time.

Nahadoth said nothing in reply and did not slow his pace. I heard the loud, echoing sound of the great latch lifting, and then the gates swung open—on their own. I groaned, realizing what he'd done. Of course there were shouts and running feet as we passed through, and as we stepped onto the grassy patch that served as Sar-enna-nem's forecourt, two clusters of guards came running forth from the ancient edifice's doors. One was the gate company—just men, since it was a lowly position that required only brute strength.

The other company was the standing guard, composed of women and those few men who had earned the honor, distinguished by white silk tunics under the armor. This one was led by a familiar face: Imyan, a woman from my own Somem tribe. She shouted in our language as she reached the forecourt, and the company split to surround us. Very quickly we were surrounded by a ring of spears and arrows pointed at our hearts.

No—their weapons were pointed at *my* heart, I noticed. Not a single one of them had aimed at Nahadoth.

I stepped in front of Nahadoth to make it easier for them, and to signal my friendliness. For a moment it felt strange to speak in my own tongue. "It's good to see you, Captain Imyan."

"I don't know you," she said curtly. I almost smiled. As girls we had gotten into all manner of mischief together; now she was as committed to her duty as I.

"You laughed the first time you saw me," I said. "I'd been trying to grow my hair longer, thinking to look like my mother. You said it looked like curly tree moss."

Imyan's eyes narrowed. Her own hair—long and beautifully Darre-straight—had been arranged in an efficient braids-and-knot behind her head. "What are you doing here, if you're Yeine-*ennu?*"

"You know I'm no longer *ennu*," I said. "The Itempans have been announcing it all week, by word of mouth and by magic. Even High North should've heard by now."

Imyan's arrow wavered for a moment longer, then slowly came down. Following her lead, the other guards lowered their weapons as well. Imyan's eyes shifted to Nahadoth, then back to me, and for the first time there was a hint of nervousness in her manner. "And this?"

"You know me," Nahadoth said in our language.

No one flinched at the sound of his voice. Darren guards are too well-trained for that. But I saw not a few exchanged looks of unease among the group. Nahadoth's face, I noticed belatedly, had begun to waver again, a watery blur that shifted with the torchlight shadows. So many new mortals to seduce.

Imyan recovered first. "Lord Nahadoth," she said at last. "Welcome back."

Back? I stared at her, then at Nahadoth. But then a more familiar voice greeted me, and I let out a breath of tension I hadn't realized that I felt.

"You are indeed welcome," said my grandmother. She came

down the short flight of steps that led to Sar-enna-nem's living quarters, and the guards parted before her: a shorter-than-average elderly woman still clad in a sleeping tunic (though she'd taken the time to strap on her knife, I noted). Tiny as she was—I had unfortunately inherited her size—she exuded an air of strength and authority that was almost palpable.

She inclined her head to me as she came. "Yeine. I've missed you, but not so much that I wanted to see you back so soon." She glanced at Nahadoth, then back at me. "Come."

And that was that. She turned to head into the columned entrance, and I moved to follow—or would have, had Nahadoth not spoken.

"Dawn is closer, here, to this part of the world," he said. "You have an hour."

I turned, surprised on several levels. "You aren't coming?"

"No." And he walked away, off to the side of the forecourt. The guards moved out of his way with an alacrity that might have been amusing under other circumstances.

I watched him for a moment, then moved to follow my grandmother.

Another tale from my childhood occurs to me here.

It is said the Nightlord cannot cry. No one knows the reason for this, but of the many gifts that the forces of the Maelstrom bestowed upon their darkest child, the ability to cry was not one of them.

Bright Itempas can. Legends say his tears are the rain that sometimes falls while the sun still shines. (I have never believed this legend, because it would mean Itempas cries rather frequently.)

Enefa of the Earth could cry. Her tears took the form of the yellow, burning rain that falls around the world after a volcano has erupted. It still falls, this rain, killing crops and poisoning water. But now it means nothing.

Nightlord Nahadoth was firstborn of the Three. Before the others appeared, he spent countless aeons as the only living thing in all of existence. Perhaps that explains his inability. Perhaps, amid so much loneliness, tears become ultimately useless.

Sar-enna-nem was once a temple. Its main entrance is a vast and vaulted hall supported by columns hewn whole from the earth, erected by my people in a time long before we knew of such Amn innovations as scrivening or clockwork. We had our own techniques back then. And the places we built to honor the gods were magnificent.

After the Gods' War, my ancestors did what had to be done. Sar-enna-nem's Twilight and Moon Windows, once famed for their beauty, were bricked up, leaving only the Sun. A new temple, dedicated exclusively to Itempas and untainted by the devotion once offered to his siblings, was built some ways to the south; that is the current religious heart of the city. Sar-enna-nem was repurposed as nothing more than a hall of government, from which our warrior council issued edicts that I, as *ennu*, once implemented. Any holiness was long gone.

The hall was empty, as befitted the late hour. My grandmother led me to the raised plinth where, during the day, the Warriors' Council members sat on a circle of thick rugs. She took a seat; I took one opposite.

"Have you failed?" she asked.

"Not yet," I replied. "But that is only a matter of time."

"Explain," she said, so I did. I will admit I edited the account somewhat. I did not tell her of the hours I wasted in my mother's chambers weeping. I did not mention my dangerous thoughts about Nahadoth. And I most certainly did not speak of my two souls.

When I was done, she sighed, the only sign of her concern. "Kinneth always believed Dekarta's love for her would safeguard you. I cannot say I ever liked her, but over the years I grew to trust her judgment. How could she have been so wrong?"

"I'm not certain she was," I said softly. I was thinking of Nahadoth's words about Dekarta, and my mother's murder: *You think it was him?*

I had spoken with Dekarta since then. I had seen his eyes while he spoke of my mother. Could a man like him murder someone he loved so much?

"What did Mother tell you, Beba?" I asked. "About why she left the Arameri?"

My grandmother frowned, taken aback by my shift from formality. We had never been close, she and I. She had been too old to become *ennu* when her own mother finally died, and none of her children had been girls. Though my father had managed against all odds to succeed her, becoming one of only three male *ennu* ever in our history, I was the closest thing to a daughter she would ever have. I, the half-Amn embodiment of her son's greatest mistake. I had given up on trying to earn her love years before.

"It was not something she spoke of much," Beba said, speaking slowly. "She said she loved my son."

"That couldn't possibly have been sufficient for you," I said softly.

Her eyes hardened. "Your father made it clear that it would have to be."

And then I understood: she had never believed my mother. "What do you think was the reason, then?"

"She was full of anger, your mother. She wanted to hurt someone, and being with my son allowed her to accomplish that."

"Someone in Sky?"

"I don't know. Why does this concern you, Yeine? It's now that matters, not twenty years ago."

"I think what happened then has bearing on now," I said, surprising myself—but it was true, I realized at last. Perhaps I had felt that all along. And with that opening, I readied my next attack. "Nahadoth has been here before, I see."

At this, my grandmother's face resumed its usual stern frown. "*Lord* Nahadoth, Yeine. We are not Amn here; we respect our creators."

"The guard have drilled in how to approach him. A shame I wasn't included; I could have used that training myself before I went to Sky. When did he come here last, Beba?"

"Before you were born. He came to see Kinneth once. Yeine, this isn't—"

"Was it after Father recovered from the Walking Death?" I asked. I spoke softly, though the blood was pounding in my ears. I wanted to reach over and shake her, but I kept control. "Was that the night they did it to me?"

Beba's frown deepened, momentary confusion becoming

alarm. "Did…to *you*? What are you talking about? You weren't even born at that point; Kinneth was barely pregnant. What did…"

And then she trailed off. I saw thoughts racing behind her eyes, which widened as they stared at me. I spoke to those thoughts, teasing out the knowledge that I sensed behind them.

"Mother tried to kill me when I was born." I knew why, now, but there was more truth here, something I hadn't discovered yet. I could feel it. "They didn't trust her alone with me for months. Do you remember?"

"Yes," she whispered.

"I know she loved me," I said. "And I know that sometimes women go mad in childbearing. Whatever it was that made her fear me then—" I nearly choked on the obfuscation. I had never been a good liar. "—it faded and she became a good mother thereafter. But you must have wondered, Beba, what it was that she feared so. And my father must have wondered…"

I trailed off then, as awareness struck. *Here* was a truth I had not considered—

"No one wondered."

I jumped and whirled. Nahadoth stood fifty feet away at the entrance of Sar-enna-nem, framed by its triangle design. With the moonlight behind him he was a stark silhouette, but as always, I could see his eyes.

"I killed anyone who saw me with Kinneth that night," he said. We both heard him as clearly as if he stood right beside us. "I killed her maid, and the child who came to serve us wine, and the man who sat with your father while he recovered from the sickness. I killed the three guards who tried to eavesdrop on this old woman's orders." He nodded toward Beba, who stiffened. "After that, no one dared to wonder about you."

So you've decided to talk? I would have asked him, but then my grandmother did something so unexpected, so incredible, so stupid, that the words stopped in my throat. She leapt to her feet and moved in front of me, drawing her knife.

"What did you do to Yeine?" she cried. I had never in my life seen her so angry. "What foulness did the Arameri put you up to? She is *mine*, she belongs to *us*, you had no right!"

Nahadoth laughed then, and the whiplashing rage in that sound sent a chill down my spine. Had I thought him merely an embittered slave, a pitiable creature burdened by grief? I was a fool.

"You think this temple protects you?" he hissed. Only then did I realize he had not actually stepped over the threshold. "Have you forgotten that your people once worshipped *me* here, too?"

He stepped into Sar-enna-nem.

The rugs beneath my knees vanished. The floor, which had been planks of wood, disintegrated; underneath was a mosaic of polished semiprecious tiles, stones of every color interspersed with squares of gold. I gasped as the columns shuddered and the bricks exploded into nothingness and suddenly I could *see* the Three Windows, not just Sun but Moon and Twilight, too. I had never realized they were meant to be viewed together. We had lost so much. And all around us stood the statues of beings so perfect, so alien, so *familiar*, that I wanted to weep for all of Sieh's lost brothers and sisters, Enefa's loyal children, slaughtered like dogs for trying to avenge their mother's murder. *I understand. All of you, I understand so much—*

And then the torchlight went out and the air creaked and I turned to see that Nahadoth had changed as well. Night's darkness now filled that end of Sar-enna-nem, but it was not like my first night in Sky. Here, fueled by the residue of ancient devotion, he showed me all he had once been: first among gods, sweet dream and nightmare incarnate, all things beautiful and terrible. Through a hurricane swirl of blue-black unlight I caught a glimpse of moon-white skin and eyes like distant stars; then they warped into something so unexpected that my brain refused to interpret it for an instant. But the library embossing had warned me, hadn't it? A woman's face shone at me from the darkness, proud and powerful and so breathtaking that I yearned for *her* as much as I had for *him*, and it did not seem strange at all that I did so. And then the face shifted again into something that in no way resembled human, something tentacled and toothed and hideous, and I screamed. Then there was only darkness where his face should have been, and that was most frightening of all.

He stepped forward again. I felt it: an impossible, invisible vastness moved with him. I heard the walls of Sar-enna-nem groan, too flimsy to contain such power. The whole world could not contain this. I heard the sky above Darr rumble with thunder; the ground beneath my feet trembled. White teeth gleamed amid the darkness, sharp like wolves'. That was when I knew I had to act, or the Nightlord would kill my grandmother right before my eyes.

Right before my—

Right before my eyes she lies, sprawled and naked and bloody
this is not flesh this is all you can comprehend

but it means the same thing as flesh, she is dead and violated, her perfect form torn in ways that should not be possible, should not be and who has done this? Who could have

what did it mean that he made love to me before driving the knife home?

and then it hits: betrayal. I had known of his anger, but never once did I imagine... never once had I dreamt... I had dismissed her fears. I thought I knew him. I gather her body to mine and will all of creation to make her live again. We are not built for death. But nothing changes, nothing changes, *there was a hell that I built long ago and it was a place where everything remained the same forever because I could imagine nothing more horrific, and* now I am there.

Then others come, our children, and all react with equal horror
in a child's eyes, a mother is god
but I can see nothing of their grief through the black mist of my own. I lay her body down but my hands are covered in her blood, our blood, sister lover pupil teacher friend otherself, and when I lift my head to scream out my fury, a million stars turn black and die. No one can see them, but they are my tears.

I blinked.

Sar-enna-nem was as it had been, shadowed and quiet, its splendor hidden again beneath bricks and dusty wood and old rugs. I stood in front of my grandmother, though I did not remember getting up or moving. Nahadoth's human mask was back in place, his aura diminished to its usual quiet drift, and once again he was staring at me.

I covered my eyes with one hand. "I can't take much more of this."

"Y-Yeine?" My grandmother. She put a hand on my shoulder. I barely noticed.

"It's happening, isn't it?" I looked up at Nahadoth. "What you expected. Her soul is devouring my own."

"No," said Nahadoth very softly. "I don't know what this is."

I stared at him and could not help myself. All the shock and fear and anger of the past few days bubbled up, and I burst out laughing. I laughed so loudly that it echoed from Sar-enna-nem's distant ceiling; so long that my grandmother peered at me in concern, no doubt wondering if I had gone mad. I probably had, because suddenly my laughter turned to screaming and my mirth ignited as white-hot rage.

"*How can you not know?*" I shrieked at Nahadoth. I had lapsed into Senmite again. "You're a god! How can you not *know?*"

His calm stoked my fury higher. "I built uncertainty into this universe, and Enefa wove that into every living being. There will always be mysteries beyond even us gods' understanding—"

I launched myself at him. In the interminable second that my mad rage lasted, I saw that his eyes flicked to my approaching fist and widened in something very like amazement. He had plenty of time to block or evade the blow. That he did not was a complete surprise.

The smack of it echoed as loud as my grandmother's gasp.

In the ensuing silence, I felt empty. The rage was gone. Horror had not yet arrived. I lowered my hand to my side. My knuckles stung.

Nahadoth's head had turned with the blow. He lifted a hand to his lip, which was bleeding, and sighed.

"I must work harder to keep my temper around you," he said. "You have a memorable way of chastising me."

He lifted his eyes, and suddenly I knew he was remembering the time I had stabbed him. *I have waited so long for you,* he had said then. This time, instead of kissing me, he reached out and touched my lips with his fingers. I felt warm wetness and reflexively licked, tasting cool skin and the metallic salt of his blood.

He smiled, his expression almost fond. "Do you like the taste?"

Not of your blood, no.

But your finger was another matter.

"Yeine," said my grandmother again, breaking the tableau. I took a deep breath, marshaled my wits, and turned back to her.

"Are the neighboring kingdoms allying?" I asked. "Are they arming for war?"

She swallowed before nodding. "We received formal notice this week, but there had been earlier signs. Our merchants and diplomats were expelled from Menchey almost two months ago. They say old Gemd has passed a conscription law to boost the ranks of his army, and he's accelerated training for the rest. The council believes he'll march in a week, maybe less."

Two months ago. I had been summoned to Sky only a short while before that. Scimina had guessed my purpose the instant Dekarta summoned me.

And it made sense she had chosen to act through Menchey. Menchey was Darr's largest and most powerful neighbor, once our greatest enemy. We had been at peace with the Mencheyev since the Gods' War, but only because the Arameri had been unwilling to grant either land permission to annihilate the other. But as Ras Onchi had warned me, things had changed.

Of course they had submitted a formal war petition. They would want the right to shed our blood.

"I would hope we had begun to muster forces as well, in the time since," I said. It was no longer my place to give orders; I could only suggest.

My grandmother sighed. "As best we could. Our treasury is so depleted we can barely afford to feed them, much less train and equip. No one will lend us funds. We've resorted to asking for volunteers—any woman with a horse and her own weapons. Men as well, if they're not yet fathers."

It was very bad if the council had resorted to recruiting men. By tradition men were our last line of defense, their physical strength bent toward the single and most important task of protecting our homes and children. This meant the council had decided that our only defense was to defeat the enemy, period. Anything else meant the end of the Darre.

"I'll give you what I can," I said. "Dekarta watches everything I do, but I have wealth now, and—"

"No." Beba touched my shoulder again. I could not remember the last time she had touched me without reason. But then, I had never seen her leap to protect me from danger, either. It pained me that I would die young and never truly know her.

"Look to yourself," she said. "Darr is not your concern, not any longer."

I scowled. "It will always be—"

"You said yourself they would use us to hurt you. Look what's happened just from your effort to restore trade."

I opened my mouth to protest that this was merely their excuse, but before I could, Nahadoth's head turned sharply east.

"The sun comes," he said. Beyond Sar-enna-nem's entry arch, the sky was pale; night had faded quickly.

I cursed under my breath. "I *will* do what I can." Then, on impulse, I stepped forward and wrapped my arms around her and held her tight, as I had never dared to do before in my whole life. She held stiff against me for a moment, surprised, but then sighed and rested her hands on my back.

"So much like your father," she whispered. Then she pushed me away gently.

Nahadoth's arm folded around me, surprisingly gentle, and I found my back pressed against the human solidity of the body within his shadows. Then the body was gone and so was Sar-enna-nem, and all was cold and darkness again.

I reappeared in my room in Sky, facing the windows. The sky here was still mostly dark, though there was a hint of pale against the distant horizon. I was alone, to my surprise, but also to my relief. It had been a very long, very difficult day. Without undressing I lay down—but sleep did not come immediately. I lay where I was awhile, reveling in the silence, letting my mind rest. Like bubbles in still water, two things rose to the surface of my thoughts.

My mother had regretted her bargain with the Enefadeh. She had sold me to them, but not without qualm. I found it perversely comforting that she had tried to kill me at birth. That seemed like her, choosing to destroy her own flesh and blood rather than let it be corrupted. Perhaps she had only decided to accept me on *her* terms—later, without the heady rush of new motherhood to color her feelings. When she could look into my eyes and see that one of the souls in them was my own.

The other thought was simpler, yet far less comforting.

Had my father known?

17

Relief

DURING THOSE NIGHTS, those dreams, I saw through a thousand eyes. Bakers, blacksmiths, scholars, kings—ordinary and extraordinary, I lived their lives every night. But as with all dreams, I now remember only the most special.

In one, I see a darkened, empty room. There is almost no furniture. An old table. A messy, half-ragged pile of bedding in one corner. A marble beside the bedding. No, not a marble; a tiny, mostly blue globe, its nearer face a mosaic of brown and white. I know whose room this is.

"Shhh," says a new voice, and abruptly there are people in the room. A slight figure, half-draped across the lap of another body that is larger. And darker. "Shhh. Shall I tell you a story?"

"Mmm," says the smaller one. A child. "Yes. More beautiful lies, Papa, please."

"Now, now. Children are not so cynical. Be a proper child, or you will never grow big and strong like me."

"I will never be like you, Papa. That is one of your favorite lies."

I see tousled brown hair. A hand strokes it, long-fingered and graceful. The father? "I have watched you grow these long ages. In ten thousand years, a hundred thousand..."

"And will my sun-bright father open his arms when I have grown so great, and welcome me to his side?"

A sigh. "If he is lonely enough, he might."

"I don't want him!" Fitfully, the child moves away from the stroking hand and looks up. His eyes reflect the light like those of some nocturnal beast. "I will never betray you, Papa. Never!"

"Shhh." The father bends, laying a gentle kiss on the child's forehead. "I know."

And the child flings himself forward then, burying his face in soft darkness, weeping. The father holds him, rocking him gently, and begins to sing. In his voice I hear echoes of every mother who has ever comforted her child in the small hours, and every father who has ever whispered hopes into an infant's ear. I do not understand the pain I perceive, wrapped around both of them like chains, but I can tell that love is their defense against it.

It is a private moment; I am an intruder. I loosen invisible fingers, and let this dream slip through them and away.

I felt the poor sleep keenly when I dragged myself awake well into the next day. The inside of my head felt muddy, congealed. I sat on the edge of the bed with my knees drawn up, gazing through the windows at a bright, clear noon sky and thinking, *I am going to die.*

I am going to DIE.

In seven days—no, six now.

Die.

I am ashamed to admit that this litany went on for some time. The seriousness of my situation had not sunk in before; impending death had taken second place to Darr's jeopardy and a celestial conspiracy. But now I had no one yanking on my soul to distract me, and all I could think of was death. I was

not yet twenty years old. I had never been in love. I had not
mastered the nine forms of the knife. I had never—gods. I had
never really *lived*, beyond the legacies left to me by my parents:
ennu, and Arameri. It seemed almost incomprehensible that I
was doomed, and yet I was.

Because if the Arameri did not kill me, I had no illusions
about the Enefadeh. I was the sheath for the sword they hoped
to draw against Itempas, their sole means of escape. If the succession ceremony was postponed, or if by some miracle I succeeded in becoming Dekarta's heir, I was certain the Enefadeh
would simply kill me. Clearly, unlike other Arameri, I had no
protection against harm by them; doubtless that was one of
the alterations they had applied to my blood sigil. And killing
me might be the easiest way for them to free Enefa's soul with
minimal harm. Sieh might mourn the necessity of my death,
but no one else in Sky would.

So I lay on the bed and trembled and wept and might have
continued to do so for the rest of the day—one-sixth of my
remaining life—if there had not come a knock at the door.

That pulled me back to myself, more or less. I was still wearing the clothes I'd slept in from the day before; my hair was
mussed; my face was puffy and my eyes red. I hadn't bathed. I
opened the door a crack to see T'vril, to my great dismay, with a
tray of food in one hand.

"Greetings, Cousin—" He paused, took a second look at me,
and scowled. "What in demons happened to you?"

"N-nothing," I mumbled, then tried to close the door. He
slapped it open with his free hand, pushing me back and stepping inside. I would have protested, but the words died in my

throat as he looked me up and down with an expression that would have made my grandmother proud.

"You're letting them win, aren't you?" he asked.

I think my mouth might have dropped open. He sighed. "Sit down."

I closed my mouth. "How do you—"

"I know nearly everything that happens in this place, Yeine. The upcoming ball, for example, and what will happen afterward. Halfbloods usually aren't told, but I have connections." He gently took me by the shoulders. "You've found out, too, I suspect, which is why you're sitting here going to rot."

On another occasion I would have been pleased that he'd finally called me by my name. Now I shook my head dumbly and rubbed my temples where a weary ache had settled. "T'vril, you don't—"

"Sit *down*, you silly fool, before you pass out and I have to call Viraine. Which, incidentally, you don't want me to do. His remedies are effective but highly unpleasant." He took my hand and guided me over to my table.

"I came because they told me you hadn't ordered breakfast or a midday meal, and I thought you might be starving yourself again." Sitting me and the tray down, he picked up a dish of some sort of sectioned fruit, speared a piece on a fork, and thrust this at my face until I ate it. "You seemed a sensible girl when you first came here. Gods know this place has a way of knocking the sense out of a person, but I never expected you to yield so easily. Aren't you a warrior, or something like that? The rumors have you swinging through trees half-naked with a spear."

I glared at him, affront cutting through my muddle. "That's the stupidest thing you've ever said to me."

"So you're not dead yet. Good." He took my chin between his fingers, peering into my eyes. "And they haven't defeated you yet. Do you understand?"

I jerked away from him, clinging to my anger. It was better than despair, if just as useless. "You don't know what you're talking about. My people...I came here to help them, and instead they're in *more* danger because of me."

"Yes, so I've heard. You do realize that both Relad and Scimina are consummate liars, don't you? Nothing you've done caused this. Scimina's plans were set in motion long before you ever arrived in Sky. That's how this family does things." He held a hunk of cheese to my mouth. I had to bite off a piece, chew it, and swallow just to get his hand out of the way.

"If that's—" He pushed more fruit at me; I batted the fork aside and the fruit flew off somewhere near my bookcases. "If that's true, then you know there's nothing I can do! Darr's enemies are preparing to attack. My land is weak; we can't fight off one army, let alone however many are gathering against us!"

He nodded, sober, and held up a new chunk of fruit for me. "That sounds like Relad. Scimina is usually more subtle. But it could be either of them, frankly. Dekarta hasn't given them much time to work, and they both get clumsy under pressure."

The fruit tasted like salt in my mouth. "Then tell me—" I blinked back tears. "What am I supposed to do, T'vril? You say I'm letting them win, but *what else can I do?*"

T'vril set down the dish and took my hands, leaning forward. I realized suddenly that his eyes were green, though a deeper shade than my own. I had never before considered the fact that we were relatives. So few of the Arameri felt human to me, much less like family.

"You fight," he said, his voice low and intent. His hands gripped my own fiercely enough to hurt. "You fight in whatever way you can."

It might have been the strength of his grip, or the urgency of his voice, but abruptly I realized something. "You want to be heir yourself, don't you?"

He blinked in surprise, and then a rueful smile crossed his face. "No," he said. "Not really. No one would want to be heir under these conditions; I don't envy you that. But..." He looked away, toward the windows, and I saw it in his eyes: a terrible frustration that must have been burning in him all his life. The unspoken knowledge that he was just as smart as Relad or Scimina, just as strong, just as deserving of power, just as capable of leadership.

And if the chance were ever given to him, he would fight to keep it. To use it. He would fight even if he had no hope of victory, because to do otherwise was to concede that the stupid, arbitrary assignment of fullblood status had anything to do with logic; that the Amn truly were superior to all other races; that he deserved to be nothing more than a servant.

As I deserved to be nothing more than a pawn. I frowned.

T'vril noticed. "That's better." He put the dish of fruit in my hands and stood up. "Finish eating and get dressed. I want to show you something."

I had not realized that it was a holiday. Fire Day; some Amn celebration I'd heard of, but never paid much attention to. When T'vril brought me out of my room, I heard the sounds of laughter and Senmite music drifting through the corridors. I had never liked the music of this continent; it was strange and arrhythmic, full of eerie minors, the sort of thing only people with refined tastes were supposed to be able to comprehend or enjoy.

I sighed, thinking we were headed in that direction. But T'vril cast a grim look that way and shook his head. "No. You don't want to attend *that* celebration, Cousin."

"Why not?"

"That party is for highbloods. You'd certainly be welcome, and as a halfblood I could go, too, but I would suggest that you avoid social events with our fullblooded relatives if you actually want to enjoy yourself. They have...odd notions of what constitutes fun." His grim look warned me off further questioning. "This way."

He led me in the complete opposite direction, down several levels and angling toward the palace's heart. The corridors were bustling with activity, though I saw only servants as we walked, all of them moving so hurriedly that they barely had time to bob a greeting at T'vril. I doubt they even noticed me.

"Where are they all going?" I asked.

T'vril looked amused. "To work. I've scheduled everyone on rotating short shifts, so they've probably waited until the last minute to leave. Didn't want to miss any of the fun."

"Fun?"

"Mmm-hmm." We rounded a curve and I saw a wide set of translucent doors before us. "Here we are; the centeryard. Now, you're friendly with Sieh so I imagine the magic will work for you, but if it doesn't—if I disappear—just return to the hall and wait, and I'll come back out to get you."

"What?" I was growing used to feeling stupid.

"You'll see." He pushed the doors open.

The scene beyond was almost pastoral—*would* have been if I hadn't known I was in the middle of a palace hovering a half mile above the earth. We looked into some sort of vast atrium at the center of the palace, in which rows of tiny cottages bordered a cobblestone path. It surprised me to realize that the cottages were made, not of the pearly material that comprised the rest of the palace, but of ordinary stone and wood and brick. The style of the cottages varied wildly from that of the palace, too—the first sharp angles and straight lines I'd seen— and from cottage to cottage. Many of the designs were foreign to my eye, Tokken and Mekatish and others, including one with a striking bright-gold rooftop that might have been Irtin. I glanced up, realizing that the centeryard sat within a vast cylinder in the body of the palace; directly above was a circle of perfectly clear blue sky.

But the whole place was silent and still. I saw no one in or around the cottages; not even wind stirred.

T'vril took my hand and pulled me over the threshold—and I gasped as the stillness broke. In a moment's flicker there were suddenly *many* people about, all around us, laughing and milling and exclaiming in a cacophony of joy that would not have startled me so much if it hadn't come out of nowhere. There was music, too, more pleasant than the Senmite but still nothing I was used to. It came from much closer, somewhere in the middle of the cottages. I made out a flute and a drum, and a babel of languages—the only one I recognized was Kenti—before someone grabbed my arm and spun me around.

"Shaz, you came! I thought—" The Amn man who'd caught

my hand started when he saw my face, then paled further. "Oh, demons."

"It's all right," I said quickly. "An honest mistake." From behind I could pass for Tema, Narshes, or half the other northern races—and it had not escaped me that he'd called me by a boy's name. That was clearly not the source of his horror. His eyes had locked on my forehead and the fullblood circle there.

"It's all right, Ter." T'vril came up beside me and put a hand on my shoulder. "This is the new one."

Relief restored color to the man's face. "Sorry, miss," he said, bobbing a greeting to me. "I just...well." He smiled sheepishly. "You understand."

I reassured him again, though I was not entirely sure that I did understand. The man wandered off after that, leaving T'vril and me to ourselves—inasmuch as we could be alone amid such a horde. I could see now that everyone present wore lowblood marks; they were all servants. There must have been nearly a thousand people in the centeryard's sprawling space. T'vril was so good at keeping them unobtrusive that I'd had no idea there were this many servants in Sky, though I suppose I should have guessed they would outnumber the highbloods.

"Don't blame Ter," T'vril said. "Today's one of the few days we can be free of rank considerations. He wasn't expecting to see that." He nodded toward my forehead.

"What is this, T'vril? Where did these people...?"

"A little favor from the Enefadeh." He gestured toward the entrance we'd just walked through, and upward. There was a faint, glasslike sheen to the air all around the centeryard, which

I had not noticed before. We stood within a huge, transparent bubble of—something. Magic, whatever it was.

"No one with a mark higher than quarterblood sees anything, even if they pass through the barrier," T'vril said. "An exception was made for me, and, as you saw, we can bring others through if we choose. This means we can celebrate without highbloods coming here to ogle our 'quaint common-folk customs' like we're animals in a zoo."

I understood at last, and smiled as I did. It was probably only one of many small rebellions that the lowblood servants quietly fomented against their higher-born relations. If I stayed in Sky longer I would probably see others...

But, of course, I would not live long enough for that.

That thought sobered me at once, despite the music and gaiety around me. T'vril flashed me a grin and let go my hand. "Well, you're here now. Enjoy yourself for a while, hmm?" And almost at the moment he let me go, a woman grabbed him and pulled him into the mass of people. I saw a flash of his red hair among other heads, and then he was gone.

I stood where he'd left me, feeling oddly bereft. The servants celebrated on around me, but I was not part of it. Nor could I relax amid so much noise and chaos, however joyous. None of these people were Darre. None of them were under threat of execution. None of them had gods' souls stuffed into their bodies, tainting all that they thought and felt.

Yet T'vril had brought me here in an attempt to cheer me up, and it would've been churlish to leave right away. So I looked around for some quiet spot where I might sit out of the way. My eyes caught on a familiar face—or at least, it seemed familiar at first. A young man watched me from the steps of one of the cottages, smiling as if he knew *me*, at least. He was a little older than me, pretty-faced and slender, Tema-looking but with completely un-Tema eyes of faded green—

I caught my breath and went over to him. "Sieh?"

He grinned. "Glad to see you out."

"You're..." I gaped a moment longer, then closed my mouth. I had known all along that Nahadoth was not the only one among the Enefadeh who could change his form. "So this is your doing?" I gestured at the barrier, which now I could see above us as well, like a dome.

He shrugged. "T'vril's people do favors for us all year; it's fitting we should pay them back. We slaves must stick together."

There was a bitterness in his tone that I had not heard before. It felt oddly comforting in comparison with my own mood, so I sat down on the steps beside him, near his legs. Together we watched the celebration in silence for a long while. After a time I felt his hand touch my hair, stroking it, and that comforted me further still. Whatever form he took, he was still the same Sieh.

"They grow and change so fast," he said softly, his eyes on a group of dancers near the musicians. "Sometimes I hate them for that."

I glanced up at him in surprise; this was a strange mood indeed for him. "You gods are the ones who made us this way, aren't you?"

He glanced at me, and for a jarring, painful instant I saw confusion on his face. Enefa. He had spoken as if I was Enefa.

Then the confusion passed, and he shared with me a small, sad smile. "Sorry," he said.

I could not feel bitter about it, given the sorrow in his face. "I do seem to look like her."

"That's not it." He sighed. "It's just that sometimes—well, it feels like she died only yesterday."

The Gods' War had occurred over two thousand years before, by most scholars' reckonings. I turned away from Sieh and sighed, too, at the width of the gulf between us.

"You're not like her," he said. "Not really."

I didn't want to talk about Enefa, but I said nothing. I drew up my knees and rested my chin on them. Sieh resumed stroking my hair, petting me like a cat.

"She was reserved like you, but that's the only similarity. She was...cooler than you. Slower to anger—although she had the same *kind* of temper as you, I think, magnificent when it finally blew. We tried hard not to anger her."

"You sound like you were afraid of her."

"Of course. How could we not be?"

I frowned in confusion. "She was your mother."

Sieh hesitated, and in it I heard an echo of my earlier thoughts about the gulf between us. "It's...difficult to explain."

I hated that gulf. I wanted to breach it, though I had no idea if it was even possible. So I said, "Try."

His hand paused on my hair, and then he chuckled, his voice warm. "I'm glad you're not one of my worshippers. You'd drive me mad with your demands."

"Would you even bother answering any prayers that I made?" I could not help smiling at the idea.

"Oh, of course. But I might sneak a salamander into your bed to get back at you."

I laughed, which surprised me. It was the first time all day that I'd felt human. It didn't last long as laughs went, but when it passed, I felt better. On impulse, I shifted to lean against his legs, putting my head on his knee. His hand never left my hair.

"I needed no mother's milk when I was born." Sieh spoke slowly, but I did not sense a lie this time. I think it was just difficult for him to find the right words. "There was no need to protect me from danger or sing me lullabies. I could hear the songs between the stars, and I was more dangerous to the worlds I visited than they could ever be to me. And yet, compared to the Three, I was weak. Like them in many ways, but obviously inferior. Naha was the one who convinced her to let me live and see what I might become."

I frowned. "She was going to ... kill you?"

"Yes." He chuckled at my shock. "She killed things all the time, Yeine. She was death as well as life, the twilight along with the dawn. Everyone forgets that."

I turned to stare at him, which made him draw his hand back from my hair. There was something in that gesture—something regretful and hesitant, not befitting a god at all—that suddenly angered me. It was there in his every word. However incomprehensible relationships between gods might be, he had been a child and Enefa his mother, and he had loved her with any child's abandon. Yet she had almost killed him, as a breeder culls a defective foal.

Or as a mother smothers a dangerous infant...

No. That had been entirely different.

"I'm beginning to dislike this Enefa," I said.

Sieh started in surprise, stared at me for a long second, then burst out laughing. It was infectious, though nonsensical; humor born of pain. I smiled as well.

"Thank you," Sieh said, still chuckling. "I hate taking this form; it always makes me maudlin."

"Be a child again." I liked him better that way.

"Can't." He gestured toward the barrier. "This takes too much of my strength."

"Ah." I wondered suddenly which was the default state for him: the child? Or this world-weary adult who slipped out whenever he let his guard down? Or something else altogether? But that seemed too intimate and possibly painful a question to ask, so I did not. We fell silent awhile longer, watching the servants dance.

"What will you do?" Sieh asked.

I laid my head back on his knee and said nothing.

Sieh sighed. "If I knew how to help you, I would. You know that, don't you?"

The words warmed me more than I'd expected. I smiled. "Yes. I know, though I can't say I understand it. I'm just a mortal like the rest of them, Sieh."

"Not like the rest."

"Yes." I looked at him. "However... *different* I might be—" I did not like saying it aloud. No one stood near enough to us to overhear, but it seemed foolish to take chances. "You said it yourself. Even if I lived to be a hundred, my life would still be only an eyeblink of yours. I should be nothing to you, like these others." I nodded toward the throng.

He laughed softly; the bitterness had returned. "Oh, Yeine. You really don't understand. If mortals were truly nothing to us, our lives would be so much easier. And so would yours."

I could say nothing to that. So I fell silent, and he did, too, and around us the servants celebrated on.

*   *   *

It was nearly midnight by the time I finally left the centeryard. The party was still in full swing, but T'vril left with me and walked me to my quarters. He'd been drinking, though not nearly as much as some I'd seen. "Unlike them, I have to be clearheaded in the morning," he said, when I pointed this out.

At the door of my apartment we stopped. "Thank you," I said, meaning it.

"You didn't enjoy yourself," he said. "I saw: you didn't dance all evening. Did you even have a glass of wine?"

"No. But it did help." I groped for the right words. "I won't deny a part of me spent the whole time thinking, *I'm wasting one-sixth of my remaining life.*" I smiled; T'vril grimaced. "But to spend that time surrounded by so much joy... it did make me feel better."

There was such compassion in his eyes. I found myself wondering, again, why he helped me. I supposed it made a difference that he had some fellow feeling for me, perhaps even liked me. It was touching to think so, and perhaps that was why I reached up to cup his cheek. He blinked in surprise, but he did not draw back. That pleased me, too, and so I yielded to impulse.

"I'm probably not pretty by your standards," I ventured. His cheek felt slightly scratchy under my fingers, and I remembered that men of the island peoples tended to grow beards. I found the idea exotic and intriguing.

A half-dozen thoughts flickered across T'vril's face in the span of a breath, then settled with his slow smile. "Well, I'm not by yours, either," he said. "I've seen those showhorses you Darre call men."

I chuckled, abruptly nervous. "And we are, of course, relatives..."

"This is Sky, Cousin." Amazing how that explained everything. I opened the door to my apartment, then took his hand and pulled him inside.

He was strangely gentle—or perhaps it only seemed strange to me because I had little experience to compare him against. I was surprised to find that he was even paler beneath his clothing, and his shoulders were covered in faint spots, like those of a leopard but smaller and random. He felt normal enough against me, lean and strong, and I liked the sounds that he made. He did try to give me pleasure, but I was too tense, too aware of my own loneliness and fear, so there were no stormwinds for me. I did not mind so much.

I was unused to having someone in my bed, so afterward I slept restlessly. Finally in the small hours of the morning I got up and went into the bathroom, hoping that a bath would settle me to sleep. While water filled the tub, I ran more in the sink and splashed my face, then stared at myself in the mirror. There were new lines of strain around my eyes, making me look older. I touched my mouth, suddenly melancholy for the girl I had been just a few months before. She had not been innocent—no leader of any people can afford that—but she had been happy, more or less. When was the last time I'd felt happiness? I could not recall.

Suddenly I was annoyed with T'vril. At least pleasure would have relaxed me and perhaps pulled my mood out of its grim track. At the same time it bothered me to feel such disappointment because I liked T'vril, and the fault was as much mine as his.

But on the heels of this, unbidden, came an even more disturbing thought—one that I fought for long seconds, caught between morbid, forbidden-thrill fascination and superstitious fear.

I knew why I had found no satisfaction with T'vril.

Never whisper his name in the dark

No. This was stupidity. No, no, no.

unless you want him to answer.

There was a terrible, mad recklessness inside me. It whirled and crashed in my head, a cacophony of not-quite-thought. I could actually see it manifest as I stared into the mirror; my own eyes stared back at me, too wide, the pupils too large. I licked my lips, and for a moment they were not mine. They belonged to some other woman, much braver and stupider than me.

The bathroom was not dark because of the glowing walls, but darkness took many forms. I closed my eyes and spoke to the blackness beneath my lids.

"Nahadoth," I said.

My lips barely moved. I had given the word only enough breath to make it audible, and no more. I didn't even hear myself over the running water and the pounding of my heart. But I waited. Two breaths. Three.

Nothing happened.

For an instant I felt utterly irrational disappointment. This was followed swiftly by relief, and fury at myself. What in the Maelstrom was wrong with me? I had never in my life done anything so foolish. I must have been losing my mind.

I turned away from the mirror—and as I did the glowing walls went dark.

"What—" I began, and a mouth settled over mine.

Even if logic hadn't told me who it was, that kiss would have. There was no taste to it, only wetness and strength, and a hungry, agile tongue that slid around mine like a snake. His mouth was cooler than T'vril's had been. But a different kind of heat coiled through me in response, and when hands began to explore my body I could not help arching up to meet them. I breathed harder as the mouth finally relinquished mine and moved down my neck.

I knew I should have stopped him. I knew this was his favorite way to kill. But when unseen ropes lifted me and pinned me to the wall, and fingers slipped between my thighs to play a subtle music, thinking became impossible. That mouth, *his* mouth, was everywhere. He must have had a dozen of them. Every time I moaned or cried out, he kissed me, drinking down the sound like wine. When I could restrain myself his face pressed into my hair; his breath was light and quick in my ear. I tried to reach up, I think to embrace him, but nothing was there. Then his fingers did something new and I was screaming, screaming at the top of my lungs, except that he had covered my mouth again and there was no sound, no light, no movement; he had swallowed it all. There was nothing but pleasure, and it seemed to go on for an eternity. If he had killed me right then and there, I would have died happy.

And then it was gone.

I opened my eyes.

I sat slumped on the bathroom floor. My limbs felt weak, shaky. The walls were glowing again. Steaming water filled the tub beside me to the brim; the taps were closed. I was alone.

I got up and bathed, then returned to bed. T'vril murmured in his sleep and threw an arm over me. I curled against him and told myself for the rest of the night that I was still trembling because of fear, nothing else.

18

The Oubliette

THERE ARE THINGS I KNOW NOW that I did not before.

Like this: In the instant Bright Itempas was born, he attacked the Nightlord. Their natures were so opposed that at first this seemed destined and unavoidable. For countless eternities they battled, each occasionally achieving victory only to be later overthrown. Only gradually did both come to understand that such battle was pointless; in the grand scale of things, it was an eternal stalemate.

Yet in the process, completely by accident, they created many things. To the formless void that Nahadoth birthed, Itempas added gravity, motion, function, and time. For every great star killed in the cross fire, each god used the ashes to create something new—more stars, planets, sparkling colored clouds, marvels that spiraled and pulsed. Gradually, between the two of them, the universe took shape. And as the dust of their battling cleared, both gods found that they were pleased.

Which of them made the first overture to peace? I imagine there were false starts at first—broken truces and the like. How long before hatred turned to tolerance, then respect and trust, then something more? And once it finally did, were they as passionate in love as they had been in war?

There is a legendary romance in this. And most fascinating to me, most frightening, is that *it isn't over yet.*

* * *

T'vril left for work at dawn. We exchanged few words and a silent understanding: the previous night had just been comfort between friends. It was not as awkward as it could have been; I got the sense he expected nothing else. Life in Sky did not encourage more.

I slept awhile longer and then lay awake in bed for a time, thinking.

My grandmother had said Menchey's armies would march soon. With so little time, I could think of few strategies that had any real chance of saving Darr. The best I could do was delay the attack. But how? I could seek allies in the Consortium, perhaps. Ras Onchi spoke for half of High North; perhaps she would know—no. I had watched both my parents and Darr's warrior council devote years to the quest for allies; if there were friends to be had, they would have made themselves known by now. The best I could do were individual sympathizers like Onchi—welcome, but ultimately useless.

So it would have to be something else. Even a few days' reprieve would be enough; if I could delay the attack until after the succession ceremony, then my bargain with the Enefadeh would take effect, earning Darr four godly protectors.

Assuming they won their battle.

So: all or nothing. But risky odds were better than none, so I would chase them with all I had. I rose and went in search of Viraine.

He was not in his laboratory. A slim young servant woman was, cleaning. "He's at the oubliette," she told me. Since I had no idea what this was, or where, she gave me directions and I set out for Sky's lowermost level. And I wondered, as I walked, at the look of disgust that had been on the servant woman's face.

I emerged from the lift amid corridors that felt oddly dim. The walls' glow was muted in a strange way—not as bright as I'd grown used to, flatter somehow. There were no windows and, most curious, no doors, either. Apparently even servants did not live this far down. My footsteps echoed from ahead as I walked, so I was not surprised to emerge from the corridor into an open space: a vast, oblong chamber whose floor sloped toward a peculiar metal grate several feet in diameter. Nor was I surprised to find Viraine near this grate, gazing steadily at me as I entered. He had probably heard me the moment I stepped off the lift.

"Lady Yeine." He inclined his head, for once not smiling. "Shouldn't you be at the Salon?"

I hadn't been to the Salon in days, or reviewed my assigned nations' records, either. It was hard to care about these duties, considering. "I doubt the world will falter for my absence, now or in the next five days."

"I see. What brings you here?"

"I was looking for you." My eyes were drawn toward the grate in the floor. It looked like an exceptionally ornate sewer grate, apparently leading to some sort of chamber under the floor. I could see light glowing from within that was brighter than the ambient light of the room Viraine and I stood in—but that odd sense of flatness, of *grayness*, was even stronger here. The light underlit Viraine's face in a way that should have sharpened the angles and shadows in his expression, but instead it stripped them away.

"What is this place?" I asked.

"We're below the palace proper, actually in the support column that elevates us above the city."

"The column is hollow?"

"No. Only this space here at the top." He watched me, his eyes trying to gauge something I could not fathom. "You didn't attend the celebration yesterday."

I was not certain whether the highbloods knew about the servants' celebration and ignored it, or whether it was a secret. In case of the latter I said, "I haven't been in a celebratory mood."

"If you had come, this would be less of a surprise to you." He gestured toward the grate at his feet.

I stayed where I was, suffused with a sudden sense of dread. "What are you talking about?"

He sighed, and abruptly I realized he was in an ugly sort of mood himself. "One of the highlights of the Fire Day celebration. I'm often asked to provide entertainment. Tricks and the like."

"Tricks?" I frowned. From what I knew, scrivening was far too powerful and dangerous to be risked on tricks. One miswritten line and gods knew what could go wrong.

"Tricks. Of the sort that generally require a human 'volunteer.'" He gave me a thin smile as my jaw dropped. "Highbloods are difficult to entertain, you see—you being the natural exception. The rest..." He shrugged. "A lifetime of indulging all manner of whims sets the bar for entertainment rather high. Or low."

From the grate at his feet, and the chamber beyond, I heard a hollow, strained moan that chilled both my souls.

"What in the gods' names have you done?" I whispered.

"The gods have nothing to do with it, my dear." He sighed, gazing into the pit. "Why were you looking for me?"

I forced my eyes, and my mind, away from the grate. "I...
I need to know if there's a way to send a message to someone,
from Sky. Privately."

The look he gave me would have been withering under ordinary circumstances, but I could see that whatever was in the
oubliette had taken the edge off his usual sardonic attitude.
"You do realize spying on such communications is one of my
routine duties?"

I inclined my head. "I suspected as much. That's why I'm
asking you. If there's a way to do it, you would know." I swallowed, then privately chided myself for allowing nervousness
to show. "I'm prepared to compensate you for your trouble."

In the strange gray light, even Viraine's surprise was muted.
"Well, well." A tired smile stretched across his face. "Lady Yeine,
perhaps you're a true Arameri after all."

"I do what's necessary," I said flatly. "And you know as well as
I do that I don't have time to be more subtle."

At that his smile faded. "I know."

"Then help me."

"What message do you want to send, and to whom?"

"If I wanted half the palace to know, I wouldn't ask how to
send it privately."

"I'm asking because the only way to send such a message is
through me, Lady."

I paused then, unpleasantly surprised. But it made sense as I
considered it. I had no idea how messaging crystals worked in
detail, but like any sigil-based magic their function simply mimicked what any competent scrivener could do.

But I did not like Viraine, for reasons I could not fully understand myself. I had seen the bitterness in his eyes, heard the contempt in his voice on those occasions that he spoke of Dekarta or the other highbloods. Like the Enefadeh, he was a weapon and probably just as much a slave. Yet there was something about him that simply made me uneasy. I suspected it was that he seemed to have no loyalties; he was on no one's side except his own. That meant he could be relied upon to keep my secrets, if I made it worth his while. But what if there was more benefit for him in divulging my secrets to Dekarta? Or worse— Relad and Scimina? Men who served anyone could be trusted by no one.

He smirked as he watched me consider. "Of course, you could always ask Sieh to send the message for you. Or Nahadoth. I'm sure *he'd* do it, if sufficiently motivated."

"I'm sure he would," I replied coolly...

The Darren language has a word for the attraction one feels to danger: *esui*. It is *esui* that makes warriors charge into hopeless battles and die laughing. *Esui* is also what draws women to lovers who are bad for them—men who would make poor fathers, women of the enemy. The Senmite word that comes closest is "lust," if one includes the variations "bloodlust" and "lust for life," though these do not adequately capture the layered nature of *esui*. It is glory, it is folly. It is everything not sensible, not rational, not safe at all—but without *esui*, there is no point in living.

It is *esui*, I think, that draws me to Nahadoth. Perhaps it is also what draws him to me.

But I digress.

"...but then it would be a simple matter for some other highblood to command my message out of him."

"Do you honestly think I would bother getting involved with your schemes? After living between Relad and Scimina for two decades?" Viraine rolled his eyes. "I don't care which of you ends up succeeding Dekarta."

"The next family head could make your life easier. Or harder." I said it in a neutral tone; let him hear promises or threats as he pleased. "I would think the whole world cares who ends up on that stone seat."

"Even Dekarta answers to a higher power," Viraine said. While I wondered what in the gods' names that meant in the context of our discussion, he gazed into the hole beyond the metal grate, his eyes reflecting the pale light. Then his expression changed to something that immediately made me wary. "Come," he said. He gestured at the grate. "Look."

I frowned. "Why?"

"I'm curious about something."

"What?"

He said nothing, waiting. Finally I sighed and went to the grate's edge.

At first I saw nothing. Then there was another of those hollow groans, and someone shuffled into view, and it took everything I had not to run away and throw up.

Take a human being. Twist and stretch his limbs like clay. Add new limbs, designed for gods know what purpose. Bring some of his innards out of his body, yet leave them working. Seal up his mouth and—Skyfather. God of all gods.

And the worst was this: I could still see intelligence and awareness in the distorted eyes. They had not even allowed him the escape of insanity.

I could not conceal my reaction entirely. There was a fine

sheen of sweat on my brow and upper lip when I looked up to meet Viraine's intent gaze.

"Well?" I asked. I had to swallow before I could speak. "Is your curiosity satisfied?"

The way he was looking at me would have disturbed me even if we hadn't stood above the tortured, mutilated evidence of his power. There was a kind of lust in his eyes that had nothing to do with sex, and everything to do with—what? I could not guess, but it reminded me, unpleasantly, of the human form Nahadoth. He made my fingers itch for a knife the same way.

"Yes," he said softly. There was no smile on his face, but I could see a high, triumphant gleam in his eyes. "I wanted to know whether you had any chance, any at all, before I assisted you."

"And your verdict is...?" But I knew already.

He gestured into the pit. "Kinneth could have looked at that thing without batting an eyelash. She could have done the deed herself and enjoyed it—"

"You lie!"

"—or pretended to enjoy it well enough that the difference wouldn't have mattered. She had what it took to defeat Dekarta. You don't."

"Maybe not," I snapped. "But at least I still have a soul. What did you trade yours for?"

To my surprise, Viraine's glee seemed to fade. He looked down into the pit, the gray light making his eyes seem colorless and older than Dekarta's.

"Not enough," he said, and walked away. He moved past me into the corridor, heading for the lift.

I did not follow. Instead I went to the far wall of the chamber, sat down against it, and waited. After what seemed an eternity of gray silence—broken only by the faint, occasional suffering sounds of the poor soul in the pit—I felt a familiar shudder ripple through the palace's substance. I waited awhile, counting the minutes until I judged that sunset's light had faded enough from the evening sky. Then I got up and went to the corridor, my back to the oubliette. The gray light painted my shadow along the floor in a thin, attenuated line. I made certain my face was in that shadow before I spoke. "Nahadoth."

The walls dimmed before I turned. Yet the room was brighter than it should have been, because of the light from the oubliette. For some reason, his darkness had no effect on it.

He watched me, inscrutable, his face even more inhumanly perfect in the colorless light.

"Here," I said, and moved past him to the oubliette. The prisoner within was looking up at me, perhaps sensing my intent. It did not bother me to look at him this time as I pointed into the pit.

"Heal him," I said.

I expected a furious response. Or amusement, or triumph; there really was no way to predict the Nightlord's reaction to my first command. What I did not expect, however, was what he said.

"I can't."

I frowned at him; he gazed into the oubliette dispassionately. "What do you mean?"

"Dekarta gave the command that caused this."

And because of his master sigil, I could countermand no orders that Dekarta gave. I closed my eyes and sent a brief prayer for forgiveness to—well. Whichever god cared to listen.

"Very well, then," I said, and my voice sounded very small in the open chamber. I took a deep breath. "Kill him."

"I can't do that, either."

That jolted me, badly. "Why in the Maelstrom not?"

Nahadoth smiled. There was something strange about the smile, something that unnerved me even more than usual, but I could not allow myself to dwell on it. "The succession will take place in four days," he said. "Someone must send the Stone of Earth to the chamber where this ritual takes place. This is tradition."

"What? I don't—"

Nahadoth pointed into the pit. Not at the shuffling, whimpering creature there, but slightly away from it. I followed his finger and saw what I had not before. The floor of the oubliette glowed with that strange gray light, so different from that of the palace's walls. The spot where Nahadoth pointed seemed to be where the light was concentrated, not so much brighter as simply *more gray*. I stared at it and thought that I saw a darker shadow embedded in the translucent palacestuff. Something small.

All this time it had been right beneath my feet. The Stone of Earth.

"Sky exists to contain and channel its power, but here, so close, there is always some leakage." Nahadoth's finger shifted slightly. "That power is what keeps him alive."

My mouth was dry. "And . . . and what did you mean about . . . sending the Stone to the ritual chamber?"

He pointed up this time, and I saw that the ceiling of the oubliette chamber had a narrow, rounded opening at its center, like a small chimney. The narrow tunnel beyond went straight up, as far as the eye could see.

"No magic can act upon the Stone directly. No living flesh can come near it without suffering ill effects. So even for a relatively simple task, like moving the Stone from here to the chamber above, one of Enefa's children must spend his life to wish it there."

I understood at last. Oh, gods, it was monstrous. Death would be a relief to the unknown man in the pit, but the Stone somehow prevented that. To earn release from that twisted prison of flesh, the man would have to collaborate in his own execution.

"Who is he?" I asked. Below, the man had managed at last to sit down, though with obvious discomfort. I heard him weeping quietly.

"Just another fool caught praying to an outlawed god. This one happens to be a distant Arameri relation—they leave a few free to bring new blood into the clan—so he was doubly doomed."

"H-he could..." I could not think. *Monstrous.* "He could send the Stone away. Wish it into a volcano, or some frozen waste."

"Then one of us would simply be sent to retrieve it. But he won't defy Dekarta. Unless he sends the Stone properly, his lover will share his fate."

In the pit, the man uttered a particularly loud moan—as close to a wail as his warped mouth could manage. Tears filled my eyes, blurring the gray light.

"Shhh," Nahadoth said. I looked at him in surprise, but he was still gazing into the pit. "Shhh. It will not be long. I'm sorry."

When Nahadoth saw my confusion, he gave me another of those strange smiles that I did not understand, or did not want to understand. But that was blindness on my part. I kept thinking that I knew him.

"I always hear their prayers," said the Nightlord, "even if I'm not allowed to answer."

We stood at the foot of the Pier, gazing down at the city half a mile below.

"I need to threaten someone," I said.

I had not spoken since the oubliette. Nahadoth had accompanied me to the Pier, me meandering, him following. (The servants and highbloods gave us both a wide berth.) He said nothing now, though I felt him there beside me.

"The Minister of Mencheyev, a man named Gemd, who probably leads the alliance against Darr. Him."

"To threaten, you must have the power to cause harm," Nahadoth said.

I shrugged. "I've been adopted into the Arameri. Gemd has already assumed I have such power."

"Beyond Sky, your right to command us ends. Dekarta will never give you permission to harm a nation which has not offended him."

I said nothing.

Nahadoth glanced at me, amused. "I see. But a bluff won't hold this man long."

"It doesn't have to." I pushed away from the railing and turned to him. "It only needs to hold him for four more days. And I can use your power beyond Sky . . . if you let me. Will you?"

Nahadoth straightened as well, to my surprise lifting a hand to my face. He cupped my cheek, drew a thumb along the bottom curve of my lips. I will not lie: this made me think dangerous thoughts.

"You commanded me to kill tonight," he said.

I swallowed. "For mercy."

"Yes." That disturbing, alien look was in his eyes again, and finally I could name it: understanding. An almost human compassion, as if for that instant he actually thought and felt like one of us.

"You will never be Enefa," he said. "But you have some of her strength. Do not be offended by the comparison, little pawn." I started, wondering again if he could read minds. "I do not make it lightly."

Then Nahadoth stepped back. He spread his arms wide, revealing the black void of his body, and waited.

I stepped inside him and was enfolded in darkness. It might have been my imagination, but it seemed warmer this time.

19

Diamonds

YOU ARE INSIGNIFICANT. One of millions, neither special nor unique. I did not ask for this ignominy, and I resent the comparison.

Fine. I don't like you, either.

We appeared in a stately, brightly lit hall of white and gray marble, lined by narrow rectangular windows, under a chandelier. (If I had never seen Sky, I would have been impressed.) At both ends of the hall were double doors of polished dark wood;

I assumed we faced the relevant set. From beyond the open windows I could hear merchants crying their wares, a baby fussing, a horse's neigh, womens' laughter. City life.

No one was around, though the evening was young. I knew Nahadoth well enough by now to suspect that this was deliberate.

I nodded toward the doors. "Is Gemd alone?"

"No. With him are a number of guards, colleagues, and advisors."

Of course. Planning a war took teamwork. I scowled and then caught myself: I could not do this angry. My goal was delay—peace, for as long as possible. Anger would not help.

"Please try not to kill anyone," I murmured, as we walked toward the door. Nahadoth said nothing in response, but the hall grew dimmer, the flickering torchlit shadows sharpening to razor fineness. The air felt heavy.

This my Arameri ancestors had learned, at the cost of their own blood and souls: the Nightlord cannot be controlled. He can only be unleashed. If Gemd forced me to call on Nahadoth's power—

Best to pray that would not be necessary.

I walked forward.

The doors flung themselves open as I came to them, slamming against the opposite walls with an echoing racket that would bring half Gemd's palace guard running if they had any competence. It made for a suitably stunning entrance as I strode through, greeted by a chorus of surprised shouts and curses. Men who had been seated around a wide, paper-cluttered table scrambled to their feet, some groping for weapons and others staring at me dumbly. Two of them wore deep-red cloaks that I recognized as Tok warrior attire. So that was one of the lands Menchey had allied with. At the head of this table sat a man of perhaps sixty years: richly dressed, salt-and-pepper-haired, with a face like flint and steel. He reminded me of Dekarta, though only in manner; the Mencheyev were High North people, too, and they looked more like Darre than Amn. He half-stood, then hovered where he was, more angry than surprised.

I fixed my gaze on him, though I knew that Menchey, like Darr, was ruled more by its council than its chieftain. In many ways we were merely figureheads, he and I. But in this confrontation, he would be the key.

"Minister," I said, in Senmite. "Greetings."

His eyes narrowed. "You're that Darre bitch."

"One of many, yes."

Gemd turned to one of his men and murmured something; the man hurried away. To supervise the guards and figure out how I'd gotten in, no doubt. Then Gemd turned back, his look appraising and wary.

"You're not among many now," he said slowly. "Or are you? You couldn't have been foolish enough to come alone."

I caught myself just before I would have looked around. Of course Nahadoth would choose not to appear. The Enefadeh had pledged to help me, after all, and having the Nightlord looming behind me like an overgrown shadow would have undermined what little authority I had in these men's eyes.

But Nahadoth was there. I could feel him.

"I have come," I said. "Not entirely alone. But then, no Arameri is ever fully alone, is she?"

One of his men, almost as richly dressed as Gemd, narrowed

his eyes. "You're no Arameri," he said. "They didn't even acknowledge you until these last few months."

"Is that why you've decided to form this alliance?" I asked, stepping forward. A few of the men tensed, but most did not. I am not very intimidating. "I can't see how that makes much sense. If I'm so unimportant to the Arameri, then Darr is no threat."

"Darr is always a threat," growled another man. "You man-eating harlots—"

"Enough," said Gemd, and the man subsided.

Good; not wholly a figurehead, then.

"So this is not about the Arameri adopting me, then?" I eyed the man Gemd had silenced. "Ah, I see. This is about old grudges. The last war between our peoples was more genera-tions back than any of us can count. Are Mencheyev memories so long?"

"Darr claimed the Atir Plateau in that war," Gemd said qui-etly. "You know we want it back."

I knew, and I knew that was a stupid, stupid reason to start a war. The people who lived on the Atir didn't even speak the Mencheyev tongue anymore. None of this made any sense, and that was enough to make my temper rise.

"Who is it?" I asked. "Which of my cousins is pulling your strings? Relad? Scimina? Some sycophant of theirs? Who are you whoring for, Gemd, and how much have you charged to bend forward?"

Gemd's jaw tightened but he said nothing. His men were not so well-trained; they bristled and glared daggers. Not all of them, though. I noted which ones looked uncomfortable, and knew that they were the ones through whom Scimina or another of my relatives had chosen to work.

"You are an uninvited guest, Yeine-*ennu*," Gemd said. "Lady Yeine, I should say. You are interrupting my business. Say what you've come to say, and then please leave."

I inclined my head. "Call off your plans to attack Darr."

Gemd waited for a moment. "Or?"

I shook my head. "There is no alternative, Minister. I've learned a great deal from my Arameri relatives these last few days, including the art of wielding absolute power. We do not give ultimatums. We give orders, and those are obeyed."

The men turned to look at one another, their expressions ranging from fury to incredulity. Two kept their faces blank: the richly dressed man at Gemd's side and Gemd himself. I could see calculation in their eyes.

"You don't have absolute power," said the man beside Gemd. He kept his tone neutral, a sign that he was uncertain. "You haven't even been named heir."

"True," I said. "Only the Lord Dekarta holds total power over the Hundred Thousand Kingdoms. Whether they thrive. Whether they falter. Whether they are obliterated and forgotten." Gemd's brow tightened at that, not quite a frown. "Grandfather has this power, but he may of course choose to delegate it to those of us in Sky who have his favor."

I let them wonder whether I had earned that favor or not. It probably sounded like a sign of favor that I had been summoned to Sky and named a fullblood.

Gemd glanced at the man beside him before saying, "You must realize, Lady Yeine, that once plans have been set in motion, they can be difficult to stop. We will need time to discuss your...order."

"Of course," I said. "You have ten minutes. I'll wait."

"Oh for—" This was from another man, younger and bigger, one of the ones I had marked for an Arameri tool. He looked at me as if I were excrement on the bottom of his shoe. "Minister, you cannot seriously be considering this ridiculous demand!"

Gemd glared at him, but the silent reprimand clearly had no impact. The younger man stepped away from the table and came toward me, his whole posture radiating menace. Every Darre woman is taught to deal with such behavior from men. It is an animal trick that they use, like dogs ruffling their fur and growling. Only rarely is there actual threat behind it, and a woman's strength lies in discerning when the threat is real and when it is just hair and noise. For now the threat was not real, but that could change.

He stopped before me and turned back to his fellows, pointing at me. "Look at her! They probably had to call a scrivener just to confirm she came out of an Arameri cunt—"

"Rish!" Gemd looked furious. "Sit down."

The man—Rish—ignored him and turned back to me, and abruptly the threat became real. I saw it in the way he positioned himself, angling his body to put his right hand near my right side. He meant to backhand me. I had an instant to decide whether to dodge or reach for my knife—

And in that sliver of time, I felt the power around me coalesce, malice-hard and sharp as crystal.

That this analogy occurred to me should have been a warning.

Rish swung. I held still, tense for the blow. Three inches from my face Rish's fist seemed to glance off something no one could see—and when it did, there was a high hard clacking sound, like stone striking stone.

Rish drew his hand away, startled and perhaps puzzled by his failure to put me in my place. He looked at his fist, on which a patch of shining, faceted black had appeared about the knuckles. I was close enough to see the flesh around this patch blistering, beading with moisture like meat cooked over a flame. Except it was not burning, but *freezing*; I could feel the waft of cold air from where I stood. The effect was the same, however, and as the flesh withered and crisped away as if it had been charred, what appeared underneath was not raw flesh, but stone.

I was surprised that Rish took so long to begin screaming.

All the men in the room reacted to Rish's cry. One stumbled back from the table and nearly fell over a chair. Two others ran over to Rish to try and help him. Gemd moved to help as well, but some powerful preservative instinct must have risen in the well-dressed man beside him; he grabbed Gemd by the shoulder to halt him. That turned out to be wise, because the first of the men who reached Rish—one of the Toks—grabbed Rish's wrist to see what was the matter.

The black was spreading swiftly; nearly the whole hand was now a glittering lump of black crystal in the rough shape of a fist. Only the tips of Rish's fingers remained flesh, and they transformed even as I watched. Rish fought the Tok, maddened with agony, and the Tok grabbed Rish's fist in an effort to hold him still. Almost immediately he jerked away, as if the stone had been too cold to touch—and then the Tok, too, stared at his palm, and the black blotch that was now spreading there.

Not merely crystal, I realized, in the part of my mind that was not frozen in horror. The black substance was too pretty to be quartz, too flawless and clear in its faceting. The stone caught the light like diamond, because that was what their flesh had become. Black diamond, the rarest and most valuable of all.

The Tok began to scream. So did several others of the men in the room.

Through it all I remained still and kept my face impassive.

He shouldn't have tried to hit me. He deserved what he got. He shouldn't have tried to hit me.

And the man who tried to help him? What did that one deserve?

They are all my enemies, my people's enemies. They should not have . . . they should not . . . Oh, gods. Gods.

The Nightlord cannot be controlled, child. He can only be unleashed. And you asked him not to kill.

I could not show weakness.

So while the two men flailed and screamed, I stepped around them and walked up to the table. Gemd looked at me, his mouth distorted with disgust and disbelief.

I said, "Take all the time you like to discuss my order." Then I turned to leave.

"W-wait." Gemd. I paused, not allowing my eyes to linger on the two men. Rish was almost half diamond now, the stone creeping over his arm and chest, down one leg and up the side of his neck. He lay on the floor, no longer screaming, though he still keened in a low, agonized voice. Perhaps his throat had turned to diamond already. The other man was reaching toward his comrades, begging for a sword so he could cut off his arm. A young fellow—one of Gemd's heirs, to judge by his features—drew his blade and edged close, but then another man grabbed him and hauled him back. Another wise decision; flecks of black no larger than a grain of sand sparkled on the floor around the two men. Bits of Rish's flesh, transformed and cast about by his flailing. As I watched, the Tok fell onto his good hand, and his thumb touched one of the flecks. It, too, began to change.

"Stop this," Gemd murmured.

"I did not start it."

He cursed swiftly in his language. "Stop it, gods damn you! What kind of monster are you?"

I could not help laughing. That there was no humor in it, only bitter self-loathing, would be lost on them.

"I'm an Arameri," I said.

One of the men behind us abruptly fell silent, and I turned. Not the Tok; he was still shrieking while blackness ate its way down his spine. The diamond had spread to encompass Rish's mouth and was consuming the whole lower half of his face. It seemed to have stopped on his torso, though it was working its way down his remaining leg. I suspected it would stop altogether once it had consumed the nonvital parts of his body, leaving him mutilated and perhaps mad, but alive. I had, after all, asked Nahadoth not to kill.

I averted my eyes, lest I give myself away by throwing up.

"Understand this," I said. The horror in my heart had crept into my voice; it lent me a deeper timbre, and a hint of resonance, that I had not possessed before. "If letting these men die will save my people, then they will die." I leaned forward, putting my hands on the table. "If killing everyone in this room, everyone in this *palace*, will save my people, then know, Gemd: I will do it. You would, too, if you were me."

He had been staring at Rish. Now his eyes jerked toward me, and I saw realization and loathing flicker through them. Was there a hint of self-loathing amid that hatred? Had he believed me when I'd said *you would, too*? Because he would. Anyone would, I understood now. There was nothing we mortals would not do when it came to protecting our loved ones.

I would tell myself that for the rest of my life.

"Enough." I barely heard Gemd over the screams, but I saw his mouth move. "Enough. I'll call off the attack."

"And disband the alliance?"

"I can speak only for Menchey." There was something broken in his tone. He did not meet my eyes. "The others may choose to continue."

"Then warn them, Minister Gemd. The next time I'm forced to do this, two hundred will suffer instead of two. If they press the issue, two thousand. You chose this war, not I. I will not fight fairly."

Gemd looked at me in mute hatred. I held his eyes awhile longer, then turned to the two men, one of whom still shuddered and whimpered on the floor. The other, Rish, seemed catatonic. I walked over to them. The glimmering, deadly black flecks did not harm me, though they crunched under my feet.

Nahadoth could stop the magic, I was certain. He could probably even restore the men to wholeness—but Darr's safety depended on my ability to strike fear into Gemd's heart.

"Finish it," I whispered.

The black surged and consumed each of the men in seconds. Chill vapors rose around them as their final screams mingled with the sounds of flesh crackling and bone snapping, then all of it died away. In the men's place lay two enormous, faceted gems in the rough shape of huddled figures. Beautiful, and quite valuable, I guessed; if nothing else, their families would live well from henceforth. If the families chose to sell their loved ones' remains.

I passed between the diamonds on my way out. The guards who had come in behind me moved out of my way, some of them stumbling in their haste. The doors swung shut behind me, quietly this time. When they were closed, I stopped.

"Shall I take you home?" asked Nahadoth. Behind me.

"Home?"

"Sky."

Ah, yes. Home, for Arameri.

"Let's go," I said.

Darkness enveloped me. When it cleared, we were in Sky's forecourt again, though at the Garden of the Hundred Thousand this time rather than the Pier. A path of polished stones wound between neat, orderly flower beds, each overhung with a different type of exotic tree. In the distance, through the leaves, I could see the starry sky and the mountains that met it.

I walked through the garden until I found a spot with an unimpeded view, beneath a miniature satinbell tree. My thoughts turned in slow, lazy spirals. I was growing used to the cool feel of Nahadoth behind me.

"My weapon," I said to him.

"As you are mine."

I nodded, sighing into a breeze that lifted my hair and set the leaves of the satinbell a-rustle. As I turned to face Nahadoth, a scud of cloud passed across the moon's crescent. His cloak seemed to inhale in that dim instant, growing impossibly until it almost eclipsed the palace in rippling waves of black. Then the cloud passed, and it was just a cloak again.

I felt like that cloak all of a sudden—wild, out of control, giddily alive. I lifted my arms and closed my eyes as another breeze gusted. It felt so good.

"I wish I could fly," I said.

"I can gift you with that magic, for a time."

I shook my head, closing my eyes to sway with the wind. "Magic is wrong." I knew that oh, so well now.

He said nothing to that, which surprised me until I thought deeper. After witnessing so many generations of Arameri hypocrisy, perhaps he no longer cared enough to complain.

It was tempting, so tempting, to stop caring myself. My mother, Darr, the succession; what did any of it matter? I could forget all of that so easily, and spend the remainder of my life— all four days of it—indulging any whim or pleasure I wanted.

Any pleasure, except one.

"Last night," I said, lowering my arms at last. "Why didn't you kill me?"

"You're more useful alive."

I laughed. I felt light-headed, reckless. "Does that mean I'm the only person in Sky who has nothing to fear from you?" I knew it was a stupid question before I finished speaking, but I do not think I was entirely sane in that moment.

Fortunately, the Nightlord did not answer my stupid, dangerous question. I glanced back at him to gauge his mood and saw that his nightcloak had changed again. This time the wisps had spun long and thin, drifting through the garden like layers of campfire smoke. The ones nearest me curled inward, surrounding me on all sides. I was reminded of certain plants in my homeland, which grew teeth or sticky tendrils to ensnare insects.

And at the heart of this dark flower, my bait: his glowing face, his lightless eyes. I stepped closer, deeper into his shadow, and he smiled.

"You wouldn't have had to kill me," I said softly. I ducked my head and looked up at him through my lashes, curving my body in silent invitation. I had seen prettier women do this all my life, yet never dared myself. I lifted a hand and moved it toward his chest, half-expecting to touch nothing and be snatched forward into darkness. But this time there was a body within the shadows, startling in its solidity. I could not see it, or my own hand where I touched him, but I could feel skin, smooth and cool beneath my fingertips.

Bare skin. Gods.

I licked my lips and met his eyes. "There's a great deal you could have done without compromising my...usefulness."

Something in his face changed, like a cloud across the moon: the shadow of the predator. His teeth were sharper when he spoke. "I know."

Something in me changed, too, as the wild feeling went still. That look in his face. Some part of me had been waiting for it.

"Would you?" I licked my lips again, swallowed around sudden tightness in my throat. "Kill me? If...I asked?"

There was a pause.

When the Lord of Night touched my face, fingertips tracing my jaw, I thought I was imagining things. There was an unmistakable tenderness in the gesture. But then, just as tenderly, the hand slid farther down and curled around my neck. As he leaned close, I closed my eyes.

"*Are* you asking?" His lips brushed my ear as he whispered.

I opened my mouth to speak and could not. All at once I was trembling. Tears welled in my eyes, spilled down my face onto his wrist. I wanted to speak, to ask, so badly. But I just stood there, trembling and crying, while his breath tickled my ear. In and out. Three times.

Then he released my neck, and my knees buckled. I fell forward, and suddenly I was buried in the soft, cool dark of him, pressed against a chest I could not see, and I began sobbing into it. After a moment, the hand that had almost killed me cupped the nape of my neck. I must have bawled for an hour, though maybe it was less. I don't know. He held me tight the whole time.

20

The Arena

ALL THAT REMAINS OF THE TIME before the Gods' War is whispered myth and half-forgotten legend. The priests are quick to punish anyone caught telling these tales. There was nothing before Itempas, they say; even in the age of the Three, he was first and greatest. Still, the legends persist.

For example: it is said that once people made sacrifices of flesh to the Three. They would fill a room with volunteers. Young, old, female, male, poor, wealthy, healthy, infirm; all the variety and richness of humanity. On some occasion that was sacred to all Three—this part has been lost with time—they would call out to their gods and beg them to partake of the feast.

Enefa, it is said, would claim the elders and the ill—the epitome of mortality. She would give them a choice: healing or gentle, peaceful death. The tales say more than a few chose the latter, though I cannot imagine why.

Itempas took then what he takes now—the most mature and noble, the brightest, the most talented. These became his priests, setting duty and propriety above all else, loving him and submitting to him in all things.

Nahadoth preferred youths, wild and carefree—though he would claim the odd adult, too. Anyone willing to yield to the moment. He seduced them and was seduced by them; he reveled in their lack of inhibition and gave them everything of himself.

The Itempans fear talk of that age will lead people to yearn for it anew and turn to heresy. I think perhaps they overestimate the danger. Try as I might, I cannot imagine what it was like to live in a world like that, and I have no desire to return to it. We have enough trouble with one god now; why in the Maelstrom would we want to live again under three?

I wasted the next day, a quarter of my remaining life. I had not meant to. But I had not returned to my rooms until nearly dawn, my second night of little sleep, and my body demanded recompense by sleeping past noon. I had dreams of a thousand faces, representing millions, all distorted with agony or terror or despair. I smelled blood and burned flesh. I saw a desert littered with fallen trees because it had once been a forest. I woke up weeping; such was my guilt.

Late that afternoon there was a knock at the door. Feeling lonely and neglected—not even Sieh had come to visit—I went to answer, hoping it was a friend.

It was Relad.

"What in the names of every useless god have you done?" he demanded.

The arena, Relad had told me. Where the highbloods played at war.

That was where I would find Scimina, who had somehow found out about my efforts to counter her meddling. He had said it between curses and profanities and much maligning of my inferior halfbreed bloodlines, but that much I understood. *What* Scimina had found out Relad did not seem to know, which gave me some hope... but not much.

I was shaking with tension when I emerged from the lift amid a crowd of backs. Those nearest the lift had made some space, perhaps after being jostled from behind by new arrivals too many times, but beyond that was a solid wall of people. Most were white-clad servants; a few were better dressed, bearing the marks of quarter- or eighthbloods. Here and there I rubbed against brocade or silk as I gave up politeness and just started pushing my way through. It was slow going because most of them towered over me, and because they were wholly riveted on whatever was happening at the center of the room.

From where I could hear screaming.

I might never have gotten there if someone hadn't glanced back, recognized me, and murmured to someone else nearby.

The murmur rippled through the crowd, and abruptly I found myself the focus of dozens of silent, pent stares. I stumbled to a halt, unnerved, but the way ahead abruptly cleared as they moved aside for me. I hurried forward, then stopped in shock.

On the floor knelt a thin old man, naked, chained in a pool of blood. His white hair, long and lank, hung 'round his face, obscuring it, though I could hear him panting raggedly for breath. His skin was a webwork of lacerations. If it had just been his back, I would have thought him flogged, but it was not just his back. It was his legs, his arms, his cheeks and chin. He was kneeling; I saw cuts on the soles of his feet. He pushed himself upright awkwardly, using the sides of his wrists, and I saw that a round red hole in the back of each showed bone and tendon clearly.

Another heretic? I wondered, confused.

"I wondered how much blood I would have to draw before someone went running for you," said a savage voice beside me, and as I turned something came at my face. I raised my hands instinctively and felt a thin line of heat cross my palms; something had cut me.

I did not pause long enough to assess the damage, springing back and drawing my knife. My hands still worked, though blood made the hilt slippery. I shifted it to a defensive grip and crouched, ready to fight.

Across from me stood Scimina, gowned in shining green satin. The flecks of blood that had sprayed across her dress looked like tiny ruby jewels. (There were flecks on her face as well, but those just looked like blood.) In her hands was something that I did not at first realize was a weapon—a long, silver wand, ornately decorated, perhaps three feet in length.

But at the tip was a short double-edged blade, thin as a surgeon's scalpel, made of glass. Too short and strangely weighted to be a spear, more like an elaborate fountain pen. Some Amn weapon?

Scimina smirked at my drawn blade, but instead of raising her own weapon, she turned away and resumed pacing around the circle that the crowd had formed, with the old man at its center. "How like a barbarian. You can't use a knife against me, Cousin; it would shatter. Our blood sigils prevent all life-threatening attacks. Honestly, you're so ignorant. What are we going to do with you?"

I stayed in my crouch and kept hold of my knife anyway, pivoting to keep her in sight as she walked. As I did so, I saw faces among the crowd that I recognized. Some of the servants who'd been at the Fire Day party. A couple of Dekarta's courtiers. T'vril, white-lipped and stiff; his eyes fixed on me in something that might have been warning. Viraine, standing forward from the rest of the crowd; he had folded his arms and stood gazing into the middle distance, looking bored.

Zhakkarn and Kurue. Why were they there? They were watching me, too. Zhakkarn's expression was hard and cold; I had never seen her show anger so clearly before. Kurue was furious, too, her nostrils flared and hands tight at her sides. The look in her eyes would have flayed me if it could. But Scimina was already flaying someone, so I focused on the greater threat for the moment.

"Sit up!" Scimina barked, and the old man jerked upright as if on strings. I could see now that there were fewer cuts on his torso, though as I watched Scimina walked past him and flicked the wand, and another long, deep slice opened on the old man's abdomen. He cried out again, his voice hoarse, and opened eyes he'd shut in reaction to the pain. That was when I caught my breath, because the old man's eyes were green and sharpfold and then I realized how the shape of his face would be familiar if he were sixty years younger and dearest gods, dearest Skyfather, it was *Sieh*.

"Ah," Scimina said, interpreting my gasp. "That does save time. You were right, T'vril; she *is* sweet on him. Did you send one of your people to fetch her? Tell the fool to be quicker next time."

I glared at T'vril, who clearly had not sent for me. His face was paler than usual, but that strange warning was still in his eyes. I almost frowned in confusion, but I could feel Scimina's gaze like a vulture, hovering over my facial expressions and ready to savage the emotions they revealed.

So I schooled myself to calmness, as my mother had taught me. I rose from my fighting crouch, though I only lowered my knife to my side and did not sheathe it. Scimina probably would not know, but among Darre, this was disrespect—a sign that I did not trust her to behave like a woman.

"I'm here now," I said to her. "State your purpose."

Scimina uttered a short, sharp laugh, never ceasing her pacing. "State my purpose. She sounds so martial, doesn't she?" She looked around the crowd; no one answered her. "So *strong*. Tiny, ill-bred, pathetic little thing that she is—*what do you THINK my purpose is, you fool?*" She shouted this last at me, her fists clenched at her sides, the odd wand-weapon quivering. Her hair, up in an elaborate coif that was still lovely, was coming undone. She looked exquisitely demented.

"I think you want to be Dekarta's heir," I said softly, "and the gods help all the world if you succeed."

Quick as wind, Scimina went from a screaming madwoman to smiling charm. "True. And I meant to begin with your land, stomping it ever so thoroughly out of existence. In fact I should have begun doing so already, if not for the fact that the alliance I so carefully put together in that region is now falling apart." She resumed pacing, glancing back at me over her shoulder, turning the wand delicately in her hands. "I thought at first the problem might be that old High North woman you've been meeting at the Salon. But I looked into that; she's only given you information, and most of it useless. So you've done something else. Would you care to explain?"

My blood went cold. What had Scimina done to Ras Onchi? Then I looked at Sieh, who had recovered himself somewhat, though he still looked weak and dazed from pain. He was not healing, which made no sense. I had stabbed Nahadoth in the heart and it had been barely a nuisance. Yet it had taken time for him to heal, I recalled with a sudden chill. Perhaps, if left alone for a while, Sieh would recover as well. Unless... Itempas had trapped the Enefadeh in human form to suffer all the horrors of mortality. They were eternal, powerful—but not invulnerable. Did the horrors of mortality include death? Sweat stung the cuts on my hands. There were things I was not prepared to endure.

But then the palace shuddered. For an instant I wondered if this tremor signified some new threat, and then I remembered. Sunset.

"Oh demons," Viraine muttered into the silence. An instant later I and every other person in the room was thrown sprawling in a blast of wind and bitter, painful cold.

It took me a moment to struggle upright, and when I did, my

knife was gone. The room was chaos around me; I heard groans
of pain, curses, shouts of alarm. When I glanced toward the lift,
I could see several people crowding its opening, trying to cram
their way in. I forgot all of this, though, when I looked toward
the center of the room.

It was difficult to see Nahadoth's face. He crouched near
Sieh, his head bowed, and the blackness of his aura was as it
had been my first night in Sky, so dark that it hurt the mind.
I focused instead on the floor, where the chains that had held
Sieh lay shattered, their tips glistening with frost. Sieh himself
I could not see entirely—only one of his hands, dangling limp,
before Nahadoth's cloak swept around him, swallowing him
into darkness.

"Scimina." There was that hollow, echoing quality to
Nahadoth's voice again. Was the madness upon him? No; this
was just pure, plain rage.

But Scimina, who had also been knocked to the floor, got
to her high-heeled feet and composed herself. "Nahadoth," she
said, more calmly than I would have imagined. Her weapon
was gone, too, but she was a true Arameri, unafraid of the gods'
wrath. "How good of you to join us at last. Put him down."

Nahadoth stood and flicked his cloak back. Sieh, a young
man now, whole and clothed, stood beside him glaring defiantly at Scimina. Somewhere deep inside me, a knot of tension
relaxed.

"We had an agreement," Nahadoth said, still in that voice
echoing with murder.

"Indeed," Scimina said, and now it was her smile that frightened me. "You'll serve as well as Sieh for this purpose. Kneel."
She pointed at the bloody space and its empty chains.

For an instant the sense of power in the room swelled, like pressure against the eardrums. The walls creaked. I shuddered beneath it, wondering if this was it. Scimina had made some error, left some opening, and now Nahadoth would crush us all like insects.

But then, to my utter shock, Nahadoth moved away from Sieh and went to the center of the room. He knelt.

Scimina turned to me, where I still half-lay on the floor. Shamed, I got to my feet. I was surprised to see that there was still an audience around us, though it was now sparse—T'vril, Viraine, a handful of servants, perhaps twenty highbloods. I suppose the highbloods took some inspiration from Scimina's fearlessness.

"This will be an education for you, Cousin," she said, still in that sweet, polite tone that I was coming to hate. She resumed pacing, watching Nahadoth with an expression that was almost avid. "Had you been raised here in Sky, or taught properly by your mother, you would know this... but allow me to explain. It is difficult to damage an Enefadeh. Their human bodies repair themselves constantly and swiftly, through the benevolence of our Father Itempas. But they *do* have weaknesses, Cousin; one must simply understand these. Viraine."

Viraine had gotten to his feet as well, though he seemed to be favoring his left wrist. He eyed Scimina warily. "You'll take responsibility with Dekarta?"

She swung on him so fast that if the wand had still been in her hand, Viraine might have suffered a mortal wound. "Dekarta will be dead in days, Viraine. *He* is not whom you should fear now."

Viraine stood his ground. "I'm simply doing my job, Scimina, and advising you on the consequences. It may be weeks before he's useful again—"

Scimina made a sound of savage frustration. *"Does it look as though I care?"*

There was a pent moment, the two of them facing each other, during which I honestly thought Viraine had a chance. They were both fullbloods. But Viraine was not in line for the succession, and Scimina was—and in the end, Scimina was right. It was no longer Dekarta's will that mattered.

I looked at Sieh, who was staring at Nahadoth with an unreadable expression on his too-old face. Both were gods more ancient than life on earth. I could not imagine such a length of existence. A day of pain was probably nothing to them...but not to me.

"Enough," I said softly. The word carried in the vaulted space of the arena. Viraine and Scimina both looked at me in surprise. Sieh, too, swung around to stare at me, puzzled. And Nahadoth— no. I could not look at him. He would think me weak for this.

Not weak, I reminded myself. *Human. I am still that, at least.*

"Enough," I said again, lifting my head with what remained of my pride. "Stop this. I'll tell you whatever you want to know."

"Yeine," said Sieh, sounding shocked.

Scimina smirked. "Even if you weren't the sacrifice, Cousin, you could never have been my uncle's heir."

I glared at her. "I will take that as a compliment, Cousin, if *you* are the example I should follow."

Scimina's face tightened, and for a moment I thought she would spit at me. Instead she turned away and resumed circling Nahadoth, though slower now. "Which member of the alliance did you approach?"

"Minister Gemd, of Menchey."

"Gemd?" Scimina frowned at this. "How did you persuade him? He was more eager for the chance than all the others."

I took a deep breath. "I brought Nahadoth with me. His persuasive powers are . . . formidable, as I'm sure you know."

Scimina barked a laugh—but her gaze was thoughtful as she glanced at me, then at him. Nahadoth gazed into the middle distance, as he had since kneeling. He might have been contemplating matters beyond human reckoning, or the dyes in T'vril's pants.

"Interesting," Scimina said. "Since I'm certain Uncle would not have commanded the Enefadeh to do this for you, that means our Nightlord decided to help you on his own. How on earth did you manage that?"

I shrugged, though abruptly I felt anything but relaxed. Stupid, stupid. I should have realized the danger in this line of questioning. "He seemed to find it amusing. There were . . . several deaths." I tried to look uneasy and found that it was not difficult. "I had not intended those, but they were effective."

"I see." Scimina stopped, folding her arms and tapping her fingers. I did not like the look in her eyes, even though it was directed at Nahadoth. "And what else did you do?"

I frowned. "Else?"

"We keep a tight leash on the Enefadeh, Cousin, and Nahadoth's is tightest of all. When he leaves the palace, Viraine knows of it. And Viraine tells me he left twice, on two separate nights."

Demons. Why in the Father's name hadn't the Enefadeh told me? Damned secret keeping— "I went to Darr, to see my grandmother."

"For what purpose?"

To understand why my mother sold me to the Enefadeh—

I jerked my thoughts off that path and folded my arms. "Because I missed her. Not that *you* would understand something like that."

She turned to gaze at me, a slow, lazy smile playing about her lips, and I suddenly realized I had made a mistake. But what? Had my insult bothered her that much? No, it was something else.

"You did not risk your sanity traveling with the Nightlord just to exchange pleasantries with some old hag," Scimina said. "Tell me why you really went there."

"To confirm the war petition and the alliance against Darr."

"And? That's all?"

I thought fast, but not fast enough. Or perhaps it was my unnerved expression that alerted her, because she *tsk*ed at me. "You're keeping secrets, Cousin. And I mean to have them. Viraine!"

Viraine sighed and faced Nahadoth. An odd look, almost pensive, passed over his face. "This would not have been my choice," he said softly.

Nahadoth's eyes flicked to him and lingered for a moment; there was a hint of surprise in his expression. "You must do as your lord requires." Not Dekarta. Itempas.

"This is not his doing," Viraine said, scowling. Then he seemed to recall himself, throwing Scimina one last glare and shaking his head. "Fine, then."

He reached into a pocket of his cloak and went to crouch beside Nahadoth, setting on his thigh a small square of paper on which had been drawn a spidery, liquid gods' sigil. Somehow—I refused to think deeply about how—I knew a line was missing from it. Then Viraine took out a brush with a capped tip.

I felt queasy. I stepped forward, lifting a bloodied hand to protest—and then stopped as my eyes met Nahadoth's. His face was impassive, the glance lazy and disinterested, but my mouth went dry anyhow. He knew what was coming better than I did. He knew I could stop it. But the only way I could do that was to risk revealing the secret of Enefa's soul.

Yet the alternative...

Scimina, observing this exchange, laughed—and then, to my revulsion, she came over to take me by the shoulder. "I commend you on your taste, Cousin. He *is* magnificent, isn't he? I have often wondered if there was some way... but, of course, there isn't."

She watched as Viraine set the square of paper on the floor beside Nahadoth, in one of the few spots unmarred by Sieh's blood. Viraine then uncapped the brush, hunched over the square, and very carefully drew a single line.

Light blazed down from the ceiling, as if someone had opened a colossal window at high noon. There *was* no opening in the ceiling, though; this was the power of the gods, who could defy the physical laws of the human realm and create something out of nothing. After the relative dimness of Sky's soft pale walls, this was too bright. I raised a hand in front of my watering eyes, hearing murmurs of discomfort from our remaining audience.

Nahadoth knelt at the light's center, his shadow stark amid the chains and blood. I had never seen his shadow before. At first the light seemed to do him no harm—but that was when I realized what had changed. I *hadn't* seen his shadow before. The living nimbus that surrounded him ordinarily did not allow it, constantly twisting and lashing and overlapping itself. It was not his nature to contrast his surroundings; he blended in. But now the nimbus had become just long black hair, draping over his back. Just a voluminous cloak cascading over his shoulders. His whole body was still.

And then Nahadoth uttered a soft sound, not quite a groan, and the hair and cloak began to boil.

"Watch closely," murmured Scimina in my ear. She had moved behind me, leaning against my shoulder like a dear companion. I could hear the relish in her voice. "See what your gods are made of."

Knowing she was there kept my face still. I did not react as the surface of Nahadoth's back bubbled and ran like hot tar, wisps of black curling into the air around him and evaporating with a rattling hiss. Nahadoth slowly slumped forward, pressed down as if the light crushed him beneath unseen weight. His hands landed in Sieh's blood and I saw that they, too, boiled, the unnaturally white skin rippling and spinning away in pale, fungoid tendrils. (Distantly, I heard one of the onlookers retch.) I could not see his face beneath the curtain of sagging, melting hair—but did I want to? He had no true form. I knew that everything I had seen of him was just a shell. But dearest Father, I had *liked* that shell and thought it beautiful. I could not bear to see the ruin of it now.

Then something white showed through his shoulder. At first I thought it was bone, and my own gorge rose. But it was not bone; it was skin. Pale like T'vril's, though devoid of spots, shifting now as it pushed up through the melting black.

And then I saw—

And did not see.

A shining form (that my mind would not see) stood over a shape-less black mass (that my mind could not see) and plunged hands into the mass again and again. Not tearing it apart. Pummeling— pounding—brutalizing it into shape. The mass screamed, struggling desperately, but the shining hands held no mercy. They plunged again and hauled out arms. They crushed formless black until it became legs. They thrust into the middle and dragged out a torso, hand up to the wrist in its abdomen, gripping to impose a spine. And last was torn forth a head, barely human and bald, unrecognizable. Its mouth was open and shrieking, its eyes mad with agony beyond any mortal endurance. But of course, this was not a mortal.

This is what you want, *snarls the shining one, his voice savage,* but these are not words and I do not hear them. It is knowledge; it is in my head. *This abomination that she created.* You would choose her over me? Then take her "gift"—take it—take it and never forget that you—chose—this—

The shining one is weeping, I notice, even as he commits this violation.

And somewhere inside me someone was screaming, but it was not me, although I was screaming, too. And neither of us could be heard over the screams of the new-made creature on the ground, whose suffering had only begun—

The arm wrenched its way out of Nahadoth with a sound that reminded me of cooked meat. That same juicy, popping sound when one tears off a joint. Nahadoth, on his hands and knees, shuddered all over as the extra arm flailed blindly and then found purchase on the ground beside him. I could see now that it was pale, but not the moon-white I was used to. This was a far more mundane, human white. This was his daytime self, tearing through the godly veneer that covered it at night, in a grisly parody of birth.

He did not scream, I noticed. Beyond that initial abortive sound, Nahadoth remained silent even though another body ripped its way out of his. Somehow that made it worse, because his pain was so obvious. A scream would have eased my horror, if not his agony.

Beside him, Viraine watched for a moment, then closed his eyes, sighing.

"This could take hours," said Scimina. "It would go faster if this were true sunlight, of course, but only the Skyfather can command that. This is just a paltry imitation." She threw Viraine a contemptuous look. "More than enough for my purposes, though, as you can see."

I kept my jaw clenched tight. Across the circle, through the shaft of light and the haze created by Nahadoth's steaming godflesh, I could see Kurue. She looked at me once, bitter, and then away. Zhakkarn kept her eyes on Nahadoth. It was a warrior's way to acknowledge suffering, and thus respect it; she would not look away. Neither would I. But gods, gods.

It was Sieh who caught and held my gaze as he walked forward into the pool of light. It did not harm him; it was not his weakness. He knelt beside Nahadoth and gathered the disintegrating head to his chest, wrapped his arms around the heaving shoulders—all three of them. Through it all Sieh watched me, with a look that others probably interpreted as hatred. I knew otherwise.

Watch, those green eyes, so like mine yet so much older, said. *See what we endure. And then set us free.*

I will, I said back, with all my soul and Enefa's, too. *I will.*

I did not know. No matter what else happened, Itempas loved Naha. I never thought that could turn to hate.

What in the infinite hells makes you think that was hate?

I glanced at Scimina and sighed.

"Are you trying to nauseate me into answering?" I asked. "Add a new mess to the floor? That's all this farce is going to do."

She leaned back from me, lifting an eyebrow. "No compassion for your ally?"

"The Nightlord is *not* my ally," I snapped. "As everyone in this den of nightmares has repeatedly warned me, he is a monster. But since he's no different from the rest of you who want me dead, I thought I might at least use his power to help my people."

Scimina looked skeptical. "And what help did he provide? You made the effort in Menchey the next night."

"None; dawn came too quickly. But..." I faltered here, remembering my grandmother's arms and the smell of the humid Darren air that night. I *did* miss her, and Darr itself, and all the peace I had once known there. Before Sky. Before my mother's death.

I lowered my eyes and let my very real pain show. Only that would appease Scimina.

"We spoke of my mother," I said, softer. "And other things, personal things—none of which should have any importance to you." With this I glared at her. "And even if you roast that creature all night, I will not share those things with you."

Scimina gazed at me for a long moment, her smile gone, her eyes dissecting my face. Between and beyond us, Nahadoth finally made another sound through his teeth, an animal snarl. There were more hideous tearing sounds. I made myself not care by hating Scimina.

Finally she sighed and stepped away from me. "So be it," she said. "It was a feeble attempt, Cousin; you must have realized it had almost no chance of succeeding. I'm going to contact Gemd and tell him to resume the attack. They'll take control of your capital and crush any resistance, though I'll tell them to hold off on slaughtering your people—more than necessary—for the time being."

So there it was, laid plain: I would have to do her bidding, or she would unleash the Mencheyev to wipe my people out of existence. I scowled. "What guarantee do I have that you won't kill them anyway?"

"None whatsoever. After this foolishness, I'm tempted to do it just for spite. But I'd rather the Darre survive, now that I think about it. I imagine their lives won't be pleasant. Slavery rarely is—though we'll call it something else, of course." She glanced at Nahadoth, amused. "But they will be alive, Cousin, and where there is life, there is hope. Isn't that worth something to you? Worth a whole world, perhaps?"

I nodded slowly, though my innards clenched in new knots. I would not grovel. "It will do for now."

"*For now?*" Scimina stared at me, incredulous, then began to laugh. "Oh, Cousin. Sometimes I wish your mother were still alive. She at least could have given me a real challenge."

I had lost my knife, but I was still Darre. I whipped around and hit her so hard that one of her heeled shoes came off as she sprawled across the floor.

"Probably," I said, as she blinked away shock and what I hoped was a concussion. "But my mother was civilized."

Fists tight enough to sting at my sides, I turned my back on the whole arena and walked out.

21

First Love

I ALMOST FORGOT. When I FIRST arrived in Sky, T'vril informed me that the highbloods sometimes gather for dinner in one of the fancier halls. This happened once during my time there, but I chose not to attend. There are rumors about Sky, you see. Some of them are exaggerations, and many are true, as I discovered. But there is one rumor I hoped never to confirm.

The Amn were not always civilized, the rumors remind us. Once, like High North, Senm was also a land of barbarians, and the Amn were simply the most successful of these. After the Gods' War they imposed their barbarian ways on the whole world and judged the rest of us by how thoroughly we adopted them—but they did not export all of their customs. Every culture has its ugly secrets. And once, the rumors say, Amn elites prized the taste of human flesh above all other delicacies.

Sometimes I am more afraid of the blood in my veins than the souls in my flesh.

When Nahadoth's torture ended, the clouds resumed moving across the night sky. They had been still, a caul over the moon that glimmered with arcs of color like weak, sickly rainbows. When the clouds finally moved on, something in me relaxed.

I had half-expected the knock at the door when it came, so I called enter. In the glass's reflection I saw T'vril, hovering uncertainly in the doorway.

"Yeine," he said, then faltered to silence.

I left him floundering in it for a while before saying, "Come in."

He stepped inside, just enough to allow the door to shut. Then he just looked at me, perhaps waiting for me to speak. But I had nothing to say to him, and eventually he sighed.

"The Enefadeh can endure pain," he said. "They've dealt with far worse over the centuries, believe me. What I wasn't sure of was *your* endurance."

"Thank you for your confidence."

T'vril winced at my tone. "I just knew you cared for Sieh. When Scimina started in on him, I thought…" He looked away, spread his hands helplessly. "I thought it would be better for you not to see."

"Because I'm so weak-willed and sentimental that I'd blabber all my secrets to save him?"

He scowled. "Because you're not like the rest of us. I thought you would do what you could to save a friend in pain, yes. I wanted to spare you that. Hate me for it if you like."

I turned to him, privately amazed. T'vril still saw me as the innocent, noble-hearted girl who had been so grateful for his kindness that first day in Sky. How many centuries ago had that been? Not quite two weeks.

"I don't hate you," I said.

T'vril exhaled, then came over to join me at the window. "Well…Scimina was furious when you left, as you might imagine."

I nodded. "Nahadoth? Sieh?"

"Zhakkarn and Kurue took them away. Scimina lost interest in us and left shortly after you did."

"'Us'?"

He paused for a second, and I could almost hear him cursing to himself under his breath. After a moment he said, "Her original plan was to play that little game with the servants."

"Ah, yes." I felt myself growing angry again. "That's when you suggested she use Sieh instead?"

He spoke tightly. "As I said, Yeine, the Enefadeh can survive Scimina's amusement. Mortals usually don't. You aren't the only one I need to protect."

Which made it no more right—but understandable. Like so much in Sky, wrong but *understandable*. I sighed.

"I offered myself first."

I started. T'vril was gazing out the window, a rueful smile on his face. "As Lady Yeine's friend, I said, if you'll forgive me for presuming. But she said I wasn't any better than the rest of the servants." His smile faded; I saw the muscles ripple along his jaw.

Dismissed again, I realized. *Not even his pain is good enough for the Central Family.* Yet he could not complain too much; his unimportance had saved him a great deal of suffering.

"I have to go," T'vril said. He lifted a hand, hesitated, then put it on my shoulder. The gesture, and the hesitancy, reminded me of Sieh. I put my own hand over his. I would miss him—ironic, since I was the one slated to die.

"Of course you're my friend," I whispered. His hand tightened for a moment, then he went to the door to leave.

Before he could, I heard a startled murmur from him; the voice that responded was familiar, too. I turned, and as T'vril stepped out Viraine stepped in.

"My apologies," he said. "May I come in?" He did not close the door, I noted, in case I said no.

For a moment I stared at him, amazed at his audacity. I had no doubt that he had magically enabled Scimina's torture of Sieh, just as he had Nahadoth's. That was his true role here, I understood now—to facilitate all the evil that our family dreamt up, especially where it concerned the gods. He was the Enefadeh's keeper and driver, wielder of the Arameri whip.

But an overseer is not solely to blame for a slave's misery. Sighing, I said nothing. Apparently deciding this constituted acceptance, Viraine let the door close and came over. Unlike T'vril, there was nothing resembling apology in his expression, just the usual guarded Arameri coolness.

"It was unwise of you to interfere in Menchey," he said.

"So I've been reminded."

"If you had trusted me—"

My mouth fell open in pure incredulity.

"If you had trusted me," Viraine said again, with a hint of stubbornness, "I would have helped you."

I almost laughed. "For what price?"

Viraine fell silent for a moment, then moved to stand beside me, almost exactly where T'vril had been. He felt very different, though. Warmer, most noticeably. I could feel his body heat from where I stood, a foot away.

"Have you chosen an escort for the ball?"

"Escort?" The question threw me entirely. "No. I've barely thought about the ball; I may not even attend."

"You must. Dekarta will compel you magically if you don't come on your own."

Of course. Viraine would be the one to impose the

compulsion, no doubt. I shook my head, sighing. "Fine, then. If Grandfather is set on humiliating me, there's nothing I can do but endure it. But I see no reason to inflict the same on an escort."

He nodded slowly. That should have been my warning. I had never seen Viraine be anything but brisk in his mannerisms, even when relaxed.

"You might enjoy the night, at least a little," he said, "if I were your escort."

I was silent for so long that he turned to face my stare and laughed. "Are you so unused to being courted?"

"By people who aren't interested in me? Yes."

"How do you know I'm not?"

"Why *would* you be?"

"Do I need a reason?"

I folded my arms. "Yes."

Viraine raised his eyebrows. "I must apologize again, then. I hadn't realized I'd made such a poor impression on you over the past few weeks."

"Viraine—" I rubbed my eyes. I was tired—not physically but emotionally, which was worse. "You've been very helpful, true, but I can't call you anything like kind. I've even doubted your sanity at times. Not that this makes you any different from other Arameri."

"Guilty as judged." He laughed again. That felt wrong, too. He was trying too hard. He seemed to realize it, because abruptly he sobered.

"Your mother," he said, "was my first lover."

My hand twitched toward my knife. It was on the side farthest from him. He did not see.

After a moment passed with no apparent reaction from me, Viraine seemed to relax somewhat. He lowered his eyes, gazing at the lights of the city far below. "I was born here, like most Arameri, but the highbloods sent me off to the Litaria—the scrivening college—at the age of four, when my gift for languages was noticed. I was just twenty when I returned, the youngest master ever approved by the program. Brilliant, if I may say, but still very young. A child, really."

I was not yet twenty myself, but of course barbarians grow up faster than civilized folk. I said nothing.

"My father had died in the interim," he continued. "My mother—" He shrugged. "Disappeared some night. That sort of thing happens here. It was just as well. I was granted fullblood status when I returned, and she was a lowblood. If she were still alive, I would no longer be her son." He glanced at me, after a pause. "That will sound heartless to you."

I shook my head, slowly. "I've been in Sky long enough."

He made a soft sound, somewhere between amusement and cynicism. "I had a harder time getting used to this place than you," he said. "Your mother helped me. She was...like you in some ways. Gentle on the surface, something entirely different underneath."

I glanced at him, surprised by this description.

"I was smitten, of course. Her beauty, her wit, all that power..." He shrugged. "But I would have been content to admire her from afar. I wasn't *that* young. No one was more surprised than I when she offered me more."

"My mother wouldn't do that."

Viraine just looked at me for a moment, during which I glared back at him.

"It was a brief affair," he said. "Just a few weeks. Then she met your father and lost interest in me." He smiled thinly. "I can't say I was happy about that."

"I told you—" I began with some heat.

"You didn't know her," he said softly. It was that softness that silenced me. "No child knows her parents, not truly."

"You didn't know her, either." I refused to think about how childish that sounded.

For a moment there was such sorrow in Viraine's face, such lingering pain, that I knew he was telling the truth. He had loved her. He had been her lover. She had gone off to marry my father, leaving Viraine with only memories and longing. And now fresh grief burned in my soul, because he was right—I *hadn't* known her. Not if she could do something like this.

Viraine looked away. "Well. You wanted to know my reason for offering to escort you. You aren't the only one who mourns Kinneth." He took a deep breath. "If you change your mind, let me know." He inclined his head, then headed for the door.

"Wait," I said, and he stopped. "I told you before: my mother did nothing without reason. So why did she take up with you?"

"How should I know?"

"What do you *think*?"

He considered a moment, then shook his head. He was smiling again, hopelessly. "I think I don't want to know. And neither do you."

He left. I stared at the closed door for a long time.

Then I went looking for answers.

I went first to my mother's room, where I took the chest of letters from behind the bed's headboard. When I turned with it in my hands, I found my unknown maternal grandmother gazing directly at me from within her portrait. "Sorry," I muttered, and left again.

It was not difficult to find an appropriate corridor. I simply wandered until a sense of nearby, familiar power tickled my awareness. I followed that sense until, before an otherwise nondescript wall, I knew I had found a good spot.

The gods' langauge was not meant to be spoken by mortals, but I had a goddess's soul. That had to be good for something.

"*Atadie*," I whispered, and the wall opened up.

I went through two dead spaces before finding Sieh's orrery. As the wall closed behind me, I looked around and noticed that the place looked starkly bare compared to the last time I'd seen it. Several dozen or so of the colored spheres lay scattered on the floor, unmoving, a few showing cracks or missing chunks. Only a handful floated in their usual places. The yellow ball was nowhere to be seen.

Beyond the spheres, Sieh lay on a gently curved hump of palacestuff, with Zhakkarn crouched beside him. Sieh was younger than I had seen him in the arena, but still too old: long-legged and lanky, he must have been somewhere in late adolescence. Zhakkarn, to my surprise, had removed her headkerchief; her hair lay in close-curled, flattened ringlets about her head. Rather like mine, except that it was blue-white in color.

They were both staring at me. I crouched beside them, setting down the chest. "Are you all right?" I asked Sieh.

Sieh struggled to sit up, but I could see in his movements how weak he was. I moved to help, but Zhakkarn had him, bracing his back with one big hand. "Amazing, Yeine," Sieh said. "You opened the walls by yourself? I'm impressed."

"Can I help you?" I asked. "Somehow?"

"Play with me."

"Play—" But I trailed off as Zhakkarn caught my eye with a stern look. I thought a moment, then stretched out my hands, palms up. "Put your hands over mine."

He did so. His hands were larger than mine, and they shook like an old man's. So much wrongness. But he grinned. "Think you're fast enough?"

I slapped at his hands, and scored. He moved so slowly that I could've recited a poem in the process. "Apparently I am."

"Beginner's luck. Let's see you do it again." I slapped at his hands again. He moved faster this time; I almost missed. "Ha! All right, third time's the charm." I slapped again, and this time did miss.

Surprised, I looked up at him. He grinned, visibly younger, though not by much. A year, perhaps. "See? I told you. You're slow."

I could not help smiling as I understood. "Do you think you might be up for tag?"

It was midnight. My body wanted sleep, not games, which made me sluggish. That worked in Sieh's favor, especially once he recovered enough to actually run. Then he chased me all over the chamber, amusing himself since I presented very little real challenge. It was doing him such noticeable good that I kept at it until he finally called a halt and we both flopped on the floor, panting. He looked, at last, normal—a spindly boy of nine or ten, beautiful and carefree. I no longer questioned why I loved him.

"Well, that was fun," Sieh said at last. He sat up, stretched, and began beckoning the dead spheres to himself. They rolled across the floor to him, where he picked them up, petted them fondly, then lifted them into the air, giving each a practiced twist before releasing it to float away. "So what's in the chest?"

I glanced at Zhakkarn, who had not joined in our play. I suspected children's games did not mesh well with the essence of battle. She nodded to me once, and this time it was approving. I flushed and looked away.

"Letters," I said, putting my hand on my mother's chest. "They are..." I hesitated, inexplicably reticent. "My father's letters to my mother, and some unsent drafts from her to him. I think..." I swallowed. My throat was suddenly tight, and my eyes stung. There is no logic to grief.

Sieh ignored me, brushing my hand out of the way before opening the chest. I regained my composure while he took out each letter, skimmed it, and laid it on the ground, eventually standing up to enlarge the pattern. I had no idea what he was doing as he finally set the last letter into the corner of a great square some five paces by five, with a smaller square off to the side for my mother's letters. Then he stood and folded his arms to stare down at the whole mess.

"There are some missing," said Zhakkarn. I started to find her looming behind me, gazing down at the pattern as well.

Puzzled, I went to look myself, but could not read either my mother's fine script or my father's more sprawling hand from this distance. "How can you tell?"

"They both refer to prior letters," Zhakkarn said, pointing here and there at certain pages.

"And the pattern is broken in too many places," Sieh added, stepping lightly between the pages to crouch and peer more closely at the letters. "Both of them were creatures of habit, your parents. Once a week they wrote, regular as clockwork, over the span of a year. But there are six—no, seven weeks missing. No apologies after the missing weeks, and that is where I see references to the prior letters." He glanced back at me over his shoulder. "Did anyone besides you know this chest was there? Wait, no, it's been twenty years; half the palace might've known."

I shook my head, frowning. "They were hidden. The place *seemed* undisturbed—"

"That might only mean it happened so long ago that the dust had time to settle." Sieh straightened, turning to me. "What is it you were expecting to find here?"

"Viraine—" I set my jaw. "Viraine says he was my mother's lover."

Sieh raised his eyebrows and exchanged a look with Zhakkarn. "I'm not certain I would use any part of the word 'love' in what she did to him."

In the face of such casual confirmation, I could not protest. I sat down heavily.

Sieh flopped down on his belly beside me, propping himself on his elbows. "What? Half of Sky is in bed with the other half at any given time."

I shook my head. "Nothing. It's just... a bit much to take."

"He's not your father or anything like that, if you're worried."

I rolled my eyes and raised my brown Darre hand. "I'm not."

"Pleasure is often used as a weapon," Zhakkarn said. "There's no love in that."

I frowned at her, surprised by this notion. I still did not like the idea of my mother lying with Viraine, but it helped to think of it as strategy. But what had she hoped to gain? What did

Viraine know that no one else in Sky knew? Or rather, what would the younger, smitten Viraine—new to Sky, overconfident, eager to please—have been more likely to say than any other Arameri?

"Something about magic," I murmured to myself. "That must be what she was trying to get out of him. Something about... you?" I glanced over at Zhakkarn.

Zhakkarn shrugged. "If she learned any such secrets, she never used them."

"Hmm. What else is Viraine in charge of, here?"

"Magic use," Sieh said, ticking off fingers. "Everything from the routine to, well, us. Information dissemination—he's Dekarta's liaison to the Itempan Order. He oversees all important ceremonies and rituals..."

Sieh trailed off. I looked at him and saw surprise on his face. I glanced at Zhakkarn, who looked thoughtful.

Ceremonies and rituals. A flicker of excitement stirred in my belly as I realized what Sieh meant. I sat up straighter. "When was the last succession?"

"Dekarta's was about forty years ago," Zhakkarn said.

My mother had been forty-five at her death. "She would have been too young to understand what was happening at the ceremony."

"She wasn't at the ceremony," Sieh said. "Dekarta ordered me to play with her that day, to keep her busy."

That was surprising. Why would Dekarta have kept my mother, his heir, away from the ceremony that she would one day have to undertake herself? A bright child could have been made to understand its purpose. Was it that they meant to kill a servant in the course of the ceremony? But this was

Sky; servants died all the time. I couldn't imagine any Arameri, much less my grandfather, denying that harsh reality even to a child.

"Did anything unusual happen at that ceremony?" I asked. "Did you make a play for the Stone that time?"

"No, we weren't ready. It was a routine succession, like the hundred others that have occurred since our imprisonment." Sieh sighed. "Or so I'm told, since I wasn't there. None of us were, except Nahadoth. They always make him attend."

I frowned. "Why just him?"

"Itempas attends the ceremony," said Zhakkarn. While I gaped at her, trying to shape my mind around the idea of the Skyfather *here, right here, coming here,* Zhakkarn went on. "He makes his greetings personally to the new Arameri ruler. Then he offers Nahadoth freedom, though only if he serves Itempas. Thus far, Naha has refused, but Itempas knows it is in his nature to change his mind. He will keep asking."

I shook my head, trying to rid myself of the lingering sense of reverence that a lifetime of training had inculcated in me. The Skyfather, at the succession ceremony. At *every* succession ceremony. He would be there to see me die. He would put his blessing on it.

Monstrous. All my life, I had worshipped him.

To distract myself from my own whirling thoughts, I pinched the bridge of my nose with my fingers. "So who was the sacrifice last time? Some other hapless relative dragged into the family nightmare?"

"No, no," said Sieh. He got up, stretched again, then bent double and began to stand on his hands, wobbling alarmingly. He spoke in between puffing breaths. "An Arameri clan head...must be willing to kill...every person in this palace... if Itempas should require it. To prove themselves, usually...the prospective head must...sacrifice someone *close*."

I considered this. "So I was chosen because neither Relad nor Scimina is close to anyone?"

Sieh wobbled too much, tumbled to the ground, then rolled upright at once, examining his nails as if the fall hadn't happened. "Well, I suppose. No one's really sure why Dekarta chose you. But for Dekarta himself, the sacrifice was Ygreth."

The name teased my memory with familiarity, though I could not immediately place it with a face. "Ygreth?"

Sieh looked at me in surprise. "His wife. Your maternal grandmother. Kinneth didn't tell you?"

22

Such Rage

ARE YOU STILL ANGRY WITH ME?

No.

That was quick.

Anger is pointless.

I disagree. I think anger can be very powerful under the right circumstances. Let me tell you a story to illustrate. Once upon a time there was a little girl whose father murdered her mother.

How awful.

Yes, you understand that sort of betrayal. The little girl was very young at the time, so the truth was hidden from her. Perhaps she was told her mother abandoned the family. Perhaps her mother vanished; in their world, such things happened. But the little girl was very clever, and she had loved her mother dearly. She pretended to believe the lies, but in reality, she bided her time.

When she was older, wiser, she began to ask questions—but not of her father, or anyone else who claimed to care for her. These could not be trusted. She asked her slaves, who hated her already. She asked an innocent young scrivener who was smitten with her, brilliant and easy to manipulate. She asked her enemies, the heretics, whom her family had persecuted for generations. None of them had any reason to lie, and between them all she pieced together the truth. Then she set all her mind and heart and formidable will on vengeance... because that is what a daughter does when her mother has been murdered.

Ah, I see. But I wonder; did the little girl love her father?

I wonder that, too. Once, certainly, she must have; children cannot help loving. But what of later? Can love turn to hate so easily, so completely? Or did she weep inside even as she set herself against him? I do not know these things. But I do know that she set in motion a series of events that would shake the world even after her death, and inflict her vengeance on all humankind, not just her father. Because in the end, we are all complicit.

All of you? That seems a bit extreme.

Yes. Yes, it is. But I hope she gets what she wants.

This, then, was the Arameri succession: a successor was chosen by the family head. If she was the sole successor, she would be required to convince her most cherished person to willingly die on her behalf, wielding the Stone and transferring the master sigil to her brow. If there was more than one successor, they competed to force the designated sacrifice to choose one or the other. My mother had been sole heir; whom would she have been forced to kill, had she not abdicated? Perhaps she had cultivated Viraine as a lover for more than one reason. Perhaps she could have convinced Dekarta himself to die for her. Perhaps this was why she had never come back after her marriage, after my conception.

So many pieces had fallen into place. More yet floated, indistinct. I could feel how close I was to understanding it all, but would I have time? There was the rest of the night, the next day, and another whole night and day beyond that. Then the ball, and the ceremony, and the end.

More than enough time, I decided.

"You can't," Sieh said again urgently, trotting along beside me. "Yeine, Naha needs to heal, just as I did. He can't do that with mortal eyes shaping him—"

"I won't look at him, then."

"It's not that simple! When he's weak, he's more dangerous than ever; he has trouble controlling himself. You shouldn't—" His voice dropped an octave suddenly, breaking like that of a youth in puberty, and he cursed under his breath and stopped. I walked on, and was not surprised when I heard him stamp the floor behind me and shout, "You are the stubbornest, most infuriating mortal I've ever had to put up with!"

"Thank you," I called back. There was a curve up ahead; I stopped before rounding it. "Go and rest in my room," I said. "I'll read you a story when I get back."

What he snarled in reply, in his own tongue, needed no translation. But the walls did not fall in, and I did not turn into a frog, so he couldn't have been that angry.

Zhakkarn had told me where to find Nahadoth. She had looked at me for a long time before saying it, reading my face with eyes that had assessed a warrior's determination since the dawn of time. That she'd told me was a compliment—or a warning. Determination could easily become obsession. I did not care.

In the middle of the lowermost residential level, Zhakkarn had said, Nahadoth had an apartment. The palace was perpetually shadowed here by its own bulk, and in the center there would be no windows. All the Enefadeh had dwellings on that level, for those unpleasant occasions when they needed to sleep and eat and otherwise care for their semimortal bodies. Zhakkarn had not mentioned why they'd chosen such an unpleasant location, but I thought I knew. Down there, just above the oubliette, they could be closer to Enefa's Stone than to Itempas's usurped sky. Perhaps the lingering feel of her presence was a comfort, given that they suffered so much in her name.

The level was silent when I stepped out of the lift alcove. None of the palace's mortal complement lived here—not that I blamed them. Who would want the Nightlord for a neighbor? Unsurprisingly, the level seemed unusually gloomy; the palace walls did not glow so brightly here. Nahadoth's brooding presence permeated the whole level.

But when I rounded the last curve, I was briefly blinded by a flash of unexpected brightness. In the afterimage of that flash I had seen a woman, bronze-skinned and silver-haired, almost as tall as Zhakkarn and sternly beautiful, kneeling in the corridor as if to pray. The light had come from the wings on her back, covered in mirror-bright feathers of overlapping precious metals. I had seen her once before, this woman, in a dream—

Then I blinked my watering eyes and looked again, and the light was gone. In its place, heavyset, plain Kurue was laboriously climbing to her feet, glaring at me.

"I'm sorry," I said, for the interruption of whatever meditations a goddess required. "But I need to speak with Nahadoth."

There was only one door in this corridor, and Kurue stood in front of it. She folded her arms. "No."

"Lady Kurue, I don't know when I'll have another chance to ask these things—"

"What, precisely, does 'no' mean in your tongue? Clearly you don't understand Senmite—"

But before our argument could escalate, the apartment door slid aside a fraction. I could see nothing through that sliver, only darkness. "Let her speak," said Nahadoth's deep voice from within.

Kurue's scowl deepened. "Naha, no." I started a little; I had never heard anyone contradict him. "It's her fault you're in this condition."

I flushed, but she was right. Yet there was no answer from within the chamber. Kurue's fists clenched, and she glared into the darkness with a very ugly look.

"Would it help if I wore a blindfold?" I asked. There was something in the air that hinted at a long-standing anger beyond just this brief exchange. Ah, but of course—Kurue hated mortals, quite rightly blaming us for her enslaved condition. She thought Nahadoth was being foolish over me. Most likely she was right about that, too, being a goddess of wisdom. I did not feel offended when she looked at me with new contempt.

"It isn't just your eyes," Kurue said. "It's your expectations, your fears, your desires. You mortals want him to be a monster and so he becomes one—"

"Then I will want nothing," I said. I smiled as I said it, but I was annoyed now. Perhaps there was wisdom in her blind hatred of humankind. If she expected the worst from us, then we could never disappoint her. But that was beside the point. She was in my way, and I had business to complete before I died. I would command her aside if I had to.

She stared at me, perhaps reading my intentions. After a moment she shook her head and made a dismissive gesture. "Fine, then. You're a fool. And so are you, Naha; you both deserve each other." With that, she walked away, muttering as she rounded a corner. I waited until the sound of her footfalls stopped—not fading, but simply vanishing—then turned to face the open door.

"Come," said Nahadoth from within.

I cleared my throat, abruptly nervous. Why did he frighten me at all the wrong times? "Begging your pardon, Lord Nahadoth," I said, "but perhaps I'd better stay out here. If it's true that just my *thoughts* can harm you—"

"Your thoughts have always harmed me. All your terrors, all your needs. They push and pull at me, silent commands."

I stiffened, horrified. "I never meant to add to your suffering."

There was a pause, during which I held my breath.

"My sister is dead," Nahadoth said very softly. "My brother has gone mad. My children—the handful who remain—hate and fear me as much as they revere me."

And I understood: what Scimina had done to him was noth-ing. What was a few moments' suffering beside the centuries of grief and loneliness that Itempas had inflicted on him? And here I was, fretting over my own small addition.

I opened the door and stepped inside.

Within the chamber, the darkness was absolute. I lingered near the door for a moment, hoping my eyes would adjust, but they did not. In the silence after the door closed I made out the sound of breathing, slow and even, some ways away.

I put out my hands and began groping my way blindly toward the sound, hoping gods had no great need of furniture. Or steps.

"Stay where you are," Nahadoth said. "I am...not safe to be near." Then, softer, "But I am glad you came."

This was the other Nahadoth, then—not the mortal, but not the mad beast of a cold winter's tale, either. This was the Nahadoth who had kissed me that first night, the one who actually seemed to like me. The one I had the fewest defenses against.

I took a deep breath and tried to concentrate on the soft empty dark.

"Kurue is right. I'm sorry. It's my fault Scimina punished you."

"She did it to punish *you*."

I winced. "Even worse."

He laughed softly, and I felt a breeze stir past me, soft as a warm summer night. "Not for me."

Point. "Is there anything I can do to help you?"

I felt the breeze again, and this time it tickled the tiny hairs on my skin. I had a sudden image of him standing just behind me, holding me close and exhaling into the curve of my neck.

There was a soft, hungry sound from the other side of the room, and abruptly lust filled the space around me, powerful and violent and not remotely tender. Oh, gods. I quickly fixed my thoughts again on darkness, nothing, darkness, my mother. Yes.

It seemed to take a long time, but eventually that terrible hunger faded.

"It would be best," he said with disturbing gentleness, "if you make no effort to help."

"I'm sorry—"

"You are mortal." That seemed to say it all. I lowered my eyes, ashamed. "You have a question about your mother."

Yes. I took a deep breath. "Dekarta killed *her* mother," I said.

"Was that the reason she gave, when she agreed to help you?"

"I am a slave. No Arameri would confide in me. As I told you, all she did was ask questions at first."

"And in return, you asked for her help?"

"No. She still wore the blood sigil. She could not be trusted."

Involuntarily I raised a hand to my own forehead. I continually forgot the mark was there. I had forgotten that it was a factor in Sky politics as well. "Then how—"

"She bedded Viraine. Prospective heirs are usually told about the succession ceremony, but Dekarta had commanded that the details be kept from her. Viraine knew no better, so he told Kinneth how the ceremony usually goes. I assume that was enough for her to figure out the truth."

Yes, it would have been. She had suspected Dekarta already— and Dekarta had feared her suspicions, it seemed. "What did she do, once she knew?"

"She came to us and asked how she might be made free of her mark. If she could act against Dekarta, she said, she would be willing to use the Stone to set us free."

I caught my breath, amazed at her daring—and her fury.

I had come to Sky willing to die to avenge my mother, and only fortune and the Enefadeh had made that possible. My mother had created her own vengeance. She had betrayed her people, her heritage, even her god, all to strike a blow against one man.

Scimina was right. I was nothing compared to my mother.

"You told me only I could use the Stone to free you," I said. "Because I possess Enefa's soul."

"Yes. This was explained to Kinneth. But since the opportunity had presented itself... We suggested to her that being disowned would get her free of the sigil. And we aimed her toward your father."

Something in my chest turned to water. I closed my eyes. So much for my parents' fairy-tale romance.

"Did she...agree from the start to have a child for you?" I asked. My voice sounded very soft in my own ears, but the room was quiet. "Did she and my father...*breed* me for you?"

"No."

I could not bring myself to believe him.

"She hated Dekarta," Nahadoth continued, "but she was still his favorite child. We told her nothing of Enefa's soul and our plans, because we did not trust her."

More than understandable.

"All right," I said, trying to marshal my thoughts. "So she met my father, who was one of Enefa's followers. She married him knowing he would help her achieve her goal, and also knowing the marriage would get her thrown out of the family. That got her free of the sigil."

"Yes. And as a test of her intentions, it proved to us that she was sincere. It also partially achieved her goal: when she left,

Dekarta was devastated. He mourned her as if she'd died. His suffering seemed to please her."

I understood. Oh, how I understood.

"But then... then Dekarta used the Walking Death to try to kill my father." I said it slowly. Such a convoluted patchwork to piece together. "He must have blamed my father for her leaving. Maybe he convinced himself that she'd come back if Father was dead."

"Dekarta did not unleash the Death on Darr."

I stiffened. "What?"

"When Dekarta wants magic done, he uses us. None of us sent the plague to your land."

"But if you didn't—"

No. Oh, no.

There was another source of magic in Sky besides the Enefadeh. Another who could wield the gods' power, albeit weakly. The Death had killed only a dozen people in Darr that year; a minor outbreak by all the usual standards. The best a mortal murderer could do.

"Viraine," I whispered. My hands clenched into fists. *"Viraine."*

He had played the martyr so well—the innocent used and abused by my scheming mother. Meanwhile he had tried to murder my father, knowing she would blame Dekarta and not him. *He* had waited in the corridors like a vulture while she came to plead with Dekarta for her husband's life. Perhaps he had revealed himself to her afterward and commiserated with her over Dekarta's refusal. To lay the groundwork for wooing her back? Yes, that felt like him.

And yet my father had not died. My mother had not returned

to Sky. Had Viraine pined for her all these years, hating my father—hating *me* for thwarting his plans? Had Viraine been the one to raid my mother's chest of letters? Perhaps he had burned any that referred to him, hoping to forget his youthful folly. Perhaps he'd kept them, fantasizing that the letters contained some vestige of the love he'd never earned.

I would hunt him down. I would see his white hair fall around his face in a red curtain.

There was a faint, skittering sound nearby, like pebbles on the hard Skystuff floor. Or claw tips—

"Such rage," the Nightlord breathed, his voice all deep crevasses and ice. And he was close, all of a sudden, so close. Right behind me. "Oh, yes. Command me, sweet Yeine. I am your weapon. Give the word, and I will make the pain he inflicted on me tonight seem kind."

My anger was gone, frozen away. Slowly I took a deep breath, then another, calming myself. No hatred. No fear of whatever the Nightlord had become thanks to my carelessness. I fixed my mind on the dark and the silence, and did not answer. I did not dare.

After a very long while I heard a faint, disappointed sigh. Farther away this time; he had returned to the other side of the room. Slowly I allowed my muscles to unclench.

Dangerous to continue this line of questioning right now. So many secrets to discover, so many pit-traps of emotion. I pushed aside thoughts of Viraine, with an effort.

"My mother wanted to save my father," I said. Yes. That was a good thing to understand. She must have grown to love him, however strangely the relationship had begun. I knew he'd loved her. I remembered seeing it in his eyes.

"Yes," said Nahadoth. His voice was as calm as before my

lapse. "Her desperation made her vulnerable. Of course we took advantage."

I almost grew angry, but caught myself in time.

"Of course. So you persuaded her then to allow Enefa's soul into her child. And..." I took a deep breath. Paused, marshaling my strength. "My father knew?"

"I don't know."

If the Enefadeh did not know what my father thought of the matter, then no one here would know. I dared not go back to Darr to ask Beba.

So I chose to believe that Father knew and loved me anyway. That Mother, beyond her initial misgivings, had chosen to love me. That she had kept the ugly secrets of her family from me out of some misguided hope that I would have a simple, peaceful destiny in Darr...at least until the gods came back to claim what was theirs.

I needed to stay calm, but I could not hold it all in. I closed my eyes and began to laugh. So many hopes had been rested on me.

"Am I allowed none of my own?" I whispered.

"What would you want?" Nahadoth asked.

"What?"

"If you could be free." There was something in his voice that I did not understand. Wistfulness? Yes, and something more. Kindness? Fondness? No, that was impossible. "What would you want for yourself?"

The question made my heart ache. I hated him for asking it. It was his fault that my wishes would never come true—his fault, and my parents', and Dekarta's, and even Enefa's.

"I'm tired of being what everyone else has made me," I said. "I want to be myself."

"Don't be a child."

I looked up, startled and angry, though of course there was nothing to see. "What?"

"You are what your creators and experiences have made you, like every other being in this universe. Accept that and be done; I tire of your whining."

If he had said it in his usual cold voice, I would have walked out in affront. But he truly did sound tired, and I remembered the price he had paid for my selfishness.

The air stirred nearby again, soft, almost a touch. When he spoke, he was closer. "The future, however, is yours to make— even now. Tell me what you want."

It was something I had never truly thought about, beyond vengeance. I wanted…all the usual things that any young woman wanted. Friends. Family. Happiness for those I loved.

And also…

I shivered, though the chamber was not cold. The very strangeness of this new thought made me suspicious. Was this some sign of Enefa's influence?

Accept that and be done.

"I…" I closed my mouth. Swallowed. Tried again. "I want… something different for the world." Ah, but the world would indeed be different after Nahadoth and Itempas were done with it. A pile of rubble, with humanity a red ruin underneath. "Something better."

"What?"

"I don't know." I clenched my fists, struggling to articulate what I felt, surprised by my own frustration. "Right now, everyone is…afraid." Closer, yes. I kept at it. "We live at the gods' mercy and shape our lives around your whims. Even when your quarrels don't involve us, we die. What would we be like if...if you just...went away?"

"More would die," said the Nightlord. "Those who worship us would be frightened by our absence. Some would decide it was the fault of others, while those who embrace the new order would resent any who keep the old ways. The wars would last centuries."

I felt the truth of his words in the pit of my belly, and it left me queasy with horror. But then something touched me—hands, cool and light. He rubbed my shoulders, as if to soothe me.

"But eventually, the battles would end," he said. "When a fire burns out, new things grow in its wake."

I felt no lust or rage from him—probably because, for the moment, he felt none from me. He was not like Itempas, unable to accept change, bending or breaking everything around him to his will. Nahadoth bent himself to the will of others. For a moment the thought made me sad.

"Are you ever yourself?" I asked. "Truly yourself, not just the way others see you?"

The hands went still, then withdrew. "Enefa asked me that once."

"I'm sorry—"

"No." There was sorrow in his voice. It never faded, for him. How terrible to be a god of change and endure grief unending.

"When I am free," he said, "I will choose who shapes me."

"But..." I frowned. "That isn't freedom."

"At the dawn of reality I was myself. There was nothing and no one else to influence me—only the Maelstrom that had given birth to me, and it did not care. I tore open my flesh and spilled out the substance of what became your realm: matter and energy and my own cold, black blood. I devoured my mind and reveled in the novelty of pain."

Tears sprang to my eyes. I swallowed hard and tried to will them away, but abruptly the hands returned, lifting my chin. Fingers stroked my eyes shut, brushing the tears away.

"When I am free I will choose," he said again, whispering, very close. "You must do the same."

"But I will never be—"

He kissed me silent. There was longing in that kiss, tangy and bittersweet. Was that my own longing, or his? Then I understood, finally: it didn't matter.

But oh gods, oh goddess, it was so good. He tasted like cool dew. He made me thirsty. Just before I began to want more, he pulled back. I fought not to feel disappointment, for fear of what it would do to us both.

"Go and rest, Yeine," he said. "Leave your mother's schemes to play themselves out. You have your own trials to face."

And then I was in my apartment, sitting on the floor in a square of moonlight. The walls were dark, but I could see easily because the moon, bright though just a sliver, was low in the sky. Well past midnight, probably only an hour or two before dawn. This was becoming a habit for me.

Sieh sat in the big chair near my bed. Seeing me, he uncurled from it and moved onto the floor beside me. In the moonlight his pupils were huge and round, like those of an anxious cat.

I said nothing, and after a moment he reached up and pulled me down so that my head rested in his lap. I closed my eyes, drawing comfort from the feel of his hand on my hair. After a time, he began to sing me a lullaby that I had heard in a dream. Relaxed and warm, I slept.

23

Selfishness

TELL ME WHAT YOU WANT, the Nightlord had said.
Something better for the world, I had replied.
But also...

In the morning I went to the Salon early, before the Consortium session began, hoping to find Ras Onchi. Before I could, I saw Wohi Ubm, the other High North noblewoman, arriving on the Salon's wide, colonnaded steps.

"Oh," she said after an awkward introduction and my inquiry. I knew then, the instant I saw the pitying look in her eyes. "You haven't heard. Ras died in her sleep just these two nights past." She sighed. "I still can't believe it. But, well; she was old."

I went back to Sky.

I walked through the corridors awhile, thinking about death.

Servants nodded as they passed me and I nodded back. Courtiers—my fellow highbloods—either ignored me or stared in open curiosity. Word must have spread that I was finished as an heir candidate, publicly defeated by Scimina. Not all of the stares were kind. I inclined my head to them anyhow. Their pettiness was not mine.

On one of the lower levels I surprised T'vril on a shadowed balcony, dangling a clipboard from one finger and watching a passing cloud. When I touched him, he started guiltily (fortunately catching the clipboard), which I took to mean he had been thinking about me.

"The ball will begin at dusk tomorrow night," he said. I had moved to stand at the railing beside him, absorbing the view and the comfort of his presence in silence. "It will continue until dawn the next morning. That's tradition, before a succession ceremony. Tomorrow is a new moon—a night that was once sacred to the followers of Nahadoth. So they celebrate through it."

Petty of them, I thought. Or petty of Itempas.

"Immediately after the ball, the Stone of Earth will be sent through the palace's central shaft to the ritual chamber, in the solarium spire."

"Ah. I heard you warning the servants about this last week."

T'vril turned the clipboard in his fingers gently, not looking at me. "Yes. A fleeting exposure supposedly does no harm, but..." He shrugged. "It's a thing of the gods. Best to stay away."

I could not help it; I laughed. "Yes, I agree!"

T'vril looked at me oddly, a small uncertain smile on his lips. "You seem...comfortable."

I shrugged. "It isn't my nature to spend all my time fretting. What's done is done." Nahadoth's words.

T'vril shifted uncomfortably, flicking a few stray windblown hairs out of his face. "I'm...told that an army gathers along the pass that leads from Menchey into Darr."

I steepled my fingers and gazed at them, stilling the voice that cried out within myself. Scimina had played her game well. If I did not choose her, I had no doubt she had left instructions for Gemd to begin the slaughter. Gemd might do it anyhow once

I set the Enefadeh free, but I was counting on the world being preoccupied with survival amid the outbreak of another Gods' War. Sieh had promised that Darr would be kept safe through the cataclysm. I wasn't sure I entirely trusted that promise, but it was better than nothing.

For what felt like the hundredth time, I considered and discarded the idea of approaching Relad. Scimina's people were on the ground; her knife was at Darr's throat. If I chose Relad at the ceremony, could he act before that knife cut a fatal wound? I could not bet my people's future on a man I didn't even respect.

Only the gods could help me now.

"Relad has confined himself in his quarters," T'vril said, obviously thinking along the same lines as me. "He receives no calls, lets no one in, not even the servants. The Father knows what he's eating—or drinking. There are bets among the highbloods that he'll kill himself before the ball."

"I suppose there's little else interesting here to bet on."

T'vril glanced at me, perhaps deciding whether to say more. "There are also bets that *you* will kill *yourself*."

I laughed into the breeze. "What are the odds? Do you think they'd let me bet, too?"

T'vril turned to face me, his eyes suddenly intent. "Yeine— if, if you—" He faltered silent and looked away; his voice had choked on the last word.

I took his hand and held it while he bowed his head and trembled and fought to keep control of himself. He led and protected the servants here; tears would have made him feel weak. Men have always been fragile that way.

After a few moments he took a deep breath. His voice was

higher than usual as he said, "Shall I escort you to the ball tomorrow night?"

When Viraine had offered the same thing, I had hated him. With T'vril, the offer made me love him a little more. "No, T'vril. I want no escort."

"It could help. To have a friend there."

"It could. But I will not ask such a thing of my few friends."

"You aren't asking. I'm offering—"

I stepped closer, leaning against his arm. "I'll be fine, T'vril."

He regarded me for a long while, then shook his head slowly. "You will, won't you? Ah, Yeine. I'll miss you."

"You should leave this place, T'vril. Find yourself a good woman to take care of you and keep you in silks and jewelry."

T'vril stared at me, then burst out laughing, not strained at all this time. "A Darre woman?"

"No, are you mad? You've seen what we're like. Find some Ken girl. Maybe those pretty spots of yours will breed true."

"Pretty—*freckles*, you barbarian! They're called freckles."

"Whatever." I lifted his hand, kissed the back of it, and let him go. "Good-bye, my friend."

I left him there, still laughing, as I walked away.

But...?

But that was not all I wanted.

That conversation helped me decide on my next move. I went looking for Viraine.

I had been of two minds about confronting him ever since the previous night's conversation with Nahadoth. I believed now that Viraine, not Dekarta, had killed my mother. I still did not understand it; if he had loved her, why kill her? And why now, twenty years after she'd broken his heart? Part of me craved understanding.

The other part of me did not care why he'd done it. This part of me wanted blood, and I knew that if I listened to it I might do something foolish. There would be blood aplenty when I got my vengeance on the Arameri; all the horror and death of a second Gods' War unleashed. That much blood should have been enough for me... but I would not be alive to see it. We are selfish that way, we mortals.

So I went to see Viraine.

He did not answer when I knocked at the door to his workshop, and for a moment I wavered, debating whether to pursue the matter further. Then I heard a faint, muffled sound from within.

Doors in Sky do not lock. For highbloods, rank and politics provide more than enough security, as only those who are immune to retaliation dare invade another's privacy. I, condemned to die in slightly more than a day, was thus immune, and so I slid the door open, just a bit.

I did not see Viraine at first. There was the workbench where I had been marked, its surface empty this time. All of the benches were empty, in fact, which seemed strange to me. So were the animal cages at the back of the room, which was stranger yet. Only then did I spot Viraine—in part because he stood so still and in part because with his white hair and garments, he matched his pristine, sterile workplace so thoroughly.

He was near the large crystal globe at the back of the chamber. I thought at first that he leaned against it in order to peer into its translucent depths. Perhaps this was how he had spied on me, in my lone, abortive communication with my assigned nations. But then I noticed that he stood slumped, one hand braced against the globe's polished surface, head hanging. I could not see his free hand through the white curtain of his hair, but there was something about its furtive movements that rang an instant note of recognition within me. He sniffed, and that confirmed it: alone in his workshop, on the eve of his god's once-in-a-lifetime reaffirmation of triumph, Viraine was crying.

It was weakness unbecoming of a Darre woman that this quieted my anger. I had no idea why he was crying. Perhaps all his evils had revived the tatters of his conscience for one moment. Perhaps he had stubbed his toe. But in the moment that I stood there, watching him weep as T'vril had managed not to, I could not help wondering: what if even one of those tears was for my mother? So few people had mourned her besides me.

I slid the door shut and left.

Foolish of me.

Yes. Even then, you resisted the truth.

Do I know it?

Now, yes. Then, you did not.

Why—

You're dying. Your soul is at war. And another memory preoccupies you.

Tell me what you want, the Nightlord had said.

Scimina was in her quarters, being fitted for her ball gown. It was white—a color that did not suit her well. There was not enough contrast between the material and her pale skin, and the overall result made her look faded. Still, the gown was lovely, made of some shining material that had been further enhanced by tiny diamonds studding the bodice and the lines of the skirt. They caught the light as she turned on her dais for the tailors.

I waited patiently while she issued instructions to them. On the far side of the room, the human version of Nahadoth sat on a windowsill, gazing out at the early-afternoon sun. If he heard me enter, he did not look up to acknowledge it.

"I confess I'm curious," Scimina said, turning to me at last. I felt a fleeting, petty sense of pleasure at the sight of a large bruise on her jaw. Was there no magic to quickly heal such small wounds? A shame. "What could bring you here to visit me? Do you plan to plead for your nation?"

I shook my head. "There would be no point."

She smiled, almost kindly. "True. Well, then. What do you want?"

"To take you up on an offer," I said. "I hope that it still stands?"

Another small satisfaction: the blank look on her face. "What offer would that be, Cousin?"

I nodded past her, at the still figure in the window. He was clothed, I saw, in a simple black shirt and pants, and a plain iron collar for once. That was good. I found him more distasteful nude. "You said that I was welcome to borrow your pet sometime."

Beyond Scimina, Naha turned to stare at me, his brown eyes wide. Scimina did, too, for a moment, and then she burst out laughing.

"I see!" She shifted her weight to one side and put a hand on her hip, much to the consternation of the tailors. "I can't argue with your choice, Cousin. He's much more fun than T'vril. But—forgive me—you seem such a small creature. And my Naha is so very…strong. Are you certain?"

Her insults wafted past me like air; I barely noticed. "I am."

Scimina shook her head, bemused. "Very well. I have no use for him at the moment anyhow; he's weak today. Probably just right for you, though—" She paused then, glancing at the windows. Checking the position of the sun. "Of course you know to beware sunset."

"Of course." I smiled, drawing a momentary frown from her. "I have no wish to die earlier than necessary."

Something like suspicion flickered in Scimina's eyes for a moment, and I felt tension in the pit of my belly. But she finally shrugged.

"Go with her," she said, and Nahadoth rose.

"For how long?" he asked, his voice neutral.

"Until she's dead." Scimina smiled and opened her arms in a magnanimous gesture. "Who am I to deny a last request? But while you're at it, Naha, see to it that she does nothing too strenuous—nothing that would incapacitate her, at least. We need her fit, two mornings from now."

The iron chain had been connected to a nearby wall. It fell away with Scimina's words. Naha picked up the loose end, then stood watching me, his expression unreadable.

I inclined my head to Scimina. She ignored me, returning her attention to the tailors' work with a snarl of irritation; one of them had pinned the hem badly. I left, not caring whether Nahadoth followed now or later.

What would I want, if I could be free?

Safety for Darr.

My mother's death given meaning.

Change, for the world.

And for myself...

I understand now. I have chosen who will shape me.

"She's right," Naha said, when we stood together in my apartment. "I'm not much use at the moment." He said it blandly, with no emotional inflection, but I guessed his bitterness.

"Fine," I said. "I'm not interested anyhow." I went to stand at the window.

Silence behind me for a long moment, and then he came over. "Something's changed." The light was wrong to see his reflection, but I could imagine his suspicious expression. "You're different."

"A lot has happened since you and I last met."

He touched my shoulder. When I did not throw off his hand, he took hold of the other, then turned me gently to face him. I let him. He stared at me, trying to read my eyes, perhaps trying to intimidate me.

Except, up close, he was anything but intimidating. Deep lines of weariness marked paths from his sunken eyes; the eyes themselves were bloodshot, even more ordinary looking than before. His posture was slouched and strange. Belatedly I understood: he could barely stand. Nahadoth's torture had taken its toll on him as well.

My face must have shown my pity, because abruptly he scowled and straightened. "Why did you bring me here?"

"Sit down," I said, gesturing to the bed. I tried to turn back to the window, but his fingers tightened on my shoulders. If he had been at his best, he would have hurt me. I understood that now. He was a slave, a whore, not even allowed part-time control of his own body. The only power he had was what little he could exert over his lovers, his users. That wasn't much.

"Are you waiting for him?" he asked. The way he said "him" held a treasure's worth of resentment. "Is that it?"

I reached up and detached his hands from my shoulders, pushing them away firmly. "Sit down. Now."

The "now" forced him to let go of me, walk the few steps to the bed, and sit down. He did it glaring the whole way. I turned back to the window and let his hate splash uselessly against my back.

"Yes," I said. "I'm waiting for him."

A stunned pause. "You're in love with him. You weren't before, but you are now. Aren't you?"

You resist the truth.

I considered the question.

"In love with him?" I said it slowly. The phrase felt strange when I thought about it, like a poem that has been read too often. "In love with him."

Another memory preoccupies you.

I was surprised to hear real fear in Naha's voice. "Don't be a fool. You don't know how often I've woken up beside a corpse. If you're strong, you can resist him."

"I know. I've said no to him before."

"Then…" Confusion.

I had a sudden epiphany as to what his life had been like: this other, unwanted Nahadoth. Every day a plaything of the Arameri. Every night—not sleep but oblivion, as close to death as any mortal can come short of the event itself. No peace, no true rest. Every morning a chilling surprise: mysterious injuries. Dead lovers. And the soul-grinding knowledge that it would never, ever end.

"Do you dream?" I asked.

"What?"

"Dream. At night, while you're...within him. Do you?"

Naha frowned for a long moment, as if he was trying to figure out the trick in my question. Finally he said, "No."

"Not at all?"

"I have...flashes, sometimes." He gestured vaguely, looking away from me. "Memories, maybe. I don't know what they are."

I smiled, feeling sudden warmth toward him. He was like me. Two souls, or at least two selves, in a single body. Perhaps that was where the Enefadeh had gotten the idea.

"You look tired," I said. "You should get some sleep."

He frowned. "No. I sleep enough at night—"

"Sleep now," I said, and he crumpled onto his side so swiftly that I might have laughed under other circumstances. I walked over to the bed, lifted his legs onto it and arranged him for comfort, then knelt beside it, putting my mouth near his ear.

"Have pleasant dreams," I commanded. The frown that had been on his face altered subtly, smoothing and softening.

Satisfied, I got to my feet and went back to the window, to wait.

Why can't I remember what happened next?

You are remembering—

No, why can't I remember it *now*? As I talk through it, it comes back to me, but only then. Without that there's an empty space. A great dark hole.

You are remembering.

The instant the sun's red curve sank below the horizon, the room shook, and with it the whole palace. This close, the vibration was powerful enough to make my teeth rattle. A line seemed to sweep the room, moving outward from behind me, and when this line passed, the room was darker. I waited, and when the hairs prickled on the back of my neck, I spoke. "Good evening, Lord Nahadoth. Are you feeling better?"

My only answer was a low, shuddering exhalation. The evening sky was still heavily stroked with sunlight, golds and reds and violets as deep as jewels. He was not himself yet.

I turned. He was sitting up. He still looked human, ordinary, but I could see his hair wafting around him, though there was no breeze. As I watched it thickened, lengthened, darkened, spinning itself into the cloak of night. Fascinating, and beautiful. He had averted his face from the lingering sunlight and did not see me approach until I was right there. Then he looked up, raising a hand as if to shield himself. *From me?* I wondered, and smiled.

The hand trembled as I watched. I took it, reassured by the cool dryness of his skin. (His skin was brown now, I noticed. My doing?) Beyond the hand his eyes watched me, black now, and unblinking. Unthinking, like those of a beast.

I cupped his cheek and willed him sane. He blinked, frowned

slightly, then stared at me as his confusion cleared. His hand in mine became still.

When I judged the moment right, I let go his hand. Unfastened my blouse, and slipped it off my shoulders. I unhitched the skirt and let it fall, along with my underclothes. Naked, I waited, an offering.

24

If I Ask

—AND THEN—THEN—

You remember.

No. No, I don't.

Why are you afraid?

I don't know.

Did he hurt you?

I don't remember!

You do. Think, child. I made you stronger than this. What were the sounds? The scents? What do the memories feel like?

Like... like summer.

Yes. Humid, thick, those summertime nights. Did you know—the earth absorbs all the day's heat, and gives it back in the dark hours. All that energy just hovers in the air, waiting to be used. It slickens the skin. Open your mouth and it curls around your tongue.

I remember. *Oh, gods, I remember.*

I knew you would.

The shadows in the room seemed to deepen as the Nightlord rose to his feet. He loomed over me, and for the first time I could not see his eyes in the dark.

"Why?" he asked.

"You never answered my question."

"Question?"

"Whether you would kill me, if I asked."

I won't pretend I wasn't afraid. That was part of it—my pounding heart, the quickness of my breath. *Esui*, the thrill of danger. But then he reached out, so slowly that I worried I was dreaming, and trailed his fingertips up my arm. Just that one touch and my fear became something entirely different. Gods. *Goddess.*

White teeth flashed at me, startling in the darkness. Oh, yes, this was far beyond mere danger.

"Yes," he said. "If you asked, I would kill you."

"Just like that?"

"You seek to control your death as you cannot control your life. I...understand this." So much unspoken meaning in that brief pause. I wondered, suddenly, whether the Nightlord had ever yearned to die.

"I didn't think you wanted me to control my death."

"No, little pawn." I tried to concentrate on his words while his hand continued its slow journey up my arm, but it was difficult. I am only human. "It is Itempas's way to force his will upon others. I have always preferred *willing* sacrifices."

He drew one fingertip along my collarbone now, and I

nearly moved away because it felt almost unbearably good. I did not because I had seen his teeth. One did not run from a predator.

"I...I knew you would say yes." My voice shook. I was babbling. "I don't know how, but I knew. I knew..." *That I was more than a pawn to you.* But no, that part I could not say.

"I must be what I am." He said it as if the words made sense. "Now. *Are* you asking?"

I licked my lips, hungry. "Not to die. But—for you. Yes. I'm asking for you."

"To have me is to die," he warned me, even as he grazed my breast with the backs of his fingers. The knuckles caught on my already-taut nipple and I could not help gasping. The room got darker.

But one thought pushed up through the desire. It was the thought that had motivated me to do this mad thing, because in spite of everything I was not suicidal. I wanted to live for whatever pittance of time I had left. In the same way I hated the Arameri, yet I sought to understand them; I wanted to prevent a second Gods' War, yet I also wanted the Enefadeh freed. I wanted so many things, each of them contradictory, all of them together impossible. I wanted them anyway. Perhaps Sieh's childishness had infected me.

"Once you took many mortal lovers," I said. My voice was more breathy than it should have been. He leaned close to me and inhaled, as if scenting it. "Once you claimed them by the dozen, and they all lived to tell the tale."

"That was before centuries of human hatred made me a monster," said the Nightlord, and for a moment his voice was sad. I had used the same word for him myself, but it felt strange and wrong to hear him say it. "Before my brother stole whatever tenderness there once was in my soul."

And just like that, my fear faded.

"No," I said.

His hand paused. I reached up and caught it, my fingers tangling in his.

"Your tenderness isn't gone, Nahadoth. I've seen it. I've tasted it." I pulled his hand up, up, to touch my lips. I felt his fingers twitch, as if in surprise. "You're right about me; if I must die, I want to die on my own terms. There are so many things I will never do—but *this* I can have. You." I kissed his fingers. "Will you show me that tenderness again, Nightlord? Please?"

From the corner of my eye I saw movement. When I turned my head there were black lines, curling and random, etching their way along the walls, the windows, the floor. The lines flowed out from Nahadoth's feet, spreading, overlapping. I caught a glimpse of strange, airy depths within the lines; a suggestion of drifting mist and deep, endless chasms. He let out a low, soughing breath, and it curled around my tongue.

"I need so much," he whispered. "It has been so long since I shared that part of myself, Yeine. I hunger—I always hunger. I devour myself with hunger. But Itempas has betrayed me, and you are not Enefa, and I . . . I am . . . afraid."

Tears stung my eyes. Reaching up, I cupped his face in my hands and pulled him down to me. His lips were cool, and this time they tasted of salt. I thought I felt him shiver. "I will give you all I can," I said, when we parted.

He pressed his forehead against mine; he was breathing hard. "You must say the words. I will try to be what I was, I will try, but—" He groaned softly, desperate. "Say the words!"

I closed my eyes. How many of my Arameri ancestors had said these words and died? I smiled. It would be a death befitting a Darre, if I joined them.

"Do with me as you please, Nightlord," I whispered.

Hands seized me.

I do not say *his* hands because there were too many of them, gripping my arms and grasping my hips and tangling in my hair. One even curled 'round my ankle. The room was almost entirely dark. I could see nothing except the window and the sky beyond, where the sun's light had finally faded completely. Stars spun as I was lifted and lowered until I felt the bed underneath my back.

Then we fed each other's hunger. Wherever I wanted to be touched, he touched; I don't know how he knew. Whenever I touched him, there was a delay. I would cup emptiness before it became a smooth muscled arm. I would wrap my legs around nothing and only then find hips settled there, taut with ready energy. In this way I shaped him, making him suit my fantasies; in this way he chose to be shaped. When heavy, thick warmth pushed into me, I had no idea whether this was a penis or some entirely different phallus that only gods possessed. I suspect the latter, since no mere penis can fill a woman's body the way he filled mine. Size had nothing to do with it. This time he let me scream.

"Yeine..." Through the haze of my own body heat I was aware of few things. The clouds, racing across the stars. The black lines, webbing the room's ceiling, widening and melding into one great yawning abyss. The rising urgency of Nahadoth's movements. There was pain now, because I wanted it. "Yeine. Open yourself to me."

I had no idea what he meant; I could not think. But he gripped my hair and slid a hand under my hips, pulling me tighter against him in a way that sent me spiraling again. "Yeine!"

Such need in him. Such wounds—two of them, raw and unhealing, for two lost lovers. So much more than one mortal girl could ever satisfy.

And yet in my madness, I tried. I couldn't; I was only human. But for that moment I yearned to be more, give more, because I loved him.

I loved him.

Nahadoth arched up, away from me. In the last starlight I caught a glimpse of a smooth, perfect body, taut-muscled and sleek with sweat all the way down to where it joined with mine. He had flung back his hair in an arc. His face was all tight-clenched eyes and open mouth and that delicious near-agony expression men make when the moment strikes. The black lines joined, and nothingness enclosed us.

Then we fell.

—no, no, we *flew*, not downward but forward, into the dark. There were streaks within this darkness, thin random lines of white and gold and red and blue. I put out my hand in fascination and snatched it back when something stung the fingertips. I looked and found them wet with glimmering stuff that spun with tiny orbiting motes. Then Nahadoth cried out, his body shuddering, and now we went *up*—

—past endless stars, past countless worlds, through layers of light and glowing cloud. Up and up we went, our speed impossible, our size incomprehensible. We left the light behind and kept going, passing through stranger things than mere worlds. Geometric shapes that twisted and gibbered. A white landscape of frozen explosions. Shivering lines of *intention* that turned to chase us. Vast, whalelike beings with terrifying eyes and the faces of long-lost friends.

I closed my eyes. I had to. Yet the images continued, because in this place I had no eyelids to close. I was immense, and still growing. I had a million legs, two million arms. I don't know what I became in that place Nahadoth took me, because there are things no mortal is meant to do or be or comprehend, and I encompassed all of them.

Something familiar: that darkness which is Nahadoth's quintessence. It surrounded me, pressed in, until I had no choice but to yield to it. I felt things in me—sanity? self?—stretch, growing so taut that a touch would break them. This was the end, then. I was not afraid, not even when I became aware of a sound: a titanic, awful roar. I cannot describe it except to say something of that roar was in Nahadoth's voice as he shouted again. I knew then that his ecstasy had taken us beyond the universe, and now we approached the Maelstrom, birthplace of gods. It would tear me apart.

Then, just when the roar had become so terrible that I knew I could bear no more, we stopped. Hovered, pent.

And then we fell again through gibbering strangeness and layered dark and whirlpools of light and dancing globes toward one globe in particular, blue-green and beautiful. There was a new roaring as we streaked down through air, trailing white-hot fire. Something glowing and pale reared up, puny then enormous, all spikes and white stone and treachery—Sky, it was Sky—and it swallowed us whole.

I think I screamed again as, naked, skin steaming, I smashed into my bed. The shock wave of impact swept the room; the sound of it was the Maelstrom come to earth. I knew no more.

25

A Chance

HE SHOULD'VE KILLED ME THAT NIGHT. It would have been easier.

That's selfish of you.

What?

He gave you his body. He gave you pleasure no mortal lover can match. He fought his own nature to keep you alive, and you wish he hadn't bothered.

I didn't mean—

Yes, you did. Oh, child. You think you love him? You think you're worthy of his love?

I can't speak for him. But I know what I feel.

Don't be a—

And I know what I hear. Jealousy does not become you.

What?

This is why you're so angry with me, isn't it? You're just like Itempas, you can't bear to share—

Be silent!

—but it isn't necessary. Don't you see? He has never stopped loving you. He never will. You and Itempas will always hold his heart in your hands.

…Yes. That is true. But I am dead, and Itempas is mad.

And I am dying. Poor Nahadoth.

Poor Nahadoth, and poor us.

*   *   *

I woke slowly, aware first of warmth and comfort. Sunlight shone against the side of my face, red through one of my eyelids. A hand rubbed my back in little arcs.

I opened my eyes and did not understand what I saw at first. A white, rolling surface. I had fleeting memories of something else like it—*frozen explosions*—and then the memories swam away, deeper into my consciousness and out of reach. For a moment understanding lingered: I was mortal, not ready for some knowledge. Then even that vanished, and I was myself again. I was wearing a plush robe. I was sitting in someone's lap. Frowning, I lifted my head.

Nahadoth's daytime form gazed back at me with frank, too-human eyes.

I did not think, half-falling and half-leaping off his lap and rolling to my feet. He rose with me and a taut moment passed, me staring, him just standing there.

The moment broke when he turned to the small nightstand, on which sat a gleaming silver tea service. He poured, the small liquid sound making me flinch for reasons I did not understand, and then held the cup forward, offering it to me.

I stood naked before him, an offering—

Gone, like fish in a pond.

"How do you feel?" he asked. I flinched again, not sure I understood the words. How did I feel? Warm. Safe. Clean. I lifted a hand, sniffed my wrist; I smelled of soap.

"I bathed you. I hope you'll forgive the liberty." Low, soft, his voice, as if he spoke to a skittish mare. He looked different from the day before—healthier for one, but also browner, like a Darre man. "You were so deeply asleep that you didn't wake. I found the robe in the closet."

I hadn't known I had a robe. Belatedly it came to me that he was still holding out the cup of tea. I took it, more out of politeness than any real interest. When I sipped, I was surprised to find it lukewarm and rich with cooling mint and calmative herbs. It made me realize I was thirsty; I drank it down greedily. Naha held out the pot, silently offering more, and I let him pour.

"What a wonder you are," he murmured, as I drank. Noise. He was staring and it bothered me. I looked away to shut him out and savored the tea.

"You were ice cold when I woke up, and filthy. There was something—soot, I think—all over you. The bath seemed to warm you up, and that helped, too." He jerked his head toward the chair where we'd been sitting. "There wasn't anywhere else, so—"

"The bed," I said, and flinched again. My voice was hoarse, my throat raw and sore. The mint helped.

For an instant Naha paused, his lips quirking with a hint of his usual cruelty. "The bed wouldn't have worked."

Puzzled, I looked past him, and caught my breath. The bed was a wreck, sagging on a split frame and broken legs. The mattress looked as though it had been hacked by a sword and then set afire. Loose goosedown and charred fabric scraps littered the room.

It was more than the bed. One of the room's huge glass windows had spiderwebbed; only luck that it hadn't shattered. The vanity mirror had. One of my bookcases lay on the floor, its contents scattered but intact. (I saw my father's book there, with great relief.) The other bookcase had been shattered into kindling, along with most of the books on it.

Naha took the empty teacup from my hand before I could drop it. "You'll need to get one of your Enefadeh friends to fix this. I kept the servants out this morning, but that won't work for long."

"I . . . I don't . . ." I shook my head. So much of what had happened was dreamlike in my memory, more metaphysical than actual. I remembered falling. There was no hole in the ceiling. Yet, the bed.

Naha said nothing as I moved about the room, my slippered feet crunching on glass and splinters. When I picked up a shard of the mirror, staring at my own face, he said, "You don't look as much like the library mural as I'd first thought."

That turned me around to face him. He smiled at me. I had thought him human, but no. He had lived too long and too strangely, knew too much. Perhaps he was more like the demons of old, half mortal and half something else.

"How long have you known?" I asked.

"Since we met." His lips quirked. "Though that can't properly be called a 'meeting,' granted."

He had stopped and stared at me, that first evening in Sky. I'd forgotten in the rush of terror afterward. Then later in Scimina's quarters— "You're a good actor."

"I have to be." His smile was gone now. "Even then, I wasn't sure. Not until I woke up and saw this." He gestured around the devastated room. "And you there beside me, alive."

I didn't expect to be. But I was, and now I would have to deal with the consequences.

"I'm not her," I said.

"No. But I'll wager you're a part of her, or she's a part of you. I know a little about these things." He ran a hand through his unruly black locks. Just hair, and not the smokelike curls of his godly self, but his meaning was plain.

"Why haven't you told anyone?"

"You think I would do that?"

"Yes."

He laughed, though there was a hard edge to the sound. "And you know me so well."

"You would do anything to make your life easier."

"Ah. Then you *do* know me." He flopped down in the chair—the only intact piece of furniture in the room—one leg tossed over one arm. "But if you know that much, Lady, then you should be able to guess why I would never tell the Arameri of your...uniqueness."

I put down the shard of mirror and went to him. "Explain," I commanded, because I might pity him, but I would never like him.

He shook his head, as if chiding me for my impatience. "I, too, want to be free."

I frowned. "But if the Nightlord is ever freed..." What did happen to a mortal soul buried within a god's body? Would he sleep and never awaken? Would some part of him continue, trapped and aware inside an alien mind? Or would he simply cease to exist?

He nodded, and I realized all of those thoughts and more must have occurred to him over the centuries. "He has promised to destroy me, should the day ever come."

And this Naha would rejoice on that day, I realized with a chill. Perhaps he had tried to kill himself before, only to be resurrected the next morning, trapped by magic meant to torment a god.

Well, if all went as planned, he would be free soon.

I rose and went to the remaining undamaged window. The sun was high in the sky, past noon. My last day of life was half over. I was trying to think of how to spend my remaining time when I felt a new presence in the room, and turned. Sieh stood there, looking from the bed to me to Naha, and back again.

"You seem well," I said, pleased. He was properly young again, and there was a grass stain on one of his knees. The look in his eyes, though, was far from childish as he focused on Naha. When his pupils turned to ferocious slits—I saw the change this time—I knew I'd have to intervene. I went to Sieh, deliberately stepping into his line of sight, and opened my arms to invite him near.

He put his arms around me, which at first seemed affectionate until he picked me up bodily and put me behind him, then turned to face Naha.

"Are you all right, Yeine?" he asked, sinking into a crouch. It was not a fighter's crouch; it was closer to the movement of an animal gathering itself to spring. Naha returned his gaze coolly.

I put my hand on his wire-tight shoulder. "I'm fine."

"This one is dangerous, Yeine. We do not trust him."

"Lovely Sieh," said Naha, and there was that cruel edge in his voice again. He opened his arms in a mockery of my own gesture. "I've missed you. Come; give your father a kiss."

Sieh hissed, and I had a moment to wonder whether I had a chance in the infinite hells of holding him. Then Naha laughed and sat back in the chair. Of course he would know exactly how far to push.

Sieh looked as though he was still considering something dire when it finally occurred to me to distract him. "Sieh." He did not look at me. "*Sieh.* I was with your father last night."

He swung around to look at me, so startled that his eyes reverted to human at once. Beyond him, Naha chuckled softly.

"You couldn't have been," said Sieh. "It's been centuries since—" He paused and leaned close. I saw his nostrils twitch delicately once, twice. "Skies and earth. You *were* with him."

Self-conscious, I surreptitiously sniffed the collar of my robe. Hopefully it was something only gods could detect. "Yes."

"But he…that should've…" Sieh shook his head sharply. "Yeine, oh, Yeine, do you know what this means?"

"It means your little experiment worked better than you thought," said Naha. In the shadows of the chair, his eyes glittered, reminding me just a little of his other self. "Perhaps you could give her a try, too, Sieh. You must get tired of perverted old men."

Sieh tensed all over, his hands forming fists. I marveled that he allowed such taunts to work on him—but perhaps that was another of his weaknesses. He had bound himself by the laws of childhood; perhaps one of those laws was *no child shall hold his temper when bullied.*

I touched his chin and turned his face back around to me. "The room. Could you…?"

"Oh. Yes." Pointedly turning his back on Naha, he looked around the room and said something in his own language, fast and high-pitched. The room was abruptly restored, just like that.

"Handy," I said.

"No one's better at cleaning up messes than me." He flashed me a quick grin.

Naha got up and went to browse one of the restored book-shelves, studiously ignoring us. Belatedly it occurred to me that he had been different before Sieh appeared—solicitous, respect-ful, almost kind. I opened my mouth to thank him for that, then thought better of it. Sieh had been careful to conceal that side of himself from me, but I had seen the signs of a crueler streak within him. There was very old, very bad blood between these two, and such things were rarely one-sided.

"Let's go somewhere else to talk. I have a message for you." Breaking my reverie, Sieh pulled me to the nearest wall. We stepped through it into the dead space beyond.

After a few chambers, Sieh sighed, opened his mouth, closed it, then finally decided to speak. "The message I carry is from Relad. He wants to see you."

"Why?"

"I don't know. But I don't think you should go."

I frowned. "Why not?"

"Think, Yeine. You aren't the only one facing death tomor-row. When you appoint Scimina heir, the first thing she'll do is kill her baby brother, and he knows it. What if he decides that killing *you*—right now, before the ceremony—is the best way to earn himself a few extra days of life? It would be futile, of course; Dekarta's seen what's happened with Darr. He'll just designate someone else the sacrifice, and tell that person to choose Scim-ina. But desperate men do not always think rationally."

Sieh's reasoning made sense—but something else did not. "Relad ordered you to bring me this message?"

"No, he asked. And he *asks* to see you. He said, 'If you see her, remind her that I am not my sister; I have never done her harm. I know she listens to you.'" Sieh scowled. "*Remind her*—that was the only part he commanded. He knows how to speak to us. He left me the choice deliberately."

I stopped walking. Sieh got a few paces ahead before he noticed, and turned to me with a puzzled look. "And why did you choose to tell me?" I asked.

A shadow of unease passed over his face; he lowered his eyes. "It's true that I shouldn't have," he said slowly. "Kurue wouldn't have allowed it, if she'd known. But what Kurue doesn't know . . ." A faint smile crossed Sieh's face. "Well, it *can* hurt her, but we'll just have to hope that doesn't happen."

I folded my arms, waiting. He still hadn't answered my question, and he knew it.

Sieh looked annoyed. "You're no fun anymore."

"Sieh."

"Fine, fine." He slid his hands into his pockets and shrugged with total nonchalance, but his voice was serious. "You agreed to help us, that's all. That makes you our ally, not our tool. Kurue is wrong; we shouldn't hide things from you."

I nodded. "Thank you."

"Thank me by not mentioning it to Kurue. Or Nahadoth or Zhakkarn, while you're at it." He paused, then smiled at me with sudden amusement. "Though it seems Nahadoth has his own secrets to hide with you."

My cheeks grew hot. "It was my decision." I blurted the words, irrationally compelled to explain. "I caught him by surprise, and—"

"Yeine, please. You're not about to try and tell me you 'took advantage of him' or anything like that, are you?"

As I had been about to say exactly that, I fell silent.

Sieh shook his head and sighed. I was startled to see an odd sort of sadness in his smile. "I'm glad, Yeine—more glad than you know. He's been so alone since the war."

"He isn't alone. He has you."

"We comfort him, yes, and keep him from completely letting go of his sanity. We can even be his lovers, though for us the experience is... well, as *strenuous* as it was for you." I blushed again, though some of that was at the disquieting thought of Nahadoth lying with his own children. But the Three had been siblings, after all. The gods did not live by our rules.

As if hearing that thought, Sieh nodded. "It's equals he needs, not pity offerings from his children."

"I'm not equal to any of the Three, Sieh, no matter whose soul is in me."

He grew solemn. "Love can level the ground between mortals and gods, Yeine. It's something we've learned to respect."

I shook my head. This was something I had understood from the moment the mad impulse to make love to a god had come over me. "He doesn't love me."

Sieh rolled his eyes. "*I* love you, Yeine, but sometimes you can be such a mortal."

Taken aback, I fell silent. Sieh shook his head and called one of his floating orbs out of nowhere, batting it back and forth in his hands. This one was blue-green, which teased my memories mercilessly. "So what do you plan to do about Relad?"

"What—oh." So dizzying, this constant switch between matters mundane and divine. "I'll meet with him."

"Yeine—"

"He won't kill me." In my mind's eye, I saw Relad's face from two nights ago, framed by the doorway of my room. He had come to tell me of Sieh's torture, which even T'vril had not done. Surely he'd realized that if Scimina forced me to give up my secrets, she would win the contest. So why had he done it?

I had a private theory, based on that brief meeting in the solarium. I believed that somewhere deep down, Relad was even less of an Arameri than T'vril—perhaps even less than me. Somewhere amid all that bitterness and self-loathing, hidden behind a thousand protective layers, Relad Arameri had a soft heart.

Useless for an Arameri heir, if it was true. Beyond useless— dangerous. But because of it, I was willing to chance trusting him.

"I could still choose him," I said to Sieh, "and he knows that. It would make no sense, because it would guarantee my people's suffering. But I could do it. I'm his last hope."

"You sound very sure of that," Sieh said dubiously.

I had the sudden urge to tousle Sieh's hair. He might even enjoy it given his nature, but he would not enjoy the thought that triggered the impulse: Sieh really was a child in one fundamental way. He did not understand mortals. He had lived among us for centuries, millennia, and yet he had never been one of us. He did not know the power of hope.

"I am very sure," I said. "But I would be grateful if you'd come with me."

He looked surprised, though immediately he took my hand. "Of course. But why?"

"Moral support. And in case I'm horribly, horribly wrong."

He grinned, and opened another wall that would take us there.

Relad's apartment was as large as Scimina's, and each was three times the size of mine. If I had seen their apartments my first day in Sky, I would have immediately understood that I was not a true contender for Dekarta's rule.

The configuration of his quarters was entirely different from Scimina's, however: a huge, open chamber with a short stair near the back leading up to a loft area. The main floor was dominated by a square depression set into the floor, in which a world map had been formed of beautifully colored ceramic tiles. Aside from this the chamber was surprisingly austere, with only a few pieces of furniture, a side bar heavily laden with alcohol bottles, and a small bookshelf. And Relad, who stood by the map looking stiff and formal and uncomfortably sober.

"Greetings, Cousin," he said as I came in, and then he paused, glaring at Sieh. "I invited only Yeine."

I put a hand on Sieh's shoulder. "He was concerned that you meant me harm, Cousin. Do you?"

"What? Of course not!" The look of surprise on Relad's face reassured me. In fact, everything about this little scene suggested he was set to charm me, and one did not charm expendable people. "Why in the Maelstrom would I? You're no good to me dead."

I set my smile and decided to let this tactless remark slide. "That's good to know, Cousin."

"Don't mind me," Sieh said. "I'm just a fly on the wall."

Relad made an effort and ignored him. "Can I get you something? Tea? A drink?"

"Well, since you asked—" Sieh began, before I squeezed his shoulder hard. I didn't want to push Relad, at least not yet.

"Thank you, no," I said. "Though I appreciate the offer. I also appreciate your warning, Cousin, the night before last." I stroked Sieh's hair.

Relad wrestled for an appropriate response for a full three seconds before finally muttering, "It was nothing."

"Why did you invite me here?"

"I have an offer to make." He gestured vaguely at the floor.

I looked down at the world map in the floor, my eyes automatically finding High North and the tiny corner of it that was Darr. Four polished, flattened white stones sat ranged around Darr's borders—one in each of the three kingdoms that I'd suspected were part of the alliance, plus a second stone in Menchey. At Darr's heart sat a single marbled-gray stone, probably representing our pathetic troop strength. But just south of Menchey, along the coast where the continent met the Repentance Sea, were three pale yellow stones. I could not guess what those were.

I looked up at Relad. "Darr is all I care about right now. Scimina has offered me my people's lives. Is that what you're offering?"

"Potentially more than that." Relad stepped down into the map-depression, walking over to stand just below High North. His feet were in the middle of the Repentance Sea, which struck me as irrationally amusing for a moment.

"The white are your enemies, as I'm certain you've guessed; Scimina's pawns. These"—he pointed at the yellow stones—"are mine."

I frowned, but before I could speak, Sieh snorted. "You have no allies in High North, Relad. You've ignored the whole continent for years. Scimina's victory is the result of your own neglect."

"I know that," Relad snapped, but then he turned to face me. "It's true I have no friends in High North. Even if I did, the kingdoms there all hate your land, Cousin. Scimina's simply facilitating what they've been itching to do for generations."

I shrugged. "High North was a land of barbarians once, and we Darre were among the most barbaric. The priests may have civilized us since, but no one can erase the past."

Relad nodded dismissively; he didn't care and it showed. He really was terrible at being charming. He pointed at the yellow stones again. "Mercenaries," he said. "Mostly Ken and Min pirates, some Ghor nightfighters, and a contingent of Zhurem City strikemen. I can order them to fight for you, Cousin."

I stared at the yellow stones and was reminded of my earlier thought about mortals and the power of hope.

Sieh hopped down into the map-depression and peered at the yellow stones as if he could see the actual forces they represented. He whistled. "You must've bankrupted yourself to hire so many and get them to High North in time, Relad. I didn't realize you'd acquired that much capital over the years." He glanced back at Relad and me over his shoulder. "But these are too far away to get to Darr by tomorrow. Scimina's friends are already on their way."

Relad nodded, watching me. "My forces are close enough to attack Menchey's capital tonight, and even stage a strike on Tokland the day after. They're fully equipped, rested, and well supplied. Their battle plans were drawn up by Zhakkarn herself." He folded his arms, a bit defensively. "With Menchey under attack, half your enemies will turn back from the assault on Darr. That will leave the Zarenne and the Atir rebels for your people to contend with, and they'll still be outnumbered two to one. But it will give the Darre a fighting chance."

I threw Relad a sharp look. He had gauged me well on this—surprisingly well. Somehow he had realized that it was not the prospect of war that frightened me; I was a warrior, after all. But an *unwinnable* war, against enemies who would not only take spoils but destroy our spirits, if not our lives...that I could not stomach.

Two-to-one odds were winnable. Hard, but winnable.

I glanced at Sieh, who nodded. My instincts told me Relad's offer was legitimate, but he knew Relad's capabilities and would warn me of any trickery. I think we were both surprised that Relad had managed this at all.

"You should abstain from drinking more often, Cousin," I said softly.

Relad smiled, utterly without humor. "It wasn't intentional, I assure you. It's just that impending death tends to sour even the best wine."

I understood completely.

There was another of those awkward silences, and then Relad stepped forward, proffering his hand. Surprised, I took it. We were agreed.

Later, Sieh and I walked slowly back to my room. He took me on a new route this time, passing through parts of Sky that I had not seen in the two weeks since my arrival. Among other wonders, he showed me a high, narrow chamber—not a dead space, but still sealed off and forgotten for some reason—whose ceiling looked like an accident in the gods' construction design. The pale Skystuff hung in attenuated extrusions like cave stalactites, though far more delicate and graceful. A few were close enough to touch; some ended barely inches below the ceiling. I could not fathom the purpose of the chamber until Sieh led me to a panel on the wall.

When I touched it, a slot opened on the ceiling, letting in a sharp, startling gust of ice-cold air. I shivered, but forgot my discomfort when the ceiling extrusions began to sing, stroked into vibration by the wind. It was like no music I'd ever heard, wavering and alien, a cacophony too beautiful to call merely noise. I didn't let Sieh touch the panel to shut off the air until I began to lose the feeling in my fingers.

In the silence that fell, during which I crouched against the wall and blew on my hands to warm them, Sieh crouched in front of me, staring at me intently. I was too cold to notice at first, but then he suddenly leaned forward and kissed me. Startled, I froze, but there was nothing unpleasant about it. It was the kiss of a child, spontaneous and unconditional. Only the fact that he was not a child made me uncomfortable.

Sieh pulled back, and sighed ruefully at the expression on my face. "Sorry," he said, and settled down beside me.

"Don't apologize," I said. "Just tell me what that was for." I realized that was an inadvertent command and added, "Will you?"

He shook his head, playing shy, and pressed his face into my arm. I liked having his warmth there, but I didn't like his silence. I pulled away, forcing him to sit up or risk falling over.

"Yeine!"

"Sieh."

He sighed, looking annoyed, and shifted to sit cross-legged. For a moment I thought he'd just sit there and sulk, but finally he said, "I just don't think it's fair, that's all. Naha got to taste you, but I didn't."

That *did* make me uncomfortable. "Even in my barbarian land, women do not take children as lovers."

The annoyance grew in his expression. "I told you before, I don't want *that* from you. I'm talking about this." He sat up on his knees abruptly and leaned toward me. I flinched away, and he stopped, waiting. It occurred to me that I loved him, trusted him with my very soul. Shouldn't I trust him with a kiss? So after a deep breath, I relaxed. Sieh waited until I gave him a minute nod, and a moment longer than that—making sure. Then he leaned in and kissed me again.

And this time it was different, because I could taste *him*— not Sieh the sweaty, slightly dirty child, but the Sieh beneath the human mask. It is…difficult to describe. A sudden burst of something refreshing, like ripe melon, or maybe a waterfall. A torrent, a current; it rushed into me and through me and back into him so swiftly that I barely had time to draw breath. Salt. Lightning. That hurt enough that I almost pulled away, but distantly I felt Sieh's hands tighten painfully on my arms. Before I could yelp, cold wind shot through me, soothing both the jolt and my bruises.

Then Sieh pulled back. I stared at him, but his eyes were still shut. Uttering a deep, satisfied sigh, he shifted to sit beside me again, lifting my arm and pulling it 'round himself proprietarily.

"What…was that?" I asked, when I had recovered somewhat.

"Me," he said. Of course.

"What do I taste like?"

Sieh sighed, snuggling against my shoulder, his arms looping around my waist. "Soft, misty places full of sharp edges and hidden colors."

I could not help it; I giggled. I felt light-headed, like I'd drunk too much of Relad's liqueur. "That's not a taste!"

"Of course it is. You tasted Naha, didn't you? He tastes like falling to the bottom of the universe."

That stopped my giggling, because it was true. We sat awhile longer, not speaking, not thinking—or at least I was not. It was, after the constant worry and scheming of the past two weeks, a moment of pure bliss. Perhaps that was why, when I did think again, it was of a different kind of peace.

"What will happen to me?" I asked. "After."

He was a clever child; he knew what I meant at once.

"You'll drift for a time," he said very softly. "Souls do that when they're first freed from flesh. Eventually they gravitate toward places that resonate with certain aspects of their nature. Places that are safe for souls lacking flesh, unlike this realm."

"The heavens and the hells."

He shrugged, just a little, so that it would not jostle either of us. "That's what mortals call them."

"Is that not what they are?"

"I don't know. What does it matter?" I frowned, and he sighed. "I'm not mortal, Yeine, I don't obsess over this the way your kind does. They're just...places for life to rest, when it's not being alive. There are many of them because Enefa knew your kind needed variety." He sighed. "That was why Enefa's soul kept drifting, we think. All the places she made, the ones that resonated best with her, vanished when she died."

I shivered, and thought I felt something else shiver deep within me.

"Will...will both our souls find a place, she and I? Or will hers drift again?"

"I don't know." The pain in his voice was quiet, inflectionless. Another person would have missed it.

I rubbed his back gently. "If I can," I said, "if I have any control over it . . . I'll take her with me."

"She may not want to go. The only places left now are the ones her brothers created. Those don't fit her much."

"Then she can stay inside me, if that's better. I'm no heaven, but we've put up with each other this long. We're going to have to talk, though. All these visions and dreams must go. They're really quite distracting."

Sieh lifted his head and stared at me. I kept a straight face for as long as I could, which was not long. Of course he managed it longer than me. He had centuries more of practice.

We dissolved into laughter there on the floor, wrapped around each other, and thus ended the last day of my life.

I went back to my apartment alone, about an hour before dusk. When I got inside, Naha was still sitting in the big chair as if he hadn't moved all day, although there was an empty food tray on the nightstand. He started as I walked in; I suspected he had been napping, or at least daydreaming.

"Go where you like for the remainder of the day," I told him. "I'd like to be alone awhile."

He did not argue as he got to his feet. There was a dress on my bed—a long, formal gown, beautifully made, except that it was a drab gray in color. There were matching shoes and accessories sitting beside it.

"Servants brought those," Naha said. "You're to wear them tonight."

"Thank you."

He moved past me on his way out, not looking at me. At the room's threshold I heard him stop for a moment. Perhaps he turned back. Perhaps he opened his mouth to speak. But he said nothing, and a moment later I heard the apartment's door open and close.

I bathed and got dressed, then sat down in front of the windows to wait.

26

The Ball

I SEE MY LAND BELOW ME.

On the mountain pass, the watchtowers have already been overrun. The Darren troops there are dead. They fought hard, using the pass's narrowness to make up for their small numbers, but in the end there were simply too many of the enemy. The Darre lasted long enough to light the signal fires and send a message: *The enemy is coming.*

The forests are Darr's second line of defense. Many an enemy has faltered here, poisoned by snakes or weakened by disease or worn down by the endless, strangling vines. My people have always taken advantage of this, seeding the forests with wise-women who know how to hide and strike and fade back into the brush, like leopards.

But times have changed, and this time the enemy has brought a special weapon—a scrivener. Once this would have been unheard of in High North; magic is an Amn thing, deemed cowardly by most barbarian standards. Even for those nations willing to try cowardice, the Amn keep their scriveners too expensive to hire. But of course, that is not a problem for an Arameri.

(Stupid, stupid me. I have money. I could have sent a scrivener to fight on Darr's behalf. But in the end, I am still a barbarian; I did not think of it, and now it is too late.)

The scrivener, some contemporary of Viraine's, draws sigils on paper and pastes these to a few trees, and steps back. A column of white-hot fire sears through the forest in an unnaturally straight line. It goes for miles and miles, all the way to the stone walls of Arrebaia, which it smashes against. Clever; if they had set the whole forest afire, it would have burned for months. This is just a narrow path. When it has burned enough, the scrivener sets down more godwords, and the fire goes out. Aside from crumbling, charred trees and the unrecognizable corpses of animals, the way is clear. The enemy can reach Arrebaia within a day.

There is a stir at the edge of the forest. Someone stumbles out, blinded and half-choked by smoke. A wisewoman? No, this is a man—a *boy*, not even old enough to sire daughters. What is he doing out here? We have never allowed boys to fight. And the knowledge comes: my people are desperate. Even children must fight, if we are to survive.

The enemy soldiers swarm over him like ants. They do not kill him. They chain him in a supply cart and carry him along as they march. When they reach Arrebaia, they mean to put him on display to strike at our hearts—oh, and how it will. Our men have always been our treasures. They may slit his throat on the steps of Sar-enna-nem, just to rub salt in the wound.

I should have sent a scrivener.

The ballroom of Sky: a vast, high-ceilinged chamber whose walls were even more vividly mother-of-pearl than the rest of the palace, and tinted a faint rose hue. After the unrelenting white of the rest of Sky, that touch of color seemed almost shockingly vivid. Chandeliers like the starry sky turned overhead; music drifted through the air, complicated Amn stuff, from the sextet of musicians on a nearby dais. The floors, to my surprise, were something other than Skystuff: clear and golden, like dark polished amber. It could not possibly have been amber since there were no seams, and that would have required a chunk of amber the size of a small hill. But that was what it looked like.

And people, filling this glorious space. I was stunned to see the enormous number present, all of them granted special dispensation to stay in Sky for this one night. There must have been a thousand people in the room: preening highbloods and the most officious of the Salon's officials, kings and queens of lands far more important than mine, famous artists and courtesans, everybody who was anybody. I had spent the past few days wholly absorbed in my own troubles, so I had not noticed carriages coming and going all day, as they must have been to bring so many to Sky. My own fault.

I would have happily gone into the room and merged with the crowd as best I could. They all wore white, which was traditional for formal events in Sky. Only I wore a color. But I wouldn't have been able to disappear in any case, because when

I entered the room and stopped at the top of the stairs, a servant nearby— clad in a strange white formal livery that I'd never seen before—cleared his throat and bellowed, loudly enough to make me wince, "The Lady Yeine Arameri, chosen heir of Dekarta, benevolent guardian of the Hundred Thousand Kingdoms! Our guest of honor!"

This obliged me to stop at the top of the steps, as every eye in the room turned to me.

I had never stood before such a horde in my life. Panic filled me for a moment, along with the utter conviction that *they knew.* How could they not? There was polite, restrained applause. I saw smiles on many faces, but no true friendliness. Interest, yes—the kind of interest one holds for a prize heifer that is soon to be slaughtered for the plates of the privileged. *What will she taste like?* I imagined in their gleaming, avid regard. *If only we could have a bite.*

My mouth went dry. My knees locked, which was the only thing that stopped me from turning on my uncomfortably high heels and running out of the room. That, and one other realization: that my parents had met at an Arameri ball. Perhaps in this very room. My mother had stood on the same steps and faced her own roomful of people who hated and feared her behind their smiles.

She would have smiled back at them.

So I fixed my eyes on a point just above the crowd. I smiled, and lifted my hand in a polite and regal wave, and hated them back. It made the fear recede, so that I could then descend the steps without tripping or worrying whether I looked graceful.

Halfway down I looked across the ballroom and saw Dekarta on a dais opposite the door. Somehow they had hauled his huge stone chair-not-throne from the audience chamber. He watched me from within its hard embrace with his colorless eyes.

I inclined my head. He blinked. *Tomorrow*, I thought. *Tomorrow.*

The crowd opened and closed around me like lips.

I made my way through sycophants who attempted to curry favor by making small talk, and more honest folk who merely gave me cool or sardonic nods. Eventually I reached an area where the crowd thinned, which happened to be near a refreshment table. I got a glass of wine from the attendant, drained it, got another, and then spotted arched glass doors to one side. Praying they would open and were not merely decorative, I went to them and found that they led outside, to a wide patio where a few guests had already congregated to take in the magically warmed night air. Some whispered to one another as I went past, but most were too engrossed in secrets or seduction or any of the usual activities that take place in the shadowy corners of such events. I stopped at the railing only because it was there, and spent a while willing my hand to stop shaking so I could drink my wine.

A hand came around me from behind, covering my own and helping me steady the glass. I knew who it was even before I felt that familiar cool stillness against my back.

"They mean for this night to break you," said the Nightlord. His breath stirred my hair, tickled my ear, and set my skin tingling with half a dozen delicious memories. I closed my eyes, grateful for the simplicity of desire.

"They're succeeding," I said.

"No. Kinneth made you stronger than that." He took the glass from my hand and lifted it out of my sight, as if he meant to drink it himself. Then he returned the glass to me. What had been white wine—some incredibly light vintage that had hardly any color and tasted of flowers—was now a red so dark that it seemed black in the balcony light. Even when I raised the glass to the sky, the stars were only a faint glimmer through a lens of deepest burgundy. I sipped experimentally, and shivered as the taste moved over my tongue. Sweet, but with a hint of almost metallic bitterness, and a salty aftertaste like tears.

"And we have made you stronger," said Nahadoth. He spoke into my hair; one of his arms slid around me from behind, pulling me against him. I could not help relaxing against him.

I turned in the half circle of his arm and stopped in surprise. The man who gazed down at me did not look like Nahadoth, not in any guise I'd ever seen. He looked human, Amn, and his hair was a rather dull blond nearly as short as mine. His face was handsome enough, but it was neither the face he wore to please me nor the face that Scimina had shaped. It was just a face. And he wore white. That, more than anything else, shocked me silent.

Nahadoth—because it *was* him, I *felt* that, no matter what he looked like—looked amused. "The Lord of Night is not welcome at any celebration of Itempas's servants."

"I just didn't think…" I touched his sleeve. It was just cloth—something finely made, part of a jacket that looked vaguely military. I stroked it and was disappointed when it did not curl around my fingers in welcome.

"I made the substance of the universe. Did you think white thread would be a challenge?"

That startled me into a laugh, which startled me silent in

the next instant. I had never heard him joke before. What did it mean?

He lifted a hand to my cheek, sobering. It struck me that though he was pretending to be human, he was nothing like his daytime self. Nothing about him was human beyond his appearance—not his movements, not the speed with which he shifted from one expression to another, especially not his eyes. A human mask simply wasn't enough to conceal his true nature. It was so obvious to my eyes that I marveled the other people out on the balcony weren't screaming and running, terrified to find the Nightlord so close.

"My children think I am going mad," he said, stroking my face ever so gently. "Kurue tells me I risk all our hopes over you. She's right."

I frowned in confusion. "My life is still yours. I'll abide by our agreement, even though I've lost the contest. You acted in good faith."

He sighed, to my surprise leaning forward to rest his forehead against mine. "Even now you speak of your life as a commodity, sold for our 'good faith.' What we have done to you is obscene."

I had no idea what to say to that; I was too stunned. It occurred to me, in a flash of insight, that *this* was what Kurue feared—Nahadoth's fickle, impassioned sense of honor. He had gone to war to vent his grief over Enefa; he had kept himself and his children enslaved out of sheer stubbornness rather than forgive Itempas. He could have dealt with his brother differently, in ways that wouldn't have risked the whole universe and destroyed so many lives. But that was the problem: when the Nightlord cared for something, his decisions became irrational, his actions extreme.

And he was beginning, against all reason, to care for me.

Flattering. Frightening. I could not guess what he might do in such a circumstance. But, more important, I realized what this meant in the short term. In only a few hours, I would die, and he would be left to mourn yet again.

How strange that this thought made my own heart ache, too.

I cupped the Nightlord's face between my hands and sighed, closing my eyes so that I could feel the person beneath the mask. "I'm sorry," I said. And I was. I had never meant to cause him pain.

He did not move, and neither did I. It felt good, leaning against his solidity, resting in his arms. It was an illusion, but for the first time in a long while, I felt safe.

I don't know how long we stood there, but we both heard it when the music changed. I straightened and looked around; the handful of guests who had been on the patio with us had gone inside. That meant it was midnight—time for the main dance of the evening, the highlight of the ball.

"Do you want to go in?" Nahadoth asked.

"No, of course not. I'm fine out here."

"They dance to honor Itempas."

I looked at him, confused. "Why should I care about that?"

His smile made me feel warm inside. "Have you turned from the faith of your ancestors so completely?"

"My ancestors worshipped *you*."

"And Enefa, and Itempas, and our children. The Darre were one of the few races who honored us all."

I sighed. "It's been a long time since those days. Too much has changed."

"*You* have changed."

I could say nothing to that; it was true.

On impulse, I stepped away from him and took his hands, pulling him into dancing position. "To the gods," I said. "All of them."

It was so gratifying to surprise him. "I have never danced to honor myself."

"Well, there you are." I shrugged, and waited for the start of a new chorus before pulling him to step with me. "A first time for everything."

Nahadoth looked amused, but he moved easily in time with me despite the complicated steps. Every noble child learned such dances, but I had never really liked them. Amn dances reminded me of the Amn themselves—cold, rigid, more concerned with appearance than enjoyment. Yet here, on a dark balcony under a moonless sky, partnered by a god, I found myself smiling as we wheeled back and forth. It was easy to remember the steps with him exerting gentle guiding pressure against my hands and back. Easy to appreciate the grace of the timing with a partner who glided like the wind. I closed my eyes, leaning into the turns, sighing in pleasure as the music swelled to match my mood.

When the music stopped, I leaned against him and wished the night would never end. Not just because of what awaited me come dawn.

"Will you be with me tomorrow?" I asked, meaning the true Nahadoth, not his daytime self.

"I am permitted to remain myself by daylight for the duration of the ceremony."

"So that Itempas can ask you to return to him."

His breath tickled my hair, a soft, cold laugh. "And this time I shall, but not the way he expects."

I nodded, listening to the slow, strange pulse of his heart. It sounded distant, echoing, as if I heard it across miles. "What will you do if you win? Kill him?"

His moment of silence warned me before the actual answer came. "I don't know."

"You still love him."

He did not answer, though he stroked my back once. I didn't fool myself. It was not me he meant to reassure.

"It's all right," I said. "I understand."

"No," he said. "No mortal could understand."

I said nothing more, and he said nothing more, and thus did the long night pass.

I had endured too many nights with little sleep. I must've fallen asleep standing there, because suddenly I was blinking and lifting my head, and the sky was a different color—a hazy gradient of soupy black through gray. The new moon hovered just above the horizon, a darker blotch against the lightening sky.

Nahadoth's fingers squeezed again gently, and I realized he'd woken me. He was gazing toward the balcony doors. Viraine stood there, and Scimina, and Relad. Their white garments seemed to glow, casting their faces into shadow.

"Time," said Viraine.

I searched inside myself and was pleased to find stillness rather than fear.

"Yes," I said. "Let's go."

Inside, the ball was still in full swing, though there were fewer people dancing now than I had last seen. Dekarta's throne stood empty on the other side of the throng. Perhaps he had left early to prepare.

Once we entered Sky's quiet, preternaturally bright halls, Nahadoth let his guise slip; his hair lengthened and his clothing changed color between one step and another. Pale-skinned again; too many of my relatives around, I supposed. We rode a lift upward, emerging on what I now recognized as Sky's topmost floor. As we exited, I saw the doors to the solarium standing open, the manicured forest beyond shadowed and quiet. The only light came from the palace's central spire, which jutted up from the solarium's heart, glowing like the moon. A fainter path ran from our feet into the trees, directly toward the spire's base.

But I was distracted by the figures who stood on either side of the door.

Kurue I recognized at once; I had not forgotten the beauty of her gold-silver-platinum wings. Zhakkarn, too, was magnificent in silver armor traced with molten sigils, her helm shining in the light. I had last seen that armor in a dream.

The third figure, between them, was at once less impressive and more strange: a sleek, black-furred cat like the leopards of my homeland, though significantly larger. And no forest had given birth to this leopard, whose fur rippled like waves in an unseen wind, iridescent to matte to a familiar, impossibly deep blackness. So he did look like his father, after all.

I could not help smiling. *Thank you,* I mouthed. The cat bared its teeth back in what could never have been misinterpreted as a snarl, and winked one green, slitted eye.

I had no illusions about their presence. Zhakkarn was not in full battle armor just to impress us with its shine. The second Gods' War was about to begin, and they were ready. Sieh—well, maybe Sieh was here for me. And Nahadoth...

I looked back at him over my shoulder. He was not watching

me or his children. Instead his gaze had turned upward, toward
the top of the spire.

Viraine shook his head, apparently deciding not to protest.
He glanced at Scimina, who shrugged; at Relad, who glared at
him as if to say *Why would I possibly care?*

(Our eyes met, mine and Relad's. He was pale, sweat beading
his upper lip, but he nodded to me just slightly. I returned the
nod.)

"So be it," Viraine said, and all walked into the solarium,
toward that central spire.

27

The Ritual of the Succession

At the top of the spire was a room, if it could be called that.

The space was enclosed in glass, like an oversize bell jar. If
not for a faint reflective sheen it would have seemed as though
we stood in the open air, atop a spire sheared flat at the tip. The
floor of the room was the same white stuff as the rest of Sky, and
it was perfectly circular, unlike every other room I'd seen in the
palace in the past two weeks. That marked the room as a space
sacred to Itempas.

We stood high above the great white bulk of the palace. From
the odd angle I could just glimpse the forecourt, recognizing it
by the green blot of the Garden and the jut of the Pier. I had
never realized that Sky itself was circular. Beyond that, the earth

was a darkened mass, seeming to curve 'round us like a great bowl. Circles within circles within circles; a sacred place indeed. Dekarta stood opposite the room's floor entrance. He was leaning heavily on his beautiful Darrwood cane, which he had doubtless needed to get up the steep spiral staircase that led into the room. Behind and above him, predawn clouds covered the sky, bunched and rippled like strings of pearls. They were as gray and ugly as my gown—except in the east, where the clouds had begun to glow yellow-white.

"Hurry up," Dekarta said, nodding toward points around the room's circumference. "Relad there. Scimina there, across from him. Viraine, to me. Yeine, here."

I did as I was bidden, moving to stand before a simple white plinth that rose from the floor, about as high as my chest. There was a hole in its surface perhaps a handspan wide; the shaft that led from the oubliette. A few inches above this shaft a tiny dark object floated, unsupported, in the air. It was withered, misshapen, closely resembling a lump of dirt. *This* was the Stone of Earth? This?

I consoled myself with the fact that at least the poor soul in the oubliette was dead now.

Dekarta paused then, glaring behind me at the Enefadeh. "Nahadoth, you may take your customary position. The rest of you—I did not command your presence."

To my surprise, Viraine answered. "It would serve well to have them here, my Lord. The Skyfather might be pleased to see his children, even these traitors."

"No father is pleased to see children who have turned on him." Dekarta's gaze drifted to me. I wondered if it was me he saw, or just Kinneth's eyes in my face.

"I want them here," I said.

There was no visible reaction from him beyond a tightening of his already-thin lips. "Such good friends they are, to come and watch you die."

"It would be harder to face this without their support, Grandfather. Tell me, did you allow Ygreth any company when you murdered her?"

He drew himself straight, which was rare for him. For the first time I saw a shadow of the man he had been, tall and haughty as any Amn, and formidable as my mother; it startled me to see the resemblance at last. He was too thin for the height now, though; it only emphasized his unhealthy gauntness. "I will not explain my actions to you, Granddaughter."

I nodded. From the corner of my eye I saw the others watching. Relad looked anxious; Scimina, annoyed. Viraine—I could not read him, but he watched me with an intensity that puzzled me. I could not spare thought for it, however. This was perhaps my last chance to find out why my mother had died. I still believed Viraine had done the deed, yet that still made no sense; he'd loved her. But if he had been acting on Dekarta's orders...

"You don't need to explain," I replied. "I can guess. When you were young, you were like these two—" I gestured to Relad and Scimina. "Self-absorbed, hedonistic, cruel. But not as heartless as they, were you? You married Ygreth, and you must have cared for her, or your mother wouldn't have designated her your sacrifice when the time came. But you loved power more, and so you made the trade. You became clan head. And your daughter became your mortal enemy."

Dekarta's lips twitched. I could not tell if this was a sign of emotion, or the palsy that seemed to afflict him now and again. "Kinneth loved me."

"Yes, she did." Because that was the kind of woman my mother had been. She could hate and love at once; she could use one to conceal and fuel the other. She had been, as Nahadoth said, a true Arameri. Only her goals had been different.

"She loved you," I said, "and I think you killed her."

This time I was certain that pain crossed the old man's face. It gave me a moment's satisfaction, though no more than that. The war was lost; this skirmish meant nothing in the grand scale of things. I would die. And while my death would fulfill the desires of so many—my parents, the Enefadeh, myself— I could not face it in such clinical terms. My heart was full of fear.

In spite of myself I turned and looked at the Enefadeh, ranged behind me. Kurue would not meet my eyes, but Zhakkarn did, and she gave me a respectful nod. Sieh: he uttered a soft feline croon that was no less anguished for its inhumanity. I felt tears sting my eyes. Foolishness. Even if I weren't destined to die today, I would be only a hiccup in his endless life. And I was the one who was dying, yet I would miss him terribly.

Finally I looked at Nahadoth, who had hunkered down on one knee behind me, framed by the gray cloud-chains. Of course they would force him to kneel, here in Itempas's place. But it was me he watched, and not the brightening eastern sky. I had expected his expression to be impassive, but it was not. Shame and sorrow and a rage that had shattered planets were in his eyes, along with other emotions too unnerving to name.

Could I trust what I saw? Did I dare? After all, he would soon be powerful again. What did it cost him to pretend love now and thus motivate me to follow through with their plan?

I lowered my eyes, pained. I had been in Sky so long that I no longer trusted even myself.

"I did not kill your mother," Dekarta said.

I started and turned to him. He'd spoken so softly that for a moment I thought I'd misheard. "What?"

"I didn't kill her. I would never have killed her. If she had not hated me I would have begged her to return to Sky, even bring you along." To my shock, I saw wetness on Dekarta's cheeks; he was crying. And glaring at me through his tears. "I would even have tried to love you, for her sake."

"Uncle," said Scimina; her tone bordered on the insolent, practically vibrating with impatience. "While I can appreciate your kindness toward our cousin—"

"Be silent," Dekarta snarled at her. His diamond-pale eyes fixed on her so sharply that she actually flinched. "You don't know how close I came to killing you when I heard of Kinneth's death."

Scimina went stiff, echoing Dekarta's own posture. Predictably she did not obey his order. "That would have been your privilege, my lord. But I had no part in Kinneth's death; I paid no attention to her or this mongrel daughter of hers. I don't even know why you chose her as today's sacrifice."

"To see if she was a true Arameri," Dekarta said very softly. His eyes drifted back to mine. It took three full heartbeats for me to realize what he meant, and the blood drained from my face as I did.

"You thought *I* killed her," I whispered. "Father of All, you honestly believed that."

"Murdering those we love best is a long tradition in our family," Dekarta said.

Beyond us, the eastern sky had grown very bright.

I spluttered. It took me several tries to muster a coherent sentence through my fury, and when I did it was in Darre. I only realized it when Dekarta looked more confused than offended by my curses. "I am not Arameri!" I finished, fists clenched at my sides. "You eat your own young, you feed on suffering, like monsters out of some ancient tale! I will never be one of you in anything but blood, and if I could burn that out of myself I would!"

"Perhaps you aren't one of us," Dekarta said. "Now I see that you are innocent, and by killing you I only destroy what remains of her. There is a part of me which regrets this. But I will not lie, Granddaughter. There is another part of me that will rejoice in your death. You took her from me. She left Sky to be with your father, and to raise you."

"Do you wonder why?" I gestured around the glass chamber, at gods and blood relatives come to watch me die. "*You killed her mother.* What did you think she would do, get over it?"

For the first time since I had met him, there was a flicker of humanity in Dekarta's sad, self-deprecating smile. "I suppose I did. Foolish of me, wasn't it?"

I could not help it; I echoed his smile. "Yes, Grandfather. It was."

Viraine touched Dekarta's shoulder then. A patch of gold had grown against the eastern horizon, bright and warning. Dawn was coming. The time for confessions had passed.

Dekarta nodded, then gazed at me for a long, silent moment before speaking. "I'm sorry," he said very softly. An apology that covered many transgressions. "We must begin."

Even then, I did not say what I believed. I did not point at Viraine and name him my mother's killer. There was still time. I could have asked Dekarta to see to him before completing the succession, as a last tribute to Kinneth's memory. I don't know why I didn't—No. I do. I think in that moment, vengeance and answers ceased to have meaning for me. What difference would it make to know why my mother had died? She would still be dead. What good did it do me to punish her killer? I would be dead, too. Would any of this give meaning to my death, or hers?

There is always meaning in death, child. You will understand, soon.

Viraine began a slow circuit of the room. He raised his hands, lifted his face, and—still walking—began to speak.

"Father of the sky and of the earth below you, master of all creation, hear your favored servants. We beg your guidance through the chaos of transition."

He stopped in front of Relad, whose face looked waxy in the gray light. I did not see the gesture that Viraine made, but Relad's sigil suddenly glowed white, like a tiny sun etched upon his forehead. He did not wince or show any sign of pain, though the light made him look paler still. Nodding to himself, Viraine moved on around the room, now passing behind me. I turned my head to follow him; for some reason it bothered me to have him out of sight.

"We beg your assistance in subduing your enemies." Behind me, Nahadoth had turned his face away from the rising dawn. The black aura around him had begun to wisp away, as it had on the night of Scimina's torture. Viraine touched Nahadoth's forehead. A sigil appeared out of nowhere, also white-hot, and Nahadoth hissed as if this caused him further pain. But the leaking of his aura stopped, and when he lifted his head, panting, the dawn's light no longer seemed to bother him. Viraine moved on.

"We beg your blessing upon your newest chosen," he said, and touched Scimina's forehead. She smiled as her sigil ignited, the white light illuminating her face in stark angles and eager, fierce planes.

Viraine came to stand before me then, with the plinth between us. As he passed behind it, my eyes were again drawn to the Stone of Earth. I had never dreamt it would look so singularly unimpressive.

The lump shivered. For just an instant, a perfect, beautiful silver seed floated there before fading back into the dark lump.

If Viraine had been looking at me in that moment, all might have been lost. I understood what had happened and realized the danger all in a single icy bolt of intuition, and it showed on my face. The Stone was like Nahadoth, like all the gods bound here on earth; its true form was hidden behind a mask. The mask made it seem ordinary, unimportant. But for those who looked upon it and expected more—especially those who knew its true nature—it would become more. It would change its shape to reflect all that they knew.

I was condemned, and the Stone was to be my executioners' blade. I should have seen it as a menacing, terrible thing. That

I saw beauty and promise was a clear warning to any Arameri that I intended to do more than just die today.

Fortunately Viraine was not looking at me. He had turned to face the eastern sky, as had everyone else in the room. I looked from face to face, seeing pride, anxiety, expectation, bitterness. The last was Nahadoth, who alone besides me did not look at the sky. His gaze found mine instead, and held it. Perhaps that was why we alone were not affected as the sun crested the distant horizon, and power made the whole world shiver like a jolted mirror.

From the instant the sun sinks out of mortal sight until the last light fades: that is twilight. From the instant the sun crests the horizon 'til it no longer touches earth: that is dawn.

I looked around in surprise, and caught my breath as before me, the Stone blossomed.

That was the only word that could fit what I saw. The ugly lump shivered, then *unfolded*, layers peeling away to reveal light. But this was not the steady white light of Itempas, nor the wavering unlight of Nahadoth. This was the strange light I had seen in the oubliette, gray and unpleasant, somehow leaching the color from everything nearby. There was no shape to the Stone now, not even the silver apricotseed. It was a star, shining, but somehow strengthless.

Yet I felt its true power, radiating at me in waves that made my skin crawl and my stomach churn. I stepped back inadvertently, understanding now why T'vril had warned off the servants. There was nothing wholesome in this power. It was part of the Goddess of Life, but she was dead. The Stone was just a grisly relic.

"Name your choice to lead our family, Granddaughter," said Dekarta.

I turned away from the Stone, though its radiance made that side of my face itch. My sight went blurry for a moment. I felt weak. The thing was killing me and I hadn't even touched it.

"R-Relad," I said. "I choose Relad."

"What?" Scimina's voice, stunned and outraged. *What did you say, you mongrel?*

Movement behind me. It was Viraine; he had come around to my side of the plinth. I felt his hand on my back, supporting me when the Stone's power made me sway, dizzy. I took it as comfort and made a greater effort to stand. As I did so, Viraine shifted a bit and I caught a glimpse of Kurue. Her expression was grim, resolute.

I thought I understood why.

The sun, as was its wont, was moving quickly. Already half of its bulk was above the horizon line. Soon it would no longer be dawn, but day.

Dekarta nodded, unruffled by Scimina's sudden spluttering. "Take the Stone, then," he commanded me. "Make your choice real."

My choice. I lifted a shaking hand to take the Stone, and wondered if death would hurt. My choice.

"Do it," whispered Relad. He was leaning forward, his whole body taut. "Do it, do it, do it..."

"No!" Scimina again, a scream. I saw her lunge at me from the corner of my eye.

"I'm sorry," Viraine whispered behind me, and suddenly everything stopped.

I blinked, not sure what had happened. Something made me look down. There, poked through the bodice of my ugly dress, was something new: the tip of a knife blade. It had emerged from my body on the right side of my sternum, just beside the swell of my breast. The cloth around it was changing, turning a strange wet black.

Blood, I realized. The Stone's light stole the color even from that.

Lead weighed my arm. What had I been doing? I could not remember. I was very tired. I needed to lie down.

So I did.

And I died.

28

Twilight and Dawn

I REMEMBER WHO I AM NOW.

I have held on to myself, and I will not let that knowledge go.

I carry the truth within myself, future and past, inseparable.

I will see this through.

In the glass-walled chamber, many things happen at once. I move among my former companions, unseen, yet seeing all.

My body falls to the floor, unmoving but for the blood spreading around it. Dekarta stares at me, perhaps seeing other dead women. Relad and Scimina begin shouting at Viraine, their faces distorted.

I do not hear their words. Viraine, gazing down at me with a peculiarly empty expression, shouts something as well, and all of the Enefadeh are frozen in place. Sieh trembles, feline muscles bunched and straining. Zhakkarn, too, quivers, her massive fists clenched. Two of them make no effort to move, I notice, and because I notice, I see them up close. Kurue stands straight, her expression calm but resigned. There is a shadow of sorrow about her, hugging close like the cloak of her wings, but it is not something the others can see.

Nahadoth—ah. The shock in his expression is giving way to anguish as he stares at me. The me on the floor bleeding out, not the me who watches him. How can I be both? *I wonder fleetingly, before dismissing the question. It doesn't matter.*

What matters is that there is real pain in Nahadoth's eyes, and it is more than the horror of a lost chance at freedom. It is not a pure pain, though; he, too, sees other dead women. Would he mourn me at all if I did not carry his sister's soul?

That is an unfair question and small-hearted of me.

Viraine crouches and yanks the knife out of my corpse. More blood spills at this, but not much. My heart has already stopped. I have fallen onto my side, half-curled as if in sleep, but I am not a god. I will not wake up.

"Viraine." Someone. Dekarta. "Explain yourself."

Viraine gets to his feet, glancing at the sky. The sun is three-quarters above the horizon. A strange look crosses his face, a hint of fear. Then it is gone, and he looks down at the bloody knife in his hand and then lets it drop to the floor. The clattering sound is distant, but my vision focuses in close on his hand. My blood has splattered his fingers. They tremble just slightly.

"It was necessary," he says, half to himself. Then he pulls himself together and says, "She was a weapon, my lord. Lady Kinneth's last

strike at you, with the collusion of the Enefadeh. There's no time to explain now, but suffice it to say that if she had touched the Stone, made her wish, all the world would have suffered for it."

Sieh has managed to straighten, perhaps because he has stopped trying to kill Viraine. His voice is lower in his cat form, a half snarl. "How did you know?"

"I told him."

Kurue.

The others stare at her, disbelieving. But she is a goddess. Even as a traitor she will not yield her dignity.

"You have forgotten yourselves," she says, looking at each of her fellow Enefadeh in turn. "We have been too long at the mercy of these creatures. Once we would never have stooped so low as to rely on a mortal—especially not a descendant of the very mortal who betrayed us." She looks at my corpse and sees Shahar Arameri. I carry the burdens of so many dead women. "I would rather die than beg her for my freedom. I would rather kill her and use her death to buy Itempas's mercy."

There is a held breath of silence, at her words. It is not shock; it is rage.

Sieh breaks it first, growling out soft, bitter laughter. "I see. You killed Kinneth."

All the humans in the room start, except Viraine. Dekarta drops his cane, because his gnarled hands have clenched into half fists. He says something. I do not hear it.

Kurue does not seem to hear him, either, though she inclines her head to Sieh. "It was the only sensible course of action. The girl had to die here, at dawn." She points at the Stone. "The soul will linger near its fleshly remnant. And in a moment Itempas will arrive to collect and destroy it at last."

"And our hopes with it," says Zhakkarn, her jaw tight.

Kurue sighs. "Our mother is dead, Sister. Itempas won. I hate it, too—but it's time we accepted this. What did you think would happen if we did manage to free ourselves? Just the four of us, against the Bright Lord and dozens of our brothers and sisters? And the Stone, you realize. We have no one to wield it for us, but Itempas has his Arameri pets. We would end up enslaved again, or worse. No."

Then she turns to glare at Nahadoth. How could I have failed to recognize the look in her eyes? It has always been there. She looks at Nahadoth the way my mother probably looked at Dekarta, with sorrow inseparable from contempt. That should have been enough to warn me.

"Hate me for it if you like, Naha. But remember that if you had only swallowed your foolish pride and given Itempas what he wanted, none of us would be here. Now I will give him what he wants, and he's promised to set me free for it."

Nahadoth speaks very softly. "You're the fool, Kurue, if you think Itempas will accept anything short of my capitulation."

He looks up then. I have no flesh in this vision, this dream, but I want to shiver. His eyes are black through black. The skin around them is crazed with lines and cracks, like a porcelain mask on the verge of shattering. What gleams through these cracks is neither blood nor flesh; it is an impossibly black glow that pulses like a heartbeat. When he smiles, I cannot see his teeth.

"Isn't that true . . . Brother?" His voice holds echoes of emptiness. He is looking at Viraine.

Viraine, half-silhouetted by the dawning sun, turns to Nahadoth—but it is my eyes he seems to meet. The watching, floating me. He smiles. The sorrow and fear in that smile is something that only I, out of this whole room, can possibly understand. I know this instinctively, though I do not know why.

Then, just before the sun's bottommost curve lifts free of the horizon, I recognize what I have seen in him. Two souls. Itempas, like both his siblings, also has a second self.

Viraine flings back his head and screams, and from his throat vomits hot, searing white light. It floods the room in an instant, blinding me. I imagine the people in the city below, and in the surrounding countryside, will see this light from miles away. They will think it is a sun come to earth, and they will be right.

In the brightness I hear the Arameri crying out, except Dekarta. He alone has witnessed this before. When the light fades, I look upon Itempas, Bright Lord of the Sky.

The library etching was surprisingly accurate, though the differences are profound. His face is even more perfect, with lines and symmetry that put mere etching to shame. His eyes are the gold of a blazing noonday sun. Though white like Viraine's, his hair is shorter and tighter-curled than even my own. His skin is darker, too, matte-smooth and flawless. (This surprises me, though it shouldn't. How it must gall the Amn.) I can see, in this first glance, why Naha loves him.

And there is love in Itempas's eyes, too, as he steps around my body and its nimbus of coagulating blood. "Nahadoth," he says, smiling and extending his hands. Even in my fleshless state, I shiver. The things his tongue does to those syllables! He has come to seduce the god of seduction, and oh, has he come prepared.

Nahadoth is abruptly free to rise to his feet, which he does. But he does not take the proffered hands. He walks past Itempas to where my body lies. My corpse is fouled with blood all along one side, but he kneels and lifts me anyhow. He holds me against himself, cradling my head so it does not flop back on my limp neck. There is no expression on his face. He simply looks at me.

If this gesture is calculated to offend, it works. Itempas lowers his hands slowly, and his smile fades.

"Father of All." Dekarta bows with precarious dignity, unsteady without his cane. "We are honored by your presence once again." Murmurs from the sides of the room: Relad and Scimina make their greetings as well. I do not care about them. I exclude them from my perception.

For a moment I think Itempas will not answer. Then he says, still gazing at Nahadoth's back, "You still wear the sigil, Dekarta. Call a servant and finish the ritual."

"At once, Father. But . . ."

Itempas looks at Dekarta, who trails off under that burning-desert gaze. I do not blame him. But Dekarta is Arameri; gods do not frighten him for long.

"Viraine," he says. "You were . . . part of him."

Itempas lets him flounder to silence, then says, "Since your daughter left Sky."

Dekarta looks over at Kurue. "You knew this?"

She inclines her head, regal. "Not at first. But Viraine came to me one day and let me know I need not be damned to this earthly hell for all eternity. Our father could still forgive us, if we proved ourselves loyal." She glances at Itempas then, and even her dignity cannot hide her anxiety. She knows how fickle his favor can be. "Even then I wasn't certain, though I suspected. That was when I decided on my plan."

"But . . . that means . . ." Dekarta pauses then, realization-anger-resignation flickering across his face in quick succession. I can guess his thoughts: Bright Itempas orchestrated Kinneth's death.

My grandfather closes his eyes, perhaps mourning the death of his faith. "Why?"

"Viraine's heart was broken." And does the Father of All realize that his eyes turn to Nahadoth when he says this? Is he aware of what this look reveals? "He wanted Kinneth back, and offered anything if I would help him achieve that goal. I accepted his flesh in payment."

"How predictable." I shift to myself, lying in Nahadoth's arms. Nahadoth speaks above me. "You used him."

"If I could have given him what he wanted, I would have," Itempas replies with a very human shrug. "But Enefa gave these creatures the power to make their own choices. Even we cannot change their minds when they're set on a given course. Viraine was foolish to ask."

The smile that curves Nahadoth's lips is contemptuous. "No, Tempa, that isn't what I meant, and you know it."

And somehow, perhaps because I am no longer alive and no longer thinking with a fleshly brain, I understand. Enefa is dead. Never mind that some remnant of her flesh and soul lingers; both are mere shadows of who and what she truly was. Viraine, however, took into himself the essence of a living god. I shiver as I realize: the moment of Itempas's manifestation was also the moment of Viraine's death. Had he known it was coming? So much of his strangeness became clear, in retrospect.

But before that, disguised by Viraine's mind and soul, Itempas could watch Nahadoth like a voyeur. He could command Nahadoth and thrill in his obedience. He could pretend to be doing Dekarta's will while manipulating events to exert subtle pressure on Nahadoth. All without Nahadoth's knowledge.

Itempas's expression does not change, but there is something about him now that suggests anger. A more burnished shade to his golden eyes, perhaps. "Always so melodramatic, Naha." He steps closer—close enough that the white glow which surrounds him clashes against Nahadoth's smoldering shadow. Where the two powers brush against each other, both light and dark vanish, leaving nothing.

"You clutch that piece of meat like it means something," Itempas says.

"She does."

"Yes, yes, a vessel, I know—but her purpose is served now. She has bought your freedom with her life. Will you not come take your reward?"

Moving slowly, Nahadoth sets my body down. I feel his rage coming before, apparently, anyone else. Even Itempas looks surprised when Nahadoth clenches his fists and slams them into the floor. My blood flies up in twin sprays. The floor cracks ominously, and some of the cracks run up the glass walls—though, fortunately, these only spiderweb and do not shatter. As if in compensation, the plinth at the center of the room shatters instead, spilling the Stone ignominiously onto the floor and peppering everyone with glittering white flecks.

"More," Nahadoth breathes. His skin has cracked further; he is barely contained by the flesh that is his prison. When he rises and turns, his hands drip something too dark to be blood. The cloak that surrounds him lashes the air like miniature tornadoes.

"She . . . was . . . more!" He is barely coherent. He lived countless ages before language. Perhaps his instinct is to forgo speech altogether in moments of extremity, and just roar out his fury. "More than a vessel. She was my last hope. And yours."

Kurue—my vision swings toward her against my will—steps forward, opening her mouth to protest. Zhakkarn catches her arm in warning. *Wise, I think, or at least wiser than Kurue. Nahadoth looks utterly demented.*

But then, so does *Itempas, as he stares down Nahadoth's rage. There is open lust in his eyes, unmistakable beneath the warrior's tension. But of course: how many aeons did they spend battling, raw violence giving way to stranger longings? Or perhaps Itempas has simply been so long without Nahadoth's love that he will take anything, even hate, in its place.*

"Naha," he says gently. "Look at you. All this over a mortal?" He sighs, shaking his head. "I'd hoped that putting you here, amid the vermin that are our sister's legacy, would show you the error of your ways. Now I see that you are merely growing accustomed to captivity."

He steps forward then, and does what every other person in the room would have considered suicide: he touches Nahadoth. It is a brief gesture, just a light brush of his fingers against the cracked porcelain of Nahadoth's face. There is such yearning in that touch that my heart aches.

But does it matter anymore? Itempas has killed Enefa; he has killed his own children; he has killed me. He has killed something in Nahadoth as well. Can he not see that?

Perhaps he does, because his soft look fades, and after a moment he takes his hand away.

"So be it," he says, going cold. "I tire of this. Enefa was a plague, Nahadoth. She took the pure, perfect universe that you and I created and fouled it. I kept the Stone because I did care for her, whatever you might think... and because I thought it might help to sway you."

He pauses then, looking down at my corpse. The Stone has fallen into my blood, less than a handbreadth from my shoulder. Despite Nahadoth's care in setting me down, my head has flopped to one side. One arm is curled upward as if to try and cup the Stone closer. The image is ironic—a mortal woman, killed in the act of trying to lay claim to a goddess's power. And a god's lover.

I imagine Itempas will send me to an especially awful hell.

"But I think it's time our sister dies completely," Itempas says. I cannot tell if he is looking at the Stone or at me. "Let her infestation die with her, and then our lives can be as they were. Have you not missed those days?"

(I notice Dekarta, who stiffens at this. Only he, of the three mortals, seems to realize what Itempas means.)

"I will hate you no less, Tempa," Nahadoth breathes, "when you and I are the last living things in this universe."

Then he is a roaring black tempest, streaking forward in attack, and Itempas is a crackle of white fire bracing to meet him. They collide in a concussion that shatters the glass in the ritual chamber. Mortals scream, their voices almost lost as cold, thin air howls in to fill the void. They fall to the floor as Nahadoth and Itempas streak away, upward—but my perception is drawn to Scimina for an instant. Her eyes fix on the knife that killed me, Viraine's knife, lying not far from her. Relad sprawls dazed amid glass shards and chunks of the broken plinth. Scimina's eyes narrow.

Sieh roars, his voice an echo of Nahadoth's battle cry. Zhakkarn turns to face Kurue, and her pike appears in one hand.

And at the center of it all, unnoticed, untouched, my body and the Stone lie still.

And here we are.

Yes.

You understand what has happened?

I'm dead.

Yes. In the presence of the Stone, which houses the last of my power.

Is that why I'm still here, able to see these things?

Yes. The Stone kills the living. You're dead.

You mean . . . I can come back to life? Amazing. How convenient that Viraine turned on me.

I prefer to think of it as fate.

So what now?

Your body must change. It will no longer be able to bear two souls within itself; that is an ability only mortals possess. I made your kind that way, gifted in ways that we are not, but I never dreamt it would make you so strong. Strong enough to defeat me, in spite of all my efforts. Strong enough to take my place.

What? No. I don't want your place. You are you. I am me. I have fought for this.

And fought well. But my essence, all that I am, is necessary for this world to continue. If I am not to be the one who restores that essence, then it must be you.

But—

I do not regret, Daughter, Little Sister, worthy heir. Neither should you. I only wish . . .

I know your wish.

Do you really?

Yes. They are blinded by pride, but underneath there is still love. The Three are meant to be together. I will see it done.

Thank you.

Thank *you*. And farewell.

I can ponder for an eternity. I am dead. I have all the time I want.

But I was never very patient.

In and around the glass room, which no longer has glass and probably no longer qualifies as a room, battle rages.

Itempas and Nahadoth have taken their fight to the skies they once shared. Above the motes they have become, dark streaks break the gradient of dawn, like strips of night layered over the morning. A blazing white beam, like the sun but a thousand times brighter, sears across these to shatter them. There is no point to this. It is daytime. Nahadoth would already be asleep within his human prison if not for Itempas's parole. Itempas can revoke that parole whenever he wishes. He must be enjoying himself.

Scimina has gotten Viraine's knife. She has flung herself on Relad, trying to gut him. He's stronger, but she has leverage and the strength of ambition on her side. Relad's eyes are wide with terror; perhaps he has always feared something like this.

Sieh, Zhakkarn, and Kurue feint and circle in a deadly metal-and-claw dance. Kurue has conjured a pair of gleaming bronze swords to defend herself. This contest, too, is foregone; Zhakkarn is battle incarnate, and Sieh has all the power of childhood's cruelty. But Kurue is wily, and she has the taste of freedom in her mouth. She will not die easily.

Amid all this, Dekarta moves toward my body. He stops and struggles to his knees; in the end he slips in my blood and half-falls on me, grimacing in pain. Then his expression hardens. He looks up into the sky, where his god fights, then down. At the Stone. It is the source of the Arameri clan's power; it is also the physical representation of their duty. Perhaps he hopes that by doing that duty, he will remind Itempas of the value of life. Perhaps he retains some smidgeon of faith. Perhaps it is simply that forty years ago, Dekarta killed his wife to prove his commitment. To do otherwise now would mock her death.

He reaches for the Stone.

It is gone.

But it was there, lying in my blood, a moment before. Dekarta frowns, looks around. His eyes are attracted by movement. The hole in my chest, which he can see through the torn cloth of my bodice: the raw lips of the wound are drawing together, pressing themselves closed. As the line of the wound shrinks, Dekarta catches a glimmer of thin gray light. Within me.

Then I am drawn forward, down—

Yes. Enough of this disembodied soul business. Time to be alive again.

I opened my eyes and sat up.

Dekarta, behind me, made a sound somewhere between choking and a gasp. No one else noticed as I got to my feet, so I turned to face him.

"Wh—what in every god's name—" His mouth worked. He stared.

"Not every god," I said. And because I was still me after all, I leaned down to smile in his face. "Just me."

Then I closed my eyes and touched my chest. Nothing beat beneath my fingers; my heart had been destroyed. Yet something was there, giving life to my flesh. I could feel it. The Stone. A thing of life, born of death, filled with incalculable potential. A seed.

"*Grow,*" I whispered.

29

The Three

As with any birth, there was pain.

I believe I screamed. I think that in that instant many things occurred. I have a vague sense of the sky wheeling overhead, cycling day through day and night and back to morning in the span of a breath. (If this happened, then what moved was not the sky.) I have a feeling that somewhere in the universe an uncountable number of new species burst into existence, on millions of planets. I am fairly certain that tears fell from my eyes. Where they landed, lichens and moss began to cover the floor.

I cannot be certain of any of this. Somewhere, in dimensions for which there are no mortal words, I was changing, too. This occupied a great deal of my awareness.

But when the changes were done, I opened my eyes and saw new colors.

The room practically glowed with them. The iridescence of the floor's Skystuff. Glints of gold from glass shards lying about the room. The blue of the sky—it had been a watery blue-white, but now it was such a vivid teal that I stared at it in wonder. It had never, at least in my lifetime, been so blue.

Next I noticed scent. My body had become something else, less a *body* than an *embodiment*, but its shape for the moment was still human, as were my senses. And something was different

here, too. When I inhaled, I could taste the crisp, acrid thinness of the air, underlaid by the metallic scent of the blood that
covered my clothing. I touched my fingers to this and tasted it.
Salt, more metal, hints of bitter and sour. Of course; I had been
unhappy for days before I died.

New colors. New scents in the air. I had never realized, before
now, what it meant to live in a universe that had lost one-third
of itself. The Gods' War had cost us so much more than mere
lives.

No more, I vowed.

Around me the chaos had stopped. I did not want to talk, to
think, but a sense of responsibility pushed insistently against
my reverie. At last I sighed and focused on my surroundings.

To my left stood three shining creatures, stronger than the
rest, more malleable in form. I recognized in them an essence of
myself. They stared at me, weapons frozen in hand or on claw,
mouths agape. Then one of them moulded himself into a different shape—a child—and came forward. His eyes were wide.
"M-Mother?"

That was not my name. I would have turned away in disinterest had it not occurred to me that this would hurt him. Why
did that matter? I didn't know, but it bothered me.

So instead I said, "No." On impulse, I reached out to stroke
his hair. His eyes got even wider, then spilled over with tears.
He pulled away from me then, covering his face. I did not know
what to make of this behavior, so I turned to the others.

Three more to my right—or rather, two, and one dying. Also
shining creatures, though their light was hidden within them,
and their bodies were weaker and crude. And finite. The dying
one expired as I watched, too many of his organs having been

damaged to sustain life. I felt the rightness of their mortality even as I mourned it.

"What is this?" demanded one of them. The younger one, the female. Her gown and hands were splattered with her brother's blood.

The other mortal, old and close to death himself, only shook his head, staring at me.

Then suddenly two more creatures stood before me, and I caught my breath at the sight. I could not help myself. They were so beautiful, even beyond the shells they wore to interact with this plane. They were part of me, kin, and yet so very different. I had been born to be with them, to bridge the gap between them and complete their purpose. To stand with them now—I wanted to throw back my head and sing with joy.

But something was wrong. The one who felt like light and stillness and stability—he was whole, and glorious. Yet there was something unwholesome at his core. I looked closer and perceived a great and terrible loneliness within him, eating at his heart like a worm in an apple. That sobered me, softened me, because I knew what that kind of loneliness felt like.

The same blight was in the other being, the one whose nature called to everything dark and wild. But something more had been done to him; something terrible. His soul had been battered and crushed, bound with sharp-edged chains, then forced into a too-small vessel. Constant agony. He had gone down on one knee, staring at me through dull eyes and lank, sweat-soaked hair. Even his own panting caused him pain.

It was an obscenity. But a greater obscenity was the fact that the chains, when I followed them to their source, were *part of me.* So were three other leashes, one of which led to the neck of the creature who had called me Mother.

Revolted, I tore the chains away from my chest and willed them to shatter.

The three creatures to my left all gasped, folding in on themselves as power returned to them. Their reaction was nothing, however, compared to that of the dark being. For an instant he did not move, only widening his eyes as the chains loosened and fell away.

Then he flung his head back and screamed, and all existence shifted. On this plane, this manifested as a single, titanic concussion of sound and vibration. All sight vanished from the world, replaced by a darkness profound enough to drive weaker souls mad if it lasted for more than a heartbeat. It passed even more quickly than that, replaced by something new.

Balance: I felt its return like the setting of a dislocated joint. Out of Three had the universe been formed. For the first time in an age, Three walked again.

When all was still, I saw that my dark one was whole. Where once restless shadows had flickered in his wake, now he shone with an impossible negative radiance, black as the Maelstrom. Had I thought him merely beautiful before? Ah, but now there was no human flesh to filter his cool majesty. His eyes glowed blue-black with a million mysteries, terrifying and exquisite. When he smiled, all the world shivered, and I was not immune.

Yet this shook me on an entirely different level, because suddenly memory surged through me. They were pallid, these memories, as of something half-forgotten—but they pushed at me, demanding acknowledgment, until I made a sound and shook

my head and batted at the air in protest. They were part of me,
and though I understood now that names were as ephemeral as
form for my kind, those memories insisted upon giving the dark
creature a name: Nahadoth.

And the bright one: Itempas.

And me—

I frowned in confusion. My hands rose in front of my face,
and I stared at them as if I had never seen them. In a way, I
had not. Within me was the gray light I had so hated before,
transformed now into all the colors that had been stolen from
existence. Through my skin I could see those colors dancing
along my veins and nerves, no less powerful for being hidden.
Not my power. But it was my flesh, wasn't it? Who was I?

"Yeine," said Nahadoth in a tone of wonder.

A shudder passed through me, the same feeling of balance I'd
had a moment before. Suddenly I understood. It *was* my flesh,
and my power, too. I was what mortal life had made me, what
Enefa had made me, but all that was in the past. From henceforth I could be whomever I wanted.

"Yes," I said, and smiled at him. "That is my name."

Other changes were necessary.

Nahadoth and I turned to face Itempas, who watched us with
eyes as hard as topaz.

"Well, Naha," he said, though the hate in his eyes was all
for me. "I must congratulate you; this is a fine coup. I thought
killing the girl would be sufficient. Now I see I should have
obliterated her entirely."

"That would have taken more power than you possess," I
said. A frown flickered across Itempas's face. He was so easy to

read; did he realize that? He still thought of me as a mortal, and mortals were insignificant to him.

"You aren't Enefa," he snapped.

"No, I'm not." I could not help smiling. "Do you know why Enefa's soul lingered all these years? It wasn't because of the Stone."

His frown deepened with annoyance. What a prickly creature he was. What did Naha see in him? No, that was jealousy speaking. Dangerous. I would not repeat the past.

"The cycle of life and death flows from me and through me," I said, touching my breast. Within it, something—not quite a heart—beat strong and even. "Even Enefa never truly understood this about herself. Perhaps she was always meant to die at some point; and now, perhaps I am the only one of us who will never be truly immortal. But by the same token, neither can I truly die. Destroy me and some part will always linger. My soul, my flesh, perhaps only my memory—but it will be enough to bring me back."

"Then I simply wasn't thorough enough," Itempas said, and his tone promised dire things. "I'll be sure to rectify that next time."

Nahadoth stepped forward. The dark nimbus that surrounded him made a faint crackling sound as he moved, and white flecks—moisture frozen out of the air—drifted to the floor in his wake.

"There will be no next time, Tempa," he said with frightening gentleness. "The Stone is gone and I am free. I will tear you apart, as I have planned for all the long nights of my imprisonment."

Itempas's aura blazed like white flames; his eyes glowed

like twin suns. "I threw you broken to the earth once before, Brother, and I can do it again—"

"Enough," I said.

Nahadoth's answer was a hiss. He crouched, his hands suddenly monstrous claws at his sides. There was a blur of movement and suddenly Sieh was beside him, a feline shadow. Kurue moved as if to join Itempas, but instantly Zhakkarn's pike was at her throat.

None of them paid any attention to me. I sighed.

The knowledge of my power was within me, as instinctive as *how to think* and *how to breathe*. I closed my eyes and reached for it, and felt it uncurl and stretch within me, ready. Eager.

This was going to be fun.

The first blast of power that I sent through the palace was violent enough to stagger everyone, even my quarrelsome brothers, who fell silent in surprise. I ignored them and closed my eyes, tapping and shaping the energy to my will. There was so much! If I was not careful, I could so easily destroy rather than create. On some level I was aware of being surrounded by colored light: cloudy gray, but also the rose of sunset and the white-green of dawn. My hair wafted in it, shining. My gown swirled about my ankles, an annoyance. A flick of my will and it became a Darren warrior's garments, tight-laced sleeveless tunic and practical calf-length pants. They were an impractical shining silver, but—well, I *was* a goddess, after all.

Walls—rough, brown, *tree-bark*—appeared around us. They did not completely enclose the room; here and there were gaps, though as I watched those filled. Branches nearby grew, split, and sprouted curling leaves. Above us the sky was still visible, though dimmer, thanks to the leafy canopy that now spread there. Through that canopy rose a titanic tree trunk, gnarling and curving high into the sky.

In fact the tree's topmost branches *pierced* the sky. If I looked down on this world from above I would see white clouds and blue seas and brown earth and a single magnificent tree, breaking the planet's smooth round curve. If I flew closer I would see roots like mountains, nestling the whole of Sky-the-city between the forks. I would see branches as long as rivers. I would see people on the ground below, shaken and terrified, crawling out of their homes and picking themselves up from the sidewalks to stare in awe at the great tree that had twined itself around the Skyfather's palace.

In fact I saw all of these things without ever opening my eyes. Then I did open them, to find my brothers and children staring at me.

"Enough," I said again. This time they paid attention. "This realm cannot endure another Gods' War. I will not permit it."

"You will not *permit*...?" Itempas clenched his fists, and I felt the heavy, blistering smolder of his power. For a moment it frightened me, and with good reason. He had bent the universe to his will at the beginning of time; he far outstripped me in experience and wisdom. I didn't even know how to fight as gods fought. He did not attack because there were two of us to his one, but that was the only thing holding him back.

Then there is hope, I decided.

As if reading my thoughts, Nahadoth shook his head. "No, Yeine." His eyes were black holes in his skull, ready to swallow worlds. The hunger for retribution curled off him like smoke. "He murdered Enefa even though he loved her. He'll have no qualms at all over you. We must destroy him, or be destroyed ourselves."

A quandary. I held no grudge against Itempas—he had murdered Enefa, not me. But Nahadoth had millennia of pain to expunge; he deserved justice. And worse, he was right. Itempas was mad, poisoned by his own jealousy and fear. One did not allow the mad to roam free, lest they hurt others or themselves.

Yet killing him was also impossible. Out of Three had the universe been made. Without all Three, it would all end.

"I can think of only one solution," I said softly. And even that was imperfect. After all, I knew from experience how much damage even a single mortal could inflict on the world, given enough time and power. We would just have to hope for the best.

Nahadoth frowned as he read my intention, but some of the hate flowed out of him. Yes; I had thought this might satisfy him. He nodded once in agreement.

Itempas stiffened as he realized what we meant to do. Language had been his invention; we had never really needed words. "I will not tolerate this."

"You will," I said, and joined my power with Nahadoth's. It was an easy fusion, more proof that we Three were meant to work together and not at odds. Someday, when Itempas had served his penance, perhaps we could truly be Three again. What wonders we would create then! I would look forward to it, and hope.

"You will serve," Nahadoth said to Itempas, and his voice was cold and heavy with the weight of law. I felt reality reshape itself. We had never really needed a separate language, either; any tongue would do, as long as one of us spoke the words. "Not a single family, but all the world. You will wander among mortals as one of them, unknown, commanding only what wealth and respect you can earn with your deeds and words. You may call upon your power only in great need, and only to aid these mortals for whom you hold such contempt. You will right all the wrongs inflicted in your name."

Nahadoth smiled then. This smile was not cruel—he was free and had no need of cruelty anymore—but neither was there mercy in him. "I imagine this task will take some time."

Itempas said nothing, because he could not. Nahadoth's words had taken hold of him, and with the aid of my power the words wove chains that no mortal could see or sever. He fought the chaining, once unleashing his power against ours in a furious blast, but it was no use. A single member of the Three could never hope to defeat the other two. Itempas had used those odds in his own favor long enough to know better.

But I could not leave it at that. A proper punishment was meant to redeem the culprit, not just assuage the victims.

"Your sentence can end sooner," I said, and my words, too, curved and linked and became hard around him, "if you learn to love truly."

Itempas glared at me. He had not been driven to his knees by the weight of our power, but it was a near thing. He stood now with back bowed, trembling all over, the white flames of his aura gone and his face sheened with a very mortal sweat. "I . . . will never . . . love you," he gritted through his teeth.

I blinked in surprise. "Why would I want your love? You're a monster, Itempas, destroying everything you claim to care for. I see such loneliness in you, such suffering—but all of it is your own doing."

He flinched, his eyes widening. I sighed, shook my head, and stepped close, lifting a hand to his cheek. He flinched again at my touch, though I stroked him until he quieted.

"But I am only one of your lovers," I whispered. "Haven't you missed the other?"

And as I had expected, Itempas looked at Nahadoth. Ah, the need in his eyes! If there had been any hope of it, I would have asked Nahadoth to share this moment with us. Just one kind word might have speeded Itempas's healing. But it would be centuries before Nahadoth's own wounds had healed enough for that.

I sighed. So be it. I would do what I could to make it easier for both of them, and try again when the ages had worked their magic. I had made a promise, after all.

"When you're ready to be among us again," I whispered to Itempas, "I, at least, will welcome you back." Then I kissed him, and filled that kiss with all the promise I could muster. But some of the surprise that passed between us was mine, for his mouth was soft despite its hard lines. Underneath that I could taste hot spices and warm ocean breezes; he made my mouth water and my whole body ache. For the first time I understood why Nahadoth loved him—and by the way his mouth hung open when I pulled back, I think he felt the same.

I looked over at Nahadoth, who sighed with too-human weariness. "He doesn't change, Yeine. He can't."

"He can if he wants to," I said firmly.

"You are naive."

Maybe I was. But that didn't make me wrong.

I kept my eyes on Itempas, though I went to Naha and took his hand. Itempas watched us like a man dying of thirst, within sight of a waterfall. It would be hard for him, the time to come, but he was strong. He was one of us. And one day, he would be ours again.

Power folded around Itempas like the petals of a great flower, scintillating. When the light faded, he was human—his hair no longer shining, his eyes merely brown. Handsome, but not perfect. Just a man. He fell to the floor, unconscious from the shock.

With that done, I turned to Nahadoth.

"No," he said, scowling.

"He deserves the same chance," I said.

"I promised him release already."

"Death, yes. I can give him more." I stroked Nahadoth's cheek, which flickered beneath my hand. His face changed every moment now, beautiful no matter how it looked—though the mortals probably would not have thought so, since some of his faces were not human. I was no longer human myself. I could accept all of Nahadoth's faces, so he had no need of any one in particular.

He sighed and closed his eyes at my touch, which both gratified and troubled me. He had been too long alone. I would have to take care not to exploit this weakness of his now, or he would hate me for it later.

Still, this had to be done. I said, "He deserves freedom, same as you."

He gave me a heavy sigh. But his sigh took the form of tiny black stars, surprisingly bright as they sparkled and multiplied and coalesced into a human form. For a moment a negative phantasm of the god stood before me. I willed it to life, and it became a man: Nahadoth's daytime self. He looked around,

then stared at the shining being who had been his other half
for so long. They had never met in all that time, but his eyes
widened with realization.

"My gods," he breathed, too awed to realize the irony of his
oath.

"Yeine—"

I turned to find Sieh beside me in his child form. He stood
taut, his green eyes searching my face. "Yeine?"

I reached for him, then hesitated. He was not mine, despite
my possessive feelings.

He reached up just as hesitantly, touching my arms and face
in wonder. "You really... aren't her?"

"No. Just Yeine." I lowered my hand, letting him choose. I
would respect his decision if he rejected me. But... "Was this
what you wanted?"

"Wanted?" The look on his face would have gratified colder
hearts than mine. He put his arms around me, and I pulled him
close and held him tightly. "Ah, Yeine, you're still such a mortal," he whispered against my breast. But I felt him trembling.

Over Sieh's head, I looked at my other children. Stepchildren,
perhaps; yes, that was a safer way to think of them. Zhakkarn
inclined her head to me, a soldier acknowledging a new commander. She would obey, which was not quite what I wanted,
but it would do for now.

Kurue, though, was another matter.

Gently disentangling myself from Sieh, I stepped toward her.
Kurue dropped immediately to one knee and bowed her head.

"I will not beg your forgiveness," she said. Only her voice
betrayed her fear; it was not its usual strong, clear tone. "I did
what I felt was right."

"Of course you did," I said. "It was the wise thing to do." As I had done with Sieh, I reached out and stroked her hair. It was long and silver in this form of hers, like metal spun into curls. Beautiful.

I let it trail through my fingers as Kurue fell to the floor, dead.

"Yeine." Sieh, sounding stunned. For the moment I ignored him, because my eyes happened to meet Zhakkarn's as I looked up. She inclined her head again, and I knew then that I had earned a measure of her respect.

"Darr," I said.

"I'll see to things," Zhakkarn replied, and vanished.

The amount of relief I felt surprised me. Perhaps I had not left my humanity so very far behind after all.

Then I turned to face everyone in the chamber. A branch was growing across the room, but I touched it and it grew in a different direction, out of the way. "You, too," I said to Scimina, who blanched and stepped back.

"No," said Nahadoth abruptly. He turned to Scimina then and smiled; the room grew darker. "This one is mine."

"No," she whispered, taking another step back. If she could have bolted—another branch had covered the stairway entrance—I'm certain she would have, though of course that would have been pointless. "Just kill me."

"No more orders," Nahadoth said. He lifted a hand, the fingers curling as if to grip an invisible leash, and Scimina cried out as she was jerked forward, falling to her knees at his feet. She clutched at her throat, fingers scrabbling for some way to free herself, but there was nothing there. Naha leaned down, taking her chin in his fingers, and laid a kiss on her lips that was no less chilling for its tenderness. "I will kill you, Scimina, never fear. Just not yet."

I felt no pity. That, too, was a remnant of my humanity.

Which left only Dekarta.

He sat on the floor, where he had been thrown during the manifestation of my tree. When I went to him, I could see the throbbing ache in his hip, which was broken, and the unstable flutter of his heart. Too many shocks. It had not been a good night for him. But he smiled as I crouched before him, to my surprise.

"A goddess," he said, then barked out a single laugh that was remarkably free of bitterness. "Ah, Kinneth never did things by half measures, did she?"

In spite of myself, I shared his smile. "No. She didn't."

"So, then." He lifted his chin and regarded me imperiously, which would have worked better if he had not been panting due to his heart. "What of us, Goddess Yeine? What of your human kin?"

I wrapped my arms around my knees, balancing on my toes. I had forgotten to make shoes.

"You'll choose another heir, who will hold on to your power as best he can. Whether he succeeds or not, we will be gone, Naha and I, and Itempas will be useless to you. It should be interesting to see what mortals make of the world without our constant interference."

Dekarta stared at me in disbelief and horror. "Without the gods, every nation on this planet will rise up to destroy us. Then they'll turn on each other."

"Perhaps."

"*Perhaps?*"

"It will definitely happen," I said, "if your descendants are fools. But the Enefadeh have never been the Arameri's sole weapon, Grandfather; you know that better than anyone. You have more wealth than any single nation, enough to hire and equip whole armies. You have the Itempan priesthood, and they will be very motivated to spread your version of the truth, since they are threatened, too. And you have your own fine-honed viciousness, which has served well enough as a weapon all this time." I shrugged. "The Arameri can survive, and perhaps even retain power for a few generations. Enough, hopefully, to temper the worst of the world's wrath."

"There will be change," said Nahadoth, who was suddenly beside me. Dekarta drew back, but there was no malice in Nahadoth's eyes. Slavery was what had driven him half mad; already he was healing. "There must be change. The Arameri have kept the world still for too long, against nature. This must now correct itself in blood."

"But if you're clever," I added, "you'll get to keep most of yours."

Dekarta shook his head slowly. "Not me. I'm dying. And my heirs—they had the strength to rule as you say, but…" He glanced over at Relad, who lay open-eyed on the floor with a knife stuck in his throat. He had bled even more than I.

"Uncle—" Scimina began, but Nahadoth jerked her leash to silence her. Dekarta glanced once in her direction, then away.

"You have another heir, Dekarta," I said. "He's clever and competent, and I believe he's strong enough—though he will not thank me for recommending him."

I smiled to myself, seeing without eyes through the layers of Sky. Within, the palace was not so very different. Bark and branches had replaced the pearly Skystuff in places, and some of the dead spaces had been filled with living wood. But even this simple change was enough to terrify the denizens of Sky, highblood and low alike. At the heart of the chaos was T'vril, marshaling the palace's servants and organizing an evacuation.

Yes, he would do nicely.

Dekarta's eyes widened, but he knew an order when he heard one. He nodded, and in return, I touched him and willed his hip whole and his heart stable. That would keep him alive a few days longer—long enough to see the transition through.

"I...I don't understand," said the human Naha, as the godly version and I got to our feet. He looked deeply shaken. "Why have you done this? What do I do now?"

I looked at him in surprise. "Live," I said. "Why else do you think I put you here?"

There was much more to be done, but those were the parts that mattered. You would have enjoyed all of it, I think—righting the imbalances triggered by your death, discovering existence anew. But perhaps there are interesting discoveries to be had where you've gone, too.

It surprises me to admit it, but I shall miss you, Enefa. My soul is not used to solitude.

Then again, I will never be *truly* alone, thanks to you.

Sometime after we left Sky and Itempas and the mortal world behind, Sieh took my hand. "Come with us," he said.

"Where?"

Nahadoth touched my face then, very gently, and I was awed and humbled by the tenderness in his gaze. Had I earned such warmth from him? I hadn't—but I would. I vowed this to myself, and lifted my face for his kiss.

"You have much to learn," he murmured against my lips when we parted. "I have so many wonders to show you."

I could not help grinning like a human girl. "Take me away, then," I said. "Let's get started."

So we passed beyond the universe, and now there is nothing more to tell.

Of this tale, anyhow.

A Glossary of Terms

Altarskirt rose: A rare, specially bred variety of white rose, highly prized.

Amn: Most populous and powerful of the Senmite races.

Arameri: Ruling family of the Amn; advisors to the Nobles' Consortium and the Order of Itempas.

Arrebaia: Capital city of Darr.

Blood sigil: The mark of a recognized Arameri family member.

Bright, the: The time of Itempas's solitary rule after the Gods' War. General term for goodness, order, law, rightness.

Darkling: Those races that adopted the exclusive worship of Itempas only after the Gods' War, under duress. Includes most High Northern and island peoples.

Darr: A High North nation.

Dekarta Arameri: Head of the Arameri family.

Demon: Children of forbidden unions between gods/godlings and mortals. Extinct.

Enefa: One of the Three. The Betrayer. Deceased.

Enefadeh: Those who remember Enefa.

Gods: Immortal children of the Maelstrom. The Three.

Godling: Immortal children of the Three. Sometimes also referred to as gods.

Gods' Realm: Beyond the universe.

Gods' War: An apocalyptic conflict in which Bright Itempas claimed rulership of the heavens after defeating his two siblings.

Heavens, Hells: Abodes for souls beyond the mortal realm.

Heretic: A worshipper of any god but Itempas. Outlawed.

High North: Northernmost continent. A backwater.

Hundred Thousand Kingdoms: Collective term for the world since its unification under Arameri rule.

Irt: An island nation.

Islands, the: Vast archipelago east of High North and Senm.

Itempan: General term for a worshipper of Itempas. Also used to refer to members of the Order of Itempas.

Itempas: One of the Three. The Bright Lord; master of heavens and earth; the Skyfather.

Ken: Largest of the island nations, home to the Ken and Min peoples.

Kinneth Arameri: Only daughter of Dekarta Arameri.

Kurue: A godling, also called the Wise.

Lift: A magical means of transportation within Sky; a lesser version of the Vertical Gates.

Maelstrom: The creator of the Three. Unknowable.

Magic: The innate ability of gods and godlings to alter the material and immaterial world. Mortals may approximate this ability through the use of the gods' language.

Menchey: A High North nation.

Mortal realm: The universe, created by the Three.

Nahadoth: One of the Three. The Nightlord.

Narshes: A High North race whose homeland was conquered by the Tok several centuries ago.

Nobles' Consortium: Ruling political body of the Hundred Thousand Kingdoms.

Order of Itempas: The priesthood dedicated to Bright Itempas. In addition to spiritual guidance, also responsible for law and order, education, and the eradication of heresy. Also known as the Itempan Order.

Relad Arameri: Nephew of Dekarta Arameri, twin brother of Scimina.

Salon: Headquarters for the Nobles' Consortium.

Sar-enna-nem: Seat of the Darren *ennu* and the Warriors' Council.

Scimina Arameri: Niece of Dekarta Arameri, twin sister of Relad.

Scrivener: A scholar of the gods' written language.

Senm: Southernmost and largest continent of the world.

Senmite: The Amn language, used as a common tongue for all the Hundred Thousand Kingdoms.

Shahar Arameri: High Priestess of Itempas at the time of the Gods' War. Her descendants are the Arameri family.

Sieh: A godling, also called the Trickster. Eldest of all the godlings.

Sigil: An ideograph of the gods' language, used by scriveners to imitate the magic of the gods.

Sky: Largest city on the Senm continent. Also, the palace of the Arameri family.

Stone of Earth: An Arameri family heirloom.

Tema: A Senmite kingdom.

Time of the Three: Before the Gods' War.

Tokland: A High North nation.

T'vril Arameri: A grandnephew of Dekarta.

Uthr: An island nation.

Vertical Gate: A magical means of transportation between Sky (the city) and Sky (the palace).

Viraine Arameri: First Scrivener of the Arameri.

Walking Death: A virulent plague that appears in frequent epidemics. Affects only those of low social status.

Yeine Darr: A granddaughter of Dekarta and daughter of Kinneth.

Ygreth: Wife of Dekarta, mother of Kinneth. Deceased.

Zhakkarn of the Blood: A godling.

APPENDIX
2

A Clarification of Terms[1]

In the name of Itempas Skyfather, most Bright and peaceful.

The Conspirators, as they are properly called,[2] are like all gods in that they possess complete mastery over the material world[3] as well as most things spiritual. Though not omnipotent—only the Three, when united, were so gifted—their individual power is so great relative to that of mortals that the difference is academic. However, the Bright Lord in His wisdom has seen fit to greatly limit the power of the Conspirators as a punishment, thus enabling their use as tools for the betterment of mortalkind.

Their disparate natures impose further limitations, different for each individual. We refer to this as *affinity*, since gods'

1. Initial compilation by First Scrivener and Order of the White Flame Ordinate Sefim Arameri, in the 55th year of the Bright. Subsequent revisions by First Scriveners Comman Knorn/Arameri (170), Latise Arameri (1144), Bir Get/Arameri (1721), and Viraine Derreye/Arameri (2224).

2. The subjects do not refer to themselves as such, but this terminology was agreed upon per the *Munae Scrivan*, 7th Reiterate, year 230 of the Bright.

3. Defined as *magic* per Litaria standard terminology, 1st progression.

language appears to have no term for it. Affinities can be either material or conceptual, or some combination thereof.[4] An example of which is the Conspirator called Zhakkarn, who holds dominion over all things combat-related including weaponry (material), strategy (conceptual), and the martial arts (both). In actual battle she has the unique ability to replicate herself thousands of times over, becoming a literal one-woman army.[5] However, she has also been observed to avoid any gathering of mortals for peaceful purposes, such as holiday celebrations. Indeed, being near religious paraphernalia symbolizing peace, such as the white jade ring worn by our order's highest devotees, causes her acute discomfort.

As the Conspirators are in fact prisoners of war, and we of the family are in fact their jailors, understanding the concept of affinity is essential as it represents our only means of imposing discipline.

Additionally, we must understand the restrictions imposed upon them by Our Lord. The primary and common means by which the Conspirators have been limited is *corporeality*. It has been observed that a god's natural state is immaterial,[6] thus permitting the god to draw upon immaterial resources (e.g., the motion of heavenly bodies, the growth of living things) for sustenance and normal function. The Conspirators, however, are not permitted to enter the aetheric state and are instead required to maintain a physical locality at all times. This restricts their range of operability to the limits of their human senses, and it

4. See *On Magic*, volume 12.
5. As observed in the Pells War, the Ulan Uprising, and other occasions.
6. Hereinafter referred to as *aetheric* per Litaria standard terminology, 4th progression.

restricts their power to that which may be contained by this material form.[7] This restriction also requires them to ingest food and drink in the mortal fashion in order to maintain strength. Experiments[8] have shown that when deprived of sustenance or otherwise physically traumatized, the Conspirators' magical abilities diminish greatly or entirely until they have returned to health. Due to the Stone of Earth's role in their imprisonment, however, they perpetually retain the ability to regenerate aged or damaged flesh and revive from apparent death, even when their bodies are virtually destroyed. Therefore it is a misnomer to say that they have "mortal forms"; their physical bodies are only superficially mortal.

In the next chapter, we will discuss the specific peculiarities of each of the Conspirators, and the means by which each might be better controlled.

7. Scrivener Pjors, in "The Limitations of Mortality" (*Munae Scrivan*, pp. 40–98), argues that no other mortals have been able to achieve comparable power, and therefore the Conspirators' abilities clearly exceed the material. Consensus within the Scriveners' College and Litaria holds that this is the purposeful doing of Our Lord, who intended that the Conspirators retain enough godly might to be of use in the aftermath of the Gods' War.

8. Family Notes, various, volumes 12, 15, 24, and 37.

APPENDIX

3

Historical Record;
Arameri Family Notes volume 1,
from the collection of
Dekarta Arameri.

(Translated by Scrivener Aram Vernm, year 724 of the Bright, may He shine upon us forever. WARNING: contains heretical references, marked "HR"; used with permission of the Litaria.)

You will know me as Aetr, daughter of Shahar—she who is now dead. This is an accounting of her death, for the records and for the easing of my heart.

We did not know there was trouble. My mother was a woman who kept her own counsel at the best of times; this was a necessity for any priestess, most of all our brightest light. But High Priestess Shahar—I will call her that and not Mother, for she was more the former than the latter to me—was always strange.

The elder brothers and sisters tell me she met the Dayfather

(HR) once, as a child. She was born among the tribeless, those outcasts who pay no heed to any god or any law. Her mother took up with a man who viewed both mother and child as his property and treated them accordingly. After one torment too many Shahar fled to an old temple of the Three (HR), where she prayed for enlightenment. The Dayfather (HR) appeared to her and gave her enlightenment in the form of a knife. She used it on her stepfather while he slept, removing that darkness from her life once and for all.

I say this not to slander her memory, but to illuminate: that was the kind of light Shahar valued. Harsh, glaring, hiding nothing. I make no wonder Our Lord treasured her so, because she was much like Him—quick to decide who merited her love, and who did not (HR).

I think this is why He appeared to her again on that terrible day when everything began to weaken and die. He simply showed up in the middle of the Sunrise Greeting and gave her something sealed in a white crystal sphere. We did not know at the time that this was the last flesh of Lady Enefa (HR), now gone to twilight Herself. We knew only that the power of that crystal kept the weakening at bay, though only within the walls of our temple. Beyond it, the streets were littered with gasping people; the fields with sagging crops; the pastures with downed livestock.

We saved as many as we could. Sun's Flame, I wish it could have been more.

And we prayed. That was Shahar's command, and we were frightened enough that we obeyed even though it meant three days on our knees, weeping, begging, hoping against all hope that Our Lord prevailed in the conflict tearing apart the

world. We took it in shifts, all of us, full ordinates and acolytes and Order-Keepers and common folk. We pushed aside
the exhausted bodies of our comrades when they sagged from
weariness, so that we could pray in their place. In between,
when we dared look outside, we saw nightmares. Giggling black
things, like cats but also monstrous children, flowed through
the streets a-hunting. Red columns of fire, wide as mountains,
fell in the distance; we saw the entire city of Dix immolated.
We saw the shining bodies of the gods' children falling from
the sky, screaming and vanishing into aether before they hit the
ground.

Through this all, my mother remained in her tower room,
gazing unflinchingly at the nightmare sky. When I went to
check on her—many of our number had begun killing themselves in despair—I found her sitting on the floor with her legs
crossed, the white sphere in her lap. She was growing old; that
position must have hurt her. But she was waiting, she said, and
when I asked her what for, she gave me her cold, white smile.

"For the right moment to strike," she said.

I knew then that she meant to die. But what could I do? I am
only a priestess, and she was my superior. Family meant nothing
to her. It is the way of our order to marry and raise children in
the ways of light, but my mother declared that Our Lord was
the only husband she would accept. She got herself with child
by some priest or another just to satisfy the elders. I and my
twin brother were the result, and she never loved us. I say that
without rancor; I have had thirty years to come to terms with it.
But because of this, I knew my words would fall on deaf ears if I
tried to talk her out of her chosen course.

So instead I closed the door and went back to my prayers.

The next morning there was an awful thunderclap of sound and force that seemed likely to blow apart the very stones of the Temple of Daylight Sky. When we picked ourselves up from this, amazed to find that we were still alive, my mother was dead.

I was the one that found her. I, and the Dayfather (HR), who was there beside her body when I opened the door.

I fell to my knees, of course, and mumbled something about being honored by His presence. But in truth? My eyes were only for my mother, who lay sprawled on the floor where I had last seen her. The white sphere was shattered beside her, and in her hands was something gray and glimmering. There was sorrow in Lord Itempas's eyes when He touched my mother's face to shut her eyes. I was glad to see that sorrow, because it meant my mother had achieved her fondest wish: pleasing her lord.

"My true one," He said. "All the others have betrayed me, save you."

Only later did I learn what He meant—that Lady Enefa (HR) and Lord Nahadoth (HR) had turned on Him, along with hundreds of their immortal children. Only later did Lord Itempas bring me His war prisoners, fallen gods in invisible chains, and tell me to use them to put the world to rights. It was too much for Bentr, my brother; we found him that night in the cistern chamber, his wrists slit in a barrel of wash water. There was only me to bear witness, and later to bear the burden, and right then to weep, because even if a god did honor my mother, what good did that do? She was still dead.

And that is how the High Priestess of the Bright, Shahar Arameri, passed on.

For you, Mother. I will live on, I will do as Our Lord

commands, I will remake the world. I will find some husband strong enough to help me shoulder the burden, and I will raise my children to be hard and cold and ruthless, like you. That is the legacy you wanted, isn't it? In Our Lord's name, it shall be yours.

Gods help us all.

Acknowledgments

So many people to thank, so little space.

Foremost thanks go to my father, who was my first editor and writing coach. I'm really sorry I made you read all that crap I wrote when I was fifteen, Dad. Hopefully this book will make up for it.

Also equal thanks to the writing incubators that have nurtured me over the years: the Viable Paradise workshop, the Speculative Literature Foundation, the Carl Brandon Society, Critters.org, the BRAWLers of Boston, Black Beans, The Secret Cabal, and Altered Fluid. Never thought I'd get this far, and I wouldn't have done it without all of you to kick me into action. (The bruises are fading nicely, thanks.)

Then to Lucienne Diver, the hardest-working agent in all the land. You believed in me; thanks. Also to Devi Pillai, my editor, who totally floored me with the realization that editors could be fun, funny people, eviscerating manuscripts with a wink and a smile. Thanks for that, and for picking such a great title.

And last but by no means least: thanks to my mother (hi, Mom!), my BFFs Deirdre and Katchan, and all the members of the old TU crew. To the staff and students of the universities I've worked at over the years; day jobs really shouldn't be so much fun. Posthumous thanks to Octavia Butler, for going first and showing the rest of us how it's done. And I always give thanks to God, for instilling the love of creation in me.

I suppose I should also thank my roommate NukuNuku, who encouraged me with headbutts, swats to the face, fur in my keyboard, incessant distracting yowls, and...um...wait, why am I thanking her again? Never mind.

THE
BROKEN
KINGDOMS

BOOK TWO OF
THE INHERITANCE TRILOGY

I REMEMBER THAT IT WAS MIDMORNING.

Gardening was my favorite task of the day. I'd had to fight for it, because my mother's terraces were famous throughout the territory, and she didn't quite trust me with them. I couldn't really blame her; my father still laughed over whatever I'd done to the laundry that one time I tried.

"Oree," she would say whenever I sought to prove my independence, "it's all right to need help. All of us have things we can't do alone."

Gardening, however, was not one of those things. It was the weeding that my mother feared, because many of the weeds that grew in Nimaro were similar in form to her most prized herbs. Fakefern had a fan-shaped frond just like sweet ire; running may was spiky and stung the fingers, same as ocherine. But the weeds and the herbs didn't *smell* anything alike, so I never understood why she had such trouble with them. On the rare occasions that both scent and feel stumped me, all I had to do was touch a leaf edge to my lips or brush my hand through the leaves to hear the way they settled into place, and I would know. Eventually, Mama had to admit that I hadn't tossed out a single good plant all season. I was planning to ask for my own terrace the following year.

I usually lost myself in the gardens for hours, but one morning something was different. I noticed it almost the moment I left the house: a strange, tinny flatness to the air. A pent-breath tension. By the time the storms began, I had forgotten the weeds and sat up, instinctively orienting on the sky.

And *I could see.*

What I saw, in what I would later learn to call *the distance,* were vast, shapeless blotches of darkness limned in power. As I gaped, great spearing shapes—so bright they hurt my eyes, something that had never happened before—jutted forth to shatter the blotches. But the remnants of the dark blotches became something else, darting liquid tendrils that wrapped about the spears and swallowed them. The light changed, too, becoming spinning disks, razor-sharp, that cut the tendrils. And so on, back and forth, dark against light, neither winning for more than an instant. Through it all, I heard sounds like thunder, though there was no scent of rain.

Others saw it, too. I heard them coming out of their houses and shops to murmur and exclaim. No one was really afraid, though. The strangeness was all up in the sky, too far above our very earthly lives to matter.

So no one else noticed what I did as I knelt there with my fingers still sunk in the dirt. A tremor in the earth. No, not quite a tremor; it was that tension I'd felt before, that *pent* feeling. It hadn't been in the sky at all.

I sprang to my feet and grabbed my walking stick, hurrying for the house. My father was out at the market, but my mother was home, and if some sort of earthquake was in the offing, I needed to warn her. I ran up the porch steps and yanked open the rickety old door, shouting for her to come out, and hurry.

Then I heard it coming, no longer confined to the earth, rolling across the land from the northwest—the direction of Sky, the Arameri city. *Someone's singing,* I thought at first. Not one someone but many—a thousand voices, a million, all vibrating and echoing together. The song itself was barely intelligible, its lyrics a single word—yet so powerful was that word that the whole world shook with its imminent force.

The word that it sang was *grow*.

You must understand. I have always been able to see magic, but Nimaro had been mostly dark to me until then. It was a placid land of sleepy little towns and villages, of which mine was no exception. Magic was a thing of the cities. I got to see it only every once in a while, and then always in secret.

But now there was light and color. It burst across the ground and the street, traced up every leaf and blade of grass and paving stone and wooden slat around the front yard. So much! I had never realized there was so much to the world, right there around me. The magic washed the walls with texture and lines so that for the first time in my life, I could see the house where I'd been born. It outlined the trees around me and the old horse cart around the side of the house—I couldn't figure out what that was at first—and the people who stood in the street with mouths hanging open. *I saw it all*—truly saw, as others did. Maybe more than they did, I don't know. It is a moment I will hold in my heart forever: the return of something glorious. The reforging of something long broken. The rebirth of life itself.

That evening, I learned my father was dead.

One month after that, I set out for the city of Sky to start my own new life.

And ten years passed.

1

"Discarded Treasure"
(encaustic on canvas)

Please help me," said the woman. I recognized her voice immediately. She, her husband, and two children had looked over—but not bought—a wall hanging at my table perhaps an hour before. She had been annoyed then. The hanging was expensive, and her children were pushy. Now she was afraid, her voice calm on the surface but tremolo with fear underneath.

"What is it?" I asked.

"My family. I can't find them."

I put on my best "friendly local" smile. "Maybe they wandered off. It's easy to get lost this close to the trunk. Where did you last see them?"

"There." I heard her move. Pointing, probably. She seemed to realize her error after a moment, with the usual sudden awkwardness. "Ah...sorry, I'll ask someone else—"

"Up to you," I said lightly, "but if you're talking about a nice clean alley over near the White Hall, then I think I know what happened."

Her gasp told me I'd guessed right. "How did you..."

I heard a soft snort from Ohn, the nearest of the other art

sellers along this side of the park. This made me smile, which I hoped the woman would interpret as friendliness and not amusement at her expense.

"Did they go *in* the alley?" I asked.

"Oh...well..." The woman fidgeted; I heard her hands rub together. I knew the problem already, but I let her muddle through. No one likes to have their errors pointed out. "It's just that...my son needed a toilet. None of the businesses around here would let him use theirs unless we bought something. We don't have a lot of money...."

She'd given that same excuse to avoid buying my wall hanging. That didn't bother me—I'd have been the first to say no one *needed* anything I sold—but I was annoyed to hear that she'd taken it so far. Too cheap to buy a wall hanging was one thing, but too cheap to buy a snack or a trinket? That was all we businesspeople asked in exchange for letting out-of-towners gawk at us, crowd out regular customers, and then complain about how unfriendly city dwellers were.

I decided not to point out that her family could have used the facilities at the White Hall for free.

"That particular alley has a unique property," I explained instead. "Anyone who enters the alley and disrobes, even partially, gets transported to the middle of the Sun Market." The market dwellers had built a stage on the arrival spot, actually—the better to point and laugh at hapless people who appeared there bare-assed. "If you go to the Market, you should find your family."

"Oh, thank the Lady," the woman said. (That phrase has always sounded strange to my ears.) "Thank *you.* I'd heard things about this city. I didn't want to come, but my husband—he's a

High Norther, wanted to see the Lady's Tree…" She let out a deep breath. "How do I get to this market?"

Finally. "Well, it's in West Shadow; this is East Shadow. Wesha, Easha."

"What?"

"Those are the names people use, if you stop to ask directions."

"Oh. But… *Shadow*? I've heard people use that word, but the city's name is—"

I shook my head. "Like I said, that's not what it's called by the people who live here." I gestured overhead, where I could dimly perceive the ghostly green ripples of the World Tree's ever-rustling leaf canopy. The roots and trunk were dark to me, the Tree's living magic hidden behind foot-thick outer bark, but its tender leaves danced and glimmered at the very limit of my sight. Sometimes I watched them for hours.

"We don't get a lot of sky here," I said. "You see?"

"Oh. I… I see."

I nodded. "You'll need to take a coach to the rootwall at Sixth Street, then either ride the ferry or walk the elevated path through the tunnel. This time of day, they'll have the lanterns at full wick for out-of-towners, so that's good. Nothing worse than walking the root in the dark—not that it makes much difference to *me*." I grinned to put her at ease. "But you wouldn't believe how many people go crazy over a little darkness. Anyway, once you get to the other side, you'll be in Wesha. There are always palanquins around, so you can either catch one or walk to the Sun Market. It's not far, just keep the Tree on your right, and—"

There was a familiar horror in her voice when she interrupted me. "This city… how am I supposed to… I'll get lost.

Oh, demons, and my husband's even worse. He gets lost all the time. He'll try to find his way back here, and I have the purse, and—"

"It's all right," I said with practiced compassion. I leaned across my table, careful not to dislodge the carved-wood sculptures, and pointed toward the far end of Art Row. "If you want, I can recommend a good guide. He'll get you there fast."

She would be too cheap for that, I suspected. Her family could've been assaulted in that alley, robbed, transformed into rocks. Was the risk really worth whatever money they'd saved? Pilgrims never made sense to me.

"How much?" she asked, already sounding dubious.

"You'll have to ask the guide. Want me to call him over?"

"I..." She shifted from foot to foot, practically reeking of reluctance.

"Or you could buy this," I suggested, turning smoothly in my chair to pick up a small scroll. "It's a map. Includes all the god spots—places magicked-up by godlings, I mean, like that alley."

"Magicked—You mean, some godling did this?"

"Probably. I can't see scriveners bothering, can you?"

She sighed. "Will this map help me reach this market?"

"Oh, of course." I unrolled it to give her a look. She took a long time staring at it, probably hoping to memorize the route to the Market without buying it. I didn't mind her trying. If she could learn Shadow's convoluted streets that easily, interrupted on the map by Tree roots and occasional notes about this or that god spot, then she deserved a free peek.

"How much?" she asked at last, and reached for her purse.

After the woman left, her anxious footsteps fading into the

general mill of the Promenade, Ohn ambled over. "You're so nice, Oree," he said.

I grinned. "Aren't I? I could have told her to just go into the alley and lift her skirts a bit, which would've sent her to her family in a heartbeat. But I had to look out for her dignity, didn't I?"

Ohn shrugged. "If they don't think of it on their own, that's their fault, not yours." He sighed after the woman. "Shame to come all the way here on a pilgrimage and spend half of it wandering around lost, though."

"Someday she'll savor the memory." I got up, stretching. I'd been sitting all morning and my back was sore. "Keep an eye on my table for me, will you? I'm going for a walk."

"Liar."

I grinned at the coarse, growly voice of Vuroy, another of the Row's sellers, as he ambled over. He stood close to Ohn; I imagined Vuroy hooking an affectionate arm around Ohn. They and Ru, another of the Row's sellers, were a triple, and Vuroy was possessive. "You just want to look in that alley, see if her dumb-as-demons man and brat dropped anything before the magic got 'em."

"Why would I do that?" I asked as sweetly as I could, though I couldn't help laughing. Ohn was barely holding in a snicker himself.

"If you find something, be sure to share," he said.

I blew a kiss in his direction. "Finders keepers. Unless you want to share Vuroy in return?"

"Finders keepers," he retorted, and I heard Vuroy laugh and pull him into an embrace. I walked away, concentrating on the *tap-tap* of my stick so that I wouldn't hear them kiss. I'd been joking about the sharing, of course, but there were still some

things a single girl didn't enjoy being around when she couldn't
have a little of it herself.

The alley, across the wide Promenade from Art Row, was
easy to find, because its walls and floor shimmered pale against
the ambient green glow of the World Tree. Nothing too bright;
by godling standards, this was minor magic, something even a
mortal could've done with a few chiseled sigils and a fortune in
activating ink. Ordinarily, I would've seen little more than a
scrim of light along the mortar between the bricks, but this god
spot had been activated recently and would take time to fade
back to its usual quiescence.

I stopped at the mouth of the alley, listening carefully.
The Promenade was a wide circle at the city's relative heart,
where foot traffic met the carriageways and came together to
encircle a broad plaza of flower beds, shade trees, and walk-
ways. Pilgrims liked to gather there, because the plaza offered
the city's best view of the World Tree—which was the same
reason we artists liked it. The pilgrims were always in a good
mood to buy our wares after they'd had a chance to pray to their
strange new god. Still, we were always mindful of the White
Hall perched nearby, its shining walls and statue of Bright
Itempas seeming to loom disapprovingly over the plaza's heretical goings-on. The Order-Keepers weren't as strict these days
as they had once been; there were too many gods now who
might take exception to their followers being persecuted. Too
much wild magic altogether in the city for them to police it all.
That still didn't make it smart to do certain things right under
their noses.

So I entered the alley only after I'd made sure there were no
priests in the immediate vicinity. (It was still a gamble—the

street was so noisy that I couldn't hear everything. I was prepared to say I was lost, just in case.)

As I moved into the relative silence of the alley, tapping my stick back and forth in case I happened across a wallet or other valuables, I noticed the smell of blood at once. I dismissed it just as quickly, because it didn't make sense; the alley had been magicked to keep itself clean of detritus. Any inanimate object dropped in it disappeared after half an hour or so—the better to lure in unwary pilgrims. (The godling who'd set this particular trap had a wicked mind for detail, I had decided.) Yet the deeper I moved into the alley, the more clearly the scent came to me—and the more uneasy I grew, because I recognized it. Metal and salt, cloying in that way blood becomes after it has grown cold and clotted. But this was not the heavy, iron scent of mortal blood; there was a lighter, sharper tang to it. Metals that had no name in any mortal tongue, salts of entirely different seas.

Godsblood. Had someone dropped a vial of the stuff here? An expensive mistake, if so. Yet the godsblood smelled...flat somehow. Wrong. And there was far, far too much of it.

Then my stick hit something heavy and soft, and I stopped, dread drying my mouth.

I crouched to examine my find. Cloth, very soft and fine. Flesh beneath the cloth—a leg. Cooler than it should have been, but not cold. I felt upward, my hand trembling, and found a curved hip, a woman's slightly poochy belly—and then my fingers stilled as the cloth suddenly became sodden and tacky.

I snatched my hand back and asked, "A-are you...all right?" That was a foolish question, because obviously she wasn't.

I could see her now, a very faint person-shaped blur occluding the alley floor's shimmer, but that was all. She should have glowed bright with magic of her own; I should have spotted her the moment I entered the alley. She should not have been motionless, since godlings had no need for sleep.

I knew what this meant. All my instincts cried it. But I did not want to believe.

Then I felt a familiar presence appear nearby. No footsteps to forewarn me, but that was all right. I was glad he'd come this time.

"I don't understand," Madding whispered. That was when I had to believe, because the surprise and horror in Madding's voice were undeniable.

I had found a godling. A *dead* one.

I stood, too fast, and stumbled a little as I backed away. "I don't, either," I said. I gripped my stick tightly with both hands. "She was like this when I found her. But—" I shook my head, at a loss for words.

There was the faint sound of chimes. No one else ever seemed to hear them, I had noticed long ago. Then Madding manifested from the shimmer of the alley: a stocky, well-built man of vaguely Senmite ethnicity, swarthy and weathered of face, with tangled dark hair caught in a tail at the nape of his neck. He did not glow, precisely—not in this form—but I could see him, contrasting solidly against the walls' shimmer. And I had never seen the stricken look that was on his face as he stared down at the body.

"Role," he said. Two syllables, the faintest of emphasis on the first. "Oh, Sister. Who did this to you?"

And how? I almost asked, but Madding's obvious grief kept me silent.

He went to her, this impossibly dead godling, and reached out to touch some part of her body. I could not see what; his fingers seemed to fade as they pressed against her skin. "It doesn't make sense," he said, very softly. That was more proof of how troubled he was; usually he tried to act like the tough, rough-mannered mortal he appeared to be. Before this, I had seen him show softness only in private, with me.

"What could kill a godling?" I asked. I did not stammer this time.

"Nothing. Another godling, I mean, but that takes more raw magic than you can imagine. All of us would have sensed that and come to see. But Role had no enemies. Why would anyone hurt her? Unless..." He frowned. As his concentration slipped, so did his image; his human frame blurred into something that was a shining, liquid green, like the smell of fresh Tree leaves. "No, why would either of them have done it? It doesn't make sense."

I went to him and put a hand on his glimmering shoulder. After a moment, he touched my hand in silent thanks, but I could tell the gesture had given him no comfort.

"I'm sorry, Mad. I'm so sorry."

He nodded slowly, becoming human again as he got a hold of himself. "I have to go. Our parents... They'll need to be told. If they don't know already." He sighed and shook his head as he got to his feet.

"Is there anything you need?"

He hesitated, which was gratifying. There are some reactions a girl always likes to see from a lover, even a former one. This former one brushed my cheek with a finger, making my skin tingle. "No. But thank you."

While we'd spoken, I hadn't paid attention, but a crowd had begun to gather at the mouth of the alley. Someone had seen us and the body; in the way of cities, that first gawker had drawn others. When Madding picked up the body, there were gasps from the watching mortals and one horrified outcry as someone recognized his burden. Role was known, then—possibly even one of the godlings who'd gathered a small following of worshippers. That meant word would be all over the city by nightfall.

Madding nodded to me, then vanished. Two shadows within the alley drew near, lingering by the place Role had been, but I did not look at them. Unless they worked hard not to be noticed, I could always see godlings, and not all of them liked that. These were probably Madding's people; he had several siblings who worked for him as guards and helpers. There would be others, though, coming to pay their respects. Word spread quickly among their kind, too.

With a sigh, I left the alley and pushed through the crowd—giving no answers to their questions other than a terse, "Yes, that was Role," and "Yes, she's dead"—eventually returning to my table. Vuroy and Ohn had been joined by Ru, who took my hand and sat me down and asked if I wanted a glass of water—or a good, stiff drink. She started wiping my hand with a piece of cloth, and belatedly I realized there must've been godsblood on my fingers.

"I'm all right," I said, though I wasn't entirely sure of that. "Could use some help packing up, though. I'm heading home early." I could hear other artists along the Row doing the same. If a godling was dead, then the World Tree had just become the second-most-interesting attraction in the city, and I could look forward to poor sales for the rest of the week.

So I went home.

I am, you see, a woman plagued by gods.

It was worse once. Sometimes it felt as if they were everywhere: underfoot, overhead, peering around corners and lurking under bushes. They left glowing footprints on the sidewalks. (I could see that they had their own favorite paths for sightseeing.) They urinated on the white walls. They didn't have to do that, urinate I mean, they just found it amusing to imitate us. I found their names written in splattery light, usually in sacred places. I learned to read in this way.

Sometimes they followed me home and made me breakfast. Sometimes they tried to kill me. Occasionally they bought my trinkets and statues, though for what purpose I can't fathom. And, yes, sometimes I loved them.

I even found one in a muckbin once. Sounds mad, doesn't it? But it's true. If I had known this would become my life when I left home for this beautiful, ridiculous city, I would have thought twice. Though I would still have done it.

The one in the muckbin, then. I should tell you more about him.

I'd been up late one night—or morning—working on a painting, and I had gone out behind my building to toss the leftover paint before it dried and ruined my pots. The muckrakers usually came with their reeking wagons at dawn, carting off the bin contents to sift for night soil and anything else of value, and

I didn't want to miss them. I didn't even notice a man there, because he smelled like the rest of the muck. Like something dead—which, now that I think about it, he probably was.

I tossed the paint and would have gone back inside had I not noticed an odd glimmer from the corner of one eye. I was tired enough that I should have ignored that, too. After ten years in Shadow, I had grown inured to godling leavings. Most likely one of them had thrown up there after a night of drinking or had spent himself in a tryst amid the fumes. The new ones liked to do that, spend a week or so playing mortal before settling into whatever life they'd decided to lead among us. The initiation was generally messy.

So I don't know why I stopped, that chilly winter morning. Some instinct told me to turn my head, and I don't know why I listened to it. But I did, and that was when I saw glory awaken in a pile of muck.

At first I saw only delicate lines of gold limn the shape of a man. Dewdrops of glimmering silver beaded along his flesh and then ran down it in rivulets, illuminating the texture of skin in smooth relief. I saw some of those rivulets move impossibly upward, igniting the filaments of his hair, the stern-carved lines of his face.

And as I stood there, my hands damp with paint and my door standing open behind me, forgotten, I saw this glowing man draw a deep breath—which made him shimmer even more beautifully—and open eyes whose color I would never be able to fully describe, even if I someday learn the words. The best I can do is compare it to things I do know: the heavy thickness of red gold, the smell of brass on a hot day, desire and pride.

Yet, as I stood there, transfixed by those eyes, I saw something else: pain. So much sorrow and grief and anger and guilt, and other emotions I could not name because when all was said and done, my life up to then had been relatively happy. There are some things one can understand only by experience, and there are some experiences no one wants to share.

Hmm. Perhaps I should tell you something about me before I go on.

I'm something of an artist, as I've mentioned. I make, or made, my living selling trinkets and souvenirs to out-of-towners. I also paint, though my paintings are not meant for the eyes of others. Aside from this, I'm no one special. I see magic and gods, but so does everyone; I told you, they're everywhere. I probably just notice them more because I can't see anything else.

My parents named me Oree. Like the cry of the southeastern weeper-bird. Have you heard it? It seems to sob as it calls, *oree,* gasp, *oree,* gasp. Most Maroneh girls are named for such sorrowful things. It could be worse; the boys are named for vengeance. Depressing, isn't it? That sort of thing is why I left.

Then again, I have never forgotten my mother's words: *it's all right to need help. All of us have things we can't do alone.*

So the man in the muck? I took him in, cleaned him up, fed him a good meal. And because I had space, I let him stay. It was the right thing to do. The human thing. I suppose I was also lonely, after the whole Madding business. Anyhow, I told myself, it did no harm.

But I was wrong about that part.

He was dead again when I got home that day. His corpse was in the kitchen, near the counter, where it appeared he'd been chopping vegetables when the urge to stab himself through the wrist had struck. I slipped on the blood coming in, which annoyed me because that meant it was all over the kitchen floor. The smell was so thick and cloying that I could not localize it—this wall or that one? The whole floor or just near the table? I was certain he dripped on the carpet, too, while I dragged him to the bathroom. He was a big man, so that took a while. I wrestled him into the tub as best I could and then filled it with water from the cold cistern, partly so that the blood on his clothes wouldn't set and partly to let him know how angry I was.

I'd calmed down somewhat—cleaning the kitchen helped me vent—by the time I heard a sudden, violent slosh of water from the bathroom. He was often disoriented when he first returned to life, so I waited in the doorway until the sounds of sloshing stilled and his attention fixed on me. He had a strong personality. I could always feel the pressure of his gaze.

"It's not fair," I said, "for you to make my life harder. Do you understand?"

Silence. But he heard me.

"I've cleaned up the worst of the kitchen, but I think there might be some blood on the living-room rugs. The smell's so thick that I can't find the small patches. You'll have to do those. I'll leave a bucket and brush in the kitchen."

More silence. A scintillating conversationalist, he was.

I sighed. My back hurt from scrubbing the floor. "Thanks for making dinner." I didn't mention that I hadn't eaten any. No way to tell—without tasting—if he'd gotten blood on the food, too. "I'm going to bed; it's been a long day."

A faint taste of shame wafted on the air. I felt his gaze move away and was satisfied. In the three months he'd been living with me, I'd come to know him as a man of almost compulsive fairness, as predictable as the tolling of a White Hall bell. He did not like it when the scales between us were unbalanced.

I crossed the bathroom, bent over the tub, and felt for his face. I got the crown of his head at first and marveled, as always, at the feel of hair like my own—soft-curled, dense but yielding, thick enough to lose my fingers in. The first time I'd touched him, I'd thought he was one of my people, because only Maroneh had such hair. Since then I'd realized he was something else entirely, something not human, but that early surge of fellow-feeling had never quite faded. So I leaned down and kissed his brow, savoring the feel of soft smooth heat beneath my lips. He was always hot to the touch. Assuming we could come to some agreement on the sleeping arrangements, next winter I could save a fortune on firewood.

"Good night," I murmured. He said nothing in return as I headed off to bed.

Here's what you need to understand. My houseguest was not suicidal, not precisely. He never went out of his way to kill himself. He simply never bothered to avoid danger—including the danger of his own impulses. An ordinary person took care while walking along the roof to do repairs; my houseguest did not. He didn't look both ways before crossing the street, either. Where most people might fleetingly imagine tossing a lighted candle onto their own beds and just as fleetingly discard that idea as mad, my houseguest simply did it. (Though, to his credit, he had never done anything that might endanger me, too. Yet.)

On the few occasions I had observed this disturbing tendency of his—the last time, he had casually swallowed something poisonous—I'd found him amazingly dispassionate about the whole thing. I imagined him making dinner this time, chopping vegetables, contemplating the knife in his hand. He had finished dinner first, setting that aside for me. Then he had calmly stabbed the knife between the bones of his wrist, first holding the injury over a mixing bowl to catch the blood. He did like to be neat. I had found the bowl on the floor, still a quarter full; the rest was splashed all over one wall of the kitchen. I gathered he'd lost his strength rather faster than expected and had struck the bowl as he fell, flipping it into the air. Then he'd bled out on the floor.

I imagined him observing this process, still contemplative, until he died. Then, later, cleaning up his own blood with equal apathy.

I was almost certain he was a godling. The "almost" lay in the fact that he had the strangest magic I'd ever heard of. Rising from the dead? Glowing at sunrise? What did that make him, the god of cheerful mornings and macabre surprises? He never spoke the gods' language—or any language, for that matter. I suspected he was mute. And I could not see him, save in the mornings and in those moments when he came back to life, which meant he was magical only at those times. Any other time, he was just an ordinary man.

Except he wasn't.

The next morning was typical.

I woke before dawn, as was my longtime habit. Ordinarily, I would just lie there awhile, listening to the sounds of morning:

the rising chorus of birds, the heavy erratic *bap-plink* of dew dripping from the Tree onto rooftops and street stones. This time, however, the urge for a different sort of morning overtook me, so I rose and went in search of my houseguest.

He was in the den rather than the small storage pantry where he slept. I felt him there the instant I stepped out of my room. He was like that, filling the house with his presence, becoming its center of gravity. It was easy—natural, really—to let myself drift to wherever he was.

I found him at the den window. My house had many windows—a fact I often lamented since they did me no good and made the house drafty. (I couldn't afford to rent better.) The den was the only room that faced east, however. That did me no good, either, and not just because I was blind; like most of the city's denizens, I lived in a neighborhood tucked between two of the World Tree's stories-high main roots. We got sunlight for a few minutes at midmorning, while the sun was high enough to overtop the roots but not yet hidden by the Tree's canopy, and a few more moments at midafternoon. Only the nobles could afford more constant light.

Yet my houseguest stood here every morning, as regular as clockwork, if he wasn't busy or dead. The first time I'd found him doing this, I thought it was his way of welcoming the day. Perhaps he made his prayers in the morning, like others who still honored Bright Itempas. Now I knew him better, if one could ever be said to know an indestructible man who never spoke. When I touched him on these occasions, I got a better sense of him than usual, and what I detected was not reverence or piety. What I felt, in the stillness of his flesh and the uprightness of his posture and the aura of peace that he exuded at no other time, was *power*. Pride. Whatever was left of the man he'd once been.

Because it was clearer to me with every day that passed that there was something broken, *shattered*, about him. I did not know what, or why, but I could tell: he had not always been like this.

He did not react as I came into the room and sat down in one of the chairs, wrapping myself in the blanket I'd brought against the house's early-morning chill. He was doubtless used to me making a show of his morning displays, since I did it frequently.

And sure enough, a few moments after I got comfortable, he began, again, to glow.

The process was different every time. This time his eyes took the light first, and I saw him turn to glance at me as if to make sure I was watching. (I had detected these little hints of phenomenal arrogance in him at other times.) That done, he turned his gaze outward again, his hair and shoulders beginning to shimmer. Next I saw his arms, as muscled as any soldier's, folded across his chest. His long legs, braced slightly apart; his posture was relaxed, yet proud. Dignified. I had noticed from the first that he carried himself like a king. Like a man long used to power, who had only lately fallen low.

As the light filled his frame, it grew steadily brighter. I squinted—I loved doing that—and raised a hand to shield my eyes. I could still see him, a man-shaped blaze now framed by the jointed lattice of my shadowy hand bones. But in the end, as always, I had to look away. I never did this until I absolutely had to. What was I going to do, go blind?

It didn't last long. Somewhere beyond the eastern rootwall, the sun moved above the horizon. The glow faded quickly after that. After a few moments, I was able to look at him again, and in twenty minutes, he was as invisible to me as every other mortal.

When it was over, my houseguest turned to leave. He did chores around the house during the day and had lately begun hiring himself out to the neighbors, giving me whatever pittance he earned. I stretched, relaxed and comfortable. I always felt warmer when he was around.

"Wait," I said, and he stopped.

I tried to gauge his mood by the feel of his silence. "Are you ever going to tell me your name?"

More silence. Was he irritated, or did he care at all? I sighed.

"All right," I said. "The neighbors are starting to ask questions, so I need something to call you. Do you mind if I make something up?"

He sighed. Definitely irritated. But at least it wasn't a no.

I grinned. "All right, then. Shiny. I'll call you Shiny. What about that?"

It was a joke. I said it just to tease him. But I will admit that I'd expected some reaction from him, if only disgust. Instead, he simply walked out.

Which annoyed me. He didn't have to talk, but was a smile too much to ask for? Even just a grunt or a sigh?

"Shiny it is, then," I said briskly, and got up to start my day.

2

"Dead Goddesses"
(watercolor)

Apparently I am pretty. Magic is all I see, and magic tends to be beautiful, so I have no way of properly judging the mundane myself. I have to take others' word for it. Men praise parts of me endlessly—always the parts, mind you, never the whole. They love my long legs, my graceful neck, my storm of hair, my breasts (especially my breasts). Most of the men in Shadow were Amn, so they also commented on my smooth, near-black Maro skin, even though I told them there were half a million other women in the world with the same feature. Half a million is not so many measured against the whole world, though, so that always got included in their qualified, fragmentary admiration.

"Lovely," they would say, and sometimes they wanted to take me home and admire me in private. Before I got involved with godlings, I would let them, if I felt lonely enough. "You're beautiful, Oree," they would whisper as they positioned and posed and polished me. "If only—"

I never asked them to complete this sentence. I knew what they almost said: *if only you didn't have those eyes.*

My eyes are more than blind; they are deformed. Disturbing. I would probably attract more men if I hid them, but why would I want more men? The ones I already attract never really want me. Except Madding, and even he wished I were something else.

My houseguest did not want me at all. I did worry at first. I wasn't stupid; I knew the danger of bringing a strange man into my home. But he had no interest in anything so mundane as mortal flesh—not even his own. His gaze felt of many things when it touched me, but covetousness was not one of them. Neither was pity.

I probably kept him around for that reason alone.

"I paint a picture," I whispered, and began.

Each morning before leaving for Art Row, I practiced my *true* art. The things I made for the Row were junk—statues of godlings that were inaccurate and badly proportioned; watercolors depicting banal, inoffensive images of the city; pressed and dried Tree flowers; jewelry. The sorts of trinkets potential buyers expected to see from a blind woman with no formal training who sold nothing over twenty meri.

My paintings were different. I spent a good portion of my income on canvas and pigment, and beeswax for the base. I spent hours—when I really lost myself—imagining the colors of air and trying to capture scent with lines.

And, unlike my table trinkets, I could see my paintings. Didn't know why. Just could.

When I finished and turned, wiping my hands on a cloth, I was not surprised to find that Shiny had come in. I tended to notice little else around me when I was painting. As if to rebuke me for this tendency, the scent of food hit my nose, and my stomach immediately set up a growl so loud that it practically filled the basement. Sheepishly I grinned. "Thanks for making breakfast."

There was a creak on the wooden stairs and the faint stir of displaced air as he approached. A hand took hold of mine and guided it to the smooth, rounded edge of a plate, heavy and slightly warm underneath. Warmed cheese and fruit, my usual, and—I sniffed and grinned in delight. "Smoked fish? Where on earth did you get that?"

I didn't expect an answer and I didn't get one. He guided me over to a spot at my small worktable, where he'd arranged a simple place setting. (He was always proper about things like that.) I found the fork and began to eat, my delight growing as I realized the fish was velly from the Braided Ocean, near Nimaro. It wasn't expensive, but it was hard to find in Shadow—too oily for the Amn palate. Only a few Sun Market merchants sold it, as far as I knew. Had he gone all the way to Wesha for me? When the man wanted to apologize, he did it right.

"Thank you, Shiny," I said as he poured me a cup of tea. He paused for just a moment, then resumed pouring with the faintest of sighs at his new nickname. I stifled the urge to giggle at his annoyance, because that would've just been mean.

He sat down across from me, though he had to push a pile of beeswax sticks out of the way to do it, and watched me eat. That sobered me, because it meant I'd been painting long enough that he'd gone ahead and eaten. And that meant I was late for work.

Nothing to be done for it. I sighed and sipped tea, pleased to find that it was a new blend, slightly bitter and perfect for the salty fish.

"I'm debating whether I should even go to the Row today,"

I said. He never seemed to mind my small talk, and I never minded that it was one-sided. "It will probably be a madhouse. Oh, that's right—did you hear? Yesterday, near the Easha White Hall, one of the godlings was found dead. Role. I was the one who found her; she was actually, really dead." I shuddered at the memory. "Unfortunately, that means her worshippers will come to pay respects, and the Keepers will be all over the place, and the gawkers will be as thick as ants at a picnic." I sighed. "I hope they don't decide to block off the whole Promenade; my savings are down to fumes as it is."

I kept eating and did not at first realize Shiny's silence had changed. Then I registered the shock in it. What had caught his attention—my worrying about money? He'd been homeless before; perhaps he feared I would turn him out. Somehow, though, that didn't feel right.

I reached out, found his hand, and groped upward until I found his face. He was a hard man to read at the best of times, but now his face was absolute stone, jaw tight and brows drawn and skin taut near the ears. Concern, anger, or fear? I couldn't tell.

I opened my mouth to say that I had no intention of evicting him, but before I could, he pushed his chair back and walked away, leaving my hand hovering in the air where his face had been.

I wasn't sure what to think of this, so I finished eating, carried my plate upstairs to wash, and then got ready to head to the Row. Shiny met me at the door, putting my stick into my hands. He was going with me.

As I had expected, there was a small crowd filling the nearby street: weeping worshippers, curious onlookers, and very snappish Order-Keepers. I could also hear a small group off at the far end of the Promenade, singing. Their song was wordless, just the same melody over and over, soothing and vaguely eerie. These were the New Lights, one of the newer religions that had appeared in the city. They had probably come looking for recruits among the dead goddess' bereft followers. Along with the Lights, I could smell the heavy, soporific incense of the Darkwalkers—worshippers of the Shadow Lord. There weren't many of them, though; they tended not to be morning people.

In addition to these were the pilgrims, who worshipped the Gray Lady; the Daughters of the New Fire, who favored some godling I'd never heard of; the Tenth-Hellers; the Clockwork League; and half a dozen other groups. Amid this rabble I could hear street-children, probably picking pockets and playing pranks. Even they had a patron god these days, or so I'd heard.

Small wonder the Order-Keepers were snappish, with so many heretics crowding their own hall. Still, they had managed to cordon off the alley and were allowing mourners to approach it in small groups, letting them linger long enough for a prayer or two.

With Shiny beside me, I crouched to brush my hand over the piles of flowers and candles and offertory trinkets that had been placed at the mouth of the alley. I was surprised to find the flowers half wilted, which meant they had been there awhile. The godling who'd marked the alley must have suspended the self-cleaning magic for the time being, perhaps out of respect for Role.

"A shame," I said to Shiny. "I never met this one, but I hear she was nice. Goddess of compassion or something like that.

She worked as a bonebender down in South Root. Anyone who could pay had to give her an offering, but she never turned away those who couldn't." I sighed.

Shiny was a silent, brooding presence beside me, unmoving, barely breathing. Thinking this was grief, I stood and fumbled for his hand and was surprised to find it clenched tight at his side. I'd completely mistaken his mood; he was angry, not sad. Puzzled by this, I slid my hand up to his cheek. "Did you know her?"

He nodded, once.

"Was she...*your* goddess? Did you pray to her?"

He shook his head, cheek flexing beneath my fingers. What had that been, a smile? A bitter one.

"You cared for her, though."

"Yes," he said.

I froze.

He had never spoken to me. Not once in three months. I hadn't even realized he *could* talk. For a moment I wondered whether I should say something to acknowledge this momentous event—and then I inadvertently brushed against him and felt the hard, tension-taut muscle of his arm. Foolish of me to fixate on a single word when something far more momentous had occurred: he had shown concern for something in the world besides himself.

I coaxed his fist open and laced my fingers with his, offering the same comfort of contact that I had given Madding the day before. For an instant, Shiny's hand quivered in mine, and I dared to hope that he might return the gesture. Then his hand went slack. He did not pull away, but he might as well have.

I sighed and stayed by him for a little while, then finally pulled away myself.

"I'm sorry," I said, "but I have to go." He said nothing, so I left him to his mourning and headed over to Art Row.

Yel, the proprietor of the Promenade's biggest food stand, allowed us artists to store things in her locked stand overnight, which made my life much easier. It didn't take long to set up my tables and merchandise, though once I sat down, it was exactly as I'd feared. For two whole hours, not a single person came to peruse my goods. I heard the others grumbling about it as well, though Benkhan was lucky; he sold a charcoal drawing of the Promenade that happened to include the alley. I had no doubt he would have ten more drawings like it by the next morning.

I hadn't gotten enough sleep the night before, since I'd been up late cleaning Shiny's mess. I was beginning to nod off when I heard a soft voice say, "Miss? Excuse me?"

Starting awake, I immediately plastered on a smile to cover my grogginess. "Why, hello, sir. See something that interests you?"

I heard his amusement, which confused me. "Yes, actually. Do you sell here every day?"

"Yes, indeed. I'm happy to hold an item if you like—"

"That won't be necessary." Abruptly I realized he hadn't come to buy anything. He didn't sound like a pilgrim; there wasn't the faintest hint of uncertainty or curiosity in his voice. Though his Senmite was cultured and precise, I could hear the slower curves of a Wesha accent underneath. This was a man who had lived in Shadow all his life, though he seemed to be trying to conceal that.

I took a guess. "Then what would an Itempan priest want with someone like me?"

He laughed. Unsurprised. "So it's true what they say about the blind. You can't see, but your other senses grow finer. Or perhaps you have some other way of perceiving things, beyond the abilities of ordinary folk?" There was the faint sound of something from my table being picked up. Something heavy. I guessed it was one of the miniature Tree replicas that I grew from linvin saplings and trimmed to resemble the Tree. My biggest-selling item, and the one that cost the most in time and effort to produce.

I licked my lips, which were abruptly and inexplicably dry. "Other than my eyes, everything about me is ordinary enough, sir."

"Is that so? The sound of my boots probably gives me away, then, or the incense clinging to my uniform. I suppose those would tell you a great deal."

Around me I could hear more of those characteristic boots, and more cultured voices, which were answered in uneasy tones by my fellow Row denizens. Had a whole troop of priests come out to question us? Usually we had to deal with only the Order-Keepers, who were acolytes in training to become priests. They were young and sometimes overzealous, but generally all right unless antagonized. Most of them hated street duty, so they did a lazy job of it, which left the people of the city to find their own ways of resolving problems—exactly as most of us pre-ferred it. However, something told me this man was no lowly Order-Keeper.

He hadn't asked a question, so I didn't speak, which he seemed to take as an answer in itself. I felt my front table shift alarmingly; he was sitting on it. The tables weren't the sturdiest things in the world, since they had to be light enough for me to carry home if necessary. My stomach clenched.

"You look nervous," he said.

"I'm not," I lied. I'd heard Order-Keepers used such techniques to throw their targets off-balance. This one worked. "But it might help if I knew your name."

"Rimarn," he said. A common name among lower-class Amn. "Previt Rimarn Dih. And you are?"

A previt. They were full-fledged priests, high-ranking ones, and they didn't leave the White Halls often, being more involved in business and politics. The Order must've decided that the death of a godling was of great importance.

"Oree Shoth," I said. My voice cracked on my family name; I had to repeat it. I thought that he smiled.

"We're investigating the death of the Lady Role and were hoping you and your friends could assist. Especially given that we've been kind enough to overlook your presence here at the Promenade." He picked up something else. I couldn't tell what.

"Happy to help," I said, trying to ignore the veiled threat. The Order of Itempas controlled permits and licenses in the city, among many other things, and they charged dearly for them. Yel's stand had a permit to sell on the Promenade; none of us artists could afford one. "It's so sad. I didn't think gods could die."

"*Godlings* can, yes," he said. His voice had grown noticeably colder, and I chided myself for forgetting how prickly devout Itempans could be about gods other than their own. I had been too long away from Nimaro, damn it—

"Their parents, the Three, can kill them," Rimarn continued. "And their siblings can kill them, if they're strong enough."

"Well, I haven't seen any godlings with bloody hands, if that's what you're wondering. Not that I see much of anything." I smiled. It was weak.

"Mmm. You found the body."

"Yes. There was no one around, though, that I could tell. Then Madding—Lord Madding, another godling who lives in town—came and took the body. He said he was going to show it to their parents. To the Three."

"I see." The sound of something being put back on my table. Not the miniature Tree, though. "Your eyes are very interesting."

I don't know why this made me more uneasy. "So people tell me."

"Are those...cataracts?" He leaned close to peer at me. I smelled mint tea on his breath. "I've never seen cataracts like those."

I've been told my eyes are unpleasant to look at. The "cataracts" that Rimarn had noticed were actually many narrow, delicate fingers of grayish tissue, layered tight over one another like the petals of a daisy yet to bloom. I have no pupils, no irises in the ordinary sense. From a distance, it looks as though I have matte, steely cataracts, but up close the deformity is clear.

"The bonebenders call them malformed corneas, actually. With some other complications that I can't pronounce." I tried to smile again and failed miserably.

"I see. Is this...malformation...common among Maroneh?"

There was a crash from two tables over. Ru's table. I heard her cry out in protest. Vuroy and Ohn started to join in. "Shut up," snapped the priest who was questioning her, and they all fell silent. Someone from the onlooking crowd—probably a Darkwalker—shouted for the priests to leave us alone, but no one else took up his cry, and he was not brave or stupid enough to repeat it.

I have never been very patient, and fear shortened my temper even more. "What is it you want, Previt Rimarn?"

"An answer to my question would be welcome, Miss Shoth."

"No, of course my eyes aren't common among Maroneh. *Blindness* isn't common among Maroneh. Why would it be?"

I felt the table shift slightly; perhaps he shrugged. "Some aftereffect of what the Nightlord did, perhaps. Legend says the forces he unleashed on the Maroland were...unnatural."

Implying that the survivors of the disaster were unnatural as well. Smug Amn bastard. We Maroneh had honored Itempas for just as long as they had. I bit back the retort that first came to mind and said instead, "The Nightlord didn't do anything to us, Previt."

"Destroying your homeland is nothing?"

"Nothing beyond that, I mean. Demons and darkness, he didn't *care* enough to do anything to us. He destroyed the Maroland only because he happened to be there at the time the Arameri let his leash slip."

There was a moment's pause. It lasted just long enough that my anger withered, leaving only horror. One did not criticize the Arameri—certainly not to an Itempan priest's face. Then I jumped as a loud crash sounded right in front of me. The miniature Tree. He'd dropped it, shattering the ceramic pot and probably doing fatal damage to the plant itself.

"Oh, dear," Rimarn said, his voice ice cold. "Sorry. I'll pay for that."

I closed my eyes and drew in a deep breath. I was still trembling from the crash, but I wasn't stupid. "Don't worry about it."

Another shift, and suddenly fingers took hold of my chin. "A shame about your eyes," he said. "You're a beautiful woman otherwise. If you wore glasses—"

"I prefer for people to see me as I am, Previt Rimarn."

"Ah. Should they see you as a blind human woman, then, or as a godling only pretending to be helpless and mortal?"

What the—I stiffened all over, and then did another thing I probably shouldn't have done. I burst out laughing. He was already angry. I knew better. But when I got angry, my nerves sought an outlet, and my mouth didn't always guard the gates.

"You think—" I had to work my hand around his to wipe a tear. "A *godling? Me?* Dearest Skyfather, is *that* what you're thinking?"

Rimarn's fingers tightened suddenly, enough to hurt the sides of my jaw, and I stopped laughing when he forced my face up higher and leaned close. "What I'm thinking is that you reek of magic," he said in a tight whisper. "More than I've ever smelled on any mortal."

And suddenly I could see him.

It was not like Shiny. Rimarn's glow was there all at once, and it didn't come from inside him. Rather, I could see lines and curlicues all over his skin like fine, shining tattoos, winding around his arms and marching over his torso. The rest of him remained invisible to me, but I could see the outline of his body by those dancing, fiery lines.

A scrivener. He was a scrivener. A good one, too, judging by the number of godwords etched into his flesh. They weren't really there, of course; this was just the way my eyes interpreted his skill and experience, or so I'd come to understand over the years. Usually that helped me spot his kind long before they got close enough to spot me.

I swallowed, no longer laughing now, and terrified.

But before he could begin the real questioning, I felt a sudden shift of the air, signaling movement nearby. That was my only warning before something yanked the previt's hand off my face. Rimarn started to protest, but before he could, another body blurred my view of him. A larger frame, dark and empty of magic, familiar in shape. Shiny.

I could not see precisely what he did to Rimarn. But I didn't have to; I heard the gasps of the other Row artists and onlookers, Shiny's grunt of effort, and Rimarn's sharp cry as he was bodily lifted and flung away. The godwords on Rimarn's flesh blurred into streaks as he flew a good ten feet through the air. He stopped glowing only when he landed in a bone-jarring heap.

No. Oh, no. I scrambled to my feet, knocking over my chair, and fumbled desperately for my walking stick. Before I could find it, I froze, realizing that though Rimarn's glow had vanished, I could still see.

I could see *Shiny*. His glow was faint, barely noticeable, but growing by the second and pulsing like a heartbeat. As Shiny interposed himself between me and Rimarn, the glow brightened still more, racheting up from a gentle burn toward that eye-searing peak that I had never seen from him outside of the dawn hour.

But it was the middle of the day.

"What the hells are you doing?" demanded a harsh voice from farther away. One of the other priests. This was followed by other shouts and threats, and I snapped back to awareness. No one could see Shiny's glow except me and maybe Rimarn, who was still groaning on the ground. They had simply seen a man—an unknown foreigner, dressed in the plain, cheap clothing that was all I'd been able to afford for him—attack a previt of the Itempan Order. In front of a full troop of Order-Keepers.

I reached out, caught one of Shiny's blazing shoulders, and instantly snatched my hand back. Not because he was hot to the touch—though he was, hotter than I'd ever felt—but because the flesh under my hand seemed to *vibrate* in that instant, like I'd touched a bolt of lightning.

But I pushed that observation aside. "Stop it!" I hissed at him. "What are you doing? You have to apologize, right now, before they—"

Shiny turned to look at me, and the words died in my mouth. I could see his face now completely, as I always could in that perfect instant before he blazed too bright and I had to look away. "Handsome" did not begin to describe that face, so much more than the collection of features that my fingers had explored and learned. Cheekbones did not have their own inner light. Lips did not curve like living things in their own right, sharing with me a slight, private smile that made me feel, for just an instant, like the only woman in the world. He had never, ever smiled at me before.

But it was vicious, that smile. Cold. Murderous. I drew back from it, stunned—and for the first time since I'd met him, afraid.

Then he glanced around, facing the Keepers who were almost surely converging upon us. He considered them and the crowd of onlookers with the same detatched, cold arrogance. He seemed to make some decision.

I kept gaping as three of the Order-Keepers grabbed him. I saw them, dark silhouettes limned by Shiny's light, throw him to the ground and kick him and haul his arms back to tie them. One of them put his knee on the back of Shiny's neck, bearing down, and I screamed before I could stop myself. The Order-Keeper, a malevolent shadow, turned and shouted for me to shut *up*, Maro bitch, or he would have some for me, too—

"*Enough!*"

At that fierce bellow, I started so badly that I lost my grip on my stick. In the silence that fell, it clattered on the Promenade's walkstones loudly, making me jump again.

Rimarn had been the one to shout. I could not see him; whatever he'd done to conceal his nature from me before, it was back in effect now. Even if I'd been able to see his godwords, I think Shiny would have drowned out his minor light.

Rimarn sounded hoarse and out of breath. He was on his feet, near the cluster of men, and spoke to Shiny. "Are you a fool? I've never seen a man do anything so stupid."

Shiny had not struggled as the priests bore him down. Rimarn waved away the Order-Keeper who'd put a knee on Shiny's neck—my own shoulder muscles unknotted in sympathetic relief—and then shoved the back of Shiny's head with a toe. "Answer me!" he snapped. "Are you a fool?"

I had to do something. "H-he's my cousin," I blurted. "Fresh from the territory, Previt. He doesn't know the city, didn't know who you were..." This was the worst lie I had ever told. Everyone, no matter their nation or race or tribe or class, knew Itempan priests on sight. They wore shining white uniforms and they ruled the world. "Please, Previt, I'll take responsibility—"

"No, you won't," Rimarn snapped. The Order-Keepers got up and hauled Shiny to his feet. He stood calmly between them, glowing so brightly that I could see half the Promenade by the light that poured off his flesh. He still had that terrible, deadly smile on his face.

Then they were dragging him away, and fear soured my mouth as I fumbled my way around my tables. Something else fell over with a crash as I groped toward Rimarn without a stick. "Previt, wait!"

"I'll be back for you later," he snapped at me. Then he, too, walked away, following the other Order-Keepers. I tried to run after them and cried out as I tripped over some unseen obstacle. Before I could fall, I was caught by rough hands that smelled of tobacco and sour alcohol and fear.

"Quit it, Oree," Vuroy breathed in my ear. "They're too pissed off to feel guilty about kicking the shit out of a blind girl."

"They'll kill him." I gripped his arm tight. "They'll beat him to death. Vuroy—"

"Nothing you can do about it," he said softly, and I went limp, because he was right.

Vuroy, Ru, and Ohn helped me get home. They carried my tables and goods, too, out of the unspoken understanding that I would not need to store my things with Yel, because I would not be going back to the Row anytime soon.

Ru and Vuroy stayed with me while Ohn went out again. I tried to keep calm and look passive, because I knew they would be suspicious. They had looked around the house, seen the pantry that served as Shiny's bedroom, found his small pile of clothes—neatly folded and stacked—in the corner. They thought I'd been hiding a lover from them. If they'd known the truth, they would've been much more afraid.

"I can understand why you didn't tell us about him," Ru was saying. She sat across the kitchen table from me, holding my hand. The night before, Shiny's blood had covered the place where our hands now rested. "After Madding...well. But I wish you had told us, sweetheart. We're your friends—we would've understood."

I stubbornly said nothing, trying not to show how frustrated I was. I had to look dejected, depressed, so they would decide that the best thing for me was privacy and sleep. Then I could pray for Madding. The Order-Keepers probably wouldn't kill Shiny immediately. He had defied them, disrespected them. They would make him suffer for a long time.

That was bad enough. But if they killed him, and he pulled his little resurrection trick in front of them, gods knew what they would do. Magic was power meant for those with other kinds of power: Arameri, nobles, scriveners, the Order, the wealthy. It was illegal for commonfolk, even though we all used a little magic now and again in secret. Every woman knew the sigil to prevent pregnancy, and every neighborhood had someone who could draw the scripts for minor healing or hiding valuables in plain sight. Things had been easier since the coming of the godlings, actually, because the priests—who could not always tell godlings and mortals apart—tended to leave us all alone.

Shiny wasn't a godling, though; he was something else. I didn't know why he'd begun to shine back at the Promenade, but I knew this: it wouldn't last. It never did. When he became weak again, he would be just a man. Then the priests would tear him apart to learn the secret of his power.

And they would come after me again for harboring him.

I rubbed my face as if I was tired. "I need to lie down," I said.

"Demonshit," Vuroy said. "You're going to pretend to go to bed, then call your old boyfriend. Think we're stupid?"

I stiffened, and Ru chuckled. "Remember we know you, Oree."

Damn. "I have to help him," I said, abandoning the pretense. "Even if I can't find Madding, I have a little money. The priests take bribes—"

"Not when they're this angry," said Ru, very gently. "They'd just take your money and kill him, anyway."

I clenched my fists. "Madding, then. Help me find Mad. He'll help me. He owes me."

I heard chimes on the heels of those words, which made my cheeks heat as I realized just how badly I'd underestimated my friends.

Someone opened the front door. I saw Madding's familiar shimmer through the walls even before he stepped into the kitchen, with Ohn a taller shadow at his side. "I heard," Madding said quietly. "Are you calling in a debt, Oree?"

There was a curious shiver in the air, and a delicate tension like something unseen holding its breath. This was Madding's power beginning to flex.

I stood up from the table, more glad to see him than I'd been in months. Then I noticed the somberness of his expression and recalled myself. "I'm sorry, Mad," I said. "I forgot . . . your sister. If there was any other way, I would never ask for your help while you're in mourning."

He shook his head. "Nothing to be done for the dead. Ohn tells me you've got a friend in trouble."

Ohn would've told him more than that, because Ohn was

an inveterate gossipper. But... "Yes. I think the Order-Keepers might have taken him somewhere other than their White Hall, though." Itempas Skyfather—*Dayfather*, I kept forgetting— abhorred disorder, and killing a man was rarely neat. They would not profane the White Hall with something like that.

"South Root," Madding said. "Some of my people saw them headed that way with your friend, after the incident at the Promenade."

I had an instant to digest that he'd had his people watching me. I decided that it didn't matter, reached for my stick, and went over to him. "How long ago?"

"An hour." He took my hand with his own smooth, warm, uncallused one. "I won't owe you after this, Oree," he said. "You understand?"

I smiled thinly, because I did. Madding never reneged on an agreement; if he owed you, he would do anything, go through anyone, to repay. If he had to go through the Itempan Order, however, that would make business in Shadow difficult for him for quite some time. There were things he could not do—kill them, for example, or leave the city except to return to the gods' realm. Even gods had their rules to follow.

I stepped closer and leaned against the comforting strength of his arm. Hard not to feel that arm without remembering other nights and other comforts and other times I'd relied on him to make all my troubles go away.

"I'd say that's worth the price of breaking my heart," I said. I spoke lightly, but I meant every syllable. And he sighed, because he knew I was right.

"Hang on, then," he said, and the whole world went bright as his magic carried us to wherever Shiny was dying.

3

"Gods and Corpses"
(oil on canvas)

THE INSTANT MADDING and I appeared in South Root, a blast of power staggered us both.

I perceived it as a wave of brightness so intense that I cried out as it washed past, dropping my stick to clap both hands over my eyes. Mad gasped as well, as if something had stricken him a blow. He recovered faster than me and took my hands, trying to pull them away from my face. "Oree? Let me see."

I let him push my hands aside. "I'm fine," I said. "Fine. Just… too bright. Gods. I didn't know these things could hurt like that." I kept blinking and tearing up, which made him peer closely into each eye.

"They're not 'things'; they're eyes. Is the pain fading?"

"Yes, yes, I'm fine, I told you. What in the infinite hells was that?" Already the brightness had vanished, subsumed into the dark that was all I usually saw. The pain was fading more slowly, but it *was* fading.

"I don't know." Madding cupped my face in his hands, thumbs grazing my underlids to brush away the tears. I allowed this at first, but abruptly his touch was too intimate, triggering memories more painful than the light had been. I pulled away, probably more quickly than I should have. He sighed a little but let me go.

There was a faint stir on either side of me, and I heard a light patter, as of feet touching the ground. Madding's tone shifted to something more authoritative, as it always did when he spoke to his underlings. "Tell me that wasn't who I thought it was."

"It was," said one voice, which I thought of as pale and androgynous even though I had seen its owner once, and she was the exact opposite, brown and voluptuous. She was also one of the godlings who didn't like it when I saw her, so I had never glimpsed her since.

"Demons and darkness," Mad said, sounding annoyed. "I thought the Arameri were keeping him."

"Not anymore, apparently," said the other voice. This one was definitively male. I had seen him, too, and he was a strange creature with long, wild hair that smelled like copper. His skin was Amn-white but with irregular darker patches here and there; I gathered the patches were his idea of decoration. I certainly found them pretty, whenever I managed to see him undisguised. This was business, though, so now he was just part of the darkness.

"Lil has come," said the woman, and Madding groaned. "There are bodies. The Order-Keepers."

"The—" Madding suddenly pulled back and looked hard at me. "Oree, please don't tell me *this* is your new boyfriend."

"I don't have a boyfriend, Mad, not that it's any of your business." I frowned, suddenly understanding. "Wait. Are you talking about Shiny?"

"Shiny? Who the—" Madding cursed, then stooped swiftly to collect my walking stick and press it into my hands. "Enough. Let's go."

His underlings vanished, and Madding began to pull me along toward wherever that white-hot power had come from.

South Root—Where Sows Root, went the local joke—was the worst neighborhood in Shadow. One of the Tree's main roots had forked off a side branch nearby, which meant the area was bracketed on three sides rather than the usual two. On rare days, South Root could be beautiful. It had been a respectable crafters' neighborhood before the Tree, so the white-painted walls were inlaid here and there with mica and smooth agate, and the streets were cobbled in patterns of large and small bricks, with gates of iron wrought in magnificent shapes. If not for the three roots, it would have gotten more sunlight than parts of Shadow closer to the Tree's trunk. I'd been told that it still did, on windy days in late autumn, for an hour or two a day. Any other time, South Root was perpetually dark.

No one lived there anymore but desperate, angry poor people. This made it one of the few places in the city where Order-Keepers might feel comfortable beating a man to death in the street.

Their consciences must've bothered them more than usual, however, because the space into which Madding finally dragged me did not feel open. I smelled garbage and mildew, and there was the bitter acridity of stale urine on my tongue. Another alley? One that had no magic to keep it clean.

And there were other smells here, stronger and even less pleasant. Smoke. Charcoal. Burned meat and hair. I could hear something still sizzling faintly.

Near this sound stood a tall, languid female figure, the only thing I could see aside from Madding. Her back was to me, so at first I noticed only her long, ragged hair, straight like a High

Norther's but an odd mottled gold in color. This was not the gold of Amn hair; it was somehow not pretty at all. She was also thin—disturbingly, unhealthily so. She wore an incongruously elegant gown with a low back, and the shoulder blades that I could see on either side of her hair were sharp-angled, like knife edges.

Then the woman turned, and I clapped both hands over my mouth to keep from crying out. Above the nose, her face was normal. Below, her mouth became a distorted, impossible monstrosity, her lower jaw hanging all the way to her knees, the too-long expanse of her gums lined with several rows of tiny, needlelike teeth. *Moving* teeth, each row marching along her jaw like a restless trail of ants. I could hear them whirring faintly. She drooled.

And when she saw my reaction, she smiled. That was the most hideous sight I had ever seen.

Then she shimmered and became an ordinary-looking woman, nondescriptly Amn, with a nondescriptly human mouth. She was still smiling, though, and there was still something disturbingly *hungry* in her expression.

"My gods," Madding murmured. (Godlings said this sort of thing all the time.) "It *is* you."

His words confused me because of their direction; he was not speaking to the blonde woman. Then I jumped at the response, because it came from another unexpected direction—above.

"Oh, yes," said this new, soft voice. "It's him."

Madding suddenly went still in a way that I knew meant trouble. His two lieutenants suddenly flickered into view, equally tense. "I see," Madding said, speaking low and carefully. "It's been a while, Sieh. Have you come to gloat?"

"A little." The voice was that of a young, prepubescent boy. I looked up, trying to gauge where he was—a rooftop, maybe, or a window on the second or third floor. I could not see him. A mortal? Or another godling who was feeling shy?

There was a sudden feel of movement before me, and abruptly the boy spoke from the ground only a few feet away. Godling, then.

"You look worn out, old man," the boy said, and belatedly I realized he, too, was addressing someone other than me, Madding, or the blonde woman. Finally I noticed that off to the side of the alley, near the wall, there was someone low to the ground. Sitting or kneeling, maybe. Panting for some reason. Something about those weary breaths was familiar.

"Mortal flesh is bound by physical laws," the boy continued, speaking to the panting person. "If you don't use sigils to channel the power, you get more, it's true—but then the magic drains your strength. Use enough and it can even kill you—for a while, anyhow. Just one of a thousand new things you'll have to learn, I'm afraid. Sorry, old man."

The blonde woman uttered a laugh like pebbles grinding underfoot. "You're not sorry."

She was right. The voice of the boy—Sieh, Madding had called him—was utterly devoid of compassion. He sounded pleased, in fact, in the way that most people would be pleased to see an enemy brought low. I cocked my head, listening close and trying to understand.

Sieh chuckled. "Of course I'm sorry, Lil. Do I look like the kind of person who would hold a grudge? That would be petty of me."

"Petty," agreed the blonde woman, "and childish and cruel. Does his suffering please you?"

"Oh, yes, Lil. It pleases me very much."

Not even the pretense of friendliness this time. There was nothing in that boyish voice but sadistic relish. I shivered, even more afraid for Shiny. I had never seen a godling child before, but I had an inkling they were not all that different from human children. Human children could be merciless, especially when they had power.

I stepped away from Madding, intending to go to the panting man. Madding pulled me sharply back, his hand like a vise on my arm. I stumbled, protesting, "But—"

"Not now, Oree," Madding said. He didn't use that tone with me often, but I had learned long ago that it meant danger when he did.

If this had been any other situation, I would have happily stepped behind him and tried to make myself as unnoticeable as possible. I was in a dark alley in the back end of beyond, surrounded by dead men and gods whose tempers were up. For all I knew, there wasn't another mortal anywhere in shouting distance. Even if there had been, what in the infinite hells could they have done to help?

"What's happened to the Keepers?" I whispered to Madding. It was an unnecessary question; they had finally stopped sizzling. "How did Shiny kill them?"

"Shiny?"

To my great dismay, it was Sieh's voice. I hadn't wanted to draw his attention or that of the blonde woman. Yet Sieh seemed honestly delighted. "*Shiny?* Is that what you call him? Really?"

I swallowed, tried to speak, then tried again when the first try failed. "He won't give me his name, so...I had to call him something."

"Did you, now?" The boy, sounding amused, came closer. I was a good deal taller than him, I guessed by the direction of his voice, but that was not as comforting as it should have been. I could still see nothing of him, not even an outline or a shadow, which meant that he was better than most godlings at concealing himself. I couldn't even smell him. I could *feel* him, though; his presence filled the whole alley in a way that none of the other godlings' did.

"Shiny," the boy said again, contemplative. "And he answers to that name?"

"Not exactly." I licked my lips and decided to take a chance. "Is he all right?"

The boy abruptly turned away. "Oh, he'll be fine. He has no *choice* but to be fine, doesn't he?" He was angrier now, I realized, my heart sinking into my stomach. I had made things worse. "No matter what happens to his mortal body, no matter how many times he abuses it—and, yes, oh yes, I know about that, did you think I didn't?" He was speaking to Shiny again, and his voice practically trembled with fury. "Did you think I wouldn't laugh at you, so proud, so *arrogant*, dying over and over because you can't be bothered to take the most basic care?"

There was a sudden jostling sound and a grunt from Shiny. And another sound, unmistakable: a blow. The boy had hit or kicked him. Madding's hand tightened on my arm, inadvertently I think. A reaction to whatever he was seeing. Sieh was barely coherent, snarling out his words. "Did you think"—another kick, this one harder; godlings were far stronger than they seemed—"I wouldn't"—Kick—"love to help you along?" *Kick*.

And an echo: the wet snap of bone. Shiny cried out, and at this I could not help myself; I opened my mouth to protest.

But before I could, another voice spoke, so softly that I almost missed it. "Sieh."

Stillness.

All at once, Sieh became visible. He was a boy, small and spindly looking, almost Maroneh-colored, though with an unkempt flop of straight hair. Not at all threatening to look at. As he appeared, he stood frozen, his eyes wide with surprise, but all at once he turned.

In the space that he faced, another godling appeared. This one was also a tiny thing, a full head shorter than me and barely larger than Sieh, yet there was something about her that hinted at strength. Possibly her attire, which was strange: a long, gray sleeveless vest that bared her slim, tight brown arms, and leggings that stopped at midcalf. Below them she was barefoot. She looked, I thought at first, the way I'd heard High Northers described, but her hair was wrong—curled and wild instead of straight, and chopped boyishly short. And her eyes were wrong, too, though I could not quite fathom how. What color was that? Green? Gray? Something else entirely?

At the corner of my vision, I saw Madding stiffen, his eyes going wide and round. One of his lieutenants uttered a swift, soft curse.

"Sieh," the quiet woman said again, her tone disapproving.

Sieh scowled, in that moment looking like nothing more than a sulky little boy caught doing something wrong. "What? It's not like he's really mortal."

Off to the side, the blonde goddess, Lil, looked at Shiny with interest. "He smells mortal enough. Sweat and pain and blood and fear, so nice."

The new goddess glanced at her, which didn't seem to bother

Lil at all, then focused on Sieh again. "This wasn't what we had in mind."

"Why shouldn't I kick him to death now and again? He's not even trying to fulfill the terms you set. He might as well entertain me."

The goddess shook her head, sighing, and went to him. To my surprise, Sieh did not resist as she pulled him into an embrace, cupping one hand at the back of his head. He held stiff against her, not reciprocating, but even I could see that he did not mind being held.

"This serves no purpose," she said in his ear, and so tender was her tone that I could not help thinking of my own mother, miles away in Nimaro Territory. "It doesn't help. It doesn't even hurt him, not in any way that matters. Why do you bother?"

Sieh turned his face away, his hands clenching at his sides. "You know why!"

"Yes, I know. Do you?"

When Sieh spoke again, I could hear the strain in his voice. "No! I hate him! I want to kill him forever!"

But then the dam broke, and he sagged against her, dissolving into tears. The quiet goddess sighed and pulled him closer, seemingly content to comfort him for however long it took.

I marveled at this for a moment, torn between awe and pity, then remembered Shiny on the ground nearby, his breathing labored now.

Surreptitiously I edged away from Madding, who was watching the tableau with the oddest look on his face, something I could not interpret. Sorrow, maybe. Chagrin. It didn't matter. While he and the others were preoccupied, I went over to Shiny. It was definitely him; I recognized his peculiar spice-and-metal scent. When I crouched to examine him, I found his back as hot as a fever and completely drenched in what I hoped was only sweat. He had bent in on himself in a huddle, his fists clenched tight, in obvious agony.

His condition enraged me. I lifted my eyes to glare at Sieh and the quiet goddess—and with a deep chill, I found her watching me over Sieh's bony shoulder. Hadn't her eyes been gray-green before? They were yellowish green now, and not at all warm.

"Interesting," she said. Beside her, Sieh turned to peer at me, too, rubbing one eye with the back of his hand. She kept a hand on his shoulder with absent affection and said to me, "Are you his lover?"

"She's not," said Madding.

The woman threw him the mildest of looks, and Madding's jaw flexed. It was as close to fear as I had ever seen him come.

"I'm not," I blurted. I didn't know what was going on, why Madding seemed so wary of this woman and the child-god, but I knew I didn't want Madding getting in trouble for my folly. "Shiny lives with me. We...he's..." What should I say? *Never lie to a godling*, Mad had warned me long ago. Some of them had spent millennia studying humankind. They could not read minds, but the language of our bodies was an open book. "I'm his friend," I said at last.

The boy exchanged a look with the goddess, and then both of them turned unnerving, enigmatic gazes on me. I noticed only then that Sieh's pupils were slitted, like those of a snake or cat.

"His friend," said Sieh. His face was expressionless now, his eyes dry, his voice without inflection. I didn't know if that was good or bad.

It sounded so weak. "Yes," I said. "It's…how I…think of myself, anyway." Another silence fell, and in it, I grew ashamed. I didn't even know Shiny's real name. "Please just stop hurting him." It was a whisper this time.

Sieh sighed, and so did the woman. The feeling that I was walking a narrow bridge over a very deep chasm began to fade.

"You call yourself his friend," the woman said. There was compassion in her voice, to my surprise. And her eyes were darker green now, shading toward hazel. "Does *he* call *you* the same?"

So they had noticed. "I don't know," I said, hating her for asking that question. I did not look at Shiny, who was still beside me. "He doesn't talk to me."

"Ask yourself why," drawled the boy.

I licked my lips. "There are many reasons why a man would hesitate to speak about his past."

"Few of those reasons are good. *His* certainly aren't." With a last contemptuous look, Sieh turned and walked away.

He paused, however, a look of surprise crossing his face, when the quiet woman suddenly moved forward, coming over to Shiny and me. When she crouched, balancing easily on her bare toes, I caught a fleeting sense of the real her, the goddess underneath her unimposing shell, and it staggered me. Where Sieh had filled the alley, she filled…what? It was too vast to grasp, too detailed. The ground beneath my knees. Every brick and speck of mortar, every struggling weed and smear of mildew. The air. The muckbins at the back of the alley. *Everything*.

And then it was gone, just as fast, and she was just a small High Norther woman with eyes that made me think of a dark, wet forest.

"You're very lucky," she said. I was confused at first; then I realized she was speaking to Shiny. "Friends are precious, powerful things—hard to earn, harder still to keep. You should thank this one for taking a chance on you."

Shiny twitched beside me. I could not see what he did, but the woman's expression changed to one of annoyance. She shook her head and got to her feet.

"Be careful of him," she said. To me this time. "Be his friend if you like—if he lets you. He needs you more than he realizes. But for your own sake, don't love him. He's not ready for that."

I could only stare at her, mute with awe. She turned away, then paused as she walked past Madding.

"Role," she said.

He nodded, as if he'd been expecting her attention. "We're doing everything we can." He threw me a quick, uneasy glance. "Even the mortals are looking into it. Everyone wants to know how this happened."

She nodded, slowly and solemnly. For an instant too long she was silent. Gods did that sometimes, contemplating the unfathomable, though they usually tried not to do it when mortals were around. Perhaps this one wasn't used to mortals yet.

"You have thirty days," she said suddenly.

Madding went stiff. "To find Role's killer? But you promised—"

"I said we wouldn't interfere in *mortal* affairs," she said sharply. Madding fell silent at once. "This is family."

After a moment, Madding nodded, though he still looked uncomfortable. "Yes. Yes, of course. And, ah—"

"He is angry," said the woman, and for the first time she looked troubled herself. "Role didn't take sides in the war. But even if she had...you're still his children. He still loves you." She paused and glanced at Madding, but Madding looked away. I guessed that she spoke of Bright Itempas, who was said to be the father of all the godlings. Naturally, He would take exception to the death of His child.

The woman continued. "So, thirty days. I've convinced him to stay out of it for that long. After that"—she paused, then shrugged—"you know his temper better than I do."

Madding went very pale.

With that, the woman turned to join the boy, both of them clearly intending to leave. From the corner of my eye, I saw one of Madding's lieutenants exhale in relief. I should have been relieved, too. I should have stayed quiet. But as I watched the woman and boy walk away, I could think of only one thing: *they knew Shiny.* Hated him, perhaps, but knew him.

I groped for my walking stick. "Wait!"

Madding looked at me like I had lost my mind, but I ignored him. The woman stopped, not turning back, but the child did, looking at me in surprise. "Who is he?" I asked, pointing at Shiny. "Will you tell me his name?"

"Oree, gods damn it." Madding stepped forward, but the woman held up a graceful hand and he went still.

Sieh only shook his head. "The rules are that he live among mortals *as* a mortal," he said, glancing beyond me at Shiny. "None of you comes into this world with a name, so neither does he. He gets nothing unless he earns it himself. Since he's not trying very hard, that means he'll never have much. Except a friend, apparently." He eyed me briefly and looked sour. "Well...like Mother said, even he gets lucky sometimes."

Mother, I noted, with the part of my mind that remained fascinated by such things even after years of living in Shadow. Godlings did mate among themselves sometimes. Was Shiny Sieh's father, then?

"Mortals don't come into the world with nothing," I said carefully. "We have history. A home. Family."

Sieh's lip curled. "Only the fortunate ones among you. He doesn't deserve to be *that* lucky."

I shuddered and inadvertently thought of how I'd found Shiny, light and beauty discarded like trash. All this time I had assumed misfortune on his part; I had speculated that he suffered from some godly disease, or an accident that had stripped all but a vestige of his power. Now I knew his condition had been deliberately imposed. Someone—these very gods, perhaps—had *done this to him,* as a punishment.

"What in the infinite hells did he *do?*" I murmured without thinking.

I didn't understand the boy's reaction at first. I would never be as good at perceiving things with my eyes as I was with my other senses, and the look on Sieh's face alone was not enough for me to interpret. But when he spoke, I knew: whatever Shiny had done, it had been truly terrible, because Sieh's hate had once been love. Love betrayed has an entirely different sound from hatred outright.

"Maybe he'll tell you himself one day," he said. "I hope so. He doesn't deserve a friend, either."

Then he and the woman vanished, leaving me alone among gods and corpses.

4

"Frustration"
(watercolor)

B<small>Y</small> NOW YOU'RE PROBABLY CONFUSED. That's all right; so was I. The problem wasn't just my misunderstanding—though that was part of it—but also history. Politics. The Arameri, and maybe the more powerful nobles and priests, probably know all this. I'm just an ordinary woman with no connections or status, and no power beyond a walking stick that makes an excellent club in a pinch. I had to figure everything out the hard way.

My education didn't help. Like most people, I was taught that there were three gods once, and then there was a war between them, which left two. One of them wasn't actually a god anymore—though he was still very powerful—so really that left just one. (And a great many godlings, but we never saw them.) For most of my life, I was raised to believe that this state of affairs was ideal, because who wants a bunch of gods to pray to when one will do? Then the godlings returned.

Not just them, though. Suddenly the priests began to say odd prayers and write new teaching poems into the public scrolls. Children learned new songs in the White Hall schools. Where once the world's people had been required to offer their praises only to Bright Itempas, now we were urged to honor two additional gods: a Lord of Deep Shadows and someone called the Gray Lady. When people questioned this, the priests simply said, *The world has changed. We must change with it.*

You can imagine how well that went over.

It wasn't as chaotic as it might have been, though. Bright Itempas abhors disorder, after all, and the people who were most upset were the ones who had taken His tenets to heart. So quietly, peacefully, and in an orderly fashion, those people just stopped attending services at the White Halls. They kept their children at home for schooling, teaching them as best they could on their own. They stopped paying tithes, even though this had once meant prison or worse. They committed themselves to preserving the Bright, even as the whole world seemed determined to turn a little darker.

Everyone else held their breath, waiting for the slaughter to begin. The Order answers to the Arameri family, and the Arameri do not tolerate disobedience. Yet no one was imprisoned. There were no disappearances, of individuals or towns. Local priests visited parents, exhorting them to bring their children back to school for the children's sake, but when the parents refused, their children were not taken away. The Order-Keepers issued an edict that everyone was to pay a basal tithe to cover public services; those who didn't do this *were* punished. But for people who chose not to tithe *to the Order*—nothing.

No one knew what to make of that. So there were other quiet rebellions, these more challenging to the Bright. Everywhere, heretics started worshipping their gods openly. Some nation up in High North—I can't recall which one—declared that it would teach children its own language first, then Senmite, instead of the other way around. There were even people who chose to worship no god at all, despite new ones appearing in Shadow every day.

And the Arameri have done nothing.

For centuries, *millennia*, the world has danced to a single flute. In some ways, this has been our most sacred and inviolable law: *thou shalt do whatever the hells the Arameri say.* For this to change... well, that's more frightening to most of us than any shenanigans the gods might pull. It means the end of the Bright. And none of us knows what will come after.

So perhaps my confusion on a few points of metaphysical cosmology is understandable.

I figured things out pretty quickly after that, thank goodness. When I turned back to the alley—

—the blonde godling was licking something on the ground.

I thought at first it was Shiny. As I came closer, though, I realized the positioning was wrong. Shiny was on *that* side of the alley. The only things on the side where she crouched were—

My gorge rose. The dead Order-Keepers.

She looked up at me. Her eyes were the same as her hair: gold mottled with irregular spots of darker color. I stared at her and suffered a pang of epiphany. When people looked at my eyes, was this what they saw? Ugliness that should have been beauty?

"Flesh freely given," the godling said, and flashed me a hungry smile.

I skirted wide around her and moved back to Shiny's side.

"You try me, Oree," Madding said, shaking his head as I passed him. "You really do."

"All I did was ask a question," I snapped, and crouched to examine Shiny. Gods knew what the Order-Keepers had done to him, even before Sieh's attack. I didn't let myself think about the bodies behind me, and who had done that.

"He was trying to keep you alive," replied Madding's lieutenant, the female one.

I ignored her, though she was probably right. I just didn't feel like admitting it. When I explored Shiny's face with my fingers, I discovered his mouth was cut, and someone had blacked his eye; it was swollen almost shut. Those wounds did not concern me. I felt my way to his ribs, trying to find the break—

Something planted itself on my chest and shoved. Hard. Startled, I cried out, flying backward with such force that my back struck the far alley wall, knocking the sense out of me.

"Oree! *Oree!*"

Hands pulled at me. I blinked away stars and saw Madding crouched before me. I didn't realize at first what had happened. Then I saw Madding swing around, his face contorting with fury—at Shiny.

"I'm all right," I said vaguely, though I was not at all sure of this. Shiny had not been gentle. My head rang dully where the back of my skull had impacted stone. I let Madding help me to my feet, grateful for his support when the shining forms of him and the blonde woman blurred unpleasantly. "I'm all right!"

Madding snarled something in the gods' singsong, guttural language. I saw the words spill from his mouth as glittering arrows that darted away to strike Shiny. Most of the words were harmless, I gathered by the way they shattered into nothing, but a few of them seemed to land and sink in.

The blonde godling's rusty laugh interrupted this tirade. "Such disrespect, little brother," she said, licking charcoal and grease from her lips. No blood; she hadn't nibbled. Yet.

"Respect is earned, Lil." Madding spat off to the side. "Did he ever try to earn ours, instead of demanding it?"

Lil shrugged, bowing her head until ragged hair obscured her face. "What does it matter? We did what we had to do. The world changes. As long as there is life to be lived and food to be savored, I am content."

With that, she abandoned her human guise. Her mouth opened wide, wider, stretching impossibly as she bent over the Order-Keepers' huddled forms.

I covered my mouth, and Madding looked disgusted. "Flesh freely given, Lil. I thought that was your creed?"

She paused. "This was given." Her mouth did not move as she spoke. It could not possibly have formed words in the human fashion, as it was.

"By whom? I doubt those men volunteered to be roasted for your pleasure."

She lifted an arm, pointing one skeletal finger at the place where Shiny huddled. "His kill. His flesh to give."

I shuddered as she confirmed my fears. Madding noticed this and leaned close to examine me, touching my shoulders and head gingerly. The soreness where he touched warned me there would be bruises come morning.

"I'm all right," I said again. My head was clearing, so I let Madding help me to my feet. "I'm fine. Let me see him."

Madding scowled. "He really tried to hurt you, Oree."

"I know." I stepped around Madding. Beyond him, I heard the unmistakable, hideous sounds of flesh being torn and bone crunching. I made certain not to move far from Madding, whose broad body blocked my view.

Instead I focused on Shiny, or where I guessed he was.

Whatever magic he'd used to kill the Order-Keepers was long
gone. He was weak now, wounded, lashing out in his pain like
a beast—

No. I had spent my life knowing the hearts of others through
the press of skin to skin. I had felt the petulant anger in that
shove. Perhaps it was only to be expected: the quiet goddess had
told him to be grateful for having me as a friend. I might never
know Shiny well, but I could tell he was too proud to take that
as anything but an insult.

He was panting again. Shoving me had spent what little
strength he'd regained. But I felt it when he managed to lift his
head and glare at me.

"My home is still open to you, Shiny," I said, speaking very
softly. "I've always helped people who needed me, and I don't
intend to stop now. You *do* need me, whether you like it or not."
Then I turned away, extending my hand. Madding put my stick
into it. I took a deep breath, tapping the ground twice to hear
the comforting clack of wood on stone.

"Find your own way back," I told Shiny, and left him there.

Madding did not delegate the task of caring for me to someone else. That was what I'd expected, since things had been
awkward between us since the breakup. Yet he stayed, bathing
me as I knelt shivering in the cold water. (Madding could have
heated the water for me—gods were handy that way—but the
cold was better for my back.) When that was done, he bundled
me into a soft, fluffy robe that he had conjured, tucked me into
bed on my belly, and settled in beside me.

I didn't protest, though I gave him an amused look. "I suppose this is just to keep me warm?"

"Well, not *just*," he said, snuggling closer and resting a hand on the small of my back. That part was unbruised. "How's your head?"

"Better. I think the cold helped." It felt nice, having him there against me. Like old times. I told myself not to get used to it, but that was like telling a child not to want candy. "There isn't even a lump."

"Mmm." He brushed aside a few coils of hair and sat up to kiss the nape of my neck. "Might be one come morning. You should rest."

I sighed. "It's hard to rest if you keep doing things like that."

Madding paused, then sighed, his breath tickling my skin. "Sorry." He lingered there for a moment with his face pressed against my neck, breathing my scent, and finally he sat up, shifting to put a few inches between us. I missed him immediately and turned my face away so that he would not see.

"I'll have someone bring...Shiny...back, if he hasn't made it on his own by morning," he said finally, after a long, uncomfortable silence. "That was what you asked me to do."

"Mmm." There was no point in thanking him. He was the god of obligation; he kept his promises.

"Be careful of him, Oree," he said quietly. "Yeine was right. He doesn't think much of mortals, and you saw what his temper's like. I have no idea why you took him in—I have no idea why you do half the things you do—but just be careful. That's all I ask."

"I'm not sure I should let you ask anything of me, Mad."

I knew I'd pissed him off when the room lit up in bright, rippling blue-green. "It doesn't all go one way between us, Oree," he snapped. His voice was softer in this form, cool and echoing. "You know that."

I sighed, started to turn over, and thought better of it when my bruises throbbed. Instead I turned just my face to him. Madding had become a shimmering, humanoid shape that was only vaguely male, but the look that boiled in his face was wholly that of an injured lover. He thought I was being unfair. He might even have been right.

"You say you still love me," I said. "But you don't want to be with me anymore. You won't share anything. You drop these vague warnings about Shiny rather than telling me anything *useful*. How do you expect me to feel?"

"I *can't* tell you anything more about him." The liquid of his form abruptly became hard crystal, delicately faceted aquamarine and peridot. I loved it when he went solid, though it usually meant stubbornness on his part. "You heard Sieh. He must wander this world, nameless and unknown—"

"Tell me about Sieh, then, and that woman. Yeine, you called her? You were afraid of them."

Madding groaned, setting all his facets ashiver. "You're like a magpie, dropping one subject to jump after a prettier one."

I shrugged. "I'm mortal. I don't have all the time in the world. Tell me." I wasn't angry anymore. Neither was he, really. I knew he still loved me, and he knew that I knew. We were just taking a hard day out on each other. It was easy to fall into old habits.

Madding sighed and leaned back against the bed's headboard, resuming his human form. "It wasn't fear."

"Looked like fear to me. All of you were afraid, except that one with the mouth. Lil."

He made a face. "Lil isn't capable of fear. And it wasn't fear. It was just…" He shrugged, frowning. "It's hard to explain."

"Everything is with you."

He rolled his eyes. "Yeine is... Well, she's very young, as our kind goes. I don't know what to think of her yet. And Sieh, despite how he looks, is the oldest of us."

"Ah," I said, though I didn't really understand. That child had been older than Madding? And why had Sieh called the woman his mother if she was younger? "The respect due a big brother—"

"No, no, that doesn't matter to us."

I frowned in confusion. "What, then? Is he stronger than you?"

"Yes." Madding grimaced in consternation. I had a momentary impression of aquamarine shading to sapphire, though he did not change; just my imagination.

"Because he's older?"

"Partly, yes. But also..." He trailed off.

I groaned in frustration. "I want to sleep tonight, Mad."

"I'm trying to say it." Madding sighed. "Mortal languages don't have words for this. He... *lives true*. He is what he is. You've heard that saying, haven't you? It's more than just words for us."

I had no idea what he was talking about. He saw that in my face and tried again. "Imagine you're older than this planet, yet you have to act like a child. Could you do it?"

Impossible to even imagine. "I... don't know. I don't think so."

Madding nodded. "Sieh does it. He does it *every day*, all day; he never stops. That makes him strong."

I was beginning to understand, a little. "Is that why you're a usurer?"

Madding chuckled. "I prefer the term *investor*. And my rates are perfectly fair, thank you."

"Drug dealer, then."

"I prefer the term *independent apothecary*—"

"Hush." I reached out, wistful, to touch the back of his hand where it rested on the sheets. "It must have been hard for you during the Interdiction." That was what he and the other godlings called the time before their coming—the time when they hadn't been permitted to visit our world or interact with mortals. Why they'd been forbidden to come, or who had forbidden them, they would not say. "I can't see gods having many obligations."

"Not true," he said. He watched me for a moment, then turned his hand over to grasp mine. "The most powerful obligations aren't material, Oree."

I looked at his hand clasped around the nothingness of my own, understanding and wishing that I didn't. I wished he had just fallen out of love with me. It would have made things easier.

His grip loosened; I had let him see more in my expression than I'd meant to. He sighed and lifted my hand, kissing the back of it. "I should go," he said. "If you need anything—"

On impulse, I sat up, though it made my back ache something awful. "Stay," I said.

He looked away, uneasy. "I shouldn't."

"No obligation, Mad. Just friendship. Stay."

He reached up to brush my hair back from my cheek. His expression, in that one unguarded moment, was the softest I ever saw it outside of his liquid form.

"I wish you were a goddess," he said. "Sometimes it feels as if you *are* one. But then something like this happens…" He brushed my robe back and grazed a bruise with his fingertip.

"And I remember how fragile you are. I remember that I'll lose you one day." His jaw flexed. "I can't bear it, Oree."

"Goddesses can die, too." I realized my error belatedly. I'd been thinking of the Gods' War, millennia before. I had forgotten Madding's sister.

But Madding smiled sadly. "That's different. We *can* die. You mortals, though...Nothing can stop you from dying. All we can do is stand by and watch."

And die a little with you. That was what he'd said before, on the night he'd left me. I understood his reasoning, even agreed with it. That didn't mean I'd ever like it.

I put my hand on his face and leaned in to kiss him. He did it readily, but I felt how he held himself back. I tasted nothing of him in that kiss, even though I pressed close, practically begging for more. When we parted, I sighed and he looked away.

"I should go," he said again.

This time I let him. He rose from the bed and went to the door, pausing in the frame for a moment.

"You can't go back to Art Row," he said. "You know that, don't you? You shouldn't even stay in town. Leave, at least for a few weeks."

"And go where?" I lay back down, turning my face away from him.

"Maybe visit your hometown."

I shook my head. I hated Nimaro.

"Travel, then. There must be somewhere else you want to visit."

"I need to eat," I said. "Rent would be nice, too, unless you intend for me to carry all my household possessions when I go."

He sighed in faint exasperation. "Then at least set up your

table at one of the other promenades. The Easha Order-Keepers don't bother with those parts of the city as much. You'll still get a few customers there."

Not enough. But he was right; it would be better than nothing. I sighed and nodded.

"I can have one of my people—"

"I don't want to owe you anything."

"A gift," he said softly. There was a faint, unpleasant shiver of the air, like chimes gone sour. Generosity was not easy for him. On another day, under other circumstances, I would've been honored that he made the effort, but I was not feeling particularly generous in that moment.

"I don't want *anything* from you, Mad."

Another silence, this one reverberating with hurt. That was like old times, too.

"Good night, Oree," he said, and left.

Eventually, after a good cry, I slept.

Let me tell you how Madding and I met.

I came to Shadow—though I still thought of it as Sky then—when I was seventeen. Very quickly I fell in with others like me—newcomers, dreamers, young people drawn to the city in spite of its dangers because sometimes, for some of us, tedium and familiarity feel worse than risking your life. With their help, I learned to make a living off my knack for crafts and to protect myself from those who would have exploited me. I slept in a tenement with six others at first, then got an apartment of my own. After a year's time, I sent a letter to my mother letting her know I was alive, and received in return a ten-page missive demanding that I come home. I was doing well.

I remember it was the end of a day, and wintertime. Snow is rare and light in the city—the Tree protects us from the worst of it—but there had been some, and it was cold enough for the cobbled paths to become icy death traps. Two days before, Vuroy had fractured his arm falling, much to the dismay of Ru and Ohn, who had to put up with his incessant complaining at home. I had no one at home to take care of me if I fell, and I couldn't afford a bonebender, so I went even more slowly than usual on the sidewalks. (Ice sounds much like stone when tapped with a walking stick, but there is a subtle difference to the air above a patch; it is not only colder but also palpably heavier.)

I was safe enough. Just slow. But because I was so intent on not breaking a limb, I paid less attention to my route than I should have, and given that I was still relatively new to the city, I got lost.

Shadow is not a good city to get lost in. The city had grown haphazardly over the centuries, springing up at the foot of Sky-the-palace, and its layout made little sense despite the constant efforts of the nobles to impose order on the mess. Long-time denizens tell me it's even worse since the growth of the Tree, which bifurcated the city into Wesha and Easha and caused other, more magical changes. The Lady had been kind enough to keep the Tree from destroying anything when it grew, but entire neighborhoods had been shifted out of place, old streets erased and new ones created, landmarks moved. Get lost and one could wander in circles for hours.

That was not the real danger, however. I noticed it quickly that chilly afternoon: someone was following me.

The steps trailed twenty feet or so behind, keeping pace. I

turned a corner and hoped, to no avail; the feet moved with me. I turned again. The same.

Thieves, probably. Rapists and killers didn't much care for the cold. I had little money on me, and I did not look wealthy by any stretch, but most likely it was enough that I looked alone and lost and blind. That made me easy pickings on a day when the pickings would be slim.

I did not walk faster, though of course I was afraid. Some thieves didn't like leaving witnesses. But to hurry would let this thief know that he had been spotted, and worse, I might still break my neck. Better to let him come, give him what he wanted, and hope that would be enough.

Except...he wasn't coming. I walked a block, two blocks, three. I heard few other people on the street, and those few were moving quickly, some of them muttering about the cold and paying no attention to anything but their misery. For long stretches, there was only me and my pursuer. *Now he will come*, I thought several times. But there was no attack.

As I turned my head for a better listen, something glinted at the corner of my vision. Startled—in those days I was not quite used to magic—I forgot wisdom, stopped, and turned to see.

My pursuer was a young woman. She was plump, short, with curly pale green hair and skin of a nearly similar shade. That alone would have alerted me as to her nature, though it was obvious in the fact that I could see her.

She stopped when I did. I noticed that her expression was very sad. She said nothing, so I ventured, "Hello."

Her eyebrows rose. "You can see me?"

I frowned a bit. "Yes. You're standing right there."

"How interesting." She resumed walking, though she stopped when I took a step back.

"If you don't mind me saying so," I said cautiously, "I've never been mugged by a godling."

If anything, her expression grew even more mournful. "I mean you no harm."

"You've been following me since that street back there. The one with the clogged sewer."

"Yes."

"Why?"

"Because you might die," she said.

I stumbled back, but only one step, because my heel slipped on a bit of ice alarmingly. *"What?"*

"You will very likely die in the next few moments. It may be difficult . . . painful. I've come to be with you." She sighed gently. "My nature is mercy. Do you understand?"

I had not met many godlings at that point, but anyone who dwelled for long in Shadow learned this much: they drew their strength from a particular thing—a concept, a state of being, an emotion. The priests and scriveners called it *affinity*, though I had never heard any godling use the term. When they encountered their affinity, it drew them like a beacon, and some of them could not quite help responding to it.

I swallowed and nodded. "You . . . You're here to watch me die. Or"—I shivered as I realized—"or to *kill* me, if something only does the job halfway. Is that right?"

She nodded. "I'm sorry." And she really did seem sorry, her eyes heavy-lidded, her brow furrowed with the beginnings of grief. She wore only a thin, shapeless shift—more proof of her nature, since any mortal would have frozen to death in that.

It made her look younger than me, vulnerable. Like someone you'd want to stop and help.

I shuddered and said, "Well, ah, maybe you could tell me what's going to kill me, and I can, ah, walk *away* from it, and then you won't have to waste time on me. Would that be all right?"

"There are many pathways to any future. But when I am drawn to a mortal, it means most paths have exhausted themselves."

My heart, already beating fast, gave an unpleasant little lurch. "You're saying it's inevitable?"

"Not inevitable. But likely."

I needed to sit down. The buildings on either side of me were not residential; I thought they might be storehouses. Nowhere to sit but the cold, hard ground. And for all I knew, doing that might kill me.

That was when I became aware of how utterly quiet it was.

There had been three other people on the street two blocks back. Only the green woman's steps had stood out to me, for obvious reasons, but now there were no other footfalls at all. The street was completely empty.

Yet I could hear...something. No—it was not a sound so much as a feeling. A pressure to the air. A lingering whiff of scent, teasingly unidentifiable. And it was...

Behind me. I turned, stumbling again, my heart leaping into my throat as I saw *another* godling standing across the street from me.

This one was paying no attention to me, however. She looked middle-aged, islander or Amn, black-haired, ordinary enough except that I could see her, too. She stood with legs apart and hands fisted at her sides, body taut, an expression of pure fury on her face. When I followed her gaze to see who this fury was directed at, I spied a third person, equally tense and still but on my side of the street, closer by. A man. Madding, though I didn't know this at the time.

The air between these two godlings was a cloud the color of blood and rage. It curled and shivered, flexing larger and flinching compact with whatever forces they were using against each other. Because that was, indeed, what I had walked into, for all that it was silent and still: a battle. One did not need magic-seeing eyes to know that.

I licked my lips and glanced back at the green-skinned woman. She nodded: this was how I might die, caught in the cross fire of a duel between gods.

Very quickly, as quietly as I could, I began to back up, toward the green woman. I didn't think she would protect me—she'd made her interest clear—but there was no other safe direction.

I'd forgotten the ice patch behind me. Of course I slipped and fell, jarring a grunt of pain from my throat and my stick from my hand. It landed on the cobblestones with a loud, echoing clatter.

The woman across the street jerked in surprise and looked at me. I had an instant to register that her face was not as ordinary as I'd thought, the skin too shiny, hard-smooth, like porcelain. Then the stones under me began to shake, and the wall behind me buckled, and my skin prickled all over.

Suddenly the man was in front of me, opening his mouth to utter a roar like surf crashing in an ocean cave. The porcelain-skinned woman screamed, flinging up her arms as something (I could not see what, exactly) shattered around her. That same force flung her backward. I heard mortar crack and crumble as her body struck a wall, then crumpled to the ground.

"What the hells are you doing?" the man shouted at her. Dazed, I stared up at him. A vein in his temple was visible, pounding with his anger. It fascinated me because I hadn't realized godlings had veins. But of course they did; I had not been in the city long, but already I had heard of godsblood.

The woman pushed herself up slowly, though the blow she had taken would have crushed half her bones if she'd been mortal. It did seem to have weakened her, as she stayed on one knee while glaring at the man.

"You can't stay here," he said, calmer now, though still visibly furious. "You're not careful enough. By threatening this mortal's life, you've already broken the most important rule."

The woman's lip curled in a sneer. "*Your* rule."

"The rule agreed upon by all of us who chose to dwell here! None of us wants another Interdiction. You were warned." He held up a hand.

And suddenly the street was *full* of godlings. Everywhere I looked, I could see them. Most looked human, but a few had either shed their mortal guises or had never bothered in the first place. I caught glimpses of skin like metal, hair like wood, legs with animal joints, tentacle fingers. There must have been two, maybe three dozen of them standing in the street or sitting on the curbs. One even flitted overhead on gossamer insect wings.

The porcelain-faced woman got to her feet, though she still looked shaky. She looked around at the assemblage of godlings, and there was no mistaking the unease on her face. But she straightened and scowled, pushing her shoulders back. "So this is how you fight your duels?" This was directed at the man.

"The duel is over," the man said. He stepped back, closer to me, and then to my surprise bent to help me up. I blinked at him in confusion, then frowned as he moved in front of me, blocking my view of the woman. I tried to lean around him to keep an eye on her, since I had a notion she'd almost killed me a moment before, but the man moved with me.

"No," he said. "You don't need to see this."

"What?" I asked. "I—"

There was a sound like the tolling of a great bell behind him, followed by a sudden swift concussion of air. Then all the god-lings around us vanished. When I craned my head around the man this time, I saw only an empty street.

"You killed her," I whispered, shocked.

"No, of course not. We opened a door, that's all—sent her back to our realm. *That's* what I didn't want you to see." To my surprise, the man smiled, and I was momentarily caught by how human this made him look. "We try not to kill each other. That tends to upset our parents."

Before I could stop myself, I laughed, then realized I was laughing with a god and fell silent. Which confused me more, so I just stared up at his strangely comforting smile.

"Everything all right, Eo?" The man didn't turn from me as he raised his voice to speak. I suddenly remembered the green woman.

When I looked at her, I started again. The green woman—Eo, apparently—was smiling at me as fondly as a new mother. Her coloring had changed, too, from green to a soft pale pink. Even her hair was pink. As I stared at her, she inclined her head to me and again to the man, then turned and walked away.

I gaped after her for a moment, then shook my head.

"I suppose I owe you my life," I said, turning back to the man.

"Since it was in danger partly because of me, let's just call it even," he said, and there was a faint ringing in the air, as of wind chimes, though there was no wind. I looked around, confused. "But I wouldn't mind buying you a drink, if you're feeling the need to celebrate life."

That startled me into another laugh as I finally realized what he was up to. "Do you try to pick up all the mortal girls you almost kill?"

"Just the ones who don't scream and run," he said. And then he startled me further by touching my face, just under one eye. I tensed just a little, as I always did when someone noticed my eyes. Bracing myself for the *if only*.

But there was no revulsion in his gaze and nothing but fascination in his touch. "And the ones with pretty eyes," he added.

You can imagine the rest, can't you? That smile, the strength of his presence, his calm acceptance of my strangeness, the fact that he was stranger still. I barely stood a chance. Two days after we met, I kissed him. He took the opportunity to pour a taste of himself into my mouth, the wretch, trying to lure me into bed. It didn't work then—I had some principles—but a few days later, I went home with him. Naked before Madding, I felt for the first time that someone saw the whole of me, not just my parts. He found my eyes fascinating, but he also waxed eloquent about my elbows. He liked it all.

I miss him. Gods, how I miss him.

I slept late the next day and woke up in agony. My back hurt all over, and because I was not used to sleeping on my belly, my neck was stiff. Between that, my sore and puffy eyes, and the headache that had returned with a vengeance, I could perhaps be forgiven for not realizing at first that there was someone new in the house.

I stumbled blearily into the kitchen, drawn by the smells and sounds of cooking breakfast. "Good morning," I mumbled.

"Good morning," said a cheery woman's voice, and I nearly fell. I caught myself against a counter, spun, and grabbed for the block of kitchen knives.

Hands caught mine and I cried out, immediately struggling. But the hands were warm, big, familiar.

Shiny, thank the gods. I stopped trying to reach for a weapon, though my heart was still racing. Shiny, and a woman. Who?

Then I recalled her greeting. That raspy, too-sweet voice. *Lil* was in my home, making me breakfast, after eating some Order-Keepers that Shiny had murdered.

"What in the Maelstrom are you doing here?" I demanded. "And show yourself, damn it. Don't hide from me in my own home."

She sounded amused. "I didn't think you liked my looks."

"I don't, but I'd rather *know* you're not standing there slavering at me."

"You won't know that even if you see me." But she appeared, facing me in her deceptively normal form. Or maybe the other shape—the mouth—was normal for her, and this was only a courtesy that she offered me. Either way, I was grateful. "As for why I'm here, I brought him home." She nodded beyond me, where I heard Shiny breathing.

"Oh." I was beginning to feel calm again. "Er. Thank you, then. But, um, Lady Lil—"

"Just Lil." She beamed and turned back to the stove. "Ham."

"What?"

"*Ham.*" She turned and looked past me, at Shiny. "I would like some ham."

"There's no ham in the house," he said.

"Oh," she said, sounding heartbroken. Her face fell, too, almost comically tragic. I hardly noticed, stunned by Shiny's response.

He moved behind me to the cupboard and took something out, setting it on the counter. "Smoked velly."

Lil brightened immediately. "Ah! Better than ham. Now we'll have a proper breakfast." She turned back to her preparations, beginning to hum some toneless song.

I was beginning to feel light-headed. I went to the table and sat down, not sure what to think. Shiny sat down across from me, watching me with his heavy gaze.

"I must apologize," he said softly.

I jumped. "You're talking *more?*"

He didn't bother to respond to that question, since the answer was obvious. "I didn't expect Lil to impose on your hospitality. That was not my intention."

For a moment I did not respond, distracted. He'd spoken at the site of Role's murder, but this was the first time I'd heard him say several sentences in a row.

And dear *gods,* his voice was beautiful. Tenor. I'd expected him to be baritone. And it was rich, every precisely enunciated word reverberating through my ears all the way down to my toes. I could listen to a voice like that all day.

Or all night... Sternly, I turned my thoughts away from that path. I had enough gods in my love life.

Then I realized I'd been staring blankly at him. "Oh, ah, I

don't mind that so much," I said at last. "Though I wish you'd asked first."

"She insisted."

That threw me. "Why?"

"I have a warning to pass on," Lil interjected, coming over to the table. She put a plate in front of me, then another in front of Shiny. My kitchen had only two chairs, so she hoisted herself up on a counter, then picked up a plate she'd apparently set aside for herself. Her eyes gleamed as she gazed at her food, and I looked away, afraid she would open her mouth wide again.

"A warning?" In spite of everything, the food smelled good. I poked it a bit and realized she'd incorporated the velly into the eggs, along with peppers and herbs I'd forgotten I had. I tried it—delicious.

"Someone is looking for you," Lil said.

It took a moment to figure out she meant me, not Shiny. Then I sobered, realizing who might be looking for me. "Everyone saw Previt Rimarn talking to me yesterday. Now that he's, um, gone, I imagine his fellow previts will come around."

"Oh, he's not dead," said Lil, surprised. "The three I ate last night were just Order-Keepers. Young, healthy, quite juicy beneath the crust." She uttered a lascivious sigh. I put down my fork, appetite gone. "There was no magic on them to spoil the taste, except that used to kill them. I imagine they were just there to do the beating."

In spite of myself, I groaned inwardly. That had been the one benefit I could see in the priests' deaths; Rimarn was the only one who knew of my magic and suspected me of being Role's killer. Now, with his men dead, he would definitely be looking for me.

Madding's words came back to me: *leave town*. Yet the problem of money haunted me. And I did not want to leave. Shadow was my home.

"He's not the one I meant, in any case," Lil said, interrupting my thoughts. Surprised, I focused on her. Her plate, faintly visible to me in the reflected glow of her body, was empty—clean, as if she'd polished it. She was licking her fork now, with long, slow strokes of her tongue that seemed obscene.

"What?"

She turned and looked at me, and abruptly I was pinned by her mottled gaze. The dark spots in her eyes *moved*, spinning about her pupils in a slow, restless dance. I found myself wondering if the spots in her hair moved, too.

"So much hunger," she said in a soft, raspy purr. "It wraps about you like a layered cloak. A previt's anger. Madding's desire." My cheeks grew warm. "And one other, more hungry than the others. Powerful. Dangerous." She shivered, and I shivered with her. "He could reshape the world with such hunger, especially if he gets what he wants. And what he wants is *you*."

I stared at her, confused and alarmed. "Who is this person? What does he want me for?"

"I don't know." She licked her lips, then regarded me thoughtfully. "Perhaps if I stay near you, I can meet him."

I frowned, too unnerved to comment on this. Why would anyone powerful want me? I was nothing, nobody. Even Rimarn would be disappointed if he knew the truth of the magic he'd sensed in me. All I could do was *see*.

And... I frowned. There were also my paintings. I kept those out of sight; only Madding and Shiny knew about them. There was something magical to those. I didn't know what, but my father had taught me long ago that it was important to keep such things hidden, and so I did.

Was it those, then, that this mysterious person wanted?

No, no, I was jumping to conclusions. I didn't even know if this person existed. All I had to go on was the word of a goddess who saw nothing wrong with eating human beings. She might see nothing wrong with lying to them, too.

Shiny was still there, though I had not heard him eat. I licked my lips, wondering if he would answer. "Do you know what she's talking about?" I asked him.

"No."

So far, so good. "Your injuries," I began.

"He's fine," Lil said. She was eyeing my unfinished plate. "I killed him, and he came back whole."

I blinked in surprise. "You healed him... by *killing* him?"

She shrugged. "Should I have left him as he was, taking weeks to heal on his own? He isn't like the rest of us. He is mortal."

"Except at sunrise."

"Even then." Lil hopped down from the counter, leaving her empty plate behind. "He has been diminished to only a fraction of his true self—enough for a pretty light show now and then, but no more. And enough to protect you." She drew close, her eyes fixed on my plate.

I was so busy pondering her words that I did not notice her approach until her expression turned... Gods, I have no words for the horror of her. It was as if her other face, the long-mouthed predator, had appeared underneath the benign one. I could not see that face, as she had warned me, but I could feel its presence and its raw, bottomles hunger. I realized it only when she lunged, not at my plate but at *me*.

I didn't even have time to cry out. Her bony, sharp-nailed hand shot at my throat and might have torn it out by the time I registered the danger. But an instant later, her hand stilled and quivered, an inch away. I stared at it, then at the dark blotch around her wrist. Just like the day before, at my table. And just as then, Shiny suddenly became visible to me, his glow rising from within, his face hard and eyes irritated as he glared at Lil.

Lil smiled at him, then at me. "You see?"

I dragged my mind back from silent screaming fits and took a deep breath to calm down. I did see. But it made no sense. I said to Shiny, "Your power comes back to you when . . . when you protect me?"

I could still see him, which made it easy to see the contemptuous look he threw at me. I nearly flinched in surprise. What had I done to merit that look? Then I remembered what Madding had said. *He doesn't think much of mortals.*

Lil grinned, reading my face. "Any mortal," she said, and eyed Shiny. " '*You will wander among mortals as one of them.*' " I blinked in surprise and saw Shiny stiffen. The words were not hers, I could tell. They did not sound like Lil at all; I heard darker echoes. " '*Unknown, commanding only what wealth and respect you can earn with your deeds and words. You may call upon your power only in great need, and only to aid these mortals for whom you hold such contempt.*' "

Shiny released her wrist and turned away from her, sitting down with a bleak expression—what little of it I could see, because his glow was fading already. Ah, he had dealt with the threat, so he no longer needed his power.

I took a deep breath and faced Lil. "I appreciate the

information. But if you don't mind, in the future, just *explain* things to me. No more demonstrations."

She laughed, which set the little hairs arise on my skin. She did not sound entirely sane. "I'm glad you can see me, mortal girl. It makes things so much more interesting." Her eyes shifted to the table. "Are you going to eat that?"

My plate—or did she mean my hand, which rested near it? Very carefully I moved my hand to my lap. "Be my guest."

Lil laughed again, delighted, and bent over the plate. There was a movement too fast for me to follow. I had the impression of whirring needles, and a quick, fetid breeze wafted past my nose. When she lifted her head half a breath later, the plate was clean. She took my napkin, too, to dab at the corners of her mouth.

I swallowed hard and pushed myself to my feet, edging around her. Shiny was a barely visible shadow across from me, eating. Lil had begun to throw glances at his plate, too. There were things I wanted to say to him, though not in front of Lil. He had been humiliated enough the night before. But we would have to reach an understanding, he and I, and soon.

I washed the dishes slowly, and Shiny ate slowly. Lil sat in my chair, glancing from one to the other of us and laughing to herself now and again.

The sun was high by the time I left the house—later than I'd hoped to set out. I had farther to go this time and tables to carry. Though I'd hoped that Shiny would join me again and perhaps help me carry things, he remained where he was after breakfast was done. He was brooding, in a darker mood than usual; I almost missed his old apathy.

Lil left when I did, to my great relief. One problematic godling houseguest was enough for me. She bid me a fond farewell
before she left, however, and thanked me so profusely for the
breakfast that I actually felt better about her. Madding had
always hinted to me that some godlings were better than others
at interacting with mortals. Some of them were too alien in
their thought processes, or too monstrous in our eyes, to fit in
easily despite their best efforts. I had an idea that Lil was among
these.

I carried my tables and the best-selling of my merchandise
to the southern promenade of Gateway Park. The northwestern promenade was where Art Row stood, the better to take
advantage of the crowds that came for the best view of the Tree
and other noteworthy sights of the city. The south promenade,
where the view was passable but not ideal and where the attrac-
tions were less impressive, was a mediocre spot. Still, it was the
only option I had left; the northeastern entrance of the park
had been occluded years ago by a root of the Tree, and the east
gate had a lovely view of Sky's freight gate.

As I entered the south promenade, I heard a few other sellers at work, calling out to passersby to hawk their wares. Not
a good sign, that—it meant potential cutomers were sparse
enough that the sellers had to compete over them. There would
be none of the companionable looking out for one another that
I was used to at the Row; this would be every seller for herself.
I could hear three—no, four—other sellers in the vicinity: one
with decorative headscarves, another selling "Tree pies" (whatever those were; they did smell nice), and two people apparently
selling books and souvenirs. I felt the glares of the latter two as
I began setting up, and I worried that I might have to deal with

unpleasantness. As often happened once they got a good look at me, however, no one bothered me. There are times—rare, I'll admit—when blindness comes in handy.

So I set up and waited. And waited. I didn't know the area and hadn't had a chance to fully explore. Although I could hear foot traffic passing relatively nearby (pilgrims remarking over how dark the city had become and how beautiful the Tree-entangled palace Sky still was), it was possible I'd managed to set myself up in a bad area. I had no doubt the other sellers had already laid claim to the best spots, so I resolved to do the best I could with what I had.

By midafternoon, however, I knew I was in trouble. My wares had lured over a few pilgrims—working folk mostly, Amn from less-prosperous towns and lands near Shadow. That was part of the problem, I realized; High Northers and island folk had always been my best customers. The faith of Itempas had always been precarious in those lands, so they bought my miniature Trees and statues of godlings eagerly. But Senmites were mostly Amn, and Amn were mostly Itempan. They were less easily impressed by the Tree and Shadow's other heretical wonders.

Which was fine. I never begrudged people their beliefs, but I needed to eat. My stomach had begun to rumble in a vocal reminder of this fact—my own fault for letting Lil's presence deter me from breakfast.

Then an idea came to me. I rummaged among my bags and was relieved to find I'd brought the sidewalk chalk. I moved around to the front of my tables, crouched, and considered what to sketch.

The idea that came to me was so fiercely powerful that I

rocked back on my toes for a moment, startled. Usually my creative urges came in the morning, when I painted in my basement. I'd meant to sketch only a few silly doodles to draw eyes toward my trinkets and goods. But the image in my head...I licked my lips and considered whether it was safe.

It was dangerous, I decided. No doubt about it. I was *blind*, for the gods' sake; I shouldn't have been able to visualize anything, much less depict it recognizably. Most people in the city wouldn't notice the paradox, or care, but to Order-Keepers and others whose job it was to watch for unauthorized magic, it would be suspect. I had survived all these years by being careful.

But...I picked up a piece of chalk, rubbing its smooth, fat length between my fingers. Colors meant little to me except as a detail of substance, but I had picked up the habit of naming my paints and chalks nevertheless. There is more to color than what can be seen, after all. The chalk smelled faintly bitter—not the bitterness of food, but the bitterness of air too rarefied to breathe, like when one climbed a high hill. I decided it was white, and perfect for the image in my head.

"I paint a picture," I whispered, and began.

I sketched the bowl of a sky. Not Sky, or any part of it—not even the sky that existed somewhere above the Tree, which I had never seen. This would be a thin, nearly empty firmament, wheeling above in layers of rising color. I laid down a thick base of white chalk, using both of my available sticks until there was just a sliver remaining. Lucky. Then I grazed in blue—not much of it, though. It felt wrong for the sky in my head—too vibrant, thick, almost greasy between my fingers. I used my hands to thin out the blue, then added another color that made a good yellow. Yes, that was right. I thickened the yellow, rolling it on, feeling its growing intensity and warmth and following it until at last it coalesced into light at the center of my composition. *Two* suns, one great and one smaller, spinning about each other in an eternal dance. Perhaps I could—

"Hey."

"Just a minute," I murmured. The clouds in this sky would be powerful things, thick and dark with impending rain. I reached for something that smelled silver and drew one, wishing I had more blue, or black.

Now birds. Of course there would be birds flying in this bright, empty sky. But they would not have feathers—

"Hey!" Something touched me and I started, dropping the chalk and blinking out of my daze.

"Wh-what?" Almost at once, my back protested, bruises and muscles twinging. How long had I been drawing? I groaned, reaching back to knead the small of my back.

"Thanks," said the voice. Male, older. No one I knew, though he reminded me vaguely of Vuroy. Then I recalled hearing his voice—one of my fellow souvenir sellers, the loudest of the three who'd been hawking his wares. "That's a nice trick," he continued. "You pulled a good crowd. But the south promenade closes at sunset, so you might want to catch a few of 'em while you can, huh?"

Crowd?

I abruptly became aware of voices around me—dozens of them, clustered around my drawing. They were murmuring, exclaiming over something. I got to my feet and hissed at the agony in my knees.

As I straightened, the cluster of people around me burst into applause.

"What—" But I knew. They were clapping for *me*.

Before I could wrap my thoughts around this, my onlookers pushed forward—I heard them jostling each other in an effort to avoid stepping on the drawing—and began asking me the price of my wares, and whether I painted professionally, and how I managed to draw such beautiful things when I couldn't see, and whether I *really* couldn't see, and, and, and. I had enough wits left to get behind the table and answer the most uncomfortable questions with silly pleasantries ("No, I really can't see! I'm glad you like it!"), before I was inundated with eager customers buying everything I had. Most of them weren't even haggling. It was the best sales day I'd ever had, and it all happened in a span of minutes.

When they were done with me, most of the customers moved on to the other tables—as they had been doing since I'd begun drawing, I realized belatedly. No wonder the hawker had come to thank me. But I could hear the distant tolling of the White Hall bells, marking sunset; the park would be closing soon.

"I thought it might be you," said a voice nearby, and I jumped, turning to smile at what I thought was yet another customer. But the man who'd spoken did not come to the table. When I oriented on him, I realized he was just beyond the chalk drawing.

"Pardon?" I asked.

"You were at the other promenade," he said, and I tensed in alarm, though he did not sound threatening at all. "The day after you found that godling's body. I saw you then, thought there was something . . . interesting . . . about you."

I began to pack up, less alarmed now; perhaps this was some sort of awkward attempt on the man's part to chat me up. "Were you in the crowd?" I asked. "One of the heretics?"

"Heretics?" The man chuckled. "Hmm. I suppose the Order would think so, though I honor the Bright Lord, too."

One of the New Lights, then; they were supposedly some other branch of Itempan. Or maybe a newer sect. I could never keep them straight. "Well . . . I'm a traditional Itempan myself." I said it to forestall any attempts on his part to convert me. "But if Role was your god, then I'm sorry for your loss."

I almost heard his eyebrows rise. "An Itempan who does not condemn the worshippers of another god or celebrate that god's death? Aren't you a bit heretical yourself?"

I shrugged, putting the last of the small boxes into my carry-sack. "Maybe so." I smiled. "Don't tell the Order-Keepers."

The man laughed and then, to my relief, turned away. "Of course not. Until later, then." He walked off, humming to himself, and that confirmed it: he was singing the New Lights' wordless song.

I sat down for a moment to recoup before starting the trip back. My pockets were full of coins, and my purse, too. Madding would be pleased; I'd have to take a few days off to replenish my stock before I could sell again, and maybe I'd take a few days beyond that, as a vacation. I'd never had a vacation before, but I could afford it now.

Boots approached from the far end of the promenade. I was so tired and dazed that I thought nothing of it; there were many people milling around the south promenade now, though the other sellers were packing up as well. If I had listened more carefully, however, I would've recognized the boots. I did, too late, when their owner spoke.

"Very good, Oree Shoth," said a voice I'd dreaded hearing all day. Rimarn Dih. Oh, no.

"Very good of you, indeed, to draw such a lovely beacon," he said, coming to stop just beyond the chalk drawing. There were three other sets of footsteps approaching beyond him, all with those horribly familiar heavy boots. I rose to my feet, trembling.

"I'd expected you to be halfway to Nimaro by now," he continued. "Imagine my surprise when I caught the scent of familiar magic, not so very far away at all."

"I don't know anything," I stammered. I gripped my stick as if that would help me. "I have no idea who killed Lady Role, and I'm not a godling."

"My dear, I don't really care about that anymore," he said, and by the cold fury in his tone, I knew he'd found whatever Lil had left of his men. That meant I was lost, utterly lost. "I want your friend. That white-haired Maro bastard; where is he?"

For a moment I was confused. Shiny's hair was white? "He didn't do anything." Oh, gods, that was a lie and Rimarn was a scrivener; he would know. "I mean, there was a godling, a woman named Lil. She—"

"Enough of this," he snapped, and turned away. "Take her."

The boots came forward, closing in. I stumbled back, but there was nowhere to go. Would they beat me to death and avenge their comrades right here, or take me to the White Hall for questioning first? I began to gasp in panic; my heart was pounding. What could I do?

And then many things happened at once.

Why? I'd asked my father long ago. Why could I not show my paintings to others? They were just paint and pigment. Not everyone liked them—some of the images were too disturbing for that—but they did no harm.

They're magic, he told me. Over and over again he told me, but I didn't listen enough. I didn't believe. *There's no such thing as magic that does no harm.*

The Order-Keepers stepped onto my drawing.

"No," I whispered as they drew closer. "Please."

"Poor girl," I heard a woman, one of those who'd wanted to know if I painted professionally, murmuring amid the crowd from some ways off. They had loved me a moment before. Now they were going to just stand there, useless, while the Keepers took their revenge.

"Put that stick down, woman," said one of the Keepers, sounding annoyed. I clutched my walking stick tighter. I couldn't breathe. Why were they doing this? They knew I hadn't killed Role, that I wasn't a godling. I had magic, but they would laugh to know what phenomenal powers I was concealing. I was no threat.

"Please, please," I said. I almost sobbed it, like my name: *please*—gasp—*please.* They kept coming.

A hand grabbed my stick, and suddenly my eyes burned. Heat boiled behind them, pushing to get out. I shut them in reflex, the pain fueling my terror.

"Get away from me!" I screamed. I tried to fight, flailed with hands and stick. My hand found a chest—

Shiny's hand on my chest, lashing out at the witness to his shame. And I pushed.

This is difficult to describe, even now. Bear with me.

Somewhere, elsewhere, there is a sky. It is a hot, empty sky, overhead as skies should be, blazing with the light of twin suns.

The sky I drew—do you understand? Somewhere it is real. I know this now.

When I screamed and pushed at the Order-Keepers, the heat behind my eyes flared into light. In my mind's eye, I saw legs fall into this sky, upside down. Legs and hips, appearing out of nowhere, kicking, twisting. Falling.

There was nothing else attached to them.

Something changed.

When I became aware of it, I blinked. Screaming all around me. Running, pounding feet. Something jostled one of my tables, knocking it over; I stumbled back. I could smell blood and something fouler: excrement and bile and stark, stinking fear.

Abruptly I realized I could not see my entire drawing anymore. It was there—I could still see the edges of it. Its glow was oddly faded and growing fainter by the second, as if its magic had been spent. However, what remained of it was occluded by three large dark blotches, spreading and overlapping. Liquid, not magical.

Rimarn Dih's voice was distraught, almost unintelligible with horror. "What did you do, Maro bitch? *What in the Father's name have you done?*"

"Wh-what?" My eyes hurt. My head hurt. The smell was making me ill. I felt wrong, off balance, all my skin aprickle. My mouth tasted of guilt, and I did not know why.

Rimarn was shouting for someone to help him. He sounded like he was exerting himself, pulling at something heavy. There was a sound, something wet... I shuddered. I did not want to know what that sound was.

Two presences suddenly appeared on either side of me. They took me by the arms, gingerly.

"Time to go, little one," said a bright male voice. Madding's lieutenant. Where the hells had he come from? Then the world flared and we were somewhere else. Quiet settled around us, along with warm, scented humidity and a blue-green feeling of calm and balance. Madding's house.

It should have been a sanctuary for me, but I did not feel safe.

"What happened?" I asked the godling beside me. "Please tell me. Something... I did something, didn't I?"

"You don't know?" Madding's other lieutenant, the female one, on my other side. She sounded incredulous.

"No." I did not want to know. I licked my lips. "Please tell me."

"I don't know how you did it," she said, speaking slowly. There was something in her tone that was almost... awed. That made no sense; she was a god. "I've never seen a mortal do anything like that. But your drawing..." She trailed off.

"It became *enarmhukdatalwasl*, though not quite *shuwao*," said the male godling, his godwords briefly stinging my eyes. I shut them in reflex. Why did my eyes hurt? It felt like I'd been punched in the back of each. "It carved a path across half a billion stars and connected one world with another, just for a moment. Damnedest thing."

I rubbed at my eyes in frustration, though this did no good; the pain was inside me. "I don't understand, damn you! Speak mortal!" *I did not want to know.*

"You made a door," he said. "You sent the Order-Keepers through it. Not all the way, though. The magic wasn't stable. It burned out before they passed through completely. Do you understand?"

"I..." No. "It was just a chalk drawing," I whispered.

"You dropped them partway into another world," snapped the female godling. "And then you closed the door. *You cut them in half.* Do you understand now?"

I did.

I began to scream, and kept screaming until one of the godlings did something, and then I passed out.

5

"Family"
(charcoal study)

I HAVE A FAVORITE MEMORY of my father that I sometimes recall as a dream.

In the dream, I am small. I have only recently learned to climb the ladder. The rungs are very far apart and I cannot see them, so for a long time I was afraid I would miss a rung and fall. I had to learn not to be afraid, which is much harder than it sounds. I am very proud of having accomplished this.

"Papa," I say, running across the small attic room. This is, by my parents' mutual agreement, *his* room. My mother does not come here, not even to clean. It is neat anyhow—my father is a neat man—yet it is permeated all over with that indefinable feeling that is *him*. Some of it is scent, but there is something more to his presence, too. Something that I understand instinctively, even if I lack the vocabulary to describe it.

My father is not like most people in our village. He goes to White Hall services only often enough to keep the priest from sanctioning him. He makes no offerings at the household altar. He does not pray. I have asked him whether he believes in the gods, and he says that of course he does; are we not Maroneh? *But that is not the same thing as honoring them,* he sometimes adds. Then he cautions me not to mention this to anyone else. Not the priests, not my friends, not even Mama. One day, he says, I will understand.

Today he is in a rare mood—and for a rare once, I can see him: a smaller-than-average man with cool black eyes and large, elegant hands. His face is lineless, almost youthful, though his hair is salt-and-pepper and there is something in his gaze, something heavy and tired, that shows his long life more clearly than wrinkles ever could. He was old when he married Mama. He never wanted a child, yet he loves me with all his heart.

I grin and lean on his knees. He's sitting down, which puts his face in reach of my searching fingers. Eyes can be fooled, I have learned already, but touch is always sure.

"You've been singing," I say.

He smiled. "Can you see me again? I thought it would have worn off by now."

"Sing for me, Papa," I plead. I love the colors his voice weaves in the air.

"No, Ree-child. Your mother's home."

"She never hears it! Please?"

"I promised," he says softly, and I hang my head. He promised my mother, long before I was born, never to expose her or me to the danger that comes of his strangeness. I am too young to understand where the danger comes from, but the fear in his eyes is enough to keep me silent.

But he has broken his promise before. He did it to teach me, because otherwise I might have betrayed my own strangeness out of ignorance. And because, I later realize, it kills him a little to stifle that part of himself. He was meant to be glorious. With me, in these small private moments, he can be.

So when he sees my disappointment, he sighs and lifts me into his lap. Very softly, just for me, he sings.

I awoke slowly, to the sound and smell of water.

I was sitting in it. The water was nearly body temperature; I barely felt it on my skin. Under me, I could feel hard, sculpted stone, as warm as the water; nearby was the smell of flowers. Hiras: a vining plant that had once been native to the Maroland. Its blooms had a heavy, distinctive perfume that I liked. That told me where I was.

If I hadn't been to Madding's place before, I would've been disoriented. Madding owned a large house in one of the richer districts of Wesha, and he had brought me here often, complaining that my little bed would give him a bad back. He had filled the ground floor of the house with pools. There were at least a dozen of them, carved out of the bedrock that underlay this part of Shadow, sculpted into pretty shapes and screened by growing plants. It was the sort of design choice godlings were infamous for; they thought first of aesthetics and lastly of convenience or propriety. Madding's guests had to either stand or strip and get into a pool. He saw nothing wrong with this.

The pools were not magical. The water was warm because Mad had hired some mortal genius to concoct a mechanism that kept boiled water in the piping system at all times. Madding had never bothered to learn how it worked, so he couldn't explain it to me.

I sat up, listening, and promptly became aware that someone was with me, sitting nearby. I saw nothing, but the breathing pattern was familiar. "Mad?"

He resolved out of the darkness, sitting at the pool's edge with one knee drawn up. His hair was loose, clinging to his damp skin. It made him look strangely young. His eyes were somber.

"How do you feel?" he asked.

The question puzzled me for a moment, and then I remembered.

I sat back against the side of the pool, barely feeling the throb of my old bruises, and turned my face away from him. My eyes still ached, so I closed them, though that didn't help much. How did I feel? Like a murderess. How else?

Madding sighed. "I suppose it does no good to point this out, but what happened wasn't your fault."

Of course it did no good. And it wasn't true.

"Mortals are never good at controlling magic, Oree. You weren't built for it. And you didn't know what your magic could do. You didn't intend to kill those men."

"They're still dead," I said. "My *intentions* don't change that."

"True." He shifted, putting the other foot into the water. "They probably intended to kill *you*, though."

I laughed softly. It echoed off the shifting surface of the water and sounded demented. "Stop trying, Mad. Please."

He fell silent for a while, letting me wallow. When he decided

I'd done enough of that, he slipped into the waist-high water and came over, lifting me against him. That was all it took, really. I buried my face in his chest and let myself turn to noodle in his arms. He rubbed my back and murmured soothing things in his language while I cried, and then he carried me out of the room of pools and up curving stairs and laid me down in the tumbled pile of cushions that served as his bed. I fell asleep there, not caring whether I ever woke up again.

Of course, I did wake up eventually, disturbed by voices talking softly nearby. When I opened my eyes and looked around, I was surprised to see a strange godling sitting beside the cushion pile. She was very pale, with short black hair molded like a cap around a pleasant, heart-shaped face. Two things struck me at once: first, that she looked ordinary enough to pass for human, which marked her as a godling who regularly did business with mortals. Second, for some reason, she sat in shadow, though there was nothing nearby that could have thrown a shadow on her, and I shouldn't have been able to see the shadow in any case.

She had been talking with Madding but paused as I sat up. "Hello," I said, nodding to her and rubbing my face. I knew all his people, and this one wasn't one of them.

She nodded back, smiling. "So you're Mad's killer."

I stiffened. Madding scowled. "Nemmer."

"I meant no insult," she said, shrugging, still smiling. "I like killers."

I glanced at Madding, wondering whether it was all right for me to tell this kinswoman of his to go to the infinite hells. He didn't seem tense, which told me she was no threat or enemy, but he wasn't happy, either. He noticed my look and sighed. "Nemmer came to warn me, Oree. She runs another organization here in town—"

"More like a guild of independent professionals," Nemmer put in.

Madding threw her a look that was pure brotherly annoyance, then focused on me again. "Oree...the Order of Itempas just contacted her, asking to commission her services. Hers specifically, not one of her people."

I picked up a big pillow and pulled it against me, not to hide my nudity but to cover my shiver of unease. Madding noticed and went to his closet to fetch something for me. To Nemmer I said, "Not that I know much about it, but I was under the impression that the Order could call upon the Arameri assassin corps whenever they had need."

"Yes," said Nemmer, "when the Arameri approve of, or care about, what they're doing. But there are a great many small matters that are beneath the Arameri's notice, and the Order prefers to take care of such matters itself." She shrugged.

I nodded slowly. "I take it you're a god of...death?"

"Oh, no, that's the Lady. I'm just stealth, secrets, a little infiltration. The sort of business that takes place under the Nightfather's cloak."

I could not help blinking at this title. She was referring to one of the new gods, the Lord of Shadows, but her term had sounded much like *Nightlord*. That could not be, of course; the Nightlord was in the keeping of the Arameri.

"I don't mind the odd elimination," Nemmer continued, "but only as a sideline." She shrugged, then glanced at Madding. "I might reconsider, though, given how much the Order is

offering. Probably a big unexploited market in taking out godlings who piss off mortals."

I gasped and whirled toward Mad, who was coming back to
the bed with a robe. He lifted an eyebrow, unworried. Nemmer
laughed and reached over to poke my bare knee, which made
me jump. "I could be here for *you*, you know."

"No," I said softly. Madding could take care of himself. There
was no reason for me to worry. "No one would send a godling to
kill me. Easier to pay some beggar twenty meri and make it look
like a robbery gone wrong. Not that they need to hide it at all;
they're *the Order*."

"Ah, but you forget," Nemmer said. "You used magic to kill
those Keepers at the park. And the Order thinks you killed
three others who'd been assigned to discipline a Maro man,
reportedly your cousin, for assaulting a previt. They couldn't
find the bodies, but word's going around about how your magic
works." She shrugged.

Oh, gods. Madding knelt behind me, putting a robe of
watered silk around my shoulders. I slumped back against him.
"Rimarn," I said. "He thought I was a godling."

"And you don't hire a mortal to kill a godling. Even one who's
apparently goddess of chalk drawings come to life." Nemmer
winked at me. But then she sobered. "It's you they want, but
you're not the one they think is behind Role's death, not ultimately. Little brother, you should've been more discreet." She
nodded toward me. "All her neighbors know about her godling
lover; half the *city* knows it. You might've been able to save her
from this otherwise."

"I know," Mad said, and there was a millennium's worth of
regret in his tone.

"Wait," I said, frowning. "The Order thinks Madding killed Role? I know a godling must have done it, but—"

"Madding is in the business of selling our blood," Nemmer said. Her tone was neutral as she said this, but I heard the disapproval in it, anyway, and heard Madding's sigh. "And I hear business is good. It's not a far stretch to think he might want to increase production, maybe by obtaining a large amount of godsblood at one time."

"Which would be a fair assumption," Madding snapped, "if Role's blood had been *gone*. There was plenty of it left in and around her body—"

"Which you took away, in front of witnesses."

"To Yeine! To see if there was any hope of bringing her back to life. But Role's soul had already gone elsewhere." He shook his head and sighed. "Why in the infinite hells would I kill her, dump her body in an alley, then *come back to fetch it*, if her blood was what I wanted?"

"Maybe that wasn't what you wanted," Nemmer said very softly. "Or at least, you didn't want *all* her blood. Some of the witnesses got close enough to see what was missing, Mad."

Madding's hands tightened on my shoulders. Puzzled, I covered one of them with my own. "Missing?"

"Her heart," said Nemmer, and silence fell.

I flinched, horrified. But then I remembered that day in the alley, when my fingers had come away from Role's body coated thickly with blood.

Madding cursed and got up; he began to pace, his steps quick and tight with anger. Nemmer watched him for a moment, then sighed and returned her attention to me.

"The Order thinks this was some sort of exotic commission,"

she said. "A wealthy customer wanting a more potent sort of godsblood. If the stuff from our veins is powerful enough to give mortals magic, how much stronger might heartblood be? Maybe even strong enough to give a blind Maroneh woman—known paramour of the very godling they suspect—the power to kill three Order-Keepers."

My mouth fell open. "That's insane! No godling would kill another for those reasons!"

Nemmer's eyebrows rose. "Yes, and anyone who knows us would understand that," she said, a note of approval in her voice. "Those of us who live in Shadow enjoy playing games with mortal wealth, but none of us *needs* it, nor would we bother to kill for it. The Order hasn't figured that out yet, or they wouldn't have tried to hire me, and they wouldn't suspect Madding—at least, not for this reason. But they follow the creed of the Bright: that which disturbs the order of society must be eliminated, regardless of whether it *caused* the disturbance." She rolled her eyes. "You'd think they'd get tired of parroting Itempas and start thinking for themselves after two thousand years."

I drew up my legs and wrapped my arms around them, resting my forehead on one knee. The nightmare kept growing, no matter what I did, getting worse by the day. "They suspect Madding because of me," I murmured. "That's what you're saying."

"No," Madding snapped. I could hear him still pacing; his voice was jagged with suppressed fury. "They suspect me because of your damned houseguest."

I realized he was right. Previt Rimarn might have noticed my magic, but that meant little in and of itself. Many mortals had magic; that was where scriveners like Rimarn came from. Only *using* that magic was illegal, and without seeing my paintings,

Rimarn would've had no proof that I'd done so. If he had questioned me that day, and if I'd kept my wits about me, he would've realized I couldn't possibly have killed Role. At worst, I might have ended up as an Order recruit.

But then Shiny had intervened. Even though Lil had eaten the bodies in South Root, Rimarn knew that four men had gone into that alley and only one had emerged, somehow unscathed. Gods knew how many witnesses there were in South Root who would talk for a coin or two. Worse, Rimarn had probably sensed the white-hot blast of power Shiny used to kill his men, even from across the city. Between that and what I'd done to the Order-Keepers with my chalk drawing, it did not seem so far-fetched a conclusion: one godling dead, another standing to profit from her death, and the mortals most intimately connected with him suddenly manifesting strange magic. None of it was proof—but they were Itempans. Disorder was crime enough.

"Well, I've said my piece." Nemmer got up, stretching. As she did so, I saw what her posture had hidden: she was all wiry muscle and acrobatic grace. She looked too ordinary to be a spy and an assassin, but it was there when she moved. "Take care of yourself, little brother." She paused and considered. "Little sister, too."

"Wait," I blurted, drawing a surprised look from both of them. "What are you going to tell the Order?"

"What I *already* told them," she said with firm emphasis, "was that they'd better never try to kill a godling again. They don't understand: it's not Itempas they have to deal with now. We don't know what this new Twilight will do. No one sane wants to find out. And Maelstrom help the entire mortal realm if they ever ignite the Darkness's wrath."

"I..." I fell silent in confusion, having no idea what she was talking about. *The Twilight* I knew; it was another name for the Lady. *The Darkness*—was that the Shadow Lord? And what had she meant by "it's not Itempas they have to deal with now"?

"They're wasting time on this stupidity," Madding snapped, "grasping at straws instead of actually trying to find our sister's killer! I could kill them for that myself."

"Now, now," said Nemmer, smiling. "You know the rules. Besides, in twenty-eight days, it will be a moot point." I wondered at this, too, then remembered the words of the quiet goddess, that day in South Root. *You have thirty days.*

What would happen when thirty days had passed?

Nemmer sobered. "Anyway... it's worse than you think, little brother. You'll hear about this soon enough, so I might as well tell you now: two of our other siblings have gone missing."

Madding started, as did I. Nemmer's sources of information were good indeed if she'd learned this before Mad's people or before the gossip vine of the streets could pass it on.

"Who?" he asked, stricken.

"Ina and Oboro."

I had heard of the latter. He was some sort of warrior-god, making a name for himself among the illegal fighting rings in the city. People liked him because he fought fair—had even lost a few times. Ina was new to me.

"Dead?" I asked.

"No bodies have been found, and none of us has felt the deaths occur. Though no one felt Role, either." She paused for a moment, growing still within her ever-present shadow, and abruptly I realized she was furious. It was hard to tell behind her jocularity, but she was just as angry as Madding. Of course;

these were her brothers and sisters missing, possibly dying. I would have felt the same in her position.

Then, belatedly, it occurred to me: I *was* in her position. If someone was targeting godlings, killing them, then every godling in the city was in danger—including Madding. And Shiny, if he still counted.

I got to my feet and went over to him. He had stopped pacing; when I took his hands in a fierce grip, he looked surprised. I turned to Nemmer and could not help the tremor in my voice.

"Lady Nemmer," I said, "thank you for telling us all this. Would you mind if Madding and I spoke in private now?"

Nemmer looked taken aback; then she grinned wolfishly. "Oh, I like this one, Mad. Shame she's mortal. And, yes, Miss Shoth, I'd be happy to leave you two alone now—on the condition that you never call me 'Lady Nemmer' again." She shuddered in mock horror. "Makes me feel old."

"Yes, L—" I bit my tongue. "Yes."

She winked, saluted Madding, and then vanished.

As soon as she was gone, I turned to Madding. "I want you to leave Shadow."

He rocked back on his heels, staring at me. "You *what*?"

"Someone is killing godlings here. You'll be safe in the gods' realm."

He gaped at me, speechless for several seconds. "I don't know whether to laugh or kick you out of my house. That you would think so little of me...that you would honestly think I'd *run* rather than find the bastards who are doing this—"

"I don't care about your pride!" I squeezed his hands again, trying to make him listen. "I know you're not a coward; I know you want to find your sister's killer. But if someone is killing godlings, and if none of the gods know how to *stop* that person…Mad, what's wrong with running? You just urged me to do the same thing to get away from the Order, right? You spent aeons in the gods' realm, and only, what, ten years in this one? Why should you care what happens here?"

"Why should I—" He shook off my hands and took hold of my shoulders, glaring at me. "Have you gone mad? You're standing here in front of me, asking me why I don't leave you behind to face the Order-Keepers and gods know what else! If you think—"

"It's *you* they want! If you leave, I'll turn myself in. I'll tell them you went back to the gods' realm; they'll draw their own conclusions from that. Then—"

"Then they'll kill you," he said. That startled me silent. "Of course they will, Oree. Scapegoats restore order, don't they? People are upset about what happened to Role; mortals don't like to think that their gods can die. They also want to see her killer brought to justice. The Order will have to give them *someone*, if not the killer. With me gone, you'd have no protection at all."

It was true, every word of it; I knew it with instinctive certainty. And I was afraid. But…

"I couldn't bear it if you died," I said softly. I could not meet his eyes. It was a variation on the same thing he'd told me months before, and it hurt to say now as much as his words had hurt to hear then. "It's different, knowing I'll lose you when I die. That's…right, natural. The way things have to be. But—" And I could not help it; I imagined *his* body in that alley, his bluegreen scent fading, his warmth cooling, his blood staining my fingers and nothing, nothing, where the sight of him should be.

No. I would rather die than allow that to happen.

"So be it," I said. "I've killed three men. It was an accident, but they're still dead. They had dreams, maybe families... You know all about debts owed, Mad. Isn't it right that I repay? As long as you're safe."

He said a word that rang of fury and fear and sour chimes, and it burst against my vision in a splash of cold aquamarine, silencing me. He let go of me then, moving away, and belatedly I realized that I had hurt him in my willingness to give my life. Obligation was his nature; altruism was its antithesis.

"You will not do this to me," he said, cold in his anger, though I heard the taut fear that lay under it. "You will not throw away your life because you were unlucky enough to be nearby when those fools started their blundering 'investigation.' Or because of that selfish bastard who lives with you." He clenched his fists. "And you will never, ever again offer to die for my sake."

I sighed. I didn't want to hurt him, but there was no reason for him to stay in the mortal realm and put up with petty mortal politics. Not even for me. I had to make him see that.

"You said it yourself," I said. "I'm going to die one day; nothing can prevent that. What does it matter whether that happens now or in fifty years? I—"

"*It matters*," he snarled, rounding on me. In two strides, he crossed the room and took me by the shoulders again. This caused a ripple in the surface of his mortal shape. For an instant, he flickered blue and then settled back, sweat sheening his face. His hands trembled. He was making himself sick to make a point. "Don't you dare say it doesn't matter!"

I knew what I should have said then, what I should have done. I had encountered this with him before—this fierce, dangerous, all-consuming need that drove him to love me no matter how much pain that caused. He was right; he needed a goddess for a lover, not some fragile mortal girl who would let herself get killed at the drop of a hat. Dumping me had been the smartest thing he'd ever done, even if letting him do it had been the hardest choice I'd ever made.

So I should have pushed him away. Said something terrible, designed to break his heart. That would've been the right thing to do, and I should've been strong enough to do it.

But I've never been as strong as I would like.

Madding kissed me. And gods, was it sweet. I felt him this time, all the coolness and fluid aquamarine of him, the edges and the ambition, everything he'd held back two nights before. I heard the chimes again as he flowed into me and through me, and when he pulled away, I clutched at him, pulling him close again. He rested his forehead on mine, trembling for a long, pent moment; he knew what he should do, too. Then he picked me up and carried me back to the pile of cushions.

We had made love before, many times. It was never perfect— it couldn't be, me being mortal—but it was always good. Best of all when Mad was needy the way he was now. He lost control at such times, forgot that I was mortal and that he needed to hold back. (By this I don't mean his strength, though that was part of it. I mean that sometimes he took me places, showed me visions. There are things mortals aren't meant to see. When he forgot himself, I saw some of them.)

I liked that he lost control, dangerous though it was. I liked knowing I could give him that much pleasure. He was one of the younger godlings, but he had still lived millennia to my decades, and sometimes I worried that I wasn't enough for him. On nights like this, though, as he wept and groaned and strained against me, and scintillated like diamond when the moment struck, I knew that was a silly fear. Of course I was enough, because he loved me. That was the whole point.

Afterward we lay, spent and lazy, in the cool humid silence of the late-night hours. I could hear others moving about in the house, on that floor and the one above: mortal servants, some of Madding's people, perhaps a valued customer who'd been given the rare privilege of buying goods direct from the source. There were no doors in Madding's home, because godlings regarded them as a nuisance, so the whole house had probably heard us. Neither of us cared.

"Did I hurt you?" His usual question.

"Of course not." My usual answer, though he always sighed in relief when I gave it. I lay on my belly, comfortable, not yet drowsy. "Did I hurt *you?*"

He usually laughed. That he stayed silent this time made me remember our earlier argument. That made me fall silent, too.

"You're going to need to leave Shadow," he said at last.

I said nothing, because there was nothing to say. He wasn't going to leave the mortal realm, because that would get me killed. Leaving Shadow might get me killed, too, but the chances were lower. Everything depended on how badly Previt Rimarn wanted me. Outside of the city, Madding had less power to protect me; no godling was permitted to leave Shadow by decree of the Lady, who feared the havoc they might cause worldwide. But the Order of Itempas had a White Hall in every sizable town, and thousands of priests and acolytes all over the world. I would be hard-pressed to hide from them if Rimarn was determined to have me.

Madding was betting Rimarn wouldn't care, however. I was easy prey, but not really the prey he wanted.

"I have a few contacts outside the city," Madding said. "I'll have them set things up for you. A house in a small town somewhere, a guard or two. You'll be comfortable. I'll make sure of that."

"What about my things here?"

His eyes unfocused briefly. "I've sent one of my siblings to take care of it tonight. We'll store your belongings here for now, then send them all to your new home by magic. Your neighbors will never even see you move out."

So neat and quick, the destruction of my life.

I rolled onto my belly and put my head down on my folded arms, trying not to think. After a moment, Mad sat up and leaned away from the pile of cushions, opening a small cabinet set into the floor and rummaging through it. I could not see what he picked up, but I saw him use it to prick his finger, at which I scowled.

"I'm not in the mood," I said.

"It'll make you feel better. Which will make *me* feel better."

"Doesn't it bother you, selling godsblood now that people think you're willing to kill over it?"

"No," he said, though his voice was sharper than usual, "because I'm *not* willing to kill over it, and I don't give a damn what others think." He held the finger out to me. A single dark drop of blood, like a garnet, sat there. "See? It's already shed. Shall I waste it?"

I sighed, but finally leaned forward and took his finger into my mouth. There was a fleeting taste of salt and metal, along with other, stranger flavors that I had never been able to name.

The taste of other realms, maybe. Whatever it was, I felt the tingle of it in my throat as I swallowed, all the way down into my belly.

I licked his finger before I let go. As I had suspected, the wound was already closed; I just liked teasing him. He let out a soft sigh.

"This is why the Interdiction happened," he said, lying back down beside me. He rubbed little circles on the small of my back with one hand; this usually meant he was thinking about sex again. Greedy bastard.

"Hmm?" I closed my eyes and shivered, just a little, as the godsblood spread its power throughout my body. Once, when Madding had given me a taste of his blood, I had begun floating precisely six inches off the floor. Hadn't been able to get down for hours. Madding was no help; he'd been too busy laughing his ass off. Fortunately, all I *usually* felt was a pleasant relaxing sensation, like drunkenness but without the hangover. Sometimes I had visions, but they were never frightening. "What are you talking about?"

"You." He brushed his lips against my ear, sending a lovely shiver down my spine. He noticed it and traced the shiver with his fingertips, making me arch and sigh. "You mortals and your intoxicating insanity. So many of us have been seduced by your kind, Oree; even the Three, long ago. I used to think anyone who fell in love with a mortal was a fool."

"But now that you've tried it, you see the error of your ways?"

"Oh, no." He sat up, straddled my legs, and slid his hands under me to cup and knead my breasts. I sighed in languid pleasure, though I couldn't help giggling when he nibbled at the back of my neck. "I was right. It *is* a kind of insanity. You make us want things we shouldn't."

My smile faded. "Like eternity."

"Yes." His hands stilled for a moment. "And more than that."

"What else?"

"Children, for one."

I sat up. "Tell me you're joking." He had promised me long before that I didn't have to take the same precautions with him that I would with a mortal man.

"Hush," he said, pressing me back down. "Of course I'm joking. But I *could* give you a child, if I wanted. If you wanted me to. And if I was willing to break the only real law the Three have ever imposed on us."

"Oh." I settled back into the cushions, relaxing as he resumed his slow, coaxing caresses. "You're talking about demons. Children of mortals and immortals. Monsters."

"They weren't monsters. It was before the Gods' War, before even I was born, but I hear they were just like us—godlings, I mean. They could dance among the stars as we do; they had the same magic. Yet they grew old and died, no matter how powerful they were. It made them... very strange. But not monstrous." He sighed. "It's forbidden to create more demons, but... ah, Oree. You'd make such beautiful children."

"Mmm." I was beginning to not pay attention to him. Madding loved to talk while his hands were doing lovely things that transcended words. He had slipped one hand between my legs during this last ramble. Lovely things. "So the Three were afraid you'd all... ah... fall in love with mortals and make more dangerous little demons."

"Not all the Three. In the end, it was only Itempas who

ordered us to stay away from the mortal realm. But he does not brook disobedience, so we did as he commanded." He kissed my shoulder, then nuzzled my temple. "I never realized how cruel that order was, before I met you."

I smiled, feeling wicked, and reached back to catch hold of the warm, hard lump that lay against my backside. I gave him a practiced stroke and he shuddered against me, his breath quickening in my ear. "Oh, yes," I teased. "So cruel."

"Oree," he said, his voice suddenly low and tight. I sighed and lifted my hips a little, and he slipped back into me like he belonged nowhere else.

Somewhere in the delicious, floating pleasure that followed, I became aware that we were being watched. I didn't think anything of it at first. Madding's siblings seemed fascinated by our relationship, so if watching us helped them whenever they decided to try a mortal, I didn't mind. But there had been something different about this gaze, I realized afterward, when I lay pleasantly exhausted and drifting toward sleep. It did not have the usual air of curiosity or titillation; there was something heavier about this. Something disapproving. And familiar.

Of course. Madding had sent someone to collect all my belongings. Naturally that would include Shiny: my brooding, arrogant, selfish bastard of a pet. I had no idea why my being with Madding angered him, and I didn't care. I was tired of his moods, tired of everything. So I ignored him and went to sleep.

Madding was gone when I woke. I sat up, bleary, and listened for a moment, trying to get my bearings. From downstairs I could hear the ceaseless ripple of water and could smell hiras perfume. Upstairs, someone was walking, making the floorboards creak.

Intuition told me it was very late, but most of Madding's people were godlings; they didn't sleep. From somewhere on the same floor, I heard a woman laughing and two men talking.

I yawned and put my head back down, but the voices impinged gently on my consciousness.

"—didn't tell you—"

"—your business, damn it! You have no—"

It sank in slowly: Shiny. And Madding. Talking? It didn't matter. I didn't care.

"You're not listening," Madding said. He spoke in a low voice but intently; that made the sound carry. "She gave you a real chance and you're throwing it away. Why would you do that when so many of us fought for you, died…" He faltered, silent for an instant. "You never consider others—only yourself! Do you have any idea what Oree has gone through because of you?"

My eyes opened.

Shiny's reply was a low murmur, unintelligible. Madding's was anything but, almost a shout: "You're destroying her! Isn't it enough that you destroyed your own family? Do you have to kill what *I* love, too?"

I got up. My stick was there on my side of the pillow pile, right where Mad had always put it. The robe was tangled in the pillows where I'd dropped it. I shook it out and put it on.

"—tell you this now—" Madding had regained some of his composure, though he was still plainly furious. He'd lowered his voice again. Shiny was silent, as he had been since Madding's outburst. Madding kept talking, but I couldn't tell what he was saying.

I stopped at the door. I didn't care, I told myself. My life was ruined and it was Shiny's fault. *He* didn't care. Why did it matter what he and Madding said to each other? Why did I still bother trying to understand him?

"—he could love you again," Madding said. "Pretend that means nothing to you, Father, if you like. But I know—"

Father. I blinked. *Father?*

"—in spite of everything," Madding said. "Believe that or not, as you will." The words had an air of finality. The argument was over, one-sided as it had been.

I stepped back against the bedroom wall and out of the doorway, though that would do me little good if Madding came back into the room. But although I heard Madding's footsteps leave whatever room they'd been in and stomp away, they headed downstairs, not back to his bedroom.

As I stood there against the wall, mulling over what I'd heard, Shiny left the room as well. He walked past Madding's room, and I braced myself for him to notice that I was out of bed and perhaps come in and find me. His footsteps didn't even slow. He headed upstairs.

Which one to follow? I wavered for a moment, then went after Madding. At least I knew he would talk to me.

I found him standing atop the largest of his pools, glowing bright enough to make the whole chamber visible as his magic reflected off walls and water. I stopped behind him, savoring the play of light across his facets, the shift and ripple of liquid aquamarine flesh as he moved, the patterned flicker of the walls. He had folded his hands together, head bowed as if to pray. Perhaps he *was* praying. Above the godlings were the gods, and above the gods was Maelstrom, the unknowable. Perhaps even it prayed to something. Didn't we all need someone to turn to sometimes?

So I sat down and waited, not interrupting, and presently Madding lowered his hands and turned to me.

"I should have kept my voice down," he said softly, amid the chime of crystal.

I smiled, drawing up my knees and wrapping my arms around them. "I find it hard not to yell at him, too."

He sighed. "If you could have seen him before the war, Oree. He was glorious then. We all loved him—competed for his love, basked in his attention. And he loved us back in his quiet, steady way. He's changed so much."

His body gave off one last liquid shimmer and then settled back into his stocky, plain-featured human shell, which I had come to love just as much over the years. He was still naked, his hair still loose, still standing on water. His eyes carried memories and sorrow far too ancient for any mortal man. He would never look truly ordinary, no matter how hard he tried.

"So he's your father." I spoke slowly. I did not want to voice aloud the suspicion I'd begun to develop. I hardly wanted to believe it. There were dozens, perhaps hundreds, of godlings, and there'd been even more before the Gods' War. Not all of them had been parented by the Three.

But most of them had been.

Madding smiled, reading my face. I'd never been able to hide anything from him. "There aren't many of us left who haven't disowned him."

I licked my lips. "I thought he was a godling. *Just* a godling, I mean, not..." I gestured vaguely above my head, meaning the sky.

"He's not just a godling."

Confirmation, unexpectedly anticlimactic. "I thought the Three would be...different."

"They are."

"But Shiny..."

"He's a special case. His current condition is temporary. Probably."

Nothing in my life had prepared me for this. I knew I was not especially knowledgeable about the affairs of gods, despite my personal association with some of them. I knew as well as anyone that the priests taught what they wanted us to know, not necessarily what was true. And sometimes even when they told the truth, they got it wrong.

Madding came over, sitting down beside me. He gazed out over the pools, his manner subdued.

I needed to understand. "What did he do?" It was the question I had asked Sieh.

"Something terrible." His smile had faded during my moment of stunned silence. His expression was closed, almost angry. "Something most of us will never forgive. He got away with it for a while, but now the debt has come due. He'll be repaying it for a long time."

Sometimes they got it *very* wrong. "I don't understand," I whispered.

He lifted a hand and drew a knuckle across my cheek, brushing a stray curl of hair aside.

"He really was lucky to find you," he said. "I have to confess, I've been a bit jealous. There's still a little of the old him left. I can see why you'd be drawn to him."

"It's not like that. He doesn't even like me."

"I know." He dropped his hand. "I'm not sure he's capable of caring for anyone now, not in any real way. He was never good at changing, bending. He broke instead. And he took all of us with him."

He fell silent, reverberating pain, and I understood then that, unlike Sieh, Madding still loved Shiny. Or whoever Shiny had once been.

My mind fought against the name that whispered in my heart.

I found his hand and laced our fingers together. Madding glanced down at them, then up at me, and smiled. There was such sorrow in his eyes that I leaned over and kissed him. He sighed through it, resting his forehead against mine when we parted.

"I don't want to talk about him anymore," he said.

"All right," I said. "What shall we talk about instead?" Though I thought I knew.

"Stay with me," he whispered.

"I wasn't the one who left." I tried for lightness and failed utterly.

He closed his eyes. "It was different before. Now I realize I'm going to lose you either way. You'll leave town, or you'll grow old and die. But if you stay, I'll have you longer." He fumbled for my other hand, not as good at doing things without his eyes as I was. "I need you, Oree."

I licked my lips. "I don't want to endanger you, Mad. And if I stay..." Every morsel of food I ate, every scrap of clothing I wore, would come from him. Could I bear that? I had traveled across the continent, left my mother and my people, scrabbled and struggled, to live as I pleased. If I stayed in Shadow, with the

Order hunting me and murder dogging my steps, would I even be able to leave Madding's house? Freedom alone, or imprisonment with the man I loved. Two horrible choices.

And he knew it. I felt him tremble, and that was almost enough. "Please," he whispered.

Almost, I gave in.

"Let me think," I said. "I have to…I can't think, Mad."

His eyes opened. Because he was so near, touching me, I could feel the hope fade in him. When he drew back, letting go of my hand, I knew he had begun to draw back his heart as well, steeling it against my rejection.

"All right," he said. "Take as long as you like."

If he had gotten angry, it would have been so much easier.

I started to speak, but he had turned away. What was there to say, anyhow? Nothing that would heal the pain I'd just caused him. Only time could do that.

So I sighed and got up, and headed upstairs.

Madding's house was huge. The second floor, where his room was located, was also where he and his siblings worked, pricking themselves to produce tiny vials of their blood for sale to mortals. He had grown wealthy from this and from his other lines of business; there were many skills godlings possessed that mortals were willing to pay a premium for. But he was still a godling, and when his business had grown, he hadn't considered opening an office; he'd simply made his house bigger and invited all his underlings to come live with him.

Most of them had taken him up on the offer. The third floor held the rooms of those godlings who liked having a bed, a few scriveners who'd slipped the Order's leash, and a handful of mortals with other useful talents—record-keeping, glassblowing, sales. The next floor up was the roof, which was what I sought.

I found two godlings lounging at the bottom of the roof stairs when I came up from below: Madding's patch-skinned male lieutenant/guard and a coolly handsome creature who'd taken the form of a middle-aged Ken man. The latter, whose gaze held wisdom and disinterest in equal measure, did not acknowledge my presence. The former winked at me and shifted closer to his sibling to let me pass.

"Up for a breath of night air?" he asked.

I nodded. "I can feel the city best up there."

"Saying good-bye?" His eyes were too sharp, reading my face like a sigil. I mustered a weak smile in response, because I did not trust myself to keep my composure if I spoke. His expression softened with pity. "It'd be a shame to see you go."

"I've caused him enough trouble."

"He doesn't mind."

"I know. But at this rate, I'll end up owing him my soul, or worse."

"He doesn't keep an account for you, Oree." It was the first time he'd used my name. I shouldn't have been surprised; he'd been with Madding for longer than I had. Perhaps they'd even come to the mortal world together, two eternal bachelors seeking excitement amid the grit and glory of the city. The idea made me smile. He noticed and smiled himself. "You have no idea how much he cares for you."

I had seen Mad's eyes when he'd asked me to stay. "I do know," I whispered, and then had to take a deep breath. "I'll see you later, ah..." I paused. All this time, I had never asked his name. My cheeks grew warm with shame.

He looked amused. "Paitya. My partner—the woman?—is Kitr. But don't tell her I told you."

I nodded, resisting the urge to glance at the older-looking godling. Some godlings were like Paitya and Madding and Lil, not caring whether mortals accorded them any particular reverence. Others, I had learned, regarded us as very much inferior beings. Either way, the older one already looked annoyed that I'd interrupted their relaxation. Best to leave him be.

"You'll have company," Paitya said as I moved past him. I almost stopped there, realizing who he meant.

But that was fitting, I decided, considering the churn of misery inside myself. I had been raised as a devout Itempan, though I'd lapsed in the years since, and my heart had never really been in it, anyhow. Yet I still prayed to Him when I felt the need. I was definitely feeling the need now, so I proceeded up the steps, wrestled the heavy metal lever open, and stepped out onto the roof.

As the metallic echoes of the door faded, I heard breathing to one side, low to the ground. He was sitting down somewhere, probably against one of the wide struts of the cistern that dominated the rooftop space. I could not feel his gaze, but he must have heard me come onto the roof. Silence fell.

Standing there, knowing who he was, I expected to feel different. I should have been reverent, nervous, awed maybe. Yet my mind could not reconcile the two concepts: the Bright Lord of Order and the man I'd found in a muckbin. Itempas and Shiny; Him and him; they did not feel at all the same, in my heart.

And I could think of only one question, out of the thousands that I should have asked.

"All that time you lived with me and never spoke," I said. "Why?"

At first I thought he wouldn't answer. But at last I heard a faint shift in the gravel that covered the rooftop and felt the solidity of his gaze settle on me.

"You were irrelevant," he said. "Just another mortal."

I was growing used to him, I realized bitterly. That had hurt far less than I'd expected.

Shaking my head, I went over to another of the cistern's struts, felt about to make sure there were no puddles or debris in the way, and sat down. There was no true silence up on the roof; the midnight air was thick with the sounds of the city. Yet I found myself at peace, anyhow. Shiny's presence, my anger at him, at least kept me from thinking about Madding or dead Order-Keepers or the end of the life I'd built for myself in Shadow. So in his own obnoxious way, my god comforted me.

"What the hells are you doing up here, anyhow?" I asked. I could not muster the wherewithal to show him any greater respect. "Praying to yourself?"

"There's a new moon tonight."

"So?"

He did not reply, and I did not care. I turned my face toward the distant, barely there shimmers of the World Tree's canopy and pretended they were the stars I'd heard others talk about all my life. Sometimes, amid the ripples and eddies of the leafy sea, I would see a brighter flash now and again. Probably an early bloom; the Tree would be flowering soon. There were people in the city who made a year's living from the dangerous work of climbing the Tree's lower branches and snipping off its silvery, hand-wide blossoms for sale to the wealthy.

"All that happens in darkness, he sees and hears," Shiny said abruptly. I wished he would stop talking again. "On a moonless night, he will hear me, even if he chooses not to answer."

"Who?"

"Nahadoth."

I forgot my anger at Shiny, and my sorrow over Madding, and my guilt about the Order-Keepers. I forgot everything but that name.

Nahadoth.

We have never forgotten his name.

These days, our world has two great continents, but once there were three: High North, Senm, and the Maroland. Maro was the smallest of the three but was also the most magnificent, with trees that stretched a thousand feet into the air, flowers and birds found nowhere else, and waterfalls so huge that it was said you could feel their spray on the other side of the world.

The hundred clans of my people—called just "Maro" then, not "Maroneh"—were plentiful and powerful. In the aftermath of the Gods' War, those who had honored Bright Itempas above other gods were shown favor. That included the Amn, a now-extinct people called the Ginij, and us. The Amn were ruled by the Arameri family. Their homeland was Senm, but they built their stronghold in our land, at our invitation. We were smarter than the Ginij. But we paid a price for our savvy politicking.

There was a rebellion of some sort. A great army marched across the Maroland, intent upon overthrowing the Arameri. Stupid, I know, but such things happened in those days. It would have been just another massacre, just another footnote in history, if one of the Arameri's weapons hadn't gotten loose.

He was the Nightlord, brother and eternal enemy of Bright Itempas. Hobbled, diminished, but still unimaginably powerful, he punched a hole in the earth, causing earthquakes and tsunamis that tore the Maroland apart. The whole continent sank into the sea, and nearly all its people died.

The few Maro who survived settled on a tiny peninsula of the Senm continent, granted to them by the Arameri in condolence for our loss. We began to call ourselves Maroneh, which meant "those who weep for Maro" in the common language we once spoke. We named our daughters for sorrow and our sons for rage; we debated whether there was any point in trying to rebuild our race. We thanked Itempas for saving even the handful of us who remained, and we hated the Arameri for making that prayer necessary.

And though the rest of the world all but forgot him outside of heretic cults and tales to frighten children, we remembered the name of our destroyer.

Nahadoth.

"I have been attempting," said Shiny, "to express my remorse to him."

That pulled me from one kind of shock into another. *"What?"*

Shiny got up. I heard him walk a few steps, perhaps over to the low wall that marked the edge of the rooftop. His voice, when he spoke, was diluted by wind and the late-night sounds of the city, but it came to me clearly enough. His diction was precise, unaccented, perfectly pitched. He spoke like a nobleman trained to give speeches.

"You wanted to know what I had done to be punished with mortality," he said. "You asked that of Sieh."

I pulled my thoughts from their endless litany of *Nahadoth, Nahadoth, Nahadoth.* "Well...yes."

"My sister," he said. "I killed her."

I frowned. Of course he had. Enefa, the goddess of earth and life, had conspired against Itempas with their brother, the Nightlord Nahadoth. Itempas had slain her for her treachery and had given Nahadoth to the Arameri as a slave. It was a famous story.

Unless...

I licked my lips. "Did she...do something to provoke you?"

The wind shifted for a moment. His voice drifted to me and away, then back again, singsong and soft. "She took him from me."

"She—" I stopped.

I did not want to understand. Obviously Itempas had been involved with Enefa at some point before their falling-out; the existence of the godlings was proof enough of that. But Nahadoth was the monster in the dark, the enemy of all that was good in the world. I didn't want to think of him as the Bright Lord's *brother*, much less—

But I had spent too much time among godlings. I had seen that they lusted and raged like mortals, hurt like mortals, misunderstood and nursed petty grudges and *killed each other over love like mortals.*

I got to my feet, trembling.

"You're saying *you* started the Gods' War," I said. "You're saying the Nightlord was your lover—that you love him *still.* You're saying *he's free now and he's the one who did this to you.*"

"Yes," said Shiny. Then, to my surprise, he let out a little laugh, so laden with bitterness that his voice wavered unsteadily for an instant. "That's precisely what I'm saying."

My hands tightened on my stick until it hurt my palms. I sank back to a crouch, planting the stick in the gravel to balance myself, pressing my forehead against the smooth old wood. "I don't believe you," I whispered. I *could not* believe him. I could not be that wrong about the world, the gods, everything. The entire human race could not be that wrong.

Could we?

I heard the gravel shift under Shiny's feet as he turned to me. "Do you love Madding?" he asked.

It was such an unexpected question, so nonsensical in the context of our discussion, that it took me several seconds to make my mouth work. "Yes. Dear gods, of course I do. Why are you asking me that now?"

More gravel, chuffing rhythmically as he came over to me. His warm hands took hold of mine where they gripped the stick. I was so surprised by this that I let him pry me loose and pull me up to stand. He did nothing then, for several moments. Just looked at me. I became aware, belatedly, that I wore nothing but a silk robe. The winter had been mild this year, and spring was coming early, but the night had begun to turn cold. Goose bumps prickled my skin, and my nipples tented the silk. I had worn as little in my own house—or less. Nudity meant nothing to me as titillation, and Shiny had never shown the slightest interest. Now, however, I was very aware of his gaze, and...it bothered me. I had never experienced this particular flavor of discomfort with him before.

He leaned closer, his hands sliding up to my arms. His hands were very warm, almost comforting. I didn't know what he meant to do until his lips brushed mine. Startled, I tried to pull away, and his hands tightened sharply—not enough to hurt, but it was a warning. I froze. He drew near again and kissed me.

I didn't know what to think. But as his mouth coaxed mine open with a skill I had never imagined he possessed, and his tongue flickered at my lips, I could not help relaxing against him. If he had forced the kiss, I would have hated it. I would have fought. Instead he was gentle—unnaturally, too-perfectly gentle. His mouth tasted of nothing, which was strange and somehow emphasized his inhumanity. It was not like kissing Madding. There was no flavor of Shiny's inner self. But when his tongue touched my own, I jumped a little, because it felt good. I had not expected that. His hands slid down to my waist, then my hips, pulling me closer. I breathed his peculiar, hot-spice smell. The heat and strength of his body—it was wholly different from Madding. Disturbing. Interesting. His teeth grazed my lower lip and I shivered, this time not wholly in fear.

He had not closed his eyes. I could feel them watching me, evaluating me, cold despite the heat of his mouth.

When he pulled back, he drew in a breath. Let it out slowly. Said, still in a terrible, soft voice, "You don't love Madding."

I stiffened.

"Even now, you want me." There was such contempt in his voice; each word dripped with venom. I had never before heard such emotion from him, and all of it hate. "His power intrigues you. The prestige of having a god for a lover. Perhaps you're even devoted to him in your small way—though I doubt that, since it seems any god will do." He let out a small sigh. "I know well the dangers of trusting your kind. I warned my children, kept them away while I could, but Madding is stubborn. I mourn the pain it will cause him when he finally realizes just how unworthy of his love you are."

I stood there, shocked to numbness. Believing him, for a long, horrifying moment. Shiny had been—still was, diminished or not—the god I had revered all my life. Of course he was right. Had I not hesitated at Madding's offer? My god had judged me and found me wanting, and it hurt.

Then sense reasserted itself, and with it came pure fury.

I was still backed against the cistern strut, which gave me perfect leverage as I planted my hands on Shiny's chest and shoved him back with all my strength. He stumbled back, making a sound of surprise. I followed, all my fear and confusion forgotten amid red-hot rage.

"*That's* your proof?" My hands found his chest and I shoved him again, throwing all my weight into it just for the satisfaction of hearing him grunt as I did so. "*That's* what makes you think I don't love Mad? You're a damned good kisser, Shiny, but do you honestly think you hold a candle to Madding in my heart?" I laughed, my own voice echoing harshly in my ears. "My gods, he was right! You really don't know anything about love."

I turned, muttering to myself, and began making my way back to the roof door.

"Wait," Shiny said.

I ignored him, sweeping my stick in a tight angry arc ahead of me. His hand caught my arm again, and this time I tried to shake him off, cursing.

"*Wait,*" he said, not letting go. He turned away from me, barely noticing my rage. "Someone's here."

"What are you—" But I heard it, too, now, and froze. Footsteps, chuffing on the rooftop gravel, beside the door hatch.

"Oree Shoth?" The voice was male, cool and dark like the late-winter night. Familiar, though I could not place it.

"Y-yes," I said, wondering if this was some customer of Madding's, and what he was doing on the roof if that was the case. And how did he know my name? Maybe he'd overheard some of Madding's people gossiping. "Were you looking for me?"

"Yes. Though I had hoped you'd be alone."

Shiny shifted suddenly, moving in front of me, and I found myself trying to hear the man through his rather intimidating bulk. I opened my mouth to shout at him, too angry for politeness or respect—and then I stopped.

It was faint. I had to squint. But Shiny had begun to glow.

"Oree," he said. Calm, as always. "Go into the house."

Fear stopped anything else I might have said. "H-he's between me and the door."

"I will remove him."

"I wouldn't advise that," said the man, unruffled. "You aren't a godling."

Shiny sighed, and under other circumstances, I would have been amused by his annoyance. "No," he snapped, "I'm not."

And before I could speak again, he was gone, the space in front of me cold in his absence. There was a glimmer of magic—something occluded by the hazy shimmer of Shiny's body. Then a flurry of movement, cloth tearing, the struggle of flesh against flesh. A spray of wetness across my face, making me flinch.

And then silence.

I held still for a moment, my own breath loud and fast in my ears as I strained to hear the sound that I knew and feared would come: bodies, hitting the cobblestones of the street three stories below. But there was only that terrible silence.

My nerves snapped. I ran to the roof door, clawed it open, and flung myself into the house, screaming.

6

"A Window Opens" *(chalk on concrete)*

THERE ARE THINGS he told me about himself. Not all of it, of course—some things I heard from other gods or remember from old stories of my childhood. But mostly he just told me. It was not his nature to lie.

In the time of the Three, things were very different. There were many temples but few holy texts, and no persecution of those with differing beliefs. Mortals loved whatever gods they wished—often several at once—and it was not called heresy. If there were disputes about a particular bit of lore or magic, it was simple enough to call on a local godling and ask about it. No point in getting possessive about one god or another when there were plenty to go around.

It was during this time that the first demons were born: offspring of mortal humans and immortal gods, neither one nor the other, possessing the greatest gifts of both. One of those gifts was mortality—a strange thing to call a gift, by my thinking, but people back then thought differently. Anyhow, all the demons possessed it.

But consider what this means: *all the demons died.* Doesn't make sense, does it? Children rarely take after just one of their parents. Shouldn't a few of the demons have inherited immortality? They certainly got the magic, in plenty—so much that they passed it on to us, when they mated with us. Scrivening and bonebending and prophecy and shadow-sending, all of this came to mortalkind through the demons. But even when the demons took godly lovers and had children with them, those children grew old and died, too.

For us, the divine inheritance was a blessing. For the gods, one drop of mortal blood doomed their offspring to death.

Apparently, no one realized what this meant for a very long time.

I scrambled downstairs much faster than I should have, given that I'd never gotten around to memorizing Madding's stairs. Behind me trailed Paitya; the middle-aged godling; Kitr, who had come out of nowhere at my shout and was visible for once; and Madding. As we reached the room of pools, two more people joined us: a tall mortal woman who shone with nearly as many godwords as Previt Rimarn, and a sleek racing dog who glowed white in my sight. As I reached the house's front door, I heard other calls upstairs; I'd woken the whole house.

I might have felt bad if my thoughts had not been filled with that awful silence.

"Oree!" Hands caught me before I got three steps out the door; I fought them. A blur of blue resolved into Madding. "You shouldn't leave the house, damn it."

"I have to—" I twisted to get around Madding. "He—"

"He who? Oree—" Madding abruptly went still. "Why is there blood on your face?"

That stopped my panic, though the hand that I lifted to my face shook badly. Wetness had splattered my face up on the roof; I'd forgotten.

"Boss?" Paitya had crouched to peer at something on the ground. I could not see what, but the grim expression on his face was unmistakable. "There's a lot more blood here."

Madding turned to look, and his eyes widened. He turned back to me, frowning. "What happened? Where were you, up on the roof?" Suddenly his frown deepened. "Did Father do something to you? So help me—"

Kitr, who had been scanning the street for danger, looked at us both sharply. "You *told* her?"

Madding ignored her, though I caught his wince of consternation. He turned me from one side to the other, checking for injuries. "I'm fine," I said, holding my stick to my chest as I grew calmer. "*I'm* fine. But, yes, I was on the roof, with...with Shiny. There was someone...a man. I couldn't see him; he must've been mortal. He knew my name, said he'd been looking for me—"

Paitya cursed and stood up, narrowing his eyes as he scanned the area. "Since when do Order-Keepers come by way of the damned roof? They usually have sense enough not to piss us off."

Madding muttered something in gods' language; it curled and spiked, a curse. "What happened?"

"Shiny," I said. "He fought with the man. There was magic..." I clutched at Madding's arms, my fingers tightening on the cloth of his shirt. "Mad, the man hit him with magic somehow, I think that's what caused the blood, I think Shiny grabbed him and pulled him off the roof, *but I didn't hear them hit the ground...*"

Madding had already begun gesturing at his companions, directing them to search around the house and nearby streets. Kitr stayed nearby, as did Paitya. Madding had no real need of bodyguards, but I did, and he had probably directed one of them to spirit me away if it came down to any sort of fight.

"I'm going to raze that White Hall to the ground," he snarled, his human shape flickering blue as he pushed me back toward the front door. "If they've dared to attack my house, my people—"

"He wasn't after Shiny," I murmured, realizing it belatedly. I stopped, clutching Madding's arm to get his attention. "Mad, that man wasn't after Shiny at all! If he was an Order-Keeper, he would've wanted Shiny, wouldn't he? They know he killed the ones in South Root." The more I thought about it, the more certain I became. "I don't think that man was an Order-Keeper at all."

I didn't mistake the swift, startled look that crossed Madding's face. He exchanged a glance with Kitr, who looked equally alarmed. Kitr then turned to look at one of the mortals, the scrivener. She nodded and knelt, taking a pad of paper out of her jacket and uncapping a thin ink-brush.

"I'll go see, too," said the middle-aged godling, vanishing. Madding pulled me against him, holding me firm with one arm and keeping the other free, in case of trouble. I tried to feel safe there, in the arms of one god and protected by half a dozen others, but all my nerves were a-jangle, and the panic would not fade. I could not push aside the feeling that something was wrong, very wrong, that someone was watching, that something was going to happen. I felt it with every ounce of intuition that I possessed.

"There's no body," said Paitya, coming over to us. Beyond him, I could see other godlings winking in and out of sight about the street, on nearby windowsills, on the edge of a roof. "Enough blood that there *should* be, but nothing. Not even, er, parts."

"Is it—" I had to struggle to be heard, half muffled against Madding's shoulder.

"It's his." Paitya glanced back at the racing dog, who was sniffing at the spot now; the dog looked up and nodded in solemn confirmation. "No doubt about it. The blood's just splattered about; it fell from above. But he didn't *land* here."

Madding muttered something in his own tongue, then switched to Senmite so I would understand. "There must have been a weapon. Or magic, as you said." He looked down at me, scowling in irritation. "He's powerless now. He must have known he couldn't take a scrivener, if that's what the man was. On the roof of a house full of godlings—why didn't he just call for help? Stubborn bastard."

I closed my eyes and leaned against Madding, suddenly weary. I could have called for help, too, I realized belatedly, though I'd been too frightened to think of doing so. Shiny, however, hadn't been afraid at all. He hadn't *wanted* help. He'd done it again— charged into a dangerous situation, spent his life like currency, all so he could have a taste of his old power. It had been for my benefit this time, but did that really make it better? Godlings respected life, including their own. They were just as immortal, but they at least tried to defend themselves or evade blows when attacked. When they fought, they tried not to kill. While Shiny slaughtered even his own kin.

"The Nightlord should've just killed him," I said, filled with sudden bitterness. Madding raised his eyebrows in surprise, but I shook my head. "There's something wrong with him, Mad. I always suspected it, but tonight…"

I remembered the little break in Shiny's voice when he'd admitted his role in the Gods' War. Just an instant of instability, a crack in the bedrock of his stoicism. But it went deeper than that, didn't it? His carelessness with his flesh—how *had* he ended up dead in my muckbin, all those months ago? That vicious kiss he'd given me. His even more vicious words afterward, blaming me for all the duplicity of the human race.

He was—or had been—the god of order, the living embodiment of stability, peace, and rationality. The man he had become, here in the mortal realm, didn't make sense. Shiny did not feel like Itempas because Shiny *wasn't* Itempas, and no part of my proper Maro upbringing would let me accept him as such.

Madding sighed. "Nahadoth wanted to kill him, Oree. A lot of my siblings did, too, after what he'd done. But the Three created this universe; if any one of them dies, it all ends. So he was sent here, where he can do the least damage. And maybe…" He paused, and again I heard that hint of longing in his voice. Hope, not quite stifled. "Maybe, somehow, he can…get better. See the error of his ways. I don't know."

"He said he was trying to apologize. Up on the roof. To… to…" I shuddered. We did not forget his name, but we didn't say it, either, not if we could help it. "The Nightlord."

Madding blinked in surprise. "Did he? That's more than I ever thought he'd do." He sobered. "But I doubt that will do any good. He *killed my mother*, Oree. Murdered her with poison, mutilated her body. Then spent the next few millennia killing or imprisoning any of us who dared to protest. It takes a little more than an apology to atone for that."

I reached up to touch Madding's face, reading his expression with my fingers. This helped me catch what I had missed. "You're still angry about it."

His brow furrowed. "Of course I am. I loved her! But"— he sighed heavily, leaning down to press his forehead against mine—"I loved him, too, once."

I cupped his face in my hands, wishing I knew how to comfort him. This was family business, though, between father and son. It was Shiny's problem to solve, if we ever found him.

There was one thing I could do, though.

"I'll stay," I said.

He started, pulling back to stare at me. Of course he knew what I meant. After a long moment, he said, "Are you sure?"

I almost laughed. I was shaky inside, not just from leftover panic. "No. But I don't think I ever will be. I just...I know what's most important to me." I did laugh then, as I realized that Shiny had helped me decide, with that horrid kiss and the challenge in his words. I did, too, love Madding. And I wanted to be with him, even though it meant the end of the life I'd worked so hard to build and the end of my independence. Love meant compromise, after all—something I suspected Shiny did not understand.

Madding's face was solemn as he nodded, accepting my decision. I liked that he did not smile. I think he knew what the decision cost me.

Instead, after a moment, he sighed and glanced at Kitr, who

had carefully paid more attention to the street than to us for the past few minutes.

"I'm calling everyone in," he said. "I don't like this. No mere scrivener should be able to hide from us." He glanced back, in the direction of the splashes of blood. "And I can't sense Father anywhere. I *especially* don't like that."

"Nor can I," said Kitr. "There are some of us with the power to hide him, but why would they? Unless…" She glanced at me, assessing and dismissing in a single sweep of her eyes. "You think this has something to do with Role? Your mortal there did find the body, but what's that got to do with anything?"

"I don't know, but—"

"Wait. There's something…" This came from the other side of the street. I followed the voice and saw the sigil-etched outline of Madding's scrivener. She stood looking up at the buildings nearby, holding a sheet of paper in her hands. A series of individual sigils had been drawn at the corners, with three rows of godwords in the middle. As I watched, one of the godwords and a sigil in the upper right corner began to glow more brightly. The scrivener, who apparently knew what this meant, gasped and took several steps back. I could not see her face, for she had no godwords written there, but terror filled her voice. "Oh, gods, I knew it! Look out! All of you, look—"

And suddenly hells filled the street.

No, not hells. *Holes.*

With a sound like tearing paper, they opened all around us, perfect circles of darkness. Some lay along the ground, some on the walls; some must've hung unsupported in midair. One of them opened right beneath the scrivener's feet, practically the instant the last word left her lips. She didn't have time to cry out before she fell into it and vanished. Another caught Kitr, who had turned to run to Madding's side. It opened before her between one step and another, and she was gone. The racing dog cursed in Mekatish and darted around the first hole that opened at his feet, but then another opened above him. I saw his short fur stand on end, pulled upward, and then with a yelp he was sucked in as well.

Before I could react, Madding suddenly shoved me away from him, into the doorway of the house. Stumbling over the doorway's raised step, I turned back, opening my mouth to speak—then saw the hole opening at his back. I felt the pull, its force powerful enough to jerk me forward a step even after I stopped.

No! I caught the door's elaborate handle in one hand to brace myself and used that leverage to raise my walking stick, hoping Madding would be able to grab it. Madding, his eyes wide and teeth bared, strained toward me. The sound of jangling chimes was barely audible, sucked away by the hole.

He mouthed something I couldn't hear. He ground his teeth, and I heard him in my head this time, in the manner of gods. *GET INSIDE!*

Then he flew backward, as if a great invisible hand had grabbed him around the waist and yanked. The hole vanished. He was gone.

I fumbled with the door handle, my breath wild and loud in my ears, my palms so sweaty that the stick slipped loose to clatter on the ground. I could hear no one else on the street; I was alone. Except for the remaining holes, which hovered all around me, darker than the black of my sight.

Then I got the door open and ran into the house, away from the holes, toward the clean, empty darkness where I was blind but where at least I knew what dangers I faced.

I got three steps into the house before the air tore behind me, and I flew backward off my feet, and a sound like trembling metal filled the world as I tumbled away.

7

"Girl in Darkness"
(watercolor)

MY DREAMS HAVE BEEN more vivid lately. They told me that might happen, but still... I remembered something.

In the dream, I paint a picture. But as I lose myself in the colors of the sky and the mountains and the mushrooms that dwarf the mountains—this is a living world, full of strange flora and fungi; I can almost smell the fumes of its alien air—the door to my room opens and my mother comes in.

"What are you doing?" she asks.

And though I am still half lost in mountains and mushrooms, I have no choice but to pull myself back into this world, where I am just a sheltered blind girl whose mother wants what's best for me, even if she and I do not agree on what that is.

"Painting," I say, though this is obvious. My belly has clenched in defensive tension; I fear a lecture is coming.

She only sighs and comes closer, putting her hand on mine to let me know where she is. She is silent for a long while. Is she looking at the painting? I nibble my bottom lip, not quite daring to hope that she is, perhaps, trying to understand why I do what I do. She has never told me to stop, but I can taste her disapproval, as sour and heavy on my tongue as old, molding grapes. She has hinted at it verbally as well, in the past. *Paint something useful, something pretty.* Something that does not entrance viewers for hours on end. Something that would not attract the sharp, gleaming interest of the priests if they saw it. Something safe.

She says nothing this time, only stroking my braided hair, and at last I realize she is not thinking about me or my paintings at all. "What is it, Mama?" I ask.

"Nothing," she says, very softly, and I realize that for the first time in my life, she has just lied to me.

My heart fills with dread. I don't know why. Perhaps it is the whiff of fear that wafts from her, or the sorrow that underlies it, or simply the fact that my garrulous, cheerful mother is suddenly so quiet, so still.

So I lean against her and put my arms around her waist. She is trembling, unable to give me the comfort that I crave. I take what I can, and perhaps give a little of my own in return.

My father died a few weeks later.

I floated in numbing emptiness, screaming, unable to hear myself. When I clasped my hands together, I felt nothing, even when I dug in my nails. Opening my mouth, I sucked in another breath to scream again but felt no sensation of air moving over my tongue or filling my lungs. I *knew* that I did it. I willed my muscles to move and believed that they responded. But I could feel nothing.

Nothing but the terrible cold. It was bitter enough to be painful, or would have been if I could feel pain. If I had been able to stand, I might have fallen to the ground, too cold to do anything but shiver. If only there had been ground.

The mortal mind is not built for such things. I did not miss sight, but touch? Sound? Smell? I was used to those. I *needed* those. Was this how other people felt about blindness? No wonder they feared it so.

I contemplated going mad.

"Ree-child," says my father, taking my hands. "Don't rely on your magic. I know the temptation will be there. It's good to see, isn't it?"

I nod. He smiles.

"But the power comes from inside you," he goes on. He opens one of my small hands and traces the whorling print of one fingertip. It tickles and I laugh. "If you use a lot of it, you'll get tired. If you use it all . . . Ree-child, you could die."

I frown in puzzlement. "It's just magic." Magic is light, color. Magic is a beautiful song—wonderful, but not a necessity of life. Not like food or water, or sleep, or blood.

"Yes. But it's also part of you. An important part." He smiles, and for the first time, I see how deeply the sadness has permeated him today. He seems lonely. "You have to understand. We're not like other people."

I cried out with my voice and my thoughts. Gods can hear the latter if a mortal concentrates hard enough—it's how they hear prayers. There was no reply from Madding, or anyone else. Though I groped around, my hands encountered nothing. Even if he'd been there, right beside me, would I have known? I had no idea. I was so afraid.

"Feel," says my father, guiding my hand. I hold a fat horsehair brush tipped with paint that stinks like vinegar. "Taste the scent on the air. Listen to the scrape of the brush. Then believe."

"Believe . . . what?"

"What you expect to happen. What you want to exist. If you don't control it, it will control you, Ree-child. Never forget that."

I should have stayed in the house I should have left the city I should have seen the previt coming I should have left Shiny in the muck where I found him I should have stayed in Nimaro and never left.

"The paint is a door," my father says.

I put out my hands and imagined that they shook.

"A door?" I ask.

"Yes. The power is in you, hidden, but the paint opens the way to that power, allowing you to bring some of it out onto the canvas. Or anywhere else you want to put it. As you grow older, you'll find new ways to open the door. Painting is just the first method you've found."

"Oh." I consider this. "Does that mean I could sing my magic, like you?"

"Maybe. Do you like singing?"

"Not like I like painting. And my voice doesn't sound good like yours."

He chuckles. "I like your voice."

"You like everything I do, Papa." But my thoughts are turning, fascinated with the idea. *"Does that mean I can do something besides make paintings? Like..."* My child's imagination cannot fathom the possibilities of magic. There are no godlings in the world yet to show us what it can do. *"Like turn a bunny into a bee? Or make flowers bloom?"*

He is silent for a moment, and I sense his reluctance. He has never lied to me, not even when I ask questions he would rather not answer.

"I don't know," he says at last. *"Sometimes when I sing, if I believe something will happen, it happens. And sometimes"*—he hesitates, abruptly looks uneasy—*"sometimes when I don't sing, it happens, too. The song is the door, but belief is the key that unlocks it."*

I touch his face, trying to understand his discomfort. *"What is it, Papa?"*

He catches my hand and kisses it and smiles, but I have already felt it. He is, just a little, afraid. *"Well, just think. What if you took a man and believed he was a rock? Something alive that you believed was something dead?"*

I try to think about this, but I am too young. It sounds fun to me. He sighs and smiles and pats my hands.

I put out my hands, closed my eyes, and *believed* a world into being.

My hands ached to feel, and so I imagined thick, loamy soil. My feet ached to stand, so I put that soil under them, solid, hollow sounding when I stomped because of the air and life teeming within it. My lungs ached to breathe, and I inhaled air that was slightly cool, moist with dew. I breathed out and the warmth of my breath made vapor in the air. I could not see that, but I *believed* it was there. Just as I knew there would be light around me, as my mother had once described—misty morning light, from a pale, early-spring sun.

The darkness lingered, resistant.

Sun. *Sun.* SUN.

Warmth danced along my skin, driving away the aching cold. I sat back on my knees, drawing deep breaths and smelling fresh-turned dirt and feeling the glaze of light against my closed eyelids. I needed to hear something, so I decided there would be wind. A light morning breeze, gradually dispelling the fog. When the breeze came, stirring my hair to tickle my neck, I did not let myself feel amazement. That would lead to doubt. I could feel the fragility of the place around me, its inclination to be *something else.* Cold, endless dark—

"No," I said quickly, and was pleased to hear my own voice. There was air now to carry it. "Warm *spring* air. A garden ready to be planted. Stay here."

The world stayed. So I opened my eyes.

I could see.

And strangely, the scene around me was familiar. I sat in the terrace garden of my home village, where I had almost always been completely blind. Not much magic in Nimaro. The only time I had ever seen the village had been—

—the day my father died. The day of the Gray Lady's birth. I had seen everything then.

I had re-created that day now, falling back on the memory

of that single, magic-infused glimpse. Silvery midmorning mists shivered in the air. I remembered that the big, boxy shape on the other side of the garden was a *house*, though I could not tell if it was mine or the neighbors' without smelling it or counting my steps. Prickly things near my feet danced in the breeze: *grass*. I had rebuilt everything.

Except people. I got to my feet, listening. In all my years in the village, I had never heard it so silent at this time of day. There were always small noises—birds, backyard goats, somebody's newborn fussing. Here there was nothing.

Like ripples in water, I felt the space around me tremble.

"It's home," I whispered. "It's home. Just early; nobody else is up yet. It's real."

The ripples ceased.

Real, yet terribly fragile. I was still in the dark place. All I'd done was create a sphere of sanity around myself, like a bubble. I would have to continue affirming its reality, believing in it, to keep it intact.

Trembling, I dropped to my knees again, pushing my fingers into the moist soil. Yes, that was better. Concentrate on the small things, the mundanities. I lifted a handful of earth to my nose, inhaled. My eyes could not be trusted, but the rest—yes. That I could do.

But I was tired suddenly, more tired than I should have been. As I squeezed the clod of dirt, I found my head nodding, my eyelids heavy. I hadn't slept much, but that did not account for this. I was in a strange place, scared out of my mind. Fear alone should have had me too tense to sleep.

Before I could fathom this new mystery, there was another of those curious rippling shivers—and then agony sizzled behind my eyes. I cried out, arching backward and clapping dirty hands to my face, my concentration broken. Even as I screamed, I felt the false Nimaro bubble shatter around me, spinning away into nothingness as the sickening, empty dark rushed in.

And then—

I landed on my side on a solid surface, hard enough that the breath was jarred from my body.

"Well, here you are," said a cool, male voice. Familiar, but I could not think. Hands touched me, turning me over and pushing my hair from my face. I tried to jerk away, but that jarred the racheting agony in my eyes, my head. I was too tired to scream.

"Is she all right?" That was a woman's voice, somewhere beyond the man.

"I'm not certain."

The words felt like godwords, slapping my ears. I clapped my hands over my ears and moaned, wishing they would all just be silent.

"This isn't the usual disorientation."

"Mmm, no. I think it's some effect of her own magic. She used it to protect herself from my power. Fascinating." He turned away from me, and I felt his smugness like a scrim of filth along my skin. "Your proof."

"Indeed." She sounded pleased as well.

At that point I passed out.

8

"Light Reveals"
(encaustic on canvas)

I AWOKE SLOWLY, and in some pain.

I was lying down. Heavy blankets covered me, soft linen and scratchy wool. I listened for a while, breathing, assessing. I was in a smallish room; my breath sounded close, though not claustrophobically so. It smelled of spent candlewax, dust, me, and the World Tree.

The lattermost scent was *very* strong, stronger than I'd ever known the Tree to smell. The air was laden with its distinctive wood resins and the bright sharp greenscent of its foliage. The Tree did not lose its leaves in autumn—a fact for which we in the city below were deeply grateful—but it did shed damaged leaves whenever they occurred, and it replaced those just before the spring flowering. It tended to smell more strongly during that time, but for the scent to be *this* strong, I had to be closer than usual.

That was not the only unusual thing. I sat up slowly, wincing as I discovered that my whole left arm was sore. I examined it and found fresh bruises there, and also on my hip and ankle. My throat was so scratchy that it hurt when I tried to clear it. And my head ached dully in a single area, from the middle of my scalp right down into my head and forward to press against my eyes—

Then I remembered. The empty place. My false Nimaro. Shattering, falling, voices. *Madding.*

Where the hells was I?

The room was cool, though I could feel watery sunlight coming from my left. I shivered a little as I got out of the warm blankets, though I was wearing clothing—a simple sleeveless shift, loose drawstring pants. Comfortable, if not the best fit. There were slippers beside the cot, which I avoided for the moment. Easier to feel the floor if I left my feet bare.

I explored the room and discovered that I had been imprisoned.

As prisons went, it was nice. The cot had been soft and comfortable, the small table and chairs were well made, and there were thick rugs covering much of the wooden floor. A tiny room off the main one contained a toilet and a sink. Yet the door I found was solidly locked, and there was no keyhole on my side. The windows were unbarred but sealed shut. The glass was thick and heavy; I would not be able to break through it easily, and certainly not without making a great deal of noise.

And the air felt strange. Not as humid as I was used to. Thinner, somehow. Sounds did not carry as well. I clapped experimentally, but the echoes came back all wrong.

I jumped when the door's lock turned, right on the heels of my thought. I was by the windows, so their solidity was suddenly comforting to me as I backed against them.

"Ah, you're awake at last," said a male voice I had never heard before. "Conveniently when I come to check on you myself, rather than sending an initiate. Hello."

Senmite, but no city accent I was familiar with. In fact, he sounded like someone rich, his every enunciation precise, his language formal. I couldn't tell more than that, since I didn't talk to many rich people.

"Hello," I said, or tried to say. My abused throat—from screaming in the empty place, I remembered now—let out a rusty squeak, and it hurt badly enough that I grimaced.

"Perhaps you shouldn't talk." The door closed behind him. Someone outside locked it. I jumped again at the sound of the latch. "Please, Eru Shoth, I mean you no harm. I imagine I can guess most of your questions, so if you'll sit down, I'll explain things."

Eru Shoth? It had been so long since I'd heard the honorific that for a moment I didn't recognize it. A Maro term of respect for a young woman. I was a bit old for it—generally it was used for girls under twenty—but that was all right; maybe he meant to flatter me. He didn't sound Maro, however.

He waited where he was, patiently, until I finally moved to sit down on one of the chairs.

"That's better," he said, moving past me. Measured steps, solid but graceful. A large man, though not as large as Shiny. Old enough to know his body. He smelled of paper and fine cloth, and a bit of leather.

"Now. My name is Hado. I'm responsible for all new arrivals here, which for the moment consists solely of you and your friends. 'Here,' if you're wondering, is the House of the Risen Sun. Have you heard of it?"

I frowned. The newly risen sun was one of the symbols of the Bright Father but was little used these days, since it was easily confused with the dawning sun of the Gray Lady. I had not heard anyone refer to the risen sun since my childhood, back in Nimaro.

"White Hall?" I rasped.

"No, not exactly, though our purpose is also votive. And we, too, honor the Bright Lord—though not in the same manner as the Order of Itempas. Perhaps you've heard the term used for our members instead: we are known as the New Lights."

That one I did know. But that made even less sense; what did a heretic cult want with me?

Hado had said he could guess my questions, but if he guessed that one, he chose not to address it. "You and your friends are to be our guests, Eru Shoth. May I call you Oree?"

Guest, hells. I set my jaw, waiting for him to get to the point.

He seemed amused by my silence, shifting to lean against the table. "Indeed, we have decided to welcome you among us as one of our initiates—our term for a new member. You'll be introduced to our doctrines, our customs, our whole way of life. Nothing will be hidden from you. Indeed, it is our hope that you will find enlightenment with us, and rise within our ranks as a true believer."

This time I turned my face toward him. I had learned that doing this drove the point home for seeing people. "No."

He let out a gentle, untroubled sigh. "It may take you some time to get used to the idea, of course."

"*No.*" I clenched my fists in my lap and forced the words out, despite the agony of speaking. "Where are my friends?"

There was a pause.

"The mortals who were brought here with you are also being inducted into our organization. Not the godlings, of course."

I swallowed, both to wet my throat and to push down a

sudden queasy fear in my belly. There was no way they had managed to bring Madding and his siblings here against their will. No way. "What about the godlings?"

Another of those telling, damning pauses. "Their fate is for our leaders to decide."

I tried to figure out whether he was lying. These were godlings I was worrying about, not mortals. I had never heard of mortal magic that could hold a godling prisoner.

But Madding had not come for me, and that meant he could not, for some reason. I *had* heard of godlings using mortals as a cover for their own machinations. Perhaps that was what was happening here—some rival of Madding's, moving to take over the godsblood trade. Or perhaps another godling had taken the commission that Lady Nemmer had declined.

If either were true, though, wouldn't only Madding have been targeted, and not his whole crew?

Just then, there was a strange movement beneath my feet, like a shiver of the floor. It rippled through the walls, not so much audible as palpable. It was as if the whole room had taken a momentary chill. One of the thick windows even rattled faintly in its frame before going still.

"Where are we?" I rasped.

"The House is attached to the trunk of the World Tree. The Tree sways slightly now and again. Nothing to be concerned about."

Dearest gods.

I'd heard rumors that some of the wealthiest folk in the city—heads of merchant cartels, nobility, and the like—had begun to build homes onto the Tree's trunk. It cost a fortune, in part because the Arameri had laid down strict requirements for aesthetics, safety, and the health of the Tree, and in part because no one with the gall to build onto the Tree would bother building a *small* house.

That a group of heretics could command such resources was incredible. That they had the power to capture and hold half a dozen godlings against their will was impossible.

These aren't ordinary people, I realized with a chill. *This is more than money; it's power too. Magical, political—everything.*

The only people in the world with that kind of power were Arameri.

"Now, I see that you're still not feeling well—not well enough to carry on a conversation, anyhow." Hado straightened, coming over to me. I flinched when I felt his fingers touch my left temple, where I was surprised to realize I had another bruise. "Better," he said, "but I think I'll recommend that you be given another day to rest. I'll have someone bring you dinner here, then take you to the baths. When you've healed more, the Nypri would like to examine you."

Yes, I remembered now. After my false Nimaro had shattered, I had been brought out of the empty place somehow. I had fallen to the floor, hard. The ache in my eyes, though—that was more familiar. I had felt the same at Madding's after I'd used magic to kill the Order-Keepers at the park.

Then I registered what Hado had said. "Nypri?" It sounded like some sort of title. "Your leader?"

"One of our leaders, yes. His role is more specific, however; he's an expert scrivener. And he's very interested in your unique magical abilities. Most likely he'll request a demonstration."

The blood drained out of my face. They knew about my magic. How? It did not matter; they knew.

"Don't want to," I said. My voice was very small, not just because of the soreness.

Hado's hand was still on my temple. He moved it down and patted my cheek, twice, in a patronizing sort of way. Both slaps were just a little too hard to be comforting, and then his hand lingered on me, an implicit warning.

"Don't be foolish," he said very softly. "You're a good Maroneh girl, aren't you? We are all true Itempans here, Oree. Why wouldn't you want to join us?"

The Arameri had ruled the world for thousands of years. In that time, they had imposed the Bright on every continent, every kingdom, every race. Those who'd worshipped other gods were given a simple command: convert. Those who disobeyed were annihilated, their names and works forgotten. True Itempans believed in one way—their way.

How like Shiny, a small, bitter voice whispered in me before I forced it silent.

Hado chuckled again, but this time he stroked my cheek approvingly at my silence. It still stung.

"You'll do well here, I see," he said.

With that, he went to the door and knocked. Someone let him out and locked the door again behind him. I sat where I was for a long while after, with my hand on my cheek.

Wordless people entered my room twice the next day, bringing me a light Amn-style breakfast and soup for lunch. I spoke to the second one—my voice was better—asking where Madding and the others were. The person did not answer. No one else appeared in the interim, so I listened at the door awhile, trying to determine whether there were guards outside and whether there was any pattern to the movement I could hear in the halls beyond. My chances of escaping—alone, from a house full of fanatics, without even a stick to help me find my way—were slim, but that was no reason not to try.

I was fiddling with the thick-glassed window when the door opened behind me and someone small came in. I straightened without guilt. They weren't stupid. They expected me to try and escape, at least for the first few days or so. True Itempans were nothing if not rational.

"My name is Jont," said a young woman, surprising me by speaking. She sounded younger than me, maybe in her teens. There was something about her voice that suggested innocence, or maybe enthusiasm. "You're Oree."

"Yes," I said. She had not given a family name, I noticed. Neither had Hado, the night before. So neither did I—a small, safe battle. "I'm pleased to meet you." My throat felt better, thank the gods.

She seemed pleased by my attempt at politeness. "The Master of Initiates—Master Hado, whom you met—says I'm to give you anything you need," she said. "I can take you to the baths now, and I've brought some fresh clothing." There was the faint *pluff* of a pile of cloth being deposited. "Nothing fancy, I'm afraid. We live simply here."

"I see," I said. "You're an . . . initiate, too?"

"Yes." She came closer, and I guessed that she was staring at my eyes. "Was that a guess, or did you sense it somehow? I've heard that blind people can pick up on things normal people can't."

I tried not to sigh. "It was a guess."

"Oh." She sounded disappointed but recovered quickly.

"You're feeling better today, I see. You slept for two whole days after they brought you out of the Empty."

"Two days?" But something else caught my attention. "The Empty?"

"The place our Nypri sends the worst blasphemers against the Bright," Jont said. She had dropped her voice, her tone full of dread. "Is it as terrible as they say?"

"You mean that place beyond the holes." I remembered being unable to breathe, unable to scream. "It was terrible," I said softly.

"Then it's fortunate the Nypri was merciful. What did you do?"

"Do?"

"To cause him to put you there."

At this, fury lanced down my spine. "I did nothing. I was with my friends when this Nypri of yours attacked us. I was *kidnapped* and brought here against my will. And my friends..." I almost choked as I realized. "For all I know, they're still in that awful place."

To my surprise, Jont made a compassionate sound and patted my hand. "It's all right. If they aren't blasphemers, he'll bring them out before too much harm is done. Now. Shall we go to the baths?"

Jont took my arm to lead me while I shuffled along, moving slowly since I had no walking stick to help me gauge floor obstacles. Meanwhile, I mulled over the tidbits of information Jont had tossed at my feet. They might call their new members initiates instead of Order-Keepers, and they might use strange magic, but in every other way, these New Lights seemed much like the Order of Itempas—right down to the same high-handed ways.

Which made me wonder why the Order hadn't yet broken them up. It was one thing to permit the worship of godlings; there was a certain pragmatism in that. But another faith dedicated to Bright Itempas? That was messy. Confusing to the layfolk. What if the Lights began to build their own White Halls, collect their own offerings, deploy their own Order-Keepers? That would violate every tenet of the Bright. The Lights' very existence invited chaos.

What made even less sense was that the Arameri allowed it. Their clan's founder, Shahar Arameri, had once been His most favored priestess; the Order was their mouthpiece. I could not see how it benefitted them to allow a rival voice to exist.

Then a thought: *maybe the Arameri don't know.*

I was distracted from this when we entered an open room filled with warm humidity and the sound of water. The bath chamber.

"Do you wash first?" Jont asked. She guided me to a washing area; I could smell the soap. "I don't know anything about Maro customs."

"Not very different from Amn," I said, wondering why she cared. I explored and found a shelf bearing soap, fresh sponges, and a wide bowl of steaming water. Hot—a treat. I pulled off my clothes and draped them over the rack I found along the shelf's edge, then sat down to scrub myself. "We're Senmite, too, after all."

"Since the Nightlord destroyed the Maroland," she said, and then gasped. "Oh, darkness—I'm sorry."

"Why?" I shrugged, putting down the sponge. "Mentioning it won't make it happen again." I found a flask beside it, which I opened and sniffed. Shampoo. Astringent, not ideal for Maroneh hair, but it would have to do.

"Well, yes, but...to remind you of such a horror..."

"It happened to my ancestors, not to me. I don't forget—we never forget—but there's more to the Maroneh than some long-ago tragedy." I rinsed myself with the bowl and sighed, turning to her. "Which way is the soak?"

She took my hand again and led me to a huge wooden tub. The bottom was metal, heated by a fire underneath. I had to use steps built into the side to climb in. The water was cooler than I liked, and unscented, though at least it smelled clean. Madding's pools had always been just right—

Enough of that, I told myself sharply as my eyes stung with the warning of tears. *You can't do him any good if you don't figure out how to get out of here.*

Jont came with me, leaning against the side of the tub. I wished she would go away, but I supposed part of her role was to act as my guard as well as my guide.

"The Maroneh have always honored Itempas first among the Three, just like we Amn," she said. "You don't worship any of the lesser gods. Isn't that right?"

Her phrasing warned me immediately. I had met her type before. Not all mortals were happy that the godlings had come. I had never understood their thinking, because—until recently—I had assumed Bright Itempas had changed His mind about the Interdiction; I thought He'd *wanted* His children in the mortal realm. Of course, more devout Itempans would realize it before I, lapsed as I was. The Bright Lord did not change His mind.

"Worship the godlings?" I refused to use her phrasing. "No. I've met a number of them, though, and some of them I even call friend." Madding. Paitya. Nemmer, maybe. Kitr—well, no, she didn't like me. Definitely not Lil.

Shiny? Yes, I had once called him friend, though the quiet goddess had been right; he would not say the same of me.

I could almost hear Jont's face screwing up in consternation. "But...they're not human." She said it the way one would describe an insect, or an animal.

"What does that matter?"

"They're not like us. They can't understand us. They're dangerous."

I leaned against the tub's edge and began to plait my wet hair. "Have you ever talked to one of them?"

"Of course not!" She sounded horrified by the idea.

I started to say more, then stopped. If she couldn't see gods as people—she barely saw *me* as a person—then nothing I could say would make a difference. That made me realize something, however. "Does your Nypri feel the way you do about godlings? Is that why he dragged my friends into that Empty place?"

Jont caught her breath. "Your friends are *godlings?*" At once her voice hardened. "Then, yes, that's why. And the Nypri won't be letting *them* out anytime soon."

I fell silent, too revolted to think of anything to say. After a moment, Jont sighed. "I didn't mean to upset you. Please, are you finished? We have a lot to do."

"I don't think I want to do anything you have in mind," I said as coldly as I could.

She touched my shoulder and said something that would keep me from ever seeing her as innocent again: "You will."

I got out of the tub and dried myself, shivering from more than the cold air.

When I was dry and wrapped in a thick robe, she led me back to my room, where I dressed in the garments she'd brought:

a simple pullover shirt and an ankle-length skirt that swirled nicely about my ankles. The undergarments were generic and loose, not a complete fit but close enough. Shoes too—soft slippers meant for indoor wear. A subtle reminder that my captors had no intention of letting me go outside.

"That's better," said Jont when I was done, sounding pleased. "You look like one of us now."

I touched the hem of the shirt. "I take it these are white."

"Beige. We don't wear white. White is the color of false purity, misleading to those who would otherwise seek the Light." There was a singsong intonation to the way Jont said this that made me think she was reciting something. It was no teaching poem I'd ever heard, in White Hall or elsewhere.

On the heels of this, a heavy bell sounded somewhere in the House. Its resonant tone was beautiful; I closed my eyes in inadvertent pleasure.

"The dinner hour," Jont said. "I got you ready just in time. Our leaders have asked you to dine with them this evening."

Trepidation filled me. "I don't suppose I could pass? I'm still a bit tired."

Jont took my hand again. "I'm sorry. It's not far."

So I followed her through what felt like an endless maze of hallways. We passed other members of the New Lights (Jont greeted most of them but did not pause to introduce me), but I paid little attention to them beyond realizing that the organization was much, much larger than I'd initially assumed. I noted a dozen people just in the corridor beyond my room. But instead of listening to them, I counted my paces as we walked so that I could find my way faster if I ever managed to escape the room. We moved from a corridor that smelled like varsmusk incense to another that sounded as though it had open windows along its length, letting in the late-evening air. Down two flights of stairs (twenty-four steps), around a corner (right), and across an open space (straight ahead, thirty-degree angle from the corner), we came to a much larger enclosed space.

Here there were many people all around us, but most of the voices seemed to be below head level. Seated, maybe. I had been smelling food for some time, mingled with the scents of lanterns and people and the omnipresent green of the Tree. I guessed it was a huge dining hall.

"Jont." An older woman's contralto, soft and compelling. And there was a scent, like hiras blossoms, that also caught my attention because it reminded me of Madding's house. We stopped. "I'll escort her from here. Eru Shoth? Will you come with me?"

"Lady Serymn!" Jont sounded flustered and alarmed and excited all at once. "O-of course." She let go of me, and another hand took mine.

"We've been expecting you," the woman said. "There's a private dining room this way. I'll warn you if there are steps."

"All right," I said, grateful. Jont had not done this, and I'd stubbed my toe twice already. As we walked, I pondered this new enigma.

Lady Serymn, Jont had called her. Not a godling, certainly, not among these godling haters. A noblewoman, then. Yet her name was Amn, one of those tongue-tangling combinations of consonants they so favored; the Amn had no nobility, except—

But, no, that was impossible.

We passed through a wide doorway into a smaller, quieter space, and suddenly I had new things to distract me, namely the scent of food. Roasted fowl, shellfish of some kind, greens and garlic, wine sauce, other scents that I could not identify. Rich people's food. When Serymn guided me to the table where this feast lay, I belatedly realized there were others already seated around it. I'd been so fascinated with the food that I'd barely noticed them.

I sat among these strangers, before their luxurious feast, and tried not to show my nervousness.

A servant came near and began preparing my plate. "Would you like duck, Lady Oree?"

"Yes," I said politely, and then registered the title. "But it's just Oree. Not 'Lady' anything."

"You undervalue yourself," said Serymn. She sat to my right, perpendicular to me. There were at least seven others around the table; I could hear them murmuring to each other. The table was either rectangular or oval-shaped, and Serymn sat at its head. Someone else sat at the other end, across from her.

"It is appropriate for us to call you Lady," Serymn said. "Please allow us to show you that courtesy."

"But I'm *not*," I said, confused. "There isn't a drop of noble blood in me. Nimaro doesn't have a noble family; they were wiped out with the Maroland."

"I suppose that's as good an opening as any to explain why we've brought you here," Serymn said. "Since I'm certain you've wondered."

"You might say so," I said, annoyed. "Hado..." I hesitated. "*Master* Hado told me a little, but not enough."

There were a few chuckles from my companions, including two low, male voices from the far end of the table. I recognized one of them and flushed: Hado.

Serymn sounded amused as well. "What we honor is not your wealth or status, Lady Oree, but your lineage."

"My lineage is like the rest of me—common," I snapped. "My father was a carpenter; my mother grew and sold medicinal herbs. *Their* parents were farmers. There's nobody fancier than a smuggler in my entire family tree."

"Allow me to explain." She paused to take a sip of wine, leaning forward, and as she did, I caught a glimmer from her direction. I turned to quickly peer at it, but whatever it was had been obscured somehow.

"How curious," said another of my table companions. "Most of the time she seems like an ordinary blind woman, not orienting her face toward anything in particular, but just now she seemed to *see* you, Serymn."

I kicked myself. It probably would've done no good to conceal my ability, but I still hated giving them information inadvertently.

"Yes," said Serymn. "Dateh did mention that she seems to have some perception where magic is concerned." She did something, and suddenly I got a clear look at what I'd glimpsed. It was a small, solid circle of golden, glowing magic. No—the circle was not solid at all. In spite of myself, I leaned closer, narrowing my eyes. The circle consisted of dozens upon dozens of tiny, closely written sigils of the gods' spiky language. Godwords. *Sentences* of them, a whole treatise's worth, spiraling and overlapping each other so densely that from a distance the circle looked solid.

Then I understood, and drew back in shock.

Serymn moved again, letting her hair fall back into place, I realized by the way the sigil-circle vanished. Yes, it would be on her forehead.

That can't be. It doesn't make sense. I don't believe it. But I had seen it with my own two magic eyes.

I licked my suddenly dry lips, folded my shaking hands in my lap, and mustered all my courage to speak. "What is an Arameri fullblood doing with some little heretic cult, Lady Serymn?"

The laughter that broke out around the table was not the reaction I'd been expecting. When it died down—I sat through it, uneasily silent—Serymn said in a voice that still rippled with amusement, "Please, Lady Oree, do eat. There's no reason we can't have a good conversation *and* enjoy a fine meal, is there?"

So I ate a few bites. Then I wiped my mouth using my best manners and sat up, making a point of waiting politely for an answer to my question.

Serymn uttered a soft sigh and wiped her own mouth. "Very well. I'm with this 'little heretic cult,' as you put it, because I have a goal to accomplish, and being here aids that purpose. But I should point out that the New Lights are neither little, nor heretical, nor a cult."

"I was given to understand," I said slowly, "that any form of worship other than that sanctioned by the Order was heretical."

"Untrue, Lady Oree. By the law of the Bright—the law as set down by my family—only the worship of *gods other than Itempas* is heretical. The form in which we choose to worship is irrelevant. It's true that the Order would prefer that the two concepts—obedience to the Bright Lord, obedience to the Order—be synonymous." There was another soft roll of chuckles from our table companions. "But to put it bluntly, the Order is a mortal authority, not a godly one. We of the Lights merely recognize the distinction."

"So you think the form of worship you've chosen is better than that of the Order?"

"We do. Our organization's beliefs are fundamentally similar to those of the Order of Itempas—indeed, many of our members are former Order priests. But there are some significant differences."

"Such as?"

"Do you really want to get into a doctrinal discussion right now, Lady Oree?" Serymn asked. "You'll be introduced to our philosophy over the next few days, like any new initiate. I thought your questions would be more basic."

They were. Still, I felt instinctively that the key to understanding the whole heaping pile of fanatics lay in understanding this woman. This *Arameri*. The fullbloods were the highest members of a family so devoted to order that they ranked and sorted themselves by how closely they could trace their lineage back to First Priestess Shahar. They were the power brokers, the decision makers—and sometimes, through the might of their god-slaves, the annihilators of nations.

Yet that had been before ten years ago, that strange and terrible day when the World Tree had grown and the godlings returned. There had always been rumors, but I knew the truth now, from Shiny's own lips. The Arameri's slaves had broken free; the Nightlord and the Gray Lady had overthrown Bright Itempas. The Arameri, though far from powerless, had lost their greatest weapons and their patron in one stunning blow.

What happened when people who'd once possessed absolute power suddenly lost it?

"All right," I said carefully. "Basic questions. Why are you here, and why am *I*?"

"How much do you know of what happened ten years ago, Lady Oree?"

I hesitated, unsure. Was it safer to play the ignorant commoner, or reveal how much I knew? Would this Arameri woman have me killed if I told her family's secret? Or was it a test to see if I would lie?

I tore off a piece of bread, more out of nervousness than hunger. "I...I know there are three gods again," I said slowly. "I know Bright Itempas no longer rules alone."

"Try 'at all,' Lady Oree," Serymn said. "But you've guessed that, haven't you? All true followers of Itempas know He would never permit the changes that have occurred in the past few years."

I nodded, inadvertently thinking of Madding's bed, and our lovemaking, and Shiny's glowering disapproval. "That's true," I said, suppressing a bitter smile.

"Then we must consider His siblings, these new gods..."

One of Serymn's companions let out a bark of laughter. "New? Come, now, Lady Serymn; we are not the gullible masses." She glanced at me, and I was not fooled by the sweetness in her tone. "Most of us, anyhow."

I set my jaw, refusing to be baited. Serymn took this with remarkable equanimity, I thought; I wouldn't have expected an Arameri to brook much in the way of ridicule, even if most of it had been at someone else's expense.

"Granted, 'the Lord of Shadows' was a feeble attempt at diversion," she replied, then returned her attention to me. "But my family has had its hands full trying to prevent a panic, Lady Oree. After all, we spent centuries filling mortal hearts with terror at the prospect of the Nightlord's release. Better that we should keep him leashed than he break loose and wreak his vengeance upon the world; that was how it went. Now only a few feeble lies keep the populace from realizing we could *all* go the way of the Maro."

She referred to the destruction of my people—her family's fault—with neither rancor nor shame, and it made me seethe. But that was how Arameri were: they shrugged off their errors, when they could even be persuaded to admit them.

"He's angry," I said. Softly, because so was I. "The Nightlord. You know that, don't you? He has given a deadline for the Arameri and the godlings to find his children's killers."

"Yes," said Serymn. "That message was delivered to the Lord Arameri several days ago, I'm told. One month, from Role's death. That leaves us approximately three weeks."

She spoke like it was nothing, a god's wrath. My hands fisted in my lap. "The Nightlord was *bored* when he destroyed the Maroland. He didn't even have his full power at the time. Can you even imagine what he'll do now?"

"Better than you can, Lady Oree." Serymn spoke very softly. "I grew up with him, remember."

The table fell silent. A clock somewhere in the room ticked loudly. All of us could hear the untold tales in her inflectionless tone—and then there was the biggest tale, lurking beneath the surface of the conversation like some leviathan: *why had a woman so powerful, so apparently fearless, fled from Sky in the first place?* And now, imagining horrors in the ticking stillness, I could not help wondering, *What the hells did the Nightlord do to her?*

"Fortunately," said Serymn at last, and I exhaled in relief when the silence broke, "his anger fits well into our plans."

I must have frowned, because she laughed. It sounded forced, though only a little.

"Consider, Lady Oree, that we have been saved once already by the third member of the Three. Consider what that means—what her presence means. Have you never wondered? Enefa of the Twilight, sister of Bright Itempas, has been dead for two thousand years. Who, then, is this Gray Lady? You're acquainted with many of the city's godlings. Did they explain this mystery to you?"

I blinked in surprise as I realized Madding had not. He had spoken of his mother's death, grief still thick in his voice. But he had also spoken of his parents, plural and present. It was just one of those contradictions that one had to accept when dealing with gods; it hadn't bothered me because I hadn't thought it was important. But then, until recently, I thought I'd understood the hierarchy of the gods.

"No," I said. "He—they never told me."

"Hmm. Then I will tell you a great secret, Lady Oree. Ten years ago, a mortal woman betrayed her god and her humanity by conspiring to set the Nightlord—her lover—free. She succeeded, and for her efforts was rewarded with the lost power of Enefa. She became, in effect, a *new* Enefa, a goddess in her own right."

I caught my breath in inadvertent surprise. I had never realized it was possible for a mortal to become a god. But that explained a great deal. The restrictions on the godlings, confining them within the city of Shadow; why the godlings so carefully policed each other to prevent mass destruction. A goddess who had once been mortal herself might take exception to the callous disregard for mortal life.

"The Gray Lady is irrelevant to us," Serymn said, "beyond the fact that we have her to thank for the current peace." She leaned forward, resting her elbows on the table. "We're counting on her intervention, in fact. Enefa—of whom this new goddess is essentially a copy—has always fought for the preservation of life. That is her nature; where her brothers are more extreme—quick to judge and quicker to wreak havoc—she *maintains*. She adapts to change and seeks stability within it. The Gods' War was not the first time Itempas and Nahadoth had fought, after all. It was simply the first time they'd done it, since the creation of life, without Enefa around to keep the world in balance."

I was shaking my head. "You mean you're counting on this new Enefa to keep us safe? Are you kidding? Even if she used to be human, she's not anymore. Now she thinks like any other god." I thought of Lil. "And some of them are crazy."

"If she'd wanted all humanity dead, she could have done it herself, many times over, during the past ten years." The table shifted slightly as Serymn made some gesture. "She is the goddess of death as well as life. And, please remember, when she was mortal, she was Arameri. We have always been predictable." I heard her smile. "I believe she will seek to channel the Nightlord's rage in the most expedient manner. He need not destroy the whole world, after all, to avenge his children. Just a part of it will do. A single city, perhaps."

I put my hands in my lap, my appetite gone.

Maroneh parents do not tell comforting bedtime tales. Just as we name our children for sorrow and rage, we also tell them stories that will make them cry and awaken in the night, shivering with nightmares. We *want* our children to be afraid and to never forget, because that way they will be prepared if the Nightlord should ever come again.

As he would soon come to Shadow.

"Why has the Order of Itempas..." I faltered, unsure of how to say it without offending a room full of former Order members. "The Nightlord. Why honor him just because he's free? He already hates us. Do they actually think an angry god would be deterred by that kind of hypocrisy?"

"The gods aren't who they're trying to deter, Lady Oree." This came from the man at the table's far end. I stiffened. "It's *us* they hope to appease."

I knew that voice. I had heard it before—three times, now. At the south promenade, just before I'd killed the Order-Keepers. On Madding's rooftop before all chaos had broken loose. And later, as I'd lain shivering and sick after my release from the Empty.

He sat at the far end of the table, opposite Serymn, radiating the same easy confidence as she. Of course he did; he was their Nypri.

As I sat there, trembling with fear and fury, Serymn chuckled. "Blunt as ever, Dateh."

"It's only the truth." He sounded amused.

"Hmm. What my husband means to say, Lady Oree, is that the Order, and through it the Arameri family, desperately hopes to convince the rest of mortalkind that the world is as it should be. That despite the presence of all our new gods, nothing *else* should change—politically speaking. That we should feel happy...safe...complacent."

Husband. An Arameri fullblood married to a heretic cultist?

"You're not making any sense," I said. I focused on the fork in my fingers, on the crackle of the dining room's fireplace in the background. Those helped me stay calm. "You're talking about the Arameri as if you're not one of them."

"Indeed. Let's just say that my activities aren't sanctioned by the rest of my family."

The Nypri sounded amused. "Oh, they might approve—if they knew."

Serymn laughed at this, as did others around the table. "Do you really think so? You're far more of an optimist than I, my love."

They bantered while I sat there, trying to make sense of nobility and conspiracy and a thousand other things that had never been a part of my life. I was just a street artist. Just an ordinary Maroneh, frightened and far from home.

"I don't understand," I said finally, interrupting them. "You've kidnapped me, brought me here. You're trying to force me to join you. What does all this—the Nightlord, the Order, the Arameri—have to do with *me*?"

"More than you realize," said the Nypri. "The world is in great danger at the moment—not just from the Nightlord's wrath. Consider: for the first time in centuries, the Arameri are vulnerable. Oh, they still have immense political and financial strength, and they're building an army that will make any rebel nation think twice. But *they can be defeated now*. Do you know what that means?"

"That someday we might have a different group of tyrants in charge?" Despite my efforts to be polite, I was growing annoyed. They kept talking in circles, never answering my questions.

Serymn seemed unoffended. "Perhaps—but which group? *Every* noble clan and ruling council and elected minister will want the chance to rule the Hundred Thousand Kingdoms. And if they all strive for it at once, what do you think will happen?"

"More scandals and intrigues and assassinations and whatever else you people do with your time," I said. Lady Nemmer would be pleased, at least.

"Yes. And coups, as weak nobles are replaced by stronger or more ambitious ones. And rebellions within those lands, as minority factions jostle for a share. And new alliances as smaller kingdoms band together for strength. And betrayals, because every alliance has a few." Serymn let out a long, weary sigh. "War, Lady Oree. There will be war."

Like the good Itempan girl I had never quite been, I nevertheless flinched. War was anathema to Bright Itempas. I had heard tales of the time before the Bright, before the Arameri had made laws to strictly regulate violence and conflict. In the old days, thousands had died in every battle. Cities had been razed to the ground, their inhabitants slaughtered as armies of warriors descended upon helpless civilians to rape and kill.

"Wh-where?" I asked.

"*Everywhere.*"

I could not imagine it. Not on such a scale. It was madness. Chaos.

Then I remembered. Nahadoth, the Lord of Night, was also the god of chaos. What more fitting vengeance could he wreak upon humanity?

"If the Arameri fall and the Bright ends, war returns," Serymn said. "The Order of Itempas fears this more than any threat the gods pose, because it is the greater danger—not just to a city, but to our entire civilization. Already there are rumors of unrest in High North and on the islands—those lands that were forcibly converted to the worship of Itempas after the Gods' War. They have never forgotten, or forgiven, what we did to them."

"High Northers," said someone else at the table, in a tone of scorn. "Darkling barbarians! Two thousand years and they're still angry."

"Barbarians, yes, and angry," said Hado, whom I had forgotten was there. "But did we not feel the same anger when we were told to start worshipping the Nightlord?" There were grumbles of assent from around the table.

"Yes," said the Nypri. "So the Order permits heresy and looks the other way when Itempas's former faithful scorn their duties. They hope the exploration of new faiths will occupy the people and grant the Arameri time to prepare for the conflagration to come."

"But it's pointless," said Serymn, a note of anger in her voice. "T'vril, the Lord Arameri, hopes to put down the war swiftly when it comes. But to prepare for earthly war, he's taken his eyes off the threat in the heavens."

I sighed, weary in more ways than one. "That's a fine thing to concern yourself with, but the Nightlord is"—I spread my hands helplessly—"a force of nature. Maybe we should all start praying to this Gray Lady, since you say she's the one keeping him in line. Or maybe we should just start picking out our personal heavens in the afterlife now."

Serymn's tone chided me gently. "We prefer to be more proactive, Lady Oree. Perhaps it's the Arameri in me, but I'm not fond of allowing a known threat to fester unchecked. Better to strike first."

"Strike?" I chuckled, certain I was misunderstanding. "What, *a god*? That isn't possible."

"Yes, Lady Oree, it is. It's been done before, after all."

I froze, the smile falling from my face. "The godling Role. *You* killed her."

Serymn laughed noncommittally. "I was referring to the Gods' War, actually. Itempas Skyfather killed Enefa; if one of the Three can die, they all can."

I fell silent in confusion, but I wasn't laughing, not any longer. Serymn wasn't a fool. I did not believe an Arameri would hint at something like a goddess's murder unless she had the power to do it.

"Which, to come to the point at last, is why we kidnapped you." Serymn lifted her glass to me, the faint crystalline sound as loud as a bell in the room's silence. Our dining companions had fallen silent, hanging on her every word. When she saluted them, they lifted their glasses in return.

"To the return of the Bright," said the Nypri.

"And the White Lord," said the woman who had commented on my sight.

" 'Til darkness ends," said Hado.

And other affirmations, from each person at the table. It had the feel of a solemn ritual—as they all committed themselves to a course of stunning, absolute insanity.

When they had all said their piece and fallen silent, I spoke, my voice hollow with realization and disbelief.

"You want to kill the Nightlord," I said.

"Yes," she said. She paused as another servant came over. I heard the cover being lifted from some sort of tray. "And we want you to help us do it. Dessert?"

9

"Seduction"
(charcoal)

THERE WAS NO FURTHER TALK of gods or insane plots after dinner. I was too stunned to think of further questions, and even if I had asked, Serymn made it clear she would answer no more. "I think we've spoken enough for tonight," she said, and then she'd laughed a rich, perfectly measured laugh. "You're looking a bit pale, my dear."

So they'd brought me back to my room, where Jont had left me nightclothes and spiced wine to drink before my evening prayers, in the Maroneh custom. Perhaps she'd looked it up in a book. Suspecting observation, I drank a glass and then prayed for the first time in several years—but not to Bright Itempas.

Instead I tried to fix my thoughts on Madding. He had told me that gods could hear the prayers of their devotees regardless of distance or circumstance, if they only prayed hard enough. I was not precisely a devotee of Madding's, but I hoped desperation would make up for it.

I know where you are, I whispered in my mind, since there might be listeners in the room. *I don't know how to get you out yet, but I'm working on it. Can you hear me?*

But though I repeated my plea, and waited on my knees for nearly an hour, there was no answer.

I knew Madding was in that dark, sensationless place—the Empty—but I wasn't sure where *that* was. For all I knew, only the Lights could open and close the way to it. Or perhaps only their scrivener-trained Nypri could. Figuring that out would be my next task.

The next morning I awoke at dawn, having slept fitfully on my cot. Already there was activity in the house. I could hear it through the door: people walking, brooms sweeping, casual chatter. I should have guessed that an organization of Itempans would start their day well before sunrise. More distantly, echoing through the corridors, I heard singing—the Lights' wordless hymn, which was far more soothing and uplifting than the Lights themselves had turned out to be. Perhaps there was some sort of morning ceremony taking place. If that was the case, then it would be only a matter of time before they came for me. Trying to quell unease, I dressed in the clothes they'd given me, and waited.

Not long afterward, the lock on my room's door opened and someone came in. "Jont?" I asked.

"No, it's Hado again," he said. My belly tightened, but I think I managed not to show my unease. There was something about this man that made me very uncomfortable. It was more than his participation in my kidnapping and forced assimilation into a cult; more than his veiled threat the night before. Sometimes I even thought I could see him, like a darker shadow etched against my vision. Mostly it was just the constant feeling, impossible to prove, that the face he showed me was just a veil, and behind it he was laughing at me.

"Sorry to disappoint you." He had caught my unease, and predictably it seemed to amuse him. "Jont has cleaning duty in the mornings. Something you'll become familiar with, too, eventually."

"Eventually?"

"It's traditional for a new initiate to be put on a work crew, but we're still trying to figure out a placement that can accommodate your unique needs."

I could not help bristling. "You mean that I'm blind? I can clean just fine, especially if you give me a walking stick." Mine, to my lament, had been left behind on the street outside Madding's house. I missed it like an old friend.

"No, Eru Shoth, I mean the fact that you'll escape first chance you get." I flinched, and he chuckled softly. "We don't usually put guards on the work crews, but until we're certain of your commitment to our way... Well, it would be foolish to leave you unsupervised."

I drew in a deep breath, let it out. "I'm surprised you have no procedures for handling recruits like me, if kidnapping and coercion are your usual practice."

"Believe it or not, most of our initiates are volunteers." He moved past me, inspecting the room. I heard him pick up a candle holder from one of the wall sconces, perhaps noting that I'd blown out the candle early. I didn't exactly need the light, and I'd never liked the idea of dying in my sleep from a fire. He continued. "We've done quite well at recruiting among certain groups—in particular, devout Itempan laity who are disaffected with the Order's recent changes. I imagine we'll do well in Nimaro when we start setting up a branch there."

"Even in Nimaro, Master Hado, there are those who feel no need to worship Itempas in the same way as everyone else. No one forces them to do what they don't want to."

"Untrue," he replied, which made me frown. "Before ten years ago, every mortal in the Hundred Thousand Kingdoms worshipped Itempas in the same way. Weekly offerings and services at a White Hall, monthly hours of service, lessons for children from three years to fifteen. Every holy day, all over the world, the same rituals were enacted and the same prayers chanted. Those who dissented..." He paused and turned to me, still radiating that cool amusement that I so hated about him. "Well. You tell me what happened to them, Lady. If there were so many dissenters in your land."

I said nothing, in consternation, because it was a pointed dig at me: a Maroneh who had fled Nimaro first chance. Worse, he was right. My own father had loathed the White Halls and the rituals and the rigid adherence to tradition. Long ago, he'd told me, the Maroneh had had their own customs for worshipping Bright Itempas—special poetic forms and a holy book and priests who had been warrior-historians, not overseers. We'd even had our own language back then. All that changed when the Arameri came to power.

"You see," said Hado. He could read my face like a book, and I hated him for it. "Itempas values order, not choice. That said"—he came over and took my hand, coaxing me up and letting me take his arm to be guided—"obviously it would be impractical to recruit many like you. We wouldn't have done it if you weren't so important to our cause."

That didn't sound good. "What exactly does that mean?"

"That instead of following the usual process of initiation, you will spend today with Lady Serymn and tomorrow with the Nypri. They'll decide how best to proceed from there." He patted my hand again, reminding me of his ungentle pats from

the night before. Yes, this, too, was a warning. If I did not somehow please the Lights' leaders, what would happen? Without
even knowing why they wanted me, I could not guess. I ground
my teeth, angry—but in truth, I was more afraid than angry.
These people were powerful and mad, and that was never a
good combination.

Hado walked me out of my room and began guiding me
through the corridors, moving at an unhurried pace. I counted
my steps for as long as I could, but there were too many twists
and turns in the House of the Risen Sun; I kept losing count.
The corridors here were all slightly curved, perhaps some function of building a house partially wrapped around a tree trunk.
And because the House's builders had been unable to extend
the structure far from the trunk—I was no architect, but even
I could see the folly in that—the House had been built narrow and high, with multiple levels and stair-connected sections,
giving the whole place an oddly disjointed feel. Hardly a monu-
ment to the Bright Lord's love of order.

Then again, perhaps this, too, was a disguise, like the New
Lights' carefully cultivated appearance of harmlessness. The
Order of Itempas saw them as just another heretic cult. Would
they feel the same if they knew this heretic cult had power
enough to challenge the gods?

Hado said nothing while we walked, and neither did I in my
preoccupation. I gauged his silence, trying to decide how much
I dared ask. Finally I braved it. "Do you know what those...
holes...are?"

"Holes?"

"The magic that was used to bring me here." I shivered. "The
Empty."

"Ah, that. I don't know, not exactly, but the Nypri was ranked Scrivener Honor Class within the Order of Itempas. That's their highest designation." He shrugged, jostling my hand on his arm. "I'm told he was even a candidate to become First Scrivener to the Arameri, though, of course, that ended when he defected from the Order."

I let out a laugh in spite of myself. "So he married an Arameri fullblood and started his own religion to remind himself of what he almost had?"

Hado chuckled, too. "Not exactly, but I understand that mutual dissatisfaction is a factor in their collaboration. I imagine it isn't a far step from mutual goals to mutual respect, and from there to love."

Interesting—or it would have been, if the happy couple hadn't kidnapped, tortured, and imprisoned me and my friends. "That's lovely," I said as blandly as I could, "but I know something about scriveners, and I've never seen a scrivener do anything like that. Overpower one godling, much less several? I didn't think that was even possible."

"Gods aren't invincible, Lady Oree. And your friends—well, nearly all of the ones who live here in the city—are the younger, weaker godlings." He shrugged, oblivious to my surprise; he had just told me something I'd never realized. "The Nypri simply found a way to exploit these facts."

I fell silent again, mulling over what he'd told me. Eventually we passed through a doorway into a smaller enclosed space, this one thickly carpeted. There were more food smells here, breakfast items—and a familiar hiras-scented perfume.

"Thank you for coming," said Serymn, coming over to us. Hado let go of my hand, and Serymn took it in a sisterly fashion, stepping close to kiss me on the cheek. I managed not to pull back at that, though it was a near thing. Serymn noticed, of course.

"Forgive me, Lady. I suppose street folk don't greet each other that way."

"I wouldn't know," I said, unable to keep a scowl off my face. "I'm not 'street folk,' whatever those are."

"And here I've offended you." She sighed. "My apologies. I have little experience with commoners. Thank you, Brightbrother Hado." Hado left, and Serymn guided me over to a large plush chair.

"Prepare a plate," she ordered, and someone off to the side of the room began doing so. Sitting down across from me, Serymn examined me in silence for a moment. She was like Shiny in that; I could feel her gaze, like the brush of moth wings.

"Did you rest well last night?"

"Yes," I said. "I appreciate your hospitality, up to a point."

"That point being your fate and the fates of your godling friends, yes. Understandable." Serymn paused as the servant came over, placing a plate in my hands. No formal service this time. I relaxed.

"And your own fate," I said. "When Madding and the others get free, I doubt they'll be very forgiving of their treatment. They're immortal; you can't hold them *forever*." Though if she could somehow kill them, that rendered my argument moot....

"True," she said. "And how convenient you mentioned this fact, as it's the cause of the mess we find ourselves in now."

I blinked, realizing she was no longer talking about Madding and the others, but another set of captive gods. "You mean the Arameri's gods. The Nightlord." Their ridiculous target.

"Not just the Nightlord, but also Sieh the Trickster." It took all my self-control not to start at this. "Kurue the Wise, and Zhakkarn of the Blood. It was inevitable they would find their way to freedom eventually. Perhaps the millennia they spent imprisoned didn't even seem like a long time to them. They are endlessly patient, our gods, but they never forget a wrong, and they never let that wrong go unpunished."

"Do you blame them? If I had power and someone harmed me, I'd get back at them, too."

"So would I. So *have* I, on more than one occasion." I heard her cross her legs. "But any person on whom I sought vengeance would be equally within her rights to try and defend herself. That's all we're doing here, Lady Oree. Defending ourselves."

"Against *one of the Three*." I shook my head and decided to try honesty. "I'm sorry, but if you're trying to convert me by appealing to...street logic, or whatever you think motivates us lowly, common folk, then there's a flaw in your reasoning. Where I come from, if someone that powerful is angry with you, you *don't* fight back. You make amends as best you can, or you go into hiding and never come out, and meanwhile you pray that no one you care about gets hurt."

"Arameri do not hide, Lady Oree. We do not make amends, not when we believe our actions to have been correct. Those are the ways of Bright Itempas, after all."

And look where that got him, I almost said, but I held my tongue. I had no idea whether Shiny was all right, or where he was. If he had managed to escape, I had little hope he would bother to help us, but on the off chance that he might, I didn't intend to tell the New Lights about him.

"I think I should warn you," I said, "that I don't consider myself much of an Itempan."

Serymn was silent for a moment. "I'd wondered about that. You left home at the age of sixteen—the year your father died, wasn't it? Only a few weeks after the Gray Lady's ascension."

I stiffened. "How in the gods' names did you know that?"

"We investigated you when you first came to our attention. It wasn't difficult. There aren't many towns on the Nimaro reservation, after all, and your blindness makes you memorable. Your White Hall priest reported that you enjoyed arguing with him during lessons, as a child." She chuckled. "Somehow that doesn't surprise me."

My stomach twisted, threatening to return my meal. They had gone to my village? Spoken with my priest? Would they threaten my mother now?

"Please, Lady Oree. I'm sorry. I didn't mean to alarm you. We mean you no harm, nor anyone in your family." There was the clink of a teapot and the sound of liquid pouring.

"You'll understand if I find that hard to believe." I found a table beside my chair and set my plate on it.

"Nevertheless, it's true." She leaned forward and put something in my hands—a small cup of tea. I held it tightly to conceal my shaking fingers. "Your priest thinks you left Nimaro because you lost your faith. Is that true?"

"That priest was *my mother's* priest, Lady, far more than he ever was mine, and neither of them knew me very damned well." My voice was just a hair too loud for polite conversation; anger had frayed my self-control. I took a deep breath and tried again to mimic her calm, cultured manner of speaking. "You can't lose faith you never had to begin with."

"Ah. So you never believed in the Bright at all?"

"Of course I believed. Even now I believe, in principle. But when I was sixteen, I saw the hypocrisy in all the things the priest had taught me. It's all very well to *say* the world values reason and compassion and justice, but if nothing in reality reflects those words, they're meaningless."

"Since the Gods' War, the world has enjoyed the longest period of peace and prosperity in its history."

"My people were once as wealthy and powerful as the Amn, Lady Serymn. Now we're refugees without even a homeland to call our own, forced to rely on Arameri charity."

"There have been losses, true," Serymn conceded. "I believe those are outweighed by the gains."

I was suddenly angry, *furious*, with her. I had heard Serymn's arguments from my mother, my priest, friends of the family— people I loved and respected. I had learned to endure my anger without protest, because my feelings were upsetting to them. But in my heart? Truly? I had never understood how they could be so…so…

Blind.

"How many nations and races have the Arameri wiped out of existence?" I demanded. "How many heretics have been executed, how many families slaughtered? How many poor people have been beaten to death by Order-Keepers for the crime of not knowing our place?" Hot droplets of tea sloshed onto my fingers. "The Bright is *your* peace. *Your* prosperity. Not anyone else's."

"Ah." Serymn's soft voice cut through my anger. "Not just lost faith, but *broken* faith. The Bright has failed you, and you reject it in turn."

I hated her patronizing, sanctimonious, knowing tone. "You don't know anything about it!"

"I know how your father died."

I froze.

She continued, oblivious to my shock. "Ten years ago—on the very day, it seems, that the Gray Lady's power swept the world—your father was in the village market. Everyone felt *something* that day. You didn't need magical abilities to sense that something momentous had just occurred."

She paused as if waiting for me to speak. I held myself rigid, so she went on.

"But it was only your father, out of all the people in that market, who burst into tears and fell to the ground, singing for joy."

I sat there, trembling. Listening to this woman, this *Arameri*, dispassionately recite the details of my father's murder.

It wasn't the singing that did him in. No one but me could detect the magic in his voice. A scrivener might have sensed it, but my village was far too poor and provincial to merit a scrivener at its small White Hall. No, what killed my father was fear, plain and simple.

Fear, and faith.

"The people of your village were already anxious." Serymn spoke more softly now. I did not believe it was out of respect for my pain. I think she just realized greater volume was unnecessary. "After the morning's strange storms and tremors, it must have seemed as though the world was about to end. There were similar incidents that day, in towns and cities elsewhere in the world, but your father's case is perhaps the most tragic. There

had been rumors about him before that day, I understand, but...
that does not excuse what happened."

She sighed, and some of my fury faded as I heard genuine
regret in her tone. It might have been an act, but if so, it was
enough to break my paralysis.

I got up from my chair. I couldn't have sat any longer, not
without screaming. I put the teacup down and moved away
from Serymn, seeking somewhere in the room with fresher, less
constricting air. A few feet away, I found a wall and felt my way
to a window; the sunlight coming through it helped to ease my
agitation. Serymn remained silent behind me, for which I was
grateful.

Who threw the first stone? It is something I have always wondered. The priest would not say, when I asked him over and
over again. No one in town could say; they did not remember.
Things had happened so quickly.

My father was a strange man. The beauty and magic that I
loved in him was an easily perceptible thing, though no one
else ever seemed to see it. Yet they noticed *something* about him,
whether they understood it or not. His power permeated the
space around him, like warmth. Like Shiny's light and Madding's chimes. Perhaps we mortals actually have more than five
senses. Perhaps along with taste and smell and the rest there is
detecting the special. I see the specialness with my eyes, but others do it in some different way.

So on that long-ago day, when power changed the world and
everyone from senile elders to infants felt it, they all discovered
that special sense, and then they noticed my father and understood at last what he was.

But what I had always perceived as glory, they had seen as a threat.

After a time, Serymn came to stand behind me.

"You blame our faith for what happened to your father," she said.

"No," I whispered. "I blame the people who killed him."

"All right." She paused a moment, testing my mood. "But has it occurred to you that there may be a cause for the madness that swept your village? A higher power at work?"

I laughed once, without humor. "You want me to blame the gods."

"Not all of them."

"The Gray Lady? You want to kill her, too?"

"The Lady ascended to godhood in that hour, it's true. But remember what else happened then, Oree."

Just Oree this time, no "Lady." Like we were old friends, the street artist and the Arameri fullblood. I smiled, hating her with all my soul.

She said, "The Nightlord regained his freedom. This, too, affected the world."

My heart hurt too much for politeness. "Lady, I don't care."

She moved closer, beside me. "You should. Nahadoth's nature is more than just darkness. His power encompasses wildness, impulse, the abandonment of logic." She paused, perhaps waiting to see if her words had sunk in. "The madness of a mob."

Silence fell. In it, a chill laced around my spine.

I had not considered it before. Pointless to blame the gods when mortal hands had thrown the stones. But if those mortal hands had been influenced by some higher power...

Whatever Serymn read on my face must have pleased her. I heard that in her voice.

"These godlings," she said, "the ones you call your friends. Ask yourself how many mortals they've killed over the ages. Far more than the Arameri ever did, I'm quite certain; the Gods' War alone wiped out nearly every living thing in this realm." She stepped closer still. I could feel her body heat radiating against my side, almost a pressure. "They live forever. They have no need of food or rest. They have no true shape." She shrugged. "How can such creatures understand the value of a single mortal life?"

In my mind, I saw Madding, a shining blue-green thing like nothing of this earth. I saw him in his mortal shape, smiling as I touched him, soft-eyed, longing. I smelled his cool, airy scent, heard the sound of his chimes, felt the purr of his voice as he spoke my name.

I saw him sitting at a table in his house, as he had often done during our relationship, laughing with his fellow godlings as they drew their blood into vials for later sale.

It was a part of his life I'd never let myself consider deeply. Godsblood was not addictive. It caused no deaths or sickness; no one ever took too much and poisoned himself. And the favors Madding did for people in the neighborhood—for those of us who were too unimportant to merit aid from the Order or the nobles, Madding and his crew were often our only recourse.

But the favors were never free. He wasn't cruel about it. He asked only what people could afford, and he gave fair warning. Anyone who incurred a debt to him knew there would be consequences if they failed to repay. He was a godling; it was his nature.

What did he do to them, the ones who reneged?

I saw Trickster Sieh's child eyes, as cold as a hunting cat's. I heard Lil's chittering, whirring teeth.

And from the deepest recesses of my heart rose the doubt that I had not allowed myself to contemplate since the day Madding had broken my heart.

Did he ever love me? Or was my love just another diversion for him?

"I hate you," I whispered to Serymn.

"For now," she replied, with terrible compassion. "You won't always."

Then she took my hand and led me back to my room, and left me there to sit in silent misery.

10

"Indoctrination" (charcoal study)

THAT AFTERNOON, Hado put me on a work crew to help clean the large dining hall. This turned out to be a group of nine men and women, a few older than me but most younger, or so I judged by their voices. They watched me with open curiosity as Hado explained about my blindness—though he did not, I noticed, tell them that I had been forced into the cult. "She's quite self-sufficient, as I'm sure you'll find, but of course there will be some tasks she can't complete," was all he said, and by that I knew what was coming. "Because of that, we've assigned several of our older initiates to shadow the work crew in case she needs assistance. I hope all of you don't mind."

They assured him that they did not in tones of such slavish eagerness that I immediately loathed all of them. But when Hado left, I made my way to the work crew's designated leader, a young Ken woman named S'miya. "Let me handle the mopping," I said. "I feel like working hard today." So she handed me the bucket.

The handle of the mop was much like a walking stick in my hands. I felt more secure with it, in control of myself for the first time since I'd come to the House of the Risen Sun. This was an illusion, of course, but I clung to it, needed it. The dining hall was huge, but I put my back into the work and paid no heed to the sweat that dripped down my face and made my shapeless tunic stick to my body. When S'miya finally touched my arm and told me we were done, I was surprised and disappointed it had gone so quickly.

"You do Our Lord proud with such effort," S'miya said in an admiring tone.

I straightened to ease my aching back and thought of Shiny. "Somehow I doubt that," I said. This earned me a moment of puzzled silence, and more when I laughed.

With that done, one of the older initiates led me to the baths, where a good soak helped ease some of the soreness I would certainly feel the next day. Then I was led back to my room, where a hot meal waited on the table. They still locked the door, and there was only a fork to eat with, no knife. But as I ate, I reflected on how quickly one could grow used to this sort of captivity—the simplicity of honest labor, soothing hymns echoing throughout the halls, free food and shelter and clothing. I had always wondered why anyone would join an organization like the Order, and now I began to see. Compared to the complexities of the outside world, this was easier on the body and the heart.

Unfortunately, this meant that once I'd bathed and eaten, the silence closed in. But as I sat miserable in my chair at the window, my head leaning against the glass as if that would somehow ease the ache in my heart, Hado returned. He had another person in tow, a woman I had not met before.

"Go away," I said.

He stopped. The woman paused as well. He said, "We're in a mood, I see. What's the problem?"

I laughed, once and harshly. "Our gods hate us. Aside from that, everything's right as rain."

"Ah. A *philosophical* mood." He moved to sit somewhere across from me. The woman, whose perfume was quite unpleasantly strong, took up position near the door. "Do you hate the gods?"

"They're gods. It doesn't matter if we hate them."

"I disagree. Hate can be a powerful motivator. Our whole world is the way it is because of a single woman's hate."

More proselytizing, I realized. I didn't feel like talking to him, but it was better than sitting alone and brooding, so I replied. "The mortal woman who became the Gray Lady?"

"One of her ancestors, actually: the founder of the Arameri clan, the Itempan priestess Shahar. Do you know of her?"

I sighed. "Nimaro might be a backwater, Master Hado, but I *did* go to school."

"White Hall lessons skim the details, Lady Oree, which is a shame, because the details are so very delicious. Did you know she was Itempas's lover, for example?"

Delicious, indeed. My mind tried to conjure an image of Shiny—stony, coldhearted, indifferent Shiny, indulging in a passionate affair with a mortal. Or anyone, for that matter. Hells, I couldn't even imagine him having sex. "No, I didn't. I'm not sure *you* know that, either."

He laughed. "For now, let's simply assume it's true, hmm? She was his lover—the only mortal he ever saw fit to honor in that way. And she truly loved him, because when Itempas fought his sibling gods, she hated them, too. Much of what the Arameri did after the war—forcing the Bright on every race, persecuting those who'd once worshipped Nahadoth or Enefa—is the result of her hate." He paused. "One of the gods we've captured is your lover. Isn't that also true?"

I made a great effort and did not react or speak.

"Apparently, you and Lord Madding were quite an item. Word is your relationship ended, but it doesn't escape me that you ran to him when you were in need."

From across the room, the woman who'd come in with Hado made a faint sound of disgust. I'd almost forgotten she was there.

"How do you feel now that someone's attacked him?" Hado asked. His voice was gentle, compassionate. Seductive. "You said the gods hate us, and for the moment I think you hate them, too, at least a little. Yet somehow I find it hard to believe your feelings have changed so completely toward the one who shared your bed."

I looked away. I didn't want to think about it. I didn't want to *think* at all. Why had Hado and the woman come, anyhow? Didn't a Master of Initiates have other duties?

Hado leaned forward. "If you could, would you fight us to save your lover? Would you risk your life to set him free?"

Yes, I thought immediately. And just like that, the doubts I'd felt since my conversation with Serymn faded.

Someday, when Madding and I were free of this place, I would ask him about his treatment of mortals. I would ask about his role in the Gods' War. I would find out what he did to people who failed to repay. I had been remiss in not doing this before. But would it make a difference, in the end? Madding had lived thousands of years to my few. In that time, he had surely done things that would horrify me. Would knowing about those things make me love him any less?

"Whore," said the woman.

I stiffened. "Excuse me?"

Hado made a sound of annoyance. "Erad, Brightsister, you will be silent."

"Then hurry up," she snapped. "He wants the sample as soon as possible."

I was already tense, ready to throw some harsh words—or the chair under me—at Erad. This caught my attention. "What sample?"

Hado let out a long sigh, plainly considering a few choice words of his own. "The Nypri's request," he said finally. "He has asked for some of your blood."

"Some of my *what*?"

"He's a scrivener, Lady Oree, and you have magical abilities no one has ever seen. I imagine he wants to study you in depth."

I clenched my fists, furious. "And if I don't want to give a sample?"

"Lady Oree, you know full well the answer to that question." There was no patience left in Hado now. I considered resisting, anyway, to see whether he and Erad were prepared to use physical force. That was stupid, though, because there were two of them and one of me, and there could easily be more of them if they just opened the door and called for help.

"Fine," I said, and sat down.

After a moment—and probably a last warning look from Hado—Erad came over and took my left hand, turning it over. "Hold the bowl," she said to Hado, and a moment later I gasped as something stabbed me in the wrist.

"Demons!" I cried, trying to jerk away. But Erad's grip was firm, as if she'd been expecting my reaction.

Hado gripped my other shoulder. "This won't take long," he said, "but if you struggle, it will take longer." I stopped fighting only because of that.

"What in the gods' names are you doing?" I demanded, yelping as Erad did something else, and it felt like my wrist was stabbed again. I could hear liquid—my blood—splattering into some sort of container. She had jabbed something into me, opening the wound further to keep the blood flowing. It hurt like the infinite hells.

"Lord Dateh requested about two hundred drams," muttered Erad. A moment passed, and then she sighed in satisfaction. "That should be enough."

Hado let go of me and moved away, and Erad took the painful thing out of my arm. She bandaged my wrist with only marginally more gentleness. I snatched my arm away from her as soon as her grip lessened. She uttered a contemptuous snort but let me go.

"We'll have someone bring you dinner shortly," Hado said as they both went to the door. "Be sure to eat; it will prevent weakness. Rest well tonight, Lady Oree." Then they closed the door behind them.

I sat where they'd left me, cradling my aching arm. The bleeding hadn't quite stopped; a stray droplet had seeped through the bandage and begun to thread its way down my forearm. I followed the sensation of its passage, my thoughts meandering in a similar way. When the droplet fell off my arm to the floor, I imagined its splatter. Its warmth, cooling. Its smell.

Its color.

There was a way out of the House of the Risen Sun, I understood now. It would be dangerous. Possibly deadly. But was it any safer for me to stay and find out whatever they planned to do with me?

I lay down, my arm tucked against my chest. I was tired—too tired to make the attempt right then. It would take too much of my strength. In the morning, though, the Lights would be busy with their rituals and chores. There would be time before they came for me.

My thoughts as dark as blood, I slept.

11

"Possession"
(watercolor)

So, there was a girl.

What I've guessed, and what the history books imply, is that she was unlucky enough to have been sired by a cruel man. He beat both wife and daughter and abused them in other ways. Bright Itempas is called, among other things, the god of justice. Perhaps that was why He responded when she came into His temple, her heart full of unchildlike rage.

"I want him to die," she said (or so I imagine). "Please, Great Lord, make him die."

You know the truth now about Itempas. He is a god of warmth and light, which we think of as pleasant, gentle things. I once thought of Him that way, too. But warmth uncooled burns; light undimmed can hurt even my blind eyes. I should have realized. We should all have realized. He was never what we wanted Him to be.

So when the girl begged the Bright Lord to murder her father, He said, "Kill him yourself." And He gifted her with a knife perfectly suited to her small, weak child's hands.

She took the knife home and used it that very night. The next day, she came back to the Bright Lord, her hands and soul stained red, happy for the first time in her short life. "I will love you forever," she declared. And He, for a rare once, found Himself impressed by mortal will.

Or so I imagine.

The child was mad, of course. Later events proved this. But it makes sense to me that this madness, not mere religious devotion, would appeal most to the Bright Lord. Her love was unconditional, her purpose undiluted by such paltry considerations as conscience or doubt. It seems like Him, I think, to value that kind of purity of purpose—even though, like warmth and light, too much love is never a good thing.

I woke an hour before dawn and immediately went to the door to listen for my captors. I could hear people moving about in the corridors beyond my door, and sometimes I caught snatches of the Lights' wordless, soothing song. More morning rituals. If they followed the pattern of previous mornings, I had an hour, maybe more, before they came.

Quickly I set to work, pushing aside the room's table as quietly as I could. Then I rolled aside the small rug to bare the wooden floor, which I inspected carefully. It was smoothly sanded, lightly finished. Dusty. It felt nothing like a canvas.

Neither had the bricks at the south promenade, though, the day I'd killed the Order-Keepers.

My heart pounded as I went through the room, collecting the items I'd marked or hidden as potentially useful. A piece of cheese and a nami-pepper from a previous meal. Chunks of melted fakefern wax from the candles. A bar of soap. I had nothing that felt or smelled like the color black, though, which was frustrating. I had a feeling I would need black.

I knelt on the floor and picked up the cheese, and took a deep breath.

Kitr and Paitya had called my drawing a doorway. If I drew a place I knew and opened that doorway again, would I be able to travel there? Or would I end up like the Order-Keepers, dead in two places at once?

I shook my head, angry at my own doubts.

Carefully, clumsily, I sketched Art Row. The cheese was more useful as texture than color, because it felt rough, like the cobbles I'd walked across for the past ten years. I yearned for black to outline the cobbles but forced myself to do without. The candlewax ran out first—too soft—but between it and the soap I managed to suggest a table, and beyond that another. The pepper ran out next, its juice stinging my fingers as I ground it to a nub trying to depict the Tree's greenscent in the air. Finally, though I used my own saliva and blood to stretch it and properly color the cobbles, the cheese crumbled to bits in my fingers. (To get my blood, I'd had to scratch off the scab from the previous night's bloodletting. Inconveniently, I was not menstruating.)

When it was done, I sat back to gaze at my work, grimacing at the ache in my back and shoulders and knees. It was a crude, small drawing, only two handspans across since there hadn't been enough "paint" to do more. More impressionistic than I liked, though I had created such drawings before and seen the magic in them nevertheless. What mattered was what the depiction evoked in the mind and heart, not how it looked. And this one, however crude, had captured Art Row so well that I felt homesick just looking at it.

But how to make it real? And then, how to step through?

I put my fingers on the edge of the drawing, awkwardly. "Open?" No, that wasn't right. At the south promenade I had been too terrified for words. I closed my eyes and said it with my thoughts. *Open!*

Nothing. I hadn't really thought that would work.

Once, I had asked Madding how it felt for him, using magic. I'd had a bit of his blood in me at the time, making me restless and dreamy; that time, the only magic that had manifested in me was the sound of distant, atonal music. (I hadn't forgotten the melody, but I'd never once hummed it aloud. All my instincts warned against doing that.) I'd been disappointed, wishing for something more grandiose, and that had gotten me wondering what it felt like to *be* magic, not just taste it in dribs and drops.

He'd shrugged, sounding bemused. "Like walking down the street feels for you. What do you think?"

"Walking down the street," I had informed him archly, "is nothing like flying into stars, or crossing a thousand miles in one step, or turning into a big blue rock whenever you get mad."

"Of course it's the same," he'd said. "When you decide to walk down a street, you flex the muscles in your legs. Right? You feel out the way with your stick. You listen, make sure there's no one in the way. And then you will yourself to move, and your body moves. You believe it will happen, so it happens. That's how magic is for us."

Will the door open, and it will open. Believe, and it will be. Nibbling my bottom lip, I touched the drawing again.

This time, I tried imagining Art Row as I would one of my landscapes, cobbling together the memories of a thousand mornings. It would be busy now, the area thick with local merchants and laborers and farmers and smiths beginning their daily business. In some of the buildings just beyond my drawing, courtesans and restaurants would be opening their books for evening appointments. The pilgrims who'd prayed with the dawn would be giving way to minstrels singing for coins. I hummed a Yuuf tune that had been a favorite of mine. Sweating stonemasons, distracted accountants; I heard their hurrying feet and tense breath and felt their purposeful energy.

I was not aware of the change at first.

The Tree's scent had been thick around me since I'd been brought to the House of the Risen Sun. Slowly, subtly, it changed—becoming the fainter, more distant scent I was used to. Then that scent mingled with the smells of the Promenade, horseshit and sewage and herbs and perfumes. I heard murmuring voices and dismissed them…but they were not coming from within the House.

I did not notice the change at all, really, until the drawing opened up beneath my hands and I nearly fell into it.

Startled, I yelped and stumbled back. Then I stared. Blinked. Leaned close and stared more.

The cloth on the nearest Row table: *it moved.* I could not see people—perhaps because I hadn't drawn any figures—but I could hear the gabble of a crowd in the distance, moving feet, rattling wheels. A breeze blew, tossing a few fallen Tree leaves across the cobbles of the Promenade, and my hair lifted off my neck, just a little.

"Intriguing," said the Nypri, behind me.

Yelping in shock, I tried to simultaneously jump to my feet and scoot away from the voice. Instead I tripped over the rolled-up rug and went sprawling. While I struggled upright, grabbing for the bed to get my bearings, I realized too late that I had heard him enter, and had dismissed it. He had been standing in the room, watching me, for quite some time.

He came over, taking my hand and helping me to my feet. I snatched my hand away as soon as I could. Beyond him, I realized in dismay, the drawing had not only stopped being real, but also it had faded from view entirely, its magic gone.

"It takes great concentration to wield magic in a controlled fashion," he said. "Impressive given that you've had no training. And you did it with nothing but food and candlewax. Truly amazing. Of course, it means we'll have to watch you eat from now on, and search your quarters regularly for anything bearing pigment."

Damn! I clenched my fists before I thought to stop myself.

"Why are you here?" I asked. It came out far more belligerent than it should have, but I couldn't help it. I was too angry over my lost chance.

"I came, ironically enough, to ask you to demonstrate your magical abilities for me. I'm still a scrivener, even if I've left the Order. Unique manifestations of inherited magic were my particular field of study." He sat down in one of the room's chairs, oblivious to my seething fury. "I should note, however, that if you meant to escape through that portal, your efforts would've ultimately been futile. The House of the Risen Sun is surrounded by a barrier that prevents magic from entering or leaving. A variation on my Empty, actually." He tapped the wooden floor with his foot. "If you had tried passing through it via that portal... Well, I'm not certain what would've happened. But you, or your remains, would not have gotten far."

Broken bowel, voices screaming... I felt ill, and defeated. "It wasn't big enough to pass through, anyway," I muttered, slumping onto the bed.

"True. With practice, however—and more paint—no doubt you *could* pass through these portals."

That got my attention. "What?"

"Your magic isn't that different from my own," he said, and abruptly I recalled the holes he'd used to capture me and Madding and the others. "Both are variants on the scrivening technique that permits instantaneous transport through matter and distance via a gate. Which is itself merely an approximation of the gods' ability to traverse space and time at will. It seems that your gift expresses itself extraversively, however, while mine is introversive."

I groaned. "Pretend I haven't spent my life studying musty old scrolls full of made-up words."

"Ah. My apologies. Let me try an analogy. Imagine that you hold a lump of gold in your hands. Gold is quite soft in its pure form; you can mold it with your fingers if you exert enough pressure. Then it can become many things: coins, a bracelet, a cup to hold water. Yet gold isn't useful for every purpose. A sword made of gold would bend easily and be too heavy to wield. For that, a different metal—say, iron—is better."

A rustle of cloth was my warning before Dateh took my hand. His fingers were dry, thick-skinned, callused at the tips. He turned over my hand, exposing my own calluses from carving wood and clipping linvin saplings, and also the stains from my makeshift paints. I did not pull away, though I wanted to. I did not like the feel of his hand.

"The magic in you is like gold," he said. "You've learned to shape it in one way, but there are others. I imagine you'll discover them with time and experimentation. The magic in me is more like iron: it can be shaped and used in similar ways, but its fundamental properties and uses are very different. And I, unlike you, have learned many ways to shape it. Now do you understand?"

I did. Dateh's holes, or portals, or whatever he called them, were like my doorways. He created them at will, perhaps using his own method to invoke them as I used painting. But while his magic opened a dark, cold space devoid of—*everything*— my magic opened the way to existing spaces...or created new spaces out of nothingness.

While I mulled this, I found myself rubbing my eyes with my free hand. They ached, though not as badly as on the previous occasions I'd used my magic. I supposed I hadn't overdone it this time.

"And your eyes," Dateh said. I stopped rubbing them, annoyed. He missed nothing. "That's even more unique. You saw Serymn's blood sigil. Can you see other magic?"

I considered lying, but in spite of myself, I was intrigued. "Yes," I said. "Any magic."

He seemed to consider this. "Can you see me?"

"No. You don't have any godwords, or you're masking them."

"What?"

I gestured vaguely with my hands, which gave me an excuse to pull away from him. "With most scriveners, I see godwords written on their skin, glowing. I can't see the skin, but I can see the words, wrapped around their arms and so on."

"Fascinating. Most scriveners do that, you know, when they've mastered a new sigil or word-script. It's tradition. They write the sigils on their skin to symbolize their comprehension. The ink washes off, but I suppose there's a magical residue."

"You don't see it?"

"No, Lady Oree. Your eyes are quite unique; I have nothing that compares. Although—"

All at once, Dateh became visible to me. I was too distracted by his looks at first to realize the significance of what I saw. I couldn't help it, because he was *not Amn*. Or at least not completely, not with hair so straight and limp that it cupped his skull as if painted on. He wore it short, probably because the priests' fashion of long hair worn in a queue would look ridiculous on him. His skin was paler than Madding's, but there were other things about him that hinted at a less than pure Amn heritage. He was shorter than me, and his eyes were as dark as polished Darrwood. Those eyes would've been more at home among my own people or one of the High North races.

How in all the gods' names had an Arameri—proudest members of the Amn race and notorious for their scorn of anyone not pure Amn—contrived to marry a *non-Amn* rebel scrivener?

But as my shock at this realization faded, a more important one finally struck me: I could see him.

Him, that was, and not the markings of his scrivener power. In fact, I saw no godwords on him at all. He was simply visible, all over, like a godling.

But the Lights hated godlings...

"What the hells are you?" I whispered.

"So you *can* see me," he said. "I'd wondered. I suppose it works only when I use magic, though."

"When you...?"

He pointed above us, off toward a corner of the room. I followed his finger, confused, but saw nothing.

Wait. I blinked, squinted, as if that would help. There was something else etched against the dark of my vision. Something small, no bigger than a ten-meri coin, or Serymn's blood sigil. It hovered, glimmering with an impossible black radiance that shimmered faintly; that was the only way I'd been able to sift it from the darkness that I usually saw. It looked just like—

I swallowed. It *was*. A tiny, almost-unnoticeable version of the same holes that had attacked us at Madding's house.

"I can enlarge it at will," he said when I finally spotted it. "I often use portals at this size for surveillance."

I understood then why he'd compared me to gold and himself to iron: my magic was prettier, but his made a better weapon.

"You haven't answered my question," I said.

"What am I?" He looked amused. "I'm the same as you."

"No," I said. "You're a scrivener. I might have a knack for magic, but lots of people have that—"

"You have far more than a 'knack' for magic, Lady Oree. This?" He gestured toward the floor, where my drawing was. "Is something that only a trained, first-rank scrivener of many years' experience could attempt. And that scrivener would need hours of drawing time and half a dozen fail-safe scripts on hand in case the activation went wrong—neither of which you seem to need." He smiled thinly. "Neither do I, I should note. I am considered something of a prodigy among scriveners because of it. I imagine you would be, too, if you had been found and trained early."

My hands clenched into fists on my knees. *"What are you?"*

"I am a demon," he said. "And so are you."

I fell silent, more in confusion than in shock. That would come later.

"Demons aren't real," I said at last. "The gods killed them all aeons ago. There's nothing left but stories to frighten children."

Dateh patted my hand where it sat on my knee. At first I thought it was a clumsy attempt on his part to comfort me; the gesture felt awkward and forced. Then I realized he didn't like touching me, either.

"The Order of Itempas punishes unauthorized magic use," Dateh said. "Have you never wondered why?"

Actually, I had not. I'd thought it was just another way for the Order to control who had power and who didn't. But I said what the priests had taught me: "It's a matter of public safety. Most people *can* use magic, but only scriveners *should*, because they have the training to keep it safe. Write even one line of a sigil wrong and the ground could open up, lightning could strike, anything might happen."

"Yes, though that isn't the only reason. The edict against wild magic actually predates the scrivening art that tamed it." He was watching me. He was like Shiny, like Serymn; I could feel his gaze. So many strong-willed people around me, all of them dangerous. "The Gods' War was not the *first* war among the gods, after all. Long before the Three fought among themselves, they fought their own children—the half-breed ones they'd borne with mortal men and women."

All of a sudden, inexplicably, I thought of my father. I heard his voice in my ears, saw the gentle wavelets of his song as they rode the air.

Serymn's voice: *there had been rumors about him.*

"The demons lost that war," Dateh said. He spoke softly, for which I was grateful, because all at once I felt unsteady. Chilled, as if the room had grown colder. "It was foolish for them to fight, really, given the gods' power. Some of the demons no doubt realized this, and hid instead."

I closed my eyes and inwardly mourned my father all over again.

"Those demons survived," I said. My voice shook. "That's what you're saying. Not many of them. But enough." My father. His father, too, he'd told me once. And his grandmother, and an uncle, and more. Generations of us in the Maroland, the world's heart. Hidden among the Bright Lord's most devout people.

"Yes," said Dateh. "They survived. And some of them, perhaps to camouflage themselves, hid among mortals with more distant, thinner gods' blood in their veins—mortals who had to struggle to use magic, borrowing the gods' language to facilitate even simple tasks. The gods' legacy is what turned the key in humankind, unlocking the door to magic, but in most mortals that door is barely ajar.

"Yet there are some few among us who are born with more. In those mortals, the door is *wide open*. We need no sigils, no years of study. Magic is ingrained in our very flesh." He touched my face just under one eye, and I flinched. "Call us throwbacks, if you will. Like our murdered ancestors, we are the best of mortalkind—and everything our gods fear."

He dropped his hand onto mine again, and it was not awkward this time. It was possessive.

"You're never going to let me go, are you?" I said it softly.

He paused for a moment.

"No, Lady Oree," he said, and I heard him smile. "We aren't."

12

"Destruction" (charcoal and blood, sketch)

I HAVE A REQUEST," I said to the Nypri when he rose to leave. "My friends, Madding and the others. I need to know what you plan to do with them."

"That isn't something you *need* to know, Lady Oree." Dateh's tone was gently chiding.

I set my jaw. "You seem to want me to join you willingly."

He fell silent for a moment, contemplating. That was gratifying, because my statement had been a gamble. I had no idea why he wanted me, beyond the fact that we were both demons. Perhaps he thought I could eventually develop magic as powerful as his, or perhaps demons had some symbolic value to the New Lights. Whatever the reason, I knew leverage when I saw it.

At last he said, "My wife believes you can be rehabilitated, made to see reason." He glanced at my drawing on the floor. "I, however, am beginning to wonder whether you're too dangerous to be worth the effort."

I nibbled my bottom lip. "I won't try that again."

"We are both Itempans here, Lady Oree. You'll try it if you think it will work. And if there is insufficient disincentive." He folded his arms, thoughtful. "Hmm. I've been trying to figure out what to do with him…."

"What?"

"Your Maroneh friend."

"My—" I started. "You mean Shiny." So he hadn't escaped. Damnation.

"Yes, whatever his name is." For once, Dateh sounded annoyed. "I thought he was a godling, too, given his intriguing ability to return from death. But I've had him in the Empty for days now, and he's shown no sign of resistance, magical or otherwise. He just keeps dying."

The small hairs along my skin prickled. I opened my mouth to say, *That's our god you're torturing, you bastard,* but then I stopped. What would Dateh do, if he knew he had the Bright Lord of Order as his prisoner? Would he even believe it? Or would he question Shiny—and be shocked to learn, as I had been, that Shiny *loved* the Nightlord and would disapprove of any action that threatened him? What would these madmen do then?

"Maybe he's...like us," I said instead. "A d-demon." It was hard to say the words.

"No. I did test him. There are distinct properties that can be observed in the blood....Aside from his peculiar ability, he's mortal in every way that I can determine." He sighed and did not see my start as I realized that was why they'd taken my blood. "The Order has discovered any number of minor magical variants over the centuries. I suppose he's just another of those." Dateh paused, long enough for the silence to unnerve me further. "This man lived with you in the city, I'm told. I can't kill him, but I think you've guessed the ways in which I can make his brief periods of life unpleasant. *You* are valuable to me; *he* is not. Do we understand each other?"

I swallowed. "Yes, Lord Dateh. I understand you perfectly."

"Excellent. I'll have him placed with you later today, then. I should warn you, though; after this much time in the Empty, he may require...assistance." I clenched my fists on my knees while he knocked on the door to be let out.

But as he did so, something changed.

It was just a momentary flicker, so fast that I thought I imagined it. For that instant, Dateh's body looked wholly different. Wrong. I saw his nearer arm, curiously doubled as he rested it on the doorsill. Two arms, not one. Two hands gripping the smooth wood.

I blinked in surprise and suddenly the image was gone. Then the door opened, and so was Dateh.

I slept. I didn't mean to, but I was exhausted after my effort to use magic. When I opened my still-twinging eyes, the light of sunset was thin and fading on my skin. Someone had been in the room during that time, which meant I'd slept hard; I was usually quick to wake at any untoward noise. My visitors had been busy. I found the furniture put back in place and a tray of food on the table. The candles were gone when I checked, replaced by a single small lantern of a design that I found odd—until I realized it held nothing more than a slow-burning moistened wick. No reservoir of oil that I could use for painting. Other items in the room had been removed or replaced, too, ostensibly because they could have been used for their pigment. The food was a bowl of some sort of porridge, as bland and textureless as they could've made it and kept it palatable. And the air smelled of floor cleanser. I felt a moment's grief for my drawing, poor as it had been.

I ate and then went to the window, wondering if I would ever escape from this place. I guessed that I had been imprisoned for five days, maybe six. Soon it would be Gebre, the spring equinox. All over the world, White Halls would deck themselves in festive ribbons and *encanda*, lanterns given a special fuel to make their flame burn white instead of red or gold. The Halls would throw open their doors to all comers, celebrating the approach of summer's long days—and even now, with so many doubting their faith, those Halls would be full. Yet at the same time, in every city, there would be ceremonies dedicated to the Nightlord, too, and to the Lady. That was something new and still strange to me.

An hour passed before the door of my cell opened again. Three men entered, carrying something heavy—two somethings, I realized, as they grunted and jostled the table and chairs out of the way. The first object they put down squeaked faintly, and I realized it was another cot, like the one I slept on.

The second object they put down was Shiny, dumped on the cot. He groaned once and then lay still.

"A present from the Nypri," said one of the men, and another laughed. They left, and I hurried to Shiny's side.

His flesh was as cold as a corpse's. I had never felt him that cold; he never stayed dead long enough to completely lose body temperature. Yet when I fumbled for his pulse, it was racing. His breath came in harsh, quick pants. They had cleaned him up; he was wearing the sleeveless white smock and pants of a new initiate. But what had they bathed him in, ice water?

"Shiny?" All thoughts of his real name fled my mind as I wrestled him onto his back, then tugged a blanket over him. I touched his face and he jerked away, making a quick animal sound. "It's Oree. Oree."

"Oree." His voice was hoarse, as mine had been, perhaps for the same reason. But he settled after that, no longer moving away from my touch.

He was mortal, Dateh had said, but I knew the truth. Beneath the mortal veneer, he was the god of light, and he had spent five days trapped in a lightless hell. Hurrying across the room, I found the lantern, which thankfully I had not yet blown out. Would such a tiny light help him? I brought it closer, putting it on the shelf above Shiny's bed. His eyes were shut tight, and all his muscles quivered like wires ready to snap. He was only a little warmer.

Seeing no better option, I slipped under the covers with him and tried to warm him with my body. This was not easy, as the cot was narrow and Shiny took up all but a few inches of it.

Finally I had to climb on top of him, resting my head on his chest. I wasn't fond of the overly intimate position, but there was nothing else to be done.

I was completely caught by surprise when Shiny suddenly wrapped himself around me and turned us over, holding me solidly in place with an arm around the waist, a hand cupping my head against his shoulder, and his leg thrown over mine. I was not quite pinned but I couldn't move much, either. Not that I tried; I was too stunned for that, wondering what had prompted this sudden gesture of affection. If that it was.

He seemed reassured by the fact that I didn't fight him. The quivering tension gradually drained out of his body, his breath against my ear slowing to something more normal. After a while, we both grew warm, and despite spending the whole day asleep, I could not quite help it; I slept again.

When I awoke, I guessed that it was late. Near midnight, give or take a few hours. I was still sleepy but had a growing need to urinate, which was a problem because I was still neatly tucked into the complicated tangle of Shiny's body. His long, slow breaths told me he was asleep, and deeply, which he probably needed after his ordeal.

Working carefully and slowly, I extricated myself from his grip and then eased my way to a sitting position, from which I managed to clamber over him to reach the floor at last. By this point, the need had grown urgent, so I stood to hurry.

A hand caught my wrist, and I yelped.

"Where are you going?" Shiny rasped.

Taking a deep breath to slow my heart, I said, "The bathroom," and waited for him to let me go.

He didn't move. I shifted from one foot to the other

uncomfortably. Finally I said, "If you don't let go, the floor is going to be very wet in a minute."

"I'm trying," he said, very softly. I had no idea what that meant. Then I realized his hand on my wrist was loosening and tightening and loosening again, as if he could not quite will it to open.

Confused, I reached out to touch his face. His brow was furrowed. He drew in another deep breath through gritted teeth, then jerkily, deliberately, released my wrist.

I puzzled over this for a moment, but nature warned me not to dawdle. I felt his eyes on me for the whole hurried walk across the room.

It was better when I came out; the room held less tension. When I went over to him, I reached for his face and found his bowed shoulders, head hanging between them, heaving like he'd just run a long and exhausting race.

I sat down beside him. "Want to tell me what that was about?"

"No."

I sighed. "I think I deserve an explanation, if only so I can plan my bathroom breaks accordingly."

Predictably, he said nothing.

Whatever lingering reverence I'd felt for him vanished. I was tired. For months I had endured his moods and his silence, his temper, his insults. Because of him, I had lost my life in Shadow. In my churlish moments, I could even blame him for my captivity. Dateh had found me because I'd killed the Order-Keepers, which wouldn't have happened if Shiny hadn't made them angry.

"Fine," I said, getting up to return to my own cot.

But when I stepped forward, his hand caught my wrist again, tighter this time. "You will stay," he said.

I tried to yank my arm free. "Let go of me!"

"Stay," he snapped. "I command you to stay."

I twisted my arm, breaking his hold, and stepped back quickly, finding the table and maneuvering so that it was between me and him. "You *can't* command me," I said, trembling with fury. "You're not a god anymore, remember? You're just a pathetic mortal as helpless as the rest of us."

"You dare—" Shiny rose to his feet.

"Of course I dare!" I gripped the table edge, hard enough to make my fingertips sting. "What's wrong with you? You think just because you say something, I'll obey? Will you kill me if I don't? You think that makes you *right*? My gods, no wonder the Nightlord hates you, if that's how you think!"

Silence fell. I had run out of rage. I waited for his, ready to throw it back at him, but he said nothing. And after a long, pent moment, I heard him sit down again.

"*Please* stay," he said at last.

"What?" But I had heard him.

For a moment, I almost walked away, anyway. I was that tired of him. But he said nothing more, and in the silence, my anger faded enough that I realized what that quiet plea must have cost. It was not the way of the Bright to *ask* for what one wanted.

So I went to him. But when he touched my hand, I pulled back. "A trade," I said. "You've taken enough from me. Give *something* back."

He let out a long sigh and touched my hand again. I was surprised to find it trembling.

"Later, Oree," he said, barely louder than a whisper. Completely confused, I reached up to touch his not-Maroneh hair with my free hand; his head was still bowed. "Later, I will tell you...everything. Not now. Please, just stay."

I didn't make a decision, not in any conscious way. I was still angry. But this time, when he tugged my hand, I let him draw me forward. I sat beside him again, and when he lay down, I let him pull me down as well, positioning me on my side and spooning himself behind me. He kept his arms loose so that I could get up if I needed to. He put his face into my hair, and I chose not to pull away.

I did not sleep for the rest of that night. I'm not certain he did, either.

"There may be a way for us to get free of this place," Shiny said the next day.

It was noon. One of the Lights' initiates had just left, after bringing us lunch and staying to see that we ate it all. He took away the leftovers and searched out my hiding places, too, to make sure there was no stored food under the mattress or rug. No chitchat this time, and no efforts to convert either of us. No one took me away for chores or lessons. I felt oddly neglected.

"How?" I asked, then guessed. "Your magic. It comes when you protect me."

"Yes."

I licked my lips. "But I'm in danger now—have been since the Lights took me." There wasn't the slightest glimmer of magic in him.

"It may be a matter of degree. Or perhaps a physical threat is required."

I sighed, wanting to hope. "That's more 'may be' and 'perhaps' than I like to hear. I don't suppose anyone thought to give you instructions on how...you...work now?"

"No."

"What do you propose, then? I pick a fight with Serymn, and when she fights back, you blow up the House and kill us all?"

There was a moment's pause. I think my levity annoyed him.

"In essence, yes. Though there would be little logic in me killing *you*, so I'll moderate the amount of force I use."

"I appreciate your consideration, Shiny, really I do."

So the rest of the day passed with aching slowness, as I waited and tried not to hope. Shiny, for all his promises to explain the previous day's bizarre behavior, said nothing more about it. I gathered he was still recovering from his ordeal in the Empty; he'd slept through dawn, which he'd never done before, though he'd glowed as usual. That, plus my company, seemed to restore him. He had been his old taciturn self since he'd woken.

Still, I felt his eyes on me more often than usual that day, and once he touched me. It was when I'd gotten up to pace, fruitlessly hoping to vent restless energy. I brushed past Shiny, and he reached out to touch my arm in passing. I would have dismissed it as a mistake or my imagination if not for the previous evening. It was as if he needed contact now and again, for some reason that made no sense to me. Though when had anything about Shiny made sense?

I didn't ask questions, preoccupied as I was with my own concerns—like Dateh's revelation that I was a demon. I did not feel much like a monster. That didn't make me eager to discuss it with Shiny, who had slaughtered my ancestors and banned his children from ever again creating more beings like me.

So I was content to let him keep his secrets for the time being.

Toward evening, I was almost relieved when there came a brisk knock at the door, followed by the arrival of another initiate. As I rose to follow the girl, Shiny simply stood and came to my side. I heard her splutter for a moment, caught off guard, but finally she sighed and took us both.

Thus we arrived in the private dining hall, where Serymn waited with Dateh. No one else this time, beyond the servants who were already busy setting out the meal and a few guards. If Serymn was bothered by Shiny's presence, she said nothing to that effect.

"Welcome, Lady Oree," she said as we sat down. I turned my face toward the faint glimmer of her Arameri blood sigil in an effort to be polite, though I was beginning to hate being called *Lady Oree*. I knew what they meant by it now. The demons of old had been the Three's offspring, too, and perhaps as deserving of respect as the godlings—and *not human*. Something I was not ready to think, about myself.

"Good afternoon, Lady Serymn," I said. "And Lord Dateh." I could not see him, but his presence was as palpable against my skin as cool moonlight.

"Lady Oree," Dateh said. Then, so subtly that I almost didn't catch it, his tone changed as he addressed Shiny. "And a good afternoon to your companion. Are you perhaps willing to introduce yourself today?"

Shiny said nothing, and Dateh let out a sigh of barely contained exasperation. I had to fight the urge to laugh, because as amusing as it was to hear Shiny drive someone else mad for a change, I was surprised at how quickly Dateh's temper broke.

For whatever reason, Dateh seemed to have taken an instant dislike to him.

"He doesn't talk to me, either," I said, keeping my tone light. "Not much, anyway."

"Hmm," said Dateh. I waited for him to ask more questions about Shiny, but he fell silent, too, radiating hostility.

"Interesting," said Serymn, which annoyed *me* now because it was exactly what I'd been thinking. "In any case, Lady Oree, I trust your day went well?"

"I was bored, actually," I said. "I'd've preferred to be on another of those work crews. Then I could've at least gotten out of my room."

"I can imagine!" said Serymn. "You seem the type of woman to prefer a more spontaneous, energetic approach to life."

"Well...yes."

She nodded, the sigil bobbing in the dark. "You may find this difficult to accept, Lady Oree, but your trials have been a necessary step in cementing you to our cause. As you found today, having no other options makes even menial labor desirable. Sever one attachment and others become more viable. It's a harsh method, but one that has been used by both the Order and the Arameri family over the centuries, to great effect."

I refrained from saying what I really thought of that effect, and covered my anger by taking a sip from my wineglass. "I thought you people were opposed to the Order's methods."

"Oh, no—only their recent change in doctrine. In most other ways, the Order's methods have been proven by time, so we adopt them gladly. We are still devoted to the ways of the Bright Father, after all."

I should have known what that would set off.

"In what way," Shiny asked suddenly, startling me in mid-swallow, "does attacking Itempas's children serve Him?"

Silence fell around the table. Mine was astonishment; so was Serymn's. Dateh's... That I could not read. But he put down his fork.

"It is our feeling," he said, his words ever so slightly clipped, "that they do not belong in the mortal realm and that they defy the Father's will by coming here. We know, after all, that they vanished from this plane after the Gods' War, when Itempas took exclusive control of the heavens. Now that His control appears to have, hmm, slipped, the godlings—like rebellious children—take advantage. Since we have the ability to correct the matter..." I heard the fabric of his robes shift; a shrug. "We do as He would expect of His followers."

"Hold His children hostage," said Shiny, and only a fool would not have heard the kindling fury in his voice. "And... kill them?"

Serymn laughed, though it sounded affected. "You assume that *we*—"

"Why not?" Dateh, too, was coldly angry. I heard some of the servants shift uneasily in the background. "During the Gods' War, their kind used this world as a battleground. Whole cities died at the godlings' hands. They cared nothing for those mortal lives lost."

At this I grew angry myself. "What is this, then?" I asked. "Revenge? That's why you're keeping Madding and the others—"

"They are nothing," Dateh snapped. "Fodder. Bait. We kill them to attract higher prey."

"Oh, yes." I couldn't help laughing. "I forgot. You actually think you can kill the Nightlord!"

I heard, but did not think about, Shiny's swift intake of breath.

"I do, indeed," Dateh said coolly. He snapped his fingers, summoning one of the servants. There was a quick murmured exchange and then the servant left. "And I shall prove it to you, Lady Oree."

"Dateh," said Serymn. She sounded... concerned? Annoyed? I could not tell. She was Arameri; perhaps Dateh's temper was spoiling some elaborate plan.

He ignored her. "You forget, Lady Oree, there is ample precedent for what we've done. Or perhaps you don't know how the Gods' War actually began? I assumed that you, having been a god's lover..."

I became acutely aware of Shiny. He sat very still; I could hardly even hear him breathe. It was ridiculous that I felt sorry for him in that instant. He had murdered his sister, enslaved his brother, bullied his children for two thousand years. He had so little concern for life in general, including mine and his own, that more deaths should have been meaningless to him.

And yet...

I had touched his hand, that day at Role's memorial. I had heard the waver in his steady, stolid voice when he'd spoken of the Nightlord. Whatever problems he had, however much of a bastard he was, Shiny was still capable of love. Madding had been wrong about that.

And how would any man feel, on learning that his daughter had been murdered in imitation of his own sins?

"I've . . . heard," I said uneasily. Shiny kept silent.

"Then you understand," said Dateh. "Bright Itempas desired, and killed to obtain that desire. Why should we not do the same?"

"Bright Itempas also embodies order," I said, hoping to change the subject. "If everyone in the world killed to get what they wanted, there would be anarchy."

"Untrue," Dateh said. "What would happen is what *has* happened. Those with power—the Arameri, and to a lesser degree the nobility and priests of the Order—kill with impunity. No others may do so without their permission. *The right to kill* has become the most coveted privilege of power in this world, as in the heavens. We worship Him not because He is the best of our gods, but because He is, or was, the greatest killer among them."

The dining room door opened then. I heard another murmur. The servant returning. Something flickered, and then abruptly a silvery, shifting gleam appeared in my vision. Startled, I peered at it, trying to figure out what it was. Something small, only an inch or so in length. Oddly shaped. Pointy, like the tip of a knife, but far too small to be used that way.

"Ah, so you *can* see it," Dateh said. He sounded pleased again. "This, Lady Oree, is an arrowhead—a very special one. Do you recognize it?"

I frowned. "I'm not exactly into archery, Lord Dateh."

He laughed, already in a better mood. "What I meant was, do you recognize the power in it? You should. This arrowhead—the substance that comprises it—was made from your blood."

I stared at the thing, which shone like godsblood. Not quite as bright. And stranger: a moving, inconstant swirl of magic, rather than the steady gleam I was used to.

My blood should have been nothing special; I was just a mortal. "Why would you make something from my blood?"

"Our blood has grown thin over the ages," said Dateh. He set the thing down on the table in front of him. "It was said that Itempas needed only a few drops to kill Enefa. These days, the quantity needed to be effective is...impractical. We therefore distill it, concentrating its power, then shape the resulting product into a more usable form."

Before I could speak, there was a sharp thump as wood hit the floor, and the dining table shook hard.

"*Demon,*" Shiny said. He was standing, his hands planted on the table. It shook with the force of his rage. "You *dare* to threaten—"

"Guards!" Serymn, angry and alarmed. "Sit down, sir, or—"

Whatever she might have said was lost. There was a crash of servingware and furniture as Shiny lunged forward, his weight making the table jolt hard against my ribs. More startled than hurt, I scrambled backward, my hand flailing for the stick that should've been beside me. Of course there was nothing, so I tripped on the dining hall's thick rug and went sprawling, practically into the fireplace. I heard shouts, a scream from Serymn, a violent scuffle of flesh and cloth. Men converged from several directions, though not on me.

I pushed myself upright to get away from the close heat of the fire, my hands scrabbling for purchase on the smooth sculpted stone of the hearth—and as I did so, my hands slipped in something warm and gritty. Ash.

Behind me, it sounded as though another Gods' War had broken out. Shiny cried out as someone hit him. An instant later, that person went flying. There were choking sounds, grunts of effort, more dishes shattering. But there was no magic,

I realized in alarm. I could see none of them—nothing except the tiny pale glimmer of the arrowhead where it had fallen to the floor, and the swift-moving bob of Serymn's blood sigil as she ran to the door to shout for help. Shiny fought for his own rage, not to protect me, and that meant he was just a man. They would overcome him soon, inevitably.

The ash. I felt around, closer to the fire, ready to snatch my hand back if I encountered something hot. My fingers fumbled over a hard, irregular lump, quite warm but not painfully so. Bits of it crumbled away as I touched it. A chunk of old wood that had been burned to charcoal, probably over several days.

The color black.

Behind me, Dateh had managed to get free of Shiny, though he was wheezing and hoarse. Serymn had him; I heard her murmuring, worried, to see if he was all right. Beyond them, a flurry of blows and shouts as more men ran in.

Inspiration struck like a kick to the gut. Scrambling back with the charcoal in my hand, I shoved aside the rug and began to scrape the charcoal against the floor, grinding it in circles. Around and around—

Someone called for rope. Serymn shouted not to bother with rope, just kill him damn it—

—and around and around and—

"Lady Oree?" Dateh, his voice rough and puzzled.

—and around and around, feverishly, sweat from my forehead dripping down to smear the blackness, blood from my scraped knuckles, too, forming a circle as deep and dark as a hole into nowhere, cold and silent and terrible and *Empty.* And somewhere in that emptiness, blue-green and bright, warm and gentle and irreverent—

"Dearest gods, stop her! *Stop her!*"

I knew the texture of his soul. I knew the sound of him, like chimes. I knew that he owed Dateh and the New Lights a debt of pain and blood, and I wanted that debt repaid with all my heart.

Beneath my fingers and my eyes, the hole appeared, its edges ragged where bits of the charcoal had broken off with the force of my grinding. I shouted into it, "*Madding!*"

And he came.

What burst from the hole was light, a scintillating blue-green mass of it that roiled like a thundercloud. After an instant, it shivered and became the shape I knew better—a man formed of living, impossibly moving aquamarine. For a moment, he hovered where the cloud had been, turning slowly, perhaps disoriented by the Empty's deprivations. But I felt rage wash the room the instant he spied Dateh and Serymn and the others, and I heard his chimes rise to a harsh, brassy jangle of dire intent.

Dateh was shouting over the guards' panicked cries, demanding something. I saw a faint flicker from his direction, almost drowned out by Madding's blaze. Madding uttered a wordless, inhuman roar that shook the whole House, and shot forward—

—then jerked back, tumbling to the floor as something struck him. I waited for him to rise, angrier. Mortals could annoy gods but never stop them. To my surprise, however, Madding gasped, the light of his facets dimming abruptly. He did not get up.

Faintly, through shock, I heard Shiny cry out, in something that sounded much like anguish.

I should not have been afraid. Yet fear soured my mouth as I scrambled to my feet, stepping onto my own drawing in my haste to reach him. It was just inert charcoal now. I tripped over the rug again, righted myself, fell over a chair that lay across the floor, and finally crawled. I reached Madding, who lay on his side, and pulled him onto his back.

There was no light in his belly. The rest of him shone as usual, though dimmer than I'd ever seen, but that part of him I could not see at all. He clutched at it, and I followed his hands to find the smooth, hard substance of his body broken by something long and thin, made of wood, that jutted up. A crossbow bolt. I grasped its shaft in both hands and yanked it free. Madding cried out, arching—and the blotch of nothingness at his middle spread farther.

I could see the arrow's tip. Dateh's arrowhead—the one made from my blood. There wasn't much left; I touched it and found that it had the consistency of soft chalk, crumbling with just the pressure of my fingers.

All at once, Madding guttered like a candle flame, his jewel facets becoming dull mortal flesh and tangled hair. *But I still couldn't see part of him.* I felt for his belly and found blood and a deep puncture. It wasn't healing.

My blood. In him. Working through his body like poison, snuffing out his magic as it went along.

No. Not just his magic.

I threw aside the arrow and touched his face, my fingers shaking. "Mad? I ... I don't know, this doesn't make sense, it's my blood, but ..."

Madding drew in a harsh breath and coughed. Blood—godsblood, which should've shone with its own light—covered his lips, but it was dark, obscuring the parts of him that I could see. Those were fading from view, too. The arrow was killing him.

No. He was a god. They did not die.

Except Role had, and Enefa had, and—

Madding choked, swallowed, focused on me. It made no sense that he laughed, but he did. "Always knew you were special, Oree," he said. "A demon! A legend. Gods. Always knew...something." He shook his head. I could barely see for his dimness and my tears. "And here I thought I'd have to watch *you* die."

"No. I...I won't. This isn't. No." I shook my head, babbling. Madding caught my hand, his own slick and hot with blood.

"Don't let him use you, Oree." He lifted his head to make sure I heard him. I could barely see his face, though I could feel it, hot and fevered. "They never understood...too quick to judge. You aren't just a weapon." He shuddered, his head falling back, his eyes drifting shut. "I would have loved you...until..."

He vanished. I could feel him beneath my hands still, but he was not there.

"Don't hide from me," I said. My voice was soft and did not carry, but he should have heard me. Should have obeyed.

Hands seized me, dragged me to my feet. I dangled limply between them, trying to will it: *I want to see you.*

"You forced my hand, Lady Oree." Dateh. He came over, visible for once; he had used magic during the struggle. He was rubbing his throat, his face bruised and bloody. Someone had torn part of his robes. He looked thoroughly furious.

I hated that I could see him and not Madding.

"A doorway into my Empty." He laughed once, without humor, then grimaced, as this hurt his bruised throat. "Amazing. Did you plan this, you and your nameless companion? I should have known better than to trust a woman who would give her body to one of *them*." He spat downward, perhaps at Madding's corpse.

not Madding *there's nothing there that isn't him*

Then he turned and snarled at one of the guards to come over. "Bring your sword," he added.

I prayed then. I had no idea if Shiny could hear me, or if he cared. I didn't care. *Bright Father, please let this man kill me.*

"Must you?" asked Serymn, her voice edged with distaste. "She might still be turned to our cause."

"It must be done within moments of death. I don't intend to let this mess go to waste." He reached over to take something from the guard. I waited, feeling nothing as Dateh turned a look on me that was as cold as the wind in the Tree's highest branches.

"When Bright Itempas killed Enefa," he said, "He also tore her body open and took from it a piece of flesh that contained all her power. Had He not done so, the universe would've ended. Killing the Nightlord runs the same risk, so I've spent years researching where the seat of a god's soul lies when they incarnate themselves in flesh."

He lifted the sword then, two-handed, so fast that for an instant I saw six arms instead of two, and three sets of teeth bared in effort.

There was the hollow *whoosh* of cloven air. I felt a stirring of wind against my face. But the impact, when it came, was not in my body, though I heard the wet *chuff* as it struck flesh.

I frowned, horror struggling up through the numbness in my mind. Madding.

Dateh tossed the sword aside, gestured at another man to help. They bent. The smell of godsblood rose around me, thick and cloying, familiar, as flat and wrong here as it had been in the alley where I'd found Role. I heard...gods. Sounds I would expect in one of the infinite hells. Meat tearing. Bone and gristle cracking apart.

Then Dateh rose. His hand had gone dark, holding something; his robes were splattered and intermittent, too. He gazed at the thing in his hand with a look that I could not interpret, not without the touch of fingers, but I guessed. Revulsion, some, and resignation. But also eagerness. Lust worthy of a god.

When he lifted Madding's heart to his lips and bit down—

I remember nothing more.

13

"Exploitation"
(wax sculpture)

IT ALL COMES DOWN to blood. Yours, mine. All of it.

No one knows how it was discovered that godsblood is an intoxicant for mortals. The godlings knew it already when they came; it had been common knowledge before the Interdiction. I suppose someone, somewhere, simply decided to try it one day. Likewise, gods have drunk mortal blood. Only a few of them, thankfully, seem to like the taste.

But some god, somewhere, eventually decided to try a demon's blood. And then the great paradox was revealed: that immortality and mortality do *not* mix.

How the heavens must have shaken at that first death! Until then, godlings had feared only each other and the wrath of the Three, while the Three feared no one. Suddenly it must have seemed to the gods that there was danger everywhere. Every poisonous drop, in every mortal vein, of every half-breed child.

There was only one way—one terrible way—that the gods' fears could be assuaged.

Yet the murdered demons had their vengeance. After the slaughter, the harmony that had once been unshakable between gods and godlings, immortals and mortals, was shattered. Those humans who'd lost demon friends and loved ones turned against humans who had aided the gods; tribes and nations fell apart under the strain. The godlings regarded their parents with new fear, aware now of what could happen should *they* ever become a threat.

And the Three? How much did it hurt them, horrify them, when the deed was done and the battle haze faded and they found themselves surrounded by the corpses of their sons and daughters?

Here's what I believe.

The Gods' War took place thousands of years after the demon holocaust. But for beings who live forever, would not the memory still be fresh? How much did the former event contribute to the latter? Would the war have even happened if Nahadoth and Itempas and Enefa had not already tainted their love for one another with sorrow and distrust?

I wonder. We all should wonder.

I stopped caring. The Lights, my captivity, Madding, Shiny. None of it mattered. Time passed.

They brought me back to my room and tied me to the bed, leaving one arm free. As an added measure, they went through the room and removed everything I might use to harm myself: the candles, the sheets, other things. There were voices, touches. Pain when something was done to my arm again. More of my blood-poison, drip, drip, dripping into a bowl. Long periods of silence. Somewhere amid this I felt the urge to urinate, and did so. The attendant who arrived next cursed like a Wesha beggar when he smelled it. He left, and presently women came. I was diapered.

I lay where they put me, in the darkness that is the world without magic.

Time passed. Sometimes I slept, sometimes I didn't. They took more of my blood. Sometimes I recognized the voices that spoke around me.

Hado, for example: "Shouldn't we at least allow her to recover from the shock first?"

Serymn: "Bonebenders and herbalists have been consulted. This won't do her any lasting harm."

Hado: "How convenient. Now the Nypri need no longer weaken himself to achieve our goals."

Serymn: "See that she eats, Hado, and keep your opinions to yourself."

I was fed. Hands put food into my mouth. I chewed and swallowed out of habit. I grew thirsty, so I drank when water was held to my mouth. Much of it spilled down my shirt. The shirt dried. Time passed.

Now and again, women returned to bathe me with sponges. Erad returned, and after some consultation with Hado, she put something into my arm that remained there, a constant niggling pain. When they came to take my blood the next time, it went faster, because all they had to do was uncap a thin metal tube.

If I could have mustered the will to speak, I would have said, *Don't cap it. Let it all run out.* But I didn't, and they didn't.

Time passed.

Then they brought Shiny back.

I heard men huffing and grunting with effort. Hado was with them. "Gods, he's heavy. We should've waited until he was alive again."

Something knocked over one of the chairs with a loud wooden clatter. "Together," said someone, and with a final collective grunt, they heaved something onto the other cot in the room.

Hado again, close by, sounding winded and annoyed. "Well, Lady Oree, it looks like you'll have company again soon."

"Much good it'll do her," said one of the other men. They laughed. Hado shushed him.

I stopped listening to them. Eventually they left. There was more silence for a time. Then, for the first time in a long while, light glimmered at the edge of my vision.

I did not turn to look at it. From the same direction, there was a sudden gasp of breath, then others, steadying after a moment. The cot creaked. Went still. Creaked again, louder, as its occupant sat up. There was more silence for a long while. I was grateful for it.

Eventually I heard someone rise and come toward me.

"You killed him."

Another familiar voice. When I heard it, something in me

changed, for the first time in forever. I remembered something. The voice had spoken softly, tonelessly, but what I remembered was a shout filled with more emotion than I'd ever heard a human voice bear. Denial. Fury. Grief.

Ah, yes. He had screamed for his son that day.

What day?

It didn't matter.

Weight bore down the side of the cot as Shiny sat beside me. "I know this emptiness," he said. "When I understood what I had done..."

The room had grown cool with the sunset. I thought of blankets, though I stopped short of wishing for one.

A hand touched my face. It was warm and smelled of skin, old blood, and distant sunlight.

"I fought, when he came for me," he said. "It is my nature. But I would have let him win. I *wanted* him to win. When he failed, I was angry. I...hurt him." The hand trembled, once. "Yet it was my own weakness that I truly despised."

It didn't matter.

The hand shifted, covering my mouth. I was breathing through my nose, anyway; it was no hardship.

"I'm going to kill you, Oree," he said.

I should have felt fear, but there was nothing.

"No demon can be permitted to live. But beyond that..." His thumb stroked my cheek once. It was oddly soothing. "To kill what you love...I know this pain. You have been clever. Brave. Worthy, for a mortal."

Deep in the murk of my heart, something stirred.

His hand slid up, covering my nose. "I would not have you suffer."

I did not care about his words, but breathing mattered. I turned my head to one side, or tried to. His hand tightened steadily, almost gently, holding my face still.

I tried to open my mouth. Had to think of the word. "Shiny." But it was muffled by his hand, unintelligible.

I lifted my left arm, the one that was free. It hurt. The area around the metal thing was terribly sore, and hot, too, with the beginnings of infection. There was a moment of resistance, and then the metal thing tore loose, sending a flash of white pain through me. Startled out of apathy, I bucked upward, reflexively catching Shiny's wrist with my hand. Blood, hot and slick, coated the inner bend of my elbow and ran down my arm.

I froze for an instant as awareness flooded through me, the instant the apathy lifted. *Madding is dead.*

Madding was dead, and I was alive.

Madding was dead and now Shiny, his father, who had cried out in anguish while my blood-arrow worked its evil, was trying to kill me.

First had come awareness. On its heels came *rage*.

I tried again to shake my head, this time scrabbling at Shiny's wrist with my fingers. It was like grabbing cordwood; his hand didn't budge. Instinctively, I sank my nails into his flesh, having some irrational thought of piercing the tendons to weaken his grip. He shifted his hand slightly—I had an instant to suck a breath—and then pushed my hand away with his free hand, easily brushing off my efforts to regain a grip.

A drop of blood landed in my eye, and red filled my thoughts. The color of pain and blood. The color of fury. The color of Madding's desecrated heart.

I put my hand against Shiny's chest. *I paint a picture, you son of a demon!*

Shiny jerked once. His hand slipped aside; I quickly caught my breath. I braced myself for him to try again, but he did not move.

Suddenly I realized I could see my hand.

For a moment, I was not certain that it *was* my hand. I had never seen my hand before, after all. It looked too small to be mine, long and slender, more wrinkly than I'd expected. There was charcoal under some of the nails. Along the back of the thumb was a raised scar, old and perhaps an inch long. I remembered getting it last year when an awl I'd been using slipped.

I turned my hand to look at the palm and found it completely coated in blood.

There was a thud as Shiny fell to the floor beside me.

I lay where I was for a moment, grimly satisfied. Then I began working at the straps that held me down. Quickly I realized the buckles were meant to be opened with two hands. My other hand was solidly strapped down with a leather cuff, padded on the inside to prevent sores. For a moment, this stymied me until it occurred to me to use the blood on my free hand. I rubbed it on the other wrist, then began working it from side to side, pulling and twisting. I had such small, slender hands. It took time, but eventually the blood and sweat on my wrist made the leather slick, and I slipped that hand free. Then I could open the rest of the buckles and sit up.

When I did, though, I fell back again. My head spun, thick queasiness rolling in its wake. I slumped against the wall, panting and trying to blink away the stars across my vision, and wondering what in the gods' names the Lights had done to me.

Only gradually did I realize: all the blood they had taken. Four times. In how many days? Time had passed, but not enough, clearly. I was in no shape to walk or even move much.

That was bad, because I would have to escape the House of the Risen Sun as soon as possible. I had no choice now.

While I lay sprawled across the bed, fighting for consciousness, light glimmered again on the floor. I heard Shiny draw breath, then slowly get to his feet. I felt his angry gaze, heavy as a lead weight.

"Don't touch me," I snapped before he could get any more ideas. "Don't you dare touch me!"

He said nothing. And did not move, looming over me in palpable threat.

I laughed at him. I felt no real amusement, just bitterness. Laughter let me vent it as well as anything else.

"Bastard," I said. I tried to sit up and face him but could not. Staying conscious and talking was the best I could do. My head had lolled to one side like a drunkard's. I kept talking, anyway. "The great lord of light, so merciful and kind. Touch me again and I'll put the next hole through your head. Then I'll bleed on you." I tried to lift my arm, but succeeded only in jerking it a bit. "See if I have enough left in me to kill one of the Three."

It was a bluff. I didn't have the strength to do any of it. Still, he stayed where he was. I could almost feel the fury in him, beating against me like insect wings.

"You cannot be permitted to live," he said. None of that fury was in his voice. He was so good at self-control. "You threaten the entire universe."

I swore at him in every language I could think of. That wasn't much: Senmite; a few epithets in old Maro, which were all I knew of the language; and a bit of gutter Kenti that Ru had taught me. When I finished, I was slurring again, on the brink of passing out. With an effort of will I fought it off.

"To the hells with the universe," I finished. "You didn't give a damn about the universe when you started the Gods' War. You don't give a damn about *anything*, including yourself." I managed to make a vague gesture with one hand. "You want to kill me? Earn it. Help me get free of this place. *Then* my life is yours."

He went very still. Yes, I'd thought that would get his attention.

"A bargain. You understand that, don't you? An *orderly*, fair thing, so you should respect it. You help me, I help you."

"Help you escape."

"Yes, damn you!" My voice echoed from the walls. There were guards outside, I remembered belatedly. I lowered my voice and went on. "Help me get away from this place and *stop these people*."

"If I kill you, they will have no more of your blood."

Such sweet words my Shiny spoke. I laughed again and felt his consternation.

"They'll still have Dateh," I said when the laughter had run out. I was tiring again. Sleepy. Not yet, though. If I didn't make this bargain with Shiny first, I would never wake up.

"With just Dateh's blood, they killed Role. With his power, they've captured others. Four times, Shiny! Four times they've taken my blood. How many more of your children have they poisoned with it?"

I heard the pause of his breath. That one had struck home, oh, yes. I had found his weakness at last, the chink in his apathy. Diminished and reviled and cold-blooded as he was, he still loved his family. So I readied my next lunge, knowing this one would cut even deeper.

"Maybe they'll even use my blood to kill Nahadoth."

"Impossible," Shiny said. But I knew him. That was fear in his voice. "Nahadoth could crush this world before Dateh blinks."

"Not if he's distracted." My eyes drifted shut while I said it. I could not open them, no matter how hard I tried. "They're killing the godlings to lure him here, to the mortal realm. Dateh kills them. *Eats* them." Madding's blood, running dark rivers down Dateh's chin as he bit into the heart like an apple. I gagged and fought the image back. "Takes their magic. I don't know how. How he." I swallowed, focused. "*The Nightlord.* I don't know how Dateh plans to do it. An arrow in the back, maybe. Who the hells knows if it'll work, but...do you want him to try? If there's even a chance he could...succeed..."

Too much. Too much. I needed rest and for no one to try and kill me for a while. Would Shiny let me have that?

One way to find out, I decided, and passed out.

I surfaced a little, bobbing beneath the threshold of consciousness.

Daytime warmth. More voices.

"...infection," said one. Male. Nice old gravelly voice like Vuroy's, oh how I missed him. More murmured words, soothing. Something about "seizure," "blood loss," and "apothecary."

"...necessary. There are signs..." Serymn. She had come to see me before, I remembered. Wasn't that sweet? She cared. "...must move quickly."

The gravelly voice rose and bobbed and dipped enough for me to hear one word, emphasized. "...*die.*"

A long sigh from Serymn. "We'll pause for a day or two, then."
More murmurs. Confusing. I was tired. I slept again.

Night again. The room felt cooler. I opened my eyes and heard
a harsh, ragged panting from the cot nearby. Shiny. His breath
bubbled and wheezed strangely. I listened to it for a while, but
then his breathing slowed. Caught once, resumed. Ceased
again. Stayed silent.

The room smelled of fresh blood again. Had they taken more
from me? But I felt better, not worse.

I fell asleep again before Shiny could resurrect and tell me
what the Lights had done to him.

Later. Still night, but deeper into it.

I opened my eyes as brightness flared against them. I glanced
over to see Shiny. He lay on the cot, curled on his side, still
shimmering from his return to life.

I tried moving and found that I had more energy. My arm
was still very sore, and thickly bandaged now, but I could move
it. The straps were back in place and cinched tight across my
chest and hips and legs, but the other wrist's cuff had been left
loose. I easily slipped my hand free.

Shiny's doing? Then he had agreed to my bargain.

I unbuckled myself and sat up slowly, cautiously. There was
an instant of dizziness and nausea, but it passed before I could
fall on my face. I sat where I was on the edge of the bed, taking deep breaths, becoming reacquainted with my body. Feet.
Shaky legs. Diaper around my hips, thankfully clean. Slouched
back. Sore neck. I lifted my head and it did not spin. With great
care, I got to my feet.

The three steps from my cot to Shiny's exhausted me. I sat down on the floor beside the cot, leaning my head on his legs. He didn't stir, but his breath tickled my fingers when I examined his face. His brow was furrowed, even in sleep. There were new lines on his face, around his sunken eyes. Not dead, but something had taken its toll on him. He usually woke as soon as he came back to life. Very strange.

As I took my hand away, it brushed against the cloth of his smock. Cooled wetness startled me. I touched, explored, and realized there was a wide patch of half-dried blood all down the lower half of his torso. Pulling up his shirt, I explored his belly. No wound now, but there had been a terrible one before.

He stirred while I was touching him, his glow fading rapidly. I saw him open his eyes and frown at me. Then he sighed and sat up beside me. We sat together, quiet, for a while.

"I have an idea," I said. "To escape. Tell me if you think it will work." I told him, and he listened.

"No," he said.

I smiled. "No, it won't work? Or no, you'd rather kill me on purpose than by accident?"

He stood up abruptly and walked away from me. I could see only a hazy outline of him as he went to the windows and stood there. His hands were clenched into fists, his shoulders high and tense.

"No," he said. "I doubt it will work. But even if it does..." A shudder passed through him, and then I understood.

My anger roiled again, though I laughed. "Oh, I *see*. I'd forgotten that day in the park. When you started this whole mess by attacking Previt Rimarn." I clenched my fists on my thighs, ignoring the twinge from the injured arm. "I remember the look on your face as you did it. That whole time I was in danger, scared out of my mind for you, but *you* were enjoying the chance to wield a bit of your old power."

He did not reply, but I was certain. I had seen his smile that day.

"It must be so hard for you, Shiny. Getting to be your old self again for so brief a time. Then it diminishes until there's nothing left of you but... *this*." I gestured toward his fading back, letting my disgust show. I didn't care what he thought of me anymore. I certainly didn't think much of him. "Bad enough you get a taste of it every morning, isn't it? Maybe it would be easier if you didn't have that little reminder of all you used to be."

He held rigid for a moment, his sullenness racheting toward anger in the usual pattern. Always predictable, he was. So satisfying.

And then, all at once, his shoulders slumped. "Yes," he said.

I blinked, thrown. That made me angrier. So I said, "You're a coward. You're afraid that it *will* work, but afterward it'll be like the last time—you'll be weaker than ever, unable even to defend yourself. Useless."

Again that inexplicable yielding. "Yes," he whispered.

I ground my teeth in thwarted rage. It gave me momentary strength to rise and glare at his back. I did not want his capitulation. I wanted... I did not know. But not this.

"Look at me!" I snarled.

He turned. "Madding," he said softly.

"What about him?"

He said nothing. I made a fist, welcoming the flash of pain as my nails cut my palm. "*What*, damn you?"

Infuriating silence.

If I'd had the strength, I would've thrown something. As it was, I had only words, so I made them count. "Let's talk about Madding, then, why don't we? Madding, your son, who died on the floor, killed by mortals who then *ripped out his heart and ate it.* Madding, who still loved you in spite of everything—"

"Be silent," he snapped.

"Or what, Bright Lord? Will you try to kill me again?" I laughed so hard that it winded me, and I had to gasp out the next words. "Do you think... I *care*... if I die anymore?" At that I had to stop. I sat down heavily, trying not to cry and hoping for the dizziness to pass. Thankfully, but slowly, it did.

"Useless," Shiny said. It was so soft, nearly a whisper, that I barely heard it over my own panting. "Yes. I tried to summon the power. I fought *for him,* and not myself. But the magic would not come."

I frowned, the back of my anger breaking. I felt nothing in its wake. We sat for a long while as the silence stretched on, and the last of his glow faded to nothingness.

Finally I sighed and lay back on Shiny's cot, my eyes closed. "Madding wasn't mortal," I said. "That's why your power didn't work for him."

"Yes," he said. He had control of himself again, his tone emotionless, his diction clipped. "I understand that now. Your plan is still a foolish risk."

"Maybe so," I breathed, drifting toward sleep. "But it's not like you can stop me, so you might as well help."

He came to the bed and stood over me for so long that I did fall asleep. He could've killed me then. Smother me, hit me, strangle me with his bare hands; he had a whole menu of options.

Instead he picked me up. The movement woke me, though only halfway. I floated in his arms, dreamlike. It felt like it took much longer for him to carry me to my cot than it should have. He was very warm.

He laid me down and strapped me back in, leaving the wrist cuff loose so that I could free myself.

"Tomorrow," he said.

I roused at the sound of his voice. "No. They might start taking my blood again. We should go now."

"You need to be stronger." Unspoken, the fact that I would be unable to count on his strength. "And my power won't come at night. Not even to protect you."

"Oh," I said, feeling stupid. "Right."

"Afternoon would be best. The sun will be unobstructed by the Tree then; that may provide some small advantage. I'll do what I can to convince them not to take more of your blood before that."

I reached up to touch his face, then trailed my hand down to his shirt and the stiff spot there. "You died again tonight."

"I have died many times in recent days. Dateh is most fascinated by my ability to resurrect."

I frowned. "What..." But, no, I could imagine all too easily what Dateh had done to him. Searching my hazy memories of the days since Madding's death, I realized this was not the first time Shiny had returned to the room dead, dying, or covered in gore. No wonder there had been no reaction from our captors when I'd blown a hole in him myself.

There were so many things I wanted to think about. So many questions unanswered. How *had* I killed Shiny? I had had no paint that time, not even charcoal. Were Paitya and the others still alive? (Madding, my Madding. No, not him, I could not think about him.) If my plan succeeded, I would try to get to Nemmer, the goddess of stealth. She would help us.

I would see Madding's killers stopped if it was the last thing I did.

"Wake me in the afternoon, then," I said, and closed my eyes.

14

"Flight"
(encaustic, charcoal, metal rubbing)

THERE WERE COMPLICATIONS.

I woke only gradually, which was fortunate, or I might have stirred and given myself away. Before I could do that, someone spoke, and I realized Shiny and I were not alone in the room.

"Let go of me."

My blood chilled. *Hado.* There was tension in the air, something that vibrated along my skin like an itch, but I did not understand it. Anger? No.

"*Let go*, or I call the guards. They're right outside the door."

A quick sound of motion, flesh and cloth.

"Who are you?" That was Shiny, though I hardly recognized his voice. It trembled, wavering from need to confusion.

"Not who you think."

"But—"

"*I am myself.*" Hado said this with such savagery that I nearly forgot myself and flinched. "Just another mortal, to you."

"Yes…yes." Shiny sounded more himself now, the emotion cooling from his voice. "I see that now."

Hado drew in a deep breath, as shaky as Shiny's voice had been, and some of the tension faded. Cloth stirred again and Hado came over to me, shadowing my face. "Has she shown any sign of recovery today? Spoken, maybe?"

"No, and no." Stiffer than usual, even for Shiny. The White Halls taught that the Bright Lord could not lie. I was relieved to hear that he could, though it plainly did not suit him.

"Everything is different now. They'll begin taking blood again tonight. Hopefully she's strong enough."

"That will likely kill her."

"Look outside, man. Two weeks have passed since Role died. Two weeks until the Nightlord's deadline—as he has so dramatically decided to remind us." He uttered a soft, humorless laugh. I wondered what he meant. "Dateh has been a man possessed since he saw it. There's no hope of my dissuading him this time."

Hado's hand stroked my face suddenly, brushing my hair back. I was surprised at such a tender gesture from him. He hadn't struck me as the type for tenderness, even to this small degree.

"In fact," he continued with a sigh, "if her mind doesn't return—or hells, even if it does—I fear he'll take *all* her remaining blood, and her heart, too."

Goose bumps prickled my skin. I prayed that Hado would not notice.

He touched the buckle across my midriff, silent now with his own thoughts—and showing no inclination to leave. I began to worry. The sunlight felt strange on my skin. *Thin*, sort of. Did that mean it was late afternoon? If Hado didn't leave soon, the sun would set and Shiny would become powerless. We needed his magic for this to work.

"You are not quite yourself," Shiny said suddenly. "Something of him lingers." Hado stiffened perceptibly beside me.

"Not the part that gives a damn about you," he snapped, and got up, stalking toward the door. "Speak of this again and I'll kill you myself."

With that he was gone, closing the door rather harder than necessary. And then Shiny was there, yanking at my midriff strap so roughly that I yelped.

"This place has been chaos all day," he said. "The guards are on edge; they keep checking the room. Every hour some interruption—servants bringing food, checking your arm, then that one." Hado, I gathered.

I pushed his hands away and fumbled with the midriff strap myself, gesturing for him to work on the leg straps, which he began to do. "What's happened to get them all upset?"

"When the sun rose this morning, it was black."

I froze, stunned. Shiny kept working.

"A warning?" I asked. The words of the quiet goddess came to me, from that day in South Root. *You know his temper better than I do.* Not Itempas, as I had assumed then. With more of his children dead or missing, it was the Nightlord whose temper would be at the breaking point. Would he even wait the full month he had promised?

"Yes. Though it seems Yeine has managed to contain his fury

to some degree. The rest of the world can see the sun clearly. Only this city cannot."

So Serymn had been right in her prediction. I could still feel sunlight on my skin, just weak. There must have been some light remaining, or Shiny wouldn't have bothered trying to free me. Perhaps it was like an eclipse. I had heard those described as the sun going black. But an eclipse that lasted all day and moved with the sun across the sky? No wonder the Lights were a-tizzy. The whole city would be in a panic.

"How much time until sunset?" I asked.

"Very little."

Gods. "Do you think you'll be able to break that window? The glass is so thick." My hands would not work as quickly as I wanted; I was still weak. But better than I had been.

"The cot legs are made of metal. I've loosened one of them, which should serve well as a club." He spoke as if that answered my question, which I supposed was an answer in itself.

We got the straps undone and I sat up. There was no dizziness this time, though I swayed when I stood. Shiny turned away from me, and I heard him positioning the table in front of the door. This was to delay the guards, who would enter as soon as they heard Shiny break the window. Every second would matter once we began.

There was a quick grunt from him, and a metallic groan as he worked the loose leg off his cot. As quietly as he could, he moved the broken cot in front of the door, too. Then we went to the window. I could still feel sunlight on my skin, but it was weak, cooling. Soon it would be gone.

"I don't know how long it will take for the magic to come," he said. *Or whether it will come at all,* he did not say, but I knew he thought it. I was thinking it myself.

"So I'll fall for a while," I said. "It's a long way down."

"Fear alone has killed mortals in moments of danger."

The anger I'd felt since Madding's death had never gone away, just quieted. It rose in me again as I smiled. "Then I won't be afraid."

He hesitated a moment more but finally lifted the cot leg.

The first blow spiderwebbed the window. It was also so loud, echoing in the partially emptied room, that almost immediately I heard men's voices through the door, raised in alarm. Someone fiddled with the lock, rattling keys.

Shiny drew back and heaved the cot leg forward again, grunting with effort as he did so. I felt the wind of the leg's passing; a truly mighty blow. It finished the window, knocking out several large pieces. A startlingly cold wind blew into the room, plastering my smock to my skin and making me shiver.

The guards had gotten the door partially open but were impeded by the table and cot. They were shouting at us, shouting for aid, trying to jostle the furniture out of the way. Shiny tossed aside the cot leg and kicked out as much of the glass as he could. Then he took my hands and guided them forward. I felt the cloth of his smock, removed to cover the jagged edges along the bottom sill.

"Try to push out, away from the Tree, as you jump," he said. As if he told women how to leap to their deaths all the time.

I nodded and leaned out over the drop, trying to figure out how best to push off. As I did so, a breeze wafted up from below, lifting a few stray strands of my hair. For an instant, my resolve faltered. I am only human, after all—or mortal, if not human.

Deliberately, I summoned the image of Madding as he had gazed at me in that last moment. He had known he was dying, known that I was the cause—but there had been no hatred or disgust in his expression. He'd still loved me.

My fear faded. I moved back, away from the window.

Shiny said over the guards' shouts, urgently, "Oree, you must—"

"Shut up," I whispered, and took a running dive through the opening, spreading my arms as I flew into the open air.

Roaring wind became the only sound I could hear. My clothes flapped around me, stinging my skin. My hair, which someone had tied back into a puff in an effort to control it, broke the tie and clouded loose behind me. Above me. I was falling, but it did not feel like falling. I floated, buoyed on an ocean of air. There was no sense of danger, no stress, no fear. I relaxed into it, wishing it would last.

A hand swatted at my leg, jarring me out of bliss. I turned onto my back, lazy, graceful. Was that Shiny? I could not see him. My plan had failed, then, and we would both die when we struck the ground. He would come back to life. I would not.

I reached up, offering my hands to him. He caught them this time, fumbling once, then drawing me close and wrapping his arms around me. I relaxed against his warm solidity, lulled by the rushing wind. Good. I would not die alone.

Because my ear was against his chest, I felt him stiffen and heard his harsh gasp. His heart thudded hard once, against my cheek. Then—

Light.

By the Three, so bright! All around me. I shut my eyes and still saw Shiny's form blazing before me, thinning the darkness of my vision. I could *feel* it against my skin, like the pressure of sunbeams. We streaked toward the earth like things I had imagined but would never see with my own eyes. Like a comet. Like a falling star.

Our descent slowed. The wind's roar grew softer, gentler. Something had reversed gravity's pull. Were we flying now? Floating. How far had we fallen, how much farther to go? How long before the sun was gone, and—

Shiny cried out. His light vanished, snuffed all at once, and with it went the force that had kept us afloat. We fell again, helpless now, with nothing left to stop us.

I felt no fear.

But Shiny was doing something. Twisting, panting with effort or perhaps the aftermath of his magic. I felt us turn in the air—

And then we hit the ground.

15

"A Prayer to Dubious Gods" (watercolor)

SOMEONE WAS SCREAMING. High, thin, incessant. Irritating. I was trying to sleep, damn it. I turned over, hoping to orient my ears away from the sound.

The instant I moved my head, nausea struck with stunning

speed and force. I had enough time to open my mouth and drag in a loud, wheezing breath before the heaves came. I vomited a thin stream of bile, but nothing more. I must not have eaten for some time.

My stomach seemed determined to dry heave nevertheless, regardless of my lungs' need for air. I fought the urge, my eyes watering and head pounding and ears ringing, until at last I managed to draw in a quick half breath. That helped. The heaving slowed; I breathed more. At last the clenching in my gut ceased—though only for the moment. I could still feel the muscles there trembling, ready to resume their onslaught.

Finally able to think, I lifted my head, trying to figure out where I was and what had happened. The ringing in my ears— which I had mistaken for screaming—was loud and incessant, maddening. The last thing I recalled was...I frowned, though this made the pain worse. Falling. Yes. I had leapt from a win-dow of the House of the Risen Sun, determined to escape or die trying. Shiny had caught me, and—

I caught my breath. *Shiny*.

Beneath me.

I scrambled off him, or tried to. The instant I moved my right arm, I screamed, which touched off another spate of stomach heaves. I fought through the pain and the retching, dragging myself off him with my left arm, which was still sore from infec-tion and whatever the Lights had inserted to draw my blood. Still, the pain in that arm was nothing compared to the agony in my right, and the clenching of my belly, and the shooting pains in my ribs, and the roiling grinding hell of my head. For a few moments I could do nothing but lie where I was, whimper-ing and helpless with misery.

At last the pain faded enough for me to function. When I finally struggled to a half-upright position, I tried again to assess my surroundings. My right arm would not work at all. I reached out with my left. "Shiny?"

He was there. Alive, breathing. I brushed his eyes, which were open. They blinked, the lashes tickling my fingertips. I wondered if he had decided to stop speaking to me again.

That was when I realized my knees and the hip I sat on were soaking wet. Confused, I felt the ground. Brick cobbles, greasy and thick with dirt. Cold dampness that grew warmer, closer to Shiny's body. As warm as—

Dearest gods.

He was alive. His magic had saved us—not completely, but enough to soften our fall. Enough that when he had turned us in the air, orienting so that he would hit the ground first, we had both survived. But if I was this injured...

My fingers found the back of his head, and I gasped, jerking my hand back. Gods, gods, gods.

Where the hells were we? How long had we been lying here? Did I dare call for help? I looked around, listened. The air felt cool and misty with deep night. Fat drops of water touched my skin now and again with the intermittent gentleness that was rain in Shadow. I could hear it, a light drizzle all around us, but in the immediate vicinity, I heard nothing, no one. I could smell a great deal, though—garbage and fermented urine and rusting metal. Another alley? No, the space around us felt more open. Wherever we were, it was isolated; if anyone had seen us land, sheer curiosity should've brought them to find us.

Shiny had begun to gasp irregularly. I put my hand on his bare chest—he had removed his shirt in the House—and almost drew it back, repelled by the unnatural *flatness* of his torso. Yet his heart still beat steadily, in contrast to the bubbling, jerky breaths that he was struggling to draw in. At this rate, his natural death might take an agonizingly long time.

I had to kill him.

Panic gripped me, though that might have been queasiness, too. I knew it was foolish. It wasn't as though he would stay dead, and when he returned to life, he would be whole. It was, as Lil had concluded, the easiest way to "heal" him. It wouldn't even be the first time I'd done it.

But it was one thing to kill in the heat of anger. Doing it in cold-blooded calculation was a whole other matter.

I wasn't even certain I *could* kill him. My right arm was useless, dislocated or broken, though thankfully it seemed to be going numb. Everything else hurt. I might've survived the fall better than him, but that didn't make me whole. At the very least, I would need two working arms to break his neck.

All at once it hit me: I was lost in some part of Shadow, helpless, with a companion as good as dead. It was only a matter of time before the Lights came looking. They knew Shiny, at least, would come back to life. I was sick, injured, weak. Terrified. And, damn it all, blind.

"Why the hells is everything so *hard* with you?" I demanded of Shiny, blinking away tears of frustration. "Hurry up and die!"

Something rattled nearby.

I gasped, my heart leaping in my chest. Frustration forgotten, I pushed myself to my knees and listened hard. It had come from my right, somewhere above me, a quick metal sound. Water falling on exposed pipe, maybe. Or someone searching for us, reacting to the sound of my voice.

On my hands and knees, I quickly felt around me. A few feet to my left I found wood, old and splintery. A barrel, its binding rings rusty, one side staved in. Above it another, and then something that felt like a wide, flat piece of roof-shingle planking, leaning against the barrels. Jammed against it, a rotted-out crate.

I was in a junkyard. The only junkyard anywhere near the Tree was Shustocks, in Wesha, where all the area's smiths and carters dumped their useless materials and carriageworks.

The roof planking formed a kind of lean-to against the barrels, with a narrow space underneath. As carefully as I could, I pushed the planking farther back, praying there was nothing balanced against it that would fall and give us away—or crush us. Nothing happened, so I felt around more, finally crawling under the planking to inspect the space.

Just enough room.

I backed out and got to my feet, and nearly fell again as another retching spasm took me. The pain in my head was truly awful, worse than it had ever been. I must've hit my head in the fall—not enough to break it, but certainly enough to rattle things around inside.

Another sound from the same direction, something thumping against wood. Then silence.

Panting my way through the pain, I stumbled back to Shiny's body. Hooking my good hand into his pants, I leaned back with my hips and pushed with my legs and whimpered through my teeth as I dragged him back, inch by inch. It took everything I had to get him into the little hiding space, and he did not fit well. His feet stuck out. I crawled in beside him, panting, and listened, hoping the rain would wash away Shiny's blood quickly.

Shiny groaned suddenly and I jumped, glaring at him in consternation. The dragging must have injured him even further. No choice now; if I didn't kill him, he would give us away.

Swallowing hard, I did as he had done to me in the House of the Risen Sun. I pressed my hand over his mouth, pinching his nose shut with my fingers.

For five breaths—I counted my own—it seemed to work. His chest rose, fell. Stilled. And then he bucked upward, fighting me. I tried to hold on, but he was too strong, even damaged as he was, jostling me loose. As soon as I let go, he sucked in air again, louder than before. *Demons, he's going to get us both killed!*

Demons. I flexed my hand, remembering.

There was plenty of blood to use as paint, at least. I reached under his neck and got a generous handful. My hand shook as I put it on his chest, gingerly. Before, I had imagined that I was painting, and then I had *believed* the painting real. Slowly I moved my hand, smoothing the blood in a wide circle on his skin. I would make another hole, like the one I had used to kill Shiny before, like the one that had pierced Dateh's Empty. Not a circle drawn with blood-paint. A hole.

His chest rose and fell beneath my hand, belying this. I scowled and lifted my hand so that I couldn't feel him breathe.

A hole. Through flesh and bone, like a grave dug in soft earth, edges neatly cut by an unseen shovel blade. Perfectly circular.

A hole.

My hand appeared. I saw it hovering in the darkness, fingers splayed, trembling with effort.

A *hole*.

Compared to the sickening throb already in my head, what

arced through my eyes was almost pleasant. Either I was getting used to it or I was already in so much pain that it didn't matter. But I noticed when Shiny stopped breathing.

My heart pounding, I lowered my hand to where his chest should have been. I felt nothing at first; then my hand drifted a little to the side. Meat and bone, cut neatly as if with a knife. I snatched my hand back, my gorge rising again all on its own.

"How peculiar!" cried a bright voice, right behind me.

I nearly screamed. Would have done it if my chest hadn't hurt. I did whirl and jump and scramble back, jarring my arm something fierce.

The creature that crouched at Shiny's feet was not human. It had a human structure, more or less, but it was impossibly squat, nearly as wide as it was tall—and it wasn't very tall. Maybe the size of a child, if that child had broad, yokelike shoulders and long arms rippling with muscle. The creature's face was not that of a child, either, though it was cheeky, with huge round eyes. It had a receding hairline, and its gaze was both ancient and half feral.

But I could see it, and that meant it was a godling—the ugliest one I had yet seen.

"H-hello," I said when my heart had stopped jumping around. "I'm sorry. You startled me."

It—he—smiled at me, a quick flash of teeth. Those were not human, either; he had no canines. Just perfectly flat squares, straight across on top and bottom.

"Didn't mean to," he said. "Didn't think you'd see me. Most don't." He leaned close, squinting at my face. "Huh. So you're that girl. The one with the eyes."

I nodded, accepting that bizarre designation. Godlings

gossipped like fishermen; enough of them had encountered me that word must've spread. "And you are?"

"Dump."

"Pardon?"

"*Dump*. That's a neat trick you did." He jerked his chin toward Shiny. "Always wanted to pop a hole or two in him myself! What're you doing with him?"

"It's a long story." I sighed, suddenly weary. If only I dared rest. Maybe... "Um. Lord D-Dump." I felt very foolish saying that. "I'm in a lot of trouble here. Please, will you help me?"

Dump cocked his head, like a puzzled dog. Despite this, the look in his eyes was quite shrewd. "You? Depends. Him? No way."

I nodded slowly. Mortals constantly asked godlings for favors; a lot of godlings were prickly about it. And this one didn't like Shiny. I would have to tread carefully, or he might leave before I could explain about his missing siblings. "First, can you tell if anyone else is around? I heard something before."

"That was me. Coming to see what had dropped into my place. Lots of people get tossed out and end up here, but never from so high up." He gave me a wry look. "Thought you'd be messier."

"Your place?" A junkyard was not my idea of a home, but godlings had no need of the material comforts we mortals liked. "Oh. Sorry."

Dump shrugged. "Not like you could help it. Won't be mine much longer, anyway." He gestured upward, and I remembered the blackened sun. The Nightlord's warning.

"You're going to leave?" I asked.

"Got no choice, do I? Not stupid enough to stick around

when Naha's this pissed. Just glad he hasn't cursed us, too." He sighed, looking unhappy. "All the mortals, though...They're marked—everybody who was in the city at the time Role and the others died. Even if they leave, they still see the black sun. I tried to send some of my kids down south to one of the coast towns, and they just came back. Said they wanted to be with me when..." He shook his head. "Kill 'em all, guilty and innocent alike. He and Itempas never were all that damn different."

I lowered my head and sighed, weary in more than body. Had it even done any good, escaping the Lights? Would it make any difference if I found a way to expose them? Would the Night-lord destroy the city anyway, for sheer spite?

Dump shifted from foot to foot, abruptly looking uncomfortable. "Can't help you, though."

"What?"

"Someone wants you. Him, too. Can't help either of you."

All at once I understood. "You're the Lord of Discards," I said. I could not help smiling. I'd grown up on tales of him, though I'd never known his true name. They'd been favorites of my childhood. He was another trickster figure, humorous, appearing prominently in stories of runaway children and lost treasures. Once something was thrown away, unwanted, or forgotten, it belonged to him.

He grinned back at me with those unnervingly flat teeth. "Yeah." Then his smile faded. "But you ain't thrown away. Someone wants you *bad*." He took a step back as if my very presence pained him, grimacing in distaste. "You're gonna have to go. I'll send you somewhere, if you can't walk—"

"I know about the missing godlings," I blurted. "I know who's been killing them."

Dump stiffened all at once, his massive fists clenching. "Who?"

"A cult of crazy mortals. Up there." I pointed back toward the Tree. "There's one of them, a scrivener who..." I hesitated, suddenly aware of the danger of naming Dateh a demon. If the gods knew there were still demons in the world...

No. I no longer cared what happened to me. Let them kill me, as long as they dealt with Madding's killers, too.

But before I could say the words, Dump suddenly caught his breath and whirled away from me, his image flaring brighter as he summoned his magic. There was a scream in the distance, and then I heard small feet come pelting around a pile of rubbish, scrabbling once as they trotted along what sounded like a loose board.

"Dump!" a young girl cried. "People in the yard! Rexy told 'em to get the hells out and they hit him! He's bleedin'!"

Abruptly I was jostled as Dump shoved the girl into the little alcove with me and Shiny. "Stay there," he commanded. "I'll go take care of 'em."

I squirmed around the girl. There wasn't much room for her, but she was small. I pushed at her; she was all lanky bones and ragged clothes. "Lord Dump, be careful! The scrivener I told you about, his magic—"

Dump made a sound of annoyance and vanished.

"Damn it!" I pounded my good fist into Shiny's unresponsive leg. If Dateh was among the Lights who had come looking for me, or if they had another arrowhead made from demons' blood...

"Hey," said the girl, annoyed. "Shove the dead guy, not me."

Dead, dead, uselessly dead. I couldn't say he hadn't warned me, though; this was why he'd wanted me stronger before we attempted the escape. So that I could leave him behind? For

a moment, the possibility turned in my thoughts. If the Lights
didn't find him, Shiny would return to life and make his own
way in the city, however he'd done it before meeting me. If they
did find him... Well, perhaps he would slow them down enough
for me to escape.

Even as I thought it, though, I knew I couldn't do it. As much
as I wanted to hate Shiny for his self-absorption and his temper
and his miserable personality, he had loved Madding, too. For
that alone, he deserved some loyalty.

In the meantime, I needed help. I couldn't count on Dump
returning. I had no way to reach mortal aid. If I could summon
another godling to help, or better still...

My first thought was so repellent that I actually had trouble considering it. I forced myself to do so, anyhow, because
Shiny had said it himself: there was one god who would want
to deal with his children's killers. Yet I also knew from my
people's history that Lord Nahadoth would not stop there. He
might decide to wipe out the Lights by wiping out the entire
city of Shadow, or perhaps the whole world. He was already
angry, and we were nothing to him—worse than nothing. His
betrayers and tormentors. It would probably please him to see us
all die.

The Gray Lady, then. She had been mortal and still showed
some concern for mortalkind. Yet how could I reach her?
I wasn't a pilgrim, though I had exploited them for years. To
pray to a god—to get a god's attention—one had to thoroughly
understand that god's nature. I didn't even know the Lady's
real name. The same went for nearly all of the godlings I could
think of, including Lady Nemmer. I didn't know enough about
any of them.

Then an idea came to me. I swallowed, my hands suddenly clammy. There was one godling whose nature was simple enough, terrible enough, that any mortal could summon her. Though the Maelstrom knew I didn't want to.

"Move," I said to the girl. Muttering, she slipped out, and I crawled one-handed out into the open. The girl started to crawl back in, but I caught her bony leg. "Wait. Is there anything around here like a stick? Something at least this long." I started to lift both arms, then gasped as the muscles of my bad arm cramped agonizingly. I finally approximated the gesture with my good arm. If I had to flee, I would need some means of finding my way.

The girl said nothing, probably glaring at me for a second or two; then she slipped out. I waited, tense, hearing the sounds of battle in the distance—adult shouts, children's screams, debris crashing and splintering. Disturbingly close. That the fight had lasted this long with a godling involved meant there were either a lot of Lights, or Dateh had already gotten him.

The girl came back, pressing something into my hand. I felt it and smiled: a broomstick. Broken off and jagged at one end, but otherwise perfect.

Now came the hard part. I knelt and bowed my head, taking a deep breath to settle my thoughts. Then I reached inside myself, trying to find one feeling amid the morass. One singular, driving need. One *hunger*.

"Lil," I whispered. "Lady Lil, please hear me."

Silence. I fixed my thoughts upon her, framed her in my mind: not her appearance, but the feel of her presence, that looming sense of so many things held in precarious containment. The scent of her, spoiling meat and bad breath. The sound of her whirring, unstoppable teeth. What did it feel like to *want* as she did, constantly? How did it feel to crave something so powerfully that you could taste it?

Perhaps a little like the way I felt, knowing Madding was lost to me forever.

I clenched my hand around the broomstick as my heart flooded with emotion. I planted the jagged end of it in the dirt and fought the urge to weep, to scream. I wanted him back. I wanted his killers dead. I could not have the former—but the latter was within my grasp, if I could only find someone to help me. Justice was so close I could taste it.

"Come to me, Lil!" I cried, no longer caring if any Lights roving the junkyard heard me. "Come, darkness damn you! I have a feast even you should like the taste of!"

And she appeared, crouching in front of me with her gold hair tangled around her shoulders, her madness-flecked eyes sharp and wary.

"Where?" Lil asked. "What feast?"

I smiled fiercely, flashing my own sharp teeth. "In my soul, Lil. Can you taste it?"

She regarded me for a long moment, her expression shifting from dubious to gradual amazement. "Yes," she said at last. "Oh, yes. Lovely." Her eyes fluttered shut, and she lifted her head, opening her mouth slightly to taste the air. "Such longing in you, for so many things. Delicious." She opened her eyes and frowned in puzzlement. "You were not so tasty before. What has happened?"

"Many things, Lady Lil. Terrible things, which is why I called you. Will you help me?"

She smiled. "No one has prayed to me for centuries. Will you do it again, mortal girl?"

She was like a bauble-beetle, scuttling after any shiny thing. "Will you help me, if I do?"

"Hey," said the girl behind me. "Who's that?"

Lil's gaze settled on her, suddenly avid. "I'll help you," she said to me, "if you give me something."

My lip curled, but I fought back disgust. "I'll give you any-thing that is mine to give, Lady. But that child is Lord Dump's."

Lil sighed. "Never liked him. No one wants his junk, but he doesn't share." Sulky, she flicked a fingertip at something I couldn't see on the ground.

I reached out and gripped her hand, making her focus on me again. "I've learned who's been killing your siblings, Lady Lil. They're hunting me now, and they may catch me soon."

She stared at my hand on hers in surprise, then at me. "I don't care about any of that," she said.

Damnation! Why did I have to be plagued by *crazy* godlings? Were the sane ones avoiding me? "There are others who do," I said. "Nemmer—"

"Oh, I like her." Lil brightened. "She gives me any bodies her people want to get rid of."

I forgot what I'd meant to say for a moment, then shook it off. "If you tell her this," I said, gambling, "I'm sure she'll give you more bodies." There would be many dead New Lights by the time this business was done, I hoped.

"Maybe," she said, suddenly calculating, "but what will *you* give me to go to her?"

Startled, I tried to think. I had no food on hand, nothing else of value. But I could not escape the feeling that Lil knew what she wanted of me; she just wanted me to say it first.

Humility, then. I had prayed to her, made her *my* goddess in a way. It was her right to demand an offering. I put my good hand on the ground and bowed my head. "Tell me what you want of me."

"Your arm," she said, too quickly. "It's useless now, worse than useless. It may never heal right. Let me have it."

Ah, of course. I looked at the arm dangling at my side. There was a swollen, hot-to-the-touch knot in the upper arm that probably meant a bad break, though fortunately it hadn't come through the skin. I had heard of people dying from such things, their blood poisoned by bits of bone, or infection and fever setting in.

It wasn't the arm I preferred to use; I was left-handed. And I had already decided that I would not need it for much longer.

I took a deep breath. "I can't be incapacitated," I said softly. "I need to... to still be able to run."

"I can do it so quickly that you'll feel no pain," Lil said, leaning forward in her eagerness. I smelled it again, that fetid whiff of breath from her real mouth, not the false one she was using to coax me. Carrion. But she preferred fresh meat. "Burn the end so it won't bleed. You'll hardly miss it."

I opened my mouth to say yes.

"No," snapped Shiny, startling us both. Leaning on one arm, I nearly fell as I tried to whirl around. I could see him; the magic of his resurrection was still bright.

Dump's girl yelped and scuttled away from us. "You was dead! What the demonshit is this?"

"Her flesh is hers to bargain with!" Lil said, her fists clenching in thwarted anger. "You have no right to forbid me!"

"I think even you would find her flesh disagreeable, Lil." I
heard wood rattle and dust grit as he climbed out of the alcove.
"Or do you mean to kill another of my children, Oree?"

I flinched. My demon blood. I had forgotten. But before I
could explain to Lil, another voice spoke that chilled every drop
of poison in my veins.

"There you are. I knew your companion would be alive, Lady
Oree, but I'm surprised—and pleased—to see you in the same
condition."

Above and behind Lil: one of the tiny, marble-sized portals
that Dateh used for spying. I had not noticed it, not with Lil
in front of me as a distraction. Too late I realized the sounds of
battle in the distance had faded into silence.

Lil turned and stood, cocking her head from one side to the
other, birdlike. I scrambled to my feet, leaning heavily on the
broomstick for balance against my deadweight arm. To the girl,
wherever she was, I hissed, "Run!"

"Now, Lady Oree." Dateh's voice was chiding, reasonable,
despite the strangeness of it issuing from the tiny hole. "We
both know there's no point in your resisting. I see that you're
injured. Must I risk hurting you further by taking you into my
Empty? Or will you come quietly?"

From my left, a startled cry. The girl. She had run—and
been caught by the people converging on us from that direction. Many sets of feet, ten or twelve. There were others moving
around the other end of the junkyard row. The New Lights had
come.

"There's no need for you to take that child," I said, trying to keep my voice from shaking. So close! We had almost done it. "Can't you let her go?"

"She's a witness, unfortunately. Don't worry; we take care of children. She won't be mistreated, so long as she joins us."

"Dump!" shouted the girl, who was apparently struggling against her captors. "Dump, help!"

Dump did not appear. My heart sank.

"You're the one!" Lil said, suddenly brightening. "I tasted your ambition weeks ago and warned Oree Shoth to beware of you. I knew if I stayed near her, I might meet you." She beamed like a proud mother. "I am Lil."

"Lil." I gripped the broomstick. "He has powerful magic. He's already killed several godlings, and"—I fought back a shudder of revulsion, which might've been enough to touch off my nausea again—"and eaten them. I don't want to see you join them."

Lil looked at me, startled. "What?"

Shiny's hand gripped my good shoulder; I felt him move in front of me.

"I don't want *you* anymore," Dateh said, cold now. To Shiny. "You're useless, whatever you are. But I have no qualms about going through you to get to her, so step aside."

Lil was still staring at me. "What do you mean, *eaten* them?"

My eyes welled with tears of grief and frustration. "He cuts out their hearts and eats them. He's been doing that to all the missing ones. Gods know how many by now."

"*Lady Oree*," Dateh said, his voice tight with anger. All at once, the hole doubled in size, tearing the air as it grew. It drifted toward us, a warning. There was no suction—yet.

"You didn't say they were being eaten. You should have said

that in the first place," Lil said, looking annoyed. Then she turned on Dateh's hole, and her expression darkened. "It is bad, very bad, for a mortal to eat one of us."

I felt the suction the instant it began. It was gentler than that night in front of Madding's, but still enough to stagger me. In front of me, Shiny grunted and set his feet, his power rising, but it dragged him forward, anyway—

Lil shoved both of us roughly aside, stepping in front of the hole.

The suction increased sharply, to full force. Shiny and I had both fallen to the ground; I was sprawled and half sensible, as the fall had jarred both my head and my broken arm. Through a haze, I saw Lil, her legs braced, her gown whipping about her scrawny form, her long yellow hair tangling in the wind. The hole was huge now, nearly as big as her body, yet somehow it had not claimed her.

She lifted her head. I was behind her, but I knew the instant her mouth lengthened, without seeing it.

"Greedy mortal boy." Lil's voice was everywhere, echoing, shrill with delight. "Do you really think that will work on *me?*"

She spread her arms wide, blazing with golden power. I heard the buzz and whir of her teeth, so loud that it made my bones rattle and my spine vibrate, so powerful that even the earth shivered beneath me. The whir rose to a scream as she lunged at the portal—and *tried to eat it.* Sparks of pure magic shot past us, each one burning where it landed. A concussion of force flattened me even more and shattered the piles of junk around us. I heard wood splintering, debris tumbling, the Lights screaming, and Lil laughing like the insane monster she was.

And then Shiny had my good arm, hauling me up. We ran, him half dragging me because my legs would not work and I kept trying to vomit. Finally he scooped me into his arms and ran, as behind us the junkyard erupted in earthquakes and chaos and flames.

16

"From the Depths to the Heights" *(watercolor)*

I GRAYED OUT FOR A TIME. The jostling, the running, and the blurring cacophony of sounds proved too much for my already-abused senses. I was vaguely aware of pain and confusion, my sense of balance completely thrown; it felt as though I tumbled through the air, unconnected to anything, uncontrolled. A blurry voice seemed to whisper into my ear: *Why are you alive when Madding is dead? Why are you alive at all, death-filled vessel that you are? You are an affront to all that is holy. You should just lie down and die.*

It might have been Shiny speaking, or my own guilt.

After what felt like a very long time, I regained enough wit to think.

I sat up, slowly and with great effort. My arm, the good one, did not obey my will at first. I told it to push me up, and instead it flailed about, scrabbling at the surface beneath me. Hard, but not stone. I sank my nails into it a little. Wood. Cheap, thin. I patted it, listening, and realized it was all around me. When I finally regained control of myself, I managed a slow, shaky exploration of my environment, and finally understood. A box. I was in some kind of large wooden crate, open at one end. Something heavy and scratchy and smelly lay upon me. A horse blanket? Shiny must have stolen it for me. It still reeked of its former owner's sweat, but it was warmer than the chilly pre-dawn air around me, so I drew it closer.

Footsteps nearby. I cringed until I recognized their peculiar weight and cadence. Shiny. He climbed into the crate with me and sat down nearby. "Here," he said, and metal touched my lips. Confused, I opened my mouth, and nearly choked as water flooded in. I managed not to splutter too much of it away, fortunately, because I was desperately thirsty. As Shiny turned up the flask for me again, I greedily drank until there was nothing left. I was still thirsty but felt better.

"Where are we?" I asked. I kept my voice soft. It was quiet, wherever we were. I heard the *bap-plink* of morning dew—such a welcome sound after days without it in the House of the Risen Sun. There were people about, but they moved quietly, too, as if trying not to disturb the dew.

"Ancestors' Village," he said, and I blinked in surprise. He had carried me across the city from the Shustocks junkyard, from Wesha into Easha. The Village was just north of South Root, near the tunnel under the rootwall. It was where the city's homeless population had made a camp of sorts, or so I'd been told. I'd never visited it. Many of the Villagers were sick in body or mind, too harmless to be quarantined, but too ugly or strange or pitiful to be acceptable in the orderly society of the Bright. Many were lame, mute, deaf…blind. In my earliest days in Shadow, I'd been terrified of joining them.

I didn't ask, but Shiny must have seen the confusion on my face. "I lived here sometimes," he said. "Before you."

It was no more than I'd already guessed, but I could not help pity: he had gone from ruling the gods to living in a box among lepers and madlings. I knew his crimes, but even so…

Belatedly I noticed more footsteps approaching. These were lighter than Shiny's, several sets—three people? One of them had a bad limp, dragging the second foot like deadweight.

"We have missed you," said a voice, elderly, raspy, of indeterminate gender, though I guessed male. "It's good to see you well. Hello, miss."

"Um, hello," I said. The first words had not been directed at me.

Satisfied, the maybe-man turned his attention back to Shiny. "For her." I heard something set down on the crate's wooden floor; I smelled bread. "See if she can get that down."

"Thank you," said Shiny, surprising me by speaking.

"Demra's gone looking for old Sume," said another voice, younger and thinner-sounding. "She's a bonebender—not a very good one, but sometimes she'll work for free." The voice sighed. "Wish Role was still around."

"That won't be necessary," said Shiny, because of course he intended to kill me. Even I could tell that these people didn't have many favors to call in; best they not spend such a precious one on me. Then Shiny surprised me further. "Something for her pain would be good, however."

A woman came forward. "Yes, we brought this." Something

else was set down, glass. I thought I heard the slosh of liquid. "It isn't good, but it should help."

"Thank you," Shiny said again, softer. "You are all very kind."

"So are you," said the thin voice, and then the woman murmured something about letting me sleep, and all three of them went away. I lay there in their wake, not quite boggling. I was too tired for real astonishment.

"There's food," Shiny said, and I felt something dry and hard brush my lips. The bread, which he'd torn into chunks so I wouldn't have to waste strength gnawing. It was coarse, flavorless stuff, and even the small piece he'd torn made my jaws ache. The Order of Itempas took care of all citizens; no one starved in the Bright. That did not mean they ate *well*.

As I held a piece in my mouth, hoping saliva would make it more palatable, I considered what I had heard. It had had the air of long habit—or ritual, perhaps. When I'd swallowed, I said, "They seem to like you here."

"Yes."

"Do they know who you are? What you are?"

"I have never told them."

Yet they knew, I was certain. There had been too much reverence in the way they'd approached and presented their small offerings. They had not asked about the black sun, either, as a heathen might have done. They simply accepted that the Bright Lord would protect them if He could—and that it was pointless to ask if He could not.

I had to clear my dry throat to speak. "Did you protect them while you were here?"

"Yes."

"And . . . you spoke to them?"

"Not at first."

With time, though, same as me. For a moment, an irrational competitiveness struck me. It had taken three months for Shiny to deem me worthy of conversation. How long had he taken with these struggling souls? But I sighed, dismissing the fancy and refusing when Shiny tried to offer me another piece of bread. I had no appetite.

"I've never thought of you as kind," I said. "Not even when I was a child, learning about you in White Hall. The priests tried to make you sound gentle and caring, like an old grandfather who's a little on the strict side. I never believed it. You sounded...well-intentioned. But never kind."

I heard the glass thing move, heard a stopper come free with a faint *plonk*. Shiny's hand came under the back of my head, lifting me gently; I felt the rim of a small flask nudge my lips. When I opened my mouth, acid fire poured in—or so it tasted. I gasped and spluttered, choking, but most of the stuff went down my throat before my body could protest too much. "Gods, no," I said when the bottle touched my lips again, and Shiny took it away.

As I lay there trying to regain the full use of my tongue, Shiny said, "Good intentions are pointless without the will to implement them."

"Mmm." The burn was fading now, which I regretted, because for a moment I had forgotten the pain of my arm and head. "The problem is, you always seem to implement your intentions by stomping all over other people's. That's pretty pointless, too, isn't it? Does as much harm as good."

"There is such a thing as greater good."

I was too tired for sophistry. There had been no greater good in the Gods' War, just death and pain. "Fine. Whatever you say."

I drifted awhile. The drink went to my head quickly, not so much dulling the pain as making me care less about it. I was contemplating sleeping again when Shiny spoke. "Something is happening to me," he said, very softly.

"Hmm?"

"It isn't my nature to be kind. You were correct in that. And I have never before been tolerant of change."

I yawned, which made my headache grow in a distant, warm sort of way. "Change happens," I said through the yawn. "We all have to accept it."

"No," he replied. "We don't. *I* never have. That is what I am, Oree—the steady light that keeps the roiling darkness at bay. The unmoving stone around which the river must flow. You may not like it. You don't like *me*. But without my influence, this realm would be cacophony, anarchy. A hell beyond mortal imagination."

Surprised into wakefulness, I blurted the first thing that came to mind. "Does it bother you that I don't like you?"

I heard him shrug. "You have a contrary nature. I suspect you are of Enefa's lineage."

I almost laughed at the sour note in his voice, though that would've hurt my head. I sobered, though, as I realized something. "You and Enefa weren't always enemies."

"We were never enemies. I loved her, too." And I could hear that, suddenly, in the soft interstices of his tone.

"Then"—I frowned—"why?"

He did not answer for a long while.

"It was a kind of madness," he said at last, "though I did not think so at the time. My actions seemed perfectly rational, until...after."

I shifted a little, uncomfortable, both from my arm and the conversation topic. "That's pretty normal," I said. "People snap sometimes. But afterward—"

"Afterward I had no recourse. Enefa was dead and could not—I thought—be restored. Nahadoth hated me and would shatter all the realms for vengeance. I dared not free him. So I committed myself to the path I had chosen." He paused for a moment. "I . . . regret . . . what I did. It was wrong. Very wrong. But regret is meaningless."

He fell silent. I knew I should have let it go then, with the echoes of his pain still reverberating in the air around me. He was ancient, unfathomable; there was so much about him I would never understand. But I reached out with my good hand and found his knee.

"Regret is never meaningless," I said. "It's not *enough*, not on its own; you have to change, too. But it's a start."

Shiny let out a long sigh of almost unbearable weariness. "Change is not my nature, Oree. Regret is all I have."

More silence then, for a long while.

"I'd like some more of that stuff," I said at length. The throb of my arm was becoming more present; the liquor had worn off. "But I think I'd better eat something beforehand."

So Shiny resumed feeding me, giving me more water, too, from among the offerings the Villagers had made. I had the presence of mind to keep a little in my mouth and use that to soften the horrid bread. "In the morning there will be soup," he said. "I'll have the others bring some to us. It would be best if neither you nor I are seen for a while."

"Right," I said, sighing. "So what do we do now? Live here among the beggars until the New Lights find us again? Hope

I don't die of infection before Mad's killers are brought to justice?" I rubbed my face with my good hand. Shiny had given me
more of the fiery liquor, and already it was making me feel warm
and feather-light. "Gods, I hope Lil is all right."

"They are both children of Nahadoth. In the end, it will be a
matter of strength."

I shook my head. "Dateh's not..." Then I understood. "Oh.
That explains a lot." I felt Shiny throw me a look. Well, too late
to take it back.

"She is my daughter, too," he said, at length. "He will not
defeat her easily."

For a moment I puzzled over this, wondering how on earth
the Lord of Night and the Bright Father had managed to have
a child together. Or was he speaking figuratively, counting all
godlings as his children regardless of their specific parentage?
Then I dismissed it. They were gods; I didn't need to understand.

We fell silent for a while, listening to the dew fall. Shiny ate
the rest of the bread, then sat back against a wall of the crate.
I lay where I was and wondered how long it would be 'til dawn
and whether there was any point in living long enough to see it.

"I know who we can go to for help," I said at length. "I don't
dare call another godling; I won't be responsible for more of
their deaths. But there are some mortals, I think, who are strong
enough to take on the Lights. If you help me."

"What do you want me to do?"

"Take me back to Gateway Park. The Promenade." The
last place I had been happy. "Where they found Role. Do you
remember it?"

"Yes. There are often New Lights in that area."

Yes. This time of year, with the Tree about to bloom, all the heretic groups would have people at the Promenade, hoping to convert some of the Lady's pilgrims to their own faiths. Easier to start with people who had already turned their backs on Bright Itempas.

"Help me get there unseen," I said. "To the White Hall."

He said nothing. All at once, tears sprang to my eyes, inexplicable. Drunkenness. I fought them back.

"I have to see this through, Shiny. I have to make sure the New Lights are destroyed. They still have my blood—they can make more of those arrow things. Madding isn't like Enefa. He won't come back to life."

I could still see him in my head. *I always knew you were special*, he'd said, and my specialness had killed him. His death had to be the last.

Shiny got up, climbed out of the crate, and walked away.

I could not help it. I gave in to the tears, because there was nothing else I could do. I didn't have the strength to make it to the Promenade on my own, or elude the Lights for much longer. My only hope was the Order. But without Shiny—

I heard his heavy footfalls and caught my breath, pushing myself up and wiping the tears off my face.

Something heavy and loose landed in front of me. I touched it, puzzled it out. A cloak. It reeked of someone's unwashed filth and stale urine, but I caught my breath as I realized what he meant for us to do.

"Put that on," Shiny said. "Let's go."

The Promenade.

Dawn had not yet come, but the Promenade was far from still. People stood in knots on streets and corners, murmuring, some weeping, and for the first time I noticed the tension that filled the city, as it must have since the sun had turned black the day before. The city was never quiet at night, but by the sounds that I could hear on the wind, many of its denizens had not slept the night before. A good number must have risen to wait for the sunrise, perhaps in hopes of seeing a change in the sun's condition. There were none of the usual vendors about— and no one at Art Row, though it was still too early for that— but I could hear the pilgrims. Many more than usual seemed to have gathered, kneeling on the bricks and murmuring prayers to the Gray Lady in her dawn guise. Hoping she would save them.

Shiny and I made our way along quietly, keeping close to buildings rather than crossing the Promenade. That would've been faster—the White Hall was directly across from us—but also more conspicuous, even amid the milling crowd. Most Villagers knew better than to enter those parts of the city frequented by visitors; doing so was a good way to get rousted by Order-Keepers. They would be tense today, and a good many of them were young hotheads who would just as soon take Shiny and me into an empty storehouse to deal with themselves. We needed to reach the White Hall itself, where they were more likely to do the proper thing and take us in.

I had discarded my makeshift stick, as it was too much of a giveaway. I barely had the strength to hold it, anyhow; a fever had sapped what little energy I'd gained from resting in the Village, forcing us to stop frequently. I walked close behind Shiny, holding on to the back of his cloak so that I could feel it when he stepped over an obstacle or skirted around milling folk. This forced me to keep low and shuffle a bit, which added to the disguise, though I could feel that Shiny hadn't done the same, walking with his usual stiff-backed, upright pride. Hopefully no one would notice.

We had to pause at one point while a line of chained people came down the street with push brooms, sweeping the bricks clean for the day's business. Debtors, most likely, only a step away from life in the Ancestors' Village themselves. Working despite the tension in the city. Of course the Order of Itempas would not disrupt the city's daily functions, even under a god's death sentence.

Then they were gone, and Shiny started forward again—and abruptly paused. I bumped into his back, and he put back an arm to push me aside, into the doorway alcove of a building. Unfortunately, he touched the broken arm in the process; I managed not to scream, but just barely.

"What is it?" I whispered, when I'd regained enough self-control to speak. I was still panting. It helped me feel cooler, given the fever.

"More Order-Keepers, patrolling," he said tersely. The Promenade must have been crawling with them. "They did not see us. Be still."

I obeyed. We waited there long enough that Shiny's morning glow began. Irrationally I worried that it would somehow draw the Lights, even though no one had ever seen the glow of his magic but me. Though perhaps it would work in our favor and draw some godling instead.

I jerked back, blinking and disoriented. Shiny held me up, bracing me against the door.

"What?" I asked. My thoughts were blurry.

"You collapsed."

I took a deep breath, shivering before I could help myself. "Just a little farther. I can make it."

"It might be best if—"

"No," I said, trying to sound firmer. "Just get me to the steps. I can crawl from there if I have to."

Shiny obviously had his doubts, but as usual he said nothing.

"You don't have to go in with me," I said as I recovered. "They'll just kill you."

Shiny sighed and took my hand, a silent rebuke. We resumed our careful movement around the circle.

That we reached the White Hall steps without trouble was so amazing that without thinking, I whispered a prayer of thanks to Itempas. Shiny turned to stare at me for a moment, then led me on up the steps.

My first knock on the big metal door got no response, but then I hadn't knocked hard. When I tried to lift my hand again and swayed on my feet, Shiny caught my hand and knocked himself. Three booming strikes, seeming to echo through the whole building. The door opened before the third blow's echoes had faded. "What the hells do you want?" asked an annoyed-sounding guard. He grew more annoyed as he assessed us. "Food distribution will be at noon, the way it is every day, *in the Village*," he snapped. "Get back there or I'll—"

"My name is Oree Shoth," I said. I tugged back the hood so he could see I was Maroneh. "I killed three Order-Keepers. You've been looking for me. For us." I gestured tiredly at Shiny. "We need to speak to Previt Rimarn Dih."

They separated us and put me in a small room with a chair, a table, and a cup of water. I drank the water, begged the silent guard for more, and when he brought no more, I put my head down on the table and slept. The guard had obviously been given no instructions about this, so he let me sleep for some time. Then I was roughly shaken awake.

"Oree Shoth," said a familiar voice. "This is unexpected. I'm told you *asked* to see me."

Rimarn. I had never been so glad to hear his cold voice.

"Yes," I said. My voice was hoarse, dry. I was hot all over and shaking a little. I probably looked like all the infinite hells combined. "There's a cult. Not heretics—Itempans. They're called the New Lights. One of their members is a scrivener. Dateh." I tried to remember Dateh's family name and could not. Had he ever told me? Unimportant. "They call him the Nypri. He's a demon, a real one, like in the stories. Demon blood is poison to gods. He's been capturing godlings and killing them. He's the one who killed Role and...and others." My strength ran out. I hadn't had much of it to begin with, which was why I'd spoken as quickly as I could. My head drooped, the table beckoning. Perhaps they would let me sleep some more.

"That's quite a tale," Rimarn said after an astonished moment. "*Quite* a tale. You do seem...distressed, though that could simply be because your protector, the god Madding, has gone missing. We keep expecting his body to turn up, like the other two we found, but so far, nothing."

He'd said it to hurt me, to see my reaction, but nothing could hurt more than the fact of Madding's death. I sighed. "Ina, probably, and Oboro. I...heard they'd gone missing." Perhaps the discovery of their bodies had triggered the Nightlord's dramatic warning.

"You'll have to tell me how you heard that, since we'd witheld that information from the public." I heard Rimarn's fingers tap against the tabletop. "I imagine you've had a difficult few weeks. Been hiding out among the beggars, have you?"

"No. Yes. Just today, I mean." I dragged my head up, trying to orient on his face. People who could see took me more seriously when I seemed to look at them. I willed him to believe me. "Please. I don't care if you go after them yourself. You probably shouldn't; Dateh's powerful, and his wife is an Arameri. A *fullblood*. They've probably got an army up there. The godlings. Just tell the godlings. Nemmer."

"Nemmer?" At that, at last, he sounded surprised. Did he know Nemmer, or perhaps know *of* her? That would figure; the Order-Keepers had to be keeping track of the various gods of Shadow. I imagined they would keep an especially close eye on Nemmer given that her nature defied the pleasant, comfortable order of the Bright.

"Yes," I said. "Madding was...they were. Working together. Trying to find their siblings." I was so tired. "Please. Can I have some water?"

For a moment, I thought he would do nothing. Then to my surprise, Rimarn rose and went to the room's door. I heard him speak to someone outside. After a moment, he returned to the table, pressing the refilled cup into my hand. Someone else came in with him and stood along the room's far wall, but I had no idea who this was. Probably just another Order-Keeper.

I spilled half the water trying to lift it. After a moment, Rimarn took it from my hands and held it to my lips. I drank it all, licked the rim, and said, "Thank you."

"How were you injured, Oree?"

"We jumped out of the Tree."

"You..." He fell silent for a moment, then sighed. "Perhaps you should begin at the beginning."

I contemplated the monumental task of talking more and shook my head.

"Then why should I believe you?"

I wanted to laugh, because I had no answer for him. Did he want proof that I'd leapt from the Tree and survived? Proof that the Lights were up to no good? What would sway him, me dying on the spot?

"Proof isn't necessary, Previt Dih." This was a new voice, and it was enough to startle me awake, because I recognized it. Oh, dear gods, how well I recognized it.

"Faith should be enough," said Hado, the New Lights' Master of Initiates. He smiled. "Shouldn't it, Eru Shoth?"

"No." I would have leapt to my feet and fled if I could have. Instead I could only whimper and despair. "No, I was so close."

"You did better than you realize," he said, coming over and patting my shoulder. It was the shoulder of the bad arm, which was now swollen and hot. "Oh, you're not well at all. Previt, why hasn't a bonebender been summoned for this woman?"

"I was just about to, Lord Hado," said Rimarn. I could hear anger in his tone, underlying the careful respect in his speech. *What...?*

Hado humphed a little, pressing the back of his hand to my forehead. "Is the other one prepared? I'm not keen on wrestling him into submission."

"If you like, my men can bring him to you later." I could actually hear Rimarn's frosty smile. "We would make certain he is sufficiently subdued."

"Thank you, but no. I have orders, and no time." A hand took my good arm and pulled me up. "Can you walk, Lady Oree?"

"Where…" I couldn't catch my breath. Fear ate at my thoughts, but I was more confused by the conversation. Was Rimarn turning me over to the Lights? Since when had the Order of Itempas been subservient to some cult? Nothing here made sense. "Where are you taking me?"

He ignored my question and pulled me along, and I had no choice but to shuffle at his side. He had to go slow, as it was the best pace I could do. Outside the little room, we were joined by two other men, one of whom grabbed my injured arm before I could evade him. I screamed, and Hado cursed.

"Look at her, you fool. Be more careful." With that, the man let me go, though his companion kept a grip on my good arm. Without that, I might not have remained standing.

"I will take her," said Shiny, and I blinked, realizing I had grayed out again. Then someone lifted me in strong arms, and I felt warm all over like I'd been sitting in a patch of sun, and though I should not have felt safe at all, I did. So I slept again.

Waking, this time, was very different.

It took a long time, for one thing. I was very conscious of this as my mind moved from the stillness of sleep to the alertness of waking, yet my body did not keep up. I lay there, aware of silence and warmth and comfort, able to recall what had happened to me in a distant, careless sort of way, but unable to move. This did not feel restrictive or alarming. Just strange. So I drifted, no longer tired, but helpless while my flesh insisted upon waking in its own good time.

Eventually, however, I did succeed in drawing a deeper

breath. This startled me because it did not hurt. The ache that had been deepening in one side where I thought the ribs were cracked was gone. So surprising was this that I drew another breath, moved my leg a little, and finally opened my eyes.

I could see.

Light surrounded me on all sides. The walls, the ceiling. I turned my head: the floor, too. All of it shone, some strange, hard material like polished stone or marble, but it glowed bright and white with its own inner magic.

I turned my head. (More surprise there: this did not hurt, either.) An enormous window, floor to very high ceiling, dominated one wall. I could not see beyond it, but the glass shimmered faintly. The furniture around the room—a dresser, two huge chairs, and an altar for worship in the corner—did not glow. I could see them only as dark outlines, silhouetted by the white of the walls and floor. I supposed not everything could be magic here. The bed that I lay on was dark, a negative shape against the pale floor. And threading up and down through the walls at random were long patches of darker material that looked like nothing I had ever seen before. This material glowed, too, in a faint green that was somehow familiar. Magic of a different sort.

"You're awake," said Hado from one of the chairs. I started, because I had not noticed the silhouette of legs against the floor.

He rose and came over, and as he did, I noticed something else strange. Though the other nonmagical objects in the room were dark to my vision, Hado was darker. It was a subtle thing, noticeable only when he moved past something that should have been equally shadowed.

Then he bent over me, reaching for my forehead, and I

remembered that he was one of the people who had killed Madding. I slapped his hand away.

He paused, then chuckled. "And I see you're feeling stronger. Well, then. If you'll get up and get dressed, Lady, you have an appointment with someone very important. If you're polite—and lucky—he may even answer your questions."

I sat up, frowning, and only belatedly realized my arm was encumbered. I examined it and found that the upper arm had been set and splinted with two long metal rods, which had then been bound tightly in place with bandages. It still hurt, I found when I tried to bend it; this triggered a deep, spreading ache through the muscles. But it was infinitely better than it had been.

"How long have I been here?" I asked, dreading the answer. I was clean. Even the blood that had been crusted under my nails was gone. Someone had bound my hair back in a single neat braid. There was no bandaging on my ribs or head; those injuries were completely healed.

That took days. Weeks.

"You were brought here yesterday," Hado said. He set clothing on my lap. I touched it and knew at once that it was not the usual New Light smock. The material under my fingers was something much finer and softer. "Most of your injuries were easily treated, but your arm will require a few more days. Don't disturb the script."

"Script?" But now I saw it as I lifted the sleeve of the nightgown I wore. Wrapped into the bindings was a small square of paper, on which had been drawn three interlinked sigils. The characters glowed against my silhouette, working whatever magic they did just by existing.

Bonebenders might use the odd sigil, generally the most commonly known or simple to draw, but never whole scripts. Anything this complex and intricate was scriveners' work—the kind that cost a fortune.

"What is this, Hado?" I turned my head to follow him as he went over to a window. Now that I knew to look for that distinctive darkness, he was easy to see. "This isn't the House of the Risen Sun. What's going on? And you—what the hells are you?"

"I believe the common term is *spy*, Lady Oree."

That hadn't been what I'd meant, but it distracted me. "Spy? *You?*"

He uttered a soft, humorless laugh. "The secret to being an effective spy, Lady Oree, is to *believe* in your role and never step out of character." He shrugged. "You may not like me for it, but I did what I could to keep you and your friends alive."

My hands tightened on the sheets as I thought of Madding. "You didn't do a very good job of it."

"I did an excellent job of it, all things considered, but blame me for your lover's death if it makes you feel better." His tone said he didn't care whether I did or not. "When you have time to think about it a little, you'll realize Dateh would have killed him, anyhow."

None of this made sense. I pushed back the covers and tried to get up. I was still weak; no amount of magical healing could fix that. But I was stronger than I had been, a clear sign of improvement. It took me two tries to stand, but when I did, I did not sway. As quickly as I could, I changed out of the nightgown and into the clothes he'd given me. A blouse and an elegantly long skirt, much more my usual style than the shapeless Light clothing. They fit perfectly, even the shoes. There was also a sling for my arm, which eased the lingering pain greatly once I worked out how to put it on.

"Ready?" he asked, then took my arm before I had a chance to answer. "Come, then."

We left the room and walked through long, curving corridors, and I could see all of it. The graceful walls, the arched ceiling, the mirror-smooth floor. As we mounted a set of shallow, wide stairs, I slowed, figuring out by trial and error how to gauge height using just my eyes and not a walking stick. Once I mastered the technique, I found that I didn't need Hado's hand on my arm to guide me. Eventually I shook him off entirely, reveling in the novelty of making my way unassisted. All my life I had heard arcane terms like *depth perception* and *panorama*, yet never fully understood. Now I felt like a seeing person—or how I had always imagined they must feel. I could see *everything*, except for the man-shaped shadow that was Hado at my side and the occasional shadows of other people passing by, most of them moving briskly and not speaking. I stared at them shamelessly, even when the shadows turned their heads to stare back.

Then a woman passed close to us. I got a good look at her forehead and stopped in my tracks.

An Arameri blood sigil.

Not the same as Serymn's—this had a different shape, its meaning a mystery to me. The servants of the Arameri were rumored to be Arameri themselves, just more distantly related. All marked, though, in some esoteric way that only other family members might understand.

Hado paused as well. "What is it?"

Compelled by a growing suspicion, I turned away from him and went to one of the walls, touching the green patch there. It was rough under my fingers, scratchy and hard. I leaned close, sniffed. The scent was faint but unmistakably familiar: the sweet living wood of the World Tree.

I was in Sky. The Arameri's magical palace. This was *Sky*.

Hado came up behind me, but this time he said nothing. Just let me absorb the truth. And at last, I did understand. The Arameri had been watching the New Lights, perhaps because of Serymn's involvement, or perhaps realizing that they were the most likely of the heretic groups to pose a threat to the Order of Itempas. I'd wondered about Hado's odd way of talking—like a nobleman. Like a man who'd spent his whole life surrounded by power. Was he Arameri himself? He had no mark, but maybe it was removable.

Hado had infiltrated the group on the Arameri's behalf. He must have warned them that the Lights were more dangerous than they seemed. But then—

I turned to Hado. "Serymn," I said. "Is she a spy, too?"

"No," said Hado. "She's a traitor. If you can call anyone in this family that." He shrugged. "Remaking society is something of a tradition with Arameri. When they succeed, they get to rule. When they fail, they get death. As Serymn will learn soon."

"And Dateh? What is he? Her unwitting pawn?"

"*Dead*, I hope. Arameri troops began attacking the House of the Risen Sun last night."

I gasped. He smiled.

"Your escape gave me the opportunity I'd been waiting for, Lady. Though my role as Master of Initiates allowed me access to the Lights' inner circle, I could not communicate beyond the House of the Risen Sun easily without rousing suspicion. Once Serymn turned out nearly the entire complement of Lights to search for you, I was able to get word to certain friends, who made sure the information reached the right ears." He paused. "The Lights were right about one thing: the gods have ample cause to be angry with mortalkind, and the deaths of their kin have done little to endear us to them. The Arameri understand this and so have taken steps to control the situation."

My hand on the Tree's bark began to tremble. I had never realized the Tree grew *through* the palace, integrated with its very substance. At the roots, its bark was rougher, with crevices deeper than the length of my hand. This bark, high on the Tree's trunk, was fine-lined, almost smooth. I stroked it absently, seeking comfort.

"Lord Arameri," I said. T'vril Arameri, head of the family that ruled the world. "Is that who you're taking me to see?"

"Yes."

I had walked among gods, wielded the magic they'd given my ancestors. I had held them in my arms, watched their blood coat my hands, feared them and been feared by them in turn. What was one mortal man to all that?

"All right, then." I turned back to Hado, who offered me his arm. I walked past him without taking it, which caused him to shake his head and sigh. Then he caught up with me, and together we continued through the shining white corridors.

17

"A Golden Chain"
(engraving on metal plate)

T'VRIL ARAMERI WAS A VERY BUSY MAN. As we walked the long hallway toward the imposing set of doors that led to his audience chamber, they opened several times to admit or release brisk-walking servants and courtiers. Most of these carried scrolls or whole stacks thereof; a few wore long sharp shapes that I assumed were swords or spears; still more were very well dressed, their foreheads bearing the marks of Arameri. No one lingered in the corridor to chat, though some spoke while on the move. I heard Senmite flavored with exotic accents: Narshes, Min, Veln, Mencheyev, others I did not recognize.

A busy man, who valued useful people. Something to keep in mind if I hoped to enlist his aid.

At the doors, we paused while Hado announced us to the two women who stood there. High Northers, I guessed by the fact that both were shorter than average and by their telltale straight hair, which hung long enough that I could see its sway. They did not appear to be guards at first glance—no weapons that I could see, though they could have had something small or close to their bodies—but something in the set of their shoulders let me know that was exactly what they were. They were *not* Arameri, or even Amn. Were they here, then, to guard the lord from his own family? Or was their presence emblematic of something else?

One of the women went inside to announce us. A moment later, a knot of other people emerged and filed past us. They stared at me with open curiosity. They looked at Hado, too, I noticed, especially the two fullbloods who emerged together and immediately fell to whispering at each other. I glanced at Hado, who seemed not even to see them. I wished I dared touch his face, because there was a pleased air about him that I wasn't sure how to interpret.

The guard emerged from the chamber and, without a word, held the door open for us. I followed Hado inside.

The audience chamber was open and airy. Two enormous windows, each many paces in width and twice Shiny's height, dominated the walls on either side of the door. As we walked, the sounds of our footsteps echoed from high overhead. I was too nervous to look up. The room's sole piece of furniture, a great blocklike chair, sat at the farthest point from the door, atop a tiered dais. And though I could not see the chair's occupant, I could hear him, writing something on a piece of paper. The scratching of his pen sounded very loud in the room's vast silence.

I could see his blood sigil, too, a stranger mark than anything I'd seen yet: a half-moon, downturned, bracketed on either side by glimmering chevrons.

We waited, silent, while he finished whatever he was doing. When the lord set his pen down, Hado abruptly dropped to one knee, his head bowed low. Quickly I followed suit.

After a moment, Lord T'vril said, "You'll both be pleased to know, I think, that the House of the Risen Sun is no more. Its threat has been removed."

I blinked in surprise. The Lord Arameri's voice was soft, low-pitched and almost musical—though the words he spoke were anything but. I wanted very much to ask what *removed* meant, but I suspected that would be a very foolish thing to do.

"What of Serymn?" asked Hado. "If I may ask."

"She's being brought here. Her husband has not yet been captured, but the scriveners tell me it's only a matter of time. We aren't the only ones seeking him, after all."

I wondered at first, then realized—of course he would have informed the city's godlings. I cleared my throat, unsure of how to pose a question without offending this most powerful of men.

"You may speak, Eru Shoth."

I faltered a moment, realizing this had been another clue I'd missed—Hado's gesture of using Maroneh honorifics. It was the sort of thing one did in dealing with folk of foreign lands, to be diplomatic. An Arameri habit.

I took a deep breath. "What about the godlings being held captive by the New Lights, ah, Lord Arameri? Have they been rescued?"

"Several bodies have been found, both in the city where the Lights dumped them and at the House. The local godlings are dealing with the remains."

Bodies. I forgot myself and stared at the man in gape-mouthed shock. More than the four I knew of? Dateh had been busy. "Which ones?" In my mind, I heard the answer to this question, too: Paitya. Kitr. Dump. Lil.

Madding.

"I haven't been given names as yet. Though I've been informed that the one who called himself Madding was among them. I believe he was important to you; I'm very sorry." He sounded sincere, if distant.

I lowered my eyes and muttered something.

T'vril Arameri then crossed his legs and steepled his fingers, or so I guessed from his movements. "But this leaves me with a dilemma, Eru Shoth: what to do with you. On the one hand, you've done a great service to the world by helping to expose the New Lights' activities. On the other, you are a weapon— and it is foolish in the extreme to leave a weapon lying about where anyone can pick it up and use it."

I lowered my head again, dropping lower than I had before, until my forehead pressed against the cold, glowing floor. I had heard this was the way to show penitence before nobles, and penitent was exactly how I felt. *Bodies.* How many of those dead, desecrated godlings had been poisoned by my blood, rather than Dateh's?

"Then again," said the Lord Arameri, "my family has long known the value of dangerous weapons."

Against the floor, my forehead wrinkled in confusion. *What?*

"The gods know now that demons still exist," said Hado, through my shock. He sounded carefully neutral. "This isn't something you'll be able to hide."

"And we will give them a demon," said the Lord Arameri. "The very one responsible for murdering their kin. That should satisfy them—leaving you, Eru Shoth, for us."

I pushed myself up slowly, trembling. "I . . . don't understand." But I did, gods help me. I did.

The Lord Arameri rose, an outline against the pale glow of

the room. As he walked down the steps of the dais, I saw that he was a slender man, very tall in the way of Amn, wearing a long, heavy mantle. Both it and his loose-curled hair, the latter tied at the tip, trailed along the steps behind him as he came to me.

"If there's one lesson the past has taught us, it is that we mortals exist at the bottom of a short and pitiless hierarchy," he said, still in that warm, almost-kind voice. "Above us are the godlings, and above those, the gods—and they *do not like us*, Eru Shoth."

"With reason," drawled Hado.

The Lord Arameri glanced at him, and to my surprise seemed to take no offense from this. "With reason. Nevertheless, we would be fools not to seek some means of protecting ourselves." He gestured away, I think toward the windows and the blackened sun beyond. "The art of scrivening was born from such an effort, initiated long ago by my forebears, though it has proven too limited to do humanity much good against gods. *You*, however, have been far more effective."

"You want to use me as the Lights did," I said, my voice shaking. "You want me to kill gods for you."

"Only if they force us to," the Arameri said. Then, to my greater shock, he knelt in front of me.

"It will not be slavery," he said, and his voice was gentle. Kind. "That time of our history is done. We will pay you as we do any of the scriveners or soldiers who fight for us. Provide you housing, protection. All we ask is that you give some of your blood to us—and that you allow our scriveners to place a mark upon your body. I will not lie to you about this mark's purpose, Eru Shoth: it is a leash. Through it we will know whenever your blood has been shed in sufficient quantity to be a danger. We will know your location in the event of another kidnapping, or if you attempt to flee. And with this mark, we will be able to kill you if necessary—quickly, painlessly, and thoroughly, from any distance. Your body will turn to ash so that no one else will be able to use its...unique properties." He sighed, his voice full of compassion. "It will not be slavery, but neither will you be wholly free. The choice is yours."

I was so tired. So very tired of all of this. "Choice?" I asked. My voice sounded dull to my own ears. "Life on a leash or death? That's your choice?"

"I'm being generous even to offer, Eru Shoth." He reached up then, put a hand on my shoulder. I thought he meant to be reassuring. "I could easily force you to do as I please."

Like the New Lights did, I considered saying, but there was no need for that. He knew precisely what a hellish bargain he'd offered me. The Arameri got what they wanted either way; if I chose death, they would take what blood they could from my body and store it against future need. And if I lived...I almost laughed as it occurred to me. They would want me to have children, wouldn't they? Perhaps the Shoths would become a shadow of the Arameri: privileged, protected, our specialness permanently marked upon our bodies. Never again to live a normal life.

I opened my mouth to tell him no, that I would not accept the life he offered. Then I remembered: I had already promised my life to another.

That would be better, I decided. At least with Shiny I would die on my own terms.

"I'd...like some time to think about it," I heard myself say, as from a distance.

"Of course," said the Lord Arameri. He rose, letting go of me. "You may remain as our guest for another day. By tomorrow evening, I'll expect your answer."

One day was more than enough. "Thank you," I said. It echoed in my ears. My heart was numb.

He turned away, a clear dismissal. Hado rose, gesturing me up, too, and as we had entered, we left in silence.

"I want to see Shiny," I said, once we were back in my room. Another cell, though prettier than the last. I did not think Sky's windows would break so easily. That was all right, though. I wouldn't need to try.

Hado, who had gone to stand at the window, nodded. "I'll see if I can find him."

"What, you aren't keeping him locked up someplace?"

"No. He has the run of Sky if he wants it, by the Lord Arameri's own decree. That has been so since he was first made mortal here ten years ago."

I was sitting at the room's table. A meal had been laid out, but it sat untouched before me. "He became mortal... here?"

"Oh, yes. All of it happened here—the Gray Lady's birth, the Nightlord's release, and Itempas's defeat, all in a single morning."

My *father's death*, my mind added.

"Then the Lady and the Nightlord left him here." He shrugged. "Afterward, T'vril extended every courtesy to him. I think some of the Arameri hoped he would take over the family and lead it on to some new glory. Instead he did nothing, said nothing. Just sat in a room for six months. Died of thirst once or twice, I heard, before he realized he no longer had a choice about eating and drinking." Hado sighed. "Then one day he simply got up and walked out, without warning or farewell. T'vril ordered a search, but no one could find him."

Because he had gone to the Ancestors' Village, I realized. Of course the Arameri would never have thought to look for their god there.

"How do you know all this?" I frowned. "You don't have an Arameri mark."

"Not yet." Hado turned to me, and I thought that he smiled. "Soon, though. That was the bargain I struck with T'vril: if I proved myself, I could be adopted into the family as a fullblood. I think bringing down a threat to the gods should qualify."

"Adopted..." I'd had no idea such a thing was even possible. "But...well...You don't seem to like these people very much."

He did chuckle this time, and again I had an odd sense about him, of someone wise beyond his years. Of something dark and strange.

"Once upon a time," he said, "there was a god imprisoned here. He was a terrible, beautiful, angry god, and by night when he roamed these white halls, everyone feared him. But by day, the god slept. And the body, the living mortal flesh that was his ball and chain, got to have a life of its own."

I inhaled, understanding, just not believing. He was speaking of the Nightlord, of course—but the body that lived by day was...?

Near the window, Hado folded his arms. I saw this easily, despite the window's darkness, because he was darker still.

"It wasn't much of a life, mind you," he said. "All the people who feared the god did *not* fear the man. They quickly learned they could do things to the man that the god would not tolerate. So the man lived his life in increments, born with every dawn, dying with every sunset. Hating every moment of it. For two. Thousand. Years."

He glanced back at me. I gaped at him.

"Until suddenly, one day, the man became free." Hado spread his arms. "He spent the first night of his existence gazing at the stars and weeping. But the next morning, he realized something. Though he could finally die, as he had dreamt of doing for centuries, he did not want to. He had been given a life at last, a whole life all his own. Dreams of his own. It would have been...wrong...to waste that."

I licked my lips and swallowed. "I..." I stopped. I had been about to say *I understand*, but that wasn't true. No mortal, and probably no god, could comprehend Hado's life. *Children of Nahadoth*, Shiny had called Lil and Dateh. Here was another of the Nightlord's children, stranger than all the rest.

"I can see that," I said. "But"—I gestured around at the walls of Sky—"*is* this life? Wouldn't something more normal—"

"I've spent my whole life serving power. And I've suffered for it—more than you can possibly imagine. Now I'm free. Should I go build a house in the country and grow vegetables? Find a lover I can endure, raise a litter of brats? Become a commoner like you, penniless and helpless?" I forgot myself and scowled. He chuckled. "Power is what I know. I would make a good family head, don't you think? Once I'm a fullblood."

He sounded sincere; that was the truly frightening thing.

"I think Lord Arameri would be a fool to let you anywhere near him," I said slowly.

Hado shook his head in amusement. "I'll go find Lord Itempas for you."

How jarring, to hear Shiny called that. I nodded absently as

Hado headed for the door. Then, when he was at the door, a thought occurred to me. "What would you do?" I asked. "If you were me. What would you choose? Life in chains or death?"

"I would be grateful to have that much of a choice."

"That's not an answer."

"Of course it is. But if you must know, I would choose life. So long as it *was* a choice, I would live."

I frowned, mulling this over. Hado hesitated a moment, then spoke again. "You've spent time among the gods, Eru Shoth. Haven't you noticed? They live forever, but many of them are even more lonely and miserable than we are. Why do you think they bother with us? *We teach them life's value.* So I would live, if only to spite them." He let out a single mirthless laugh, then sighed and offered me a sardonic bow. "Good afternoon."

"Good afternoon," I said. After he was gone, I sat thinking for a long time.

I ate something, more out of habit than necessity, and then eventually I took a nap. When I woke up, Shiny was there.

I heard him breathing as I sat up, bleary and stiff. Still weary from my ordeals, I'd fallen asleep at the table beside the remains of my meal, cradling my head on my good arm. I bumped the sling-bound arm against the table as I lifted my head, but this elicited only a mild twinge. The sigil had nearly finished its work.

"Hello," I said. "Thank you for letting me sleep." He said nothing, but that didn't bother me. "What happened to you?"

He shrugged. He was sitting across from me, near enough that I could hear his movements. "I was questioned at the White Hall; then we came here."

Obviously. I did not say it, because one took what one could get with him. "Where did you go after they brought you here?" Silently I made a wager with myself that he would say *nowhere*.

"Nowhere that matters."

I could not help smiling. It felt good, because it had been a long time since I'd felt the urge to genuinely smile. It reminded me of days long past, a life long gone, when my only worries had been putting food on the table and keeping Shiny from bleeding on my carpets. I almost loved him for reminding me of that time.

"Does anything matter to you?" I asked, still smiling. "Anything at all?"

"No," he said. His voice was flat, emotionless. Cold. I was beginning to understand just how wrong that was for him, a being who had once embodied warmth and light.

"Liar," I said.

He fell silent. I picked up the paring knife they'd given me for my meal, liking the slightly rough texture of its wooden hilt. I would have expected something finer to be used in Sky— porcelain, maybe, or silver. Nothing so common and utilitarian as wood. Maybe it was expensive wood.

"You care about your children," I said. "You feared Dateh would harm your old love, the Nightlord, so it seems you still care about him. You could probably even get to like this new Lady, if you gave her half a chance. If she's willing to take a chance on you."

More silence.

"I think you care about a great many things, more than you want to. I think life still holds some potential for you."

"What do you want from me, Oree?" Shiny asked. He sounded...not cold, not anymore. Just tired. I heard Hado's words again: *they're even more miserable than we are.* With Shiny, I could believe it.

At his question, I shook my head and laughed a little. "I don't know. I keep hoping you'll tell me. You're the god, after all. If I prayed to you for guidance, and you decided to answer, what would you tell me?"

"I wouldn't answer."

"Because you don't care? Or because you wouldn't know what to say?"

More silence.

I put the knife down and got up, walking around the table. When I found him, I touched his face, his hair, the lines of his neck. He sat passive, waiting, though I felt the tension in him. Did it bother him, the idea of killing me? I dismissed the thought as vain on my part.

"Tell me what happened," I said. "What made you like this? I want to understand, Shiny. See, Madding loved you. He—" My throat tightened unexpectedly. I had to look away and take a deep breath before continuing. "He hadn't given up on you. I think he wanted to help you. He just didn't know how to begin." Silence before me. I stroked his cheek. "You don't *have* to tell me. I won't break my promise; you helped me escape, and now you can remove one more demon from the world. But I deserve that much, don't I? Just a little bit of the truth?"

He said nothing. Beneath my fingers, his face was marble-still. He was looking straight ahead, through me, beyond me. I waited, but he did not speak.

I let out a sigh, then reached for an empty soup bowl. It wasn't very big, but there was a glass, too, which had held the best wine I'd ever tasted. I was slightly tipsy because of it, though mostly I had slept that off. I set the bowl and glass in front of me and carefully shrugged my right arm out of the sling. I could use it now, though there was still an ache in the muscles of my upper arm. They had healed, but the memory of pain was still fresh.

"Wait until I'm unconscious before you do it," I said. I couldn't tell if he was paying any attention to me. "Then pour the blood down the toilet. Don't leave any for them to use, if you can."

That same stubborn silence. It didn't even make me angry anymore; I was so inured to it.

I sighed and raised the knife to make the first cut to my wrist.

Then the glass broke against the floor, and a hand gripped my wrist tight, and suddenly we were across the room, against the wall, me pinned by the wire-taut weight of Shiny's body.

He pressed against me, breathing hard. I tried to pull my wrist from his hand, and he made a tight sound of negation, shaking my arm until I stilled. So I waited. I had managed to graze my wrist, but nothing more. A drop of my blood welled around his gripping hand and fell to the floor.

He bent. Slow, slow, like a tall old tree in the wind, fighting it every inch of the way. Only when he had bent to his fullest did he stop, his face pressed against the side of mine, his breath hot and harsh in my ear. It must have been an uncomfortable posture for him. But he stopped there, torturing himself, trapping me, and only in this manner was he able, at last, to speak. It was a whisper the whole time.

"They did not love me anymore. He was born first, I came next. I was never alone because of him. Then she came and I did not mind, I did not mind, as long as she understood that he was mine, too. It was not the sharing, do you see? It was good having her with us, and then the children, so many of them, all perfect and strange. I was happy then, *happy*, she was with us and we loved her, he and I, but I was first in his heart. I knew that. She respected it. It was never the sharing that troubled me.

"But they changed, changed, they always changed. I knew the possibility, but after so long, I did not believe. He had been alone for eternities before me. I did not understand. Even when we were enemies, he thought of me. How could I know? In all the time of my existence, it had never occurred, not once! Even apart from them, I knew their presence, felt their awareness of me. But then…but then…"

At this point, he pulled me against him. His free hand, the one that wasn't holding my wrist, fisted in the cloth at the small of my back. It wasn't a hug; that much I was sure of. It didn't feel like a gesture of comfort. It was closer to the way he'd held me after his release from the Empty. Or the way I sometimes gripped my walking stick when I was adrift in some place I didn't know, with no one to help me if I stumbled. Yes, very much like that.

"I didn't think it possible. Was it a betrayal? Had I offended them somehow? I didn't think they could forget me so completely.

"But they did.

"They forgot me.

"They were together, he and she, yet I could not feel them. They thought only of each other. I was not part of it.

"They left me alone."

I have always understood bodies better than voices or faces or words. So when Shiny whispered to me of horror, of a single moment of solitude after an eternity of companionship, it was not his words that conveyed the devastation this had wreaked on his soul. He was pressed against me as intimately as a lover. There was no need for words.

"I fled to the mortal realm. Better human company than nothing. I went to a village, to a mortal girl. Better any love than none. She offered herself and I took her, I needed her, I have never felt such need. After, I stayed. Mortal love was safer. There was a child, and I did not kill him. I knew he was demon, forbidden, I had written the law myself, but I needed him, too. He was... I had forgotten how beautiful they could be. The mortal girl whispered to me, in the night when I was weak. My siblings were wrong, wicked, hateful to have forgotten me. They would betray me again if I went back to them. Only she could love me truly; I needed only her. I needed to believe it, do you understand? I needed something certain. I lived in dread of her death. Then *they* came for me, found me. They apologized— apologized! Like it was nothing."

He laughed once, here. It was half a sob.

"And they brought me home. But I knew: I could no longer trust them. I had learned what it meant to be alone. It is the opposite of all that I am, that emptiness, that... *nothing*. I fought ten thousand battles before time began, burned my soul to shape this universe, and never before have I experienced such agony.

"The mortal girl warned me. She said they would do it again. That they would forget they loved me. That they would turn to each other and I would be alone—*left* alone—forever.

"They would not.

"They would *not*.

"Then the mortal girl killed our son."

He fell silent here for just a moment, his body utterly still.

" 'Take it,' she told me, and offered me the blood. And I thought...I thought...I thought...*when there were only two of us, I was never alone.*"

A final silence, fortelling the story's end.

Slowly, he let me go. All the tension and strength ran out of him, like water. He slid down my body to his knees, his cheek pressed to my belly. He had stopped trembling.

I have spent time studying the nature of light. It is part curiosity and part meditation; someday I hope to understand why I see the way I do. Scriveners have studied light, too, and in the books that Madding read to me, they claimed that the brightest light—true light—is the combination of all other kinds of light. Red, blue, yellow, more; put it all together and the result is shining white.

This means, in a way, that true light is dependent on the presence of other lights. Take the others away and darkness results. Yet the reverse is not true: take away darkness and there is only more darkness. Darkness can exist by itself. Light cannot.

And thus a single moment of solitude had destroyed Bright Itempas. He might have recovered from that in time; even a river stone wears into new shapes. But in the moment of his greatest weakness, he had been manipulated, his already-damaged soul struck an unrecoverable blow by the mortal woman he'd trusted to love him. That had driven him so mad that he had murdered his sister to keep from ever experiencing the pain of betrayal again.

"I'm sorry," he said. It was very soft, and not meant for me. But the next words were. "You don't know how much I've thought of taking your blood for myself."

I folded my arm around his shoulders and bent down to kiss his forehead. "I do know, actually." Because I did.

So I straightened, took his hand, and pulled him up. He came without resistance, letting me lead him to the bed, where I pulled him to lie down. When we'd settled, I snuggled into the crook of his arm, resting my head on his chest as I'd so often done with Madding. They felt and smelled very different—sea salt to dry spice, cool to hot, gentle to fierce—but their heartbeats were the same. Steady, slow, reassuring. Could a son inherit such a thing from a father? Apparently so.

I could always die tomorrow, I supposed.

18

"The Gods' Vengeance" *(watercolor)*

I THINK MADDING ALWAYS SUSPECTED THE TRUTH.

Throughout my childhood, I had a strange memory of being someplace warm and wet and enclosed. I felt safe, yet I was lonely. I could hear voices, yet no one spoke to me. Hands would touch me now and again, and I would touch back, but that was all.

Many years later, I told this story to Madding, and he looked at me oddly. When I asked him what was wrong, he didn't answer at first. I pressed him, and finally he said, "It sounds like you were in the womb."

I remember laughing. "That's crazy," I said. "I was thinking. Listening. *Aware*."

He shrugged. "So was I, before I was born. I guess that happens sometimes with mortals, too."

But it isn't supposed to, he did not say.

"What do you intend to do?" Shiny asked me the next morning.

He stood at the window across the room, glowing softly with the dawn. I sat up blearily, stifling a yawn.

"I don't know," I said.

I wasn't ready to die. That was easier to admit than I'd thought. I had killed Madding; to live with that knowledge would be—had been—almost unbearable. But killing myself, or letting Shiny or the Arameri do it, felt worse somehow. In the wake of Madding's death, it felt like throwing away a gift.

"If I live, the Arameri will use me for the gods know what. I won't have more deaths on my conscience." I sighed, rubbing my face with my hands. "You were right to want to kill us. You should've gotten us all, though. That was the only mistake the Three made."

"No," said Shiny. "We were wrong. Something had to be done about the demons—that I will not deny—but we should have sought a different solution. They were our children."

I opened my mouth. Closed it. Stared, though he was now little more than a pale relief against the dimmer sheen of the window. I wasn't really sure what to say. So I changed the subject. "What do *you* plan to do?"

He stood as he had on so many mornings at my house, facing the rising sun with back straight and head high and arms folded. Now, however, he let out a soft sigh and turned to me, leaning against the window with an almost palpable weariness. "I have no idea. Nothing in me is whole or right, Oree. I am the coward you named me, and the fool you did not. Weak." He lifted his hand as if he'd never seen it before and made a fist. It didn't look weak to me, but I imagined how a god might see it. Bones that could be broken. Skin that would not instantly heal if torn. Tendons and veins as fine as gossamer.

And underneath this fragile flesh, a mind like a broken teacup, badly mended.

"It's solitude, then?" I asked. "That's your true antithesis, not darkness. You didn't realize?"

"No. Not until that day." He lowered his hand. "But I should have realized. Loneliness is a darkness of the soul."

I got up and went over to him, stumbling once over the rugs. Finding his arm, I reached up to touch his face. He allowed this, even turning his cheek against my hand. I think he was feeling alone in that very moment.

"I'm glad they put me here in this mortal form," he said. "I can do no harm when I go mad. When I was trapped in that realm of darkness, I thought I would. Having you there afterward...Without that, I would have broken again."

I frowned, thinking of the way he'd clung to me that day, barely able to let go even for a moment. No human being could bear solitude forever—I would've gone mad in the Empty, too—but Shiny's need was not a human thing.

I thought of something my mother had said to me, many times during my childhood. "It's all right to need help," I said. "You're mortal now. Mortals can't do everything alone."

"I wasn't mortal then," he said, and I could tell he was thinking of the day he'd killed Enefa.

"Maybe it's the same for gods." I was still tired, so I turned to lean against the window beside him. "We're made in your image, right? Maybe your siblings didn't send you here so you'd do no harm as a mortal, but rather so that you could learn to deal with this as mortals do." I sighed and closed my eyes, tired of Sky's constant glow. "Hells, I don't know. Maybe you just need friends."

He fell silent, but I thought I felt him look at me.

Before I could say anything more, there was a knock at the door. Shiny went to answer it.

"My lord." A voice that I did not recognize, with the professional briskness of a servant. "I bear a message. The Lord Arameri requests your presence."

"Why?" Shiny asked—something I would never have done myself. The messenger was taken aback, too, though he paused for only a beat before answering.

"Lady Serymn has been captured."

As before, the Lord Arameri had dismissed his court. I suppose making bargains with demons and disciplining wayward full-bloods were not matters for public consumption.

Serymn stood between four guards—Arameri as well as High Norther—though they were not actually touching her. I could not tell if she looked any worse for the wear, but her silhouette stood as straight and proud as any other time I'd met her.

Her hands had been bound in front of her, which seemed to be the only concession made to her status as a prisoner. She, the guards, Shiny, and I were the only people in the room.

She and the Lord Arameri regarded each other in stillness and silence, like elegant marble statues of Defiance and Mercilessness.

After a moment of this perusal, she looked away from him— even blind, I could tell this was dismissive—and faced me. "Lady Oree. Does it please you to stand beside those who let your father die?"

Once, those words would have bothered me, but now I knew better. "You misunderstood, Lady Serymn. My father didn't die because of the Nightlord, or the Lady, or the godlings, or anyone who supports them. He died because he was different— something ordinary mortals hate and fear." I sighed. "With reason, I'll admit. But give credit where credit is due."

She shook her head and sighed. "You trust these false gods too much."

"No," I said, growing angry. Not just angry but furious, *incandescent* with rage. If I'd had a walking stick, there would have been trouble. "I trust the gods to be what they are, and I trust mortals to be mortals. *Mortals*, Lady Serymn, stoned my father to death. *Mortals* trussed me up like livestock and milked me of blood until I nearly died. Mortals killed my love." I was very proud of myself; my throat did not close and my voice did not waver. The anger buoyed me that far. "Hells, if the gods *do* decide to wipe us out, is it such a bad thing? Maybe we've earned a little annihilation." At that, I couldn't help looking at Lord T'vril, too.

He ignored me, sounding bored when he spoke. "Serymn,

stop toying with the girl. This rhetoric might have swayed your poor, lost spiritual devotees, but everyone here sees through you." He gestured at her, a graceful hand wave encompassing all that she was. "What you may not understand, Eru Shoth, is that this whole affair is a family squabble gotten out of hand."

I must have looked confused. "Family squabble?"

"I am a mere halfblood, you see—the first who has ever ruled this family. And though I was appointed to this position by the Gray Lady herself, there are those of my relatives, particularly the fullbloods, who still question my qualifications. Foolishly, I counted Serymn among the less dangerous of those. I even believed she might be useful, since her organization seemed to give direction to those members of the Itempan faith who have been disillusioned lately." I could not see him glance at Shiny, but I guessed that he did. "I did not believe they could do true harm. For this, you have my apologies."

I stiffened in surprise. I knew nothing of nobles or Arameri, but I knew this: they did not apologize. Ever. Even after the destruction of the Maroland, they had offered the Nimaro peninsula to my people as a "humanitarian gesture"—not an apology.

Serymn shook her head. "Dekarta appointed you his heir only under duress, T'vril. Ordinarily you'd do well enough, halfblood or not. But in these dark times, we need a family head strong in the old values, someone who will not waver from devotion to Our Lord. You lack the pride of our heritage."

I felt the Lord Arameri smile, because it was a brittle, dangerous thing, and the whole room felt less safe for it.

"Have you anything else to say?" he asked. "Anything worthy of my time?"

"No," she replied. "Nothing worthy of *you*."

"Very well," said the Lord Arameri. He snapped his fingers, and a servant appeared from a curtain behind T'vril's seat. He crouched beside T'vril's chair, holding something; there was the faint clink of metal. T'vril did not take it, and I could not see what it was. I did, however, see Serymn's flinch.

"This man," said the Lord Arameri. He gestured toward Shiny. "You left Sky before the last succession. Do you know him?"

Serymn glanced at Shiny, then away. "We were never able to determine *what* he was," she said, "but he is the Lady Oree's companion and perhaps lover. He had no value to us, except as a hostage against her good behavior."

"Look again, Cousin."

She looked, radiating disdain. "Is there something I should be seeing?"

I reached for Shiny's hand. He had not moved—did not seem to care at all.

The Lord Arameri rose and descended the steps. At the foot of the steps, he abruptly turned toward us in a swirl of cloak and hair and dropped to one knee, with a grace I would never have expected of a man so powerful. From this, he said in a ringing tone, "Behold Our Lord, Serymn. Hail Itempas, Master of Day, Lord of Light and Order."

Serymn stared at him. Then she looked at Shiny. There had been no sarcasm in T'vril's tone, no hint of anything other than reverence. Yet I could guess what she saw when she looked at Shiny: the soul-deep weariness in his eyes, the sorrow beneath his apathy. He wore borrowed clothing, as I did, and said nothing at T'vril's bow.

"He's Maroneh," Serymn said, after a long perusal.

T'vril got to his feet, flicking his long tail of hair back with practiced ease. "That is a bit of a surprise, isn't it? Though it would not be the first lie our family has told until it forgot the truth." He turned and went to her, stopping right in front of her. She did not step back from his nearness, though I would have. There was something about the Lord Arameri in that moment that made me very afraid.

"You knew he had been overthrown, Serymn," he said. "You've seen many gods take mortal form. Why did it never occur to you that your own god might be among them? Hado tells me that your New Lights were not kind to him."

"No," Serymn said. Her strong, rich voice wavered with uncertainty for the first time since I'd met her. "That's impossible. I would have...Dateh...We would have *known*."

T'vril glanced back at the servant, who hurried forward with the metal object. He took it and said, "I suppose your pure Arameri blood doesn't entitle you to speak for our god after all. Just as well, then. Hold her mouth open."

I didn't realize the last part was a command until the guards suddenly took hold of Serymn. There was a struggle, a jumble of silhouettes. When they stilled, I realized the guards had taken hold of Serymn's head.

T'vril lifted the metal object so that I could see it at last, outlined by the glow of the far wall. Scissors? No, too large and oddly shaped for that.

Tongs.

"Oh, gods," I whispered, understanding too late. I turned away, but there was no avoiding the horrible sounds: Serymn's gagging cry, T'vril's grunt of effort, the wet tear of flesh. It took only a moment. T'vril handed the tongs back to the servant with a sigh of disgust; the servant took them away. Serymn made a single, raw sound, not so much a scream as a wordless protest, and then she sagged between the guards, moaning.

"Hold her head forward, please," T'vril cautioned. I heard him as if from a distance, through fog. "We don't want her to choke."

"W-wait," I said. Gods, I could not think. That sound would echo in my nightmares.

"Yes, Eru Shoth?" Other than sounding a bit winded, the Lord Arameri's tone was the same as always: polite, soft-spoken, warm. I wondered if I would throw up.

"Dateh," I said, "and the missing godlings. She…she could have told us…." Now Serymn would say nothing, ever again.

"If she knew, she would never tell," he said. He mounted the steps and sat down again. The servant, having disposed of the tongs behind the curtain, hurried back out and handed him a cloth for his hands, which he used to wipe each finger. "But most likely, she and Dateh agreed to separate in order to protect each other. Serymn is a fullblood, after all; she would have known to expect harsh questioning in the event of capture."

Harsh questioning. Noble language for what I'd just witnessed.

"And unfortunately, the matter is out of my hands," he continued. I caught a hint of a gesture. The main doors opened and another servant entered, carrying something that caught my eye at once because it glowed as brightly as the rest of this so-magical palace. And unlike the walls and floor, the object that the servant carried was a bright, cheerful rose color. A small rubber ball, like something a child might play with.

T'vril took this ball from the servant and continued. "Not

only has my cousin forgotten that Bright Itempas no longer rules the gods, but she has also forgotten that we Arameri now answer to several masters rather than one. The world changes; we must change with it or die. Perhaps, after hearing of Serymn's fate, more of my fullblood cousins will remember this."

He turned his hand and let the pink ball fall. It bounced against the floor beside his chair and he caught it, then bounced it twice more.

A boy appeared before him. I recognized him at once and gasped. Sieh, the child-godling who had once tried to kick Shiny to death. The Trickster, who had once been an Arameri slave.

"What?" he asked, sounding annoyed. He glanced toward my gasp once, then looked away with no change in his expression. I prayed to no god in particular that he had not recognized me—though with Shiny standing beside me, that was a thin hope.

T'vril inclined his head respectfully. "Here is one of the killers of your siblings, Lord Sieh," he said, gesturing at Serymn.

Sieh raised his eyebrows, turning to her. "I remember her. Dekarta's third-removed niece or something, left years ago." A wry, unchildlike smile crossed his face. "Really, T'vril, the tongue?"

T'vril handed the pink ball back to the servant, who bowed and took it away. "There are those in the family who believe I am...too gentle." He shrugged, glancing at the guards. "An example was necessary."

"So I see." Sieh trotted down the steps until he stood before Serymn, though I saw him fastidiously step around the blood that darkened the floor. "Having her will help, but I don't think Naha will restore the sun until you have the demon. Do you?"

"No," said T'vril. "We're still looking for him."

Serymn made a sound then, and the little hairs on my skin prickled. I could feel her attention, could see her straining toward me as she made the sound again. There was no way to make out words, or even be certain she had tried to speak, but somehow I knew: she was trying to tell Sieh about me. She was trying to say, *There is a demon.*

But T'vril had seen to it she would never tell my secret, not even to the gods.

Sieh sighed at Serymn's struggles to speak. "I don't care what you have to say," he said. Serymn went still, watching him in fresh apprehension. "Neither will my father. If I were you, I'd save my strength to pray he's not in a creative mood."

He waved a hand, lazy, careless, and perhaps only I saw the flood of black, flamelike raw power that lashed out from that hand, coiling for a moment like a snake before it lunged forward and swallowed Serymn whole. Then it vanished, and Serymn went with it.

And then Sieh turned to us.

"So you're still with him," he said to me.

I was very aware of my hand, holding Shiny's. "Yes," I replied. I lifted my chin. "I know who he is now."

"Do you really?" Sieh's eyes flicked to Shiny, stayed there. "Somehow I doubt that, mortal girl. Not even his children know him anymore."

"I said I know him *now*," I said, annoyed. I had never liked being patronized, regardless of who was doing it—and I had been through enough in recent weeks to no longer fear a godling's temper. "I don't know what he was like before. That person is gone, anyway; he died the day he killed the Lady. *This* is just what's left." I jerked my head toward Shiny. His hand had gone slack, I think with shock. "It's not much, I'll grant you. Sometimes I want to kick him senseless myself. But the more I get to know him, the more I realize he's not as much of a lost cause as all of you seem to think."

Sieh stared at me for a moment, though he recovered quickly. "You don't know anything about it." He clenched his fists. I half expected him to stamp his feet. "He killed my mother. *All* of us died that day, and he's the one who killed us! Should we forget that?"

"No," I said. I could not help it; I pitied him. I knew how it felt to lose a parent in a way that defied all sense. "Of course you can't forget. But"—I lifted Shiny's hand—"*look* at him. Does it look like he spent the centuries gloating?"

Sieh's lip curled. "So he regrets what he did. Now, *after* we've freed ourselves, and *after* he's been sentenced to humanity for his crimes. So very remorseful."

"How do you know he didn't regret it before?"

"Because he didn't set us free!" Sieh thumped a hand against his chest. "He left us here, let humans do as they pleased with us! He tried to *force* us to love him again!"

"Maybe he couldn't think of another way," I said.

"*What?*"

"Maybe that was the only thing that made sense, mad as it was, after the mad thing he'd already done. Maybe he wanted time to fix things, even though it was impossible. Even though he was making things worse." My anger had already faded. I remembered Shiny the night before, on his knees before me, empty of hope. "Maybe he thought it was better to keep you prisoner and be hated than lose you entirely."

I knew it was a pointless argument. Some acts were beyond forgiveness; murder, unjust imprisonment, and torture were probably among them.

And yet.

Sieh closed his mouth. He looked at Shiny. His jaw tightened, eyes narrowing. "Well? Does this mortal speak for you, Father?"

Shiny said nothing. His whole body radiated tension, but none of that found its way into words. I wasn't surprised. I loosened my hand from his to make it easier for him to let me go when he walked away.

His hand snapped closed on mine, suddenly, tightly. I couldn't have pulled away if I'd wanted to.

While I blinked and wondered at this, Sieh sighed in disgust. "I don't understand you," he said to me. "You don't seem stupid. He's a waste of your energy. Are you the sort of woman who tortures herself to feel better or who takes only lovers who beat her?"

"Madding was my lover," I said quietly.

At that, Sieh actually looked chagrined. "I forgot. Sorry."

"So am I." I sighed and rubbed my eyes, which were aching again. Too much magic in Sky; I wasn't used to being able to see like this. I missed the familiar magic-flecked darkness of Shadow.

"It's just that...all of you will live forever." Then I remembered and amended myself, smiling bleakly. "Barring murder, I mean. You'll have forever with one another." *As Madding and I could never have had, even if he hadn't been killed.* Oh, I was tired; it was harder to keep the sorrow at bay. "I just don't see the point of spending all that time full of hate. That's all."

Sieh gazed at me, thoughtful. His pupils changed again,

becoming catlike and sharp, but this time there was no sense of threat accompanying the transformation. Perhaps, like me, he needed strange eyes to see what others couldn't. He turned those eyes on Shiny then, for a long, silent perusal. Whatever he saw didn't make his anger fade, but he didn't attack again, either. I counted that as a victory.

"Sieh," Shiny said suddenly. His hand tightened more on mine, on the threshold of pain. I set my teeth and bore it, afraid to interrupt. I felt him draw in a breath.

"Never apologize to me," Sieh said. He spoke very softly, perhaps sensing the same thing that I did. His face had gone cold, devoid of anything but a skein of anger. "What you did can never be absolved by mere words. To even attempt it is an insult—not just to me, but to my mother's memory."

Shiny went stiff. Then his hand twitched on mine, and he seemed to draw strength from the contact, because he spoke at last.

"If not words," he said, "will deeds serve?"

Sieh smiled. I was almost sure his teeth were sharp now. "What deeds can make up for your crimes, my bright father?"

Shiny looked away, his hand loosening on my own at last. "None. I know."

Sieh drew in a deep breath and let it out heavily. He shook his head, glanced at me, shook his head again, and then turned away.

"I'll tell Mother you're doing well," Sieh said to T'vril, who had sat silent throughout this conversation, probably holding his breath. "She'll be glad to hear it."

T'vril inclined his head, not quite a bow. "And is she well, herself?"

"Very well, indeed. Godhood suits her. It's the rest of us who are a mess these days." I thought I saw him hesitate for a moment, almost turning back to us. But he only nodded to T'vril. "Until the next time, Lord Arameri." He vanished.

T'vril let out a long sigh in his wake. I felt that this spoke for all of us.

"Well," he said. "With that business out of the way, we are left with only one matter. Have you considered my proposal, Eru Shoth?"

I had latched on to one hope. If I lived and let the Arameri use me, I might someday find a way free. Somehow. It was a thin hope, a pathetic one, but it was all I had.

"Will you settle things with the Order of Itempas for me?" I asked, trying for dignity. Now it was I who clung to Shiny for support. It was easier, somehow, to give up my soul with him there beside me.

T'vril inclined his head. "Already done."

"And"—I hesitated—"can I have your word that this mark, the one I must wear, will do nothing *but* what you said?"

He lifted an eyebrow. "You have little room to bargain here, Eru Shoth."

I flinched, because it was true, but I clenched my free hand, anyhow. I hated being threatened. "I could tell the godlings what I am. They'll kill me, but at least they won't use me the way you mean to."

The Lord Arameri sat back in his chair, crossing his legs. "You don't know that, Eru Shoth. Perhaps the godling you tell will have her own enemies to get rid of. Would you really risk exchanging a mortal master for an immortal one?"

That was a possibility that had never occurred to me. I froze, horrified by it.

"You will not be her master," Shiny said.

I jumped. T'vril drew in a deep breath, let it out. "My lord. I'm afraid you weren't privy to our earlier conversation. Eru Shoth is aware of the danger if she remains free." *And you are in no position to negotiate on her behalf,* his tone said. He did not have to say it aloud. It was painfully obvious.

"A danger that remains if *you* lay claim to her," Shiny snapped. I could hardly believe my ears. Was he actually trying to fight for me?

Shiny let go of my hand and stepped forward, not quite in front of me. "You cannot keep her existence a secret," he said. "You can't kill enough people to safely make her your weapon. It would be better if you had never brought her here—then at least you could deny knowledge of her existence."

I frowned in confusion. But T'vril uncrossed his legs.

"Do you intend to tell the other gods about her?" he asked quietly.

And then I understood. Shiny was not powerless. He could not be killed, not permanently. He could be imprisoned, but not forever, because he was supposed to be wandering the world, learning the lessons of mortality. At some point, inevitably, one of the other gods would come looking for him, if only to gloat over his punishment. And then T'vril's plan to make me the Arameri's latest weapon would come apart.

"I will say nothing," Shiny said softly, "if you let her go."

I caught my breath.

T'vril was silent for a moment. "No. My greatest concern

hasn't changed: she's too dangerous to leave unprotected. It would be safer to kill her." Which would erase Shiny's leverage, besides ending my life.

It was a game of *nikkim*: feint against feint, each trying to outplay the other. Except I had never paid attention to such games, because I could not see them, so I had no idea what happened if there was a draw. I definitely didn't like being the prize.

"She *was* safe until the Order began to harass her," Shiny said. "Anonymity has protected her bloodline for centuries, even from the gods. Give that to her again, and all will be as it was." Shiny paused. "You still have the demon blood you took from the House of the Risen Sun before you destroyed it."

"He took—" I blurted, then caught myself. But my hands clenched. Of course they would never have let such a valuable resource go to waste. My blood, Dateh's blood, the arrowheads— perhaps they had even learned Dateh's refining method. The Arameri had their weapon, with or without me. Damn them.

Shiny was right, though. If the Lord Arameri had that, then he didn't need me.

T'vril rose from his chair. He descended the steps and walked past the guards, moving to stand at one of the long windows. I saw him pause there, gazing out at the world that he owned— and at the black sun, warning sign of the gods who threatened it. He clasped his hands behind his back.

"Make her anonymous, you say," he said, and sighed. At that sigh, my heart made an uneasy leap of hope. "Very well. I'm willing to consider it. But how? Shall I kill anyone in the city who knows her? As you say, that would require more deaths than is practical."

I shuddered. Vuroy and the others from Art Row. My land-lord. The old woman across the street who gossiped to the neighbors about the blind girl and her godling boyfriend. Rimarn, the priests of the White Hall, a dozen nameless ser-vants and guards, including the ones standing here listening to all this.

"No," I blurted. "I'll leave Shadow. I was going to do it any-way. I'll go somewhere no one knows me, never talk to anyone, just don't—"

"Kill her," Shiny said.

I flinched and stared at his profile. He glanced at me. "If she is dead, her secrets no longer matter. No one will look for her. No one can use her."

I understood then, though the idea made me shiver. T'vril turned to look at us over his shoulder. "A false death? Interest-ing." He thought for a moment. "It would have to be thorough. She could never speak to her friends again, or even her mother. She could no longer be Oree Shoth at all. I can arrange for her to be sent elsewhere, with resources and a concocted past. Perhaps even hold a magnificent funeral for the brave woman who gave her life to expose a plot against the gods." He glanced at me. "But if my spies hear any rumor, any *hint* of your survival, then the game ends, Eru Shoth. I will do whatever is necessary to prevent you from falling into the wrong hands again. Is that understood?"

I stared at him, and at Shiny, and then at myself. At the body that I could see, as a shadowy outline against the constant glow of Sky's light. Breasts, gently rolling. Hands, fascinatingly com-plex as I lifted them, turned them, flexed the fingers. The tips of my feet. A spiraling curl of hair at the edge of my vision. I had never seen myself so completely before.

To die, even in this false way, would be terrible. My friends would mourn me, and I would mourn even more the life I'd already lost. My poor mother: first my father and now this. But it was the magic, the strangeness of Shadow, all the beautiful and frightening things that I had learned and experienced and *seen*, that would hurt most to leave behind.

I had once wanted to die. This would be worse. But if I did it, I would be free.

I must have stayed silent too long. Shiny turned to me, his heavy gaze more compassionate than I had ever imagined it could be. He understood; of course he did. It was a hard thing, sometimes, to live.

"I understand," I said to the Lord Arameri.

He nodded. "Then it shall be done. Remain here another day. That should be sufficient time for me to make the arrangements." He turned back to the window, another wordless dismissal.

I stood there unmoving, hardly daring to believe it. I was free. *Free*, like old times.

Shiny turned to leave, then turned back to me, radiating irritation at my failure to follow. Like old times.

Except that he had fought for me. And won.

I trotted after him and took his arm, and if it bothered him that I pressed my face against his shoulder as we walked back to my room, he did not complain.

19

"The Demons' War"
(charcoal and chalk on black paper)

It should have ended there. That would have been best, wouldn't it? A fallen god, a "dead" demon, two broken souls limping back toward life. That would have been the end that this tale deserved, I think. Quiet. Ordinary.

But that wouldn't have been good for you, would it? Too lacking in closure. Not dramatic enough. I will tell myself, then, that what happened next was a fortunate thing, though even now it feels anything but.

I slept deeply that night, despite my fear of what was to come, despite my worry about Paitya and the others, despite my cynical suspicion that the Lord Arameri would find some other way to keep me under his graceful, kindly thumb. My arm had healed completely, so I stripped off the bandages and the sling and the sigil-script, took a long, deep bath to celebrate the absence of pain, and curled up against Shiny's warmth. He shifted on the bed to make room for me, and I felt him watching me as I fell asleep.

Sometime after midnight, I woke with a start, blinking in disorientation as I rolled over. The room was quiet and still; Sky's magical walls were too thick to let me hear movement in the halls beyond, or even the sound of the wind that must surely be fierce outside, up so high. In that, I preferred the House of the Risen Sun, where at least there had been small sounds of life all around me—people walking through the corridors, chanting and songs, the occasional creaking and groaning of the Tree as it swayed. I would not miss the House, or its people, but being there had not been wholly unpleasant.

Here there was only the quiet, bright-glowing stillness. Shiny was asleep beside me, his breathing deep and slow. I tried to remember if I'd had a nightmare but could recall nothing. Pushing myself up, I looked around the room because I could. There would be things I'd miss about Sky, too. I saw nothing, but my nerves still jumped and my skin still tingled, as if something had touched me.

Then I heard a sound behind me like tearing air.

I whirled, my thoughts frozen, and it was behind me: a hole the height of my body, like a great, open mouth. Stupid, stupid. I had known he was still out there but thought myself safe in the stronghold of the Arameri. Stupid, stupid, stupid.

I was halfway across the bed, dragged by the hole's power, before I could open my mouth to cry out. Convulsively, my hands locked on the sheets, but I knew it was futile. In my mind's eye, I saw the sheets simply pull free of the bed, fluttering uselessly as I disappeared into whatever hell Dateh had built to hold me.

There was a jerk, so hard that friction heat burned my knuckles. The sheets had caught on something. A hand wrapped around my wrist. *Shiny.*

I shot backward into the terrible metal roar, and he came with me. I felt his presence even as I screamed and flailed, even as the feel of his hand on my wrist faded into cold numbness. We tumbled through trembling darkness, falling sideways into—

Sensation and solidity. I struck the ground—ground?—first, hard enough to jar the breath from my body. I *felt* the breath. Shiny landed nearby, uttering a grunt of pain, but at once he rolled to his feet, pulling me up, too. I caught my breath and looked around wildly, though I could see only darkness.

Then my eyes caught on something: a faint, blurry form, curled and fetal, hovering amid the dark. Dateh? But it did not move, and then I saw the shimmer of something between me and the form. Like glass. I turned again, trying to comprehend, and saw another murky form, hovering in the dark beyond the glass. This one I recognized by her brown skin: Kitr. She did not move. I reached for her, but when my hands encountered the glassy dark, they stopped. It was solid, enclosing us entirely above and around, a bubble of normality carved out of the Empty's hellish substance.

I turned again, and there was Dateh.

He was closer to us than the blurry forms, on the other side of the wide room that the bubble formed. I wasn't sure he knew we were there (though his will had brought us here), because his back was to us, and he crouched amid sprawled bodies. I could not see the bodies, except where their dimness occluded my view of Dateh, but I could taste blood in the air, thick and sickly and fresh. I heard the sounds I had hoped never to hear again: tearing flesh. Chewing teeth.

I stiffened and felt Shiny's hand tighten on my wrist. So he, too, could see Dateh, which meant there was light in this empty world. And it meant Shiny could see which of his children lay around us, sprawled and desecrated, the magic of their lives long gone.

Tears of helpless rage pricked my eyes. Not again. *Not again.* "Gods damn you, Dateh," I whispered.

Dateh paused in whatever he was doing. He turned to us, still in a crouch, moving in an odd, scuttling manner. His mouth, robes, and hands were stained dark, and his left hand was closed around a dripping lump. He blinked at us like a man coming out of a fugue. I could not see the demarcation between pupil and iris in his eyes; they looked like a single dark pit, too large, carved into the white.

He seemed to recall himself slowly. "Where is Serymn?" he asked.

"Dead," I snapped.

He frowned at this, as if confused. Slowly he rose to his feet. He drew a breath to speak again, then paused as he noticed the heart in his hand. Frowning, he tossed it aside and stepped closer to us. "Where is my wife?" he asked again.

I scowled, but behind my bravado, I was terrified. I could feel power sluicing off him like water, pressing against my skin, making it crawl. It shimmered around him, making the whole chamber flicker unsteadily. He had been missing since the Arameri raid on the House of the Risen Sun. Had he spent all that time hiding here, killing and eating godlings, making himself stronger? And madder?

"Serymn is *dead*, you monster," I said. "Didn't you hear me? The gods took her to their realm for punishment, and she deserved it. They'll find you, too, soon."

Dateh stopped. His frown deepened, and he shook his head. "She isn't dead. I would know."

I shuddered. So the Nightlord had been in a creative mood

after all. "Then she will be. Unless you mean to challenge the Three now?"

"I have always meant to challenge them, Lady Oree." Dateh shook his head again, then smiled with bloody teeth. It was the first hint of his old self I had seen, but it chilled me nevertheless. He had eaten the godlings in hope of stealing their power, and it seemed he had managed to do so. But something else had gone very, very wrong. That was plain in his smile and in the emptiness of his eyes.

It is bad, very bad, for a mortal to eat one of us, Lil had said.

He turned, surveying his handiwork. The bodies seemed to please him, because he laughed, the sound echoing within the space of his bubble. "We demons are the gods' children, too, are we not? Yet they have hunted us nearly to extinction. *How is that right?*" I jumped at the last, because he shouted it. But when he spoke again, he laughed. "I say that if they fear us so, we should give them something to fear: their despised, persecuted children, coming to take their place."

"Don't be absurd," said Shiny. He still gripped my wrist; through this I felt the tension in his body. He was afraid—but along with the fear, he was *angry*. "No mortal can wield a god's power. Even if you could defeat the Three, the very universe would unravel under your feet."

"I can create a new one!" Dateh cried, delighted, demented. "You hid yourself within my Emptiness, didn't you, Oree Shoth? Untrained, in terror, with nothing but instinct, you carved out a safer realm for yourself." To my horror, he held his hand out as if he actually expected me to take it. "It is why Serymn hoped to win you to our cause. I can create only this one realm, but you've already built dozens. You can help me build a world where mortals need never live in fear of their gods. Where you and I will *be* gods, in our own right, as we should be."

I stumbled back from his outstretched hand and stopped as I felt the solid curve of Dateh's barrier behind me. Nowhere to run.

"Your gift has existed before among our kind," said Dateh. He gave up reaching for me but watched me around Shiny's shoulder with a hunger that was almost sexual. "It was rare, though—even when there were hundreds of us. Only Enefa's children possessed it. I need that magic, Lady Oree."

"What in the Maelstrom are you talking about?" I demanded. I frantically groped along the hard surface behind me, half hoping to find a doorknob. "You've already made me kill for you. What, you expect me to eat godling flesh and go mad with you, too?"

He blinked, startled. "Oh...no. No. You were a godling's lover. *I* never believed you could be trusted. But your magic need not be lost. I can consume *your* heart and then wield your power myself."

I froze, my blood turning to ice. Shiny, however, stepped forward, in front of me.

"Oree," he said softly. "Use your magic to leave this place."

I started out of horror and fumbled for him, finding his shoulder. To my confusion, he was not tense at all, unafraid. "I...I don't—"

He ignored my babbling. "You've broken his power before. Open a door back to Sky. I will make certain he doesn't follow."

I could see him, I realized. He had begun to glow, god-power rising as he committed himself to protecting me.

Dateh bared his teeth and spread his arms. "Get out of my way," he snarled.

I blinked, squinted, flinched. *He* had begun to glow as well, but with a jarring, sickening clash of colors, more than I could name. It made my stomach churn to look at him. The colors were bright, though, so bright. He was more powerful than I had ever dreamt.

I did not understand why until I blinked and my eyes made that strange, involuntary adjustment that hurt so much—and suddenly I *saw* Dateh, through whatever veil he'd cast around himself with his scrivening skills.

And I screamed. Because what stood there, enormous and heaving, rocking on twenty legs and flailing with as many arms—*and oh gods, oh gods, his FACE*—was too hideous for me to take without some outlet for my horror.

Shiny rounded on me. "Do as I say! Now!"

And then he charged forward, blazing, to meet Dateh's challenge.

"No," I whispered, shaking my head. I could not take my eyes from the great gabbling thing Dateh had become. I wanted to deny what I had seen in Dateh's face: Paitya's gentle smile, Dump's square teeth, *Madding's eyes*. And many others. There was almost nothing left of Dateh himself—nothing but will and hate. How many godlings had he consumed? Enough to over-whelm his humanity and grant him unimaginable power.

No one could fight such a creature and hope to survive. Not even Shiny. Dateh would kill him and then come eat my heart. I would be trapped within him, my very soul enslaved, forever.

"*No!*" I ran for the wall of the bubble, slapping its cold shim-mering surface with my hands. I could not think through my terror. My breath came in gasps. I wanted nothing more than to escape.

My hands suddenly became visible. And between my hands, something new flickered into view.

I stopped, startled out of panic. The new thing rotated before me, flickering faintly, a bauble of silvery light. As I stared at it, I realized there was a face in its surface. I blinked, and the face blinked, too. It was *me*. The image—a mirror reflection, I realized, something else I had heard of but never seen—was distorted by the bubble's shape, but I could make out the curve of cheekbones, lips open in a sob, white teeth.

But most clearly, I could see my eyes.

They were not what I expected. Where my irises should have been, dull disks of twisted gray, I saw instead brilliance: tiny winking, wavering lights. My malformed corneas had withdrawn, opening like a flower, to reveal something even stranger inside.

What—?

There was a cry behind me and the sound of a blow. As I turned, something streaked across my vision like a comet. But this comet screamed as it fell, trailing fire like blood. Shiny.

Dateh uttered a rattling hiss, raising two of his stolen arms. Light, sickly mottled, dripped from his hands like oil and splattered the floor of the Empty realm. Where it fell, I heard hissing.

The small bubble winked out of existence between my hands.

Escape and strange magic forgotten, I ran to where Shiny lay, not so shiny now, and not moving. He was alive, I found as I pulled him onto his back; breathing, at least, though raggedly. But crossing his chest from shoulder to hip was a streak of darkness, an obscene obliteration of his light. I touched it, my hand trembling, but there was no wound. No magic, either.

Then I understood: whatever it was that made demon blood negate the magic of a god's life-essence, Dateh had found a way to channel it—or perhaps this was simply the culmination of what he had become. Not just a demon but a god whose very nature was mortality. He was turning Shiny back into an ordinary man, piece by piece. And once that was done, he would tear Shiny apart.

"Lady Oree," breathed the thing that had been Dateh. I could no longer think of it as a man. Its voice overlapped upon itself: I heard him echo in female registers, other males, older, younger. It wheezed as it lumbered toward me. Perhaps it had developed multiple lungs, or whatever godlings shaped within their bodies to simulate breath.

It said, "We are the last of our kind, you and I. I was wrong, wrong, wrong to threaten you." It paused, shook its massive head as if to clear it. "But I need your power. Join me, use it for me, and I'll do you no harm." It took a step closer, six feet shuffling at once.

I did not, dared not, trust the Dateh creature. Even if I agreed to its plan, its sanity was as distorted as the rest of its form; it might still kill me on a whim. It would kill Shiny regardless, I was certain—permanently, irreversibly. What would happen to the universe if one of the Three died? Would this god-eating madman even care?

Unthinking, I clutched at Shiny, a bulwark against fear. He stirred under my hands, semiconscious, no protection at all. Even his light had begun to fade. But he was not dead. Perhaps if I stalled for time, he could recover.

"J-join you?" I asked.

Dateh's form shivered, then resolved again into the ordinary, mortal shape that I had known in the House of the Risen Sun. It was an illusion. I could *feel* the warped reality still present, even if it had found a way to fool my eyes. Dateh was like Lil, safe on the surface, horror underneath.

"Yes," it said, and this time it spoke in a single voice. It gestured behind itself, toward the corpses I knew were there. "I could train you. Make you st-st-strong." The Dateh-creature paused then, eyes unfocusing for a moment, and there was that curious blurring again, the outward mask cracking for an instant. The effort needed to hold that mask in place was a taut, palpable thing. No wonder the Dateh-creature hesitated to devour me; one more heart, one more stolen soul, might be too much to contain.

Shiny groaned, and the creature's face hardened. "But you must do something for me." Its voice had changed. I choked back a sob. It spoke with Madding's voice, gentle and persuasive. Its hands flexed from fists to claws and back. "That creature in your lap. I thought he had no true magic, but now I see I underestimated him."

My vision blurred with tears as I shook my head, and I reached across Shiny's body as if I could somehow protect him. "No," I blurted. "I won't let you kill him, too. No."

"I want *you* to kill him, Oree. Kill him, and take his heart."

I froze, staring at Dateh, my mouth falling open.

It smiled again, its teeth flickering from Dateh's to Dump's back to Dateh's. "You love too many of these gods," it said. "I need proof of your commitment. So kill him, Oree. Kill him and take that shining power for your own. When you've done it, you'll understand how much more you were meant to be."

"I can't." I was trembling all over. I barely heard myself. "I can't."

The Dateh-creature smiled, and this time its teeth were sharp, like a dog's. "You can. Your blood will work, if you use enough of it." He gestured, and a knife appeared on Shiny's chest. It was black, shimmering like solid mist—a piece of the Empty given form. "I will have your power one way or another, Lady Oree. Eat him and join me, or I eat you. Choose."

You may think me a coward.

You'll remember that I fled when Shiny told me to, instead of staying to fight at his side. You will remember that throughout this final horror, I was useless, helpless, too terrified to be any good to anyone, including myself. It may be that by telling you this, I have earned your contempt.

I won't try to change your mind. I'm not proud of myself or the things I did in that hell. I can't explain it, anyhow—no words can capture the terror that I felt in those moments, faced with the starkest, ugliest choice that any creature on this earth must face: kill, or die. Eat, or be eaten.

I will say this, though: I think I made the choice that any woman would when confronted by the monster that murdered her beloved.

I set the knife aside. Didn't need it. Shiny's chest heaved like a bellows. Whatever Dateh had done had hurt him badly, despite the magic that still wavered around him. Unnecessarily, I smoothed the cloth across his chest, then rested my hands there, one on either side of his heart.

My tears fell onto my hands in a patter of threes: one two

three, one two *three*, one two *three*. Like the weeper-bird's cry. *Oree, oree, oree.*

I chose to live.

The paint was the door, my father had taught me, and belief was the key that unlocked it. Beneath my hands, Shiny's heart beat steady, strong.

"I paint a picture," I whispered.

I chose to fight.

Dateh let out a rattling sigh of pleasure as the shimmering bubble formed again between my hands, hovering just above Shiny's heart. I knew what it was at last—the visible manifestation of my will. My power, inherited from my god ancestors and distilled through generations of humanity, given shape and energy and *potential*. That was all magic was, really, in the end. Possibility. With it I could create anything, provided I believed. A painted world. A memory of home. A bloody hole.

I willed it into Shiny's body. It passed through his flesh harmlessly, settling amid the steady, strong pulses of his heart.

I looked up at Dateh. Something changed in me then; I don't know what. All at once, Dateh hissed in alarm and stepped back, staring at my eyes as if they had turned to stars.

Perhaps they had.

I chose to believe.

"*Itempas*," I said.

Lightning blazed out of nothingness.

The concussion of it stunned both Dateh and me. I was flung backward, slamming against Dateh's barrier with enough force to knock the breath from my body. I fell to the ground, dazed but laughing, because this was so familiar to me and because I was no longer afraid. I *believed*, after all. I knew it was over, even if Dateh had yet to learn that lesson.

A new sun blazed in the middle of Dateh's Empty, too bright to look upon directly. The heat of it was terrible even from where I lay, enough to tighten my skin and take my breath away. Around this sun glimmered an aura of pure white light— but it did not merely glow in every direction, this aura. Lines and curves seared my sight before I looked away, forming rings within rings, lines connecting, circles overlapping, godwords forming and marching and fading out of thin air. The sheer complexity of the design would have stunned me in itself, but each of the rings turned in dizzying, graceful gyroscopic patterns around a human form.

I stole a series of sweeping glances through the brilliance and made out a corona of glowing hair, a warrior's garments done in shades of pale, and a slender, white-metaled straightsword held in one perfect black hand. I could not see his face—too bright—but it was impossible not to see his eyes. They opened as I watched, piercing the unrelenting white with colors I had only heard of in poetry: fire opal. Sunset's cloak. Velvet and desire.

I could not help remembering a day, so long ago, when I'd found a man in a muckbin. They had been the same eyes then, but so much more beautiful now, incandescent, assured, that there was no sense in comparing.

"Itempas," I said again, reverent.

Those eyes turned to me, and it did not bother me that I saw no recognition in them. He saw me and knew me for one of His children, but no more than that. An entity so far beyond humanity had no need of human ties. It was enough for me that He saw, and His gaze was warm.

Before Him huddled the Dateh-creature, thrown by the same blast of power that had flattened me. As I watched, it clambered unsteadily to its many feet, the mask of its humanity shattered.

"What the hells are you?" the Dateh-creature demanded.

"A shaper," said the Lord of Light. He raised his sword of white steel. I saw hundreds of godwords in filigreed patterns along the blade's length. "I am all knowledge and purpose defined. I strengthen what exists and cull that which should not."

His voice made the darkness of the Empty tremble. I laughed again, filled with inexpressable joy. Pain suddenly blossomed in my eyes, grinding, terrible. I clung to my joy and fought back against it, unwilling to look away. My god stood before me. No Maroneh had seen Him since the earliest days of the world. I would not let a simple thing like physical weakness interfere.

The Dateh-creature shouted with its many voices and let loose a wave of magic so tainted that the air turned brown and foul. Itempas batted this aside with all the effort of an afterthought. I heard a clear ringing note in the wake of His movement.

"Enough," He said, His eyes turning dark and red like a cold day's sunset. "Release my children."

The creature stiffened all over. Its eyes—Madding's eyes—grew wide. Something stirred at its midriff, then bulged obscenely in its throat. It fought this with an effort of sheer will, setting its teeth and straining. I felt it struggling to hold all the power it had swallowed into itself. This was futile, however, and a moment later it threw back its head and screamed, streams of viscous color fountaining from its throat.

Each color evaporated in the blaze of Itempas's white heat, becoming thin, shimmering mist. The mists flew to Him, swirling and entwining until they formed a new ring of His multilayered aura, this one turning in front of Him.

He lifted a hand and the mists contracted to encircle it. Even through my agony I felt their delight.

"I'm sorry," He said, His beautiful eyes full of pain. (So familiar, that.) "I have been a poor father, but I will do better. I will become the father you deserve." The ring coalesced further, becoming a swirling sphere that hovered over His palm. "Go and be free."

He blew on the gathered souls, and they scattered into nothingness. Did I imagine that one of them, a green-blue helix, lingered a moment longer? Perhaps. Even so, it vanished, too.

Then Dateh stood alone, half slumped and knees buckling, just a man again.

"I didn't know," he whispered, gazing at the shining figure in wonder, in fear. He fell to his knees, his hands shaking as if palsied. "I didn't know it was *you*. Forgive me!" Tears ran down his face, some caused by fear, but some, I understood, were tears of awe. I knew, because the same tears ran slow and thick down my own face.

Bright Itempas smiled. I could not see His face through the glory of His light, or my hot tears, but I felt that smile along every inch of my skin. It was a warm smile—loving, benevolent. Kindly. Everything I had always believed Him to be.

The white blade flashed. That was the only way I knew that it moved; otherwise I would have thought it had simply appeared, conjured from one place to another, through the center of Dateh's chest. Dateh did not cry out, though his eyes widened. He looked down and saw his lifeblood begin threading the Bright Lord's narrow blade in pulses: one-one, two-two, three-three. The sword was so fine, the strike so precise even through bone, that his pierced heart just kept beating.

I waited for the Bright Lord to withdraw the sword and let Dateh die. But He reached out then, with the hand that did not hold the sword. The smile was still on His face, warm and gentle and utterly merciless. There was no contradiction in this as He took hold of Dateh's face.

I had to look away then. The pain in my eyes had grown too great. I saw only red now, and it was not anger. I *heard* it, though, when Dateh began to scream. I *felt* reverberations in the air as bones cracked and ground together, as Dateh flailed and struggled and finally just twitched. I smelled fire, smoke, and the greasy acridity of burned flesh.

I tasted satisfaction then. It was not sweet, or filling, but it would do.

Then the Empty was gone, shattering around us, but I was barely aware of it. There was only the red, red pain. I thought I saw Sky's glowing floor beneath me, and I tried to push myself up, but the pain was too great. I fell, curling in on myself, too sick to retch.

Warm hands lifted me, so familiar. They touched my face,

brushing away the strange thick tears that issued from my eyes. I worried, irrationally, about staining His perfect white garments with blood.

"You have given me back myself, Oree," said that shining, knowing voice. I wept harder and loved it helplessly. "To be whole again, after all these centuries... I had forgotten the feeling. But you must stop now. I would not add your death to my crimes."

It hurt so much. I had believed, and belief had become magic, but I was only mortal. The magic had limits. Yet how could I stop myself from believing? How did one find a god, and love Him, and let Him go?

The voice changed, becoming softer. Human. Familiar. "Please, Oree."

My heart called him Shiny even though my mind insisted on something else. That was enough to stop me doing whatever I was doing, and I felt the change in my eyes. Suddenly I could no longer see the glowing floor, or anything else, but the pain in my head immediately diminished from a shriek to a chronic moan. My whole body went limp with relief.

"Rest now." The disordered bed beneath me. Sheets came up to my chin. I began to shiver violently—shock. A big hand stroked the soft mass of my hair. I whimpered because this made my head hurt worse. "Shhh. I will care for you."

I did not plan what I said then. I was in too much pain, half delirious. But I asked through chattering teeth, "Are you my friend now?"

"Yes," he replied. "As you are mine."

I could not help smiling all the way into dreams.

20

"Life"
(oil study)

MORE THAN A YEAR it took me to heal.

The first two weeks of that I spent in Sky, comatose. The Lord Arameri, summoned to my room to find a barely alive demon, an exhausted fallen god, several dead and nearly dead godlings, and a human-shaped pile of ash, reacted remarkably well. He sent for Sieh again and apparently spun a magnificent tale of Dateh attacking Sky only to be repelled and ultimately destroyed by Shiny, the latter acting to defend mortal lives. Which was more or less true, as the Lord Arameri had learned long ago that it was difficult to lie to gods. (Not for nothing was he ruler of the world.)

I slept right through the restoration of the sun. I'm told the whole city celebrated for days. Wish I could have been there.

Later, when I regained consciousness and the scriveners at last pronounced me well enough to travel, I was quietly relocated to the city of Strafe, in a small barony called Ripa on the northeastern coast of the Senm continent. There I became Desola Mokh, a tragically blind young Maroneh woman who had been fortunate enough to come into money after the death of her only remaining relative. Strafe was a midsized city, really a large small town, best known for cheap fishskin leather and mediocre wine. I had a modest town house near the ocean, with—I am told—a lovely view of both the placid town center and the churning Repentance Sea. I liked the sea, at least; the smell reminded me of good days in Nimaro.

With me traveled Enmitan Zobindi, a taciturn Maro man who was neither my husband nor a relative. (This was the talk of the town for weeks.) He earned the not-unfriendly nickname of Shadow, as in Desola's Shadow, because he was most often seen running errands around town for me. The town ladies, who eventually overcame their nervousness about approaching us, dropped polite hints during their weekly visits that I should just go ahead and marry the man, since he was doing the work of a husband, anyhow. I merely smiled, and eventually they got over it.

If they had asked, I might have felt contrary enough to tell them: Shiny wasn't doing *all* the work of a husband. At night we shared a bed, as we had done since the House of the Risen Sun. It was convenient, since the town house was drafty; I saved a lot of money on firewood. It was comforting, too, since more often than not, I awoke crying or screaming in the night. Shiny held me, and often caressed me, and occasionally kissed me. That was all I needed to regain my emotional equilibrium, so it was all I asked of him, and all he offered. He could not be Madding for me. I could not be Nahadoth or Enefa. Still, each of us managed to fulfill the other's basic needs.

He talked more, I should note. In fact, he told me many things about his former life, some of which I've now told you. Some of what he told me I'll never tell.

And—oh, yes. I had become blind, fully and truly.

My ability to see magic never returned after the battle with

Dateh. My paintings were just paint now, nothing special. I still enjoyed creating them, but I could not see them. When I went for walks in the evening, I went slower, because there was no Tree glimmer or godling leavings to see by. Even if I'd still been able to perceive such things, there would have been nothing to see. Strafe was not Shadow. It was a very unmagical town.

It took me a long while to get used to this.

But I was human, and Shiny was more or less the same, so it was inevitable that things would change.

I had been in the garden planting, since it was finally full springtime. I had some winter onions cradled in my skirt, and my hands and clothes were stained with soil and grass. I'd put a kerchief on my head to hold back my hair and was thinking about anything but Shadow and old times. This was a good thing. A new thing.

So I was less than pleased to walk into my toolshed and find a godling waiting for me.

"Don't you look good," said Nemmer. I recognized her voice, but it still startled me. I dropped the onions. They thumped to the floor and rolled around for what sounded like an obscene amount of time.

Not bothering to pick them up, I stared in her direction. She may have thought I was astonished. I wasn't. It was just that I remembered the last time I'd seen her, at Madding's house. With Madding. It took me a moment to master my feelings.

Finally I said, "I thought godlings weren't allowed to leave Shadow."

"I'm the goddess of stealth, Oree Shoth. I do a lot of things that I'm not supposed to." She paused in surprise. "You can't see me, can you?"

"No," I said, and left it at that.

So did she, thankfully. "Wasn't easy to find you. The Arameri did a good job of covering your tracks. I honestly thought you were dead for a while. Lovely funeral, by the way."

"Thank you," I said. I hadn't attended. "Why are you here?"

She whistled at my tone. "You certainly aren't happy to see me. What's wrong?" I heard her push aside some of the tools and pots on my workbench and sit down. "Afraid I'll out you as the last living demon?"

I had lived without fear for more than a year, so it was slow to awaken in me. I only sighed and knelt to begin collecting the spilled onions. "I suppose it was inevitable you would find out *why* the Arameri 'killed' me."

"Mmm, yes. Nummy secrets." I heard her kick her feet idly, like a little girl nibbling a cookie. "I promised Mad, after all, that I'd find out who was killing our siblings."

At that, I sat back on my heels. I still felt no fear. "I had nothing to do with Role. That was Dateh. The rest, though..." I had no idea, so I shrugged. "It could have been either of us. They started taking my blood not long after they kidnapped me. The only one I'm sure was my fault was Madding."

"I wouldn't say it was your *fault*—" Nemmer began.

"I would."

An uncomfortable silence fell.

"Are you going to kill me now?" I asked.

There was another pause that told me she'd been considering it. "No."

"Do you want my blood for yourself, then?"

"Gods, no! What do you take me for?"

"An assassin."

I felt her stare at me, her consternation churning the air of the small room. "I don't want your blood," she said finally. "In fact, I'm planning to do all I can to make sure anyone *else* who figures out your secret dies before they can act on it. The Arameri were right about anonymity being your surest protection. I intend to make sure even *they* don't remember your existence for long."

"Lord T'vril—"

"Knows his place. I'm sure he could be persuaded to remove certain records from the family archive in exchange for my silence about his carefully hidden stash of demons' blood. Which isn't hidden as well as he thinks it is."

"I see." My head was beginning to hurt. Not from magic, just pure irritation. There were aspects of life in Shadow that I did not miss. "Why did you come, then?"

She kicked her feet again. "I thought you'd want to know. Kitr runs Madding's organization now, with Istan."

I didn't know the latter name, but I was relieved—more than I'd ever expected to be—to hear that Kitr was alive. I licked my lips. "What about . . . the others?"

"Lil is fine. The demon couldn't take her." With the clarity of intuition, I realized Dateh had become "the demon" for Nemmer. I was something else. "She almost killed him, in fact; he fled from their battle. She's taken over the Shustocks junkyard—Dump's old place?—and Ancestors' Village." At my look of alarm, she added, "She doesn't eat anyone who doesn't want to be eaten. In fact, she's rather protective of the children; their hunger for love seems to fascinate her. And for some reason, she's gained a taste for being worshipped lately."

I couldn't help laughing at that. "What about—"

"None of the others survived," she said. My laughter died.

After a moment of silence, Nemmer added, "Your friends from Art Row are all fine, though."

That was very good, but it hurt me most of all to think about that part of my old life, so I said, "Did you have a chance to check on my mother?"

"No, sorry. Getting out of the city is difficult enough. I could make only one trip."

I nodded slowly and resumed picking up onions. "Thank you for doing it. Really."

Nemmer hopped down and helped me. "You seem to have a good life here, at least. How is, ah..." I smelled her discomfort, like a toe of garlic amid the onions.

"He's better," I said. "Do you want to talk to him? He went to the market. Should be back soon."

"Went to the market." Nemmer weakly let out a little laugh. "Will wonders never cease."

We got the onions into a basket. I sat back, mopping my now-sweaty brow with a dirty hand. She sat there beside me on her knees, thinking a daughter's thoughts. "I think he'd be happy if you stayed," I said softly. "Or came back at some point in the future. I think he misses all of you."

"I'm not sure I miss him," she said, though her tone said something entirely different. Abruptly she got to her feet, brushing off her knees unnecessarily. "I'll think about it."

I rose as well. "All right." I considered whether to invite her to stay for dinner, then decided against it. Despite what it might have meant to Shiny, I didn't really want her to stay. She didn't really want to, either. An awkward silence descended between us.

"I'm glad you're well, Oree Shoth," she said finally.

I extended my hand to her, not worrying about the dirt. She was a god. If dirt bothered her, she could will it away. "It was good seeing you, Lady Nemmer."

She laughed, easing the awkwardness. "I told you not to call me 'Lady.' You mortals all make me feel so *old*, I swear." But she took my hand and squeezed it before vanishing.

I puttered about in the shed awhile, then went into the house and upstairs to bathe. After that, I put my hair back in a braid, donned a thick, warm robe, and curled up in my favorite chair, thinking.

Evening fell. I heard Shiny come in downstairs, wipe his feet, and begin putting away the supplies he'd bought. Eventually he came upstairs and stopped, standing in the doorway, looking at me. Then he came over to the bed and sat down, waiting for me to tell him what was wrong. He talked more these days, but only when the mood took him, and that was rare. For the most part, he was just a very quiet man. I liked that about him, especially now. His silent presence soothed my loneliness in a way that talking would only have irritated.

So I got up and went over to the bed. I found his face with my hands, traced its stern lines. He shaved his head bald every morning. That kept people from realizing it was completely white, which was too striking for the low profile we were trying to keep. He was handsome enough without it, but I missed pushing my fingers into his hair. I ran my fingers across his smooth scalp instead, wistful.

Shiny regarded me for a moment, thoughtful. Then he reached up and untied the sash of my robe, tugging it open. I froze, startled, as he gazed at me—nothing more than that. But as he had somehow done long ago, on a rooftop in another life, just that look made me incredibly aware of my body, and his nearness, and all the potential that lay therein. When he took hold of my hips, there was absolutely no doubt as to what he intended. Then he pulled me closer.

I pulled back instead, too stunned to react otherwise. If my skin hadn't still tingled where he'd touched me, I would have thought I'd imagined the whole thing. But that, and the roaring-awake of certain parts of me that had been mostly asleep for a long while, told me it was very real.

Shiny lowered his hands when I stepped back. He didn't seem upset, or concerned. He just waited.

I laughed weakly, suddenly nervous. "I thought you weren't interested."

He said nothing, of course, because it was obvious that had changed.

I fidgeted, pushing up my sleeves (they fell back down immediately), tucking back a stray curl of hair, shifting from foot to foot. I didn't close the open robe, though.

"I don't know—" I began.

"I have decided to live," he said quietly.

That, too, was obvious from the way he'd changed in the past year. I felt his gaze as he spoke, heavier than usual along my skin. He had been my friend, and now offered more. Was *willing to try* more. But I knew: he was not the sort of man who loved easily, or casually. If I wanted him, I would have all of him, and he wanted all of me. All or nothing; that was as fundamental to his nature as light itself.

I tried to joke. "It took you a year to decide that?"

"Ten, yes," Shiny replied. "This last year was for *you* to decide."

I blinked in surprise, but then I realized he was right. *Such a strange thing*, I thought, and smiled.

Then I stepped forward again, found his face, and kissed him. It was much better than that long-ago night on Madding's roof, probably because he wasn't trying to hurt me this time. The same incredible gentleness without malice—nice. He tasted of apples, which he must've eaten on his way back from town, and radishes, which were not so pleasant. I didn't mind. I felt his eyes on me the whole time. *He would be the type*, I thought, but then I hadn't closed mine, either.

It did feel strange, though, and until he'd taken hold of my waist again, pulling me where he wanted so he could do all the things his gaze had implied, I didn't realize what it was that had me confused. Then he did something that made me gasp, and I realized Shiny's kiss had been just a kiss. Just one mouth on another, with no impression of colors or music or soaring on unseen winds. It had been so long since I'd kissed a mortal that I'd forgotten we couldn't do that.

That was all right, though. There were other things we could do just fine.

I slept well into the small hours, until a dream made me start awake. I kicked Shiny in the shin inadvertently, but he did not react. I touched his face and realized he was awake, untroubled by my thrashing.

"Did you sleep at all?" I yawned.

"No."

I couldn't remember the dream, but the feeling of unease it had given me lingered. I pushed myself up from his chest and rubbed my face, bleary and painfully aware of the unlovely taste of my mouth. Outside I could hear a few determined birds beginning their morning song, though the chill in the air told me it wasn't yet dawn. Otherwise it was quiet—that eerie, not-quite-comforting quiet one finds in small towns before dawn. Not even the fishermen were up. In Shadow, I thought with fleeting sadness, the birds would not have been so alone.

"Everything all right?" I asked. "I can make some tea."

"No." He reached up then to touch my face, as I so often did with him. Since his eyes worked just fine, I wondered if I dared take it as a gesture of affection. Maybe the room was just dark. He was always a hard man to read, and now I had to learn a whole new set of interpretations for the things he did.

"I want you," he said.

Or he could just tell me. I couldn't help laughing, though I nuzzled his hand to let him know his advance wasn't unwelcome. "We're going to have to work on your bedroom talk, I think."

He sat up, shifting me easily to his lap, and pulled me into a kiss before I could warn him about my breath. His was no better. But it was my turn to be surprised, because as he deepened the kiss and smoothed his hands down my arms, gently pulling them behind me, I felt something. A flicker. A trickle of heat— real heat. Not passion, but *fire*.

I gasped, my eyes widening as he pulled back.

"I want to be inside you," he said, his voice low, implacable. One of his hands pinned my wrists behind my back; the other massaged elsewhere, just right. I think I made a sound. I'm not sure. "I want to watch the dawnlight break across your skin. I want you to scream as the sun rises. I don't care what name you call."

That has to be the most unromantic thing I've ever heard, I thought giddily. He touched me more then, kissing, tasting, caressing. He had learned much about me in our previous session, which this time he used to ruthless effect. When his teeth grazed my throat, I cried out and arched backward, not quite voluntarily. The way he was holding my wrists meant that I bent how he wanted me to bend. He wasn't hurting me—I could feel the care he took to avoid that—but I couldn't break his grip. I trembled, my eyelids fluttering shut, fear and arousal making me light-headed as I finally understood.

Sunrise was coming. I had made love to a godling, but this was different. I could no longer see the glow rise in Shiny's body, but I had tasted the first stirrings of magic in his kiss. He was not quite my Shiny, not anymore, and he would be nothing like my cool, carefree Madding. He would be a thing of heat and intensity and absolute power.

Could I lie down with something like that and get up whole?

"I want to be myself for you, Oree," he whispered against my skin. "Just once." Not a plea—never that. An explanation.

I closed my eyes and made myself relax. I couldn't bring myself to speak, but I didn't have to. My trust was enough.

So he lifted us, turning to put me under him on the bed, this time pinioning my arms above my head. I lay passive, knowing that he needed this. The control. He had so little power these days; what he could claim was precious to him. For some moments, he simply looked at me. His gaze was like feathers on my skin, a torment. When he actually touched me, it had the weight of command. I arched and shuddered and opened myself to him. I could not help it. As he pressed against me, into me, I felt the impossible heat of his body rise. He moved slowly at first, concentrating, whispering something. Godwords, like a prayer, almost at the threshold of my ability to hear them. The magic would not work for him, would it?

but he is different now, this is different—

and then I felt the words on my skin. I don't know how I knew they were words. I shouldn't have. Usually only my fingers were that sensitive, but now my thighs made out the arcs and curves and jagged turns of gods' language, each character perfectly clear in my mind. It was more than words; there were strange tilted lines, too, and numbers, and other symbols whose purpose I could not decipher. Too complex. He had created language at the beginning of time, and it had always been his most subtle instrument. The words slid along my skin, wending down my legs, circling my breasts—gods. There are no mortal words for how it felt, but I writhed, how I writhed. He watched me, heard me whimper, and was pleased. I felt that, too.

"Oree," he said. Only that. I heard whispers behind it, a dozen voices—all his—overlapping. The word took on a dozen different layers of meaning, encompassing lust, fear, dominance, tenderness, reverence.

Then he kissed me again, fiercely this time, and I would have cried out if I could have because it *burned*, like lightning arcing down my throat and setting all my nerves afire. It made me writhe anew, which he generously permitted. It made me cry, but the tears dried almost at once.

My sweat became steam. I felt the heat of the encroaching sun soak in and then gather within me, rising close to the skin, boiling. It would either find an outlet or it would burn me up; it did not care. *I* did not care. I was shouting wordlessly, straining against him, begging for just that little bit extra, just that final touch, just a taste of the god within the man, because he was both, and I loved them both, and I needed both with all my soul.

Then came the day, and with it the light, and all my awareness dissolved amid the rush and roar and incomprehensible glory of ten thousand white-hot suns.

21

"Still Life"
(oil on canvas)

THIS PART IS HARD FOR ME, harder than all the rest. But I will tell it, because you need to know.

When I awoke, it was early evening. I'd slept all day, but as I sat up, kicking my way free of the entangling sheets, I gave serious thought to lying back down. I could have slept a week more, so tired was I. Still, I was hungry, thirsty, and in sore need of a toilet, so I got up.

Shiny, asleep beside me, didn't stir, even when I tripped over my discarded robe and cursed loudly. I supposed the magic had worn him out even more than it had me.

In the bathroom, I took stock, having reached the conclusion that I was alive and had not been burned to a crisp. I felt fine, in fact, other than the tiredness and a bit of soreness here and there. More than fine. It struck me as I stood there rubbing my face: I was happy again, perhaps for the first time since I'd left Shadow. Truly, completely, happy.

So when the first tickle of cold air brushed my ankles, I barely noticed. Not until I left the bathroom, and walked into a space of coldness so sharp and alien that it made me stop short, did I realize Shiny and I were not alone.

There was only silence, at first. Only a growing feeling of presence and *immensity*. It filled the bedroom, oppressive, making the walls creak faintly. Whatever had come to visit us, it was not human.

And it did not like me. Not one whit.

I stood very still, listening. I heard nothing—and then something inhaled, very near the back of my neck.

"You still smell of him."

Every nerve in my body screamed. I stayed silent only because fear had robbed me of breath. I knew who this was. I had not heard his approach, didn't dare speak his name, but *I knew who he was*.

The voice behind me—soft, deep, malevolent—chuckled. "Prettier than I expected. Sieh was right; you were a lucky find for him." A hand stroked my hair, which was a mess, the braid half undone. The finger that snaked out to graze the back of my neck was ice cold. I could not help jumping. "But so delicate. So soft a hand to hold his leash."

I was not surprised, not at all, when those long fingers suddenly gripped my hair, pulling my head back. I barely registered the pain. The voice, which now spoke into my ear, was of far greater concern.

"Does he love you yet?"

I could not process the words. "Wh-what?"

"Does he." The voice moved closer. "Love you." I should have felt his body by now, leaning against my shoulder, but there was only a feeling of stillness and cool, like midnight air. "*Yet.*"

The last word was so close to my ear that I felt the caress of his breath. I expected to feel his lips in the next instant. When I did, I would start screaming. I knew this as surely as I knew he would kill me when I did it.

Before I could doom myself, however, another voice spoke from across the room.

"That's not a fair question. How could she know?" This one was a woman, a cultured contralto, and I recognized her voice. I'd heard it a year before, in an alley, with the scents of piss and burned flesh and fear heavy in the air. The goddess Sieh had called Mother. I knew, now, who she really was.

"It's the only question that matters," said the man. He released my hair, and I stumbled forward to a trembling halt, wanting to run and knowing there was no point.

Shiny was not awake. I could hear him in the bed, still breathing slow and even. Something was very wrong with that.

I swallowed. "Do you prefer Y-Yeine, Lady? Or, ah—"

"Yeine will do." She paused, a hint of amusement in her voice. "Aren't you going to ask my companion's name?"

"I think I know it already," I whispered.

I felt her smile. "Still, we should at least observe the formalities. You are Oree Shoth, of course. Oree, this is Nahadoth."

I made myself nod, jerkily. "Very nice to meet you both."

"Much better," said the woman. "Don't you think?"

I didn't realize this wasn't directed at me until the man—*not a man, not a man at all*—replied. And I jumped again, because suddenly his voice was farther away, over near the bed. "I don't care."

"Oh, be nice." The woman sighed. "I appreciate your asking, Oree. I suppose someday my own name will be better known, but until then, I find it irritating when others treat me and my predecessor as interchangeable."

I could guess her location now: over by the windows, in the big chair where I sometimes sat to listen to the town. I imagined her sitting daintily, one leg crossed over the other, her expression wry. Her feet would still be bare, I felt certain.

I tried not to imagine the other one at all.

"Come with me," said the woman, rising. She came closer, and I felt a cool hand take my own. Though I had gotten a taste of her power on that long-ago day in the alley, I felt nothing of her right then, even this close. It was all the Nightlord's cold that filled the room.

"Wh-wha—" I turned to go with her out of sheer unthinking self-preservation. But as she tugged my hand, my feet stopped moving. She stopped as well, turning to me. I tried to speak and could not muster words. Instead I turned, not wanting to but *needing* to. I faced the Nightlord, who stood near the bed, looming over Shiny.

There was a hint of kindness in the Lady's voice. "We will do him no harm. Not even Naha."

Naha, I thought dizzily. *The Nightlord has a pet name.* I licked my lips. "I don't...he's." I swallowed again. "Usually a light sleeper."

She nodded. I couldn't see her, but I knew it. I didn't need to see her to know anything she did.

"The sun has just set, though it still lights the sky," she said, taking my hand again. "This is my time. He'll wake when I let him—though I don't intend to let him until we're gone. It's better that way."

She led me downstairs. In the kitchen, she sat with me at the table, taking the other chair. Here, away from Nahadoth, I could feel something of her, but it was restrained somehow, nothing like that moment in the alley. She had an air of stillness and balance.

I debated whether I should offer her tea.

"Why is it better that Shiny stay asleep?" I asked at last.

She laughed softly. "I like that name, Shiny. I like *you*, Oree Shoth, which is why I wanted to talk to you alone." I started as her fingers, gentle—and strangely, callused—tilted my face down so she could see me more clearly. I remembered she was much shorter than me. "Naha was right. You really are lovely. Your eyes accentuate it, I think."

I said nothing, worried that she hadn't answered my question.

After a moment, she let me go. "Do you know why I prohibit the godlings from leaving Shadow?"

I blinked in confusion. "Um...no."

"I think you do know—better than any other, perhaps. Look what happens when even one mortal gets too closely involved with our kind. Destruction, murder...Shall I let the whole world suffer the same?"

I frowned, opened my mouth, hesitated, then finally decided to say what was on my mind.

"I think," I said slowly, "that it doesn't matter whether you restrict the godlings or not."

"Oh?"

I wondered if she was genuinely interested, or whether this was some sort of test.

"Well...I wasn't born in Shadow. I went there because I had heard about the magic. Because..." *I would be able to see there,* I had intended to say, but that wasn't true. In Shadow I had seen wonders on a daily basis, but in practical terms, I hadn't been much better off than I was in Strafe; I'd still needed a stick to get around. I hadn't cared about being able to see, anyway. I had come because of the Tree and the godlings, and the rumors of still greater strangeness. I had yearned to find a place where my father could have felt at home. And I had not been the only one. All my friends, most of whom were not demons or godlings or magic-touched in any way, had come to Shadow for the same reason: because it had been a place like no other. Because...

"Because the magic called to me," I said at last. "That will happen wherever magic is. It's part of us now, and some of us will always be drawn to it. So unless you take it away completely, which even the Interdiction never managed to do"—I spread my hands—"bad things will happen. And good."

"Good?" The Lady sounded thoughtful.

"Well...yes." I swallowed again. "I regret some of what's happened to me. But not all of it."

"I see," she said.

Another silence fell, almost companionable.

"Why is it better that Shiny stay asleep?" I asked, very softly this time.

"Because we've come to kill you."

My innards turned to water. Yet strangely, I found it easier to talk now. It was as if my anxiety had passed some threshold, beyond which it became pointless.

"You know what I am," I guessed.

"Yes," she replied. "You bent the chains we placed on Itempas and released his true power, even if only for a moment. That got our attention. We've been watching you ever since. But"—she shrugged—"I was a mortal for longer than I've been a god. The possibility of death is nothing new or especially frightening to me. So I don't care that you're a demon."

I frowned. "Then what...?"

But I remembered the Nightlord's question. *Does he love you yet?*

"Shiny," I whispered.

"He was sent here to suffer, Oree. To grow, to heal, to hopefully rejoin us someday. But make no mistake—this was also a punishment." She sighed, and for an instant I heard the sound of distant rain. "It's unfortunate that he met you so soon. In a thousand years, perhaps, I could have persuaded Nahadoth to let this go. Not now."

I stared at her with my sightless eyes, stunned by the monstrosity of what she was saying. They had made Shiny nearly human, the better to experience the pain and hardship of mortal life. They had bound him to protect mortals, live among them, understand them. Like them, even. But he could not love them.

Love *me*, I realized, and ached with both the sweetness of the knowledge and the bitterness that followed.

"That isn't fair," I said. I wasn't angry. I wasn't that stupid. Still, if they were going to kill me, anyway, I was damn well going to speak my mind. "Mortals love. You can't make him one of us and keep him from doing that. It's a contradiction."

"Remember why he was sent here. He loved Enefa—and murdered her. He loved Nahadoth and his own children, yet tormented them for centuries." She shook her head. "His love is dangerous."

"It wasn't—" *His fault*, I almost said, but that was wrong. Many mortals went mad; not all of them attacked their loved ones. Shiny had accepted responsibility for what he'd done, and I had no right to deny that.

So I tried again. "Have you considered that having mortal lovers may be what he needs? Maybe—" And again I cut myself off, because I had almost said, *Maybe I can heal him for you*. That was too presumptuous, no matter how kind the Lady seemed.

"It may be what he needs," said the Lady, evenly. "It isn't what *Nahadoth* needs."

I flinched and fell silent then, lost. It was as Serymn had guessed: the Lady knew what another Gods' War would cost humanity, and she had done what she could to prevent it. That meant balancing the needs of one damaged brother against the other—and for the time being, at least, she had decided that the Nightlord's rage deserved more satisfaction than Shiny's sorrow. I didn't blame her, really. I had felt that rage upstairs, that hunger for vengeance, so strong that it ground against my senses like a pestle. What amazed me was that she actually thought there was some hope of reconciling the three of them. Maybe she was as crazy as Shiny.

Or maybe she was just willing to do whatever it took to fill the chasm between them. What was a little demon blood, a little cruelty, compared to another war? What were a few ruined mortal lives, so long as the majority survived? And if all went well, then in a thousand years or ten thousand, the Nightlord's wrath might be appeased. That was how gods thought, wasn't it?

At least Shiny will have forgotten me by then.

"Fine," I said, unable to keep the bitterness out of my voice. "Get it over with. Or do you mean to kill me slowly? Give Shiny's knife an extra turn?"

"He'll suffer enough knowing *why* you died; *how* makes little difference." She paused. "Unless."

I frowned. Her tone had changed. "What?"

She reached across the table and cupped my cheek, her thumb brushing my lips. I nearly flinched but managed to master the reflex in time. That seemed to please her; I felt her smile.

"Such a lovely girl," she said again, and sighed with what might have been regret. "I might be able to persuade Nahadoth to let you live, provided Itempas still suffers."

"What do you mean?"

"If, perhaps, you were to leave him…" She trailed off, letting her fingers trail away from my face. I stiffened, sick with understanding.

When I finally managed to speak, I was shaking inside. I was angry at last, though; that steadied my voice. "I see. It's not enough for you to hurt him; you want *me* to hurt him, too."

"Pain is pain," said the Nightlord, and all the small hairs on my skin prickled, because I had not heard him come into the room. He was somewhere behind the Lady, and already the room was turning cold. "Sorrow is sorrow. I don't care where it comes from, as long as it is all he feels."

Despite my fear, his careless, empty tone infuriated me. My free hand tightened into a fist. "So I'm to choose between letting you kill me and stabbing him in the back myself?" I snapped. "Fine, then—kill me. At least he'll know *I* didn't abandon him."

Yeine's hand brushed mine, which I suspected was meant to be a warning. The Nightlord went silent, but I felt his rigid fury. I didn't care. It made me feel better to hurt him. He had taken my people's happiness and now he wanted mine.

"He still loves you, you know," I blurted. "More than me. More than anything, really."

He hissed at me. It was not a human sound. In it I heard snakes and ice, and dust settling into a deep, shadowed crevice. Then he started forward—

Yeine stood, turning to face him. Nahadoth stopped. For a span of time that I could not measure—perhaps a breath, perhaps an hour—they stared at one another, motionless, silent. I knew that gods could speak without words, but I was not certain that was happening here. This felt more like a battle.

Then the feeling faded and Yeine sighed, stepping closer to him. "Softly," she said, her voice more compassionate than I could have imagined. "Slowly. You're free now. Be what you choose to be, not what they made you."

He let out a long, slow sigh, and I felt the cold pressure of him fade just a little. When he spoke, however, his voice was just as hard as before. "I am of my choosing. But that is *angry*, Yeine. They burn in me, the memories . . . They hurt. The things he did to me."

The room reverberated with betrayals unspoken, horrors and loss. In that silence, my anger crumbled. I had never been able to truly hate anyone who'd suffered, no matter what evils they'd done in the aftermath.

"He has not earned such happiness, Yeine," the Nightlord said. "Not yet."

The Lady sighed. "I know."

I heard him touch her, perhaps a kiss, perhaps just taking her hand. It reminded me at once of Shiny and the way he often touched me, wordlessly, needing the reassurance of my nearness. Had he done that with Nahadoth, once upon a time? Perhaps Nahadoth—underneath the anger—missed those days, too. He had the Lady to comfort him, however. Shiny would soon have no one.

Silently, the Nightlord vanished. Yeine stayed where she was for a moment, then turned back to me.

"That was foolish of you," she said. I realized she was angry, too, with me.

I nodded, weary. "I know. Sorry."

To my surprise, that actually seemed to mollify her. She returned to the table, though she didn't sit. "Not wholly your fault. He's still...fragile, in some ways. The scars of the War, and his imprisonment, run deep. Some of them are still raw."

And I remembered, with some guilt, that this was Shiny's fault.

"I've made my decision," I said, very softly.

She saw what was in my heart—or perhaps it was just obvious. "If what you said was true," she said, "if you do care about him, then ask yourself what's best for him."

I did. And in that moment I imagined Shiny, what he might become, long after I died and had turned to dust. A wanderer, a warrior, a guardian. A man of soft words and swift decisions and little in the way of kindness—yet he would have some, I understood. Some warmth. Some ability to touch, and be touched by, others. I could leave him that much, if I did it right.

But if I died, if his love killed me, there would be nothing in him. He would distance himself from mortalkind, knowing the consequences of caring too deeply for us. He would snuff that small ember of warmth in himself, fearful of the pain it brought. He would live among humanity yet be wholly alone. And he would never, ever heal.

I said nothing.

"You have one day," Yeine said, and vanished.

I sat at the table for a long while.

Whatever the Lady had done to still time, it faded once she was gone. Through the kitchen windows, I felt night fall, the air turning cool and dry. I could hear people walking outside, cicadas in the distant fields, and a carriage rattling along a cobbled street. There was the scent of flowers on the wind...though not the flowers of the World Tree.

In time, I heard movement upstairs. Shiny. The pipes rattled as he ran a bath. Strafe was not Shadow, but it had better plumbing, and I shamelessly wasted wood and coal to give us hot water whenever we wanted it. After a time, I heard him let the water out, moving around some more; then he came downstairs. As before, he stopped in the doorway of the room, reading something in my stillness. Then he came over to the table and sat down—where the Lady had sat, though that meant nothing. I didn't have many chairs.

I had to hold very still as I spoke. Otherwise, I would break, and it would all be for nothing.

"You have to leave," I said.

Silence from Shiny.

"I can't be with you. It never works between gods and mortals; you were right about that. Even to try is foolish."

As I spoke, I realized with a shock that I believed some of what I was saying. I had always known, in part of my heart, that Shiny could not stay with me forever. I would grow old, die, while he stayed young. Or would he grow old, too, die of old age, and then be reborn young and handsome again? Not good for me, either way. I wouldn't be able to help resenting him, feeling guilty for burdening him. I would cause him unimaginable pain as he watched me fail, and in the end we would be separated forever, anyway.

But I had wanted to try. Gods, how I'd wanted to try.

Shiny sat there, gazing at me. No recriminations, no attempts to change my mind. That was not his way. I had known from the moment I began this that it wouldn't take much. Not in words, anyhow.

Then he got up, came around the table, and crouched in front of me. I turned, moving slowly and oh so carefully to face him. Control. That was his way, wasn't it? I tried for it and held myself still. I fought the urge to touch his face and learn how badly he now thought of me.

"Did they threaten you?" he asked.

I froze.

He waited, then when I did not answer, sighed. He got to his feet.

"That isn't why," I blurted. Suddenly it was powerfully important that he know I was not acting out of fear for my own life. "I didn't...I would rather have let them—"

"No." He touched my cheek then, once and briefly. It hurt.

Like breaking my arm all over again. Worse. That was all it took to shatter my careful control. I began to tremble, so much that I could barely get the words out.

"We can fight them," I blurted. "The Lady, she doesn't really want to do this. We can run or—"

"No, Oree," he said again. "We can't."

At this, I fell silent. It was not the inability to think this time, just the utter certainty of his words. They left me with nothing to say.

He rose. "You should live, too, Oree," he said.

Then he went to the door. His boots were there, neatly placed beside mine. He pulled them on, his movements neither swift nor slow. Efficient. He put on the lambskin coat I'd bought for him at the beginning of the winter, because he kept forgetting he could get sick, and I hadn't felt like nursing him through pneumonia.

I inhaled to say something. Let the breath out. Sat there, trembling.

He walked out of the house.

I had known he would go like that, too, with nothing but the clothes on his back. He wasn't human enough to care about possessions or money. I heard his heavy tread move down the steps, then down the dusty street. They faded into the distance, lost in the sounds of night.

I went upstairs. The bathroom was spotless as usual. I took off my robe and had a long soak, as hot as I could bear the water. I steamed even after I dried off.

It did not hit me until I picked up a sponge to clean the tub. Now that Shiny was gone, I would have to do that myself from now on.

I finished the tub, then sat down in it and wept for the rest of the night.

So now you know it all.

You needed to know it, and I needed to tell it. I've spent the past six months trying not to think about all that's happened, which wasn't the wisest thing to do. It was easier, though. Better to go to bed and simply sleep, rather than lie there all night feeling lonely. Better to concentrate on the *tap-tap* of my stick as I walk, rather than think of how, once, I could have navigated by the faint outline of some godling's footprints. I've lost so much.

But I've gained some things, too. Like you, my little surprise.

On some level I knew it was a risk. Gods don't breed as easily as us, but they made him more mortal than any god has ever been. I don't know what it means that they left him this ability when they took so much else. I suppose they just forgot.

Then again, I can't help remembering that evening, at my kitchen table, when the Lady Yeine touched me. She is the Mistress of Dawn, the goddess of life; surely she sensed you, or at least your imminence, while we sat there. That makes me wonder: did she notice you and let you live? Or did she...?

She's a strange one, the Lady.

Even more strangely, she listened to me.

I've now heard the news from too many merchants and gossips to discount: there are gods everywhere. Singing in rain forests, dancing atop mountains, staking out beaches and flirting with the clam-boys. Most large cities have a resident godling these days, or two or three. Strafe is trying to attract one right now; the town elders say it's good for business. I hope they succeed.

Soon the world will be a far more magical place. Just right, I think, for you.

And—

No.

No, I know better than to think it.

No.

And yet.

I lie here in my lonely bed, watching for the sunrise. I feel it coming—the light warms its way along the blankets and my skin. The days are getting shorter with the coming of winter. I'm guessing you'll be born around the solstice.

Are you still listening? Can you hear me in there?

I think you can. I think you were made that second time, when Shiny became his true self for me, just a little. Just enough. I think he knew it, too, like the Lady knew it, and maybe even the Nightlord. This isn't the sort of thing he would do by accident. He'd seen that I missed my old life. This was his way of helping me focus on the new one. And also... his way of making up for past mistakes.

Gods. *Men.* Damn him; he should've asked me. I could die giving birth to you, after all. Probably not, but it's the principle of the thing.

Well.

I hope you're listening, because sometimes gods—and demons—do that. I think that you're awake, aware, and that you understand everything I've said.

Because I think I saw you, yesterday morning when I woke

up. I think my eyes worked again, just for a moment, and you were the light I saw.

I think that if I wait 'til dawn and watch closely, I'll see you again this morning.

And I think that if I wait long enough and listen carefully, one day I'll hear footsteps on the road outside. Maybe a knock at the door. He'll have learned basic courtesy by then from someone. We can hope for that, can't we? Either way, he'll come inside. He'll wipe his feet, at least. He'll hang his coat.

And then you and I, together, will welcome him home.

APPENDIX

1

A Glossary of Terms

Amn: Most populous and powerful of the Senmite races.

Arameri: Ruling family of the Amn; advisors to the Nobles' Consortium and the Order of Itempas.

Art Row: Artists' market at the Promenade, in East Shadow.

Blood sigil: The mark of a recognized Arameri family member.

Bonebender: A healer, often self-taught, with knowledge of herbalism, midwifery, bonesetting, and basic surgical techniques. Some bonebenders illegally utilize simple healing sigils.

Bright, the: The time of Itempas's solitary rule, after the Gods' War. General term for goodness, order, law, righteousness.

Darkwalkers: Worshippers of the Lord of Shadows.

Dateh Lorillalia: A scrivener, formerly of the Order of Itempas. Husband of Serymn Arameri.

Dekarta Arameri: Most recent former head of the Arameri family.

Demon: Children of forbidden unions between gods/godlings and mortals. Mortal, though they may possess innate magic that is equivalent, or greater, to that of godlings in strength.

Dump: A godling who dwells in West Shadow, overseeing the Shustocks junkyard. The Lord of Discards.

Easha: Local term for East Shadow.

Enefa: One of the Three. Former Goddess of Earth, creator of godlings and mortals, Mistress of Twilight and Dawn (deceased).

Eo: A godling who dwells in Shadow. The Merciful.

Gateway Park: A park built around Sky and the World Tree's base, in East Shadow.

God: Immortal children of the Maelstrom. The Three.

Godling: Immortal children of the Three. Sometimes also referred to as gods.

Godsblood: A popular and expensive narcotic. Confers heightened awareness and temporary magical abilities on consumers.

God spots: Local/colloquial name for locations in Shadow that have been temporarily or permanently made magical by godlings.

Gods' Realm: All places beyond the universe.

Gods' War: An apocalyptic conflict in which Bright Itempas claimed rulership of the heavens after defeating his two siblings.

Hado: A member of the New Lights. Master of Initiates.

Heavens, Hells: Abodes for souls beyond the mortal realm.

Heretic: A worshipper of any god but Itempas.

High North: Northernmost continent. A backwater.

House of the Risen Sun: A mansion. One of several attached to the World Tree's trunk.

Hundred Thousand Kingdoms, the: Collective term for the world since its unification under Arameri rule.

Ina: A godling who dwells in Shadow.

Interdiction, the: The period during which no godlings appeared in the mortal realm, per order of Bright Itempas.

Islands, the: Vast archipelago east of High North and Senm.

Itempan: General term for a worshipper of Itempas. Also used to refer to members of the Order of Itempas.

Itempas: One of the Three. The Bright Lord; master of heavens and earth; the Skyfather.

Kitr: A godling who dwells in Shadow. The Blade.

Lil: A godling who dwells in Shadow. The Hunger.

Madding: A godling who dwells in Shadow. The Lord of Debts.

Maelstrom: The creator of the Three. Unknowable.

Magic: The innate ability of gods and godlings to alter the material and immaterial world. Mortals may approximate this ability through the use of the gods' language.

Maroland, the: Smallest continent, which once existed to the east of the islands; site of the first Arameri palace. Destroyed by Nahadoth.

Mortal realm: The universe, created by the Three.

Nahadoth: One of the Three. The Nightlord. Also called the Lord of Shadows.

Nemmer: A godling who dwells in Shadow. The Lady of Secrets.

Nimaro Reservation: A protectorate of the Arameri, established after the Maroland's destruction to provide a home for survivors. Located at the southeast edge of the Senm continent.

Nobles' Consortium: Ruling political body of the Hundred Thousand Kingdoms.

Oboro: A godling who dwells in Shadow.

Order of Itempas: The priesthood dedicated to Bright Itempas. In addition to spiritual guidance, also responsible for law and

order, education, public health and welfare, and the eradication of heresy. Also known as the Itempan Order.

Order-Keepers: Acolytes (priests in training) of the Order of
Itempas, responsible for maintenance of public order.

Order of New Light: An unauthorized priesthood dedicated to
Bright Itempas, comprised mainly of former members of the
Order of Itempas. Colloquially known as the "New Lights."

Paitya: A godling who dwells in Shadow. The Terror.

Pilgrim: Worshippers of the Gray Lady who journey to Shadow
to pray at the World Tree. Generally High Northers.

Previt: One of the higher rankings for priests of the Order of
Itempas.

Promenade, the: Northernmost edge of Gateway Park in East
Shadow. A site popular with pilgrims, due to its view of the
World Tree. Also the site of Art Row and the city's largest
White Hall.

Role: A godling who dwells in Shadow. The Lady of Compassion.

Salon: Headquarters for the Nobles' Consortium.

Script: A series of sigils, used by scriveners to produce complex
or sequential magical effects.

Scrivener: A scholar of the gods' written language.

Senm: Southernmost and largest continent of the world.

Senmite: The Amn language, used as a common tongue for all
the Hundred Thousand Kingdoms.

Serymn Arameri: An Arameri fullblood, husband of Dateh
Lorillalia. Owner of the House of the Risen Sun.

Shadow: Local/colloquial name for the largest city on the
Senm continent (official name is Sky).

Shahar Arameri: High priestess of Itempas at the time of the
Gods' War. Her descendants are the Arameri family.

Shustocks: A neighborhood in Wesha.

Sieh: A godling, also called the Trickster. Eldest of all the godlings.

Sigil: An ideograph of the gods' language, used by scriveners to imitate the magic of the gods.

Sky: Official name of the largest city on the Senm continent. Also, the palace of the Arameri family.

Strafe: A city along the northwestern coast of the Senm continent.

Teman Protectorate, the: A Senmite kingdom.

Time of the Three: Before the Gods' War.

T'vril Arameri: Current head of the Arameri family.

Velly: A cold-water fish, normally smoked and salted. A Maroneh delicacy.

Wesha: Local term for West Shadow.

White Hall: The Order of Itempas's houses of worship, education, and justice.

World Tree, the: A leafy evergreen tree estimated to be 125,000 feet in height, created by the Gray Lady. Sacred to worshippers of the Lady.

Yeine: One of the Three. The current Goddess of Earth, Mistress of Twilight and Dawn. Also called the Gray Lady.

Historical Record;
First Scriveners' notes, volume 96;
from the collection of T'vril Arameri.

(Interview conducted and originally transcribed by First Scrivener Y'li Denai/Arameri, at Sky, year 1512 of the Bright, may He shine upon us forever. Recorded in fixed messaging sphere. Secondary transcription completed by Librarian Sheta Arameri, year 2250 of the Bright. WARNING: contains heretical references, marked "HR." Used with permission of the Litaria.)

FIRST SCRIVENER Y'LI ARAMERI: Are you comfortable?
NEMUE SARFITH ENULAI:[1] Should I be?
YA: Of course. You are a guest of the Arameri, Enulai Sarfith.
NS: Exactly! (laughs) I suppose I should enjoy it while I can. I doubt you'll have many more Maro guests here in the future.

1. Interviewer's note: "Enulai" (HR) is apparently a hereditary title among the Maro.

YA: I see you've decided not to use the new word. Maroneh[2]—

NS: Three words, actually, in the old tongue. *Maro n neh.* Nobody says it right. Too much of a mouthful. I was Maro all my life; I'll be Maro 'til I die. Not long, now.

YA: For the record, would you be willing to state your age?

NS: The Father has blessed me with two hundred and two years.

YA: (laughs) I was told you liked to claim that age.

NS: You believe I'm lying?

YA: Well...madam—I mean, Enulai...

NS: Call me what you like. But remember that enulai always speak the truth, boy. Lying is dangerous. And I wouldn't bother lying about something so trivial as my age. So write it down!

YA: Yes, madam. I have done so.

NS: You Amn never listen. In the days following the War,[3] we warned you to respect the Dark Father (HR). He is not our enemy—we told you—even if he is Bright Itempas's. Before the War, he loved us better than Enefa (HR) herself. The things you must have done to him, to fill his heart with such rage.

YA: Madam, please. We do not speak...that name you mentioned, the—

NS: What? Enefa? (shouts) Enefa, Enefa, Enefa!

YA: (sighs)

2. Reference: The Survivors' Provisional Council of Nimaro Territory issued an official pronouncement on behalf of their royal family (deceased), indicating that their people were henceforth to be known as "Maroneh," not "Maro."

3. Interviewers' note: The Gods' War.

NS: Roll your eyes at me one more time.

YA: My apologies for disrespecting you, madam. It is only... The absolute dominance of Itempas is the fundamental principle of the Bright.

NS: I love the White Lord as much as you do. It was my people He chose as the model for His mortal appearance (HR), and we were the first to receive His blessing of knowledge (HR). Mathematics and astronomy and writing and—all of that, all of it, we did it before any of you Senmites, or those ignorant bastards up in the north, or that bunch of pirates on the islands. Yet for all He gave us, we have always remembered that He is one of *Three*. Without His siblings, He is nothing (HR).

YA: Madam!

NS: Report me to your family head if you like. What will he do, kill me? Destroy my people? I have nothing left to lose, boy. That's the only reason I came.

YA: Because the Maro royal family is gone.[4]

NS: No, fool, because the *Maro* are gone. Oh, if we get to making babies, there might be enough of us to limp along for a while longer, but we'll never be what we were. You Amn will never let us get that strong again.

YA: Er, yes, madam. But specifically, it was the duty of the enulai to serve the royal family, was it not? As, ah, let's see, bodyguards and storytellers—

NS: Historians.

YA: Well, yes, but much of that history... I have a list here... legends and myths...

---

4. Interviewers' note: See *Post-Cataclysm Maro: Census.*

NS: It was all true.

YA: Madam, really.

NS: Why did you bother to invite me here?

YA: Because I am a historian as well.

NS: Then *listen*. That's the most important thing any historian can do. Hear clearly with just your ears, not with ten
thousand Amn lies garbling everything—

YA: But, madam, an example, one of the enulai stories
recorded...the tale of the Fish Goddess.

NS: Yes. Yiho, of the Shoth clan, though they're all dead
now, too, I suppose.

YA: The tale speaks of her sitting by a river for three days
during a famine and causing schools of ocean fish to swim
up the river—from salt water to fresh water—and fling
themselves into nets.

NS: Yes, yes. And ever since then, those breeds of fish have
continued to swim up the river to spawn, every year. She
changed them forever.

YA: But that's...Is the tale from before the War? Was this
Yiho a godling?

NS: No, of course not. She dies an old woman at the end of
the tale, doesn't she?

YA: Well, then—

NS: Though the gods had many children.

YA: (pause) My gods. (sound of a blow) Ah!

NS: That's for blaspheming.

YA: I don't believe this. (sighs) You're right, my apologies.
I forgot myself. I was only...You're suggesting that the
woman described in the tale was...was a half-breed, a
child of the gods—

NS: All of us are children of the gods. But Yiho was special.

YA: (silence)

NS: (laughs) What's that I see in your pale eyes, boy? Have you suddenly started listening? Figures.

YA: Remembering, actually. Many of the Maro stories in my records prominently feature enulai themselves.

NS: Yes, go on...

YA: Every member of the royal family had an enulai. The enulai would educate them, advise them, protect them from danger.

NS: (laughs) Get to the point, boy. I'm not getting any younger.

YA: Protect them, often using strange abilities that the Litaria has designated unlikely or impossible—

NS: Because you scriveners don't make your own magic. You borrow it, secondhand, using the gods' language. But if you spoke the magic yourselves—if that didn't kill you— or, better still, if you could simply *will* a thing into being, you could do all that the gods do. And more.

YA: Enulai Sarfith, I wish you had not told me this.

NS: (laughs)

YA: You know what I must do.

NS: (more laughter) Ah, boy. What does it matter? I am the last descendant of Enulai—daughter of Enefa, last-born of the mortal gods who chose to spend their brief days among humankind. All the Maro's kings and queens are dead. All my children and grandchildren are dead. All of us who carried the Gray Mother's blood—we're as dead as she is. Why should I bother hiding anymore?

YA: (speaks to a servant, sending for guards)

NS: (while he speaks, softly) All gone, demonkind. All gone. No need to search for more. None left.[5]

YA: I'm sorry. (garbled)

NS: Don't be. (garbled) destroyed the last of demonkind. No need to search for more now.

YA: No need to search for more.

NS: There are no demons left in the world, anywhere.

YA: None left. (garbled, until the guards come) Farewell, Enulai. I'm sorry it had to turn out this way.

NS: (laughing) I'm not. Good-bye, boy.

[Interview ends][6]

5. Librarian's note: Original transcript ends here. The message sphere recording is partially inaudible from this point on. There appears to be no damage to the sphere's controlling script; however, consultation with scriveners suggests magical interference. I have transcribed the remainder of the interview as best I could.

6. Librarian's note: This transcript and sphere were misfiled by First Scrivener Y'li Arameri in the Library of Sky and thus lost for some 600 years. Recovered when an exhaustive search of the Library vaults was conducted per order of Lord T'vril Arameri.

Acknowledgments

Since I thanked everybody and everybody's sister in the acknowledgments of *The Hundred Thousand Kingdoms*, here I'll offer some literary/artistic acknowledgments. Fitting, since *The Broken Kingdoms* is a more, hmm, *aesthetic* book than its predecessor.

For the vocabulary of encaustic painting, sculpture, and watercolor used herein, I again thank my father, artist Noah Jemisin, who taught me more of his craft than I ever realized, given that I can't draw a straight line. (No, Dad, fingerpainting when I was five doesn't count.)

For the city of Shadow, I owe an obvious debt to urban fantasy—both the Miéville kind and the "disaffected hot chick with a weapon" kind (to quote a detractor of the latter, though I'm a fan of both). But a lot of it I owe to a lifetime spent in cities: Shadow's Art Row is the Union Square farmers' market in New York, maybe with a bit of New Orleans's Jackson Square thrown in.

For several of the godlings, particularly Lil, Madding, and Dump, I thank my subconscious, because I had a dream about them (and several godlings you'll meet in the third book of the Inheritance Trilogy). Lil tried to eat me. Typical.

Oh—and for a taste of how people in a major city might cope with a giant tree looming overhead, I acknowledge my past as an anime fangirl. In this case, the debt is owed to a lovely little shoujo OAV and TV series called *Mahou Tsukai Tai*, which I highly recommend. The problems caused by the giant tree were handled in a much more lighthearted manner there, but the beauty of the initial image lingers in my mind.

THE
KINGDOM
OF GODS

BOOK THREE OF THE
INHERITANCE TRILOGY

BOOK ONE

Four Legs in the Morning

SHE LOOKS SO MUCH LIKE ENEFA, *I think, the first time I see her.*

Not this moment, as she stands trembling in the lift alcove, her heartbeat so loud that it drums against my ears. This is not really the first time I've seen her. I have checked in on our investment now and again over the years, sneaking out of the palace on moonless nights. (Nahadoth is the one our masters fear most during those hours, not me.) I first met her when she was an infant. I crept in through the nursery window and perched on the railing of her crib to watch her. She watched me back, unusually quiet and solemn even then. Where other infants were fascinated by the world around them, she was constantly preoccupied by the second soul nestled against her own. I waited for her to go mad, and felt pity, but nothing more.

I next visited when she was two, toddling after her mother with great determination. Not mad yet. Again when she was five; I watched her sit at her father's knee, listening raptly to his tales of the gods. Still not mad. When she was nine, I watched her mourn her father. By that point, it had become clear that she was not, and would never go, insane. Yet there was no doubt that Enefa's soul affected her. Aside from her looks, there was the way she killed. I watched her climb out from beneath the corpse of her first man, panting and covered in filth, with a bloody stone knife in her hand. Though she was only thirteen years old, I felt no horror from her—which I should have, her heart's fluctuations amplified by her double souls. There was only satisfaction in her face, and a very familiar coldness at her core. The warriors' council women, who had expected to see her suffer, looked at each other in unease. Beyond the circle of older women, in the shadows, her watching mother smiled.

I fell in love with her then, just a little.

So now I drag her through my dead spaces, which I have never shown to another mortal, and it is to the corporeal core of my soul that I take her. (I would take her to my realm, show her my true soul, if I could.) I love her wonder as she walks among my little toy worlds. She tells me they are beautiful. I will cry when she dies for us.

Then Naha finds her. Pathetic, isn't it? We two gods, the oldest and most powerful beings in the mortal realm, both besotted by a sweaty, angry little mortal girl. It is more than her looks. More than her ferocity, her instant maternal devotion, the speed with which she lunges to strike. She is more than Enefa, for Enefa never loved me so much, nor was Enefa so passionate in life and death. The old soul has been improved, somehow, by the new.

She chooses Nahadoth. I do not mind so much. She loves me, too, in her way. I am grateful.

And when it all ends and the miracle has occurred and she is a goddess (again), I weep. I am happy. But still so very alone.

1

Trickster, trickster
Stole the sun for a prank
Will you really ride it?
Where will you hide it?
Down by the riverbank!

THERE WILL BE NO TRICKS in this tale. I tell you this so that you can relax. You'll listen more closely if you aren't flinching every other instant, waiting for the pratfall. You will not reach the end and suddenly learn I have been talking to my other soul or making a lullaby of my life for someone's unborn brat. I find such things disingenuous, so I will simply tell the tale as I lived it.

But wait, that's not a real beginning. Time is an irritation, but it provides structure. Should I tell this in the mortal fashion? All right, then, linear. Slooooow. You require context.

Beginnings. They are not always what they seem. Nature is cycles, patterns, repetition—but of what we believe, of the beginning I understand, there was once only Maelstrom, the unknowable. Over a span of uncountable aeons, as none of us were here yet to count, It churned forth endless substances and concepts and creatures. Some of those must have been glorious, because even today the Maelstrom spins forth new life with regular randomness, and many of those creations are indeed beautiful and wondrous. But most of them last only an eyeblink or two before the Maelstrom rips them apart again, or they die of instant old age, or they collapse in on themselves and become tiny Maelstroms in turn. These are absorbed back into the greater cacophony.

But one day the Maelstrom made something that did not die. Indeed, this thing was remarkably like Itself—wild, churning, eternal, ever changing. Yet this new thing was ordered enough to think, and feel, and dedicate itself to its own survival. In token of which, the first thing it did was get the hells away from the Maelstrom.

But this new creature faced a terrible dilemma, because away from the Maelstrom there was nothing. No people, no places, no spaces, no darkness, no dimension, no EXISTENCE.

A bit much for even a god to endure. So this being—whom we shall call *Nahadoth* because that is a pretty name, and whom we shall label male for the sake of convenience if not completeness—promptly set out to create an existence, which he did by going mad and tearing himself apart.

This was remarkably effective. And thus Nahadoth found himself accompanied by a formless immensity of separate substance. Purpose and structure began to cohere around it simply as a side effect of the mass's presence, but only so much of that could occur spontaneously. Much like the Maelstrom, it churned and howled and thundered; unlike the Maelstrom, it was not in any way *alive*.

It was, however, the earliest form of the universe and the gods' realm that envelops it. This was a wonder—but Nahadoth likely did not notice, because he was a gibbering lunatic. So let us return to the Maelstrom.

I like to believe that It is aware. Eventually It must have noticed Its child's loneliness and distress. So presently, It spat out another entity that was aware and that also managed to escape the havoc of its birth. This new one—who has always and only been male—named himself Bright Itempas, because he was an arrogant, self-absorbed son of a demon even then. And because Itempas is also a gigantic screaming twit, he attacked Nahadoth, who...well. Naha very likely did not make a good conversation partner at the time. Not that they talked at all, in those days before speech.

So they fought, and fought, and fought times a few million jillion nillion, until suddenly one or the other of them got tired of the whole thing and proposed a truce. Both of them claim to have done this, so I cannot tell which one is joking. And then, because they had to do *something* if they weren't fighting and because they were the only living beings in the universe after all, they became lovers. Somewhere between all this—the fighting or the lovemaking, not so very different for those two—they had a powerful effect on the shapeless mass of substance that Nahadoth had given birth to. It gained more function, more structure. And all was well for another Really Long Time.

Then along came the Third, a she-creature named Enefa, who should have settled things because usually three of anything is better, more stable, than two. For a while this was the case. In fact, EXISTENCE became the universe, and the beings soon became a family, because it was Enefa's nature to give meaning to anything she touched. I was the first of their many, many children.

So there we were: a universe, a father and a mother and a Naha, and a few hundred children. And our grandparent, I suppose—the Maelstrom, if one can count It as such given that It would destroy us all if we did not take care. And the mortals, when Enefa finally created them. I suppose those were like pets—part of the family and yet not really—to be indulged and disciplined and loved and kept safe in the finest of cages, on the gentlest of leashes. We only killed them when we had to.

Things went wrong for a while, but at the time that this all began, there had been some improvement. My mother was dead, but she got better. My father and I had been imprisoned, but we'd won our way free. My other father was still a murdering, betraying bastard, though, and nothing would ever change that, no matter how much penance he served—which meant that the Three could never be whole again, no matter that all three of them lived and were for the most part sane. This left a grating, aching void in our family, which was only tolerable because we had already endured far worse.

That is when my mother decided to take things into her own hands.

I followed Yeine one day, when she went to the mortal realm and shaped herself into flesh and appeared in the musty inn room that Itempas had rented. They spoke there, exchanging inanities and warnings while I lurked incorporeal in a pocket of silence, spying. Yeine might have noticed me; my tricks rarely worked on her. If so, she did not care that I watched. I wish I knew what that meant.

Because there came the dreaded moment in which she looked at him, really *looked* at him, and said, "You've changed."

And he said, "Not enough."

And she said, "What do you fear?" To which he said nothing, of course, because it is not his nature to admit such things.

So she said, "You're stronger now. She must have been good for you."

The room filled with his anger, though his expression did not change. "Yes. She was."

There was a moment of tension between them, in which I hoped. Yeine is the best of us, full of good, solid mortal common sense and her own generous measure of pride. Surely she would not succumb! But then the moment passed and she sighed and looked ashamed and said, "It was...wrong of us. To take her from you."

That was all it took, that acknowledgment. In the eternity of silence that followed, he forgave her. I knew it as a mortal creature knows the sun has risen. And then he forgave himself—for what, I cannot be sure and dare not guess. Yet that, too, was a palpable change. He suddenly stood a little taller, grew calmer, let down the guard of arrogance he'd kept up since she arrived. She saw the walls fall—and behind them, the him that used to be. The Itempas who'd once won over her resentful predecessor, tamed wild Nahadoth, disciplined a fractious litter of child-gods, and crafted from whole cloth time and gravity and all the other amazing things that made life possible and so interesting. It isn't hard to love that version of him. I know.

So I do not blame her, not really. For betraying me.

But it hurt so much to watch as she went to him and touched his lips with her fingers. There was a look of dazzlement on her face as she beheld the brilliance of his true self. (She yielded so easily. When had she become so weak? Damn her. Damn her to her own misty hells.)

She frowned a little and said, "I don't know why I came here."

"One lover has never been enough for any of us," said Itempas, smiling a sad little smile, as if he knew how unworthy he was of her desire. Despite this, he took her shoulders and pulled her close and their lips touched and their essences blended and I hated them, I hated them, I despised them both, how dare he take her from me, how dare she love him when I had not forgiven him, how dare they both leave Naha alone when he'd suffered so much, how could they? I hated them and I loved them and gods how I wanted to be with them, why couldn't I just be one of them, it wasn't fair—

—no. No. Whining was pointless. It didn't even make me feel better. Because the Three could never be Four, and even when the Three were reduced to two, a godling could never replace a god, and any heartbreak that I felt in that moment was purely my own damned fault for wanting what I could not have.

When I could bear their happiness no more, I fled. To a place that matched the Maelstrom in my heart. To the only place within the mortal realm I have ever called home. To my own personal hell ... called Sky.

I was sitting corporeal at the top of the Nowhere Stair, sulking, when the children found me. Total chance, that. Mortals think we plan everything.

They were a matched set. Six years old—I am good at gauging ages in mortals—bright-eyed, quick-minded, like children who have had good food and space to run and pleasures to stimulate the soul. The boy was dark-haired and -eyed and -skinned, tall for his age, solemn. The girl was blonde and green-eyed and pale, intent. Pretty, both of them. Richly dressed. And little tyrants, as Arameri tended to be at that age.

"You will assist us," said the girl in a haughty tone.

Inadvertently I glanced at their foreheads, my belly clenched for the jerk of the chains, the painful slap of the magic they'd once used to control us. Then I remembered the chains were gone, though the habit of straining against them apparently remained. Galling. The marks on their heads were circular, denoting full-bloods, but the circles themselves were mere outlines, not filled in. Just a few looping, overlapping rings of command, aimed not at us but at reality in general. Protection, tracking, all the usual spells of safety. Nothing to force obedience, theirs or anyone else's.

I stared at the girl, torn between amazement and amusement. She had no idea who—or what—I was, that much was clear. The boy, who looked less certain, looked from her to me and said nothing.

"Arameri brats on the loose," I drawled. My smile seemed to reassure the boy, infuriate the girl. "Someone's going to get in trouble for letting you two run into me down here."

At this they both looked apprehensive, and I realized the problem: they were lost. We were in the underpalace, those levels beneath Sky's bulk that sat in perpetual shadow and had once been the demesne of the palace's lowblood servants—though clearly that was no longer the case. A thick layer of dust coated the floors and decorative moldings all around us, and aside from the two in front of me, there was no scent of mortals anywhere nearby. How long had they been wandering down here alone? They looked tired and frazzled and depleted by despair.

Which they covered with belligerence. "You will instruct us in how we might reach the overpalace," said the girl, "or guide us there." She thought a moment, then lifted her chin and added, "Do this now, or it will not go well with you!"

I couldn't help it: I laughed. It was just too perfect, her fumbling attempt at hauteur, their extremely poor luck in meeting me, all of it. Once upon a time, little girls like her had made my life a hell, ordering me about and giggling when I contorted myself to obey. I had lived in terror of Arameri tantrums. Now I was free to see this one as she truly was: just a frightened creature parroting the mannerisms of her parents, with no more notion of how to *ask* for what she wanted than how to fly.

And sure enough, when I laughed, she scowled and put her hands on her hips and poked out her bottom lip in a way that I have always adored—in children. (In adults it is infuriating, and I kill them for it.) Her brother, who had seemed sweeter-natured, was beginning to glower, too. Delightful. I have always been partial to brats.

"You have to do what we say!" said the girl, stamping her foot. "You will help us!"

I wiped away a tear and sat back against the stair wall, exhaling as the laughter finally passed. "You will find your own damn way home," I said, still grinning, "and count yourselves lucky that you're too cute to kill."

That shut them up, and they stared at me with more curiosity than fear. Then the boy, who I had already begun to suspect was the smarter if not the stronger of the two, narrowed his eyes at me.

"You don't have a mark," he said, pointing at my forehead. The girl started in surprise.

"Why, no, I don't," I said. "Imagine that."

"You aren't…Arameri, then?" His face screwed up, as if he had found himself speaking gibberish. *You curtain apple jump, then?*

"No, I'm not."

"Are you a new servant?" asked the girl, seduced out of anger by her own curiosity. "Just come to Sky from outside?"

I put my arms behind my head, stretching my feet out in front of me. "I'm not a servant at all, actually."

"You're dressed like one," said the boy, pointing.

I looked at myself in surprise and realized I had manifested the same clothing I'd usually worn during my imprisonment: loose pants (good for running), shoes with a hole in one toe, and a plain loose shirt, all white. Ah, yes—in Sky, servants wore white every day. Highbloods wore it only for special occasions, preferring brighter colors otherwise. The two in front of me had both been dressed in deep emerald green, which matched the girl's eyes and complemented the boy's nicely.

"Oh," I said, annoyed that I'd inadvertently fallen prey to old habit. "Well, I'm not a servant. Take my word for it."

"You aren't with the Teman delegation," said the boy, speaking slowly while his eyes belied his racing thoughts. "Datennay was the only child with them, and they left three days ago, anyway. And they dressed like Temans. Metal bits and twisty hair."

"I'm not Teman, either." I grinned again, waiting to see how they handled that one.

"You *look* Teman," said the girl, clearly not believing me. She pointed at my head. "Your hair barely has any curl, and your eyes are sharp and flat at the corners, and your skin is browner than Deka's."

I glanced at the boy, who looked uncomfortable at this comparison. I could see why. Though he bore a fullblood's circle on his brow, it was painfully obvious that someone had brought non-Amn delicacies to the banquet of his recent heritage. If I hadn't known it was impossible, I would have guessed he was some variety of High Norther. He had Amn features, with their long-stretched facial lines, but his hair was blacker than Nahadoth's void and as straight as windblown grass, and he was indeed a rich all-over brown that had nothing to do with a suntan. I had seen infants like him drowned or head-staved or tossed off the Pier, or marked as lowbloods and given over to servants to raise. Never had one been given a fullblood mark.

The girl had no hint of the foreign about her—no, wait. It was there, just subtle. A fullness to her lips, the angle of her cheekbones, and her hair was a more brassy than sunlit gold. To Amn eyes, these would just be interesting idiosyncracies, a touch of the exotic without all the unpleasant political baggage. If not for her brother's existence, no one would have ever guessed that she was not pure-blooded, either.

I glanced at the boy again and saw the warning-sign wariness in his eyes. Yes, of course. They would have already begun to make his life hell.

While I pondered this, the children fell to whispering, debating whether I looked more of this or that or some other mortal race. I could hear every word of it, but out of politeness I pretended not to. Finally the boy stage-whispered, "I don't think he's Teman at *all*," in a tone that let me know he suspected what I really was.

With eerie unity they faced me again.

"It doesn't matter if you're a servant or not, or Teman or not," said the girl. "*We're* fullbloods, and that means you have to do what we say."

"No, it doesn't," I said.

"Yes, it does!"

I yawned and closed my eyes. "Make me."

They fell silent again, and I felt their consternation. I could have pitied them, but I was having too much fun. Finally, I felt a stir of air and warmth nearby, and I opened my eyes to find that the boy had sat down beside me.

"Why won't you help us?" he asked, his voice soft with honest concern, and I nearly flinched beneath the onslaught of his big dark eyes. "We've been down here all day, and we ate our sandwiches already, and we don't know the way back."

Damnation. I'm partial to cuteness, too. "All right," I said, relenting. "Where are you trying to go?"

The boy brightened. "To the World Tree's heart!" Then his excitement flagged. "Or at least, that was where we *were* trying to go. Now we just want to go back to our rooms."

"A sad end to a grand adventure," I said, "but you wouldn't have found what you were looking for anyhow. The World Tree was created by Yeine, the Mother of Life; its heart is her heart. Even if you found the chunk of wood that exists at the Tree's core, it would mean nothing."

"Oh," said the boy, slumping more. "We don't know how to find her."

"I do," I said, and then it was my turn to sag, as I remembered what had driven me to Sky. Were they still together, she and Itempas? He was mortal, with merely mortal endurance, but she could renew his strength again and again for as long as she liked. How I hated her. (Not really. Yes, really. Not really.)

"I do," I said again, "but that wouldn't help you. She's busy with other matters these days. Not much time for me or any of her children."

"Oh, is she your mother?" The boy looked surprised. "That sounds like our mother. She never has time for us. Is your mother the family head, too?"

"Yes, in a way. Though she's also new to the family, which makes for a certain awkwardness." I sighed again, and the sound echoed within the Nowhere Stair, which descended into shadows at our feet. Back when I and the other Enefadeh had built this version of Sky, we had created this spiral staircase that led to nothing, twenty feet down to dead-end against a wall. It had been a long day spent listening to bickering architects. We'd gotten bored.

"It's a bit like having a stepmother," I said. "Do you know what that is?"

The boy looked thoughtful. The girl sat down beside him. "Like Lady Meull, of Agru," she said to the boy. "Remember our genealogy lessons? She's married to the duke now, but the duke's children came from his first wife. His first wife is the mother. Lady Meull is the stepmother." She looked at me for confirmation. "Like that, right?"

"Yes, yes, like that," I said, though I neither knew nor cared who Lady Meull was. "Yeine is our queen, sort of, as well as our mother."

"And you don't like her?" Too much knowing in both the children's eyes as they asked that question. The usual Arameri pattern, then, parents raising children who would grow up to plot their painful deaths. The signs were all there.

"No," I said softly. "I love her." Because I did, even when I hated her. "More than light and darkness and life. She is the mother of my soul."

"So, then..." The girl was frowning. "Why are you sad?"

"Because love is not enough." I fell silent for an instant, stunned as realization moved through me. Yes, here was truth, which they had helped me find. Mortal children are very wise, though it takes a careful listener or a god to understand this. "My mother loves me, and at least one of my fathers loves me, and I love them, but that just isn't *enough*, not anymore. I need something more." I groaned and drew up my knees, pressing my forehead against them. Comforting flesh and bone, as familiar as a security blanket. "But what? What? I don't understand why everything feels so wrong. Something is changing in me."

I must have seemed mad to them, and perhaps I was. All children are a little mad. I felt them look at each other. "Um," said the girl. "You said *one* of your fathers?"

I sighed. "Yes. I have two. One of them has always been there when I needed him. I have cried for him and killed for him." Where was he now, while his siblings turned to each other? He was not like Itempas—he accepted change—but that did not make him immune to pain. Was he unhappy? If I went to him, would he confide in me? Need me?

It troubled me that I wondered this.

"The other father..." I drew a deep breath and raised my head, propping my folded arms on my knees instead. "Well, he and I never had the best relationship. Too different, you see. He's the firm disciplinarian type, and I am a brat." I glanced at them and smiled. "Rather like you two, actually."

They grinned back, accepting the title with honor. "We don't have any fathers," said the girl.

I raised my eyebrows in surprise. "*Someone* had to make you." Mortals had not yet mastered the art of making little mortals by themselves.

"Nobody important," said the boy, waving a hand dismissively. I guessed he had seen a similar gesture from his mother. "Mother needed heirs and didn't want to marry, so she chose someone she deemed suitable and had us."

"Huh." Not entirely surprising; the Arameri had never lacked for pragmatism. "Well, you can have mine, the second one. I don't want him."

The girl giggled. "He's your father! He can't be ours."

She probably prayed to the Father of All every night. "Of course he can be. Though I don't know if you'd like him any more than I do. He's a bit of a bastard. We had a falling-out some time ago, and he disowned me, even though he was in the wrong. Good riddance."

The girl frowned. "But don't you miss him?"

I opened my mouth to say *of course I don't* and then realized that I did. "Demonshit," I muttered.

They gasped and giggled appropriately at this gutter talk. "Maybe you should go see him," said the boy.

"I don't think so."

His small face screwed up into an affronted frown. "That's silly. Of course you should. He probably misses you."

I frowned, too taken aback by this idea to reject it out of hand. "What?"

"Well, isn't that what fathers do?" He had no idea what fathers did. "Love you, even if you don't love them? Miss you when you go away?"

I sat there silent, more troubled than I should have been.

Seeing this, the boy reached out, hesitating, and touched my hand. I looked down at him in surprise.

"Maybe you should be happy," he said. "When things are bad, change is good, right? Change means things will get better."

I stared at him, this Arameri child who did not at all look Arameri and would probably die before his majority because of it, and I felt the knot of frustration within me ease.

"An Arameri optimist," I said. "Where did you come from?"

To my surprise, both of them bristled. I realized at once that I had struck a nerve, and then realized which nerve when the girl lifted her chin. "He comes from right here in Sky, just like me."

The boy lowered his eyes, and I heard the whisper of taunts around him, some in childish lilt and some deepened by adult malice: *where did you come from did a barbarian leave you here by mistake maybe a demon dropped you off on its way to the hells because gods know you don't belong here.*

I saw how the words had scored his soul. He had made me feel better; he deserved something in recompense for that. I touched his shoulder and sent my blessing into him, making the words just words and making him stronger against them and putting a few choice retorts at the tip of his tongue for the next time. He blinked in surprise and smiled shyly. I smiled back.

The girl relaxed once it became clear that I meant her brother no harm. I willed a blessing to her, too, though she hardly needed it.

"I'm Shahar," she said, and then she sighed and unleashed her last and greatest weapon: politeness. "Will you *please* tell us how to get home?"

Ugh, what a name! The poor girl. But I had to admit, it suited her. "Fine, fine. Here." I looked into her eyes and made

her know the palace's layout as well as I had learned it over
the generations that I had lived within its walls. (Not the dead
spaces, though. Those were mine.)

The girl flinched, her eyes narrowing suddenly at mine. I
had probably slipped into my cat shape a little. Mortals tended
to notice the eyes, though that was never the only thing that
changed about me. I put them back to nice round mortal pupils,
and she relaxed. Then gasped as she realized she knew the way
home.

"That's a nice trick," she said. "But what the scriveners do is
prettier."

*A scrivener would have broken your head open if they'd tried
what I just did*, I almost retorted, but didn't because she was
mortal and mortals have always liked flash over substance and
because it didn't matter, anyway. Then the girl surprised me further, drawing herself up and bowing from the waist. "I thank
you, sir," she said. And while I stared at her, marveling at the
novelty of Arameri thanks, she adopted that haughty tone she'd
tried to use before. It really didn't suit her; hopefully she would
figure that out soon. "May I have the pleasure of knowing your
name?"

"I am Sieh." No hint of recognition in either of them. I stifled
a sigh.

She nodded and gestured to her brother. "This is Dekarta."

Just as bad. I shook my head and got to my feet. "Well, I've
wasted enough time," I said, "and you two should be getting
back." Outside the palace, I could feel the sun setting. For a
moment I closed my eyes, waiting for the familiar, delicious
vibration of my father's return to the world, but of course there
was nothing. I felt fleeting disappointment.

The children jumped up in unison. "Do you come here to play often?" asked the boy, just a shade too eagerly.

"Such lonely little cubs," I said, and laughed. "Has no one taught you not to talk to strangers?"

Of course no one had. They looked at each other in that freakish speaking-without-words-or-magic thing that twins do, and the boy swallowed and said to me, "You should come back. If you do, we'll play with you."

"Will you, now?" It *had* been a long time since I'd played. Too long. I was forgetting who I was amid all this worrying. Better to leave the worry behind, stop caring about what mattered, and do what felt good. Like all children, I was easy to seduce.

"All right, then," I said. "Assuming, of course, that your mother doesn't forbid it"—which guaranteed that they would never tell her—"I'll come back to this place on the same day, at the same time, next year."

They looked horrified and exclaimed in unison, "Next *year*?"

"The time will pass before you know it," I said, stretching to my toes. "Like a breeze through a meadow on a light spring day."

It would be interesting to see them again, I told myself, because they were still young and would not become as foul as the rest of the Arameri for some while. And, because I had already grown to love them a little, I mourned, for the day they became true Arameri would most likely be the day I killed them. But until then, I would enjoy their innocence while it lasted.

I stepped between worlds and away.

The next year I stretched and climbed out of my nest and stepped across space again, and appeared at the top of the Nowhere Stair. It was early yet, so I amused myself conjuring little moons and chasing them up and down the steps. I was winded and sweaty when the children arrived and spied me.

"We know what you are," blurted Deka, who had grown an inch.

"Do you, now? Whoops—" The moon I'd been playing with made a bid to escape, shooting toward the children because they stood between it and the corridor. I sent it home before it could put a hole in either of them. Then I grinned and flopped onto the floor, my legs splayed so as to take up as much space as possible, and caught my breath.

Deka crouched beside me. "Why are you out of breath?"

"Mortal realm, mortal rules," I said, waving a hand in a vague circle. "I have lungs, I breathe, the universe is satisfied, hee-ho."

"But you don't sleep, do you? I read that godlings don't sleep. Or eat."

"I can if I want to. Sleeping and eating aren't that interesting, so I generally don't. But it looks a bit odd to forgo breathing— makes mortals very anxious. So I do that much."

He poked me in the shoulder. I stared at him.

"I was seeing if you were real," he said. "The book said you could look like anything."

"Well, yes, but all of those things are *real*," I replied.

"The book said you could be fire."

I laughed. "Which would also be real."

He poked me again, a shy grin spreading across his face. I liked his smile. "But I couldn't do *this* to fire." He poked me a third time.

"Watch it," I said, giving him A Look. But it wasn't serious, and he could tell, so he poked me again. With that I leapt on him, tickling, because I cannot resist an invitation to play. So

we wrestled and he squealed and struggled to get free and complained that he would pee if I kept it up, and then he got a
hand free and started tickling me back, and it actually did tickle
awfully, so I curled up to escape him. It was like being drunk,
like being in one of Yeine's newborn heavens, so sweet and so
perfect and so much delicious fun. I *love* being a god!

But a hint of sour washed across my tongue. When I lifted my
head, I saw that Deka's sister stood where he had left her, shifting from foot to foot and trying not to look like she yearned to
join us. Ah, yes—someone had already told her that girls had
to be dignified while boys could be rowdy, and she had foolishly
listened to that advice. (One of many reasons I'd settled on a
male form myself. Mortals said fewer stupid things to boys.)

"I think your sister's feeling left out, Dekarta," I said, and she
blushed and fidgeted more. "What shall we do about it?"

"Tickle her, too!" Dekarta cried. Shahar threw him a glare,
but he only giggled, too giddy with play-pleasure to be repressed
so easily. I had a fleeting urge to lick his hair, but it passed.

"I'm not feeling left out," she said.

I petted Dekarta to settle him and to satisfy my grooming
urge, and considered what to do about Shahar. "I don't think
tickling would suit her," I said at last. "Let's find a game we can
all play. What about, hmm...jumping on clouds?"

Shahar's eyes widened. "What?"

"Jumping on clouds. Like jumping on a bed but better. I can
show you. It's fun, as long as you don't fall through a hole. I'll
catch you if you do—don't worry."

Deka sat up. "You can't do that. I've been reading books
about magic and gods. You're the god of childhood. You can
only do things children do."

I laughed, pulling him into a headlock, which he squealed and struggled to get free of, though he didn't struggle all that hard. "Almost anything can be done for play," I said. "If it's play, I have power over it."

He looked surprised, going still in my arms. I knew then that he had read the family records, because during my captivity, I had never once explained to the Arameri the full implications of my nature. They had thought I was the weakest of the Enefadeh. In truth, with Naha swallowed into mortal flesh every morning, I had been the strongest. Keeping the Arameri from realizing this had been one of my best tricks ever.

"Then let's go cloud jumping!" Deka said.

Shahar looked eager, too, as I offered her my hand. But just as she reached for my hand, she hesitated. A familiar wariness came into her eyes.

"L-Lord Sieh," she said, and grimaced. I did, too. I hated titles, so pretentious. "The book about you—"

"They wrote a book about me?" I was delighted.

"Yes. It said…" She lowered her eyes, then remembered that she was Arameri and looked up, visibly steeling herself. "It said you liked to kill people, back when you lived here. You would do tricks on them, sometimes funny tricks…but sometimes people would die."

Still funny, I thought, but perhaps this was not the time to say such things aloud. "It's true," I said, guessing her question. "I must've killed, oh, a few dozen Arameri over the years." Oh, but there had been that incident with the puppies. A few hundred, then.

She stiffened, and Deka did, too, so much that I let him go. Headlocks are no fun when they're real. "Why?" asked Shahar.

I shrugged. "Sometimes they were in the way. Sometimes to prove a point. Sometimes just because I felt like it."

Shahar scowled. I had seen that look on a thousand of her ancestors' faces, and it always annoyed me. "Those are bad reasons to kill people."

I laughed—but I had to force it. "Of course they're bad reasons," I said. "But how better to remind mortals that keeping a god as a slave is a bad idea?"

Her frown faltered a little, then returned in force. "The book said you killed *babies*. Babies didn't do anything bad to you!"

I had forgotten the babies. And now my good mood was broken, so I sat up and glared at her. Deka drew back, looking from one to the other of us anxiously. "No," I snapped at Shahar, "but I am the god of *all* children, little girl, and if I deem it fitting to take the lives of some of my chosen, then who the hells are you to question that?"

"I'm a child, too," she said, jutting her chin forward. "But *you're* not my god—Bright Itempas is."

I rolled my eyes. "Bright Itempas is a coward."

She inhaled, her face turning red. "He is not! That's—"

"He is! He murdered my mother and abused my father—and killed more than a few of his own children, I'll thank you to know! Do you think the blood is any thicker on my hands than on his? Or for that matter, on your own?"

She flinched, darting a look at her brother for support. "I've never killed anyone."

"*Yet.* But it doesn't matter, because everything you do is stained with blood." I rose to a crouch, leaning forward until my face was inches from hers. To her credit, she did not shrink away, glaring back at me—but frowning. Listening. So I told her. "All your family's power, all your riches, do you think they come from nowhere? Do you think you *deserve* them, because you're smarter or holier or whatever they teach this family's spawn these days? Yes, I killed babies. Because their mothers and fathers had no problem killing the babies of other mortals, who were heretics or who dared to protest stupid laws or who just didn't breathe the way you Arameri liked!"

Appropriately, I ran out of breath at that point and had to stop, panting for air. Lungs were useful for putting mortals at ease but still inconvenient. Just as well, though. Both children had fallen silent, staring at me in a kind of horrified awe, and belatedly I realized I had been ranting. Sulking, I sat down on a step and turned my back on them, hoping that my anger would pass soon. I liked them—even Shahar, irritating as she was. I didn't want to kill them yet.

"You...you think we're bad," she said after a long moment. There were tears in her voice. "You think *I'm* bad."

I sighed. "I think your family's bad, and I think they're going to raise you to be just like them." Or else they would kill her or drive her out of the family. I'd seen it happen too many times before.

"I'm not going to be bad." She sniffed behind me. Deka, who was still within the range of my eyesight, looked up and inhaled, so I guessed that she was full-out crying now.

"You won't be able to help it," I said, resting my chin on my drawn-up knees. "It's your nature."

"It isn't!" She stamped a foot on the floor. "My tutors say mortals aren't like gods! We don't have *natures*. We can all be what we *want* to be."

"Right, right." And I could be one of the Three.

Sudden agony shot through me, firing upward from the

small of my back, and I yelped and jumped and rolled halfway down the steps before I regained control of myself. Sitting up, I clutched my back, willing the pain to stop and marveling that it did so only reluctantly.

"You kicked me," I said in wonder, looking up the steps at her.

Deka had covered his mouth with both hands, his eyes wide; of the two of them, only he seemed to have realized that they were about to die. Shahar, fists clenched and legs braced and hair wild and eyes blazing, did not care. She looked ready to march down the steps and kick me again.

"I *will* be what I want to be," she declared. "I'm going to be head of the family one day! What I say I'll do, I'll do. I *am* going to be good!"

I got to my feet. I wasn't angry, in truth. It is the nature of children to squabble. Indeed, I was glad to see that Shahar was still herself under all the airs and silks; she was beautiful that way, furious and half mad, and for a fleeting instant I understood what Itempas had seen in her foremother.

But I did not believe her words. And that put me in an altogether darker mood as I went back up the steps, my jaw set and tight.

"Let's play a game, then," I said, and smiled.

Deka got to his feet, looking torn between fear and a desire to defend his sister; he hovered where he was, uncertain. There was no fear in Shahar's eyes, though some of her anger faded into wariness. She wasn't stupid. Mortals always knew to be careful when I smiled a certain way.

I stopped in front of her and held out a hand. In it, a knife appeared. Because I was Yeine's son, I made it a Darre knife, the kind they gave to their daughters when they first learned to take lives in the hunt. Six inches straight and silvery, with a handle of filigreed bone.

"What is this?" she asked, frowning at it.

"What's it look like? Take it."

After a moment she did, holding it awkwardly and with visible distaste. Too barbaric for her Amn sensibilities. I nodded my approval, then beckoned to Dekarta, who was studying me with those lovely dark eyes of his. Remembering one of my other names, no doubt: *Trickster*. He did not come at my gesture.

"Don't be afraid," I said to him, making my smile more innocent, less frightening. "It's your sister who kicked me, not you, right?"

Reason worked where charm had not. He came to me, and I took him by the shoulders. He was not as tall as I, so I hunkered down to peer into his face. "You're really very pretty," I said, and he blinked in surprise, the tension going out of him. Utterly disarmed by a compliment. He probably didn't get them often, poor thing. "In the north, you know, you'd be ideal. Darre mothers would already be haggling for the chance to marry you to their daughters. It's only here among the Amn that your looks are something to be ashamed of. I wish they could see you grown up; you would have broken hearts."

"What do you mean, 'would have'?" asked Shahar, but I ignored her.

Deka was staring at me, entranced in the way of any hunter's prey. I could have eaten him up.

I cupped his face in my hands and kissed him. He shivered, though it had been only a fleeting press of lips. I'd held back the force of myself because he was only a child, after all. Still, when I pulled back, I saw his eyes had glazed over; blotches of color warmed his cheeks. He didn't move even when I slid my hands down and wrapped them around his throat.

Shahar went very still, her eyes wide and, finally, frightened. I glanced over at her and smiled again.

"I think you're just like any other Arameri," I said softly. "I think you'll want to kill me rather than let me murder your brother, because that's the good and decent thing to do. But I'm a god, and you know a knife can't stop me. It'll just piss me off. Then I'll kill him *and* you." She twitched, her eyes darting from mine to Deka's throat and back. I smiled and found my teeth had grown sharp. I never did this deliberately. "So I think you'll let him die rather than risk yourself. What do you think?"

I almost pitied her as she stood there breathing hard, her face still damp from her earlier tears. Deka's throat worked beneath my fingers; he had finally realized the danger. Wisely, though, he held still. Some predators are excited by movement.

"Don't hurt him," she blurted. "Please. Please, I don't—"

I hissed at her, and she shut up, going pale. "Don't beg," I snapped. "It's beneath you. Are you Arameri or not?"

She fell silent, hitching once, and then—slowly—I saw the change come over her. The hardening of her eyes and will. She lowered the knife to her side, but I saw her hand tighten on its hilt.

"What will you give me?" she asked. "If I choose?"

I stared at her, incredulous. Then I burst out laughing. "That's my girl! Bargaining for your brother's life! Perfect. But you seem to have forgotten, Shahar, that that's not one of your options. The choice is very simple: your life or his—"

"No," she said. "That's not what you're making me choose. You're making me choose between being bad and, and being myself. You're trying to *make* me bad. That's not fair!"

I froze, my fingers loosening on Dekarta's throat. In the Maelstrom's unknowable name. I could feel it now, the subtle lessening of my power, the greasy nausea at the pit of my belly. Across all the facets of existence that I spanned, I diminished. It was worse now that she had pointed it out, because the very fact that she understood what I had done made the harm greater. Knowledge was power.

"Demonshit," I muttered, and grimaced ruefully. "You're right. Forcing a child to choose between death and murder—there's no way innocence can survive something like that intact." I thought a moment, then scowled and shook my head. "But innocence never lasts long, especially for Arameri children. Perhaps I'm doing you a favor by making you face the choice early."

She shook her head, resolute. "You're not doing me a favor; you're cheating. Either I let Deka die, or I try to save him and die, too? It's not fair. I can't win this game, no matter what I do. You better do something to make up for it." She did not look at her brother. He was the prize in this game, and she knew it. I would have to revise my opinion of her intelligence. "So...I want you to give me something."

Deka blurted, "Just let him kill me, Shar; then at least you'll live—"

"Shut up!" She snapped it before I would have. But she closed her eyes in the process. Couldn't look at him and keep herself cold. When she looked back at me, her face was hard again. "And you don't have to kill Deka, if I...if I take that knife and use it on you. Just kill me. That'll make it fair, too. Him or me, like you said. Either he lives or I do."

I considered this, wondering if there was some trick in it. I could see nothing untoward, so finally I nodded. "Very well. But you *must choose*, Shahar. Stand by while I kill him, or attack me, save him, and die yourself. And what would you have of me, as compensation for your innocence?"

At this she faltered, uncertain.

"A wish," said Dekarta.

I blinked at him, too surprised to chastise him for talking. "What?"

He swallowed, his throat flexing in my hands. "You grant one wish, anything in your power, for... for whichever one of us survives." He took a shaky breath. "In compensation for taking *our* innocence."

I leaned close to glare into his eyes, and he swallowed again. "If you dare wish that I become your family's slave again—"

"No, we wouldn't," blurted Shahar. "You can still kill me— or... or Deka—if you don't like the wish. Okay?"

It made sense. "Very well," I said. "The bargain is made. Now *choose*, damn you. I don't feel like being—"

She lunged forward and shoved the knife into my back so fast that she almost blurred. It hurt, as all damage to the body does, for Enefa in her wisdom had long ago established that flesh and pain went hand in hand. While I froze, gasping, Shahar let go of the knife and grabbed Dekarta instead, yanking him out of my grasp. "Run!" she cried, pushing him away from the Nowhere Stair toward the corridors.

He stumbled a step away and then, stupidly, turned back to her, his face slack with shock. "I thought you would pick... you should have..."

She made a sound of utter frustration while I sagged to my knees and struggled to breathe around the hole in my lung. "I *said* I would be good," she said fiercely, and I would have laughed in pure admiration if I'd been able. "You're my brother! Now go! Hurry, before he—"

"Wait," I croaked. There was blood in my mouth and throat. I coughed and fumbled behind me with one hand, trying to reach the knife. She'd put it high in my back, partially through my heart. Amazing girl.

"Shahar, come with me!" Deka grabbed her hands. "We'll go to the scriveners—"

"Don't be stupid. They can't fight a god! You have to—"

"*Wait*," I said again, having finally coughed out enough blood to clear my throat. I spat more into the puddle between my hands and still couldn't reach the knife. But I could talk, softly and with effort. "I won't hurt either of you."

"You're lying," said Shahar. "You're a trickster."

"No trick." Very carefully I took a breath. Needed it to talk. "Changed my mind. Not going to kill...either of you."

Silence. My lung was trying to heal, but the knife was in the way. It would work its way free in a few minutes if I couldn't reach it, but those minutes would be messy and uncomfortable.

"Why?" asked Dekarta finally. "Why did you change your mind?"

"Pull this...mortalfucking knife, and I'll tell you."

"It's a trick—" Shahar began, but Dekarta stepped forward. Bracing a hand on my shoulder, he took hold of the knife hilt and yanked it free. I exhaled in relief, though that almost started me coughing again.

"Thank you," I said pointedly to Dekarta. When I glared at Shahar, she tensed and took a step back, then stopped and inhaled, her lips pressed tightly together. Ready for me to kill her.

"Oh, enough with the martyrdom," I said wearily. "It's lovely, just lovely, that you two are all ready to die for each other, but it's also pretty sickening, and I'd rather not throw up more than blood right now."

Dekarta had not taken his hand from my shoulder, and I realized why when he leaned to the side to peer at my face. His eyes widened. "You weakened yourself," he said. "Making Shahar choose... It hurt you, too."

Far more than the knife had done, though I had no intention of telling them that. I could have willed the knife out of my flesh or transported myself away from it, if I had been at my best. Shaking off his hand, I got to my feet, but I had to cough one or two times more before I felt back to normal. As an afterthought, I sent away the blood from my clothing and the floor.

"I destroyed some of her childhood," I said, sighing as I turned to her. "Stupid of me, really. Never wise to play adult games with children. But, well, you pissed me off."

Shahar said nothing, her face hollow with relief, and my stomach did an extra turn at this proof of the harm I'd done her. But I felt better when Dekarta moved to her side, and his hand snaked out to take hers. She looked at him, and he gazed back. Unconditional love: childhood's greatest magic.

With this to strengthen her, Shahar faced me again. "Why did you change your mind?"

There had been no reason. I was a creature of impulse. "I think because you were willing to die for him," I said. "I've seen Arameri sacrifice themselves many times—but rarely by choice. It intrigued me."

They frowned, not really understanding, and I shrugged. I didn't understand it, either.

"So, then, I owe you a wish," I said.

They looked at each other again, their expressions mirrors of consternation, and I groaned. "You have no idea what you want to wish for, do you?"

"No," said Shahar, ducking her eyes.

"Come back in another year," said Dekarta, quickly. "That's more than enough time for us to decide. You can do that, can't you? We'll…" He hesitated. "We'll even play with you again. But no more games like this one."

I laughed, shaking my head. "No, they're not much fun, are they? Fine, then. I'll be back in a year. You'd better be ready."

As they nodded, I took myself away to lick my wounds and recover my strength. And to wonder, with dawning surprise, what I'd gotten myself into.

2

Run away, run away
Or I'll catch you in a day
I can make you scream and play
'Til my father goes away
(Which one? Which one?
That one! That one!)
Just run, just run, just run.

As always when I was troubled, I sought out my father, Nahadoth.

He was not difficult to find. Amid the vastness of the gods' realm, he was like a massive, drifting storm, terrifying for those in his path and cathartic in his wake. From any direction, one could look into the distance and there he was, defying logic as a matter of course. Almost as noticeable were the lesser presences that drifted nearby, drawn toward all that heavy, dark glory even though it might destroy them. I beheld my siblings in all their variety and sparkling beauty, elontid and mnasat and even a few of my fellow niwwah. Many lay prostrate before our dark father or strained toward the black unlight that was his core, their souls open for the most fleeting droplets of his approval. He played favorites, though, and many of them had served Itempas. They would be waiting a long time.

For me, however, there was welcome on the wind as I traveled through the storm's outermost currents. The layered walls of his presence shifted aside, each in a different direction, to admit me. I caught the looks of envy from my less-favored siblings and gave them glares of contempt in return, staring down the stronger ones until they turned away. Craven, useless creatures. Where had they been when Naha needed them? Let them beg his forgiveness for another two thousand years.

As I passed through the last shiver, I found myself taking corporeal form. A good sign, that; when he was in a foul mood, he abandoned form altogether and forced any visitors to do the same. Better still, there was light: a night sky overhead, dominated by a dozen pale moons all drifting in different orbits and waxing and waning and shifting from red through gold through blue. Beneath it, a stark landscape, deceptively flat and still, broken here and there by line-sketched trees and curving shapes too attenuated to qualify as hills. My feet touched ground made of tiny mirrored pebbles that jumped and rattled and vibrated like frenzied living things. They sent a delicious buzz through my soles. The trees and hills were made of the glittering pebbles, too—and the sky and moons, for all I knew. Nahadoth was fond of playing with expectations.

And beneath the sky's cool kaleidoscope, shaping himself in an aimless sort of way, my father. I went to him and knelt, watching and worshipping, as his shape blurred through several forms and his limbs twisted in ways that had nothing to do with grace, though occasionally he grew graceful by accident. He did not acknowledge my presence, though of course he knew I was there. Finally he finished, and fell, purposefully, onto a couch-like throne that formed itself as I watched. At this, I rose and went to stand beside him. He did not look at me, his face turned toward the moons and shifting only slightly now, mostly just reacting to the colors of the sky. His eyes were shut, only the long dark lashes remaining the same as the flesh around them changed.

"My loyal one," he said. The pebbles hummed with the low reverberations of his voice. "Have you come to comfort me?"

I opened my mouth to say yes—and then paused, startled, as I realized this was not true. Nahadoth glanced at me, laughed softly and not without cruelty, and widened his couch. He knew me too well. Shamed, I climbed up beside him, nestling into the drifting curve of his body. He petted my hair and back, though I was not in the cat's shape. I enjoyed the caresses anyhow.

"I hate them," I said. "And I don't."

"Because you know, as I do, that some things are inevitable."

I groaned and flung an arm over my eyes dramatically, though this only served to press the image into my thoughts:

Yeine and Itempas straining together, gazing at each other in mutual surprise and delight. What would be next? Naha and Itempas? All three of them together, which existence had not seen since the demons' time? I lowered my arm and looked at Nahadoth and saw the same sober contemplation on his face. Inevitable. I bared my teeth and let them grow cat-sharp and sat up to glare at him.

"You *want* that selfish, thickheaded bastard! Don't you?"

"I have always wanted him, Sieh. Hatred does not exclude desire."

He meant the time before Enefa's birth, when he and Itempas had gone from enemies to lovers. But I chose to interpret his words more immediately, manifesting claws and digging them into the drifting expanse of him.

"Think of what he did to you," I said, flexing and sheathing. I could not hurt him—would not even if I could—but there were many ways to communicate frustration. "To us! Naha, I know you will change, must change, but you need not change *this* way! Why go back to what was before?"

"Which before?" That made me pause in confusion, and he sighed and rolled onto his back, adopting a face that sent its own wordless message: white-skinned and black-eyed and emotionless, like a mask. The mask he had worn for the Arameri during our incarceration.

"The past is gone," he said. "Mortality made me cling to it, though that is not my nature, and it damaged me. To return to myself, I must reject it. I have had Itempas as an enemy; that holds no more appeal for me. And there is an undeniable truth here, Sieh: we have no one but each other, he and I and Yeine."

At this I slumped on him in misery. He was right, of course;

I had no right to ask him to endure again the hells of loneliness he had suffered in the time before Itempas. And he would not, because he had Yeine and their love was a powerful, special thing—but so had been his love with Itempas, once. And when all Three had been together…How could I, who had never known such fulfillment, begrudge him?

He would not be alone, whispered a small, furious voice in my most secret heart. *He would have me!*

But I knew all too well how little a godling had to offer a god.

Cold white fingers touched my cheek, my chin, my chest. "You are more troubled by this than you should be," said Nahadoth. "What is wrong?"

I burst into frustrated tears. "I don't know."

"Shhhh. Shhhh." She—Nahadoth had changed already, adapting to me because she knew I preferred women for some things—sat up, pulling me into her lap, and held me against her shoulder while I wept and hitched fitfully. This made me stronger, as she had known it would, and when the squall passed and nature had been served, I drew a deep breath.

"I don't know," I said again, calm now. "Nothing is right anymore. I don't understand the feeling, but it's troubled me for some while now. It makes no sense."

She frowned. "This is not about Itempas."

"No." Reluctantly I lifted my head from her soft breast and reached up to touch her more rounded face. "Something is changing in me, Naha. I feel it like a vise gripping my soul, tightening slowly, but I don't know who holds it or turns it, nor how to wriggle free. Soon I might break."

Naha frowned and began to shift back toward male. It was a warning; *she* was not as quick to anger as *he* was. He was male most of the time these days. "Something has caused this." His eyes glinted with sudden suspicion. "You went back to the mortal realm. To Sky."

Damnation. We were all, we Enefadeh, still sensitive to the stench of that place. No doubt I would have Zhakkarn on my doorstep soon, demanding to know what madness had afflicted me.

"*That* had nothing to do with it, either," I said, scowling at his overprotectiveness. "I just played with some mortal children."

"Arameri children." Oh, gods, the moons were going dark, one by one, and the mirror-pebbles had begun to rattle ominously. The air smelled of ice and the acrid sting of dark matter. Where was Yeine when I needed her? She could always calm his temper.

"Yes, Naha, and they had no power to harm me or even to command me as they once did. And I felt the wrongness *before* I went there." It had been why I'd followed Yeine, feeling restless and angry and in search of excuses for both. "They were just children!"

His eyes turned to black pits, and suddenly I was truly afraid. "You love them."

I went very still, wondering which was the greater blasphemy: Yeine loving Itempas, or me loving our slavemasters?

He had never hurt me in all the aeons of my life, I reminded myself. Not intentionally.

"Just children, Naha," I said again, speaking softly. But I couldn't deny his words. *I loved them.* Was that why I had decided not to kill Shahar, breaking the rules of my own game? I hung my head in shame. "I'm sorry."

After a long, frightening moment, he sighed. "Some things are inevitable."

He sounded so disappointed that my heart broke. "I—"
I hitched again, and for a moment hated myself for being the
child I was.

"Hush now. No more crying." With a soft sigh, he rose,
holding me against his shoulder effortlessly. "I want to know
something."

The couch dissolved back into the shivering bits of mirror,
and the landscape vanished with it. Darkness enclosed us, cold
and moving, and when it resolved, I gasped and clutched at
him, for we had traveled via his will into the blistering chasm
at the edge of the gods' realm, which contained—insofar as the
unknowable could be contained—the Maelstrom. The monster
Itself lay below, far below, a swirling miasma of light and sound
and matter and concept and emotion and moment. I could hear
Its thought-numbing roar echoing off the wall of torn stars that
kept the rest of reality relatively safe from Its ravenings. I felt
my form tear as well, unable to maintain coherence under the
onslaught of image-thought-music. I abandoned it quickly. Flesh
was a liability in this place.

"Naha…" He still held me against him, yet I had to shout to
be heard. "What are we doing here?"

Nahadoth had become something like the Maelstrom,
churning and raw and formless, singing a simpler echo of Its
toneless songs. He did not answer at first, but he had no sense
of time in this state. I schooled myself to patience; he would
remember me eventually.

After a time he said, "I have felt something different
here, too."

I frowned in confusion. "What, in the Maelstrom?" How
he could comprehend anything of this morass was beyond

me—quite literally. In my younger, stupider days, I had dared to play in this chasm, risking everything to see how deeply I could dive, how close I could get to the source of all things. I could go deeper than all my siblings, but the Three could go deeper still.

"Yes," Nahadoth said at length. "I wonder..."

He began to move downward, toward the chasm. Too stunned to protest at first, I finally realized he was actually taking me in. "Naha!" I struggled, but his grip was steel and gravity. "Naha, damn you, do you want me dead? Just kill me yourself, if so!"

He stopped, and I kept shouting at him, hoping reason would somehow penetrate his strange thoughts. Eventually it did, and to my immense relief, he began to ascend.

"I could have kept you safe," he said with a hint of reproof.

Yes, until you lost yourself in the madness and forgot I was there. But I was not a complete fool. I said instead, "Why were you taking me there anyhow?"

"There is a resonance."

"What?"

The chasm and the roar vanished. I blinked. We stood in the mortal realm, on a branch of the World Tree, facing the unearthly white glow of Sky. It was nighttime, of course, with a full moon, and the stars had shifted fractionally. A year had passed. It was the night before I was to meet the twins a third time.

"There is a resonance," Nahadoth said again. He was a darker blotch against the Tree's bark. "You, and the Maelstrom. The future or the past, I cannot tell which."

I frowned. "What does that mean?"

"I don't know."

"Has it ever happened before?"

"No."

"Naha…" I swallowed my frustration. He did not think as lesser beings did. It was necessary to move in spirals and leaps to follow him. "Will it hurt me? I suppose that's all that matters."

He shrugged as if he did not care, though his brows had furrowed. He wore his Sky face again. This close to the palace where we had both endured so many hells, I did not like it as much.

"I will speak to Yeine," he said.

I shoved my hands into my pockets and hunched my shoulders, kicking at a spot of moss on the bark beneath my feet. "And Itempas?"

To my relief, Nahadoth uttered a dry, malicious laugh. "*Inevitable* is not the same as *immediate*, Sieh—and love does not mandate forgiveness." With that he turned away, his shadows already blending with those of the Tree and the night horizon. "Remember that, with your Arameri pets."

Then he was gone. The clouds above the world wavered for an instant with his passing, and then reality became still.

Troubled beyond words, I became a cat and climbed the branch to a knot the size of a building, around which clustered several smaller branches that were dotted with the Tree's triangle-shaped leaves and silvery flowers. There I curled up, surrounded by Yeine's comforting scent, to await the next day. And I wondered—with no surcease since I no longer had to sleep—why my insides felt hollow and shaky with dread.

With time to kill before the meeting, I amused myself—if one can call it amusing—by wandering the palace in the hours before dawn. I started in the underpalace, which had so often been a haven for me in the old days, and discovered that it had indeed been entirely abandoned. Not just the lowest levels, which had always been empty (save the apartments I and the other Enefadeh had inhabited), but all of it: the servants' kitchens and dining halls, the nurseries and schoolrooms, the sewing salons and haircutters'. All the parts of Sky dedicated to the lowbloods who made up the bulk of its population. By the look of things, no one had been in the underpalace to do more than sweep in years. No wonder Shahar and Dekarta had been so frightened that first day.

On the overpalace levels, at least, there were servants about. None of them saw me as they went about their duties, and I didn't even bother to shape myself an Amn form or hide in a pocket of silence. This was because even though there were servants, there weren't *many* of them—not nearly as many as there had been in my slave days. It was a simple matter to step around a curve of corridor when I heard one walking toward me, or spring up to cling to the ceiling if I was caught between two. (Useful fact: mortals rarely look up.) Only once was I forced to use magic, and that not even my own; faced with an inescapable convergence of servants who would surely spot me otherwise, I stepped into one of the lift alcoves, where some long-dead scrivener's activation bounced me up to another level. Criminally easy.

It should not have been so easy for me to stroll about, I mused as I continued to do so. I had reached the highblood levels by this point, where I did have to be a bit more careful. There were fewer servants here, but more guards, wearing the ugliest white livery I'd ever seen—and swords, and crossbows, and hidden daggers, if my fleshly eyes did not deceive me. There had always been guards in Sky, a small army of them, but they had taken pains to remain unobtrusive in the days when I'd lived here. They had dressed the same as the servants and had never worn weapons that could be seen. The Arameri preferred to believe that guards were unnecessary, and they hadn't been, in truth, back then. Any significant threat to the palace's highbloods would have forced us Enefadeh to transport ourselves to the site of danger, and that would've been the end of it.

So, I considered as I stepped through a wall to avoid an unusually attentive guard, it seemed the Arameri had been forced to protect themselves more conventionally. Understandable—but how did that account for the diminished number of servants?

A mystery. I resolved to find out, if I could.

Stepping through another wall, I found myself in a room that held a familiar scent. Following it—and tiptoeing past the nurse dozing on the sitting room couch—I found Shahar, asleep in a good-sized four-poster bed. Her perfect blonde curls spread prettily over half a dozen pillows, though I stifled a laugh at her face: mouth open, cheek mashed on one folded arm, and a line of drool down that arm forming a puddle on the pillow. She was snoring quite loudly and did not stir when I went over to examine her toy shelf.

One could learn a great deal about a child from her play. Naturally I ignored the toys on the highest shelves; she would want her favorites within easy reach. On the lower shelves, someone had been cleaning the things and keeping them in good order, so it was hard to spot the most worn of the items. Scents revealed much, however, and three things in particular drew me closer. The first was a large stuffed bird of some sort. I touched my tongue to it and tasted a toddler's love, fading now.

The second was a spyglass, light but solidly made so as to withstand being dropped by clumsy hands. Perhaps she used it to look down at the city or up at the stars. It had an air of wonder that made me smile.

The third item, which made me stop short, was a scepter.

It was beautiful, intricate, a graceful, twisting rod marbled with bright jewel tones down its length. A work of art. Not made of glass, though it appeared to be; glass would have been too fragile to give to a child. No, this was tinted daystone, the same substance as the palace's walls—very difficult to shatter, among its other unique properties. (I knew that very well, since I and my siblings had created it.) Which was why, centuries ago, a family head had commissioned this and other such scepters from his First Scrivener, and had given it to the Arameri heir as a toy. *To learn the feel of power*, he had said. And since then, many little Arameri boys and girls had been given a scepter on their third birthday, which most of them promptly used to whack pets, other children, and servants into painful obedience.

The last time I had seen one of these scepters, it had been a modified, adult version of the thing on Shahar's shelf. Fitted with a knife blade, the better to cut my skin to ribbons. The perversion of a child's toy had made each slice burn like acid.

I glanced back at Shahar—fair Shahar, *heir* Shahar, someday Lady Shahar Arameri. A very few Arameri children would not have used the scepter, but Shahar, I felt certain, was not so gentle. She would have wielded it with glee at least once. Deka had probably been her first victim. Had her brother's cry of pain cured her of the taste for sadism? So many Arameri learned to treasure the suffering of their loved ones.

I contemplated killing her.

I thought about it for a long time.

Then I turned and stepped through the wall into the adjoining room.

A suite, yes; that, too, was traditional for Arameri twins. Side-by-side apartments, connected by a door in the bedroom, ostensibly so that the children could sleep together or apart as they desired. More than one set of Arameri twins had been reduced to a singlet thanks to such doors. So easy for the stronger twin to creep into the weaker one's room unnoticed, in the dark of the night while the nurses slept.

Deka's room was darker than Shahar's, as it was positioned on the side of the palace that did not get moonlight. It would get less sunlight, too, I realized, for through the window-wall I could see one of the massive, curling limbs of the World Tree stretching into the distance against the night horizon. Its spars and branches and million, million leaves did not completely obscure the view, but any sunlight that came in would be dappled, unsteady. Tainted, by Itempan standards.

There were other indicators of Deka's less-favored status: fewer toys on the shelves, not as many pillows on the bed. I went to the bed and gazed down at him, thoughtful. He was curled on his side, neat and quiet even in rest. His nurse had done his long black hair in several plaits, perhaps in an awkward bid to give it some curl. I bent and ran my finger along one plait's smooth, rippling length.

"Shall I make you heir?" I whispered. He did not wake, and I got no answer.

Moving away, I was surprised to realize none of the toys on his shelves tasted of love. Then I understood when I came to the small bookcase, which practically reeked of it. Over a dozen books and scrolls bore the stamp of childish delight. I ran my fingers along their spines, absorbing their mortal magic. Maps of faraway lands, tales of adventure and discovery. Mysteries of the natural world—of which Deka probably experienced little, stuck here in Sky. Myths and fancies.

I closed my eyes and lifted my fingers to my lips, breathing the scent and sighing. I could not make a child with such a soul heir. It would be the same as destroying him myself.

I moved on.

Through the walls, underneath a closet, over a jutting spar of the World Tree that had nearly filled one of the dead spaces, and I found myself in the chambers of the Arameri head.

The bedroom alone was as big as both the children's apartments combined. Large, square bed at the center, positioned atop a wide circular rug made from the skin of some white-furred animal I could not recall ever having hunted. Austere, by the standards of the heads I had known: no pearls sewn into the coverlet, no Darren blackwood or Kenti hand carving or Shuti-Narekh cloudcloth. What little other furniture there was had been positioned about the edges of the vast room, out of the way. A woman who did not like impediments in any part of her life.

The Lady Arameri herself was austere. She lay curled on her side, much like her son, though that was as far as the similarity went. Blonde hair, surprisingly cut short. The style framed her angular face well, I decided, but it was not at all the usual Amn thing. Beautiful, icy-pale face, though severe even in sleep. Younger than I'd expected: late thirties at a guess. Young enough that Shahar would come of age long before she was elderly. Did she intend for Shahar's children to be the true heirs, then? Perhaps this contest was not as foregone as it seemed.

I looked around, thoughtful. No father, the children had said, which meant the lady had no husband in the formal sense. Did she deny herself lovers, too, then? I bent to inhale her scent, opening my mouth slightly for a better taste, and there it was, oh, yes. The scent of another was embedded deep in her hair and skin, and even into the mattress. A single lover of some duration—months, perhaps years. Love, then? It was not unheard of. I would hunt amid the palace denizens to see if I could find the match to that lilting scent.

The lady's apartment told me nothing about her as I visited its other chambers: a substantial library (containing nothing interesting), a private chapel complete with Itempan altar, a personal garden (too manicured to have been cared for by anything but a professional gardener), a public parlor and a private one. The bath alone showed signs of extravagance: no mere tub here but a pool wide and deep enough to swim, with separate adjoining chambers for washing and dressing. I found her toilet in another chamber, behind a crystal panel, and laughed. The seat had been inscribed with sigils for warmth and softness. I could not resist; I changed them to ice-cold hardness. Hopefully I could arrange to be around to hear her shout when she discovered them.

By the time I finished exploring, the eastern sky was growing light with the coming dawn. So with a sigh I left Lady Arameri's chambers, returned to the Nowhere Stair, and lay down at the bottom to wait.

It seemed an age before the children arrived, their small feet striking a determined cadence as they came through the silent corridors. They did not see me at first, and exclaimed in dismay—then, of course, they came down the steps and found me. "You were hiding!" Shahar accused.

I had arranged myself on the floor, with my legs propped up against the wall. Smiling at her upside down, I said, "Talking to strangers again. Will you two never learn?"

Dekarta came over to crouch beside me. "Are you a stranger to us, Sieh? Even still?" He reached out and poked my shoulder again, as he had done before he learned I was dangerous. He smiled shyly and blushed as he did it. Had he forgiven me, then? Mortals were so fickle. I poked him back and he giggled.

"*I* don't think so," I said, "but you lot are the ones who worship propriety. The way I see it, a stranger feels like a stranger; a friend feels like a friend. Simple."

To my surprise, Shahar crouched as well, her small face solemn. "Would you mind, then?" she asked with a peculiar sort of intent that made me frown at her. "Being our friend?"

I understood all at once. The wish they'd earned from me. I'd expected them to choose something simple, like toys that never broke or baubles from another realm or wings to fly. But they were clever, my little Arameri pets. They would not be bribed by paltry material treasures or fleeting frivolities. They wanted something of real worth.

Greedy, presumptuous, insolent, *arrogant* brats.

I flipped myself off the wall with an awkward, ugly movement that no mortal could have easily replicated. It startled the children and they fell back with wide eyes, sensing my anger. On my hands and toes, I glared at them. "You want *what*?"

"Your friendship," said Deka. His voice was firm, but his eyes looked uncertain; he kept glancing at his sister. "We want you to be our friend. And we'll be yours."

"For how long?"

They looked surprised. "For as long as friendship lasts," said

Shahar. "Life, I guess, or until one of us does something to break it. We can swear a blood oath to make it official."

"Swear a—" The words came out as a bestial growl. I could feel my hair turning black, my toes curling under. "How dare you?"

Shahar, damn her and all her forbears, looked innocently confused. I wanted to tear her throat out for not understanding. "What? It's just friendship."

"*The friendship of a god.*" If I'd had a tail, it would have lashed. "If I did this, I would be obligated to play with you and enjoy your company. After you grow up, I'd have to look you up every once in a while to see how you're doing. I'd have to *care* about the inanities of your life. At least *try* to help you when you're in trouble. My gods, do you realize I don't even offer my worshippers that much? I should kill you both for this!"

But to my surprise, before I could, Deka sat forward and put his hand on mine. He flinched as he did it, because my hand was no longer fully human; the fingers had shortened, and the nails were in the process of becoming retractable. I kept the fur off by an effort of will. But Deka kept his hand there and looked at me with more compassion than I'd ever dreamt of seeing on an Arameri's face. All the swirling magic inside me went still.

"I'm sorry," he said. "We're sorry."

Now two Arameri had apologized to me. Had that ever happened when I'd been a slave? Not even Yeine had said those words, and she had hurt me terribly once during her mortal years. But Deka continued, compounding the miracle. "I didn't think. You were a prisoner here once—we read about it. They made you act like a friend then, didn't they?" He looked over at Shahar, whose expression showed the same dawning understanding. "Some of the old Arameri would punish him if he wasn't nice enough. We can't be like them."

My desire to kill them flicked away, like a snuffed candle.

"You...didn't know," I said. I spoke slowly, reluctantly, forcing my voice back into the boyish higher registers where it belonged. "It's obvious you don't mean...what I think you meant by it." A backhanded route to servitude. Unearned blessings. I moved my nails back into place and sat up, smoothing my hair.

"We thought you would like it," Deka said, looking so crestfallen that I abruptly felt guilty for my anger. "I thought...we thought..."

Yes, of course, it would have been his idea; he was the dreamer of the two.

"We thought we were almost friends anyway, right? And you didn't seem to mind coming to see us. So we thought, if we asked to be friends, you would see we weren't the bad Arameri you think we are. You would see we weren't selfish or mean, and maybe"—he faltered, lowering his eyes—"maybe then you would keep coming back."

Children could not lie to me. It was an aspect of my nature; they could lie, but I would know. Neither Deka nor his sister were lying. I didn't believe them anyway—didn't want to believe them, didn't trust the part of my own soul that tried to believe them. It was never safe to trust Arameri, even small ones.

Yet they meant it. They wanted my friendship, not out of greed but out of loneliness. They truly wanted me for myself. How long had it been since anyone had wanted me? Even my own parents?

In the end, I am as easy to seduce as any child.

I lowered my head, trembling a little, folding my arms across my chest so they would not notice. "Um. Well. If you really want to ... to be friends, then ... I guess I could do that."

They brightened at once, scooching closer on their knees. "You mean it?" asked Deka.

I shrugged, pretending nonchalance, and flashed my famous grin. "Can't hurt, can it? You're just mortals." Blood-brother to mortals. I shook my head and laughed, wondering why I'd been so frightened by something so trivial. "Did you bring a knife?"

Shahar rolled her eyes with queenly exasperation. "You can make one, can't you?"

"I was just asking, gods." I raised a hand and made a knife, just like the one she'd used to stab me the previous year. Her smile faded and she drew back a little at the sight of it, and I realized that was not the best choice. Closing my hand about the knife, I changed it. When I opened my hand again, the knife was curved and graceful, with a handle of lacquered steel. Shahar would not know, but it was a replica of the knife Zhakkarn had made for Yeine during her time in Sky.

She relaxed when she saw the change, and I felt better at the grateful look on her face. I had not been fair to her; I would try harder to be so in the future.

"Friendships can transcend childhood," I said softly when Shahar took the knife. She paused, looking at me in surprise. "They can. If the friends continue to trust each other as they grow older and change."

"That's easy," said Deka, giggling.

"No," I said. "It isn't."

His grin faded. Shahar, though—yes, here was something

she understood innately. She had already begun to realize what it meant to be Arameri. I would not have her for much longer.

I reached up to touch her cheek for a moment, and she blinked. But then I smiled, and she smiled back, as shy as Deka for an instant.

Sighing, I held out my hands, palms up. "Do it, then."

Shahar took my nearer hand, raising the knife, and then frowned. "Do I cut the finger? Or across the palm?"

"The finger," said Deka. "That was how Datennay said you do blood oaths."

"Datennay is an idiot," Shahar said with the reflexiveness of an old argument.

"The palm," I said, more to shut them up than to take any real stance.

"Won't that bleed a lot? And hurt?"

"That's the idea. What good is an oath if it doesn't cost you something to make?"

She grimaced, but then nodded and set the blade against my skin. The cut she made was so shallow that it tickled and did not make me bleed at all. I laughed. "Harder. I'm not a mortal, you know."

She threw me an annoyed look, then sliced once across the palm, swift and hard. I ignored the flash of pain. Refreshing. The wound tried to close immediately, but a little concentration kept the blood welling.

"You do me, I do you," Shahar said, giving the knife to Dekarta.

He took the knife and her hands and was not at all hesitant or shy about cutting his sister. Her jaw flexed, but she did not cry out. Nor did he when she made the cuts for him.

I inhaled the scent of their blood, familiar despite three generations removed from the last Arameri I had known. "Friends," I said.

Shahar looked at her brother, and he gazed back at her, and then they both looked at me. "Friends," they said together. They took each other's hands first, then mine.

Then—

Wait. What?

They held my hands, tight. It hurt. And why were both children crying out, their hair whipping in the wind? Where had the wind—

I didn't hear you. Speak louder.

This made no sense, our hands were *sealed, sealed together*, I could not let them go—

Yes, I am the Trickster. Who calls...?

They were screaming, the children were screaming, both of them had risen off the floor, only I held them down and why was there a grin on my face? Why—

Silence.

3

I SLEPT, and while I did, I dreamt. I did not remember some of these dreams for a long time. I was aware of very little, in fact, aside from

something

being

wrong

and perhaps a little bit of

wait

I

thought

what.

Vague awareness, in other words. A most unpleasant state for any god. None of us is all knowing, all seeing—that is mortal nonsense—but we know *a lot* and see *quite a bit*. We are used to a near-constant infusion of information by means of senses no mortal possesses, but for a time there was nothing. Instead, I slept.

Suddenly, though, in the depths of the silence and vagueness, I heard a voice. It called my name, my *soul*, with a fullness and strength that I had not heard in several mortal lifetimes. Familiar pulling sensation. Unpleasant. I was comfortable, so I rolled over and tried to ignore it at first, but it pricked me awake, slapped me in the back to prod me forward, then shoved. I slid through an aperture in a wall of matter, like being born—or like entering the mortal realm, which was pretty much the same thing. I emerged naked and slippery with magic, my form reflexively solidifying itself for protection against the soul-devouring ethers that had once been Nahadoth's digestive fluids, in the time before time. My mind dragged itself out of stupor at last.

Someone had called my name.

"What do you want?" I said—or tried to say, though the words emerged from my lips as an unintelligible growl. Long before mortals had achieved a form worthy of imitation, I had taken the likeness of a creature that loved mischief and cruelty in equal measure, as quintessential an encapsulation of my nature as my child shape. I still tended to default to it, though I preferred the child shape these days. More fine control and nuance. But I had not been fully conscious when I took form in the mortal realm, and so I had become the cat.

Yet that shape was clumsy when I tried to rise, and something about it... felt wrong. I wasted no time trying to understand it, simply became the boy instead—or tried to. The change did not go as it should have. It took real effort, and my flesh remolded itself with molasses-slow reluctance. By the time I had clothed myself in human skin, I was exhausted. I flopped where I had materialized, panting and shaking and wondering what in the infinite hells was wrong with me.

"*Sieh?*"

The voice that had summoned me from the vague place. Female. Familiar and yet not. Puzzled, I tried to lift my head and turn to face the voice's owner, and found to my amazement that I could not. I had no strength.

"It *is* you. My gods, I never imagined..." Soft hands touched my shoulders, pulled at me. I groaned softly as she rolled me onto my side. Something pulled at my head, painful. Why the hells was I cold? I was never cold.

"By the endless Bright! This is..."

She touched my face. I turned toward her hand instinctively, nuzzling, and she gasped, jerking away. Then she stroked me again and did not pull away when I pressed against her this time.

"Sh-Shahar," I said. My voice was too loud and sounded wrong. I opened my eyes as wide as I could and stared at her, buglike. "Shahar?"

She was Shahar. I was certain of it. But something had happened to her. Her face was longer, the bones finer, the nose bridge higher. Her hair, which had been shoulder length when I'd last seen her—a moment ago? The day before?—now tumbled around her body, disheveled as if she'd just woken from sleep. Waist length at least, maybe longer.

Mortal hair did not grow so quickly, and not even Arameri would waste magic on something so trivial. Not these days, anyhow. Yet when I tried to find the nearby stars to know how much time had passed, what came back to me was only a blank, unintelligible rumble, like the jabbering of memory-worms.

"Cold," I murmured. Shahar got up and went away. An instant later, something covered me, warm and thick with the scents of her body and bird feathers. It should not have warmed me, any more than my body should have been cold to begin with, but I felt better. By this point I could move a little, so I curled up under it gratefully.

"Sieh..." She sounded like she was regaining her composure after a deep shock. Her hand fell on my shoulder again, comforting. "Not that I'm not glad to see you"—she did not sound glad, not at all—"but if you were ever going to come back, why now? Why here, like this? This...gods. Unbelievable."

Why now? I had no idea, since I had no idea what *now* meant. Of *then*, I remembered less thoughts than impressions: holding her hand, holding Deka's hand. Light, wind, something out of control. Shahar's face, wide-eyed with panic, mouth open and—

Screaming. She had been screaming.

Some of my strength had returned. I used it to reach for her knee, which was a few inches from my face. My fingers slid over smooth, hot skin to reach thin, fine cloth—a sleep shift. She gasped and jerked away. "You're freezing!"

"I'm *cold*." So cold that I could feel the room's moisture beginning to cling to my skin, wherever the blanket didn't cover it. I pulled my head under the blanket, or tried to. That pulling sensation again. It held my head in place, though I could move somewhat against its tension. "Demonshit! What is that?"

"Your hair," said Shahar.

I froze, staring up at her.

She pushed at my arm, then pulled up a lock of hair for me to see. Loose-waved, dark brown, thick, and longer than her arm. *Feet* long. I couldn't move because I was half tangled in it.

"I didn't tell my hair to get that long," I said. It was a whisper.

"Well, tell it to get short again. Or quit flopping about so I can get you loose." She flipped up the blanket and started gathering my hair, tugging and finger combing. When she turned me onto my side, my head was freed. I'd been lying on the bulk of it.

My hair should not have grown. *Her* hair should not have

grown. "Tell me what's happened," I said as she shifted me about like an oversized doll. "How much time has passed since we took the oath?"

"Took the oath?" She stared down at me, an incredulous look on her face. "Is that all you remember? My gods, Sieh, you broke the oath almost the instant you made it—"

I cursed in three mortal languages, loudly, to cut her off. "Just tell me how much time has passed!"

Fury reddened her cheeks, though the pale light around us— Sky's glowing walls—made this difficult to see. "Eight years."

Impossible. "I would have remembered eight years."

I should have understood the anger in her voice as she snapped, "Well, that's how long it's been. Not my fault if you don't remember it. I suppose you must have so many important things to do, you gods, that mortal years pass like breaths for you."

They did, but we were *aware* of the breaths. I wanted to know more, like why she sounded so angry and hurt. Those things called to me like the sting of broken innocence, and they felt important. But they also felt like the sorts of things that needed to be softened with silence before they were brought forth sharp, so I pushed them aside and asked, "Why am I so weak?"

"How should I know?"

"Where was I? While I was gone?"

"Sieh"—she let out a hard exhalation—"I don't know. I haven't seen you once since the day eight years ago when you and I and Deka agreed to become friends. You tried to kill us and disappeared."

"Tried—I didn't try to kill you." Her face hardened further, full of hate. That meant I *had* tried to kill her, or at least she believed I had. "I didn't *intend* to. Shahar—" I reached for her again, instinctive this time. I could pull strength from mortal children if I had to, but when I touched her knee again, there was only a trickle of what I needed. Of course; eight years. She would be sixteen now—not yet a woman, but close. I whimpered in frustration and pulled away.

"I remember nothing from that moment until now," I said, to take my mind off fear. "I took your hands and then I was here. Something is wrong."

"Obviously." She pinched the bridge of her nose between her fingers and let out a heavy sigh. "Hopefully your arrival didn't trip the boundary scripts in the walls, or there will be a dozen guards breaking down the door in a minute. I'm going to have to think of some way to explain your presence." She paused, frowning at me hopefully. "Or can you leave? That would really be the easiest solution."

Yes, good for me and for her. It was obvious she didn't want me here. I didn't want to be here, either, weak and heavy and wrong-feeling like this. I wanted to be with, with, wait, was that—Oh, no.

"No," I whispered, and when she sighed in exasperation, I realized she thought I'd been responding to her question. I made a heroic effort and grabbed her hand as tight as I could, startling her. "*No*. Shahar, how did you bring me here? Did you use scrivening, or—or did you command it somehow?"

"I didn't bring you here. You just showed up."

"No, you made me come, I felt it, you pulled me out of him—" And oh demons, oh hells, I could feel him coming. His fury made the whole mortal realm throb like an open wound. How could she not feel it? I shook her hand in lieu of shouting at her. "You pulled me out of him and *he's going to kill you if you don't tell me right now what you did!*"

"Who—" she began. And then she froze, her eyes going wide, because even she could feel it now. Of course she could, because he was in the room with us, taking shape as the glowing walls went suddenly dark and the air trembled and hushed in reverence.

"Sieh," said the Lord of Night.

I closed my eyes and prayed Shahar would stay silent.

"Here," I said. An instant later he was beside me, the drifting dark of his cloak settling around him as he knelt. Chilly fingers touched my face, and I fought the urge to laugh at my own obtuseness. I should have realized at once why I was so cold.

He turned my face from side to side, examining me with more than eyes. I permitted this, because he was my father and it was his right to be concerned, but then I caught his hand. It solidified beneath my touch, and strength flowed into me from the limitless furnace of his soul. I exhaled in relief. "Naha. Tell me."

"We found you adrift, like a soul with no home. Damaged. Yeine attempted to heal you and could not. I took you into myself to do the same."

And Nahadoth's womb was a cold, dark place. "I don't feel healed."

"You aren't. I could not find a cure for your condition, nor could I preserve you." His voice, usually inflectionless, turned bitter. It was Itempas's gift to halt the progression of processes that depended on time; Nahadoth lacked this power entirely. "The best I could do was keep you safe while Yeine sought a cure. But you were taken from me. I had no idea where you had gone . . . at first."

And then his dark, dark eyes lifted to settle on Shahar. She flinched, quite reasonably.

I had no reason to want to save her, other than my own childish sense of honor. I had taken her innocence; I owed her. And however wrong it seemed to have gone, I had taken an oath to be her friend. So I sat up carefully—not into his line of sight, because that was never safe, but enough to get his attention. "Naha, whatever she did, she didn't do it intentionally."

"Her intentions do not matter," he said very softly. He did not look away from her. "When you were pulled from me, it felt much like the days of our incarceration. A summons that could be neither ignored nor denied."

Shahar made a soft sound, not quite a whimper, and Nahadoth's expression turned sharp and hungry. I did not blame him for his anger, but Shahar was not like the Arameri of old; she had not been raised to know the ways of gods. She did not realize that her fear could spur him to attack, because night was the time of predators and she was acting too much like prey.

Before I could think of some way to distract him, the worst occurred: she spoke.

"L-Lord Nahadoth," she said. Her voice shook, and he leaned closer to her, his breath quickening and the room growing darker. Demonshit. But then, to my surprise, she drew a deep breath and her fear receded. "Lord Nahadoth," she said again. "I assure you, I did nothing to . . . to *summon* Lord Sieh here. I was thinking of him, yes...." She glanced at me, her expression suddenly bleak, which confused me. "I spoke his name. But not because I wanted him here—quite the opposite. I was angry. It was a curse."

I stared at her. A *curse?* But her shift of mood had done what I could not; Naha exhaled and sat back.

"A curse is much like a prayer," he said, thoughtful. "If you knew his nature well enough..."

"A prayer wouldn't have snatched me from your void," I said, looking down at myself. The length of my limbs was obscene. My palms were half again as large as they had been! I was meant to have small, clever child fingers, not these monstrous paws. "And it couldn't have done *this* to me. Nothing should have done this." Now that Naha had renewed my strength, I could correct the error. I willed myself back to normal.

"Stop." Nahadoth's will clamped down on mine like a vise before I could begin the shaping. I froze, startled. "It is no longer safe for you to alter your form."

"No longer *safe?*"

He sighed. "You do not understand." So he looked into my eyes and made me know what he and Yeine had come to realize in the eight years since everything had gone wrong.

There is a line between god and mortal that has nothing to do with immortality. It is *material*: a matter of substance, composition, flexibility. This was what ultimately made the demons weaker than us, though some of them had all our power: they could cross this line, become godstuff, but it took great effort, and they could not do it for long. It was not their natural state. Other mortals could not cross the line at all. They were locked to their flesh, aging as it aged, drawing strength from its strength and growing weak with its failure. They could not shape it or the world around them, save with the crude power of their hands and wits.

The problem, Nahadoth willed me to know, was that I was no longer quite like a god. The substance of me was somewhere between godstuff and mortality—but I was becoming more mortal as time passed. I could still shape myself if I wished, as I had done when I arrived as the cat. But it would not go easily. There might be pain, damage to my flesh, permanent distortion. And there would come a day, perhaps today, perhaps another, when I would no longer be able to shape myself at all. If I tried then, I would die.

I stared at him and felt truly afraid.

"What are you saying?" I whispered, though he had said nothing. Mortal figure of speech. "Naha, what are you saying?"

"You are becoming mortal."

I was breathing harder. I had not willed myself to breathe harder. Or tremble, or sweat, or grow larger, or mature into manhood. My body was doing all that on its own. My body: alien, tainted, out of control.

"I'm going to die," I said. My mouth was dry. "Naha, growing older defies my nature. If I stay like this, if I keep aging, if I *trip and fall* hard enough, I'll die the way mortals do."

"We will find a way to heal you—"

My fists clenched. *"Don't lie to me!"*

Naha's mask cracked, replaced by sorrow. I remembered ten million nights in his lap, begging him for stories. His beautiful lies, I had called them. He had held me and told me of wonders real and imagined, and I had been so happy to never grow up. So that he could keep lying to me forever.

"You will grow older," he said. "As you leave childhood behind, you will grow weaker. You will begin to require sustenance and rest as mortals do, and your awareness of things beyond mortal senses will fade. You will become...fragile. And, yes, if nothing is done, you will die."

I could not bear the softness of his voice, no matter how hard the words. He was always so soft, always yielding, always tolerant of change. I did not want him to tolerate this.

I threw off the blanket and got to my feet—awkwardly, as my limbs were longer than I was used to and I had too much hair—and stumbled over to Shahar's windows. I put my hands on the glass and leaned on it with all my weight. Mortals rarely did this, I had observed during my centuries in Sky. Even though they knew that Sky's glass was reinforced by magic and inhumanly precise engineering, they could not rid themselves of the fear that just once, the glass might break or the pane come loose. I braced my feet and shoved. I needed *something* in my presence to be unmoving and strong.

Something touched my shoulder and I turned fast, irrationally aching for hard sunset eyes and harder brown arms and brick-wall flexibility. But it was only the mortal, Shahar. I glared at her, furious that she wasn't who I wanted, and thought of batting her aside. It was somehow her fault this had happened to me. Maybe killing her would free me.

If she had looked at me with compassion or pity, I would have done it. There was none of that in her face, though—just resentment and reluctance, nothing at all comforting. She was Arameri. That wasn't something they did.

Itempas had failed me, but Itempas's chosen had been magnificently predictable for two thousand years. I yanked her closer and locked my arms around her, so tight that it couldn't have been comfortable for her. She turned her face away and her cheek pressed against my shoulder. She did not bend, though—didn't speak, didn't return my embrace. So I held her and trembled and ground my teeth together so that I would not simply start screaming. I glared at Nahadoth through the screen of her curls.

He gazed back at me, still and rueful. He knew full well why I had turned away from him, and he forgave me for it. I hated him for that, just as I'd hated Yeine for loving Itempas and just as I hated Itempas for going mad and not being here when I needed him. And I hated all three of them for squandering each other's love when I would give anything, *anything*, to have that for myself.

"Go away," I whispered through Shahar's hair. "Please."

"It isn't safe for you here."

I laughed bitterly, guessing his intent. "If I'm to have only a few more decades of life, Naha, I won't spend them asleep inside you. Thanks."

His expression tightened. He was not immune to pain, and I supposed I was driving the knives in deeper than usual. "You have enemies."

I sighed. "I can take care of myself."

"I will not lose you, Sieh. Not to death, and not to despair."

"Get out!" I clutched Shahar like a teddy bear and shut my eyes, shouting, "Get out, demons take you, go away and leave me the hells alone!"

There was an instant of silence. Then I felt him go. The walls resumed their glow; the room felt suddenly looser, airy. Shahar relaxed, minutely, against me. But not all the way.

I kept her against me anyway because I was feeling selfish and I did not want to care what she wanted. But I was older now, more mature whether I wanted to be or not, so after a moment I stopped thinking solely about myself. She stepped back when I let her go, and there was a distinctly wary look in her eyes.

"What are you going to do?" she asked.

I laughed, leaning back against the glass. "I don't know."

"Do you want to stay here?"

I groaned and put my hands on my head, tangling my fingers in all my unwanted hair. "I don't know, Shahar. I can't think right now. This is a bit much, all right?"

She sighed. I felt her come to stand beside me at the window, radiating thought. "You can sleep in Deka's room for tonight. In the morning I'll speak with Mother."

I was so soul-numb that this did not bother me nearly as much as it should have. "Fine," I said. "Whatever. I'll try not to wake him as I pace the floors and cry."

There was a moment's silence. That did not catch my attention so much as the ripple of hurt that rode in the silence's wake. "Deka isn't here. You'll have the room to yourself."

I looked at her, frowning. "Where is he?" Then it occurred to me: Arameri. "Dead?"

"No." She didn't look at me and her expression didn't change, but her voice went sharp and contemptuous of my assumption. "He's at the Litaria. The scriveners' college? In training."

I raised both eyebrows. "I didn't know he wanted to become a scrivener."

"He didn't."

Then I understood. Arameri, yes. When there was more than one potential heir, the family head did not *have* to pit them against one another in a battle to the death. She could keep both alive if she put one in a clearly subordinate position. "He's meant to be your First Scrivener, then."

She shrugged. "If he's good enough. There's no guarantee. He'll prove himself if he can, when he comes back. *If* he comes back."

There was something more here, I realized. It intrigued me enough to forget my own troubles for a moment, so I turned to her, frowning. "Scrivener training lasts years," I said. "Ten or fifteen, usually."

She turned to face me, and I flinched at the look in her eyes. "Yes. Deka has been in training for the past eight years."

Oh, no. "Eight years ago..."

"Eight years ago," she said in that same clipped, edged tone, "you and I and Deka took an oath of friendship. Immediately upon which you unleashed a flare of magic so powerful that it destroyed the Nowhere Stair and much of the underpalace— and then you vanished, leaving Deka and me buried in the rubble with more bones broken than whole."

I stared at her, horrified. She narrowed her eyes, searching my face, and a flicker of consternation diluted her anger. "You didn't know."

"No."

"How could you not know?"

I shook my head. "I don't remember anything after we joined

hands, Shahar. But…you and Deka were wise to ask for my friendship; it should have made you safe from me for all time. I don't understand what happened."

She nodded slowly. "They pulled us out of the debris and patched us up, good as new. But I had to tell Mother about you. She was furious that we'd concealed something so important. And the heir's life had been threatened, which meant someone had to be held accountable." She folded her arms, holding her shoulders ever-so-slightly stiff. "Deka had fewer injuries than I. Our fullblood relatives started to hint that Deka—only Deka, never me—might have done something to antagonize you. They didn't come right out and accuse him of plotting to use a godling as a murder weapon, but…"

I closed my eyes, understanding at last why she had cursed my name. I had stolen her innocence first and then her brother. She would never trust me again.

"I'm sorry," I said, knowing it was wholly inadequate.

She shrugged again. "Not your fault. I see now that what happened was an accident."

She turned away then, pacing across her room to the door that adjoined her suite to the one that had been Dekarta's. Opening it, she turned back to look at me, expectant.

I stayed by the window, seeing the signs clearly now. Her face was impassive, cool, but she had not completely mastered herself yet. Fury smoldered in her, banked for now, but slow burning. She was patient. Focused. I would think this a good thing, if I hadn't seen it before.

"You don't blame me," I said, "though I'll wager you did, until tonight. But you still blame *someone*. Who?"

I expected her to dissemble. "My mother," she said.

"You said she was pressured into sending Deka away."

Shahar shook her head. "It doesn't matter." She said nothing for a moment more, then lowered her eyes. "Deka... I haven't heard from him since he left. He returns my letters unopened."

Even with my senses as muddled as they were, I could feel the raw wound in her soul where a twin brother had been. A wound like that demanded redress.

She sighed. "Come on."

I took a step toward her and stopped, startled as I realized something. Arameri heads and heirs had loathed one another since the Bright's dawning. Unavoidable, given circumstances: two souls with the strength to rule the world were rarely good at sharing or even cohabitating, for that matter. That was why the family's heads had been as ruthless about controlling their heirs as they were about controlling the world.

My eyes flicked to Shahar's odd, incomplete blood sigil. None of the controlling words were there. She was free to act against her mother, even plot to kill her, if she wanted.

She saw my look and smiled. "My old friend," she said. "You were right about me, you know, all those years ago. Some things are my nature. Inescapable."

I crossed the room to stand beside her on the threshold. I was surprised to find myself uncertain as I considered her. I should have felt vindicated to hear her plans of vengeance. I should have said, and meant it, *You'll do worse before you're done.*

But I had tasted her childish soul, and there had been something in it that did not fit the cold avenger she seemed to have become. She had loved her brother, enough to sacrifice herself for him. She had sincerely yearned to be a good person.

"No," I said. She blinked. "You're different from the rest of them. I don't know why. You shouldn't be. But you are."

Her jaw flexed. "Your influence, maybe. As gods go, you've had a greater impact on my life than Bright Itempas ever could."

"That should've made you worse, actually." I smiled a little, though I did not feel like it. "I'm selfish and cruel and capricious, Shahar. I've never been a good boy."

She lifted an eyebrow, and her eyes flicked down. I wore nothing but my ridiculously long hair, which fell to my ankles now that I was standing. (My nails, however, had kept to my preferred length. Partial mortality, partial growth? I would live in dread of my first manicure.) I thought Shahar was looking at my chest, but my body was longer now, taller. Belatedly I realized her gaze had settled lower.

"You're not a *boy* at all anymore," she said.

My face went hot, though I did not know why. Bodies were just bodies, penises were just penises, yet she had somehow made me feel keenly uncomfortable with mine. I could think of nothing to say in reply.

After a moment, she sighed. "Do you want food?"

"No…" I began, but then my belly churned in that odd, clenching way that I had not felt in several mortal generations. I had not forgotten what it meant. I sighed. "But I will by morning."

"I'll have a double tray brought up. Will you sleep?"

I shook my head. "Too much on my mind, even if I was exhausted. Which I'm not." Yet.

She sighed. "I see."

Suddenly I realized *she* was exhausted, her face lined and

paler than usual. My time sense was returning—murky, sluggish, but functional—so I understood it had been well past
midnight when she'd summoned me. Cursed me. Had she been
pacing the floor herself, her mind cluttered with troubles? What
had caused her to remember me, however hatefully, after all this
time? Did I want to know?

"Does our oath stand, Shahar?" I asked softly. "I didn't mean
to harm you."

She frowned. "Do you want it to stand? I seem to recall you
were less than thrilled by the idea of two mortal friends."

I licked my lips, wondering why I was so uneasy. *Nervous.*
She made me nervous. "I think perhaps . . . I could use friends,
under the circumstances."

She blinked, then smiled with one side of her mouth. Unlike
her earlier smiles, this one was genuine and free of bitterness.
It made me see how lonely she was without her brother—and
how young. Not so far removed, after all, from the child she had
been.

Then she stepped forward, putting her hands on my chest,
and kissed me. It was light, friendly, just a warm press of her lips
for an instant, but it rang through me like a crystal bell. She
stepped back and I stared at her. I couldn't help it.

"Friends, then," she said. "Good night."

I nodded mutely, then went into Deka's room. She shut the
door behind me, and I slumped back against it, feeling alone
and very strange.

4

Sleep, little little one
Here is a world
With hate on every continent
And sorrow in the fold.
Wish for a better life
Far, far from here
Don't listen while I talk of it
Just go there.

I DIDN'T SLEEP THAT NIGHT, though I could have. The urge was there, itchy. I imagined the craving for sleep as a parasite feeding on my strength, just waiting for me to grow weak so that it could take over my body. I had liked sleep, once, before it became a threat.

But I did not like boredom, either, and there was a great deal of that in the hours after I left Shahar. I could only ponder my troubling condition for so long. The only way to vent my frustration was to do something, anything, so I got up from the chair and wandered about Deka's room, peering into the drawers and under the bed. His books were too simple to interest me, except one of riddles that actually contained a few I hadn't heard before. But I read it in half an hour and then was bored again.

There is nothing more dangerous than a bored child—and though I had become a bored adolescent, that old mortal adage still rang true. So as the small hours stretched into slightly longer hours, I finally got up and opened a wall. That much, at least, I could do without expending any of my remaining strength; all it took was a word. When the daystone had finished rolling aside to make room for me, I went through the resulting opening into the dead spaces beyond.

Roaming my old territory put me in a better mood. Not everything was the same as it had been, of course. The World Tree had grown both around and through Sky, filling some of its old corridors and dead spaces with branchwood and forcing me to make frequent detours. This, I knew, had been Yeine's intent, for without the Enefadeh, and more importantly without the constant empowering presence of the Stone of Earth, Sky needed the Tree's support. Its architecture broke too many of Itempas's laws for the mortal realm; only magic kept it in the sky and not smashed on the ground.

So down seventeen levels, around a swirling rise of linked globules that only resembled a tunnel in dreams, and underneath an arched branch spur, I found what I'd sought: my orrery. I moved carefully between the protective traps I'd set, out of habit stepping around the patches of moonstone that lined the floor. It looked like daystone—mortals had never been able to tell the difference—but on cloudy, new-moon nights, the pieces of moonstone transformed, opening into one of Nahadoth's favorite hells. I had made it as a little treat for our masters, to remind them of the price to be paid for enslaving their gods, and we had all seeded it through the palace. They had blamed—and punished—Nahadoth for it, but he'd thanked me afterward, assuring me the pain was worth it.

But when I spoke *atadie* and the orrery opened, I stopped on its threshold, my mouth falling open.

Where there should have been more than forty globes floating through the air, all turning around the bright yellow sphere
at the orrery's center, there were only four still floating. *Four*,
counting the sun sphere. The rest lay scattered about the floor
and against the walls, corpses in the aftermath of a systemic
carnage. The Seven Sisters, identical small goldenworlds I
had collected after searching billions of stars, lay strewn about
the edges of the room. And the rest—Zispe, Lakruam, Ama-
naiasenre, the Scales, Motherspinner with its six child moons
linked by a web of rings, and oh, Vaz, my handsome giant. That
one, once a massive stark-white sphere I had barely been able to
get my arms around, had hit the floor hard, splitting down the
middle. I went to the nearer of the shattered halves and picked
it up, moaning as I knelt. Its core was exposed, cold, still. Planets were resilient things, far more than most mortal creatures,
but there was no way I could repair this. Even if I'd had the
magic left to spare.

"No," I whispered, clutching the hemisphere to myself and
rocking over it. I couldn't even weep. I felt as dead as Vaz inside.
Nahadoth's words had not driven home the horror of my condition, but this? This I could not deny.

A hand touched my shoulder, and so great was my misery
that I did not care who it was.

"I'm sorry, Sieh." Yeine. Her voice, a soft contralto, had deepened further with grief. I felt her kneel beside me, her warmth
radiant against my skin. For once, I took no comfort in her
presence.

"My fault," I whispered. I had always meant to disperse the
orrery, returning its worlds to their homes when I'd tired of
them. Only I never had, because I was a selfish brat. And when

I'd been incarcerated in mortal form, desperate to feel like a god because my Arameri masters treated me like a thing, I had brought the orrery here despite the danger that they might be discovered. I had spent strength I didn't have, killing my mortal body more than once, to keep the orrery alive. And now, after all that, I hadn't even noticed that I'd failed them.

Yeine sighed and looped her arms around my shoulders, pressing her face to my hair for a moment. "Death comes to all, in time."

But this had been too soon. My orrery should have lasted a sun's lifetime. I drew a deep breath and set the hemisphere down, turning to look up at her. Her face did not show the shock that I knew she felt at the sight of my older shape. I was grateful for that, because she could have flinched at my withered beauty, but of course that was not her way. She still loved me, would always love me, even if I could no longer be her little boy. I lowered my eyes, ashamed that I had ever begrudged Itempas her affection.

"There are some survivors," I said softly. "They..." I drew a deep breath. What would I do without them? I would truly be alone then...but I would do what was right. They deserved that, these truest friends of mine. "Will you help them, Yeine? Please?"

"Of course." She closed her eyes. One by one, the planets that still floated about the sun sphere, and a couple of the ones on the floor, vanished. I followed with her as best I could, watching her carefully deposit each where I had found it: this one spinning around a bright golden sun, which was delighted to have it back; that one near twin suns that sang in harmony; that one in the heart of a stellar nursery, surrounded by howling infant planets and hissing, cranky magnetars, where it sighed and resigned itself to the noise.

But when Yeine reached for the sun sphere, En, it fought her. Surprised, we both opened our eyes back in the orrery to find that En had shed its ordinary yellow kickball disguise. It had begun to spin and burn, expending itself in a dangerous way given that I could not replenish it. At this rate, it would fail and die like the rest in minutes.

"What the hells are you doing?" I demanded of it. "Quit that; you're being rude."

It responded by darting out of its place and whisking over to boot me in the stomach. I *oof*ed in surprise, wrapping my arms around it inadvertently, and felt its outrage. How dare I try to send it away? It was older than many of my siblings. Had it not always been there when I needed it? It would not be sent away like some disgraced servant.

I touched its hot, pale-yellow surface, trying not to cry. "I can't take care of you anymore," I said. "Don't you understand? If you stay with me, you'll die."

It would die, then. Did not care it would die did not care.

"Stubborn ball of hot air!" I shouted, but then Yeine touched my hand where it rested on En's curve. When she did, En glowed brighter; she was feeding it as I could not.

"A true friend," she said gently, with only a hint of censure, "is something to be treasured."

"Not to death," I said, looking up at her for support. "Yeine, please; it's crazy. Send it away."

"Shall I deny its wishes, Sieh? Force it to do what you want? Am I Itempas now?"

And at that I faltered, silent, because of course she knew

of my earlier anger. Perhaps she had even known I was there, spying on her with Itempas until I'd flounced off. I hunched, ashamed of myself and then ashamed that I felt ashamed.

"You use force when it suits you," I muttered, trying to cover the shame with sullenness.

"And when I must, yes. But it doesn't suit me now."

"I don't want more death on my conscience," I said, both to her and to En. "Please, En. I couldn't bear to lose you. Please!"

En—the demonshitting, lightfarting gasbag—responded by turning red and bloating with each passing second. Gathering itself to explode, as if that was somehow better than starving to death! I groaned.

Yeine rolled her eyes. "A tantrum. I suppose that's to be expected, given your influence, but really..." She shook her head and sat back on her knees, looking around thoughtfully. For an instant her eyes darkened, from their usual faded green to something deep and shadowed, like a thick, wet forest, and then suddenly the orrery chamber was empty. All my dead toys vanished. En, too, for which I felt sudden regret.

"I'll keep the rest safe for you," she said, reaching up to smooth a hand over my hair as she had always done. I closed my eyes and relaxed into the comfort of familiarity, pretending for a moment that I was still small and all was well. "Until the day you can reclaim them and send them home yourself."

I exhaled, grateful despite the bitterness her words triggered in me. It hurt her to make dead things live again; it went against her nature, a perversion of the cycle Enefa had designed at the beginning of life. She did not do it often, and we never asked it of her. But...I licked my lips. "Yeine...this thing that's happening to me..."

She sighed, looking troubled, and belatedly I realized there was no need to ask. If she'd had the power to reverse my transformation into a mortal, she would have used it, no matter what harm it did her. But what did it mean, then, that the goddess who had supreme power over mortality could not erase mine?

"If I were older," she said, and I felt guilty for making her doubt herself. She lowered her eyes, looking small and vulnerable, like the mortal girl she resembled. "If I knew myself better, perhaps I would be able to find some solution."

I sighed and shifted to lie on my side, putting my head in her lap after awkwardly pushing my hair out of the way. "This may be beyond all of us. Nothing like it has ever happened before. It's pointless to rail against what you can't stop." I scowled. "*That* would make you Itempas."

"Nahadoth is unhappy," she said.

I suspected she wanted to change the subject. I sighed. "Nahadoth is overprotective."

She stroked my hair again, then lifted the tangled mass and began to finger comb it. I closed my eyes, soothed by the rhythmic movements.

"Nahadoth loves you," she said. "When we first found you in this...condition...he tried so hard to restore you that it damaged him. And yet..." She paused, her tension suddenly prickling the air between us.

I frowned, both at her description of Nahadoth's behavior and at her hesitation. "What?"

She sighed. "I'm not certain you can be any more reasonable about this than Naha."

"*What*, Yeine?" But then I understood, and as she had

predicted, I grew unreasonably angry. "Oh gods and demons, no, no you don't. You want to talk to Itempas."

"Resisting change is his nature, Sieh. He may be able to do what Nahadoth could not: stabilize you until I find a cure. Or if we joined again, as Three—"

"No! You'd have to set him free for that!"

"Yes. For your sake."

I sat up, scowling. "I. Don't. Care."

"I know. Neither does Nahadoth, to my surprise."

"Naha—" I blinked. "What?"

"He is willing to do anything to save you. Anything, that is, except the one thing that might actually work." Abruptly she was angry, too. "When I asked, he said he would rather let you die."

"Good! He knows *I* would rather die than ask for that bastard's help! Yeine"—I shook my head but forced the words out—"I understand why you're drawn to him, even though I hate it. Love him if you must, but don't ask the same of me!"

She glared back, but I did not back down, and after a moment, she sighed and looked away. Because I was right, and she knew it. She was still so young, so mortal. She knew the story, but she had not *been there* to see what Itempas had done to Nahadoth, or to the rest of us Enefadeh. She lived with the aftermath—as did we all, as would every living thing in the universe, forever and ever—but that was entirely different from knowing firsthand.

"You're as bad as Nahadoth," she said at last, more troubled than angry. "I'm not asking you to forgive. We all know there's no forgiving what he did, the past can't be rewritten, but someday you're going to have to *move on.* Do what's necessary for the world, and for yourselves."

"Staying angry is necessary for me," I said petulantly, though I forced myself to take a deep breath. I did not want to be angry with her. "One day, maybe, I'll move on. Not now."

She shook her head, but then took me by the shoulders and guided me down so that my head lay in her lap again. I had no choice but to relax, which I wanted to do, anyway, so I sighed and closed my eyes.

"It's irrelevant in any case," she said, still sounding a bit testy. "We can't find him."

I did not want to talk about him, either, but I dredged up interest. "Why not?"

"I don't know. But he's been missing for several years now. When we seek his presence in the mortal realm, we feel nothing, find nothing. We aren't worried...yet."

I considered this but could offer no answer. Even together, the Three were not omniscient, and Yeine and Nahadoth alone were not the Three. If Itempas had found some scrivener to craft an obscuration for him...But why would he do that?

For the same reason he does anything else, I decided. *Because he's an ass.*

"I don't," Yeine said softly after a while. I frowned in confusion. She sighed and stroked my hair again. "Love him, I mean."

So many unspokens in her words. *Not yet* the most obvious among them, and perhaps a bit of *not ever, because I am not Enefa,* though I did not believe that. She was too drawn to him already. Most relevant was *not until you love him, too,* which I could live with.

"Right." I sighed, weary again. "Right. I don't love him, either."

We both fell silent at that, for a long while. Eventually she began to touch my hair here and there, causing the excess length to fall away. I closed my eyes, grateful for her attention, and wondered how many more times I would be privileged to experience it before I died.

"Do you remember?" I asked. "The last day of your mortal life. You asked me what would happen when you died."

Her hands went still for a moment. "You said you didn't know. Death wasn't something you'd thought much about."

I closed my eyes, my throat tightening for no reason I could fathom. "I lied."

Her voice was too gentle. "I know."

She finished my hair and gathered the shed length of it in one hand. I felt the flick of her will, and then she put her hand in front of my face to show me what she'd done. My hair had become a thin woven cord short enough to loop about my neck, and threaded onto this cord was a small, yellow-white marble. A different size and substance, but I would recognize its soul anywhere: En.

I sat up, surprised and pleased, lifting the necklace to grin at my old friend. (It did not like being smaller. It missed being a kickball, bouncy and fat. Did it have to be this puny, rigid shape just because I wasn't a child anymore? Surely adult mortals liked to kick balls sometimes. I stroked it to still its whining.) Then I touched my shorter hair and found that she'd reshaped that, too, giving me a style that suited the older lines of my face.

I looked up at her. "You've made me very pretty—thank you. Did you play with dolls as a mortal girl?"

"I was Darre. Dolls were for boys." She got to her feet, unnecessarily dusting off her clothes, and looked around the now-empty chamber. "I don't like you being here, Sieh. In Sky."

I shrugged. "This place is as good as any other." Nahadoth had been right about that. I couldn't leave the mortal realm in my condition; too much of the gods' realm was inimical to flesh. Naha could have kept me safe by taking me into himself, but I would not tolerate that again.

"This place has Arameri."

Resisting the urge to bat at the marble on its cord, I slipped it over my head and let it settle under my shirt instead. (En liked that, being near my heart.) "I'm not a slave anymore, Yeine. They're no threat to me now." She shot me a look of such disgust that I recoiled. "What?"

"Arameri are *always* a threat."

I raised my eyebrows. "Really, daughter of Kinneth?"

At this she looked truly annoyed, her eyes turning a yellowy, acid peridot. "They cling to power by a thread, Sieh. Only their scriveners and armies allow them to keep control—mortal magic, mortal strength, both of which can be subverted. What do you think they'll do, now that they have a god in their power again?"

"I can't see how a weak, dying god will do them much good. I can't even take another form safely. I'm pathetic." She opened her mouth to protest again, and I sighed to interrupt her. "I will be careful. I promise. But truly, Yeine, I have more important concerns right now."

She sobered. "Yes." After another moment's silence, she uttered a heavy sigh and turned away. "See that you are careful, Sieh. A mortal lifetime may seem like nothing to you...." She paused, blinked, and smiled to herself. "To me, too, I suppose. But don't squander it. I mean to use every moment of yours to try and find a cure."

I nodded. So lucky I was to have such devoted, determined parents. Two out of three of them, anyhow.

"I will see you again when I know more," she said. She leaned forward to pull me into an embrace. I was still sitting on my knees; I did not rise as she did this. If I had, I would have been taller than her, and that did not feel at all right.

Then she vanished, and I sat alone in the empty orrery for a long time.

Judging by the angle of the sun, it was well into the afternoon when I returned to Dekarta's room. I didn't care about that for long, however, because as I stepped through the hole in the wall, I found that I had visitors. They rose to greet me as I stopped in surprise.

Shahar, more demure than I had ever seen her, stood near the door to her own room. She was dressed in what passed for daily wear among fullbloods: a long gown of honey-lattice, bright blue satin slippers, and a cloak, with her hair tucked and looped into an elaborate chignon. Beside Shahar stood a woman whose demeanor immediately cried *steward* to me. She stood the tallest of the three women in the room, broad-shouldered and handsome and marvelously direct in her gaze, with a churning avalanche of thick, coily black hair falling about her shoulders and back. Yet despite her commanding presence, she was not as well dressed as the other two, and her mark was only that of a quarterblood. She kept silent and looked through me with her hands behind her back, in the posture of detached attention that all her successful predecessors had mastered.

Between these two stood a third woman: the most high Lady Arameri herself, head of the family and ruler of the Hundred

Thousand Kingdoms, resplendent in a deep red shawl-collared gown. Then to my further shock, all three women dropped to one knee—the steward smoothly, the lady and her heir somewhat less so. At the sight of their bowed heads, I couldn't help laughing.

"Well!" I said, putting my hands on my hips. "Now *this* is a welcome. I had no idea I was so important. Have you actually been waiting here all day for me to come back?"

"It's no less a welcome than we would offer to any god," said the lady. Her voice was low, surprisingly like Yeine's. She looked older awake, with a ruler's troubles and her own personality influencing the lines of her face, but she was still beautiful in a chilly, powerful way. And she was not afraid of me at all.

"Yes, yes, I know," I said, going to stand before her. I had not bothered to conjure or steal clothing for myself, which put certain parts of me right at the lady's eye level, should she choose to look up. Could I needle her into doing so? "Very diplomatic, Lady Arameri, given that half my family wants to kill you and the other half couldn't care less if the first half did. I assume Shahar told you everything?"

She didn't take the bait, damn her, keeping her gaze downcast. "Yes. My condolences on your loss of immortality, Lord Sieh."

Bitch. I scowled and folded my arms. "It's not *lost*; it's just mislaid for a while, and I am still a god whether I live forever or die tomorrow." But now I sounded petulant. She was manipulating me, and I was a fool for letting her do it. I went to the windows, turning my back on them to hide my annoyance. "Oh, get up. I hate pointless formality, or false humility, whichever this is. What's your name, and what do you want?"

There was a whisper of cloth as they rose. "I am Remath Arameri," the lady said, "and I want only to welcome you back to Sky—as an honored guest, of course. We will extend you every courtesy, and I have already set the scrivener corps to the task of researching your...condition. There may be little we mortals can do that the gods haven't already attempted, but if we learn anything, we will share it with you, naturally."

"Naturally," I said, "since if you can figure out how it happened to me, you might be able to do it to any god who threatens you."

I was pleased that she did not attempt to deny it. "I would be remiss in my duties if I didn't try, Lord Sieh."

"Yes, yes." I frowned as something she'd mentioned caught my attention. "Scrivener *corps*? You mean the First Scrivener and his assistants?"

"The mortal world has changed since you last spent time among us, Lord Sieh," she said. A nice touch, that, making my centuries of slavery sound like a vacation. "As you might imagine, the loss of the Enefadeh—of your magic—was a great blow to our efforts to maintain order and prosperity in the world. It became necessary that we assume greater control over all the scriveners that the Litaria produces."

"So you have an army of scriveners, in other words. To go with your more conventional army?" I hadn't paid attention to the mortal realm since T'vril's death, but I knew he'd been working on that.

"The Hundred Thousand Legions." She did not smile—I got the impression she didn't do that often—but there was a hint of wry irony in her voice. "There aren't really a hundred thousand, of course. It just sounds impressive that way."

"Of course." I had forgotten what a pain it was, dealing with Arameri family heads. "So what do you *really* want? Because I highly doubt you're actually glad to have me here."

She did not dissemble, either, which I liked. "I'm neither glad nor displeased, Lord Sieh—though, yes, your presence does serve several useful purposes to the family." There was a pause, perhaps while she waited to see my reaction. I did wonder why the Arameri could possibly want me around, but I imagined that would become clear soon enough. "To that end, I have informed Morad, our palace steward, to ensure that all your material needs are met while you're here."

"It would be my honor and pleasure, Lord Sieh." This from the black-haired woman. "We could begin with a wardrobe."

I snorted in amusement, liking her already. "Of course."

Remath continued. "I have also informed my daughter Shahar that you are now her primary responsibility. For the duration of your time here in Sky, she is to obey you as she would me and see to your comfort at any cost."

Wait. I frowned, turning back to Remath at last. The expression on Remath's face—or rather, the intent lack of expression—made it clear that she knew full well what she had just done. The shocked look that Shahar threw at her back confirmed it.

"Let me be sure I understand you," I said slowly. "You're offering me *your daughter* to do with as I please." I glanced at Shahar again, who was beginning to look murderous. "What if it pleases me to kill her?"

"I would prefer that you not do so, naturally." Remath delivered this with sculptured calm. "A good heir represents a substantial investment of time and energy. But she is Arameri,

Lord Sieh, and our fundamental mission has not changed since the days of our founding Matriarch. We rule by the grace of the gods; therefore, we serve the gods in all things."

Shahar threw me a look more raw than anything I'd seen since her childhood, full of betrayal and bitterness and helpless fury. Ah—now that was the Shahar I remembered. Not that this was as terrible as she seemed to think; our oath meant she had nothing to fear from me. Had she told Remath about that? Was Remath counting on a childhood promise to keep her heir safe?

No. I had lived among the Arameri for a hundred generations. I had seen how they raised their children with careful, calculated neglect; that was why Shahar and Dekarta had been left to wander the palace as children. They believed any Arameri stupid enough to die in a childhood accident was too stupid to rule. And I had also seen, again and again, how Arameri heads found ways to test their heirs' strength, even at the cost of their heirs' souls.

This, however . . . I felt my fists clench and had to work hard not to become the cat. Too dangerous, and a waste of magic.

"How dare you." It came out a snarl, anyway. "You think I'm some petty, simpleminded mortal, delighting in the chance to turn the tables? You think I need someone else's humiliation to know my own worth? *You think I'm like you?*"

Remath lifted an eyebrow. "Given that mortals are made in the gods' image, no, I think *we* are like *you.*" That infuriated me into silence. "But very well; if it doesn't please you to use Shahar, then don't. Tell her what *will* please you. She'll see it done."

"And is this to take precedence over my other duties, Mother?" Shahar's voice was as cool as Remath's, though higher pitched; they sounded much alike. But the fury in her eyes could have melted glass.

Remath glanced over her shoulder and seemed pleased by her daughter's anger. She nodded once, as if to herself. "Yes, until I inform you otherwise. Morad, please make certain Shahar's secretary is informed." Morad murmured a polite affirmative, while Remath kept watching Shahar. "Have you any questions, Daughter?"

"No, Mother," Shahar replied quietly. "You've made your wishes quite clear."

"Excellent." In what I considered a brave gesture, Remath turned her back on her daughter and faced me again. "One more thing, Lord Sieh. Rumors are inevitable, but I would advise that you not make your presence—or rather, your nature—known during your time here. I'm sure you can imagine what sort of attention that would draw."

Yes, every scrivener and godphile in the palace would drive me to distraction with questions and worship and requests for blessings. And since this was Sky, there would also be the inevitable highbloods who wanted a little godly assistance with whatever schemes they had going, and a few who might try to harm or exploit me to gain prestige for themselves, and... I ground my teeth. "Obviously it would make sense for me to keep a low profile."

"It would, yes." She inclined her head—not the bow of a mortal to a god, but a respectful gesture between equals. I wasn't sure what she meant by that. Was she insulting me by not bothering to show reverence, or was she paying me the compliment of honesty? Damn, I couldn't figure this woman out at all. "I'll take my leave of you now, Lord Sieh."

"Wait," I said, stepping closer so that I could look her in the eye. She was taller than me, which I liked; it made me feel more my old self. And she was at least wary of me, I saw when I stood closer. I liked that, too.

"Do you mean me harm, Remath? Say you don't. *Promise* it."

She looked surprised. "Of course I don't. I'll swear any oath you like on that."

I smiled, showing all my teeth, and for the barest instant I did smell fear in her. Not much, but even an Arameri is still human, and humans are still animals, and animals know a predator when one draws near.

"Cross your heart, Remath," I said. "Hope to die. Stick a needle in your eye."

She lifted an eyebrow at my nonsense. But the words of a god have power, regardless of what language we speak, and I was not quite mortal yet. She felt my intent, despite the silly words.

"Cross my heart," she replied gravely, and inclined her head. Then she turned and swept out, perhaps before she could reveal more fear, and certainly before I could say anything else. I stuck my tongue out at her back as she left.

"Well." Morad drew a deep breath, turning to regard me. "I believe I can find suitable garments for your size, though a proper fitting with the tailor would make things easier. Would you be willing to stand for that, Lord Sieh?"

I folded my arms and conjured clothing for myself. A small and petty gesture, and a waste of magic. The slight widening of her eyes was gratifying, though I pretended nonchalance as I said, "I suppose it wouldn't hurt to work with a tailor, too. Never been much for keeping up with fashion." Then I wouldn't need to expend more magic.

She bowed—deeply and respectfully, I was pleased to see. "As for your quarters, my lord, I—"

"Leave us," snapped Shahar, to my surprise.

After the slightest of startled pauses, Morad closed her mouth. "Yes, lady." With a measured but brisk stride, she, too, left. Shahar and I gazed at each other in silence until we heard the door of Dekarta's apartment shut. Shahar closed her eyes, drawing a deep breath as if for strength.

"I'm sorry," I said.

I expected her to be sad. When she opened her eyes, however, the fury was still burning. Coldly. "Will you help me kill her?"

I rocked back on my heels in surprise and slid hands into my pockets. (I always made clothes with pockets.) Considering for a moment, I said, "I could kill her for you right now, if you want. Better to do it while I still have magic to spare." I paused, reading the telltale signs in her posture. "But are you sure?"

She almost said yes. I could see that, too. And I was willing to do it, if she asked. It had never been my way to kill mortals before the Gods' War, but my enslavement had changed everything. Arameri weren't ordinary mortals, anyway. Killing them was a treat.

"No," she said at last. Not reluctantly. There was no hint of squeamishness in her—but then, I had been the one to teach her to kill, long ago. She sighed in frustration. "I'm not strong enough to take her place, not yet. I have only a few allies among the nobles, and some of my fullblood relatives...." She grimaced. "No. I'm not ready."

I nodded slowly. "You think she knows that?"

"Better than I do." Shahar sighed and slumped into a nearby chair, putting her head in her hands. "It's always like this with her, no matter what I do. No matter how well I prove myself. She thinks I'm not strong enough to be her heir."

I sat down on the edge of a beautifully worked wooden desk. My butt settled more heavily than I intended, partly because my butt was bigger now and partly because I was feeling a little winded. Why? Then I remembered: the clothing I'd conjured.

"That's standard for Arameri," I said to distract myself. "I can't remember how many times I saw family heads put their children through all manner of hells to make sure they were worthy." Fleetingly I wondered what the Arameri did for a succession ceremony now, since the Stone of Earth no longer existed and there was no need for a life to be spent in its inheritance. Remath's master sigil, I'd noticed, had been the standard kind, complete with the old commanding language even though it was now useless. Clearly they maintained at least a few of the old traditions, however unnecessarily. "Well, it should be easy enough to prove you're not weak. Just order the annihilation of a country or something."

Shahar threw me a scathing look. "You think the slaughter of innocent mortals is funny?"

"No, it's horrific, and I will hear their screams in my soul for the rest of existence," I said in my coldest tone. She flinched. "But if you're afraid of being seen as weak, then you have limited options. Either do something to prove your strength—and in Arameri terms, *strength* means *ruthlessness*—or quit now and tell your mother to make someone else heir. Which she should do, in my opinion, if she's right and you aren't strong enough. The whole world will be better off if you never inherit."

Shahar stared at me for a moment. Hurt, I realized, because I'd been deliberately cruel. But I'd also told the truth, however unpleasant she might find it. I'd seen the carnage that resulted when a weak or foolish Arameri took over the family. Better for the world and for Shahar, because otherwise her relatives would eat her alive.

She rose from the chair and began to pace, folding her arms and nibbling her bottom lip in a way that I might have found endearing on another day and under better circumstances.

"What I don't understand is why your mother wants me here," I said. I stretched out my offensively long legs and glared down at them. "I'm not even a good figurehead, if that's what she's thinking. My magic is dying; anyone who looks at me can see that something's wrong. And she wants me to keep my god-hood secret anyhow. This makes no sense."

Shahar sighed, stopping her pacing and rubbing her eyes. "She wants to improve relations between the Arameri and the gods. It's a project her father began—mostly because *you* stopped visiting Sky when her grandfather, T'vril Arameri, died. She's been sending gifts to the city's godlings, inviting them to events and so on. Sometimes they actually show up." She shrugged. "I'm told she even courted one as a potential husband. He didn't accept, though. They say that's why she never married; after being turned down by a god, she couldn't settle for anything less without being seen as weak."

"Really?" I grinned at the idea of cold Remath trying to win one of my siblings' love. Some of them might have been amused enough to allow a seduction. Which one had she propositioned? Dima, maybe; he would mount anything that held still long enough. Or Ellere, who could match any Arameri for hauteur and preferred stiff types like Remath—

"Yes. And I suspect that's why she tried to give me to you." I blinked in surprise, and Shahar smiled thinly. "Well, you're too young for her tastes. But not mine."

I leapt to my feet, taking several quick steps back from her. "That's insane!"

She stared at me, surprised by my vehemence. "Insane?" Her jaw tightened. "I see. I had no idea you found me so repellent."

I groaned. "Shahar, I'm the god of *childhood*. Would you please think about that for a moment?"

She frowned. "Children are perfectly capable of marriage."

"Yes. And some of them even have children themselves. But childhood doesn't last long under those conditions." I shuddered before I could stop myself, folding my arms over my chest to match her posture. Paltry, inadequate protection. Impossible not to think of groping hands, grunting breaths. So many of Shahar's forbears had loved having a pretty, indestructible, never-aging boy around—

Gods, I was going to be sick. I leaned against the desk, trembling and panting.

"Sieh?" Shahar had drawn near, and now she touched me, her hand warm against my back. "Sieh, what's wrong?"

"What do you do for fun?" I took deep breaths.

"What?"

"Fun, damn you! Do you do anything but scheme in your spare time, or do you actually have a life?"

She glowered at me, and her petulance made me feel just a little better. I turned and grabbed her hand and dragged her across the room, onto Deka's modestly sized bed. She gasped and tried to pull free of me. "What the hells are you doing?"

"Jumping on the bed." I didn't take my shoes off. Worked better with them on. I stood awkwardly in the soft middle of the mattress and hauled her up with me.

"*What?*"

"You're supposed to try and keep me happy, right?" I took her by the shoulders. "Come on, Shahar. It's only been eight years. You used to love trying new things, remember? I offered to take you cloud jumping once and you leapt at the chance, until you remembered that I was a baby-killing monster." I grinned, and she blinked, outrage fading as she remembered that day. "You kicked me down the stairs so hard I actually got bruises!"

She uttered a weak, uncertain laugh. "I'd forgotten about that. Kicking you."

I nodded. "It felt good, didn't it? You didn't care that I was a god, that I might get angry and hurt you. You did what you wanted, damn the consequences."

Yes, at last, the old light was in her eyes. She was older, wiser, she would never do something so foolish today—but that didn't mean she didn't *want* to. The impulse was there, buried but not dead. That was enough.

"Now try it again," I said. "Do something fun." I bounced a little on the bed's soft, springy surface. She yelped and stumbled, trying to get her footing—but she laughed. I grinned, the nausea gone already. "Don't think! Just do what feels good!"

I jumped, really jumped this time, and the force of my landing nearly threw her off the bed. She shrieked in terror and excitement and sheer giddy release, and finally jumped in self-defense, wobbling badly because my jumping had thrown her off. I laughed and grabbed her and made her jump with me, as high as I could go without using magic. She cried out again when we actually got within arm's reach of the room's arched ceiling. Then we came down fast and hard, and something in Deka's bed groaned in protest and I took us up again and she was laughing, laughing, her face alight, and on impulse I pulled her close and we overbalanced and went sideways and I had to use magic to make sure we landed safely on our backs, but that was fine because suddenly magic was easy again and I felt so good that I laughed and kissed her.

I truly hadn't meant anything by it. Jumping felt good and laughing felt good and she felt good and kissing her felt good. Her mouth was soft and warm, her breath a tickle against my upper lip. I smiled as I let it end and sat up.

But before I could, her hands gripped the cloth at the back of my shirt, pulling me down again. I started as her mouth found mine again, more delicious sweetness like flower nectar; then her tongue slipped between my lips. Now the sweetness turned to honey, thick and golden, sliding down my throat in a slow caress, spreading molten through my body. She shifted a little to press her small breasts against my chest. (Wait, little girls didn't have breasts, did they?) Oh, gods, her hands on my back felt so good, I hadn't liked a mortal this much in ages, could it be the love that Remath schemed for? No, I loved Shahar already, had loved her since childhood, oh yes oh yes oh yes. *Exquisite mortal, here is my soul; I want you to know it.*

We parted then, her gasping and jerking away, me letting out a slow, trembling sigh.

"Wh-what…" She put a hand to her mouth, her green eyes wide and so clear in the afternoon sunlight that I could count every spoke of her irises. "Sieh, what—"

I cupped her cheek, sighing languidly. "That was me." I closed my eyes, relaxing into the moment. "Thank you."

"For what?"

I didn't feel like explaining, so I didn't. I just rolled onto my back and let myself drift. Thankfully, she said nothing for a long while, lying still beside me.

Such moments of peace never last, so I didn't mind when she finally spoke. "It's your antithesis, isn't it? Marriage, things like that. Anything to do with adulthood."

I yawned. "Duh."

"Just talking about it made you sick."

"No. Finding out that I'm dying *and* worrying about my orrery *and* talking about marriage made me sick. If I'm already strong, a little thing like that can't hurt me."

"Your orrery?" I felt the bed shift as she sat up on her elbows, her breath tickling my face.

"Nothing important. It's gone now."

"Oh." She was silent a moment longer. "But how do you keep yourself from thinking about things like dying?"

I opened my eyes. She was on her side now, head propped on her fist. Her hair had come partially loose from its swept-up chignon, and her eyes were softer than I'd ever seen them. She looked thoroughly rumpled and a bit naughty, not at all the poised and controlled family heir.

"How do *you* keep yourself from thinking about death?" I touched her nose with a fingertip. "You mortals have to live with that fear all the time, don't you? If you can do it, I can, too." I would have to, or I would die even sooner. But I did not say this aloud; it would have spoiled the mood.

"I see." She lifted a hand, hesitated, and then yielded to

impulse, resting it on my chest. I couldn't purr in this form, but I could sigh in pleasure and arch a little beneath her hand, which I did. "So...what was that, just now?"

"Why, Lady Shahar, I believe it's called a *kiss* in Senmite. In Teman it's *umishday*, and in Oubi it's—"

She swatted my chest hard enough to sting, then blanched as she realized what she'd done, then got over it. Her cheeks had gone that blotchy pink that either meant sickness or strong emotion in Amn; I guessed she was feeling shy. "What I mean is, *why* did you do it?"

"Why did you kiss me last night?"

She frowned. "I don't know. It felt right."

"Same for me." I yawned again. "Damn. I think I need to sleep."

She sat up, though she did not immediately leave the bed. Her back was to me, so I could see the tension in her shoulders. I thought she was going to ask another question, and perhaps she meant to. But what she said instead was, "I'm glad you came back, Sieh. Really. And I'm glad...what happened that day wasn't..." She drew a deep breath. "I hated you for a long time."

I folded my hands under my head, sighing. "You probably still hate me a little, Shahar. I took your brother from you."

"No. Mother did that." But she did not sound wholly certain, and I knew the mortal heart was not always logical.

"Wounds need time to heal," I said, thinking of my own.

"Maybe so." After another moment, she stood with a sigh. "I'll be in my room."

She left. I was tempted to lie there awhile longer and fight the urge to sleep, but there are times to be childish and times when wisdom takes precedence. Sighing, I rolled over and curled up, giving in.

5

ABOVE MORTALS ARE THE GODS, and above us is the unknowable, which we call Maelstrom. For some reason It likes the number three. Three are Its children, the great gods who made the rest of us, who named themselves and encompass existence. Three also are the rankings of us lesser gods—though that is only because we killed the fourth.

First came the niwwah, the Balancers, among whose ranks I am honored to be counted. We were born of the Three's earliest efforts at intercourse, for they had other ways of lovemaking long before reproduction had anything to do with it. They did not know how to be parents then, so they did many things wrong, but it was long ago and most of us have forgiven them for it.

We are called Balancers not because we balance anything, mind, but because each of us has two of the Three as parents in what we have come to realize is a balanced combination: Nahadoth and Enefa in my case, Itempas and Enefa in others. We do not like each other much, Nahadoth's children and our half siblings who belong to Itempas, but we do love each other. So it goes with family.

Next are the elontid, the Imbalancers. Again, this name is not because they take any active role in the maintenance or destruction of existence, but because they were born of *imbalance*. We did not know at first that certain mixes among us are dangerous. Nahadoth and Itempas, first and foremost— Enefa made them able to breed together, but they are both too similar and too different to do so easily. (Gender has nothing to do with this difficulty, mind you; that is only a game for us, an affectation, like names and flesh. We employ such things because you need them, not because we do.) On the rare occasions that Naha and Tempa bear children together, the results are always powerful, and always frightening. Only a few have lived to adulthood: Ral the Dragon, Ia the Negation, and Lil the Hunger. Also counted among the elontid are those born of unions between gods and godlings, reflecting the inequity of the merging that created them. They are gods of things that ebb and wane, like the tides, fashion, lust and liking.

Nothing is wrong with them, I must emphasize, though some among my fellow niwwah treat them as pitiable creatures. This is a mistake; they are merely different.

Third we count the mnasat: those children we godlings have produced among ourselves. Here there is weakness, in the relative sense of things, for even the mnasat can destroy a world if pressed. Countless numbers have been born over the aeons, but most are culled in their first few centuries—caught in the cross fire of the Three's endless battling and copulating, or dragged into the Maelstrom by accident, or lost through any of the other legion hazards that might befall a young god. The War in particular decimated their ranks—and I will admit that I took my share of their lives. Why shouldn't I have, if they were so foolish as to interfere in the concerns of their betters? Yet there were a few whom I could not kill, and who proved themselves worthy through that trial-by-apocalypse. The mnasat have shown us by the harsh example of their deaths that it is *living true*, not mere strength, which dictates matters among us. Those who submitted to their natures gained power to match even the strongest of us niwwah—and those who forgot themselves, no matter how much innate power they possessed, fell.

There is another lesson in this: life cannot exist without death. Even among gods there are winners and losers, eaters and eaten. I have never hesitated to kill my fellow immortals, but I sometimes mourn the necessity.

The demons were the fourth ranking of us, if you're wondering. But there is no point in speaking of them.

I awakened with a rude snarfle and a groan. Dreams. I had forgotten those, a plague of mortal flesh. Bad enough mortals wasted so much of their lives insensible, but Enefa had also given them dreams to teach them about themselves and their universe. Few of them ever listened to the lessons—a total waste of creation in my eyes—but thanks to that, I would have to endure these mind-farts every time I slept. Lovely.

It was late in the night, nowhere near morning. Though I had been asleep for only three or four hours, I felt no further urge to rest, perhaps because I wasn't yet fully mortal. So what to do with the hours until Shahar was awake to entertain me?

I got up and went roaming again in the palace, this time not bothering to conceal myself. The servants and guards said nothing when I passed them, despite my nondescript clothing and unmarked forehead, but I felt their eyes on my back. What had Morad, or whoever served as the captain of the guard now, told them about me? There was no flavor of adoration or revulsion to their stares. Just curiosity—and wariness.

I went into the underpalace first, to the Nowhere Stair. Which no longer existed, to my shock.

In its place was an open atrium. Three levels of wide circular balconies ringed a space that had been reworked with sculptures and potted plants of the sort that needed little care. (At least it wasn't dusty anymore. The Arameri no longer neglected the underpalace, having realized it could hide secrets.) The atrium lacked the intentionally carefree feel of most Sky architecture, and I could see where the edges of each balcony had been too-hastily molded by the scriveners, leaving them uneven and not as smooth as they should have been. Servants had cleaned up the rubble, but signs of the disaster were still there, for one who knew how to see.

I crouched at the edge of one of the balconies, bracing one hand on the thin railing, and touched the rough daystone of the floor. Echoes still reverberated in the stone—not echoes of sound, since those had long since moved on, but echoes of *event*. I closed my eyes and saw again what the stone had witnessed.

The Nowhere Stair. At the bottom of it, three children holding hands. (I marveled at how small Shahar had been then; already I had grown used to her older shape.) I watched the mortals' faces change from smiles to alarm, felt the rising rush of wind, saw their hair and clothing begin to whip about as if they'd been caught in a tornado. They screamed as their feet rose from the floor; then they flipped entirely, twisting upside down. Only I did not budge, my feet seemingly rooted to the ground. Only their grip on each other and me held them down.

And the look on my face! In the memory, I stood with mouth slack, eyes distant and confused, brow ever-so-slightly furrowed and head cocked, as if I heard something no one else could, and whatever I heard had obliterated my wits.

Then my body blurred, flesh interspersing with white lines.

My mouth opened and the stone beneath my fingertips gave one last microscopic shiver as a concussion of force tore loose from my throat. The Nowhere Stair shattered like glass, as did all the daystone around it and beneath it and above it. What saved the children was that the energy blasted outward in a spherical wave; they fell amid the rubble, bleeding and still, but not much of the rubble landed on them.

And when the dust cleared, I had vanished.

Taking my fingers off the stone, I frowned to myself. Then I said to the mortal who had hovered somewhere behind me, watching for the past ten minutes, "What do you want?"

He came forward, preceded by the familiar mingled scent of books and chemical phials and incense; by that I knew what he was before he ever spoke. "My apologies, Lord Sieh. I did not mean to disturb you."

I rose, dusting off my hands, and turned to take his measure. An island man of late middle years, with salt-sprinkled red hair and a lined saturnine face that showed a hint of beard stubble. There was a fullblood mark on his brow, but he didn't look Arameri or even Amn. And fullbloods rarely smelled of hard work. An adoptee, then.

"You the First Scrivener?" I asked.

He nodded, obviously torn between fascination and unease. Finally he offered me an awkward bow—not deep enough to be properly respectful but too deep for the kind of disdain a devout Itempan should have shown. I laughed, remembering Viraine's cool, nuanced poise, and then sobered as I remembered why Viraine had been so good at things like that.

"Forgive me," the man said again. "But the servants passed word that you were abroad in the palace, and...I thought...

well, it seems natural that you would come to the scene of the crime, so to speak."

"Mmm." I slipped my hands into my pockets, trying very hard not to feel uneasy in his presence. These were not the old days. He had no power over me. "It's late, First Scrivener, or early. Don't you Itempans believe in a full night's rest before your dawn prayers?"

He blinked; then his surprise faded into amusement. "They do, but I'm not Itempan, Lord Sieh. And I wanted to meet you, which necessitated staying up late, or so my research suggested. You were known to be decidedly nocturnal during your"—his confidence faltered again—"time here."

I stared at him. "How can you not be Itempan?" All scriveners were Itempan priests. The Order gave anyone with a knack for magic a single choice: join or die.

"About—hmm—fifty years ago? The Litaria petitioned the Nobles' Consortium for independence from the Order of Itempas. The Litaria is a secular body now. Scriveners may devote themselves to whichever god, or gods, they wish." He paused, then smiled again. "As long as we serve the Arameri, regardless."

I looked him up and down, opened my mouth a little to get a better taste of his scent, and was stymied. "So which god do you honor?" He certainly wasn't one of mine.

"I *honor* all the gods. But in terms of spirituality, I prefer to worship at the altars of knowledge and artistry." He made an apologetic little gesture with his hand, as if he worried about hurting my feelings, but I had begun to grin.

"An atheist!" I put my hands on my hips, delighted. "I haven't seen one of you since before the War. I thought the Arameri wiped all of you out."

"As well as they did all the other gods' worshippers, Lord Sieh, yes." I laughed at this, which seemed to hearten him. "Heresy is actually rather fashionable among the commonfolk, though here in Sky I am more circumspect about it, of course. And the, ah, *polite* term for people like me is *primortalist.*"

"Ugh, what a mouthful."

"Unfortunately, yes. It means 'mortals first'—neither an accurate nor complete representation of our philosophy, but as I said, there are worse terms. We believe in the gods, naturally." He nodded to me. "But as the Interdiction has shown us, the gods function perfectly well whether we believe in them or not, so why devote all that energy to a pointless purpose? Why not believe most fervently in mortalkind and its potential? We, certainly, could benefit from a little dedication and discipline."

"I agree wholeheartedly!" And if I didn't miss my guess, there were probably a few of my siblings involved in his mortal-worshipping movement. But I refrained from pointing this out, lest it disturb him. "What's your name?"

He bowed again, more easily this time. "Shevir, Lord Sieh."

I waved a hand. "I make the Arameri call me 'lord.' It's just Sieh."

He looked uneasy. "Er, well—"

"Arameri is a state of mind. I've known some adoptees who fit right into this family. You, sir, are a die among the jacks." I smiled to let him know that had been meant as a compliment, and he relaxed. "Remath told you all about me, then?"

"The Lady Arameri informed me of your...condition, yes. I and my staff, including those in the city below, are already hard at work trying to determine what might have caused the change. We'll inform Lady Remath at once if we find anything."

"Thank you." I refrained from pointing out that telling Remath wouldn't do me any good unless Remath chose to pass the information along. He probably knew that and was just letting me know where his loyalties lay. Mortals first. "Were you here in Sky, eight years ago?"

"Yes." He came to stand beside me, staring avidly at my profile, my posture, everything. Studying me. Knowing his beliefs, I did not mind for once. "I was head of the healing squadron then; it was I and my colleagues who treated Lord Dekarta and Lady Shahar after their injury. I was promoted to First Scrivener for saving their lives." He hesitated. "The previous First Scrivener was removed from office for failing to realize that a god had visited Sky."

I rolled my eyes. "There is no scrivening magic that can detect a god's presence if we don't want to be detected." I had never wanted to be detected.

"The lady was informed of this." He was smiling thinly, not bitter at least. I supposed there was no point in laying blame.

"If you were here back then, you—or your predecessor— would have conducted an investigation."

"Yes." He straightened as if giving a report. "The incident occurred in early afternoon. There was a tremor throughout the palace, and all of the boundary scripts sounded an alarm, indicating unauthorized active magic within the palace's walls. Guards and service staff arrived to find this." He gestured at the atrium. The debris had been removed, but that changed nothing; it was painfully clear to anyone who had seen it before that the atrium was really just an enormous sunken pit. "No one knew what had happened until three days later, when first Dekarta, then Shahar awakened."

More than enough time for rumors to gain traction and ruin Deka's life. Poor boy, and his sister, too.

"What sort of magic was it?" I asked. Scriveners loved to classify and categorize magic, which somehow helped them grasp it with their unmagical mortal minds. There might be something in their convoluted logic that would help me understand.

"Unknown, Lord—" He caught himself. "Unknown."

"*Unknown?*"

"Nothing like it has been observed in the mortal realm, at least not within recorded history. The Litaria's best scholars have confirmed this. We even consulted several of the friendlier godlings of the city; they weren't able to explain it, either. If *you* don't know—" He shut his mouth with an audible snap, in palpable frustration. He had plainly hoped I would have more answers.

I understood entirely. Sighing, I straightened. "I didn't intend to hurt them. Nothing that happened makes any sense."

"The children's hands were bloody," Shevir said, his tone neutral. "Both hands, cut in the same way, inflicted on each other to judge by the angles and depth. Some of my colleagues believed they may have attempted some sort of ritual...."

I scowled. "The only ritual involved was one that children the world over have enacted to seal promises." I lifted my hand, gazing at my own smooth, unscarred palms. "If *that* could cause what happened, there would be a great many dead children lying about."

He spread his hands in that apologetic gesture again. "You must understand, we were desperate to come up with some explanation."

I considered this and hoisted myself up onto the railing,

reveling in the ability to kick my feet at last. This seemed to make Shevir very uncomfortable, probably because the drop into the atrium was far enough to kill a mortal. Then I remembered that I was becoming mortal, and with a heavy sigh, I dropped back to the floor.

"So you decided one of the children—Deka—had summoned me, annoyed me, and I blew them to the hells in retaliation."

"*I* didn't believe that." Shevir grew sober. "But certain parties would not be put off, and ultimately Dekarta was sent to the Litaria. To learn better control of his innate talents, his mother announced."

"Exile," I said softly. "A punishment for getting Shahar hurt."

"Yes."

"What's he like now? Deka."

Shevir shook his head. "No one here has seen him since he left, Lord Sieh. He doesn't come home at holidays or vacation breaks. I'm told he's doing well at the Litaria; ironically, he turned out to have a genuine talent for the art. But...well... rumor has it that he and Lady Shahar hate each other now." I frowned, and Shevir shrugged. "I can't say I blame him, really. Children don't see things the way we do."

I glanced at Shevir; he was lost in thought and hadn't noticed the irony of talking about childhood to me. He was right, though. The gentle Deka I'd known would not have understood that he was being sent away for reasons that had very little to do with Shahar being injured. He would have drawn his own conclusions about why the friendship oath had gone wrong and why he'd been separated from his beloved sister. Self-blame would have been only the beginning.

But why had Remath even bothered exiling him? In the old

days, the family had been quick to kill any member who'd transgressed in some way or another. They should have been even quicker with Deka, who broke the Arameri mold in so many ways.

Sighing heavily, I straightened and turned away from the atrium railing. "Nothing in Sky has ever made sense. I don't know why I keep coming here, really. You'd think being trapped in this hell for centuries would've been enough for me."

Shevir shrugged. "I can't speak for gods, but any mortal who spends enough time in a place grows... acclimated. One's sense of what is normal shifts, even if that place is filled with unpleasantness, until separation feels wrong."

I frowned at this. Shevir caught my look and smiled. "Married seventeen years. Happily, I might add."

"Oh." This reminded me, perversely, of the previous night's conversation with Shahar. "Tell me more about her," I said.

I hadn't specified the "her," but of course Shevir was as good at parsing language as any scrivener. "Lady Shahar is very bright, very mature for her age, and very dedicated to her duties. I've heard most of the other fullbloods express confidence in her ability to rule after her mother—"

"No, no," I said, scowling. "None of that. I want to know..." Suddenly I was uncertain. Why was I asking him about this? But I had to know. "About *her*. Who are her friends? How did she handle Deka's exile? What do you think of her?"

At this flood of questions, Shevir raised his eyebrows. Suddenly I realized two horrifying things: first, that I was developing a dangerous attraction to Shahar, and second, that I had just revealed it.

"Ah... well... she's very private," Shevir began awkwardly.

It was too late, but I waved a hand and tried to repair the damage I'd done. "Never mind," I said, grimacing. "These are mortal affairs, irrelevant. All I should concentrate on now is finding the cure for whatever's happened to me."

"Yes." Shevir seemed relieved to change the subject. "Er, to that end...the reason I sought you out was to ask if you might be willing to provide some samples for us. My fellow scriveners—that is, of the palace contingent—thought we might share this information with the previts in Shadow and the Litaria."

I frowned at this, unpleasantly recalling other First Scriveners and other examinations and other samples over the centuries. "To try and figure out what's changed in me?"

"Yes. We have information on your, ah, prior tenure...." He shook his head and finally stopped trying to be tactful. "When you were a slave here, immortal but trapped in mortal flesh. Your present state appears to be very different. I'd like to compare the two."

I scowled. "Why? To tell me that I'm going to die? I know that already."

"Determining *how* you're turning mortal may give us some insight into what caused it," he said, speaking briskly now that he was in his element. "And perhaps how to reverse it. I would never presume that mortal arts can surpass godly power, but every bit of knowledge we can gather might be useful."

I sighed. "Very well. You'll want my blood, I presume?" Mortals were forever after our blood.

"And anything else you would be willing to give. Hair, nail parings, a bit of flesh, saliva. I'll want to record your current measurements, too—height and weight and so forth."

I could not help growing curious at this. "How could that possibly matter?"

"Well, for one thing, you appear to be no more than sixteen years old to my eye. The same age as Lady Shahar and Lord Dekarta, now—but initially, I understand, you looked significantly older than both of them. Approximately ten years to their eight. If you had merely aged eight years in the intervening time—"

I caught my breath, understanding at last. I had grown up before, hundreds of times; I knew the pattern that my body normally followed. I should have been heavier, taller, more finished, with a deeper voice. Eighteen years old, not sixteen. "Shahar and Dekarta," I breathed. "My aging has slowed to match theirs."

Shevir nodded, looking pleased at my reaction. "You do seem rather thin, so perhaps you lacked nourishment while you were . . . away . . . and this stunted your growth. More likely, however—"

I nodded absently, quickly, because he was right. How had such a crucial detail escaped me?

Because it is the sort of thing only a mortal would notice.

I had suspected that my condition was somehow linked to the friendship oath I'd taken with Shahar and Dekarta. Now I knew: their mortality had infected me, like a disease. But what kind of disease slowed its progress to match that of other victims? There was something *purposeful* about that sort of change. Something intentional.

But whose intent, and for what purpose?

"Let's go to your laboratory, Scrivener Shevir," I said, speaking softly as my mind raced with inferences and implications. "I believe I can give you those samples right now."

I was getting hungry by the time I left Shevir's laboratory, just after dawn. It wasn't bad yet—not the sort of raw, precarious ache I'd known a few times during my slave years, whenever my masters had starved me—but it made me irritable, because it was more proof of my oncoming mortality. Would I starve to death if I ignored it now? Could I still sustain myself with games and disobedience, as I normally did? I was tempted to find out. Then again, I considered as I rubbed my upper arm, where a bandage and healing script concealed the divot of flesh Shevir had taken from me, there was no point in making myself suffer unnecessarily. As a mortal, there would be pain enough in my life, whether I sought it out or not.

Noise and commotion distracted me from grimness. I stepped quickly to the side of a corridor as six guardsmen ran by, hands on their weapons. One of them carried a messaging sphere, and through this I heard the speaker—their captain, I assumed— issuing rapid commands in a low tone. Something about "clear the north-seven corridors" and "forecourt," and most clearly, "Tell Morad's people to bring something for the smell."

I could no more resist such temptation than I could Shahar's summons—maybe less so. So I hummed a little ditty and slid my hands into my pockets and skipped as I headed down a different corridor. When the guards were out of sight, I opened a wall and tore off running.

I was almost thwarted by the Tree, which had grown through one of the most useful junctures in the dead spaces, and by my stupid, infuriatingly lanky body, which could no longer squeeze through the tighter passages. I knew plenty of alternate routes but still arrived at the courtyard late and out of breath. (That annoyed me, too. I was going to have to make my mortal body stronger, or it would be completely useless at this rate.)

It was worth it, however, for what I saw.

Sky's forecourt had been designed by my late sister, Kurue, who had understood two key elements of the mortal psyche: they hate being reminded of their own insignificance, yet they simultaneously and instinctively expect their leaders to be overwhelmingly dominant. This was why visitors were confronted with magnificence at four cardinal points as they arrived on the Vertical Gate. To the north was Sky's vaulted, cavernous entryway, taller than many buildings in the city below. To the east and west lay the twin lobes of the Garden of the Hundred Thousand, a mosaic of ordered flower beds each crowned by an exotic tree. Beyond these one could see a branch of the World Tree, wild and miles vast, spreading a million leaves against the blue sky. Kurue had never planned for the Tree, but it was a testament to her skill that it looked like she had. For those who dared to look south, there was nothing. Only the lonely Pier and an otherwise unimpeded view of the landscape and very, very distant horizon.

Now the forecourt had been defiled by something hideous. As I emerged from the garden via the servants' ground entrance, no one noticed me. Soldiers were all over the place, disorganized, in a panic. I saw the captain of the guard on one side of the gate mosaic, shouting at the coach driver to take the coach away, away, away for the Father's sake, take it to the ground station at the cargo gate and let no one touch it.

I ignored all this as I walked forward through the hubbub, my eyes on twin lumps on the ground. Someone had had the sense to lay them on a square of cloth, but that barely contained the mess. Pieces of the lumps spilled and scattered every which way, not helped at all by soldiers who stumbled around retching even as they tried to scrape everything back onto the cloth. As I got close enough to get a good look at the mess—flesh gone gelatinous, so rotten the only thing solid in it was spongy bone—the captain turned and spotted me. He was warrior enough to drop his hand to the sword at his side, but sensible enough to avoid drawing it as he realized who I must be. He cursed swiftly, then caught himself and threw a quick glance to be sure his men weren't looking before he bowed quickly. Not a subtle man.

"Sir," he said carefully, though I could see he would rather have used *my lord*. He was no Itempan, either, though his forehead bore an Arameri mark. He held up a hand, and I stopped a few feet from the outermost edges of the foulness. "Please, it's dangerous."

"I don't think the maggots are likely to attack, do you?" My joke fell flat because there were no maggots. It was easy to see that what lay on the blanket were the remains of two very, very dead mortals, but that peculiarity did puzzle me. And the smell was wrong. I stepped closer, opening my mouth a little, though the last thing I wanted was a better taste of it. I had never liked carrion. But that taste gave me nothing but ammonia and sulfur and all the usual flavors of death.

"Arameri, I take it?" I crouched for a better look. I could not make out marks on their foreheads, or their faces at all for that matter, which were oddly blackened and featureless. Almost flat. "Who were they? These look long-enough dead that I might've known them."

Stiffly, the captain said, "They are—we believe—Lord Nevra and Lady Criscina, second cousins of Lady Remath. Fullbloods. And they died—we believe—last night."

"*What?*"

He didn't repeat himself, though he did stir from his pose in order to kick over a globule of Nevra. Or Criscina. The soldiers had by now managed to get all the scattered bits onto the cloth and were wrapping it carefully for transport. I could see smears along the ground between the Vertical Gate and the cloth. They had brought the bodies up to Sky in the coach, but they hadn't bothered to wrap them first? That made no sense ... unless they hadn't realized the couple inside were dead before they'd opened the door.

I went over to the captain, who stiffened again at my approach, but held firm. I was surprised to see a lowbloods' simple bar symbol on his forehead, though it was also hollowed out at the center in the manner of all the blood sigils I'd seen, except Remath's. It was rare for lowbloods to achieve high rank within Sky. That meant this man either had a powerful patron—not a parent, or he wouldn't be a lowblood—or he was very competent. I hoped the latter.

"I must admit I pay little attention to mortals once they're dead," I said, keeping my voice low. "No fun, corpses. But I was under the impression it normally took them a few months, if not years, to reach this state."

"Normally, yes," he said tersely.

"Then what caused this?"

His jaw flexed. "Please forgive me, sir, but I am under orders to keep this matter private. This *family* matter." Which meant that Remath had ordered his silence, and nothing short of my dangling him off the Pier would make him talk. Perhaps not even that; he seemed the stubborn type.

I rolled my eyes. "You know as well as I do that only magic could cause such a horror. A scrivener's activation gone wrong, or perhaps they aggravated one of my siblings." Though I doubted that. Any godling was capable of such a thing, even the ones with gentler natures, but I could think of no godling who *would*. We killed; we did not desecrate. We respected death. To do otherwise was an offense to Enefa, and probably Yeine, too.

"I cannot say, sir."

Stubborn, indeed. "Why did you say it was dangerous?"

He looked hard at me then, to my surprise. Not angrily, though I was pestering him and I knew it. He had the most remarkable gray eyes. Rare in Sky, and almost unheard of among Maroneh, though he looked brown enough to be fully of that race. Probably part Amn, if he was Arameri.

"As you said, my lord." He spoke softly but emphatically. "Only magic could have done such a thing. This magic works on contact."

He lifted his chin in the direction of the bodies' faces, which were still visible as the soldiers worked to wrap the loose limbs. I peered closer and realized that what I had taken for just more decay was something different. The blackness of their faces was not rot, but char. Not faces at all, in fact: each of the dead mortals wore some sort of mask over their features. The masks had burned so badly as to fuse with the flesh, leaving only eyes and a line of jaw of the original faces.

Then the soldiers were done bundling. Six of them set off, carrying the bodies slowly between them. As they reached the palace entrance, a phalanx of servants emerged, carrying cleaning implements and censers. They would cleanse the forecourt of its taint quickly so that no highblood would know such horror had ever lain here.

"I must make my report to the Lady Arameri," said the captain, turning.

"What's your name?" I asked.

The captain paused, looking wary, and by that I guessed he'd heard something of my reputation. I grinned.

"No singsongs, I promise," I said. "No games or tricks. You've done nothing to offend me, so you have nothing to fear."

He relaxed minutely. "Wrath Arameri."

Definitely Maroneh, with a name like that. "Well, Captain Wrath, since you're going to tell the lady I turned up here, anyway, you might also tell her that I'd be happy to assist in determining the cause of... this." I gestured vaguely at the place where the corpses had lain.

He frowned again. "Why?"

"Boredom." I shrugged. "Curiosity killed the cat. I'm too old to play with toys now."

A flicker of confusion crossed his face, but he nodded. "I will convey your message, sir." He turned on his heel and left, heading into the palace, but he paused on the steps and bowed as a slim, white-clad figure appeared in the entryway. Shahar.

I followed him more slowly, nodding to the servants out of habit (which seemed to startle them) and stopping at the foot of the wide steps. Shahar wore a simple morning robe of plush white fur, and a forbidding expression that made me hunch sheepishly, out of long habit.

"I awoke to find you missing," she said, "and since I'm now

judged on how well I serve your needs"—oh, marvelous, just the lightest glaze of venom on those words; she was very good—"it became imperative that I find you before completing any of my other, many, duties. I was at a loss, however, until I was informed of this incident. I knew you would be wherever there was trouble."

I flashed her my most winning smile, which made her eyes even colder. Perhaps I was too old for that to work anymore. "You could simply have called me," I said. "Like you did two nights ago."

She blinked, distracted from her own anger so easily that I knew she wasn't that upset. "Do you think that would work?"

I shrugged, though I was less nonchalant about it than I let her see. "We're going to have to try it sometime, I suppose."

"Yes." She let out a deep sigh, but then her eyes drifted to the servants now assiduously attacking the soiled area around the Vertical Gate. One of them was even cleaning the gate itself, though carefully, using a clear solution and taking great pains not to step on any of the black tiles.

"You knew them?" I asked. Softly, in case she'd cared for them.

"Of course," she said. "Neither was any threat to me." As near a declaration of friendship as it got with this family. "They managed our shipping concerns in High North and on the islands. They were competent. Sensible. Brother and sister, like—" *Deka and me*, I suspected she would have said. "A great loss to the family. Again."

By the bleakness of her expression, I realized suddenly that she was not surprised by the manner of their deaths. And her wording had been another clue, as had Wrath's warning.

"I'm hungry," I said. "Take me somewhere with food and eat with me."

She glared. "Is that a command?"

I rolled my eyes. "I'm not forcing you to obey it, so no."

"There are many kinds of force," she said, her gaze as hard as stone. "If you tell my mother—"

I groaned in exasperation. "I'm not a tattletale! I'm just hungry!" I stepped closer. "And I want to talk about this somewhere private."

She blinked, then flushed—as well she should have, because she should've caught my hints. Would have, if her pride hadn't interfered. "Ah." She hesitated, then looked around the forecourt as if it were full of eyes. It usually was, one way or another. "Meet me at the cupola of the library in half an hour. I'll have food brought." With that she turned away in a swirl of fur and whiteness, her shoes clicking briskly on the daystone as she walked.

I watched her walk away, amused until I realized my eyes were lingering on the slight curves of her hips and their even slighter sway, thanks to her stiff, haughty walk. That unnerved me so badly that I stumbled as I backed down the steps. Though there were only servants to see me—and they were carefully not looking, probably on Morad's orders—I still quickly righted myself and slipped into the garden as a cover, pretending to look at the boring trees and flowers with great fascination. In truth, however, I was shaking.

Nothing to be done for it. Shevir had gauged my age at sixteen, and I knew full well what that age meant for mortal boys. How long before I found myself curled in a sweating knot, furiously caressing myself? And now I knew whose name I would groan when the moment struck.

Gods. How I *hated* adolescence.

Nothing to be done for it, I told myself again, and opened a hole in the ground.

It did not take long to reach the library. I emerged between two of the massive old bookshelves in a disused corner, then made my way along the stacks until I reached the half-hidden spiral staircase. Kurue had built the library's cupola as a reward for those palace denizens who loved the written word. They usually found it only by browsing the stacks and sitting quietly for a while, losing themselves in some book or scroll or tablet. It made me obscurely proud that Shahar had found it—and then I grew annoyed at that pride and more annoyed at my annoyance.

But as I reached the top of the staircase, I stopped in surprise. The cupola was already occupied, and not by Shahar.

A man sat on one of its long cushioned benches. Big, blond, dressed in a suggestively martial jacket that would have looked more so if it hadn't been made out of pearlescent silk. The cupola's roof was glass, its walls open to the air (though as magically protected from the winds and thinner air as the rest of the palace). A shaft of sunlight made a churning river of the man's curly hair, and jewels of his jacket buttons, and a sculpture of his face. I knew him at once for Arameri Central Family even without looking at the mark on his brow, because he was too beautiful and too comfortable.

But when he turned to me, I saw the mark and stared, because it was *complete*. All the scripts I remembered: the contract binding the Enefadeh to the protection and service of Shahar's direct descendants, the compulsion that forced Arameri to remain loyal to their family head…all of it. But why did only this man, out of all the Central Family, wear the mark in its original form?

"Well, well," he said, his eyes raking me with the same quick analysis.

"Sorry," I said uneasily. "Didn't know anyone was up here. I'll try someplace else."

"You're the godling," he said, and I stopped in surprise. He smiled thinly. "I think you must remember how difficult it is to keep a secret in this place."

"I managed, in my day."

"Indeed you did. And a good thing that was, or you would never have gotten free of us."

I lifted my chin, feeling annoyed and belligerent. "Is that really a good thing in the eyes of a fullblood?"

"Yes." He shifted then, setting aside the large, handsomely bound book that had been in his lap. "I've just been reading about you and your fellow Enefadeh, actually, in honor of your arrival. My ancestors really had a monster by the tail, didn't they? I feel exceedingly fortunate that you were released before I had to deal with you."

I narrowed my eyes at him, trying to understand my own wariness. "Why don't I like you?"

The man blinked in surprise, then smiled again with a hint of irony. "Maybe because, if you were still a slave and I your master, *you're* the one I would put the shortest leash on."

I wasn't sure if that was it, but it didn't help. I had never trusted mortals who guessed at how dangerous I was. That usually meant they were just as dangerous. "Who are you?"

"My name is Ramina Arameri."

I nodded, reading the lines of his face and the frame of his bones. "Remath's brother?" No, that wasn't quite right.

"Half brother. Her father was the last family head. Mine wasn't." He shrugged dismissively. "How could you tell?"

"You look Central Family. You smell like her. And you feel"— I glanced at his forehead—"like power that has been leashed."

"Ah." He touched his forehead with a self-deprecating little smile. "This does make it obvious, doesn't it? True sigils were the norm in your day, I understand."

"*True* sigils?" I frowned. "What do they call those trimmed-down ones, then?"

"Theirs are called semisigils. Aside from Remath, I am the only member of the family who currently wears a true sigil." Ramina looked away, his gaze falling on a flock of birds swirling around a Tree branch in the distance. They took off, gliding away, and he followed their slow, steady flight. "It was given to me when my sister took her place as head of the family."

I understood then. The true sigil enforced loyalty to the family head at the cost of the wearer's will. Ramina could no more act against his sister's interests than he could command the sun to set.

"Demons," I said, feeling an unexpected pity for him. "Why didn't she just kill you?"

"Because she hates me, I suppose." Ramina was still watching the birds; I couldn't read his expression. "Or loves me. Same effect either way."

Before I could reply, I heard footsteps on the spiral staircase. We both fell silent as two servants came up, bowing quickly toward Ramina and throwing me uncomfortable looks as they set up a wooden tray and put a large platter of finger foods on it. They left quickly, whereupon I went over to the tray and crammed several items into my mouth. Ramina lifted an eyebrow; I bared my teeth at him. He sniffed a bit and looked away. Good. Bastard.

I was full after only that mouthful, which made me happy because it proved I wasn't fully mortal yet. So I belched and began licking my fingers, which I hoped would disgust Ramina. Alas, he did not look at me. But a moment later, he glanced toward the steps again as Shahar emerged from the floor entrance. She nodded to me, then spotted Ramina and brightened. "Uncle! What are you doing up here?"

"Plotting to take over the world, obviously," he said, smiling broadly at her. She went over and hugged him with real affection, which he returned with equal sincerity. "And having a lovely conversation with my new young friend here. Did you come to meet him?"

Shahar sat down beside him, glancing from him to me and back. "Yes, though it's just as well you're here. Do you know what's happened?"

"Happened?"

She sobered. "Nevra and Criscina. They—Soldiers brought the bodies this morning."

Ramina grimaced, closing his eyes. "How?"

She shook her head. "The masks, again. This time it..." She made a face. "I didn't see the result, but I smelled it."

I sat down on a bench opposite them, in the cupola's shadows, and watched them. The light making an aura of their curls. Their identical looks of sorrow. Yes, it was so obvious I wondered why Remath bothered to try and keep it secret.

Ramina got to his feet and began pacing, his expression ferocious. "Demons and darkness! All the highbloods will be livid, and rightly so. They'll blame Remath for not finding these bastards." He stopped abruptly and turned to Shahar, his eyes narrowing. "And you will be in greater danger than ever, Niece, if these attackers have grown that bold. I wouldn't advise travel for some time."

She frowned a little at this, but not in a surprised way. No doubt she had been thinking the same thing since the forecourt. "I'm scheduled to go to the Gray this evening, to meet with Lady Hynno."

The Gray? I wondered.

"Reschedule it."

"I can't! I asked for the meeting. If I reschedule, she'll know something's wrong, and Mother has decreed that any news of these murders is to remain secret."

Ramina stopped and looked pointedly at me. I flashed him a winning smile.

Shahar made a sound of exasperation. "She also decreed that I'm to give him whatever he wants." She glowered at me. "He saw the bodies, anyway."

"Yes," I said, "but I would appreciate an explanation to go with those bodies. I take it this sort of thing has happened before?"

Ramina frowned at my forwardness, but Shahar only slumped, not bothering to hide her despair. "Never a fullblood before. But others, yes."

"Other *Arameri?*"

"And those who support our interests, sometimes, yes. Always with the masks and always deadly. We're not even sure how the culprit gets the victims to put the mask on. The effects are different every time, and the masks burn up afterward, as you saw."

Amazing. In the old days, no one would have dared to kill an Arameri, for fear of the Enefadeh being sent to find and punish the killers. Had the world overcome its fear of the Arameri to that degree in just a few generations? The resilience—and vindictiveness—of mortals would never cease to astound me.

"Who do you think is doing it, then?" I asked. They both threw me irritated looks, and I raised my eyebrows. "Obviously you don't *know*, or you would have killed them. But you must *suspect* someone."

"No," said Ramina. He sat down, crossing his legs and tossing his long mane of hair over the back of the seat. He regarded me with active contempt. "If we suspected someone, we would kill them, too."

I grew annoyed. "You have the masks, however damaged. Have the scriveners forgotten how to craft tracking scripts?"

"This is not the same," said Shahar. She sat forward, her eyes intent. "This isn't scrivening. The scriveners have no idea how this, this...false magic works, and..." She hesitated, glancing at Ramina, and sighed. "They can't stop it. We are helpless against these attacks."

I yawned. I didn't time it that way, didn't do it deliberately to suggest that I didn't care about their plight, but I saw them both scowl at me, anyway. When I closed my mouth, I glowered back. "What do you want me to say? 'I'm sorry'? I'm not, and you know it. The rest of the world has had to live with this kind of terror—murders without rhyme or reason, magic that strikes without warning—for centuries. Thanks to you Arameri." I shrugged. "If some mortal has figured out a way to make you know the same fear, I'm not going to condemn them for it. Hells, you should be glad I'm not cheering them on."

Ramina's expression went blank, in that way Arameri think is so inscrutable when it really just means they're pissed and trying not to show it. Shahar, at least, was honest enough to give me the full force of her anger. "If you hate us so much, you know what to do," she snapped. "It should be simple enough for you to kill us all. Or"—her lip curled, her tone turning nasty—"ask Nahadoth or Yeine to do it, if you don't have the strength."

"Say that again!" I shot to my feet, feeling quite strong enough to slaughter the whole Arameri family because she was being a brat. If she'd been a boy, I would have slugged her one. Boys could beat each other and remain friends, however; between boys and girls the matter was murkier.

"Children," said Ramina. He spoke in a mild tone, but he was looking at me, palpably tense despite that oh-so-calm face. I appreciated his acknowledgment of my nature. It did help to calm me, which was probably what he'd hoped for.

Shahar looked sulky, but she subsided, and after a moment I, too, sat down, though I was still furious.

"For your information," I spat, crossing my legs and *not* sulking, thank you, "what you're describing isn't false magic. It's just *better* magic."

"Only the gods' magic is better than scrivener magic," Shahar said. I could hear her trying for calm dignity, which immediately made me want to torment her in some way.

"No," I said. To alleviate the urge to annoy her, I shifted to lie down on the bench, putting my feet up on one of the delicate-looking columns that supported the roof. I wished my feet had been dirty, though I supposed that would only have inconvenienced the servants. "Scrivening is only the best thing you mortals—pardon me, you *Amn*—have come up with thus far. But just because *you* haven't thought of anything better doesn't mean there can't *be* anything better."

"Yes," said Ramina with a heavy sigh, "Shevir has already explained this. Scrivening merely approximates the gods' power, and poorly. It can only capture concepts that are communicated via simple written words. Spoken magic works better, when it works."

"The only reason it doesn't work is because mortals don't say it right." The bench was surprisingly comfortable. I would try sleeping up here some night, in the open air, beneath the waning moon. It would feel like resting in Nahadoth's arms. "You get the pronunciation right, and the syntax, but you never master the *context*. You say the words at night when you should only say them by day. You speak them when we're on this side of the sun, not that side—all you have to do is consider the seasons, for gods' sake! But you don't. You say *gevvirh* when you really mean *das-ankalae*, and you take the *breviranaenoket* out of the . . ." I glanced at them and realized they weren't following me at all. ". . . You say it wrong."

"There's no way to say it better," said Shahar. "There's no way for a mortal to understand all that . . . context. You know there isn't."

"There's no way for you to speak as we do, no. But there are other ways to convey information besides speech and writing. Hand signs, body language"—they glanced at each other and I pointed at them—"meaningful looks! What do you think magic is? *Communication.* We gods call to reality, and reality responds. Some of that is because we made it and it is like limbs, the outflow of our souls, we and existence are one and the same, but the rest..."

I was losing them again. Stupid, padlock-brained creatures. They were smart enough to understand; Enefa had made certain of that. They were just being stubborn. I gave up and sighed, tired of trying to talk to them. If only some of my siblings would come to visit me... but I dared not risk word getting out about my condition. As Nahadoth had said, I had enemies.

"Would you consent to work with Shevir, Lord Sieh?" asked Ramina. "To help him figure out this new magic?"

"No."

Shahar made a harsh, irritated sound. "Oh, of course not. We're only giving you a roof over your head and food and—"

"You have *given* me nothing," I snapped, turning my head to glare at her. "In case you've forgotten, *I built the roof.* If we're going to get particular about obligations, Lady Shahar, how about you tell your mother I want two thousand years of back wages? Or offerings, if she prefers; either will keep me in food for the rest of my mortal life." Her mouth fell open in pure affront. "No? Then shut the hells up!"

Shahar stood so fast that on another world she would have shot into the sky. "I don't have to take this." In a flurry of fur and smolder, she went down the steps. I heard the click of her shoes along the library's floors, and then she was gone.

Feeling rather pleased with myself, I folded my arms beneath my head.

"You enjoyed that," said Ramina.

"Whatever gave you that impression?" I laughed.

He sighed, sounding bored rather than frustrated. "It might amuse you to bicker with her—in fact, I'm sure it does amuse you—but you have no idea of the pressure she's under, Lord Sieh. My sister has not been kind to her in the years since you almost killed her and caused her brother to be sent away."

I flinched, reminded of the debt I owed to Shahar—a reminder that Ramina had no doubt meant to deliver. Uncomfortable now, I took my feet off the column and turned onto my belly, propping myself up on my elbows to face him.

"I understand why Remath sent the boy away," I said, "though I'm still surprised that she did it. Usually, when there's more than one prospective heir, the family head pits them against each other."

"That wasn't possible in this case," Ramina said. He had turned his gaze away again, this time toward the vast open landscape on the palace's other side. I followed his eyes, though I had seen the view a million times myself: patchwork farmland and the sparkling blot of the Eyeglass, a local lake. "Dekarta has no chance of inheriting. He's safer away from Sky, quite frankly."

"Because he's not fully Amn?" I gave him a hard look. "And how, exactly, did that happen, *Uncle* Ramina?"

He turned back to me, his eyes narrowing, and then he sighed. "Demonshit."

I grinned. "Did you really lie with your own sister, or did a scrivener handle the fine details with vials and squeeze bulbs?"

Ramina glared at me. "Is tact simply not in your nature, or are you this offensive on purpose?"

"On purpose. But remember that incest isn't exactly unknown to gods."

He crossed his legs, which might have been defensiveness or nonchalance. "It was the politic solution. She needed someone she could trust. And we are only half siblings, after all." He shrugged, then eyed me. "Shahar and Dekarta don't know."

"Shahar, you mean. Who's Deka's father?"

"I am." When I laughed, his jaw tightened. "The scriveners were most careful in their tests, Lord Sieh. Believe me. He and Shahar are full siblings, as Amn as I am."

"Impossible. Or you aren't as Amn as you think."

He bristled, elegantly. "I can trace my lineage unbroken back to the first Shahar, Lord Sieh, with no taint of lesser races at any point. The problem, however, is Remath. Her half-Ken grandfather, for one..." He shuddered dramatically. "I suppose we're lucky the children didn't turn up redheads on top of everything else. But that wasn't the only problem."

"His soul," I said softly, thinking of Deka's smile, still shy even after I'd threatened to kill him. "He is a child of earth and dappled shadows, not the bright harsh light of day."

Ramina looked at me oddly, but I was tired of adapting myself to mortals' comfort. "If by that you mean he's too gentle... well, so is Shahar, really. But she at least looks the part."

"When will he be allowed to return?"

"In theory? When his training is complete, two years from now. In actuality?" Ramina shrugged. "Perhaps never."

I frowned at this, folding my arms and resting my chin on them. With a heavy sigh, Ramina got to his feet as well. I thought he would leave and was glad for it; I was tired of plodding mortal minds and convoluted mortal relationships. But he stopped at the top of the stairwell, gazing at me for a long moment.

"If you won't help the scriveners find the source of these attacks," he said, "will you at least agree to protect Shahar? I feel certain she will be a target for our enemies—or those among our relatives who may use the attacks as a cover for their own plots."

I sighed and closed my eyes. "She's my friend, you fool."

He seemed annoyed, probably because of the "you fool." "What does that—" He paused, then sighed. "No, I should be grateful. The one thing we Arameri have always lacked is the gods' friendship. If Shahar has managed to win yours... well, perhaps she has a better chance of surviving to inherit than I'd first thought."

With that, Ramina left. I still didn't like him.

6

I sent a letter to my love
And on the way I dropped it,
A little puppy picked it up
And put it in his pocket.
It isn't you,
It isn't you,
But it is you.

Sᴋʏ ɪs ʙᴏʀᴇᴅᴏᴍ. That was the thing I had hated the most about it, back when I'd been a slave. It is a massive palace, each spire of which could house a village; its chambers contain dozens of entertainments. All of these become tedious to the point of torment after two thousand years. Hells, after twenty.

It was quickly becoming obvious that I would not be able to

endure Sky for much longer. Which was fine; I needed to be out in the world anyhow, searching for the means to cure myself, if such a thing existed in the mortal realm. But Sky was a necessary staging ground for my efforts at life, allowing me relative safety and comfort in which to consider important logistical questions. Where would I live when I left? *How* would I live, if my magic would soon desert me? I had no resources, no particular skills, no connections in mortal society. The mortal realm could be dangerous, especially given my new vulnerability. I needed a plan, to face it.

(The irony of my situation did not escape me; it was the nature of all mortal adolescents to experience such anxiety at the prospect of leaving their childhood home for the harsh adult world. Knowing this did not make me feel better.)

I had come to no conclusion by the afternoon, but since I guessed that Shahar might have gotten over her fury with me by this point, I went in search of her.

When I walked into Shahar's quarters, I found her surrounded by three servants who seemed to be in the middle of dressing her. As I appeared in the parlor doorway, she turned around so fast that her half-done hair whipped loose; I saw a flash of dismay cross one servant's face before the woman masked it.

"Where in the infinite hells have you been?" Shahar demanded as I leaned against the doorjamb. "The servants said you left the cupola hours ago."

"Good to see you, too," I drawled. "What are you getting all polished up for?"

She sighed, submitting once again to the servants' attentions. "Dinner. I'm meeting with Lady Hynno of the Teman Protectorate's ruling Triadice, and her *pymexe*."

She pronounced the word perfectly, which was fitting, as she'd probably been taught to speak Teman since childhood. The word meant something like "heir," though with a masculine suffix. "Prince," then, in Amn parlance, though unless the Temans had rewritten their charter again in the centuries since I'd last paid attention to them, it was not a hereditary role. They chose their leaders from among their brighter young folk, then trained them for a decade or so before actually letting them be in charge of anything. That sort of sensible thinking was why I'd chosen the Temans as my model, back when I'd first crafted a mortal appearance for myself.

Then I noticed the gown they were wrapping around Shahar. Quite literally: the gown seemed to consist of bands of subdued gold cloth, palm wide, being woven over and under other bands until a herringbone pattern had been achieved. The overall effect was very elegant and cleverly emphasized Shahar's still-developing curves. I whistled, and she threw a wary look at me. "If I didn't know any better," I said, "I would think you were courting this prince. But you're too young, and since when have Arameri *married* foreigners? So this must be something else."

She shrugged, turning to gaze at herself in the bedroom mirror; the dress was almost done. They needed to wrap only the bottom few layers around her legs. But how was she going to get out of the thing? Perhaps they would cut it off her.

"The Triadic likes beauty," she said, "and she controls the tariffs on shipping from High North, so it's worthwhile to impress her. She's one of the few nobles who can actually make things difficult for us." She turned to the side, inspecting her profile; now that the servant had repaired her hair, she looked perfect and knew it. "And Prince Canru is an old childhood friend, so I don't mind looking nice for him."

I raised my eyebrows in surprise. Arameri usually didn't let their children have friends. Though I supposed friends were necessary, now that they had no gods. I went over to the parlor's couch and flopped onto it, not caring about the servants' glances. "So your dinner will be business and pleasure, then."

"Mostly business." The servants murmured something, and there was a pause as Shahar examined herself. Satisfied, she nodded, and the servants filed out. Once they were gone, Shahar slid on a pair of long, pale yellow gloves. "I mean to ask her about what happened to my cousins, in fact."

I rolled onto my side to watch her. "Why would she know?"

"Because the Temans are part of a neutral group in the Nobles' Consortium. They support us, but they also support progressive efforts like a revised tithe system and secular schools. The Order of Itempas can no longer afford to educate children beyond the age of nine, you see—"

"Yes, yes," I said, rubbing my eyes. "I don't care about the details, Shahar. Just tell me the important part."

She sighed in exasperation, coming over to the couch to gaze haughtily at me. "I believe Hynno has alliances with those High Norther nobles who consistently vote against the interests of the Arameri in the Consortium," she said. "And *they*, I believe, are the source of the attacks on my family."

"If you think that, then why haven't you killed them?" Not even a handful of generations ago, her forbears would have done it already.

"Because we don't know which nations are involved. The

core of it is in High North, that much we're certain of, but that still encompasses two dozen nations. And I suspect some involvement by Senmite nations as well, and even some of the islands." She sighed, putting her hands on her hips and frowning in consternation. "I want the head of this snake, Sieh, not just its fangs or scales. So I'm taking your advice and issuing a challenge. I'm going to tell them to kill me before I assume leadership of the family, or I will destroy the whole of High North to deal with the threat."

I rocked back, duly impressed, though a knot of cold anger tightened in my stomach as well. "I see. I assume you're bluffing in order to lure them out into the open."

"Of course I am. I'm not even certain we *can* destroy a continent anymore, and the attempt would certainly exhaust the scrivener corps. Weakening ourselves at a time like this would be foolish." Looking pleased with herself, Shahar sat down beside me. Her dress made a pleasant harmony of sounds as it flexed with her body, a carefully designed effect of its peculiar construction. It probably cost the treasury of a small nation. "Still, I've already spoken with Captain Wrath, and we will coordinate an operation that can put on a suitably threatening display—"

"So you won't use your ancestors' methods," I snapped, "because you still want to be a good Arameri. But you're not above using their *reputation* to advance your goals. Do I have that right?"

She stared at me, startled into momentary silence. "What?"

I sat up. "You threaten people with genocide, and then you wonder why they scheme against you. Really, Shahar; I thought you wanted to change things."

Her face darkened at once. "I would never actually do it, Sieh. Gods, that would make me a monster!"

"And what does it make you to threaten all that they know and love?" She fell silent in confusion and growing anger, and I leaned close so that my breath would caress her cheek. "A monster too cowardly to accept her own hideousness."

Shahar went pale, though two flaring spots of color rose on her cheeks as fury warred with shock in her eyes. To her credit, however, she did not launch an immediate attack, and she did not move away from me. Her nostrils twitched. One of her hands tightened, then relaxed. She lifted her chin.

"Clearly you aren't suggesting that I actually inflict some calamity on them," she said. Her voice was soft. "What, then, do you suggest, Trickster? Let them continue with these assassination attempts until every fullblood is dead?" Her expression tightened further. "Never mind. I don't know why I'm even asking. You don't care whether any of us live or die."

"Why should I?" I gestured around us, at Sky. "It's not as though there aren't plenty of Arameri—"

"No, there aren't!" Her temper broke with an almost palpable force. She shifted to her hands and knees, glowering. "You've looked around this place, Sieh. They tell me the underpalace was full, back in your day. They tell me there were once as many Arameri living abroad as there were here in Sky, and we could take our pick from among the best of the family to serve us. These days we've actually been adopting people into the family who aren't related at all! Tell me what that means to you, O eldest of godlings!"

I frowned. What she was saying made no sense. Humans bred like rabbits. There had been thousands of Arameri in the days when I'd been a slave...but she was right. The underpalace should never have been empty. No mostly-Maroneh lowblood should have been able to rise to captain of the guard. And Remath had mated with her own brother—that had never happened in the old days. Incest, certainly, constantly, but never *for children*. Yet if Remath, herself diluted in some hidden way, sought to concentrate the Central Family's strengths...

The signs had been there since I'd first returned to Sky, but I hadn't seen them. I was so used to thinking of the Arameri as powerful and numerous, but in fact they were dwindling. Dying.

"Explain," I said, inexplicably troubled.

Shahar's anger faded; she sat down again, her shoulders slumping. "The targeting of highbloods is a recent thing," she said, "but the attacks were happening for a long time before that. We just didn't notice until the problem became acute." Her expression grew sour.

"Lowbloods," I guessed. Those Arameri least-closely related to the Central Family, lacking in resources or social status to give them greater value to the family head. The servants, the guards. The expendable ones.

"Yes." She sighed. "It started long ago. Probably a few decades after you and the other Enefadeh broke free. All the collateral lines of the family, the ones we left free to manage businesses or simply bring in new blood—It was subtle at first. Children dying of odd diseases, young wives and husbands turning up infertile, accidents, natural disasters. The lines died out. We apportioned their estates to allies or resumed control of them ourselves."

I was already shaking my head. "No. Accidents can be arranged, gods know children are easy to kill, but *natural disasters*, Shahar? That would mean…" Could a scrivener do it? They knew the scripts for wind and rain and sunlight, but storms were demonishly hard to control. Too easy to trigger a tsunami when trying for a flash flood. But the alternative— no. No.

She smiled, following my worst thoughts. "Yes. It *could* mean that a god has been working to kill us for the past fifty years or more."

I leapt to my feet, beginning to pace. My mortal skin suddenly felt constricting, choking; I wanted to shed it. "If I wanted to kill the Arameri, I would *do* it," I snapped. "I would fill this place with soap bubbles and bury you in bath toys. I would put spiked holes in all the floors and cover them with rugs. I would will every Arameri under twelve to just fall down and die—I can do it, too!" I rounded on her, daring her to challenge me.

But Shahar was still nodding, wearily, her smile gone. "I know, Sieh."

Her capitulation bothered me. I was not used to seeing her despair. I was not used to regarding any Arameri as helpless or vulnerable, let alone all of them.

"Yeine forbade any of us to retaliate against the Arameri," I said softly. "She didn't care about you—she hates you as much as the rest of us do—but she didn't want war everywhere, and…" The Arameri, foul as they were, had been the best hope for keeping the world from collapsing into chaos. Even Nahadoth had gone along with Yeine, and none of my siblings would defy her.

Would they?

I turned away, going to the window so that Shahar would not see my fear.

She sighed and got to her feet. "I've got to go. We're leaving early so as to fool any potential assassins...." She paused, noticing my stillness at last. "Sieh?"

"Go on," I said softly. Beyond the window, the sun had begun to set, scattering a crimson spectrum across the sky. Did Itempas feel the end of day, wherever he was, the way Nahadoth had once died with every dawn? Did some part of him quail and gibber into silence, or did he fade slowly, like the bands of color in the sky, until his soul went dark?

At my silence, Shahar headed for the door, and I roused myself enough to think. "Shahar." I heard her stop. "If something happens, if you're in danger, call me."

"We never tested that."

"It will work." I felt that instinctively. I didn't know how I knew, but I did. "I don't care if most of the Arameri die, it's true. But you are my friend."

She went still behind me. Surprised? Touched? Once upon a time, I would have been able to taste her emotions on the air. Now I could only guess.

"Get some rest," she said at last. "I'll have food sent up. We'll speak again when I return." Then she left.

And I leaned back against the window, trembling now that she was gone, left alone to ponder the most terrible of possibilities.

A godling defying a god. It seemed impossible. We were such low things compared to them; they could kill us so easily. Yet we were not powerless. Some among us—myself, once upon a time—were strong enough to challenge them directly, at least for a few moments. And even the least of us could keep secrets and stir up trouble.

One godling's mischief did not trouble me. But if *many* of us were involved, conspiring across mortal generations, implementing some complex plan, it was no longer mischief. It was a revolt. One far more dangerous than whatever the northerners planned for the Arameri.

Because if the godlings revolted against the gods, the gods would fight back, as they had done when threatened by the demons long ago. But godlings were not as fragile as demons, and many of us had no vested interest in keeping the mortal realm safe. That would mean a second Gods' War, worse than the first one.

This had been brewing right under my nose for fifty years, and I hadn't had a clue.

Beyond me, in silent rebuke, the bloody sky went gradually black.

7

How many miles to Babylon?
Three score and ten.
Can I get there by candlelight?
Aye, and back again.
If your feet are nimble and light,
You'll get there by candlelight.

I NEEDED HELP. But not from Nahadoth or Yeine; I dared not chance their tempers. Not until I knew more.

Who could I trust among my siblings? Zhakkarn, of course,

but she was never subtle and would be no help in uncovering a conspiracy. The rest—hells. Most of them I had not spoken to in two thousand years. Before that I had tried to kill some of them. Bridges burned, ashes scattered, ground strewn with salt.

And there was the small problem of my inability to return to the gods' realm in my current state. That was less of a problem than it seemed, because fortunately the city beneath Sky was teeming with my youngest siblings, those for whom the novelty of the mortal realm had not yet worn off. If I could convince one of them to help me...But which one?

I turned from the window, frustrated, to pace. The walls of Sky had begun to glow again, and I hated them, for they were more proof of my impotence; once upon a time, they would have dimmed, just a bit, in my presence. I was no Nahadoth, but there was more than a little of his darkness in me. Now, as if to mock me, the walls stayed bright, diffusing every shadow—

—shadow.

I stopped. There was one of my siblings, just maybe, who would help me. Not because she liked me; quite the opposite. But secrets were her nature, and that was something we shared. It was always easier to relate to those of my siblings with whom I had something in common. If I appealed to that, would she listen? Or would she kill me?

"No reward without risk," I murmured to myself, and headed for the apartment door.

I took the lift down to the penultimate level of the under-palace. The corridors here were as quiet as always—and dim, compared to the brighter glow of all the other levels. Yes, this was the place.

For nostalgia's sake, I touched each door as I passed it, remembering. Here were my sisters' rooms: Zhakkarn's with cannon shot embedded in the floor and the walls hung with shields; her hammock of blood-soaked slings and whips. (Very comfortable, I knew from experience, though a little scratchy.) Dear traitor Kurue's, with pearls and coins scattered over nearly every surface, and books stolen from the library stacked atop the rest. The coins would be tarnishing now.

I avoided my own quarters, for fear of how they would make me feel. How long before I ended up living there again? I steered my thoughts off this path with a heavy hand.

This left the fourth chamber, at the center of the level. The one that had been Nahadoth's.

It was pitch-black within, but I could still see a little in the dark even without cat's eyes. The chamber was completely empty. No furnishings, no decorations, no hint that the room had ever been used. Yet every inch of its structure screamed defiance of our onetime jailors: the permanently lightless walls. The ceiling, which dipped toward the center of the room; the floor rose in the same spot, as if some terrible force had sucked the very stone toward itself. The sharp corners, which no other room in Sky had. If I stared hard enough into the dark, I could almost see Nahadoth's silhouette etched against it and hear his soft, deep voice. *Have you come for another story? Greedy child.*

It had been cruel of me to push him away. I would pray an apology to him after this.

Reaching into my shirt, I pulled up the necklace of my own woven hair. Tugging En off the cord, I willed it to hover in the space between the floor and ceiling extrusions. To my relief, this worked; En stayed in the air and began turning at once, happily.

This reminded it of the orrery, though it was lonely without planets.

"Sorry," I said, reaching out to stroke its smooth surface with a fingertip. "I'll give you more planets someday. In the meantime, will you give me light?"

In answer, En flared bright yellow-white for me, a gleeful candle. Suddenly Nahadoth's chamber became smaller, stark with shadows. My own loomed behind me, a big-headed apparition that seemed to taunt me with the shape of the child I should have been. I ignored it and focused on the task at hand.

"Lady of Secrets," I said, extending a hand; my shadow did the same. Shaping my fingers just so, I made the profile of a face on the wall and spoke with it. "Shadow in the dark. Nemmer Jru Im, my sister; do you hear me?"

There was a pause. Then, though I did not move, my hand shadow cocked its head.

"Well, this is unexpected," it said in a woman's voice. "Big brother Sieh. It's been some time."

I added my other hand, working the shadow into the shape of a donkey's head. *I've been an ass.* "I hear interesting things about you, Nemmer. Will you speak with me?"

"I answered, didn't I?" The first shadow shifted, impossibly manifesting its own arms and hands, the latter of which were set on its hips. "Though I'll admit that's because I've heard some very interesting things about you, too. I'm *dying* to know if they're true."

Damn. I might have known. "I'll tell you every juicy detail, but I want something in return."

"Do you, now?" I tensed at the wariness in her tone. That she did not trust me was irrelevant; she trusted no one. She did not like me, though, which was another matter entirely. "I'm not certain I'm interested in making any bargains with you, *Trickster*."

I nodded; no more than I had expected. "I mean no harm to you, Nemmer. Cross my heart and hope to die." I heard the bitterness in my own voice and angled my fingers into the shape of an old man's head. "You did not turn on us in the War. I bear no grudge toward you."

"That I do not believe," she said, folding her arms. "Everyone knows you hate the ones who stood by doing nothing as much as the ones who fought for Itempas."

"*Hate* is a strong word—"

Her silhouette tossed its head in the universal gesture of rolled eyes. "Resent us, then. *Yearn to kill* us. Is that more accurate?"

I stopped and dropped my hands with a sigh. The talking shadows remained. "You know my nature, Sister. What do you want from me—maturity?" I wanted to laugh, but I was too soul-weary. "Fine, I'll say it: I hate you and I wouldn't have contacted you if I had a choice, and we both know it. Now, will you speak with me, or shall we just tell each other to go to the infinite hells and leave it at that?"

She was silent for a moment. I had time enough to worry: who could I contact if she refused to help me? The other choices were worse. What if—

"All right," she said at last, and the knot that had been tightening in my belly loosened. "I need time to set things up. Come here, a week from today. Noon." The location made itself present in my consciousness, as if I had always known it. A house somewhere in the city below Sky. South Root. "Come alone."

I folded my arms. "Will *you* be alone?"

"Oh, of course."

I made the shape of a cat's head with my hands: ears back, teeth bared. She laughed.

"I don't care if you believe me. You asked for this meeting, not I. Be there in a week, or not at all." With that, her shadow leaned down and blew hard. With a surprised flare, En went dark and dropped to the floor. Then Nemmer was gone.

In the dark, I retrieved En, who was quite put out. I murmured soothing words and tucked it back into my shirt, all the while thinking.

If Nemmer knew what had happened to me—and it was her nature to know such things; not even the Three could keep her out of their business, though she wasn't foolish enough to flaunt that—then when I arrived in a week, I might find her and a group of my least-favorite siblings, some of whom had been waiting for a chance to repay me for the Gods' War for two thousand years.

But Nemmer had never been one to play the games of our family. I didn't know why she'd sat out the war. Had she been torn, like so many of our siblings, between our fathers? Had she been one of those working to save the mortal realm, which had nearly been destroyed by our battling? I sighed in frustration, realizing that *this* was the sort of thing I should have occupied myself with as eldest, not our parents' sordid dramas. If I had bothered to reconcile with my siblings, perhaps tried to understand their reasons for betraying Nahadoth—

"If I had done that, I would not be who I am." I sighed into the dark.

Which, ultimately, was why I would risk trusting Nemmer.

She, too, was only what her nature made her. She kept her own counsel, gathering secrets and doling out knowledge where she deemed best and making alliances only as it suited her—briefly, if at all. If nothing else, that meant she was not my enemy. Whether she became my friend would be up to me.

On returning to Deka's room, I was surprised to find that I had visitors again: Morad, the ample-haired palace steward, and another servant, who was busy making the bed and tidying up. Both bowed to me at once, as they would to any Arameri highblood. Then the servant promptly resumed his cleaning duties while Morad looked me up and down with an expression of unconcealed distaste.

Frowning at her scrutiny, I looked at myself—and then, belatedly, realized why the servants had all stared at me on my way to the underpalace. I still wore the clothing I had conjured for myself two days before. It had been nondescript then, but it was filthy now, after all my scrabbling through dusty corridors and Tree-choked dead spaces. And...I sniffed one of my armpits and wrinkled my nose, appalled that I had not noticed. I had not bathed since my return to this world, and apparently my adolescent body had a greater capacity for generating reek than I had done as a child.

"Oh," I said, smiling sheepishly at Morad. She sighed, though I thought I saw a hint of amusement on her face.

"I'll run you a bath," she said, and paused, looking particularly at my head. "And summon a stylist. And the tailor. And a manicurist."

I touched my stringy, gritty hair with a weak laugh. "I suppose I deserve that."

"As you like, my lord." Morad touched the servant, who had almost finished the bed, and murmured something. He nodded and exited the apartment at once. To my surprise, Morad then rolled up her sleeves and finished tucking the sheets. When that was done, she went into the bathroom; a moment later, I heard water run.

Curious, I followed her into the room and watched while she sat on the tub's edge, testing the water with her fingers. It was even more noticeable with her back turned and all that hair of hers visible in full riot. It was clear that she was not fully Amn; her hair had the kind of tight, small coils that wealthy Amn spent hours and fortunes to achieve, and it was as black as my father's soul. Her skin was pale enough, but the marks of *other* were in her features, plain to anyone who looked. It was also plain that she was not ashamed of her mixed blood; she sat as straight and graceful as a queen. She could not have been raised in Sky or any Amn territory; they would have beaten her spirit down with cruel words long before now.

"Maroneh?" I guessed. "You must've gotten the hair from them, at least. The rest... Teman, maybe? Uthre, a bit of Ken?"

Morad turned to me, lifting one elegant eyebrow. "Two of my grandparents were part Maroneh, yes. One was Teman, another Min, and there are rumors that my father was actually a half-Tok who pretended to be Senmite to get into the Hunthou Legions. My mother was Amn."

More proof of the Arameri's desperation. In the old days, they would barely have acknowledged a woman with such jumbled bloodlines, let alone make her Steward. "Then how..."

She smiled wryly, as if she got such rude questions all the time. "I grew up in southern Senm. When I came of age, I petitioned to come here on the strength of my fourth grandparent—an Arameri highblood." At my grimace, she nodded. It was an old story. "Grandmama Atri never knew my grandfather's name. He was passing through town on a journey. Her family had no powerful friends, and she was a pretty girl." She shrugged, though her smile had faded.

"So you decided to come find Grandpapa the rapist and say hello?"

"He died years ago." She checked the water once more and stopped the taps. "It was Grandmama's idea that I come here, actually. There's not much work in that part of Senm, and if nothing else, her suffering could bring me a better life." She rose and went to stand pointedly beside the washing area's bench, picking up the flask that held shampoo.

I got up and undressed, pleased that my nudity didn't seem to bother her. When I sat down, before I could warn her, she lifted the cord that held En from around my neck and set it on a counter. I was relieved that En tolerated this without protest. It must have been tired after its earlier exertion. Plus, it had always had odd taste in mortals.

"You didn't have to come *here* for a better life," I said, yawning as she wet my hair and began washing it. Sending the message to Nemmer had left me tired, too, and Morad's fingers were skillful and soothing. "There must be a thousand other places in the world where you could've made a living and where you wouldn't have had to deal with this family's madness."

"There were no other places that paid as much," she said.

I swung around to stare at her. "They *pay* you?"

She nodded, amused at my reaction, and gently pushed my head back into place so that she could resume work. "Yes. Old

Lord T'vril's doing, actually. As a quarterblood, I can retire in five more years with enough money to take care of my whole family for the rest of my life. I'd say that's worth dabbling in madness, wouldn't you?"

I frowned, trying to understand. "They are your family," I said. "The ones you left behind, in the south. The Arameri are just employers to you?"

Her hands paused. "Well. I've been here fifteen years at this point; it's home now. Some aspects of life in Sky aren't so terrible, Lord Sieh. I suspect you know that. And...well, there are people I love here, too."

I knew then. She resumed work in silence, pouring warm water over me and then lathering again, and when she leaned past me to pick up the flask of shampoo, I got a good mouthful of her scent. Daystone and paper and patience, the scents of efficient bureaucracy, and one thing more. A complex scent, layered, familiar, with each element supporting and enriching the other. Dreams. Pragmatism. Discretion. Love.

Remath.

It was my nature to use the keys to a mortal's soul whenever they fell into my hands. If I had still been myself, the child or the cat, I would have found some way to torment Morad with my knowledge. I might even have made a song of it and sung it everywhere until even her friends found themselves humming the tune. The refrain would have been *see wow, you silly cow, how dare you lose your heart.*

But though I would always be the child, and the child was a bully, I could not bring myself to do this to her. I was going soft, I supposed, or growing up. So I kept silent.

Presently Morad finished with my hair, whereupon she

handed me a soapy sponge and stepped back, plainly unwilling to wash the rest of my body. She had wrapped my hair in a damp towel that was tied like a beehive atop my head, which made me giggle when I finished and stood and caught a glimpse of myself in the mirror. Then my eyes drifted down. I saw the rest of me and fell silent.

It was the same body I had shaped for myself countless times, sometimes deliberately, sometimes in helpless response to moments of weakness. Short for "my age"; I would grow another two or three inches but would never be tall by Amn standards. Thinner than I usually made myself, perhaps from years of not eating while I gradually became mortal within Nahadoth. Long-limbed. Beneath my brown skin, there were bones poking out at every juncture, like blemishes. The muscles that lined them were attenuated and not very strong.

I leaned closer to the mirror, peering at the lines of my face critically. Not very attractive, either, though I knew that would improve. Too disproportionate for now. Too tired-eyed. Shahar was much prettier. And yet she had kissed me, hadn't she? I traced the outline of my lips with a finger, remembering the feel of her mouth. What had she thought of mine, on hers?

Morad cleared her throat.

Did Shahar ever think of—

"The water will get cold," Morad said gently. I blinked, blushing, and was abruptly glad I hadn't made fun of her. I got into the tub, and Morad exited the bathroom to go speak with the tailor, who'd just arrived and announced himself.

When I emerged in a fluffy robe—I looked ridiculous—the tailor measured me, murmuring to himself that I would need looser clothing to conceal my thinness. Then came the manicurist, and the shoemaker, and one or two others whom Morad had somehow summoned, though I hadn't seen her use magic. By the time it was done, I was exhausted—which Morad thankfully noticed. She dismissed all the craft servants and turned to head for the door herself.

Belatedly it occurred to me that she'd been unbelievably helpful. Who knew how many duties she had as steward, and how many of those had she neglected to see to my comfort? "Thank you," I blurted as she opened the door.

She paused and looked back at me in surprise, then smiled in such a genuine, generous way that I suddenly knew what Remath saw in her.

Then she was gone. I sat down to eat the meal the servants had left. Afterward, I sprawled naked across Deka's bed, for once looking forward to sleep so that I could perhaps dream of love and

forget

I stood upon a plain like a vast glass mirror. Mirrors again. I had seen them in Nahadoth's realm, too. Perhaps there was meaning in this? I would ponder it some other time.

Above me arced the vault of the heavens: an endlessly turning cylinder of clouds and sky, vast and limitless and yet somehow enclosed. Clouds drifted across it from left to right, although the light—from no source I could ascertain—shifted in the opposite direction, waxing light and waning dark in a slow and steady gradient.

The gods' realm, or a dream manifestation of it. It was an approximation, of course. All my mortal mind could comprehend.

Before me, rising from the plain, a palace lay impossibly on its side. It was silver and black, built in no recognizable mortal architectural style and yet suggesting all of them, a thing of lines and shadow without dimension or definition. An impression, not reality. Below, instead of a reflection, its opposite shone in the mirror: white and gold, more realistic but less imaginative, the same yet different. There was meaning in this, too, but it was obvious: the black palace ascendant, the white palace nothing but an image. The silvery plain reflecting, balancing, and separating both. I sighed, annoyed. Had I already become as tiresomely literal as most mortals? How humiliating.

"Are you afraid?" asked a voice behind me.

I started and began to turn. "No," the speaker snapped, and such was the force of his command—commanding reality, commanding my flesh—that I froze. *Now* I was afraid.

"Who are you?" I asked. I didn't recognize his voice, but that meant nothing. I had dozens of brothers and they could take any shape they chose, especially in this realm.

"Why does that matter?"

"Because I want to know, duh."

"Why?"

I frowned. "What kind of question is that? We're family; I want to know which one of my brothers is trying to scare the hells out of me." And succeeding, though I would never admit such a thing.

"I'm not one of your brothers."

At this, I frowned in confusion. Only gods could enter the gods' realm. Was he lying? Or was I simply too mortal to understand what he really meant?

"Should I kill you?" the stranger asked. He was young, I

decided, though such judgments meant little in the grand scale of things. He was oddly soft-spoken, too, his voice mild even as he delivered these peculiar not-quite-threats. Was he angry? I thought so, but couldn't be sure. His tone was all flat emotionlessness edged in cold.

"I don't know. Should you?" I retorted.

"I've been contemplating the matter for most of my life."

"Ah," I said. "I suppose you and I must have gotten off on the wrong foot from the beginning, then." That happened sometimes. I'd tried to be a good elder brother for a long time, visiting each of my younger siblings as they were born and helping them through those first, difficult centuries. Some of them I was still friends with. Some of them I'd loathed the instant I'd laid eyes on them, and vice versa.

"From the very beginning, yes."

I sighed, slipping my hands into my pockets. "Must be a difficult decision, then, or you'd have done it already. Whatever I did to make you angry, either it can't have been all that bad, or it's unforgivable."

"Oh?"

I shrugged. "If it was really bad, you wouldn't be waffling about whether to kill me. If it was unforgivable, you'd be too angry for revenge to make any difference. There'd be no *point* in killing me. So which is it?"

"There's a third option," he said. "It was unforgivable, but there *is* a point in killing you."

"Interesting." In spite of my unease, I grinned at the conundrum. "And that point is?"

"I don't simply *want* vengeance. I require and embody and evolve through it."

I blinked, sobering, because if vengeance was his nature, then that was another matter entirely. But I did not remember a sibling who was god of vengeance.

"What have I done to earn your wrath?" I asked, troubled now. "And why are you even asking the question? You have to serve your nature."

"Are you offering to die for me?"

"No, demons take you. If you try to kill me, I'll try to kill you back. Suicide isn't *my* nature. But I want to understand this."

He sighed and shifted, the movement drawing my eye toward the mirror below our feet. It didn't help much. The angle of the reflection was such that I could see little beyond feet and legs and a hint of elbow. His hands were in his pockets, too.

"What you have done is unforgivable," he said, "and yet I *must* forgive it, because you did not know."

I frowned, confused. "What does my knowledge have to do with anything? Harm committed unknowingly is still harm."

"True. But if you had known, Sieh, I'm not certain you would have done it."

At his use of my name, I grew more confused, because his tone had changed. For an instant, the coldness had broken, and I heard stranger things underneath. Sorrow. Wistfulness? Perhaps a hint of affection. But I did not know this god; I was certain of it.

"Irrelevant," I said finally, turning my head as much as I could. Beyond a certain point, my neck simply would not bend; it was like trying to turn with two pillows braced on either side of my head. Pillows formed of nothing but solid, unyielding will. I tried to relax. "You can't base decisions on hypotheticals. It doesn't matter what I *would have* done. You know only what

I *did*." I paused meaningfully. "Perhaps you could tell me." For once I wasn't in the mood for games.

Unfortunately, my companion was. "You chose to serve your nature," he said, ignoring my hint. "Why?"

I wished I could look at him. Sometimes a look is more eloquent than any words. "*Why?* What the hells—are you kidding?"

"You are the oldest of us and must pretend to be the youngest."

"I don't pretend anything. I am what I must be, and I'm damn good at it, thanks."

"So we are weaker than the mortals, then." His voice grew soft, almost sad. "Slaves to fate, never to be freed."

"Shut the hells up," I snapped. "You don't know slavery if you think *this* is the same thing."

"Isn't it? Having no choice—"

"You have a choice." I lifted my gaze to the shifting firmament above. The gradient—night to day, day to night—did not change at a constant rate. Only mortals thought of the sky as a reliable, predictable thing. We gods had to live with Nahadoth and Itempas; we knew better. "You can accept yourself, take control of your nature, make it what you *want* it to be. Just because you're the god of vengeance doesn't mean you have to be some brooding cliché, forever cackling to yourself and totting up what you owe to whom. Choose how your nature shapes you. Embrace it. Find the strength in it. Or fight yourself and remain forever incomplete."

My companion fell silent, perhaps digesting my advice. That was good, because it was clear that I'd done him a disservice, besides whatever wrong he felt I'd committed. I did not remember him; that meant I hadn't bothered to find him, guide him, after his birth. And he'd needed such guidance, because it was painfully clear that he did not like the hand fate, or the Maelstrom, had dealt him. I didn't blame him for that; I wouldn't have wanted to be god of vengeance, either. But he was, and he was going to have to find a way to live with that.

In the mirror, I saw the man behind me step closer, raising a hand. I braced myself to fight—purely on principle, since I already knew there was nothing I could do. It was clear his power superseded what little god-magic I had left, or I would have been able to break his compulsion and turn around.

But his hand touched my hair, to my utter shock. Lingered there a moment, as if memorizing the texture. Then fingers grazed the back of my neck, and I jumped. Was this some kind of threat? But he made no attempt to harm me. His finger traced the knots of spine along the back of my neck, stopping only when my clothing interfered. Then—reluctantly, I thought—his hand pulled away.

"Thank you," he said at last. "That was something I needed to hear."

"Sorry I didn't say it sooner." I paused. "So are you going to kill me now?"

"Soon."

"Ah. Good vengeance takes time?"

"Yes." The coldness had returned to his voice, and this time I recognized it for what it was. Not anger. Resolve.

I sighed. "Sorry, too, to hear that. I think I might've liked you."

"Yes. And I you."

There was that, at least. "Well, don't dither too long about it. I've only got a few decades left."

I thought he smiled, which I counted as a victory. "I have already begun."

"Good for you." I hoped he didn't think I was mocking him. It always made me feel good to see the young ones do well, even if that meant they would inevitably threaten me. That was the way of things, after all. Children had to grow up. They did not always become what others wanted. "Do me a favor, though?"

He said nothing, in keeping with his newfound resolve. That was all right. I could be his enemy, if that was what he needed from me. I just didn't see any point in being an ass about it.

"I don't belong here anymore." I gestured around us at the mirrored plain, the palaces, the sky. "Not even in this watered-down dream of reality. Wake me up, will you?"

"All right."

And suddenly a hand ripped through me from behind. I cried out in surprise and agony, looking down to see my mortal heart clenched in a sharp-nailed hand—

I jerked awake to the sound of my own cry, echoing from the vaulted ceiling.

Glowing vaulted ceiling. It was night. Above me loomed Shahar, who had a hand on my chest and a worried look on her face. I was still sleepy, disoriented. A quick check of my chest verified that my heart was still there. Inadvertently, I looked at Shahar's chest, thinking muzzily that my dream-enemy might have tried to harm her, too. Her dress lay in cut strips down to her waist, half undone, and she held a loose sleep shift over her breasts with her free arm, which she must have grabbed to cover herself when she'd come into my room. This did nothing to hide the other beautiful parts of her: the gentle sweep of neck into shoulder, the slight curve of her waist. Of her breasts, I could still see one rounded shadow near her elbow.

I reached up to pull her arm out of the way and stopped with my fingers two inches from her arm. It took her a moment to realize. She stared at my reaching hand uncomprehendingly; then her eyes widened and she jerked away.

I lowered my hand. "Sorry," I muttered.

She glared at me. "You started screaming so loud I could hear you through the adjoining door. I thought something was *wrong* with you."

"A dream."

"Not a pleasant one, obviously."

"Actually, it wasn't so bad, 'til the end." The fear was fading quickly. My dream-companion hadn't been gentle about it, but he'd chosen an excellent way to send me back to the mortal realm. I felt none of the heartrending sorrow that I might have on realizing that the gods' realm was now forbidden to me. Instead I was just annoyed. "Little mortalfucking bastard. If I ever get my magic back, I'm going to break every bone in whatever body he manifests. Let him avenge *that*."

I paused then, because Shahar was looking at me oddly. "What in every god's name are you talking about?"

"Nothing. I'm babbling." I yawned, my jaw cracking with the effort. "Sleep makes me stupid. Never liked it."

"Mortalfuck," she said, looking thoughtful. "Is that—" She paused, grimacing, too refined to say the word beyond repeating my term. "*Being with* a mortal. Is it such an anathema among gods that you use it as a curse?"

I blushed, though it bothered me that I did. I had nothing to be ashamed of. Pushing myself up on my elbows, I said, "No, it's not anathema at all. Far from it."

"What, then?"

I tried to seem nonchalant. "It's just that mortals are dangerous to love. They break easily. In time, they die. It hurts." I shrugged. "It's easier, safer, to just use them for pleasure. But that's hard, too, because it's impossible for us to take pleasure without giving back something of ourselves. We are not..." I groped for the words in Senmite. "We do not...It isn't our way. No, it isn't *natural* to do things that way, to be nothing but body, contained only within ourselves, so when we are with another, we reach out and the mortal gets inside us—we cannot help it—and then it hurts to push them out, too..." I trailed off, because Shahar was staring at me. I'd been talking faster and faster, the words tumbling together in my effort to convey how it felt. I sighed and forced myself back to human speed. "*Being with* mortals isn't anathema, but it's not good, either. It never ends well. Any god with sense avoids it."

"I see." I wasn't sure I believed that, but she sighed. "Well. Give me a moment." She stepped back into her room, not shutting the door, and I heard her wrestle with the cloth of her dress for a few moments. Then she returned, wearing the sleep shift instead of holding it in front of herself this time. By this point I had sat up, rubbing my face to try and banish the dregs of sleep and the memory of my bloody, torn-out heart. When Shahar sat down on the bed, she did so gingerly, at its edge, out of my arms' reach. I didn't blame her for that or the fact that she seemed more relaxed after my speech about avoiding sex.

Still, there was something odd about her manner, something

I couldn't put my finger on. She seemed jittery, tense. I wondered why she hadn't just stayed in her room and gone to bed, once she'd seen that I wasn't dying.

"How did your meeting with, ah..." I waved a hand vaguely. Some noble.

She chuckled. "It went well, though that depends on your definition of *well*." She sobered, her eyes darkening with a hint of her earlier anger. "You'll be pleased to know that I did not follow through on my plan to challenge the resistance, per your advice. The message I sent instead—I hope, if I'm right about Lady Hynno—was that I would like to negotiate. Find out more about their demands and determine whether there's some way that we might meet them. Without throwing the world into chaos, that is." She glanced at me warily.

"I'm impressed," I said truthfully. "And surprised. Negotiation—compromise—is usually anathema to Itempans. And you changed your mind because of me?" I laughed a little. There were some good things about being older. People listened to me more.

Shahar sighed, looking away. "We'll see what happens when my mother hears of it. She already thinks I'm weak; after this, I may not be heir for much longer." With a heavy sigh, she lay back on the bed, stretching out her arms over her head. I could not help myself; my eyes settled on the very noticeable contrast of her areolae under the sheer shift. They were surprisingly dark, given her pale coloring. Perfect brown circles, with soft little cylinders at their centers—

Useless stupid animal mortaling body. My penis had reacted before I could stop it, jabbing me in the belly and forcing me to sit up from my usual slouch. It hurt, and I felt hot all over, as if I'd come down sick. (I had. It was called *adolescence*, an evil,

evil disease.) But it was not just her flesh that drew me. I could barely see it with my withering senses, but her soul gleamed and whispered like rubbed silk. We have always been vulnerable to true beauty.

I dragged my eyes away from her breasts to find her watching me—watching me watch her? I did not know, but the hunger in me sharpened at the unalarmed, contemplative look in her eyes. I fought the reaction back, but it was difficult. Another symptom of the disease.

"Don't be stupid," I said, focusing on mundanities. "It takes great strength to compromise, Shahar. More than it does to threaten and destroy, since you must fight your own pride as well as the enemy. You Arameri have never understood this— and you didn't have to, when you had us at your beck and call. Now, perhaps, you can learn to be true rulers and not merely bullies."

She rolled onto her belly, which brought her to lie between my legs, propped on her elbows. At this I frowned, growing suspicious, and then wondering at my own unease. She was just a girl testing the waters of womanhood. An older version of *I'll show you mine if you show me yours.* She wanted to know if I found her desirable. Did I not owe her the courtesy of an honest response? I lowered my knees and sat back on my elbows so that she could see the evidence of my admiration in the tented sheet and the heat of my gaze. She immediately blushed, averting her eyes. Then she looked at me again, and away again, and eventually looked down at her folded arms, which were fidgeting on the covers.

"I think Mother wants me to marry Canru," she said. Her words had an air of effort. "The Teman heir I told you about. I think that's why she's let me be friends with him. She's never let anyone else close to me."

I shrugged. "So marry him."

She glared at me, forgetting her prudishness. "I don't want to."

"Then *don't*. Shahar, for the gods' sakes. You're the Arameri heir. Do what you damn well please."

"I can't. If Mother wants this—" She bit her lower lip and looked away. "We have never sold our sons or daughters into marriage before now, Sieh. We didn't have to, because we didn't have anything to gain. We didn't need alliances or money or land. But now...I think...I think Mother understands that the Temans might prove pivotal, given High North's increasing restlessness. I think that's why she's letting me handle things with Lady Hynno. She's putting me on display."

All at once she looked up at me, and there was such ferocity in her expression that it struck me like a blow. Why?

"I want to succeed Mother, Sieh," she said. "I want to be head after her. Not just because I want power; I know the evil our family's done to you and to the world. But we've done good, too, great good, and I want *that* to be our legacy. I will do whatever it takes to achieve that."

I stared at her, taken aback. And mourning. Because what she wanted was impossible. Her childhood promise, to be both a good person and an Arameri, to use her family's power to make the world better—it was naïveté of the highest order. I had seen others like her, a few, one every handful of generations within Itempas's chosen family. They were always the brightest lights, the most glorious souls of the whole grimy bunch. The ones I could not hate, because they were special.

But it never lasted, once they gained power. They streaked

through life like falling stars across the heavens, brilliant but ephemeral. The power killed the glory, dulled the specialness into despair. It hurt so much to watch their hopes die.

I could say nothing. To let her see my sorrow would start the process early. So I sighed and turned onto my side, pretending boredom, when in fact I was trying hard not to cry.

Her frustration flared like a struck match. She got up on her hands and knees and crawled over to me, bracing her arms on either side of my body so she could glare into my face. "*Help* me, damn you! You're supposed to be my friend!"

I stifled a yawn. "What do you want me to do? Tell you to marry a man you don't love? Tell you *not* to marry him? This isn't a bedtime tale, Shahar. People marry people they don't love all the time, and it isn't always terrible. He's already your friend; you could do worse. And if it's something your mother wants, you don't have a choice, anyway."

Her hand, braced on the covers in front of me, trembled. My senses throbbed with the waver of her conflicting yearnings. The child in her wanted to do as she pleased, cling to impossible hopes. The woman in her wanted to make sound decisions, succeed even if it meant sacrifice. The woman would win; that was inevitable. But the child would not go quietly.

With that same trembling hand, she touched my shoulder, pushing until I twisted my torso to face her. Then she leaned down and kissed me.

I permitted it, more out of curiosity than anything else. It was clumsy this time and did not last long. She was off the center of my mouth, covering mostly the bottom lip. I did not share myself with her, and she sat up, frowning.

"Does that make you feel better?" I asked. I honestly wanted to know. Shahar's expression crumpled. She turned away and lay down behind me, her back to mine. I felt her fighting tears.

Troubled, and worried that I had somehow harmed her, I turned to her and sat up. "What is it that you want?"

"My mother to love me. My brother back. The world not to hate us. Everything."

I considered this. "Shall I fetch him for you? Deka?"

She tensed, turning over. "Could you do that?"

"I don't know." I could not change my shape anymore. Traveling across distances was not so very different, save that it involved changing the shape of reality to make the world smaller. If I could not do one, I might not be able to do the other.

As I watched, however, the eagerness faded from her expression. "No. Deka may not love me anymore."

I blinked in surprise. "Of course he does."

"Don't patronize me, Sieh."

"I'm not," I snapped. "I can feel the bond between us, Shahar, as clear as this." I took a curl of her hair in my fingers and pulled on it, gentle but steady. She made a sound of surprise and I let the curl go; it bounced back prettily. "You both pull at me and at each other. Neither of you likes me very much now, but otherwise nothing has changed between the two of you since those days in the underpalace, years ago. You still love him, and he still loves you just as much. I'm a god, all right? I know."

I was not strictly telling the truth. It was true that Shahar's feelings toward me had waned, though they grew stronger with every hour I spent in her presence. Deka's, however, had grown stronger, too, even with no contact between us for half his lifetime. I didn't quite know how to interpret that, so I didn't mention it.

Her eyes went wide at my words—and then welled with tears. She made a quick, abortive sound: *buh.* As soon as she uttered it, she clapped a hand to her mouth, but her hand was trembling.

I sighed and pulled her against me, her face against my chest. It was only when I did this—only when she felt safe from eyes that might look upon her humanity and judge it a weakness— that she let herself break into deep, racking sobs so loud that they echoed from the walls of the apartment. Her tears were hot, though they cooled rapidly on my skin and as they pattered onto the sheets. Her shoulders heaved against my arms, and as the sobs grew worse, her arms went hard around me, squeezing me as if her life depended on my solidity and stillness. So I gave her both, stroking her hair and murmuring soothing things in the language of creation, letting her know that I loved her, too. For I did, fool that I was.

When her tears finally stopped, I kept stroking her, liking the way her curls went flat and sprang up again as my hand passed, and thinking of nothing. I barely noticed when her arms loos- ened, her hands coming to stroke my sides and back and hip. I kept thinking of nothing when she eased my shirt up and laid the lightest of kisses on my belly. It tickled; I smiled. Then she sat up to look at me, her eyes red-rimmed but dry, a peculiar intent in her eyes.

When she kissed me this time, it was wholly different. She nudged my lips apart and touched my tongue with her own, sweet and wet and sour. When I did not react, she slid her hands under my shirt, exploring the flat strangeness of a body that was not her own. I liked this until one of her hands went far- ther down, her fingers tickling hair and cloth at the edge of my pants, and then I caught her wrist. "No," I said.

She closed her eyes and I felt her aching emptiness. It was not lust. Missing her brother had made her feel alone. "I love you," she said. Not even an admission, this; it was simply a statement of fact, like *the moon is pretty* or *you're going to die*. "I've always loved you, since we were children. I tried not to."

I nodded, stroking her hand. "I know."

"I want to choose. If I have to sell myself for power, I want to give myself first. For love. For a friend."

I sighed, closing my eyes. "Shahar, I told you, it's not good—"

She scowled and lunged forward and kissed me again. I was stunned silent, the objection dying in my throat. Because this time it was like kissing a god. The quintessence of her came through the opening of my lips and drove itself into my soul before I could stop it. I gasped and inhaled a white shivering sun that pulsed strong and weak but never went out and never blew up. A rocky determination, jumbled but sharp-edged, with the potential to become as solid as bedrock. When I opened my eyes, I was lying back and she was above me, still kissing me, her hands coaxing sighs from me despite my reluctance. I did not stop her because I am supposed to be a child but really I am not and my body was too old to provide me with a child's defenses against reality. Children do not think about how magnificent it would be to become one with another person. They do not yearn to lose themselves in force and sensation and panting. Children think about consequences, if only to try and avoid them. It takes an adult to abandon such thoughts entirely.

So when her hand slipped into my pants this time, I did not stop her. And I did not protest while she explored me, first with her fingers and then, oh gods, oh yes, her mouth, her mortal husband could have the rest but I would marry her mouth and fingertips. I murmured without thinking and the walls went dark because there was mischief in what we were doing and that gave me strength. Despite this, I lay there helpless in the dark as she learned to make me whimper. She tormented me with this, tasting every part of my body. She even licked En, where it lay on my chest. Greedy thing, it rolled so that she might try its other side, too, but she didn't notice.

I touched her, too. She liked that lots.

Then she straddled me. There came a moment of lucidity in which I caught her hips and looked up at her and said, "Are you sure—" but she pushed herself down and I cried out because it was so wonderful that it hurt, flesh is not at all a terrible thing, I had forgotten that it could feel good and not just grotesque, it was so nice not to be used. She felt the same as a goddess inside. I whispered this to her and she smiled, rising and falling above me, her mouth open and teeth reflecting the moon, her hair a pale moving shadow. Then we shifted and I was on her, not out of any paltry mortal need on my part to dominate but simply because I liked the sweet mewling sounds she made as I angled my way into her, and also because I was still a god and even a weak god is dangerous to mortals. Matter is such tenuous stuff. So I controlled myself by focusing on her flesh, on her hands stroking my back (inadvertently I purred), on my own clenching tightening quickening excitement, on carrying her only into the good parts of existence and none of the bad ones.

And when she could bear no more, when I knew it was safe to bring her back to herself, when I was sure I could stay corporeal...only then did I let her go, and myself as well.

She fainted. That is normal when one of us mates with a mortal. Only the very extraordinary can touch the divine without being overwhelmed by it. I fetched a damp towel from the bathroom and mopped up the sweat and saliva and so forth, then tucked her against me under the covers so that I could breathe the scent of her hair.

I felt no regret, but I was sad. She was farther from me now, and I was the one who had sent her away.

8

Tell me a story
Fast as you can
Make the world and break it
And catch it in your hand

I SLEPT AGAIN. This time, though, since Shahar had renewed my godly strength—experimentation and abandon are close enough to childish impulses to suit me—I was able to sleep as gods do, and keep the dreams at bay.

When I woke, Shahar was not beside me, and it was noon. I sat up to find her near the window, wrapped in one of the sheets, her slim form still and shadowed against the bright blue sky.

I hopped up, assessed myself to see whether I needed to piss or shit—not yet, though clearly I needed to brush my teeth—and then went over to her. (I was cold again. Damnation.) When she did not move at my approach, lost in thought, I grinned and leaned close and licked a bare spot on the back of her neck, where her hair had not come completely undone during the previous night.

She jumped and whirled and frowned at me, at which point I belatedly realized that perhaps she was not in a playful mood.

"Hello," I said, feeling suddenly awkward.

Shahar sighed and relaxed. "Hello." Then she lowered her eyes and turned back to the window.

I felt very stupid. "Oh, demons. Did I hurt you? That was the first time . . . I tried to be careful, but—"

She shook her head. "There was no pain. I . . . could tell you were being careful."

If she wasn't hurt, then why did she radiate such an ugly, clotted mix of emotions? I struggled to remember my handful of experiences with mortal women from before the War. Was this sort of behavior normal? I thought it might be. What, then, should a lover say at a time like this? Gods, it had been easier when I was a slave; my rapists had never expected me to give a damn about them afterward.

I sighed and shifted from foot to foot and folded my arms so I would not be so cold. "So . . . I take it you don't like what we did."

She sighed, and if anything, her mood turned darker. "I loved what we did, Sieh."

I was beginning to feel very tired, and it had nothing to do with my mortality affliction. Something had gone wrong; that was obvious. Would she have liked it better if I had become female for her? I wasn't sure I could do that anymore, but it was such a small change. I would try, for her sake, if that would help. "What, then? Why do you look like you just lost your best friend?"

"I may have," she whispered.

I stared at her as she turned back to me. The sheet had slipped off one of her shoulders, and most of her hair was a fright. She looked out of control and out of her element and lost. I remembered her wildness the night before. She had discarded all thought of propriety or position or dignity, and flung herself into the moment with perfect zeal. It had been glorious, but clearly such abandon had cost her something.

Then I noticed, below the hand that held the sheet about herself, her free hand. She held it over her belly, fingering the skin there as if measuring its strength. I had seen ten thousand mortal women make the same gesture, and still I almost missed its meaning. Such things are not normally within my demesne.

Pleased to have finally figured out the problem, I smiled and stepped closer, taking her hand off her belly and coaxing her to open the sheet so that I could step into it. She did so, clumsily adjusting the sheet so that she could hold it around both of us, and I sighed in grateful pleasure at the warmth of her nearness. Then I addressed the unease in her eyes that I thought I understood. Because I was who I was, and I am not always wise, I made it a tease. "Are you planning to kill me?"

She frowned in confusion. I realized for the first time that she was as tall as I was, growing long and lean like a good Amn girl. I slid an arm around her waist and pulled her close, noting that she did not fully relax.

"A child," I said. I put a hand on her belly as she had done, rubbing circles to tease her. "It would kill me, you know." Then I remembered my current condition and my amusement faded a little. "Kill me faster, anyway."

She stiffened, staring at me. "What?"

"I told you already." Her skin felt good beneath my hands.

I bent and kissed her smooth shoulder right on the divot of bone and thought of biting her there as I rode her like a cat. Would she yowl for me? "Childhood cannot survive some things. Sex is fine, between friends." I smiled on her skin. "Done without consequences. But consequences—like making a child—change everything."

"Oh, gods. It's your antithesis."

I hated that word. Scriveners had come up with it. The word was like them, cold and passionless and precise and overly logical, capturing nothing of what truly made us what we were. "It corrupts my nature, yes. Many things can harm me—I'm just a godling, alas, not a god—but that one is the most sure." I licked at her neck again, really trying this time, though not holding any great hope of success. Nahadoth had never managed to teach me how to seduce with any real degree of mastery.

"Sieh!" She pushed at me, and when I lifted my head, I saw the horror in her eyes. "I didn't use any...preventative...when we were together last night. I..." She looked away, trembling. I regretted my teasing when I realized she was genuinely upset, but it made me happy that she cared so much.

I laughed gently, relenting. "It's all right. My mother Enefa realized the danger long ago. She changed me. Do you understand? No children."

She did not look reassured—did not *feel* reassured, her anguish tainting the very air around us. I have siblings who cannot endure mortal emotions. They are sad creatures who haunt the gods' realm, devouring tales of mortal life and pretending they are not jealous of the rest of us. Shahar would have killed half of them by now.

"Enefa is dead," she said.

That was more than enough to sober me. "Yes. But not all her works died with her, Shahar, or neither you nor I would be standing here."

She looked up at me, tense and afraid. "You're different now, Sieh. You're not really a god anymore, and mortals—" Her face softened so beautifully. It made me smile, despite the conversation. "*Mortals grow up.* Sieh, I want you to be sure there's no child. Can you check somehow? Because...because..." She lowered her eyes, and suddenly it was shame that she felt, sour and bitter on the back of my tongue. Shame, and fear.

"What?"

She drew a deep breath. "I didn't try to prevent a baby. In fact"—her jaw flexed— "I've been to the scriveners. They used a script." She blushed, but forged ahead. "To make it easier, more likely, for three or four days. And once I, with you, I, I'm supposed to go to them. They have other scripts that they say... Even with a god, fertility magic works the same way."

Her stammering embarrassment confused me; I couldn't figure out what she was trying to say at first. And then, like a comet's icy plume, understanding slashed through me.

"You *wanted* a child?"

She laughed once, bitter. When she turned back to the window, her eyes were hard and older than they should be, and so perfectly Arameri. Then I knew.

"Your mother."

Shahar nodded, still not meeting my eyes. " 'If we cannot *own* gods, then perhaps we can *become* gods,' she said. The demons of old had great magic despite their mortality. Or, at the very least, we can gain the greatest demon magic: the power to *kill* gods."

I stared at her, feeling sick, because I should have known. The Arameri had been trying to get their hands on a demon for decades. I should have seen it in Remath's quest for a godly lover; I should have realized why she'd been so pleased to have me in Sky. Why she'd tried to give me her daughter.

I shrugged off the sheet and walked away from Shahar, manifesting clothing about myself. Black this time, like my fur when I was a cat. Like my father's wrath.

"Sieh?" Shahar blurted the words, cursed, dropped the sheet and grabbed for a robe. "Sieh, what are you—"

I stopped and turned back to her, and she froze at the look in my eyes. Or perhaps at my eyes themselves, because I could not become this angry, even in my weakened half-mortal state, without a little of the cat showing.

I would save the claws, however, for Remath.

"Why did you tell me?" I asked, and she went pale. "Did you wait until now for a reason?" Some of my magic had come back to me. I touched the world, found Remath within it. Her audience chamber, surrounded by courtiers and petitioners. "Were you hoping I would kill her in front of witnesses so the other highbloods would think you weren't involved? Was that what you told yourself so it wouldn't feel like matricide?"

Her lips turned white as she pressed them together. "How dare you—"

"Because this wasn't necessary." I rode over her words with my own, with my grief, and that drove the anger from her face in an instant. "I told you I would kill her for you, if you asked. All I ever wanted was to be able to trust you. If you had given me that, I would have done anything for you."

She flinched as if I'd struck her. Her eyes welled with tears, but this was not like last night. She stood in the slanting afternoon light of Itempas's sun, proud despite her nakedness, and the tears did not fall, because Arameri do not cry. Not even when they have broken a god's heart.

"Deka," she said at last.

I shook my head, mute, too consumed with my own nature to follow her insane mortal reasoning.

She drew another breath. "I agreed to do this because of Deka. We made a bargain, Mother and I: one night with you, in exchange for him. The scriveners would take care of the rest. But when you said that a child would kill you . . ." She faltered.

I wanted to believe she had betrayed her mother for my sake. But if that was true, then it meant she had also agreed to sacrifice my love in exchange for her brother.

I remembered the look in her eyes when she'd said she loved me. I remembered the feel of her body, the sound of her sighs. I had tasted her soul and found it sweeter than I could ever have imagined. Nothing in what she'd done with me had been false. But would she have followed through on her desire now, so soon, if not for her mother's bargain? Would she have done it at all if she hadn't wanted someone else more than she wanted me?

I turned my back on her.

"Remath has perverted something that should have been pure," I said. For the first time since I'd joined hands with two bright-eyed mortal children, something of my true self had slipped through the space between worlds to fill me. My voice grew deeper, becoming the man's tenor that I had not quite achieved physically yet. I could have taken any shape I wanted in that moment; it was not beyond me anymore. But the part of me that hurt was the man, not the child or the cat, and it was the man whose pain needed assuaging. The man was the weakest part of me, but it would do for this purpose.

"Sieh," she whispered, and then fell silent. Just as well. I was in no mood to listen.

"I cannot protect children from all the evils of the world," I said. "Suffering is part of childhood, too. But this…" It came out more sibilant than it should have. I fought the change back with a soft snarl. "This, Shahar, is *my* sin. I should have protected you, from your own nature if nothing else. I have betrayed myself, and someone will die for that."

With that, I left. Her apartment door shivered into dust before me. When I stepped into the corridor, the daystone groaned and cracked beneath my feet, sending branching faults up the walls. The handful of guards and servants who stood unobtrusively about the corridor tensed in alarm as I strode toward them. Four of them stopped, sensing with whatever rudimentary awareness mortals have that I was not to be trifled with. The fourth, a guard, stepped into my path. I have no idea whether he meant to stop me or whether he was just moving to the other side of the corridor, where there was more room. I do not think at such times; I do what feels good. So I slashed my will across him like claws and he fell in six or seven bloody pieces to the floor. Someone screamed; someone else slipped in the blood; they did not get in my way again. I walked on.

The floors opened and bent around me, forming steps, slopes, a new path. I stepped into the midday brilliance of the corridor that led to Remath's audience chamber. I walked toward the ornate double doors at the end of the corridor, in front of which stood two Darren women. The warriors of Darr are famous for their skill and wits, which they use to make up for their lack of physical strength. Since the time of our escape, they had been tasked with protecting the Arameri family head, even from other Arameri. But as I came down the hall, spiderwebbing the windows with every step, they looked at each other. There was pride to consider, but stupid Darre do not last long in their culture, and they knew there was no way they could fight me. They could, however, attempt to appease me, which they did by kneeling before the door, heads bowed, praying for my mercy. I showed it by sweeping them off to either side, probably bruising them a little against the walls but not killing them. Then I tore apart the doors and went in.

The room was full of courtiers, more guards, servants, clerks, scriveners. And Remath. She, on her cold stone throne, folded her hands and waited as if she'd been expecting me. The rest stared at me, stunned and silent.

I pulled En loose from its cord. "Kill for me, beloved," I murmured, and dropped it to the floor. It bounced, then shot around the room, ricocheting off walls and windows and the stone of Remath's chair. It did not bounce off mortal flesh. When En had punched holes in enough of them and the screaming stopped, it came back to me, flaring hot to cook off the blood and then dropping cool and satisfied into my hand. I slipped it into my pocket.

Remath had not been touched; En knew my heart well. She had not moved throughout the slaughter and showed no hint of concern that I had just killed thirty or so of her relatives.

"I take it you're unhappy about something," she said.

I smiled and saw her eyes flicker for an instant as she registered my sharp teeth. "Yes," I said, raising my hand. In it, conjured out of possibility, lay ten thick, silver knitting needles.

Each was longer than my hand. "But I will feel better in a moment. Cross your heart and hope to die, Remath. Here are my needles for your eyes."

To her credit, she kept her voice even. "I kept my promise. I've done you no harm."

I shook my head. "Shahar was my friend, and you have taken her from me."

"A minor harm," she said, and then she surprised me with a small smile. "But you are a trickster, and I know better than to try and argue with you."

"Yes," I agreed. And then I stepped forward, plucking the first of the needles from my palm and rolling it between my fingers in anticipation, because I am a bully, too, when all is said and done.

I heard Shahar's cry before she ran in, though I ignored it. She gasped as she reached the chamber and saw blood and bodies everywhere, but then she ran forward—slipping once in someone's viscera—and grabbed my arm. This did nothing to slow my advance, since for the moment I was much stronger than any mortal, and after being dragged forward a step or two, she abandoned that effort. But then she ran around me and put herself in my path, just as I put my foot on the first step of the dais that held Remath's throne. "Sieh, don't do this."

I sighed and pushed her aside as gently as I could. This made her stumble off the steps, and she fell into the blood of some cousin or another of hers. I could smell the Arameri in him. Or not *in* him, not anymore; I laughed at my own joke.

As I stopped in front of Remath—who remained where she was, calm as death loomed—Shahar appeared again, this time flinging herself directly in front of her mother's throne. Her gold satin robe was drenched with blood down one side of her body, and somehow she'd gotten it on the side of her face as well. Half her hair hung limp and dripping with it. I laughed again and tried to think up a rhyme that would properly make fun of her. But what rhymed with *horror*? I would ponder it later.

I stopped, however, because Shahar was in the way. "Move," I said.

"No."

"You wanted her dead, anyway."

"Not like *this*, damn you!"

"Poor Shahar." I made a singsong of it. "*Poor little princess, how is she to see? With her fingers and her toes, once her eyes are with me.*" I held the needle forward so that she could see it. "You have betrayed me, sweet Shahar. It is nothing to me to kill you, too."

Her jaw tightened. "I thought you loved me."

"I thought you loved *me*."

"You swore not to harm me!"

She was right. Her failure to keep her word did not mean I should stoop to the same level. "Very well. I won't kill you—just her."

"She's my mother," she snapped. "How much do you think it will harm me if you kill her right before my eyes?"

As much as she'd harmed me by betraying my trust. Maybe a bit more. "I'm not interested in bargains right now, Shahar. Move, or I'll move you. I won't be gentle this time."

"Please," she said, which ordinarily would only have goaded me further—bully—but this time it did not. This time, to my own great surprise, the churning vortex of my rage slowed, then went still. In the sudden storm-calm, I gazed at her and realized another truth that she had hidden from me all this time. And perhaps not just from me. I glanced at Remath, who was staring at Shahar, surprised into an expression of astonishment at last. Yes.

"You love her," I said.

And because Shahar was Arameri, she flinched as if struck and looked away in shame. But she did not move out of my way.

I let out a long, heavy sigh, and with it my power began to fade. I couldn't have kept it up much longer anyhow; I was too old for tantrums.

Shaking my head, I let the needles drop to the floor. They scattered over the steps with tinny metal sounds, loud in the chamber's silence. Listening to the nearby world, I could hear shouts and running feet—Captain Wrath and his men racing to save Remath and die in the trying because they were not sensible like Darre. Even the scriveners were marshaling, bringing their most powerful scripts, though they were disorganized because Shevir was here, his corpse cooling among the others I'd killed. I turned and looked at him, his face frozen in a look of surprise beneath the gaping hole in his forehead, and felt regret. He hadn't been a bad man as First Scriveners went. And I had been a very bad boy.

On the strength of that, I took myself away from Sky, not really caring where I went instead, just wanting comfort and silence and a place to be miserable in peace.

I would not see Shahar again for two years.

BOOK TWO

Two Legs at Noon

I AM A FLY ON THE WALL, or a spider in a bush. Same difference, except that the spider is a predator and suits my nature better.

I sit in a web that would give me away in an instant if he saw it, because I have woven a smiling face into the tiny dewdrop-beaded strands. It has never been his nature to notice the minutia of his surroundings, however, and the web is half hidden by leaves anyhow. With my many eyes, I observe as Itempas, the Bright Sky, Daybringer, sits on a whitebaked clay rooftop waiting for the sun to rise. It surprises me that he sits to observe this, but then many things have surprised me today. Like the fact that the rooftop is part of a mortal dwelling, and inside it are the mortal woman he loves and the mortal—but half-god—child she has borne him.

I knew something was wrong. There had been a day of change in the gods' realm not long before. The hurricane that was Nahadoth met the earthquake that was Enefa, and they found stillness in each other. A beautiful, holy thing—I know, I watched. But in the distance, the immovable white-capped mountain that was Itempas shimmered and went away. He has been gone ever since.

Ten years, in mortal reckoning. An eyeblink for us, but still unusual for him. He does not sulk. More commonly he confronts a source of disruption, attacks it, destroys it if he can, or settles into some equilibrium with it if he cannot—but he has done neither this time. Instead he has fled to this realm with its fragile creatures and tried to hide himself among them, as if a sun can fit in among match flames. Except he isn't hiding, not exactly. He's just . . . living. Being ordinary. And not coming home.

The rooftop door opens, and the child comes out. Strange-looking creature, disproportionate with his big head and long legs. (*Do I look like that in my mortal form? I resolve to make my head smaller.*) He is brown-skinned and blond, freckled. From here, I can see his eyes, as green as the leaves that hide me. He is eight or nine years old now—a good age, my favorite age, old enough to know the world yet young enough to still delight in it. I have heard his name, Shinda, whispered by the other children of this dusty little village; they are frightened of him. They can tell, as I can with just a glance, that he might be mortal, but he will never be one of them.

He comes to stand behind Itempas and wraps his arms around Itempas's shoulders, resting his cheek against his father's densely curled hair. Itempas does not turn to him, but I see him reach up to touch the boy's arms. They watch the sun rise together, never saying a word.

When the day is well begun, there is another movement at the rooftop door; a woman comes to stand there. She is Remath's age, similarly blonde, similarly beautiful. In two thousand years, I will join hands with her descendant and namesake and become mortal. They look much alike, this Shahar, that Shahar, except for the eyes. This Shahar watches Itempas with an unblinking steadiness that I would find frightening if I had not seen it in the eyes of my own worshippers. When her son straightens and comes over to greet her, she does not look at him, though she absently touches his shoulder and says something. He goes inside and she remains there, watching her lover with a high priestess's fanaticism. But he does not turn to her.

I leave, and report back to Nahadoth and Enefa as I have been bidden. Parents often send children as spies and peacemakers when there is trouble between them. I tell them that Itempas is not angry, if anything he seems sad and a bit lonely, and, yes, they should go and bring him home because he has been away too long. And if I do not tell them of his mortal woman, his mortal son, what of it? Why should it matter that the woman loves him, needs him, will probably go mad without him? Why should we care that his return means the destruction of that family and the peace he seems to have found with them? We are gods and they are nothing. I am a far better son than some half-breed demon boy. I will show him, as soon as he comes home.

9

I FELL.

It happens like that sometimes, when one travels through life without a plan. In this case I was traveling through space, motion, conceptualization—same difference, except that mortals cannot survive it. Half mortal that I was, I shouldn't have. But I did, possibly because I did not care.

So it was that I drifted through Sky's white layers, passing through some of the Tree's wooden flesh in the process, down, down, down. Past the lowest layer of clouds, damp and cold. Because I was incorporeal, I saw the city with both mortal and godly eyes: humped silhouettes of buildings and streets aglow with flickers of mortal light, interspersed now and again by the brighter, colored plumes of my brothers and sisters. They could not see me because I had not lost all sense of self-preservation and because even when I am not sulking, my soul's colors are shadowy. That is my father's legacy and a bit of my mother's as well. I am good at sneaking about because of it. Or hiding, when I do not wish to be found.

Down. Past a ring of mansions attached to the World Tree's trunk, devastatingly expensive tree houses, these, without even ladders or GIRLZ KEEP OWT signs to make them interesting. Below this was another layer of city, this one new: houses and workshops and businesses built atop the Tree's very roots,

perched precariously on wildly sloping streets and braced plat-
forms. Ah, of course; the esteemed personages of the mansions
above could not be left without servants and chefs and nan-
nies and tailors, could they? I witnessed bizarre contraptions,
gouting steam and smoke and metallic groans, connecting this
halfway city to the elegant platforms above. People rode up
and down in them, trusting these dangerous-looking things to
convey them safely. For a moment, admiration for mortal inge-
nuity nearly distracted me from my misery. But I kept going,
because this place did not suit me. I had heard Shahar refer to
it, and understood its name now: the Gray. Halfway between
the bright of Sky and the darkness below.

Down. And now I blended with the shadows, because there
were so many here between the Tree's roots and beneath its
vast green canopy. Yes, this suited me better: Shadow, the city
that had once been called Sky, before the Tree grew and made
a joke of that name. It was here at last that I felt some sense of
belonging—though only a little. I did not belong anywhere in
the mortal realm, really.

I should have remembered that, I thought in bitterness as I
came to rest and turned to flesh again. *I should never have tried
to live in Sky.*

Well. Adolescence is all about making mistakes.

I landed in a stinking, debris-strewn alley, in what I would
later learn was South Root, considered to be the most violent
and depraved part of the city. Because it was so violent and
depraved, no one bothered me for the better part of three days
while I sat amid the trash. This was good, because I wouldn't
have had the strength to defend myself. My paroxysm of rage in
Sky and subsequent magical transit had left me too weak to do

much but lie there. As I'd been hungry before leaving Sky, I ate: there were some moldy fruit rinds in the bin nearest me, and a rat came near to offer me its flesh. It was an old creature, blind and dying, and its meat was rank, but I have never been so churlish as to disrespect a sacred act.

It rained, and I drank, tilting my head back for hours to get a few mouthfuls. And then, adding the ultimate insult to injury, my bowels moved for the first time in a century. I had enough strength to get my pants down, but not enough to move away from the resulting mess, so I sat there beside it and wept awhile, and just generally hated everything.

Then on the third day, because three is a number of power, things finally changed.

"Get up," said the girl who'd entered the alley. She kicked me to get my attention. "You're in the way."

I blinked up at her to see a small figure, clad in bulky, ugly clothing and a truly stupid hat, glaring down at me. The hat was a thing of beauty. It looked like a drunken cone on top of her head and had long flaps to cover her ears. The flaps could be buttoned under her chin, though she hadn't done so, perhaps because it was late spring and as hot as the Dayfather's temper, even in this city of noontime shadows.

With a sigh, I pulled myself laboriously to my feet, then stepped aside. The girl nodded too curtly for thanks, then brushed past me and began rummaging through the pile of garbage I'd sat beside. I started to warn her about my small addition to the refuse, but she avoided it without looking. Deftly plucking two halves of a broken plate out of the trash, she made a sound of pleasure and stuck them into the satchel hanging off her shoulder, then moved on. As she shuffled away, I saw one of her feet scrape the ground even though she'd lifted it; it was larger than the other and misshapen, and she'd made it larger still by bundling rags about the ankle.

I followed her down the alley as she poked through the piles, picking up the oddest of items: a handleless clay pot, a rusted metal canister, a chunk of broken windowpane. This last seemed to please her the most, by the look of delight on her face.

I leaned in to peer over her shoulder. "What will you do with it?"

She whipped about and I froze, as she had placed the tip of a long and wickedly sharp glass dagger at my throat.

"This," she said. "Back off."

I did so quickly, raising my hands to make it clear that I meant no harm, and she put the knife away, resuming her work.

"Glass," she said. "Grind it down for knives, use the leftovers to grind other things. Get it?"

I was fascinated by her manner of speaking. Shadow dwellers' Senmite was rougher than that of the people in Sky, and quicker spoken. They had less patience for long, flowery verbal constructions, and their new, briefer constructions contained additional layers of attitude. I began adjusting my own speech to suit.

"Got it," I said. "Then?"

She shrugged. "I sell them at the Sun Market. Or give 'em away, if people can't pay." She glanced at me, looking me up and down, and then snorted. "You could pay."

I looked down at myself. The black clothing I had manifested back in Sky was filthy and stank, but it was made of fine-quality cloth, and the shirt and pants and shoes all matched, unlike her clothes. I supposed I did look wealthy. "But I don't have any money."

"So get a job," she replied, and resumed work.

I sighed and moved to sit down on a closed muckbin, which squelched when my weight bore down on it. "Guess I'll have to. Know anyone who might need"—I considered what skills I had that might be valuable to mortals. "Hmm. A thief, a juggler, or a killer?"

The girl stopped again, looking hard at me, and then folded her arms. "You a godling?"

I blinked in surprise. "Yes, actually. How did you know?"

"Only they ask those kinds of crazy questions."

"Oh. Have you met many godlings?"

She shrugged. "A few. You going to eat me?"

I frowned, blinking. "Of course not."

"Fight me? Steal something? Turn me into something else? Torture me to death?"

"Dear gods, why would I—" But then it occurred to me that some of my siblings were capable of all that and worse. We were not the gentlest of families. "None of those things are my nature, don't worry."

"All right." She turned back to examine something she'd found, which I thought might be an old roof shingle. With an annoyed sigh, she tossed it aside. "You're not going to get many worshippers, though, just sitting there like that. You should do something more interesting."

I sighed and drew my legs up, wrapping arms around them. "I don't have a lot of interesting left in me."

"Hmm." Straightening, the girl pulled off her stupid hat and mopped her brow. Without it, I saw that she was Amn, her white-blonde curls cropped short and held back with cheap-looking barrettes. She looked ten or eleven, though I saw more years than that in her eyes. Fourteen, maybe. She hadn't eaten enough in those years, and it showed, but I could still feel the childhood in her.

"Hymn," she said. A name. My skepticism must have shown, because she rolled her eyes. "Short for Hymnesamina."

"I like the longer name, actually."

"I don't." She looked me up and down perfunctorily. "You're not bad-looking, you know. Skinny, but you can fix that."

I blinked again, wondering if this was some sort of flirtation. "Yes, I know."

"Then you've got another skill besides thieving, juggling, and killing."

I sighed, feeling very tired. "No whoring."

"You sure? You'd make a lot more money than with the rest, except killing, and you don't look very tough."

"Looks mean nothing for a god."

"But they do mean something to mortals. You want to make money as a killer, you need to look like one." She folded her arms. "I know a place where they'd let you pick your clients, you being what you are. If you can make yourself look Amn, you'd make even more." She cocked her head, considering this. "Or maybe the foreign look is better. I don't know. Not my thing."

"I just need enough to buy food." But I would need more mortal things as I grew older, wouldn't I? There would come a time—soon, probably—when I would no longer be able to con-jure clothing or necessities, and someday shelter would be more than just a pleasant accessory. Winters in central Senm could kill mortals. I sighed again, resting my cheek on my knees.

Hymn sighed, too. "Whatever. Well...see you." She turned and headed toward the mouth of the alley—then froze, her gaze going sharp and alarmed. Her tension thickened the already-ripe air further when she stepped back, out of the alley's entrance and into the shadows.

This was just enough to pull me out of my mood. I uncurled and watched her. "Muggers, bullies, or parents?"

"Muckrakers," she said, so softly that no mortal would have heard her, but she knew I could.

By the way she said it, I realized she expected me to know what muckrakers were. I could guess, though. There was money to be made from any city's refuse, from charging to get rid of it to selling its useful bits. Curious, I hopped up and came over to where she was standing, out of the slanting light from the torchlamps. When I peeked around her at the street beyond, I saw a group of men near an old mulecart, on the other side of the potholed street. Two of them were laughing and hefting muckbins, dumping them into the cart; two more stood idle, talking, while a fifth was in the cart with a pitchfork and a mask over his face, stirring something that steamed.

I glanced down at the junk in Hymn's bag. "Would they really begrudge you a few small things?"

She glared at me. "The muckrakers don't care if it's just a little bit; it's *theirs*. They pay the Order for the rights, and they don't like it when anybody messes with what's theirs. They warned me once already." Despite her show of anger, I could smell the fear underneath. She looked past me, around the alley, but there was no way out. It stood at the intersection of three buildings, and the nearest window was twenty feet up. She could try to sneak out of the alley, and there was a chance the men wouldn't see her. They were preoccupied with their work and chatter. But if they spotted her, she would not get far with her misshapen foot.

The men were a rough-smelling crew, even without the stench of refuse, and had the unmistakable look of people who have no qualms against harming a child. I bared my teeth at them, for I had always hated such mortals.

At this stirring of my old self, I began to grin.

"Hey!" I shouted. Beside me, Hymn jumped and gasped, whirling to try and escape. I caught her arm and held her in place so they would see her. Sure enough, when the muckrakers looked around, they spotted me—but it was the sight of Hymn that made them scowl.

"What the hells are you doing?" she cried, trying to jerk free.

"It's all right," I murmured. "I won't let them hurt you." The men near the wagon were turning now, heading toward us with purposeful strides and dire intent. Only three of them, though; the two who'd been working had stopped to watch. I grinned at them and raised my voice again. "Hey, you like shit, right? Have some!" And I turned and yanked my pants down to flash my backside. Hymn moaned.

The muckrakers shouted, and even the two who'd been watching ran around the wagons, the whole lot charging toward our little alley. Laughing, I pulled my pants up and grabbed Hymn's arm again. "Come on!" I said, and hauled her toward the back of the alley.

"Where—" She couldn't get out more than that, stumbling over a pile of fungus-covered firewood that someone had dumped between the muckbins. I helped her stay upright, then hauled her back until we were pressed against the alley's rear wall. A moment later, the alley, already dim, went darker still as the men's silhouettes blocked the torchlamps.

"What the hells is this?" one of the men asked Hymn. "We warn you not to steal our stuff, and you not only come back but also bring a friend? Huh?" He stepped over the funguswood, clenching his fists; the others closed in behind him.

"I didn't mean..." Hymn's voice trembled as she started to speak to the men.

"This girl is under my protection," I said, stepping in front of her. I was grinning like a madman; I felt power around me like a wafting shroud. Mischief is a heady thing, sweeter than any wine. "Never touch her again."

The lead man stopped, staring at me in disbelief. "And who in demons are you, brat?"

I closed my eyes and inhaled in pleasure. How long had it been since anyone had called me a brat? I laughed and let go of Hymn and spread my arms, and at the touch of my will, the lids blasted off every bin and crate in the alley. The men cried out, but it was too late; they were mine to toy with.

"I am the son of chaos and death," I said. They all heard me, as intimately as if I'd spoken into their ears, despite the noise of their startled cries and the falling lids. A brisk wind had begun to blow through the alley, stirring the looser refuse and blowing dust into all our eyes. I squinted and grinned. "I know all the rules in the games of pain. But I will be merciful now, because it pleases me. Consider this a warning."

And I curled my fingers into claws. The bins exploded, the refuse contained in each rising into the air and swirling and

churning in a circle, a hurricane of debris and foulness that
surrounded the five men and herded them together. When I
brought my hands together in a clap, all of it sucked inward—
plastering them from head to toe with every disgusting substance mortalkind has ever produced. I made sure a bit of my
own ordure was in there, too.

I could have been truly cruel. They'd meant to hurt Hymn,
after all. I could have shattered the fungus log and speared them
with spore-covered splinters. I could have broken their bodies
into pieces and stuffed the whole mess back into the bins, muck
and all. But I was having fun. I let them live.

They screamed—though some of them had the wit to keep
their mouths closed for fear of what the scream would let in—
and flailed at themselves with remarkable vigor given what their
jobs entailed. But I supposed it was one thing to shovel and haul
shit; quite another to bathe in it. I had made certain the stuff
went into their clothes and various crevices of their bodies. A
good trick is all about the details.

"Remember," I said, stalking forward. Those who could see
me, because they had managed to get the muck out of their eyes,
yelled and grabbed their still-blind companions and stumbled
back. I let them go and grinned, and made a chunk of wood
spin like a top on one of my fingertips. A waste of magic, yes,
but I wanted to enjoy being strong for however long it lasted.
"Never touch her again, or I will find you. Now go!" I stomped
at them, mock-threatening, but they were horrified and wise
enough to scream and turn and run out of the alley, some of
them tripping and slipping in the slime. They fled down the
street, leaving behind their wagon and mule. I heard them
yelling in the distance.

I fell to the ground—we were still at the back of the alley, where the ground was relatively clean—and laughed and laughed, until my sides ached. Hymn, however, began picking her way over the tumbled debris, trying to find a way out of the alley that would not require her to walk through a layer of filth.

Surprised at being abandoned, I stopped laughing and sat up on one elbow to watch her. "Where are you going?"

"Away from you," she said. Only then did I realize she was furious.

Blinking, I got to my feet and went to her. Strong as I was feeling after that trick, it was nothing to grab her about the waist and leap over the front half of the alley, landing in the brighter-lit, fresher air of the street. There were a few people about, standing and murmuring in the wake of the muckrakers' spectacle, but there was a collective gasp as I landed on the cobblestones. Quickly—hurriedly, in some cases—all of the onlookers turned and left, some of them glancing back as if in fear that I would follow.

Puzzled by this, I set Hymn down, whereupon she immediately began hurrying away, too. "Hey!"

She stopped, and turned back to me with a look of such wariness that I flinched. "What?"

I put my hands on my hips. "I saved you. What, not even a thanks?"

"Thank you," she said tightly, "though I wouldn't have been in danger if you hadn't called out to them."

This was true. But…"They won't bother you again," I said. "Isn't that what you wanted?"

"What I *wanted*," she said, turning red in the face now, "was to do my business in peace. Should've left when I figured out you

were a godling! And you're worse somehow. You seemed so sad, I
thought for a moment that you were more"—she spluttered, too
apoplectic to speak for a moment—"*human.* But you're just like
the rest of them, screwing up mortal lives and thinking you're
doing us a favor." She turned away, walking briskly enough that
the limp made her gait into an ugly sort of half hop. I'd been
wrong; the bad foot didn't slow her down at all.

I stared in the direction she had gone until it became clear she
would not stop, and then finally I sighed and trotted after her.

I had nearly caught up when Hymn heard my footsteps and
stopped, rounding on me. "*What?*"

I stopped, too, putting my hands in my pockets and trying
not to hunch my shoulders. "I need to make it up to you." I
sighed, wishing I could just leave. "Is there something you want?
I can't fix your foot, but...I don't know. Whatever."

I could almost hear her teeth grinding together, though she
did not speak for a moment. Perhaps she needed to master her
rage before she started shouting at a god.

"I don't want my foot fixed," she said with remarkable calm. "I
don't want anything from you. But if it's your nature that you're
trying to serve, and you won't leave me alone until you've done
it, then here's what I need: money."

I blinked. "Money? But—"

"You're a god. You should be able to make money."

I tried to think of a game or toy that might allow me to
produce money. Gambling was an adult game; it did not suit
my nature at all. Perhaps I could act out a children's tale or
lullaby, that one about the golden ropes and the pearl lanterns..."Would you take jewelry instead?"

She made a sound of utter disgust and turned to leave. I

groaned and trotted after her. "Listen, I said I could make things that are valuable, and you can sell them! What's wrong with that?"

"I *can't* sell them," she snapped, still walking. I hurried to keep up. "Trying to sell something valuable would get me killed. If I took it to a pawnbroker, everyone in South Root would know I had money before I left the shop. My house would get robbed, or my relatives would be kidnapped, or something. I don't know anyone in the merchant cartels who could fence it for me, and even if I did, they'd take half or more in 'fees.' And I don't have the status to impress the Order of Itempas, so they'd take the rest in tithes. I could go to one of the godlings around town, maybe, but then I'd have to deal with *more* of you." She threw me a scathing look. "My parents are old, and I'm the only child. What I need is money for food and rent and to get the roof fixed and maybe to buy my father a bottle of wine now and again so he can stop worrying so much about how we're going to survive. Can you give me any of that?"

I stumbled after this litany, a little stunned. "I . . . no."

Hymn stared at me for a long moment, then sighed and stopped, reaching up to rub her forehead as if it pained her. "Look, which one are you?"

"Sieh."

She looked surprised, which was a welcome change from contempt and exasperation. "I don't recognize your name."

"No. I used to live here"—I hesitated—"a long time ago. But I only came back to the mortal realm a few days ago."

"Gods, no wonder you're such a horror. You're new in town." This seemed to ease some of her anger, and she looked me up and down. "All right, what's your nature?"

"Tricks. Mischief." These were always easier to explain to mortals. They found "childhood" difficult to grasp as a specific concept. Hymn nodded, though, so I took a chance and added, "Innocence."

She looked thoughtful. "You must be one of the older ones. The younger ones are simpler."

"They're not simpler. Their natures are just more attuned to mortal life, since they were born after mortals were created—"

"I know that," she said, looking annoyed again. "Look, people in this city have lived with your kind for a long time now. We get how you work; you don't need to lecture." She sighed again and shook her head. "I know you need to serve your nature, all right? But I don't need tricks; I need money. If you want to conjure something, sell it yourself, and bring me that later, that would be fine. Just try and be discreet, will you? And leave me alone until then. *Please.*"

With this, Hymn turned to walk away, slower this time as she had calmed somewhat. I watched her go, feeling altogether out of sorts and wondering how in the infinite hells I was going to get money for her. Because she was right; *playing fair* was as fundamental to my nature as being a child, and if I allowed the wrong I had done her to stand, it would erode a little more of whatever childhood she had remaining. Doing that prior to my transformation would've made me ill. Doing it now? I had no idea what would happen, but it would not be pleasant.

I would have to obtain money by mortal means, then. But if there were jobs to be had, would Hymn have been digging through muckbins and making knives from broken crockery? Worse, I had no knowledge of the city in its current incarnation, and no inkling of where to begin my search for employment.

So I began walking after Hymn again.

The streets were quiet and empty as I walked, taking on a dim, twilightish aspect as the morning progressed. Dawn had come and gone while I tormented the muckrakers, and all around me I could feel the city awakening, its pulse quickening with the start of day. Ghostly white buildings, long unpainted but soundly made and still beautiful in a run-down way, loomed out of the dark on either side of the street. I saw faces peering through the windows, half hidden by the curtains. Through gaps in the buildings I could see the mountainous black silhouette of a Tree root. Roots hemmed in this part of the city, while the Tree itself loomed above all to the north. There would be no sunlight here, no matter how bright the day grew.

Then I turned another corner and stopped, for Hymn stood there glaring at me.

I sighed. "I'm sorry. I really am! But I need your help."

We sat in the small common room of her family's home. An old inn, she explained, though they hardly ever had travelers through anymore and survived by taking in long-term boarders when they could. For the time being, there were none.

"It's the only way," I said, having reached this conclusion by my second cup of tea. Hymn's mother had served it to me, her hand shaking as she poured, though I'd tried my best to put her at ease. When Hymn murmured something to her, she'd withdrawn into another room, though I could hear her still lurking near the door, listening. Her heartbeat was very loud.

Hymn shrugged, toying with the plate of dry cheese and stale bread her mother had insisted upon serving. She ate only a little of it, and I ate none, for it was easy to see this family had almost nothing. Fortunately this behavior was considered polite for a godling, since most of us didn't need to eat.

"Your choice, of course," she said.

I did not like the choices laid before me. Hymn had confirmed my guess that there was little in the way of work, as the city's economy had lost ground in recent years to innovations coming out of the north. (In the old days, the Arameri would have unleashed a plague or two to kill off commoners and increase the demand for labor. Unemployment, frustrating as it was, represented progress.) There was still money to be made from serving the mortals who came to the city on pilgrimage, to pray for one of any dozen gods' blessing, but not many employers would be pleased to hire a godling. "Bad for business," Hymn explained. "Too easy to offend someone by your existence."

"Of course," I sighed.

Since the city's legitimate business was closed to me, my only hope was its illegitimate side. For that, at least, I had a possible way in: Nemmer. I was to meet her in three more days, according to our agreement. I no longer cared that some sibling of ours was targeting the Arameri. Let them all die, except perhaps Deka, whom I would geld and put on a leash to keep him sweet. But the conspiracy against our parents meant I should still see her. I could ask her help in finding work then.

If I could stomach the shame. Which I could not. So I had decided to try another way into the city's shadier side. Hymn's way: the Arms of Night. The brothel she had already tried to convince me to join.

"A friend of mine went to work there a couple of years ago," she said. "Not as a prostitute! She's not their type. But they need servants and such, and they pay a good wage." She shrugged. "If you don't want to do the one thing, you could always do the other. Especially if you can cook and clean."

I was not fond of that idea, either. Enough of my mortal years in Sky had been spent serving one way or another. "I don't suppose any of their customers would like a nice game of tag?" Hymn only looked at me. I sighed. "Right."

"We should go now, if you want to talk to them," she said. "They get busy at night." She spoke with remarkable compassion given how tired she already was of me. I supposed the misery in my expression had managed to penetrate even her cynical armor. Which might have been why she tried again to dissuade me. "I don't care, you know. If you make up for nearly getting me killed. I told you that."

I nodded heavily. "I know. This isn't really about you, though."

She sighed. "I know, I know. You must be what you are." I looked up in surprise, and she smiled. "I told you. Everyone here understands gods."

So we left the inn and headed up the street, which was bustling now that I'd been out of sight for a while. Carters rattled past with their rickety old wagons while vendors pushed along rolling stands to sell their fruit and fried meat. An old man sat on a blanket on one corner, calling out that he could repair shoes. A middle-aged man in stained laborer's clothes went over to him, and they crouched to dicker.

Hymn limped easily through this chaos, waving cheerfully to this or that person as we passed, altogether more comfortable amid her fellow mortals than she'd been in my company. I watched her as we walked, fascinated. I could taste a solid core of innocence underneath her cynical pragmatism, and just the faintest dollop of wonder, because not even the most jaded mortal could spend time in a god's presence without feeling *something*. And she was amused by me, despite her apparent annoyance. That made me grin—which she caught when she looked around and caught a glimpse of my face. "What?" she asked.

"You," I said, grinning.

"What about me?"

"You're one of mine. Or you could be, if you wanted." That thought made me cock my head in consideration. "Unless you've pledged yourself to another god?"

She shook her head, though she said nothing, and I thought that I sensed tension in her. Not fear. Something else. Embarrassment?

I remembered Shevir's term. "Are you a primortalist?"

She rolled her eyes. "Do you ever stop talking?"

"It's very hard for me to be quiet and well behaved," I said honestly, and she snorted.

The road we were on went uphill for a ways. I guessed there might be a root of the Tree underground somewhere, close to the surface. As we went up, we passed gradually into a zone of relative brightness, which would probably receive direct sunlight at least once a day, whenever the sun sank below the Tree's canopy. The buildings grew taller and better maintained; the streets grew busier, too, possibly because we were traveling inward toward the city's heart. Hymn and I now had to shift to the sidewalk to avoid coaches and the occasional finely made palanquin borne along by sweating men.

At last we reached a large house that occupied the majority

of a bizarrely triangular block, near the intersection of two brisk-moving streets. The house was triangular as well, a stately six-story wedge, but that was not what made it so striking. What made me stop, half in the street, and stare was the fact that someone had had the audacity to paint it *black*. Aside from wooden lintels and white accents, the whole structure from roof edge to foundation was stark, unrelenting, unabashed blackness.

Hymn grinned at my openmouthed expression and pulled me forward so I wouldn't get run over by a human-drawn carriage. "Amazing, isn't it? I don't know how they get away with breaking the White Law. My papa says the Order-Keepers used to kill homeowners as heretics if they refused to paint their houses white. They still issue fines sometimes—but nobody bothers the Arms of Night." She poked me in the shoulder, making me look at her in surprise. "You be polite, if you really care about making it up to me. These people are into more than whorehouses. No one crosses them."

I smiled weakly, though my stomach had tightened in unease. Had I fled Sky only to put myself in the hands of other mortals with power? But I owed Hymn, so I sighed and said, "I'll be good."

She nodded, then led me through the house's gate and up to its wide, plain double doors.

A servant—conservatively dressed—opened the door at her knock. "Hello," said Hymn, inclining her head in a polite bow. (She glared at me, and I hastily did the same.) "My friend here has business with the proprietor."

The servant, a stocky Amn woman, swept a quick assessing glance over me and apparently decided I was worthy of further attention. Given that I wore three days' worth of alley filth, this made me feel quite proud of my looks. "Your name?"

I considered half a dozen, then decided there was no point in hiding. "Sieh."

She nodded and glanced at Hymn, who introduced herself as well. "I'll let him know you're here," the woman said. "Please, wait in the parlor."

She led us to a small, stuffy little room with wood-paneled walls and an elaborately patterned Mencheyev carpet on the floor. It had no chairs, so we stood while the woman closed the door behind us and left.

"This place doesn't feel much like a whorehouse," I said, going to the window to peer out at the bustling street. I tasted the air and found nothing I would have expected—no lust, though that could only have been because there were no clients present. No misery either, though, or bitterness or pain. I could smell women, and men, and sex, but also incense and paper and ink, and fine food. Far more businesslike than sordid.

"They don't like that word," Hymn murmured, coming near so that we could speak. "And I told you, the people who work here aren't whores—not people who will do anything for money, I mean. Some of the ones here don't work for money at all."

"What?"

"That's what I've heard. And more, the people who run this place are taking over all the brothels in the city and making them work the same way. I hear that's why the Order-Keepers give them so much leeway. Darkwalker tithe money is just as shiny as anyone else's, when it comes down to it."

"Darkwalkers?" My mouth fell open. "I don't believe it. These people—the proprietors or whatever—they worship *Nahadoth*?" I could not help thinking of Naha's worshippers of old, in the days before the Gods' War. They had been revelers and dreamers and rebels, as resistant to the idea of organization as cats to obedience. But times had changed, and two thousand years of Itempas's influence had left a mark. Now the followers of Nahadoth opened businesses and paid taxes.

"Yes, they worship Nahadoth," said Hymn, throwing me a look of such challenge that I instantly understood. "Does that bother you?"

I put my hand on her bony shoulder. If I could have, I would have blessed her, now that I knew who she belonged to. "Why would it? He's my father."

She blinked but remained wary, her tension shifting from one shoulder to the other. "He's the father of most godlings, isn't he? But not all of them seem to like him."

I shrugged. "He's hard to like sometimes. I get that from him." I grinned, which pulled a smile from her, too. "But anyone who honors him is a friend of mine."

"That's good to know," said a voice behind me, and I went stiff because it was a voice that I had never, ever expected to hear again. Male, baritone-deep, careless, cruel. The cruelty was most prominent now, mingled with amusement, because here I was in his parlor, helpless, mortal, and that made him the spider to my fly.

I turned slowly, my hands clenching into fists. He smiled with almost-perfect lips and gazed at me with eyes that weren't quite dark enough. "*You*," I breathed.

My father's living prison. My tormentor. My victim.

"Hello, Sieh," he said. "Nice to see you again."

10

I⟶ SHOULD NEVER HAVE HAPPENED.

Itempas's madness, Enefa's death, Nahadoth's defeat. The War. The sundering of our family.

But it had, and I had been chained within a sack of meat that slurped and leaked and thumped about, clumsy as a cudgel, more helpless than I had been even as a newborn. Because newborn gods were free, and I? I was nothing. Less than nothing. A slave.

We had sworn from the beginning to look out for one another, as slaves must. The first few weeks were the worst. Our new masters worked us to the bone repairing their broken world—which, in all honesty, we had helped to break. Zhakkarn went forth and rescued all the survivors, even the ones buried under rubble or half crisped by lava or lightning. I, better than anyone at clearing up messes, rebuilt one village in every land for the survivors' housing. Meanwhile, Kurue made the seas live and the soils fruitful again.

(They had ripped off her wings to force her to do it. It was too complex a task to be commanded, and she was too wise; she could easily find the loopholes in it. The wings grew back and they tore them away again, but she bore the pain in cold silence. Only when they'd driven heated spikes into her skull, threatening to damage her now-vulnerable brain, had she capitulated. She could not bear to be without her thoughts, for those were all she had left.)

Nahadoth, that awful first year, was left alone. This was partly necessity, as Itempas's betrayal had left him silent and broken. Nothing stirred him; not words, not whippings. When the Arameri commanded, he would move and do as he was told—no more, no less. Then he would sit back down. This stillness was not his nature, you understand. There was something so obviously wrong with it that even the Arameri let him be.

But the other problem was Naha's unreliability. By night he had power, but send him to the other side of the world, past the dawnline of the sun, and he turned to drooling, senseless meat. He had no power at all in that form—could not even manifest his own personality. The meat's mind was as empty as a newborn babe's. Still dangerous, though, especially when sunset came.

Because it was, in its own way, a child, I was given charge of it.

From the first I hated this. It shat itself every day, sometimes more than once. (One of the mortal women tried to show me how to use a diaper; I never bothered. Just left the creature on the ground to do its business.) It moaned and grunted and screamed, incessantly. It bit me bloody when I tried to feed it— newborn or not, it had a man's flesh, and that man had a full set of strong, sharp teeth. The first time it did this, I knocked several of those teeth out. They grew back the next night. It didn't bite me again.

Gradually, though, I came to be more accepting of my duty, and as I warmed toward the meat, so it regarded me with its own simple species of affection. When it began to walk, it followed me everywhere. Once Zhakka and Rue and I had built the first White Hall—the Arameri still pretended to be priests back then—the creature filled the shining corridors with jabbering as it learned to talk. Its first word was my name. When

I grew weak and lapsed into the horrifying state that mortals called *sleep*, the meat creature snuggled against me. I tolerated this because sometimes, when dusk fell and it became my father again, I could snuggle back and close my eyes and imagine that the War had never happened. That all was as it should be.

But those dreams never lasted. The thin, lifeless dawn, and my mindless charge, always returned.

If only it had stayed mindless. But it did not; it began to think. When the others and I probed inside it, we found that it had begun, like any thinking, feeling being, to grow a soul. Worst of all, it—he—began to love me.

And I, as I should never, ever have done, began to love him back.

Hymn and I stood now in the creature's large, handsomely furnished office, wreathed in disgusting smoke.

"I'd ask you to sit," he said, pausing to take another long drag on the burning thing in his mouth, exhaling the smoke with a languid air, "but I doubt you would." He gestured at the equally handsome leather chairs that faced his desk. He sat in a fine chair across from these.

Hymn, who had been glancing uneasily at me since we'd come upstairs from the parlor, sat. I did not.

"My lord—" she began.

"*Lord?*" I spat this, folding my arms.

He looked at me with amusement. "Nobility these days has less to do with bloodlines and friendships with the Arameri, and more to do with money. I have plenty of that, so yes, that makes me a lord." He paused. "And I go by the name 'Ahad' now. Do you like it?"

I sneered. "You can't even bother to be original."

"I have only the name you gave me, lovely Sieh." He hadn't changed. His words were still velvet over razors. I ground my teeth, bracing for cuts. "Speaking of loveliness, though, you're rather lacking at the moment. Did you piss off Zhakkarn again? How is she, by the way? Always liked her."

"What in the fifty million hells are you doing alive?" I demanded. This earned a little gasp from Hymn, but I ignored her.

Ahad's smile never flagged. "You know precisely why I'm alive, Sieh. You were there, remember? At the moment of my birth." I stiffened at this. There was too much knowing in his eyes. He saw my fear. "'Live,' she said. She was newborn herself; maybe she didn't know a goddess's word is law. But I suspect she did."

I relaxed, realizing that he referred to his rebirth as a whole and separate being. But how many years had passed since then? Ahad should have grown old and died years before, yet here he was, as hale and healthy as he'd been on that day. Better, in fact. He was smug and well dressed now, his fingers heavy with silver rings, his hair long and straight and partially braided like a barbarian's. I blinked. No, like a Darre's, which was what he looked like now: a mortal, Darren man. Yeine had remade him to suit her then-tastes.

Remade him. "What are you?" I asked, suspicious.

He shrugged, setting that shining black hair a-ripple over his shoulders. (Something about this movement nagged me with its familiarity.) Then he lifted a hand, casually, and turned it into black mist. My mouth fell open; his smile widened just a touch. His hand returned, still holding the smelly cheroot, which he raised for another long inhalation.

I went forward so swiftly and intently that he rose to face

me. An instant later, I stopped against a radiant cushion of his power. It was not a shield; nothing so specific. Just *his will* given force. He did not want me near him and this became reality. Along with the scent that I'd drawn near him to try and detect, this confirmed my suspicions. To my horror.

"You're a godling," I whispered. "She made you a *godling*."

Ahad, no longer smiling, said nothing, and I realized I was still closer than he wanted me. His distaste washed against me in little sour-tasting tides. I stepped back, and he relaxed.

I did not understand, you see. What it meant to be mortal— relentlessly, constantly, without recourse to the soothing aethers and rarefied dimensions that are the proper housing for my kind. Years passed before I realized that to be bound to mortal flesh is more than just magical or physical weakness; it is a degradation of the mind and soul. And I did not handle it well, those first few centuries.

So easy to endure pain and pass on in turn to those weaker than oneself. So easy to look into the eyes of someone who trusted me to protect him—and hate him, because I could not.

What he has become is my fault. I have sinned against myself, and there is no redeeming that.

"So it appears," Ahad said. "I have such peculiar abilities now. And as you've noticed, I grow no older." He paused, looking me up and down. "Which is more than I can say for you. You smell like Sky, Sieh, and you look like some Arameri have been torturing you again. But"—he paused, his eyes narrowing—"it's more than that, isn't it? You feel . . . wrong."

Even if he had not become a god, he was the last person to

whom I would have willingly revealed my condition. Yet there was no hiding it, now that he'd seen me. He knew me better than anyone else in this realm, and he would be that much more vicious if I tried to hide it.

I sighed and waved a hand to clear some of the drifting smoke from my vicinity. It came right back. "Something has happened," I said. "I was in Sky, yes, for a few days. The Arameri heir—" No. I didn't want to talk about that. Better to get to the worst of it. "I seem to be"—I shifted, put my hands into my pockets, and tried to seem nonchalant—"dying."

Hymn's eyes widened. Ahad—I hated that stupid name of his already—looked skeptical.

"Nothing can kill a godling but demons and gods," he said, "and the world's fresh out of demons, last I heard. Has Naha finally grown tired of his little favorite?"

I clenched my fists. "He will love me until time ends."

"Yeine, then." To my surprise, the skepticism cleared from Ahad's face. "Yes, she is wise and good-hearted, but she didn't know you back then; you played the innocent boy so well. She could make you mortal, couldn't she? If so, I commend her for giving you a slow, cruel death."

I would have gotten angrier, if my own cruel streak hadn't come to the fore. "What's this? Have you got a baby-god crush on Yeine? It's hopeless, you know. Nahadoth's the one she loves; you're just his leftovers."

Ahad kept smiling, but his eyes went black and cold. He had more than a little of my father still in him; that much was obvious.

"You're just mad neither of them wants *you*," he said.

The room went gray and red. With a wordless cry of rage,

I went for him—meaning, I think, to rip him open with my claws, and forgetting for the moment that I had none. And forgetting, far more stupidly, that he was a god and I was not.

He could have killed me. He could have done it by accident; newborn godlings don't know their own strength. Instead he simply caught me by the throat, lifted me bodily, and slammed me onto the top of his desk so hard that the wood cracked.

While I groaned, dazed by the blow and the agony of landing on two paperweights, he sighed and sucked more smoke from the cheroot with his free hand. He kept me pinned, easily, with the other.

"What does he want?" he asked Hymn.

As my vision cleared, I saw she had gotten to her feet and was half ducked behind her chair. At his question, she straightened warily.

"Money," she said. "He got me into trouble earlier today. Said he needed to make it up to me, but I don't need any of his tricks."

Ahad laughed, in the humorless way he had done for the last dozen centuries. I couldn't remember the last time I'd felt true amusement from him. "Isn't that just like him?" He smiled down at me, then lifted a hand. A purse appeared in it; I heard heavy coins jingle within. Without looking at Hymn, he tossed it. Without blinking she caught it.

"That enough?" he asked when she tugged open the pouch's string to look inside. Her eyes widened, and she nodded. "Good. You can go now."

She swallowed. "Am I in trouble for this?" She glanced at me as I struggled to breathe around Ahad's tightening hand.

"No, of course not. How could you have known I knew him?"

He threw her a significant look. "Though you still don't know anything, you understand. About me being what I am, him being what he is. You never met him, and you never came here. Spend your money slowly if you want to keep it."

"I know that." Scowling, Hymn made the pouch disappear. Then to my surprise, she glanced at me again. "What are you going to do with him?"

I had begun to wonder that myself. His hand was tight enough to feel the pounding of my pulse. I reached up and scrabbled at his wrist, trying to loosen it, but it was like trying to loosen the roots of the Tree.

Ahad watched my efforts with lazy cruelty. "I haven't decided yet," he said. "Does it matter?"

Hymn licked her lips. "I don't do blood money."

He looked up at her and let the silence grow long and still before he finally spoke. His words were kinder than his eyes. "Don't worry," he said. "This one is a favorite of two of the Three. I'm not stupid enough to kill him."

Hymn took a quick, deep breath—for strength, I thought. "Look, I don't know what's happened between you two, and I don't care. I never would have...I didn't mean to—" She stopped, took a deep breath. "I'll give you back the money. Just let him come with me."

Ahad's hand tightened until I saw stars at the edges of my vision. "Don't," he said, sounding far too much like my father in that instant, "*ever* command me."

Hymn looked confused, but of course mortals do not realize how often they speak in imperatives—that is, ordinary mortals do not. Arameri long ago learned that lesson when we killed them for forgetting.

I fought back fear so that I could concentrate. *Leave her alone, damn you! Play your games with me, not her!*

Ahad actually started, throwing a sharp glance at me. I had no idea why—until I remembered just how young he was, in our terms. And that reminded me of my one advantage over him.

Closing my eyes, I fixed my thoughts on Hymn. She was a hot bright point on the darkening map of my awareness. I had found the power to protect her when the muckrakers came. Could I now protect her from one of my own?

Wind shot through the hollows of my soul, cold and electric. Not much; not nearly as much as there should have been. But enough. I smiled.

And reached up to grip Ahad's hand. "Brother," I murmured in our tongue, and he blinked, surprised that I could talk. "Share yourself with me."

Then I took him into my self. We blazed, white green gold, through a firmament of purest ebony, down, down, down. This was not the core of me, for I would never trust him in that sweet, sharp place, but it was close enough. I felt him struggle, frightened, as all that I was—a torrent, a current—threatened to devour him. But that was not my intention. As we swirled downward, I dragged him closer to me. Here without flesh, I was the elder and the stronger. He did not know himself and I overpowered him easily. Gripping the front of his shirt, I grinned into his wide, panicked eyes.

"Let's see *you* now," I said, and thrust my hand into his mouth.

He screamed—a stupid thing to do under the circumstances. That just made it easier. I compacted myself into a single curved claw and plunged into the core of him. There was an instant of resistance, and pain for both of us, because he was not me and all gods are antithetical to each other on some level. Then there was the briefest plume of strangeness as I tasted his nature, dark but not, rich in memory yet raw with his newness, craving, desperate for something that he did not want and did not know that he needed—but it latched on to me with a ferocity I had not expected. Young gods are not usually so savage. Then I was the one being devoured—

I came out of him with a cry and twisted away, curling in on myself in agony while Ahad stumbled and fell across the empty chair. I heard him utter a sound like a sob, once. Then he drew deep breaths, controlling himself.

Yes, I had forgotten. He was not truly new. He wasn't even young, like Yeine. As a mortal, he had seen thousands of years before his effective rebirth. And he had endured hells in that time that would have broken most mortals. It had broken *him*, but he'd put himself back together, stronger. I laughed to myself as the pain of nearly becoming something else finally began to recede.

"You never change, do you?" My voice was a rasp. He'd left finger marks in the flesh of my neck. "Always so difficult."

His reply was a curse in a dead language, though I was gratified to hear weariness in his voice as well.

I pushed myself up, slowly. Every muscle in my body ached, along with the bump to the back of the head I'd taken. At the corner of my vision there was movement: Hymn. Coming back into the room, after quite sensibly vacating it while two godlings fought. I was surprised, given her knowledge of us, that she hadn't vacated the house and neighborhood, too.

"You done?" she asked.

"Very," I said, pulling myself to sit on the edge of the desk. I would need to sleep again soon. But first I had to make my peace with Ahad, if he would allow that.

He was glaring at me now, from the chair. Nearly recovered already, though his hair was mussed and he had lost his cheroot. I hated him more for a moment, and then sighed and let that go. Let it all go. Mortal life was too short.

"We are no longer slaves," I said softly. "We need no longer be enemies."

"We weren't enemies because of the Arameri," he snapped.

"Yes, we were." I smiled, which made him blink. "You wouldn't have even existed if not for them. And I—" If I allowed it, the shame would come. I had never allowed it before, but so much had changed since those days. Our positions had reversed: he was a god; I wasn't. I needed him; he didn't need me. "I would have at least... would have tried to be a better..."

But then he surprised me. He had always been good at that.

"Shut up, you fool," he said, getting to his feet with a sigh. "Don't be any more of an ass than you usually are."

I blinked. "What?"

Ahad stalked over to me, surprising me further. He hadn't liked being near me for centuries. Planting his hands on the desk on either side of my hips, he leaned down to glare into my face. "Do you really think me so petty that I would still be angry after all this time? Ah, no—that isn't it at all." His smile flickered, and perhaps it was my imagination that his teeth grew sharper for a moment. I *hoped* it was, because the last thing he needed was an animal nature. "No, I think you're just so gods-damned certain of your own importance that you haven't figured it out. So let me make this clear: *I don't care about you.* You're irrelevant. It's a waste of my energy even to hate you!"

I stared back at him, stunned by his vehemence and, I will admit, hurt. And yet.

"I don't believe you," I murmured. He blinked.

Then he pushed away from the desk with such force that it scooched back a little, nearly jostling me off. I stared as he went over to Hymn, grabbed her by the scruff of her shirt, and half dragged her to the door, opening it.

"I'm not going to kill him," he said, shoving her through hard enough that she stumbled when he let her go. "I'm not going to do a damned thing other than gloat over his prolonged, humiliating death, which I have no reason whatsoever to hasten. So your money's clean and you can wash your hands of him in good conscience. Be glad you escaped before he could ruin your life. Now get out!" And he slammed the door in her face.

I stared at him as he turned to regard me, taking a long, slow breath to compose himself. Because I knew his soul, I felt the moment that he made a decision. Perhaps he had already guessed at mine.

"Would you like a drink?" he asked at last, with brittle politeness.

"Children shouldn't drink," I said automatically.

"How fortunate that you're not a child anymore."

I winced. "I, ah, haven't had alcohol in a few centuries." I said it carefully, testing this new, fragile peace beneath us. It was as thin as the tension on a puddle's surface, but if we tread delicately, we might manage. "Do you have anything, er..."

"For the pathetic?" He snorted and went over to a handsome wood cabinet, which turned out to hold a dozen or so bottles.

All of them were full of strong, richly colored liquids. Stuff for men, not boys. "No. You'll have to sink or swim, I'm afraid."

Most likely I would sink. I looked at the bottles and committed myself to the path of truce with a heavy sigh.

"Pour on, then," I said, and he did.

Some while later, after I had unfortunately remembered too late that vomiting is far, far more unpleasant than defecating, I sat on the floor where Ahad had left me and took a long, hard look at him. "You want something from me," I said. I believe I said it clearly, though my thoughts were slurred.

He lifted an eyebrow in genteel fashion, not even tipsy. A servant had already taken away the wastebasket splattered with my folly. Even with the windows open, the stench of Ahad's cheroot was better than the alternative, so I did not mind it this time.

"So do you," he said.

"Yes," I said, "but my wants are always simple things. In this case I want money, and since I really wanted it for Hymn and you've already given it to her, that essentially solves the problem. *Your* wants are never simple."

"Hmm." I didn't think this statement pleased him. "And yet you're still here, which implies you want something more."

"Care during my feeble senescence. It will take me another fifty or sixty years to die, during which I will require increasing amounts of food and shelter and"—I looked at the bottle on the desk between us, considering—"and other things. Mortals use money to obtain these things; I am becoming mortal; therefore, I will need a regular source of money."

"A job." Ahad laughed. "My housekeeper thought you might make a good courtesan, if you cleaned up a little."

Affront penetrated the alcohol haze. "I'm a god!"

"Nearly a third of our courtesans are godlings, Sieh. Didn't you feel the presence of family when you came in?" He gestured around the building, his hand settling on himself, and I flushed because in fact, I had not sensed him or anyone else. More evidence of my weakness. "A goodly number of our clients are, too—godlings who are curious about mortals but afraid or too proud to admit it. Or who simply want the release of meaningless, undemanding intercourse. We aren't so different from them, you know, when it comes to that sort of thing."

I reached out to touch the world around me as best I could, my senses numbed and unsteady as they were. I could feel a few of my siblings then. Mostly the very youngest. I remembered the days when I had been fascinated by mortalkind—especially children, with whom I had loved to play. But some of my kind were drawn to adults, and with that came adult cravings.

Like the taste of Shahar's skin.

I shook my head—a mistake, as the nausea was not quite done with me. I said something to distract myself. "We've never needed such things, Ahad. If we want a mortal, we appear somewhere and point at one, and the mortal gives us what we want."

"You know, Sieh, it's all right that you haven't paid attention to the world. But you really shouldn't *talk* as though you have."

"What?"

"Times have changed." Ahad paused to sip from a square glass of fiery red liquid. I had stopped drinking that one after the first taste because mortals could die of alcohol poisoning. Ahad held it in his mouth a moment, savoring the burn, before continuing. "Mortalkind, heretics excepted, spent centuries believing in Itempas and nothing else. They don't know what happened to him—the Arameri keep a tight grip on that information, and so do we godlings—but they know *something* has changed. They aren't gods, but they can still see the new colors of existence. And now they understand that our kind are powerful, admirable, but fallible." He shrugged. "A godling who wants to be worshipped can still find adherents, of course. But not many—and really, Sieh, most of us don't *want* to be worshipped. Do you?"

I blinked in surprise, and considered it. "I don't know."

"You could be, you know. The street children swear by you when they speak any god's name at all. Some of them even pray to you."

Yes, I had heard them, though I'd never done anything to encourage their interest. I'd had thousands of followers once, but these days it always surprised me that they remembered. I drew up my knees and wrapped my arms around them, understanding finally what Ahad meant.

Nodding as if I'd spoken my thoughts aloud, Ahad continued. "The rest of our clients are nobles, wealthy merchants, very lucky commoners—anyone who's ever yearned to visit the heavens before death. Even our mortal courtesans have been with gods enough to have acquired a certain ethereal technique." He smiled a salesman's smile, though it never once touched his eyes.

"That's what you're selling. Not sex, but divinity." I frowned. "Gods, Ahad, at least worship is *free*."

"It was never free." His smile vanished. It hadn't been real, anyway. "Every mortal who offered a god devotion wanted *something* in exchange for it—blessings, a guaranteed place in the heavens, status. And every god who demanded worship expected loyalty and more, in exchange. So why shouldn't we be honest about what we're doing? At least here, no god lies."

I flinched, as he had meant me to. Razors. Then he went on.

"As for our residents, as we call them, there is no rape here, no coercion. No pain, unless that's mutually agreed upon by both client and resident. No judgments, either." He paused, looking me up and down. "The housekeeper usually has a good eye for new talent. It will be a shame to tell her that she was so far off in your case."

It was not entirely due to the alcohol that I straightened in wounded pride. "I could be a *marvelous* whore." Gods knew I had enough practice.

"Ah, but I think you would be unable to keep yourself from contemplating the violent murder of any client who claimed you. Which, given your nature and the unpredictability of magic, might actually cause such death to occur. That's not good for business." He paused, and I did not imagine the cold edge to his smile. "I have the same problem, as I discovered quite by accident."

There was a long silence that fell between us. This was not recriminating. It was simply that such statements stirred up sediment of the past, and it was natural to wait for that to settle before we moved on.

Changing the subject helped, too. "We can discuss the matter of my employment later." Because I was almost certain he would hire me. Unreasoning optimism is a fundamental element of childishness. "So what is it, then, that you want?"

Ahad steepled his fingers, propping his elbows on the arms of the handsome leather chair. I wondered whether this was a sign of nerves. "I should think you'd have guessed. Considering how easily you defeated me in—" He paused, frowning, and then I finally did catch on.

"No mortal tongue has words for it," I said softly. I would have to speak diplomatically, and that was never easy for me. "In our realm there is no need for words. Naturally you will have picked up some of our tongue over the centuries...." I let the question ask itself, and he grimaced.

"Not much of it. I couldn't hear...feel..." He struggled to say it in Senmite, probably out of stubbornness. "I was like any other mortal before Yeine did this to me. I tried speaking your words a few times, died a few times, and stopped trying."

"*Your* words now." I watched Ahad absorb this, his expression going unreadably blank. "I can teach you the language, if you want."

"There are several dozen godlings living in Shadow," he replied stiffly. "If and when I deem it valuable, I can learn from them."

Idiot, I thought, but kept it behind my teeth, nodding as if I thought deliberate ignorance was a good idea. "You have a bigger problem, anyway."

He said nothing, watching me. He could do that for hours, I knew; something he'd learned during his years in Sky. I had no idea whether he knew what I was about to say.

"You don't know your nature." That was how I'd known I could best him, or at least get him off me, in the contest of our wills. His reaction to the touch of my thoughts had given it away: I had seen mortal newborns do the same at the brush of a fingertip. A quick, startled jerk, a flailing look to determine *what and how and why*, and *will it hurt me?* Only learning oneself better, and understanding one's place in the world, made the touch of another mundane.

After a moment, Ahad nodded. This, too, was a gesture of trust between us. In the old days he would never have revealed so much weakness to me.

I sighed and got up, swaying only a little as I gained my feet, and went over to his chair. He did not rise this time, but he grew palpably less relaxed as I got closer, until I stopped.

"I will do you no harm," I said, scowling at his skittishness. Why couldn't he just be a coldhearted bastard all the time? I could never truly hate him, for pity. "The Arameri hurt you worse than I ever did."

Very, very quietly he replied, "*You let them.*"

There was nothing I could say to that, because it was true. So I just stood there. This would never work if we began to rehash old hurts. He knew it, too. Finally he relaxed, and I stepped closer.

"All gods must learn who and what they are for themselves," I said. As gently as I could—my hands were rough and dirty from my days in the alley—I cupped his face and held it. "Only you can define the meaning and limit of your existence. But sometimes, those of us who have already found ourselves can give the new ones a clue."

I had already gained that clue during our brief metaphysical struggle. That fierce, devouring need of his. For what? I looked into his strangely mortalish eyes—strange because he had never really been mortal, yet mortality was all he knew—and tried to understand him. Which I should have been able to do because I had been there at the moment of his birth. I had seen his first steps and heard his first words. I had loved him, even if—

The nausea struck faster than ever before, because the alcohol had already made me ill. I barely managed to whirl away and collapse onto the floor before I was retching, screaming through the heaves, wobbling because my legs were trying to jerk and my spine was trying to bow backward even as my stomach sought to cast out the poison I had taken in. But this poison was not physical.

"Still a child after all." Ahad sighed into my ear, his voice a low murmur that easily got through my strangled cries. "Shall I call you big brother or little brother? I suppose it doesn't matter. You will never grow up fully, no matter how old you look. Brother."

Brother. Brother. Not child, not

forget

Ahad was not my son, not even figuratively, because

forget

Because a god of childhood could not be a father, not if he wanted to *be* at all, and

forgetforgetforget

Brother. Ahad was my brother. My new little brother, Yeine's first child. Nahadoth would be . . . well, not proud, probably. But amused.

My body unknotted. The agony receded enough that I stopped screaming, stopped spasming. There was nothing in my stomach anyhow. I lay there, returning gradually to myself as the horror faded, then drew one cautious breath. Then another.

"Thank you," I whispered.

Ahad, crouching over me, sighed. He did not say *you're welcome*, because I was not welcome and we both knew it. But he had done me a kindness when he hadn't had to, and that deserved acknowledgment.

"You smell," he said, "and you're filthy, and you look like horseshit. Since you're too useless to take yourself out of here as you should, I have no choice but to put you up for the night. But don't get used to it; I want you living somewhere else after this." He got up and went away, I assume to find a servant and make arrangements for my stay.

When he came back, I had managed—barely—to sit on my knees. I was still shaky. Insanely, my stomach now insisted that it needed to be filled again. *In or out*, I told it, but it did not listen.

Ahad crouched in front of me again. "Interesting."

I managed to lift my eyes to him. His expression betrayed nothing, but he lifted a hand and conjured a small hand mirror. I was too tired even for envy. He lifted the mirror to show me my face.

I had grown older. The face that gazed back at me was longer, leaner, with a stronger jawline. The hair on my chin was no longer downy and barely visible; it had grown darker, longer, the wispy precursors of a beard. Late adolescence, rather than the middling stage of it I'd been in. Two years of my life gone? Three? Gone, regardless.

"I should be flattered, perhaps," Ahad said. "That you remember the old days with such fondness." His words skirted the edge of danger, but I was too tired for true fear. He could kill me anytime he wanted, and would've done it by now if he'd really meant to. He just liked flaunting his power.

Suddenly this seemed monumentally unfair. "I hate this," I whispered, not caring if he heard me. "I hate that I'm nothing now."

Ahad shook his head, less annoyed than unsurprised. His hand seized the back of my shirt and pulled me to my feet. "You're not 'nothing.' You're mortal, which is far from nothing. The sooner you accept that, the better off you'll be." He took one of my arms, holding it up, and made a sound of disgust. "You need to *eat*. Start taking care of your body if you want it to last for the few years you have left. Or would you rather die now?"

I closed my eyes, letting myself dangle from his grasp. "I don't want to be mortal." I was whining. It felt good to realize I still could, however much I'd grown up. "Mortals lie when they say they love you. They wait until you trust them, then shove the knife in, and then they work it around to make sure it kills you."

There was a moment of silence, during which I closed my eyes and honestly contemplated having a good cry. It ended when the office door opened and two servants came in, and when Ahad gave me a slap on the cheek that was not *quite* gently chiding.

"Gods do that, too," he snapped, "so you're damned whichever way you turn. Shut up and deal with it."

Then he shoved me into the servants' waiting arms and they hauled me away.

11

I L-O-V-E, love you
I'll K-I-S-S, kiss you
Then I pushed him in a lake
And he swallowed a snake
And ended up with a tummy ache

THE SERVANTS TOOK ME to a large sumptuous bathchamber with lovely benches that reeked of sex despite their freshly laundered cushions. They stripped me, throwing my old clothes into a pile to be burned, and scrubbed me with careless efficiency, rinsing me in perfumed water. Then they put me into a robe and took me to a room and let me sleep the whole day and well into the night. I did not dream.

I woke up thinking that my sister Zhakkarn was using my head as a pike target, though she would never do such a thing. When I managed to sit upright, which took doing, I contemplated nausea again. A long-cold meal and a pitcher of room-temperature water sat on a sideboard of the room, so I decided on ingestion rather than ejection and applied myself grimly. It helped that the food tasted good. Beside this sat a small dish holding a dab of thick white paste and a paper card, on which elegant blocky letters had been written: EAT IT. The hand was familiar, so I sighed and tasted the paste. The alley rat had been more rancid but not by much. Still, as I was a guest in Ahad's home, I held my breath and gulped the rest down, then quickly ate more food in an attempt to disguise the bitter taste. This did not work. However, I began to feel better, so I was pleased to confirm it was medicine, not poison.

Fresh clothing had been set out for me, too. Pleasantly non-descript: loose gray pants, a beige shirt, a brown jacket, brown boots. Servant attire, most likely, since I suspected that would suit Ahad's sense of cruelty. Thus arrayed, I opened the door of the room.

And promptly stopped, as the sounds of laughter and music drifted up from downstairs. Nighttime. For a moment the urge to play a dozen bawdy, vicious tricks was almost overwhelming, and I felt a tickle of power at the thought. It would be so easy to change all the house's sensual oils into hot chili oil or make the beds smell of mildew rather than lust and perfume. But I was older now, more mature, and the urge passed. I felt a fleeting sadness in its wake.

Before I could close the door, however, two people came up the steps, giggling together with the careless intimacy of old friends or new lovers. One of them turned her head, and I froze as our eyes met. Egan, one of my sisters—with her arm around the waist of some mortal. I assessed and dismissed him in a glance: richly dressed, middle-aged, drunk. I turned back to meet Egan's frowning gaze.

"Sieh." She looked me up and down and smirked. "So the rumors are true; you're back. Two thousand years wasn't enough mortal flesh to satisfy you?"

Once upon a time, Egan had been worshipped by a desert tribe in eastern Senm. She had taught them to play music that could bring rain, and they had sculpted a mountain face to make a statue of her in return. Those people were gone now, absorbed into the Amn during one of that tribe's endless campaigns of conquest before the War. After the War, I had destroyed Egan's statue myself, under orders from the Arameri to eliminate anything that blasphemed against Itempas, no matter how beautiful. And here stood the original in mortal flesh, with an Amn man's hand on her breast.

"I'm here by accident," I said. "What's your excuse?"

She lifted a graceful eyebrow, set into a beautiful Amn face. It was a new face, of course. Before the War, she had looked more like the people of the desert tribe. Both of us ignored the mortal, who had by now begun trying to nibble at her neck.

"Boredom," she said. "Experience. The usual. During the War, it was the ones who'd spent the most time among mortalkind, defining their natures, who survived best." Her eyes narrowed. "Not that you helped."

"I fought the madman who destroyed our family," I said wearily. "And yes, I fought anyone who helped him. I don't understand why everyone acts like I did a horrible thing."

"Because you—all of you who fought for Naha—lost yourselves in it," Egan snapped, her body tensing so with fury that her paramour lifted his head to blink at her in surprise. "He infected you with his fury. You didn't just kill those who fought; you killed anyone who tried to stop you. Anyone who pleaded for calm, if you thought they should've been fighting. Mortals, if they had the temerity to ask you for help. In the Maelstrom's name, you act like Tempa was the only one who went mad that day!"

I stared at her, fury ratcheting higher in me, and then, suddenly, it died. I couldn't sustain it. Not while I stood there with my head still aching from alcohol and Ahad's beating the day before, and my skin crawling as infinitesimal flecks of it died—some renewed, some lost forever, all of it slowly becoming dryer and less elastic until one day it would be nothing but wrinkles and liver spots. Egan's lover touched her shoulder to try and soothe her, a pathetic gesture, but it seemed to have some effect, because she relaxed just a little and smiled ruefully at him, as if to apologize for destroying the mood. That made me think of Shahar, and how lonely I was, and how lonely I would be for the rest of my mercilessly brief life.

It is very, very hard to sustain a two-thousand-year-old grudge amid all that.

I shook my head and turned to go back into my room. But just before I could close the door, I heard Egan. "Sieh. Wait."

Warily I opened the door again. She was frowning at me. "Something's different about you. What is it?"

I shook my head again. "Nothing that should matter to you. Look…" It occurred to me suddenly that I would never have a chance to say this to her or to any of my siblings. I would die with so much unfinished business. It wasn't fair. "I'm sorry, Egan. I know that means nothing after everything that's happened. I wish…" So many wishes. I laughed a little. "Never mind."

"Are you going to be working here?" She smoothed a hand over her mortal man's back; he sighed and leaned against her, happy again.

"No." Then I remembered Ahad's plans. "Not…like this." I gestured toward her with my chin. "No offense, but I'm not overly fond of mortals right now."

"Understandable, after all you've been through." I blinked in surprise, and she smiled thinly. "None of us liked what Itempas did, Sieh. But by then, imprisoning you seemed the only sane choice he'd made, after so much insanity." She sighed. "We all had a long time to think about how wrong that decision was. And then…well, you know how he is about changing his mind."

By which she meant *he didn't*. "I know."

Egan glanced at her mortal, thoughtful, and then at me. Then at the mortal again. "What do you think?"

The man looked surprised but pleased. He looked at me, and abruptly I realized what they were considering. I couldn't help blushing, which made the man smile. "I think it would be nice," he said.

"No," I said quickly. "I—er—thank you. I can see you mean well…but no."

Egan smiled then, surprising me, because there was more compassion in it than I'd ever expected to see. "How long since you've been with your own?" she asked, and it threw me. I couldn't answer, because I couldn't remember the last time I'd made love to another god. Nahadoth, but that was not the same. He'd been diminished, stuffed into mortal flesh, desperate in his loneliness. That hadn't been lovemaking; it had been pity. Before that, I thought it might have been—

forget

Zhakka, maybe? Selforine? Elishad—no, that had been ages ago, back when he'd still liked me. Gwn?

It would be good, perhaps, to lose myself in another for a while. To let one of my kind take my soul where she would and give it comfort. Wouldn't it?

As I had done for Shahar.

"No," I said again, more softly. "Not now…not yet. Thank you."

She eyed me for a long moment, perhaps seeing more than

I wanted her to see. Could she tell I was becoming mortal? Another reason not to accept her offer; she would know then. But I thought maybe that wasn't the reason for her look. I wondered if maybe, just maybe, she still cared.

"The offer stands for whenever you change your mind," she said, and then flashed me a smile. "You might have to share, though." Turning her smile on the mortal, she and he moved on, heading up to the next floor.

My stirrings had been noticed. When I turned from watching Egan leave, the servant man who had quietly come upstairs bowed to me. "Lord Sieh? Lord Ahad has asked that you come to his office, when you're ready."

I put a hand on my hip. "I know full well he didn't *ask*."

The servant paused, then looked amused. "You probably don't want to know the word he actually used in place of your name, either."

I followed the servant downstairs. During these evening hours, he explained quietly, only the courtesans were to be visible; this was necessary to maintain the illusion that the house contained nothing but beautiful creatures offering guiltless pleasure. The sight of servants reminded the clientele that the Arms of Night was a business. The sight of people like me—servants of a different kind, he did not say, but I could guess—reminded them that the business was one of many, whose collective owners had fingers in many pots.

So he took me into what looked like a closet, which proved to lead into a dimly lit, wide back stairwell. Other servants and the occasional mortal courtesan moved back and forth along this, all of them smiling or greeting each other amiably in passing. (So different from servants in Sky.) When we reached the ground floor, the servant led me through a short convoluted passage that reminded me a bit of my dead spaces, and then opened a door that appeared to have been cut from the bare wooden wall. "In here, Lord Sieh." Unsurprisingly, we were back in Ahad's office. Surprisingly, he was not alone.

The young woman who sat in the chair across from him would have been striking even if she hadn't been beautiful. This was partly because she was Maroneh and partly because she was very tall for a woman, even sitting down. The roiling nimbus of black hair about her head only added to the inches by which she topped the chair's high back. But she was also elegant of form and bearing, her presence accented by the faint fragrance of hiras-flower perfume. She had dressed herself like a nobody, in a nondescript long skirt and jacket with worn old boots, but she carried herself like a queen.

She had been smiling at something Ahad said when I entered. As I stepped into the room, her eyes settled on me with a disconcertingly intent gaze, and her smile faded to something cooler and more guarded. I had the sudden acute feeling of being sized up, and found wanting.

The servant bowed and closed the door behind me. I folded my arms and watched her, waiting. I was not so far gone that I didn't know power when I smelled it.

"What are you?" I asked. "Arameri by-blow? Scrivener? Noblewoman in disguise so you can visit a brothel in peace?"

She did not respond. Ahad sighed and pinched the bridge of his nose.

"Glee is part of the group that owns and supports the Arms of Night, Sieh," he said. "She's come to see you, in fact—to make certain you won't jeopardize the investment she and her partners have already made. If she doesn't like you, you ridiculous ass, you don't stay."

This made me frown in confusion. "Since when does a godling do a mortal's bidding? Willingly, that is."

"Since godlings and mortals began to have mutual goals," said the woman. Her voice was low and rolling, like warm ocean waves, yet her words were so precisely enunciated that I could have cut paper with them. Her smile was just as sharp when I turned to her. "I imagine such arrangements were quite common before the Gods' War. In this case, the relationship is less supervisory and more . . . partnership." She glanced at Ahad. "Partners should agree on important decisions."

He nodded back, with only a hint of his usual sardonic smile. Did she know he would gut-knife her in a moment if it benefitted him more than cooperation did? I hoped so and held out my hands to let her get a good look at me. "Well? *Do* you like me?"

"If it were a matter of looks, the answer would be no." I dropped my arms in annoyance and she smiled, though I didn't think she'd been kidding. "You don't suit my tastes at all. Fortunately, looks are not the means by which I judge value."

"She has a job for you," Ahad said. He swiveled in his chair to face me and leaned back, propping one foot on the desk. "A test, of sorts. To see if your unique talents can be put to some use."

"What the hells kind of test?" I was affronted by the very idea.

The woman—Glee? oddly cheerful for a Maroneh woman's name—lifted one perfectly arched eyebrow in a way that felt inexplicably familiar. "I would like to send you to meet Usein Darr, scion of the current baron. Are you, perhaps, familiar with recent political events in the North?"

I tried to remember the things I'd overheard or been told while in Sky. But then, the image of Nevra and Criscina Arameri's bodies came to mind.

"You want me to find out what this new magic is all about," I said. "These masks."

"No. We know what they are."

"You do?"

Glee folded her hands, and the sense of familiarity grew. I had never met her before; I was certain of it. Very strange.

"The masks are art," she said. "Specifically derived from a Mencheyev-Darren method of prayer that long predates the Bright, which they kept up in secret to avoid persecution. Once, they danced their exhortations to and praises of the gods, with each dancer donning a mask in order to act out specific, contextualized roles. Each dance required certain interactions of these roles and a common understanding of the archetypes represented. The Mother, for example, symbolized love, but also justice; it was actually a representation of death. The Sorrowful was worn by an angry, prideful person, who would eventually commit great wrongs and come to regret what they had done. Do you understand?"

I fought to stifle a yawn. "Yeah, I get the idea. Someone takes an archetype, mixes it with common symbology, carves it out of wood from the World Tree using the blood of a slaughtered infant or something—"

"The blood of a godling, actually."

I fell silent in surprise. Glee smiled.

"We don't know whose. Perhaps just godsblood bought off the street; the specific originator of the blood may not matter, just its inherent power. We're looking into that as well. And I don't

know about wood from the Tree, but I wouldn't be surprised."
She sobered. "Finding out how the masks work isn't what I want
you to do in Darr. We're less concerned with the tool, more
concerned with the wielder. I would like you to approach Usein
Darr with an offer from our group."

I could not help perking up. There was great potential for
mischief in any negotiation. "You want their magic?"

"No. We want peace."

I started. *"Peace?"*

"Peace serves the interests of both mortals and gods," Ahad
said when I looked at him to see if this Glee was a madwoman.

"I have to agree." I frowned at him. "But I didn't think
you did."

"I have always done whatever makes my life easier, Sieh." He
folded his hands calmly. "I am not Nahadoth, as you're so fond
of pointing out. I'm rather fond of predictability and routine."

"Yes. Well." I shook my head and sighed. "But *mortals* are part
Nahadoth, and it sounds like the ones up north would rather
live in chaos than endure the Arameri's world order any longer.
It's not our place to tell this woman she's wrong, if she's the head
of it."

"Usein Darr is not the sole force behind the northern rebellion," Glee said. "And it must be called a rebellion at this point.
Darr is now one of five northern nations that have ceased to
tithe to the White Halls within its borders, though they instead
offer schooling, care for the elderly, and so forth to their citizens
directly. That keeps the Nobles' Consortium from censuring
them for failure to govern—though since no High Northern
noble has attended a Consortium session in over a year, it hardly
matters. The whole of High North has, effectively, refused to

recognize the Consortium's authority." She sighed. "The only thing they haven't done is raise an army, probably because that would bring the Arameri's wrath down on them. Everything but open defiance—but still, defiance. And Darr is, if not its head, most certainly its heart."

"So what am I to offer *this* Darre, then, if her heart's set on freeing the world from Arameri tyranny? A goal I don't at all disagree with, mind you." I considered. "I suppose I could kill her."

"No, you could not." Glee did not raise her voice, but then she didn't have to. Those paper-cutting words suddenly became knives, sharp enough to flense. "As I said, Usein Darr is not the sole motivator of these rebels. Killing her would only martyr her and encourage the rest."

"Besides that," said Ahad, "those godlings who dwell in the mortal realm do so on the sufferance of Lady Yeine. She has made it clear that she values mortal independence and is watching closely to see whether our presence proves detrimental. And please remember that *she* was once Darre. For all we know, Usein is some relative of hers."

I shook my head. "She's not mortal anymore. Such considerations are meaningless to her now."

"Are you sure?"

I paused, suddenly uncertain.

"Well, then." Ahad steepled his fingers. "Let's kill Usein and see. Should be a delight, pissing off someone who had an infamous temper *before* she became the goddess of death."

I rolled my eyes at him but did not protest. "Fine, then," I said. "What *is* my goal in Darr?"

Glee shrugged, which obliquely surprised me because she

hadn't seemed like the kind to be that casual. "Find out what Usein wants. If it's within our power, offer it."

"How the hells do I know what's within you people's power?"

Ahad made a sound of exasperation. "Just assume anything and promise nothing. And lie, if you must. You're good at that, aren't you?"

Mortalfucking son of a demon. "Fine," I said, slipping my hands into my pockets. "When do I go?"

I should have known better than to say that, because Ahad sat a little straighter, and his eyes turned completely black. Then he smiled with more than a bit of his old cruelty and said, "You realize I've never done this before."

I tried not to show my alarm. "It's not much different from any other magic. A matter of will." But if his will faltered...

"Ah, but, Sieh, I would so happily will you out of existence."

Better to let him see my fear. He had always cultivated that in the old days; he liked to feel powerful. So I licked my lips and met his eyes. "I thought you didn't care about me. Didn't hate me, didn't love me."

"Which compounds the problem. Perhaps I don't care enough to make sure I do this right."

I took a deep breath, glancing at Glee. *See what you're dealing with?* But she showed no reaction, her beautiful face as serene as before. She would have made a good Arameri.

"Perhaps not," I said, "but if you do care at all about... craftsmanship, or whatever, then could you please be sure to just wipe me out of existence? And not, instead, spread my innards thinly across the face of reality? I've seen that happen before; it looks painful."

Ahad laughed, but a feeling that had been in the air—an

extra measure of heaviness and danger that had been thickening around us—eased. "I'll take care, then. I do like being neat."

There was a flicker. I felt myself disassembled and pushed out of the world. Despite Ahad's threats, he was actually quite gentle about it. Then a new setting melted together around me.

Arrebaia, the largest city amid the collection of squabbling tribes that had grown together and decided to fight others instead of each other. I could remember when they had not been Darre, just Somem and Lapri and Ztoric, and even further back when they had been families, and before that when they had been wandering bands lacking names of any kind. No more, however. I stood atop a wall near the city's heart and privately marveled at how much they'd grown. The immense, tangled jungle that dominated this part of High North shone on the distant horizon, as green as the dragons that flew through other realms and the color of my mother's eyes when she was angry. I could smell its humidity and violent, fragile life on the wind. Around me spread a maze of streets and temples and statues and gardens, all rising in stony tiers toward the city's center, all carpeted in the paler green of the ornamental grass that the Darre cultivated. It made their city glow like an emerald in the slanting afternoon light.

Before me, in the near distance, loomed the hulking, squared-off pyramid of Sar-enna-nem. My destination, I guessed, since Ahad did not strike me as the subtle type.

My arrival had not gone unnoticed, however. I glanced down from the wall on which I stood to find an old woman and a boy-child of four or five years staring up at me. Amid the crowded street, they alone had stopped; between them was a rickety-looking cart bearing a few tired-looking vegetables and fruits.

Ah, yes, the end of the market day. I sat down on the wall, dangling my feet over it and wondering how the hell I was supposed to get down, since it was a good ten feet high and I now had to worry about breaking bones. Damn Ahad.

"Hey, there," I said in Senmite. "You know whether this wall runs all the way to Sar-enna-nem?"

The boy frowned, but the old woman merely looked thoughtful. "All things in Arrebaia lead to Sar-enna-nem," she said. "But you may have trouble getting in. Foreigners are more welcome in the city than they used to be, but they are barred from the temple by declaration of our *ennu*."

"Temple?"

"Sar-enna-nem," said the boy, his expression suddenly scornful. "You don't know anything, do you?"

He spoke with the thickest accent I'd heard in centuries, his Senmite inflected by the gulping river flow of the Darren tongue. The woman's Senmite bore only a trace of this. She had learned Senmite early, probably before she'd learned Darre. The boy had done it the other way around. I glanced up as a pack of children near the boy's age ran past, shrieking as children always seem to. They were shrieking in Darre.

"I know a lot of things," I said to the boy, "but not everything. I know Sar-enna-nem *used to be* a temple, long ago, back before the Arameri made the world over. So it's a temple again?" I grinned, delighted. "Whose?"

"All the gods', of course!" The boy put his hands on his hips, having clearly decided I was an idiot. "If you don't like that, you can leave!"

The old woman sighed. "Hush, boy. I didn't raise you to be rude to guests."

"He's a Teman, Beba! Wigyi from school says you can't trust those eyes of theirs."

Before I could retort, the old woman's hand shot out and cuffed the boy. I winced in sympathy at his yelp, but really, a smart child would've known better.

"We will discuss proper comportment for a young man when we get home," she added, and the boy looked chastened at last. Then she focused on me again. "If you didn't know the temple is a temple again, then I doubt you've come looking to pray. What is it that you really want here, stranger?"

"Well, I was looking for your *ennu*—or his daughter Usein, rather." I had vague memories of someone mentioning a Baron Darr. "Where might she be found?"

The old woman narrowed her eyes at me for a long moment before answering. There was an attentiveness in her posture, and I noted the way she shifted her stance back, just a little. She moved her right hand to her hip, too, for easy access to the knife that was almost surely sheathed at the small of her back. Not all of Darr's women were warriors, but this one had been, no doubt about it.

I flashed her my broadest, most innocent smile, hoping she would dismiss me as harmless. She didn't relax—my smile didn't work as well as it had when I'd been a boy—but her lips did twitch in an almost-smile.

"You want the Raringa," she said, nodding westward. The word meant something like "seat of warriors" in one of the older High Northern trade tongues. Where the warriors' council met, no doubt, to advise the young ennu-to-be on her dangerous course of action. I looked around and spotted a low, dome-shaped building not far from Sar-enna-nem. Not nearly so majestic, but then the Darre were not much like the Amn. They judged their leaders by standards other than appearance.

"Anything else?" the old woman asked. "The size and armament of her guard contingent, maybe?"

I rolled my eyes at this, but then paused as a new thought occurred to me. "Yes," I said. "Say something in Darre for me."

Her eyebrows shot toward her hairline, but she said in that tongue, "It's a shame you're mad, pretty foreign boy, because otherwise you might sire interesting daughters. Though perhaps you're just a very stupid assassin, in which case it's better if someone kills you before you breed."

I grinned, climbing to my feet and dusting grass off my pants. "Thanks much, Auntie," I said in Darre, which made both her and the boy gape. The language had changed some since I'd last spoken it; it sounded more like Mencheyev now, and they'd lengthened their vowels and fricatives. I probably still sounded a little strange to them, and I would definitely have to watch my slang, but already I could do a passable imitation of a native speaker. I gave them both a flourishing bow that was probably long out of fashion, then winked and sauntered off toward the Raringa.

I was not the only foreigner about, I saw as I came onto the wide paved plaza that led into the building. Knots of people milled about the area: some locals, others wearing fancy attire from their own lands. Diplomats, perhaps—ah, yes, come a-courting the new power in the region, feeling out the woman who would soon hold its reins. Maybe they were even coming to probe the possibility of an alliance—discreetly, of course. Darr was still very small, and the Arameri were still the Arameri. But it had escaped no one's notice that the world was changing, and this was one of the epicenters of transformation.

Luck favored me as I approached the gates, for the guards there were men. Doubtless because so many of the foreigners hailed from lands ruled by men; a bit of unspoken diplomacy to make them more comfortable. But in Darr, men became guards if they were not handsome enough to marry well or clever enough to serve in some more respected profession, like hunting or forestry. So the pair who watched the Raringa's gates did not notice what smarter men might have, such as my Teman face but lack of Teman hair cabling or the fact that I wore plain clothing. They simply looked me over to be certain I had no obvious weapons, then nodded me onward.

Mortals notice that which stands out, so I didn't. It was simple enough to match my gait and posture to that of other foreigners heading toward this or that meeting, or aides moving in and out of the Raringa's vaulted main doors. The place was not large and had clearly been designed in days when Darr had been a simpler society and its people could just walk in and talk to their leaders. So I found the main council chamber through the biggest set of doors. And I figured out which one of the women seated on the council dais was Usein Darr by the simple fact that her presence practically filled the building.

Not that she was a large woman, even by Darren standards. She sat cross-legged on a low, unadorned divan at the farthest end of the council circle, her head above theirs as they all slouched or reclined on piles of cushioning. If not for that, she would not have been visible at all, hidden by their taller frames. Several feet of long, defiantly straight hair draped her shoulders, night-black, some of it gathered atop her head in an elaborate series of looped and knotted braids; the rest hung free. Her face was a thing of high umber planes and glacial, unadorned slopes: beautiful by any standard, though no Amn would ever have admitted it. And strong, which meant that she was beautiful by Darren standards as well.

The council dais had a gallery of curved benches around it, for the comfort of any spectators who chose to sit through the proceedings. A handful of others, mostly Darre, sat here. I chose an unoccupied bench and settled onto it, watching for a while. Usein said little but nodded now and again as the members of the council each took their turn to talk. She'd propped her hands on her knees in such a way that her elbows jutted out, which I thought was an overly aggressive posture until I belatedly noticed the swell of her belly above her folded legs: she was well into a pregnancy.

I quickly grew bored as I realized that the matter Usein and her councillors were discussing so intently was whether to clear a section of forest to allow coffee growing. Thrilling. I supposed it had been too much to hope that they would discuss their war plans in public. Since I was still tired and just a little hungover, I fell asleep.

Someone shook me an uncountable time later, pulling me from a hazy dream dominated by a woman's bulging belly. Naturally I thought I was still dreaming when I opened my eyes to find another belly hovering in front of me, and naturally I put out a hand to stroke it. I have always found pregnancy fascinating. When mortal women permit, I hover near them, listening for the moment when the child's soul ignites out of nothingness and begins to resonate with mine. The creation of souls is a mystery that we gods endlessly debate. When Nahadoth was born, his soul was fully formed even though no mother ever carried him within her body. Did the Maelstrom give it to him? But only things with souls can bestow souls, or so we have come to believe over the aeons. Does this mean It has a soul? And if so, where did Its soul come from?

All irrelevant questions, because an instant after my hand touched Usein Darr's belly, her knife touched the skin beneath my eye. I came very much awake.

"My apologies, Usein-*ennu*," I said, lifting my hand very carefully. I tried to lift my eyes, too, to focus on her, but it was the knife that dominated my attention. She had been much faster than Hymn, which I supposed was not surprising. I seemed to attract women who were good with a blade.

"Just Usein," she said in Darre. A rude thing to do to an obvious foreigner, and unnecessary, since her knife made its own silent point. "My father is in poor health, but he may live years more, despite the ill wishes of others." Her eyes narrowed. "I imagine women in Tema are no happier to have strangers pawing them, so I see no reason to excuse your behavior."

Swallowing, I finally forced my gaze upward to her face. "My apologies," I said again, also in Darre. One of her eyebrows lifted. "Would you excuse me if I said I'd been dreaming about a woman like you?"

Her lips twitched, considering a smile. "Are you a father already, little boy? You should be at home knitting blankets to warm your babies, if so."

"Not a father and never a father, actually, not that any woman would want children who took after me." (My own smile faltered as I remembered Shahar; then I pushed her out of my mind.) "Congratulations on your conception. May your delivery be swift and your daughter strong."

She shrugged, after a moment taking her knife from my skin. She did not sheathe it, however—a warning. "This babe will be what it is. Probably another son, given that my husband seems to produce nothing else." With a sigh, she put her free hand on her hip. "I noticed you during our council session, pretty boy, and came over to find out more about you. Especially as Temans don't bother coming here anymore; they've made their allegiance to the Arameri clear. So, are you a spy?"

Casting an uneasy glance at her still-naked blade, I considered several lies—then decided the truth was so outrageous that she might believe it more readily. "I'm a godling, sent by an organization of godlings based in Shadow. We think you might be trying to destroy the world. Could you, perhaps, stop?"

She did not react quite as I'd expected. Instead of gaping at me, or laughing, she gazed at me in solemn silence for a long, taut moment. I couldn't read her face at all.

Then she sheathed her knife. "Come with me."

We went to Sar-enna-nem.

Night had fallen while I napped, the moon rising high and full over the branching stone streets. I had only a few moments to glimpse this before Usein Darr and I—accompanied by two sharp-eyed women and a handsome young man who'd greeted Usein with a kiss and me with a threatening look—stepped inside the temple. One of the guardswomen was pregnant, too, though not overtly so because she was stocky and heavyset. Her child's soul had grown, though, so I knew.

The instant I crossed the threshold, I knew why Usein had

brought me here. Magic and faith danced along my skin like raindrops on a pond's surface. I closed my eyes and reveled in it, soaking it in as I walked over the glimmering mosaic stones, letting my reawakened sense of the world steer my feet. It had been months since I'd last felt the world fully. Listening now, I heard songs that had last been sung before the Gods' War, echoing from Sar-enna-nem's ceiling arches. I licked my lips and tasted the spiced wine that had once been used for offerings, tinged with occasional drops of blood. I put out my hands, stroking the air of the place, and shivered as it returned the caress.

Illusions and memories; all I had left. I savored them as best I could.

There had been only a few people in the temple when we'd entered: a man in priest garb, a portly woman carrying two fretting babes, a few worshippers kneeling in a prayer area, and a few unobtrusive guards. I navigated around these and between the small marble statues that stood on plinths all about the chamber, letting resonance guide me. When I opened my eyes, the statue at which I'd stopped gazed back at me with uncharacteristic solemnity on its finely wrought features. I reached up to touch its small, cheeky face, and sighed for my lost beauty.

There was no surprise in Usein Darr's voice. "I thought so. Welcome to Darr, Lord Sieh. Though I heard you stopped involving yourself in mortal affairs after T'vril Arameri's death."

"I had, yes." I turned away from the statue of myself and put one hand on my hip, adopting the same pose. "Circumstances have forced my hand, however."

"And now you help the Arameri who once enslaved you?" She did not, to her credit, laugh.

"No. I'm not doing this for them."

"For the Dark Lord, then? Or my exalted predecessor, Yeine-*ennu*?"

I shook my head and sighed. "No, just me. And a few other godlings and mortals who would rather not see a return to the chaos of the time before the Gods' War."

"Some would call that time 'freedom.' I would think *you* would call it so, given what happened after."

I nodded slowly and sighed. This was a mistake. Glee should never have sent me on a mission like this. I wasn't going to be able to do a very good job of negotiating with Usein, because I didn't really disagree with her goals. I didn't care if the mortal realm descended back into strife and struggle. All I cared about was—

Shahar, her eyes soft and full of a tenderness I'd never expected to see as I taught her everything I knew of pleasure. Deka, still a child, blushing shyly and moving close to me whenever he could—

Distraction. A reminder. I had sworn an oath.

"I remember what your world was like then," I said softly. "I remember when Darre infants starved in their cribs because enemies burned your forests. I remember rivers with water tinted red, fields that bloomed greener and richer because the soil had soaked up so much blood. Is that really what you want to return to?"

She came over, gazing up at the statue's face rather than at me. "Were you the one who made the Walking Death?"

I twitched in surprise and sudden unease.

"It seems like the sort of disease you would create," she said with brutal softness. "Tricksy. There hasn't been an outbreak since Yeine-*ennu*'s day, but I've read the accounts. It lurks for weeks before the symptoms appear, spreading far and wide in the meantime. At its height, the victims of the disease seem more alive than ever, but their minds are dead, burned away by the fever. They walk, but only to carry death to new victims."

I could not look at her, for shame. But when she spoke again, I was surprised to hear compassion in her voice.

"No mortals should have as much power as the Arameri had when they owned you," she said. "No mortals should have as much power as they have *now*: the laws, the scriveners, their army, all their pet nobles, the wealth they've claimed from peoples destroyed or exploited. Even the history taught to our children in the White Hall schools glorifies them and denigrates everyone else. *All civilization*, every bit of it, is made to keep the Arameri strong. That is how they've survived after losing you. That is why the only solution is to destroy everything they've built. Good and bad, all of it is tainted. Only by starting fresh can we truly be free again."

At this, however, I could only smile.

"Start fresh?" I asked. I looked up at the statue of myself. Its blank eyes. I imagined them green, like my own. Like those of Shinda, Itempas's dead demon son.

"For that," I said, "you would have to go further back than the Bright. Remember what caused it, after all—the Gods' War, which was what put me and the other Enefadeh under the Arameri's control in the first place. And remember what caused that: our bickering. Our love affairs gone horribly, horribly wrong." Usein grew silent behind me, in surprise. "To really start fresh, you need to get rid of the gods, not just the Arameri. Then burn every book that mentions us. Smash every statue, including this pretty one here. Raise your children to be ignorant of the world's creation or our existence; let them come up with stories of their own to explain it all. For that matter, kill any child who even *thinks* about magic—because that is how deeply we have tainted mortalkind, Usein Darr." I turned to her and reached out. This time when I put my hand on her swollen belly, she did not draw her knife; she flinched. I smiled. "We're in your blood. Because of us, you know all the wonders and horrors of possibility. And someday, if you don't kill yourselves, if we don't kill you, you might *become* us. So how fresh of a start do you really want?"

Her jaw twitched, the muscles flexing once. I felt her fight for something—courage, maybe. Resolve. Beneath my fingers, her child shifted, pressing briefly against my hand. I felt its shiny new soul thrum in concert with my own for a moment. *His* soul, alas for her poor husband.

After a moment, Usein drew a deep breath. "You wish to know our plans."

"Among other things, yes."

She nodded. "Come, then. I'll show you."

Sar-enna-nem is a pyramid; only the topmost hall of it held prayer space and statues. The next levels down held much more interesting things.

Like masks.

We stood in a gallery of sorts. Our escort had left us at Usein's unseen signal, though her glowering husband had brought an oddly shaped stool so that she could sit. She watched while I strolled about, looking at each mask in turn. The masks lined every shelf; they were set into the walls between the shelves; they were artfully positioned on display tables in front of the shelves. I even glimpsed a few attached to the ceiling. Dozens of them, maybe hundreds, every size and color and configuration, though they had some commonalities. All of them were oval shaped, as a base. All had open eyeholes and sealed mouths. All of them were beautiful, and powerful in ways that had nothing to do with magic.

I stopped at one of the tables, gazing down at a mask that made something inside me sing in response. There, on the table, was Childhood: smooth, fat cheeks; a mischievously grinning mouth; great wide eyes; broad forehead waiting to be filled with knowledge. Subtle inlays and painting around the mouth had been applied, some of it realistic and some pure abstraction. Geometric designs and laugh lines. Somehow, it hinted that the mask's grin could have been simple joy or sadistic cruelty, or joy in cruelty. The eyes could have been alight with the pleasure of learning or aghast at all the evils mortals inflict on their young. I touched its stiff lips. Just wood and paint. And yet.

"Your artist is a master," I said.

"Artists. The art of making these masks isn't purely a Darre thing. The Mencheyev make them, too, and the Tok—and all of our lands got the seed of it from a race called the Ginij. You may remember them."

I did. It had been a standard Arameri extermination. Zhakkarn, via her many selves, had hunted down every last mortal of the race. Kurue erased all mention of them from books, scrolls, stories, and songs, attributing their accomplishments to others. And I? I had set the whole thing in motion by tricking the Ginij king into offending the Arameri so that they had a pretext to attack.

She nodded. "They called this art *dimyi*. I don't know what the word means in their tongue. We call it *dimming*." She shifted to Senmite to make the pun. The word was meaningless in itself, though its root suggested the mask's purpose: to diminish its wearer, reduce them to nothing more than the archetype that the mask represented.

And if that archetype was *Death*...I thought of Nevra and Criscina Arameri, and understood.

"It started as a joke," she continued, "but over time the word has stuck. We lost many of the Ginij techniques when they were destroyed, but I think our dimmers—the artists who make the masks—have done a good job of making up the difference."

I nodded, still staring at Childhood. "There are many of these artists?"

"Enough." She shrugged. Not wholly forthcoming, then.

"Perhaps you should call these artists *assassins* instead." I turned to look at Usein as I said this.

Usein regarded me steadily. "If I wanted to kill Arameri," she said, slowly and precisely, "I wouldn't kill just one, or even a few. And I wouldn't take my time about it."

She wasn't lying. I lowered my hands and frowned, trying to understand. How could she not be lying? "But you *can* do magic with these things." I nodded toward Childhood. "Somehow."

She lifted an eyebrow. "I don't know these people you work for, Lord Sieh. I don't know your aims. Why should I share my secrets with you?"

"We can make it worth your while."

The look she threw me was scornful. I had to admit, it had been a bit clichéd.

"There is nothing you can offer me," she said, getting to her feet with pregnant-woman awkwardness. "Nothing I want or need from anyone, god or mortal—"

"Usein."

A man's voice. I turned, startled. The gallery's open doorway framed a man, standing between the flickering torch sconces. How long had he been there? My sense of the world was fading already. I thought at first it was a trick of the light that he seemed to waver; then I realized what I was seeing: a godling, in the last stages of configuring his form for the mortal realm. But when his face had taken its final shape—

I blinked. Frowned.

He stepped farther into the light. The features he'd chosen certainly hadn't been meant to help him blend in. He was short, about my height. Brown skin, brown eyes, deep brown lips—these were the only things about him that fit any mortal mold. The rest was a jumble. Teman sharpfolds with orangey red islander hair and high, angular High Northern cheekbones. Was he an idiot? None of those things fit together. Just because we could look like anything didn't mean we *should*.

But that was not the biggest problem.

"Hail, Brother," I said uncertainly.

"Do you know me?" He stopped, slipping his hands into his pockets.

"No..." I licked my lips, confused by the niggling sense that I *did* know him, somehow. His face was unfamiliar, but that meant nothing; none of us took our true shape in the mortal realm. His stance, though, and his voice...

Then I remembered. The dream I'd had a few nights before. I'd forgotten it thanks to Shahar's betrayal. *Are you afraid?* he'd asked me.

"Yes," I amended, and he inclined his head.

Usein folded her arms. "Why are you here, Kahl?"

Kahl. The name wasn't familiar, either.

"I won't be staying long, Usein. I came only to suggest that you show Sieh the most interesting of your masks, since he's so curious." His eyes never left mine as he spoke to her.

From the corner of my eye, I saw a muscle in Usein's jaw flex. "That mask isn't complete."

"He asked you how far you were willing to go. Let him see."

She shook her head sharply. "How far *you* are willing to go, Kahl. We have nothing to do with your schemes."

"Oh, I wouldn't call it nothing, Usein. Your people were eager enough for my help when I offered it, and some of you likely guessed what that help would cost. I never deceived you. *You* were the one who chose to renege on our agreement."

There was a curious shiver to the air, and something about Kahl wavered again, not quite visibly. Some aspect of his nature? Ah, but of course; if Usein had indeed reneged on some deal with him, he would consider her a target for vengeance, too. I looked at her, wondering if she knew just how dangerous it was to cultivate a godly enemy. Her lips were tight and her face sheened lightly with sweat as she watched him, her knife hand twitching. Yes. She knew.

"You used us," she said.

"As you used me." He lifted his chin, still watching me. "But that's beside the point. Don't you want your gods to see how powerful you've become, Usein? Show him."

Usein made a frustrated sound, part fear and part annoyance. But she went to one of the wall shelves and pushed aside a book, exposing a previously hidden hole. She reached into it and pulled something. There was a low clack from somewhere behind the shelves, as of an unseen latch opening, and then the whole wall swung outward.

The power that flooded forth staggered me. I gasped and tried to stumble back from it, but I had forgotten the new size of my feet. I tripped and fell against a nearby table, which was the only thing that kept me upright. The radiating waves felt like... like Nahadoth at his worst. No, worse. Like all the weight of every realm pressing down, not on my flesh but on my mind.

And as I panted there, sweat dropping onto my forearms where they trembled on the table, I realized: I had felt this horror before.

There is a resonance, Nahadoth had said.

I managed to force my head upright. My flesh wanted to let go of itself. I fought to remain corporeal, since I wasn't sure I'd be able to re-form if I didn't. Across the room I saw that Kahl had stepped back, too, bracing his hand against the door frame; his expression was unsurprised, grimly enduring. But elated, too.

"What...?" I tried to focus on Usein, but my sight blurred. "What is..."

She stepped into the hidden alcove that had been revealed by the opened wall. There, on a darkwood plinth, sat another mask—one that was nothing like the others. It seemed to be made of frosted glass. Its shape was more elaborate than an oval, the edges fluted and geometric. I thought it might hurt the face of whoever donned it. It was larger than a standard mask, too, bearing flanges and extensions at jawline and forehead that reminded me, somehow, of wings. Of flight. Of falling, down, down, through a vortex whose walls churned with a roar that could shatter the mortal realm—

Usein picked it up, apparently heedless of its power. Couldn't she feel it? How could she bring her child near something so terrible? There were no torches in the alcove; the thing glowed with its own soft, shifting light. Where Usein's fingers touched it, I saw a hint of movement, just for an instant. The glass turned to smooth brown flesh like the hand that held it, then faded back to glass.

"This mask—or so Kahl tells me—has a special power," she said, glancing at me. Then she narrowed her eyes at Kahl, who nodded in return, though he was looking decidedly uncomfortable, too. Hard to tell anything, looking at that stoic face of his. "When it's complete, if it works as predicted, it will confer godhood upon its wearer."

I stiffened. Looked at Kahl, who merely smiled at me. "That's not possible."

"Of course it is," he said. "Yeine is the proof of that."

I shook my head. "She was special. Unique. Her soul—"

"Yes, I know." His gaze was glacially cold, and I remembered the moment he'd committed himself to being my enemy. Had the same expression been on his face then? If so, I would have tried harder to earn his forgiveness. "The conjunction of many elements, all in just the right proportion and strength, all at just the right time. Of such a recipe is divinity made." He gestured toward the mask; his hand shook and grew blurry before he lowered it. "Godsblood and mortal life, magic and art and the vagaries of chance. And more, all bound into that mask, all to impress upon those who view it, an *idea*."

Usein set the thing down on the carved wooden face that served as its stand. "Yes. And the first mortal who put it on burned to death from the inside out. It took three days; she screamed the whole time. The fire was so hot that we couldn't get near enough to end her misery." She turned a hard look on Kahl. "That thing is evil."

"Merely incomplete. The raw energy of creation is neither good nor evil. But when that mask is ready, it will churn forth something new... and wondrous." He paused, his expression turning inward for a moment; he spoke softer, as if to himself, but I realized that his words were actually aimed at me. "I will not be a slave to fate. I will embrace it, control it. I will be what I *wish* to be."

"You're mad." Usein shook her head. "You expect us to put this kind of power into your hands, for demons know what purpose? No. Leave this place, Kahl. We've had enough of your kind of help."

I hurt. The incomplete mask. It was like the Maelstrom: potential gone mad, creation feeding upon itself. I was not mortal enough to be immune to it. Yet that was not the sole source of my discomfort; something else beat against me like an oncoming tide, trying to drive me to my knees. The mask had heightened my god-senses, allowing me to feel it, but my flesh was only mortal, too weak to endure so much power in one place.

"What are you?" I asked Kahl in our words, between gasps. "Elontid? Imbalance..." That was the only explanation for the seesaw flux I felt from him. Resolve and sorrow, hatred and longing, ambition and loneliness. But how could there be another elontid in the world? He could not have been born during the time of my incarceration, not with Enefa dead and all gods rendered sterile for that time. And who were his parents? Itempas was the only one of the Three who could have made him, but Itempas did not mate with godlings.

Kahl smiled. To my surprise, there was no hint of cruelty in it—only that curious, resolute sorrow I'd heard in my dream.

"Enefa is dead, Sieh." His voice was soft now. "Not all her works vanished with her, but some did. *I* remembered. You will, too, eventually."

Remember what?

forget

Forget what?

Kahl staggered suddenly, bracing himself against the door and sighing. "Enough. We'll finish this later. In the meantime, a word of advice, Sieh: find Itempas. Only his power can save you; you know this. Find him, and live for as long as you can." When he pushed himself upright, his teeth were a carnivore's, needle-sharp. "Then if you must die, die like a god. At my hands, in battle."

Then he vanished. And I was alone, helpless, being churned to pieces by the mask's power. My flesh tried, again, to fragment; it *hurt*, the way disintegration should. I screamed, reaching out for someone, anyone, to save me. Nahadoth—No, I didn't want him or Yeine anywhere near that mask, no telling what it would do to them. But I was so afraid. I did not want to die, not yet.

The world twisted around me. I slid through it, gasping—

Rough hands grasped me, hauled me over onto my back. Above me, Ahad's face. Not Nahadoth but close enough. He was frowning, examining me with hands and other senses, actually looking concerned.

"You care," I said dizzily, and stopped thinking for a while.

12

Wᴴᴇɴ I ᴡᴏᴋᴇ, I told Ahad what I had seen in Darr, and he got a very odd look on his face. "That was not at all what we suspected," he muttered to himself. He looked over at Glee, who stood by the window, her hands clasped behind her back, as she gazed out over the quiet streets. It was nearly dawn in this part of the world. The end of the working day for the Arms of Night.

"Call the others," she said. "We'll meet tomorrow night."

So Ahad dismissed me for the day, ordering the servants to give me food and money and new clothing, because the old set no longer fit well. I had aged again, you see—perhaps five years this time, passing through my final growth spurt in the process. I was two inches taller and even thinner than before, unpleasantly close to skeletal. My body had reconfigured its existing substance to forge my new shape, and I hadn't had much substance to go around. I was well into my twenties now, with no hint of childhood remaining. Nothing but human left.

I went back to Hymn's house. Her family ran an inn, after all, and I had money now, so it made sense. Hymn was relieved to see me, though she puzzled over my changed appearance and pretended to be annoyed. Her parents were not at all pleased, but I promised to perform no impossible feats on their premises, which was easy because I couldn't. They put me in the attic room.

There, I ate the entire basket of food Ahad's servants had packed for me. I was still hungry when the food was gone— though the basket had been generously packed—but had sated myself enough that I could attend to other needs. So I curled up on the bed, which was hard but clean, and watched the sun rise beyond my lone window. Eventually I considered the topic of death.

I could kill myself now, probably. This was not normally an easy thing for any god to do, as we are remarkably resilient beings. Even willing ourselves into nonexistence did not work for long; eventually we would forget that we were supposed to be dead and start thinking again. Yeine could kill me, but I would never ask it of her. Some of my siblings, and Naha, could and would do it, because they understood that sometimes life is too much to bear. But I did not need them anymore. The past two nights' events had verified what I'd already suspected: those things that had once merely weakened me before could kill me now. So if I could steel myself to the pain of it, I could die whenever I wished simply by continuing to contemplate antithetical thoughts until I became an old man, and then a corpse.

And perhaps it was even simpler than that. I needed to eat and drink and pass waste now. That meant I could starve and thirst, and that my intestines and other organs were actually necessary. If I damaged them, they might not grow back.

What would be the most exciting way to commit suicide?

Because I did not want to die an old man. Kahl had gotten that much right. If I had to die, I would die as myself—as Sieh, the Trickster, if not the child. I had blazed bright in my life. What was wrong with blazing in death, too?

Before I reached middle age, I decided. Surely I could think of something interesting by then.

On that heartening note, I finally slept.

* * *

I stood on a cliff outside the city, gazing upon the wonder that was Sky-in-Shadow and the looming, spreading green of the World Tree.

"Hello, Brother."

I turned, blinking, though I was not really surprised. When the first mortal creatures grew the first brains that did more than pump hearts and think of meat, my brother Nsana had found fulfillment in the random, spitting interstices of their sleeping thoughts. He had been a wanderer before that, my closest playmate, wild and free like me. But sad, somehow. Empty. Until the dreams of mortals filled his soul.

I smiled at him, understanding at last the sorrow he must have felt in those long empty years before the settling of his nature.

"So this is the proof of it," I said. I had pockets for the moment, so I slipped my hands into them. My voice was higher pitched; I was a boy again. In dreams, at least, I was still myself.

Nsana smiled, strolling toward me along a path of flowers that stirred without wind. For a moment his truest shape flickered before me: faceless, the color of glass, reflecting our surroundings through the distorting lenses of limbs and belly and the gentle featureless curve of his face. Then he filled in with detail and colors, though not those of a mortal. He did nothing like mortals if he could help it. So he had chosen skin like fine fabric, unbleached damask in swirling raised patterns, with hair like the darkest of red wine frozen in midsplash. His irises were the banded amber of polished, petrified wood—beautiful, but unnerving, like the eyes of a serpent.

"The proof of what?" he asked, stopping before me. His voice was light, teasing, as if it had been only a day since we'd seen each other and not an aeon.

"My mortality," I said. "I wouldn't have seen you otherwise." I smiled, but I knew he would hear the truth in my voice. He had abandoned me for mortalkind, after all. I'd gotten over it; I was a big boy. But I would not pretend it hadn't happened.

Nsana let out a little sigh and walked past me, stopping on the edge of a cliff. "Gods can dream, too, Sieh. You could have found me here anytime."

"I hate dreaming." I scuffed the ground with a foot.

"I know." He put his hands on his hips, his expression frankly admiring as he gazed over the dreamscape I'd created. This one was not merely a memory, as my dream of the gods' realm had been. "A shame, too. You do it so well."

"I don't *do* anything. It's a dream."

"Of course you do. It comes from you, after all. All of this"— he gestured expansively around us, and the dreamscape rippled with the passage of his hands—"is you. Even the fact that you let me come here is your doing, because you certainly never allowed it before." He lowered his arms and looked at me. "Not even during the years you spent as an Arameri slave."

I sighed, tired, even asleep. "I don't want to think right now, Nsa. Please."

"You never want to think, you silly boy." Nsana came over, wrapping an arm around my shoulders and pulling me close. I put up a token resistance, but he knew it was token, and after a moment I sighed and let my head rest on his chest. Then it was not his chest—it was his shoulder—because suddenly I was taller than him and not a child anymore. When I lifted my head in surprise, Nsana let out a long sigh and cupped my face in his hands so that he could kiss me. He did not share himself with me that way because there was no point; I already stood encompassed within him, and he within me. But I did remember other kisses, and other existences, when innocence and dreams had been two halves of the same coin. Back then, I'd thought we would spend the rest of eternity together.

The dreamscape changed around us. When we parted, Nsana sighed, the fabric patterns of his face shifting into new lines. They hinted at words, but meant nothing.

"You're not a child anymore, Sieh," he said. "Time to grow up now."

We stood on the streets of the First City. Everything that mortals will or might become is foreshadowed in the gods' realm, where time is an accessory rather than a given, and the essences of the Three mingle in a different balance depending on their whims and moods. Because Itempas had been banished and diminished, only the barest remnant of his order held sway now. The city, which had been recognizable just a few years before, was only barely so now, and it shifted every few moments in some cycle we could not fathom. Or perhaps that was because this was a dream? With Nsana, there was no telling.

So he and I walked along cobblestoned streets that turned into smoothly paved sidewalks, stepping onto moving metal pathways now and again as they grew from the cobblestones and then melted away, as if tired. Pathways of mushrooms grew and withered in our wake. Each block, some of which were circular, held squat buildings of painted wood, and stately domes of hewn marble, and the occasional thatched hut. Curious, I peered into one of these buildings through its slanted window. It was dim, full of hulking shapes too distorted and uncomfortable-looking to be furniture, its walls decorated with blank paintings. Something within moved toward the window, and I backed up quickly. I wasn't a god anymore. Had to be careful.

We were shadowed now and again by great towers of glass and steel that floated, cloudlike, a few meters off the ground. One of them followed us for two blocks, like a lonely puppy, before it finally turned with a foggy groan and drifted down another avenue. No one walked with us, though we felt the presence of others of our brethren, some watching, some uncaring. The City attracted them because it was beautiful, but I could not understand how they endured it. What was a city without inhabitants? It was like life without breathing, or friendship without love; what was the point?

But there was something in the distance that caught my attention, and Nsana's, too. Deep in the City's heart, taller and more still than the floating skyscrapers: a smooth, shining white tower without windows or doors. Even amid the jumbled, clashing architecture of that place, it was clear: this tower did not belong.

I stopped and frowned up at it, as a mushroom taller than Nsa spread its ribbed canopy over our heads. "What is that?"

Nsana willed us closer, folding the city until we stood at the tower's feet. This confirmed there were no doors, and I curled my lip as I realized the thing was made of daystone. A little piece of Sky amid the dreams of gods: an abomination.

"You have brought this here," said Nsana.

"The hells I did."

"Who else would have, Sieh? I touch the mortal realm only through its dreams, and it does not touch me. It has never marked me."

I threw a sharp look at him. "Marked? Is that how you think of me?"

"Of course, Sieh. You *are*." I stared at him, wondering whether to feel hurt or angry or something else entirely, and Nsana sighed. "As I am marked by your abandonment. As we are all marked by the War. Did you think the horrors you've endured would simply slough away when you became a free god? They have become part of you." But before I could muster a furious retort, Nsana frowned up at the tower again. "There is more to this, though, than just bad experiences."

"What?"

Nsana reached out, laying a hand on the surface of the white tower. It glowed like Sky at night beneath his touch, becoming translucent—and within the tower, suddenly, I could see the shadow of some vast, twisting shape. It filled the tower, brown and indistinct, like ordure. Or a cancer.

"There's a secret here," said Nsana.

"What, in my dreams?"

"In your soul." He looked at me, thoughtful. "It must be old, to have grown so powerful. Important."

I shook my head, but even as I did so, I doubted.

"My secrets are small, silly things," I said, trying to ignore that worm of doubt. "I kept the bones of the Arameri I killed in a stash beneath the family head's bedroom. I piss in the punch bowl at weddings. I change directions on maps so they make no sense. I stole some of Nahadoth's hair once, just to see if I could, and it almost ate me alive—"

He looked hard at me. "You have childish secrets and adult ones, Sieh, because you have never been as simple as you claim or wish to be. And this one—" He slapped the tower, making a sound that echoed from the empty streets around us. "This one is something you've kept even from yourself."

I laughed, but it was uneasy. "I can't keep a secret from myself. That doesn't make any sense."

"When have you ever made sense? It's something you've forgotten."

"But I—"

forget

I faltered, silent. It was cold all of a sudden. I began shivering, though Nsana—who wore only his hair—was fine. But his eyes had narrowed suddenly, and abruptly I realized he'd heard that odd little burp of my thoughts.

"That was Enefa's voice," he said.

"I don't . . ." But it had been. It had always been Mother whispering in my soul, nudging my thoughts away from this place when they got too close. Her voice: *forget*.

"Something you've forgotten," Nsana said softly, "but perhaps not by your own will."

I frowned, torn between confusion and alarm and fear. And above us, in the white tower, the dark thing shifted with a low rumbling groan. There was the faintest sound of stone shifting, and when I looked up at the tower, I spied a series of fine, barely noticeable cracks in its daystone surface.

Something I had forgotten. Something Enefa had *made me* forget. But Enefa was gone now, and whatever she had done to me was beginning to wear off.

"Gods and mortals and demons in between." I rubbed my face. "I don't want to deal with this, Nsa. My life is hard enough right now."

Nsana sighed, and his sigh transformed the City into a

playground of delights and horrors. A high, steep slide ended in a pit of chewing, flensing, disembodied teeth. The chains on a nearby swing set were wet with oil and blood. I could not see the trap in the seesaw, but I was certain there was one. It was too innocent-looking—like me, when I am up to something.

"Time for you to grow up," he said again. "You ran away from me rather than do it before. Now you have no choice."

"I had no choice before!" I rounded on him. "Growing old will kill me!"

"I didn't say grow old, you fool. I said grow *up*." Nsana leaned close, his breath redolent of honey and poisonous flowers. "Just because you're a child doesn't mean you have to be immature, for the Maelstrom's sake! I have known you long and well, my brother, and there's another secret you hide from yourself, only you do a terrible job so everyone knows: you're lonely. You're always lonely, even though you've left more lovers in your wake than you can count. You never want what you have, only what you can't!"

"That's not—"

He cut me off ruthlessly. "You loved me before I learned my nature. While I needed you. Then when I found my strength and became whole, when I no longer *needed* you but still *wanted* you—" He paused suddenly, his jaw flexing as he choked back words too painful to speak. I stared back at him, rendered speechless. Had he really felt this way, all this time? Was that how he'd seen it? I had always thought *he* had left *me*. I shook my head in wonder, in denial.

"You cannot be one of the Three," he whispered. I flinched. "It's long past time you accepted that. You want someone you can never leave behind. But *think*, Sieh. Not even the Three are like that. Itempas betrayed all of us and himself. Enefa grew self-ish, and Nahadoth has always been fickle. This new one, Yeine, she'll break your heart, too. Because you want something that she can never give you. You want perfection."

"Not perfection," I blurted, and then felt ill as I realized I had confirmed everything else he'd said. "Not...perfection. Just..." I licked my lips, ran my hands through my hair. "I want someone who is *mine*. I...I don't even know..." I sighed. "The Three, Nsana, they are *the Three*. Three facets of the same diamond, whole even when separate. No matter how far apart they drift, they always, always, come back together eventually. That closeness..."

It was what Shahar had with Deka, I realized: a closeness that few outsiders would ever comprehend or penetrate. More than blood-deep—soul-deep. She hadn't seen him for half her life and she'd still betrayed me for him.

What would it be like to have that kind of love for myself?

I wanted it, yes. Gods, yes. And I did not really want it from Yeine or Nahadoth or Itempas, because they had each other and it would have been wrong to interfere with that. But I wanted something like it.

Nsana sighed. Here in my dream, he was supreme; he could know my every thought and whim if he wanted, without even trying. So of course he knew now that he had never been enough for me.

"I'm sorry," I said, very softly.

"You certainly are." Looking sour, Nsana turned away for a moment, contemplating his own thoughts. Then he sighed and faced me again.

"Fine," he said. "You need help, and I'm not so churlish that

I'd ignore your need. So I'll try to find out more about this secret of yours. At the rate you're going, you'll be dead before you figure it out."

I lowered my eyes. "Thank you."

"Don't thank me, Sieh." He gestured, and I followed this movement to see a little patch of flowers on one side of the playground. Amid dozens of black daisies that bobbed and swayed in the cool breeze, a single white-petaled flower stood utterly still. It was not a daisy. I had seen such a flower before: an altarskirt rose, one of a rare variety bred in High North. The white tower of my secret, repeating itself across theme and form.

"This secret will hurt when it is finally revealed," he said.

I nodded slowly, my eyes on that single frightening flower. "Yes. I can see that."

The hand on my shoulder caught me by surprise, and I turned to see that Nsana's mood had changed again: he was no longer exasperated with me, but something closer to pitying. "So many troubles," he said. "Impending death, our parents' madness, and I see someone has broken your heart recently, too."

I looked away at this. "It's no one. Just a mortal."

"Love levels the ground between us and them. When they break our hearts, it hurts the same as if the deed were done by one of our own." He cupped the back of my head, ruffling my hair companionably, and I smiled weakly and tried not to show how much I really wanted a kiss instead. "Ah, my brother. Do stop being stupid, will you?"

"Nsana, I—"

He put a finger over my lips, and I fell silent.

"Hush," he murmured, then leaned close. I closed my eyes, waiting for the touch of his lips, but they came where I had not been expecting them: on my forehead. When I blinked at him, he smiled, and it was full of sorrow.

"I'm a god, not a stone," he said. I flushed in shame. He stroked my cheek. "But I will love you always, Sieh."

I woke in the dark and cried myself back to sleep. If I dreamt again before morning, I did not remember it. Nsa was kind like that.

My hair had grown again, though not as much as before. Only a couple of feet. Nails, too, this time; the longest was four inches, jagged and beginning to curl. I begged scissors from Hymn and chopped off both as best I could. I had to get Hymn's father to teach me how to shave. This so amused him that he forgot to be afraid of me for a few minutes, and we actually shared a laugh when I cut myself and yelled out a very bad word. Then he started to worry that I would cut myself and blow up the house someday. We don't read minds, but some things are easy for anyone to guess. I excused myself then and went off to work.

I offended the Arms of Night's housemistress immediately by coming in through the main door. She took me back out and showed me the servants' door, an unobtrusive entrance at the house's side, leading to its basement level. It was a better door, quite frankly; I have always preferred back entrances. Good for sneaking. But my pride was stung enough that I complained, anyway. "What, I'm not good enough to come in the front?"

"Not if you're not paying," she snapped.

Inside, another servant greeted me and let me know that Ahad had left instructions in case of my arrival. So I followed him through the basement into what appeared to be a rather

mundane meeting room. There were stiff-backed chairs that
looked as though they had absorbed years' worth of boredom,
and a wide, square table on which sat an untouched platter of
meats and fruits. I barely noticed all this, however, for I had
stopped, my blood going cold as I registered who sat at the
room's wide table with Ahad. Nemmer.

And Kitr. And Eyem-sutah. And Glee, the only mortal. And,
of all the insanities, Lil.

Five of my siblings, sitting about a meeting table as though
they had never spun through the vortices of the outermost
cosmos as laughing sparkles. Three of the five hated me. The
fourth might; no way of knowing with Eyem-sutah. The fifth
had tried to eat me more than once. She would very likely try
again, now that I was mortal.

*If there's anything edible left when the others get done with me,
that is.* I set my jaw to hide my fear, which probably telegraphed
it clearly.

"About time," said Ahad. He nodded to the servant, who
closed the door to leave us alone. "Please, Sieh, sit down."

I did not move, hating him more than ever. I should have
known better than to trust him.

With a sigh of mild annoyance, Ahad added, "None of us
are stupid, Sieh. Harming you means incurring Yeine's and
Nahadoth's displeasure. Do you honestly think we would do
that?"

"I don't know, Ahad," said Kitr, who was smiling viciously at
me. "I might."

Ahad rolled his eyes. "You won't, so be silent. Sieh, sit *down*.
We have business to discuss."

I was so startled by Ahad's shutdown of Kitr that I forgot my fear. Kitr, too, looked more astonished than affronted. Any fool could tell that Ahad was the youngest of us, and inexperience meant weakness among our kind. He *was* weak, lacking the crucial means of making himself stronger. Yet there was no hint of fear in his eyes as he met her glare, and to my amazement—and everyone else's, to judge by their expressions—Kitr said nothing in reply.

Feeling vaguely unimportant in the wake of this, I came to the table and sat down.

"So what the hells is this?" I asked, choosing a chair with no one on either side of me. "The weekly meeting of the Godlings' Auxiliary, Lower Shadow Chapter?"

They all glowered. Except Lil, who laughed. Good old Lil. I had always liked her, when she wasn't asking for my limbs as snacks. She leaned forward. "We are *conspiring*," she said. Her raspy voice was filled with such childlike glee that I grinned back.

"This is about Darr, then." I looked at Ahad, wondering if he had told them about the mask already.

"This is about many things," he replied. He alone had a comfortable chair; someone had carted in the big leather chair from his office. "All of which may fit into a larger picture."

"Not just the pieces you've discovered." Nemmer smiled sweetly. "Isn't that why you contacted me, Brother? You're turning mortal, and it's making you pay attention to more than your own ass for a change. But I thought you were staying in Sky. Did the Arameri throw you out?"

Kitr laughed hard enough to make the hairs on the back of my neck bristle. "Gods, Ahad, you said he was powerless, but I never dreamt it would be this bad. You're *mortal*, Sieh. What good can you do in all this? Nothing but run to Daddy and Mommy—who aren't here now to protect you." Her eyes fixed on me, her smile fading, and I knew she was remembering the War. I was remembering it, too. Beneath the table, my hands clenched into fists and I wished I had my claws.

Eyem-sutah, who had not fought because he'd loved a mortal and had nearly killed himself protecting her, let out a long, weary sigh. "Please," he said. "Please. This helps nothing."

"Indeed, it does not," said Ahad, looking at all of us with contempt. "So if we are agreed that no one is a child here, not even the one who should be, can we then please focus on events of *this* millennium?"

"I don't like your tone—" began Kitr, but then to my greater surprise, Glee cut her off.

"I have limited time," she said. She seemed so completely at ease in a room full of godlings that I wondered again if she might be Arameri. It was far back in her lineage if so; she looked to be pure-blooded Maroneh.

To my surprise, all my siblings fell silent at her words, looking at her with a combination of consternation and unease. This made me even more curious—so Ahad was not the only one who deferred to her?—but that curiosity would have to remain unsatisfied for the moment.

"All right, then," I said, addressing Ahad because he seemed to be at least trying to stay focused. "Who's going to go take that mask and destroy it?"

"No one." Ahad steepled his fingers.

"Excuse me?" Kitr spoke before I could. "Based on what you've told us, Ahad, nothing so powerful should be left in mortal hands."

"And what better hands are there for it?" He looked around the table, and I flinched as I realized what he meant. Nemmer, too, sighed and sat back. "One of us? Nahadoth? Yeine?"

"It would make more sense—" Kitr began.

"No," said Nemmer. "No. Remember what happened the last time a god got hold of a powerful mortal weapon." At this, Eyem-sutah, who had chosen to resemble an Amn, went pale.

Kitr's face tightened. "You don't know that this mask is even dangerous to us. It hurt *him*." She jabbed a thumb at me, her lip curling. "But harsh language could hurt him now."

"It hurt Kahl, too," I said, scowling. "The thing is broken, incomplete. Whatever it's supposed to do, it's doing it wrong. But as powerful as it is now, I see no reason why we should wait for the mortals to *complete* it before we act." I glared at Ahad, and at Glee, too. "You know what mortals are capable of."

"Yes, the same things as gods, on a smaller scale," Ahad replied, his voice bland.

Glee glanced at him, but I could not read the look on her face before she turned to me. "There is more to this than you know."

"So tell me!" Ahad I was used to. He kept secrets like I kept toys, and he did it mostly out of spite. Glee hadn't seemed the type, however.

"You aren't a child anymore, Sieh. You should learn patience," Ahad drawled. His smirk faded. "But you're right; an explanation may be in order since you're new, both to our organization and to Shadow. This group's original purpose was merely to police our own behavior and prevent another Interdiction. To a degree, that is still our purpose. Things changed, however, when a few mortals used demons' blood to express their displeasure at our arrival." He sighed, crossing his legs and leaning back in his chair. "This was a few years back. You may recall the time."

Of course I did. A handful of my siblings had been killed, and Nahadoth had come very close to turning Sky-in- Shadow into a large smoking crater. "Hard to forget."

He nodded. "This group had already organized in order to protect *them* from *us*. After that incident, it became clear that we should also work to protect *us* from *them* as well."

"That's stupid," I said, frowning around the table. Glee lifted an eyebrow, and I grimaced but ignored her. "The demon was taken care of; the menace has ended. What is there to fear? Any one of you could smash this city, melt down the surrounding mountains, make the Eyeglass's water burn—"

"No," said Eyem-sutah. "We cannot. If we do, Yeine will revoke our right to dwell here. You don't understand, Sieh; you didn't *want* to come back after your incarceration ended. I don't blame you, given circumstances. But would you truly prefer never to visit the mortal realm again?"

"That's beside the—"

Eyem-sutah shook his head and leaned forward, cutting me off. "Tell me you have never nestled into some mortal woman's breast to be held, Sieh, and loved unconditionally. Or felt adoration when some mortal man tousles your hair. Tell me they mean nothing to you. Look into my eyes and say it, and I will believe you."

I could have done it. I am a trickster. I can look into anyone's eyes and say anything I need to say and be completely believable in the process. Only Nahadoth, who knows me better than any other, and Itempas, who always knows falsehood, have ever been able to catch me out when I truly want to lie.

But even tricksters are not without honor, as Eyem-sutah well knew. He was right, and it would have been wrong of me not to acknowledge that. So I lowered my eyes, and he sat back.

"Out of such debate was this organization born," Ahad said, with only a hint of dryness. "Not all godlings have chosen to participate, but most adhere to the rules we set, out of mutual self-interest." He shrugged. "Those who do not, we deal with."

I propped my chin on my fist, pretending boredom to hide the unease Eyem-sutah's questions had left in me. "Fine. But how'd you end up in charge? You're an infant."

Ahad smiled by curling his upper lip. "No one else wanted the task, after Madding died. Lately, however, our structure has changed. Now I'm merely the organizer, at least until such time as our actual leader chooses to take a more active role."

"And your leader is...?" Not that I thought he'd tell me.

"Does it matter?"

I considered. "I guess not. But this is all awfully...*mortal*, don't you think?" I gestured around at the meeting room, the table and chairs, the tray of bland finger foods. (I restrained my urge to reach for a piece of cheese, out of pride.) "Why not come up with some sinister-sounding name, too, if you're going to go this far? 'The Organization' or something original like that. Whatever, if we're going to act like a bunch of mortals."

"We have no need of a name." Ahad shrugged, then glanced pointedly at Glee. "And our group consists of more than just gods, which requires some concession to mortal convention." Glee inclined her head to him in silent thanks. "In any case, we dwell in the mortal realm. Should we not at least attempt to think like mortals from time to time, in order to anticipate our adversaries more easily?"

"And then do nothing when we actually discover a threat?" Kitr clenched a fist on the table.

Ahad's expression went Arameri-neutral. "What, precisely, would you have us do, Kitr? Go and take this mask? We don't know who created it, or how; they could simply make another. We don't know what it does. Sieh said this Kahl seemed to be using the Darre to create it. Doesn't that imply it's something mortals can touch but that might strike a god dead?"

I frowned, unwilling to concede the point. "We have to do *something*. The thing is dangerous."

"Very well. Shall we capture Usein Darr, torture her to learn her secrets? We could threaten to give her unborn child to Lil, perhaps." Lil, who had been staring at the plate of food, smiled and said "Mmmmm" without taking her eyes away from it. "Or shall we dispense with subtlety and smite Darr with fire and pestilence and erasure, until its cities are in ruins and its people forgotten? Does that sound at all familiar to you, *Enefadeh*?"

Every voluntary muscle in my body locked in fury. En pulsed once, questioningly, against my chest—did I want it to kill someone again? It was still tired from my rage at Remath, but it would try.

That, and that alone, calmed me. I put my hand over En, stroking it through my shirt. No more killing now, but it was a good little star for wanting to help. With another pulse of pleasure, En cooled back into sleep.

"We are not the Arameri," Ahad said, speaking softly, though his eyes stayed on me. Demanding my acknowledgment. "We are not Itempas. We cannot repeat the mistakes of the past. Again and again our kind have tried to dominate mortalkind and have harmed ourselves in the doing. This time, if we choose to dwell among mortals, then we must share the risks of mortality. We must *live* in this world, not merely visit it. Do you understand?"

Of course I did. *Mortals are as much Enefa's creations as we ourselves.* I had argued this with my fellow prisoners a century ago as we contemplated using a mortal girl's life to achieve our freedom. We'd done it anyway, and the plan had been successful—more in spite of our efforts than because of them—but I had felt the guilt keenly back then. And the fear: for if we did as Itempas and his pet Arameri had done, did we not risk becoming just like them?

"I understand," I said, very softly.

Ahad watched me a moment longer, then nodded.

Glee sighed. "I'm more concerned about this Kahl than any mortal magic. No godling by that name is on any city registry. What do the rest of you know of him?" She looked around the table.

No one responded. Kitr and Nemmer looked at each other, and at Eyem-sutah, who shrugged. Then they all looked at me. My mouth fell open. "*None* of you knows him?"

"We thought you would," Eyem-sutah said. "You're the only one who was around when all of us were born."

"No." I chewed my lip in consternation. "I could swear I've heard the name before, but..." The memory danced on the edge of my consciousness, closer than ever before.

forget, whispered Enefa's voice. I sighed in frustration.

"He's elontid," I said, staring at my own clenched fist. "I'm sure of that. And he's young—I think. Maybe a little older than the War." But Madding had been the last godling born before the War. Even before him, Enefa had made few children in the last aeon or so—certainly no elontid. She had lost the heart for childbearing after seeing so many of her sons and daughters murdered in the battle against the demons.

Would that you were a true child, she would say to me sometimes while stroking my hair. I lived for such moments. She was not much given to affection. *Would that you could stay with me forever.*

But I can, I would always point out, and the look in her eyes would turn inward and sad in a way that I did not understand. *I will never grow old, never grow up. I can be your little boy forever.*

Would that this were true, she would say.

I blinked, frowning. I had forgotten that conversation. What had she meant by—

"Elontid," said Ahad, almost to himself. "The ones borne of god and godling, or Nahadoth and Itempas." He turned a speculative look on Lil. She had begun to stroke one of the strawberries on the platter, her bony, jagged-nailed finger trailing back and forth over its curve in a way that would have been sensual in anyone else. She finally looked away from the platter but kept fingering the strawberry.

"I do not know a Kahl," she said, and smiled. "But we do not always wish to be known."

Glee frowned. "What?"

Lil shrugged. "We elontid are feared by mortals and gods alike. Not without reason." She threw me a glance that was pure lasciviousness. "You smell delicious now, Sieh."

I flushed and deliberately took something off the platter. Cucumber slathered with maash paste and comry eggs. I made a show of stuffing it into my mouth and swallowing it barely chewed. She pouted; I ignored her and turned to Glee.

"What Lil means," I said, "is that the elontid are different. They aren't quite godlings, aren't quite gods. They're"—I thought a moment—"more like the Maelstrom than the rest of us. They flux and wane, create and devour, each in their own way. It makes them...hard to grasp." I glanced at Lil, and when I did, she scooped up a cucumber slice and downed it in a blur, then stuck her tongue out at me. I laughed in spite of myself. "If any god could conceal his presence in the world, it would be an elontid."

Glee tapped a finger on the table, thoughtful. "Could they hide even from the Three?"

"No. Not if they united. But the Three have had their own problems to worry about for some time now. They are incomplete." I blinked then, as something new occurred to me. "And the Three could be *why* none of us remembers this Kahl. Enefa, I mean. She might have made all of us—"

forget

Shut up, Mother, I thought irritably.

"—forget."

"Why would she do that?" Eyem-sutah looked around, his eyes widening. "That makes no sense."

"No," said Nemmer softly. She met my eyes, and I nodded. She was one of the older ones among us—nowhere near my age, but she had been around to see the war against the demons. She knew the many strange configurations that could result among the children of the Three. "It makes perfect sense. Enefa—" She grimaced. "She had no problem killing us. And she would do it, if any of her children were a threat to the rest. After the demons, she wasn't willing to take more risks. But if a child *could* survive without harming others, and if that child's survival depended for some reason on others not knowing of its existence…" She shook her head. "It's possible. She might have even created some new realm to house him, apart from the rest of us. And when she died, she took the knowledge of that child with her."

I thought of Kahl's intimation. *Enefa is dead now. I remembered.* Nemmer's theory fit, but for one thing.

"Where's this elontid's other parent? Most of us wouldn't just leave a child to rot in some heaven or hell forever. New life among our kind is too precious."

"It has to be a godling," Ahad mused. "If it were Itempas or Nahadoth, this Kahl would just be"—his mouth began to shape the word *normal*, but then Lil turned a glare on him to make Itempas proud, and he amended himself—"niwwah, like the rest of you."

"I am mnasat," Kitr snapped, glaring herself.

"Whatever," Ahad replied, and I was suddenly glad the platter's paring knife was out of Kitr's reach. Hopefully Ahad would find his nature soon; he wasn't going to last long among us otherwise.

"Many godlings died in the War," said Glee, and we all sobered as we realized what she meant.

"Gods," murmured Kitr, looking horrified. "To be raised in exile, forgotten, orphaned…Did this Kahl even know how to find us? How long was he alone? I can't imagine it."

I could. The universe had been much emptier once. There had been no word for *loneliness* back then, in my true childhood, but all three of my parents—Nahadoth in particular— had worked hard to protect me from it. If Kahl had lacked the same…I could not help but pity him.

"This complicates things to an unpleasant degree," said Ahad, sighing and rubbing his eyes. I felt the same. "From what you reported, Sieh, it sounds as though the High Northers and Kahl are working at cross-purposes. He's using their dimmers to create a mask that turns mortals into gods, for some reason I can't fathom. And they are using the same art to create masks that somehow kill Arameri."

"Or else *Kahl* has been killing the Arameri, using the masks, and doing it to cast suspicion on the northerners," I said, remembering the dream conversation I'd had with him. *I have already begun*, he had said then. It was the oldest of tricks, to sow dissension between groups that had common interests. Good for deflecting attention from greater mischief, too. I contemplated it more and scowled. "And there's another thing. The Arameri destroy any land that injures them—which guarantees that their enemies will strike decisively, if and when they ever do." I thought of Usein Darr, proudly stating that she would never kill just *a few* Arameri. "The High Northers wouldn't bother with assassins and a lowblood here, a highblood there. They'd bring an army and try to destroy the whole family at once."

"There's no evidence that they're building an army at all," said Nemmer.

There was, but it was subtle. I thought of Usein Darr's pregnancy and that of her guardswoman, and the woman in Sarenna-nem who'd had two babies with her, both too young to be eating solid food yet. I thought of the children I'd seen there—belligerent, xenophobic, barely multilingual, and every one of them four or five years old at the most. Darr was famous for its contraceptive arts. Even before scrivening, the women there had long ago learned to time childbearing to suit their constant raiding and intertribal wars. Their war crop, they called it, making a joke of other lands' reliance on agriculture. In the years preceding a war, every woman under thirty tried her best to make a child or two. The warriors would nurse the babes for a few days, then hand them over to the nonwarriors in the family—who, having also recently borne children, would simply nurse two or three, until all the children could be weaned and handed over to grandmothers or menfolk. Thus the warriors could go off to fight knowing that their replacements were growing up safe, should they fall in battle.

It was a bad sign to see so many Darre breeding. It was a worse sign that the children hated foreigners and weren't even trying to ape Senmite customs. They certainly weren't preparing those children for *peace*.

"Even if they were building an army," said Ahad, "there would be no reason for us to interfere. What mortals do to each other is their business. Our concern lies solely with this godling Kahl and the strange mask Sieh saw."

At this, Glee's already-grim look grew positively forbidding. "So you will do nothing if war breaks out?"

"Mortals have warred with one another since their creation," Eyem-sutah said with a soft sigh. "The best we can do is try to prevent it…and protect the ones we love, if we fail. It is their nature."

"Because it is *our* nature," snapped Nemmer. "And because of us, they now have magic as a weapon for their warring. They'll use soldiers and swords like before the Gods' War, but also scriveners and these masks, and demons know what else. Do you have any idea how many could die?"

It would be worse than that, I knew. Most of mortalkind had

no idea what war really meant anymore. They could not imagine the famine and rapine and disease, not on such a scale. Oh, they feared it of old, and the memory of the ultimate war—*our War*—had burned itself into the souls of every race. But that would not stop them from unleashing its full fury again and learning too late what they had done.

"This will do more than kill," I murmured. "These people have forgotten what humanity can be like at its worst. Rediscovering this will shock them; it will wound their souls. I have seen it happen before, here and on other worlds." I met Ahad's eyes, and he frowned, just a little, at the look on my face. "They'll burn their histories and slaughter their artists. They'll enslave their women and devour their children, and they'll do it in the gods' names. Shahar was right; the end of the Arameri means the end of the Bright."

Ahad spoke with brutal softness. "It will be worse if we get involved."

He was right. I hated him more than ever for that.

In the silence that fell, Glee sighed. "I've stayed too long." She rose to leave. "Keep me informed of anything else you discover or decide."

I waited for one of the gods at the table to chastise her for giving them orders. Then I realized none of them were planning to. Lil had begun to lean toward the platter, her eyes gleaming. Kitr had taken the small paring knife and was spinning it on her fingertip, an old habit that meant she was thinking. Nemmer rose to leave as well, nodding casually to Ahad, and suddenly I couldn't stand it anymore. I shoved back my chair and marched around the table and got to the door just as Glee started to open it. I slammed it shut.

"Who in the suppurating bright hells are you?" I demanded.

Ahad groaned. "Sieh, gods damn it—"

"No, I need to know this. I swore I'd never take orders from a mortal again." I glared up at Glee, who didn't look nearly as alarmed by my tantrum as I wanted her to be. What ignominy; I couldn't even make mortals fear me anymore. "This doesn't make sense! Why are all of you *listening* to her?"

The woman lifted an eyebrow, then let out a long, heavy sigh. "My full name is Glee Shoth. I speak for, and assist, Itempas."

The words struck me like a slap—as did the name, and the odd familiarity of her manner, and her Maroneh heritage, and the way my siblings all seemed uneasy in her presence. I should have seen it at once. Kitr was right; I really was losing my touch.

"You're his daughter." I whispered it. I could barely make my mouth form the words. Glee Shoth—daughter of Oree Shoth, the first and, as far as I knew, only mortal friend Itempas had ever had. Clearly they had gone beyond friendship. "His...dear gods, his *demon* daughter."

Glee did not smile, but her eyes warmed in amusement—and now that I knew, all those tiny niggling familiarities were as obvious as slaps to the face. She didn't look like him; in features, she'd taken more after her mother. But her mannerisms, the air of stillness that she wore like a cloak... It was all there, as plain as the risen sun.

Then I registered the implications of her existence. A demon. A demon *made by Itempas*—he who had declared the demons forbidden in the first place and led the hunt to wipe them out. A daughter, allied to him, *helping* him.

I considered what it meant, that he loved her.

I considered his reconciliation with Yeine.

I considered the terms of his imprisonment.

"It's him," I whispered. I nearly staggered, and would have if I had not leaned on the door for support. I focused on Ahad to marshal my shaken thoughts. "*He's* the leader of this crazy group of yours. *Itempas.*"

Ahad opened his mouth, then closed it. "'You will right all the wrongs inflicted in your name,'" he said at last, and I twitched as I remembered the words. I had been there, the first time they'd been spoken, and Ahad's voice was deep enough, had just the right timbre, to imitate the original speaker perfectly. He shrugged at my stare and finally flashed his usual humorless smile. "I'd say the Arameri, and all they've done to the world, count as one great whopping wrong, wouldn't you?"

"And it is his nature." Glee threw Ahad an arch look before returning her attention to me. "Even without magic, he will fight the encroachment of disorder in whatever way he can. Is that so surprising?"

I resisted out of stubbornness. "Yeine said she couldn't find him lately."

Glee's smile was paper-thin. "I regret concealing him from Lady Yeine, but it's necessary. For his protection."

I shook my head. "Protection? From—Gods, this makes no sense. A mortal can't hide from a god."

"A demon can," she said. I blinked, surprised, but I shouldn't have been. I'd already known that some demons had survived their holocaust. Now I knew how. Glee continued. "And fortunately, some of us can hide others when we need to. Now, if you'll excuse me..." She looked pointedly at my hand on the door, which I let fall.

Ahad had taken out a cheroot and was rummaging absently

in his pockets. He threw a lazy glance at Glee, and there was a hint of the old evil in his eyes. "Tell the old man I said hi."

"I will not," she replied promptly. "He hates you."

Ahad laughed, then finally remembered he was a god and lit the cheroot with a moment's concentration. Sitting back in his chair, he regarded Glee with steady lasciviousness as she opened the door. "But you don't, at least?"

Glee paused on the threshold, and the look in her eyes was suddenly as familiar as her not-quite-smile had been a moment before. Of course it was. I had seen that same easy, possessive arrogance all my life. The absolute assurance that all was as it should be in the universe, because all of it was hers—if not now, then eventually.

"Not yet," she said, and not-smiled again before leaving the room.

Ahad sat forward as soon as the door shut, his eyes fixed on the door in such obvious interest that Lil began staring at him, finally distracted from the food. Kitr made a sound of exasperation and reached for the platter, probably out of irritation rather than any actual hunger.

"I'll see if I can get one of my people into Darr," said Nemmer, getting to her feet. "They're suspicious of strangers, though... might have to do it myself. Busy, busy, busy."

"I will listen harder to the sailors' and traders' talk," said Eyem-sutah. He was the god of commerce, to whom the Ken had once dedicated their magnificent sailing vessels. "War means shipments of steel and leather and march-bread, back and forth and back and forth..." His eyelids fluttered shut; he let out a soft sigh. "Such things have their own music."

Ahad nodded. "I'll see all of you next week, then." With that,

Nemmer, Kitr, and Eyem-sutah disappeared. Lil rose and leaned over the table for a moment; the platter of food vanished. So did the platter, though Ahad's table remained untouched. Ahad sighed.

"You have become interesting, Sieh," Lil said to me, grinning beneath her swirling, mottled eyes. "You want so many things, so badly. Usually you taste only of the one endless, unfulfillable longing."

I sighed and wished she would go away, though that was pointless. Lil came and went as she pleased, and nothing short of a war could dislodge her when she took an interest in something. "What are you doing here?" I asked. "I didn't think you cared about anything but food, Lil."

She shrugged with one painfully bony shoulder, her ragged hair brushing the cloth of her gown with a sound like dry grass. "This realm changed while we were away. Its taste has grown richer, its flavors more complex. I find myself changing to suit." Then to my surprise, she came around the table and put her hand on mine. "You were always kind to me, Sieh. Be well, if you can."

She vanished as well, leaving me even more perplexed than before. I shook my head to myself, not really noticing that I was alone with Ahad until he spoke.

"Questions?" he asked. The cheroot hung between his fingers, on the brink of dropping a column of ash onto the carpet.

I considered all the swirling winds that blew around me and shook my head.

"Good," he said, and waved a hand. (This flung ash everywhere.) Another pouch appeared on the table. Frowning, I picked it up and found it heavy with coins.

"You gave me money yesterday."

He shrugged. "Funny thing, employment. If you keep doing it, you keep getting paid."

I glowered at him. "I take it I passed Glee's test, then."

"Yes. So pay that mortal girl's family for room and board, buy some decent clothing, and for demons' sake, eat and sleep so you stop looking like all hells. I need you to be able to blend in, or at least not frighten people." He paused, leaning back in his chair and taking a deep draw from the cheroot. "Given the quality of your work today, I can see that I'll be making good use of you in the future. That is, by the way, the standard salary we offer to the Arms of Night's top performers." He gave me a small, malicious smile.

If the day hadn't already been so strange, I would have marveled at his praise, laced with insults as it was. Instead I merely nodded and slipped the pouch into my shirt, where pickpockets wouldn't be able to get at it easily.

"Well, get out, then," he said, and I left.

I was five years older, several centuries chastened, and more hated than ever by my siblings, including the one I'd apparently forgotten. As first days on the job went... well. I was still alive. It remained to be seen whether this was a good thing.

BOOK THREE

Three Legs in the Afternoon

I DRIFT THROUGH DREAMING. Since I am not mortal, there are no nightmares. I never find myself naked in front of a crowd, because that would never bother me. (I would waggle my genitals at them, just to see the shock on their faces.) Most of what I dream is memory, probably because I have so many of them.

Images of parents and children. Nahadoth, shaped like some sort of great star-flecked beast, lies curled in a nest of ebon sparks. This is in the days before mortals. I am a tiny thing half hidden in the nest's glimmers. An infant. I huddle against her for comfort and protection, mewling like a new kitten, and she strokes me and whispers my name possessively—

Shahar again. The Matriarch, not the girl I know. She is younger than in my last dream, in her twenties perhaps, and she sits in a window with an infant at her breast. Her chin is propped on her fist; she pays little attention to the babe as it sucks. Mortal, this child. Fully human. Another human child sits in a basket behind her— twins—tended by a girl in priest's robes. Shahar wears robes, too, though hers are finer. She is high ranking. She has borne children as her faith demands, but soon she will abandon them, when her lord needs her. Her eyes are ever on the horizon, waiting for dawn—

Enefa, in the fullest glory of her power. All her experiments, all the tests and failures, have reached the pinnacle of success at last. Merging life and death, light and dark, order and chaos, she brings mortal life to the universe, transforming it forever. She has been giving birth for the past billion years. Her belly is an earth of endless vastness and fecundity, rippling as it churns forth life after life after life. We who have already been born gaze upon this geysering wonder in worshipful adoration. I come to her, bringing an offering of love, because life needs that to thrive. She devours it greedily and arches, crying out in agony and triumph as another species bursts forth. Magnificent. She gropes for my hand because her brothers have gone off somewhere, probably together, but that's all right. I am the oldest of her god-children, a man grown. I am there for her when she needs me. Even if she does not need me very often—

Myself. How strange. I sit on a bed in the first Sky, in mortal flesh, confined to it by mad Itempas and my dead mother's power. This is in the early years, I can tell, when I fought my chains at every turn. My flesh still bears the red weals of a whip, and I am older than I like, weakened by the damage. A young man. Yet I sit beside a longer, larger form whose back is to me. Male, adult, naked. Mortal: black hair a tangled mass. Sickly white skin. Ahad, who had no name back then. He is weeping, I know the way shoulders shake during sobs, and I—I do not remember what I have done to him, but there is guilt as well as despair in my eyes—

Yeine. Who has never borne a child as mortal or goddess, yet who became my mother the instant she met me. She has the nurturing instincts of a predator: choose the most brutal of mates, destroy anything that threatens the young, raise them to be good killers. Yet compared to Enefa, she is a fountain of tenderness, and I drink her love so thirstily that I worry she will run out. (She never has.) In mortal flesh we curl on the floor of the Wind Harp chamber, laughing, terrified of the dawn and the doom that seems inevitable, yet which is, in fact, only the beginning—

Enefa, again. The great quickening is long done. These days she makes few new children, preferring to observe and prune and transplant the ones she already has, on the nonillion worlds where they grow. She turns to me and I shiver and become a man by her will, *though by this point I have realized that* child *is the most fundamental manifestation of my nature. "Don't be afraid," she says when I dare to protest. She comes to me, touches me gently; my body yields and my heart soars. I have yearned for this, so long, but—*

I am dying, this love will kill me, get it away oh gods I have never been so afraid—

Forget.

13

One for sorrow
Two for joy
Three for a girl
Four for a boy
Five for silver
Six for gold
Seven for a secret
Never to be told.

MORTAL LIFE IS CYCLES. Day and night. Seasons. Waking and sleep. This cyclical nature was built into all mortal creatures by Enefa, and the humans have refined it further by building their cultures to suit. Work, home. Months become years, years shift from past to future. They count endlessly, these creatures. It is this which marks the difference between them and us, I think, far more than magic and death.

For two years, three months, and six days, I lived as ordinary a life as I could. I ate. I slept. I grew healthier, taking pains to make myself sleek and strong, and dressed better. I contemplated asking Glee Shoth to arrange a meeting between myself and Itempas. I chose not to, because I hated him and would rather die. Perfectly ordinary.

The work was ordinary, too, in its way. Each week I traveled wherever Ahad chose to send me, observing what I could, interfering where I was bidden. Compared to the life of a god... well. It was not boring, at least. It kept me busy. When I worked hard, I thought less. That was a good and necessary thing.

The world was not ordinary, either. Six months after I'd met her, and three months after the birth of her latest lamented son, Usein Darr's father died of the lingering illness that had incapacitated him for some while. Immediately afterward, Usein Darr got herself elected as one of the High North delegates. She traveled to Shadow in time for the Consortium's voting season, whereupon her first act was to give a fiery speech openly challenging the existence of Shadow's delegate. No other single city had a delegate on the Consortium. "And everyone knows why," Usein declared, then dramatically (according to the news scrolls) turned to glare into the eyes of Remath Arameri, who sat in the family box above the Consortium floor. Remath said nothing in reply—probably because everyone *did* know why, and there was no point in her confirming the obvious. Shadow's delegate was in fact Sky's delegate, little more than another mouthpiece through which the Arameri could make their wishes known. This was nothing new.

What *was* new was that Usein's protest was not struck down by the Consortium Overseer; and that several other nobles—*not* all northerners—rose to voice agreement with her; and that in the subsequent secret vote, nearly a third of the Consortium agreed that Shadow's delegate should be abolished. A loss, and yet a victory. Once upon a time, such a proposal would never have even made it to vote.

It was not a victory so much as a shot across the bow. Yet the Arameri did not respond in kind, as the whispers predicted in the Arms of Night's parlor and the back of the bakery and even at the dinner table with Hymn's family each evening. No one tried to kill Usein Darr. No mysterious plagues swept through the stone-maze streets of Arrebaia. Darren blackwood and herbal rarities continued to fetch high prices on the open and smugglers' markets.

I knew what this meant, of course. Remath had drawn a line somewhere, and Usein simply had yet to cross it. When she did, Remath would bring such horrors to Darr as the land had never seen. Unless Usein's mysterious plans reached fruition first.

Politics would never be interesting enough to occupy the whole of my attention, however, and as the days became months and years, I felt ever more the weight of unfinished, childishly avoided business upon my soul. Eventually one particular urge became overwhelming, and on a slow day, I begged a favor of Ahad. Surprisingly, he obliged me.

Deka was still at the Litaria. That I hadn't expected. After Shahar's betrayal, I had braced myself to find him in Sky somewhere. She had done it to get him back, hadn't she? Yet when Ahad's magic settled, I found myself in the middle of a classroom. The chamber was circular—a remnant of the Litaria's time as part of the Order of Itempas—and the walls were lined by slate covered in chalk renderings: pieces of sigils with each stroke carefully numbered, whole sigils lacking only a stroke or two, and strange numerical calculations that apparently had something to do with how scriveners learned our tongue.

I turned and blinked as I realized I was surrounded by

white-clad children. Most were Amn, ten or eleven years old; all sat cross-legged on the floor, with their own slates or pieces of reed paper in their laps. All of them gaped at me.

I put my hands on my hips and grinned back. "What? Your teacher didn't tell you a godling was dropping by?"

An adult voice made me turn, and then I, too, gaped as the children did.

"No," drawled Dekarta from the lectern. "We're doing show-and-tell *next* week. Hello, Sieh."

Deka wore black now.

I had been surprised by this, but that was not the only shock. I stole little looks up at him—he was much taller than me now—as we walked through a brightly lit, carpeted corridor lined with the busts of dead scriveners. His stride was easy, unhurried, confident. He did not look at me, though he must have noticed me watching him. I tried to read his expression and could not. Despite his exile from Sky, he had still mastered the classic Arameri detachment. Blood told.

Oh, yes, it did. He looked like Ahad.

Demonshitting, hells-spawned, Yeine-loving ratbastard *Ahad*.

So many things made sense now; so many more did not. The resemblance was so strong as to be undeniable. Deka was an inch or two shorter than Ahad, leaner and somewhat unfinished in the manner of young men. He wore his hair short and plain, where Ahad's was long and elaborate. Deka looked more Amn, too; Ahad's features leaned more toward the High Norther template. But in every other way, and particularly in this new aura of easy, dangerous strength, Deka might as well have been made as Ahad had: sprung to life full grown from his progenitor, with no mother in the way to gum things up.

Yet that could not be. Because if Ahad was some recent ancestor of Dekarta's, then that meant Dekarta, and Shahar, and whichever of their parents carried Ahad's blood, were demons. Demons' blood should have killed me the day we'd made the oath of friendship.

And not like this, slowly, cruelly. I had seen what demons' blood did to gods. It should have snuffed out the light of my soul like water on a candleflame. Why was I still alive at all, much less in this hobbled form?

I groaned softly, and at last Deka glanced over at me. "Nothing," I said, rubbing my forehead, which felt as though it *should* ache. "Just...nothing."

He uttered a low chuckle of amusement. My sweet little Deka was a baritone now, and not at all little anymore. Was he still sweet? That was something only time could tell.

"Where are we going?" I asked.

"My laboratory."

"Oh, so they let you use one by yourself?"

He had not stopped smiling; now he developed a smug air. "Of course. All teachers have their own."

I slowed, frowning up at him. "You mean you're a full scrivener? Already?"

"Shouldn't I be? The course of study isn't that difficult. I finished it a few years back."

I remembered the wistful, shy child he had been—so unsure of himself, so quick to let his sister take the lead. Could it be that here, beyond the shadow of his family's disapproval, he had unleashed that wild cleverness of his? I smiled. "Still the arrogant Arameri, in spite of everything."

Deka glanced at me, his smile fading just a little. "I'm not Arameri, Sieh. They threw me out, remember?"

I shook my head. "The only way to truly leave the Arameri is to die. They'll always come back for you, otherwise—if not for you, for your children."

"Hmm. True enough."

We had turned a corner in the meantime and headed down another carpeted corridor, and now Deka led me up a wide, banistered stairwell. Three girls carrying reed pens and scrolls bobbed in polite greeting as they came down the stairs and passed us. All three blushed or batted their eyes at Deka. He nodded back regally. As soon as they were out of sight around the corner, I heard their burst of excited giggling and felt a flicker of my old nature respond. Crushes: like butterfly wings against the soul.

At the top of the stairs, Deka unlocked and opened a pair of handsome wooden doors. Inside, the room was not what I expected. I had seen the First Scrivener's laboratory in Sky: a stark, forbidding place of white gleaming surfaces that held only ephemeral touches of color, like black ink or red blood. Deka's lab was Darrwood, deep and brown, and gold Chellin marble. Octagonal in shape, four of its walls were nothing but books—floor-to-ceiling shelves, each stacked two or three deep with tomes and scrolls and even a few stone or wooden tablets. Wide flat worktables dominated the center of the room, and something odd, a sort of glass-enclosed booth, stood on the room's edge at the juncture of two walls. Yet there were no tools or implements in sight, other than those used for writing. No cages along the wall, filled with specimens for experiments. No lingering scent of pain.

I looked around the room in wonder and confusion. "What the hells kind of scrivener are you?"

Deka closed the door behind me. "My specialty is godling lore," he said. "I wrote my concluding thesis on you."

I turned to him. He stood against the closed doors, watching me. For an instant, in his stillness, he reminded me of Nahadoth as much as Ahad. All three had that same habit of unblinking intensity, which in Ahad covered nihilism and in Nahadoth covered madness. In Deka, I had no idea what it meant. Yet.

"You don't think I tried to kill you, then," I said.

"No. It was obvious something went wrong with the oath."

One knot of tension eased inside me; the rest stayed taut. "You don't seem surprised to see me."

He shrugged, ducking his eyes, and for a moment I saw a hint of the boy he'd been. "I still have friends in Sky. They keep me informed of events that matter."

Very much still the Arameri, whatever his protestations to the contrary. "You knew I would be coming, then."

"I guessed. Especially when I heard about your leaving, two years ago. I expected you then, actually." He looked up, his expression suddenly unreadable. "You killed First Scrivener Shevir."

I shifted from one foot to another, slipping my hands into my pockets. "I didn't mean to. He was just in the way."

"Yes. You do that a lot, I've realized from studying your history. Typical of a child, to act first and deal with the consequences later. You're careful to do that—act impulsively—even though you're experienced and wise enough to know better. This is what it means to live true to your nature."

I stared at him, flummoxed.

"My contacts told me you were angry with Shahar," he said. "Why?"

I set my jaw. "I don't want to talk about it."

"You didn't kill her, I see."

I scowled. "What do you care? You haven't spoken to her for years."

Deka shook his head. "I still love her. But I've been used as a weapon against her once already. I will not let that happen again." He pushed away from the door abruptly and came toward me, and so flustered was I by his manner that I took a step back before I caught myself.

"*I will be her weapon instead,*" he said.

It took me a shamefully long time, all things considered, to realize that he had spoken to me in the First Tongue.

"What the hells are you doing?" I demanded, clenching my fists to keep from clapping a hand over his mouth. "Shut up before you kill us both!"

To my shock, he smiled and began to unfasten his overshirt. "I've been speaking magic for years, Sieh," he said. "I can hear the world and the stars as gods do. I know when reality listens closest, when even the softest word will awaken its wrath or coax it into obedience. I don't know how I know these things, but I do."

Because you are one of us, I almost said, but how could I be sure of that? His blood hadn't killed me. I tried to understand even as he continued undressing in front of me.

Then he got his overshirt open. I knew before he'd unlaced

the white shirt underneath; the characters glowed dark through the fabric. Black markings, dozens of them, marched along most of his upper torso and shoulders, beginning to make their way down the flat planes of his abdomen. I stared, confused. Scriveners marked themselves whenever they mastered a new activation; it was the way of their art. They put our powerful words on their fragile mortal skin, using will and skill alone to keep the magic from devouring them. But they used ordinary ink to do it, and they washed the marks off once the ritual was done. Deka's marks, I saw at once, were like Arameri blood sigils. Permanent. Deadly.

And they were not scrivening marks. The style was all wrong. These lines had none of the spidery jaggedness I was used to seeing in scrivener work: ugly, but effective. These marks were smooth and almost geometric in their cleanliness. I had never seen anything like them. Yet they had power, whatever they were; I could read that in the swirling interstices of their shapes. There was meaning in this, as multilayered as poetry and as clear as metaphor. Magic is merely communication, after all.

Communication, and conduits.

This is something we have never told mortals. Paper and ink are weak structures on which to build the framework of magic. Breath and sound aren't much better, yet we godlings willingly confine ourselves to those methods because the mortal realm is such a fragile place. And because mortals are such dangerously fast learners.

But flesh makes for an excellent conduit. This was something the Arameri had learned by trial and error, though they'd never fully understood it. They wrote contracts with us onto their foreheads for protection, calling them blood sigils as if that was all they were, and *we could not kill them*, no matter how badly worded they were. Now Deka had written demands for power into his own skin, and his flesh gave the words meaning. He had written it in a script of his own devising, more flexible and beautiful than the rough speech of his fellow scriveners, and *the universe would not deny him.*

He had made himself not quite as powerful as a god—his flesh was still mortal, and the marks had only limited meaning—but surely more powerful than any scrivener who had ever lived. I had an inkling that his markings would be more effective than even the northerners' masks; those were only wood and gods-blood, after all. Deka was more than that.

My mouth fell open, and Deka smiled. Then he closed his undershirt.

"H-how...?" I asked. But I could guess. Demon and scrivener. A combination we had already learned to fear, channeled here toward a new purpose. *"Why?"*

"You," he said, very softly. "I was planning to go find you."

There was, fortunately, a small couch nearby. I sat down on it, dazed.

We exchanged stories. This was what Deka told me.

Shahar had been the one to suggest his exile. In the tense days after our oath and the children's injury, the clamors for Deka's execution had run loud in the halls of Sky. There were still a dozen or so fullbloods and twenty or thirty highbloods altogether. In the old days, they had not mattered because the family head's rule had been absolute. These days, however, the highbloods had power of their own. Some of them had their own pet scriveners, their own pet assassins. A few had their own pet armies. If enough of them banded together and acted against Remath, she could be overthrown. This had never happened in all the two-millennia history of the Arameri, but it could happen now.

But when they had demanded Deka's death, Shahar had spoken for him, as soon as she was well enough to talk. She had gone toe-to-toe with Remath—an epic debate, Deka called it, all the more impressive because one of its combatants was eight years old—and gotten her to acknowledge that exile was a more suitable punishment than death. Deka could never win enough support to become heir now, even if his looks could somehow be overcome. He would be forever branded by the stigma of failure. And Shahar needed him alive, she had argued, so as to have one advisor whose prospects were so truncated, so hopeless, that he would have no choice but to serve her faithfully in order to survive. Remath had agreed.

"I imagine dear Sister will fill this in when I go back," Deka said then, touching his semisigil with a soft sigh. I nodded slowly. He was probably right.

So Deka had left Sky for the Litaria. The first few months of his exile had been misery, for with a child's eyes, he had seen only his mother's rejection and his sister's betrayal. He had not reckoned, however, on one crucial thing.

"I am happy here," he said simply. "It isn't perfect; there are cliques and bullies, politics, unfairness, like anywhere. But compared to Sky, this is the gentlest of heavens."

I nodded again. Happiness has healing power. Between that and the wisdom brought by maturity, Deka had come to realize what Shahar had done for him, and why. By then, however, several years had passed during which he'd returned all her letters, until she'd finally stopped sending them. It would have been dangerous in the extreme to resume communication at that point, because any of Shahar's rivals—who were surely watching her mailings—would know that Deka was once again her weakness. There was strength in the fact that she could pretend not to love him and point to her hand in his exile as proof. And as long as Deka pretended not to love her back, they were both safe.

I shook my head slowly, though, troubled by his plan. Love could not be conditional. I had seen the danger of that too often. Conditions created a chink in otherwise unbreakable armor, left a fatal flaw in the perfect weapon. Then the armor broke, at precisely the wrong time. The weapon turned against its wielder. Deka and Shahar's game could so easily turn real.

But it was not my place to say that, because they were still children enough to learn best through experience. I could only pray to Nahadoth and Yeine that they would not learn this lesson in the most painful way.

After our talk, Deka rose. An hour or so had passed. Beyond the laboratory windows, the sun had moved through noon into afternoon. I was hungry again, damn it, but no one had brought food. Perhaps there were no servants in this place where learning created its own hierarchy.

As if guessing my thought (though my stomach had also rumbled loudly), Deka went to a cabinet and opened a drawer, taking out several flat loaves of bread and a chub of dry sausage. He began slicing this on a board. "So why have you come? It can't just have been to see an old friend."

He still thought of me as a friend. I tried not to let him see how this affected me. "I did just want to see you, believe it or not. I wondered how you'd turned out."

"You can't have wondered all that hard, since it took you two years to come."

I winced. "After Shahar, what happened with her, I mean... I didn't want to see you, because I was afraid that you would be...like her." Deka said nothing, still working on the food. "I thought you would be back in Sky by now, though."

"Why?"

"Shahar. She made a deal with your mother to bring you home."

"And you thought I would go as soon as my sister snapped her fingers?"

I faltered silent, confused. As I sat there, Deka turned back to me and brought the sausage and bread over, setting it before me as if he were a servant and not an Arameri. No poor man's gristle-and-scraps here, I found when I took a slice. The sausage was sweet and redolent of cinnamon, bright yellow in color per the local style. The Litaria might make Remath Arameri's son serve his own food, but the food was at least suited to his station. He'd brought a flask of wine, too, light and strong, of equal quality.

"Mother sent a letter shortly after you left Sky, inquiring as to when I might return," Deka said, sitting in the chair across from me and taking a slice of meat for himself. He swallowed and uttered a short, sour laugh. "I responded with a letter of my own, explaining that I intended to remain until I'd completed my research."

I burst out laughing at his audacity. "You told her you'd come back when you were good and ready, is that it? And she didn't force you home?"

"No." Deka's expression darkened further. "But she had Shahar write to me, asking the same question."

"And you said?"

"Nothing."

"Nothing?"

He sat back in his chair, crossing his legs and toying with the glass of wine in his fingers. I didn't like that pose for him; it reminded me too much of Ahad. "There was no need. It was a warning. Shahar's letter said, 'I am told the standard course of study at the Litaria is ten years. Surely you can finish your research within that time?'"

"A deadline."

He nodded. "Two years to wrap up my affairs here and go back to Sky—or, no doubt, Mother's willingness to let me return would expire." He spread his hands. "This is my tenth year."

I thought of what he'd told me and shown me. The strange new magic he'd developed, his vow to become Shahar's weapon. "You're going back, then."

"I leave in a month." He shrugged. "I should arrive by midsummer."

"Two months' traveling time?" I frowned. The Litaria was a sovereign territory within the sleepy agrarian land of Wiru, in southern Senm. (That way only a few farmers would die if the place ever blew to the heavens.) Sky was not that far. "You're a scrivener. Draw a gate sigil."

"I don't actually need to; the Litaria has a permanent gate that can be configured to Sky's. But to travel that way would make it seem as though I was afraid of assault. There is the family pride to consider. And more importantly, I will not slink to Sky quietly, like a bad dog finally allowed back into the house."

He sipped from his glass of wine. Over the rim, his eyes were dark and colder than I'd ever expected to see. "Let Mother and the rest of them see what they have chosen to create by sending me here. If they will not love me, fear is an acceptable substitute."

For a moment I was stunned. This was not at all the Deka I remembered, but then, he was no longer a child, and he had never been a fool. He knew as well as I did what he was going back to in Sky. I could not blame him for hardening himself to prepare for it. But I did mourn, just a little, for the sweet boy I'd first known.

At least he had not become what I'd feared, though: a monster, worthy only of death.

Yet.

At my silence, Deka glanced up, gazing at me just a moment too long. Did he sense my unease? Did he *want* me to feel uneasy?

"So...what will you do?" I asked. I fought the urge to stammer.

He shrugged. "I informed Mother that I would be traveling overland and made note of the route. Then I sent it by standard courier, with only the usual privacy sigils in the seal."

I whistled with a lightheartedness that I didn't feel. "Every highblood in Sky will have seen it, then." I frowned. "These mask-wielding assassins, though...And gods, Deka, if any of *your relatives* want you dead, you've given them a map for the best places to ambush you!"

"And if Mother stints me on an appropriate guard complement, that's precisely what will happen." He shrugged. "As head, she must be seen to at least *try* to protect the Central Family, the Matriarch's bloodline. To do any less would make her unfit to lead. So she'll likely send a whole legion to escort me—thus the two months of travel."

"Caught in your own trap. Poor Deka." He smiled, and I grinned back. Yet I found myself sobering. "What if there *is* an attack, though? Assassins, regardless who sends them? A legion of enemy soldiers?"

"I'll be fine."

There was arrogance, and there was stupidity. "You should be afraid, Deka, no matter how powerful you've become. I've seen this mask magic. It's like nothing the Litaria has prepared you for."

"I've seen Shevir's notes, and the Litaria has been closely involved in the investigation into this new magical form. The masks are like scrivening, like the gods' language: merely a symbolic representation of a concept. Once one understands this, it is possible to develop a countermeasure." He shrugged. "And these mask makers don't know anything about *my* new magical form. No one does but me. And now you."

"Um. Oh." I fell silent again, awkwardly.

Abruptly, Deka smiled. "I like this," he said, nodding toward me. "You're different now, not just physically. Not so much the brat. Now you're more . . ." He thought a moment.

"Heartless bastard?" I smiled. "Obnoxious ass?"

"Tired," he said, and I sobered. "Unsure of yourself. The old you is still there, but it's almost buried under other things. Fear, most noticeably."

Inexplicably, the words stung. I stared back at him, wondering why.

His expression softened, a tacit apology. "It must be hard for you. Facing death, when you're a creature of so much life."

I looked away. "If mortals can do it, I can."

"Not all mortals do, Sieh. You haven't drunk yourself to death yet, or flung yourself into dangerous situations, or killed yourself in any of a hundred other ways. Considering that death is a new reality for you, you're handling it remarkably well." He leaned forward, resting his elbows on his knees, his eyes boring into my own. "But the biggest change is that you're not happy anymore. You were always lonely; I saw that even as a child. But the loneliness wasn't destroying you back then. It is now."

I flinched back from him, my thoughts moving from stunned toward affronted, but they lacked the strength to go all the way there, instead flopping somewhere in between. A lie came to my lips, and died. All that remained was silence.

A hint of the old self-deprecation crossed Deka's face; he smiled ruefully. "I still want to help you, but I'm not sure if I can. You aren't sure you like me anymore, for one thing."

"I—" I blurted. Then I got up and walked away from him, over to one of the windows. I had to. I didn't know what to say or how to act, and I didn't want him to say anything else. If I'd still had my power, I would have simply left the Litaria. Maybe the mortal realm entirely. As it was, the best I could do was flee across the room.

His sigh followed me, but he said nothing for a long while. In that silence, I began to calm down. Why was I so agitated? I felt like a child again, one with jittery buttons dancing on his skin, like in an old Teman tale I'd heard. By the time Deka spoke, I was almost myself again. Well, not *myself*. But human, at least.

"You came to us all those years ago because you needed something, Sieh."

"Not two little mortal brats," I snapped.

"Maybe not. But we gave you something that you needed, and you came back for it twice more. And in the end, I was right. You *did* want our friendship. I've never forgotten what you said that day: '*Friendships can transcend childhood, if the friends continue to trust each other as they grow older and change.*'" I heard him shift in his chair, facing my back. "It was a warning."

I sighed, rubbing my eyes. The meat and bread sat uneasily in my belly. "It was sentimental rambling."

"Sieh." How could he know so much, so young? "You were planning to kill us. If we became the kind of Arameri who once made your life hell—if we betrayed your trust—you knew you would *have* to kill us. The oath, and your nature, would have required it. You told us that because you didn't want to. You wanted real friends. Friends who would last."

Had that been it? I laughed hopelessly. "And now I'm the one who won't last much longer."

"Sieh—"

"If it was like you say, I would have killed Shahar, Deka. Because she betrayed me. She knew I loved her, and she used me. She..." I paused, then looked up at the reflection in the window. My own face in the foreground, pinched and tired, too big as always, shaped wrong, old. I had never understood why so many mortals found me attractive in this shape. In the background, watching me from the couch on which he sat, Deka. His eyes met mine in the glass.

"I slept with her," I said, to hurt him. To shut him up. "I was her first, in fact. Little Lady Shar, so perfect, so cute. You should have heard her moan, Deka; it was like hearing the Maelstrom itself sing."

Deka only smiled, though it seemed forced. "I heard about

Mother's plan." He paused. "Is that why you didn't kill Shahar? Because it was Mother's plan and not hers?"

I shook my head. "I don't know why I didn't kill her. There was no why. I do what feels good." I rubbed my temples, where a headache had begun.

"And you didn't feel like murdering the girl you loved."

"Gods, Deka!" I rounded on him, clenching my fists. "Why are we talking about this?"

"So it was just lust? The god of childhood leaps on the first half-grown woman he meets who's willing?"

"No, of course not!"

He sighed and got to his feet. "She was just another Arameri, then, forcing you into her bed?" The look on his face showed that he didn't remotely believe that. "You wanted her. You loved her. She broke your heart. And you didn't kill her because you love her still. Why does that trouble you so?"

"It doesn't," I said. But it did. It shouldn't have. Why did it matter to me that some mortal had done precisely what I'd expected her to do? A god should not care about such things. A god . . .

. . . should not need a mortal to be happy.

Gods. Gods. What was wrong with me? Gods.

Deka sighed and came over to me. There were many things in his eyes: compassion. Sorrow. Anger, though not at me. Exasperation. And something more. He stopped in front of me, and I was not as surprised as I should have been that he lifted a hand to cup my cheek. I did not pull away, either. As I should have.

"I will not betray you," he murmured, much too softly. This was not the way a friend spoke to a friend. His fingertips rasped along the edge of my jaw. This was not the touch of a friend. But—I did not think—Oh, gods, was he...

"I'm not going anywhere, either. I have waited so long for you, Sieh."

I started, confused, remembering. "Wait, where did you hear—"

Then he kissed me, and I fell.

Into him. Or he enveloped me. There are no words for such things, not in any mortal language, but I will try, I will try to encapsulate it, confine it, define it, because my mind does not work the way it once did and I want to understand, too. I want to remember. I want to taste again his mouth, spicy and meaty and a little sweet. He had always been sweet, especially that first day, when he'd looked into my eyes and begged me to help them. I craved his sweetness. His mouth opened and I delved into it, meeting him halfway. I had blessed him that day, hadn't I? Perhaps that was why, now, the purest of magic surged through him and down my throat, flooding my belly, overflowing my nerves until I gasped and tried to cry out, but he would not let my mouth go. I tried to back away but the window was there. We could not travel to other realms safely. My only choice was to release the magic or be destroyed. So I opened my eyes.

Every lantern in the room flared like a bonfire, then burst in a cloud of sparks. The walls shook, the floor heaved. One of the shelves on a nearby bookcase collapsed, spilling thick tomes to the floor. I heard the window frame rattle ominously at my back, and someone on the floor above cried out in alarm. Then Deka ended the kiss, and the world was still again.

Darkness and damnation and eighth-blooded unknowing Arameri *demons*.

Deka blinked twice, licked his lips, then flashed me the sort of elated, look-what-I-did grin I'd once been famous for. "That went better than expected."

I nodded beyond him. "You were expecting this?"

He turned, and his eyes widened at the fallen shelf, the now-smoldering lanterns. One lay on the floor, its glass shattered. As he stared, a scroll that had not dropped with the others fluttered to the shelf below, forlorn.

I touched his shoulder. "You need to send me back to Shadow." This made him turn around, a protest already on his lips. I gripped his shoulder to make him listen. "No. I won't do this again, Deka. I can't. You were right about Shahar. But that's why... I, with you, I—" I sighed, inexpressibly weary. Why did mortal troubles never wait for convenient times? "Gods, I can't do this right now."

I saw Deka struggle for a mature response, which heartened me because it meant that he had not somehow outgrown me at a mere eighteen years. He took a deep breath and moved away from me, running a hand through his hair. Finally he turned to one of the tables in the room and pulled out a large sheet of the thick, bleached paper that scriveners used for their work. He took a brush, inkstone and stick, and reservoir from a nearby table, and said with his back to me, "The way you appeared was gods' magic."

"One of my siblings." *Your great-grandfather.* Ahad was going to love this.

"Ah." He prepared the ink, his fingers grinding the sigil-marked inkstone back and forth slowly, meditatively. "Do you think, next time, I'll be able to summon you to me the way Shahar did?"

He was too tense to even attempt subtlety. I sighed and gave him what he wanted. "There's only one way to find out, I suppose."

"May I attempt it? At an appropriate time, of course."

I leaned against the window again. "Yes."

"Good." The tension in his broad shoulders eased, just a touch. He began to sketch the sigil for a gate with quick, decisive movements—stunningly fast, compared to most scriveners I had seen. Every line was perfect. I felt the power of it the instant he drew the final line.

"I may be able to help you." He said this briskly, with a scrivener's matter-of-fact detachment. "I can't promise anything, of course, but the magic I've been designing—my body-marking— accesses the potential hidden within an individual. Whatever's happening to you, you're still a god. That should give me something to work with."

"Fine."

Deka set the sigil on the floor and stepped back. When I went to stand beside it, his expression was as carefully blank as if he stood before Remath. I could not leave things that way between us.

So I took his hand, the one I'd held ten years before, when his demon blood had mingled with mine and failed to kill me. His palm was unmarked, but I remembered where the cut had been. I traced a line across it with a fingertip, and his hand twitched in response.

"I'm glad I came to see you," I said.

He did not smile. But he did fold his hand around mine for a moment.

"I'm not Shahar, Sieh," he said. "Don't punish me for what she did."

I nodded wearily. Then I let go of him, stepped onto the sigil, and thought of South Root. The world blurred around me, leaping to obey Deka's command and my will. I savored the momentary illusion of control. Then, when the walls of my room at Hymn's snapped into place around me, I lay down on the bed, threw an arm over my eyes, and thought of nothing but Deka's kiss for the rest of the night.

14

I⊤ FELT GOOD TO RUN up sand dunes. I put my head down and took care to churn the sand behind me and scuff up the perfect wave patterns the wind had etched around the sparse grasses. By the time I reached the top of the dune, I was out of breath, and my heart was pumping steadily within its cage of bones and muscle. I stopped there, putting my hands on my hips, and grinned at the beach and the spreading expanse of the Repentance Sea. I felt young and strong and invincible, even though I really wasn't any of those things. I didn't care. It was just nice to feel good.

"Hello, Sieh!" cried my sister Spider. She was down at the water's edge, dancing in the surf. Her voice carried up to me on the salty ocean breeze, as clear as if I stood beside her.

"Hello, there." I grinned at her, too, and spread my arms. "All the oceans in the world, and you had to pick the *boiled* one?"

One of my siblings, the Fireling, had fought a legendary battle here during the Gods' War. She'd won, but not before the Repentance was a bubbling stewpot filled with the corpses of a billion sea creatures.

"It has nice rhythms." She was doing something strange in her dance, squatting and hopping from one foot to another with no recognizable semblance of rhythm. But that was Spider; she made her own music if she needed to. So many of Nahadoth's children were like her, just a little mad but beautiful in their madness. Such a proud legacy our father had given us.

"All the dead things here scream in time with each other," she said. "Can't you hear them?"

"No, alas." It almost didn't hurt anymore, acknowledging that my childhood was gone and would never return. Mortals are resilient creatures.

"A shame. Can you still dance?"

In answer, I ran down the dune, side-sliding so that I wouldn't overbalance. When I reached level ground, I altered my steps into a side-to-side sort of hop that had been popular in upper Rue once, centuries before the Gods' War. Spider giggled and immediately came out of the water to join my dance, her steps alternating to complement mine. We met at the tideline, where dry sand turned to hard-packed wet. There she grabbed my hands and pulled me into a new dance, formal and revolving and slow. Something Amn, or possibly just something she'd made up on the spot. It never mattered with her.

I grinned, taking the lead and turning us in a looping circle, toward the water and away. "I can always dance for you."

"Not so well anymore. You have no rhythm." We were in northern Tema, the land whose people we had both watched over long ago. She had taken the shape of a local girl, small and lithe, though her hair was bound up in a bun at the back of her head as no self-respecting Teman would have done. "You can't hear the music at all?"

"Not a note." I pulled her hand close and kissed the back of it. "But I can hear my heart beating, and the waves coming in, and the wind blowing. I may not be exactly on the beat, but you know, I don't have to be a *good* dancer to love dancing."

She beamed, delighted, and then spun us both, taking control of the dance so deftly that I could not mind. "I've missed you, Sieh. None of the others ever loved to move like you do."

I twirled her once more so that my arms could settle around her from behind. She smelled of sweat and salt and joy. I pressed my face into her soft hair and felt a whisper of the old magic. She was not a child, but she had never forgotten how to play.

"Oh—" She stopped, her whole body going taut with attention, and I looked up to see what had interested her so. A few dozen feet away on the beach, lurking near a dune as if ready to duck back behind it: a young man, slim and brown and handsome, fascinating in his shy eagerness. He wore no shirt or shoes, and his pants were rolled up to his knees. In one hand he carried a bucket full of sandy clams.

"One of your worshippers?" I murmured in her ear, and then I kissed it.

Spider giggled, though her expression was greedy. "Perhaps. Move away from me, Brother. He's shy enough as it is, and you're not a little boy anymore."

"They're so beautiful when they love us," I whispered. I pressed against her, hungry, and thought for the umpteenth time of Deka.

"Yes," she said, reaching back to cup my cheek. "But I don't share, Sieh, and I'm not the one you want anyway. Let go now."

Reluctantly I did so and stepped back, bowing extravagantly to the young man so that he would know he was welcome. He blushed and ducked his head, the long cabled locks of his hair falling forward. Because he was poor, he had wrapped the locks with some sort of threadlike seaweed and ornamented them with seashells and bits of bright coral, rather than the metal bands and gemstones most Temans preferred. He did begin to walk closer at our tacit invitation, holding the bucket in both hands with an air of offering. His whole day's income, most likely—a sincere mark of devotion.

While he approached, Spider glanced back at me, her eyes gleaming. "You want to know about Kahl, don't you?"

I blinked in surprise. "How did you know?"

She smiled. "*I* can hear the world just fine, Brother. The wind says you're playing errand boy for Ahad, the new one. Everyone knows who *he* works for."

"I didn't." I could not keep the sourness out of my voice.

"That's because you're selfish and flighty. Anyhow, of course that's why you came. There's nothing else in Tema that could be of interest to you."

"Maybe I just wanted to see you."

She laughed, high and bright, and I grinned, too. We had always understood each other, she and I.

"For the past, then," she said. "Only for you, Sieh."

Then, turning a little pirouette that marked a strange and powerful pattern into the sand, Spider stopped on one toe and dipped toward me, her other leg extending gracefully above her in a perfect arabesque. Her eyes, which had been brown and ordinary until then, suddenly glimmered and became different. Six additional tiny-pupilled irises swirled out of nowhere and settled into place around her existing irises, which shrank a bit to make room for them. The clam boy stopped where he was a few feet away, his eyes widening at the sight. I didn't blame him; she was magnificent.

"Time has never been as straightforward as Itempas wished," she said, stroking my cheek. "It is a web, and we all dance along its threads. You know that."

I nodded, settling cross-legged in front of her. "No one dances like you, Sister. Tell me what you can."

She nodded and fell silent for a moment. "A plains fire has been lit." For an instant as she spoke, I glimpsed fingerlike palps wiggling behind her human teeth. She used magic to speak when she was in this state, or else she would have lisped badly. She had always been vain.

"A fire?" I prompted when she fell silent. Her eyes flickered, searching realms I had never been able to visit, even as a god. This was what I had come for. It was difficult to convince Spider to scry the past or future, because she didn't like dancing those paths. They made her strange and dangerous, when all she really wanted to do was spin and mate and eat. She was like me; once, we had both had other shapes and explored our natures in other ways. We liked the new ways better, but one could never leave the past entirely behind.

"The Darre's new ennu, I think, is the kindling. But this fire will burn far, far beyond this realm."

I frowned at this. "How can mortal machinations affect

anything more than mortal life?" But that was a foolish question. I had spent two thousand years suffering because of one mortal's evil.

She shivered, her eyes glazing, though she never once lost her balance on that single toe. The clam boy frowned from where he knelt on the sand, his bucket set before him. When this was done, I knew, Spider would demand a dance with him. If he pleased her, and was lucky, she would make love with him for a few hours and then send him on his way. If he was not lucky... well. The clams would make a fine appetizer. Those mortals who choose to love us know the risks.

"A seashell." Her voice dropped to a murmur, flat and inflectionless. "It floats on green wood and shining white bones. Inside is betrayal, love, years, and more betrayal. Ah, Sieh. All your old mistakes are coming back to haunt you."

I sighed, thinking of Shahar and Deka and Itempas, to name a few. "I know."

"No. You don't. Or rather, you do, but the knowledge is buried deep. Or rather, it was." She cocked her head, and all her dozen pupils expanded at once. Her eyes, speckled with holes, pulled at me. I looked into them and glimpsed deep chasms bridged by gossamer webs. Quickly I leaned back, averting my eyes. Anyone drawn into Spider's world became hers, and she did not always let them go. Not even if she loved them.

"The wind blows louder by the moment," she whispered. "*Sieh, Sieh, Sieh*, it whispers, in the halls of the unknowable. Something stirs in those halls, for the first time since Enefa's birth. *It is alive. It thinks. It considers you.*"

This nonsense was not at all what I had expected, and not really what I wanted to hear. I frowned and licked my lips, wondering how to steer her back toward the knowledge I needed. "What of Kahl, Sister? The Arameri's enemy?"

She shook her head suddenly, vehemently, closing her eyes. "He is *your* enemy, Sieh, not theirs. They are irrelevant. Innocent—ha!—bystanders." She shuddered, and to my surprise she abruptly tottered on her toe, nearly losing her balance. The clam boy looked up suddenly, his face taut with fervor; I heard him utter a low, intent prayer. We have never needed prayers, but we do like them. They feel much like...hmm. Like a push, or a supporting hand on the back. Even gods need encouragement sometimes. After a moment, Spider steadied.

"Itempas," she said at last, sounding abruptly weary. "He is the key. Stop being stubborn, Sieh; just talk to him."

"But—" I clamped my teeth down on what I would have said. This was what I'd asked her to give me. I had no right to complain just because it wasn't what I wanted to hear. "Fine."

With a sigh she opened her eyes, which were human again. When she straightened and stepped off the pattern, carefully removing her toe from its center without disturbing it, I saw the lingering sheen of magic within its lines.

"Go away now, Brother," she said. "Come back in a million years, or whenever you think of me again."

"I won't be able to," I said softly. In a million years I would be less than dust.

She glanced at me, and for just an instant her eyes flickered strange again. "No. I suppose you won't, will you? But don't forget me, Brother, amid all the new mysteries you'll have to explore. I'll miss you."

With that, she turned to her clam boy and offered him her hand. He came and took it, rising, his face alight even as she suddenly grew four additional arms and wrapped all six of them about him tightly. She would probably let him live, given that he had helped her. Probably.

I turned and headed back over the dunes, leaving my sister to her dance.

It had been a busy month since my trip to see Deka. A week later had come the expected announcement: Remath Arameri was bringing her beloved son home at last. Dekarta had begun his journey toward Sky amid great fanfare and three whole legions of soldier escorts. They would make a tour of the procession, visiting a dozen of the southern Senm kingdoms before reaching Sky-in-Shadow on the auspicious summer solstice. I had laughed on hearing about the tour. Three legions? That went beyond any need to protect Deka. Remath was showing off. Her message was clear: if she could spare three legions just to protect a less-favored son, imagine how many she could bring to bear for something that mattered?

So Ahad had kept me on the move visiting this noble or that merchant, spending a night on the streets in a few cities to hear what the commonfolk thought, sowing rumors and then listening to see what truths sprang up as a result. There had been more meetings, too, though Ahad invited me only when he had to. Nemmer and Kitr had complained after I loosened the legs of their chairs one time. I couldn't see what they were so upset about; neither had actually fallen. *That* would have been worth the broken collarbone Kitr gave me in recompense. (Ahad sent me to a bonebender for healing and told me not to speak to him for a week.)

So, left to my own devices, I'd spent the last few days tooling about Tema. Beyond the beach dunes stood a city, shimmering through the heat haze: Antema, capital city of the Protectorate. It had been the greatest city in the world before the Gods' War and was one of the few cities that had managed to survive that horror mostly unscathed. These days it was not quite as impressive as Sky—the World Tree and the palace were just too stunning for any other city to top—but what it lacked in grandeur it made up in character.

I admired the view again, then sighed and finally fished in my pocket for the messaging sphere Ahad had given me.

"What," he said, when the sphere's soft thrum had finally gotten his attention. He knew exactly how long to keep me waiting; an instant longer and I would've stilled the activation.

I had already decided not to tell him about my visit with Spider, and I was still considering whether to request a meeting with Itempas. So I said, "It's been a week. I'm getting bored. Send me somewhere."

"All right," he said. "Go to Sky and talk to the Arameri."

I stiffened, furious. He knew full well that I didn't want to go there, and why. "Talk to them about what, for demons' sake?"

"Wedding gifts," he said. "Shahar Arameri is getting married."

It was the talk of the town, I discovered, when I got to Antema and found a tavern in which to get very, very drunk.

Teman taverns are not made for solitary drunkenness. The Teman people are one of the oldest mortal races, and they have dealt with the peculiar isolation of life in cities for longer than the Amn have even had permanent houses. Thus the walls of the tavern I'd fallen into were covered in murals of people paying attention to me—or so it seemed, as each painted figure sat facing strategic points where viewers might sit. They leaned forward and stared as if intent upon anything I might say. One got used to this.

One also got used to the carefully rude way in which the taverns were furnished, so as to force strangers together. As I sat on a long couch nursing a hornlike cup of honey beer, two men joined me because there were only couches to sit on and I was not churl enough to claim one alone. Naturally they began talking to me, because the tavern's musician—an elderly twin-ojo player—kept taking long breaks to nap. Talking filled the silence. And then two women joined us, because I was young and handsome and the other two men weren't bad-looking themselves. Before long, I was sitting among a laughing, raucous group of utter strangers who treated me like their best friend.

"She doesn't love him," said one of the men, who was well into his own honey horn and growing progressively more slurred in his speech because of it. Temans mixed it with something, aromatic sea grass seed I thought, that made it a fearsomely strong drink. "Probably doesn't even like him. An Amn, Arameri no less, marrying a Temaboy? You just know she looks down her pointy white nose at all of us."

"I heard they were childhood friends," said a woman, whose name was Reck or Rook or possibly Rock. Ruck? "Datennay Canru passed all the exams with top marks; the Triadice wouldn't have confirmed him as a *pymexe* if he wasn't brilliant. It's an honor to the Protectorate, the Arameri wanting him." She lifted her Amn-style glass, which contained something bright green, and out of custom, all of us raised our drinks to answer her toast.

But as soon as our arms came down, her female companion scowled and leaned forward, her locks swinging for emphasis. "It's an insult, not an honor. If the damned Arameri thought so much of our Triadice, they would've deigned to marry in before now. All they want's our navy to guard against the crazy High Northers—"

"It's an insult only if you make it one," said one of the men, who spoke rather hotly because there were three men and two women and he was the homeliest of the group, and he knew that he was most likely to go home alone. "They're still Arameri. They don't need us. And she genuinely likes him!"

This triggered a chorus of agreement and protest from the whole group, during which I alternated my attention between them and a set of peculiar masks hanging on one of the tavern's walls. They reminded me a bit of the masks I'd seen in Darr, though these were more elaborately styled and decorated, in the Teman fashion. They all had hair locks and jolly faces, yet somehow they were even more distracting than the staring mural people. Or perhaps I was just drunk.

After the argument had gone back and forth a few times, one of the women noticed that I had been quiet. "What do you think?" she asked, smiling at me. She was a bit older, relatively speaking, and seemed to think I needed the encouragement.

I finished the last of my horn, gave a discreet nod to the waiter for more, and sat back, grinning at the woman. She was pretty, small and dark and wiry as Teman women tended to be, with the most beautiful black eyes. I wondered if I was still god enough to make her faint.

"Me?" I asked, and licked spoiled honey from my lips. "I think Shahar Arameri is a whore."

There was a collective gasp—and not just from my couch, because my voice had carried. I looked around and saw shocked stares from half the tavern. I laughed at all of them, then focused on my own group.

"You shouldn't say that," said one of the men, who had also been giving me the eye—though now, I suspected, he was rethinking that. "The Order doesn't care what you say about the gods anymore, except Itempas, but the Arameri..." He darted a look around, as if afraid Order-Keepers would appear out of nowhere to beat me senseless. In the old days they would have. Lazy sots. "You shouldn't say that."

I shrugged. "It's true. Not her fault, of course. Her mother's the problem, see. She gave the girl to a god once, as a broodmare, hoping to make a demon-child. Probably let your *pymexe* have a free ride, too, to seal the deal. You say he's a smart man. I'm sure he wouldn't mind treading in the footsteps of gods."

The waiter, who had been on his way to me with another horn, stopped just beyond the couch, his eyes wide and horrified. The man who had been thinking about me stood up, quickly, almost but not quite before his third companion, who'd ignored me entirely up to that point, leapt to his feet. "Canru is my second cousin, you green-eyed half-breed nobody—"

"Who's a half-breed?" I drew myself up to my full sitting height, which made me nowhere near as tall as he was. "There's not a drop of mortal in me, damn it, no matter how old I look!"

The man, already opening his mouth to roar at me, faltered to silence, staring at me in confusion. One of the women leaned away, the other closer; both had wide, wondering eyes. "What did you say?" asked the closer-leaner. "Are you a godling?"

"I am," I said gravely, and belched. "Pardon me."

"You're as godly as my left testicle," snapped the furious man.

"Is that very godly?" I laughed again, feeling full of mischief and rage and joy. The rage was strongest, so before the man could react, I shot out my free hand and grabbed at his crotch, correctly guessing precisely where his left testicle would be. It was child's play—for a mean child, anyway—to grasp the thing and give it a sharp, expert twist. He screamed and doubled over, his face purpling with shock and agony as he grabbed at my arm, but dislodging me would've necessitated a harder pull on his tender bits. With his face inches from mine, I flashed my teeth and hissed at him, tightening my fingers just enough for warning. His eyes went wide and terrified for some reason, which I could tell had nothing to do with the threat to his manhood. I doubted that my eyes had changed; there wasn't enough magic left in me for that. Something else, maybe.

"These don't seem very godly to me," I said, giving his balls another jiggle. "What do you think?"

He gaped like a fish. I laughed again, loving the flavor of his terror, the thrill of even this paltry, pointless sort of power—

"Let him go."

The voice was familiar, and female. I craned my neck back, blinking in surprise to see that Glee Shoth stood behind my couch. She stood with her hands on her hips, tall and imposing and so very Maroneh in that room full of Temans. The look on her face was somehow disapproving and serene at once. If I hadn't spent several billion years trying to provoke that precise expression on another's face, I would have found it wholly disconcerting.

I beamed at her upside down and let the man go. "Oh, you are *so* his child."

She lifted an eyebrow, proving my point. "Would you care to join me outside?" Without waiting to see if I agreed, she turned and walked out.

Pouting, I got to my feet and swayed a bit. My companions were still there, to my surprise, but they were silent, all of them regarding me with a mixture of fear and distaste. Ah, well.

"May both my fathers smile upon you," I said to them, gesturing expansively and making a genuine effort to bless them, though nothing happened. "If you can manage to get a smile out of them, anyway, the ill-tempered bastards. And may my mother kill you all gently in your sleep, at the end of a long and healthy span. Farewell!"

The whole tavern was silent as I stumbled out after Glee.

She turned to walk with me as I reached the foot of the steps. I had not drunk so much that I couldn't walk, but steadiness was another matter. As I had expected, Glee made no compensation for my weaving and stumbling, and for the first block or so, I lagged about three paces behind her. "Your legs are very long," I complained. She was almost a foot taller than me.

"Make yours longer."

"I can't. My magic is gone."

"Then move them faster."

I sighed and did so. Gradually I drew alongside her. "Did you inherit anything from your mother? Or are you just him done over with breasts?"

"I have my mother's sense of humor." She glanced at me, contempt clear in her face. "I expected rather more of *you*, though."

I sighed. "I've had a hard day."

"Yes. When you cut off the messaging sphere, Ahad asked

me to find you. He suggested I search the gutters. I suppose I should be glad he was wrong about that."

I laughed, though a moment later my laughter faltered silent and I glared at her, affronted. "Why are you doing his bidding? Aren't you his boss? And what does it matter if I relax a little? I've spent the past two years running that bastard's errands, trying to help that pathetic little group of his keep this world from falling apart. Don't I deserve a night off?"

She stopped. By this point we stood on a quiet street corner in a residential neighborhood. It was late enough that no one was about. Which is perhaps why, for just an instant, her eyes seemed to flare red-gold like a struck match. I started, but then they were brown again, and more than a little angry.

"I have spent nearly this past *century* trying to keep this world from falling apart," she snapped. I blinked in surprise; she looked no older than thirty. I had forgotten that demons usually lived longer than humans, though both were mortal. "I'm not a god. I have no choice but to live in this realm, unlike you. I will do whatever I must to save it—including working with godlings like you who claim to despise Itempas, though in reality you're just as selfish and arrogant as him at his worst!"

She resumed walking, leaving me behind because I was too stunned to follow. By the time I recovered, she had disappeared around a corner. Furious, I ran after her, only to nearly trip when I rounded the corner and found her there, waiting.

"How dare you!" I hissed the words. "I am nothing like him!"

She sighed, shaking her head, and to my greater fury she decided not to argue with me. That sort of thing has always driven me mad. "Has it even occurred to you to ask why I came? Or are you too inebriated to think that far?"

"*I don't*—" I blinked. "Why are you here?"

"Because, as Ahad would have told you if you'd given him the chance to finish, we have work to do. Dekarta Arameri is altering and accelerating his route to proceed directly to Shadow in light of the engagement. When he and his escort arrive at Shadow—*tomorrow*, to foil potential troublemakers—there will be a grand procession through the city. Shahar Arameri is scheduled to appear publicly, on the steps of the Salon, for the first time since she gained her majority. The official announcement of the engagement will be made then, before the Nobles' Consortium and half the city, and Dekarta will be officially welcomed home at the same time. It should be quite the event."

Despite Glee's needling, I was not, in fact, too inebriated to think. The Arameri were not given to public spectacle—or at least they hadn't been during my time of servitude—mainly because it hadn't been necessary. What could top the glory of their unstated, rarely seen, utterly devastating power? And Sky was symbol enough of who they were. But times had changed, and their power now derived at least partially from their ability to awe the masses who had once been beneath their notice.

And...I shivered as I realized it. What better opportunity could there be for the Arameri's enemies to strike?

Glee nodded as she saw that I understood at last. "We will need everyone in the city, to watch for trouble."

I licked my lips, which were suddenly dry. "I don't have any magic left," I said. "Not a drop. I can do a few tricks, things maybe scriveners can do, but that's nothing much. I'm just a mortal now."

"Mortals have their uses." She said this with such delicate

irony that I grimaced. "And you love them, don't you? Shahar and Dekarta."

I remembered the mask-decayed bodies I had seen two years before, during my disastrous few days in Sky. I tried to imagine Shahar's and Dekarta's corpses laid out in the same way, their faces obscured by burned masks and their flesh too destroyed even to rot.

"Take me there," I said softly. "Wherever you're going. I want to help."

She inclined her head and extended a hand to me. I took it before it occurred to me to wonder what she could do. She wasn't a godling, just a demon. A mortal.

Then her power clamped down on the world around us, taking us in and out of reality with a god's deft strength. I could not help admiration; she had our father's touch.

Glee had rented an inn room in the northern Easha section of Shadow, a thriving business district near the city's center. I realized at once that it was one of the nicer inns—the kind of place I couldn't afford even on the salary Ahad gave me, and especially not before a major event in the city. It sounded as though there was a large and raucous crowd in the common room downstairs. Every inn in the city was probably filling up as people from the surrounding lands poured in to see the spectacle. Even Hymn's place would be getting some business amid this; I was glad, if so. Though hopefully they wouldn't be so crass as to rent out *my* room.

Glee went to the window and opened the shutters, revealing the reason she'd brought us here. I went to stand beside her and saw that the window overlooked the Avenue of Nobles, at the distant end of which stood the imposing white bulk of the Salon. We had a good view: I could see the tiny figures of people milling about the avenue near the Salon's wide steps and Order-Keepers in their conspicuously white uniforms setting up barriers to keep the onlookers back. Arameri did not appear in public often, though their faces were known thanks to the Order's news scrolls and the currency. Everyone in a hundred-mile radius had probably traveled to the city, or was on their way, to catch a once-in-a-lifetime glimpse.

Glee pointed along the avenue in the opposite direction, since it ran past the building we were in. "Dekarta's procession will enter the city from there. The route hasn't been published, but it will be in the news scrolls tomorrow morning. That makes it difficult for assassins to plan. But the procession will have to travel along the avenue this far; there's no other way for a large party to reach the Salon."

"Which means they might strike anywhere along this street?" I shook my head, incredulous. Even if I'd still had magic, it was an impossible scenario to try and plan for. In the morning, the dozens of mortals around the Salon would have grown to hundreds; by afternoon, when the event was to take place, there would be thousands. How to find just one amid the morass? "Do you know how the assassins get their victims to don the masks?"

"No." She sighed, and for an instant her stoic face slipped. I realized she was very tired, and troubled. Was Itempas doing nothing, fobbing all the work of protecting the world off on her? Bastard.

Turning from the window, Glee went to the room's handsome leather chair and sat down. I turned to sit on the windowsill, because I have always been more comfortable on such perches than in any conventional seat.

"So, we stay here until tomorrow, and then ... what?" I asked.

"Nemmer has a plan in place," she said. "Her people have done such things before. She knows how best to utilize the strengths of both godlings and mortals. But since you and I are neither, she's suggested that perhaps we could contribute most usefully by circulating through the crowd and keeping watch for anything unusual."

I shifted to prop one leg against the window frame, sighing at her characterization of me. "I still *think* like a godling, you know. I've tried to adjust, be more mortal, but—" I spread my hands. "I have been the Trickster for more years than most mortals know how to count. I'm not sure I'll live long enough to become anything else, in my head."

She rested her head on the chair back and closed her eyes, evidently planning to sleep there. "Even gods have limits; yours are just different. Do what you can within them."

Silence fell between us, but for the soft stir of a night breeze through the open window and the mortals in the common room below, who were singing some sort of song in lusty and off-beat cadence. I listened to them for a while, smiling as I recognized the song as a variation on one I'd taught their ancestors. I hummed the tune along with them until I grew bored, and then I glanced at Glee to see if she was asleep—to find her eyes open, watching me.

So I sighed and decided to address the matter directly. "So, little sister." She lifted an eyebrow at this, and I smiled. "How old are you?"

"Older than I look, like you."

Nearly a century, she'd said. "You're Oree Shoth's daughter." I vaguely remembered her. A beautiful mortal girl, blind and brave. She had loved one of my younger brothers, who'd died. And she'd loved Itempas, too, apparently. I couldn't see him coupling with her otherwise. Ephemeral intimacy offended him.

"Yes."

"She still call him 'Shiny'?"

"Oree Shoth is dead."

"Oh." I frowned. Something about her phrasing was odd, but I couldn't figure out what. "I'm sorry."

Glee was silent for a moment, her gaze disconcertingly direct. Another thing she'd gotten from him. "Are you really?"

"What?"

She crossed her legs primly. "I was always told that you were one of mortalkind's champions, in the old days. But now you don't seem to like mortals much." She shrugged as I scowled. "Understandably. But given that, I can't see you getting especially upset about one more death."

"Well, that would mean you don't know me very well, wouldn't it?"

To my surprise, she nodded. "That's precisely what it means. Which is why I asked: are you sorry for my mother's death? Honestly."

Surprised, I closed my mouth and considered my answer. "I am," I said at last. "I liked her. She had the kind of personality that I think I could've gotten along with, if she hadn't been so devoted to Itempas." I paused, considering. "Even so, I never would've expected him to *respond* to that devotion. Oree Shoth must've been pretty special to make him take a chance on a mortal woman again…"

"He left my mother before I was born."

"He—" Now I stared at her, flummoxed, because that was not at all like him. His heart did not change. But then I remembered another mortal lover and child he'd left behind, centuries ago. It was not his nature to leave, but he could be persuaded to do so, if it was in the best interests of those he cared for.

"Lord Nahadoth and Lady Enefa demanded it," Glee said, reading my face. "He left only to save her—our—lives. So, later, when I was old enough, I went looking for him. Eventually I found him. I've traveled with him ever since."

"I see." A tale worthy of the gods, though she wasn't one of us. And then, because it was in my mind and she knew it was there and there was no point in my trying to conceal the obvious, I asked the question that had hovered between us for the whole two years since we'd met. "What is he like now?"

She took her time answering, appearing to consider her words carefully. "I don't know what he was like before the War," she said, "or even during the years of your…incarceration. I don't know if he's the same as he was then, or different."

"He doesn't change."

Another of those odd silences. "I think he may have."

"He *can't* change. It's anathema to him."

She shook her head, with familiar stubbornness. "He can. He did when he killed Enefa, and I believe he's changed again since. He's *always* been able to change, and he's always done it, however slowly or reluctantly, because he's a living being and change is part of life. Enefa didn't make it that way; she just took the common qualities her brothers already possessed and put those into the godlings and mortals she created."

I wondered if she'd had this conversation with Itempas. "Except she made mortalkind complete, unlike us."

She shook her head again, the soft curls of her hair wafting gently as if in a breeze. "Gods are just as complete as mortals. Nahadoth isn't wholly dark. Father isn't wholly light." She paused, her eyes narrowing at me. "*You* haven't been a true child since the universe was young. And for that matter, the War in part began because Enefa—the preserver of balance—*lost* her balance. She loved one of her brothers more than the other, and that broke them all."

I stiffened. "How *dare* you blame her! You don't know anything about it—"

"I know what he told me. I know what I've learned, from books and legends and conversations with godlings who were there when the whole mess began, who watched from the sidelines and tried to think how to stop it, and wept as they realized they could not. You were too close, Sieh; you were hip-deep in the carnage. You decided Itempas was to blame without ever asking *why*."

"He killed my mother! Who cares why?"

"His siblings abandoned him. Only for a brief time, but solitude is his antithesis; it weakened him. Then Shahar Arameri murdered his son, and that drove him over the edge. In this case, the 'why' matters a great deal, I think."

I laughed, bitter, sick with guilt and trying to hide my shock. Solitude? *Solitude?* I had never known that—No, none of that mattered. It could not matter. "A mortal! Why in the Maelstrom's name would he mourn a single mortal so powerfully?"

"Because he loves his children." I flinched. Glee was glaring at me, her eyes plainly visible in the dim room. Neither of us had bothered to put on a light, because the light from the street lanterns was more than enough to see by. "Because he's a good father, and good fathers do not stop loving if their children are merely mortal. Or if those children hate them."

I stared at her and found myself trembling. "He didn't love us when he fought us in the War."

Glee folded her hands in front of her, steepling her fingers. She'd been spending too much time with Ahad. "From what I understand, your side was winning until Shahar Arameri used the Stone of Earth. Weren't you?"

"What the hells does that matter?"

"You tell me."

And of course I thought back to the worst days of my life. Shahar had not been the first to use the Stone. I had sensed a godling's controlling hand first, sending searing power— the power of life and death itself—in a terrible wave across the battlefield of earth. Dozens of my siblings had fallen in that attack. It had nearly caught me, too. That had been the first warning that the tide was turning. Until then, the taste of triumph had been thick in my mouth. Who had that god-ling been? One of Tempa's loyalists; he'd had his own, same as Nahadoth. Whoever it was had died trying to wield the power of Enefa.

Then Shahar had gotten the Stone, and she hadn't both-ered attacking mere godlings. She went straight for Nahadoth, whom she hated most because he had taken Itempas from her. I remembered watching him fall. I had screamed and wept and known then that it was my fault. All of it.

"He…didn't have to…" I whispered. "Itempas. If he was so sorry, he could have just—"

"That isn't his nature. Order is cause and effect, action and reaction. When attacked, he fights back."

I heard her shift to get comfortable in the chair. I heard this, because I could not look at her anymore, with her fine dark skin and too-keen eyes. She was not as obviously alien as Shinda had been, all those centuries ago. She could hide among mortalkind more easily because her peculiar heritage did not immediately announce itself and because the last thing anyone noticed about a six-foot-tall black woman was the aura of magic. There was something about her that made me think she was quite capable of defending herself, too—and I sensed Itempas's hand in that. Action and reaction. *This* mortal child would not die so easily; her father had made sure of that.

Our father.

"Many things triggered the War," said Glee, speaking softly. "Shahar Arameri's madness, Itempas's grief, Enefa's jealousy, Nahadoth's carelessness. No one person is to blame." She lifted her chin belligerently. "However much you might like to believe otherwise."

I stayed silent.

Itempas had never been like Nahadoth. Naha plucked lovers from the mass of mortality like flowers from a meadow, and he discarded them as easily when they wilted or a more interesting flower came along. Oh, he loved them, in his own erratic way, but steadfastness was not his nature.

Not so Itempas. He did not love easily—but when he did, he loved forever. He had turned to Shahar Arameri, his high priestess, when Nahadoth and Enefa stopped wanting him.

They'd never stopped loving him, of course; they'd just loved each other a little more. But to Itempas, it must have felt like the darkest of hells. Shahar had offered her love, and he had accepted it, because he was a creature of logic, and *something* was better than *nothing*. And because he had chosen to love her and please her, he had bent his own rules enough to give her a son. Then he'd loved that son and stayed with his mortal family for ten years. He could have easily been content with them for the remainder of their mortal lives. An eyeblink in a god's eternity. No great matter.

He had left them only because Naha and Nefa had convinced him that the mortals would be better off without him. And Naha and Nefa had done that only because someone had lied to them.

Just a harmless trick, I had thought then. It harmed only the mortals, and then only a little. Shahar had status and wealth, and mortals were adaptable. They did not need him.

Just a harmless trick.

No one person is to blame, Itempas's daughter had said.

I closed my mouth against the taste of old, ground-in guilt.

In my silence, Glee spoke again. "As for what kind of man he is now..." I thought she shrugged. "He's stubborn, and proud, and infuriating. The kind of man who will move the earth and skies to get what he wants. Or to protect those he cares for."

Yes. I remembered that man. How minute of a change was sanity to insanity and back? Not much, across the expanse of time.

"I want to see him," I whispered.

She was silent for a moment. "I will not allow you to harm him."

"I don't want to harm him, damn it—" Though I had, I remembered, on one of the last occasions I'd seen him. She must have heard about that. I grimaced. "I won't do anything this time, I promise."

"The promise of a trickster."

I forced myself to take a deep breath against my own temper, releasing that held breath rather than the furious words in my thoughts. It was not right, the way I thought of her. Mortal. Inferior. It was not right that I struggled to respect her. She was as much a child of the Three as I.

"There's no promise I can offer that you'll trust," I said, and was relieved that my voice stayed soft. "You shouldn't, really. I only *have* to keep promises to children. And honestly, I don't know if even that applies anymore. Everything I am has changed." I leaned my head back on the window and gazed out at the night-lit city below.

Nahadoth could hear any words spoken at night, if he wanted.

"Please let me see him," I said again.

She watched me steadily. "You should know that his magic works only in certain circumstances. It's not powerful enough to stop whatever's happened to you—not in his current form."

"I know. And I know you have to keep him safe. Do what you have to do. But if it's possible..."

I could see her, very faintly, beyond my reflection. She nodded to herself slowly, as if I'd passed some sort of test. "It's possible. I can't promise anything, of course; he may not want to see *you*. But I'll speak to him." She paused. "I'd appreciate it if you didn't tell Ahad."

Surprised, I glanced at her. My senses were not so dull that I couldn't still distinguish scents, and the faint whiff of Ahad—cheroots and bitterness and emotions like long-clotted blood—clung to her like stale perfume. It was a few days old, but she had been in his presence, close to him, touching him. "I thought you had a thing with him."

She had the grace to look abashed. "I find him attractive, I suppose. That's not 'a thing.'"

I shook my head, bemused. "I'm still amazed that he had enough of a soul to be made into a complete and separate being. I don't know what you see in him."

"You don't know him," she said, with a hint of sharpness that told me there was more to the "thing" than she was letting on. "He does not reveal himself to you. He loved you once; you can hurt him as no one else can. What you think of him, and what he truly is, are very different things."

I rocked back a little, surprised at her vehemence. "Well, clearly you don't trust him—"

She flicked a hand impatiently, dismissively. Gods, she was so much like Itempas that it hurt. "I'm not a fool. It may be a long time before he sheds the habits of his former life. Until then, I'm cautious with him."

I was tempted to warn her further: she needed to be more than cautious with Ahad. He had been created from the substance of Nahadoth in his darkest hour, nurtured on suffering and refined by hate. He liked to hurt people. I don't think even he realized what a monster he was.

But that impatient little flick had been a warning for *me*. She wasn't interested in whatever I had to say about Ahad. Clearly she intended to judge him for herself. I couldn't really blame her; I wasn't exactly unbiased.

I wasn't tired, but clearly Glee was. She fell silent after that, and I turned back to the window to let her sleep. Presently her breathing evened out, providing a slow and curiously soothing background noise for my thoughts. The people in the common room had finally shut up. There was no one but me and the city.

And Nahadoth, appearing silently in the window reflection behind me.

I was not surprised to see him. I smiled at the pale glimmer of his face, not turning from the window. "It's been a while."

The change to his face was minute; a slight drawing together of those fine, perfect brows. I chuckled, guessing his thoughts. A while; two years. Barely noticeable, to a god. I'd taken longer naps. "Every passing moment shortens my life, Naha. Of course I feel it more now."

"Yes." He fell silent again, thinking his unfathomable thoughts. He didn't look well, I decided, though this had nothing to do with his actual appearance, which was magnificent. But that was just his usual mask. Beneath that mask, which I could just barely perceive, he felt . . . strange. Off. A storm whose winds had faltered at the touch of colder, quelling air. He was unhappy—very much so.

"When you see Itempas," he said at last, "ask him to help you."

At this I swung around on the windowsill, frowning. "You're not serious."

"Yeine can do nothing to erase your mortality. I can neither cure nor preserve you. I meant it, Sieh, when I said I would not lose you."

"There's nothing he can *do*, Naha. He's got less magic than me!"

"Yeine and I have discussed the matter. We will grant him a single day's parole if he will agree to help you."

My mouth fell open. It took me several tries to speak. "He's endured barely a century of mortality. Do you really think we can trust him?"

"If he attempts to escape or attack us, I will kill his demon."

I flinched. "Glee?" I glanced at her. She had fallen asleep in the chair, her head slumped to one side. Either she was a heavy sleeper, an excellent faker, or Naha was keeping her asleep. Most likely the latter, given the subject of our conversation.

She had tried to help me.

"Are we Arameri now?" I asked. My voice was harsher than usual in the dimness, deep and rough. I kept forgetting that it was not a child's voice. "Are we willing to pervert love itself to get what we want?"

"*Yes*." I knew he meant it by the fact that the room's temperature suddenly dropped ten degrees. "The Arameri are wise in one respect, Sieh: they show no mercy to their enemies. I will not risk unleashing Itempas's madness again. He lives only because the mortal realm cannot exist without him and because Yeine has pleaded for his life. I permitted him to keep his daughter only for this purpose. Demon, beloved...she is a weapon, and I mean to use her."

I shook my head in disbelief. "You regretted what you did to the demons, Naha. Have you forgotten that? They are our children, too, you said—"

He stepped closer, reaching for my face. "You are the only child who matters to me now."

I recoiled and struck his hand away. His eyes widened in surprise. "What the hells kind of father are you? You always say things like that, treat some of us better than others. Gods, Naha! How twisted is that?"

Silence fell, and in it my soul shriveled. Not in fear. It was simply that I knew, or had known, precisely why he did not love all his children equally. Differentiation, variation, appreciation of the unique: this was part of what he was. His children were not the same, so his feelings toward each were not the same. He loved us all, but differently. And because he did this, because he did not pretend that love was fair or equal, mortals could mate for an afternoon or for the rest of their lives. Mothers could tell their twins or triplets apart. Children could have crushes and outgrow them; elders could remain devoted to their spouses long after beauty had gone. The mortal heart was fickle. Naha made it so. And because of this, they were free to love as they wished, and not solely by the dictates of instinct or power or tradition.

I had understood this once. All gods did.

My hand dropped into my lap. It was shaking. "I'm sorry," I whispered.

He lowered his hand, too, saying nothing for a long, bruised moment.

"You cannot remain in mortal flesh much longer," he said at last. "It's changing you."

I lowered my head and nodded once. He was my father, and he knew best. I had been wrong not to listen.

With a night-breeze sigh, Nahadoth turned away, his substance beginning to blend into the room's shadows. Sudden, irrational panic seized me. I sprang to my feet, my throat knotting in fear and anguish. "Naha—please. Will you…"

Mortal, mortal, I was truly mortal now. I was his favorite, he was my dark father, his love was fickle, and I had changed almost beyond recognition. "Please don't leave yet."

He turned back and swept forward all in one motion, and all at once I was adrift and cradled in the soft dark of his innermost self, with hands I could not see stroking my hair.

"You will always be mine, Sieh." His voice was everywhere. He had never let anyone but me and his siblings into this part of himself. It was the core of him, vulnerable, pure. "Even if you love him again. Even if you grow old. I am not wholly dark, Itempas is not wholly light, and there are some things about me that will never change, not even if the walls of the Maelstrom should fall."

Then he was gone. I lay on the patterned rug, shivering as the inn room began to warm up in Nahadoth's wake, watching the silver curls of my own breath. I was too cold to cry, so I tried to remember a lullaby that Nahadoth had once sung to me, so that I could sing myself to sleep. But the words would not come. The memory was gone.

In the morning I woke to find Glee standing over me with a mixture of confusion and contempt on her face. But she offered me a hand to help me up from the floor.

A new little sister. And Ahad was a new sibling, too. I vowed to try and be a better brother to them both.

Dekarta's procession was spotted on the outskirts of the city around midmorning. At the rate they were wending their way through the streets—passing through South Root, of all things; Hymn's parents would make a killing—they would reach the Avenue of Nobles at twilight.

Auspicious timing, I decided. Then I followed Glee out of the inn and we slipped into the crowd to try and keep Shahar and Dekarta alive for a few paltry years more.

15

The soldiers go a-marching
pomp pomp pomp
The catapults are flinging
whomp whomp whomp
The horses come a-trotting
clomp clomp clomp
And down falls the enemy
stomp stomp stomp!

THE STEPS OF THE SALON were impressive on their own: white marble, wide and colonnaded, gently curving around the building's girth. Clearly they were not impressive enough for Arameri tastes, however, and so the steps had been embellished. Two additional stairwells—immense and unsupported—curved off the Salon's steps to the left and right like wings poised in flight. They were made of daystone so that they glowed faintly; only a scrivener could have built them. They were magnificent even against the looming backdrop of the Tree, which tended to diminish any mortal effort at grandeur to pointlessness. In fact, the twin stairwells seemed to come from the Tree itself, suggesting a divine connection for the people who descended them. Which was probably the point.

I could not see the platforms at the tops of the daystone stairways, but it was not hard to guess that the scriveners had etched gates into each. Shahar, Remath, and perhaps a few others of the Central Family would arrive by this means, then descend to the Salon's actual steps. Revoltingly predictable, but they were Itempans; I couldn't expect better.

Sighing, I craned my neck again from my vantage point: the lid of a muckbin at the corner of a dead-end street, about a block away from the Salon building. The Avenue of Nobles was a sea of mortal heads, thousands of people standing about or walking, laughing, talking, the aura of excitement wafting off them like a warm summer breeze. The city's street artists had taken shameless advantage of the opportunity to make festive ribbon pennants, dancing puppets with the faces of famous folk, and small contraptions that blatted out a few flakes of sparkling white confetti when blown hard. Already the air was thick with the glittering motes, which did a marvelous job of capturing the thin, dappled light that passed for daytime in Shadow. Adults and children alike seemed to love the things. I shivered now and again as their pleasure in the toys stirred whatever was left of the god in me.

Hard to focus, amid so many distractions. (My hands itched to play with one of the puppets. It had been so long since I'd had a new toy.) But I had a job to do, so I kept scanning the crowd, holding on to a gutter pipe as I leaned this way and that. I would know when I found what I was looking for. It was only a matter of time.

Then, just as I had begun to worry, I spotted my quarry. Moving past a tightly packed group of middle-aged women who looked both thrilled and terrified to be among such a crowd:

a boy of nine or ten years old. Amn, wearing old clothing that had the look of garments taken from a White Hall tithe pile, with unkempt hair that hadn't seen a comb in days. He passed one of the women and stumbled, bracing one hand on her back to right himself and apologizing quickly. It was nicely done; he had bowed himself away and into the current of foot traffic almost before the woman realized he'd touched her.

I grinned, delighted. Then I hopped down from the bin lid (another man immediately claimed my place atop it, throwing a belligerent look at my back) and hurried after him.

Took half a block to catch up with him; he was small and wove among the members of the crowd as deftly as a river snake among reeds. I was a grown-up and had to be polite. But I'd guessed his destination—a pack of children milling about a stall that sold tamarind-lime juice—and that made it easy to head him off a few feet before he reached them. I caught his thin, wiry arm and stayed ready, because boys his age were not defenseless. They had no compunctions against biting, and they tended to run in packs.

The boy swore at me in polyglot profanity, immediately trying to pull free. "Leggo!"

"What'd you take?" I asked, genuinely curious. The woman hadn't had a purse visible, probably fearing exactly what had happened to her, but there could have been one beneath her clothing. "Jewelry? A shawl or something? Or did you actually manage to get into her pocket?" If the latter, he was a master of his craft and would be perfect for my needs.

His eyes grew wide. "'In't take nothin'! Who th' hells—" He jumped suddenly and grabbed at my wrist, which was already emerging from *his* pocket. I'd gotten only one coin; my hands were too damned big now for proper pocket-picking. But his face turned purple with fury and consternation, and I grinned.

I lifted the hand that held the coin and closed my fingers around it. Didn't even need magic for this trick: when I opened my hand again, two coins lay there, his and one from my own pocket.

The boy froze, staring at this. He did not take either coin, turning a suddenly shrewd and wary look on me. "Wh'you want?"

I let him go, now that I'd gotten his attention. "To hire you, and any friends you've got with similar inclinations."

"We don't want trouble." The slangy, contracted Senmite he'd been using vanished as swiftly as he had, after lifting the woman's purse. "Keepers don't bother us as long as we stick to pockets and wallets. Anything more and they'll hunt us down."

I nodded, wishing I could bless him with safety. "All I want you to do is look," I said. "Move through the crowd, see what you usually see, do what you usually do. But if you let me, I can look through your eyes."

He caught his breath, and for a moment I couldn't read his face. He was astonished and skeptical and hopeful and frightened, all at once. But he searched my face with such sudden intensity that I realized, far later than I should have, what he was thinking. When I did, I started to grin, and that did it: his eyes got as big as twenty-meri coins.

"Trickster, trickster," he whispered. "Stole the sun for a prank." En pulsed on my breast, pleased to be mentioned.

"No prayers, now," I said, cupping his cheek with one hand. Mine. "I'm not a god today, just a man who needs your help. Will you give it?"

He inclined his head just a hair more formally than he needed to. Ah, he was marvelous. "Your hand," I said, and he offered it to me at once.

I still had a few ways of using magic, though they were crude and weak and a betrayal of my pride to employ. The universe did not listen to me the way it once had, but as long as I kept the requests simple, it would grudgingly obey. "Look," I said in our tongue, and the air shivered around us as I traced the shape of an eye into the boy's palm with my fingertip. "Hear. Share."

The outline flickered briefly, a silver flash like drifting confetti, and then the boy's flesh was just flesh again. He peered at it, fascinated.

"Find your friends," I said. "Touch as many of them as you can with this hand, and send them out among the crowd. The magic will end when the Arameri family head returns to Sky." Then I closed my free hand and opened it again. This time a single coin sat in my palm: a hundred-meri piece, more than the boy could have stolen in a week, unless he'd gotten very bold or very lucky.

The boy's eyes fixed on it, but he did not reach for it, swallowing. "I can't take money from you."

"Don't be stupid," I said, and tucked the coin into his pocket before I let him go. "No follower of mine should ever do something for nothing. If you need to change it safely, go to the Arms of Night in South Root and tell Ahad I sent you. He'll be an ass about it, but he won't cheat you. Now go." And because he was staring at me, awe stunting his wits, I winked at him and then stepped back, letting myself vanish amid the crowd. There was no magic to this. It just took an understanding of how mortals moved when they gathered together in great herds like this. The boy did the same thing as part of his pickpocketing, but I had several thousand years' experience on him. From his perspective, I seemed to disappear. I caught a final glimpse of his mouth falling open, and then I let the traffic carry me elsewhere.

"Smoothly done," said Glee when I found her again. She had been waiting in front of a small café, standing as still and striking as a pillar amid the flow of babbling mostly Amn.

"You were watching?" The café had a bench, which was packed; I didn't even try to sit. Instead I leaned against a wall, half in Glee's shadow. Though neither of us were Amn, I was betting no one would notice me with her there. After five minutes I knew I was right; half the people who had passed us glanced at her, and the other half ignored us altogether.

"Some," she replied. "I'm not a god. I can't see without my eyes like you do. But I can see magic, even in a crowd."

"Oh." Demon magic was always strange. I slipped my hands into my pockets and yawned loudly, not bothering to cover my mouth despite the disgusted glances of a passing couple. "So, Itempas around here somewhere, too?"

"No."

I snorted. "What exactly is it that you're protecting him *from*? Nothing short of demons' blood can kill him, and who would do that, given the consequences?"

She said nothing for a long moment, and I thought she would ignore me. Then she said, "How much do you know about godsblood?"

"I know the mortals drink it, when they can, for a taste of magic." My lip curled. During my first few decades in Sky, some of the Arameri had taken blood from me. It had done nothing for them, since my flesh then was more or less mortal, but that hadn't stopped them from trying. "I know some of my siblings sell it to them, gods know why."

Glee shrugged. "Our organization, via Kitr's group, keeps an eye on such sales. A few months ago, Kitr received a request for some very unusual godsblood. More unusual, anyway, than the standard requests for menstrual flow or heart blood."

Now it was my turn to be surprised, mostly because I hadn't realized any of my sisters bothered menstruating. Why in darkness—Well, it didn't matter. "Itempas is mortal now. His flesh is, anyway. His blood would only sour some poor mortal's stomach."

"He's still one of the Three, Sieh. Even without magic, his blood has value. And who's to say that these mask users can't find a way to eke magic out of Father's blood even in his current state? Remember that there is godsblood in the northerners' masks...and remember that Kahl's mask is yet incomplete."

I cursed as I understood. I did this strictly in Senmite—too dangerous to speak our tongue under these conditions. No way to know who was listening or what strange magics slept nearby. "*This* is what comes of gods selling pieces of themselves to mortals." My stupid, stupid younger siblings! Hadn't they seen, again and again, that mortals would always find a way to use gods, hurt us, control us, if they could? I slammed a fist against the unyielding stone of the wall behind me and gasped as, instead of cracking the wall, my hand reminded me of its fragility with a white, breathtaking flash of pain.

Glee sighed. "Stop that." Coming over, she took my hand

and lifted it, turning it this way and that to see whether I'd broken the bone. I hissed and tried to pull away, but she threw me such a quelling glare at me that I stopped squirming and meekly held still. She would be a terrifying mother someday, if she ever had children.

"For what it's worth, I agree with you," she said quietly. "Though I don't limit my condemnation to mortals. Remember what gods have done with the blood of demons, after all."

I flinched at this, my anger evaporating into shame.

"Not broken," she pronounced, and let me go. I cradled my hand to my chest since it still hurt, and sulking made me feel better.

"Gods are not truly creatures of flesh," Glee continued, nodding toward my injured hand. "I understand this. But the vessels that you wear in this realm contain something of the real you—enough to access the greater whole." She let out a long, heavy breath. "The Arameri had Nahadoth in their possession for centuries. You know, better than I, how much of his body they might have taken in that time. And while I doubt they have anything of Yeine, they *did* have a piece of Enefa in their keeping."

I inhaled. The Stone of Earth. The last remnant of my mother's flesh, taken from the corporeal form that had died when Itempas poisoned her with demons' blood. It was gone now, because Yeine had incorporated it into herself. But for two thousand years it had been a physical object, kept in the exclusive possession of mortals who had already developed a taste for the power of gods.

"A pound of the Nightlord's flesh," Glee said, "and perhaps nothing more than a speck of the Gray Lady's. Add to that some portion of the Dayfather, and use mortal magic to stir the mix..." She shrugged. "I cannot imagine what would result from such a recipe. Can you?"

Nothing good. Nothing *sane*. To mingle the essences of the Three was to invoke a level of power that no mortal, and few godlings, could handle safely. The crater that would be left by such an attempt would be immense—and it would be a crater not on the face of the world but on reality itself.

"No god would do this," I murmured, shaken. "This Kahl... he has to know how dangerous this is. He can't be planning what we think he's planning." Vengeance was his nature, but this went beyond vengeance. This was madness.

"Nevertheless," Glee said. "The worst case is what we must prepare for. And this is why I don't intend to let anyone have my father." The familiar look was there again, in the cold implacability of her voice and the stubborn set of her shoulders. For a moment I imagined a circle of light revolving about her, a white sword in her hands... but no.

"You're mortal," I said softly. "Even if you can somehow keep Itempas hidden from a god, you won't be able to do it forever. If nothing else, Kahl can wait you out."

She looked at me, and for an instant I was painfully aware that only the fragile shield of her skin stood between me and her deadly, demonic blood.

"Kahl will die before I do," she said. "I'll make certain of that." With that, she turned and walked into the crowd, leaving me alone with my wonder and fear.

I bought a tamarind juice to console myself.

After a while, I decided to see whether the seed I'd planted had borne any fruit. Closing my eyes and sitting down on the steps of a closed bookstore, I sought out the boy who bore my mark. It took only a moment, and to my delight I found that he had spread the mark to eight others already, all of whom were now roving through the crowd on both sides of the barricaded street. I could hear through them, too—mostly the ever-present murmur of the crowd, punctuated by the occasional variance: horse hooves as a mounted Order-Keeper passed on the street, music as a busker plied his trade. All of the sights were from a child's point of view. I sighed in longing and settled in to wait for the festivities to begin.

Two hours passed. Glee eventually came back and reported that Nemmer—who hadn't bothered to speak to me—had sent a message that there was no sign of trouble thus far. Better still, Glee handed me a cup of savory ice flavored with rosemary and serry flowers that she'd bought from some vendor; for that alone I would love her forever.

As I licked my fingers, the crowd abruptly grew tense, and their noise trebled all at once. I had to keep my eyes closed in order to focus on the children's vision, but through their eyes I saw the first white, waving banners of Dekarta's procession, which had reached the Avenue of Nobles at last. There came a marching column of soldiers first, several hundred deep. In their midst rode a massive palanquin, gliding smoothly along on the shoulders of dozens of men. Mounted soldiers and Order-Keepers flanked this, some with an air that made me suspect they were scriveners, and more soldiers followed behind. The palanquin was simple and graceful in its design, little more than a railed platform, but it had been constructed of daystone, too, and shone like noonday in this perpetually twilit city.

And atop this, stunning and stark in black, stood Dekarta.

He'd added a heavy mantle to his outfit, which suited his broad shoulders perfectly, and he stood with legs apart and his hands gripping the forward rail as if it were the yoke of the world. No detached gaze for him; his eyes scanned the crowd as the procession traveled, his expression as cool and challenging as I'd ever seen. When the palanquin stopped and the men lowered it to the ground, he did not wait for it to touch the street stones before he stepped off its side and strode forward, purposeful and swift. The soldiers parted clumsily, and his guards scrambled to follow. Deka stopped, however, on reaching the foot of the steps. There he flicked back his cloak and waited, his eyes trained on the World Tree—or perhaps he was gazing at the palace nestled in the lowest fork of its trunk. It was his first sight of home in ten years, after all. If he still considered Sky home.

The crowd, meanwhile, had gone mad for him. People on either side of the street barriers cheered, shouted, and waved their white pennants. Through one of my spy-children's eyes, I saw a gaggle of well-dressed merchant girls scream and point at Deka and scream again, clutching each other and jumping up and down. It was more than his beauty, I realized. It was everything: his hauteur, the implied defiance of his clothing, the confidence that seemed to issue from his very pores. Everyone knew his story—born an outsider, the spare who could never be heir. That was part of it, too. He was more like them than a true Arameri, and he was stronger, not weaker, for his difference. They certainly seemed to love him for it.

But then there was a stir at the other end of the avenue. From somewhere within the Salon, two people emerged. Ramina Arameri, magnificent in a white uniform with the full sigil stark on his brow, and another man I didn't recognize. Well dressed, Teman, tall for one of that race, with waist-length locks wrapped in silver cuffs and studded with what had to be diamonds. He wore white, too, though not completely. The centerline of his uniform, which otherwise matched Ramina's, had been accented by a double line of green fabric edged in gold. The colors of the Teman Protectorate. Datennay Canru, Shahar's husband-to-be.

They moved to the center of the steps and then stood waiting, their presence enough of a warning that no one missed what followed.

There was a flicker atop both sets of daystone steps, and in the same instant two women appeared. To the right was Remath, clad in a deceptively simple white satin gown, carrying an object that made my belly clench: a glass scepter, tipped with a spadelike sharp blade. To the left...

In spite of everything that had happened, in spite of my resolve to be a man and not a boy about it, I had to open my own eyes to see her for myself. Shahar.

It was clear that Remath intended for her daughter to be the center of attention. This was not difficult, as like Dekarta, Shahar had only grown in beauty over the years. Her figure had filled out, her hair was longer, and the lines of her face seemed more settled and mature—the face of a woman, at last, rather than a girl. The dress she wore seemed barely attached to her flesh. The base garment was a translucent tube, thin enough that all of Shadow could see her pale skin through its fabric—but at her breasts and hips, enormous silvery flower petals, loose and curling and long as a man's arm, had been adhered to the material. They drifted behind her like clouds as she came down the steps. There was a collective gasp from the crowd as everyone realized: the petals were real and taken from the World Tree's flowers. Given the size, however, they could only have been blossoms from very high on the Tree, where the Tree pierced the world's envelope. No mortal flower collector could climb to such airless heights, and the Arameri no longer had god-slaves. How had they gotten them? Regardless, the effect was perfect: Shahar had become a mortal woman swathed in the divine.

Shahar's expression, unlike Remath's, was everything an Arameri heir's should be: proud, arrogant, superior. But when she turned to face her mother and they walked toward each other, she lowered her gaze with just the perfect touch of humility. The world was not hers, not yet, not quite. Mother and daughter met between the steps, and Remath took Shahar's left hand in her right. Then—with such casual grace that they had to have practiced it dozens of times—both women turned toward the Avenue of Nobles and raised their free hands toward Dekarta, in clear welcome.

Showing no hint of the reticence or resentment that I suspected he felt, Dekarta climbed the steps to reach them, then knelt at their feet. Both women bent, offering him their hands, each of which he took in his own. Then he rose, moving to Remath's left, and all three turned to face the waiting masses, raising their joined hands for the world to see.

The crowd was a many-headed beast, screaming, stamping, cheering. The air was so full of glittering confetti that the city seemed to have been struck by a silver snowstorm. And as this little show took place, I redoubled my concentration and straightened from my slouch against the wall. I caught a glimpse of Glee, not far off: she stood tense, scanning the street with whatever peculiar senses a demon could bring to bear. This was the moment, I felt with certainty. If Usein Darr or Kahl or some ambitious Arameri rival meant to strike, they would do it now.

Sure enough, one of my spy-children saw something.

It might have been nothing. The busker I had noticed earlier near the public well had stopped playing a battered old brass lunla to peer at something. I would have dismissed the image if it had not come from my clever one, the pickpocket I'd marked. If he was paying such sudden and close attention to the busker, then there was something about the busker worth seeing.

I noticed the busker's open lunla case, which he'd set out before him as a silent appeal to passersby. Atop the layer of coins and notes scattered on the worn velvet, someone had tossed a larger object. I saw the busker pick it up, frowning in puzzlement. I saw the eyeholes and caught a quick glimpse of lacing lines on the inside of the thing before the busker turned it around, trying to figure out what it was.

A mask.

I was moving before I opened my eyes. Glee was beside me, both of us rudely shoving our way through the crowd as needed. She had taken out the small messaging sphere again, and this time it glowed red instead of white, sending some wordless signal. For an instant my god-senses actually worked, and in that span, I felt the faint tremor of my siblings' movements, folding and unfolding the world as they converged on the area.

Through the eyes of my boy, I saw the busker's face go suddenly slack, as though a brain fit had seized him. Instead of twitching or slumping, however, he moved the mask forward, like a man moving in a dream. He put it over his face. As he tied it at the back, I caught a glimpse of white lacquer and starkly drawn shade lines. The suggestion of an entirely different face: implacable, serene, frightening. I had no idea what archetype it had been meant to symbolize. Through the eyeholes of this, the busker blinked once, sudden awareness and confusion coming into them as though he couldn't fathom why he'd put the demonshitting thing on. He reached up to pull it off.

The designs of the mask flickered, as if they'd caught the light for a moment. A breath later, the man's eyes went dead. Not closed, not dazed. I am a son of Enefa; I know death when I see it.

Yet the busker got to his feet and looked around, pausing as his white-masked face oriented on the top of the Salon steps. I expected him to begin walking in that direction. Instead he charged toward the steps, running faster than any mortal should have been able, plowing down or flinging aside—*far* aside—anyone unfortunate enough to get in his way.

I also did not expect the cobblestones that edged the Salon steps to suddenly flare white, revealing themselves to be bricks of daystone that someone had painted gray to match the surrounding granite. Through this translucent layer of paint, I could see the darker, starker lines of an etched sigil, the characters on each stone together commanding immobility in the harshest gods' pidgin and addressed to any living thing that tried to cross it. A shield, of sorts, and it should have worked. The Arameri on the steps had no fear of knives or arrows; their blood sigils could deflect such things easily. All they needed to fear were the mask-wielding assassins, whose strange magic could somehow circumvent their sigils. Keep them out of reach and the Arameri would be safe—so the scrivener corps had reasoned.

The busker staggered, then stopped as he reached the ring of stones. The mask swung from side to side, not in negation, and not with any movement that could be interpreted as human. I had seen gravel lizards do the same, swaying back and forth over a carcass.

Too late I remembered the simplistic literalness of scrivening magic. Any *living* thing, the stones commanded. But even if the busker's heart still beat and his limbs still moved, that alone did not qualify as life. The mask had dimmed his soul to nothingness.

The busker stopped swaying, the rounded eyeholes fixed on a target. I followed its gaze and saw Shahar frozen at the top of the steps, her eyes wide and her expression still.

"Oh, demons," I groaned, and ran for the steps as fast as I could.

The busker stepped closer to the sigil-stones.

"There!" cried Glee, pointing.

She could not have been talking to me. As the crowd's cheers turned to screams and stamping became stampeding, Kitr appeared at the foot of the steps, just in front of the Arameri guard. A line of twelve glowing red knives appeared in the air before her, hovering and ready. I had seen her fling those knives through armies, leaving fallen mortals like scythed wheat. She could have done that here, risking the crowd to get her target, but like most of the godlings of the city, she would not. They had all taken an oath to respect mortal life. So she waited for the fleeing mortals to scatter more, giving her a clear shot.

I saw the danger before she did, for she had ignored the Arameri's guards behind her. Faced with a strange godling and a mad mortal, they reacted to both. Half of them fired cross-bows at the masked man; the other half fired at Kitr. This could not do her any lasting harm, but it did throw her off balance as her body jerked with the impact of the bolts. She recovered in an instant, shouting at them in fury—and as she did so, the masked man pushed past the barrier, as if the air had turned fleetingly to butter. Slowed, but not stopped.

I thought Kitr would miss her chance, distracted by the mortals. Instead she hissed, her form flickering for just an instant. In her place curled an enormous red-brown snake, its cobralike hood flared. Then she was a woman again, and the knives streaked at the man with the speed of spat poison, all twelve of them thudding into his body with such force that he should have been flung halfway to the city limits.

Instead he merely stopped for a moment, rocking back on his heels. That was the first evidence that the mask had its own protective magic. I saw a glimmer around the edges of his mask, against his skin, underneath. What was it doing? Strengthening his flesh, certainly, or Kitr's knives would've torn it apart. Displacing the force of the blows. Before I could fathom it, the busker started forward again, running slower because of the knives in his thighs. But running.

And in that instant, a second masked man, this one bigger and heavier, raced out of the crowd and plowed into the guards from the side.

Two of them. *Two* of them.

Glee cursed. We were too far from the madness, going too slow as we fought our way through the panicked crowd. She grabbed my shoulder. "Get them to Sky!" she said, and flung me through the ether. Startled, I materialized atop the Salon steps, in front of an equally stunned cluster of Arameri and soon-to-be-Arameri eyes.

"Sieh," said Shahar. She stared at me, oblivious to the chaos twenty steps away, and I knew in that instant that she still loved me.

"Get the hells out of here," I snapped at her, stifling my fury at Glee. Why in heavens had she sent me? What could I do, with no useful magic? "Why are you just standing here? Go back to Sky, damn it!"

There was a crackle, and lightning arced up from somewhere within the crowd, twisting back down to strike the second masker and a handful of guards, who were flung away screaming. Idiot scriveners. Like the first masker, this one stumbled. Stopped. A moment later he lurched forward, his hands scrabbling for purchase on the steps until he could manage to run upright again.

The guards had had enough time to recoup, however. Wrath Arameri, a naked sword in his hand, swept past us at the head of twin lines of soldiers. One line split and converged around us to protect Remath and the rest of us. The other line Wrath directed to assist the guards at the foot of the steps. Wrath fell in at Remath's side, daring to put a hand on her shoulder as he urged her back toward the daystone steps. Both maskers ran right into a thicket of pikes and swords. From the men's reactions, however—or lack thereof—it was already clear the blows would only slow them down, not stop them or kill them. They were already dead.

"What in demons?" murmured Datennay Canru. I followed his gaze, and my mouth went dry: a third masker had appeared, this one on the steps of the nearby Itempan White Hall. He wore the uniform of an Order-Keeper, but unlike the first two, his mask was the deep splashy crimson of blood, with stylized white and gold designs and an open mouth that suggested a roar of vengeful fury. This man, too, began to run toward us—and with the crowd thinning and the guards occupied, nothing stood in his way.

Nothing but me.

"Oh gods, no," I whispered. What could I do? En pulsed hot against the skin of my chest. I grabbed for it; then I remembered. En's power was mine; when I was strong, so was it. But I was only mortal now. If I used En, drained the last of its strength...

No. I would not kill my oldest friend, not for this. And I would not let my new friends, even if one of them had betrayed me, die. I was still a god, damn it, even without magic. I was still the wind and caprice, even bound into dying flesh. I would fear no mere mortal, no matter how powerful.

So I bared my teeth and lashed the tail I no longer possessed. Shouting a challenge, I ran down the steps to meet the crimson masker.

My words had been in the First Tongue, a command, though I hadn't expected the man to listen. But to my shock, the crimson masker stopped and turned toward me.

This mask was beautiful and horrid, the runnels and paint suggesting fouled rivers, the strange-angled eyes like crooked mountains. Its mouth—a stylized thing of lips and teeth with a dark pit of an opening beyond which I could not see its wearer's face—was twisted, a wail of utmost despair. *Murderer*, its markings whispered to me, and suddenly I thought of all the evils I'd done during the Gods' War. I thought of the evils I'd done since—sometimes at the Arameri's bidding, sometimes out of my own rage or cruelty. Forgetting my own challenge amid crushing guilt, I stumbled to a halt.

I felt a jolt. Sudden restriction and pain. Blinking, I looked down and found that the man had made a blade of his hand and had thrust it into my body at the midriff, nearly up to the wrist.

I was still staring down at this when Dekarta reached me. He grabbed my arm and spoke without words, whipping his head in a wide, vicious arc. Sound and force flooded from his throat, a roar of denial powered by the living energy of his skin and blood and bone. Better than many gods could have done. Where the power struck the crimson-masked man, I saw it cancel the mask's message. The mask split down the center with a faint crack, and an instant later he flew backward a good fifty feet, vanishing amid the fleeing crowd. I could not see precisely where he landed because then Deka's power struck the steps of the Salon, which erupted, shattering into rubble and bursting upward in an arcing spray.

There could be no precision to such a strike. Guards and soldiers went flying, screaming, along with the enemy. Through all this I saw another white-masked man, one I hadn't noticed, run into the barrier of broken, flying stone and tumble back. But as the dust and rubble returned to earth, he sat up.

Nemmer appeared swathed in shadows, facing me. I saw her eyes widen at the sight of my wound. Beyond her, I saw the fallen white-masked man get to his feet and come charging again, this time leaping with godlike strength over the channel of rubble that Deka had created. I willed a warning, since I could not muster the breath, and to my astonishment Nemmer seemed to hear me. She turned and met the man as he struck.

Then I was in Deka's arms, being carried like a child, *bump te bump te bump*. It was nice that he was so much bigger than me. He ran up the steps to the rest of the Arameri party, who had finally—finally!—begun to hurry up the curving steps toward the nearer gate. From Deka's embrace, I tried to shout at them to go faster, but I couldn't lift my head. So strange. It was like my first day as a mortal, when Shahar had summoned me to this realm as the cat, or the day two thousand years before that, when Itempas had thrown me down in chains of flesh and given my leash to a woman, one of Shahar's daughters, who looked equal parts horrified and elated at the power she held.

Then we reached the top of the steps, and the world folded into a blur, and I passed out in its rippling crease.

16

I SEE SOMETHING I should not.

I see as gods do, absorbing all the world around us whether we have eyes to see it or ears to hear it or a body at all present. I know things because they happen. This is not a mortal thing, and it should not happen while I am in the mortal realm, but I suppose it is proof that I am not completely mortal yet.

We have reached Sky. The forecourt is chaos. The captain of the guard is shouting and gesturing at a gaggle of men who crossed the gate with us. Soldiers and scriveners are running, the former to surround the Vertical Gate with spears and swords in case the maskers follow, the latter bringing brushes and inkpots so that they can seal it off before that happens. While this occurs, Wrath and Ramina try to pull Remath into the palace, but she shakes them off. "I will not retreat in my own home," she says, so the soldiers and scriveners make ready to defend her with their lives.

Amid all this running and shouting, I flop about in Deka's arms, dying. Dying faster, that is, instead of the decades-long death that aging has imposed on me. The crimson masker has punched a hole through many of my organs and a good chunk of my spine. If I somehow survive, which is highly unlikely, I will never walk again. Yet my heart still beats, and my brain still fires sparks within its wrinkled meat, and as long as those things continue, there is an anchor for my soul to hold on to.

I'm glad it will be like this. I died protecting those I cared for, facing an enemy, like a god.

Deka has carried me off the Vertical Gate, onto the unblemished white daystone of Sky's forecourt. He falls to his knees, shouting for someone to hold me, he can save me if he has help, help him, damn it.

It is Shahar who comes to her brother's call. She kneels at my other side, and their long-awaited reunion is a quick and panicked meeting of eyes across the gore of my open belly. "Get his clothes open," he commands, though she is the heir and he is nothing, just a fancy servant. (I am useless, aside from the part of me that watches. My eyes have rolled back in my head, and my mouth hangs open, ugly and inelegant. Some god.) While she struggles to lift my shirt— she tried to tear it first, thinking that would disturb the wound less, but the cheap material is surprisingly strong—Deka pulls a square of paper and a capped brush from wherever scriveners keep such things, and sketches a mark that means hold. He means for

*it to hold in my blood, hold back the filth that is already poisoning
my body. That will give him time to write more sigils, which might
actually heal me. (Has he only painted offensive magic into his skin?
Silly boy.)*

*But as he completes the mark and reaches for me, putting his hand
on Shahar's to brace himself so that he can lay the sigil in place,
something happens.*

*The universe is a living, breathing thing. Time, too. It moves,
though not as mortals imagine. It is restless, twitchy. Mortals don't
notice because they're restless and twitchy, too. Gods notice, but we
learn to ignore these things early on, the same way mortal newborns
eventually ignore the lonely silence of a world without heartbeats.
Yet suddenly I notice everything. The slow, aeons-deep inhalation
of the stars. The crackle of the sun's power against this planet's veil
of life. The minute scratching of mites too small to see on Shahar's
pristine white skin. The lazy, buzzy jolt of hours and days and
centuries.*

*And between them, beneath their hands, I open my eyes. My
mouth opens. Am I shouting? I cannot hear the words. I reach up,
my hands covering Shahar's and Dekarta's, and there is a flicker
of something, like lightning, along their skins. Shahar gasps, her
eyes going wide. Dekarta stares at her, opening his mouth to cry out.*

*There is a blurring. White lines, like the streaking of comets, run
through the shapes of our flesh. It is like before, the watching-me
realizes—like the time of our oath, when we touched and they
made me mortal. But this is different. This time, when the power
comes, it is not a wild concussion. There is a will at work: two wills,
with one purpose. Something bursts within me and is funneled to a
fine point.*

Then

it

becomes

I flopped about in Deka's arms, pissed. "Put me down, Maelstrom, damn you. I'm a god, not a sack of potatoes—"

He stumbled to a halt just beyond the Vertical Gate. A few paces ahead, Shahar had done the same. Eight of Captain Wrath's men surrounded her, trying to hurry her into the palace as they had already done Remath, but she shook them off. "I will not retreat in my own—"

She paused. Deka did, too. He set me on my feet. I swept marble dust off my clothes and hair and straightened my clothing, and then froze.

Oh.

Oh.

I understood, and did not. Many combinations in existence had meaning, and meaning has always imbued power—whether purely of an existential nature, or materially, or magically. There were the Three, of course, omnipotent on the infinitely rare occasions that they worked together. Twins. Male and female. God and mortal and the demons between.

But there was no reason for this. No precedent. They'd changed the universe. A pair of mortals.

They'd changed the universe *to heal me.*

They had changed the universe.

I stared at them. They stared back. Around us the chaos continued. All the other mortals seemed oblivious to what had happened, which was unsurprising. To them, it *hadn't* happened. There was no blood on the ground where I'd lain. My clothes weren't torn, because there had never been a wound. If I tried to remember, my mind conjured a glimpse of the crimson masker, hand poised before the blow, flying backward as Deka's blast of raw magic struck. But I could also remember the blow happening first.

A moment later Nemmer appeared, dropping something heavy to the ground. A body. I blinked. No, a masker; one of the white ones. Trussed up in what looked like huge writhing snakes formed of translucent shadow. This was Nemmer's magic. The instant she appeared, half of Wrath's soldiers moved to attack, and the other half realized the mistake and tried to stop them. There was a flurry of shouts and aborted lunges and then a great deal of confused milling. I suspected that if Wrath got through this day with his position intact, he would soon put his soldiers through a heavy training course on Gods, the Quick Recognition and Not Attacking Of.

"Got them," she said, putting her hands on her hips. She glanced at me and grinned. "Tell your mortals to stand down, Sieh. The danger has passed."

I stared at her, mute with shock. Her grin faltered. She glared at me, then snapped her fingers at my face. I jumped.

"What the hells is wrong with you?" Her smile turned vicious. "Were you so frightened by your first taste of mortal danger, big brother?"

I felt no real anger at her taunt because I had been in mortal danger a thousand times more than she had ever been. And I had far stranger things to occupy my thoughts.

But I was not the Trickster for nothing, and my mouth moved automatically while my brain continued to churn. "I was frightened by the incompetence I saw down there," I snapped. "Did you *plan* to let them nearly achieve their goal, or were your much-vaunted professionals caught napping?"

Nemmer did not lose her temper, but it was a near thing. At least she stopped smiling. "There were ten of them," she said, which broke some of my shock and brought me back to the present. "Counting the one your pet scrivener killed. All coming from different directions, all unstoppable—unless their bodies are completely destroyed or the masks are broken. You're lucky only one got through. We weren't prepared for a strike of this magnitude."

Ten of them. Ten mortals, tricked into donning the masks and turning themselves into living weapons. I shook my head, sickened.

"All the mortals up here are fine?" She spoke in a neutral tone. We were back to the unspoken truce, then.

I looked around, noting Shahar and Dekarta standing together nearby, listening to our conversation. Not far beyond them was Canru, looking uncomfortable and alone. Across the courtyard, Remath had stopped on the steps and seemed to be arguing with Ramina. Wrath faced us, his hand on his sword hilt, his gaze riveted on the masked creature at Nemmer's feet.

"The mortals who matter are fine," I said, feeling weary and full of grief. Ten who did not matter had died. And how many soldiers and innocents among the crowd? "We are all fine."

She looked uneasy at my wording but nodded, gesturing at the trussed-up man in the white mask. He was not dead; I saw him fighting the bonds, panting with the effort. "This one's for you, then. I figure the scrivener boy might be able to figure out something about this magic. Mortals understand how mortals think better than I ever will." She paused, then lifted her hand; something else appeared in it. "I'll give you this, too. Be careful of the intact masks, but once they're broken, the magic dies."

She held it out: the broken halves of the crimson mask.

I felt hard fingers punch through my flesh.

I took the mask pieces from her.

"Got to go," she said. She sounded just like a common mortal, right down to the Wesha accent. "Things to do, secrets to gather. We'll talk soon." With that, she vanished.

Remath was walking back, unhurried, as if she strolled through the aftermath of an attack on her family every day. While I could speak without her hearing, I went to Shahar and Dekarta, handing the pieces of the mask to Deka. He did not take them with his bare hands, quickly pulling his sleeves down to take the halves, gingerly, by the edges.

"Say nothing of what happened," I said, speaking low and quickly.

"But—" Shahar began, predictably.

"*No one remembers but us*," I said, and she shut up. Not even Nemmer, whose nature it was to sense the presence of secrets, had noticed anything. Dekarta caught his breath; he understood what this meant as well as I had. Shahar flicked a glance at him and at me, and then—as if she had not spent ten years apart from him, and as if she had not once broken my heart— she covered for us both, immediately turning to face her oncoming mother.

"The situation has been controlled," she said as Remath drew to a halt before us. Wrath positioned himself directly between me and Remath, his hard brown gaze fixed on me. (I winked at him. He did not react.) Ramina remained behind her, his arms folded, showing no hint of relief that his son and daughter were alive and well.

"Lady Nemmer reported there were ten assailants in all," Shahar continued. "Her organization captured the rest and will be conducting its own investigation. She would like mortal input, however." With a look of distaste, Shahar glanced at the immobilized masker.

"How considerate of her," said Remath, with only the faintest hint of sarcasm. "Wrath." He flinched and left off glaring at me. "Return to the city and oversee the investigation there. Be certain to find out why so many of these creatures were able to make it through our lines."

"Lady..." Wrath began. He glanced at me.

Remath lifted an eyebrow and faced me as well. "Lord Sieh. Are you planning to try and kill me again?" She paused, and added, "Today?"

"No," I said, letting my voice and face show that I still hated her, because I was not an Arameri and I saw no point in hiding the obvious. "Not today."

"Of course." To my surprise, she smiled. "Do stay awhile, Lord Sieh, since you're here. If I recall, you are prone to boredom, and I have plans of my own to set in motion, now that this unpleasantness has occurred." She glanced at the masker again, and there was an odd sort of sorrow in her expression for the most fleeting of moments. If it had lasted, I might have begun to pity her. But then it vanished and she smiled at me and I hated her again. "I believe you will find the next few days most interesting. As will my children."

While Shahar and I digested this in silence, Remath glanced at Deka, who stood just behind Shahar, his expression so neutral that he reminded me, at once, of Ahad. There was a long, silent moment. I saw Shahar, wearing her own careful mask, glance from one to the other.

"Not the homecoming you were expecting, I imagine." Remath's tone surprised me. She sounded almost affectionate.

Deka almost smiled. "Actually, Mother, I *was* expecting someone to try and murder me the instant I arrived."

The look that crossed Remath's face in that instant would have been difficult for anyone to interpret, mortal or immortal, if they were not familiar with Arameri ways. It was one of the ways they trained themselves to conceal emotion. They smiled when they were angry and showed sorrow when they were over-joyed. Remath looked wryly amused, skeptical of Deka's apparent nonchalance, mildly impressed. To me her feelings might as well have been written into the sigil on her forehead. She was glad to see Deka. She was very impressed. She was troubled—or bitterly empathetic, at least—to see him so cold.

Shahar loved her. I wasn't sure about Deka. Did Remath love either of her children back? That I could not say.

"I'll see both of you tomorrow," she said to Shahar and Dekarta, then turned and walked away. Wrath bowed to her back, then strode off with a final glance at us before raising his voice to call his men. Ramina, however, lingered.

"Interesting stylistic choice," he said to Deka. As if in response to his words, a stray breeze lifted Deka's black cloak behind him like a living shadow.

"It seemed fitting, Uncle," Deka replied. He smiled thinly. "I am something of a black sheep, am I not?"

"Or a wolf, come to feast on tender flesh—unless someone tames you." Ramina's eyes drifted to Deka's forehead, then to

Shahar, in clear implication. Shahar's brows drew down in the beginnings of a frown, and Ramina flashed a loving smile at both of them. "But perhaps you're more useful with sharp teeth and killer instincts, hmm? Perhaps the Arameri of the future will need a whole *pack* of wolves." And with this, he glanced at me. I frowned.

With studied boredom in her tone, Shahar said, "Uncle, you're being even more obscure than usual."

"My apologies." He didn't look apologetic at all. "I merely came to mention a detail about the meeting Sister asked that you attend tomorrow. She's ordered full privacy—no guards, no courtiers beyond the ones invited. Not even servants will be present."

At this, Shahar and Dekarta both looked at each other, and I wondered what in the infinite hells was going on. Remath should never have declared her intention for a private meeting in advance; too easy for other Arameri or interested parties to slip in a listening sphere. Or an assassin. But Ramina was marked with a full sigil; he could not act against his sister even if he wanted to. Which meant that he was speaking on Remath's behalf. But why?

Then I realized Ramina was still looking at me. So it was something Remath wanted *me* to know, in particular. To make sure I'd be there.

"Damned twisty-headed Arameri," I said, scowling at him. "I've had a horrid day. Say what you mean."

He blinked at me with such blatant surprise that he fooled no one. "I should think it would be obvious, Trickster. The Arameri are about to implement a trick that should impress even you. Naturally we would welcome your blessing for such an endeavor." With that, he smiled and strode after his sister.

I stared after him in confusion, as if that would help. It didn't. And now I spied Morad approaching at the head of a phalanx of servants, all of them pausing to bow as Ramina walked past in the palace archway.

Shahar turned to me and Deka, speaking low and quickly. "I must attend to Canru and the Teman party down at the Salon; they'll be very put out about this. Both of you, request quarters that can be reached through the dead spaces. Sieh knows what I mean." With that, she, too, left us, heading over to join her fiancé.

"Are you all right?" I heard Canru ask her. I tightened my jaw against inadvertent approval and turned to Deka.

"I suppose you'll want to settle in, too," I said. "Order the scrivener corps about and start dissecting your new prize, or whatever it is you people do." I looked over at the trussed-up masker.

"I'd much rather go somewhere and have a long talk with you about what just happened," he said, and there was something in his voice, a smoothness, that made me blush inadvertently. He smiled, missing nothing. "But I suppose that will have to wait. I'll be taking one of the spire rooms—Spire Seven, most likely, if it's still available. Where will you be?"

I considered. "The underpalace." There was no place more private in all of Sky. "Deka, the dead spaces—"

"I know what they are," he said, surprising me, "and I can guess which room you'll be in. We'll come around midnight."

Flustered, I watched Deka as he turned to greet Morad. I heard him issue orders as easily as if he had not just returned from a ten-year exile, and I heard Morad answer with, "At once, my lord," as if she had never missed him.

All around the courtyard, everyone spoke with someone else. I stood alone.

Obscurely troubled, I went over to the masker and prodded him with a toe, sighing. He grunted and struggled toward me in response. "Why must all you mortals be so difficult?" I asked. The dead man, predictably, did not answer.

My old room.

I stood in the open doorway, unsurprised to see that it had not been touched in the century since I'd left. Why would any servant, or steward for that matter, have bothered? No one would ever want to dwell in a chamber that had housed a god. What if he'd left traps behind or woven curses into the walls? Worse, what if he came back?

The reality was that I had never intended to come back, and it had never occurred to me to weave curses into anything. If I had, I would never have burdened the walls with anything so trivial as a curse. I would have created a masterwork of pain and humiliation and despair from my own heart, and I would have forced any mortal who invaded the space to share those horrors. Just for a moment or two, rather than the centuries I endured, but none of it blunted.

An old wooden table stood on one side of the room. On its surface were the small treasures I had always loved to gather, even when they had no life or magic of their own. A perfect dried leaf, now probably too fragile to touch. A key; I did not remember what it opened or if its lock still existed. I just liked keys. A perfectly round pebble that I had always meant to turn into a planet and add to my orrery. I had forgotten about it after I'd gotten free, and now I had no power to correct the error.

Beyond the table was my nest—or so I had styled it, though it had none of the comfort or beauty of my true nest in the gods' realm. This was just a pile of rags, gray and dry-rotted and dusty now, and probably infested with vermin to boot. Some of the rags were things I had stolen from the fullbloods: a favorite scarf, a baby's blanket, a treasured tapestry. I'd always tried to take things they cared about, though they'd punished me for it whenever they'd caught me. Every blow had been worth it—not because the thefts caused them any great hardship, but because I was *not* a mortal, *not* just a slave. I was still Sieh, the mischievous wind, the playful hunter, and no punishment could ever break me. To remind myself of that, I had been willing to endure anything.

Dust and mite food now. I slid my hands into my pockets, sat down against a wall, and sighed.

I was dozing when they arrived, through the floor. Shahar, to my surprise, was the first one through. I smiled to see that she held a small ceramic tablet, on which had been drawn a single, simple command in our language. *Atadie*. Open. I had shown her the door, and she'd had someone make her a key.

"Have you been wandering the dead spaces by yourself these past few years?" I asked as she climbed out of the hole and dusted herself off. She or Dekarta had made steps out of the reshaped daystone. He came up behind her, looking around in fascination.

She looked at me warily, no doubt remembering that the last time I'd seen her, really spoken to her, had been two years before, the morning after we'd made love.

"Some," she said, after a moment. "It's useful to be able to go where I want with none the wiser."

"Indeed it is," I said, smiling thinly. "But you should be careful, you know. The dead spaces were mine once—and any place that was mine for so long is likely to have taken on some of my nature. Step into the wrong corridor, open the wrong door, and you never know what might jump out and bite you."

She flinched, as I'd meant her to, and not just at my words. *Betrayer*, I let my eyes say, and after a moment she looked away.

Deka looked warily at us both, perhaps only now realizing how bad things were between us. Wisely, he chose not to mention it.

"There's panic in Shadow," he said, "and we're getting reports of unrest from elsewhere in the world. There have been riots, and the Order has instituted extra services at all White Halls to accommodate the Itempans who suddenly feel compelled to pray. Mother's called an emergency session of the Consortium in three days' time, and she's authorized the Litaria to facilitate travel by gate for all the representatives. Rumor has the Arameri all dead and a new Gods' War impending."

I laughed, though I shouldn't have. Fear was like poison to mortals; it killed their rationality. Somewhere, there would be deaths tonight.

"That's Remath's problem, not mine," I said, sitting forward, "or yours. We have a more significant concern."

They looked at each other, then at me, and waited. Belatedly I realized they thought I was about to explain something.

"I haven't got a clue what happened," I said, raising my hands quickly. "Never seen anything like that in my life! But I have no idea why anything happens the way it does around you two."

"It didn't come from us." Shahar spoke softly, with the barest hint of hesitation. I scowled at her and she blanched, but then tightened her jaw and lifted her chin. "We felt it, Deka and I, and this time you did, too. We have felt that power before, Sieh. It was the same as the day the three of us took our oath."

Silence fell, and in it I nodded slowly. Trying not to be afraid. I had already guessed that the power was the same. What frightened me was my growing suspicion as to *why*.

Deka licked his lips. "Sieh. If the three of us touch, and it somehow causes this... this *thing* to occur, and if that power can be directed... Sieh, Shahar and I—" He took a deep breath. "We want to try it again. See if we can turn you back into a godling."

I caught my breath, wondering if they had any idea of how much danger we were all in.

"No," I said. I stood and stepped away from the wall, too tense to maintain my pose of indifference.

"Sieh—" Deka began.

"*No.*" Gods. They really had no idea. I turned and began to pace, nibbling a thumbnail. All that happened in darkness. Sky's glowing halls had been designed specifically to thwart Nahadoth's nature, and Itempas was diminished to mortality. Yeine, though... every creature that had ever lived could be her eyes and ears, if she so chose. Was she observing us now? Would she...?

"*Sieh.*" Shahar. She stepped in front of me and I stopped, because it was either that or run into her. I hissed, and she glared back. "You're making no sense. If we can restore your magic—"

"They'll kill you," I said, and she flinched. "Naha, Yeine. If the three of us have that kind of power, they'll kill us all."

They both looked blank. I groaned and rubbed my head. I had to make them understand.

"The demons," I said. More confusion. They did not know they were Ahad's descendants. I cursed in three languages, though I made sure none of them were my own. "The demons, damn it! Why did the gods kill them?"

"Because they were a threat," said Deka.

"No. No. Gods, do both of you only ever listen to teaching poems and priests' tales? You're Arameri; you know that stuff is all lies!" I glared at them.

"But that *was* why." Deka was looking stubborn again, as he'd done as a child, as he'd probably done in every Litaria lesson since. "Their blood was poison to gods—"

"And they could pass for mortals, better than any god or godling. They could, and did, blend in." I stepped closer and looked into his eyes. If I wasn't careful, if I did not work hard to keep the years hidden, mortals were not fooled by my outward appearance. Now, however, I let him see all I had experienced. All the aeons of mortal life, all the aeons before that. I had been there nearly from the beginning. I understood things Deka would never comprehend, no matter how brilliant he was and no matter how diminished I became as a mortal. I *remembered.* So I wanted him to believe my words now, without question, the way ordinary mortals believed the words of their gods. Even if that meant making him fear me.

Deka frowned, and I saw the awareness come over him. And though he loved me and had wanted me since he was too young to know what desire meant, he stepped back. I felt a moment's sorrow. But it was probably for the best.

Shahar, sweet, beautiful betrayer that she was, leapt to my point before her brother did.

"They made *mortalkind* a threat," she said very softly. "They fit in among us, yes. Interbred with us. Passed on their magic, and sometimes their poison, to all their mortal descendants."

"Yes," I said. "And though it was the poison that was of immediate concern—one of my brothers died of demon poison, which set the whole thing off—there was also the fear of what would happen to our magic, filtered and distorted through a mortal lens. We saw that some of the demons were just as powerful as pure godlings." I looked at Deka as I said it. I couldn't help myself. He stared back at me, still shaken to discover that his childhood crush was something frightening and strange, oblivious to my real implication. "It wasn't hard to guess that someday, somehow, a mortal might be born with as much power as one of the Three. The power to change reality itself on a fundamental level." I shook my head and gestured around us, at the room, Sky, the world, the universe. "You don't understand how fragile all this is. Losing one of the Three would destroy it. Gaining a Fourth, or even something close to a Fourth, would do the same."

Deka frowned, concern overwhelming shock. "And what we did... you think the Three would see that as the culmination of their fears?"

"But it's not as though we did anything harmful—" Shahar began.

"Changing reality *is* harmful! If you tried it again, even to help me—Deka, you understand how magic works. What happens if you misdraw a sigil or misspeak a godword? If the two of you try to use this power to remake me..." I sighed, and faced the truth I hadn't wanted to admit. "Well, think of what happened last time. You wanted me to be your friend, a true friend—something that I could never have been as a god. You would have grown up and understood how different I was. You would have become proper Arameri and wondered how you could use me." Now I looked at Shahar, whose lips tightened ever so slightly. "If I had stayed a god, our friendship would never have survived this long. So you, some part of you, made me into something that *could* be your friend."

Deka took another step back, horror filling his face. "You're saying *we* did this? The collapse of the Nowhere Stair, your mortality...?"

At this I sighed and went back to the wall, sliding down to sit against it. "I don't know. This is all guesses and conjecture. Your will, if it had this strange magic behind it, may have focused the magic just enough to cause a change, but then it backlashed... or something. None of that answers the fundamental question of *why* you have this power."

"It isn't just us, Sieh." Shahar again, quiet again. "Deka and I have touched many times, and nothing came of it. It's only when we touch *you* that there's any change."

I nodded bleakly. I had figured that out as well.

Silence fell as they digested everything I'd said. It was broken by the loud grumbling of my empty belly and my louder yawn. At this, Dekarta shifted uncomfortably. "Why did you come here, Sieh? There are no servants this far down, and this room is... foul." He looked around, his lip curling at the pile of ancient rags.

A foul place for a fouled god, I thought. "I like it here," I said. "And I'm too tired to go anywhere else. Go away now, both of you. I need to rest."

Shahar turned toward the hole in the floor, but Deka lingered. "Come with us," he said. "Have something to eat, take a bath. There's a couch in my new quarters."

I looked up at him and saw the bravery of his effort. I had jarred his fantasies badly, but he would try, even now, to be the friend he'd promised to be.

You are the one who did this to me, beautiful Deka.

I smiled thinly, and he frowned at the sight.

"I'll be all right," I said. "Go on. Let's all be ready to face your mother in the morning."

So they left.

As the daystone of the floor resealed itself, I lay down and curled up to sleep, resigning myself to stiffness by morning. But as soon as I closed my eyes, I realized I was no longer alone.

"Are you really afraid of me?" asked Yeine.

I opened my eyes and sat up. She sat cross-legged in my old nest, dainty as always, beautiful even amid rags. The rags were no longer dry-rotted, however. I could see color and definition returning to what had been a gray mass and could hear the faint tightening of the thread fibers as they regained cohesion and strength. Along one of Yeine's thighs, a line of barely visible mites had begun to crawl, vanishing over the rise of her flesh. Sent packing, I imagined, or she might be killing them. One never knew with her.

I said nothing in response to her question, and she sighed.

"I don't care if mortals grow powerful, Sieh. If they do, and they threaten us, I'll deal with that then. For now"—she shrugged—"maybe it's a good thing that some of them have magic like this. Maybe that's what they really need, power of their own, so they can stop being jealous of ours."

"Don't tell Naha," I whispered. At this she sobered and grew silent.

After a moment, she said, "You used to come to me whenever we were alone."

I looked away. I wanted to. But I knew better.

"Sieh," she said. Hurt.

And because I loved her too much to let her think the problem was her, I sighed and got up and went over to the nest. Climbing into it brought back memories, and I paused for an instant, overwhelmed by them. Holding Naha on a moonless night—the one time he was safe from both Itempas and the Arameri—as he wept for the Three that had been. Endless hours I'd spent weaving new orbits for my orrery and polishing my Arameri bones. Grinding my teeth as another guard-captain, this one a fullblood and cruel, ordered me to turn over for him. (I had gotten his bones, too, in the end. But they had not made as good toys as I'd hoped, and eventually I'd tossed them off the Pier.)

And now Yeine, whose presence burned away the bad and burnished the good. I wanted to hold her so much, but I knew what would happen. It amazed me that she didn't. She was so very young.

She frowned at me in puzzlement, reaching out to cup my cheek. My self-control broke, and I flung myself against her as I had done so many times, burying my face in her breast, gripping the cloth at the back of her vest. It felt so good, too, at first. I felt warm and safe and young. Her arms came around me, and her face pressed into my hair. I was her baby, her son in all but flesh, and the flesh didn't matter.

But there is always a moment when the familiar becomes strange. It is always there, just a little, between any two beings who love one another as much as she and I. The line is so fine. In one moment I was her child, my head pillowed on her breast in all innocence. In the next I was a man, lonely and hungry, and her breasts were small but full. Female. Inviting.

Yeine tensed. It was barely perceptible, but I had been expecting it. With a long sigh I sat up, letting her go. When her eyes—troubled, uncertain—met mine, I turned away. I am not a complete bastard. For her, I would stay the boy that she needed and not the man I had become.

To my surprise, however, she caught my chin and made me look at her again.

"There is more to this than you being mortal," she said. "More than you wanting to protect those two children."

"I want to protect *mortalkind*," I said. "If Naha finds out what those two can do..."

Yeine shook her head, and shook mine a little, refusing to be distracted. Then she searched my face so intently that I began to be afraid again. She was not Enefa, but...

"You've been with Nahadoth and many of your siblings," she said. Her revulsion crawled along my skin like the evacuating mites. She was trying to resist it, and failing. "I know...things are different, for godkind."

If she had only been older. Just a few centuries might have been enough to reduce the memory of her mortal life and her mortal inhibitions. I mourned that I would not have time to see her become a true god.

"I was Enefa's lover, too," I said softly. I did not look at her at first. "Not...not often. When Itempas and Nahadoth were off together, mostly. When she needed me."

And because there would be no other time, I looked up at her and let her see the truth. *You might have needed me, too, in time. You're stronger than Naha and Tempa, but you're not immune to loneliness. And I have always loved you.*

To her very great credit, she did not recoil. I loved her more than ever for that. But she did sigh.

"I've felt no urge to have children," she said, grazing her knuckles along my cheek. I leaned into her touch, closing my eyes. "With so many angry, damaged stepchildren already, it seems foolish to complicate matters further. But also..." I felt her smile, like starlight on my skin. "You are my son, Sieh. It makes no sense. I should be your daughter. But... that's how I feel."

I caught her hand and pulled it against my chest so she could feel my mortal heartbeat. I was dying; it made me bold. "If I can be nothing else to you, I am glad to be your son. Truly."

Her smile turned sad. "But you want more."

"I always want more. From Naha, from Enefa... even from Itempas." I sobered at that, shifting to lie against her side. She permitted this, even though it had gone wrong before. A sign of trust. I did not abuse it. "I want things that are impossible. It's my nature."

"Never to be satisfied?" Her fingers played with my hair gently.

"I suppose." I shrugged. "I've learned to deal with it. What else can I do?"

She fell silent for so long that I grew sleepy, warm and comfortable with her in the softness of the nest. I thought she might sleep with me—just sleep, nothing more—which I wanted desperately and no longer knew how to ask for. But she, goddess that she was, had other things in mind.

"Those children," she said at last. "The mortal twins. They make you happy."

I shook my head. "I barely know them. I befriended them on a whim and fell in love with them by mistake. Those are things children do, but for once I should have thought like a god, not a child."

She kissed my forehead, and I rejoiced that there was no reticence in the gesture. "Your willingness to take risks is one of the most wonderful things about you, Sieh. Where would you and I be, if not for that?"

I smiled in spite of my mood, which I think was what she'd wanted. She stroked my cheek and I felt happier. Such was her power over me, which I had willingly given.

"They are not such terrible people to love," Yeine said, her tone thoughtful.

"Shahar is."

She pulled back a little to look at me. "Hmm. She must have done something terrible to make you so angry."

"I don't want to talk about it."

She nodded, allowing me to sulk for a moment. "Not the boy, though?"

"Dekarta." She groaned, and I chuckled. "I did the same thing! He's nothing like his namesake, though." Then I paused as I considered Deka's body-markings, his determination to be Shahar's weapon, and his relentless pursuit of me. "He's Arameri, though. I can't trust him."

"*I'm* Arameri."

"Not the same. It isn't an inborn thing. You weren't raised in this den of weasels."

"No, I was raised in a different den of weasels." She shrugged, jostling my head a little. "Mortals are the sum of many things, Sieh. They are what circumstance has made them and what they wish to be. If you must hate them, hate them for the latter, not the former. At least they have some say over that part."

I sighed. Of course she was right, and it was nothing more than I had argued with my own siblings over the aeons, as we debated—sometimes more than philosophically—whether mortals deserved to exist.

"They are such fools, Yeine," I whispered. "They squander every gift we give them. I..." I trailed off, trembling inexplicably. My chest ached, as though I might cry. I was a man, and men did not cry—or at least Teman men did not—but I was also a god, and gods cried whenever they felt like it. I wavered on the brink of tears, torn.

"You gave this Shahar your love." Yeine kept stroking my hair with one hand, absently, which did not help matters. "Was she worthy of it?"

I remembered her, young and fierce, kicking me down the stairs because I'd dared to suggest that she could not determine her own fate. I remembered her later, making love to me on her mother's orders—but how hungry she'd looked as she held me down and took pleasure from my body! I had not abandoned myself so completely with a mortal for two thousand years.

And as I remembered these things, I felt the knot of anger in me begin to loosen at last.

With a soft, amused chuckle, Yeine disentangled herself from me and sat up. I watched her do this wistfully. "Be a good boy and rest now. And don't stay up all night thinking. Tomorrow will be interesting. I don't want you to miss any of it."

At this I frowned, pushing myself up on one elbow. She ran

fingers through her short hair as if to brush it back into place. A hundred years and still so much the mortal: a proper god would simply have willed her hair perfect. And she did not bother to hide the smug look on her face as I peered at her now.

"You're up to some mischief," I said, narrowing my eyes.

"Indeed I am. Will you bless me?" She got to her feet and stood smirking with one hand on her hip. "Remath Arameri is as interesting as her children, is all I'll say for now."

"Remath Arameri is evil, and I would kill her if Shahar did not love her so." As soon as I said this, however, Yeine raised an eyebrow, and I grimaced as I realized how much I had revealed— not just to her, but also to myself. For if I loved Shahar enough to tolerate her horror of a mother, then I loved Shahar enough to forgive her.

"Silly boy," Yeine said with a sigh. "You never do things the easy way, do you?"

I tried to make a joke of it, though the smile was hard to muster. "Not if the hard way is more fun."

She shook her head. "You almost died today."

"Not really." I flinched as she leveled A Look at me. "Everything turned out all right!"

"No, it didn't. Or rather, it shouldn't have. But you still have a god's luck, however much the rest of you has changed." She sobered suddenly. "A good mother desires not only her children's safety, but also their happiness, Sieh."

"Er..." I could not help tensing a little, wondering what she was going on about. She was not as strange as Naha, but she thought in spirals, and sometimes—locked in a mortal's linear mind as I was—I could not follow her. "That's good, I suppose...."

Yeine nodded, her face still as unfathomable thoughts churned behind it. Then she gave me another Look, and I blinked in surprise, for this one held a ferocity that I hadn't seen from her in a mortal lifetime.

"I will see to it that you know happiness, Sieh," she said. "We will do this."

Not she and Naha. I knew what she meant the way I knew the Three merited capital-letter status. And though the Three had never joined in the time since her ascension, she was still one of them. Part of a greater whole—and when all three of them wanted the same thing, each member spoke with the whole's voice.

I bowed my head, honored. But then I frowned as I realized what else she was saying. "Before I die, you mean."

She shook her head, just herself again, then leaned over to put a hand on my chest. I felt the minute vibration of her flesh for just an instant before my dulled senses lost the full awareness of her, but I was glad for that taste. She had no heart, my beautiful Yeine, but she didn't need one. The pulse and breath and life and death of the whole universe was a more than sufficient substitute.

"We all die," she said softly. "Sooner or later, all of us. Even gods." And then, before her words could bring back the melancholy that I'd almost shed, she winked. "But being my son should get you *some* privileges."

With that she vanished, leaving behind only the cooling tingle of warmth where her fingers had rested on my chest and the renewed, clean rags of my nest. When I lay down, I was glad to find she'd left her scent, too, all mist and hidden colors and a mother's love. And a whiff—no more than that—of a woman's passion.

It was enough. I slept well that night, comforted.

But not before I'd disobediently lain awake for an hour or so, wondering what Yeine was up to. I could not help feeling excited. Every child loves a surprise.

"Thank you all for coming," said Remath. Her eyes touched on each of us in turn: me, Shahar, Dekarta, and, oddly, Wrath and Morad, alone of Remath's full court. The latter two knelt behind Shahar and Deka, conceding right of prominence to the fullbloods. Ramina was present, too, standing behind and to the left of Remath's throne. I leaned against the wall nearby, my arms folded as I pretended boredom.

It was late afternoon. We'd expected Remath's summons earlier in the day—in the morning, when she took her usual audience, or after that. But no one had come to fetch us, so Shahar and Deka had done whatever it was Arameri fullbloods did all day, and meanwhile I had slept until noon, mostly because I could. Morad, bless her, had sent brave servants to beard me in my lair with food and clothing, then bring me to Remath.

From the blocky stone chair that had been an Itempan altar before the Gods' War, and that still smelled faintly of Shinda Arameri's demon blood, Remath smiled at us.

"In light of yesterday's disturbing events," she said, "it seems the time has come to implement a plan that I hoped I would never need. Dekarta." He twitched in surprise and looked up. "Your teachers at the Litaria assure me that you are without doubt the finest young scrivener they have ever graduated, and as my spies at the Litaria confirm your accomplishments, it appears this is not just toadying praise. This pleases me more than you can know."

Dekarta stared at her in obvious surprise for a full second before answering. "Thank you, Mother."

"Do not thank me yet. I have a task for you and Shahar, one that will take substantial time and effort, but upon which the family's future will entirely depend." She folded her legs and glanced at Shahar. "Do you know what that task is, Shahar?"

It had the feel of an old question. Perhaps Remath quizzed Shahar in this manner all the time. Shahar seemed unfazed by it as she lifted her head to reply.

"I'm not certain," she said, "but I have suspicions, as my own sources have informed me of some very curious activities on your part."

"Such as?"

Shahar narrowed her eyes, perhaps considering how much she wanted to divulge in front of the mixed audience. Then, bluntly, she said, "You've had parties examining remote locations around the world, and you've had several of the scriveners—in secret, on pain of death—researching the building techniques used to create Sky." She glanced at me briefly. "Those that can be replicated with mortal magic."

I blinked in surprise. Now *that* I hadn't been expecting. When I frowned at Remath, I was even more disturbed to find her smiling at me, as if my shock pleased her.

"What in the heavens are you up to, woman?" I asked.

She ducked her eyes almost coyly, reminding me, suddenly, of Yeine. Remath had that same smug look Yeine had worn the evening before. I did not like being reminded that they were relatives.

"The Arameri must change, Lord Sieh," she said. "Is that not what the Nightlord told us, on the day you and the other

Enefadeh broke free from your long captivity? We have kept the world still too long, and now it twists and turns, reveling in sudden freedom—and risking its own destruction by changing too far, too fast." She sighed, the smugness fading. "My spies in the north gave me a report last year that I did not understand. Now, having seen the power of these masks, I realize we are in far greater danger than I ever imagined...."

Abruptly she trailed off, falling silent, and for a breath-held moment there were hells in her eyes—fears and weariness that she had not let us see up to now. It was a stunning lapse on her part. It was also, I realized as she lifted her gaze to Shahar, deliberate.

"My spies have seen hundreds of masks," she said softly. "Perhaps *thousands*. In nearly every High North nation there are *dimyi* artists; the northerners have been spreading knowledge of the form and nurturing youngsters with the talent for more than a generation. They sell them to foreigners as souvenirs. They give them to traders as gifts. Most people hang them on their walls as decoration. There is no way to know how many masks exist—in the north, on the islands, throughout Senm. Even in this city, from Sky to the Gray to Shadow beneath. No telling."

I inhaled, realizing the truth of her words. Gods, I had *seen* the masks myself. On the walls of a tavern in Antema. In the Salon once, right below Sky, when I'd pretended to be the page of some noble in order to eavesdrop on a Consortium session. Stern, commanding faces arranged on a wall in the bathroom; they'd drawn my eye while I took a piss. I hadn't known what they were then.

Remath continued. "I have, of course, requested the aid of

the Order-Keepers in locating and neutralizing this threat. They have already begun searching homes and removing masks—without touching them," she added, as Deka looked alarmed and had opened his mouth to speak. "We are aware of the danger."

"No," Deka said, and we all blinked in surprise. One did not interrupt the Arameri family head. "No one is aware of the danger, Mother, until we've had a chance to study these masks and understand how they work. They may function through more than contact."

"We must nevertheless try," she said. "If even one of those masks can turn an ordinary mortal into a nigh-unstoppable creature like the ones that attacked us yesterday, then we are *already surrounded* by our enemies. They need not muster soldiers, or train them, or feed them. They can create their army at any time, in any place, through whatever mechanism or spell they use to control the masks. And the defenses our scriveners have devised have proven woefully inadequate."

"The corps have only now obtained examples of these masks in their undamaged state to study," said Shahar. "It would seem too soon—"

"I cannot risk this family's fortunes on uncertainties. We've lost too much already, relying on tradition and our reputation. We believed we were unassailable, even as our enemies winnowed our ranks." She paused for a moment, a muscle flexing in her jaw, her eyes going dark and hard. "You will make stranger choices, Shahar, when the time comes for you to lead. Not for nothing did I give you our Matriarch's name." Her eyes flicked to Deka. "Though I know already that you have the strength to do what's right."

Shahar tensed, her eyes narrowing. In suspicion? Or anger? I cursed my paltry mortal awareness of the world.

Remath took a deep breath. "Shahar. With the aid of Dekarta, and our family's most capable members, you are to oversee the preparation of a new home for the Arameri."

Utter silence fell. I stared along with the rest of them. Unknowable Maelstrom, she'd actually sounded serious.

"A *new palace?*" Shahar did not bother to hide her incredulity. "Mother…" She trailed off, shaking her head. "I don't understand."

Remath extended a graceful hand. "It is very simple, Daughter. A new palace will soon be built for us—in a hidden location, far more defensible and isolated than Sky. Captain Wrath and the White Guard, Steward Morad, and any others whom you trust implicitly will reside in this new palace—alone, until such time as you can make it ready for the whole family. Unlike Sky, the location of this new palace shall be secret. Dekarta, you are to ensure that this remains the case, utilizing whatever magical means are at your disposal. Create new ones if you must. Ramina, you are to advise my children."

I could see which people in the room had known about this by their reactions. Shahar's eyes were bigger than En; so were Deka's. Wrath's mouth hung open, but Morad continued to watch Remath, impassive. So Remath had told her lover. And Ramina smirked at me; he, too, had known.

But it made no sense. The Arameri had built a new palace before, but only when the old one had been destroyed, thanks to Nahadoth and an especially stupid Arameri family head. The current Sky was fine, and safer than any location in the world, seated as it was within a *giant tree*. There was no need for this.

I stepped away from the wall, putting my hands on my hips.

"And what orders do you have for me, Remath? Will you command me to hew the stones and lay the mortar for this new palace? After all, I and my siblings built *this* one."

Remath's gaze settled on me, inscrutable. She was silent for so long that I actually began to wonder if she would try to kill me. It would be utterly stupid on her part; nothing short of the Maelstrom would be able to stop Nahadoth's fury. But I put nothing past her.

Try me, I thought at her, and bared my teeth in a grin. En pulsed on my breast in hot agreement. At my smile, however, Remath nodded slightly, as if I'd confirmed something.

"You, Lord Sieh," she began, "are to look after my children."

I froze. Then, before I could muster a thought, Shahar sprang to her feet, abandoning protocol. Her hands were fists at her sides, her expression suddenly fierce. She rounded on all of us.

"Out," she said. "*Now.*"

Wrath alone looked at Remath, who said nothing. Ramina and Morad held still for a breath, perhaps also waiting to see if Remath would counter Shahar's command, but they carefully did not look at either woman. It was never wise to take sides in a battle between the head and heir. As soon as it was clear that Remath would not intervene, they left. The chamber's heavy doors swung shut with an echoing silence.

Shahar glared at Dekarta, who had gotten to his feet as well but remained where he was, his face set and hard. "No," he said.

"How dare you—"

"Mark me," he snapped, and she flinched, silent. "Put a true sigil on me, geld me like Ramina. Do this if you want me to obey. Otherwise, *no.*"

Shahar's lips tightened so much that I saw them turn white

under the rouge. She was angry enough to say the words—in front of Remath, who might not let her take them back. Fools, her and Deka both. They were too young to play this game yet.

With a sigh I strode forward, stopping between and to one side of them. "You took the oath to each other as well," I said, and they both glared at me. If Remath had not been there, I would have cuffed them like the squabbling brats they were, but for the sake of their dignity, I merely glared back.

With a dismissive *hmmph*, Shahar turned her back on us, striding up to the foot of the dais that held her mother's chair. She stopped when they were eye to eye.

"You will not do this," she said, her voice low and tight. "You will not make plans for your own death."

Remath sighed. Then, to my surprise, she stood and walked down the steps until she stood before Shahar. They were of a height, I saw. Shahar might never be as full in breast or hip, but she did not turn aside as her mother drew near, her gaze clear and angry. Remath looked her up and down and slowly, smiled.

Then she embraced Shahar.

I gaped. So did Deka. So did Shahar, who stood stiff within her mother's arms, her face a study in shock. Remath's palms pressed flat against Shahar's back. She even rested her cheek on Shahar's shoulder, closing her eyes for just a moment. At last, with a reluctance that could not be feigned, she spoke.

"The Arameri must change," she said again. "This is too little, and perhaps too late—but you have always had my love, Shahar. I am willing to admit that, here, in front of others, because that, too, is part of the change we must make. And because it is true." She pulled back then, her hands lingering on Shahar's arms until distance forced her to let go. I had the sense that she would have preferred not to. Then she glanced at Deka.

Deka's jaw flexed, his hands clenching into fists at his sides, and though I doubt anyone else saw it, the marks on his body, beneath his clothing, flared in black warning. Remath would get no welcome there. She sighed, nodding to herself as if she'd expected nothing more. Her sorrow was so plain that I didn't know what to think. Arameri did not show their feelings so honestly. Was this some sort of trick? But it did not feel like one.

Her eyes fell on me then, and lingered. Uneasily I wondered if she would try to hug me, too. If she did, I decided I would goose her.

"You will not distract me, Mother," Shahar said. "Are you mad? Another *palace*? Why are you sending me away?"

Remath shook off the moment of candor, her face resuming its usual family head mask. "Sky is an obvious and valuable target. Anyone who wants to damage Arameri influence in the world knows to come here. Just one masked assassin through the Gate would be sufficient; even if no one is harmed, the fact that our privacy can be breached would show our every potential enemy that we are vulnerable." She turned away from us, heading over to the windows, and sighed at the city and mountains beyond. A branch of the Tree arced away, miles long. The blossoms had begun to disintegrate, the Tree's time of flowering having ended. Petals floated away from the branch, dancing along an air current in a winding trail.

"And our enemies include a god," she said. "So we must take radical steps to protect ourselves, for the world still needs us. Even if it thinks otherwise." She glanced back at us over her shoulder. "This *is* a contingency, Shahar. I have no intention of dying anytime soon."

Shahar—stupid, gullible girl—actually looked relieved.

"That's all well and good," I said, rolling my eyes, "but building a secret palace is impossible. You'll need workers, crafters, suppliers, and unless you mean for Shar and Deka to scrub their own toilets, servants. You don't exactly have enough of those to go around here in Sky, so that means hiring locals from wherever your new palace is situated. There's no way to keep a secret with that many people involved, even with magic." Then it occurred to me how she could keep the secret. "And you can't have them *all* murdered."

Remath lifted an eyebrow. "I could, actually, but as you've guessed, that would leave its own trail of questions to be answered. Such crimes are more difficult to hide these days." She nodded sardonically to me, and I smiled bitterly back, because once it had been my job to help erase the evidence of Arameri atrocities.

"In any case," Remath said, "I have found another way."

Beyond the windows, the sun had begun to set. It hadn't touched the horizon yet, and there were still a good twenty minutes or so to go before twilight officially began. This, I would later realize, when I recovered from the shock, was why Remath murmured a soft prayer of apology before she spoke aloud.

"Lady Yeine," she said, "please hear me."

My mouth fell open. Shahar gasped.

"I hear," Yeine said, appearing before us all.

And Remath Arameri—head of the family that had remade the world in Bright Itempas's name, great-granddaughter of a man who had thrown Enefa's worshippers off the Pier for fun, many-times-great-granddaughter of the woman who had brought about Enefa's death—dropped to one knee before Yeine, with her head bowed.

I went over to Remath. My eyes were defective; they had to be. I leaned closer to peer at her but detected no illusion. I hadn't mistaken someone else for her.

I looked up at Yeine, who looked positively gleeful.

"No," I said, stunned.

"Yes," she replied. "A fine trick, wouldn't you say?"

Then she turned to Shahar and Dekarta, who kept looking from her to their mother and back at Yeine. They didn't understand. I didn't want to.

"I will build your new palace," she said to all of us. "In exchange, the Arameri will now worship me."

17

IT WAS SIMPLE, really.

The Arameri had served Itempas for two thousand years. But Itempas was now useless as a patron, and Yeine was family, of a sort. I suppose that was how Remath rationalized it to herself— if she'd needed to. Perhaps it had been nothing more than pragmatism for her. Devout Arameri had always been rare. In the end, all most of them truly believed in was power.

We would travel to the site of the new palace at dawn, Remath told us. There Yeine would build it according to Remath's specifications, and the Arameri would enter a new era in their long and incredible history.

I exited the audience chamber with the rest of them, leaving Remath and Yeine alone to discuss whatever family heads discussed with their new patron goddesses. Wrath, Morad, and Ramina, who had waited in the corridor outside, were called in as Shahar, Deka, and I left, probably to make their obeisance to Yeine as well. No doubt they would have tasks to complete by morning, as they would be traveling to the new palace with us. We would also take a minimal complement of guards, courtiers, and servants, because—according to Remath—we would need no more than that to establish ourselves. Shahar and Deka, respectively, were to choose those members of the family and the various corps who would accompany us. Unspoken in all of this was the fact that anyone who traveled to the new palace, for reasons of secrecy, might never be permitted to return.

I informed Shahar that I had business in Shadow for a few hours and left. The Vertical Gate had been reconfigured in the days since the attack. Now it was set by default to transport in one direction only—away from the palace—and returning required a password sent via a special messaging sphere, which I was given as I prepared to leave. The scrivener on duty, who stood among the soldiers guarding the gate, solemnly reminded me not to lose the sphere, because I would be killed by magic the instant I stepped onto the Gate without it, or killed by the soldiers should I survive and somehow manage the transit, anyway. I made sure I didn't lose the sphere.

That done, I traveled to South Root, where I notified first Hymn and then Ahad that I would be staying at Sky for the time being.

Hymn was more subdued about this than I'd expected, though her parents were plainly overjoyed to see the back of me. Hymn said little as she helped me pack my meager belongings; everything I owned fit into a single cloth satchel. But when I turned to go, she caught my hand and pressed two things into it. The first was a glass knife, the same faded-leaves color as my eyes. She had clearly worked on it for some time; the blade had been polished to mirror smoothness, and she'd even managed to fit it with a brass kitchen-knife handle. The other thing she gave me was a handful of tiny beads in different sizes and colors, each made from glass or polished stone, each etched with infinitesimal lines of clouds or continents. They had holes bored through them to go onto my necklace alongside En.

"How did you know?" I asked as she spilled them into my hand.

"Know what?" She looked at me as though I'd gone mad. "I just remembered that old rhyme about you. About how you stole the sun for a prank? I figured, suns need planets, don't they?"

Pathetic, compared to my lost orrery. Magnificent, given the love that had gone into making them. She turned away when I clutched them to my chest, though I managed—just—not to cry in front of her.

Ahad was in an odder state when I found him at the Arms of Night. As it was afternoon at the time, and the house was about to open for its usual leisurely business, I had expected to find him in his offices. He was on the back porch, however, and instead of his usual cheroot, he held a plucked flower, turning it contemplatively in his fingers. By the troubled expression on his face, the contemplations were not going well.

"Good," was all he said when I informed him that I was

moving back to Sky, and that the Arameri had become Yeinans instead of Itempans, and that, by the way, there was going to be a new palace somewhere.

"*Good?* That's all you have to say?"

"Yes."

I thought of the half-dozen slurs and insults he should've thrown at me in place of that quiet affirmative, and frowned. Something was wrong. But I could not exactly ask him whether he was all right. He would laugh at my attempted concern.

So I tried a different tack. "They're yours, you know. Shahar, Dekarta. Your grandchildren. Great-grand, actually."

This, at least, drew his attention. He frowned at me. "What?"

I shrugged. "I assume you slept with T'vril Arameri's wife before you left Sky."

"I slept with *half* of Sky before I left. What does that have to do with anything?"

I stared at him. "You really don't know." And here I'd thought he'd done it as part of some scheme. I frowned, putting my hands on my hips. "Why the hells did you leave Sky anyhow? Last I saw, you were on the brink of being adopted into the Central Family, maneuvering your way toward becoming the next family head. A bare century later, you're a whoremonger, living among the commonfolk in the seediest part of town?"

His eyes narrowed. "I got tired of it."

"Got tired of what?"

"All of it." Ahad looked away now, toward the center of town—and the great omnipresent bulk of the World Tree, a brown and green shadow limned by the slanting afternoon sun. Almost hidden in the first crotch of the trunk was a glimmer of pearlescent white: Sky.

"I got tired of the Arameri." Ahad turned the flower again. It looked like something common—a dandelion, one of the few flowers that still bloomed in Shadow's dimness. He'd apparently plucked it from between the walkway stones that led up to the back door. I wondered why he was so fascinated by it. "T'vril married a fullblood to cement his rule. She was his third cousin on his father's side or something. Didn't give a damn about him, and the feeling was mutual. I seduced her on behalf of a branch family from outside Sky; they wanted their own girl married to T'vril instead. I needed the capital to boost my investments. So I took the money that they offered and made sure he found out about the affair. He wasn't even upset." His lip curled.

I nodded, slowly. It amazed me that it had taken so much for him to understand. "Not much different from what you did when we were slaves."

Ahad's glare was sharp and dangerous. "It was by my choice. That makes all the difference in the world."

"Does it?" I leaned against one of the porch columns, folding my arms. "Being used one way or another—does it really feel all that different?"

He fell silent. That, and the fact that he'd left Sky afterward, was answer enough. I sighed.

"T'vril's wife must've been pregnant when you left." I would look up the timing when I got back to Sky, though that was hardly necessary. Deka was all the evidence that mattered.

"I can't have children." He said it wearily, with the air of something often repeated. Did so many women want his bitter, heartless seed? Amazing.

"You *couldn't*," I said, "not while there was no goddess of life and death. Not while you were part of Naha, just a half-time reflection of him. But Yeine made you whole. She gave you the gift that gods lost when Enefa died. We all regained it when Yeine took Enefa's place." Except me, I did not add, but he already knew that.

Ahad frowned at the flower that dangled in his fingers, considering. "A child . . . ?" He let out a soft chuckle. "Well, now."

"A son, I'm told."

"A son." Was there regret in his voice? Or just a different sort of apathy? "Come unknown and gone already."

"A *demon*, you fool," I said. "And Remath, Shahar, and Dekarta are probably demons as well." How far removed from a godly forbear did mortals have to be before their blood lost its deadly potency? Shahar and Dekarta were one-eighth god, and their blood had not killed me. Could only a few generations make such a difference? We had all overestimated the danger of the demons, if that was the case—but then, no god would ever have been stupid enough to sample a possible demon's blood and find out.

Ahad chuckled again. This time it was low and malicious. "Are they, now? From god-enslavers to god-killers. The Arameri are so endlessly interesting."

I stared at him. "I will never understand you."

"No, you won't." He sighed. "Keep me apprised on everything. *Use* the damned messaging sphere I gave you; don't just play with it or whatever it is you do."

As this was positively friendly by his standards, and I was tired of the flower silliness, I finally gave in to my curiosity. "You all right?"

"No. But I'm not interested in talking about it."

Ordinarily I would have left him to his brooding. But there

was something about him in that moment—a peculiar sort of weight to his presence, a taste on the air—that intrigued me. Because he wasn't paying any attention to me, I touched him. And because he was so absorbed in whatever he was thinking about, he allowed this.

A lick of something, like fire without pain. The world breathed through both of us, quickening—

At this point, Ahad noticed me and knocked my hand away, glaring. I smiled back. "So you've found your nature?"

His glare became a frown so guarded that I couldn't tell whether he was confused or just annoyed again. Had I guessed correctly, or had he not realized what he was feeling? Or both?

Then something else occurred to me. I opened my mouth to breathe his scent, tasting the familiar disturbed ethers as best I could with my atrophied senses. Particularly around that flower. Yes, I was sure.

"Glee's been here," I said, thoughtful. She had worn the flower in her hair, to judge by the scent. I could tell more than that, actually—such as the fact that she and Ahad had recently made love. Was that what had him in such a mood? I held off on teasing him about this, however, because he already looked ready to smite.

"Weren't you going somewhere?" he asked, pointedly and icily. His eyes turned darker, and the air around us rippled in blatant warning.

"Back to Sky, please," I said, and before I finished the sentence, he'd thrown me across existence. I chuckled as I detached from the world, though he would hear it and my laughter would only piss him off. But Ahad had his revenge. I appeared ten feet above the daystone floor, in one of the most remote areas of the underpalace. The fall broke my wrist, which forced me to walk half an hour for a healing script from the palace scriveners.

There had been no progress on determining who had sent the assassins, the scriveners informed me in terse, monosyllabic responses when I questioned them. (They had not forgotten that I'd killed their previous chief, but there was no point in my apologizing for it.) They were hard at work, however, determining how the masks functioned. In the vast, open laboratory that housed the palace's fifty or so scriveners, I could see that several of the worktables had been allocated to the crimson mask pieces, and an elaborate framework had been set up to house the white mask. I did not see the mortal to whom the white mask had been attached, but it was not difficult to guess his fate. Most likely the scriveners had the corpse somewhere more private, dissecting it for whatever secrets it might hold.

Once my wrist was done, I returned to my quarters and stuffed the clothes and toiletries Morad had given me into Hymn's satchel and was thus packed.

The sun had set while I did my business in Shadow. Night brought forth Sky's glow in unmarked stillness. I left my room, feeling inexplicably restless, and wandered the corridors. I could have opened a wall, gone into the dead spaces, but those weren't wholly mine anymore; I did not want them now. The servants and highbloods I passed in the corridors noticed me, and some recognized me, but I ignored their stares. I was only one murderous god, and a paltry one at that. Once, four had walked the halls. These mortals didn't know how lucky they were.

Eventually I found myself in the solarium, the Arameri's private garden. It was a natural thing to follow the white-pebbled path through the manicured trees. After a time I reached the foot of the narrow white spire that jutted up from the palace's heart. The stairway door was not locked, as it had normally been in the old days, so I climbed the tight, steep twist of steps until I emerged onto the Altar—the flattened, enclosed top of the spire where, for centuries, the Arameri had conducted their Ritual of Succession.

Here I sat on the floor. Countless mortals had died in this chamber, spending their lives to wield the Stone of Earth and transfer the power of gods from one Arameri generation to the next. The spire was empty now, as dusty and disused as the underpalace. I supposed the Arameri did their successions elsewhere. The hollow plinth that had once stood at the center of the room was gone, shattered on the day Yeine and the Stone became one. The crystal walls had been rebuilt, the cracked floors repaired, but there was a still lifelessness to the room that I did not remember feeling during the days of my incarceration.

I pulled En off its chain and set it on the floor before me, rolling it back and forth and remembering what it had felt like to ride a sun. Aside from that, I thought of nothing. Thus I was as ready as I could have been when the daystone floor suddenly changed, brightening just a little. The room felt more alive, too.

He had always had that effect, in the old days.

I looked up. The glow of the daystone made for a nice reflection in the glass, so it was easy to see the two figures behind me: Glee and someone the same height. Broader. Male. Glee nodded to me in the reflection, then vanished, leaving the two of us alone.

"Hi," I said.

"Hello, Sieh," said Itempas.

I waited, then smiled. "No 'It's been a while,' or 'You're look-ing well'?"

"You aren't looking well." He paused. "Does it seem a long time to you?"

"Yes." It wouldn't have, before I'd turned mortal. He had been mortal for a century himself, though; he understood.

Footsteps, heavy and precise, approached me from behind. Something moved on the periphery of my vision. For an instant I thought he would sit beside me, but that would have been too strange for both of us. He walked past me and stopped at the edge of the Altar, gazing through the glass at the night-dark, branch-shrouded horizon beyond.

I gazed at his back. He wore a long leather coat that had been bleached almost white. His white hair was long, too, twisted into a heavy mane of thick cords, like Teman cable-locks but bare of ornamentation other than a clasp that kept them neat and controlled. White trousers and shirt. *Brown* boots. I found myself perversely pleased that he'd been unable to find boots in white.

"I will, of course, accept Nahadoth's offer," he said. "If it is within my power to heal you, or at least stop your aging, I will do all I can."

I nodded. "Thanks."

He returned the nod. Though he faced the horizon, his eyes were on me in the glass reflection. "You intend to stay with these mortals?"

"I suppose. Ahad wants me to keep him informed of what the Arameri are doing." Then I remembered. "Of course, *you're* Ahad's boss, so..."

"You may stay." His gaze was intent, lacking none of its old power despite his mortal condition. "And you *should* stay, to be near the mortals you love."

I frowned at him. His eyes flicked away from mine. "Their lives are too brief," he added. "One should not take that time for granted."

He meant Glee's mother. And perhaps the first Shahar Arameri, too. He had loved her despite her obsessive, destructive madness.

"How do you feel about the Arameri dumping you?" I asked, a bit nastily. I didn't have the energy for real nastiness. I was just trying to change the subject.

I heard the creak of leather and the rasp of hair as he shrugged. "They are mortal."

"No tears shed, hmm?" I sighed, lying back on the stone and stretching my arms above my head. "The whole world will follow them, you know, and turn away from you. It's already happening. Maybe they'll keep calling it the Bright, but it'll really be the Twilight."

"Or the Dawn."

I blinked. Something I hadn't considered. That made me sit up on one elbow and narrow my eyes at him. He stood the way he always had: legs apart, arms folded, motionless. Same old Dayfather, even in mortal flesh. He did not change.

Except.

"Why did you allow Glee Shoth to live?" I asked.

"For the same reason I allowed her mother to live."

I shook my head in confusion. "Oree Shoth? Why would you have killed her?" I scowled. "She wouldn't put up with your shit, is that it?"

If I hadn't been watching him in the glass, I would never

have believed what I saw. He *smiled*. "She wouldn't, no. But that wasn't what I meant. She was also a demon."

This rendered me speechless. In the silence that fell, Itempas finally turned to me. I flinched in shock, even though he looked the same as the last time I'd seen him, apart from the hair and the clothes. And yet something about him—something I could not define—was different.

"Do you plan to kill Remath Arameri and her children?" he asked.

I stiffened. He knew. I said nothing, and he nodded, point made.

Suddenly I was full of nervous tension. I got to my feet, shoving En into a pocket. The Altar was too small for real pacing, but I tried anyway, walking over to him—and then I stopped, seeing my own reflection beside his in the glass. He turned, too, following my gaze, and we looked at ourselves. Me, short and wiry and defensive and confused. I had developed a slouch in my manifest maturity, mostly because I did not like being so tall. Him: big and powerful and elegant, as he had always been. Yet his eyes were so full of knowing and yearning that almost, almost, I wanted him to be my father again.

Almost, almost, I forgave him.

But that could not be, either. I hunched and looked away. Itempas lowered his eyes, and a long, solid silence formed in the enclosed space.

"Tell Glee to come back and get you," I said at last, annoyed. "I've said all I'm going to say."

"Glee is mortal, and I have no magic. We cannot speak as gods do; we must use words. And actions."

I frowned. "What, then, you're staying here?"

"And traveling with you to the new palace, yes."

"Yeine will be here, too." At this I clenched my fists and resumed pacing, in tight angry arcs. "Oh, but you must know that. You came here for her." The two of them, entwined, his lips on the nape of her neck. I forced this image from my mind.

"No. I came for you."

Words. Actions.

Both meaningless. They should not have made my throat clench the way they did. I fought them with anger, glaring at his back. "I could call Naha. I could ask him to kill you over and over, until you beg to truly die." And because I was a brat, I added, "He'll do it, too, for me."

"Is that truly what you wish?"

"Yes! I'd do it myself if I could!"

To my surprise, Itempas pivoted and came toward me, opening his coat. When he reached into one of the inner-breast pockets, I tensed, ready to fight. He pulled out a sheathed dagger, and I grabbed for En. But then he handed the dagger to me, hilt-first. It was a small, light thing, I found when I took it; a child's weapon, in those parts of the world where mortals gave their children sharp toys. Not altogether different from the dagger I'd used to damage Shahar's innocence, ten years before— except this dagger was strapped securely into the leather sheath, held in place by a loop about the guardpiece. No one would be able to draw this blade by accident.

As I turned the thing in my fingers, wondering why in his own name Itempas had given it to me, my nose caught the faint whiff of old, dried blood.

"A gift from Glee," he said. "To me. If death ever becomes preferable to living."

I knew what it was, then. *The gift of mortality*, Enefa had called it. Glee's blood was on the knife—her terrifying, poisonous demon blood. She had given Itempas a way out of his imprisonment, if he ever found the courage to take it.

My hand clenched convulsively around the knife's hilt. "If you ever use this, the mortal realm will die."

"Yes."

"*Glee* will die."

"If she hasn't already died by then, yes."

"*Why would she give this to you?*"

"I don't know."

I stared at him. He wasn't being deliberately obtuse. He must have asked her. Either he hadn't believed her answer, or—more likely, given how much she'd taken after him—she hadn't bothered to answer. And he had accepted her silence.

Then he knelt before me, flicking his coat behind himself in the process, so that it spread out gracefully along the white stone floor. He lifted his head, too, partly because he was an arrogant son of a demon and partly to give me easy access to his chest and throat. Such a handsome, proud offering.

"Bastard," I said, clenching my fist around the knife hilt. Death. I held the death of the universe in my fist. "Arrogant, selfish, evil *bastard*."

Itempas merely waited. The knife was small, but I could angle it just so, get it between the ribs easily to prick his heart. Hells, if Oree Shoth had been a demon, too, then her daughter was more than half god. Even a scratch tainted with her blood might do the trick.

I unfastened the loop, but my fingers were shaking. When I took the hilt in my hand to draw it, I couldn't. My hands just wouldn't move. Eventually I let them—and the dagger—drop to my sides.

"If you want me to die—" he began.

"Shut up," I whispered. "Shut up, gods damn you. I hate you."

"If you hate me—"

"*Shut up!*" He fell silent, and I cursed and threw the dagger to the floor between us. The sound of leather on daystone made an echoing *crack* from the chamber's walls. I had begun to cry. I raked my hands through my hair. "Just shut up, all right? Gods, you're so insufferable! You can't *make me* choose something like that! I'll hate you if I damn well please!"

"All right." His voice was soft, soothing. Against my will, I remembered times—rare but precious—when we had sat together in his placid realm, watching time dance. I had always been conscious of the fact that he and I would never be friends. Lovers was out of the question. But father and son? That much we could do.

"All right, Sieh," he said now, so gently. He did not change. "Hate me if you like."

The urge to love him was so powerful that I shook with it.

I turned and stormed over to the stair entrance, trotting down the steps. When I looked up, just before my head passed beyond the floor's threshold, I saw Itempas watching me. He had not picked up the knife. He had, however, changed: his face was wet with tears.

I ran. I ran. I ran.

The door to Deka's apartment was not locked. No servant would invade his privacy unannounced, and no highblood would come near him as yet. He was an unknown commodity. His family feared him, as he'd wished. I should have, too, because he was more powerful than me, but I had always loved strong people.

He rose from the worktable at which he'd been sitting—not a standard furniture item in Sky. Already he'd made changes. "Who the—Sieh?" He looked exhausted. He'd been up most of the night before, working with the scrivener corps to examine the assassins' masks. Yet here he was, barefoot and tunicless, hair mussed, still awake. I saw sketches on several scrolls and a stack of sheets marked with the Litaria's official sigil. Personnel for the new palace, perhaps. "Sieh, what...?"

"There's no need to fear me," I said, coming around the work-table at him. I held his eyes as I would those of any prey. He stared back. So easy to catch them when they wanted to be caught. "I may be older than the world, but I'm also just a man; no god is ever only one thing. If the whole of me frightens you, love whichever part you like."

He flinched, confusion and desire and guilt all rising and sinking out of sight in his face. Finally he sighed as I reached him. His shoulders slumped a little in defeat. "Sieh."

So much meaning in that one word. The wind, but also light-ning, and need as raw as an open wound. I put my arms around him. The power written into his skin pulsed once, whispering warningly to me of pain and slaughter. I pressed my face to his shoulder and clenched my fists on the back of his shirt, wishing it was gone so I could touch those deadly marks.

"Sieh..." Deka began. He'd gone stiff at my embrace, holding his arms out as if afraid to touch me. "Sieh, gods—"

"Just let me do this," I breathed into his shoulder. "Please, Deka."

His hands landed on my shoulders, too light, hesitant. That

wouldn't do. I pulled him harder against me and he made a soft, strained sound. Then his arms slid around me, tightening. I felt the scrape of nails through my shirt. His face pressed into my hair. A hand cupped the back of my neck.

There was a time of stillness. It wasn't long, because nothing in the mortal realm lasts long. It felt long, however, which was all that really mattered.

When I'd finally had enough, I pulled back and waited for the questions. Mortals always asked questions. *Why did you come here?* would be first, I was certain, because he wanted me and probably hoped that I wanted him. That wasn't it at all, but I would tell him what he wanted to hear.

A long, awkward silence fell. Deka fidgeted and said, "I need at least a few hours of sleep."

I nodded, still waiting.

He looked away. "You don't have to leave."

So I didn't.

We lay in his bed, side by side, chaste. I waited, expecting his hands, his mouth, the weight of his body. I would give him what he wanted. Might even enjoy it. Anything not to be alone.

He shifted closer and put his hand over mine. I waited for more, but a long while passed. Eventually, I heard long, even breaths from his side of the bed. Surprised, I turned my head. He was dead asleep.

I gazed at him until I slept, too.

Cycles.

Deka woke some time before dawn and shook me awake. Quite without planning, we did what mortal lovers have done since time immemorial, stumbling blearily around each other as we each prepared for the day. While he spoke to the servants, ordering tea and summoning a clerk to distribute messages to the scriveners, assassins, and courtiers he'd chosen to accompany us, I went into the bathroom and made myself presentable. Then while he did the same, I drank the tea and peeked at his desk, where he'd scribbled notes about defensive magic and begun penning some sort of request to the Litaria. He caught me doing this as he emerged from his bedroom, but he didn't seem to care, walking past me and checking to see how much tea I'd left him. (Not much. This earned me a glower. I shrugged.)

We proceeded to the forecourt. A group of thirty or so scriveners, soldiers, and various highbloods were already there, including Shahar, who stood dressed in a furred traveling cloak against the brisk morning air. She nodded to us as we arrived, and I nodded back, which made her blink. Servants were arriving, too, carrying trunks and satchels that probably contained more of the highbloods' belongings than their own. As the eastern horizon grew more solidly pale with the imminence of dawn, Remath arrived—and with her, to my great surprise, came Itempas and Yeine. I saw many of the other assembled folk peer at the latter in confusion, since they were obviously not of the family. Yeine stopped some ways back, turning toward the distant horizon as if hearing its call; this was her time. Itempas broke off from Remath as they reached the group, coming to stand near the rest of us, though not close enough for conversation. He watched Yeine.

Deka turned, staring at Itempas, and then abruptly his eyes widened. "Sieh, is that—"

"Yes," I snapped. I folded my arms and carefully ignored both of them.

Ramina was there as well, clearly awaiting Remath, as was Morad, who was dressed for travel. That surprised me. Was Remath willing even to give up her lover to this madness? Perhaps they were not so close after all. Morad's face was impassive, but I suspected she was less than happy about it.

"Good morning, my friends," Remath said, though aside from Morad, no one there was her friend. "By now matters have been explained to you. Naturally you will be unhappy at the short notice, but this was necessary for the sake of secrecy and safety. I trust there are no objections."

In any other circumstance, there would have been, but these were Arameri, and particularly ones who had been chosen for their wits and value. Silence greeted her in response.

"Very well. We await one final guest, and then we will proceed."

Abruptly the world gave a faint, and deliciously familiar, shudder. It was a delicate thing, yet powerful; even the mortals could feel it. The daystone beneath our feet creaked ominously, while the satinbell trees in the nearby Garden of the Hundred Thousand shivered, shedding some of their perfect dangling blossoms. And I closed my eyes, inhaling so that I would not whoop for joy.

"Sieh?" Shahar's voice, alarmed and puzzled. Her ancestors had known this sensation, but no Arameri in a hundred years had felt it. I opened my eyes and smiled at her, so fondly that she blinked and almost smiled back.

"My father returns," I whispered.

Beyond us, Yeine turned; she was smiling, too. Itempas—he had turned away from us, gazing off toward the palace as if it was suddenly the most interesting of sights. But I saw the stiffness in his shoulders, the effort that it took him to stay relaxed.

Nahadoth faded into view near Yeine, a storm weaving itself from nothingness into a semblance of mortal flesh. The shape that he took was an homage to his time of suffering: male, pale, the tendrils of his substance bleeding away like drifting, living smoke. (There had been a mortal body within that smoke once: Ahad. Did he shiver now, somewhere in the city below, feeling the nearby presence of his old prisoner?) Nahadoth's shape was the only thing that had not changed since the days of his enslavement, for I felt his power now, gloriously whole and terrible, a weight upon the very air. Chaos and darkness, pure and unleashed.

There were murmurs and cries of alarm within the group of Arameri as Nahadoth manifested, though Remath quelled them with a glare. Making an example of herself, she stepped forward. I did not think less of her for pausing to steel herself.

I did think better of Shahar, though, who took a deep breath and moved away from us, hurrying to her mother's side. Remath glanced back at her, forgetting to hide her surprise. Shahar inclined her head in taut reply. She had, after all, met Nahadoth before. Together, both women proceeded to join the two gods.

Deka did not attempt to join them. He had folded his arms and begun to shift from foot to foot, throwing frowns at Itempas and then at me, generally radiating unhappiness. It was not difficult to guess at the source of his distress: the Three walked among us, even if they were not quite complete, and Deka was not stupid enough to believe they had all come merely to build the Arameri's vacation home. No doubt he guessed now why I had been so upset the night before.

I came for you, Itempas had said.

I folded my arms across my chest as well, but this was not defensive. It just took effort to steel myself against hope.

Then the conversation was done, and Yeine looked up at all of us, nodding once in absent reply to something Remath said. Her eyes met mine across the forecourt just as, beyond her, the horizon flared gold with the sun's first delicate rays. For just an instant—as fleeting as the dawn itself—her form changed, becoming something indescribable. My mind tried to define it anyway, using images and sensations that its mortal perceptions could encompass. A phantasm of herself drawn in silver-pastel mist. A vast and impossible landscape, dominated by a whole forest of trees as great as the one that cradled us now. The scent and taste of ripe fruit, tooth-tender and succulently sweet. For a moment I ached with most unfilial yearnings: lust for her, jealousy for Naha, and pity for Tempa because he had gotten to taste her only once.

Then the moment passed, and Yeine was herself again, and her smile was for me alone, her first and favorite son. I would not give up that specialness for all the world.

"Time to go," she said.

And suddenly we were no longer in Sky.

"We" being all of us, gods and Arameri, right down to the servants and baggage. One moment we were in Sky's forecourt, and the next, the forty or so of us were somewhere else in the world, transported by a flick of Yeine's will. It was later here; the dawn had advanced into full morning, but I paid little attention to this. I was too busy laughing at the Arameri, most of whom were stumbling or gasping or otherwise trying not to panic, because *we stood atop an ocean*. Waves surrounded us, an endless plain of gently heaving emptiness. When I looked down, I saw that our feet dented the water, as though some-one had laid a thin and flexible coating between the liquid and our shoes. When the waves bobbed beneath us, we bobbed with them but did not sink. Some of the Arameri fell over, unable to adjust. I chuckled and braced my feet apart, balancing easily. The trick was to lean forward and rely on one's core, not the legs. I had skated oceans of liquefied gas, long ago. This was not so different.

"Bright Father help us!" cried someone.

"You need no help," Itempas snapped, and the man fell over, staring at him. Tempa, of course, was rock-steady upon the waves.

"Will this do?" Yeine asked Remath. Remath, I was amused to see, had solved the problem of maintaining balance and dignity by dropping to one knee again.

"Yes, Lady," Remath replied. A swell passed beneath us, mak-ing everyone rise and then drop several feet. Yeine, I noted, did not move as this occurred; the dent beneath her feet sim-ply deepened as the water rose and flowed around her. And the swell died the instant it drew near Nahadoth, the wave's force dissipating into scattered, pointless motion.

"Where are we?" Shahar asked. She had knelt as well, follow-ing Remath's lead, but even this seemed difficult for her. She did not look up as she spoke, concentrating on remaining at least somewhat upright.

It was Nahadoth who answered. He had turned to face the sun, narrowing his eyes with a faint look of distaste. It did not harm him, however, because it was just one small star, and it was always night somewhere in the universe.

"The Ovikwu Sea," he said. "Or so it was last called, long ago."

I began to chuckle. Everyone nearby looked at me in confusion. "The Ovikwu," I said, letting my voice carry so they could all share the joke, "was a landbound sea in the middle of the Maroland—the continent that once existed where we now stand." The continent that had been destroyed by the Arameri when they'd been foolish enough to try and use Nahadoth as their weapon. He'd done what they wanted, and then some.

Deka inhaled. "The *first* Sky. The one that was destroyed."

Nahadoth turned—and paused, gazing at him for far too long a breath. I tensed, my belly clenching. Did he notice the familiarity of Deka's features, so clearly etched with Ahad's stamp? If he realized what Deka was, what Remath and Shahar were... Would he listen if I pleaded for their lives?

"The first Sky is directly below," he said. And then he looked at me. *He knew.* I swallowed against sudden fear.

"Not for long," said Yeine.

She raised a hand in a graceful beckoning gesture toward the sea beneath us. The Three can bring new worlds into existence at will; they can set galaxies spinning with a careless breath. It took Yeine no effort to do what she did then. She didn't need to gesture at all. That was just her sense of theater.

But I think she'd overestimated the mortal attention span. No one noticed *her* once the first stones burst from the sea.

It was Deka who murmured for a bubble of air to form around all of us, warding off the now-churning waves and spray. Thus we were safe, able to watch in undisturbed awe as jagged, seaweed-draped and coral-encrusted chunks of daystone—the smallest the size of the Arms of Night—rose beneath and around us. Rubble undisturbed for centuries: it rose now, tumbling upward, stone piling atop stone and fusing, walls forming and shedding debris, courtyards rising beneath our feet to take the place of the heaving waves, structure shaping itself from nothingness.

Then it was done, and the spray cleared, and we looked around to find ourselves standing atop glory.

Take a nautilus shell; cut it cross section. Gently elevate its swirling, chambered tiers as they approach the tight-bound center, culminating at last in a pinnacle on which we all stood. Note its asymmetrical order, its chaotic repetition, the grace of its linkages. Contemplate the ephemerality of its existence. Such is the beauty that is mortal life.

This was not Sky, old or new. It was smaller than both its predecessor palaces and deceptively simpler. Where those earlier structures had been built compact and high, this palace hugged the ocean's surface. Instead of sharp spires piercing the sky, here there were low, smoothly sloping buildings, joined by dozens of lacy bridges. The foundation—for the palace had been built atop a kind of convex platform—was many-lobed and odd, with spars and indentations jutting out in every direction. Its surface gleamed in the dawn light, white and nacreous as pearl, the only similarity between it and Sky.

I could feel the power woven into every sweeping balustrade, keeping the massive edifice afloat—but there was more to it than magic. Something about the structure itself worked to maintain its buoyancy. If I had still been a god, I might have understood it, for there are rules even where we are concerned, and it was Yeine's nature to seek balance. Perhaps the magic harnessed the ocean's waves in some new way or absorbed the power of the sun. Perhaps the foundation was hollow. Regardless, it was clear this new palace would float, and with some assistive magic would travel readily across the ocean. It would defend the precious cargo within its walls, if only because no mortal army could assail it.

While the mortals turned about, most of them speechless with awe, the rest making sounds of shock and delight and incomprehension, I strode across the drying daystone of the central platform. Yeine and Nahadoth turned to face me.

"Not bad," I said. "Bit *white*, though, isn't it?"

Yeine shrugged, amused. "You were thinking gray walls? Do you *want* them all to kill themselves?"

I looked around, considering the vast but monotonous surrounding oceanscape. Faintly I could hear surf and wind; aside from that there was silence. I grimaced. "Point. But that doesn't mean they should have to endure the same boring, austere sameness of the previous two palaces, does it? They're yours now. Find some way to remind them of that."

She thought a moment. Nahadoth, however, smiled. Suddenly the daystone beneath our feet softened, turning to thick black loam. Everywhere I looked—on railings, edging the bridges—the daystone had remolded itself into troughs of soil.

Yeine laughed and went to him, a teasing look in her eye. "A hint?" She extended her hand, and he took it. I could not help noticing the easy camaraderie between them and the sudden softness of Nahadoth's cabochon eyes when he gazed at her. His ever-changing face grew still, too, becoming a different kind of familiar: brown-skinned and angular and Darren. I fought the urge to glance at Deka, to see if he had noticed.

"We have always built better together than alone," Naha

said. Yeine leaned against him, and the soft dark tendrils of his aura swept forward to surround her. They did not touch her, but they did not have to.

A movement at the corner of my vision drew my attention. Itempas had turned away from his siblings' intimacy, watching me instead. I gazed back at him in his solitude, surprised to feel sympathy instead of the usual anger. We two outcasts.

Then I spied Shahar, standing near Dekarta. He was alight as I had never seen him, turning and turning to try and take in the whole of the palace. It looked as though he would never stop grinning. I thought of the adventure novels he'd loved so as a child and wished I was still god enough to enjoy this pleasure with him.

Shahar, more subdued, was smiling, too, glancing now and again at the spirals, but mostly she was just watching him. Her brother, whom she'd lost for so long, come back to her at last.

And purely by chance as I watched them, they noticed me. Deka's grin grew wider; Shahar's small smile lingered. They did not join hands as they walked over to me, stepping carefully over the soft soil, but the bond between them was obvious to anyone who knew how love looked. That this bond included me was equally obvious. I turned to them, and for a long and wondrous moment, I was not alone.

Then Yeine said, "Come, Sieh," and the moment ended.

Shahar and Deka stopped, their smiles fading. I saw understanding come. They had made me mortal so I could be their friend. What would happen to us once I was a god again?

A hand touched my shoulder, and I looked up. Itempas stood there. Ah, yes; he had loved mortals, too, over the years. He knew how it felt to leave them behind.

"Come," he said gently.

Without another word, I turned my back on Dekarta and Shahar and went with him.

Yeine and Nahadoth met us, and their power folded around us, and we vanished just as the first green shoots began to push up from the soil.

18

In the name of Itempas
We pray for light.
We beg the sun for warmth.
We diffuse the shadows.
In the name of Itempas
We speak to give meaning to sound.
We think before we act.
We kill, but only for peace.

THE CHAMBER IN WHICH WE APPEARED was not far from the others. Still in the new palace, in fact—one of the smaller, delicate nautilus chambers that had formed on the palace's outermost edges, covered over by prism glass. As soon as we appeared in it, I knew what it really was: a pocket of space made different from the world around it, ideal for scrivening or channeling magic without spreading the magic's effects to the surrounding structure. Deka would love these when he found them.

Nahadoth and Yeine faced Itempas, who gazed back at them. No expression on any face, though this meant little, I knew, for they had never needed words to speak. Too much of what they needed to exchange was emotion in any case. Perhaps that was why, when Nahadoth spoke, he kept his words brief and his manner cool.

"Until sunset," he said. "You will have that much parole."

Itempas nodded slowly. "I will attend to Sieh at once, of course."

"When sunset comes and you return to mortal flesh, you will be weak," Yeine added. "Be sure you prepare."

Itempas only sighed, nodding again.

It was an intentional cruelty. They had granted him parole for my sake, but we needed his power for only a moment. For them to allow a whole day of freedom beyond that, when they would only snatch it back at the day's end, was just their way of turning the knife again. He deserved it, I reminded myself, deserved it in spades.

But I will not pretend it didn't trouble me.

Then there was a shimmer, all that my mortal mind could perceive, and the whole world sang clean when they stripped the mortal covering from him and cast it away. Itempas did not cry out, though he should have. I would have. Instead he only shuddered, closing his eyes as his hair turned to an incandescent nimbus and his clothes glowed as if woven from stars and—I would have laughed, if this had not been sacred—his boots turned white. Even with my dull mortal senses, I felt the effort he exerted to control the sudden blaze of his true self, the wash of heat that it sent across the surface of reality, tsunamis in the wake of a meteor strike. He stilled it all, leaving only profound silence.

Would I do as well, when I was a god again? Probably not.

Most likely I would shout and jump up and down, and maybe start dancing across any planets nearby.

Soon, now.

When the blaze of Itempas's restoration had passed, he paused for a moment longer, perhaps composing himself. I braced myself when he focused on me, as he had promised. But then, almost imperceptibly—I would not have noticed if I hadn't known him so well—he frowned.

"What is it?" asked Yeine.

"There is nothing wrong with him," Itempas replied.

"Nothing wrong with me?" I gestured at myself, with my man's hand. I'd had to shave again that morning and had nicked my jaw in the process. It still *hurt*, damn it. "What is there about me that *isn't* wrong?"

Itempas shook his head slowly. "It is my nature to perceive pathways," he said. An approximation of what he meant, since we were speaking in Senmite out of respect for my delicate mortal flesh. "To establish them where none exist and to follow those already laid. I can restore you to what you are meant to be. I can halt that which has gone wrong. But nothing about you, Sieh, is wrong. What you have become…" He looked at Yeine and Nahadoth. He would never have done anything so undignified as throw up his hands, but his frustration was a palpable thing. "He is as he should be."

"That cannot be," said Nahadoth, troubled. He stepped toward me. "This is not his nature. His growth damages him. How can this be *meant*?"

"And who," asked Yeine, speaking slowly because she was not as practiced as the other two at rendering our concepts into mortal speech, "has meant it?"

They looked at each other, and belatedly I realized the gist of their words. I would not be regaining my godhood today. Sighing, I turned away from them and went over to the curving nacre wall. I sat down against it and propped my arms on my knees.

And, quite predictably, things went very bad, very fast.

"This cannot be," Nahadoth said again, and I knew his anger by the way the little chamber suddenly dimmed despite the bright morning sunlight filtering through its glass ceiling. Only the chamber dimmed, however, rather than the whole sky. Clever Yeine, planning for her brothers' tempers. If only I had not been trapped in the chamber with them.

Nahadoth stepped toward Itempas, his aura weaving itself darker and thinner, becoming a glow that no mortal eyes should have been able to see by any law of nature—but of course he defied such laws, so the blackness was plain to all.

"You have always been a coward, Tempa," he said. The words skittered around the chamber's walls, darting, striking in echoes. "You pressed for the demons' slaughter. You fled this realm after the War and kept our children away, leaving us to deal with the mess. Shall I believe you now when you say you cannot help my son?"

I waited for the explosion of Itempas's fury and all the usual to follow. They would fight, and Yeine would do as Enefa had always done and keep their battle contained, and only when they were both exhausted would she try to reason with them.

I was so tired of this. So tired of all of it.

But the surprise was mine. Itempas shook his head slowly. "I would do no less than my best by our child, Naha." Only the faintest of emphasis on *our*, I noticed, where once he would have made a show of possession. He did not look at me, but he didn't have to. Every word that Itempas spoke had meaning, often in multiple layers. He knew, as I did, that his claim on me was precarious at best.

I frowned at him, wondering at this newfound humility; it did not at all seem like the Tempa I knew. Nor did his calm in the face of Nahadoth's accusation. Nahadoth frowned at this, too, more in suspicion than surprise.

And then something else unexpected happened: Yeine stepped forward, looking at Nahadoth with annoyance. "This serves no purpose," she snapped. "We did not come here to rehash old grievances." And then, before Nahadoth could flare at her, she touched his arm. "Look to our son, Naha."

Startled out of anger, Nahadoth turned to me. All three of them looked at me, in fact, radiating a combination of pity and chagrin. I smiled back at them, bleak in my despair.

"Nicely done," I said. "You only forgot I was here for half a minute."

Nahadoth's jaw tightened. I took an obscure pride in this.

Yeine sighed, stepping between her taller brothers with a glare at each, and came to my side. She crouched beside me, balancing on her toes; as usual she wore no shoes. When I did not move, she shifted to sit against me, her head resting on my shoulder. I closed my eyes and pressed my cheek against her hair.

"There is another option," Nahadoth said at last, breaking the silence. He spoke slowly, reluctantly. Change should not have been difficult for him, but I could see that this was. "When we are of one accord, all things become possible."

Again, I expected a reaction that Itempas did not provide. "Sieh's restoration is something we all desire." He spoke stiffly because change *was* difficult for him. Yet he made the effort anyway, even though it was an extreme suggestion: to bring together the Three as they had not done since the dawning of the universe. To remake reality, if that was what it took to remake *me*.

To this, I had no snide remark. I stared at them, Naha and Tempa, standing side by side and trying, for my sake, to get along.

Yeine lifted her head, which forced me to do the same. "I am willing, of course," she said to them, though she sounded concerned. "But I have never done this before. Is there danger to Sieh?"

"Some," said Itempas.

"Perhaps," said Nahadoth.

At Yeine's frown, I touched her hand, explaining as I had done for Shahar and Deka. "If the Three's accord is not total"— I nodded toward Itempas and Nahadoth, not needing to be subtle in my meaning—"if there is any hint of discord between you, things could go very wrong."

"How wrong?"

I shrugged. I had not seen it happen myself, but I understood the principle. It was simple: their will became reality. Any conflicts in their respective desires manifested as natural law—inertia and gravity, time and perception, love and sorrow. Nothing that the Three did was subtle.

Yeine considered this for a long moment. Then she reached up to caress my hair. As a boy, I had loved for her to do this. As a man, I found it awkward. Patronizing. But I tolerated it.

"Then there is danger," she said, troubled. "I want what *you* want. And it seems to me that what you want is not entirely clear."

I smiled sadly. Itempas's eyes narrowed. He and Nahadoth exchanged a knowing look. That was nice, actually. Like old times. Then they remembered that they hated each other and focused on me again.

It was ironic, really, and beautiful in its way. The problem was not them but me. The Three walked the world again and had come together in the hope of saving me. And I could not be saved, because I was in love with two mortals.

Yeine sighed. "You need time to think." She got to her feet, brushing unnecessarily at her pants, and faced Nahadoth and Itempas. "And we have business of our own to discuss, Sieh. Where shall we send you?"

I shook my head, rubbing my head wearily. "I don't know. Somewhere else." I gestured vaguely at the palace. "I'll make my own way." I always did.

Yeine glanced back at me as if she'd heard that last thought, but like a good mother, she let it pass unremarked. "Very well."

Then the world blurred, and I found myself sitting in a large open chamber of the new palace. Templelike, its ceiling arched high overhead, thirty or forty feet away. Vines dangled from its cornices and wended down the curving pillars. In the handful of minutes since we'd left, Yeine's power had thoroughly permeated the palace and covered it in green. The daystone was no longer precisely white, either: one wall of the chamber faced the sun, translucent, and against the bright backdrop I saw white stone marbled with something darker, gray shading to black. The black was studded with tiny white points, like stars. Perhaps they would glow, too, come night.

Deka sat there on his knees, alone. What had he been doing, praying? Holding vigil while my mortality passed away? How quaint. And how unsubtle of Yeine, to send me to him. I would never have figured her for a matchmaker.

"Deka," I said.

He started, turned, and frowned at me in surprise. "Sieh? I thought—"

I shook my head, not bothering to get up. "I have unfinished business, it seems."

"What—" No. Deka was too smart to ask that question. I saw understanding, elation, guilt, and hope flow across his face in a span of seconds before he caught himself and put his Arameri mask in place instead. He got to his feet and came over, offering a hand to help me up, which I took. When I was up, however, there was a moment of awkwardness. We were both men now, and most men would have stepped apart after such a gesture, putting distance between themselves so as to maintain the necessary boundaries of independence and camaraderie. I did not move away, and neither did Deka. Awkwardness passed into something entirely different.

"We were thinking about what to name this palace," he said softly. "Shahar and I."

I shrugged. "Seashell? Water?" I had never been much for creative naming. Deka, who had taste, grimaced at my suggestions.

"Shahar likes 'Echo.' She'll have to run it past Mother, of course." So fascinating, this conversation. Our mouths moved, speaking about things neither of us cared about, a verbal mask for entirely different words that did not need to be said. "She thinks this will make a good audience chamber." Another grimace, this one more delicate.

I smiled. "You disagree?"

"It doesn't feel like an audience chamber. It feels…" He shook his head, turning to face a spot beneath the translucent swirl-wall. I took his meaning. There was a votive atmosphere to this chamber, something difficult to define. There should have been an altar in that spot.

"So tell her," I said.

He shrugged. "You know how it is. Shahar is still...Shahar." He smiled, but it faded.

I nodded. I didn't really want to talk about Shahar.

Deka's hand brushed mine, tentative. This was something he could have played off as an accident, if I let him. "Perhaps you should bless this place. It's a trick, of a sort, or it will be. The real home of the Arameri, leaving Sky as a decoy..."

"I can't bless anything anymore, except in the poetic sense." I took his hand, growing tired of the game. No semblance of just-friends anymore. "Shall I become a god again, Deka? Is that what you want?"

He flinched, thrown by my directness, his mask cracking. Through it I saw need so raw that it made me ache in sympathy. But he abandoned the game, too, because that was what the moment deserved. "No."

I smiled. If I had still been a god, my teeth would have been sharp. "Why not? I could still love you, as a god." I stepped closer, nuzzling his chin. He did not take this bait or the verbal bait I offered next. "Your family would love you better, if I were a god. *Your* god."

Deka's hands gripped my arms, tight. I expected him to thrust me away, but he didn't. "I don't care what they want," he said, his voice suddenly low, rough. "*I want* an equal. I want to be *your* equal. When you were a god, I couldn't be that, so...So help me, yes, some part of me wished you were mortal. It wasn't deliberate, I didn't know what would happen, but I don't regret it. So Shahar's not the only one who betrayed you." I flinched, and his hands tightened, to the threshold of pain. He leaned closer, intent. "As a child, I was nothing to you. A game to pass the time." When I blinked in surprise, he laughed bitterly. "I told you, Sieh. I know everything about you."

"Deka—" I began, but he cut me off.

"I know why you've never taken a mortal lover as more than a passing whim. Even before mortals were created, you'd lived so long, seen so much, that no mortal could be anything but an eyeblink in the eternity of your life. That's if you were willing to try, and you weren't. *But I will not be nothing to you*, Sieh. And if I must change the universe to have you, then so be it." He smiled again, tight, vicious, beautiful. Terrifying.

Arameri.

"I should kill you," I whispered.

"Do you think you could?" Unbelievable, his arrogance. Magnificent. He reminded me of Itempas.

"You sleep, Deka. You eat. Not all my tricks need magic."

His smile grew an edge of sadness. "Do you really *want* to kill me?" When I didn't answer—because I didn't know—he sobered. "What *do* you want, Sieh?"

And because I was afraid, and because Yeine had asked the same question, and because Deka really did know me too well, I answered with the truth.

"N-not to be alone anymore." I licked my lips and looked away—at the altar-less floor, at a nearby pillar, at the sun diluted by swirls of white and black and gray. Anywhere but at him. I was so very, very tired. I had been tired for an age of the world. "To have...I want...something that is *mine*."

Deka let out a long, shaky sigh, pressing his forehead against mine as if he'd just won some victory. "Is that all?"

"Yes. I want—"

And then there was no repeating what I wanted, because his mouth was on mine and his soul was in me and it was frightening to be invaded—and exhilarating and agonizing. Like racing comets and chasing thoughtwhales and skating along freezing liquid air. It was better than the first time. He still kissed like a god.

Then his mouth was on my throat, his hands tugging open my shirt, his legs pushing us back back back until I stopped against one of the vine-covered pillars. I barely noticed despite the breath being knocked out of me. I was gasping now because he'd bitten me just over my lower rib cage, and that was the most erotic sensation I'd ever felt. I reached out to touch him and found hot mortal skin and humming tattooed magic, free of the encumbering cloth as he stripped himself. There are so many ways to make magic. I tapped a cadence over his shoulders, and hot, raw power seared up my arms in response. I drank it in and moaned. He had made himself strong and wise, a god in mortal flesh, for me, me, me. Was he right? I had always avoided mortals. It made no sense for a being older than the sun to want a creature that would always be less than a child, in relative terms. But I did want him; oh gods, how I wanted him. Was that the solution? It was not my nature to do what was wise; I did what felt good. Why should that not apply to love as well as play?

Had I truly been fighting myself all this time?

Movement on the edge of my vision pulled me out of the haze of Deka's teeth and hands. I focused on reality and saw Shahar, in the entryway of the marbled chamber. She had stopped there, framed by the corridor beyond, illuminated by the swirling sun. Her eyes were wide, her face paler than ever, her lips a flat white line. I remembered those lips soft and open, welcoming, and in spite of everything, I craved her again. I stroked Deka's straight hair and thought of hers coiling round my fingers and—Gods, no, I would go mad if I kept this up.

Something that was mine. I looked down at Deka, who'd crouched at my feet, licking the bite on my ribs as I shuddered. His hands cupped my waist, as gentle as if I were made of eggshell. (I was. It was called mortal flesh.) Beautiful, perfect boy. Mine.

"Prove it," I whispered. "Show me how much you love me, Deka."

He looked up at me. I realized he knew Shahar was there. Of course; the bond between us. Perhaps that was why she'd come here, too, at this precise moment, out of the whole vast empty palace. I was lonely. I needed. That need drew them to me now, just as my need had drawn them on a long-ago day in Sky's underpalace. We had shared something powerful when we took our oath, but the connection had been there even beforehand. That could not be broken by something so paltry as betrayal.

All this was in Deka's eyes as he gazed up at me. I do not know what he saw in mine. Whatever it was, though, he nodded once. Then he rose, never taking his hands off me, and turned me gently to face the pillar. When he spoke into my ear, the words were gods' language. That made me believe them, and trust him, because they could be nothing but true.

"I'll never hurt you," he said, and proved it.

Shahar left sometime during what followed. Not immediately.

She stayed for a long while, in fact, listening to my groans and watching while I stopped caring about her, or even being aware of her presence. Perhaps she even lingered after I pulled her little brother to the floor and made a proper altar of it, wringing sweat and tears and songs of praise from him, and blessing him with pleasure in return. I didn't know. I didn't care. Deka was my only world, my only god. Yes, I used him, but he wanted me to. I would worship him forever.

I was exhausted afterward. Deka wasn't tired at all, the bastard. He sat up awhile, using the floor to idly trace the outlines of sigils that he intended to draw into the new palace's substance as part of its first layer of arcane protection. Apparently teams of soldiers and scriveners had already begun exploring the palace and mapping its wonders. He told me about this while I lay in a stupor. It was as though he'd gorged himself on my vitality, leaving me little better than a husk. Then it occurred to me that during our lovemaking, it had been he who'd drawn us out of the world and back; his kisses, not mine, had woven our souls together. He was still one-eighth of a god. I was all mortal.

If this was how mortals usually felt when a god was done with them, I felt fresh guilt for all my past dalliances.

Eventually I recovered, however, and told Deka that I needed to leave. All the highbloods were selecting apartments in the uppermost central spirals of the palace—the old pattern from Sky. It would be easy for me to find him later. There was an uncomfortable moment when Deka gave me a long and silent perusal before replying, but whatever he saw in my face satisfied him. He nodded and rose to get dressed himself.

"Be careful," was all he said. "My sister may be dangerous now."

I thought that was probably true.

I found Itempas less than a half hour before sunset. As I'd suspected, he'd taken up residence on the wide central platform where we'd first arrived, which had become a meadow of bobbing sea grass in the meantime. This palace had not been configured to exalt him; nevertheless, the highest center point of anything was a natural place for him to settle.

He stood facing the sun, his legs braced apart and arms folded, unmoving, though he must have sensed my approach. The grass whispered against my pant legs as I walked, and I saw that the grass nearest Itempas had turned white. Typical.

I did not see Nahadoth or Yeine or feel their presence nearby. They had abandoned him again.

"Want to be alone?" I asked, stopping behind him. The sun had almost touched the sea in the distance. He could count the remaining moments of his godhood on one hand. Maybe two.

"No," he said, so I sat down in the grass, watching him.

"I've decided that I want to remain mortal," I said. "At least until...you know. Close to. Ah. The end. Then the three of you can try to change me back." Unspoken was the fact that I might change my mind again then and choose to die with Deka. It was a choice that not every god got to make. I was very fortunate.

He nodded. "We felt your decision."

I grimaced. "How unromantic. And here I was thinking that was an orgasm."

He ignored my irreverence out of long habit. "Your love for those two has been clear to all of us since your transformation into mortal, Sieh. Only you have resisted this knowledge."

I hated it when he got sanctimonious, so I changed the subject. "Thanks for trying, by the way. To help me."

He sighed gently. "I wonder, sometimes, why you think so little of me. Then I remember."

"Yes. Well." I shrugged, uncomfortable. "Is Glee coming to fetch you?" Unspoken: *when you are mortal again?*

"Yes."

"She really loves you, you know."

He turned, just enough so that I could see his face. "Yes."

I was babbling, and he had noticed. Annoyed, I stopped talking. The silence collected around us, comfortable. In the old days, I had only ever liked being quiet around him. With anyone else, the urge to fill the silence with chatter or movement was overwhelming. He had never needed to command me to be still. Around him, I just wanted to.

We watched the sun inch toward the horizon. "Thank you," he said suddenly, surprising me.

"Hmm?"

"For coming here."

At this, I sighed and shifted and rubbed a hand over my hair. Finally I got up, coming to stand beside him. I could feel the radiant warmth of his presence, skin tightening even from a foot away. He could blaze with the fire and light of every sun in existence, but most times he kept the furnace banked so that others could be near him. His version of a friendly invitation— because naturally he would never, ever just *say* he was lonely, the fool.

And somehow, I had never, ever noticed that he did this. What did that make me? His twice-fool son, I supposed.

So I stayed there beside him while we watched the last

curve of the sun flatten into an oblong, then puddle against the edge of the world, and finally melt away. The instant this happened, Itempas gasped, and I felt a sudden swift wave of heat, as of something rushing away. What remained in its wake was human, ordinary, just a middle-aged man in plain clothes and worn boots (brown again, ha ha!) with too much hair for practicality. And when he toppled backward like an old broken tree, unconscious in the aftermath of godhood, it was I who caught him, and eased him to the floor, and cradled his head in my lap.

"Stupid old man," I whispered. But I stroked his hair while he slumbered.

Would that things could have ended there.

A moment after I'd settled down with Itempas, I felt a presence behind me and did not turn. Let Glee think what she would of me with her father. I was tired of hating him. "Make him decorate his hair," I said, more to make conversation than anything else. "If he's going to wear his hair in a Teman style, he ought to do it right."

"So," said Kahl, and I went rigid with shock. His voice was soft, regretful. "You have forgiven him."

What—

Before the thought could form, he was in front of me, on Itempas's other side, with one hand poised in a way that made no sense to me—until he plunged it down, and too late I remembered that Glee had been protecting him from this very thing.

By that point, Kahl's hand was up to the wrist in Itempas's chest.

Itempas jerked awake, rigid, his face a rictus of agony. I did not waste time screaming denial. Denial was for mortals. Instead I grabbed Kahl's arm with all my strength, trying to keep him from doing what I *knew* he was about to do. But I was just a mortal, and he was a godling, and not only did he rip Itempas's heart out in a blur of splattering red, but he also threw me across the platform in the process. I rolled to a halt amid the salt-sweet stench of bruised sea grass, barely three feet from the edge. There were steps wending around the platform, but if I'd missed those, it was a long way—several hundred feet—to the base of the palace.

Dazed, I struggled upright and discovered that my arm was dislocated. As I finished screaming from this, I looked up and found Kahl standing between me and Itempas's corpse. The heart was in his hand, dripping; his expression was implacable.

"Thank you," he said. "I've been hunting him for years now. His demon daughter is good at hiding. I knew that if I watched *you*, however, I would eventually get my chance."

"What—" Hard to think around pain. If mortals could do it, I could, damn it. I ground my teeth and spoke through them. "What in the infinite hells is *wrong* with you? You know that won't kill him. And now Naha and Yeine will be after you." I was not a god anymore. I could not call them with my thoughts. What could I do, as a mortal, facing the god of vengeance in the moment of his triumph? Nothing. Nothing.

"Let them come." So familiar, that arrogance. Where had I seen it before? "They haven't found me yet. I can complete the mask now and take it back from Usein." He lifted Itempas's heart, peering intently at it, and for the first time I saw him smile in unreserved pleasure. His lips drew back, showing a hint of canine—

—sharp teeth, so much like—

"Only a spark left. Just enough, though."

I understood then, or thought I did. What Kahl had sought was not Itempas's mere blood or flesh, but the pure bright power of the god of light. As a mortal, Itempas had none, and in his true form he was too powerful. Only now, in the space between mortality and immortality, was Itempas both vulnerable and valuable—and I, powerless, was no sufficient guardian. Glee had been right not to trust me with him, though not for the reasons she feared.

"You're going to take the mask from Usein?" I struggled to sit up, holding my arm. "But I thought..."

No. Oh, no. I had been so wrong.

A mask that conferred the power of gods. But Kahl had never meant for a mortal to wear it.

"You can't." I could not even imagine it. Once upon a time, there were three gods who had created all the realms. Less than three and it would all end. *More* than three and—"You can't! If the power doesn't rip you apart—"

"Are you concerned?" Kahl lowered the heart, his smile fading. There was anger in him now; all his earlier reticence and sadness had vanished. He had accepted his nature at last, waxing powerful in the moment of his triumph. Even if I had been my old self, I would have felt fear. One did not challenge the elontid at such times. "Do you care about me, Sieh?"

"I care about *living*, you demonshitting fool! What you're planning..." It was a nightmare that no godling would admit dreaming. The Maelstrom had given birth to three gods down the course of eternity. Who knew if—or when—it might suddenly belch forth another? What we thought of as the universe, the collection of realities and embodiments that had been born from the Three's warring and loving and infinitely careful craft, was too delicate to survive the onslaught of a Fourth. The Three themselves would endure, and adapt, and build a new universe that would incorporate the new one's power. But everything of the old existence—including godlings and the entire mortal realm—would be gone.

There was a blur and suddenly Kahl was before me. To be more precise, his foot was on my chest, and I was on the ground being crushed beneath it. With my good hand I scrabbled for his booted foot but could gain no purchase on the fine, god-conjured leather. The only reason I could still breathe at all was the soil beneath my back: my torso had sunk into it rather than simply collapsing.

Kahl leaned over me, adding pressure to my lungs. Through watering eyes I saw his: narrow, deep-set slashes in the plane of his face, like Teman eyes. Like mine, though far colder. And they were green, too, like mine.

—*like Enefa's*—

"Are you afraid?" He cocked his head as if genuinely curious, then leaned closer. I could almost hear my ribs groan, on the brink. But when I forced my face back up, muscles straining, throat bulging, I forgot all about my ribs. Because now Kahl was close enough that I could see his eyes clearly, and when his pupils flickered into narrow, deadly slits—

—*eyes like Enefa's no no EYES LIKE MINE*—

I tried to scream.

"It's far too late for you to care about me, Father," he said.

The word fell into my mind like poison, and the veil on my memory shredded into tatters.

Kahl vanished then, and I do not remember what happened after that. There was a lot of pain.

But when I finally awoke, I was thirty years older.

BOOK FOUR

No Legs at Midnight

*H*ERE IS WHAT HAPPENED.

In the beginning there were three gods. Nahadoth and Itempas came first, enemies and then lovers, and they were happy for all the endless aeons of their existence.

Enefa's coming shattered the universe they had built. They recovered, and welcomed her, and built it again—newer, better. They grew strong together. But for most of that time, Nahadoth and Itempas remained closer to each other than to their younger sister. And she, in the way of gods, grew lonely.

So she tried to love me. But because she was a god and I merely a godling, our first lovemaking nearly destroyed me. I tried again—I have always been hardheaded, as the Maro say—and would have kept trying if Enefa, in her wisdom, had not finally realized the truth: a godling cannot be a god. I was not enough for her. If she was ever to have something of her own, she would have to win one of her brothers away from the other.

She succeeded, many centuries later, with Nahadoth. This was one of the events that led to the Gods' War.

But in the meantime, she did not wholly spurn me. She was not a sentimental lover, but a practical one, and I was the best of the godchildren she had yet produced. I would have been honored, when she decided to make a child from my seed—

—if the existence of that child had not almost killed me.

So she took steps to save both of us. First she tended to me, as I lay disintegrating within the conflagration of my own unwanted maturity. A touch, a reweaving of memory, a whisper: forget. As the knowledge that I was a father vanished, so, too, did the danger, and I was cured.

Then she took the child away. I do not know where; some other realm. She sealed the child into this place so that it—he—Kahl—could grow up in safety and health. But he could not escape, and he was alone there, because keeping the secret from me meant keeping Kahl unknown to the other gods.

Perhaps Enefa visited him to prevent the madness that comes of isolation. Or perhaps she ignored and observed him while he cried for her, one of her endless experiments. Or perhaps she took him as a new lover. No way to know, now that she is dead. I am just father enough to wonder.

Still, because the fact of Kahl's existence did not change, this has led to our current problem. Her delicate chains in my mind, the heavy bars on Kahl's prison: both were loosened when Enefa died in Tempa's trembling hands. Those protections held, however, until Yeine claimed the remnant of Enefa's body and soul for her own. This "killed" Enefa at last. The chains were broken, the bars snapped. Then Kahl, son of death and mischief, Lord of Retribution, was loosed upon the realms to do as he would. And it was only a matter of time before my memory returned.

Just as well, I suppose, that I am already dying.

19

I DID NOT FEEL at all well when I woke.

I lay in a bed, somewhere in the new palace. It was night-time, and the walls glowed, though far more strangely than they had in Sky. Here the dark swirls in the stone reduced the light, though the flecks of white within each indeed gleamed like tiny stars. Beautiful, but dim. Someone had hung lanterns from looping protrusions on the walls, which seemed to have been created for that purpose. I almost laughed at this, because it meant that after two thousand years, the Arameri would now have to use candles to see by, like everyone else.

I didn't laugh because something had been shoved down my throat. With some effort I groped about my face and found some sort of tube in my mouth, held in place with bandages. I tried to tug it loose and gagged quite unpleasantly.

"Stop that." Deka's hand came into my view, pushing mine away. "Be still, and I'll remove it."

I will not describe what the removal felt like. Suffice it to say that if I had still been a god, I would have cursed Deka to three hells for putting that thing in me. Though only the nicer hells, since he'd meant well.

Afterward, as I sat panting and trying to forget the fear that I might die choking on my own vomit, Deka moved to the edge of the bed beside me. He rubbed my back gently and slowly. A warning. "Feel better?"

"Yes." My voice was rough, and my throat dry and sore, but that would fade. I was more troubled by the awful weakness in every limb and joint. I looked at one of my hands and was stunned: the skin was dry and loose, more wrinkled than smooth. "What..."

"You needed nourishment." He sounded very tired. "Your body had begun to devour itself. One of my scriveners came up with this. I think it saved your life."

"Saved—"

And then I remembered. Kahl. My—

forget

My mind shied away from both the thought and my mother's warning, though it was too late for either. The knowledge was free, the damage done.

"Mirror." I whispered it, hoarse.

One appeared nearby: full-length, on a wheeled wooden pivot stand. I had no idea how it had been conjured. But when Deka got up and tilted it toward me, I forgot the mystery of the mirror. I stared at myself for a long, long time.

"It could have been much worse," Deka said, while I sat there. "We—the scriveners—didn't know what was wrong with you. Our warning-scripts led us to you. Then Lord Itempas revived and told us what needed to be done. I was able to design a negation-script to work in tandem with a loop-interrupt..." He trailed off. I wasn't listening, anyway. It had worked; that was all that mattered. "We stopped the age acceleration. Then we repaired what we could. Three of your ribs were broken, your sternum was cracked, one lung punctured. There was some bruising to your heart, a dislocated shoulder..."

He stopped again when I reached out to touch the mirror.

My face was still handsome, at least, though no longer boy-ishly pretty. This was not my doing. My body was growing how it wanted now, and I could have ended up pudgy and bald. I'd gone gray mostly at the temples, though there was plenty threaded through the rest of my hair, which was long again, tangling into knots on the sheets behind me. The shape of my face was not so different, just softer. Temans tended to age well in that respect. The texture of my skin, however, was thicker, dryer, weathered, even though it had seen little of the outdoors. There were deep-set lines around my mouth, finer ones at the corners of my eyes, and I was looking decidedly grizzled, though thankfully someone had shaved me. If I kept my mouth shut and dressed right, I might be able to do "distinguished."

When I lowered my hand, it took more effort to move. Slower reflexes, softer muscles. I was skinny again, though not nearly as bad as after the last mortaling. The food tube had kept me in healthy flesh, but it was definitely weaker, less resilient flesh.

"I'm too old for you now," I said, very softly.

Deka pushed aside the mirror, saying nothing. That silence hurt, because I took it to mean he agreed with me. Not that I blamed him. But then Deka lay down beside me and pulled me to lie with him, draping an arm across my chest. "You need to rest."

I closed my eyes and tried to turn away from him, but he wouldn't let me, and I was too tired to struggle. All I could do was turn my face away.

"Aren't you too old to sulk, too?"

I ignored him and sulked anyway. It wasn't fair. I had wanted so much to make him mine.

Deka sighed, nuzzling the back of my neck. "I'm too tired

to talk sense into you, Sieh. Stop being stupid and go to sleep. There's a lot going on right now, and I could use your help."

He was the strong one, young and brilliant, with a bright future. I was nothing. Just a fallen god and a terrible father. (Even to think this hurt, grinding agony throughout my body like a headache with serrated teeth. I bit my lip and focused on loneliness and self-pity instead, which was better.)

But I was still tired. Deka's arm, draped over my chest, made me feel safe. And though it was an illusion, doomed like all things mortal, I resolved to enjoy it while I could, and slept again.

When I woke next, it was morning. Sunlight shone through the walls; the bedroom was illuminated in shades of white and green. Deka was gone from beside me. Glee was in the room instead, sitting beside the bed in a big chair.

"I knew it was a mistake to trust you," she said.

I was feeling stronger, and my temper, at least, had not mellowed with age. I sat up, creaky, stiff, and glared at her. "Good morning to you, too."

She looked as tired as Deka, her clothing more disheveled than I had ever seen it, though still neat by the standards of average mortals. But when the daughter of Itempas wears unmatched clothing with her blouse half undone at the top, she might as well be a beggar from the Ancestors' Village. She had, as perhaps a final concession to exhaustion, bottled her thunderstorm of hair rather than style it with her usual careless confidence: a tie pulled it into a fluffy bun at the nape of her neck. It did not suit her.

"All you had to do," she said tightly, "was shout Yeine's name.

It was twilight; she would have heard you. She and Naha would have come and dealt with Kahl, and that would have been that."

I flinched, because she was right. It was the sort of thing a mortal would have thought to do. "Well, where the hells were you?" This was a weak riposte. Her failure did not negate mine.

"I am not a god. I didn't know he'd been attacked." She sighed, lifting a hand to rub her eyes. Her frustration was so palpable that the very air tasted bitter. "Father didn't use his sphere to summon me until Kahl was long gone. His first thought, upon returning to life, was of *you*."

If I had still been a child, I would have felt a small and petty pleasure at this hint of her jealousy. But my body was older now; I could no longer be childish. I just felt sad.

"I'm sorry," I said. She only nodded, bleak.

Because I felt stronger, I took in more of my surroundings this time. We were in the bedchamber of an apartment. I could see another room beyond the doorway, brighter lit; there must have been windows. The walls and floors were bare of personal touches, though I glimpsed clothes hanging neatly in a large closet across the room. Some of them were the ones Morad had given me before we'd left Sky. Apparently Deka had told the servants I was living with him.

Pushing aside the covers, I got to my feet, slowly and carefully, as my knees hurt. I was naked, too, which was unfortunate as I seemed to have sprouted hair from an astonishing variety of body parts. Glee would just have to endure, I decided, and made my way to the closet to dress.

"Did Dekarta explain what has happened?" Glee had composed herself; she sounded brisk and professional again.

"Aside from me taking a great flying leap toward death? No."
All my clothes had been made for a younger man. They would
look ridiculous on me now. I sighed and pulled on the most boring of what I found and wished for shoes that might somehow
ease the ache in my knees.

Something flickered at the edge of my vision. I turned, startled, and saw a pair of boots sitting on the floor. Each had good,
stiff leather about the ankles, and when I picked one up, I saw it
had thick padding in the sole.

I turned to Glee and held up the boot in wordless query.

"Echo," she said. "The palace's walls listen."

"I... see." I did not.

She looked fleetingly amused. "Ask for something—or even
think of it with enough longing—and it appears. The palace
seems to clean itself as well, and it even rearranges furniture and
decor. No one knows why. Some remnant of the Lady's power,
perhaps, or some property that has been permanently built in."
She paused. "If it is permanent, there will be little need for servants here, going forward."

And little need for the age-old divisions between highbloods
and low, among Arameri family members. I smiled down at the
boot. How like Yeine.

"Where is Deka?" I asked.

"He left this morning. Shahar has kept him busy since Kahl's
attack. He and the scriveners have been setting up all manner
of defensive magics, internal gates, and even scripts that can
move the palace, though not with any great speed. When he
hasn't been here, tending you, he's been working."

I paused in the middle of pulling on pants. "How long have I
been, er, incapacitated?"

"Almost two weeks."

More of my life slept away. I sighed and resumed dressing.

"Morad has been busy organizing the palace's operations and preparing sufficient living quarters for the highbloods," Glee continued. "Ramina has even put the courtiers to work. Remath has begun transferring power to Shahar, which requires endless paperwork and meetings with the military, the nobles, the Order…" She shook her head and sighed. "And since none of those are permitted to come here, the palace's gates and message spheres have seen heavy use. Only Remath's orders keep Shahar here, and no doubt if Deka were not First Scrivener and essential to making the palace ready, she would have him visiting fifty thousand kingdoms as her proxy."

I frowned, going to the mirror to see if anything could be done about my hair. It was far too long, nearly to my knees. Someone had cut it already, I suspected, because given my usual pattern it should have been long enough to fill the room by this point. I willed scissors to appear on a nearby dresser, and they did. Almost like being a god again.

"Why the urgency?" I asked. "Has something happened?" I hacked clumsily at my hair, which of course offended Glee. She made a sound of irritation, coming over to me and taking the scissors from my hand.

"The urgency is all Remath's." She worked quickly, at least. I saw hanks of hair fall to the floor around my feet. She was leaving it too long, brushing my collar, but at least I wouldn't trip on it now. "She seems convinced that the transition must be completed sooner rather than later. Perhaps she has told Shahar the reason for her haste; if so, Shahar has not shared this knowledge with the rest of us." Glee shrugged.

I turned to her, hearing the unspoken. "How has Shahar been, then, as queen of her own little kingdom?"

"Sufficiently Arameri."

Which was both reassuring and troubling.

Finishing, Glee brushed off my back and set the scissors down. I looked at myself in the mirror and nodded thanks, then immediately ran fingers through my hair to make it look messier. This annoyed Glee further; she turned away, her lips pursed in disapproval. "Shahar wanted to be informed when you were up and about, so I let a servant know when you began to stir. Expect a summons shortly."

"Fine. I'll be ready."

I followed Glee out of the bedchamber and into a wide, nicely apportioned room of couches and sidebars that smelled of Deka, though it did not at all *feel* like him. No books. One whole wall of this room was a window, overlooking the bridge-linked tiers of the palace and the placid ocean beyond. The sky was blue and cloudless, noonday bright.

"So what now?" I asked, going to stand at the window. "For you and Itempas? I assume Naha and Yeine are searching for Kahl."

"As are Ahad and his fellow godlings. But the fact that they have not yet found him—and did not, prior to his attack— suggests he has always had some means of hiding from us. Perhaps he simply retreats to wherever Enefa kept him hidden before now. That worked well enough for millennia."

"Darr," I said. "The mask was there."

"Not anymore. Immediately after leaving here, Kahl went to Darr and took the mask. To be precise, he forced a young Darren man to pick up the mask, and took *him*. The Darre are furious; when Yeine arrived, searching for Kahl, they told her everything." Glee folded her arms, the expression on her face very familiar. "Apparently Kahl approached Usein Darr's grandmother, more than fifty years ago. He showed them how to combine the art of mask making with scrivening techniques and godsblood, and they took it further still. In exchange, he claimed the best of their mask makers and had them work on a special project for him. He *killed* them, Sieh, when they'd done whatever work he needed. The Darre say the mask grew more powerful—and Kahl grew less able to approach it himself—with every life he gave it."

I knew what Kahl was doing now. That sickening churn of wild, raw power I'd felt near the mask, like a storm—the Three had been born from something like that. A new god could be made from something similar.

But he'd killed mortals to give it power? That I didn't understand. Mortals were children of the Maelstrom, it was true; we all were, however distant. But the power of the Three was as a volcano to mortals' candleflames. Mortal strength was so much lesser than ours as to be, well, nothing. If Kahl wanted to create himself anew as a god, he would need far more power than that.

I sighed, rubbing my eyes. Didn't I have enough to worry about? Why did I have to deal with all these mortal issues, too?

Because I am mortal.

Ah, yes. I kept forgetting.

Glee said nothing more, so I experimented with wishing for food, and the precise meal I wanted—a bowl of soup and cookies shaped like cute prey animals—appeared on a nearby table. No need for servants indeed, I mused as I ate. That would serve the family's security interests well, as they would have no need to hire non-Arameri. There would always be a need for certain tasks to be done, though, like running errands, and the Arameri were the Arameri. Those with power would always find some way to exert it over those who didn't. Yeine was naïve to hope that such a simple change might free the family of its historic obsession with status.

Still...I was glad for her naïveté. That was always the nicest thing about having a newborn god around. They were willing to try things the rest of us were too jaded even to consider.

The knock at the door came just as I finished eating. "Come."

A servant stepped inside, bowing to both of us. "Lord Sieh. Lady Shahar requests your presence, if you are feeling better."

I looked at Glee, who inclined her head to me. This could have meant anything from *hurry up* to *hope she doesn't kill you*. With a sigh, I rose and followed the servant out.

Shahar had not chosen the Temple as her seat of power. (Already it had acquired capital-letter status in my heart, because what I had done with Deka there was holy.) The servant led us instead to a chamber deep within the palace's heart, directly below the central high platform that had already come to be called the Whorl. Deka and his crew had been busy, I saw as we walked. Transport-sigils had been painted at intervals throughout the palace's corridors and painted over with resin in order to protect them from scuffing or wear. They did not work quite like the lifts in Sky—standing on one sent a person anywhere they willed themselves to go within the palace, not merely up and down. This was awkward if one had never been to a particular location. When I asked the servant about this, he smiled and said, "The first time we go anywhere, we go on foot. Steward Morad's orders." Just the kind of eminently sensible thing I expected of her, especially given that with servants so sparse, she could not afford to lose even one to oblivion.

Since the servant had been to the audience chamber before, I allowed him to control the magic, and we appeared in a space of cool, flickering light. Echo was more translucent than Sky, reflecting more of whatever colors surrounded it. By this I guessed immediately that we were somewhere beneath the waterline of the palace—which was confirmed as we passed a row of windows. I saw a great expanse of glimmering, shadow-flickering blueness and a passing curious fish. I grinned in delight at Shahar's cleverness. Not only would her audience chamber be safer underwater than the rest of the palace, but also any visitors—the few who would be permitted to see her in person—would instantly be awed by the alien beauty of the fishes'-eye view. There was a certain symbolism to the choice as well, as the Arameri now served the Lady of Balance. Shahar's safety would depend on the strength of the walls and windows and the equilibrium they could maintain against the weight of the water. It was perfect.

And even though I am a god, it was I who stopped when we entered the audience chamber, staring about in awe.

The chamber was small, as befit a space that would never be used by many people. Echo would have little need of the tricks that Sky had employed to intimidate and impress visitors, like vaulted ceilings and proportions meant to make supplicants feel unimportant before the great stone throne. This room was shaped like Echo itself: a descending spiral, though with small alcoves surrounding the depressed central space. In the alcoves, I glimpsed some of the soldiers who had come with us, at guard. Then I noticed more shadowy figures interspersing them, these crouched and oddly still. The ever-elusive Arameri assassins.

A poor choice, I decided. They made it too obvious that Shahar felt the need to guard herself from her own family.

When I finally stopped boggling, I noticed that Deka had preceded me. He knelt before the chamber's depression, not looking up, though he'd probably heard me. I stopped beside him, emphatically *not* kneeling. The seat we faced was almost humble: just a wide, curving stool lined with a cushion, low-backed. Yet the room was structured so that every eye was drawn to it, and all of the flickering oceanlight coming through the chamber's windows met in overlapping waves there. Had Shahar been sitting on the stool, she would have seemed unworldly, especially if she sat still. Like a goddess herself.

Instead, she stood near one of the room's windows, her hands behind her back. In the cool light she was almost unnoticeable, the folds of her pale gown lost amid flickering blueness. Her stillness troubled me—but then, what about this little scene didn't? I had spent centuries in chambers like this, facing Arameri leaders. I knew danger when I sensed it.

When the servant knelt to murmur to Shahar, she nodded and then raised her voice. "Guards. Leave."

They exited with no hesitation. The assassins did so by slipping out through small doors in each alcove, which the servant also used to leave at Shahar's quiet command. Presently, she and I and Dekarta were alone. Deka rose to his feet then, glancing once at me; his face was unreadable. I nodded to him, then slipped my hands into my pockets and waited. We had not seen

Shahar since that moment in the Temple, when she had witnessed our claiming of each other.

"Mother has accelerated the schedule again," Shahar said, not turning to us. "I asked her to reconsider, or at least send more help. She has agreed to do the latter; you will receive ten scriveners from the Sky complement by tomorrow afternoon."

"That will do more harm than good," Deka said, scowling. "New people need to be trained, shown around, supervised. Until they're ready, that will slow down my teams, not speed up the work."

Shahar sighed. I could hear the weariness in her voice, though I also heard her struggle to contain it. "It was the only concession I could gain, Deka. She's like a heretic these days, filled with a fervor no rational person can comprehend."

In this I also heard a hint of sourness that I was certain she only revealed because we would have detected it anyway. Was she upset about Remath's decision to turn from the Itempan faith? A pointless concern, given all our other troubles.

"Why?"

"Who can say? If I had the time to conspire against her, I might accuse her of madness and seek backers within the family for a coup. Though perhaps that's why she's sent me here, where I'm less of a danger." She laughed once, then turned— and paused, staring at me. I sighed while she took in my new, middle-aged shape.

It surprised me that she smiled. There was nothing malicious in it, just compassion and a hint of pity. "You *should* look like my father," she said, "but with that look of disgust on your face, it's clear you're still the same bratty little boy we met all those years ago."

I smiled in spite of myself. "I don't mind so much," I said. "At least I'm done with adolescence. Never could stand it; if I don't want to kill someone, I want to have sex with them."

Her smile faded, and I remembered: I had lain with her while we were both adolescents. Perhaps she had fond memories of what I now joked about. A mistake on my part.

She sighed, turning to pace. "I will have to rely on you, both of you, more than ever. What is happening now is unprecedented. I've checked the family archives. I truly don't know what Mother is thinking." She stopped at last, pressing fingers against her forehead as if she had a terrible headache. "She's making me the family head."

There was a moment of silence as we both processed her words. Deka reacted before I did, stricken. "How can you be head if she still lives?"

"Precisely. It's never been done." She turned to us suddenly, and we both flinched at the raw misery in her face. "Deka...I think she's preparing to die."

Deka went to her at once, ever the loving brother, taking her elbow. She leaned on him with such utter trust that I felt unexpected guilt. Had she come seeking us for comfort that night, only to find us comforting one another, uninterested in her? What had she felt, watching us make love while she stood alone, friendless, hopeless?

For just an instant, I saw her again at the window, stock-still, her hands behind her back. I saw Itempas gazing at the horizon, stock-still, too proud to let his loneliness show.

I went to them and reached for her, hesitating only at the last moment. But I had not stopped loving her, either. So I laid a hand on her shoulder. She started and lifted her head to look at me, her eyes bright with unshed tears. They searched mine, seeking—what? Forgiveness? I wasn't certain I had that in me to give. But regret—yes, that I had.

Naturally, I could not let such a powerful moment pass without a joke. "And here I thought *I* had problem parents." It wasn't a very good joke.

She chuckled, blinking quickly against the tears and trying to compose herself. "Sometimes I wish I still wanted to kill her." It was a better joke, or would have been if there had been a grain of truth in it. I smiled anyway, though uncomfortably. Deka did not smile at either joke—but then Remath had no interest in him, and he probably *did* want to kill her.

It seemed Deka was thinking along the same lines. "If she steps down in favor of you," he said, all seriousness, "you will have to exile her."

Shahar flinched, staring at him. *"What?"*

He sighed. "No beast can function with two heads. To have two Arameri palaces, two Arameri rulers…" He shook his head. "If you cannot see the potential danger in that, Shahar, you aren't the sister I remember."

She was, and she could. I saw her expression harden as she understood. She turned away from us, going back to the window and folding her arms across her breasts. "I'm surprised you've suggested only exile. I would have expected a more permanent solution from you, Brother."

He shrugged. "Mother doubtless expects something along those lines herself. She's not a fool, and she's trained you well." He paused. "If you didn't love her, I would suggest it. But under the circumstances…"

She laughed once, harshly. "Yes. Love. So inconvenient."

She turned then, looking at both of us, and suddenly I tensed again, because I *knew* that look. I had worn it too many times, in too many shapes, not to recognize it on another being. She was up to no good.

Yet when she focused on me, the look softened. "Sieh," she said. "Are we friends again?"

Lie. The thought came to me so strongly that for an instant I thought it was not my own. Deka, perhaps, sending his words into my mind as gods could. But I knew the flavor of my own thoughts, and this had the particular bitter suspicion that came of years spent with this mad family and aeons of life amid my own madder one. She wanted the truth, and the truth would hurt her. And she was too powerful now, too dangerous, for me to hurt with impunity.

For the sake of what we'd once had, however, she deserved the truth, painful or not.

"No," I said. I spoke softly, as if that would ease the blow. She stiffened, and I sighed. "I can't trust you, Shahar. I need to trust the people I call friend." I paused. "But I understand why you betrayed me. Perhaps I would even have made the same choice, in your position; I don't know. I'm not angry about it anymore. I can't be, given the result."

And then I did something stupid. I looked at Deka and let my love for him show. He blinked, surprised, and I added insult to injury by smiling. It would hurt so much, leaving him, but he did not need an old man for a lover. Such things mattered for mortals. I would do the mature thing, preserve my dignity, and step aside before our relationship grew too awkward.

I have always been a selfish fool. I thought only of myself in that moment, when I should have thought of protecting him.

Shahar's face went utterly blank. It was as though someone had thrust a knife into her and cut out her soul, leaving only a cold and implacable statue in her place. But it was not empty, this statue. Anger had filled its hollows.

"I see," she said. "Very well. If you cannot trust me, then I can hardly allow myself to trust you, can I?" Her eyes flicked over to Deka, still cold. "That puts me in a difficult position, Brother."

Deka frowned, puzzled by the change in Shahar's manner. I, however, was not. It was all too easy to see what she meant to do to her brother, in her rage at me.

"Don't," I whispered.

"Dekarta," she said, ignoring me, "it pains me to say this, but I must ask that you accept a true sigil."

When Deka stiffened, she smiled. I hated her for that.

"I, of course, would never presume to dictate your choice of lover," she said, "but in light of Sieh's history, the many Arameri he has slain through his tricks and deceptions—"

"I don't believe this." Deka was trembling, fury clawing through the shock on his face. But beneath that fury was something much worse, and again I knew it by experience. Betrayal. He had trusted her, too, and she had broken his heart as she'd broken mine.

"Shahar." I clenched my fists. "Don't do this. Whatever you feel toward me, Deka is your brother—"

"And I am being generous even to let him live," she snapped. She walked away from us, going to sit on the stool. There, she was poised and implacable, her slim form washed in ice-water light. "He just implied that I should kill the head of this family. Clearly he needs the restrictions of a true sigil, lest he plot further treachery."

"*And this would have nothing to do with me fucking your little brother instead of you*—" My fists clenched. I stepped forward, intending…gods, I didn't know. To grab her arm and make her see reason. To shout into her face. She tensed as I came near, though, and the sigil on her brow turned to white light. I knew what that meant, had felt the whip's sting too often in the past, but that had been a mortal lifetime ago. I was not prepared when a slash of raw magic threw me across the room.

It didn't kill me. Didn't even hurt much, compared to the agony that Kahl's revelation had caused. The blast threw me upside down against the window; a passing squid seemed fascinated by my shoelaces on the glass. What amused me, even as I lay there dazed and struggling to right myself, was that Shahar's sigil had only treated me as a threat *now*, in my useless mortal form. She had never truly feared me when I was a god.

Deka pulled me up. "Tell me you're all right."

"Fine," I said muzzily. My knees hurt more, and my back was killing me, but I refused to admit that. I blinked and managed to focus on Shahar. She hovered, half standing, above her seat. Her eyes were wide and stricken. That made me feel better, at least. She hadn't meant it.

Deka meant it, however, as he let me go and got to his feet. I felt the black pulse of his magic, heavy as a god's, and thought for a moment that I heard the echoing sibilance of the air as he turned to face his sister.

"Deka," she began.

He spoke a word that cracked the air, and thunder roiled in its wake. She cried out, arching backward and clapping both hands over her forehead, half falling over her seat. When she struggled upright a moment later, there was blood on her fingers and streaking her face. She lowered her trembling hand, and I saw the raw, scorched wound where her semisigil had been.

"Mother is a fool," Deka said, his voice echoing and cold. "I love you, and she thinks that keeps you safe from me. But I would rather kill you myself than watch you become the kind of monster this family is infamous for producing." His right arm levered away from his side, stick-straight, though his hand hung loose, the backs of his fingers caressing the air like a lover. I remembered the meaning of the markings on that arm and realized he really was going to kill her.

"Deka..." Shahar shook her head, trying to clear blood from her eyes. She looked like the victim of some disaster, though the disaster had not yet struck. "I didn't...Sieh, is he all...I can't see."

I touched Deka's other arm and found the muscles as tight as woven rope. Power tingled against my fingers, through his shirt. "Deka. Don't."

"You would do the same, if you still could," he snapped.

I considered this. He knew me so well. "True. But it would be wrong for you."

That caused his head to whip toward me. "*What?*"

I sighed and stepped in front of him, though the power that coiled around him pressed warningly against my skin. Scriveners were not gods. But Deka was not just a scrivener, and it was as a brother-god that I touched his arm and gently, firmly, guided it back to his side. Gestures were a form of communication. Mine said, *Listen to me*, and his power withdrew to consider my suggestion. I saw his eyes widen as he realized what I had done.

"She is your sister," I said. "You're strong, Deka, so strong, and they are fools to forget that you're Arameri, too. Murder is in your blood. But I know you, and if you kill her, it will destroy you. I can't let you do that."

He stared at me, trembling with warring urges. I have never before seen such deadly rage mingled with loving sorrow, but I think it must have been what Itempas felt when he killed Enefa. A kind of madness that only time and reflection can cure—though by then, usually, it is too late.

But he listened to me and let the magic go.

I turned to Shahar, who had finally gotten the blood out of her eyes. By the look on her face, she had only just begun to realize how close she'd come to death.

"We're leaving," I said. "I am, anyway, and I'm going to ask Deka to come with me. If you've decided that we're your enemies, we can't stay here. If you're wise, you'll leave us be." I sighed. "You haven't been very wise today, but I suspect that's a onetime aberration. I know you'll come to your senses eventually. I just don't feel like waiting around for it to happen."

Then I took Deka's hand, looking up at him. His expression had gone bleak; he knew I was right. But I would not press him. He'd spent ten years trying to get back to his sister, and she'd undone that in ten minutes. Such things were not easy for any mortal to bear. Or any god, for that matter.

Deka's hand squeezed mine, and he nodded. We turned to leave the audience chamber. Shahar stood behind us. "Wait," she said, but we ignored her.

When I opened the door, however, everything changed.

We stopped in surprise at the noise of many voices, raised

and angry. Beyond the main corridor, I glimpsed soldiers running and heard shouts. Immediately before us was Morad, her face red with fury. She was shouting at the guards, who'd crossed pikes in front of the chamber's entrance. When the door opened, the guards started, and Morad grabbed at one of the pikes, half yanking it away before the guard cursed and tightened his grip.

"Where is Shahar?" she demanded. "I *will* see her."

Shahar came up behind us. It was a measure of Morad's agitation that she did not blink at the sight of the heir's bloody face. "What has happened, Morad?" I heard the thinness of the calm veneer on Shahar's voice. She had composed herself, just.

"Maskers have attacked Shadow," Morad said.

We stood there, stunned into silence. Behind her, a troop of soldiers came tearing around the corner, running toward us. Wrath was behind them, walking with the ominous deliberation of a general preparing for war. All around us I could feel a hollow thrum as whatever protective magics Deka's scriveners had put into place came alive. Seals for the gates, invisible walls to keep out foreign magics, who knew what else.

"How many maskers?" asked Shahar. She spoke more briskly now, all business.

After the worst had passed, I would remember this moment. I would see the false calm on Morad's face, and hear the real anguish in her voice, and pity her all the more. A servant and a queen were as doomed as a mortal and a god. Some things could not be helped.

"*All of them,*" Morad said.

20

Ashes, ashes, we all fall DOWN!

IT WAS THE STILLNESS that made them so frightening.

It was not easy to view city streets and crowds via a seeing sphere. The spheres were made to display nearby faces, not vast scenes. And what Wrath's lieutenant in Shadow had to show us, by slowly panning his sphere in a circle, was vast.

There were dozens of maskers.

Hundreds.

They filled the streets. In the Promenade, where normally pilgrims jostled with street performers and artists for space, there were only maskers. Along the Avenue of Nobles, right up to the steps of the Salon: maskers. Just visible amid the trees and flowers of Gateway Park: maskers. Approaching from South Root, their shoes stained by street muck: maskers.

We could see many fleeting forms that were not maskers, most of them hurrying in the opposite direction, some of them carrying whatever they could on horses or wheelbarrows or their own hunched backs. The people of Shadow were no strangers to magic, having lived among godlings for decades and in the shadow of Sky for centuries. They knew trouble when they smelled it, and they knew the appropriate response: run.

The maskers did not molest the unmasked. They moved in silence and unison, when they moved. Most of them stopped moving when they reached the center of Shadow, then just stood there, utterly still. Men and women, a few children—not many, thank me—a few elders. No two masks were alike: they came in white and black; some were marbled like Echo's substance; some were red and cobalt blue and stony gray. Some were painted porcelain, some clay and straw. Many were in the High Northern style, but quite a few displayed the aesthetics and archetypes of other lands. The variation was astonishing.

And they were all looking up at Sky.

We—Shahar and Dekarta and I, and a good number of the highbloods and servants—stood in what would doubtless come to be called the Marble Hall, given the usual Amn naming conventions. For some reason known only to Yeine, the walls of the chamber were streaked with a deep rust color, interspersing white and gray, which made the whole room look washed in blood. There was some wry symbolism in this, I suspected; some element of Yeine's morbid sense of humor. I was apparently too mortal to get the joke.

Wrath was gone, though his soldiers were present, guarding the doors and the balcony. It had been his suggestion to gather all the highbloods together; easier to guard. While we waited for him to say when we could leave—no time soon, I gathered—some servant had brought the large seeing sphere from the scriveners' storage, setting it up on the room's single long table. Through this, we were able to behold the ominous stillness in the streets of Shadow.

"Are they waiting for something?" asked a woman who bore a halfblood mark. She stood near Ramina. He put a comforting hand on her back while she stared at the hovering image.

"Some signal, perhaps," he replied. For once, he was not smiling. But long minutes passed, and there was no movement on the part of the maskers. The person panning the sphere stood atop the Salon's steps. On either end of the arc swing we could glimpse Arameri soldiers, clad in the white armor of the Hundred Thousand Legions, hastily setting up barricades and preparing for a defensive battle. Even in such brief glimpses, however, we saw enough to despair. The bulk of the Arameri army was outside the city, in a vast complex of permanent barracks and bases stationed a half day's ride away. Everyone had assumed that the attack, when it came, would be from beyond the city. The army was no doubt marching and riding and gating into the city as fast as it could now, but those of us who had seen the maskers in action knew that it would take more than soldiers to stop them.

I turned to Shahar, who stood on one of the elevated tiers around the chamber's edge. She had wrapped her arms around herself as if cold; her expression was too blank to be intentional. In the whole room, where her relatives clustered in twos and threes and comforted each other, she stood alone.

I considered for a moment, then stepped away from Deka and went to her. Her head turned sharply toward me as I approached. She was not at all in shock. A subtle shift transformed her posture from the lost girl of a moment before to the cold queen who had tried to enslave her brother. But I saw the wariness in her. She had lost that battle.

Deka watched me go to her but did not join us.

"Shouldn't you contact Remath?" I asked. I kept my tone neutral.

She relaxed fractionally, acknowledging my unspoken offer of truce. "I've tried. Mother hasn't answered." She looked away, through the translucent walls, at the lowering sun. West, toward Sky. "There's no point, in any case. The army is there and under

Mother's command as it should be, along with the bulk of the scrivener and assassin corps and the nobles' private forces. Echo is barely functional and understaffed as it is. We have no help to offer."

"Not all support must be material, Shahar." It still felt strange to remember that Remath and Shahar loved each other. I would never get used to Arameri behaving like normal people.

She glanced at me again, not so sharply this time. Considering. Then Ramina said, "Something's happening," and we all grew tense.

There was a blur in the air, a few feet above and to one side of the image we'd been watching. The soldiers reached for their weapons. The highbloods gasped and one cried out. Deka and the other scriveners tensed, some pulling out premade, partially drawn sigils.

Then the image resolved, and we saw Remath. The image was angled oddly—over her shoulder and slightly behind her. The sphere must have been set into her stone seat.

Facing her, in Sky's audience chamber, was Usein Darr.

Shahar caught her breath and moved down the steps, as if she meant to step through the image and aid her mother. The soldiers in Sky's audience chamber had drawn their weapons, swords and pikes and crossbows. They did not attack, however. Remath must have warned them off, though two of her guards, Darre women, had moved to stand between Remath and Usein, crouching with hands on their knives. Usein stood proud and fearless at the center of the room, ignoring the guards. She had come unarmed, though she did wear traditional Darre battle dress: a leather-wrapped waist, a heavy fur mantle that marked her as a battlefield commander, and armor made of thin plates of flakespar—a light, strong material the Darre had invented a few decades back. She looked taller when she wasn't pregnant.

"I take it we have you to thank for the spectacle below," said Remath. She drawled the words, sounding amused.

Usein inclined her head. I thought she would speak in Darre, given her nationalism, but she used clear, ringing Senmite instead. "It is not our preferred way of doing battle, we in the north. To use magic, even our own, feels cowardly." She shrugged. "But you Arameri do not fight fair."

"True," said Remath. "Well, then. I expect you have demands?"

"Simple ones, Arameri." Family name only was the way Darre addressed formidable opponents, a mark of respect by her terms. To Amn, of course, it was blatant disrespect. "I—and my allies, who would be here if it had not taken all our dimmers and magicians to get even one person through your barriers—demand that your family give up its power and all trappings thereof. Your treasury: fifty percent of it is to be given to the Nobles' Consortium, to be distributed equally among the nations of the world. Thirty percent will go to the Order of Itempas and all established faiths that offer public services. You may retain twenty percent. You may no longer address the Nobles' Consortium. It is for them to say whether Sky-in-Shadow can retain its representative. Disband your army and distribute its generals among the kingdoms; relinquish your scriveners and spies and assassins and all your other little toys." Her eyes flicked toward the Darre guards, full of contempt. I did not see whether the women reacted to this or not. "Send your son back to the Litaria; you don't want him anyway." (Nearby, Deka's jaw flexed.) "Send your daughter to foster in some other kingdom for ten years so that she can learn the ways of some people other than you murderous, high-handed Amn. I will leave the choice of kingdom to you." She smiled thinly. "But Darr would welcome her and treat her with such respect as she is capable of earning."

"*Like hells* will I live among those tree-swinging barbarians," snapped Shahar, and the other highbloods murmured in angry agreement.

Usein went on. "In short, we demand that the Arameri become just another family and leave the world to rule itself." She paused, looking around. "Oh. And leave this palace. Sky's presence profanes the Lady's Tree—and frankly, the rest of us are tired of looking up at you. You will henceforth dwell on the ground, where mortals belong."

Remath waited a moment after Usein fell silent. "Is that all?"

"For now."

"May I ask a question?"

Usein lifted an eyebrow. "You may."

"Are you responsible for the murders of my family members?" Remath spoke lightly, but only a fool would not have heard the threat underneath. "*You* in the plural, obviously."

For the first time, Usein looked unhappy. "That was not our doing. Wars of assassination are not our way." Left unspoken was that wars of assassination were very much the Amn way.

"Whose, then?"

"Kahl." Usein smiled, but it was bleak. "Kahl Avenger, we call him—a godling. He has been of great help to us, me and my forbears and our allies, but it has since become clear that this served his own agenda. He merely used us. We have broken ways with him, but I'm afraid the damage is done." She paused, her jaw tightening briefly. "He has killed my husband

and numerous members of our Warriors' Council. Perhaps that will seem a consolation to you."

Remath shook her head. "Murder is never a thing to be celebrated."

"Indeed." Usein regarded Remath for a long moment, then bowed to her. It was not a deep bow, but the respect in the gesture was plain. An apology, unspoken. "Kahl has been declared an enemy by the peoples of the north. But that does not negate our quarrel with you."

"Naturally." Remath paused, then inclined her head, a show of great respect in Amn terms, since the ruler of the Amn had no need to bow to anyone. By Darre standards, it was probably an insult.

"Thank you for your honesty," Remath added. "Now, as to the rest, your demands regarding my family: no."

Usein raised her eyebrows. "That's all? 'No'?"

"Were you expecting anything else?" I could not see Remath's face well, but I guessed that she smiled.

Usein did, too. "Not really, no. But I must warn you, Arameri: I speak for the people of this world. Not all of them would agree with me, I will admit, as they have spent too many centuries under your family's control. You have all but crushed the spirit of mortalkind. It is for their sake that I and my allies will now fight to revive it—and we will not be merciful."

"Are you certain that's what you want?" Remath sat back, crossing her legs. "The spirit of mortalkind is contentious, Usein-ennu. Violent, selfish. Without a strong hand to guide it, this world will not know peace again for many, many centuries. Perhaps ever."

Usein nodded, slowly. "Peace is meaningless without freedom."

"I doubt the children who starved to death, before the Bright, would agree."

Usein smiled again. "And I doubt the races and heretics your family have destroyed would consider the Bright *peace*." She made a small gesture of negation with her hand. "Enough. I have your answer, and you will soon have mine." She lifted a small stone that bore a familiar mark. A gate sigil. She closed her eyes, and a flicker later she was gone.

The lower image—of Shadow and the silent maskers—jolted abruptly, drawing our eyes. There was a brief blur of motion, which grew still as the soldier who held the sphere set it down. We saw him then, a young man in heavy armor marked with seven sigils: one on each limb, one on his helmet, one on his torso, and one on his back. Simple magic of protection. He held a pike at the ready, as did the other men—all in the same armor—that we could see. Their armor was white. I suppose Remath hadn't gotten around to reequipping her army to symbolize the family's new divine allegiance.

And beyond them, the maskers had begun to move. Slowly, silently, they walked toward the soldiers that we could see. I could only assume that beyond the image, the scene was being repeated throughout Shadow. All of the masks that we could see, in every color, were tilted upward, paying no attention to the soldiers before them. Fixed on Sky.

"How does she command them?" Deka murmured, frowning as he peered at the image. "We were never able to determine..."

His musings were drowned out by noise from both images. Out of view, someone shouted to the soldiers, and the battle began as volleys of crossbow bolts shot toward the masked ranks. Already we could see that the bolts did almost nothing.

The maskers continued forward with arrows jutting from chests, legs, abdomens. A handful went down as their masks were split or cracked, but not enough. Not nearly enough.

In the higher image, Remath barked orders to the soldiers in her audience chamber. We saw hurried movement, chaos. Amid this, however, Remath rose from her throne and turned to face it. She leaned forward and touched something we could not see. "Shahar."

Shahar started, coming forward. "Mother? You must come here, of course. We are ready to accommodate—"

"No." Her quiet negative struck Shahar silent, but Remath smiled. She was calmer than I had ever seen her. "I have had dreams," she said, speaking softly. "I've always had them, for whatever reason, and they have always, always, come true. I have dreamt this day."

I frowned in confusion. Dreams that came true? Was that even possible for mortals? Remath *was* a godling's grand-daughter...

In the image below her face, the maskers charged forward, running now. The sphere's range was too small to capture more than a segment of chaos. For brief stretches there was nothing to see, interspersed with blurring glimpses of shouting men and still, inhuman faces. We barely noticed. Shahar stared at her mother, her face written with anguish as if there were no one else in the room, nothing else that she cared about. I put a hand on her shoulder because for a moment it looked as though she might climb onto the table to reach Remath. Her shoulder, beneath my hand, was taut and trembling with suppressed tension.

"You must *come here*, Mother," she said tightly. "No matter what you've seen in some dream—"

"I have seen Sky fall," said Remath, and Shahar jerked beneath my hand. "And I have seen myself die with it."

In the other image, the one in the large sphere, there were screams. A sudden loud concussion that I thought might have been an explosion. And suddenly the sphere was jostled from its place, falling toward the Salon steps. We heard the crunch as it broke, and then the image vanished. The other image—Remath's image—shuddered a moment later, and she looked around as people exclaimed in alarm behind her. They had felt the explosion, too.

"Why did you have the Lady build Echo, if not to come here?" Shahar was shaking her head as she spoke, wordless negation despite her effort to speak reasonably. *"Why would you do this, Mother?"*

"I have dreamt of more than Sky." Remath suddenly looked away from Shahar, her gaze settling on me and Deka. "I have seen *all existence* fall, Lord Sieh. Sky is merely the harbinger. Only you can stop it. You and Shahar and you, my son. All three of you are the key. I built Echo to keep you safe."

"Mother," said Deka in a strained voice. "This—"

She shook her head. "There's no time." She paused suddenly, looking away as a soldier came close and murmured to her. At her nod, he hurried away, and she looked at us again, smiling. "They are climbing the Tree."

Someone in the Marble Hall cried out. Ramina, his face taut, stepped forward. "Remath, gods damn it, there's no reason for you to stay if—"

Remath sighed, with a hint of her usual temper. "I told you, I have seen how this must go. If I die with Sky, there is hope. My death becomes a catalyst for transformation. There is a future beyond it. If I flee, it all ends! The Arameri fall. The *world* falls. The decision is quite simple, Ramina." Her voice softened again. "But...will you tell her...?"

I wondered at this as Ramina's jaw flexed. Then I remembered: Morad. She wasn't present, no doubt trying to assist Wrath in preparing for the possibility of an attack. I hadn't realized Ramina knew about them, but then, I supposed, he was the only one Remath could have trusted with the secret. No doubt Morad knew about Ramina fathering Remath's children, too. The three of them were bound together by love and secrets.

"I'll tell her," Ramina said at last, and Remath relaxed.

"I will, too," I said, and she started. Then, slowly, she smiled at me.

"Lord Sieh, are you beginning to like me?"

"No," I said, folding my arms. It was Morad whom I liked. "But I'm not a *complete* ass."

She nodded. "You love my son."

It was my turn to flinch. Very carefully I avoided looking at Deka. What the hells was she doing? If any of us got through this, the whole family would find some way to use my relationship with Deka against him. Perhaps she simply thought he could handle it.

"Yes," I said.

"Good." She glanced at Deka, then away, as if she could not bear to look at him. From the corner of my eye, I saw his fists clench. "I could protect only one of them, Lord Sieh. I had to make a choice. Do you understand? But I...I did what I could. Perhaps someday, you..." She faltered silent, throwing another of those darting glances at her son. I looked away so that I wouldn't see what passed between them, and saw others doing the same around the room. This was too intimate. The Arameri had changed indeed since the old days; they no longer liked to see pain.

Then Remath sighed and faced me again, saying nothing. But she knew, I felt certain. I nodded, minutely. *Yes, I love Shahar, too.* For whatever good that did.

It seemed to satisfy Remath. She nodded back. As she did this, there was another shudder in Sky, and the image began to flicker. Deka muttered something in gods' language and the image stilled, but I could see the instability of the message. Color and clarity wisped away from the image's edges like smoke.

"Enough." Remath rubbed her eyes, and I felt sudden sympathy for her. When she lifted her head again, her expression held its usual briskness. "The family and the world are yours now, Shahar. I have no doubt that you will do well by both."

The image vanished, and silence fell.

"No," Shahar whispered. Her knuckles, where her hands gripped the chair, were a sickly white. "*No.*"

Deka relented at last and came over. "Shahar—"

She rounded on him, her eyes wild. My first thought was, *She's gone mad.*

My second thought, when she grabbed Deka's hand, then mine, and I realized her intent in the same instant that magic washed through me like the arc of light that heralds a star's birth—

—was *demonshit, not again.*

We became We.

As one, We reached forth with Our hand, unseen and yet vast, and picked up the bobbing, lonely mote that was Echo.

And it was as one that We sent that mote west, hurtling across the world so rapidly that it should have killed everything inside. But part of Us (Deka) was smart enough to know that such speed was fatal for mortals, and We shaped the forces of motion around the mote accordingly. And another part of Us (me) was wise in the ways of magic, and that part murmured soothingly to the forces so they would be appeased, or else they would have backlashed violently against such abuse. But it was the will— Shahar, Shahar, O my magnificent Shahar—who drove us forward, her soul fixed on a singular intent.

Mother.

We all thought this—even I, who hated Remath, and even Deka, whose feelings toward her were such a morass that no mortal language could encompass it. (The First Tongue could: *maelstrom.*) And for all of Us, *mother* meant different things. For me it was a soft breast, cold fingers, the voice of a god with two faces—Naha, Yeine—whispering words of love. For Shahar it was fear and hope and cold eyes warming, fleetingly, with approval, and a single hug that would reverberate within her soul for the rest of her life. For Deka—ah, my Deka. For Deka, *mother* meant Shahar, a fierce little girl standing between him and the world. It meant a child-godling with old, tired eyes, who had nevertheless taken the trouble to smile kindly at him, and stroke his hair, and help him be strong.

For this, We kept control.

The palace slowed as We approached Sky-in-Shadow. We saw everything, everywhere within the scope of Our interest. On the ground just outside the city: a small force of warriors, northerners from many nations. Usein Darr was among these, sitting on the back of a small, swift horse, watching the city through a long contraption of lenses that made the distant seem closer. Like a nautilus spiral, We cycled inward, seeing all the sane folk of the city evacuating, bottlenecks of traffic on every major street. Further in: a dead masker. Beside his body crouched a woman, alone, weeping. (*Mother.*) In. Godlings in the streets, helping their chosen, helping any who asked, doing what they could, not doing enough. We have always been far better at destroying than protecting. Further in. Maskers now, the ones whose bodies had been old or infirm; they straggled behind their more able comrades, hobbling toward the Tree. In, in. Dead soldiers here, in the sigil-marked white of the Hundred Thousand Legions. They littered the Salon steps, lay disemboweled on the Promenade stones, hung from the windows of nearby buildings—one with a crossbow still in his hand, though his head was gone. In.

The World Tree.

Its trunk was infested with tiny, crawling mites that had once been thinking mortals. The maskers climbed with a strength that mortal flesh should not have possessed—and indeed, a few of them did not. We saw them fall, the magic burning out their bodies. But more of them clung securely to the thick, rough bark, and more still made the climb, steadily. It was only a half-mile to Sky, straight up. Some of the maskers were more than halfway there.

Shahar saw this and screamed DIE and We screamed with her. We swept Our infinite hand over the Tree, knocking the insects away: dozens, hundreds. Because they were already dead, some got up and began climbing again. We crushed them. Then We turned outward again, rushing, raging, toward Usein and her warriors. We were greedy for the taste of their fear.

They were afraid, We saw when We reached them, but not of Us.

We whirled and saw what they saw: Kahl. He stood in the air over the city, gazing down at what his machinations had wrought. He looked displeased.

We were much stronger. Exulting, We raised Our hand to destroy—

—*my son*—

—and stopped, frozen. Indecisive, for the first time, because of me.

We had no flesh, so Kahl did not see Us. His lips tightened at the scene below. In one hand, We saw, was the strange mask. It was complete now—and yet not. Kahl could hold it with no apparent discomfort, but the thing had no power. Certainly nothing that could forge a new god.

He raised a hand, and it is my fault, not Ours, *mine*, for I am a god and I should have *known* what he was about to do. But I did not think it, and the lives lost will haunt my eternal soul.

He sent forth power as a hundred whipcord serpents. Each wove through buildings and stone and sought its lair: a tiny, barely visible notch in all of the masks, so small as to be sub-liminal. (We knew across time. We saw Kahl doing a god's work, whispering into the dreams of the sleeping *dimyi* artists, inspiring them, influencing them. We saw Nsana the Guide turn, sensing the intrusion upon his realm, but Kahl was subtle, subtle. He was not discovered.)

We saw all of the masks glow blue-white—

—and then *explode*.

Too many. Too close to the base of the Tree, where We had

swept the bodies. We screamed as We understood and rushed back, but even gods are not omnipotent.

Roiling fire blossomed at the World Tree's roots. The shock wave came later, like thunder, echoing. (Echo, Echo.) The great, shuddering groan of the Tree rose slowly, so gradually that We could deny it. We could pretend that it was not too late right up until the World Tree's trunk split, sending splinters like missiles in every direction. Buildings collapsed, streets erupted. The screams of dying mortals mingled with the Tree's mournful cry, then were drowned out as the Tree listed slowly, gracefully, monstrously. It fell away from Shadow, which We thought was a blessing—until the Tree's crown, massive as mountains, struck the earth.

The concussion rippled outward in a wave that destroyed the land in every direction as far as mortal eyes could see.

We saw Sky shatter into a hundred thousand pieces.

And high above Us, his face a mask of savage triumph to contrast the mask in his hands: Kahl. He raised the mask over his head, closing his eyes. It shone now, glimmering and shivering and changing—replete, at last, with the million or more mortal lives he had just fed it. Its ornamentation and shape flared to form a new archetype—one suggesting implacability and fathomless knowledge and magnificence and quintessential power. Like Nahadoth and Itempas and Yeine, if one could somehow strip away their personalities and superficialities to leave only the distilled meaning of them. That meaning was God: the mask's ultimate form and name.

We felt the mask call out, and We felt something answer, before Kahl vanished.

We dissolved then. Shahar's grief, Deka's anguish, my horror—all the same emotion, but the respective reverberations were too powerful individually to meld into the whole of Us. With what remained of Us, We (I) remembered belatedly that We were in a flying palace that had been built as a floating palace, and either way it would not do well as a falling palace. So We (I) looked around and spied the Eyeglass Lake, a boring little body of water in the middle of even more boring farmland. It would do. Into this, carefully, We deposited the delicate shell that was Echo. Usein would be pleased, at least: the Eyeglass was small and unassuming, nothing compared to the ocean's vast grandeur. Only a mile of distance would now separate the palace from the shore; people could swim to it if they wanted. Remath's plan to isolate the Arameri had backfired. The Arameri, such as remained, would be henceforth more accessible than ever, and far, far closer to the earth.

Then We were gone, leaving only Deka and Shahar and I, who stared at one another as the power drained away. We fell as one and sought solace in the void together.

21

THINGS CHANGED.

Deka and Shahar woke a day later. I, for reasons I can only guess at, slept for a week. I was reinstalled in Deka's quarters and reintroduced to my old friend the feeding tube. I had aged again. Not much this time; just ten years or so. This put me in my early to mid-sixties, by my guess. Not that a few years really mattered, at that age.

In the week that I slept through, the war ended. Usein sent a message to Echo the day after Skyfall. She did not surrender, but in light of the tragedy, she and her allies were willing to offer a truce. It was not difficult to read between the lines of this. Her faction had intended the deaths of the Arameri and their soldiers, and perhaps some abstract deaths in the future as mortalkind devolved to its endless warring. No one, not even a hardened Darre warrior, had been prepared for the fallen Tree, the shattered city, or the wasteland that was now central Senm. I am told that the northerners joined in the rescue operations, and they were welcome—even though they'd inadvertently caused the disaster. Everyone who could help was welcome, in those first few days.

The city's godlings did what they could. They had saved many by transporting them out of the area when the first explosions began. They saved more by mitigating the damage. The Tree's roots had nearly torn free of the earth when it fell. If the stump had uprooted, there would have been no rubble from which to rescue survivors, only a city-sized freshly turned grave. The godlings worked tirelessly thereafter, entering the most damaged parts of the city and sniffing out the fading scents of life, holding up sagging buildings, teaching the scriveners and bonebenders magic that would save many lives in the days to follow. Godlings from other lands came to help, and even a few from the gods' realm.

Despite this, of all the mortals who had once populated Sky-in-Shadow, only a few thousand survived.

Shahar, in her first act as the family head, did something at once stupid and brilliant: she ordered that Echo be opened to the survivors. Wrath protested this vehemently and finally prevailed in getting Shahar and the rest of the highbloods to relocate to the center of the palace—the Whorl and its surrounding buildings, which could be guarded by Wrath's men and the handful of remaining soldiers who had come with the survivors. The rest of Echo was ceded to wounded, heart-lost mortals, many of them still covered in dust and blood, who gratefully slept in beds that made themselves and ate food that appeared whenever they wished for it. These were small comforts, and no consolation, given what they had suffered.

In the days that followed, Shahar convened an emergency session of the Nobles' Consortium and blatantly asked for help. The people of Shadow could rebuild, she said, with time to heal and sufficient assistance. But more than goods and food, they would need something the Arameri could not provide: *peace*. So she asked the assembled nobles to put aside their differences with each other and the Arameri and to remember the best principles of the Bright. It was, I am told, an amazing, stirring speech. The proof of this lies in the fact that they listened to her. Caravans of supplies and troops of volunteers began arriving within the week. There was no more talk of rebellion—only for the time being, but even that was a significant concession.

They may have been motivated by more than Shahar's words, however. There was a new object in the sky, and it was drawing closer.

A week after I woke, when I was feeling strong enough, I left Echo. Some godling—don't know which—had stretched a tongue of daystone from the palace's entrance to the lakeshore, wide enough for carriages and pack animals. Nowhere near as elegant as Sky's Vertical Gate, but it worked. Deka, who needed a break from the frenetic work of the past few weeks, decided to come with me. I considered trying to persuade him otherwise, but when I turned to him and opened my mouth, he gave me such a challenging look that I closed it again.

It took us an hour to walk over the bridge, and we spoke little on the way. In the distance we could see the humped, distorted shape of the fallen Tree through the morning haze. Neither of us looked in that direction often. Closer by, a fledgling city had already begun to develop around Echo and its lake. Not all the survivors wanted to live in Echo, so they had built tents and makeshift huts on the shore in order to stay close to family or new-made friends in the palace. A kind of market had developed amid this camp as a result, not far from the bridge's terminus. Deka and I rented two horses from a caravanner who'd set up a stall—two fine mounts for the young man and his grandfather, the proprietor said, trying to be friendly—and began our journey, which would supposedly take only a day. We had no escorts or guards. We were not that important. Just as well; I wanted privacy to think.

The road we'd chosen to take, once the main thoroughfare between the city and its surrounding provinces, was badly damaged. We rode across humped pavement and patches of rubble that forced us to dismount frequently and check the horses' hooves for stones. In one place the road simply split, falling away into a chasm that was unpleasantly deep. I was fine with going around it; there was nothing but ruined farmland in the vicinity, so it wasn't as though the detour would take long. Deka, however, in a rare show of temper, spoke to the rocks and got them to form a narrow, solid bridge across the gap. We crossed before I muttered something to Deka along the lines that he should really be less quick to use magic to solve problems. He only looked at me, and I hunched. It had just seemed like the sort of thing an older man should say to a younger one.

We moved on. By afternoon, we reached the outskirts of the city. It was harder going here, and the damage slowed us down. Every street that had once been cobbled was rubble; the sidewalks were death traps, where we could even find streets. I caught a glimpse of the utter ruin that was South Root and despaired. There was a chance, a slim one, that Hymn and her family had gotten out before Skyfall. I would pray for Yeine to watch over them, alive or dead.

We did not want the city itself in any case, so it was easier to skirt around the worst parts, using the outlying districts to make our way. These had been the homes and estates of the middling wealthy—too poor to build onto the World Tree's trunk but rich enough to buy the better sunlight that could be had farther from the roots. This made things easier, because they had wide lawns and dirt paths that the horses could manage. There was plenty of sunlight now.

Eventually we reached the trunk itself, a long, low mountain laid along the earth, as far as the eye could see. We surprised our first survivors here, since the rest of the area had been thoroughly abandoned: scavengers, picking through the ruins of the mansions that had once been attached to the Tree. They glared at us and pointedly fingered hatchet handles and machetes. We courteously gave them a wide berth. Everyone was happy.

Then we reached Sky. Where, to my surprise, we were not alone.

We smelled Ahad's reeking cheroot before we saw him, though the scent was different this time. My nose was not what it had been, so it was only when I got close that I understood he'd put cloves in the thing to make the smell less offensive. I realized why when I noticed that the smoke was mingled with Glee Shoth's hiras-flower perfume.

They likely heard the horses before we came into sight but did not bother to alter their position, so we found Ahad draped atop one of the nearer, smaller piles of rubble as though it was a throne. Behind him was Glee. He leaned back against her, his head pillowed on her breasts. She had propped one elbow on a smooth piece of daystone, her free hand idly combing his loose hair. His expression was as cold as usual, but I didn't buy it this time. There was too much vulnerability in his posture, too much trust in the way he'd let Glee hold his weight. I saw too much wariness in his eyes. He could not hide some things from me, which was probably why he hadn't bothered to try. But he would kill me, I suspect, if I dared to comment on it. So I didn't.

"If you've come to dance on this grave, you're too late," he said as we dismounted and came to look up at them. "I already did it."

"Good," I said, nodding to Glee, who nodded silently back. (She, unlike Ahad, did not bother to hide the pride she felt in him. And there was a decided smug possessiveness in the way she stroked his hair that reminded me fleetingly of Itempas, back when he'd held Nahadoth's affections.) I stretched and grimaced as my knees twinged after the long ride. "I'm not really up to dancing anymore."

"Yes, you do look like shit, don't you?" He exhaled a long, curling stream of smoke, and I saw him consider whether to hurt me further. There were so many ways he could have done it with a casual comment. *So it turns out you're an even worse father than I thought,* or perhaps *Glad to know I wasn't your first mistake.* I braced myself as best I could, though there was really nothing I could do. According to Deka, I was still aging faster than I should have been, perhaps ten days for every one. Merely knowing that I was a father was a relentless poison that would kill me in a year, two at the most. Not that any of us had so long to wait.

Ahad said nothing, to my relief. Either he was feeling magnanimous, or Glee had begun to mellow him. Or perhaps he simply saw no point under the circumstances.

"Hello," said Deka. He was staring at Ahad, and belatedly I remembered that I'd never gotten around to telling him about his origins. My long-lost son's attempt to destroy the universe had been a bit distracting.

Ahad sat up, eyeing the boy. After a moment, a slow smile spread across his face. "Well, well, well. You would be Dekarta Arameri."

"I am." Deka said this stiffly, trying and failing to conceal his fascination. They did not look wholly alike, but the resemblance was close enough to defy coincidence. "And you are?"

Ahad spread his arms. "Call me 'Grandpa.'"

Deka stiffened. Glee threw an exasperated look at the back of Ahad's head. I sighed and rubbed my eyes. "Deka...I'll explain later."

"Yes," he said. "You will." But he folded his arms and looked away from Ahad, and Ahad uttered a sigh of disappointment. I wasn't sure whether he really minded Deka's disinterest or was just using another opportunity to needle the boy.

We fell silent then, as was proper at graveside.

I gazed at the great piles of tumbled daystone and slipped my hands into my pockets, wondering at the feelings within me. I had loathed Sky for all the years of my incarceration. Within its white walls I had been starved, raped, flayed, and worse. I had been a god reduced to a possession, and the humiliation of those days had not left me despite a hundred years of freedom.

And yet... I remembered my orrery, and En pulsed in gentle sympathy against my chest. I remembered running through Sky's wild, curving dead spaces, making them my own. I had found Yeine here; without thinking, I began to hum the lullaby I had once sung her. It had not been all suffering and horror. Life is never only one thing.

Ahad sighed above me. Sky had been his home once. Deka touched my hand; same for him. None of us mourned alone, for however long that mourning might last.

Above us, halfway between the sun and the faint, early risen moon, we could all see the peculiar smudge that had grown steadily larger since the day of Kahl's victory. It was not a thing that could be described easily, in either Senmite or the gods' language. A streaking transparency. A space of wavering nothingness, leaving nothingness in its wake. We could feel it, too, like an itch on the skin. Hear it, like words sung just out of hearing— but it would not be long now before we all heard it, more clearly than any sane being would want. Its roar would eclipse the world.

The Maelstrom. Kahl had summoned It, and It was coming.

After a time, during which the sun set and the early stars began to show, Ahad sighed and got to his feet, turning to help Glee to hers. They flickered to the ground, which made Deka start, then inhale as his suspicions were confirmed. Ahad winked at him, then sobered as he turned to me.

"The others think they can ride out whatever happens in the gods' realm," he said softly. "I have my doubts, but I can't blame them for trying." He hesitated, then glanced at Glee. "I'm staying here."

It was an admission I would never have expected from him. Glee was mortal; she could not survive in our realm. When I glanced at Glee, to see if she understood how profound a change she had worked on him, she nodded minutely, lifting her chin in a blatantly protective challenge. Ahad was not the only one of us who could cause pain with a comment.

I had no interest in hurting Ahad, however. I'd done enough to him.

"Perhaps a more productive line of conversation is *saving* this realm, rather than fleeing it," said Deka, and by the edge in his voice, I knew I would get an earful when we were alone. But Ahad shook his head, growing uncharacteristically serious.

"There's no saving it," he said. "Not even the Three can command the Maelstrom. At best, they can stand aside while It punches through the realms, and rebuild from whatever's left. Not that that does us much good." He shrugged and sighed, looking up at the sky. The smudge was just as visible at night, a waver against the carpet of stars. Beyond It, however, the stars were gone. There was nothing but black void.

"My father believes it is worthwhile to try and save this realm," said Glee. Deka stared at her, probably guessing more secrets. I really should have told him everything beforehand. More stupidity on my part.

"Yeine and Nahadoth, too, if I know them at all." I sighed. "But if they could have stopped it, they would have done so by now."

I did not add that I had prayed to both, more than once, in the preceding nights. They had responded with silence. I tried not to worry about what that meant.

"Well, we'd better get going. Just came to wish the old hell good-bye." Ahad's cheroot had finally burned down. He dropped the butt to the ground and stubbed it out with his toe, throwing one final glance at Sky's tumbled bulk behind us. The daystone still glowed at night, ghostly soft radiance to contrast the torn emptiness in the sky above. A fitting marker for mortalkind's grave, I decided. Hopefully Yeine and Naha would find some way to preserve it when the world was gone.

And Itempas, my mind added to Yeine's and Naha's names, though of course that was less certain. Perhaps they would let him die with the rest of us. If they were going to, this would be the time.

"We will see you again," Glee said. I nodded, noticing at last that they were holding hands.

Then they vanished, leaving me alone with Deka. "Explain," he snapped.

I sighed and looked around. It was well and truly night. I hadn't figured on the journey taking as long as it had. We had no supplies with which to make camp. It would be horse blankets on the ground instead. My old bones were going to love that.

"Let's get comfortable first," I said. His jaw flexed as though he would have preferred to argue, but instead he turned to the horses, bringing them closer to the daystone pile so that they could have some shelter from the wind.

We set up on what had been the foundation of a house, blown

clean away by the force of the Tree's fall. A few small pieces of daystone had landed here, so we gathered them into a pile for light, and Deka murmured a command that made them generate heat as well. I laid out our blankets separately, whereupon Deka promptly moved his over next to mine and pulled me into his arms.

"Deka," I began. We had shared his bed since my last mortaling, but both of us had been too tired for anything but sleep. Convenient for putting off necessary conversations, but they could not be put off forever. So I took a deep breath and prayed briefly to one of my brothers for strength. "You don't have to pretend. I know how it is for young men, and—"

"I think," he said, "you've been stupid enough lately, Sieh. Don't make things worse."

At this I tried to sit up. I couldn't because he wouldn't let me and because my back complained fiercely when I tried. Too much time on horseback. "What?"

"You are still the child," he said quietly, and I stopped struggling. "And the cat, and the man, and the monster who smothers children in the dark. So you're an old man, too; fine. I told you, Sieh, I'm not going anywhere. Now lie down. I want to try something."

More out of shock than any real obedience, I did as he bade me.

He slid a hand under my shirt, which made me blush and splutter. "Deka, gods—"

"Be still." His hand stopped, resting on my chest. It was not a caress, though my stupid old body decided that it was and further decided that perhaps it was not so old after all. I was grateful; at my age there were no guarantees that certain bodily processes still worked.

Deka's expression was still, intent. I had seen the same concentration from him when he spoke magic or drew sigils. This
time, however, he began to whisper, and his hand moved in
time with his words. Puzzled, I listened to what he was saying,
but they were not words. It was not our language, or any language. I had no idea what he was doing.

I felt it, though, when words began tickling their way along
my skin. When I jumped and tried to sit up, Deka pressed me
down, closing his eyes so that my twitching would not distract
him. And I *did* twitch, because it was the most peculiar sensation. Like ants crawling over my flesh, if those ants had been flat
and made of sibilance. That was when I noticed the soft black
glow of Deka's marks—which were more than tattoos, I realized
at last. They always had been.

But something was not right. The marks he whispered into
my flesh did not linger. I felt them wend around my limbs
and down my belly, but as soon as they settled into place,
they began to fade. I saw Deka's brow furrow, and after a few
moments of this he stopped, his hand on my chest tightening
into a fist.

"I take it that didn't go as expected," I said quietly.

"No."

"What *did* you expect?"

He shook his head slowly. "The markings should have tapped
your innate magic. You're still a god; if you weren't, your antithesis wouldn't affect you. I should be able to remind your flesh
that its natural state is young, malleable, embodied only by your
will...." His jaw tightened, and he looked away. "I *don't* understand why it failed."

I sighed. There had been no real hope in me, probably

because he hadn't told me what he was doing ahead of time. I was glad for that. "I thought you wanted me mortal."

He shook his head again, his lips thinning. "Not if it means you dying, Sieh. I never wanted that."

"Ah." I put my hand over his fist. "Thank you for trying, then. But there's no point, Deka, even if you could fix me. Godlings are fragile compared to the Three. When the Maelstrom breaks this universe, most likely we—"

"Shut up," he whispered, and I did, blinking. "Just shut up, Sieh." He was trembling and there were tears in his eyes. For the first time since his childhood, he looked lost and lonely and more than a little afraid.

I was still a god, as he had said. It was my nature to comfort lost children. So I pulled him to me, intending to hold him while he wept.

He pushed my hands aside and kissed me. Then, as though the kiss had not been sufficient reminder that he was no child, he sat up and began tugging my clothes off.

I could have laughed, or said no, or pretended disinterest. But it was the end of the world, and he was mine. I did what felt good.

We would all die in three days, but there was so much that could be done in that time. I was not a true mortal; I knew better than to take Enefa's gift for granted. I would savor every moment of my life that remained, suck its marrow, crunch its bones. And when the end came... well, I would not be alone. That was a precious and holy thing.

In the morning, we returned to Echo. Deka went to look in on his scriveners and ask again whether they had found some miracle that could save us all. I went in search of Shahar.

I found her in the Temple, which had finally been dedicated as such. Someone had put an altar in it, right on the spot where Deka and I had first made love. I tried not to think lewd thoughts about human sacrifice as I stopped before it, because I refused to be a *dirty* old man.

Shahar stood beyond the altar, beneath the colored swirl that now cast faintly blue light on us, like that of the cloudless sky outside. Her back was to me, though I was certain she'd heard me approach. I'd had to speak to four guards just to get into the room. She did not move until I spoke, however, and then she started, coming out of whatever reverie she'd lapsed into.

"Friends lie," I said. I spoke softly, but my voice echoed in the high-ceilinged chamber. It was deeper now, with a hoarse edge that would only get worse as I grew older. "Lovers, too. But trust can be rebuilt. You *are* my friend, Shahar. I shouldn't have forgotten that." She said nothing. I sighed and shrugged. "I'm a bastard, what do you expect?"

More silence. I saw the tightness of her shoulders. She folded her arms across her chest. I had seen enough women cry that I recognized the warning signs and decided to leave. But just as I reached the doorway, I heard, "Friends."

I stopped and looked back. She held up her right hand—the one that had held mine, years ago when we'd taken our oath. I rubbed a thumb across my own tingling palm and smiled.

"Friends," I said, raising my own. Then I left, because there was something in my eyes. Dust, probably. I would have to be more careful in the future. Old men had to take good care of their eyes.

22

. . . and they all lived happily ever after.
The end.

THE WORLD REMAINED SURPRISINGLY calm as the Maelstrom grew to dwarf the sun in the sky. This was not at all what I had expected. Mortal humans are only a few languages and eccentricities removed from mortal beasts, and it is the nature of beasts to panic at the approach of danger.

There were some beastly acts. No looting—the Order-Keepers had always been quick to execute thieves—but many cases of arson and vandalism as mortals destroyed property to vent their despair. And there was violence, of course. In one of the patriarchal lands, so many men slaughtered their wives and children before killing themselves that one of my siblings got involved. She appeared in the capital wreathed in falling leaves and let it be known that she would personally carry the souls of such murderers to the worst of the infinite hells. Even then the killings did not stop entirely, but they did decrease.

All this was nothing to what could have been. I had expected...I don't know. Mass suicide, cannibalism, the total collapse of the Bright.

Instead, Shahar married Datennay Canru of Tema. It was a small and private ceremony, as there had not been time to prepare for anything better. At my prompting, she asked Deka to administer the rites as First Scrivener, and at my prompting, Deka agreed. There were no apologies exchanged. They were both Arameri. But I saw that she was contrite, and I saw that Deka forgave her. Then Shahar had the Order of Itempas spread word of the event by crier and runner and news scroll. She hoped to send a message by her actions: *I believe there will be a future.*

Canru agreed readily to the marriage, I think, because he was more than a bit in love with her. She...well, she had never stopped loving me, but she genuinely liked him. We all sought our own forms of comfort in those days.

I spent my nights in Deka's arms and was humbly grateful for my fortune.

So the world went on.

Until its end.

We gathered at dawn on the final day: Arameri, notables from Tema and other lands, commonfolk from Shadow, Ahad and Glee, Nemmer and a few of the other godlings who had not fled the realm. The Whorl was not as high as Sky had been, but it was as good a vantage point as any. From there, the heavens were a terrible, awe-inspiring sight. More than half of the sky had been devoured by the swirling, wavering transparency. As the sun rose and passed into the space of change, its shape turned sickly and distorted, its light flickering on our skins like a campfire. This was not an illusion. What we saw was literal, despite the impossibility of the angles and distance. Even Tempa's rules for physics and time had been distorted by the Maelstrom's presence. Thus we beheld the slow and tortured end of our sun as it was torn apart and drawn into the great maw. There would be light for a while longer, and then darkness such as no mortal had ever seen. If we lasted that long.

I held Deka's hand as we stood gazing at it, unafraid.

Alarmed gasps from the center of the Whorl meadow drew my attention: Nahadoth and Yeine had appeared there amid the bobbing sea grass. The gathered folk stumbled back from them, though some quickly knelt or began weeping or calling out to them. No one shushed them, for hope had never been a sin.

I dragged Deka with me as I pushed through the crowd. Between Nahadoth and Yeine was Itempas; they had brought him. All three of them looked grim, but they would not have come without reason. Nahadoth might act without purpose, but Yeine tended not to, and Itempas had never done so.

They turned to me as I reached them, and I was suddenly sure of it. "You have a plan," I said, squeezing Deka's hand hard.

They looked at each other. Beyond the Three, Shahar stepped out of the crowd as well, Canru in her wake. He stopped, gazing at them in awe. Shahar came forward alone, her fists tight at her sides.

Itempas inclined his head to me. "We do."

"What?"

"Death."

If I had not spent countless eternities enduring his manner, I would have screamed at this. "Can you be more specific?"

There was the faintest twitch of Itempas's lips. "Kahl has called the Maelstrom to join with him," he said. "He will have to appear in order to take It into himself and—he hopes—use Its power to become a god. We will kill him and offer It a new seat of power instead." He spread his hands, indicating himself.

I caught my breath, horrified as I understood. "No. Tempa, you were born from the Maelstrom. To return to It—"

"I have chosen this, Sieh." His voice cut across mine, sooth-ing, definitive. "It is the fate my nature demands. I have felt the possibility since Kahl's summoning. Yeine and Nahadoth have confirmed it." Behind him, Yeine's face was unreadable, serene. Nahadoth...he was almost the same. It was not his nature to contain himself, however. He could not hide his unease entirely, not from me.

I scowled at Itempas. "What is this, some misguided attempt at atonement? I told you a century ago, you stubborn fool, noth-ing can make up for your crimes! And what good does it do for you to sacrifice yourself, if your death will cause everything to end anyway?"

"The Maelstrom may cease Its approach if It fulfills Kahl's purpose," Itempas replied. "In this case, creating a new god. We believe the form that this new god takes will depend on the nature and will of the vessel." He shrugged. "I will see that what is created is a fitting replacement for myself."

I stumbled back, and Deka put a hand on my shoulder in concern. It was the same conjunction of power and will that had forged Yeine into a new Enefa, and where that had been wild, a series of not-quite-accidental coincidences, now Itempas hoped to control a similar event. But whatever god was created in his place, however stick-in-the-mud that new one might turn out to be, *Itempas* would die.

"No," I said. I was trembling. "You can't."

"It's the only solution, Sieh," said Yeine.

I stared at the two of them, so set in their resolve, and did not know what I felt in that moment. Not so long before, I would have rejoiced at the idea of a new Itempas. Even now it was a temptation, because I might have forgiven him and I might still love him, but I would never forget what he had done to our family. Nothing would ever be the same for any of us. Would it not be easier, somehow—*cleaner*—to start over with someone new? Knowing Itempas, the idea had some appeal for him, too. He did like things neat.

I turned to Nahadoth, hoping for—something. I didn't know what. But Nahadoth, damn him, wasn't paying attention to any of us. He had turned away to gaze at the swirling sky. Around him, the dark wreathing tendrils of his presence wheeled in a slow, matching dance. Inching higher, in random increments, as I watched. Toward the Maelstrom.

Wait—

Itempas spoke his name sharply, before my thoughts could crystallize into fear. Yeine, surprised by this, frowned at both her brothers. For a moment, I saw incomprehension in her face, and then her eyes widened. But Naha only smiled, as if it amused him to frighten us. And he kept looking up at the Maelstrom, as if It was the most beautiful sight in the mortal realm.

"Perhaps we should do nothing," Nahadoth said. "Worlds die. Gods die. Perhaps we should let *all* of it go, and start anew."

Start anew. My eyes met Yeine's across the drift of Naha's blackness. Deka's hand tightened on my shoulder; he understood, too. The unsteady tremor of sorrow that edged Nahadoth's voice. The way his shape kept blurring in time with the Maelstrom's perturbations, resonating with its terrible, churning song.

But there was no fear in Itempas's face as he took a step toward Nahadoth. He was smiling, in fact—and I marveled, because even though he was trapped in mortal flesh, his smile somehow had all the old power. Nahadoth, too, reacted to this. He lowered his gaze to focus on Itempas, his own smile fading.

"Perhaps we should," Itempas said. "That *would* be easier than repairing what's broken."

The drifting curls of Nahadoth's substance grew still. They shifted aside as Itempas approached Nahadoth, allowing him near—but also curving inward, and sharpening into jagged, irregular scythes. Fanged jaws ready to close on Itempas's so-powerless flesh. Itempas ignored this blatant threat, continuing forward and, finally, stopping before him.

Behind him, Glee stood stiff and wide-eyed. I held my breath.

"Will you die with me, Nahadoth?" he asked. His voice was low, but it carried; we all heard it, even over the twisting, growing shriek of the Maelstrom. "Is that what you want?"

Beyond them, perhaps only I saw Yeine's expression tighten, though she said nothing. Anyone could see the delicacy of the spell Tempa had woven, more fragile still because it was nothing but words. He had no magic. No weapons at all for this battle, save the history between them, good and ill.

Nahadoth did not answer, but then he didn't need to. There were faces he wore only when he meant to kill. They are beautiful faces—destruction is not his nature, just an art he indulges—but in my mortal shape I could not look upon them without wanting to die, so I fixed my eyes on Itempas's back. Somehow, despite *his* mortal shape, Tempa could still bear Naha's worst.

"The new one," Tempa said, very softly. "I'll make certain he's worthy of both of you."

Then he lifted his hands—I clamped down on my tongue to keep from blurting a warning—and cupped Nahadoth's face. I expected his fingers to fall off, for the black depths around Naha had grown lethal, freezing flecks of snow from the air and etching cracks into the ground beneath their feet. It probably did hurt Itempas; they always hurt each other. This did not stop him from leaning close and touching his lips to Nahadoth's.

Nahadoth did not return the kiss. Itempas might as well have pressed his mouth to stone. Yet the fact that it had occurred at all—that Nahadoth permitted it, that it was Itempas's farewell—made it something holy.

(I clenched my fists and fought back tears. I was too old for sentimentality, damn it.)

Itempas pulled away, his sorrow plain. But as he stood there, his hands hiding Nahadoth's face from any view but his own, Naha showed him something. I couldn't see what, but I could guess, because there were faces Naha wore for love, too. I had never seen the one he'd shaped for Itempas, because Itempas guarded that face jealously, as he had always done with Naha's love. But Itempas inhaled at the sight of whatever Naha showed him now, closing his eyes as if Naha had stricken him one last, terrible blow.

Then he stepped back, and as his hands fell away, Nahadoth's face resumed its ordinary, shifting nature. With this, Naha turned his back on all of us, his cloak retracting sharply to form a tight, dark sheath around him. Itempas might as well not have been there anymore.

But he did not look up at the sky again.

When Itempas mastered himself, he glanced at Yeine and nodded. She regarded him for a long, weighted moment, then finally nodded in return. I let out a breath, and Deka did, too. I thought perhaps even the Maelstrom grew quieter for a moment, but that was probably my imagination.

But before I could digest my own relief and sorrow, Nahadoth's head jerked sharply upward—but not toward the Maelstrom, this time. The blackness of his aura blazed darker.

"*Kahl,*" he breathed.

High above—the same place from which he'd struck down the World Tree—a tiny figure appeared, wreathed in magic that trembled and wavered like the Maelstrom.

Before I could think, however, I was nearly floored by the furnace blast of Yeine's rage. She wasted no time in deciding to act; the air simply rippled with *negation of life*. I flinched, in spite of myself, as death struck Kahl, my son—

—my unknown, unwanted, unlamented son, whom I would have mentored and protected if I had been able, whose love I would have welcomed if I'd been given the choice—

—did *not* die. Nothing happened.

Nahadoth hissed, his face twitching reptilian. "The mask protects him. He stands outside this reality."

"Death is reality everywhere," Yeine said. I had never heard such murderousness in her voice.

There was a shudder beneath us, around us. The towns-folk cried out in alarm, fearing another cataclysm. I thought I knew what was happening, though I could no longer sense it: the earth beneath us had shifted in response to Yeine's hate, the whole planet turning like some massive, furious bodyguard to face her enemy. She spread her hands, crouching, the loose curls of her hair whipping in a gale that no one else felt, and her eyes were as cold as long-dead things as they fixed on Kahl.

On my son. But—

Nahadoth, his face alight, laughed as her power rose, even as the inimical nature of it forced him to step back. Even Itempas stared at her, pride warring with longing in his gaze.

This was it should be. It was what I had wanted all along, really, for the three to reconcile. But—

—*to kill my son!*

No. That I hadn't wanted.

Deka glanced at me and caught my hand suddenly, alarmed. "Sieh!" I frowned, and he lifted a lock of my hair for me to see. It had been brown streaked thickly with white; now the white predominated. The few remaining brown strands faded to colorlessness as I watched. It was longer, too.

I looked up at Deka and saw the fear in his eyes. "I'm sorry," I said. And I truly was, but... "I never wanted to be a poor father, Deka. I—"

"*Stop it.*" He gripped my arm. "Stop speaking, stop thinking about him. You're killing yourself, Sieh."

So I was. But it would have happened anyway. Damn Enefa; I would think what I liked, mourn as I wished for the son I had never known. I remembered his fingers on the back of my neck. He would have forgiven me if he could have, I think, if forgiveness had not been counter to his nature. If my weakness had not left him to suffer so much. Everything he'd become was my fault.

There was a crack of displaced air as Yeine vanished. I could not see what followed—my eyes were not what they had been, and I seemed to be developing cataracts. But there was another crack from high above, a thunder of echoes, and then Nahadoth tensed, his smile fading. Itempas stepped up beside him quickly, his fists clenched. "No," he breathed.

"No," Nahadoth echoed, and then he, too, was gone, a flicker of shadow.

"What's happening?" I asked.

Deka squinted above us, shaking his head. "Kahl. It isn't possible. Dear gods, how is he—" He caught his breath. "Yeine has fallen. Now Nahadoth—"

"*What?*"

But there was no time to consider this, because suddenly the space where Nahadoth and Yeine had been was filled again, and we all fell to our knees.

Kahl wore the God Mask, and the power that it radiated was the worst thing I had ever felt in my life. Worse, even, than the day Itempas forced me into mortal flesh, and that had been like having all my limbs broken so that I could be stuffed into a pipe. Worse than seeing my mother's body, or Yeine's when she died her mortal death. My skin crawled; my bones ached. All around me I heard others falling, crying out. The mask was *wrong*—the emulation of a god, extraneous and offensive to existence itself. In its incomplete form, only godlings had been able to feel the wrongness, but now the God Mask radiated its hideousness to all children of the Maelstrom, mortal and immortal alike.

Deka moaned beside me, trying to speak magic, but he kept stuttering. I struggled to stay on my knees. It would have been easier to just lie down and die. But I forced my head up, trembling with the effort, as Kahl took a step toward Itempas.

"You're not the one I would have chosen," he said, his voice shivering. "Enefa was the original target of my vengeance. I would thank you for killing her, in fact, but here and now, you are the easiest of the Three to kill." He stepped closer, raising a hand toward Itempas's face. "I'm sorry."

Itempas did not back up or drop to the ground, though I saw how the ripple of power around Kahl pressed at him. It likely took everything he had to stay upright, but that was my bright father. If pride alone had been his nature, no force in the universe could ever have stopped him.

"Stop," I whispered, but no one heard me.

"*Stop*," said another voice, loud and sharp and furious.

Glee.

Even with my failing eyesight, I could see her. She was on her feet as well, and it was not a trick of the light: a pale, faint nimbus surrounded her. It was easier to see this because the sky had grown overcast, stormclouds boiling up from the south as a brisk wind began to blow. We could no longer see the Maelstrom, except in snatches when the clouds parted, but we could hear It: a hollow, faint roar that would only grow louder. We could feel It, too, a vibration deeper than the earth that Yeine had shaken. A few hours, a few minutes; no telling when It would arrive. We would know when It killed us.

Itempas, who had not stepped away from Kahl, stumbled now as he turned to stare at his daughter. There were many things in Glee's eyes in that moment, but I did not notice them for staring at her eyes themselves, which had gone the deep, baleful ember of a lowering sun.

Kahl paused, the God Mask turning slightly as he peered at her. "What is it that you want, mortal?"

"*To kill you*," she replied. Then she burst into white-hot flame.

All the mortals nearby screamed, some of them fleeing for the stairs. Itempas threw up an arm as he was flung farther back. Ahad, beside her, cried out and vanished, reappearing near me. Even Kahl staggered, the blur around him bending away from the sheer blazing force of her. I could feel the heat of her fire tightening my skin from where I was, ten feet away. Anyone closer was probably risking burns. And Glee herself...

When the flames died, I marveled, for she stood clad all in white. Her skirt, her jacket—dear gods, even her *hair*. The light that surrounded her was almost too bright to look at. I had to squint through watering eyes and the shield of my hand. For an instant I thought I saw rings, words marching in the air, and in her hands... no. It could not be.

In her hands was the white-bladed sword that Itempas had used to cleave apart Nahadoth's chaos and bring design and structure to the earliest iteration of the universe. It had a name, but only he knew it. No one could wield it but him; hells, no one else had ever been able to get *near* the damned thing, not in all the aeons since he'd created time. But Itempas's daughter held it before her in a two-handed grip, and there was no doubt in my mind that she knew how to use it.

Kahl saw this, too, his eyes widening within the mask's slits. But of course he feared it; he had disrupted the order of all things, bringing the Maelstrom where it did not belong and claiming power he had no right to possess. In a contest of strength, he could endure, even against Nahadoth and Yeine— but there is more to being a god than strength.

"Control," said Itempas. He had drawn as close as he could, anxious to advise his daughter. "Remember, Glee, or the power will destroy you."

"I will remember," she said.

And then she was gone, and Kahl was, too, both of them leaving a melted, glowing trough across the Whorl's grassy plain.

Then two more streaks shot across the horizon in that direction, moving to join the battle: Nahadoth and Yeine.

Without Kahl's power to crush me, I struggled to my feet. Damned knees hurt like someone had lined the joints with broken glass. I ignored the pain and grabbed for Deka, then dragged him over to Ahad. "Come on," I said to both of them.

Ahad tore his eyes from the dwindling, shining mote that his lover had become. In the distance, plates of spinning darkness swirled out of nowhere, converging on a point. A massive, jagged finger of stone shot up from the earth, hundreds of feet into the sky in seconds. The second Gods' War had begun, and it was an awesome sight—even if, this time, it would leave far more than just the mortal realm in ruins.

"What?" Ahad looked dazed when I gripped his arm.

"Help me get Itempas," I said. When he simply stared at me, I jabbed him in the ribs with my gnarled fist. He glared; I stepped closer to shout into his face. "Pay attention! We have to go. With that kind of power in play, Glee won't last long. Nahadoth and Yeine might be able to stop him, I hope, we can pray, but if not, he's going to come back here." I pointed at Itempas, who was also staring after Glee, his fists clenched.

Finally understanding, Ahad caught my arm. I was holding Deka. There was a flicker as we moved through space, and then Ahad had Itempas by the arm as well. Itempas looked startled, but cottoned on faster than Ahad had; he did not fight. But then Ahad frowned. "Where can we go that he won't find us?"

I almost wailed the words. "Anywhere, anywhere, you fool!" The planet was going to die. All reality was beginning to falter, bleeding out through the mortal wound that the Maelstrom had punched into its substance. All we could do was start running, anywhere we could, and hope that Kahl did not catch up. Though if he did … "Dear gods, I hope you've found your nature by now."

Ahad's face went too impassive. "No."

"Demonshitting *brak'skafra*—" There was a hollow whoosh behind me, louder even than the Maelstrom's growing roar, and Deka turned quickly, barking a command to counter whatever I'd stupidly unleashed. The sound went silent; Deka glared at me. "Sorry," I muttered.

"Anywhere," Ahad said, but he was looking away from us. Something bloomed against the horizon like a round, white sun. I wanted to cheer for magnificent demon girls, but the light died too quickly for me to feel comfortable, and then Ahad took us away from the palace.

With his attention so thoroughly divided, I should have realized where we would end up. When the world resolved around us, we stood on tumbled white stones littered with the debris of everyday life: torn bedsheets, broken perfume bottles, an overturned toilet. Looming high overhead: broken, wilting limbs as thick as buildings.

"*Sky?*" I rounded on Ahad, wishing for once that I had a cane. I had to shout to be heard over the rising cacophony, but that was fine, because I was furious. "You brought us to *Sky*, you stupid son of a demon? What were you *thinking?*"

"I—"

But whatever Ahad might have retorted died in his mouth as his eyes widened. He whirled, looking north, and we all saw it. A great amorphous blotch of blackness was fading from view, but against its contrast we could see a tiny, blazing white star.

Falling, and winking out of sight as it fell.

Ahad took a great, shuddering breath, and the air around him turned the color of a bruise. The sound that he made was less a word than an animal, maddened shriek. For an instant he became *something else*, shapeless and impossible, and then we were all flung sprawling as daystone and Tree wood and the air itself whipped into an instant tornado around him. He was a god, and his will forged reality. All the matter nearby hastened to do his bidding.

Then he was gone, and all the debris that had been blasted away in his wake pelted onto whatever body parts we'd been foolish enough to turn upright.

I pushed myself up slowly, trying to get a broken Tree branch off my back and daystone dust out of my mouth. My hands hurt. Why did my hands hurt? I'd never had arthritis on any of the previous occasions I'd become old. Then again, that had been old age as I'd imagined it; perhaps the reality was simply more unpleasant than I'd thought.

Hands grabbed me, helping me up: Deka. He pushed the branch away, then pushed my hair out of my face; it was waist-long now, though thin and stringy white. No matter how old I got, the stuff kept growing. Why couldn't I go bald, damn it?

"Should've seen that coming," I muttered as he helped me to my feet.

"Seen what?"

Then Itempas was there, also helping me. Between the two of them, I was able to scramble over the jagged, unstable stones of the fallen Sky. "That one." Itempas nodded in the direction Ahad had gone. In another life I would have laughed at his refusal to use Ahad's borrowed name. "Apparently, his nature has something to do with love."

No wonder it had taken Ahad so long to find himself. He had lived the past century in the antithetical prison of his own apathy—and his centuries of suffering in Sky had probably not predisposed him to attempt love, even when the opportunity came along. But Glee...I bit my lip. In spite of everything, I prayed that she would be all right. I did not want to lose my newest sister, and I did not want this other, surrogate son of mine to discover himself through grief.

It is not an easy thing to climb a pile of rubble the size of a small city. It is harder when one is a half-blind old man of eighty or so. I kept having to stop and catch my breath, and my coordination was so poor that after a few close calls and nearly broken ankles, Itempas stepped in front of me and told me to climb onto his back. I would have refused, out of pride, but then Deka, damn him, picked me up bodily and forced me to do it. So I locked my arms and legs round Itempas, humiliated, and they ignored my complaints and resumed climbing.

We did not speak as the Maelstrom's roar grew louder. This was not merely because of the noise but also because we were waiting, and hoping, but as we kept climbing and the moments passed, that hope faded. If Yeine and the others had been able to defeat Kahl, they would have done it by now. The universe still existed; that meant the two gods were alive at least. Beyond that, no news was not good news.

"Where can we go?" Deka had to shout to be heard. All around us was a charging, churning monstrosity of sound. I made out bird whistles and men shouting as if in agony, ocean surf and rock grating against metal. It did not hurt our ears— not yet—but it was not pleasant either.

"I can take us away once, maybe twice," he said, and then looked ashamed. "I don't have a god's strength, or even..." He looked toward where Glee had fallen. I hoped Ahad had managed to catch her. "But anywhere in the mortal realm, Kahl will find us. Even if he doesn't—"

We all paused to look up. High above, the clouds had begun to boil and twist in a way that had nothing to do with weather patterns. Would the great storm stop there in the sky, once It reached the place from which It had been summoned? Or would It simply plow through and leave a void where the earth had been?

Back to Echo, then. Deka and I could join with Shahar again, attempt to control what we had done only by instinct before...but even as I thought this, I dismissed it. Too much discord between Shahar and Deka now; we might just make things worse. I leaned my head on Itempas's broad shoulder, sighing. I was tired. It would be easier, so much easier, if I could just lie down now and rest.

But as I thought this, suddenly I knew what could be done.

I lifted my head. "Tempa." He had already stopped, probably to catch his breath, though he would never admit such a thing. He turned his ear toward me to indicate that he was listening. "How long does it take you to return to life when you die?"

"The time varies between ten and fifty minutes." He did not ask why I wanted to know. "Longer if the circumstances that caused me to die remain present—I revive, then die again immediately."

"Where do you go?" He frowned. It was hard to make my voice work at this volume. "While you're dead. Where do you go?"

He shook his head. "Oblivion."

"Not the heavens? Not the hells?"

"No. I am not dead. But I am not alive, either. I hover between."

I wriggled to get down, and he set me on my feet. I nearly fell at once; the circulation in my legs had been cut off by his arms, and I hadn't even felt it. Deka helped me to sit on a rough piece of what—I think—had once been a part of the Garden of the Hundred Thousand. Groaning, I massaged one of my legs, nodding irritably for Deka to take the other, which he did.

"I need you to die," I said to Tempa, who lifted an eyebrow. "Just for a while." And then, using as few words as I could to save my voice, I told them my plan.

Deka's hands tightened on my calf. He made no protest, however, for which I was painfully grateful. He trusted me. And if he helped me, I would be able to pull my biggest trick ever.

My last trick.

"Please," I said to Tempa.

He said nothing for a long moment. Then he sighed, inclining his head, and took off his coat, handing it to me.

Then, as coolly as though he did such things every day, he looked around, spying a thin, fine extrusion jutting up from the pile. A piece of the Wind Harp: it was a wickedly sharp spear perhaps four feet long, angled straight up in the air. Tempa examined it, flicked away a scrap of faded cloth that had wrapped around its tip, and yanked it to the side, jostling loose a good bit of rubble while he positioned it to his liking. When he'd gotten it to about a forty-five degree angle, he nodded in satisfaction—and fell forward onto it, sliding down its shaft until friction or bone or gods knew what stopped him short. Deka cried out, leaping to his feet, though it was too late and he'd known it was going to happen anyhow. He protested because that was just the kind of man he was.

I reached up to take Deka's hand, and he turned to me, his face still writ in lines of horror. How had an Arameri been born with a soul as perfect as his? I was so glad I'd lived to see it, and to know him.

He proved his worth again when grim determination replaced horror in his eyes. He helped me to my feet, handing me Tempa's coat, which I put on. The wind had risen to a gale, and I was a skinny, frail old man.

We both looked up then, startled, as a sound like wailing horns filled the sky and the clouds tore apart. Above us, filling the sky, a new and terrible god appeared: the Maelstrom. What we saw was not Its true self, of course, which was vaster than all existence, let alone a single world. Like everything that entered the mortal realm, It had shaped an approximation of Itself: churning clouds, the sun stretched into glowing candy, a string of floating pieces of worlds and shattered moons trailing in Its wake. In Its boiling surface, we could see ourselves and the world around us, a reflection distorted and magnified. Our faces screamed; our bodies broke and bled. The imminent future.

Deka turned his back to me and crouched. Speech was no longer possible now. Soon our ears would rupture, which would be a blessing, because otherwise the roar would destroy our sanity. I climbed onto Deka's back, pressing my face into his neck so that I could breathe his scent one last time. Ignoring my sentimentality, he closed his eyes and murmured something. I felt the markings on his back grow hot and then cold against my chest.

Gods do not fly. Flying requires wings and is inefficient in any case. We leap, and then stick to the air. Anyone can do it; most mortals just haven't learned how. There's a trick to it, see.

Deka's first leap took us nearly into the Maelstrom. I groaned and clung to him as the thunder of the storm above us grew so great that I lost the feeling in my hands, nearly lost my grip entirely. But then, somehow, Deka corrected his error, arcing down now toward the gods' battle.

Which was not over. There was a flash of darkness, and we passed through a space of coldness: Nahadoth. Then warm air, redolent of spores and rotting leaves: Yeine. Both still alive, and still fighting—and winning, I was glad to see. They had dissipated their forms, corralling Kahl in a thickening sphere of combined power so savage that I urged Deka to stop well away, which he did. At the center of this sphere was Kahl, raging, blurring, but contained. The God Mask had made him one of them, temporarily, but no false god could challenge two of the Three for long. To win, Kahl would have to make his transformation permanent. To do that, he would need strength he didn't have.

Which was why I, his father, offered that to him now. I closed my eyes and, with everything that I was, sent my presence through the ethers of this world and every other.

The swirling, searing forms of Yeine and Nahadoth stopped, startled. Kahl spun within the shell that held him, and I thought that his eyes marked me from within the mask.

Come, I said, though I had no idea whether he could hear my voice. I prayed it, shaping my thoughts around fury, to make sure. My poor Hymn, whom I'd never been able to bless. All the dead of Sky-in-Shadow Glee and Ahad. And he wanted Itempas, my father! No. It was not difficult to summon a craving for vengeance in my own heart. Then, carefully, I masked this with sorrow. That wasn't hard to dredge up either.

Come, I said again. *You need power, don't you? I told you to accept your nature. Enefa threw you in a hole somewhere, left you forgotten and forsaken, for me. You cannot forgive me for that. Come, then, and kill me. That should give you the strength you need.*

Within his glimmering prison, Kahl stared at me—but I knew I'd baited the trap well. He was Vengeance, and I was the source of his oldest and deepest pain. He could no more resist me than I could a ball of string.

He hissed and flexed what remained of his power, a minia-ture Maelstrom straining to break free. Then I felt the unstable surge of his elontid nature, amplifying the God Mask and wax-ing powerful enough that the shell Naha and Yeine had woven around him cracked into smoking fragments. Then he came for me.

This was my gift to him, father to son. The least I could offer, and far less than I should have done.

My Deka; he never wavered, not even when the outermost edges of Kahl's blurring rage struck and began to shred his skin. We both screamed as our bones snapped, but Deka did not drop me. Not even when Kahl wrapped his arms around both of us, tearing us apart by sheer proximity, in an embrace that he'd probably intended as a parody of love. Perhaps there was even a bit of real love in it. Vengeance was nothing if not predictable.

Which was why, with the last of my strength, I reached into Itempas's coat, pulled out the dagger coated with Glee Shoth's blood, and shoved it into Kahl's heart.

He froze, his green, sharpfold eyes going wide within the God Mask. The power around him went still, as the calm within a storm.

My hands were bleeding, mangled claws, but thankfully they were still the hands of a trickster. I snatched the God Mask from Kahl's face. This was easy, as he was already dead. As it came away, his face, so like mine, stared at me with empty eyes. Then all three of us began to fall, separating. Kahl slid off the knife as we twisted in the air. I hung on to it by sheer force of will.

But there came a jolt, and I found Yeine leaning into the diminishing plane of my vision.

"Sieh!" Such was her voice that I could hear her even over the great storm. I felt her power gather to heal me.

I shook my head, having no strength to talk. I had enough left, just, to raise the God Mask to my face. I saw her eyes widen when I did this, and she tried to grab my arms. Silly former mortal. If she had used magic, she could have stopped me.

Then the mask was on me.

It was on me.

IT WAS ON ME AND I—

I—

—smiled. Yeine had released me, crying out. I'd hurt her. I hadn't meant to. We gods just have opposing natures.

She fell, and Deka fell. Yeine would be all right. Deka would not, but that was fine, too. It had been his choice. He had died like a god.

Nahadoth coalesced before me, just beyond the range of my painful, vibrating aura. His face was a study in betrayal. "Sieh," he said. I had hurt him, too. He looked at me the way he looked at Itempas these days. That was worse than what I'd done to Yeine. I felt sudden pity for my bright father and prayed—to no one in particular—that Nahadoth would forgive him soon.

"What have you done?" he demanded.

Nothing, yet, my dark father.

I won't say I wasn't tempted. I had what I'd yearned for. It would be easy, so easy, to go and kill Tempa with the knife, as he had killed Enefa long ago. Easy, too, to absorb the Maelstrom, make the transformation permanent, take Itempas's place. I could be Naha's lover in earnest then, and share him with

Yeine, and make all of us a new Three. I heard a song promising this in the Maelstrom's ratcheting scream.

But I was Sieh, the whim and the wind, the Eldest Child and Trickster, source and culmination of all mischief. I would not tolerate being some cheap imitation of another god.

So I turned, the power coming easily as my flesh remembered itself. A beautiful feeling, greater than anything I had ever known, and this wasn't even real godhood. Closing my eyes, I spread my arms and turned to face the Maelstrom.

"Come," I whispered with the voice of the universe.

And It came, Its wild substance passing into me through the filter of the God Mask. Remaking me. Fitting me into existence like a puzzle piece—which worked only because Itempas's temporary absence had left a void. Without that, my presence, a *Fourth*, would have torn it all apart. In fact, when Itempas next awoke, the sundering would begin.

Thus I raised the knife coated with my son's blood. There was plenty of Glee's left, too, I hoped—though really, there was only one way to find that out.

I drove the knife into my breast, and ended myself.

23

IN THE SKY ABOVE, just when it seemed the Maelstrom would crush everything, It suddenly winked out of existence, leaving a painful silence.

As I pushed myself up from where I'd been curled on the ground, my hands clamped over my ears, Lord Nahadoth appeared, carrying my brother. Then came Lord Ahad, bringing a newly revived Lord Itempas and a badly wounded Glee Shoth. A moment later, Lady Yeine arrived, bearing Sieh.

I am Shahar Arameri, and I am alone.

I issued an edict to the Consortium, summoning them to Echo, and to this I added a personal invitation for Usein Darr, and any allies that she chose to bring. To make my position clear, I phrased the note thus: *To discuss the terms of the Arameri surrender.*

Mother always said that if one must do something unpleasant, one should do it wholeheartedly and not waste effort on regret.

I invited representatives from the Litaria as well, and the Merchants' Guild, and the Farmers' Collective, and the Order of Itempas. I even summoned a few beggars from Ancestors' Village, and artists from Shadow's Promenade. As Lord Ahad was indisposed—he would not leave the bedside of Glee Shoth, who had been healed but slept in deep exhaustion—I included an invitation to several of the gods of Shadow, where they could be located. Most of them, not entirely to my surprise, had remained in the mortal realm as the disaster loomed. It was not the Gods' War again; they cared about us this time. To wit, Ladies Nemmer and Kitr responded in the affirmative, saying that they would attend.

The Litaria's involvement meant that all parties could gather quickly, as they sent scriveners forth to assist those mortals who could not hire their own. Within less than a day, Echo played host to several hundred of the world's officials and influencers, decision makers and exploiters. Not everyone who mattered, of course, and not enough of those who didn't. But it would do. I had them gather in the Temple, the only space large enough to hold them all. To address them, I stood where my brother and my best friend had shown me how to love. (I could not think of that and function, so I thought of other things instead.)

And then I spoke.

I told everyone there that we, the Arameri, would give up our power. Not to be distributed among the nobles, however, which would only invite chaos and war. Instead, we would give the bulk of our treasury, and management of our armies, to a single new governing body that was to consist of everyone in the room or their designated representatives. The priests, the scriveners, the godlings, the merchants, the nobles, the common folk. All of them. This body—by vote, edict, or whatever method they chose—would rule the Hundred Thousand Kingdoms in our place.

To say that this caused consternation would be understating the case.

I left as soon as the shouting began. Unconscionable for an Arameri ruler, but I no longer ruled. And like most mortals who had been near the Maelstrom that day, my ears were sensitive, still ringing despite my scriveners' healing scripts. The noise was bad for my health.

So I sought out one of the piers of Echo. A few hadn't been damaged by the palace's precipitous flight from ocean to lake. The view from here was of the lakeshore, with its ugly, sprawling survivors' encampment—not the ocean I craved or the drifting clouds I would never stop missing. But perhaps those were things I should never have gotten used to in the first place.

A step behind me. "You actually did it."

I turned to find Usein Darr standing there. A thick bandage covered her left eye and that side of her face; one of her hands had been splinted. There were probably other injuries hidden by her clothing and armor. For once I saw none of Wrath's constantly hovering guards about, but Usein did not have a knife in her good hand, which I took as a positive sign.

"Yes," I said, "I did it."

"Why?"

I blinked in surprise. "Why are you asking?"

She shook her head. "Curiosity. A desire to know my enemy. Boredom."

By my training, I should never have smiled. I did it anyway, because I no longer cared about my training. And because, I was certain, it was what Deka would have done. Sieh, I suspected, would have gone a step further, because he always went a step further. Perhaps he would have offered to babysit her children. Perhaps she would even have let him.

"I'm tired," I said. "The whole world isn't something one woman should bear on her shoulders—not even if she wants to. Not even if she has help." And I no longer did.

"That's it?"

"That's it."

She fell silent, and I turned back to the railing as a light breeze, redolent of algae and rotting crops and human sorrow, wafted over the lake from the land beyond. The sky was heavily overcast as if threatening a thunderstorm, but it had been so for days without rain. The lords of the sky were in mourning for their lost child; we would not see the sun or the stars for some time.

Let Usein knife me in the back, if she wished. I truly did not care.

"I am sorry," she said at length. "About your brother, and your mother, and..." She trailed off. We could both see the Tree's corpse in the distance; it blocked the mountains that had once marked the horizon. From here, Sky was nothing more than tumbled white jewels around its broken crown.

"'I was born to change this world,'" I whispered.

"Pardon?"

"Something the Matriarch—the first Shahar—reportedly said." I smiled to myself. "It isn't a well-known quote outside the family, because it was blasphemous. Bright Itempas abhors change, you see."

"Hmm." I suspected she thought I was mad. That was fine, too.

After a time, Usein left, probably returning to the Temple to battle for Darr's fair share of the future. I should have gone, too. The Arameri were, if nothing else, the royal family of the numerous and fractious tribes of the Amn race. If I did not fight for my people, we might be shortchanged in the time to come.

So be it, I decided, and hitched up my gown to sit against the wall.

It was Lady Yeine who found me next.

She appeared quietly, seated on the railing I had just leaned against. Though she looked the same as always—relentlessly Darren—her clothing had changed. Instead of pale gray, the tunic and calf-pants she usually wore were darker in color. Still gray, but a color that matched the lowering stormclouds above. She did not smile, her eyes olive with sorrow.

"What are you doing here?" she asked.

If one more person, mortal or god, asked me that question, I was going to scream.

"What are *you* doing here?" I asked in return. An impertinent question, I knew, for the god to whom my family now owed its allegiance. I would never have dared it with Lord Itempas. Yeine was less intimidating, however, so she would have to deal with the consequences of that.

"An experiment," she said. (I was privately relieved that my rudeness did not seem to bother her.) "I am leaving Nahadoth and Itempas alone together for a while. If the universe comes apart again, I'll know I made a mistake."

If my brother had not been dead, I would have laughed. If her son had not been dead, I think she would have, too.

"Will you release him?" I asked. "Itempas?"

"It has already been done." She sighed, drawing up one knee and resting her chin on it. "The Three are whole again, if not wholly united, and not exactly rejoicing at our reconciliation. Perhaps because there *is* no reconciliation; that will take an age of the world, I imagine. But who knows? It has already gone faster than I expected." She shrugged. "Perhaps I'm wrong about the rest, too."

I considered the histories I had read. "He was to be punished for as long as the Enefadeh. Two thousand years and some."

"Or until he learned to love truly." She said nothing more. I had seen Itempas weep beside the body of his son, silent tear tracks cleansing the blood and dirt from his face. This had been nothing meant for a mortal's eyes, but he had permitted me to see it, and I was keenly conscious of the honor. At the time, I'd had no tears of my own.

And I had seen Lord Itempas put a hand on the shoulder of

Lord Nahadoth, who knelt beside Sieh's corpse without moving. Nahadoth had not shaken that hand off. By such small gestures are wars ended.

"We will withdraw," Lady Yeine said, after a time of silence. "Naha and Tempa and I, completely this time. There is much work to be done, repairing the damage that the Maelstrom did. It takes all our strength to hold the realms together, even now. The scar of Its passage will never fade completely." She sighed. "And it has finally become clear to me that our presence in the mortal realm does too much harm, even when we try not to interfere. So we will leave this world to our children—the godlings, if they wish to stay, and you mortals, too. And the demons, if there are any left or any more born." She shrugged. "If the godlings get out of hand, ask the demons to keep them in line. Or do it yourselves. None of you are powerless anymore."

I nodded slowly. She must have guessed my thoughts, or read them in my face. I was slipping.

"He loved you," she said softly. "I could tell. You drove him half mad."

At that, I did smile. "The feeling was mutual."

We sat then, gazing at the clouds and the lake and the broken land, both of us thinking unimaginable thoughts. I was glad for her presence. Datennay tried, and I was growing to care for him, but it was hard to keep the pain at bay some days. The Mistress of Life and Death, I feel certain, understood that.

When she got to her feet, I did, too, and we faced each other. Her tiny size always surprised me. I thought she should have been like her brothers, tall and terrible, showing some hint of her magnificence in her shape. But that was what I got for thinking like an Amn.

"Why did it begin?" I asked. And because I was used to how gods thought and that question could have triggered a conversation about anything from the universe to the Gods' War and everything in between, I added, "Sieh. How did we make him mortal? Why did we have such power over him, with him? Was it because..." It was difficult for me to admit, but I'd had the scriveners test me, and they had confirmed my suspicions. I was a demon, though the god-killing potency of my blood was negligible, and I had no magic, no specialness. Mother would have been so disappointed.

"It had nothing to do with you," Yeine said softly. I blinked. She looked away, sliding her hands into her pockets—a gesture that tore at my heart, because Sieh had done it so often. He'd even looked like her, a little. By design? Knowing him, yes.

"But what—"

"I lied," she said, "about us staying wholly out of the mortal realm. There will be times in the future when we'll have no choice but to return. It will be our task to assist the godlings, you see, when the time of metamorphosis comes upon them. When they become gods in their own right."

I jerked in surprise. "Become...what? Like Kahl?"

"No. Kahl sought to force nature. He wasn't ready for it. Sieh was." She let out a long sigh. "I didn't begin to understand until Tempa said that whatever Sieh had become, he was *meant* to become. His bond with you, losing his magic—perhaps these are the signs we'll know to watch for next time. Or perhaps those were unique to Sieh. He was the oldest of our children, after all, and the first to reach this stage." She looked at me and shrugged. "I would have liked to see the god he became. Though I still would have lost him then, even if he'd lived."

I digested this in wonder and felt a little fear at the implications. Godlings could grow into gods? Did that mean gods, then, could grow into things like the Maelstrom? If they could somehow live long enough, would mortals become godlings?

Too many things to think about. "What do you mean, you would have lost him if he'd lived?"

"This realm can abide only three gods. If Sieh had survived and become whatever he was meant to be, his fathers and I would have had to send him away."

Death or exile. Which would I have preferred? *Neither. I want him back, and Deka, too.* "But where could he have gone?"

"Elsewhere." She smiled at my look, with a hint of Sieh's mischief. "Did you think this universe was all there was? There's room out there for so much more." Her smile faded then, just a little. "He would have enjoyed the chance to explore it, too, as long as he didn't have to do it alone."

The Goddess of Earth looked at me then, and suddenly I understood. Sieh, Deka, and I; Nahadoth, Yeine, and Itempas. Nature is cycles, patterns, repetition. Whether by chance or some unknowable design, Deka and I had begun Sieh's transition to adulthood— and perhaps, when the chrysalis of his mortal life had finally split to reveal the new being, he would not have transformed alone.

Would I have wanted to go with him and Deka, to rule some other cosmos?

Just dreams now, like broken stone.

Yeine dusted off her pants, stretched her arms above her head, and sighed. "Time to go."

I nodded. "We will continue to serve you, Lady, whether you're here or not. What prayers shall we say for you at the dawn and twilight hour?"

She threw me an odd look, as if checking to see if I was joking. I wasn't. This seemed to surprise and unnerve her; she laughed, though it sounded a bit forced.

"Say whatever you want," she said finally. "Someone might be listening, but it won't be me. I have better things to do."

She vanished.

Eventually I wandered back into the palace, and to the Temple, where the assembly was breaking up at last. Merchants and nobles and scriveners drifted down the hall in knots, still arguing with each other. They ignored me completely as I came to the Temple entrance.

"Thanks for leaving," said Lady Nemmer as she emerged looking thoroughly disgruntled. "We got exactly one thing done, aside from setting a date for a future useless meeting."

I smiled at her annoyance; she scowled back, the room growing oddly shadowed. But she wasn't really angry, so I asked, "And the thing you got done was?"

"We chose a name." She waved a hand, irritable. "A pretentious and needlessly poetic one, but the mortals outnumbered Kitr and I, so we couldn't vote it down. *Aeternat*. It's one of our words. It means—"

I cut her off. "I don't need to know, Lady Nemmer. Please convey to whoever's speaking for this Aeternat that they should inform me when they're ready for the transfer of military command and funds."

She looked at me in real surprise, then finally nodded. We turned at the sound of someone calling my name from down the corridor: Datennay. He'd sat in on the Aeternat's session. I would have to quickly dissuade him from doing that, now that he was my husband. Beyond him was Ramina, who watched me

with a solemn sorrow in his expression that I understood completely. He caught my eye over the heads of a gaggle of shouting
priests and smiled, however, inclining his head in approval. It
warmed me. I would need to have his true sigil removed sometime soon.

And I would need to send a note to Morad, I reminded
myself. She'd quit her position and gone home to southern
Senm, to no one's surprise. I still hoped to entice her back eventually; competent stewards were hard to find. I would not press
Morad, however. She deserved the time and space to mourn in
her own way.

While Datennay approached, I inclined my head to Nemmer
in farewell. "Welcome to ruling the world, Lady Nemmer. I wish
you enjoyment of it."

She spoke a godword so foul that one of the nearby lanterns
turned to melted metal-and-oil sludge and crashed to the floor.
As I walked away, I heard her cursing again—in some mortal
tongue this time, more softly, as she bent to clean up the mess.

Datennay met me halfway down the hall. He hesitated
before offering me his hand. Once, I had discouraged him from
displaying affection in public. Now, however, I took his hand
firmly, and he blinked in surprise, flashing a smile.

"These people are all mad," I said. "Take me away from here."

As we walked away, something pulsed hot between my
breasts, and I remembered I had forgotten to tell Lady Yeine
about the necklace we'd found on Sieh's body. The cord had
been broken, half the smaller beads lost to whatever had
snapped it, but the central bead—the peculiar yellow one—
was fine. It was surprisingly heavy, and sometimes, if I was not
imagining things, it became oddly warm to the touch. I had put

the thing on a chain around my own neck, because I felt better wearing it. Less alone.

Lady Yeine would not mind if I kept it, I decided. Then I stroked the little sphere as if to comfort it, and walked on.

CODA

Shahar Arameri died in bed at the age of seventy, leaving two daughters and a son—half-Teman fullbloods unmarked by any sigil—to carry on the family. The Arameri still owned many businesses and properties, and they remained one of the most powerful clans on the Senm continent. They just had less. Shahar's children immediately began scheming to get more upon her death, but that is a matter for other tales.

The godling Ahad, called Beloved by his fellow godlings, watched over Glee Shoth for the entire year that she slept after her legendary battle with Kahl. When she finally awoke, he took her away from Echo and the new city developing around its lake. They settled in a small northwestern Senm town, where they spent some years looking after an elderly, blind Maro woman until her death. There they remained for another hundred years or so, never marrying, raising no children, but always together. She lived a long time for a mortal, and gave him a proper name of his own before she died. He tells no one that name, it is said, guarding it like something precious and rare.

Those mortals who worshipped the Goddess of Earth claimed ownership of the corpse of the World Tree. By the time of Shahar's death, they had excavated and preserved enough of its trunk to house a small city, which began to call itself World. They lived in the Tree and on it, said their prayers at the skeleton of its roots, dedicated their sons and daughters to its broken branches. Fires, and fire-godlings, were not allowed in this city. They lit their chambers at night with pieces of Sky.

The Aeternat...well. It was not eternal. But that, too, is a matter for other tales.

So many tales, really. They are sure to be exciting. A shame that I will get to hear none of them.

I? Oh, yes.

When Shahar exhaled her last breath I awakened, midwifed into existence by her mortality. My first act was to turn in space and time and kiss Deka awake, beside me. Then I called to my En, and it shot across realities and blazed into joyous, welcoming life somewhere far, far beyond the realms of the Three. It would be the seed-star of a new realm. *Our* realm. It sent out great arcing plumes of fire, silly little ball of gas, and I petted it silent and promised it worlds to warm just as soon as I'd taken care of other business.

Then we found Shahar, and gathered her up, and took her with us. She was, to say the least, surprised. But not displeased. We are together now, the three of us, for the rest of forever. I will never be alone again.

My name is not Sieh, and I am no longer a trickster. I will think of a new name and calling, eventually—or some one of you, my children, will name me. Make of me, of us, whatever you wish. We are yours until time ends, and perhaps a little beyond.

And we will all create such wonderful new things, you and we, out here beyond the many skies.

A Glossary of Terms

(handwritten: FOR IDIOTS. 3 books and you still don't know this stuff?)

~~Ahad~~: A niwwah godling living in Shadow; proprietor of the Arms of Night brothel.

Amn: Most populous and ~~powerful~~ *(handwritten: its)* of the Senmite races.

Antema: Capital of the largest province of the Teman Protectorate.

A~~ramer~~i: R~~uling family of the Am~~n; advis~~ors to the N~~o *(handwritten overwriting: ASSHOLES ASSHOLES ASSHOLES ASSHOLES ASSHOLES ASSHOLES assholes)* ~~bles and advisors to~~ Itemp~~as.~~

Arms of Night: A brothel in the South Root neighborhood of Shadow, known to cater to an exclusive clientele. *(handwritten: shooty shooty smell like)*

Blood sigil: The mark of a recognized Arameri family member.

Bright, the: The time of Itempas's solitary rule, after the Gods' War. General term for goodness, order, law, righteousness. *(handwritten: HA, HA, HA)*

Darkwalkers: Worshippers of the Nightlord.

Datennay Canru: Pymexe (heir) to Lady Hynno of the Teman Triadice; a friend of Shahar and Dekarta Arameri.

Dekarta Arameri: Twin brother of heir Shahar Arameri. Named for a former head of the family. *DO YOU LOVE ME?*

Demon: Children of ~~forbidden~~ unions between gods/ *COME AND I WILL SHOW YOU* godlings and mortals. Mortal, though they ~~may~~ possess innate magic equivalent to that of godlings in strength, or greater.

Dimmer: An artist skilled in dimyi.

Dimyi: The art of mask making; a specialty of High North.

Easha: East Shadow.

Echo: A palace.

Elontid: The second ranking of godling. The Imbalancers, born of the inequality between gods and godlings, or the instability of Nahadoth and Itempas. Sometimes as powerful as gods, sometimes weaker than godlings. *SCRVNRS SUCK* *BLAH BLAH BLAH BLAH BLAH*

EN! The best friend a godling ever had.

Enefa: One of the Three. ~~Former~~ Goddess of Earth, creator of godlings and mortals, Mistress of Twilight and Dawn (deceased).

Eyem-sutah: A niwwah godling living in Shadow. Lord of the Lanes (of commerce).

Gateway Park: A park built around Sky and the World Tree's base.

Glee Shoth: A Maroneh woman; ~~business partner~~ *CRAZY girlfriend* of Ahad. *WHO HAS NO TASTE.*

God: Immortal children of the Maelstrom. The Three.

Godling: Immortal children of the Three. Sometimes also referred to as *gods.* *?*

Godsblood: A popular and expensive narcotic. Confers heightened awareness and temporary magical abilities on consumers. *EAT OF MY FLESH AND THY SOUL SHALL BE FORFEIT*

Gods' realm: All places beyond the universe.

you are here

Gods' War: An apocalyptic conflict in which Bright Itempas claimed rulership of the heavens after defeating his two siblings.

Gray, the: The "middle city" of Sky-in-Shadow, situated atop the World Tree's roots. Includes servants, suppliers, and crafters, and the mansions they serve (which encircle the Tree's trunk) by means of a network of steam-driven escalators.

Heavens, Hells: Abodes for souls beyond the mortal realm.

High North: Northernmost continent. A backwater.

Hundred Thousand Kingdoms, the: Collective term for the world since its unification under Arameri rule.

Hymnesamina: A girl living in the South Root neighborhood of Shadow. *with a truly stupid hat.*

Interdiction, the: The period after the Gods' War when no godlings appeared in the mortal realm, per order of Bright Itempas.

Islands, the: Vast archipelago east of High North and Senm.

Itempan: General term for a worshipper of Itempas. Also used to refer to members of the Order of Itempas.

Itempas: One of the Three. The Bright Lord; master of heavens and earth; the Skyfather.

Kitr: A masat godling who lives in Shadow. The Blade.

Lil: An elontid godling who lives in Shadow. The Hunger.

Maelstrom: The creator of the Three. Unknowable.

Magic: The innate ability of gods and godlings to alter the material and immaterial world. Mortals may approximate this ability through the use of the gods' language.

Maroland, the: Smallest continent, which once existed to the east of the islands; site of the first Arameri palace. Destroyed by Nahadoth.

Mnasat: The third ranking of godlings; godlings born of godlings. Generally weaker than godlings born of the Three.

Mortal realm: The universe, created by the Three.

Nahadoth: One of the Three. The Nightlord.

Nemmer: A niwwah godling who lives in Shadow. The Lady of Secrets.

Nimaro Reservation: A protectorate of the Arameri, established after the Maroland's destruction.

Niwwah: The first ranking of godlings, born of the Three; the Balancers. More stable but sometimes less powerful than the elontid.

Nobles' Consortium: Ruling political body of the Hundred Thousand Kingdoms.

Nsana: A niwwah godling; the Dreammaster.

Order of Itempas: The priesthood dedicated to Bright Itempas. In addition to spiritual guidance, also responsible for law and order, education, public health, and welfare. Also known as the Itempan Order.

Order-Keepers: Acolytes (priests-in-training) of the Order of Itempas, responsible for maintenance of public order.

Pilgrim: Worshippers of the Gray Lady who journey to Shadow to pray at the World Tree.

Previt: One of the higher rankings for priests in the Order of Itempas.

Promenade, the: Northernmost edge of Gateway Park in East Shadow.

Pymexe: (masculine; feminine is *pymoxe*) Heir to one of the three ruling positions in the Teman Triadice. Not hereditary; Triadic heirs are chosen at an early age, after a rigorous selection process involving official examinations and interviews.

Ramina Arameri: A fullblood; half brother of Remath Arameri.

Remath Arameri: Current head of the Arameri family; mother of Shahar and Dekarta.

Salon: Headquarters for the Nobles' Consortium.

Script: A series of sigils, used by scriveners to produce complex or sequential magical effects.

Scrivener: A scholar of the gods' written language.

Semisigil: A modern version of the Arameri blood sigil, modified to remove anachronistic scripts.

Senm: Southernmost and largest continent of the world.

Senmite: The Amn language, used as a common tongue for all the Hundred Thousand Kingdoms.

Shadow: The city beneath Sky.

Shahar Arameri: Current heir of the Arameri Family. Also high priestess of Itempas at the time of the Gods' War. Matriarch of the Arameri family.

Sieh: A godling, also called the Trickster. Eldest of all the godlings.

Sigil: An ideograph of the gods' language, used by scriveners to imitate the magic of the gods.

Sky: The palace of the Arameri family.

Sky-in-Shadow: Official name for the palace of the Arameri and the city beneath it.

Teman Protectorate, the: A Senmite kingdom.

Time of the Three: Before the Gods' War.

True sigil: An Arameri blood sigil in the traditional style.

T'vril Arameri: A former head of the Arameri family.

Usein Darr: A Darren warrior; heir to the Baron Darr.

Wesha: West Shadow.

White Hall: The Order of Itempas's houses of worship, education, and justice.

World Tree, the: An evergreen tree estimated to be 125,000 feet in height, created by the Gray Lady. Sacred to worshippers of the Lady.

Wrath Arameri: Captain of the White Guard in Sky.

Yeine: One of the Three. The current Goddess of Earth, Mistress of Twilight and Dawn.

Acknowledgments

Going to keep it short this time. This is the longest novel I've ever written, after all, and I'm plum tuckered out.

I need to thank you.

Seriously. That's not just pretentious "I'd like to thank all the little people" bullshit. A writer is a writer whether she's read or not, but no writer can have a career in this business unless she satisfies her readers. And really, even that's not enough, not in these days of the long tail and a quarter-million new titles published per year in the United States alone. A writer needs readers who will find other readers, and grab them by the arm, and say to them, *Read this book right now.* She needs readers who will post reviews on retailer sites and argue with other readers over their ratings; readers who will select her work for their monthly book club meetings and discuss it over tea and cake; readers who will tweet about the book's surprises; readers who'll put the book on a literature syllabus. She even needs people who'll rant that they hate the book—because those kinds of strong reactions make people curious.

The opposite of liking is not disliking, after all. The opposite of liking is apathy.

All new writers have Something to Prove—me more than most, maybe. But because so many of you have been anything but apathetic, I know I've done a good job. So thank you. Thank you. Thank you.

THE

AWAKENED
KINGDOM

A SEQUEL NOVELLA TO THE
INHERITANCE TRILOGY

I am born! Hello!
Many things happen.
The end!

Hello again! How are you? I am fine. I have learned more about
Proper Ways from Papa Tempa. Papa said that what I did before
was not the Proper Way to tell a story, so I will do it over. I do
not like the way he says I should tell it, though. That is BOR-
ING. I want to make you feel like I feel! So I will talk like I
thinked when stuff was happening, and I will start from the
very beginning, when my thinking was not so good because I
was extra new.

I am glad you are with me. You are new, too, and now we can
be new together! We have much to learn, everyone says, but I
have learned a great deal already! I will share it with you. See,
here is what I learned today: how to speak to others without
making them angry and how to run if I do make them angry
and how not to blur myself into another so that both of us are
lost and how to come close to MAELSTROM without dissolu-
tion and how to name all the names of all the pieces of EXIS-
TENCE. I learned that besides Maelstrom and existence there
is also NOTHINGNESS and it goes on for a long long way.
Forever! It is not safe to go there, says Naha. She took me to the
edge of the gods' realm and showed me. It is very scary, but then
so is Naha.

Do you know Naha? And Papa Tempa and Mama Yeine?
You should know them! They encompass all the fullness of

existence that the soul can grasp. I will take you to meet them.
They will like you, you'll see!

Hello! Mama Yeine says I do not have to say hello every time I
see someone I already know.

Also, Papa Tempa tells me I am doing a wrong thing again.
I am supposed to respect TIME, because that is a thing he has
made for the place where mortals live, and you come from there.
You might forget this if I tell it to you now, so I will tell it to you
later and you will remember it when you reach now. That will
happen in the gods' realm, when you go there, which is where
you are now, so don't forget!

I do not know why you are confused. I explained it fine. OK!
Now I will tell my story.

Imagine that you have just been born.

It is very confusing. (Not like time. Time is easy.) There is a
lot of pain and messiness and then suddenly everything is new
and different and cold and bright! And then something says *Be*
and there you are. And while you lie there screaming there are
hands that touch you, and warmth that folds around you, and
there are voices, and they are familiar because you have heard
them since long before your birth. So you are comforted.

But you scream again because the world blurs and that is
when suddenly you discover words like *agoraphobia* and *vertigo*
and *you* and *other*. You do not want to learn these words, but
you have no choice! You know *world*, too, which you sort of
knew before, except it once meant something entirely different.
Once *world* was warm and dark and close. Now world is different, and you must start all over again learning how it works.
This is not fair, but world—*the* world—is often unfair.

And then a really bad thing happens.

You were wanted! Mama and Papa and Naha wanted you lots. You know this, and you know there is a space carved into existence which is shaped like a godling, and that godling is supposed to be you! The hole was left when Biggest Sibling went away. By that I mean, he died. His name was Sieh. Now imagine you are supposed to be Sieh! Well, not really. Sieh is dead. But you were made to fill the hole he left behind—to be the Trickster and the wind, mischief and cruelty, the cat and the boy and the cranky old man. Imagine the Three have shaped you so, so carefully to match the hole. You will be different from Sieh-that-was, but you will be important in the same way. You will be powerful in the same way. The planets will follow you and the mortals will tell tales of you and you will steal all the suns, but only keep the ones that want to be your friend. Without a Trickster the universe will not end, but it will be a much duller place.

But when you are born, things are…different. Wrong. You do not feel quite of caprice and wind and man-ness. You try these things, and because you are a god things happen, but they are not the things that should happen, and they do not nourish you. They do not *inform* you. You are something steadier than caprice. Heavier than wind. And when you curl yourself into various shapes, it is woman-ness that calls to you, except when you make shapes that do not have woman-ness. (Like amoebas. I like being an amoeba! Glurgle glurgle squishchomp.)

You are not what your parents want you to be.

You are not what *you* want to be, because you love them, your parents, and you want to make them happy, and you just… can't. In fact, now you have no idea what you should be, instead. You are incomplete.

It is. It is very. Sad. I was very sad.

But then something changed and I got mad. Because it was so *unfair*. I did everything right. I was born, and everything! Life should have been perfect for me and suddenly it was not and everything was just, just awful.

So I went around for a while, mad. I made hells and kicked them and did not feel any better so I let them fade away. I asked Mama to help me make some life to kick instead, and she looked at me in a scary way and said that life was not mine to play with. She gave me some knowledge to study, though, and that made me bigger which is why I am not talking in quite so many exclamations now. But once I had learned it I was bored again and mad again so I went off looking for something else to do.

I talked to some siblings. Some of them did not want to talk to me but others did. One called the Dreamer told me that he had not been able to find himself for a long, long time—so long that he gave up trying, and thought it would never happen, and resolved to just be sad and empty forever. But then it happened. "It *will* happen," he said, which made me feel better. I asked him how he'd made himself be less empty during that long time, and he said he had filled the emptiness with other people's love for a little while. "But without love of the self, others' love will never be enough." I didn't understand that part so I just nodded and went away.

Then I tried to talk to Spider Manysighted, and she just laughed and threw webs around me and talked gibberish and I almost died! I went away before I could. I don't think I like her much.

Then I talked to Ral the Dragon, which was hard because all it does is spit fire and roar. So I tried spitting fire and roaring along with it, and it didn't spit any fire *at* me, so I guess that was OK.

When I was done I felt even more better, but I was still mad. So finally I went to the wall of torn stars which is at the edge of the Maelstrom, and I just sat there and felt bad for a while.

And I thought: *This is so unfair! I should be Sieh!*

And then I thought: *Why can't I be Sieh?*

And then I thought, ooh, I thought: *Maybe I can* make *me be Sieh.*

Oooooh!

There isn't any rule against it. It's what the Three wanted, and it's important to obey them, isn't it? Nobody said I couldn't.

So I went back to Spider and I played a trick. I tied her realm to Ral the Dragon's and ran away before either of them could see what I'd done. They started fighting! And I tried to laugh at them, to feel proud of what I had done, because it was good mischief! And that is what Sieh would have done.

Except... it wasn't funny. Spider had been mean to me, but Ral had been nice, and... I didn't like being mean.

I decided maybe I was doing mischief wrong. I tried again, this time sneaking into Elhodi's Infinite Garden and switching things around so they bloomed out of season and grew next to things that would eat them and making all the flowers be polka-dotted. And then I waited nearby to see what would happen when Elhodi found it. I thought he would get angry, and then I would laugh, and it would be OK because I hadn't met Elhodi at all and he hadn't been either mean or nice.

But when Elhodi came in, he started to *cry*. Really! I felt bad then. I realized his garden had been beautiful, and I'd made it ugly, and... and... being mischievous wasn't any fun at all.

I came out of hiding and said I was sorry. He let me help him put everything back, which made us both feel better. Then he said, "Why?" Or rather, he rustled a little, because Elhodi only speaks in plant, but I figured it out.

"I thought I could make me be Sieh," I said. "This is what he would do. Isn't it?"

Elhodi just stared at me for a moment, then shook his head in a bobbing, windblown sort of way. Then he touched me and took me back to the center of the gods' realm, where the Three were just finishing whatever they had been doing before. When he spoke to them and left me there I thought I would be in trouble, so I stood before them and bowed my head and waited to be punished for being bad.

They sort of looked at each other and then all of them sort of sighed and then Naha and Yeine vanished and Itempas took my hand and sat me down.

"You do not understand your purpose," he said, which I thought was silly because duh, I knew that, it was kind of the whole point.

He shook his head. "Not nature. *Purpose.* Why, not what. You misunderstand the reason for your creation."

I frowned. "To be Sieh," I said. "I mean, to be what he was."

"No."

Now I was very confused. "Why did you make me, then?"

"To live."

I was even more confused! "I'm alive, but I'm not what you want me to be."

"There is nothing that we want you to be, besides yourself. You are everything we desired of you."

I really, really, really didn't understand, so I shut up and tried to think about it and still didn't understand. Itempas sighed and conjured an image of Sieh in his favorite mortal shape: tiny, mammalian, wavering a little between big-headed boy and spindly old man and sleek black cat. Shapes, plural; I had heard that mortals did not blur themselves the way we did. As if to emphasize this, Itempas fixed the image on the boy, who stared back at us with Yeine's lively, deadly eyes. And because this was Itempas and he liked to be precise, I did more than see Sieh; I *felt* him, as he must have seemed to everyone who met him in life. There was so much of him! He'd been nothing like I thought. His soul was so heavy that everything was pulled toward him, everyone thought about him, every event involved him to at least a tiny degree. Wow! He didn't feel like a godling at all.

I got really ashamed, then, because that was when I knew I hadn't done my tricks *wrong*; I just wasn't enough to do them right.

"What you detect in us is something called *grief*," Itempas said, speaking very softly for a moment. "That is the wound left behind when something integral to the self is taken away."

I gasped, finally understanding. "The hole! I didn't fit it!"

Itempas is good at words, and he knew what I meant even if I didn't know how to say it right. "It is a kind of void, yes. No one can fit the one left by a specific soul, however. Such a void is unique."

So I wasn't even supposed to try to fit it? I fidgeted. "Wounds get better. What makes grief get better?"

"Nothing. Time can ease it, but nothing ends it."

That sounded awful! "Grief sounds like a bad thing," I said, frowning. "Why don't you and Naha and Mama get rid of it?"

"That would require removing love from existence. Do you believe it would be a good thing to do so?"

I thought hard. I loved Mama and Papa and Naha. I loved some of my siblings. I loved the wall of torn stars and the tiny glowing flowers in Elhodi's garden that I'd helped him replant. I did not want to stop loving things. "No."

He inclined his head, which made me feel very grown up. "Such things are better endured than avoided."

I tried to imagine having a wound that would never heal. I couldn't. I knew what pain was—I had felt lots of that when I was born—and it was a terrible, scary thing, but usually pain went away after a while. "How do you endure something that never ends?"

"That is something many of us are still learning. Gods are particularly bad at it." He sighed and let Sieh's image vanish into the swirls of ether. "Our grief suppurates unchecked and unfading for eternities. We invariably inflict new pain in an effort to ease the old. That tendency has caused so much harm to existence that we now understand we can no longer afford to indulge it."

"Oh? What do you do instead?"

He conjured another image: a planet, smaller than most, wet, green with life. "We learn from mortals. They are small and weak creatures in so many ways—but in love, they are our equals. In grief, they are stronger."

"Stronger!" Everything everyone had told me about mortals made them sound like funny little pets.

"Yes. They were made to endure death on a scale we cannot imagine." Abruptly Itempas made a funny face. I had never seen his face be like this. "So lately, we have...attempted to...

change. It is a mortal technique to...to counter death with life."

Life. *Me*. Oh! Finally I understood, which was good because Papa Tempa was hurting himself to make me understand. He was trying, though, because sometimes it is better to change than to do bad things. And that was what he was trying to tell me! (It's hard for Papa Tempa to change. But not as hard as it was for him to be alone, my siblings had told me, so we tried always to make sure he was not.)

But I squirmed, because something he had said bothered me. "You made me so you wouldn't do more bad things?" Siblings had told me all about the Gods' War.

"No," Itempas said, and now he sounded strong again. "We made you because you are a *good* thing."

This made me curl up and want to go back to the wall of torn stars. "I don't know what that means, though."

He inclined his head. "Your confusion and frustration are normal. This is part of life."

"Well, I don't like life, then!"

Itempas's eyes sort of crinkled and his mouth sort of curved and he touched me for a moment, all proudwarm and firm. "Don't let your mother hear you say that." He considered. "Or Nahadoth, if she is bored." Then he pulled away and gathered himself to leave.

I jumped up. "Wait! Papa—" If there was a Proper Way to be alive, he would know how to get started, at least. "I don't know what to do next!"

Itempas paused, considering, and then he lowered his sun-colored gaze. "Perhaps it was the right choice for you to study Sieh's life," he said. "He lived better than most of us." Abruptly he leveled a hard look at me. "Do not *emulate* him, however. That is easy, and foolish. *Learn* from him—his mistakes as well as his accomplishments. Then become yourself."

He went away then. I still didn't understand, but at least I felt better! That is why I like Papa Tempa best.

So I made myself some feet and kicked them for a while, and thought and thought and thought. And finally I decided what you probably know I decided because I have already done it and if I hadn't I wouldn't be here talking to you. I decided to go to the mortal realm.

This was really bad, because Naha had said the mortal realm was a terrible place where bad things happened to gods. Then she'd held me for a long time without talking at all, which I understood better now that Papa Tempa had told me about GRIEF. I didn't really want to go to a place that was full of grief! But Sieh had spent a lot of time there, and the things that had happened to him there had been really, really important. Everyone said he'd gotten stronger there. And Mama Yeine had come from there, and she was terrible but also really amazing, so obviously the mortal realm was not all bad. So I decided I would go there, too, and maybe get stronger, and try not to die. I did not want to make more GRIEF.

In the mortal realm there is a world that is very special! This was the planet Papa Tempa had shown me. It is special for bad reasons, mostly, like killing a lot of us. But it is also the world most of us go to when we visit the mortal realm, so I packed myself up and wrapped myself in skin and some bones and stuff. I picked stuff that was different from Sieh's, just like Itempas had said, which meant that when I became a big-headed human I made myself smaller and browner and girlier, and I gave myself pretty gold eyes like Papa's instead of green ones like Mama's. Then I took a deep breath with my brand-new lungs, and I went! There!

Now I will skip over some stuff that is not very important.

I did not mean to break that planet it was just in the way when I came into being and I fixed it and I said I was sorry and the planet said OK so since I'm supposed to learn from stuff like that I will tell you *don't break planets*, especially the ones with living things on them, or at least fix them if you do break them. Also, *don't go in black holes*, no matter how much they look like cute little Nahas. They are not cute! They are actually very bitey and kind of mean. Also just OK I do not want to talk about any of this anymore.

Hello! That's better. Now I will tell you where you came from, so you can know what it was like for me.

I went to the scary Planet Where Gods Die. (It did not have a better name, it told me, sadly. I promised I would make up a good name for it before I left.) It has two big continents; since Sieh spent most of his time on the bigger one, I picked the smaller one. There was a big city there, and a place in the city where there were many mortals shuffling about doing mortally things. I made myself be in the middle of them all, and then I put my hands on my hips and said, "Hello!"

Also, do not do this to mortals.

OK well it is a good thing to say hello. But you should maybe say it at the same volume little human-mortals speak, not the volume that big sun-mortals use. And you should maybe use a human language, because the universe doesn't care about those and doesn't try to say hi back.

So, um. The city. Broke, a little. And a lot of people. They broke, too.

That was really, really, really, soooooo many reallys, bad. People are not as strong as planets, and they cannot be put back together as easily. Once the Yeine of them is gone, oops I mean the life, it can't come back. Which meant that I had made a lot of mortals *die*. Become grief. I felt the holes torn by their goneness! I knew they would not come back, and I knew I had been so terribly awfully bad that I might not ever be good again.

So I stood there in what remained of the market, staring at flat bodies and flat buildings and cracked streets and burning air, and I started to cry, because I didn't know what else to do and everything was already *wrong*.

"Stop," said someone, and I blinked and lifted my face out of my hands because I hadn't thought there was anybody left to talk to me. When I looked up, though, there was a mortal still standing! He had pretty long black hair and wore pretty bright-colored blankety things and he had his hands out in front of him with his eyes shut tight like he was trying to do something hard. There was something in one of his hands, a rolled-up piece of paper on two sticks, but that wasn't what he was trying hard at. What he was doing was keeping the air still and cool and the ground steady beneath himself. But that isn't hard! Silly mortal. It was why he was still standing, though.

"*Stop*," he said again, this time baring his teeth, "*sniveling*."

I was very, very careful to make my voice more like his as wiped my face with the back of one fist. "What?"

His eyes opened a crack; they were very very black and reminded me a little of Naha's. "Shut *up*," he snapped again. He was really mad! At me! "Stop crying and *fix* this."

Oh.

I tried. I put the air and ground and buildings back to the way they were supposed to be, maybe they were a little crooked but at least they weren't in pieces anymore, and then I tried to figure out how to fix the mortals. A lot of them could not be fixed. But the ones who were still breathing—I was scared to try and fix them. What if I made them a little crooked, too? Mortals weren't very malleable. But if I did nothing, they would stop. I mean, die.

There was a kind of shiver and a folding and one of my siblings appeared! He shaped himself out of ether into something that looked like a tall, pale human man with flatyellowshort hair and eyes like methane ice planets, and there were weird things on his face, little circles of glass held in place with wire. But none of that mattered because *he* was wrong, too, and I didn't really understand why at first.

"What, precisely, are you doing, Sibling?" he asked.

I had to try really hard not to start crying again. "I broke them and I don't know how to fix them! I didn't mean to!"

His eyes narrowed. "Ah," he said at last. "You're the *new* one. That explains a great deal." He sighed and pushed the wire-glass things up his face with one finger. "One moment."

Then everything sort of *un*-everythinged. Some of what happened was too fast for me to see, and that is saying a lot because, you know, I am a god. Something vast and incomprehensible as the Maelstrom passed near, and for a minute I got really scared! But then there was a *shoop* and a *slurbt* and reality shook some, and all of a sudden everything was back to normal! The mortals were all fixed, shuffling about again as mortals did, but they weren't upset or anything, which was strange. The buildings were uncrooked, because—oh! oh, I got it!—they had never fallen in the first place! And the streets were uncracked! And the city was unbroked!

I turned to my sibling, who had folded his arms and was now looking around the marketplace through his glass things. I was so happy I wanted to cry again, in a different way. "That was amazing!"

"Yes." This came from the mortal, who exhaled and let his bubble of cool stillness go away. Except it was still there, just a little, in a way that I did not understand. I felt it when he looked at me, still angry and lip-curled, and it made me stop smiling and remember that I had been really bad. The mortal smoothed the cloth that was wrapped around him. "Thank you, Lord Ia. May I also rely upon you to deal with your...companion? I'd rather not take up the matter with my grandmother."

Something happened that I didn't understand. Ia looked at the mortal. The mortal looked away, but I could tell that he had seen Ia looking at him. It was almost like they were trying to talk without words, but I had heard mortals couldn't do that.

"Very well," said Ia, after a moment. He folded his arms across his chest. He was wearing cloth, too, all in straight lines and white. It looked stark compared to the mortal's flowing, draped colors, and uncomfortable! "Please give my regards to Fahno-enulai, then, should you ever deem it appropriate to speak to her of this incident."

The mortal nodded, looked at me in an angry way one more time, then turned and walked away. "But I said I was sorry," I said, in his wake. I did not like that the mortal had gone away still angry.

"Your regret doesn't negate what he saw," said Ia, "which

was a godling abusing her power—destroying mortal lives out of sheer carelessness—and then doing nothing whatsoever to remedy the situation until prompted."

He sounded a lot like Papa Tempa. Except, he sounded like Papa Tempa *mad*. I squirmed. "I tried to fix things."

"Things. Not people."

"I didn't know how!"

"Then you should have called someone who did. Yeine would have been able to repair the damage easily; why did you not summon her?"

Oh. I. "I, um, didn't think of that."

"No, you didn't. Instead you had a meltdown." He took a deep breath. "You shouldn't be here, Sibling. Go somewhere else and grow up a bit before you return."

"But—" He was turning to go! He was so mad he didn't even want to talk to me. I stood where he'd left me, with my hand upraised to try and get his attention, but he didn't look back. After a moment he was gone down the street.

Everything was awful and I hadn't even been on the planet five minutes.

Should I leave, like Ia had told me? I didn't want to, but maybe he was right. Maybe I needed to learn how to handle mortals better if I was going to be here in a place full of them. But how was I to learn anything about mortals better if I didn't meet some?

That was it! I would go and meet the boy who was mad at me, again. I would find out how to make him less mad.

So I ran in the direction he had gone. He wasn't far; mortals are very slow! I caught up to him on a street that had a lot fewer people on it, but more walls and statues and an air of importance. The mortal boy was standing in the shadows against a wall, across the street from a big domed building that felt more important than everything else around.

"Hello," I said when I stopped beside him. I said it very carefully this time, in a whisper!

He jumped and stared at me, first surprised and then—oh. He was still mad. Still really mad. "Go *away*, godling."

I bit my lip. "But I want to show you I can be good and not hurt mortals! Please? I'm really sorry."

His jaw flexed. "You should apologize to the people you injured and killed!"

"But I can't! They got NEGATED." That was the word for what I'd seen Ia do. "You're the only one that remembers. It was scary, wasn't it? I'm sorry I scared you, even if I didn't hurt you."

He stared at me again, then sighed and rubbed his forehead with the back of the hand that held the paper-on-sticks I'd seen before. "By all the infinite hells. Fine; apology accepted. Now leave. I have important—" Abruptly he paused. Looked at me. His eyes narrowed. "Huh."

"Huh?" I straightened; I could tell he was thinking better thoughts about me! "Huh!"

That seemed to stop him from thinking better thoughts. "Gods, you're a strange thing."

"I'm not strange." I scowled. "I just don't know what I'm doing; that's different."

He blinked, then chuckled. "Well, at least you're honest." He took a deep breath, considered a moment longer, then said, "If you truly want to apologize, do me a favor, godling. Then I'll consider all debts paid between us."

I perked up. "OK! What favor?"

He held forth the paper thing. "I need you to take this scroll and put it somewhere."

I took it carefully. It was even more fragile than most mortal stuff. "Where?"

"Look at me." I did, and he took a deep breath, then *yelled at me with his mind.* I saw a place inside the big dome-building. A circle near its center, where a group of important-feeling women sat on cushions and stools and talked about important-sounding stuff. Not far from them, sitting in a basket nearby, were lots of scrolls just like the one I held. "There. Do you see it?"

I grimaced. "Yes. You didn't have to yell it, though. I was right here."

He blinked, then smiled. "Forgive me; I've never spoken without words to a godling before. I just knew it could be done."

"Well, you should not be rude when you do it." But then he raised his eyebrows, and I remembered I had been much ruder, so I felt bad again. "...Sorry."

"Gods. Maybe I'm a fool to involve you in this."

"No!" I inhaled and held up the scroll. "I can put it there! I promise!"

"*Without being seen.* You will need to—" He frowned, as if trying to remember something. "Dissipate your presence, I think is the wording you godlings use. Yes? Become your true immaterial self, take this scroll there, and make it material when no one's watching, so that it's just another scroll in the pile. All right?"

"OK! And then I'll come back and tell you—"

"No. I won't be here when you get back. I'll know you did it successfully if... certain things happen. But I need to be able to say, honestly, that I know nothing of what you did within

the Raringa's walls." Oh, yes; that was the big domed building. I could feel the truth of its name, spoken over centuries by
many mortal voices, shaped by many mortal thoughts. "Seat of
warriors"? I was not sure what that meant. "Just go, and do it,
and like I said, apology accepted even if I never see you again.
Especially if I never see you again. All right?"

"Um. OK!" He still did not like me, but at least if I did this, it
would mean I had been good some, and not all bad. "OK, I am
going now."

"Good luck, godling." That was a nice thing for him to say!
I grinned as I dissipated myself. I was getting better at dealing
with mortals!

It was extra easy to go through the domed place's walls and
into the big room with the circle of cushions. Nobody was looking at the pile of scrolls, so it was extra easy to put the boy's
scroll in among the rest. Then I stayed for a while, trying to
figure out what the women were saying, but it was boring stuff
about something called tariffs. I got tired from hearing it,
and finally left.

The boy was gone like he'd said he would be, which was sad.
But I had learned at least that bad things could be countered
by good things! So then I decided to go find Ia. Maybe I could
apologize to him, too, do him a favor, and be good again!

It was sort of hard to find him. I could feel other siblings of
mine all over the planet, all glowy-bright and magic-smelling,
but Ia's glow was sort of subdued and fuzzy. He was close by,
though, so I took shape again and ran to catch up, trying very
hard not to bump into any mortals. That was hard because
they were everywhere and kept bumping into me. I made sure I
bumped into them *gently*, at least.

He was at the edge of town on the roof of a small building, looking out over the city with his arms folded. He reminded me of Papa Tempa, standing like that! I appeared beside him and said, "Hello?"

He didn't even look at me, though his jaw flexed the same way the mortal boy's had. "I told you, Sibling. You don't know enough to be here safely. Must I force you home?"

"I...I want to learn how to be safe!"

"Not at the mortals' expense. Learn it elsewhere. And *grow up.*"

"But..." How could I make him know what I was thinking? He was all bristly and fuzzy; I couldn't mesh with him and share thoughts in the way I would have in the gods' realm. I wasn't even sure if it was polite to speak as gods spoke in this realm. I had to use words. "That's why I came here! I want to grow up!"

Ia shook his head. "This world has suffered much at the hands of our kind. It does not need more gods who will view its lives as playthings."

I gasped. I had never thought of it that way! The Planet Where Gods Die was also the Planet Whose Mortals Were Killed by Gods, Lots. "But mortals die all the time anyway, don't they?" Then Ia turned to look at me.

OK. I will tell you now why Ia is scary. He's *really* scary. He is one of the scariest godlings ever and I did not know this before I met him, and he gets really mad so that is why I'm telling you how not to make him mad and why you should be careful.

Remember waaaaay back at the beginning of the story when I told you about EXISTENCE and MAELSTROM and NOTH-INGNESS? And I told you the nothingness is the scariest part because at least if existence kills you there is something, and at least if the Maelstrom kills you there *was* something, but if the nothing gets you then it is like you never were in the first place?

Oh, I forgot that part. Sorry! OK, if the nothing kills you then you *become* nothing. You go away, from whereness and whatness and thenness. You stop being. You never were. Nobody will even get the griefs, because there was never anything to remember. Understand?

I don't know why not. I explained it fine.

Anyway, *that is what is in Ia*. He is negation; not just the end of something but the never-was of it. That was how he'd made the bad thing I'd done in the market go away; he made it never-be. He looked at me and suddenly I saw beneath the mortal shell he wore, and the fuzzy outline of him that had warned me against looking further. Now he let me see past the shell, and *all the nothing of him was right there*. Waiting. So scary that even the mortals nearby stumbled and looked around and started walking wider circles around us, with big scared looks on their faces. They could feel the scary, same as me, even if they could not see the scary of him or know what it meant. They could feel that the scary was super really *extra* mad.

"Mortals indeed die often, relatively speaking," he said. I was shaking. I was so scared. "So do godlings. So many, really, that I've forgotten."

I made my voice very small, and myself—the me that was me, not just the me he could see—small, too. "I didn't mean I was going to kill anybody," I said. "Um, anybody *else*, I mean. I was just asking!"

"Some questions are dangerous, Sibling. It's time you learned that."

Oh. Oh. So scared. "H-how will I know which ones I shouldn't ask if I don't ask them?"

"That comes with wisdom. Which you can gain *anywhere else*, with no one the worse off for your fumblings as you grow."

"That's not true!" I said. And then I stopped and clapped my hands over my mouth because, um. I hadn't meant to say that. I hadn't wanted to get in trouble again.

Ia is very scary, but Ia is also very wise, because Ia is really old. So he sort of squinched his eyes at me, and I knew that he knew something about me I didn't know. "Hmm."

"Huh?"

Ia didn't say anything. But right then he took hold of the world and folded it and pulled me along without bothering to ask if I wanted to go. I was so scared that I didn't complain, because I didn't want to be nothinged. The place we went to was a between-place. When the world is folded and we are not here or there but both, that is between. I saw the market and another place, gray and stony, overlapping. Ia stopped us there, where it was suddenly quiet because mortals cannot be between, and where we could talk like gods without doing any damage.

"What isn't true?" he asked. I didn't think he was mad anymore. He seemed thoughtful instead, and when he folded his arms to listen I thought maybe he was really listening now, and not just trying to get rid of me.

So I took a deep breath and said everything the best way I could. "I can't learn wisdom anywhere else," I said, because suddenly I didn't just want to stay in the mortal realm, I *needed* to. I knew it the way mortals with teeth know how to bite. "This place is, is… it's right. I can feel it making me better even now! And, and I know you don't want me to be here, even Naha told me not to come, but—but I have to stay. If I go back—" Suddenly I was unhappy. My eyes tried to get wet again, but I didn't let them because I didn't want him to think I was doing the meltdown thing again. It was really hard not to cry, though. I bit my lip instead. I hurt all over! It was worse than being scared.

Ia lifted one yellow eyebrow. "Go on."

"I was supposed to be Sieh. But I'm not Sieh. And I tried to be Sieh, except Sieh is dead so I mean I wanted to be the space that was Sieh but I didn't *fit*." I was babbling, still trying not to cry. "And everybody knows there needs to be a Sieh, the planets and suns keep calling for him, it's all wrong without him, but I'm not the one, see? I asked Papa Tempa and he said I should be myself and that the Three are happy with me but I know it's not *completely* true. They have grief over him, and I'm not enough to make it go away. He was so special, and I'm... just...me."

There weren't any other words I knew that would explain it, not even in our language. So I just stood there, looking at the blurred ground and wishing I could go to the wall of torn stars and cry where nobody would see me.

But Ia got really quiet for a moment. I didn't know why. He said, "You embody some aspect of mortality, then."

"Maybe?" I could only shrug. "Doesn't everybody?"

"Some of us predate mortality, Sibling. Our natures are those of existence itself—or things beyond existence." Yeah, like *nothing*. Ia was probably one of the really old ones, from back when the Three first learned how to make children. Like Sieh had been.

"Very well," Ia said, after a long time that felt longer. "You may remain."

"Really?" I caught my breath and bounced a little, excited. "You mean it?"

"Provided," he said, and he was all sharp and just a little mad again, "that you take the greatest of care never to cause harm to any mortal."

"I won't! I promise I'll never hurt—"

He flicked his hand. "You cannot promise that. You don't know yourself yet; you may be unable to help it. And there is danger in any interaction between gods and mortals, for both parties. This is not a safe realm, Sibling. But beyond that, I must insist that you *try* to avoid harm."

I tried to stand really tall, which was how I knew mortals showed each other they really meant a thing, but it didn't work because I was shaped like a little girl and he was twice as big. "I promise to *try*," I said. "I'll try hard! I don't want to ever hurt mortals like I did before."

"If you do," said Ia, scary again, "you will answer for it, to more than just me. Do you understand?" After I nodded hard, Ia unfolded the world so that we finally stood firmly in the gray place.

The gray place was a thing mortals called a HOUSE, which is what they used to keep their flesh safe and dry and comfortable. Some mortals carried their houses around with them, or made new ones wherever they slept, but human-mortals made places that stayed. (Sometimes they moved around, though, and swapped houses between them.) This house was bigger than the ones around it, and it had lots of space inside and a wide flat thing on top. The wide flat thing was meant to keep rain outside, but someone had also put furniture and a frame and drapes on it, so maybe it was also for living, too. The frame and drapes made a shady place underneath, and in this shady place were two mortals, who looked at us in surprise. I was surprised, too, so I asked Ia without words where we were and why.

"We are in the house of Fahno dau she Miu tai wer Tellomi kanna Enulai," Ia said aloud. "Someone you will need to know, if you mean to stay here."

In the mortals' language her name meant that Fahno was the daughter of Miu and of the clan Tellomi, and she was also part of some group of people called enulai. I didn't know what a clan or an enulai was—maybe like niwwah and elontid and mnasat, which were the different kinds of godlings? Maybe a family, like all us gods? If so, I liked that she was a daughter. I was a daughter, too! Maybe we could be friends.

But I needed to be polite now to prove to Ia that I could be here and not do bad things. I took a deep breath and spoke really softly this time when I said, "Hello!"

The two mortals looked really confused. Ia made a sound that was annoyed. "Don't *whisper.*"

"I don't want to be bad again!"

"Just speak at the same volume they do."

I whispered louder, because I was getting annoyed, too. "They haven't *said* anything."

"Then speak at the volume *I* am using," he snapped, so I tried that and said hello again, very carefully.

One of the mortals was sitting in a big, wide chair, and she was big and wide, too. The other stood beside her, because he had been showing her something on a scroll before we appeared. He was tall and narrow. I thought maybe he was younger, too, but both of them were so much older than me that I couldn't tell! I could tell that both of them wanted to laugh, though. I don't know what was so funny.

"Hello," said the wide one back. She showed her teeth; that was good! I grinned back. I was doing hello right! Then she looked at Ia and raised her eyebrows.

"*Not* mine," Ia said, looking more annoyed, which I hadn't thought was possible. "The Three have at last blessed the realms with another godling."

"That is a wondrous thing," the wide one said, looking very surprised and pleased. "And may I assume the task of raising her has been given to you? I did not think godlings did things like us mortals, but I have always thought you would father fine children, Ia."

Ia pushed his glass things up. "Godlings raise themselves, Fahno-enulai. I'm simply providing…guidance. And attempting to minimize the damage."

"That sounds like raising children, to me." She tilted her head and looked at the narrow mortal. "Arolu? Men know more of these things."

The narrow mortal, Arolu, had the laughing look, too, although he put a hand inside his sleeve and covered his mouth while he did it. "I would say no, Fahno. A child is both joy and pain, and I see only pain in Lord Ia's face."

"Yes, well." Ia turned back to the wide woman. "An expert concurs."

The wide woman shook her head. (Was she Fahnodaushe-MiutaiwerTellomikannaEnulai, or was she Fahno-enulai? I had not known that mortals had lots of names the way gods did. How did they decide which to use when?) "Enough with your chattering, both of you. You've interrupted us, Lord Ia, but since

I hadn't felt like discussing the household accounts anyway, I don't mind so much." She waved, and the narrow man sighed and straightened, tucking the scroll into his arm. Then she focused on me, and I got scared again, because I had not realized mortals could feel like gods but this one really really did. She had a big, strong presence, and I was suddenly aware that she was trying to decide if I was worth her time. I straightened up, hoping she would think so.

"Please introduce your sibling, Lord Ia," she said. "We must teach her good manners, after all."

Ia pushed up his round eye-things. "That might be difficult, Fahno—the name, that is, and not the manners. She has no name as yet."

"No name?" Fahnosomething frowned.

"We create those for ourselves, too, or choose a name from what others call us. Generally later, once we're more certain of who we are—but that is why this sibling of mine has come, in fact. She seeks to learn her nature, and thinks she might find it here among your kind."

"Fascinating." To me, Fahnosomething said, "What do your parents call you, little one?"

I jumped. "They call me You, FahnoIDon'tKnowWhichOth- erNamesToCallYou. I don't mind if you call me that, too!" Even though the mortal word for *you* was so thin and flat. It contained nothing of my essence or experiences, nothing of what Fahnosomething thought of me. It was just a syllable.

Fahno twitched, which was a funny sort of thing for her to do. "You may call me Fahno-enulai. And—I'm sorry, but we'll need something more than You to work with. Can you just choose a temporary name for now?"

I looked at Ia, frowning and trying to understand why this was so important. "Mortals cannot perceive one another's souls," he explained. "They need names, and sight and other things, to tell one another apart."

"That is so sad!" I looked at Fahno and put a hand to my mouth, because that was one of the worst things I'd ever heard. "You poor things."

"We get by," said Fahno in a wry tone. "But names are one of the, ah, coping mechanisms we use."

"Oh. OK, then." I thought really hard for a minute. Well, I was in a mortal shell, so I would start with that word. "Shell? Ssss. Ssss...shhh. Sh." I liked the roundness of the *sh* sound, and the languor of the *ll*. "Shrill?" No, but—"Shill?" It had... weight. And even meaning: in their language it was *decoy*. I was pretending to be mortal, wasn't I? "Shill." I looked at Ia, who ignored me. I looked at Fahno. "Shill? I like Shill."

"Shill it is, then." She looked me up and down. "Interesting."

"Huh?"

"Well, you appear to be a healthy Darren girl of perhaps six or seven years old. Except for your eyes—oh!" I had just made my eyes brown instead of gold, like Fahno's; she chuckled. "Ah, yes. Now you could pass for some niece or granddaughter of mine. Did you do that on purpose?"

I shrugged, because I hadn't, except the eyes, which I had, and I didn't know how to answer. "It's what other mortals on this continent look like. Also, it just felt right."

"Ah. And why did you choose that name?"

"I just picked things that sounded pretty and put them together."

"Why those syllables, though?" I blinked, and Fahno sat

forward, propping her elbows on her knees. "Even for gods, a name encapsulates some proportion of who you are. There's a reason those syllables sounded pleasant to your ear. There's a reason you combined them in that particular manner, and a reason the whole appealed to you. Perhaps you should think about that."

I inhaled and stared at her. "You know *a lot* about gods!"

She chuckled. "Thank you for noticing. That was just observation, though. I've never met a godling child before." She took a deep breath and turned to Ia again, her smile fading. "Which is why, old friend...I'm going to turn you down."

Ia frowned. "You are the best of the enulai, Fahno. If anyone can manage a newborn godling—"

"I am also the *oldest* of the enulai, Ia. I've retired! All the godlings I once looked after have been assigned to others. I haven't the energy to keep an eye on a mortal child, let alone one who can gallivant about the universe at will. I'm sorry, old friend, but I just can't."

Ia looked surprised and sad and sort of...scared? I didn't know why. It was weird that somebody so scary could be scared too! I would ask him about it later. To Fahno I said, "What's all that mean?"

I don't think Ia heard me. Fahno had a weird sad look on her face while she looked at Ia, but she said to me, "We call it the Compact, little one. An agreement made some three hundred years ago, when mortalkind finally grew weary of being caught in the gods' cross fire, and the Three left us to manage our own affairs. If you mean to do more than just visit this world now and again, if you would live among us, you must have a minder to see that you wreak a minimum of havoc. An enulai." She touched her own breast. "But I cannot be your enulai; I am too old." She paused for a moment, her gaze flicking back to Ia again. "I think my dear friend forgot that even we demons eventually grow old, and die."

And that is when I screamed and ran away to another galaxy.

OK that was not my fault. Naha told me all about demons! She said they were full of POISON and they can make me die and they are as bad as NOTHINGNESS and MAELSTROM except they have killed way more gods and that is why I ran away!

But Ia came and got me and told me I was being stupid and rude and I should stop. He told me how enulai are, yes, demons who have agreed to keep an eye on godlings so they don't do bad things, and how that is only fair because it is the mortals' planet, after all, even if we have earned the right to be on it by fighting for it and dying on it and making children there. (*Demon* children!) And he said the demons will not kill me unless I do bad things to mortals, so don't do bad things and everything will be fine.

I was still scared until Ia finally got mad and made himself scarier and so finally I went back to Fahno and said I was sorry. Ia is mean and I do not like him at all, and it's not fair that he's so strong because I don't think he should be, I don't care how old he is.

Anyway. Fahno accepted my apology and told me I could stay with her and her family while she tried to find another enulai for me. I was happy then because I would see what it was like to live like a mortal! And that is when I realized Fahno had said it to distract me so I wouldn't be so scared anymore, but she meant it, too, so that is OK. It worked and I was happy again.

"You really are just a child," she said after all this, shaking her head.

"Well, of *course* I am," I said. Mortals were very strange.

After that Ia said he was tired of dealing with me and went away. Arolu took me to another part of the house and showed me a room that had things for me to use while I was staying there. One of them was called a BED and it was for lying on during sleep! But godlings do not sleep so I asked Arolu what I should do instead.

"I'm sure you can find some way to occupy yourself," he said. "But do it quietly, please, because the mortals of the house will be sleeping."

Then he told me about the house's library, and I was really happy because I had heard of books! I sat down to teach myself to read and promised to be very quiet all night. I was, too, once Arolu left. OK, I got bored and made up a song to sing but I sang it in sounds mortals can't hear. The song went *Hey hey hey hello hello hello how are you I am fine I have a name it is Shill.* But nobody heard me.

(I liked Arolu. He was big and his voice was always warm and he had lots and lots of long black hair, which reminded me a little of Naha. I asked him if anybody ever got lost in his hair, and he sort of blushed and said that was a question only a wife should ask. I didn't know what that meant.)

Some time passed. It was not even a year, but it felt much longer. Time in the mortal realm is very strange! All the mortals went to bed and got very quiet, so I dissipated my body and went to go look at them. Mortal sleep is not very interesting to watch. They just lie there and fart and dream. One of the bedrooms in the house was empty, but there was a familiar smell all over it. I wasn't sure what made it familiar, so I went back to wandering through the house.

And then I got annoyed. Everything was boring! The mortal realm was supposed to be fun! I decided I just wasn't seeing enough of it, and jumped out the window to go exploring.

The city we were in was called ARREBAIA. It told me its name with the wind and the mortals' thoughts. It was really old! Way older than me, but everything was older than me so that didn't matter. It had big stone walls all over the place, holding dirt in terraces for the mortals' gardens and streets and markets, and it was full of heavy old cubes and pyramids that the mortals lived in. It was a perfect city for playing in.

So I ran down a pyramid! I ran up a cube! I jumped into a penned-in place and there was an animal called an ALPACA! I petted it; it liked me. I ran down the street with my arms out, which made the mortals turn and stare, but I did not care because it was nighttime and I missed Naha. (I was really fast, anyway, so the mortals did not have to look at me for very long.) There was bright shiny moonlight on my skin and nice cool air and I think I ate a bug. It tasted awful! There were all sorts of things everywhere, and they were amazing! I loved them all.

But then! I heard something!

Something jumpy and beaty and steady and off-steady. I did not know what it was! It was way over on the other side of town, not too far from Fahno's house, so I ran back as fast as I could (and maybe I folded spacetime a little, but just a little, so that is not cheating). The beaty sound was coming from the forest outside town, right where its edge stopped against the city's outermost terrace-wall. I hopped over the wall and went into the trees, which was hard because the trees were big and tangly and wet and I was making so much noise that I worried I would scare the beaty sound. I turned into a lizard, and that made it easier. The smell of humans got thick, and then I saw a campfire through the trees, and the beaty sound was a *feeling* too now, all heavy and pounding down in my lizard-guts.

Then I got through the trees and gasped—because it was another city! A little bitty city, just a few buildings and they were empty, just a few streets and they were made of dirt, just two terraces and they grew wild, not planted or lived on at all. But it was a real city, because it was fierce and angry and it said *who are you* so I said who I was and then I asked who it was. It had a little bitty name, too: YUKUR. Arrebaia means "the city of the conquerors," but Yukur is just "the men's place." Still, I told the city that Yukur was a very pretty name, because I wanted to be nice.

Yukur sort of huffed and told me I was not supposed to be there because I was not really a boy, but it was maybe OK because I was shaped like a lizard, and anyway I was a godling so it could not stop me. I could tell that it did not like me being there, though, so I made my lizard body into a boy lizard body, and promised I would only wear a boy body, or no body at all, while I was in the city's limits. Then it was happy, and I was glad, because I had done the hello thing right again.

I skittered down a wall and up some steps and then jumped into some bushes when people went by: two boys, all aflutter in their pretty robes and long hair, rushing up the steps like they were late for something. I could hear one of them whisper to the other, "It's Eino tonight!" I didn't know what that meant.

(I know *you* know, but I am telling the story! Shut up! Interrupting is rude.)

The other boy giggled and then they both were gone up the steps. I followed them but it was slow because I was only a little lizard. I decided to be human instead, but since I had said I would be a boy, I made a boy body. Every boy I had seen since coming to the mortal realm—except Ia, but he was weird—wore heavy drapey robes and long hair, so I made myself like that, too, and ran after the two I had seen. It is hard to run when you are covered from neck to toe in robes, though, and when your hair is four feet long, and also when you have stuff between your legs that dangles and flops around! I did not like any of it, but I had made a promise. Eventually I figured out that I had to hold my head really high and gather up my robes, and run in this weird very straight way or I would hurt the dangly bits—but if I did all this, I could run like those other boys.

And I wanted to run! There was another sound over the beats that had drawn me to Yukur: deep and rough and rhythmic mortal voices. I did not know what it was, but it made me bouncy; I wanted to make the sounds, too, and move with the beats. I could have just dissipated and gone to see as a godling, but this was a mortal thing, all body-stuff, pounding blood and tingly skin and heavy breath. I needed mortalness to know what it all meant.

Finally I got to the top of the terrace. And! I saw!

Fires and smoke! And lots of boys all gathered in a circle! Some of them were to the side of the group, hitting things made of wood and leather which is what made the beaty noise—drums; Itempas had told me all about them. The rest of the boys were trotting about for a better position in the circle, or already in the circle, moving all together and making sounds in time with the beats, some high and some low and all of it together beautiful. Exciting! So this was MUSIC! It is not like the music in the gods' realm, which is why I did not recognize it at first. Only two beats overlapping, no harmonies or clicks or static or interweaving thoughts, and the beats were not even as fast as pulsar-beats. The boys' singing was not especially interesting, either, just words chanted over and over, a couple of tones harmonizing. It was catchy, though, and I liked it even if it was very simple. I moved forward a few feet behind the boys I had seen before, who were still whispering as they edged into the circle of other boys. Most of the boys around us were bigger, older, with heavy jaws and deep voices and big shoulders beneath their robes. They moved aside as us younger ones came through, though, grinning down at us in welcome, and I could not help smiling shyly back. One of the big boys patted me on the back. "It's all right," he said. "You don't have to, if you don't want to. Just do what feels right."

"OK," I said, not really knowing what else to say. It must have been right, because the big one pushed me forward, closer to the circle's center, so I could see.

And then it was WOW I had never seen COOL I really liked WHEE there was stuff going SWISH and legs going KICK and IT WAS AMAZING.

What? Oh, fine, I will say it better. OK. The boys in the circle were *fighting*.

It did not look like fighting, not at first, because everything was swirling robes and looping rivers of hair. It looked like dancing, or what Papa Tempa had said dancing looked like. It was harder than dancing, though, faster, and the feel of it was not about the music. The boys rode the music, but they were focused on each other, and everything in them was all fierce! And wanting to win! One boy's foot came out from a swirl of robe and swept the other's ankle and that one fell back but caught himself to turn the fall into a flip. He swirled away, always swirling, everything a circle. Suddenly I understood: it was *supposed* to look like a dance, even if it was really a fight!

And I wanted to fight-dance, too, watching them! I did dance a little, because the drums were so nice, and because the boys' song pulled me along like the Maelstrom when It is hungry. But I wanted to do the other dance, too!

Then somebody called out, and the drums stopped, and the boys at the center ended their swirls and faced each other. I could feel how much they wanted to keep fighting, but instead each one of them crossed a big wide sleeve over his face and dipped down on one leg for a minute, which said *respect* in the language without words. Then they went back into the circle, and all the boys around us cheered and stamped and the air got hot with joy!

But then everybody got quiet, shushing and elbowing each other, more excited for some reason. I turned to look where everyone else was looking, and gasped when they gasped as another boy stepped through the crowd. I don't know why they gasped. *I* gasped because even though this boy was just a mortal like all the rest, he wasn't wearing any of the robey things boys in Darr liked to wear. He had on loose pants, and the slipper-shoes boys wear, but above the pants he didn't have on anything except brown skin! The boy had a lot of hair like all the others, too, but his was all clipped up on top of his head in big loopy knots. The starkness of him was like a slap in the eyeballs.

I also gasped because I recognized him! It was the boy from the market. His was the scent I had detected in the empty room of Fahno's house; there had been echoes of Fahno in it because they were related somehow. And now I knew why he hadn't been there, even though all the mortals in Fahno's house were supposed to be asleep. He looked different from that day in the market in other ways: *darker,* somehow. More vibrant, more fierce, with more of his true self showing through the skin— like Naha when the wildness comes. When the boy stepped forward, holding up his arms to get everyone's attention, all the other boys breathed together, ensnared. Of course they were! In that moment, I was, too. He felt like another god.

"Eino," said one of the boys I'd followed. He said it the same way I said, *the Three.*

"Comes the midnight," Eino said, turning with his arms still spread. "Comes the moondown. 'Tis the Nightlord's time, all deepfine and cool and scary. 'Tis the time when boys—*men*— come out to play."

Laughter rippled through the boys, and someone whooped on the other side of the circle; there were other shouts, stamping feet, raised fists trailing colored robe-sleeves. Eino laughed, too, throwing his head back so that the cords of his long neck stood out. I had never realized mortals could be like this. I had no idea why he was talking so funny, either, but it was perfect for the moment, for the moonlight, for the boys' excitement. When he hissed and ran forward and leapt into the middle of the circle, landing in a crouch, everyone hissed, too, some of them crouching, too, moving to Eino's rhythm the same way they'd moved to the drums before. "Time for the midnight dance!" cried one, and others took up the cry, punching the air and swirling and swaying even without music. When Eino drew himself up, though, straight and taut with one hand held out in invitation, everyone got quiet again.

"Go on," whispered one boy nearby to another. But that one shook his head.

"It's Eino!" That was another boy. I think it was supposed to make everyone excited, and it did. "Eino!"

"I don't know." "You can!" "You can do it!" "Look at how strong he is." "He's one of us." "Do it and see!" So much wanting, from all the boys around me. So many whispers, so many hopes, so much fear. That was when I finally understood: everybody was excited because Eino was offering to dance with one of them. He just wanted a volunteer!

Well, that was easy.

"I'll do it!" I jumped up and down, waving my hand. Everybody got quiet, then moved aside so there was nothing between me and Eino.

Eino tilted his head and lowered his hand. He was so still, all shining skin and muscle in the firelight. His eyes were very black, too. "Haven't seen you before. Or have I?" His eyes narrowed, and even though I was wearing a different body, I got nervous. Maybe he could see my soul? Mortals weren't supposed to be able to do that. He shook his head, finally, and I relaxed. "Shed those window-drapes the women have put on you, baby boy. Here in our place we dance like Nahadoth, shadows and chaos, feeling the dark with our skin."

Eagerly I threw off the robes, which I didn't like anyway, until I had on nothing but pants and slippers like him. He grinned when I tried to stand like him, mostly failing because he was much bigger and prettier, almost a man. I was shaped like a boy, but still just a little one. "Nice. You're feeling it." He jerked his head toward my head, though, and I remembered the long hair. Hastily I tied it in a big knot at the back of my head, and he nodded approval. "Let's dance, then."

He came at me, no pause and no preparation—not straight on, though. It was the circling of before, the swirling dance, in and out and revolving. Since he wasn't wearing robes or hair I could see it better now. I stood for a minute, getting the feel of it, then clumsily tried to move like he did; everyone laughed, at first.

But then—oh. Ohhhh. The chanting started again. The foot-stomping shook the fires, making the light jump, sound and sight in rhythm, cacophony given meaning, and that made it just the tiniest bit like the gods' realm. Then it became easy to mimic the way Eino sort of jog-jumped into the circle and back, and to use the momentum the way he did, turning and turning, arms out, legs flying. At once I could feel the way moving in circles made the center of me almost unshakable. I could dart in unpredictable directions even while seeming to follow a pattern! Eino was circling on his side of the circle, waiting for me to get the hang of it, but that was no fun! I darted toward him and back. *Come at me!* Eino puffed out an approving sort of laugh, and then the dance really got started.

Oh, it was perfect. No drums this time, but none were needed; the boys' voices were heavy and deep, their movements in unison like a guide. I went to the ground when Eino did, planting my hands in the dust and kicking out with my legs, laughing and breathless when he dodged me effortlessly with a backflip, delighted even when he leapt back and slammed me to the ground. It hurt, but what was pain? The dance became everything. The dance was worship, and strength, and better magic than anything I'd ever known in my short life. "I am!" I cried, and maybe it was boy-language and maybe it was god-language but it did not matter because it had the same meaning either way! Eino felt it, too, and he answered me in kind with sweat and ferocity and magic. Now when he threw a fist at me the movement said FORCE and it hit me really hard! If I had been mortal I would've gone flying; several of the boys in the ring behind me cried out and fell. But I laughed and said back WIND, silly! And I spun the force away in a gust that made everybody's pretty long hair whip around. Then Eino stomped the ground and I felt the verb of his muscles shout SHATTER, and the ground cracked in a line of rubble from his feet toward mine. (His eyes got really big, but the dance had him; he had no time to react, beyond this.) So I jumped up high, like ten feet into the air, and I said WHEE without words and he stopped staring at the ground and stared at me instead. The dance! He started to grin. Then he jumped, too, not as high but just right, and we both landed in a spin. We spun and *spun*, our circle getting wider as the other boys backed away, the earth shaking harder, the chanting growing louder and harsher and faster until—

Everything stopped.

I was mid-leap when the world suddenly narrowed to a fine point, and my whole self shifted and flexed and rang like a bell.

I understood. I *understood something new*!

"Power," I said softly. I uncurled myself from the leap and stuck to the air in surprise. "That must be part of it!"

"Yes," said Nahadoth, who curled out of the shadows of the crowd.

I turned happily. "Naha!" She materialized in grace and silence and movement, the swirls of her substance licking and flickering round every boy nearby. Their abandon fed her and she fed them in turn, for this was her time and they had invoked her spirit. The fire went out as she passed, the logs pop-hissing as they frosted over—but the moonlight above, and that from her face, was more than enough to see by.

"Look how you've grown," she said. "Multiple shapes, new perspectives, new languages... *Shill*."

I beamed, putting my hands on my hips. "Yes, Naha! Hello, hello! I made that name up myself. Do you like it?"

"It is beautiful." I could not be sure if she was talking about me, though, because she had stopped to stare at Eino, frozen as he was in mid-lunge. For a moment a look that was avid, almost greedy, came over Nahadoth's face, and I started to get worried. Eino had spoken Naha's name in the dark. Even I knew that was never safe.

Maybe I could make her think about something else. "Naha, I think I found a little bit of my nature! It's power!"

"Yes." She was reaching out to touch Eino's face. I got really nervous, because I liked Eino—but she just drew a finger over his lips, so I relaxed. "Not *your* power, though."

"I—" Oh. "Huh?"

"Can you not see?" Naha was behind Eino now, staring intently at his back like she wanted to hollow him out and live in his skin. "Look, Shill. We made your eyes from the stuff of the Maelstrom Itself. See *everything*."

So I looked again, really hard, and then I looked some more, and then I got bored and started thinking about whether power had anything to do with being a trickster like I wanted, I mean what if I ended up being something weird like the godling of lizards or something, I didn't want to be weird, and then all of a sudden I saw all the realms and all the paths and all the lines of meaning that mortals could not.

"Oh!" I dropped to the ground and trotted over to one of the boys standing frozen around us. There it was: a little *bloorp* of intention, of devotion, running from him to Eino. "And oh!" I ran over to another boy; another *bloorp*, like a thread made of bubbles, or maybe heat haze. A tie. A web. They were all of them, every boy at that camp, fixed on Eino. Every one of them had given him something of themselves, making him stronger; every one of them would die for him. Because of the dance? I did not know. But even I had a little, thin link to him. Mine, however, glowed gold-white, and it ran in both directions. I was making him stronger, but he was making me stronger at the same time. I didn't know what that meant.

"We make them in our image," Nahadoth breathed, "and they replicate us endlessly in their own."

I didn't understand at all, but that was pretty normal when talking to Naha. I just shrugged.

When Naha stepped out from behind Eino, I finally noticed how the little city Yukur was shivering, the very bricks of it radiating awe and fear at her presence. It did not protest her being there, though the shape she wore was female now, because she was even less a she than I was the he I seemed to be. It would not have mattered much if Yukur had protested, though; Nahadoth was Nahadoth. Rules meant nothing to the god of chaos and change.

I trotted over to stand before her; at once the tendrils of her swept round me, possessive. "I know you didn't want me to come here, Naha," I said, earnestly. "I . . . I hope you're not mad."

She looked amused, cupping my face in her hands. "I have no interest in *obedient* children." Then the light of her face dimmed, and for some reason she looked away, southward. There was nothing south except that other continent of the planet; what was she thinking about, looking that way? "But beware, Shill. Never underestimate mortals—especially not where power is involved. Not even when they have power of their own already." She looked at Eino again, and this time the look was cold. "They always crave more."

I nodded solemnly, even though I did not understand this, either. I was *more* now, smarter maybe, but some things were not about smarts.

Naha left off glaring at Eino to look up at the moon, which echoed her face, quick-switch as always. "'Comes the moon-down,'" she said, thoughtful. It could have meant lots of things. "You should warn them, by the way."

And then, because that was how Naha said good-bye, she faded away.

A moment later time snapped back into place. The chanting boys resumed and then faltered, startled; the leaping blur that was Eino landed and stumbled; the boys nearest the fire gasped and jerked in surprise when they found it suddenly extinguished and icy-cold.

And suddenly Eino stared at me, recognizing me at last through the boy-flesh and the dance-haze. "*You.*"

Whoops. "Oh. Um. Hello." Everyone stared at me; for the

first time, this was really uncomfortable. To distract them, I added, "I'm, um, supposed to warn you about something."

Everything was quiet for long enough to make me squirm. Then Eino suddenly flinched and inhaled and looked away, toward the entrance to Yukur. His eyes widened. "Oh, slippy-dicked *hells*."

Everyone looked where he was looking. There was nothing to see—but I didn't need eyes to see, and clearly Eino didn't, either. Along the half-hidden road that led to Yukur came a bunch of women, all skintight and teeth-bared and cruel-cold. I could not hear their thoughts because they weren't thinking very loud, but I could taste their intent anyway, because that was not a thought but a feeling: anticipation. Hunting-lust, and maybe other kinds, too. For... for... I inhaled. They were coming for all the boys here!

Right in that moment, one of the boys near the edge of the terrace saw the women's torches through the trees. We all heard his broken-voiced shout, though I couldn't make out the words, and suddenly boys in that direction cried out and began to scatter—some down another set of steps toward the trees on Yukur's other side, some toward us and away from the women, some down the main terrace steps and right toward them.

"No!" Eino's voice had the deepness of a near man; most of them heard him. "No, don't run! We have to stand together—face them—demonshit!"

No one was listening. I had no idea what was happening, but I thought maybe people should listen to Eino. *HEY!* I said with god-talk into all the boy-heads around. Not all of them heard me even then; some of them were too afraid. But most of the boys stopped or stumbled, and turned back to stare at Eino as if he'd been the one to yell at them.

Eino threw me a quick glance; I didn't know if he was mad or what. But he waved his arms at the boys. "Here! To me!" He turned to the boys nearby, herding them toward the rear of the dance-terrace where the firelight did not reach and the shadows of the surrounding forest were flickery and subtle. Oh! I saw what he meant to do! I grinned and trotted along with him, as more of the boys who had heard me ran to join him, huddling together and whispering in harsh, fearful voices.

"Hush!" Eino's hiss stilled them. He stepped in front of them, facing the stairs and spreading his arms as if to cloak the boys behind him, though there were at least twenty of them and he did not have hair that moved like Naha's. And yet—hee! After a moment the shadows around us stretched, weaving together and becoming less dappled, more solid, more obscure... until when the first woman came up the steps, dragging a panting boy with her, she saw nothing. We were invisible to mortal eyes.

More women came up, some of them also hauling boys who struggled or stumbled along with heads bowed or faces tear-streaked. But as the first woman looked around and didn't see us even though we were standing right there, her brows drew together in a scowl. "This is it?"

Another woman crouched by the boys' fire, which had thawed out and looked as though it hadn't been lit in ages. Clever Naha! "Looks like. Unless the others fled into the forest?"

"Bunch of untrimmed boys in the forest, at night, in a tither? We'll never see them again," muttered another woman.

"Demonshit. I don't want to hear it in Council if one of them gets eaten by a jaguar. Spread out beyond the city, try to pick up trails." The first woman glared at the cold fire. Then she yanked around the boy she held, to face her. "I heard more voices than just you few. Where'd the rest go?"

"I . . . I do not know, medre."

She did something to his arm that I couldn't see because of all his robes. He made a sound that was tight and terrible. She was hurting him! I almost gasped, but that would have given away Eino's group—and already Eino was dripping sweat, his face tight with concentration and his arms trembling with effort. I did not know why. It was not a hard thing he was doing.

"I don't know!" The boy did not show his pain much, but even the little that tightened his jaw and thinned his lips was terrible. "I didn't see!"

"*Stop* that," said the woman by the fire, glowering. "You want to explain away bruises to his mother or sisters?"

The first woman rolled her eyes, but stopped doing whatever she was doing; I relaxed as the boy did. Then she grinned. "Well, there's other ways to find out what you've been up to. Right, pretty?" She stepped closer and put a hand down between them, feeling for something amid his robes; he gasped and jerked away, but she pulled him back. "No telling what you boys do when you're alone, trying to play woman for each other. Maybe I should check to see if you're still intact? Maybe I should make you less intact, take you to my house instead of yours." She fumbled with his robes, trying to pull them up. He went rigid, his eyes full of tears. I did not like it *at all* and I wanted to do bad things to her! But if I did, it would give away Eino's group.

"Brightness and shadows, Veiba." The woman by the fire,

who felt like a leader, came over and dragged the boy away from her; Veiba laughed, as the boy turned his face away and trembled. "We don't have time for that sort of foolishness."

With that, the leader turned and whistled in two tones. From steps and terraces and the nearby woods around Yukur—Yukur was really mad! All those womenfeet on its stones!—other whistles answered her in different tones, different tunes. The woman sighed. "No trails out of the site but those of the few we've caught. We lost them."

"These few are enough," said Veiba. "It's proof they've been sneaking out, coming here."

The other women murmured agreement; finally the leader sighed. Raising her voice, she called, "Hear the decree of the Warriors' Council! By their word is this place of traitors forbidden now and henceforth. Come again and we *will* catch you, and name you traitors, too. Come forth now for amnesty; we will see you escorted home." She glanced at Veiba in plain warning. "*Safely.*"

She paused for a moment, listening. That's when I heard Eino panting really hard! He was going to give us away! I didn't understand why, but he was almost out of magic. That was weird, so I touched his back and gave him some more. He jumped and looked at me in a surprised way, but it was enough. He stopped panting, and when the moment of silence passed, the leader shook her head and held up her fist in a signal. All the women turned and started heading back down the steps, bringing the boys they'd caught with them. But those were only a few of the boys who'd been in the dance-circle! We were *the best* at hide-and-seek.

When the strange women were finally gone, Eino let the

magic go and sagged to the ground on his hands and knees. The other boys hugged each other and some of them cried a little and the rest went down next to Eino, praying or rubbing his back or whispering quiet, *Thank the gods.* (I poked my lip out at this. They should be thanking the godling! Stupid mortals.)

"Hey," I said, hunkering down next to Eino to peer at him once some of the other boys had withdrawn. "You want some more magic? I have lots."

He looked up at me with the strangest look on his face. "Wh-why?"

"Huh?"

"*Why?* Why are you here? Why did you help us?"

I blinked, but I didn't know how to answer the questions, so I just kind of shrugged. "I'm really sorry," I said, partly also to Yukur. Yukur just sent a wave of snittiness back; it would be mad for a century about this. I sighed. "I didn't mean to interrupt the thing you and the others were doing."

Eino's jaw tightened. He sat back on his knees abruptly. "You at least joined in and didn't break the spirit of it. That lot, though"—he nodded after the strange women—"were probably retaliation for that little trick I pulled on the Council this afternoon. We've danced out here before, many times, and no one ever troubled us." He shook his head, sobering. "Gods. An actual raid. I must have really pissed them off."

"What do you mean?" I hunkered forward; he was speaking softly, like he didn't want the other boys to know, so I did it, too. "What was in that paper thing you made me take into the Raringa?"

"An idea they clearly didn't want to consider. I'll tell you later." He looked around at the other boys, who had withdrawn into knots and were talking quietly to each other now. "Can you send them home? The hunters will be watching the trails, after that."

"Huh? Oh! Yeah!"

"A moment, then." Eino got to his feet, taking a deep breath and turning to the other boys. "You weren't here, friends. If the ones they caught say that you were, you'll be home safe in your beds in a moment to belie them. There's no proof; remember that."

Some of the boys let out relieved sighs. But another one who was tall and older like Eino frowned. "Eino, I can't do this anymore. If I'd been caught... my mother's carting business depends on me marrying into Selu-medre's clan. The scandal—"

"Scandal!" A younger boy made an angry gesture. "You weren't out here cavorting with foreign women or siring daughters for free, for gods' sake—"

"Enough." Eino looked weary and angry and some other stuff besides. "There'll be time for recriminations later. If you don't want to come next time, then don't come. It'll be some time before I do this again, anyway, to let things cool down." His expression turned bitter. "I never dreamt they would find something so simple so threatening."

The older boy frowned, but before he could ask, Eino glanced at me. I looked at the other boys and felt the places in the world where they were supposed to be, the place each called home, and I made little folds to put each of them in those places. (Some of them were surprised! I giggled at them.) After a moment, only me and Eino remained at the top of the terrace. He stared out over Yukur, the edges of his thoughts tasting thick and bitter. "There," I said. "You want to go now, too? I have to go back to

Fahno-enulai's anyway; I'm staying with her 'til she finds me an enulai."

He drew back a little at this, then sighed. "Of course you are. But I don't want to go back yet." His jaw tightened. "How did you do that?"

"Do what?"

He made an odd gesture with his hand, and I felt it: a tiny wave of the FORCE he had thrown during the dance. "I've never been able to do that before."

I shrugged. "I dunno why you *didn't*, but you *could*. Isn't that what the dance was for?"

He turned his head a little, so I saw how he frowned. "It was just a dance. I found descriptions of it in a book, images of it in an old sphere. Nothing I learned said it was supposed to be magical."

"Well, it was." I shrugged. "The moves were not magic by themselves, but you made them magic because you told them to be, and the universe listened. Together you and the dance said stuff like *sha ejuviat*, and *wahek akekkipu*."

Eino twitched. "You're speaking godwords."

"Um, yeah! 'Cause I'm a god?" I tried not to roll my eyes. Papa Tempa told me that mortals don't believe things even when they see them, sometimes, so you had to say stuff that was obvious. Silly mortals. "Oh. Do you need me to tell you what I said in mortal?" I tried to think of how to translate, but mortal words are all wrong for stuff like that.

"No," he said, slowly, frowning to himself. "I...understood what you said."

Oh, well then. "So, you were speaking godwords yourself in the dance—just, you know, without godwords. Probably because you're a demon, too, if you're related to Fahno-enulai? I dunno. But that's why the dance was full of magic. You were dancing with a god, and everything we do is magic, and you're more magic than most mortals, so you danced it, too." It had been so much fun! I did a little hop, remembering the dance, and stomped the ground once—but only a little, because Yukur didn't need anybody else messing it up.

He turned to face me, looking troubled. "I know some magic," he said, slowly. "My grandmother taught me enough to control myself, and to protect myself. But that takes concentration, practice. I've never done magic *by accident*."

I stopped play-dancing, puzzled. "You didn't do it by accident. You *wanted* to hit me, even though we were only play-hitting. You wanted the ground to shatter beneath your feet."

"That's it? I want something enough, and it happens?"

"Well, that's how it works when *I* do it. But I don't need the dancing. And I never saw anybody run out of magic before! Maybe because you're mortal?"

He stared at me without answering for so long that I got bored and started spinning around, humming the boys' chant.

"I need to know if you're going to tell my family about this," he said finally. "Since you're staying with us."

I stopped humming, although I kept spinning, because it was fun. "Tell them about what?"

Having become more sophisticated, now I could tell better when mortals were wary or surprised or disbelieving, and he was all three. "About *this*. Some of the boys they caught will talk." His jaw flexed. "They'll have to. Some of them will say that this was my gathering. But like I told the others, without corroboration, it will just be rumor. Rumors can't—" He paused, then laughed in an angry sort of way. "Well, they can hurt me. But not as much as proof, and they won't have that."

"Oh." I shrugged. "I won't tell if you don't want me to. But why aren't you supposed to be here, if that's the problem? And why were those women so mean?" I stopped spinning and scowled after them, and wished that bad things would happen to Veiba. My first curse! I didn't know if it would work, but I sure hoped it would.

Eino shook his head. "They were cruel because that's what people are, sometimes. And we weren't supposed to be here because good clan-sons don't do such things. We stay home where it's safe. We obey without question. We don't go out late at night unchaperoned to cavort like barbarians. And we don't demand, via unsigned proposals slipped unseen into the Council's 'new business' docket, that men be granted again the rights that we justifiably lost centuries ago!"

I was really confused. "Huh?"

Eino sighed and looked around, finding his discarded robes and shaking them out. Some of the other boys had trampled them; he grimaced and brushed ineffectually at the footprints until I willed them all away. He let out a little wry chuckle, then nodded thanks and began to put on the robes in layers: first a long narrow sleeveless sheath of the same stuff as his loose pants, then a simple black robe, then the voluminous, brightly dyed outer robe, which had strange seams and extra lengths of cloth and weird unnecessary leather belts. It was very complicated. I grimaced over at my own discarded robes, disliking them just because of watching him.

"We come to Yukur," he said, as he got dressed, "because once, a long time ago, a rebellion started here."

I knew what a rebellion was! A long long time ago, like a whole three hundred years, a godling called Kahl Avenger had tried to do bad things. Everybody was still upset about it. "And everybody is still upset about it." I was trying to sound wise.

"No, it was ages ago; everyone who lived through that time is long dead. And the rebels were fools." Eino scowled, stepping into his slippers. "They hoped that a few weapons and help from Tokken and Menchey—nations that were our enemies back then—would allow them to overthrow the government and establish a different rule. *Male* rule, in the foreign fashion of things. But the Darre were warriors then, much more than now, and the rebellion was put down. Harshly."

Well, that wasn't a very good story! "What happened to them?"

"Tried as traitors and executed or exiled. And then, even though men had helped to fight back against the rebels, even though a man was ennu, the nation's leader, at the time . . . the women took away any rights the men possessed." Eino shook his head, flicking at wrinkles and making minute adjustments to his robes. "To vote, to hold property, to occupy any positions of worth, even to be counted adults in their own right. It was a reaction against everything seen as a contribution to the rebellion: the weak ennu, a war that had decimated the country a few decades before, foreign influences. But that's why now, a bunch of boys gathering to have fun brings down fifty hells' worth of wrath." He sighed and shook his head. "Or maybe that was me. That scroll I had you deliver—it was a proposal to grant men inheritance rights. It probably had no chance of passing, but I just wanted them to *consider* it, for gods' sake. Instead, it just seems to have made them angry. Hells." He began to take the combs out of his hair, letting it fall back into its usual black river.

I felt really sad and flat then, all the fun of the dance gone. "Why do you do things like this, then? Dance when you're not supposed to, ask for things that make people mad? Wouldn't it be easier to just..." I shrugged. I didn't really know how to say it.

He let out a sharp sort of laugh that didn't sound like he actually thought anything was funny. "You really *are* new to this realm, aren't you? You don't know mortals very well."

I nodded, glad to finally have the conversation return to something I understood. "I'm new to everything. You are the first mortal I ever met."

"The first—" Eino frowned. "You do seem...inexperienced. And, well, young. But one can never tell with godlings; forgive me if you're actually a billion years old."

I had to count on my fingers, and multiply by the spins of this galaxy's wheel, and then by the expansion of the universe, and some other things. Time is annoying. "I'm almost a thousand hours old!"

"A thousand—" He got an odd look on his face. "Hours?"

Oh, wait, he had used years. But I needed the next thing smaller than a year. "Um, a month?"

He stared at me. "You're *one month old?*"

"And, like, ten days." It wasn't like I was still a *baby*.

After a long, silent stretch he burst out laughing, and it was almost a mean laugh but not quite. "Gods, this is my luck! But I suppose I should thank you—er."

"Shill! My name is Shill!"

He inclined his head in a formal sort of way. "Eino mau Tehno tai wer Tellomi, Shill-medre." Son of Tehno, of the same clan as Fahno, and he'd given my name a suffix that just meant he wanted to be polite to a strange woman. I beamed, delighted, especially since I was still wearing a boy body. "Lady Shill, rather. I don't know if I would've been able to keep the others hidden, without you."

"You're welcome! I would have done it for you, though, if you'd asked, so then you wouldn't be so tired. That would be my thank-you for the dancing. Or fighting." I frowned, confused.

Eino smiled. "Both. In the days before the traitors, that was how men fought to hide their strength from—and display their beauty to—women. It was called *anatun*, the battle-dance."

"I like anatun! I became more of myself while dancing with you." Eagerly I grabbed one of the dangly parts of his sleeve; this, finally, was what I needed to talk to him about. "Will you help me?"

His expression grew wary. "Help you do what?"

"I don't know what I am." I bit my lip. Mortals had different ways of saying it. How had Ia explained it to Fahno? "I don't know my . . . nature. But lots of godlings, they come to this realm and meet mortals who help them figure themselves out. I think you can be that person for me!"

Eino flinched and glared at my hands until I let go of his robes. "No," he said, in a cold scary way that made me think of Mama Yeine. "*You destroyed the city by accident*, Lady Shill. You think I don't remember, just because Lord Ia cleaned up your mess? I'm grateful for your help, but go find your nature with someone else as your prop. I have my own troubles."

"But it only happened with you! And I only found a little bit of me!" He set his jaw and turned away, starting toward and down the terrace steps; anxiously I trotted after him, trying desperately to think of how I could convince him. "Maybe—um—maybe I can help you?"

Eino stopped. Fully robed, with his hair perfect, he was so different from the wild master of the dance that he seemed like a whole other person. I didn't know which was the real him, and which wasn't. Maybe he was both. In this shape, however, his expression didn't change; his whole face was like a mask. "What do you mean?"

"I...I don't know." I twisted some grass beneath my toe; it didn't mind. "I could do more god-stuff for you, I guess?" He had so little magic. "Anything you want, if I know how to do it."

His eyes narrowed. "You'd do my bidding? In exchange for... what, exactly?"

Oh, this! I inhaled. "Let me follow you around and do stuff like you do and talk to you and watch how you do things and maybe be your friend!"

Eino's expression turned sardonic. "Just that."

"Well...yes. I need to *understand* you." This, I felt sure, was the key to learning my nature. And then I gasped. "Oh! Maybe you could be my enulai, too!"

Something changed minutely in his expression. "No."

"Why not? You're a d-demon, aren't you?" I still shivered when I said it.

"Yes, I am." He smiled, but it was another not-happy smile. "I am the only child or grandchild of Fahno, greatest enulai of the age, who's inherited her gift. But I'm told I don't have the *temperament* to be an enulai."

I remembered Eino yelling at me in the market when I'd stood there blubbering. "Uh, I don't think whoever told you that was right."

He blinked, then for the first time since the raid, he smiled in a good way.

After a moment he sighed. "Very well, then, Lady Shill." He extended his hand; not quite sure what else to do, I took it. "I suppose you've been helping me all along, lately. We might as well formalize the relationship. Only until Beba assigns you a proper enulai, though. And only if you tell no one; I'm in enough trouble as it is."

I gasped in delight. An enulai! A *secret* enulai, all mine! "OK!"

"In the meantime—" He tilted his head with perfect grace. "Home, please?"

"OK!" I was so happy that I took his hand and did exactly what he wanted, right then and there.

OK OK OK OK WAAAAAIT. (This is how Mama Yeine likes to tell stories. I don't tell Papa Tempa that I like her storying, too, even if it is not the Proper Way.)

Now I will tell you about other stuff that was happening, because mortal stuff is very tiny stuff compared to everything else that's always going on. And this other stuff is important! You need to know it, too, because you are really new, like me.

THERE IS A BIG HOLE IN EXISTENCE. Can you see it? Mortals can't, but you can. Look right there. Look look look! Now tilt your head and squint. And now *laheelishrinjael jyama, shu enwa owamehikach. Ashkayeerikajishge ichttu. Ichttu, ichttu!* No, your other left. See it now?

Yes, it is really big. That is where the Maelstrom punched through. The Three have patched over the hole, and it is healing; Naha says it should be fine in a couple billion years. But right now it is still a big hole and actually you should not ever go too close to that hole because there are still bits of Maelstrom stuck in it and they will eat you. That is why I told you about it. I'm a good teacher!

Now look here and here and here and here, and there. Those are smaller holes. They will not hurt you. They're hard to see, even, right? But they hurt existence. Those are the holes that are left behind when godlings die. We are not very important, not like the Three. The universe does not come apart if we die. It does get kind of messed up, though. Especially when one of the very old ones dies, because they've been around long enough that existence has sort of grown around them, and leaned on them a little. Without them, it cracks and maybe stumbles. Then in a few eons it's fine again.

Everything was already stumbly when the Maelstrom came. The Demons' War killed demons, and they do not leave holes the way godlings do, but maybe they left little itchy bumps because then later everybody got cranky and had the Gods' War. That one was really bad, because lots of godlings died in it—mostly young ones, but a few old ones, too. And maybe that is why it was so easy for Kahl to call the Maelstrom, and why Sieh changed and died—because when existence is shaky, all kinds of things can happen, good and bad.

(Like me! OK, that is not really why I happened. I happened because my parents had sex.)

Anyway so when Sieh died and the hole was there, every-thing in the universe got...drifty. Galaxies spun loose, with stars flying everywhichway. Wandering planets barged into solar systems without even asking! Even the dark matter has been getting snitty; it keeps shrinking down and trying to make pocket universes. The Three have to keep telling it to settle down.

Some of that was because of the big hole. But some of it was because Sieh was gone. All the planets and moons used to like Sieh. The suns didn't like him as much because he stole planets sometimes, but they listened to him, and did what he asked. Every other god, they give attitude.

That is what a trickster does, see. Shifts things around, stirs things up, makes the strong weak and the weak strong, makes people mad in good times so they won't get madder in bad ones.

Tricksters are important. They are not always funny, not always cruel, not always childish; there are many kinds of tricksters, and Sieh was not the only one. But he was *the* Trickster, the one who keeps existence on its toes, and without him, things keep going, but they don't go *well*.

Tricksters are really, *really* important. OK so there.

WHEEEEEEE WHEEEEEEEE WHEEEEEEwhat? But that part was fun! I wanted to tell you about it so you would know how fun!

Oh, *fine*. I will skip the stuff that is not important, but I think you are being a storybully, and you should maybe just relax. OK. So Eino slept really really late the next day and I got bored with watching him, so I went to a couple of other planets nearby and found a big gassy one that had really fast winds that were fun to skate on. There were little dancing creatures in the wind so I danced with them, and deeper inside the planet there were big boxes floating that had lots of long-dead mortals inside but you are BORING and don't want to know about that so I will skip ahead.

After I came back Eino was still asleep, so I sat down outside his room because I thought there might be more interesting
things to look at in the hallway, and that is how I found out
I was not supposed to be near his room. When people in the
house began to stir, a boy I did not know saw me sitting in front
of Eino's door. He gasped really loud and ran off. (I was pretty
sure that was not my fault.) Then Arolu came and found me
and asked me to come with him.

We sat down in the house's kitchen, where all the mortal
food kept distracting me because it smelled so interesting, so
finally Arolu asked another boy to get me a plate of food, and
while I tried to figure out how to eat it, he talked. "I see you've
met my son, Eino."

"Oh! He's your son?" I watched the other boy, who sat at the
far end of the long table from me and Arolu. He used a small
knife and a fork to shovel food into his mouth, so I tried to imitate him. Also I wondered why nobody had introduced me to
him or to the boy who'd tattled on me. Maybe they were waiting
for me to say hi first? "You and he aren't much alike, though.
He's not very nice."

Arolu chuckled. "Boys that age do tend to be...high-strung."
He spread his hands, as if in apology. "But along those lines...
Lady Shill, it's important that you not be seen alone with him.
Especially not in intimate places, like his bedchamber."

Bedchambers were intimate? "Why?" A piece of fruit slid off
the knife; I giggled.

"Because you are female, Lady Shill, and he is male, and
because you look older today than you did yesterday. I would
have put you at seven then; now you look, hmm, ten."

I looked down at myself, pleased to find that I had, indeed, gotten bigger. Being in the mortal realm was making me so much better! But—"Why does it matter that I look older now?"

"Because it is a reminder to everyone who meets you that your childlike appearance does not necessarily make you a *child*."

"But I am a child!"

"For now." Arolu reached over to a pot of liquid and poured some into a little cup, which he then offered to me. I sipped it and then kicked my feet because it was amazing! Sweet and sort of bitey, which made me grin at him. He smiled back. "Ginger juice, with a bit of serry-flower pulp. A Darren specialty; I'm told we sell quite a lot of it in northern Senm."

"It's good! Thank you!" He really was nice. I hoped Eino grew up to be more like him.

He inclined his head with perfect grace. "What I mean, Lady Shill, is that not only could you choose to become an adult in appearance, but you are maturing in fact—rapidly, as your recent change suggests. That is a dangerous thing."

I stopped in the middle of sipping my juice, frowning. "I'm going to try really hard not to hurt anybody."

His smile was suddenly sad. "I'm glad to hear that. But the fact remains you *might* hurt someone, for all your best intentions. Eino is impressionable, and even a young godling can be...impressive."

I put my juice down, completely mystified. "Eino's really strong, though. He's even stronger than me in a lot of ways." I felt this instinctively. "That's why I want to stay near him, so I can get strong like that."

"Yes." Arolu stopped smiling. "You *could* use him that way. But what does he gain from the exchange? Will he grow stronger too?" When I inhaled, because I had never thought of it as *using*, Arolu sighed. "Study the history of gods and mortals on this world, Lady Shill. I suspect I cannot keep you from Eino; I've lived among enulai too long not to understand something of your kind and your natures. You must be what you are—but please, try not to make the same mistakes as others of your kind. That's all I ask."

With that, he patted my hand and got up and went away upstairs. I sat there a little while longer, trying to understand what that whole conversation had been about, but I didn't. Then one of the boys came over and said, "May I take your plate, Lady?"

I blinked up at him. He was small, almost as small as me, and his hair was only to his shoulders; he'd braided it back. He didn't have on a complicated robey thing the way Eino and Arolu did; his was simpler and plainer-colored, with narrow sleeves that had been pushed up to the elbow. He kept his eyes turned down, which I didn't like, so I said, "Hello! I'm Shill. Who are you?"

He looked surprised. "Oh—um. I'm Juem, Lady. Just a servant."

I knew the word *servant*. It was sort of like the way some mortals tried to do things we wanted, except we never asked them to. I wondered why. And I really wished he would look up! "Hey, do you want some juice?" I picked up the pot Arolu had used. There wasn't much left so I made more until the pot was full, and then I made some cups, and then I stood up to try and pour the juice into them the way Arolu had done. The other boy was over by the fire, looking at me oddly; Juem just stared, gape-mouthed. I don't know why. It was hard pouring the juice.

I spilled some, then gasped and tried to find something to wipe it up with, and Juem reached for a rag on another table, but then I just vanished it away and tried to pretend I hadn't spilled it. Juem started laughing behind his hand, and I ducked my head. "Um. Sorry."

The other boy—the one who'd told Arolu about me being outside Eino's room—came over and took the pot from my hands with a graceful little bow. "It's all right, Lady. That's our job, anyway. It takes practice."

"It's a hard job!" They both giggled at this, but I felt better, because I didn't think they were laughing at me. "Um, hello. I'm Shill."

The other boy looked amused. He was older than Juem, but looked a lot like him, and I could feel the kinship between them. Siblings! "I heard. I'm Erem. Honored to meet you, Lady."

"OK." I wasn't sure what else to say when people said stuff like that. "Do you want some too?" So we all sat down and had juice together.

"This is good," Juem said as we relaxed. "We should do a fermented version for the wedding feast."

"What?" Erem looked shocked.

"What?" I asked, confused.

Juem chuckled at Erem. "The old lady announced it yesterday; didn't you hear? She's picked Mikna. 'S'why Eino stormed out all afire before mid-meal. She said who she'd picked, he asked her for a private talk in her study, all prim and calm as you please—and then Heshna at the Dallaq clan house said he could hear Eino yelling. That's two houses away." He grinned at both of us; I blinked. "They say he didn't even come home 'til the middle of the night!"

Anything about Eino interested me. I knew that mid-meal was a time when humans liked to feed themselves in the middle of the day. I had appeared in the market around midday! So I had met Eino right after he had yelled at Fahno, then gone looking for a way to sneak his scroll into the Raringa.

Erem inhaled, sitting forward. "Only he could get away with that."

"Maybe. Rumor has it he was at Yukur with a bunch of other boys breaking curfew, all of 'em cavorting like traitors of old!"

"No!"

I was not supposed to tell, so I bit my bottom lip. But I was so curious! Maybe I could ask about things that weren't about the anatun? "I don't understand," I said, carefully. "Why was Eino upset? What is a Mikna?"

They looked at each other, Erem suddenly squirming. "This is just servant gossip, Lady," Erem said. "We shouldn't have brought it up in front of you. It's nothing of import."

"I'm forty days old," I said solemnly, and they blinked. "Oh! Forty-one. Everything is important to me."

They stared, then giggled behind their hands. I smiled, too, even though I didn't think it was that funny. Finally Juem sighed. "Mikna's a who, not a what," he said. "She's another enulai practicing in Darr, one of Fahno's protégés."

"But not the only other enulai practicing in Darr," Erem interjected. "Darr is blessed with three, though we've only got maybe seven godlings altogether living in the country."

"Two again," said Juem. "Fahno's retired."

"Oh. Right."

"Mikna," I said, hoping they would get to the point.

Juem chuckled at me. "Mikna is by all accounts the better

enulai. Older, stronger, with a bigger stable of godlings. And she's old Darre—from an old clan, that is, with conqueror roots and traditional ways. Always had a bit of magic, but a few years back a godling took up with a boy from the clan, and decided to make a daughter with him. Godlings aren't much for raising demons, so she gave the child to the clan, and they've been enulai ever since."

I nodded. "Eino."

"I was getting there!" He huffed at my impatience. "Eino's old enough to be married off, see. More than, but Fahno-enulai's better than most clan matriarchs; she didn't want him going off to be a father when he was barely more than a boy himself. But he's just gotten prettier with the extra years, and word's out about how strong his magic is. That usually means his demon blood is strong, too—which makes our Eino the perfect sire for the next generation of enulai, in any clan."

"But then there's the other enulai clan in Darr," said Erem, leaning forward so I would know that what he had to say was important, too. "That's Lumyn's people. Lumyn's not much for the enulai art; the blood runs weak in her, probably because they've been breeding with foreigners for years. Amn and such." They both grimaced; I nodded, though I had only the vaguest idea of what he was talking about. "Lumyn even trained outside Darr, down somewhere in Senm. But she's of marrying age, too, and she came a-courting Eino as well—and Eino seems to like her better."

It was a little confusing, but I understood. Sort of. "If they both want babies from Eino, why doesn't he just give them both babies?" It seemed the simplest solution.

They both stared at me. "They want husbands, not just the

children those husbands will make," said Juem, finally, once he stopped looking appalled. "Who else is going to bathe the children and feed them and teach them the ways of two clans, and protect them if the home's invaded? Women risk their lives enough to bear children and provide for them by tool or by blade; the least men can do is handle things after that."

"Oh." I frowned, wondering if Eino was much interested in feeding babies. He would be really good at protecting them, though!

"So," Juem continued, reaching for more serry juice, "now there's two clans fighting hard for our little Eino. And he doesn't want the one his beba's picked."

"It's done," said Erem, shaking his head. "If you said she's picked Mikna—"

"Now, when have you ever known Eino to give in to what somebody else wanted?"

Yeah, that didn't sound like Eino at all.

But—"I don't know if Eino wants either of them," I said, frowning to myself. I thought maybe Eino really just wanted to dance, and maybe be an enulai himself, and do other things that men long ago used to do. Maybe men got married back then, but if so they got married when they wanted, and it sounded like Fahno and these other women wanted Eino to marry now.

Erem belched. "He doesn't have a choice. Fahno's got no heirs, see."

I must have frowned in confusion, because Juem explained: "She had three sons, but they went off to marry into other families, like boys do. She had a daughter, Tehno, but Tehno didn't get much of the blood—the demon blood, you know? Not enough to become enulai after Fahno. But Tehno married

Arolu, and they made Eino, who did have it. It's a throwback sort of thing like that sometimes."

"OK," I said, trying to parse it all.

"And that would be fine; Tehno wasn't an enulai, but she'd proven herself capable of bearing children with the gift, and that would've been enough for her to inherit. But then Tehno went off and got herself killed a few years ago, trying to do business with the Litaria." He sighed. "Damned criminals."

"What's a Litaria?"

"Bad people." He scowled.

Erem nodded. "Back in the days of the Bright, they were the only people allowed to use magic. Nowadays there's lots of people and godlings to do magic—but the Lit's still got the strongest mortal stuff, called scrivening. So they throw their weight around, run a lot of black market and shady magic ventures. Tehno wasn't demon enough to become an enulai, but she was demon enough that her blood was still poison to gods—if enough of it was taken, and distilled." His face hardened. "So they lured her to a meeting place for some deal they'd worked out, and then they killed her for her blood. It was a big scandal because enulai are supposed to keep the Lit from running amok, not make deals with them." He sighed. "Poor Fahno. She wiped out the branch of the Lit that did it, but..." He spread his hands.

I inhaled. "Enulai have to be demons so they can kill gods if they have to... but people try to hurt them for being demons?"

Juem nodded. "Another reason why enulai look after godlings; they help godlings and their godlings help them, usually. But Tehno didn't have any watching her back." He sighed heavily. "And if Fahno can't make or adopt another heir, then her clan will dissolve when she dies. The house and all her assets will go to the Council, and Arolu and Eino will end up on the street with nothing. Fahno's only chance is to marry Eino off, adopt one of their daughters, and continue the clan that way."

It was too much mortally stuff. I was getting bored. Only one thing mattered. "Eino could be Fahno's heir," I said, carefully. "He's got lots of magic, and probably the scary blood, too."

Juem coughed, in a polite sort of way. "He's a boy, Lady Shill. There are boy enulai, of course, but not here in Darr."

Ohhhh!! Was that why they'd told Eino he didn't have the temperament to be an enulai? But boy-temperaments were not different from girl-temperaments, or whatever mortals called Naha-temperaments. And was that why Eino wanted the people in the Raringa to consider letting boys inherit stuff? If they changed the rules, he would be able to stay with his own clan.

We finished the ginger-serry juice, talking about nothing after that. Then I left the kitchen and went to see if Eino was awake yet. His room was empty, so I followed his scent-feel to the bathroom, where there was water still on the floor with some of the sweat from his dance the night before in it. After that I tracked him to another room where there were lots of pretty, elaborate robes hanging on racks. One of them was gone, and the scent of perfume was in the air, with Eino's smell still strong underneath. I grinned, because Find Eino was a fun game even if it was kind of easy! I followed his smell to another room, where he'd eaten some things—and then finally down a long corridor I saw him! He was standing at the end of it, looking into a big room beyond; he did not see me. His shoulders were very tight and his face had gone hard and blank like a mask again.

I was thinking about running up behind him and surprising him, when suddenly people started yelling in the room beyond!

"—completely improper—" That was Arolu. He sounded mad!

"I think I'm done with propriety, thank you, Arolu-wo." A strange woman!

"Fahno-enulai will not approve!"

"Let her proceed," said *another* strange woman. She sounded bored, and maybe annoyed. "It's a pitiful gesture, but if she feels compelled to make it, who are we to stand in her way?"

Confused, I came to the doorway beside Eino. He didn't look at me, though Arolu did. Only for a second, though; he was focused on the two strange women in front of him. I wasn't sure why at first—until I caught both the women's scents, and realized they smelled a little like Eino, and Fahno: their own scents were underlain by a peculiar bitterness, like something maybe a little bit dangerous. Did that mean they were demons, too? And probably enulai, too! That meant these must be the women that the servants had told me about: Mikna, who had been chosen to marry Eino, and Lumyn, whom Eino liked better.

One of the women was stocky and darker-skinned, standing near the door with one hand on her hip and a look of contempt on her face. The other woman was already crossing the room to Eino and pressing something into his hands. She was older than him—they both were—and taller than any Darren woman I'd seen, paler brown and narrower in frame. She dressed in more colors than most Darren women, too: usually they stuck to tight-fitting blacks and grays, while boys wore loose color. But above her black leggings she had on a vest that was as green as the forest. It was very pretty, and almost matched her eyes, which were a pale version of the same shade.

"For you," she said firmly, to Eino. Her voice shook with emotion as she held Eino's hands. "Gods grant that one day we can use it together." Just as quickly she pulled away, and turned to face the other woman.

Eino stared back at the woman in green in a way that...I frowned and touched his arm, and he jumped and stared at me as if it had hurt. No one but him and Arolu had even noticed me. He was almost crying! And he felt awful inside, buzzy and angryhurt like there were bees in his soul. He clutched the thing she'd given him, a small cloth-wrapped parcel, to his breast.

I didn't know what it meant that he was so upset! I didn't like that these strange women had hurt him. Then Fahno-enulai came into the room from the other doorway, and everything got way, way worse. Um, and maybe some of that was my fault.

"Lumyn-enulai," she said to the tall woman. I had never seen Fahno look so angry. "If you had a courting-gift to offer for Eino, the traditional thing to do would have been to give it to his father, or me."

The tall woman let out a harsh laugh. "If I had, he'd never have received it. I've no patience for tradition, Fahno-enulai; didn't you tell me that was my failing, once? And it wasn't a courting-gift." She shrugged; it felt like a lie, somehow, and I did not like her for that. "It was simply a trinket I found, and which I thought your grandson might like. Will you begrudge him something so unimportant?"

"Nevertheless. I did not invite you to this house."

Lumyn inclined her head as if conceding something. "You did, however, inquire via the union about available enulai who might attend the newborn godling, Lady Shill. Did you not? Forgive me, but I thought you were looking for help."

I frowned, because she was lying again. Whatever she had given Eino had made him sad; it was obviously more than a trinket. I really did not like her at all.

"I summoned Mikna for that purpose," Fahno said, moving slowly closer to Lumyn. She was old and wide and I could feel how her back hurt, but in that moment she was like a big old bear, lumbery and scary. "You lack the strength to deal with a godling like Shill, and now I see you lack the discipline as well."

"'Managing gods is as much a matter of compatibility and temperament as sheer strength,'" said Lumyn, and Fahno stopped, wincing. Lumyn smiled. "That is from your teachings, is it not? I came because this godling of yours is a free and glorious creature, like all her kind, and she should have choices—rather than having others' wills foisted upon her."

Another lie! I clenched my fists. But now the stocky woman—Mikna?—spoke. "Foolishness," she said. "The godling is but a child, according to Fahno's description. 'Free and glorious creatures' who don't understand the world cannot be trusted to make such important choices on their own. To attempt it may seem like kindness, but in truth, it is cruel." She stepped forward, and her whole posture said GO AWAY. "Do you truly want to help, Lumyn? Are you enulai enough, *Darre* enough, to truly care? Then let the people who know the situation best make the decision—and be mature enough to abide by it."

But now I was confused, and angrier! Because this was somehow a lie, too.

Lumyn shook her head. "A godling child isn't some helpless, mindless creature!" she said. "She can be shown the world, and helped to make the decision in full knowledge. To treat her otherwise—like an object to be fought over, like a pet—is a fundamental misjudgment of who and what she is. *That* is cruelty."

None of them had even noticed me, so focused were they on each other. I looked at Eino, worried. He had fixed his eyes on the floor, and he was stiff and tight all over. I got madder, seeing how upset he was. I wasn't sure how, but I was sure they were being mean! And even if they were all scary demons, I could not let them be mean to Eino!

So I marched into the space between them, my fists tight. "Hey! I'm *right here!*"

All three women flinched and stared at me as if it was the first time they'd even realized I was in the room. And that was how I finally figured out the lie. My mouth fell open.

"You aren't even really talking about me, are you? None of you!" I looked over at Eino, who hadn't moved. "Everything you're saying is really about him!"

Fahno sighed and pinched the bridge of her nose. "Gods. Lady Shill, I wish…" She shook her head. "Yes. This is about Eino's future."

"But he doesn't like it!" I pointed at Eino again. "He's all upset! All three of you are mad at each other, about him, and none of you are even *looking* at him!"

Fahno looked, and her expression grew pained. "Yes…yes. Arolu, ah, please take Eino back to his rooms—" Arolu nodded and moved toward Eino.

"No," said Eino. He was still staring at the floor; the bundle that Lumyn had given him was still in his hand. "You're right, Beba; this is about my future. Shouldn't I hear this?" All of a sudden he looked up, and Fahno flinched at his glare. "Since

I'm not permitted to choose my fate, I should at least face it with open eyes. Is that not the way of the Darre?"

Fahno's jaw muscles flexed, and then she focused on me again. "This *is* about you, Lady Shill—though I will allow that it's not just about you. I had invited Mikna-enulai here to meet you, because I felt she would be an appropriate match for you."

Mikna inclined her head. "And it is a pleasure to meet you, Lady Shill."

"I don't like you," I said. She raised her eyebrows. Then to Lumyn I said, "And I don't like you, either. You both made Eino get sad. You shouldn't have made him sad!"

Lumyn took a deep breath. "Lady Shill, I see that you consider Eino a friend. It troubles you that he's unhappy right now, and *I feel the same way.* My gift, believe it or not, was meant to cheer him." She glanced at Eino. "I'm sorry that it didn't."

"That's not *your* doing," Eino said softly. His voice was thicker than usual, and rough. Arolu sort of *tsk*ed and came over, taking Eino's shoulder.

"Enough," Arolu said to the women. "Please." At this, they all sort of shifted or looked away, and then Fahno sighed.

"There's still the matter of Lady Shill's disposition," she said, which I guess was a way of changing the subject. She folded her arms. "I . . . appreciate that you felt it appropriate to come here, Lumyn-enulai, but I remain convinced that Mikna-enulai is the better choice."

Lumyn sort of smirked. "Lady Shill has made it clear she dislikes both of the options she's been presented."

"That's right," I said. I was annoyed! They kept talking about me like I wasn't there! "I don't want either of you!"

Fahno scowled. "You must have an enulai, Lady Shill, or

leave this world per the Compact between your kind and mortalkind. Have you decided to leave?"

"I'm not leaving!" Now I was scared she would make me go, or call Ia, who would make me go. That made me madder still. "I just don't like any of this! I don't want somebody who's going to talk about me like I'm not here, or say things about one person when they really mean it about another person, or, or—" I couldn't articulate it. I was shaking, I was so mad—but at the same time, I felt weird. Sort of ugly inside, shaking, too, wibbly and kind of gross. I wanted to cry, and I didn't know why. "I want Eino!"

Fahno inhaled; Mikna threw a sharp look at him, then back at me. Lumyn frowned. "Eino?"

"*Eino!*" I yelled it, and everybody jumped, because I had slipped and my voice had gotten too loud again—not loud enough to damage anything, but enough that the windows rattled and a vase shivered on the side of the room. I bit my lip and pushed my voice down to soft again. "Sorry. But I don't understand why he can't be my enulai. Everybody says it's because he's a boy, but he's not a boy, he's a *demon*, and he's full of magic, and I know he'd be a really good enulai for me because I actually like him! Why not him?"

Fahno was staring at me, and then she looked at Eino. That was when I realized I'd done a bad thing, because I'd promised Eino I wouldn't tell about him going out to dance and stuff. And I hadn't—but now Fahno knew that we'd met before, somehow, and my words were maybe getting Eino in trouble. I bit my lip, but it was too late.

But then Eino spoke behind me, and his voice was so harsh and bitter that it made me feel even more bad inside, because suddenly I knew I had done the same thing as the other women. I had been selfish, and used him without even doing anything good for him, just like Arolu feared.

"You can't have me, Shill," he said. He sounded both sad and angry, but I looked at him without eyes and saw that he was smiling. I didn't understand it. "It's like I told you: an enulai is a person trained in an art demanding great skill. I cannot be a person; I am chattel, instead. I am nothing." He turned to go.

"You're not nothing," I said, stricken. He was so hurt. *I* had helped hurt him, and it was terrible! I ran forward a few steps, holding up a hand after him, but he didn't see me as Arolu sighed and guided him away.

But it was all wrong! He was worse! I had made him worse and IT WAS ALL WRONG.

"You're not nothing!" I shouted it, not with my voice this time but everything else, and the planet shook. I set my feet and crouched and yelled at the ground without a voice, because I didn't want to hurt anybody but I was hurting, too, like nothing I had ever felt before, and I had to stop it! I had to make Eino know! "You're not! You're not! You're not nothing and *I won't ever let you be nothing!*"

"Shill!" Fahno cried, but I didn't hear her. I didn't *want* to hear her. I didn't want the mortal realm to be like this. It shouldn't be like this! I understood now: Eino was like me, not the right shape for the role his parents needed him to fill. He was not the decorative, obedient thing that everyone in Darr wanted him to be, and it was *hurting* him that he couldn't be. Nobody should try to make children be what they aren't. Everyone should just be what they were supposed to be! Everything was wrong and terrible! ALL EXISTENCE WAS WRONG AND TERRIBLE AND IT SHOULD BE BETTER!

I screamed this at the ground, at existence, and tried to make it be, but I was not one of the Three or even a particularly strong godling. Nothing got any better.

And then soft, perfumed hands took hold of me, and big colored sleeves folded round me, and Eino's hard chest pressed against my face. "Hush, Shill," he said. "Hush, you silly creature. It's all right."

It was... it was not all right. But I felt better anyway. So I stopped screaming, and I pressed my face into his chest and realized only then that I'd been crying, and when he hugged me I *felt* like everything would be all right, even if that was probably a lie, too.

"I'm sorry," I said into his chest. "I didn't mean to treat you like nothing, too."

"Did you?" His hand stroked my hair; it felt nice. He would be a good father if he ever did make babies.

I swallowed hard, hitched, and then took a deep breath so I could talk. "I said what I wanted from you and I didn't even *ask* you."

"Ah. Well, I'm used to that." He sighed. Then he said, not to me, "Relax. It was just a little tantrum, and it's over already."

"I'd hardly call that 'little,'" said Ia, who I hadn't even realized had come. "And it isn't a tantrum, strictly. Fahno-enulai, is anyone hurt?"

"No," said Fahno. I could tell she was trying to be calm; why? Because I had scared her. I felt worse, realizing it, but Eino stroked my back and I felt better. "She was quite careful to avoid doing anything that harmed mortals, I noticed."

"Ah. Then there's hope for her yet."

I pulled my teary face away from Eino and glared at him. "Don't be mean, Sibling."

Ia, who stood among the three women looking pale and strange and so out of place, lifted an eyebrow. But then he pushed up his glasses and glanced at Fahno. "If you don't mind," he said, "I'd like to take my sibling away for a talk. I'll return her by nightfall. Hopefully you and your fellow enulai will have worked out your... jurisdictional issues by then."

Fahno grimaced. "I appreciate your delicate phrasing, Ia." She looked at me. "Forgive me, Shill. We shouldn't have fought in front of you. And..." She hesitated, then faced her grandson. "I hope that you too will forgive me, Eino. I just want to help you. I know you don't believe that."

Eino only sighed. I pushed away from Eino and stood up to glare at all of them. "You shouldn't have *hurt Eino* in front of me. But..." I bit my lip. "I did it, too. And the thing is, Eino's really strong. He can fight for himself." I turned to him. "If you do, I'll help you."

Eino was staring at me, half amused and half still sadhurt. "I don't think I'm ready to declare war on my family and friends, Shill." His smile faded, and he faced Fahno again. "I know you mean well, Beba. Believe me, this would be easier if you hated me."

With that, a deeply uncomfortable silence fell. Arolu resumed urging Eino to come with him, and this time Eino obeyed. Fahno shook her head in their wake, in between glaring at both Mikna and Lumyn. Lumyn all but ignored her, gazing longingly after Eino. Mikna, at least, looked abashed—and then she turned a thoughtful gaze on me.

With an annoyed glare round the room, Ia stepped forward and summoned me away with a flick of his eyes.

We appeared in a place that was almost-nothing: a big wide grassy hill, overlooking a big flat stretch of more grass and flowers and stuff. There was nothing in the sky but blue, and nothing walking on the grass but bugs and tiny mice and a snake or two, except snakes do not walk. It was quiet and it made me feel quiet inside, so I sat and drew up my knees and wrapped my arms around them and put my head down.

"What you felt, just now, was your antithesis," Ia said. He stood next to me, watching the grass wave in the wind. "That's what mortals call it, and the word serves well enough. Something in that room was the opposite of what you are—not just its negation, but its active obliteration. They wounded you and didn't even realize it. That will always be the danger, Sibling. They think of us as powerful, and we are, but...they can damage us so easily, in ways they barely understand. If we let them."

That was what an antithesis felt like? "It hurt," I said, rubbing my tummy. My head hurt, too, and bits of my soul were all achy and tender. "I tried not to hurt them back, though."

"Commendable, given your youth. Many older gods would not have been able to resist lashing out in reaction." I perked up a little, and felt better, at hearing I was *commendable*. He'd never said anything nice about me before. But then he sighed. "Shill, I'm going to ask you again to return to our realm."

I gasped, hurt again but in a different way. "Why? Why, Ia, I've been really good—"

"Yes. You have been." That stopped me. If he thought I was good, then why? "But Shill, you've been in this realm barely more than a day, and look at what's happened."

"I—" I frowned, more confused. "What's happened?"

"You *care* about them." I looked up at him finally, and he looked at me, and his face was heavy and sad in a way I had never seen before. "It's impossible not to, if you stay here long enough, but for you it took only one day. And in that day they've damaged you. That means you're vulnerable to them, Sibling— more so than most of us. Something in your nature must make you that way, or maybe it's simply that you're a child. But we can die, Shill, of the things they do to us. You do not understand yet what that means, but...I've seen too many of us die, lately."

It was nice that Ia did not want me to die. But I did not like that he wanted me to leave the mortal realm.

"Maybe," I said, trying to understand even as I spoke, "if I understand what happened, I might understand what my antithesis is, and then I won't get hurt by it again."

Ia shook his head. "This entire realm is inimical to us in so many ways, Shill. Everything is so...*concentrated*. There's no way to escape the threat completely while you remain here."

"I don't care! I knew it was dangerous before I came. Even Naha told me not to come, and she's not scared of anything."

"Untrue, Shill. She fears the loss of those she loves." Ia sobered. "I thought he would never stop mourning Sieh. In the end, he went beyond the edges of our realm, into the nothingness. I followed him for a time, because I can, and because I worried he would...well." He shrugged a little, but he did not have to say it. Everybody can see that one day, Naha might become a Maelstrom. It is a *maybe* and not a *probably*, or worse an *eventually*, but that it is even a maybe is a scary thing. That's Naha, though: a scary, changeable thing.

"But he just mourned," Ia continued. He gazed into the

distance without really seeing it; there was nothingness in his eyes. "Mourned and wandered, as if he was...searching for something. I don't know what. Eventually he went farther than even I could follow, and there's no telling how long he was gone. There's no time in the nothing, you see. When he returned... she was different, in many ways. Perhaps that's what she needed to heal." He looked at me. "Nahadoth has had time enough to love you, too, Shill. Will you make her mourn again for a lost child, so soon?"

I bit my lip and squirmed and looked at my knees. I had learned from the mortals, though, and instead of answering this really hard question, I changed the subject. "Um, Ia? Who is your enulai?"

He said nothing for a moment. I was scared he would make me answer the Naha question. But he said, "I don't have one."

I frowned. "Fahno said all godlings—"

"I know." He seemed to hesitate. "I'm not like other godlings, Shill. Haven't you noticed?"

The question confused me because no two godlings were alike. "No?"

I felt him look at me, like he didn't quite believe me. But then he shook his head, almost to himself. "It has been so long since a new godling walked among us. I'd forgotten that you *don't* see it. Not at first."

Then there was a new voice behind us, and I jumped, but Ia only went very still and narrowed his eyes at the sound of it.

"He is a monster," said the woman. Said the godling, I realized, even as I turned and looked up—and up—to take in all of her mortal shape. She was like seven feet tall! And wider than me and Ia put together! Her fists were great big, and her bones were great big, and her headkerchief was great big; everything was great big!

I inhaled, grinning, and stood to face her. "I want to get *that* big." Her eyebrows lifted a little, I think in amusement.

"A monster even among our kind, like all the elontid," she continued. "Nahadoth, for all her chaos, is *something*. Ia alone among us is the abyss: no god can stare into him long without losing themselves, in terror. So he lives here in the mortal realm, among beings who cannot grasp the horror of him. He never comes to our realm, where the facade would not last. He needs no enulai to keep him in check, for who would foul his only home?"

Ia, face so composed that I thought at once it was another kind of lie, finally stood and turned to her. "Zhakkarn," he said, calmly. "To what do we owe the pleasure?"

She turned aside to reveal Mikna, walking up behind her. "I asked Lady Zhakkarn to come," Mikna said. I bristled at once, but she held up a hand. "Please, Lady Shill. We've begun on the wrong foot, and for that I apologize. I ask, however, that you hear me out."

I folded my arms. "I don't want to. I don't like you."

"She didn't ask you to like her," Ia snapped. "I don't like *you*, but I listen to you, don't I?"

Because grown-up godlings listened, even if they did not always agree. I sighed very hard but unfolded my arms. I did not try to smile, though, because I was so mad that my bottom lip poked out instead.

"Stop *sulking*," Ia said.

I stamped my foot at him. "Stop yelling at me!"

"I didn't—" Ia's teeth clamped shut with an audible click, and he looked away.

"You should have spent more time around Sieh, Sibling," Zhakkarn said to him. Her voice was big, too, though most of it did not show its bigness. You could feel it, though, underneath the softness of her words. Inside her was a great big bloodthirsty *roar.* "He would have taught you patience."

"Thank you, Zhakkarn, but I didn't because I have little interest in children. Or rather, no interest." He pushed his glasses up and put his hands behind his back.

Mikna grimaced. "I too have little experience with children, I'm afraid. But Shill—I *do* work with godlings, which is why I asked Lady Zhakkarn to join me in greeting you. She has... rather more experience of mortals than I do of godlings." An odd, uncomfortable look passed over her face; beside her, Zhakkarn was still and calm as the cloudless sky, though of course we could all hear that huge awful roar. Ia sighed faintly. "I hoped that she might help to bridge the gap between us, if she was willing, and fortunately she is."

"I told you I didn't want you," I said, getting a little mad again. I didn't like that she sounded all reasonable. I didn't feel like being polite. "Tell me what you want or go away."

Nobody said anything, though Mikna raised an eyebrow— and Zhakkarn looked at me. Just that. But all at once I changed my mind about being rude to Mikna.

"What I want," Mikna said after a moment, "is to show you something. Will you come with us?"

I was more polite this time, because Zhakkarn. "Um, where?"

"To the Proving Ground," said Zhakkarn.

I frowned. "What's that? Why?"

Mikna said, "Because, as I realized after you left, you are a girl of proving age—or you would be, if you were human and actually the age that you resemble." She paused. "You've been trying to understand Eino, haven't you? Eino is Darre. If you want to understand him better, you need to understand his people."

I blinked. Oh. *Ohhhh.* "Um." But she was right. I'd only met a handful of mortals so far, and I could see already that all their little strangenesses—what language they spoke and how they dressed and what they looked like and what they called themselves—were *important* to them. To Eino. So... "OK."

With that, Zhakkarn took us somewhere else. I thought at first she would take Ia and me and Mikna, but when we appeared in a big dusty courtyard surrounded by high walls and a circle of wooden railings, Ia was nowhere to be seen. "Ia is male," Mikna said, when she saw me looking around. "This place isn't for them."

"He's not really a boy," I said, folding my arms.

"He is as much male as you are female," said Mikna. Which made me bristle, until...oh. Well, OK. "And there is...history, between him and Lady Zhakkarn, as you probably gathered. It's probably for the best."

Something to do with the Gods' War, probably, I decided. Lots of my older siblings were still mad about that. "OK."

She nodded and backed up, spreading her arms so I would look around, which I did. "In Darr, a girl's ninth year is considered sacred. Three times three, you see, and we have always honored the Three and all their children, not merely Itempas or any single one. But that doesn't mean we can't have a special, hmm, *affinity* for any godling." She glanced at Zhakkarn, who had pulled off her kerchief to reveal close-cropped curls of bright blue-white hair. Zhakkarn regarded her in stoic silence, which would have scared me, but Mikna just smiled again.

"Well, I'm not nine," I said, folding my arms. Honestly, though, I was curious.

"I know. And by the time you are nine in truth you will understand more of creation than any mortal child—but for convenience's sake, let's treat you as nine years old now. At nine, a Darren girl—at least in the old days—" At this she faltered a little, her expression turning grim; I wondered why. Then she recovered. "A Darren girl would face her first foe in battle. Come."

She beckoned, and I came forward to where she pointed: a square of black bricks set into the dusty ground, near the wooden railing. There was another black square across the circle from it. When I was standing on the square, Mikna nodded. "Good. Let's get started."

And then Zhakkarn got up and moved to stand on the black square opposite me.

My mouth fell open. "But I can't beat you!" I could feel it: her very nature was fighting, blood, pain. I glared at Mikna. "I thought you wanted me to fight *you*."

Mikna looked amused. "You're still a god, Lady Shill, and one who as yet lacks a great deal of self-control. I have no wish to die. But more importantly, a nine-year-old Darren girl's first foe would generally be an adult woman of the same clan. The goal of this contest is not to win; it is to learn how to face a foe who is larger, stronger, and more experienced."

"And lose!"

"That is possible," said Zhakkarn. She had taken a stance with her fists upraised and ready; suddenly I did not like that her fists were so great big. I was not really afraid of her body; that was just mortal stuff, like mine. What made me swallow and sweat was that—oh, no—I could feel how the great big roar inside her was quiet suddenly. Focused. On *me*.

I swallowed hard, then took a deep breath. OK. This was scary, but maybe it would be like when I had gone to talk to Ral the Dragon, who never did anything except roar so I'd had to roar with it. Zhakkarn was full of battle, so I would have to battle with her. And then maybe we could be friends! This made me be not scared anymore. And anyway, I had battled before with Eino, right? The dance had been a kind of fight. The moment I thought of that, I got excited. Maybe I would like this, too!

Zhakkarn lowered her chin, her eyes suddenly sharp. "There seems to be a bit of the warrior in you already, Sibling."

Was there? "I was in a fight last night!" I said. "It was fun."

Zhakkarn smiled. "Let's hope this one is, too, little Sibling."

Then she came at me. It was so fast I didn't have time to be scared, except it was also so fast I couldn't think, so I sort of squeaked and scrambled backward and hit the wooden railing. But she was still coming! So I folded myself over to the other side of the ring, where she had been.

And SHE DID IT, TOO.

So then her fist was up and she punched like WHAM and it hurt lots, like A WHOLE LOT, like OH HELLS I DIDN'T KNOW MORTAL STUFF COULD HURT LIKE THAT. I tried to will it not to hurt and it kept hurting, even! The mortal realm is not nice at all. Before I could get up she KICKED me. That wasn't fair! It hurt lots more. I yelled, because I couldn't help it. Stuff was broken inside me. Then I tried to crawl and she grabbed me by the ankle and THREW ME ACROSS THE RING! I went into the wall some, because the bricks were not very sturdy. And she was STILL COMING.

"Hey!" I yelled, as she walked toward me. It took me a minute to push myself even partially out of the wall, and then I had to spit out some teeth along with rocks. I clung to the edges of the hole I was in, panting. "That is not fair! How am I supposed to fight when you don't *wait?*"

"Do you think a real enemy will politely wait for you to recover?" Zhakkarn was still coming, and oh, was her face scary. Eyes like hard steel and jaw tight like, like, like I dunno SCARY TIGHT THINGS what did it even matter she was gonna KILL me. "Do you think battle is *fair?*"

I blinked, because well, I had. The dance with Eino...but now I knew that hadn't really been battle. It had just been play. Eino dreamt of fighting the way the men of long ago had fought, but if that had been how they'd really fought, no wonder they'd lost.

But—

(I had to stop thinking for a bit, because Zhakkarn grabbed me out of the wall and a lot of bad things happened for a while. I do not want to talk about them.)

OK, so. But.

I lay on the ground where Zhakkarn had thrown me the last time, trying to understand something that had occurred to me earlier. My eyes were swollen shut, but I could feel Zhakkarn coming again—and also, I could feel that she was disappointed in me, because I hadn't managed to put up much of a fight. That was worse than the pain, actually, because the pain would go away, but a sibling's disappointment would not.

But. This was important!

But it bugged me that Eino's kind of fighting wasn't real fighting. It *should* have been. It *could* have been, maybe, if Eino knew more about how to do it than what he'd learned in musty old spheres and scrolls. Or if Eino had been taught the Proper Way to fight, by someone who had worked with him and sparred with him from when he was small! There was no reason for men's fighting to be any worse than women's fighting. Women were not magic or anything; they just knew something the men didn't.

Zhakkarn picked me up by the neck and held me up in the air with one hand. Also, she was choking me. "Do you yield, Sibling?"

I felt like I was on the edge of something—something besides passing out. Oh, right! Darren women knew other women had learned to fight, so they tried. They got good at it because they believed they could. But the men did not try. They did not believe.

(Something cracked in my neck. Ow.)

And no one else believed in them, either. That was why Fahno wanted Eino to be married, was *making* him be married, when he didn't want to be. It was because Fahno didn't think boys could be strong. But boys *could* be strong! And girls could be strong! Everybody could be strong, if they all got the same knowledge, and if they tried. If they all believed!

I gasped, which was really saying something because my throat was all closed up. And I opened my eyes some, because all of a sudden they were not so bruised and hurt. I stared at Zhakkarn, who blinked.

I get it now! I said into her head, since I couldn't talk. And then I grabbed her arm to brace myself, and curled up, and kicked her in the chest with both feet as hard as I could!

We both went down, because she still had hold of me, and

because Papa Tempa had filled the mortal realm with MOMEN-TUM which was annoying. She did stagger, though, and let me back down to the ground by accident. That was good, because suddenly I was strong again, or at least not weak! And even if I didn't know how to fight well, I believed that I *could* fight, and really that is what matters. And! I did kind of know how to fight because of Eino's dance, which was too fair and pretty to be proper fighting but only because nobody had used it for proper fighting in godsknewhowlong, and nobody ever would if I didn't *try*, so I spun and whirled my arms like I would have in the dance and that made Zhakkarn let go and I was free!

...To fall down, because lots of stuff was broken in me. Mortal realm, mortal rules. I said some bad words.

Zhakkarn straightened, looking down at me, and all of a sudden she didn't look disappointed anymore.

"More than a bit of the warrior," she said. "That you scored even one blow is excellent, Sibling. I look forward to our next battle if you fight like this from the outset."

"*I ab nebba fahdig you agan,*" I said through messed-up teeth, glaring at her.

"Never say never," said Mikna, coming into the narrow range of my sight. She crouched, smiling. "I get the feeling you're stubborn, Lady Shill. You should probably yield, though, unless you want this battle to contin—"

"YIELD." I did not yell it loud enough to hurt anybody, but it was pretty loud. Mikna grimaced, but laughed. And—oh, thank our parents—Zhakkarn folded her arms to wait for me to heal.

It took a few minutes. Once my stomach-muscles could work again I sat up and glared at them some more. *Not fun.*

"Battles rarely are," said Zhakkarn, shrugging.

"Well now I know that!" I had just grown some new teeth, so I could talk better now. I was so mad at Mikna! "That didn't have any point!"

"Didn't it?" Mikna raised her eyebrows. "But you've learned so much, Lady Shill."

"Like what?"

"Enough that you seem to have grown. Fahno said that might happen, particularly when you got closer to discovering your nature." At this I blinked, and looked down, but it was true! Now I was long and leggy, and there were little bumps on my chest where my body was thinking about growing breasts.

"I don't get it," I said, staring down at all that leg. "I only took this shape so I could be around you mortals. I turned into a lizard already, and some other stuff. Why is it only this shape that changes without me meaning it to?"

Zhakkarn crouched, not that that helped much; she still loomed over us both. But now her expression was a little sad, though she was smiling. "This happened to Sieh in his last few years," she said. "Not quite in the same way, or for similar reasons—but Sibling, we are living creatures, immortal or not. Life...grows."

Didn't it! I got to my feet and stood wobbling for a moment. "I'm so tall!" I grinned at Mikna, who stood, too; she was the same height.

"Perhaps you'll match Lady Zhakkarn someday after all." She shrugged. "But if you'll think about it, Lady Shill, you've grown in other ways, too. A girl's first battle teaches her that the world is not fair." I blinked and sobered; she nodded, seeing that I understood. "It teaches her to fight *despite* this, because a true enemy will not relent, and because it is a simple matter of survival. Claim what ground you can and hold it. Get back up if you're knocked down. A woman's strength has always lain in *not giving up*."

I thought about this. I didn't hate her anymore, but— "Everybody should learn this, though," I said, troubled. "Why do you only teach it to women?"

The look on Mikna's face turned—I don't know. Pitying? She turned, putting her hands on her hips, and gazed toward the walls of the arena, though it was clear that her thoughts lay far beyond it. "You're so young, Lady Shill. You've had only the barest taste of what we mortals do to each other. Look around this world for a few years, then ask me that question again."

I frowned. "What do you mean?"

"Once we shared this knowledge with our men. Once men honed their skills against women in battle, and had at least some small chance at proving themselves worthy in the way of warriors. A few even became ennu, the figurehead for all that makes us strong as a people. Those were simpler times—the days when Yeine walked among women as a mortal." I perked up at this. "Back then, we thought that all we had to fear were foreigners. And the gods, of course."

A demon spoke of fearing gods. "Of course," I said, really softly.

"But not long after Skyfall," Mikna continued, "in the new golden age that Darr had begun to enjoy with the ending of the Bright, and the rebuilding after the war—our men turned on us. Not all, certainly, but enough to pose a real threat. They wanted to *take over*." A muscle in her jaw tightened. "That's the way of men, you see, when women don't keep them in check.

They want *all*, not just *some*. Nature made them weak: slaves to their impulses, helpless against pain, barely capable of making it out of the womb. Their weakness makes them fearful. Nothing is more dangerous than fearful people with a fresh taste of power."

I frowned. This did not feel... I wasn't sure. I was more sophisticated now, able to think bigger thoughts, but maybe I still wasn't big enough to understand.

Mikna tossed some of her long hair back over her shoulder. "So we crushed the dangerous ones, and made the fateful decision to protect the rest of the men from themselves. But Eino is the proof that Darren flames cannot be smothered so easily. Gods, the fight in him!" She smiled, almost to herself. "How could I not want him? I am a true Darre."

I looked up at Zhakkarn, who watched me impassively, then back at Mikna. "If you make him do something he doesn't want, he'll fight *you*. Real battle, not fun. Or"—it suddenly occurred to me, and this thought was terrible—"or you'll make him so hurt and sad inside that he won't care about fighting anymore. He... he won't be Eino, if you do that."

Mikna looked uncomfortable for a moment, then took a deep breath. "Darr is changing. The forests are shrinking, the seasons going strange. We have changed, as we must, but there's almost nothing left of the warrior Darr anymore. Now we're merchants." She said this like it made her mouth taste bad. "A wealthy nation! And with every passing generation, we forget a little more of who we were."

I looked at Zhakkarn again, because I wasn't sure what to say. Of course Mikna's people were changing; that was what life did. And of course their climate was all strange; even now

I could hear this world's moon muttering to itself, disgruntled and unhappy. It had been wandering since Sieh's end, pulling the tides and the winds with it, changing where rain fell and rivers ran. The forests shrank and the animals learned to eat different things or died and other things ate them and thrived and everything kept on, dying and borning endlessly, in cycles and patterns and repetition. All these things were mortality.

They don't understand, Zhakkarn said to me without words. *Their lives are too short to see the wholeness of it.*

I scowled. *I'm not even two months old and I understand.*

You are a god.

And being a god was more than just being immortal. I sighed, suddenly feeling lonely on a planet teeming with living beings. Zhakkarn got to her feet after a moment, then came over and put a big hand on my shoulder. I wasn't mad at her anymore after that.

Mikna exhaled, oblivious to us.

"You think Fahno cruel to give Eino to me," she said. I blinked. "You think me cruel to take him, when he doesn't want me."

"Well, yes," I said. Then I sighed. "But Arolu says you can take care of him, if Fahno dies without an heir."

She smiled in a lopsided way. "Take care of him? I want nothing of the sort. I'd be a fool not to recognize the strength in him, Shill; that's precisely why I want him. Call me selfish for it, but I want daughters—and sons, too—with his spirit. It's as simple as that."

I started to get mad again; Zhakkarn squeezed my shoulder, gently. "Well, maybe you should *ask* him to give you some spirit and babies, then!"

She blinked, then laughed. "You have such an odd way of phrasing things." She sighed. "I will be—careful with him. I'm no brute; I want a helpmeet, not just some stud-beast to be chained away between uses. But, Shill...I did *ask* him to marry me. And Lumyn asked him. He hasn't answered either of us... which is why Fahno is forcing the issue."

"Oh!" Why hadn't Eino answered her? I would have to ask him. I was beginning to think that understanding this whole mess might be the key to understanding *him*. And myself.

I had grown, though, and I understood now how important good manners were. "Thank you," I said. "You made me bigger. I'll, um, I'll go think about what you said." Then I shifted from foot to foot, but I was too grown up now not to acknowledge when I'd been wrong. "And I, uh, I'm sorry I was mean to you."

She smiled cheerfully. "That's fine. I got to watch Lady Zhakkarn beat you senseless, after all. Let's call it even."

I was surprised into a laugh, though it was not a very good laugh. (Suddenly I understood why so many mortals laughed without really meaning it.) "Um, I'm gonna go find Eino and talk to him now. Bye."

She nodded, as did Zhakkarn. "Until later, Lady Shill."

I will stop here to tell you another thing you should know. That day with Mikna was when I realized that it is not their poison that makes enulai powerful. Also, I started to know that *having power* does not make a person—or a god—*better*, or *right*. I did not dislike Mikna anymore, and I probably would even like Lumyn if I gave her a chance...but I thought they were both wrong about a lot of things.

Yes yes OK I know you knew that already you do not have to be obnoxious about it OK.

So I went back to Fahno's house, not bothering with a body as I moved through it. Lumyn was gone. Fahno was in her study, and the whole room felt of weary frustration; I did not invade her privacy. The servants were just going about their business as usual. Arolu was in a pretty room with a glass skylight where there were comfortable seats and flowers and books and lengths of cloth and thread on skeins. At first I thought he was working on a small embroidered blanket with a hood and little feet, which was in his lap. But he just sat there, unmoving, and after a moment I realized he had something else in his lap: a small ceramic circle which bore a portrait of a woman's face. I could see her resemblance to Eino in the strength of her jaw and the determination in her gaze. Tehno, Eino's mother, and Arolu's lost wife.

"I'm sorry," he said after a moment. I was confused, because he could not see me; how did he know I was there? But then he touched the circle, and I realized he wasn't talking to me. I wondered what he was sorry about. Whether he'd gone through this at some point, being given to a woman he maybe didn't love, made to stuff himself into floofy clothes and quiet rooms when maybe he was the kind of man who wanted to run and shout. Somewhere along the way he had grown to love Tehno, obviously, but when? How? Had it been worth it?

I was a big girl now; I didn't bother him.

Eino was up on the roof, lounging beneath the canopy of the chair I'd first seen Fahno in. A whole day had passed since that moment; it made me feel nostalgic for how young and silly I'd been back then. He didn't sit like Fahno, though, who liked to be forward-leaning and intent; instead Eino sat sprawled in the chair, his legs crossed, his arms draped over the rests, an expression of distant boredom in his face. But his face was another kind of lie; mortals did that a lot, I was beginning to see. He was not bored, he was brooding. Angry, with perfect grace. I shaped myself out of ether and settled on the ground beside his chair; he did not seem at all surprised when I did.

"The word is out, Shill," he said quietly. "Everyone in town is talking about me. How I somehow got the Council to discuss male property inheritance. How I lured a group of innocent, good-hearted boys to Yukur for unnatural revels in the middle of the night. How I'm the reason a boy ran away to Menchey rather than marry the woman his clan had chosen for him. How I've been seen talking to men in the sharing houses, and foreigners. How I've been gathering an army, and soon it will be the Men's Rebellion all over again."

I leaned against his chair. "What's a sharing house?"

"Where men go when they have no clan to care for them, and when they are not so homely that they are completely without value. They get meals and a bed to sleep in, provided they share it with any woman who wants them." He smiled thinly. "Father fears I'll end up in one, at the rate I'm going. I'm beginning to think I might not mind."

I frowned. Sharing houses did not sound very nice. "Is any of that other stuff true, about you?"

"Does it matter? Home and tradition are threatened. Everywhere, young men of previously honorable character are acting out. Someone must be to blame."

He sounded sad, too, underneath the mad. Maybe I should

not have left, while Lumyn and Fahno and Mikna were still arguing. As I watched him, Eino reached into one of his sleeves and took out something small. I heard the echo of Lumyn's voice and realized it was the thing she'd given him. A small box. He opened it, tilting it so I could see: inside was a very curvy knife. A *beautiful* knife, its handle wrapped in shiny white stuff and its sharp blade inlaid with small plates of black stone and red-and-green lacquer, done up in patterns like forest vines. I *ooh*ed. "I like that knife!"

"Do you?" Eino was smiling again, but it was still mad and sad and bitter. "I do, too, in spite of myself. Such a pretty threat."

"Huh?"

He turned the knife over, setting his thumb against its edge. "Not how she sees it, of course. Lumyn is Darre through and through, whatever anyone else thinks. Of course she would give me a circumcision knife, and think it a romantic gesture; that's how most Darre think of it, after all. It's how I thought of it, really, until I *thought*, and realized just how grotesque the whole custom is."

I knew the word because Papa Tempa had taught it to me. But—"She wants to *cut* you?"

"Of course. It's how marriage goes, for Darre. A woman takes a man to her home, and there in solemn, intimate ceremony..." He shrugged. He'd cut his finger. A fat drop of blood welled up as I watched; I cringed away inwardly even as I stayed still and stared, hypnotized. Demon blood. "I suppose I should be glad these aren't ancient times, when women would just kidnap the men they wanted, cut them to establish their claim, and rape them. We are civilized now. A proper woman gets permission from the boy's clan head, first."

I set my jaw. "No one's going to do anything to you that you don't want." The air rang with my words. I was only a little godling; I couldn't change the universe by word alone. But I could mean it, and Eino felt that. He blinked and looked at me as if finally noticing I was there, though he'd been talking to me all along. This time his smile was not as sad, and more genuine.

"I'm glad I have you for a friend, Shill," he said, gently. "At least what you want from me is something I'm willing to give." He reached for me, perhaps to pet my hair, but I flinched away from the blood on his finger, and he blinked. "...Sorry." He put his hand back in his lap.

I was just proud of myself for not running away this time. I drew up my knees, wrapped my arms around them. "What do you want to do?" I asked. "Are you going to marry Lumyn, or Mikna?"

His voice hardened and his smile faded. "Not you, too, Shill."

I shrugged, awkwardly. "I don't care *which*. I just want to understand how you think about it."

"Ah. Your quest for understanding." Abruptly he got up, pacing with the knife in his hand. "What I think is that I don't want to think about this, Shill. I think there are other problems in the world, other things I could be worrying about, besides who gets to slice me up and ride me! Like how to help you." He stopped, glaring at me. "I want to be your enulai. But I don't know my own magic. And you just saw—I haven't been trained in how to be careful around gods! *You* should choose Mikna; at least she won't kill you by accident."

I wanted to say, *I don't want Mikna*, but he was right; she was a better enulai. Maybe only because she'd been trained and he hadn't, but I didn't know how to make anyone train him. "She isn't terrible," I said, grudgingly.

Eino laughed, pacing again. "No, she isn't. I'd probably fall in love with either of them if I had half a moment to think about it. But no one will give me that moment, and all I can think about is how unfair all this is. If I'd just been born with the right stuff between my legs..." He shook his head.

I knew how that felt, kind of. "I was supposed to be different, too," I said, shifting to sit cross-legged. "Everybody thought I would be the new Trickster when I was born. But I'm not. I even thought I could *make* myself be the Trickster, but none of that has worked. I'm still just me."

Eino stopped again, his back to me this time. It was sunset now, and he stood stock-still in the slanting red light; it made me think of Papa Tempa. "What do you intend to do about that?"

"Do?" I considered, then finally shrugged. "I don't know. I can't be what everyone wanted me to be. I can't even be what I want to be. I'm going to have to find a way to live with what I *am*, I guess." As soon as I figured that out.

"And if you can't? Live with it, I mean."

I had never thought of that. "I don't know. I guess...if I really want to, I can always go to Mama—um, Yeine, that is. Or, or find a demon. When gods want to die, that's what they have to do."

"Poor creatures." It sounded like a joke, the way Eino said it, but it didn't seem very funny. "That you must rely on someone else for the privilege of taking your own life."

I shrugged a little, not really liking the conversation anymore. "Yeine calls mortality a gift. I think it's scary, but when you put it that way, maybe it is."

"Yes." Eino fell silent. I watched him, and worried. He was so still, just like Papa. But mortals are not meant to be like Itempas. They're supposed to bend; if they get too much like him, they break.

I could hear some noise downstairs in the house, but I'd sort of pushed it away as unimportant. A moment later, though, I heard footsteps on the stairs that led up to the roof, and then Arolu opened the door. He was breathing hard, his handsome face stark with worry. "Eino," he said, then seemed to run out of things to say. A moment later, however, he was pushed forward and out of the doorway, and three women in black uniforms stepped out onto the rooftop with Fahno in tow looking worried.

"Eino mau Tehno?" This was one of the uniformed women. As weapons went she had only a knife strapped across the small of her back, but her hand was on the hilt of this. "You are summoned. The Council would like a word with you."

"Would they?" asked Eino, as I got to my feet. He didn't sound alarmed, and suddenly he was smiling. It was a strange smile. "Good. I'd like to talk to them, too."

I did not know this at the time, but later I showed my older siblings a memory of this smile, and they said it was a lot like Sieh's had been, when he was up to something scary.

The women in the uniforms took Eino back to the place I'd visited on my first day in the mortal realm: the Raringa, a great domed building where the Warriors' Council held court and decided the fate of the Darre.

I tried to stay with Eino, because I did not know what was going on but it seemed to be bad. Fahno made me walk with her and Arolu instead, though, because—she said—it would make the Council more prejudiced against Eino if I misbehaved. I wasn't sure if I believed her, but I stayed quiet and near her anyway, just in case. Mikna and Lumyn were there at the Raringa, too, arriving when we did; Lumyn glanced at us but moved to the other side of a gathering knot of women moving into the chamber, while Mikna came over and nodded briskly to Fahno, her jaw set and tight. She saw me and nodded again. Even Ia was there, appearing quietly beside us as we claimed a spot amid the gathering crowd of onlookers.

"What's happening?" I whispered to him. A lot of people looked at us; I'd been too loud again.

"I don't know," he said, frowning slightly. That made me worry more, and I was already worried lots. I didn't like the look on Ia's face. I didn't like that Eino had said *And if you can't? Live with it.*

I especially didn't like that I knew Eino still had Lumyn's knife, hidden somewhere in his robes.

At the door of the Council chamber the uniformed women tried to put shackles on Eino. I bared my teeth and made them go away. They looked at him like *he* had done it. He smiled and said, "There's no need for that, is there?" And they did not try to put shackles on him again.

Fahno looked at me very hard and suspiciously! But she did not know for sure, and that was what mattered. I had learned a lot from Eino.

Now Eino knelt at the center of a wide circle of some fifty or sixty old women seated on cushions, and one much younger woman who sat on an elevated stool facing him. He was quiet and still, his eyes downcast, his robes a swirl of bright burgundy-emerald jewel tones around him; the women were stark and restless in black and gray, murmuring to one another and glaring over pursed lips and sniffing noses. I didn't like any of them.

But it was Fahno who made a rumbly sound that made me think of stormclouds, and Fahno who pushed me aside so she could stalk forward and stand in front of Eino, glaring back at the women around her.

"This is a full Council," she said. Her voice was really quiet; that was how everyone could tell just how mad she was. "Is there some reason why *I* was not informed of this meeting?"

The young woman took a deep breath; I didn't blame her. "You're too close to the situation, Fahno-enulai. You would've had to recuse yourself in any case, so we bypassed that step for efficiency's sake."

"I would've appreciated the chance to recuse myself," she said, glowering, "especially as then you would've had to tell me what the hells this is all about."

"This isn't about *you*, Fahno," said one of the other women, from the far side of the circle.

"Not about me?" Fahno's voice was big and wide, like she was; when she used it fully, it almost filled the domed chamber. Several of the women nearest her flinched. "You drag *my grandson* here, on the eve of his marriage, and this has nothing to do with me?"

Another woman leaned forward, looking as angry as Fahno. "If you want us to consider you, Fahno—and your permissiveness, your indulgence, how this boy's wildness is due to your *incompetence as a clan matriarch*, we certainly will—"

"If I may," said Eino, from where he knelt behind Fahno. He

said it lightly, in a pleasant tone, but his voice was just as deep
and resonant as Fahno's; everyone started and turned to him,
Fahno included. He smiled and ducked his eyes demurely. "If I
may, great warriors, Kitke-ennu, my beba. I would like to speak
for myself."

"This isn't the time," Fahno snapped.

"There will be no better, Beba. Please."

She stared at him; he stared back. For the first time I realized
they had the same eyes, just as deepwater black and implacable,
even though Eino's were lined with kohl and silver-lidded and
Fahno's were deep-set and ringed from worry. She shook her
head just a little, and I almost heard the speech-without-words
between them! Or maybe I imagined it? *I won't be able to protect
you,* she said, I thought.

I'll protect myself, he said back, and I shivered all over without
knowing why. But at the end of the exchange, Fahno sighed
and stepped aside. She lingered in the circle, though, her arms
folded, making clear by her presence that Eino was not without
his supporters.

I pushed forward through the crowd, too, before Mikna could
grab me, and I took Fahno's hand. She glanced down at me in
surprise, and some of the old women gave me bad looks. I did
not give them bad looks back! I was being very mature.

"Please," said Eino. He spoke quietly now, but his back was
very straight, his hands very flat in his lap. "May I know why I
have been brought here?"

The young woman seemed to consider whether to answer.
"There has been an accusation," she said, finally—and then she
eyed Fahno. "One that we have already dismissed as ground-
less, mind you. It was unofficial in any case, made by Luud mau

Esuum, a young unproven man of one of the merchant clans. We are aware that young men can be...excitable."

Many of the women in the circle nodded, some indulgently, some maliciously. Eino bore it all without a twitch and said, "And what was the nature of the accusation, Kitke-ennu, if I—or my clan matriarch—may know?"

"Sedition." Kitke-ennu said this flatly, but there was a rustle around the chamber again—not amid the ring of Council-women this time, but the watching crowd, most of whom apparently hadn't known. Kitke scowled. "But we have dismissed it out of respect for Fahno-enulai, who has served Darr well in all her years."

"Sedition!" Eino laughed then, stilling the murmurs; women stared at him, shocked. He shook his head to himself. "Oh, poor Luud. He'd have done better to accuse me of luring him into iniquity; you would have believed that. What did you do to him, to scare him so badly that he told the truth?"

Fahno flinched. Arolu gasped and put his sleeve to his mouth. Several women in the circle tried to speak at once; Kitke quickly held up a hand and leaned forward, her eyes narrowing. "Are you saying the charge is true?"

"That depends on what you think of as sedition." Eino shrugged, no longer demure or serene. The look on his face was openly contemptuous now; he looked around at the Warriors' Council the same way Ia had looked at me on that first day, or Zhakkarn on the second—like he *knew* they were beneath him. He lifted his chin, as if to emphasize this. "I believe the Darre are stronger as a whole people, not with half of our kind reduced to possessions and treated like children. I act in accordance with this belief. Is that sedition?"

"It is!" yelled one of the women behind us, and there were other murmurs in the room, some of them from the circle, others from beyond it. Kitke-ennu glanced around at them without moving her head; her jaw flexed.

"I do not believe so," she said—and there were murmurs in agreement with this, too, which made me happy. But then Kitke added, "Yet if men would be treated as women, then they must carry themselves as women, and exercise sound judgment, comport themselves with dignity. You cannot act the barbarian, Eino mau Tehno, and expect civilized folk to listen."

"The men of Darr have been civilized for two hundred years and more," Eino said, his voice sharp and words quick. "It has gotten us nowhere. Perhaps barbarism will be more effective."

And he drew his hands into his sleeves for a moment, then slipped them out again; with his left hand he raised Lumyn's mosaic knife.

There were murmurs again, and gasps, and Fahno froze. "Eino—"

He glanced at her, then set his jaw and drew his hands into his robes again. "I will not be bartered, Beba," he said. "Not even for your sake."

"What are you doing?" Arolu, behind us, was trying to come forward; Mikna and Ia held him back. "No, no, he is my son, I cannot let him—"

"There is no need for anything drastic," Kitke-ennu said, holding up her hands in alarm; she'd half risen to her feet already. "To kill yourself—"

"*Kill* myself?" Eino laughed again, so harshly that I jumped. "No. I do this with the Warriors' Council itself as witness, in a house that belongs to all Darre. I am *claiming* myself."

We could not see what he did, there inside his robes, but we saw the sudden, sharp jerk of his movement. Saw how his face tightened, his lips drawing back from his teeth. He did not cry out, though I flinched, and so did Ia, at the white flare of his pain. I smelled his demon blood then, a lot of it! And a moment later, spots of darker color appeared on the cloth across his lap.

There were SCREAMS! I was almost one of them! Fahno staggered back, staring at Eino; beyond her, Mikna and Arolu were just as shocked. Ia—he stared, too, but there was the tiniest of admiring smiles on his lips. Lumyn looked ill.

. Eino's face had gone sallow. He swayed where he knelt, and I saw his eyes roll back. He was going to fall! So I ran over and caught him, and held him against me while everyone around us just kept on freaking out.

"I don't suppose . . . you can heal me," he murmured, through the screams and chaos. "Sweet bright hells, this hurts."

"I don't know how," I said, anxiously. "I still haven't learned that. Ia's coming, though—"

"No. He can only n-negate what I've done. I don't want it negated." Eino's eyes fluttered shut; he'd begun shaking, his skin turning cool and clammy. "I will be . . . what I choose to be. If they cannot make a p-place for me, I will carve my own."

I blinked. Oh.

Ia and Arolu reached us, Arolu's eyes wide and white; at once he tore off one of his sleeves, twisted it, and then pushed Eino back so he could get his robes up. Someone was calling for a bonebender. Eino, however, had started to laugh through his shaking. He murmured something; I leaned close to hear it.

"I *am* a warrior," he said, through gritted teeth, "and I will not fight fair."

I sat up, staring down at him. Ia, standing at the edge of my vision, suddenly looked sharply at me.

Oh. I understood a new thing, all of a sudden:

Power is not a thing that can be given.

The men of Darr had tried to give up theirs, to prove their loyalty after their fellows' betrayal, but they were still Darre. The Darre as a whole kept trying to let go of their warrior selves, but they couldn't; it was what had made them strong for so long, and they knew it. Even Ia—he had chosen to live among the mortals because they did not fear him, but that did not make him anything less than he was: the greatest and most terrifying of the Three's remaining children.

Everyone treated Eino like less than he was, but that did not make him so. Even when he tried to fit himself in with their thinking, when he let them use him, he was still not their thing. He was still himself: a great mortal temporarily folding himself small, *choosing* to bend and smile behind his sleeve and refrain from dancing in others' presence. He might allow others to forget his worth, might have to remind them, might have to fight and bleed to make them recognize it—but as long as he remembered who and what he was, none of them could diminish him. He was, would forever be, glorious.

Oh!

And all he would ever have to do, to claim his true glorious self—

OH! OH! OH!

—was *take his power back.*

I lifted my hands without quite knowing why. Just felt right. I made cups of my hands. Something filled them now, brimming gold and bright-hot and strange. Where had it come from? Mostly Eino—but there was some of me in there, too, just a little, just enough. A spark of myself. Why had I added that to Eino's shining power?

Because I had to. Because it was...it was why I was there! Why I *was*, at all.

All around us the mortal realm seemed to swirl, as if something had set it spinning around an axis that was us. But here, here which had become the center of all things, everything was suddenly still.

"Shill?" Ia's voice was sharp.

"This is yours," I whispered to Eino, who squinted up at me, panting. "You took it back from them."

Eino looked utterly confused. "Mine?"

I grinned. "Here!"

"Wha—" he began, before I plunged both hands up to the wrists into his body.

Into him! Into the he-that-was-Eino, not the flesh, not just the soul! Oh, there are no words for it, not even in my sophisticated big-girl vocabulary, but it was beautiful and perfect, all the whatness and howness of existence pouring through me, finding all the whoness and whyness of him and filling it up, blowing it open, setting us both on fire like baby stars! And I was all swirly, WE were swirly together, there is nothing to describe it except

YOU

ARE

And also, also:

I

AM

Because I am! Because THAT IS WHAT I AM!

Many things happened.

There was light like morning all around me. In the light, my hair lifted and whipped. I rose—no, I *grew*, limbs and face getting longer, breasts and hips becoming more than thoughts, hair stretching into a whipping banner. As I grew I pulled the shining, screaming thing that was Eino with me, dragging him by his soul; I was laughing. *We* were laughing, him through his screams and me through my tears, as all around us gathered a ring of power so vicious and intense that the Raringa's floor peeled apart in splinters and rubble and its roof shattered and flew outward and most of the mortals screamed and fled.

And high above us the moon moved back into the place that it had held for eons, and the sun gasped and turned to see what was happening, and all the planets, everywhere, suddenly paid attention and got excited. All over existence I could feel all the incomprehensible members of my family perk up, or inhale, or sparkle, or ripple as they perceived the change.

It is the best feeling I have ever had. I wanted to share it! So I sent the light forth in spreading-ring wavelets, seeking, feeling, knowing:

An old woman in a place that does not revere old women the way the Darre do. She has nothing—no home, no family, no money, not even her full mind—but she has stood to scream at the cruel boys who've tried to take the little dog she loves, stood to fight them, because even she deserves to have something that loves her back—

Yes.

*A young man who is smaller than he should be, visibly weaker;
others have smelled his weakness. They hurt him, as they have done
over and over, for no reason other than their own pleasure, but in
this lone moment he is sick of it, he is done, and he balls his fists and
launches himself at them even though he knows it is futile—*
Yes, this one, too.

*A child, a girl, the least valued of her many siblings, the one who
seems like nothing so her parents treat her like nothing, give her
nothing that she does not take first, and she demands nothing except
the one thing they owe her, which is that they look at her, look at her,
LOOK AT ME RIGHT NOW—*
Oh, yes, yes, yes!

And more, and more, new fires igniting as the wave of power
circled the globe. Nothing special about any of them, nothing
unique, just the right confluence of circumstance in the right
moment of my maturation, and that was all it took. It hurt every
time this happened, took that spark of me that seemed as necessary as their own strength—but I grew, too! Their power made
me powerful even as I diminished. It was theirs! *I* was theirs!
They took what they should always have had, and I made it real
for them, made it right for me!

"Shill!" Ia came through the light and grabbed me flesh and
soul; I laughed wildly, wanting him to laugh with me. "Look
at what you're doing to yourself! Stop this!" But I did not care
about his concern. I wanted more: to be more, to give more.
This was me, and I had found myself at last, and I would revel in
it 'til I no longer could!

So Ia did the only thing possible: he surrounded me with
the quintessence of himself so that the *nothing* of him clashed
against the *everything* of me.

And then, only then, did I stop doing what I was doing—whatever that was—and settle back into myself.

I sagged to the floor, confused, because...because...what? I felt glorious. I also felt almost dead. This was a very strange combination of feelings.

"No, Shill." Ia held me still, stroking my hair back from my face. "No. Make them *earn* what you can give them. Make sure they're worthy, little Sibling."

"Wh-what?" I couldn't think. Why was Ia being so nice, all of a sudden? What had happened, exactly? I tried to sit up and could not. Ia helped me. I would think about that later, though, because suddenly there were more important mysteries to ponder.

Like: what had wrecked the Raringa? There was rubble everywhere around me, a burst pipe at the back of the room spraying a flood, fallen lanterns smoldering and and torn scrolls fluttering and broken record-spheres rolling about. Most of the people in the chamber were not hurt, for which I was relieved. But—suddenly I remembered what I had done, what I had been *compelled* to do to Eino, and I gasped, looking around for him. "Where—" Then I saw him, and my mouth fell open.

Because Eino floated unconscious at the center of the room in a slow-curling funnel of hair and robe. He *glowed*, blacklit and shivery—and all around him, swirling too in a delighted dance, were dozens of small colored balls. Some of them had clouds. As I watched, down through the hole in the Raringa's ceiling came a tiny sun, which circled Eino once and then passed into Eino's flesh, vanishing. I could feel other suns out there, queuing up to do the same thing: at least ten of them, happily giving themselves over to remake him into what they'd yearned for: a new god of mischief and troublemaking and stirring things up just for shits and giggles—or maybe because tradition had held sway for too long.

A new... trickster. *The* Trickster.

And elsewhere, everywhere around the mortal realm, all over this planet—there were others. One... two... six... a dozen... more. Newborn gods: mortals suddenly and shockingly turned immortal, all of them still forging the selves they would become, solidifying in power... but all of them made by me.

"Oh," I said, blinking. "Whoops."

It was Yeine, later when we had all gone back to Fahno's house, who explained what had happened.

"It's something I thought might take place eventually," she said. She sat at the kitchen table; everyone in the house had gathered round in awe. Juem, with shaking hands, had offered her a roasted gran banana, and to everyone's surprise she had grinned and enthusiastically accepted. It had been her favorite, apparently, when she was mortal.

She looked at me, where I sat across from her. My mortal shape was taller than hers now, all grown up, with nice strong arms and long fast legs and nice white teeth, which I used to grin back at her.

"I turn my back on you for *three days*, Shill." She shook her head, amused and wry. "Well, that will teach me to assume I know what the universe needs. I thought it lacked... something. I thought that something might be what it had lost—and that was indeed the case." She turned now to Eino.

Eino, who floated in the middle of the room, because he could not figure out how to make himself stand on the ground.

Everyone was giving him a wide berth, and he looked distinctly worried, himself. Poor baby god! At least he'd finally figured out how to make the planets stop bothering him.

"Welcome to the family," she said gently, and Eino flinched.

"Please," he said, fidgeting; his robes kept swirling around him in an unfelt wind, and his hair kept getting into his face. "Please, great Lady of Twilight—"

"Yeine will do."

He looked distinctly uncomfortable. I leaned over to whisper to Yeine, "Boys aren't supposed to get *familiar* with strange women." Then I winked at Arolu, so he would know I had listened to him. He groaned from where he sat, looking faint as he had all afternoon.

Yeine coughed, though I could tell she was really laughing. "Ah. Things have changed a bit since my day, I see; back then we couldn't shut men up around strange women. But I think you'll find, Eino mau Tehno, that the rules of mortality no longer apply to you now. Speak to whomever you like."

He stared at her, and gradually began to sag toward the ground. "It's true, then. I'm...this is..." He lifted his hands, stared at them. "I'm a godling."

She regarded him for a long moment, thoughtful. I stared at him. "*Yeah*," I said. I couldn't believe he actually seemed upset about it. "You're a godling, and now you'll live forever, and you've got all kinds of magic! Now nobody can make you get married, or keep you from dancing. Now, if you wanted, you could make every man in Darr free, just like that!"

I snapped my fingers—or tried to. But as I lifted my hand, there was a terrible, vertiginous moment in which my stomach dropped and the room spun and I felt myself diminish. I shuddered and closed my eyes. Yeine, however, touched my hand, and a moment later I felt better. Not good. Just not awful anymore.

"No, he can't," she said, sternly. "Or rather, he can, but if he does so in your presence, he will harm you. Power cannot be given, Shill; isn't that what you finally understood? People can only take it—and then only what is already theirs by right. Only what they can claim, and hold, with their own hands. Anything more is dangerous to them and others. Anything less, however..." She squeezed my hand, and I looked up to see her smile. "Well, that's where you come in, my big girl. Nahadoth and Itempas will be so proud."

I grinned back, dizzyingly happy. I was myself at last, which was all the Three had ever really wanted me to be.

"Every man in Darr has the right to be free," Eino said. He was on his feet now. A persistent little moon orbited his head; he couldn't seem to get rid of it. This in no way diminished the grave determination in his face.

"Not at the expense of Darr's women," said Mikna. He rounded on her, and she lifted her chin, even though he was a god now and she was just a mortal. I felt that this was very brave of her.

"...No," he agreed after a moment, to her obvious surprise. "But our strength should not diminish yours. It makes us *all* powerful, together." He inclined his head to her.

Mikna seemed to consider this, and then after a moment she nodded back in silent acknowledgement.

"Then tell everybody this," I said. It seemed so obvious all of a sudden. "You see it now, Eino; help all of the Darre see it, too. Show them who they were, and who they could become!" Then I would grow as they grew, and everything would be better!

"And yet," Ia said, dampening my glee, because *Ia*, "Shill has done precisely what she claims should not be done; she has given power beyond imagining to mortals who cannot possibly be ready for it." He stood on the edge of the room with his arms folded, beyond the clustering of folk around Yeine. For the first time I realized how lonely he seemed, over there by himself.

"Yes." Yeine grew grave as well. "A plethora of new gods who haven't a clue of what they are, or why this has happened; there will be trouble from it, I am certain. From many quarters, since our family was not ready for so many new additions, so soon." She sighed. "And yet it is something I expected, as I said. Just... not now."

"Mortals becoming gods." Fahno, at the table with us, rubbed her eyes. "You *expected* this, Lady? Before you, no one had ever done it. And the confluence of circumstances required to make it happen—"

"Established a precedent," Yeine said. "Made a path. Opened a door. It is the nature of this universe that once a thing becomes possible, it *will* happen somewhere, for however brief a time. Life spawns from lifelessness, gods from godlings; why should there not be a bridge in between, from the mortal to the immortal?" She abruptly looked pleased. "A new cycle of life. Fascinating."

Ia grimaced. Maybe he was not fascinated. "It almost killed her, though." He was looking at me.

"True." Yeine watched me as well. "And what that means is that you cannot just empower any mortal, Shill, nor can you do it frequently. Certain conditions and circumstances must obviously be met, first, to facilitate the change; what those are, you will have to discover. So from here on, do try to exercise some discretion, why don't you?"

I inhaled, delighted, because this was part of me, too. "I'm going to get really good at it." And as I got better—"Oh, wow. I'll be *strong*, one day."

"One day, yes." Yeine looked thoughtful. "Mortal life has always been, well, mortal. This universe that Nahadoth and Itempas and I have built is not eternal. There may be others, but when this one ends, mortalkind ends with it. But perhaps it need not end with *death*."

We all fell silent at that, in wonder, in fear. I couldn't imagine such a time ever coming to pass. But I understood this instinctively: because I existed, the end of mortal life—the *rebirth* of mortal life, into immortality—was possible. And if it was possible...

"I'll work to make that happen," I said, and even just this thought made me feel happy and right and full of light again.

Then I thought of something and glanced at Ia, and bit my lip. "But, um, maybe you could help me, Sibling, until then? I mean—you stopped me, when I would've spun myself away to nothing."

He drew back, with an offended air. "I've done enough baby-sitting, Shill, thank you." And with that he vanished.

I slumped, disappointed. Yeine shook her head and got to her feet, then leaned down to murmur in my ear.

"How convenient that you're not a baby anymore. Isn't it?"

I blinked, and then a slow grin spread across my lips. She winked, and straightened again. Well, then.

I put my hands on the table and pushed to my feet. "OK," I said. "There's lots to do! You mortals have to fix all the stuff that's wrong with your realm, if you're going to make it to the end of the universe." I waggled a finger at Mikna, who lifted an eyebrow skeptically. Then I pointed at Eino. "You! Come with me. We have to find the other babies and make sure they do not wreck stuff."

A pained look crossed his face; his little pet moon glowed white with amusement. "You barely know what you're doing yourself, Shill."

"That is beside the point. I know more than you do; that means it's my job to teach." I put my hands on my hips, pleased with this plan. "I can help them find their natures, too! That's what I do now, see."

"I'm not certain this is wise," said Fahno; she had the same look on her face as Eino.

"Empowerment does not always wait for wisdom," said Yeine, "though that will doubtless come with time in Shill's case. Hopefully soon."

"Yes, but will we survive until then?"

"Hey! I'm *right here*." I shook my head, then went over to Eino. "OK. Calm down about being a god. You can still do mortal stuff if you want. Marry and make babies and lead revolutions all you want. Right?"

Eino blinked in surprise, then looked at Fahno, who stared back at him as well. He bit his lip and looked away for a moment. "Beba."

Fahno took a deep breath and stood. "If you want nothing more to do with us, I will understand."

He flinched. "No! I'm still Darre, Beba. I'm still *clan*."

She hesitated, lowered her eyes. "You have a new clan now."

He set his jaw. "I have an old clan." He went over to her, took her hands. She squeezed his hands, her eyes overbright, and Arolu came over, too. Eino folded his arms round them both, shaking, and there were lots of tears and whispers of things that probably should have been said long before.

Quietly, beyond us all, I felt Yeine vanish, and knew why. Eino might be Darre now, but Fahno was right; his attachment to his mortal life would not last long. It was as Zhakkarn had said, and as Yeine had learned herself: they were too small, too ephemeral, to grasp the whole of what we were. In the end, we would always leave them behind.

But that would happen on its own, with Eino. I didn't need to push. Let him make his own farewells to mortality; he had forever, after all. And after all, someday mortalkind would be better. I wouldn't push them, either—but when they were ready, I would be there, waiting. I would help them all I could.

I won't push any of you, see? I didn't give you anything, and you don't owe me anything. Your power is yours; it has always been there. I'm just going to help you reach it. What you do with it, from there on, is up to you.

Now come along, babies! Today I will teach you how not to smash planets by accident. Oh! And also: how to tell stories the Proper Way. You always have to finish with THE END, or Papa will give you *such* a look.

THE END.

extras

orbit

meet the author

N. K. Jemisin

N. K. JEMISIN is a career counselor, political blogger, and would-be gourmand living in New York City. She's been writing since the age of ten, although her early works will never see the light of day. Find out more about the author at nkjemisin.com.

introducing

If you enjoyed
THE AWAKENED KINGDOM,
look out for

THE FIFTH SEASON

Book One of the Broken Earth

by N. K. Jemisin

THIS IS THE WAY THE WORLD ENDS. AGAIN.

Three terrible things happen in a single day.

*Essun, masquerading as an ordinary schoolteacher in a
quiet small town, comes home to find that her husband has
brutally murdered their son and kidnapped their daughter.
Mighty Sanze, the empire whose innovations have been civilization's bedrock for a thousand years, collapses as its greatest city
is destroyed by a madman's vengeance. And worst of all, across
the heartland of the world's sole continent, a great red rift is torn
that spews enough ash to darken the sky for years. Or centuries.*

*But this is the Stillness, a land long familiar with struggle,
where orogenes—those who wield the power of the earth as a*

weapon—are feared far more than the long cold night. Essun has remembered herself, and she will have her daughter back.

She does not care if the world falls apart around her. Essun will break it herself, if she must, to save her daughter.

The first novel in a new series by award-winning author N. K. Jemisin, where a mother struggles to find her daughter in a post-apocalyptic world.

1

The straw is so warm that Damaya doesn't want to come out of it. Like a blanket, she thinks through the bleariness of half-sleep. Like the quilt her great-grandmother once sewed for her out of patches of uniform cloth. Years ago Muh Dear had worked for the Brevard militia as a seamstress, and got to keep the scraps from any repairs that required new cloth. The blanket she made for Damaya is mottled and dark, blue and green in rippling bands like columns of marching men, but it came from Muh Dear's hands, so Damaya doesn't care that it's ugly. It smells sweet and gray and a bit fusty, so it is easy to imagine that the straw—which smells mildewy and like old manure with a hint of fruity, fungal sweetness—is Muh's blanket. Even though the actual blanket is back in Damaya's room, on the bed where she left it, and in which she will never sleep again.

She can hear voices outside the straw pile now: Mama and someone else talking as they draw closer. A rattle-creak as the barn door is unlocked, and they come inside; another rattle as the door shuts behind them. Then Mother raises her voice and calls, "DamaDama?"

Damaya curls up tighter, clenching her teeth. She hates that stupid nickname. She hates the way Mother says it, all light and sweet, like it's actually a term of endearment and not a lie.

When Damaya doesn't respond, Mother says: "She can't have gotten out. My husband checked all the barn locks himself."

"Nothing is secure for her kind." This voice belongs to a man. Not her father or older brother, or the comm headman, or anyone she recognizes. This man's voice is deep, and he speaks with an accent like none she's ever heard: sharp and heavy, with long drawled *o*'s and *a*'s and crisp beginnings and ends to every word. Smart-sounding. Dangerous. He jingles faintly as he walks, so much that she wonders whether he's wearing a big set of keys. Or perhaps he has a lot of money in his pockets? This thought makes Damaya curl in on herself, sick and trembling, because of course she's heard the other children in creche whisper of child-markets in faraway cities of beveled stone. Not all places in the world are as civilized as the Nomidlats. She laughed off the whispers then, but everything is different now.

"Here," says the man's voice, not far off now. "Fresh spoor, I think."

Mother makes a sound of disgust, and Damaya burns in shame as she realizes they've seen the corner she uses for a bathroom. It smells terrible there, even though she's been throwing straw over it each time. "Squatting on the ground like an animal. I raised her better."

"Is there a toilet here?" asks the child buyer, in a tone of polite curiosity. "Did you give her a bucket?"

Silence from Mother, which stretches on, and belatedly Damaya realizes the man has *reprimanded* Mother with those quiet questions. It isn't the sort of reprimand Damaya is used to. The man hasn't raised his voice or called anyone names. Yet Mother stands still and silenced as surely as if he'd followed the words with a smack to the head.

A giggle bubbles up in her throat, and at once she crams her fist into her mouth to stop it from spilling out. They'll hear Damaya laugh at her mother's embarrassment, and then the child buyer will know what a terrible child she really is. But is that such a bad thing? Maybe then her parents will get less for her. That alone almost makes her let the giggles loose—or screams so the buyer will think there's something wrong with her—because Damaya hates her parents, she *hates* them, and anything that will make them suffer makes her feel better.

Then she bites down on her hand, hard, and hates herself, because *of course* they're selling Damaya if she can think such thoughts.

Footsteps nearby. "Cold in here," says the man.

"Not freezing," says Mother, and Damaya almost giggles again at her sullen, defensive tone. Maybe the child buyer will smack Mother for giving him attitude.

But the child buyer ignores Mother. His footsteps come closer. Damaya can feel each step the way she feels everyone else's steps, a beat against her eardrums with a faint echo that goes down into the barn's dirt floor. She has always felt things in this two-layered way, and only lately has she come to understand what it means. His steps are heavier than most, though, echoing through the rock that lies a few feet below the soil, almost like he's *trying* to make the earth shake. She's never felt anyone whose steps go that deep.

And now he's coming up the ladder, to the loft where she lies under the straw.

"Ah," he says, reaching the top. "It's warmer up here."

"Dama!" Mother sounds furious now. "Get down here!"

Damaya scrunches herself up tighter under the straw and says nothing. The child buyer's footsteps pace closer.

"You needn't be afraid," he says in that rolling voice. Closer. She feels the reverberation of his voice through the wood and down to the ground and into the rock and back again. Closer. "I've come to help you, Damaya Strongback."

Another thing she hates, that he calls her by her use-name. She doesn't have a strong back at all, and neither does Mother. All Strongback means is that some of her female ancestors were lucky enough to join a comm but too undistinguished to earn a more secure place within it. *Strongbacks get dumped same as commless when times get hard*, her brother Chaga has told her, to tease her. Especially if a comm has too much labor and not enough specialization, and especially during a Season. Of course, Chaga is a Resistant, like Father. All comms like to have them around no matter how hard the times, in case of sickness and famine and such.

The man's footsteps stop just outside the straw pile. "You needn't be afraid," he says again, more softly now. Mother is still down on the ground level; she probably can't hear him. "I won't let your mother hurt you."

Damaya inhales.

She's not stupid. The man is a child buyer, and child buyers do terrible things. But because he has said these words, and because some part of Damaya is tired of being afraid and angry, she uncurls. She pushes her way through the soft warm pile and sits up, peering out at the man through loose strands of hair and dirty straw.

He is as strange-looking as he sounds, and not from anywhere near Palela. His skin is almost white, it's so paper-pale; he must smoke and curl up in strong sunlight. He has long limp hair, which together with the skin might mark him as an Arctic, though the color of it—a deep heavy black, like the soil near an old blow—doesn't fit. Damaya's creche teacher says Arctics go in more for brown or orange or yellow hair. Eastern Coasters' hair is black like that, and when it's curly it's the next best thing to ashblow hair, but people from the east have black skin. And he's big, not small like Arctics are supposed to be—taller and with broader shoulders than Father. But where Father's big shoulders join a big chest and a big belly, this man sort of *tapers*. Everything about the stranger seems lean and elongated. Nothing about him makes racial sense.

But what strikes Damaya most is the child buyer's eyes. They're *white*, or nearly so. She can see the whites of his eyes, and then a silvery-gray disk of color that she can barely distinguish from the white, even up close. The pupils of his eyes are wide in the barn's dimness, and startling amid the desert of colorlessness.

She's heard of eyes like these, which are called *icewhite* in stories and stonelore. They're rare, and always an ill omen. But then the child buyer smiles at Damaya, and she doesn't even think twice before she smiles back. She trusts him immediately. She knows she shouldn't, but she does.

"And here we are," he says, still speaking softly so that Mother won't hear. "Damaya Strongback, I presume?"

"Dama," she says, automatically. People she likes get to call her that. "Just once, not DamaDama. I hate that."

He inclines his head gracefully, and extends a hand to her. "So noted. Will you join us, then, Dama?"

Damaya doesn't move and he does not grab her. He just stays where he is, patient as stone, offering and not taking. Ten breaths pass. Twenty. Damaya knows she'll have to go with him, but she likes that he makes it *feel* like a choice. So at last she takes his hand and lets him pull her up. He keeps her hand while she dusts off as much of the straw as she can, and then he tugs her closer, just a little. "One moment."

"Hnh?" But the child buyer's other hand is already behind her head, pressing two fingers into the base of her skull so quickly and deftly that she doesn't startle. He shuts his eyes for a moment, shivers minutely, and then exhales, letting her go.

"Duty first," he says, cryptically. She touches the back of her head, confused and still feeling the lingering sensation of his fingers' pressure. "Now let's head downstairs."

"What did you do?"

"Just a little ritual of sorts. Come now; I need to tell your mother you'll be leaving with me."

So it really is true. Damaya bites her lip, and when the man turns to head back to the ladder, she follows a pace or two behind.

"Well, that's that," says the child buyer as they reach Mother on the ground floor. "If you could assemble a package for her—one or two changes of clothing, any travel food you can provide, a coat—we'll be on our way."

Mother stops glaring at Damaya, in surprise. "We gave away her coat."

"Gave it away?"

He speaks mildly, but Mother looks abruptly uncomfortable. "She's got a cousin who needed it. We don't all have wardrobes full of fancy clothes to spare. And—" Here Mother hesitates, glancing at Damaya. Damaya just looks away. She doesn't want to see if Mother looks sorry for giving away the coat. She especially doesn't want to see if Mother's *not* sorry.

"And you've heard that orogenes don't feel cold the way the rest of us do," says the man, with a weary sigh. "That's a myth. I assume you've seen your daughter take cold before."

"Yes, but." Mother catches Damaya looking back this time. Both of them flinch. "But I thought…"

That Damaya might be faking it. That was what she'd said to Damaya that first day, after they got home from creche and while they were setting her up in the barn. Mother had raged, her face streaked with tears, while Father just sat there, silent and grim. Damaya had hidden it from them, Mother said, hidden everything, pretended to be a child when she was really a monster, that was what monsters *did*, she had always known there was something *wrong* with Damaya, she had always been such a little *liar*—

The man shakes his head. "Nevertheless, she will need some protection against the cold. It will grow warmer as we approach the Equatorials, but we'll be weeks on the road getting there."

Mother's jaw flexes. "So you're really taking her to Yumenes, then."

"Of course I—" And then the man stares at her. "Ah." He glances at Damaya. They both look at Damaya, their gazes like an itch. She squirms. "And even thinking I was coming to kill your daughter, you had the comm headman summon me."

Mother tenses. "Don't. It wasn't, I didn't—" At her sides, her hands flex. Then she bows her head, as if she is ashamed, which Damaya knows is a lie. Mother isn't ashamed of anything she's done. If she were, why did she do it?

"Ordinary people can't take care of…of children like her," says Mother, very softly. Her eyes dart to Damaya's, once, and away, fast. "She almost killed a boy at school. We've got another child, and neighbors, and…she's *dangerous*. I have to think of what's best for the whole family, the whole comm…" She trails off. Then abruptly she squares her shoulders, lifting her chin. "That's any citizen's duty, isn't it?"

"Mmm. And the Empire thanks you for your sacrifice and service." The words are praise. The tone is not. Damaya looks at the man again, confused now. Child buyers don't kill children. And what's this about going to the Equatorials? Those lands are far, far to the south.

Then the child buyer glances at Damaya and, somehow, understands that she does not understand. His face softens, which should be impossible with those frightening eyes of his.

"To Yumenes," the man says to Mother, to Damaya. "Yes. She's young enough, and therefore I'm taking her to the Fulcrum, where she will be trained to use her curse."

Damaya stares back at him, realizing just how wrong she's been. Mother has not sold Damaya. She and Father have *given* Damaya away. And Mother does not hate her; actually, she *fears* Damaya. Does that make a difference? Maybe. Damaya doesn't know how to feel, in response to these revelations.

And the man, the man is not a child buyer at all. He is—

"You're a Guardian?" she asks, even though by now she knows. He smiles again. She did not think Guardians were like this. In her head they are tall, cold-faced, bristling with weapons and secret knowledge. He's tall, at least.

In most of the stories she's been told, though, Guardians *kill* roggas like her.

"I am," he says, and takes her hand. He likes to touch people a lot, she thinks. "I'm *your* Guardian."

She frowns, but this is because she's more confused than ever.

Mother sighs. "I can give you a blanket for her."

"That will do, thank you." And then the man falls silent, waiting. After a few breaths of this, Mother realizes he's waiting for *her*. She nods jerkily, then leaves, her back stiff the whole way out of the barn. So then the man and Damaya are alone.

"Here," he says, reaching up to his shoulders. He's wearing something that must be a uniform: blocky shoulders and long stiff lines of sleeve and pant leg, burgundy cloth that looks sturdy but scratchy. Like Muh's quilt. It has a short cape, more decorative than useful, but he pulls it off and wraps it around Damaya. It's long enough to be a dress on her, and warm from his body.

"Thank you," she says. "Who are you?"

"My name is Schaffa Guardian Warrant."

She's never heard of a place called Warrant, but it must exist, because what good is a comm name otherwise? "Guardian is a use-name?"

"It is for Guardians." He drawls this, and her cheeks grow warm with embarrassment. "We aren't much use to any comm, after all, in the ordinary course of things. It's appropriate that we advertise this."

Damaya frowns in confusion. "What, so they'll kick *you* out when a Season comes? But..." Guardians are many things, she knows from the stories, but they are not unimportant. They must be strong to do what they do; they must be great warriors and hunters and sometimes—often—assassins. Comms need such people when hard times come.

Schaffa shrugs, moving away to sit on a bale of old hay. There's another bale behind Damaya, but she keeps standing, because she likes being on the same level with him. Even sitting he's taller, but at least not by so much.

"The orogenes of the Fulcrum serve the world," he says. "You will have no use-name from here forth, because your usefulness lies in what you are, not merely some familial aptitude. From birth an orogene child can stop a shake; even without training, you are orogene. Within a comm or without one, *you are orogene*. With training, however, and with the guidance of other skilled orogenes at the Fulcrum, you can be useful not merely to a single comm, but the whole world." He spreads his hands. "As a Guardian, via the orogenes in my care, I have taken on a similar purpose, with a similar breadth. It's fitting that I share my charges' possible fate."

Damaya is so curious, so full of questions, that she doesn't know which to ask first. "Do you have—" She stumbles over the concept, and the words, and the acceptance of herself. "Others, l-like me, I." And she runs out of words.

Schaffa laughs, as if he senses her eagerness and it pleases him. "I am Guardian to six right now," he says, inclining his head to let Damaya know that this is the right way to say it, to think it. "Including you."

"And you brought them all to Yumenes? You found them all like this, like me—"

"Not exactly. The first three were given into my care when I became a Guardian. Later, when I had more experience, I was assigned to ride circuit in this part of the Nomidlats." He spreads his hands. "When your parents reported their orogene child to Palela's headman, he telegraphed word to Brevard, which sent it to Geddo, which sent it to Yumenes—and they in turn telegraphed word to me." He sighs. "It's only luck that I checked in at the node station near Brevard the day after the message arrived. Otherwise I wouldn't have seen it for another two weeks."

Damaya knows Brevard, though Yumenes is only legend to her, and the rest of the places Schaffa has mentioned are just words in a creche textbook. Brevard is the town closest to Palela, and it's much bigger. It's where Father and Chaga go to sell farmshares at the beginning of every growing season. Then she registers his words. Two more weeks in this barn, freezing and peeing in a corner. She's glad he got the message in Brevard, too.

"You're very lucky," he says, perhaps reading her expression. His own has grown sober. "Not all parents do the right thing. Sometimes they don't keep their child isolated as the Fulcrum and we Guardians recommend. Sometimes they do, but we get the message too late, and by the time a Guardian arrives a mob has carried the child off and beaten her to death. Don't think too unkindly of your parents, Dama. You're alive and well, and that is no small thing."

Damaya squirms a little, unwilling to accept this. He sighs. "And sometimes," he continues, "the parents of an orogene will try to hide the child. To keep her, untrained and without a Guardian. That always goes badly."

This is the thing that's been in her mind for the past two weeks, ever since that day at school. If her parents loved her, they would not have locked her in the barn. They would not have called this man. Mother would not have said those terrible things.

"Why can't they—" she blurts, before she realizes he has said this on purpose. To see if *Why can't they just hide me and keep me here* is something she's been thinking—and now he knows the truth. Damaya's hands clench on the cape where she's holding it closed around herself, but Schaffa merely nods.

"First because they have another child, and anyone caught harboring an unregistered orogene is ejected from their comm as a minimum punishment." Damaya has heard this, though she resents the knowledge. Parents who cared about her would *risk*, wouldn't they? "Your parents could not have wanted to lose their home, their livelihood, and custody of *both* their children. But the greatest danger lies in what you are, Dama. You can no more hide that than you can the fact that you are female, or your clever young mind." She blushes, unsure if this is praise. He smiles so she knows it is.

He continues: "Every time the earth moves, you will hear its call. In every moment of danger you will reach, instinctively, for the nearest source of warmth and movement. The ability to do this is to you as fists are to a strong man. It's harder than you can imagine to not fight back, especially when the threat is imminent. Of course you'll do what you must to protect yourself. And when you do, people will die."

Damaya flinches. Schaffa smiles again, as kindly as always.

And Damaya thinks about that day.

It was after lunch, in the play-yard. She had eaten her bean roll while sitting by the pond with Limi and Shantare as she usually did while the other children played or threw food at each other. Some of the other kids were huddled in a corner of the yard, scratching in the dirt and muttering to each other; they had a geomesting test that afternoon. And then Zab had come over to the three of them, though he'd looked at Damaya in particular as he said, "Let me cheat off you."

Limi giggled. She thought Zab liked Damaya. Damaya didn't like *him*, though, because he was awful—always picking on Damaya, calling her names, poking her until she yelled at him to stop. So she said to Zab, "I'm not getting in trouble for you."

And he'd said, "You won't, if you do it right. Just move your paper over—"

"*No*," she'd said again. "I'm not going to do it right. I'm not going to do it *at all*. Go away." And then she'd turned back to Shantare, who had been talking before Zab interrupted.

Next thing Damaya knew, she was on the ground. Zab had shoved her off the rock using both hands, and she'd tumbled head over heels, literally, landing on her back. Later—she'd had two weeks in the barn to think about it—she would recall the look of shock on his face, as if he hadn't realized she would go over so easily. But at the time, all she had known was that she was on the ground. The *muddy* ground. Her whole back was cold and wet and foul, everything smelled of fermenting bog and crushed grass, it was in her *hair* and that was her best *uniform* and Mother was going to be furious and *she* was furious and so she'd grabbed the air and—

Damaya shivers. *People will die.* Schaffa nods as if he has heard this thought.

"You're firemountain-glass, Dama." He says this very softly. "You're a gift of the earth—but Father Earth hates us, never forget, and his gifts are neither free nor safe. If we pick you up, hone you to sharpness, treat you with the care and respect you deserve, then you become useful. More than useful: valuable. But if we just leave you lying about, you'll cut to the bone the first person who blunders across you. Or worse—you'll shatter, and hurt many."

Damaya remembers the look on Zab's face. The air had gone cold for only an instant, billowing around her like a burst balloon. That was enough to make a crust of ice on the grass beneath her, and to make the sweatdrops go solid on Zab's skin. They'd stopped and jerked and stared at each other.

She remembers his face. *You almost killed me,* she had seen there.

Schaffa, watching her closely, smiles.

"It isn't your fault," he says. "Most of what they say about orogenes isn't true. There's nothing you did to be born like this, nothing your parents did. Don't be angry with them, or with yourself."

And she begins to cry. Because, well. He's right. All of it, everything he says, it's right. She has hated Mother for putting her in here, she's hated Father and Chaga for letting Mother do it, she hates herself for having been born what she is and disappointing them all. And now Schaffa knows just how weak and terrible she is.

"Shh," he says, standing and coming over to her. He kneels and takes her hands; she starts crying harder. She can't hold it in anymore. But Schaffa squeezes her hands sharply, enough to hurt, and she starts and draws breath and blinks at him through the blur. "You mustn't, little one. Your mother will return soon. Never cry where they can see you."

"Wh-what?"

He looks so sad—for Damaya?—as he reaches up and cups her cheek. "It isn't safe."

So she stops, though she doesn't really understand. Once she's wiped her cheeks, he examines her and thumbs away a tear that she's missed, then nods after this inspection. "Your mother will probably be able to tell, but that will do for everyone else."

The barn door creaks and Mother is back, this time with Father in tow. Father's jaw is tight, and he doesn't look at Damaya even though he hasn't seen her since Mother put her in the barn. Both of them focus on Schaffa, who stands and moves a little in front of Damaya, nodding thanks as he accepts the folded blanket and twine-wrapped parcel that Mother gives him.

"We've watered your horse," Father says, stiffly. "You want provender to carry?"

"No need," says Schaffa. "If we make good time, we should make Brevard just after nightfall."

Father frowns. "A hard ride."

"Yes. But in Brevard, no one from this village will get the fine idea to come seek us out along the road, and make their farewells to Damaya in a ruder fashion." Schaffa smiles thinly.

It takes a moment for Damaya to understand, and then she realizes: people from Palela want to kill Damaya. But that's wrong, isn't it? They can't really, can they? She thinks of all the people she knows. The teachers from creche. The other children. The old ladies at the wellhouse who used to be friends with Muh.

Father thinks of this, too, she can see that in his face, and he frowns and opens his mouth to say what she's thinking: *They wouldn't do something like that.* But he stops before the words leave his mouth. And he glances at Damaya, once and with his face full of anguish, before remembering to look away again.

"Here you are," Schaffa says to Damaya, holding out the blanket. It's Muh's. She stares at it, then looks at Mother, but Mother won't look back.

Damaya swallows back tears because it isn't safe to cry. Even when she pulls off Schaffa's cloak and he wraps the blanket around her instead, familiar-fusty and scratchy and perfect, she keeps her face completely still. Schaffa's eyes flick to hers; he nods, just a little, in approval. Then he takes her hand and leads her toward the barn door.

Mother and Father follow, but they don't say anything. Damaya doesn't say anything. She does glance at the house once, catching a glimpse of someone through a gap in the curtains before they flick shut. Chaga, her big brother, who taught her how to read and how to ride a donkey and how to skip rocks on a pond. He doesn't even wave good-bye...but maybe this is not because he hates her.

Then Schaffa is lifting Damaya onto a horse bigger than any she's ever seen, a big glossy bay with a long neck, and then Schaffa's in the saddle behind her, tucking the blanket around her legs and shoes so she won't chafe or get chilblains, and then they are away.

"Don't look back," Schaffa advises. "It's easier that way." So she doesn't.

But later, she wishes that she had.